SPIT
THREE
TIMES

Davide Reviati

Translated by Jamie Richards

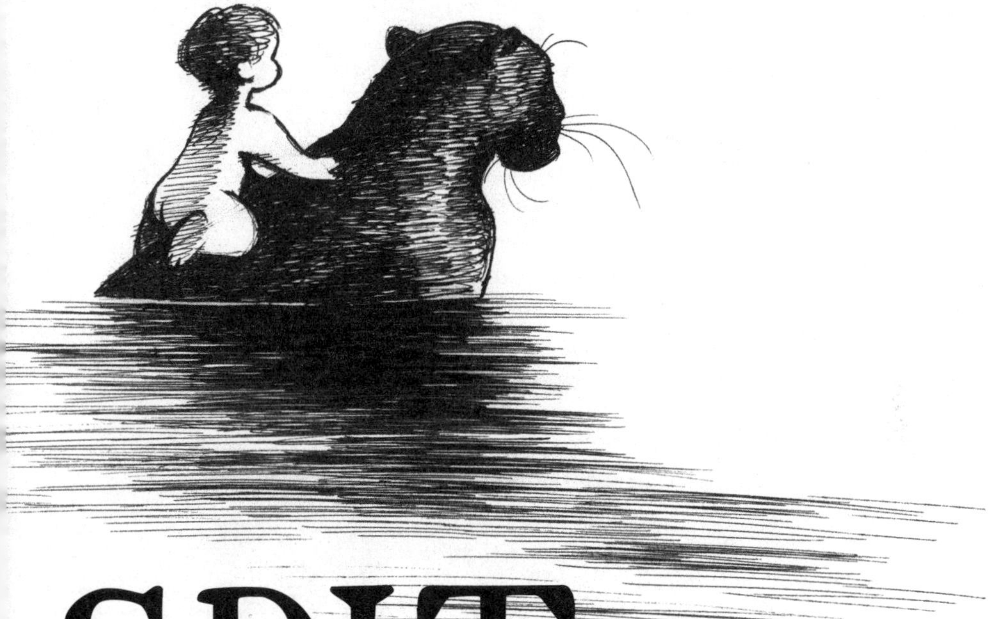

SPIT THREE TIMES

SEVEN STORIES PRESS
New York • Oakland • Liverpool

Translation made in arrangement with
Am-Book (www.am-book.com)

SEVEN STORIES PRESS
140 Watts Street
New York, NY 10013
www.sevenstories.com

Library of Congress Card Number: 2020932915
ISBN 978-1-60980-909-6 (pbk)
ISBN 978-1-60980-910-2 (e-book)

College professors and high school and middle school teachers may order free examination copies of Seven Stories Press titles. To order, visit www.sevenstories.com or send a fax on school letterhead to 212-226-1411.

English edition design: Abigail Miller

Printed in the USA.

9 8 7 6 5 4 3 2 1

My whole life I've snuck through my landscape,
carrying my bit of life under my arm
like stolen goods.

Mariella Mehr, *Steinzeit*

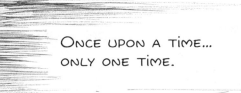

ONCE UPON A TIME...
ONLY ONE TIME.

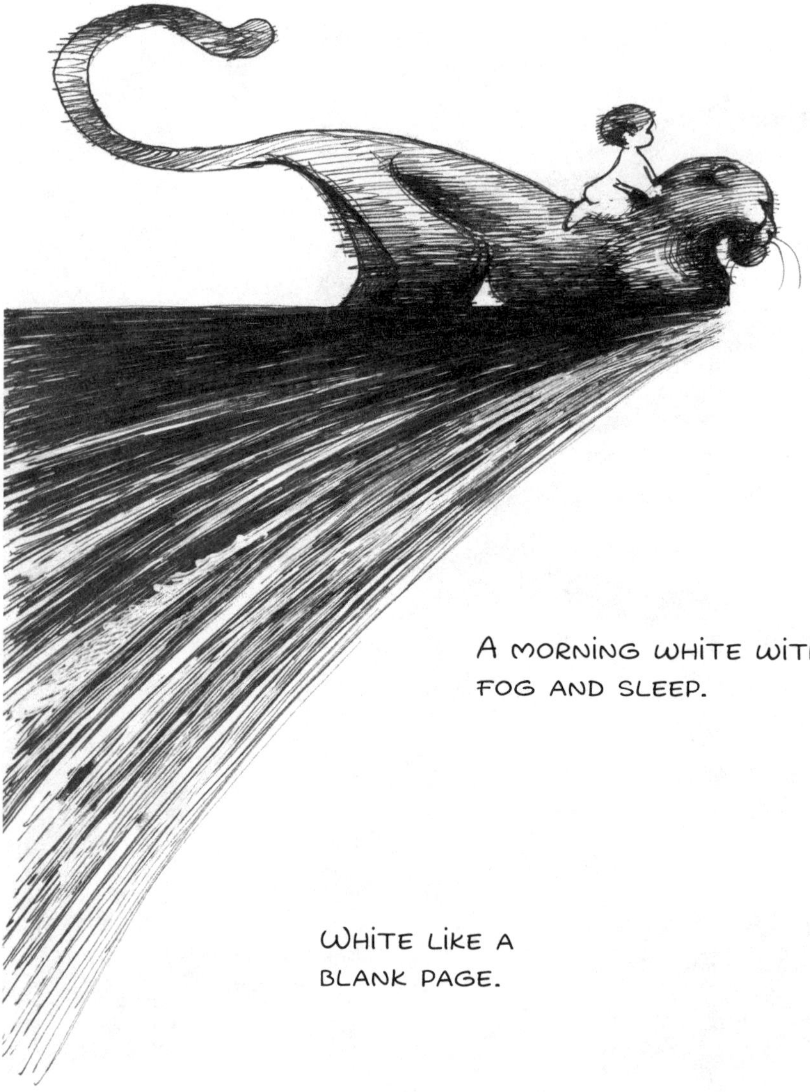

A MORNING WHITE WITH
FOG AND SLEEP.

WHITE LIKE A
BLANK PAGE.

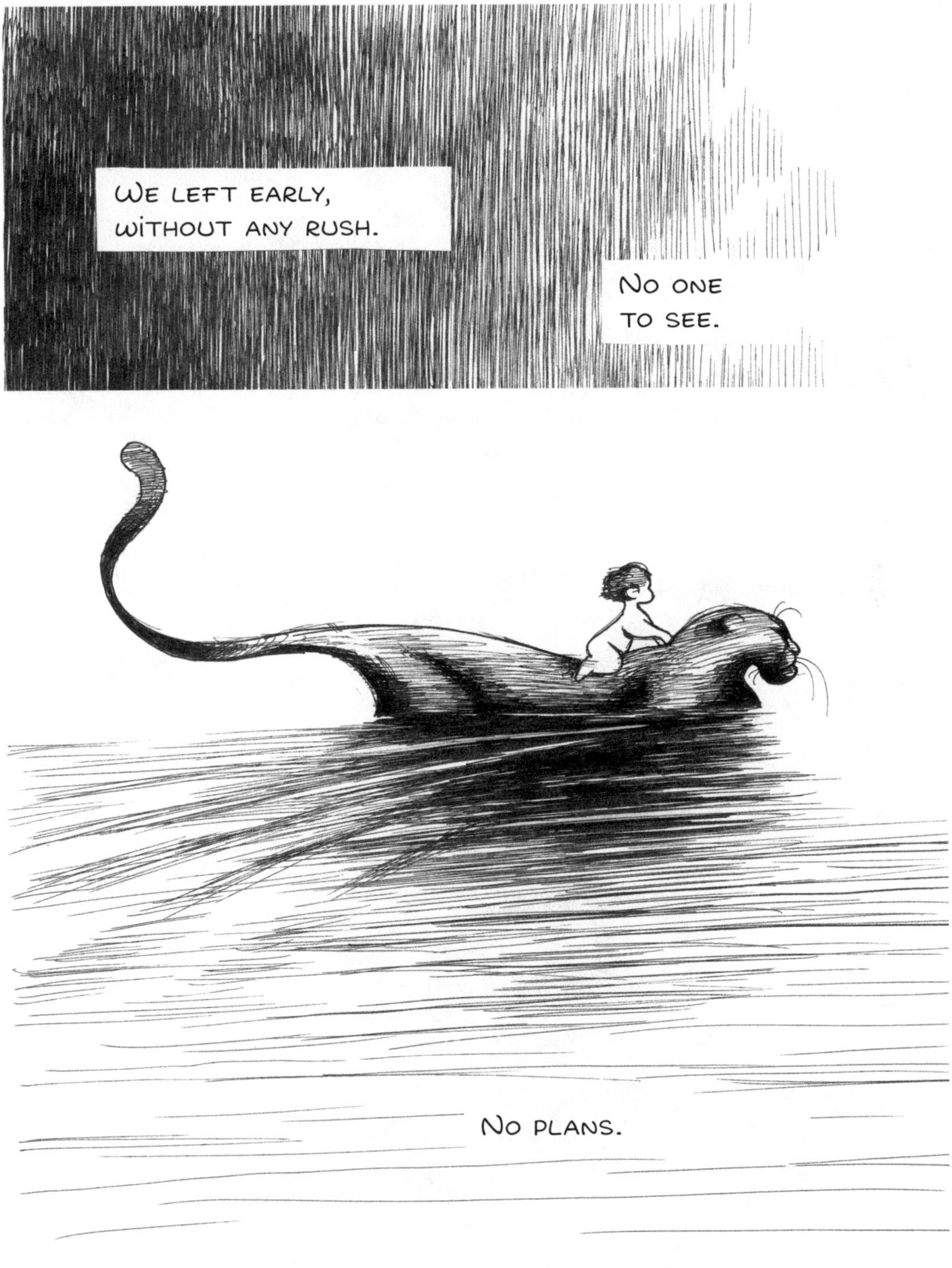
We left early,
without any rush.
No one
to see.
No plans.

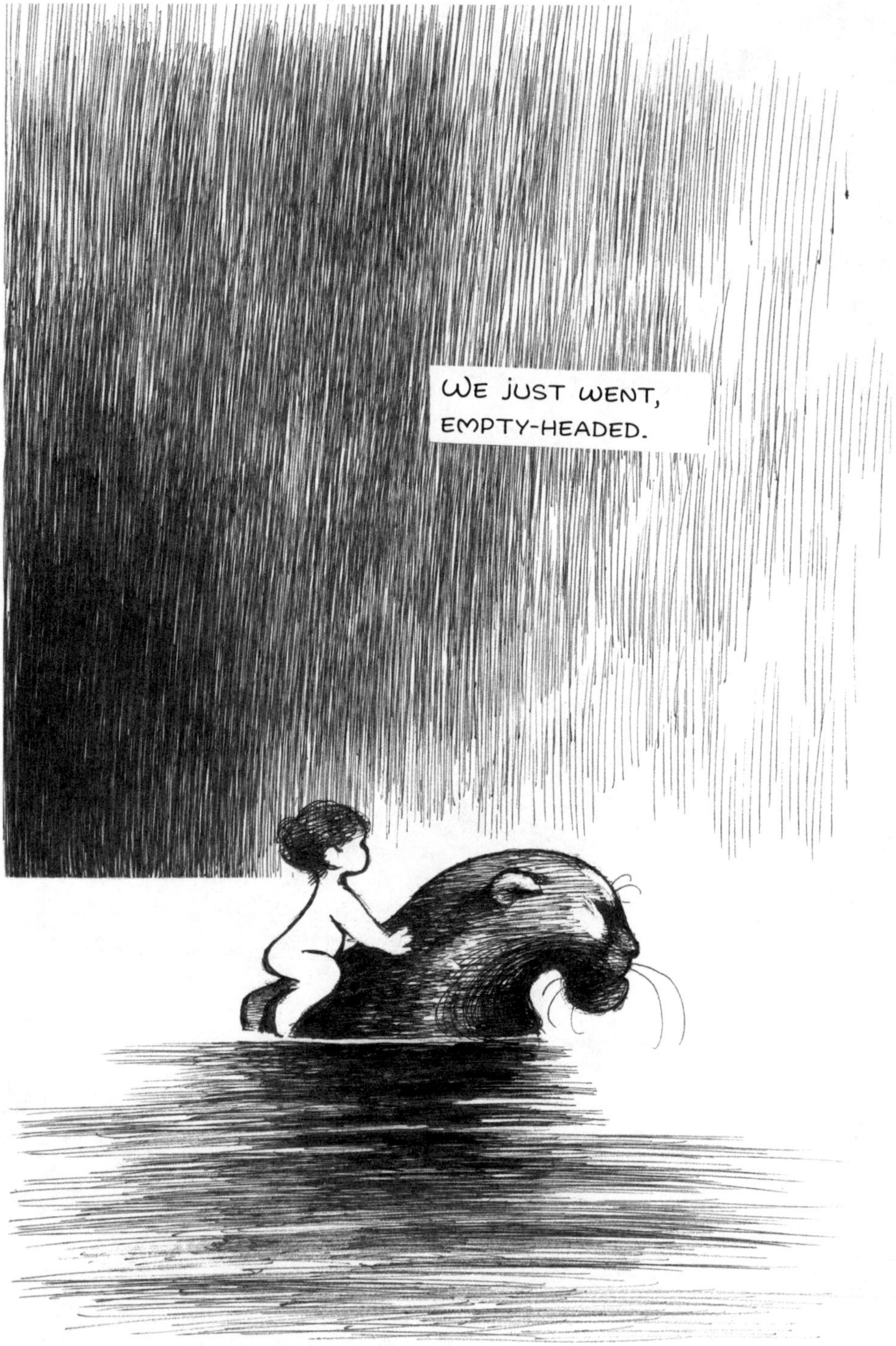
WE JUST WENT,
EMPTY-HEADED.

LIGHT.

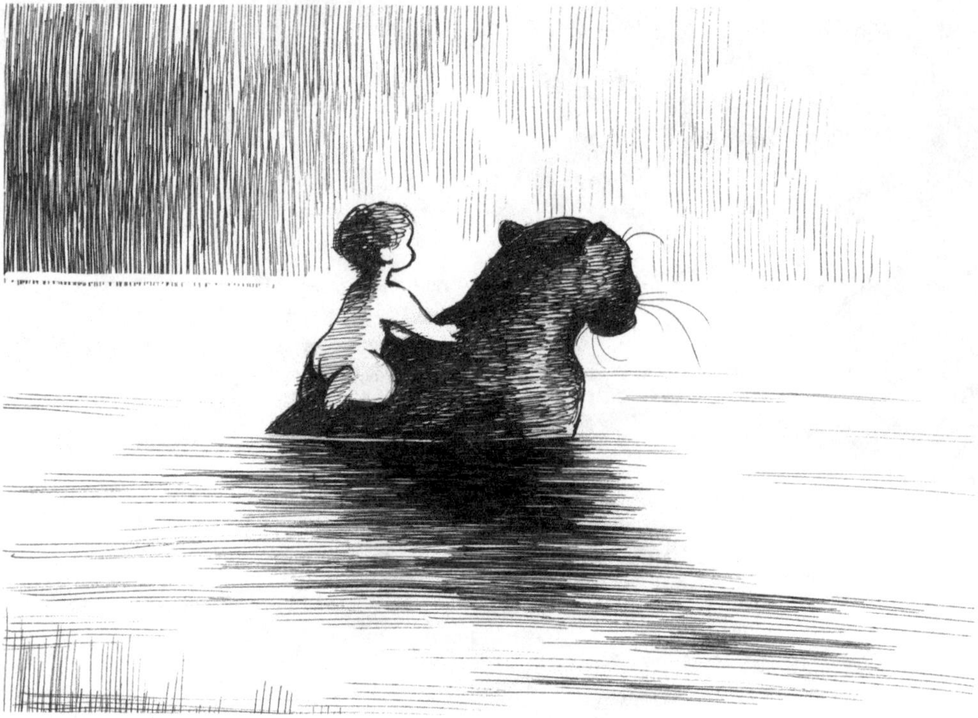

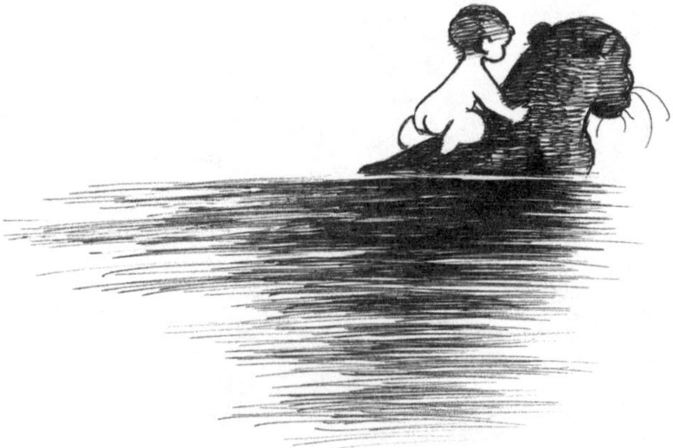

Once upon a morning,
without wants or
cares, Blank.

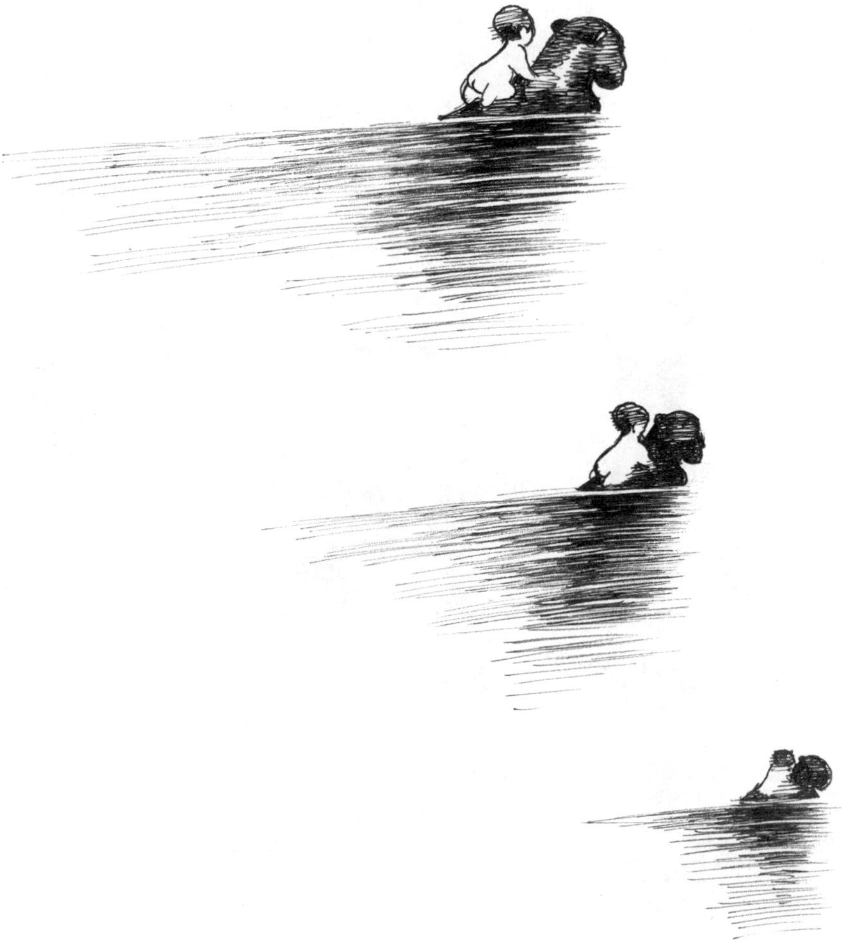

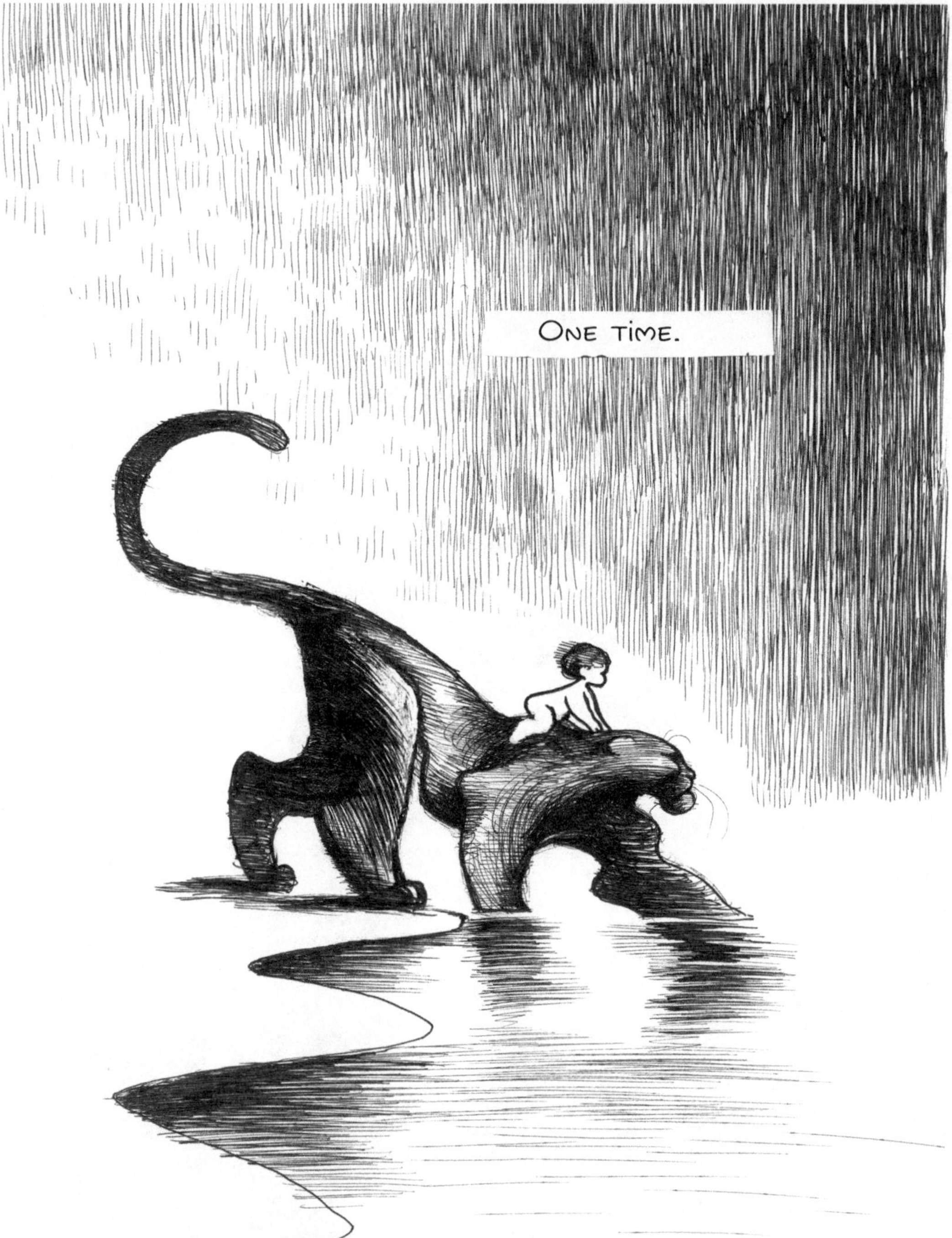
One time.

I

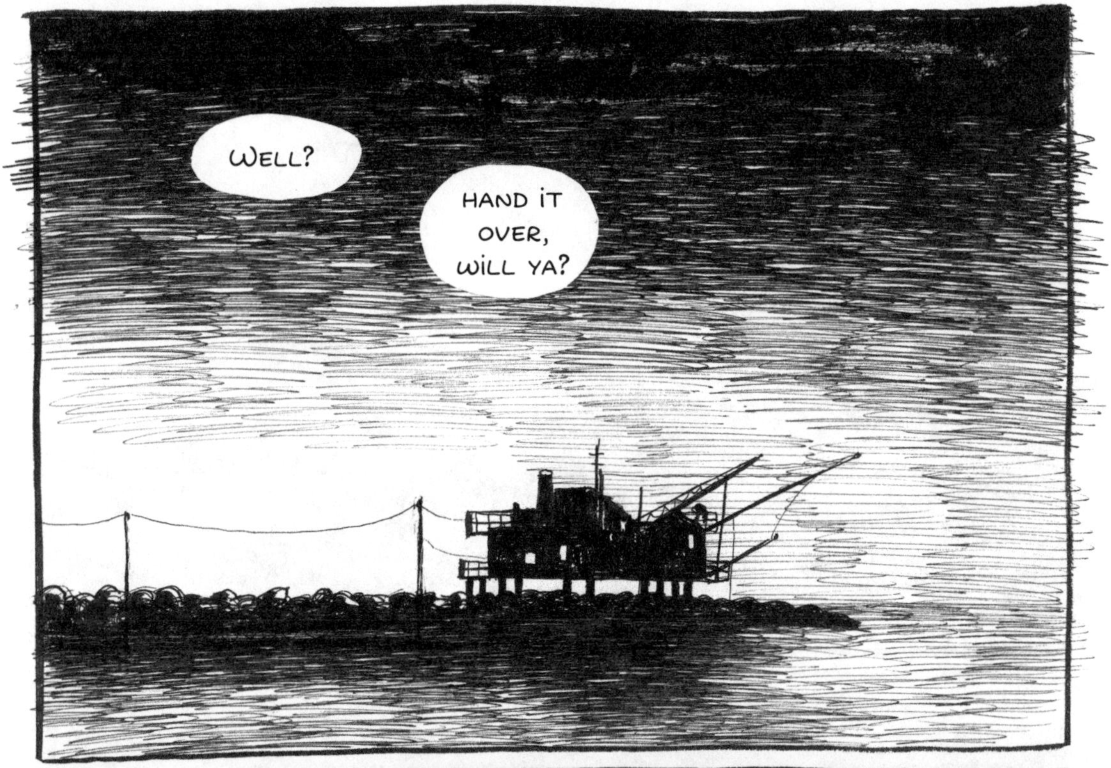
WELL?
HAND IT OVER, WILL YA?

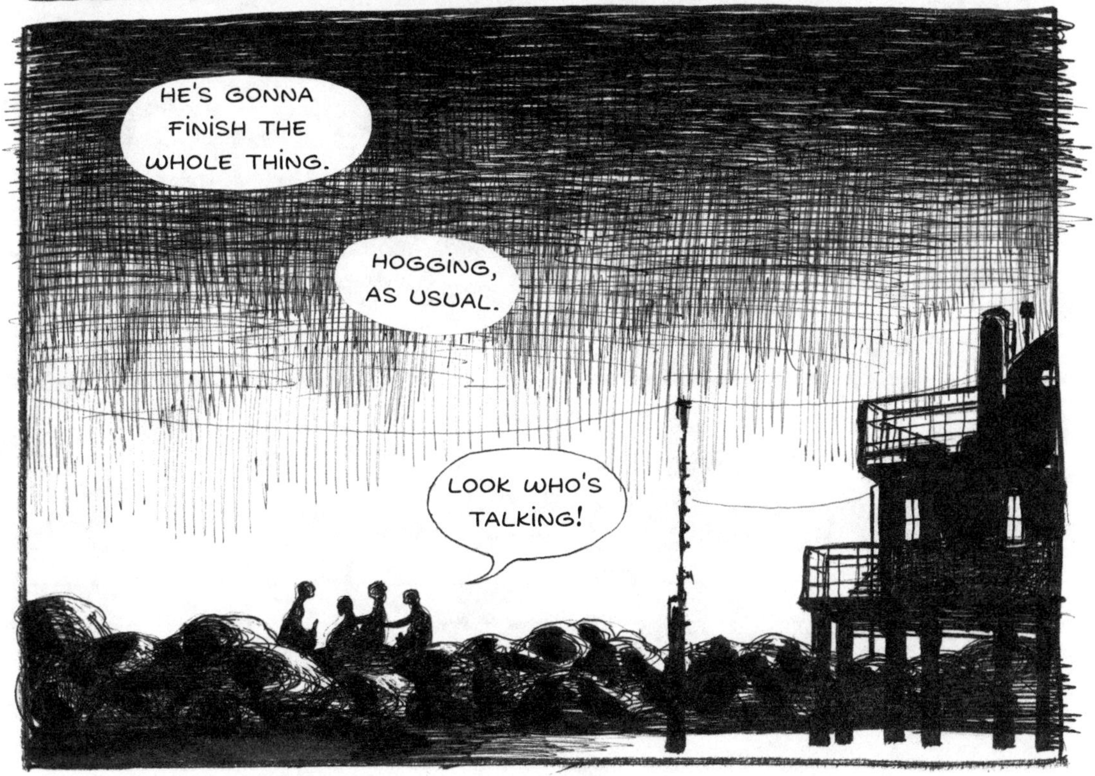
HE'S GONNA FINISH THE WHOLE THING.
HOGGING, AS USUAL.
LOOK WHO'S TALKING!

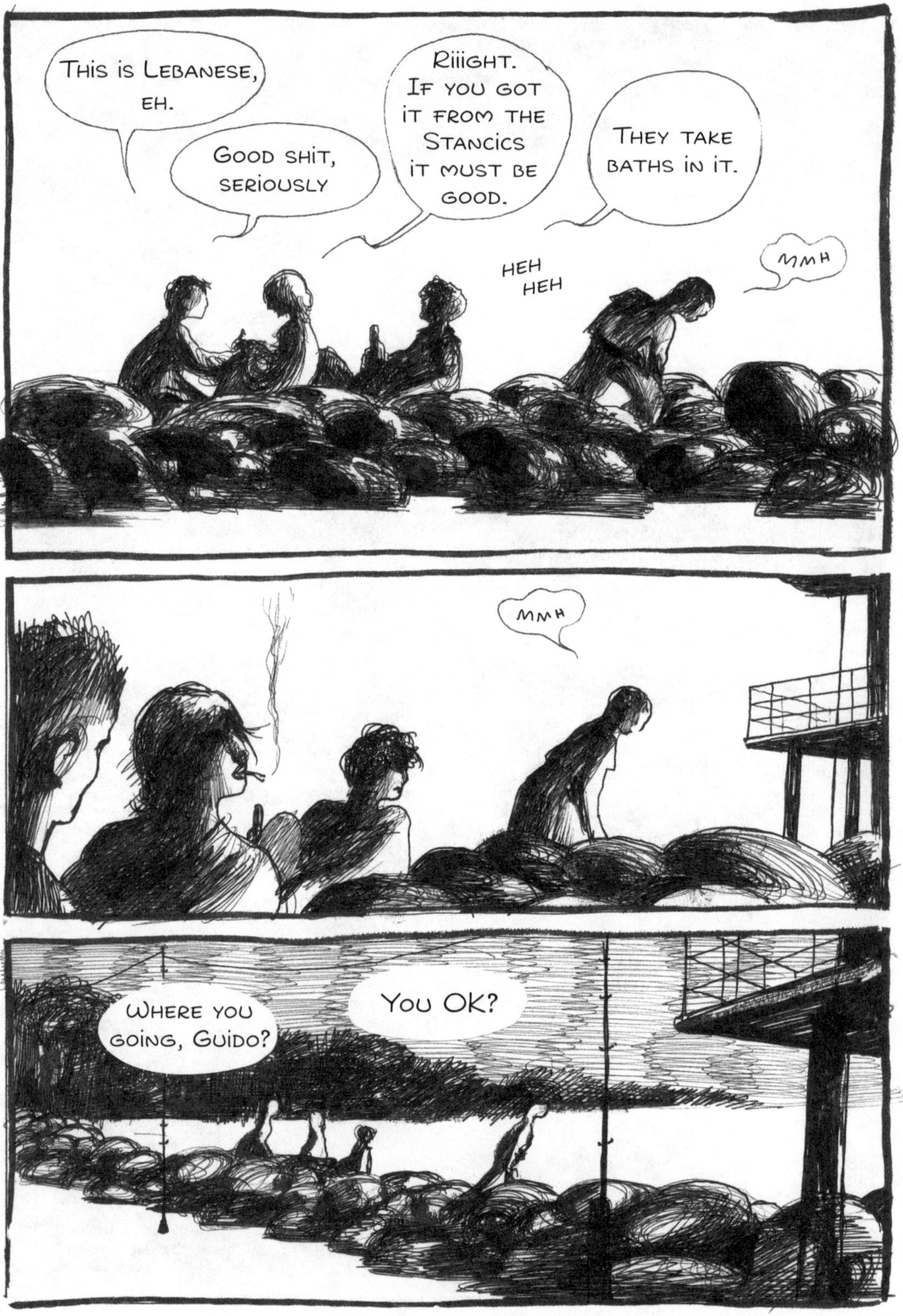
This is Lebanese, eh.
Good shit, seriously
Riiight. If you got it from the Stancics it must be good.
They take baths in it.
heh heh
mmh
mmh
Where you going, Guido?
You OK?

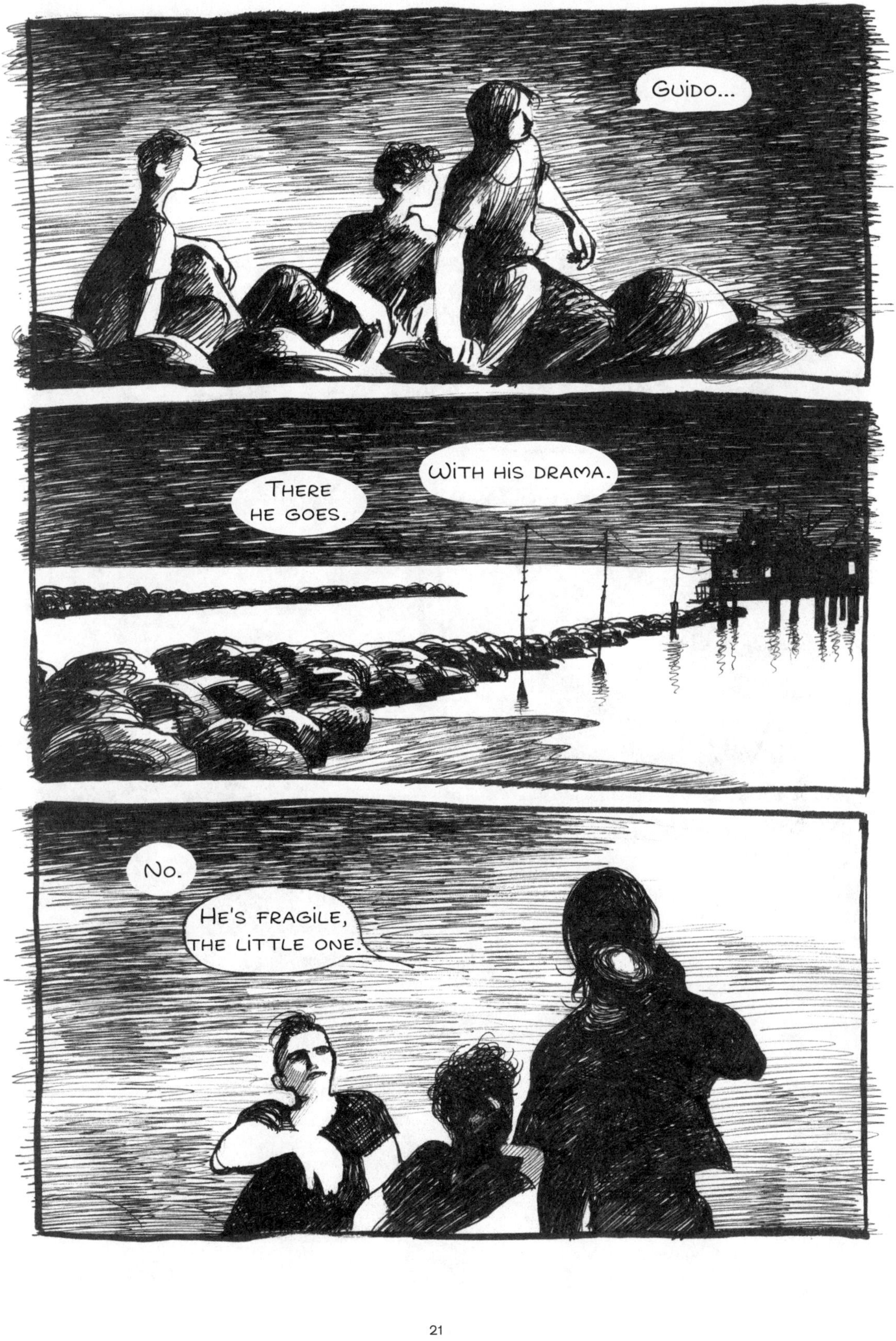
GUIDO...
THERE HE GOES.
WITH HIS DRAMA.
NO.
HE'S FRAGILE, THE LITTLE ONE.

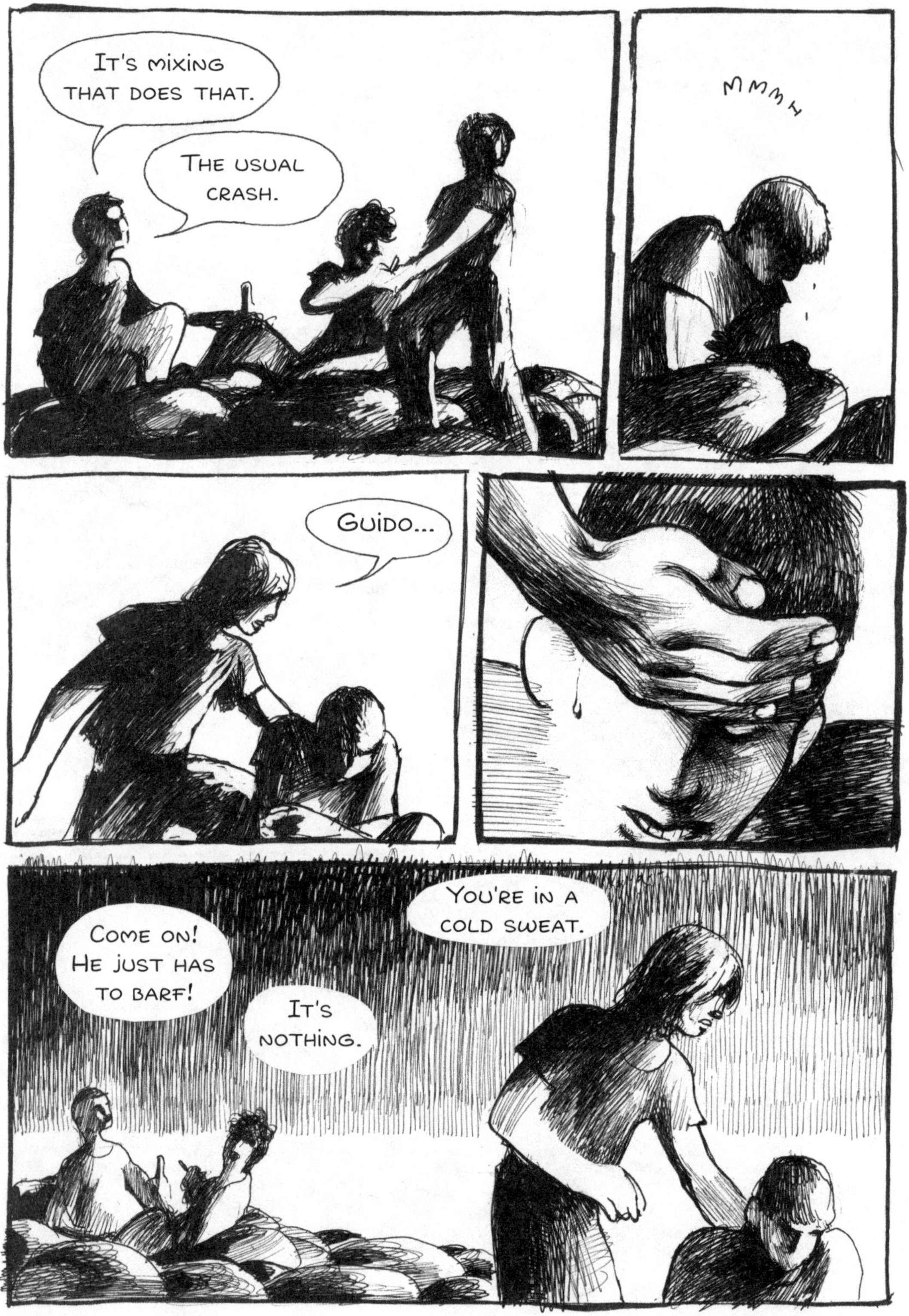
It's mixing that does that.
The usual crash.
MMMH
Guido...
You're in a cold sweat.
Come on! He just has to barf!
It's nothing.

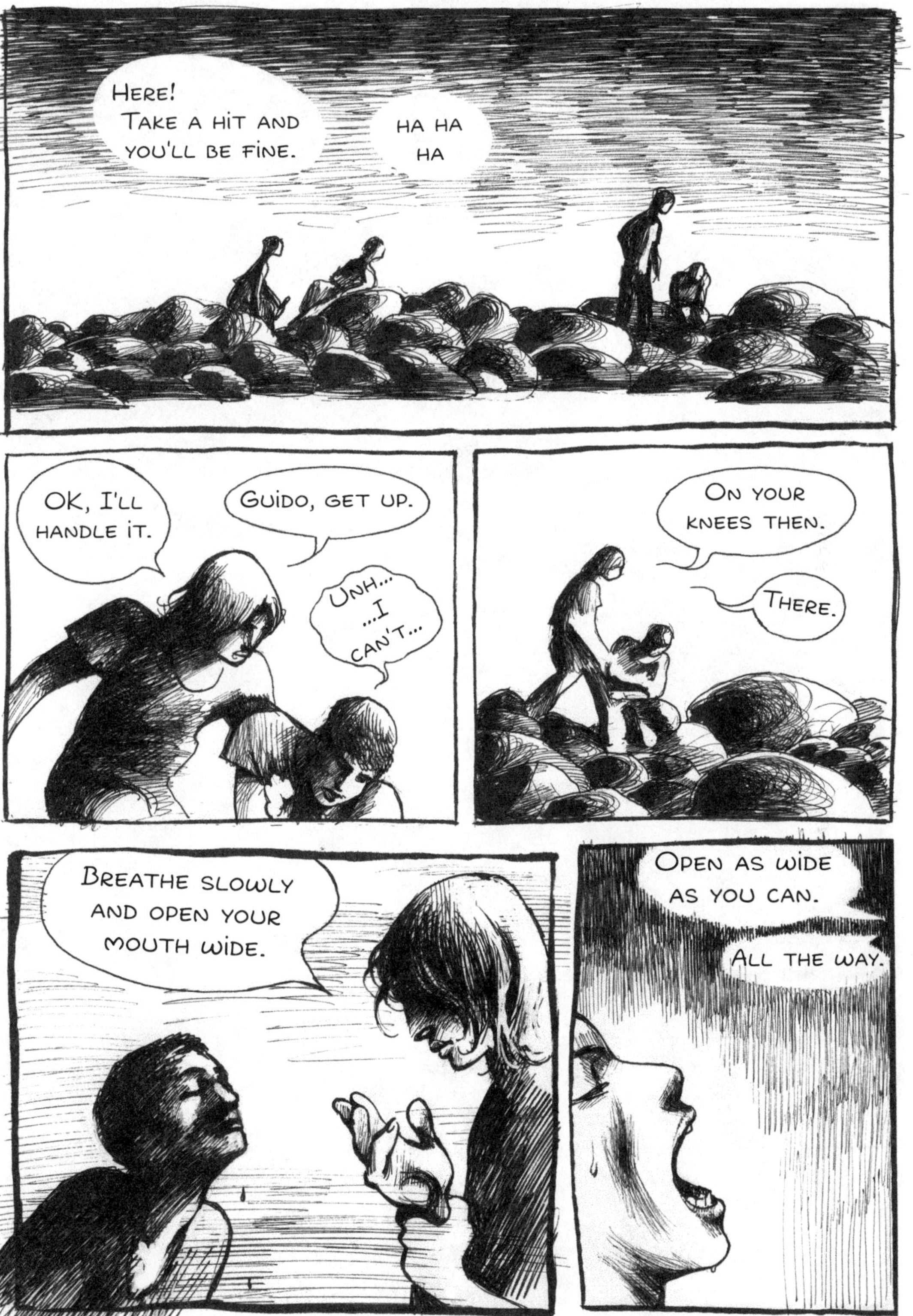
Here! Take a hit and you'll be fine.
Ha ha ha
OK, I'll handle it.
Guido, get up.
Unh... ...I can't...
On your knees then.
There.
Breathe slowly and open your mouth wide.
Open as wide as you can.
All the way.

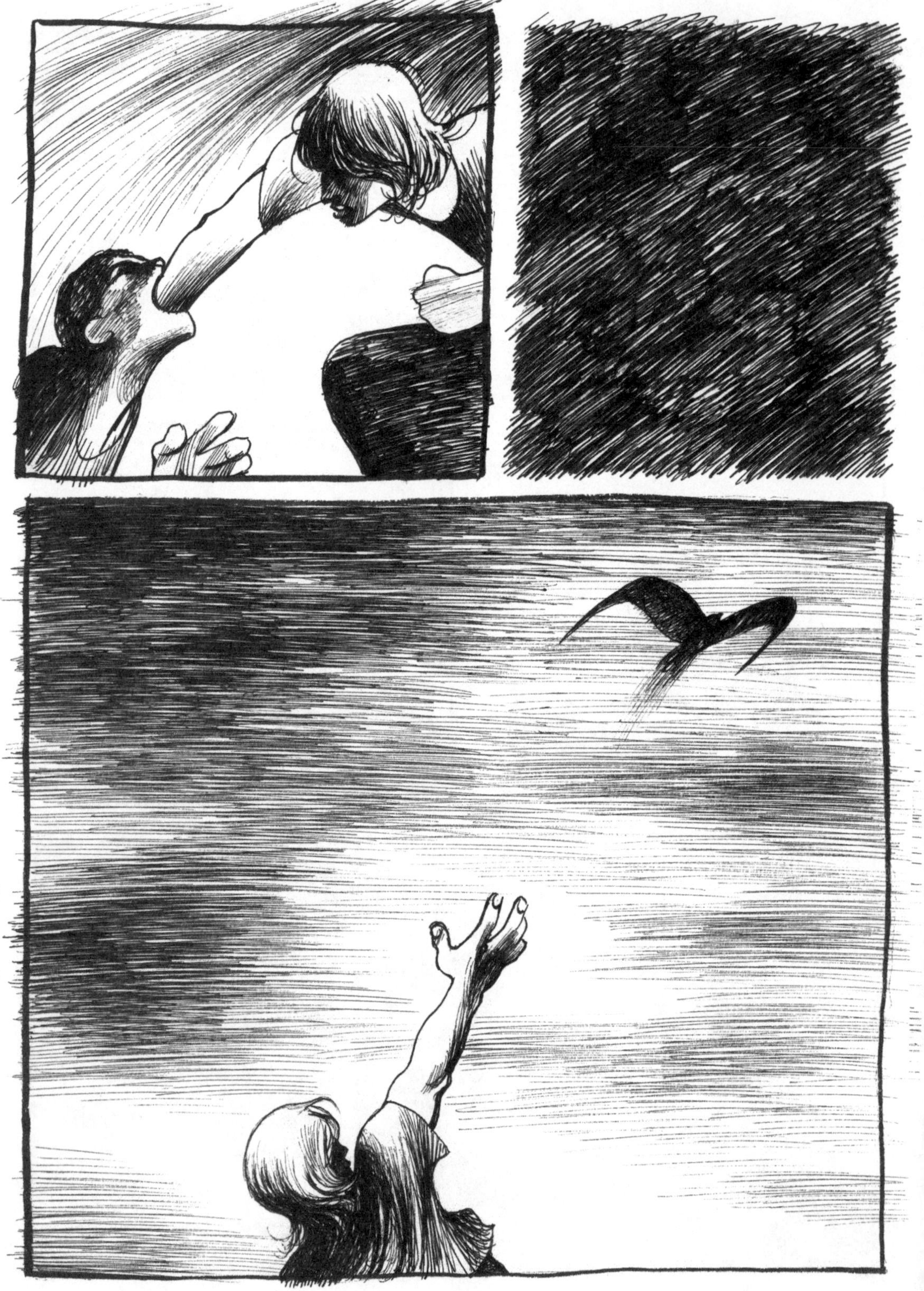

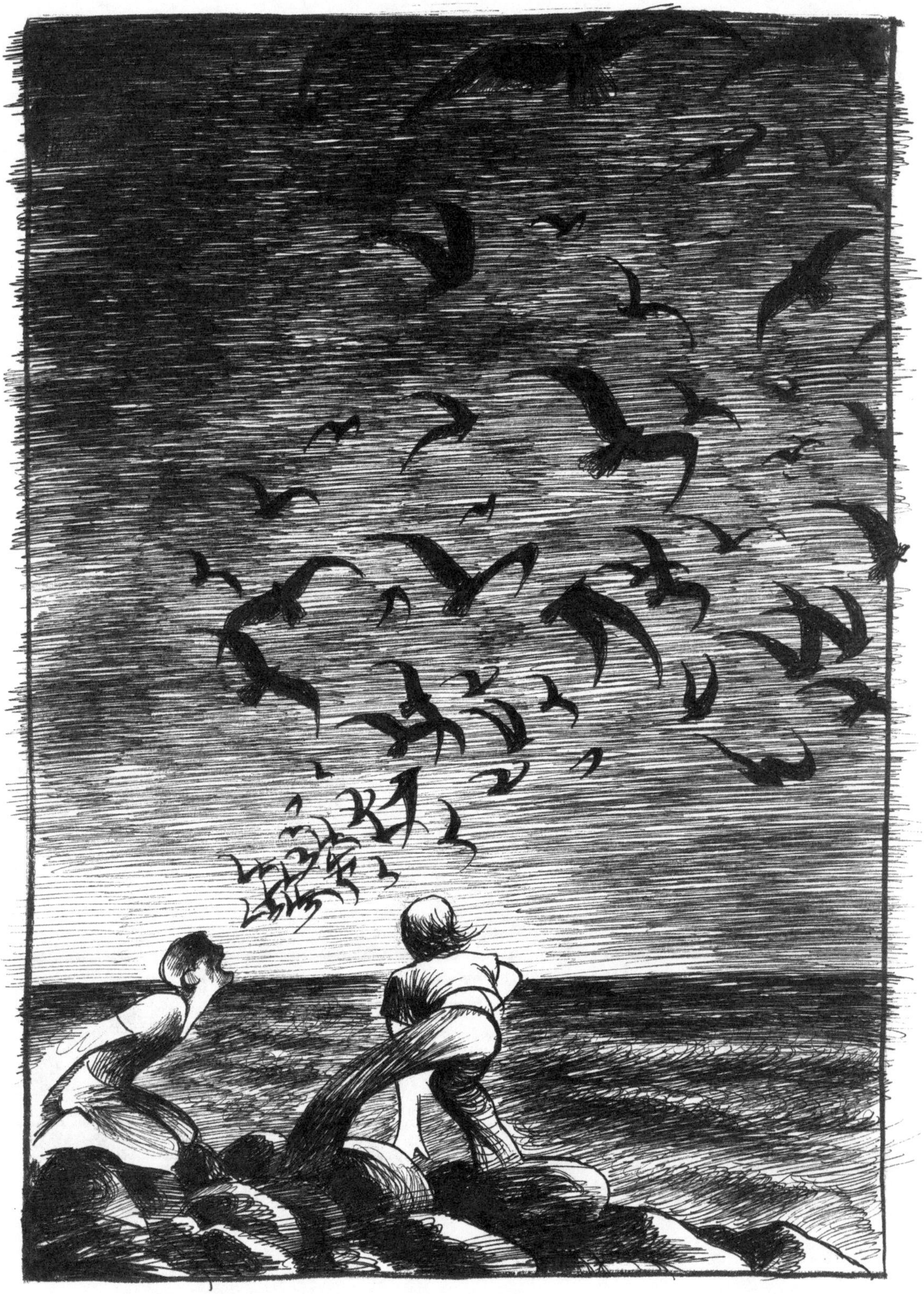

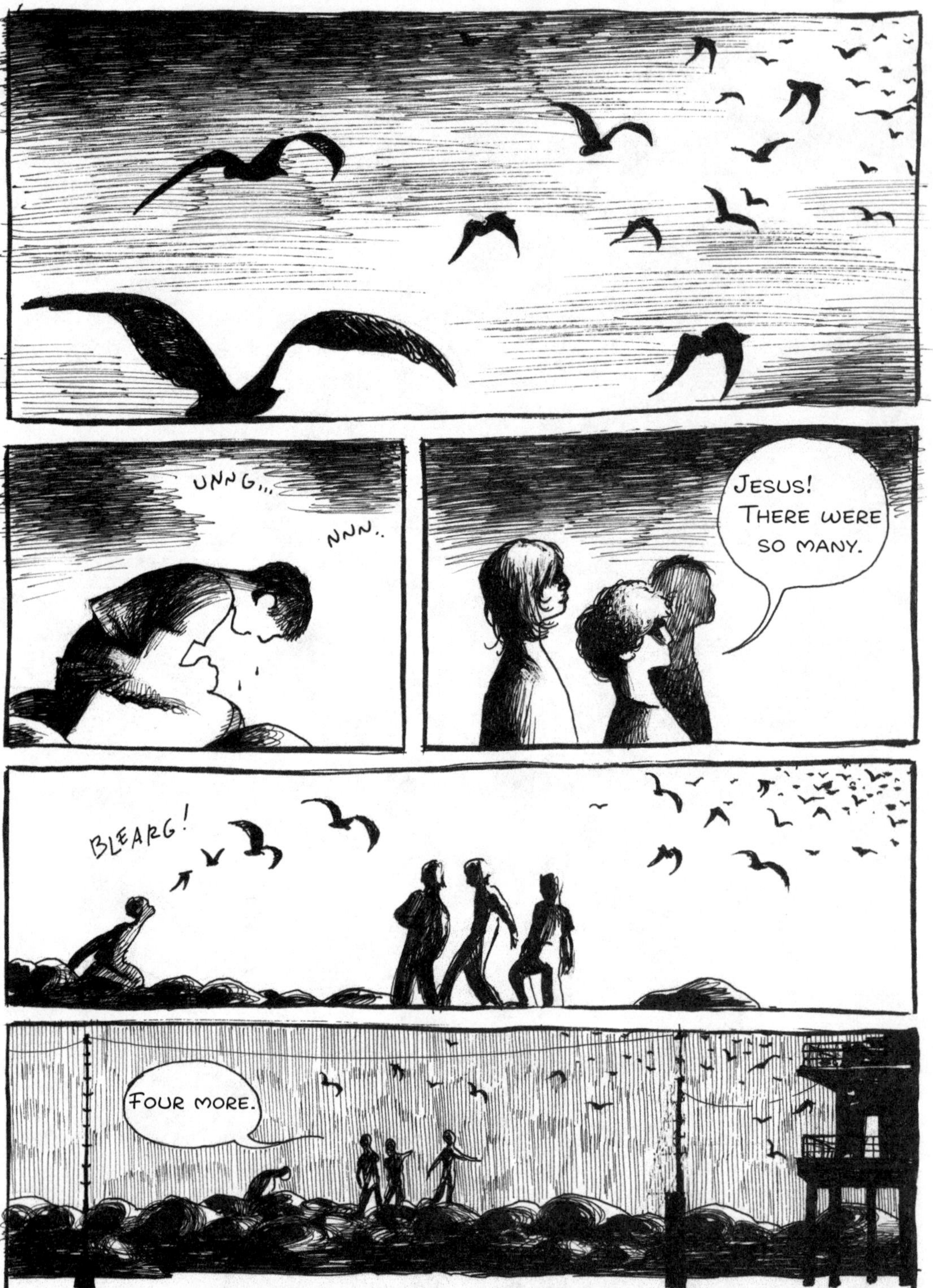
UNNG...
NNN..
JESUS! THERE WERE SO MANY.
BLEARG!
FOUR MORE.

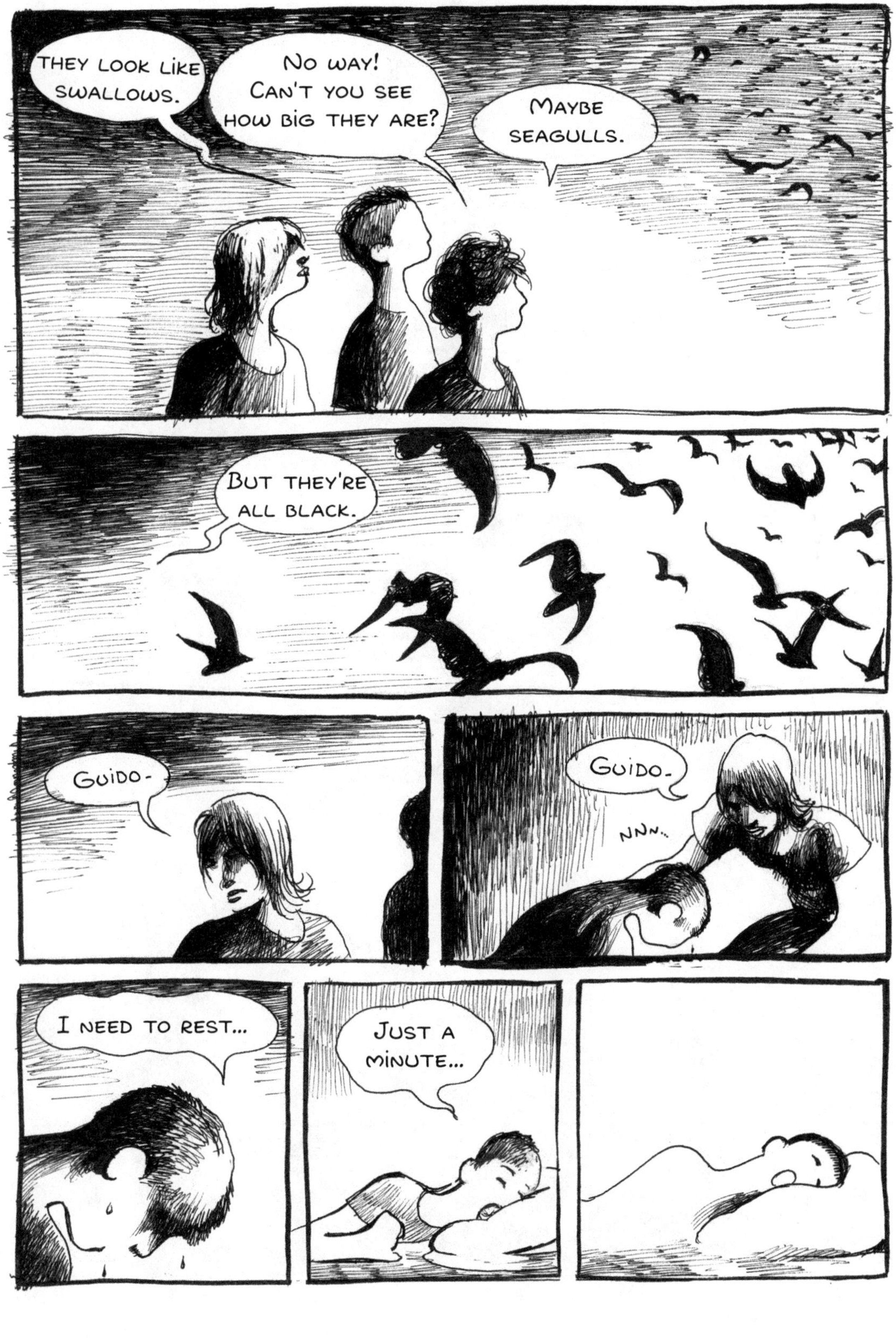
THEY LOOK LIKE SWALLOWS.
NO WAY! CAN'T YOU SEE HOW BIG THEY ARE?
MAYBE SEAGULLS.
BUT THEY'RE ALL BLACK.
GUIDO-
GUIDO-
NNN...
I NEED TO REST...
JUST A MINUTE...

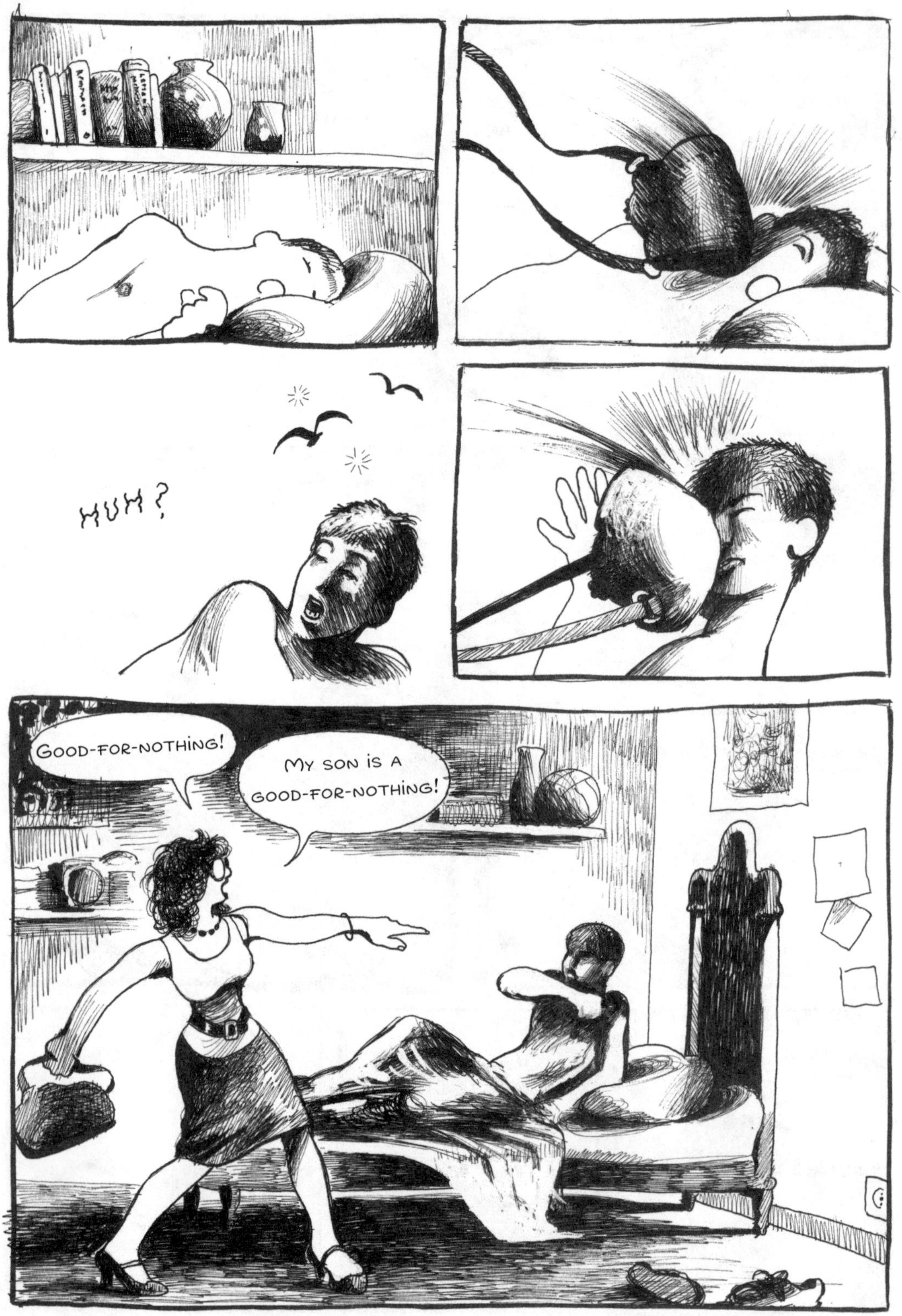
HUH?
GOOD-FOR-NOTHING!
MY SON IS A GOOD-FOR-NOTHING!

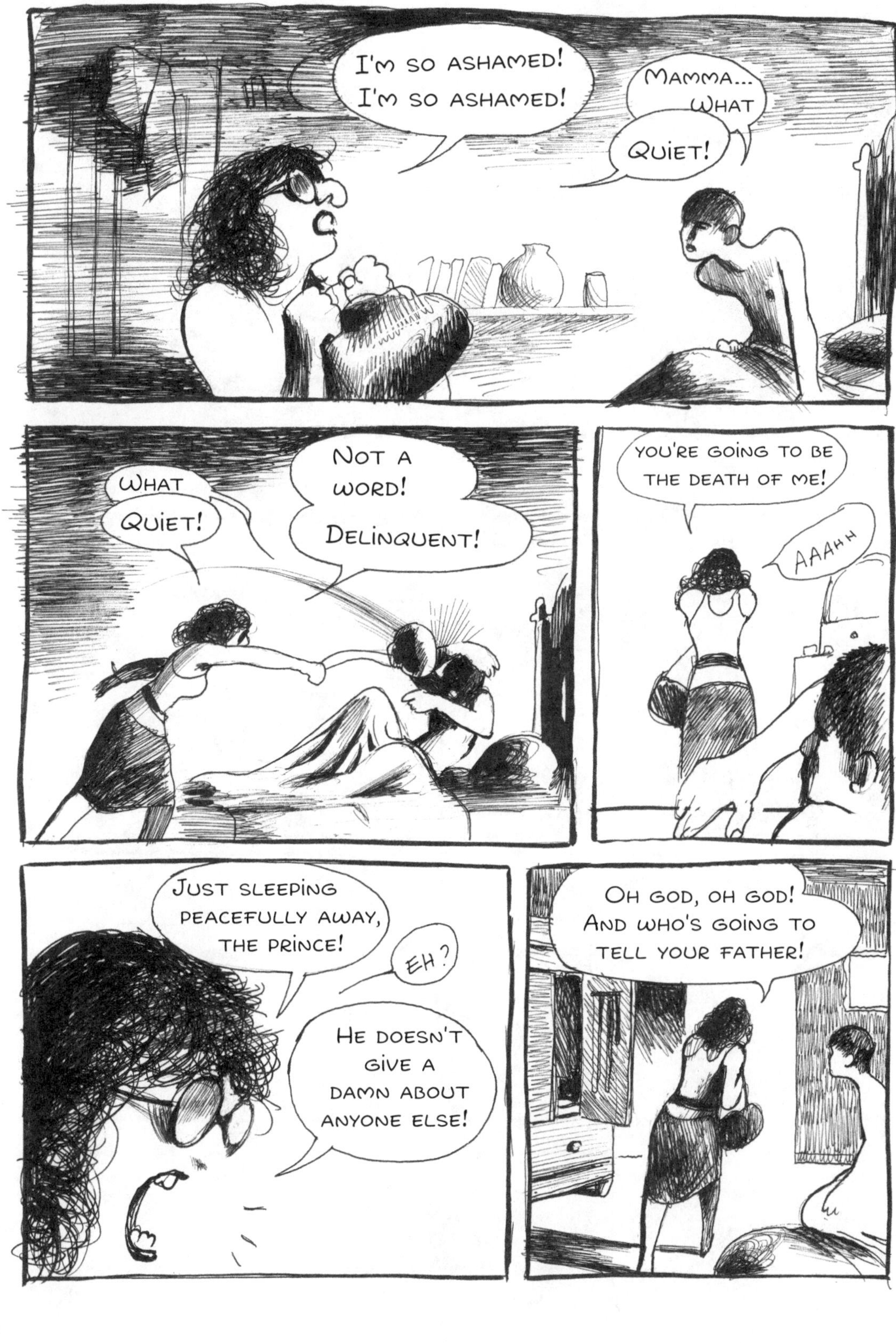
I'm so ashamed!
I'm so ashamed!
Mamma... what
Quiet!
What
Quiet!
Not a word!
Delinquent!
You're going to be the death of me!
AAAhh
Just sleeping peacefully away, the prince!
Eh?
He doesn't give a damn about anyone else!
Oh god, oh god! And who's going to tell your father!

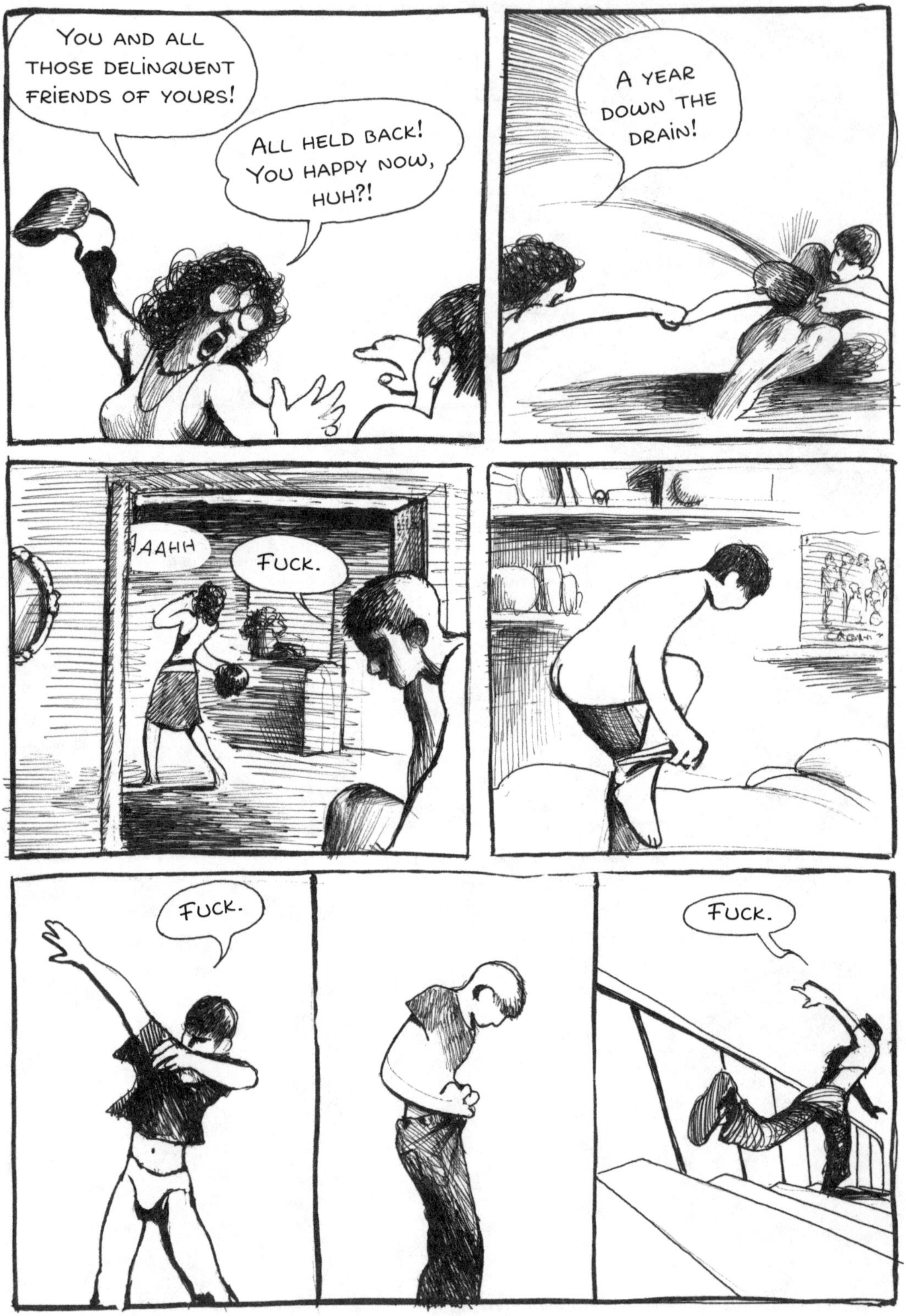

YOU AND ALL THOSE DELINQUENT FRIENDS OF YOURS!
ALL HELD BACK! YOU HAPPY NOW, HUH?!
A YEAR DOWN THE DRAIN!
AAAHH
FUCK.
FUCK.
FUCK.

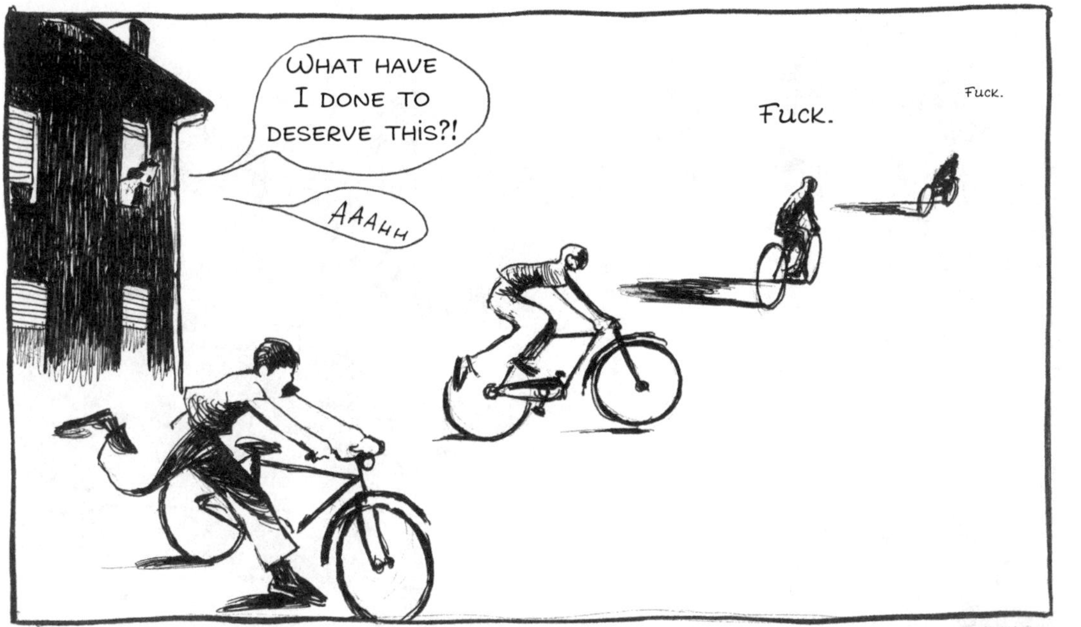
WHAT HAVE I DONE TO DESERVE THIS?!
AAAHH
FUCK.
FUCK.

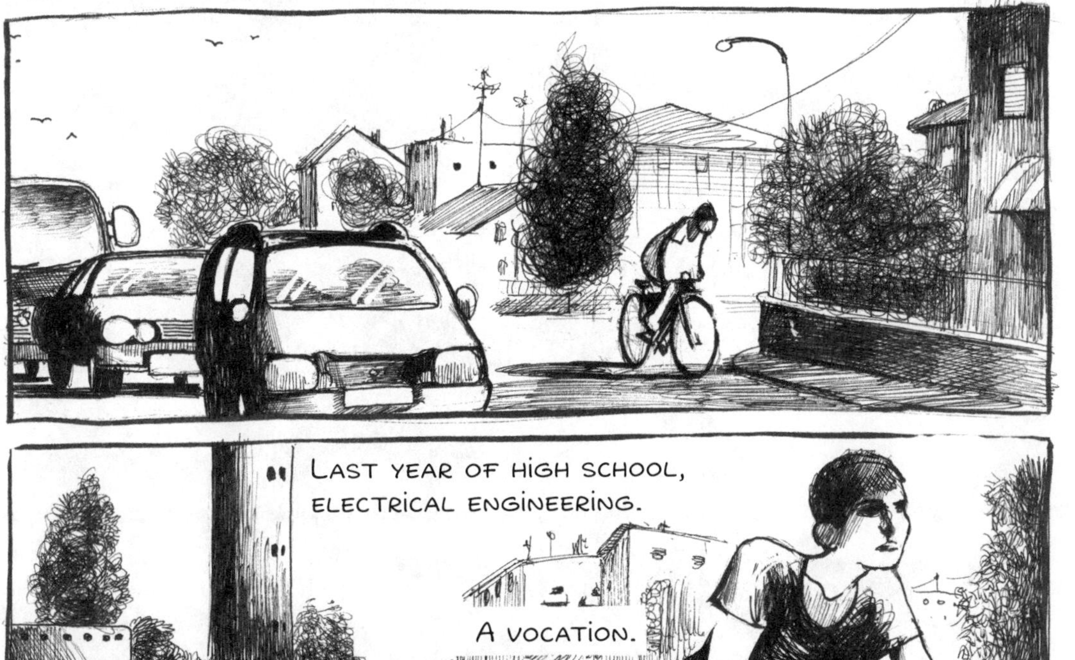

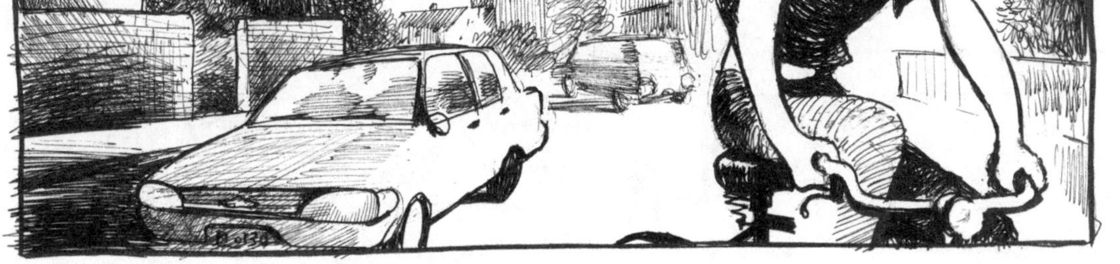
LAST YEAR OF HIGH SCHOOL, ELECTRICAL ENGINEERING.
A VOCATION.

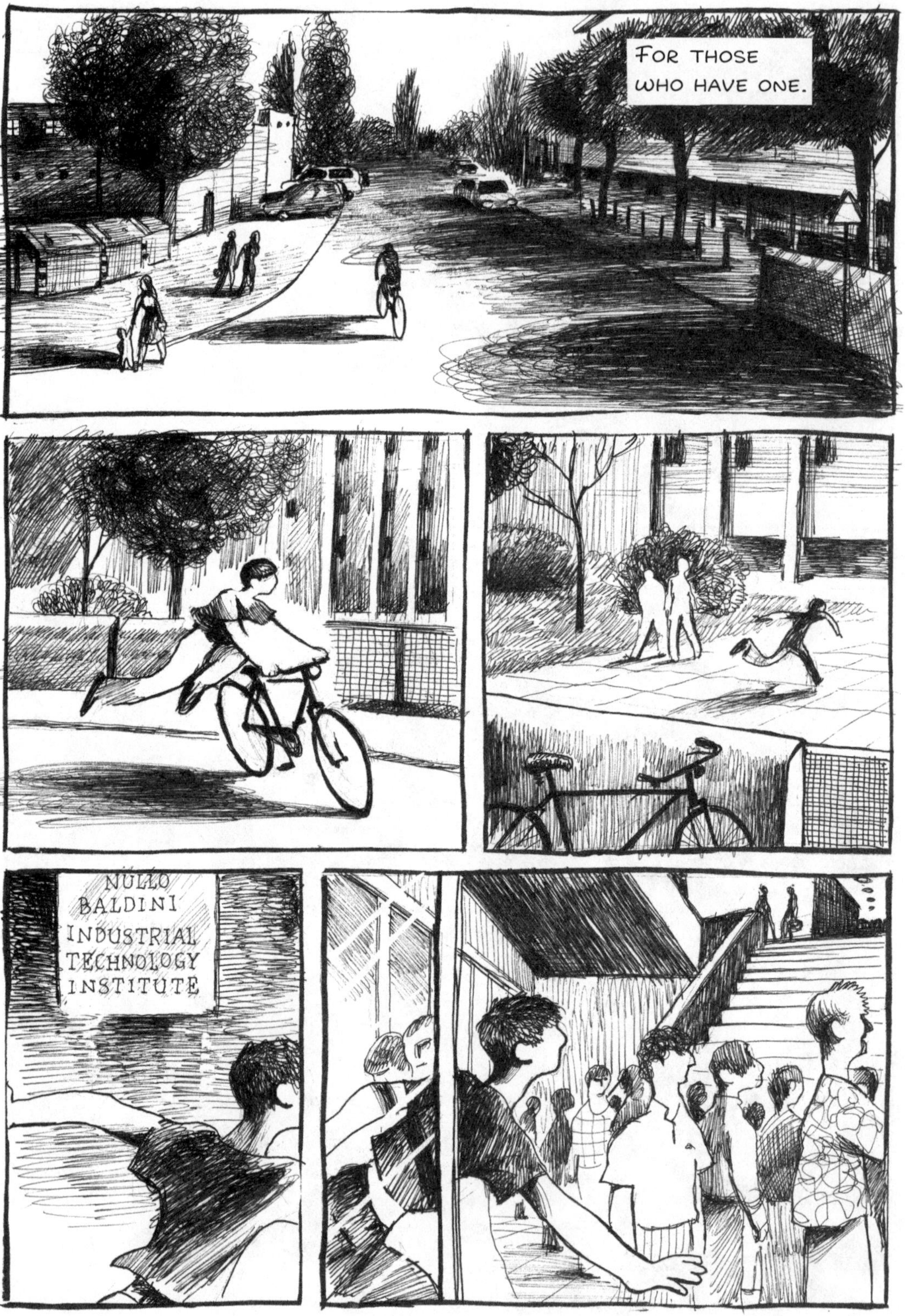
FOR THOSE WHO HAVE ONE.
NULLO BALDINI INDUSTRIAL TECHNOLOGY INSTITUTE

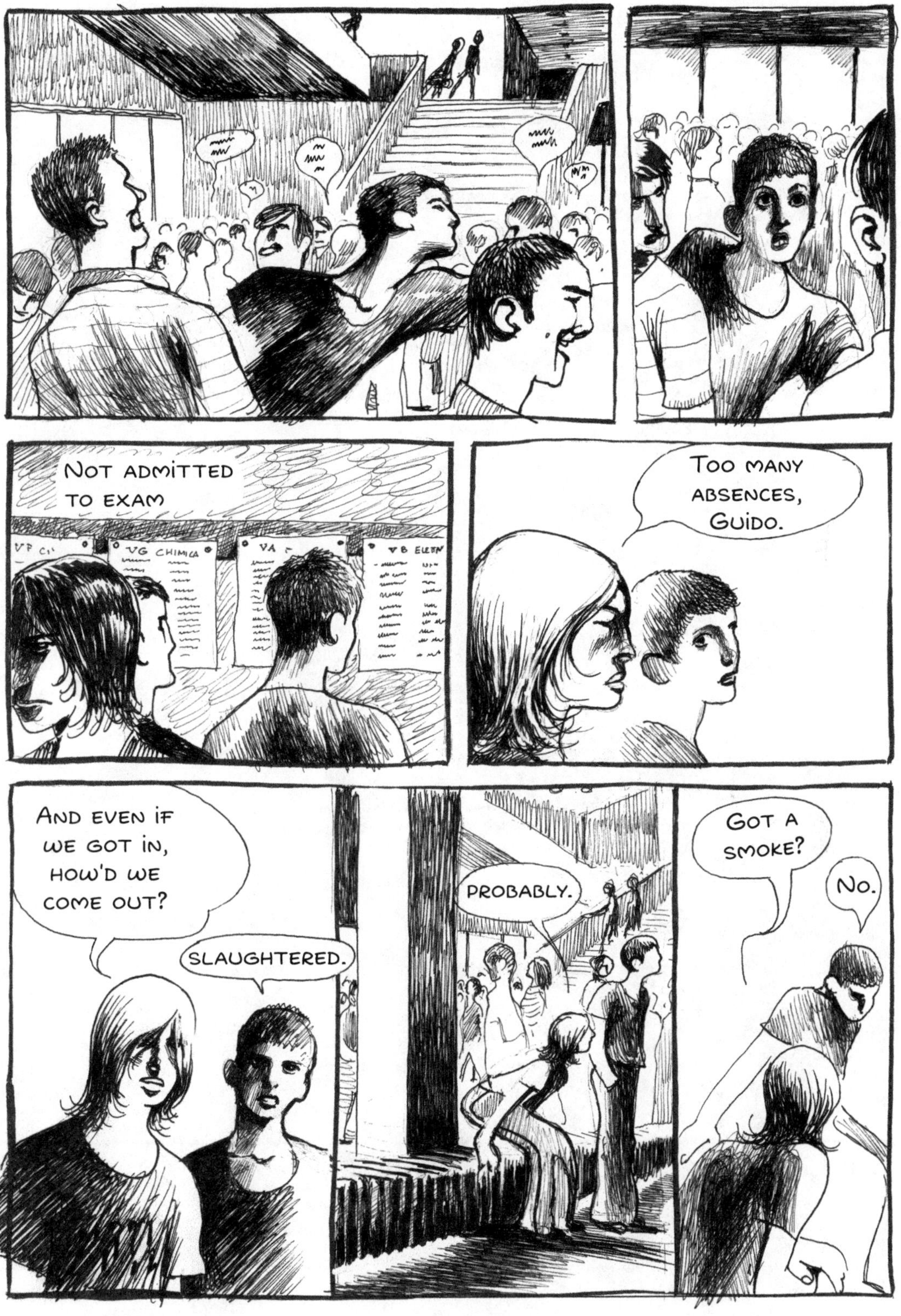
Not admitted to exam
VG Chimica
Too many absences, Guido.
And even if we got in, how'd we come out?
Slaughtered.
Probably.
Got a smoke?
No.

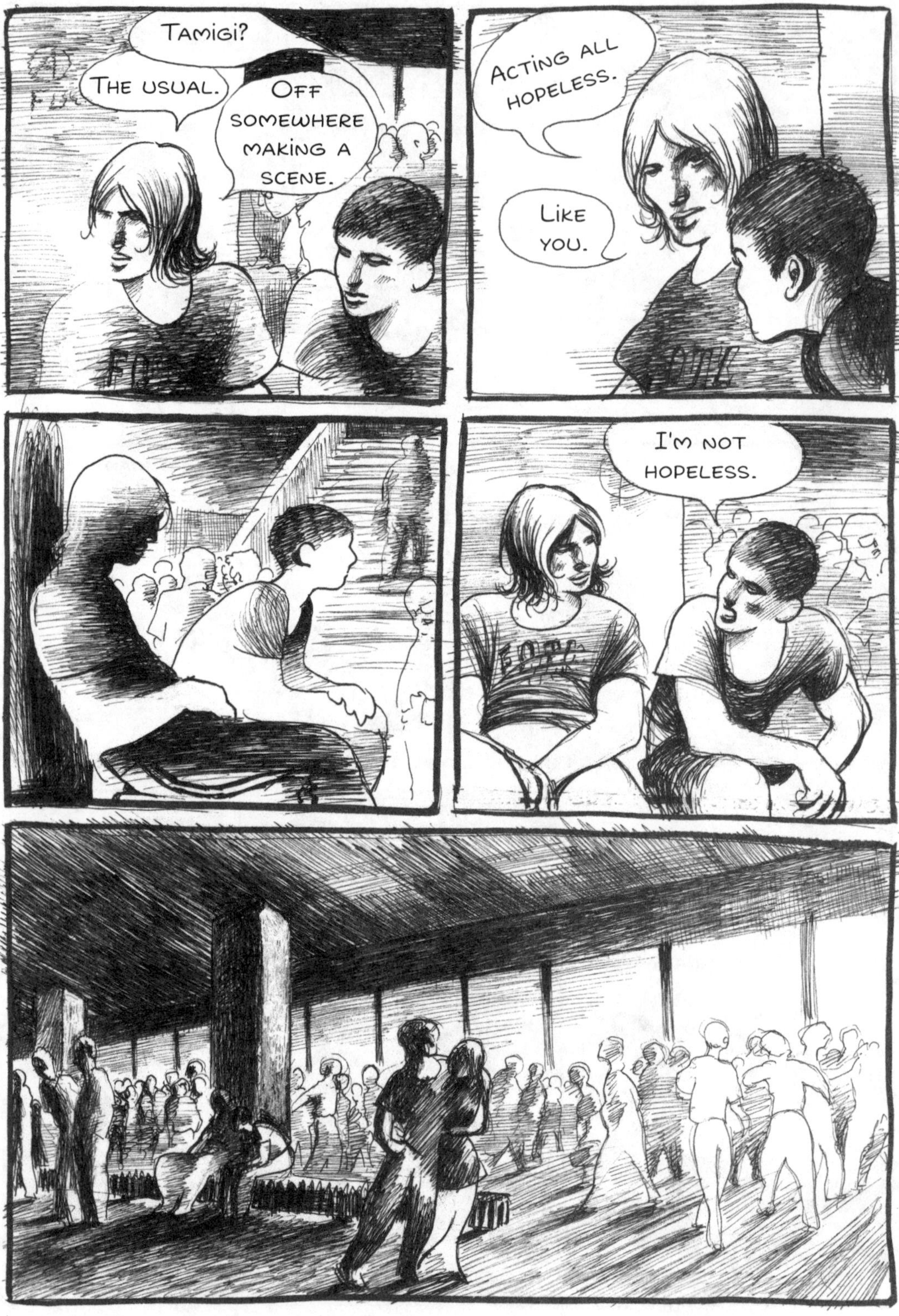
Tamigi?
The usual.
Off somewhere making a scene.
Acting all hopeless.
Like you.
I'm not hopeless.

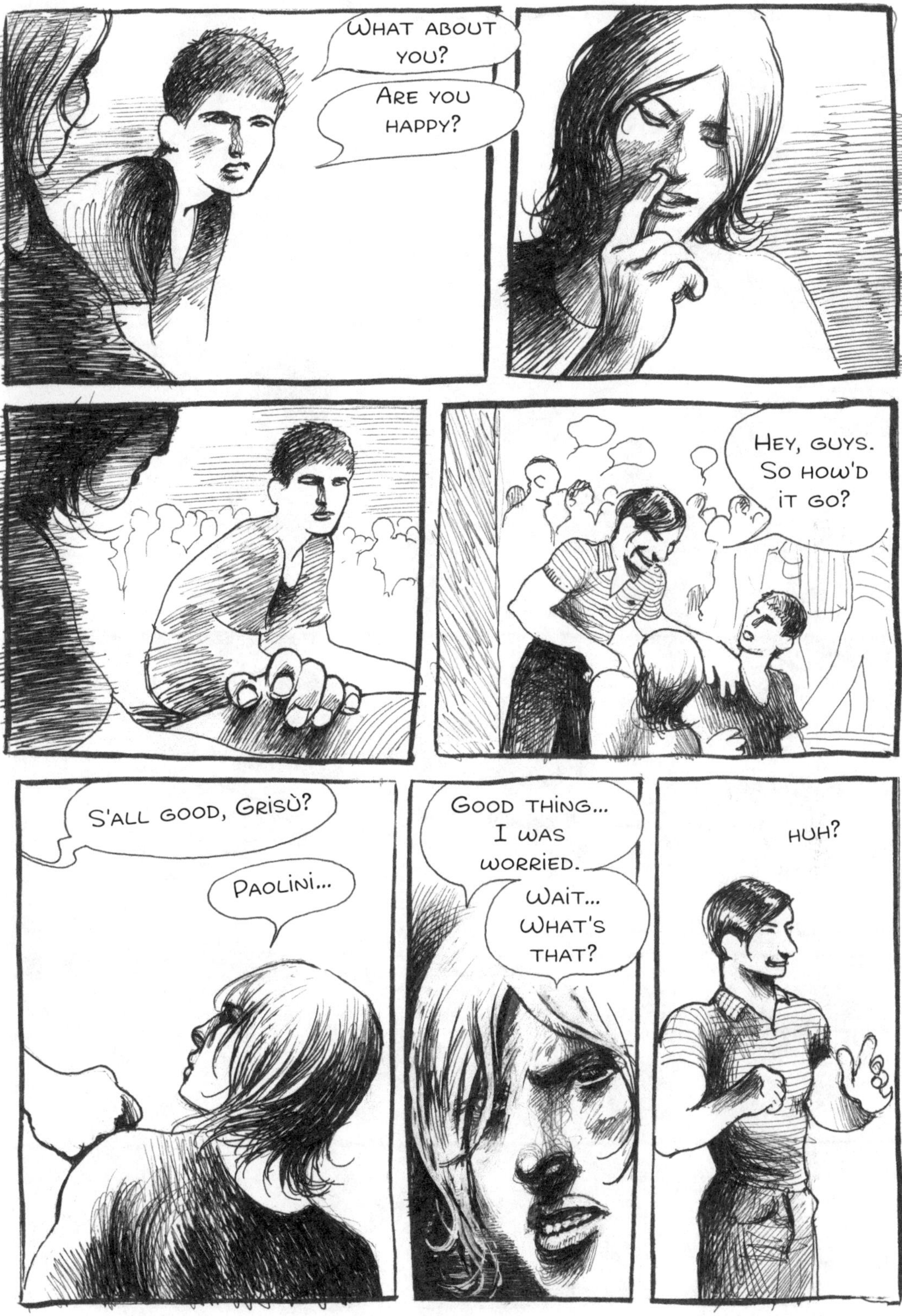
WHAT ABOUT YOU?
ARE YOU HAPPY?
HEY, GUYS. SO HOW'D IT GO?
S'ALL GOOD, GRISÙ?
PAOLINI...
GOOD THING... I WAS WORRIED.
WAIT... WHAT'S THAT?
HUH?

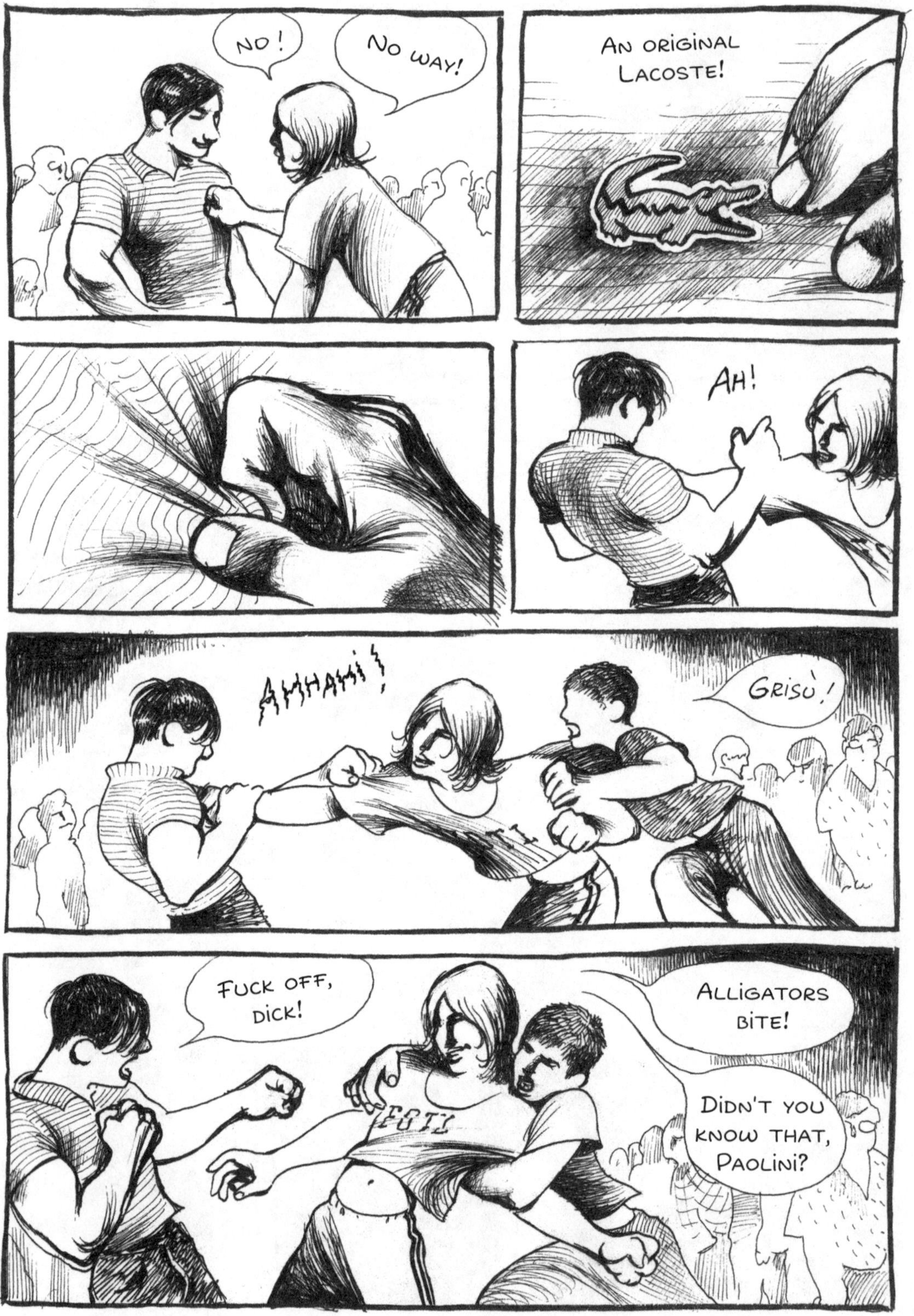
No!
No way!
An original Lacoste!
Ah!
Ahhahh!
Grisù!
Fuck off, dick!
Alligators bite!
Didn't you know that, Paolini?

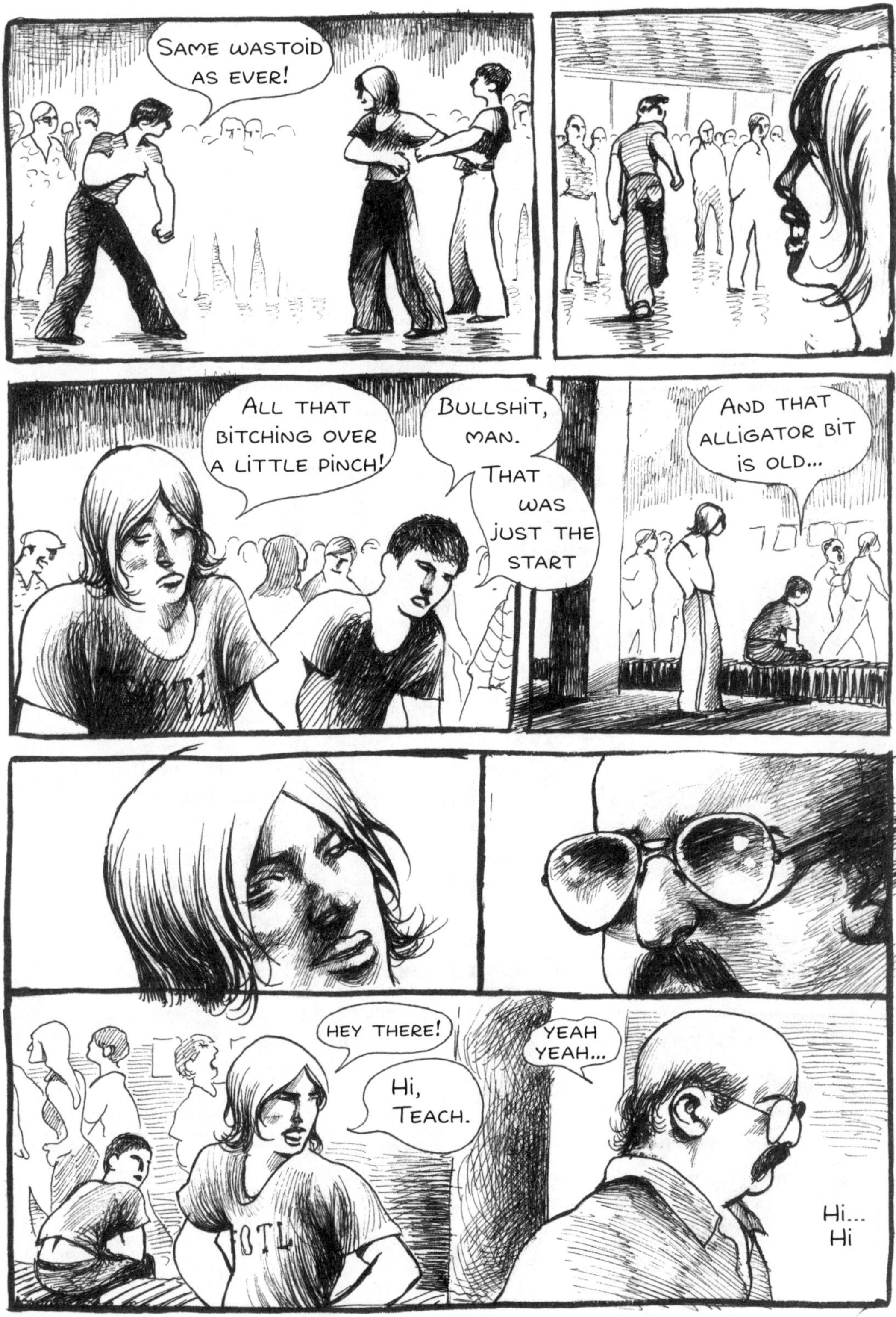
Same wastoid as ever!
All that bitching over a little pinch!
Bullshit, man.
That was just the start
And that alligator bit is old...
Hey there!
Hi, Teach.
Yeah yeah...
Hi... Hi

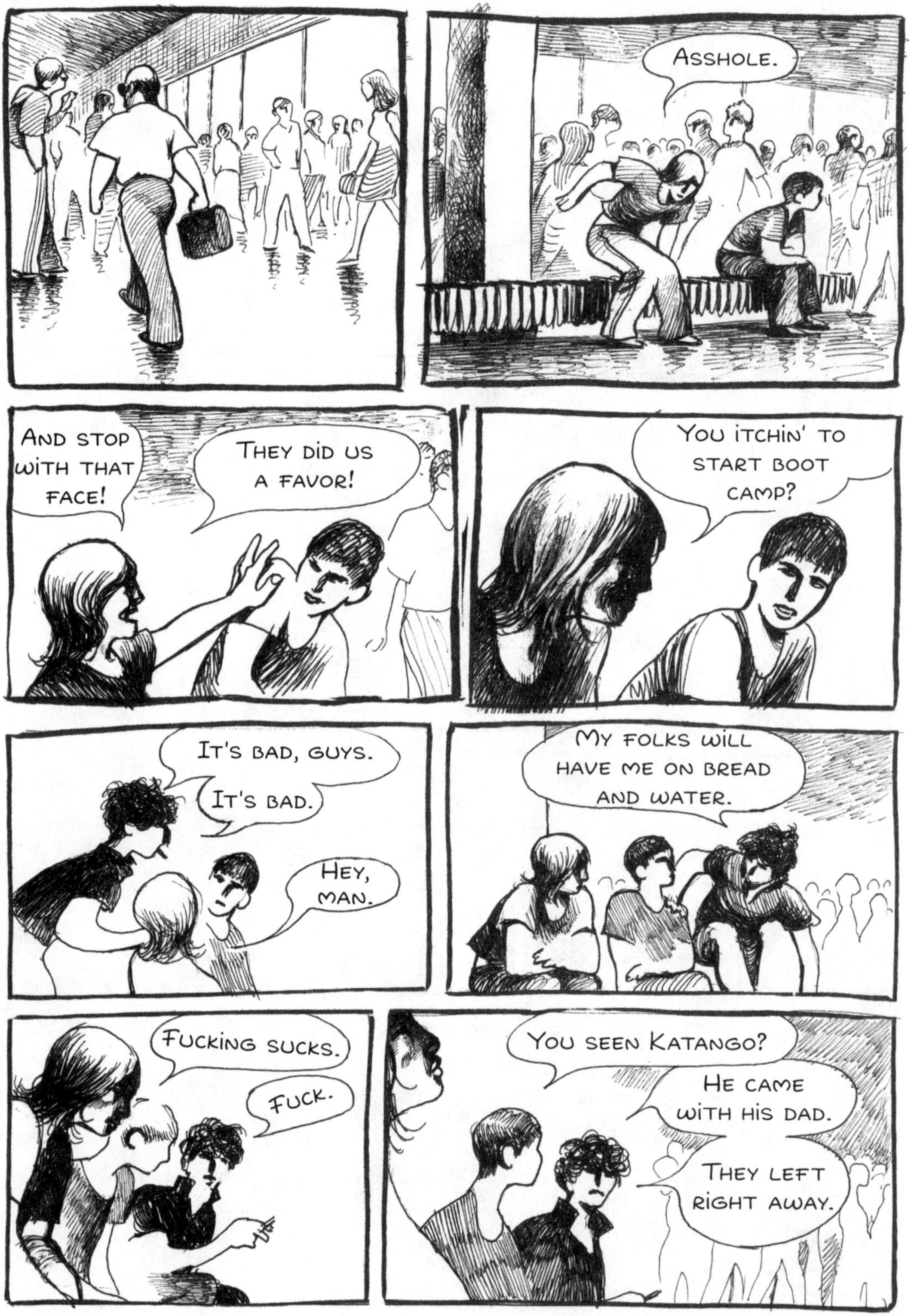
Asshole.
And stop with that face!
They did us a favor!
You itchin' to start boot camp?
It's bad, guys.
It's bad.
Hey, man.
My folks will have me on bread and water.
Fucking sucks.
Fuck.
You seen Katango?
He came with his dad.
They left right away.

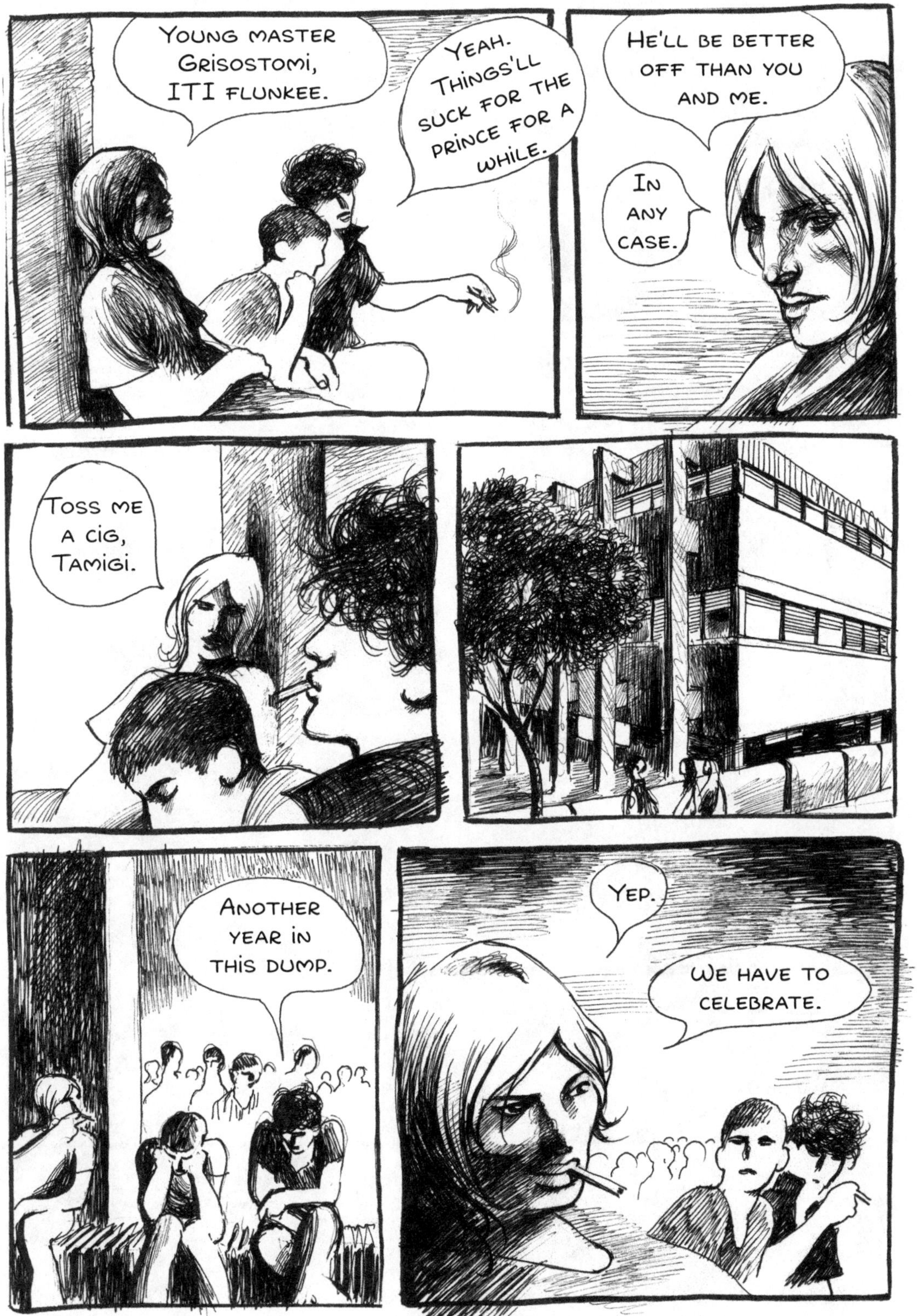
Young master Grisostomi, ITI flunkee.
Yeah. Things'll suck for the prince for a while.
He'll be better off than you and me.
In any case.
Toss me a cig, Tamigi.
Another year in this dump.
Yep.
We have to celebrate.

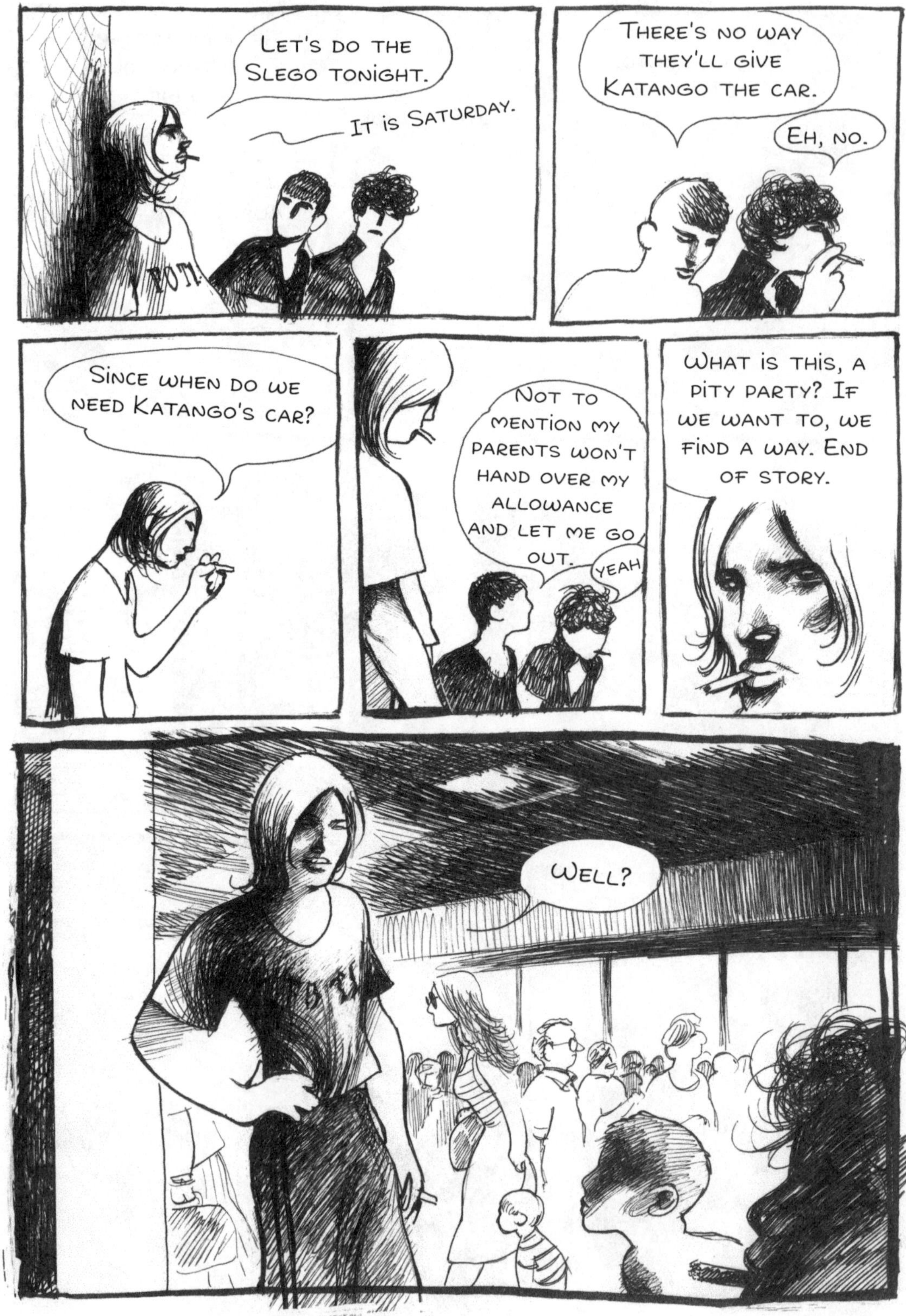
Let's do the Slego tonight.
It is Saturday.
There's no way they'll give Katango the car.
Eh, no.
Since when do we need Katango's car?
Not to mention my parents won't hand over my allowance and let me go out.
Yeah
What is this, a pity party? If we want to, we find a way. End of story.
Well?

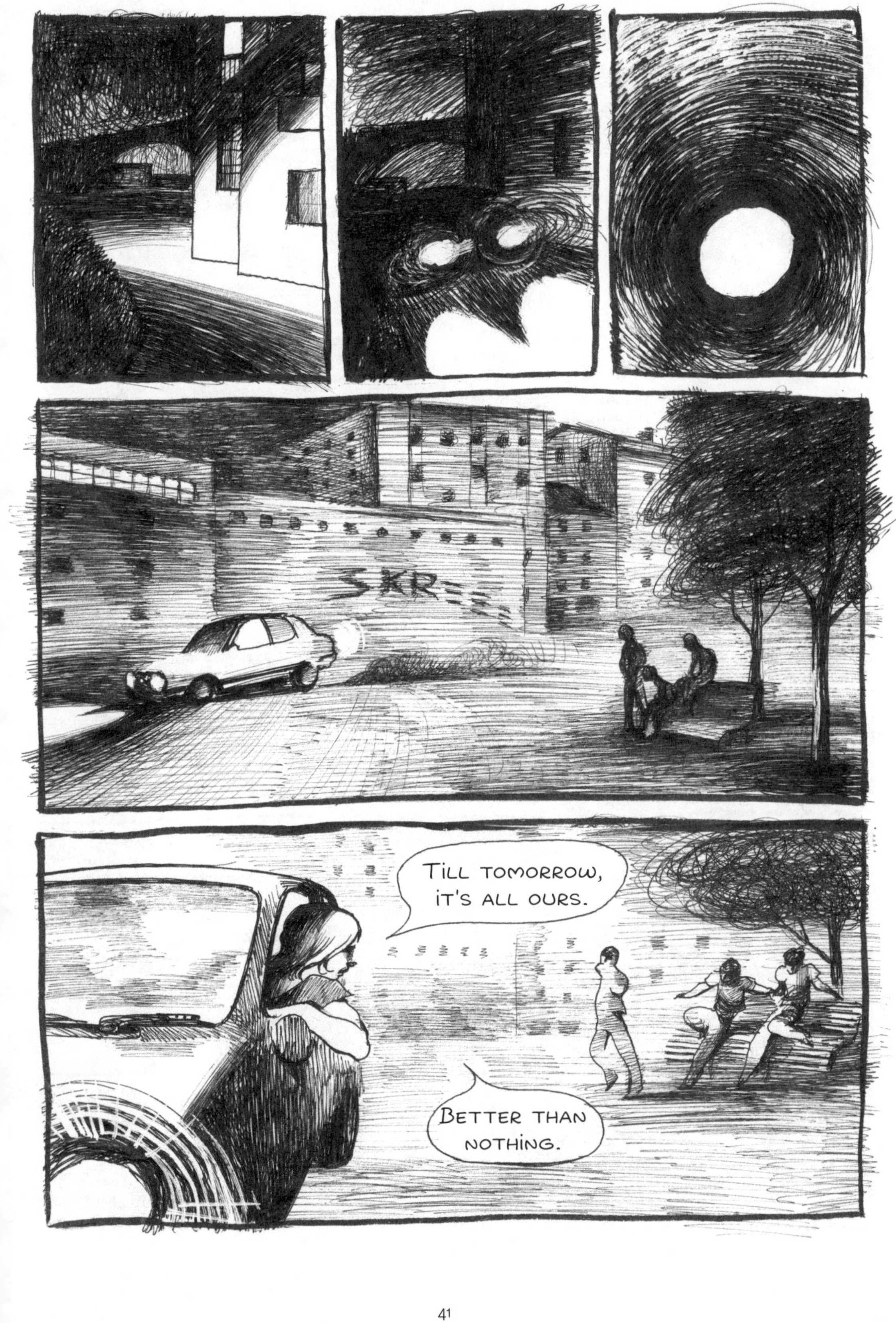
Till tomorrow, it's all ours.
Better than nothing.

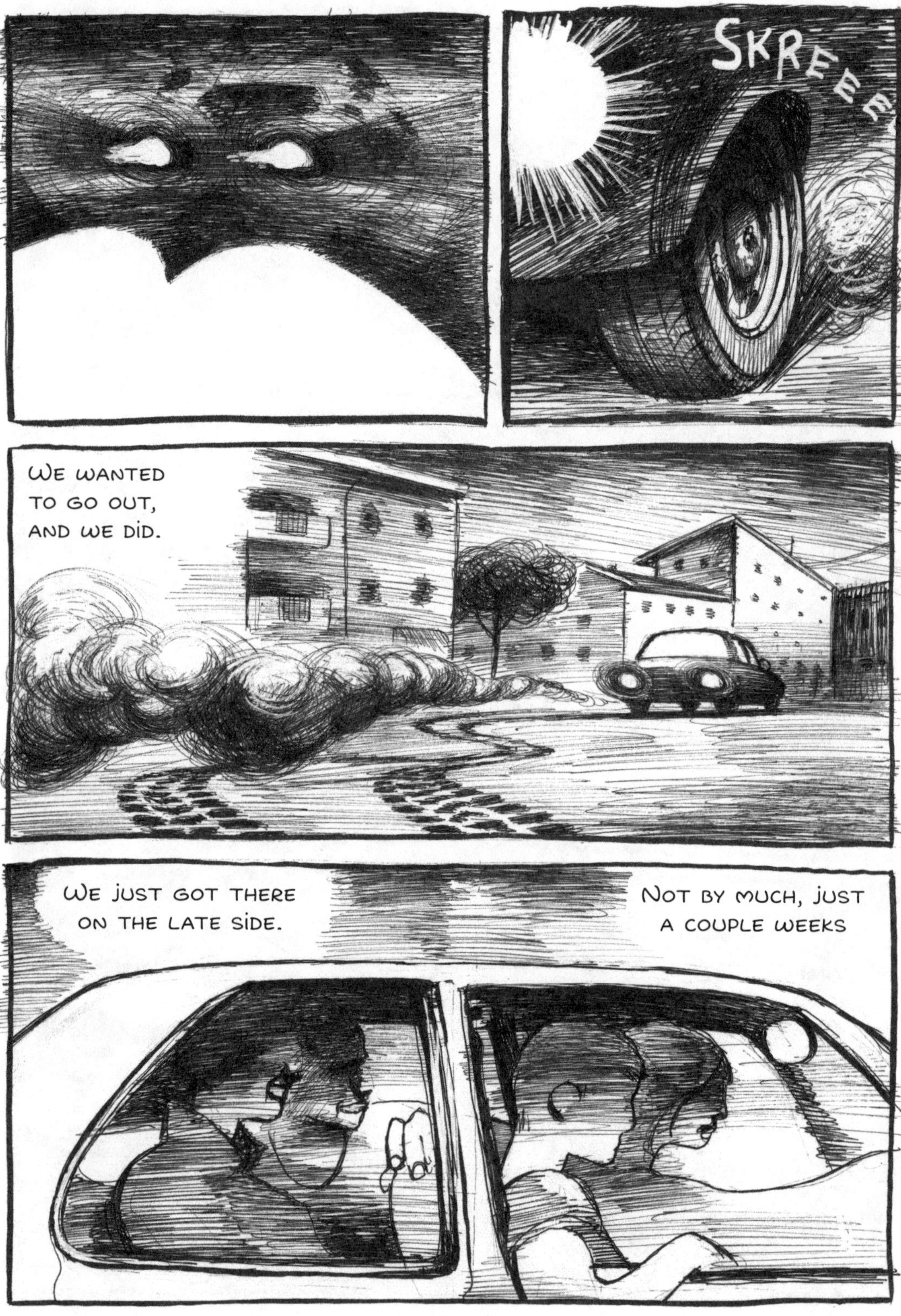
SKREEE
WE WANTED TO GO OUT, AND WE DID.
WE JUST GOT THERE ON THE LATE SIDE.
NOT BY MUCH, JUST A COUPLE WEEKS

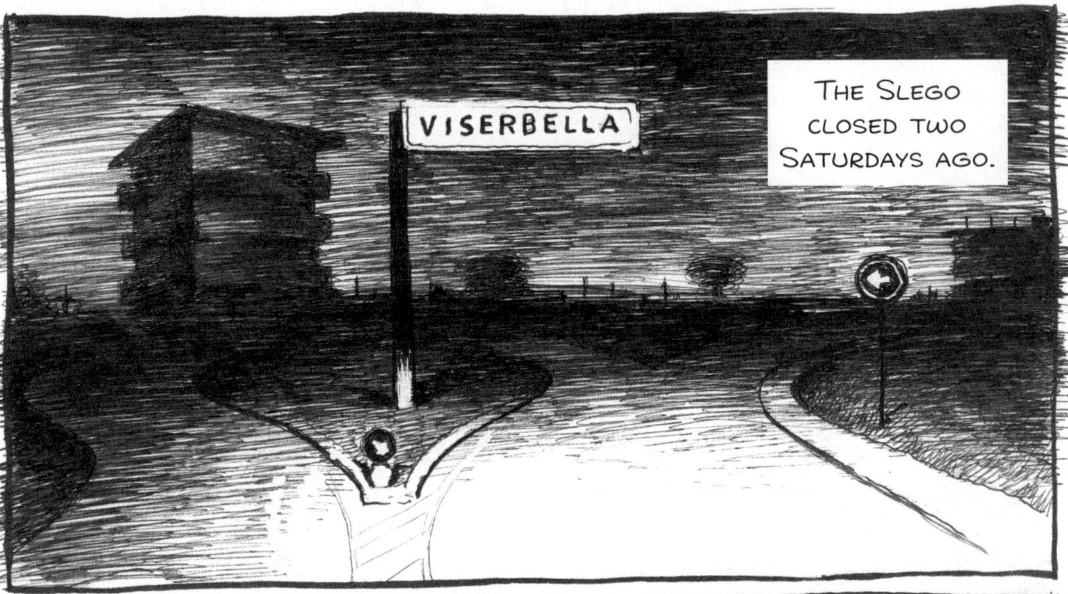
VISERBELLA
The Slego closed two Saturdays ago.

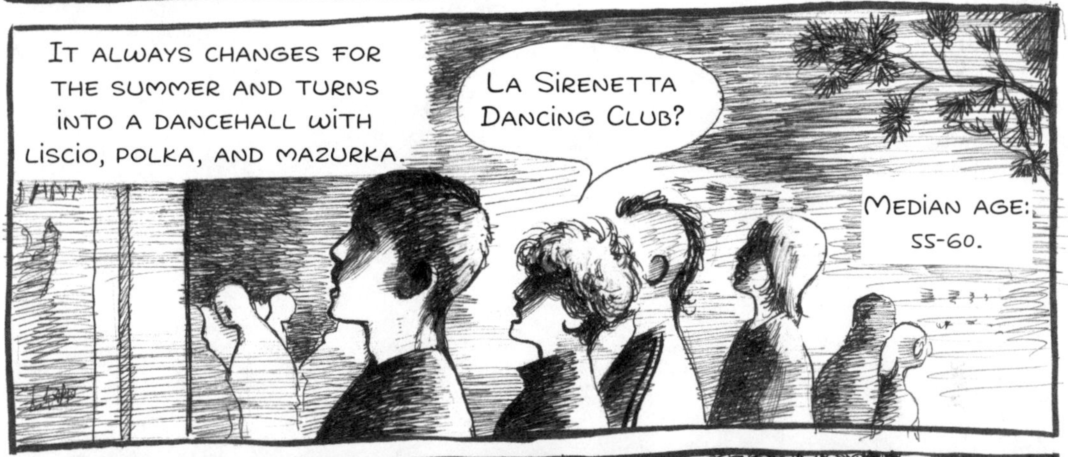
It always changes for the summer and turns into a dancehall with liscio, polka, and mazurka.
La Sirenetta Dancing Club?
Median age: 55-60.

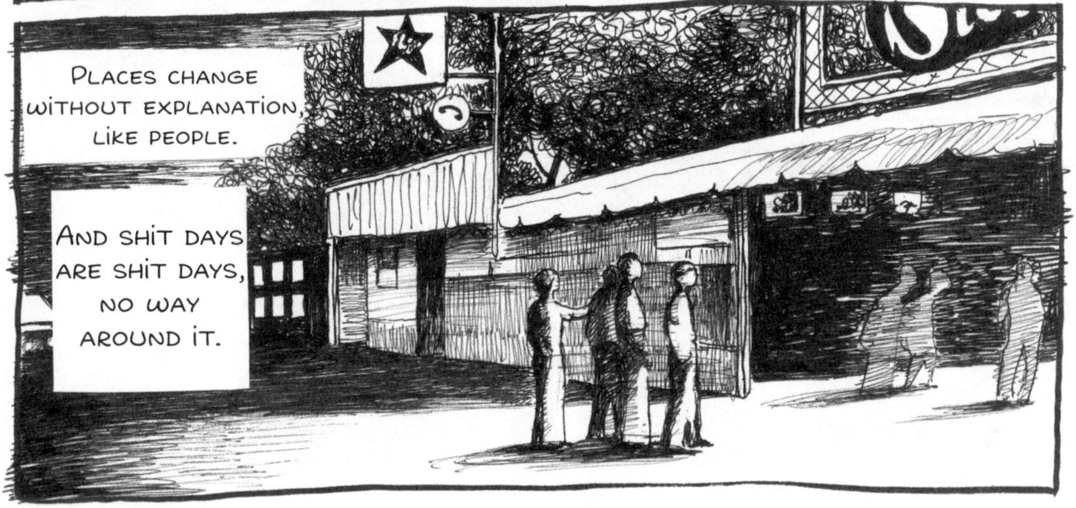
Places change without explanation, like people.
And shit days are shit days, no way around it.

II

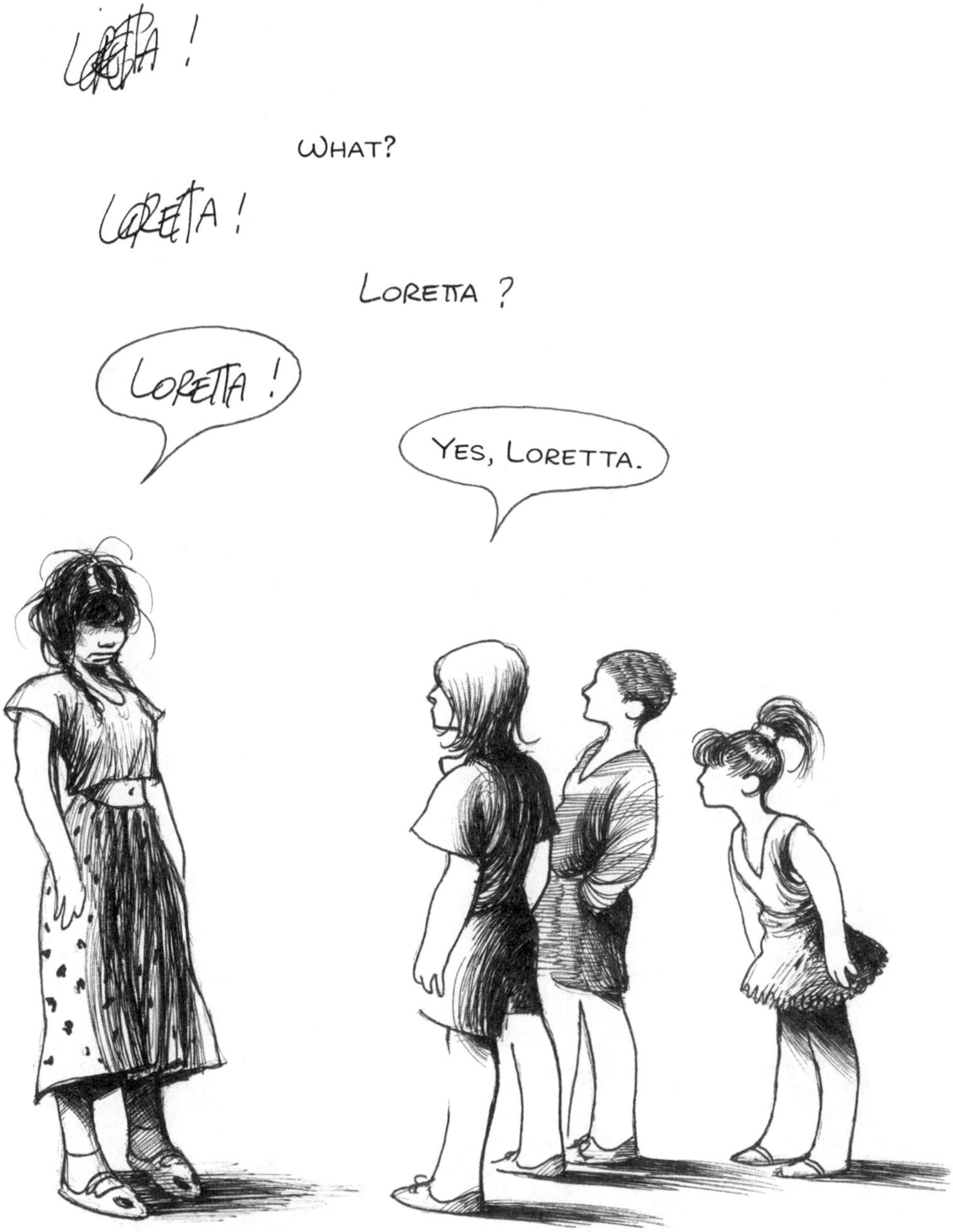
WHAT?
LORETTA!
LORETTA?
LORETTA!
YES, LORETTA.

MUTILATED TOYS.

ALL KINDS OF
BITS AND PIECES.

CARTRIDGES AND
CASINGS.

RUSTED COPPER POTS.

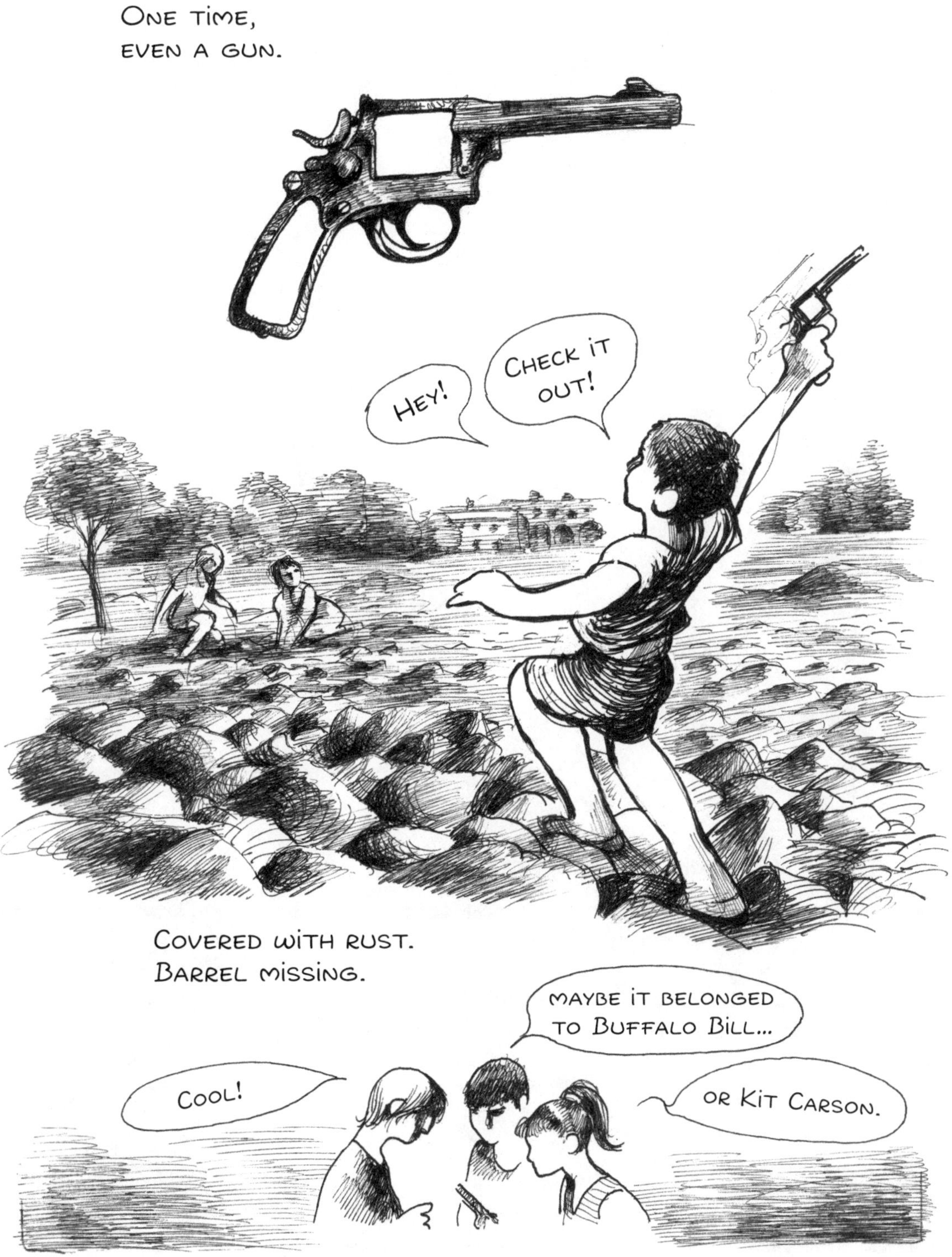
ONE TIME,
EVEN A GUN.
HEY!
CHECK IT OUT!
COVERED WITH RUST.
BARREL MISSING.
MAYBE IT BELONGED TO BUFFALO BILL...
COOL!
OR KIT CARSON.

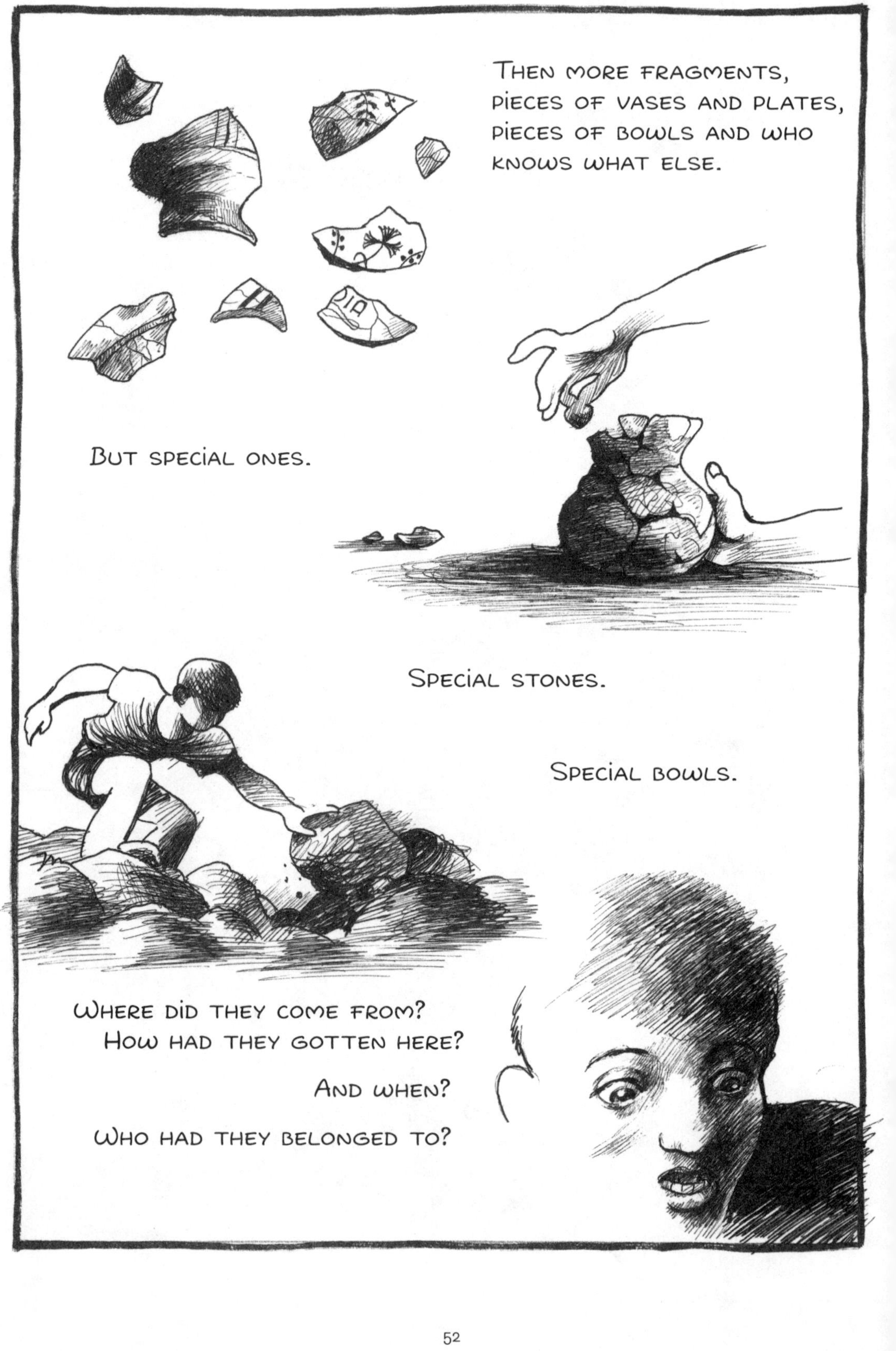
Then more fragments, pieces of vases and plates, pieces of bowls and who knows what else.
But special ones.
Special stones.
Special bowls.
Where did they come from?
How had they gotten here?
And when?
Who had they belonged to?

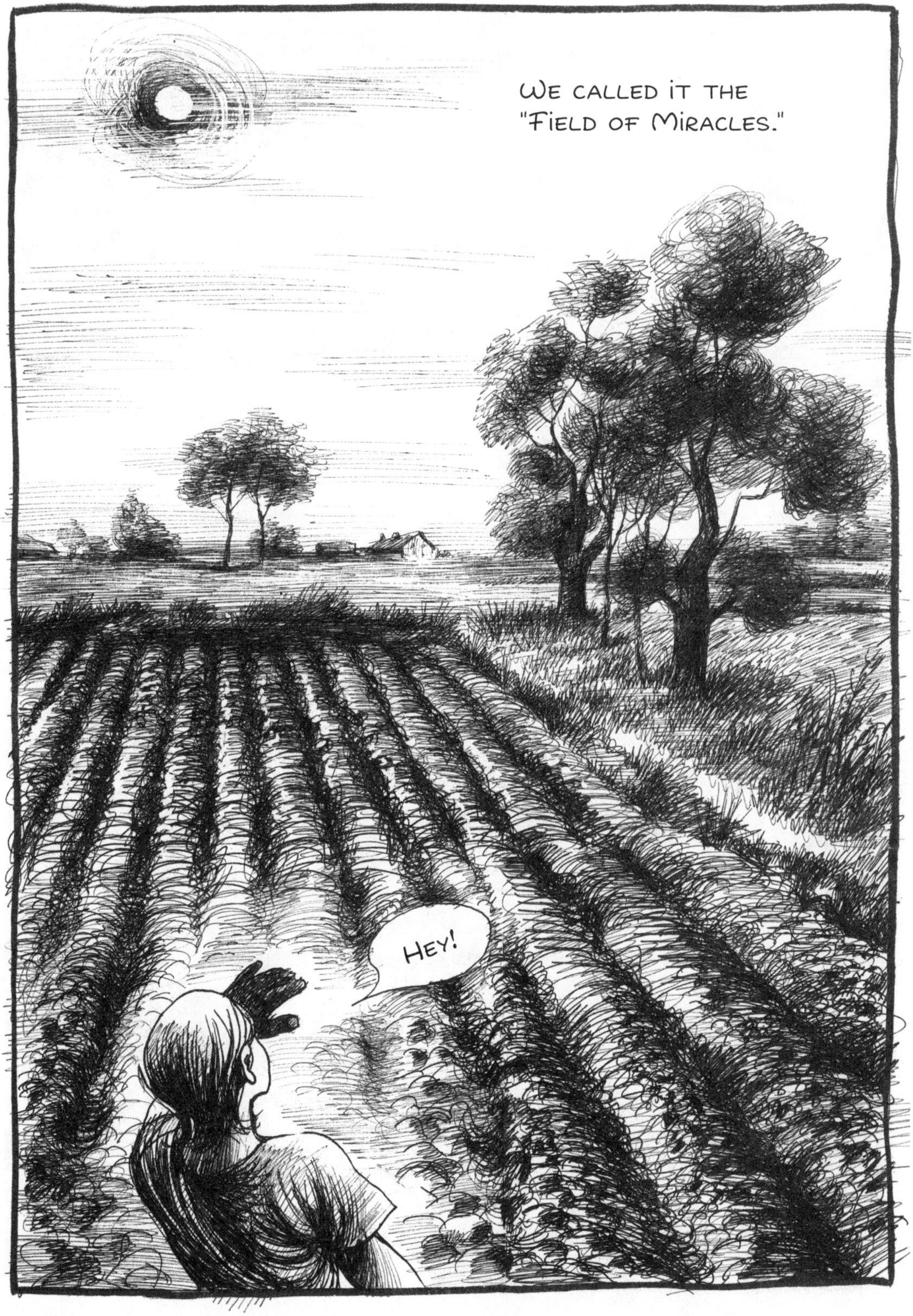
We called it the "Field of Miracles."
Hey!

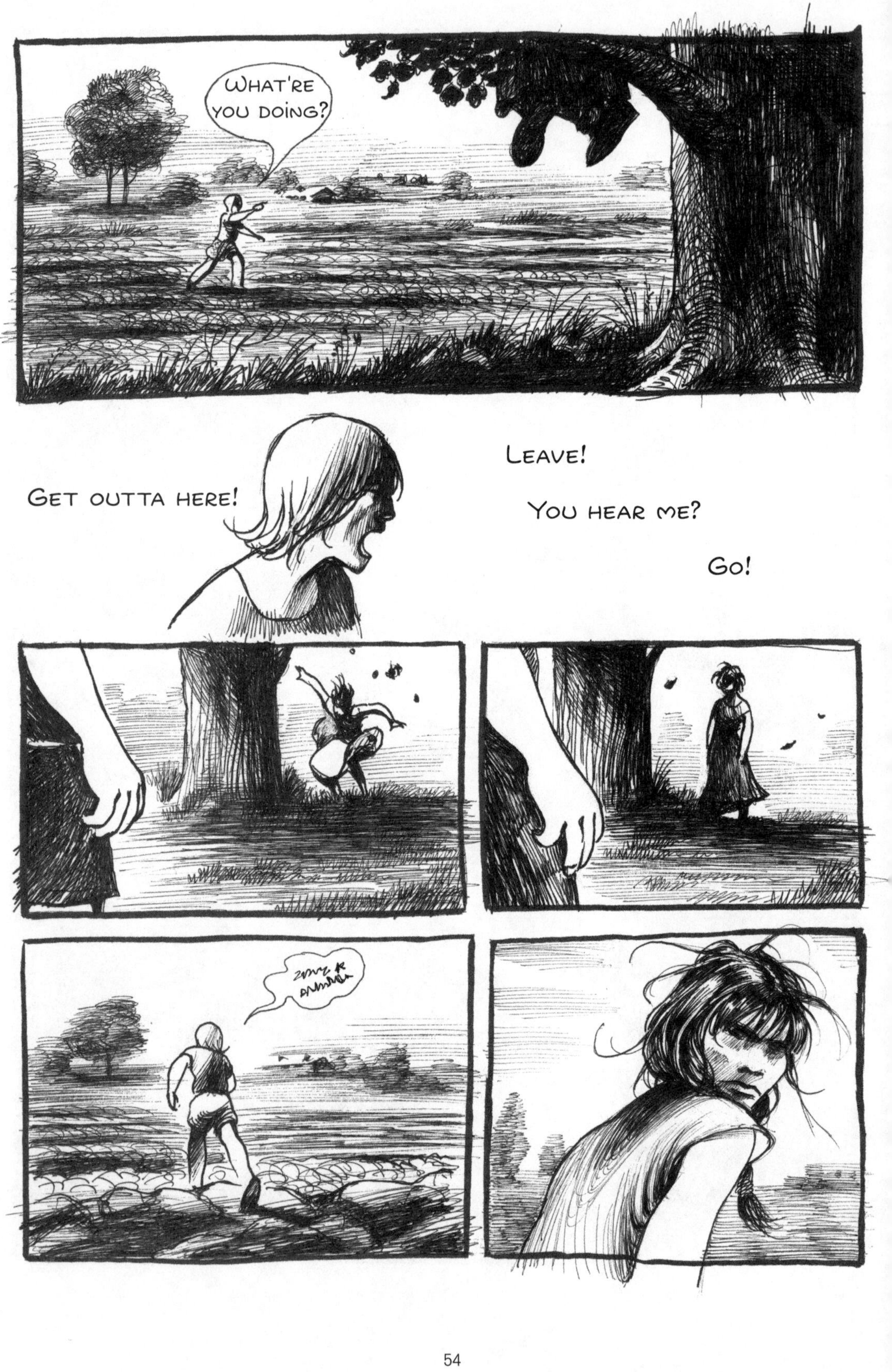
WHAT'RE YOU DOING?
GET OUTTA HERE!
LEAVE!
YOU HEAR ME?
GO!

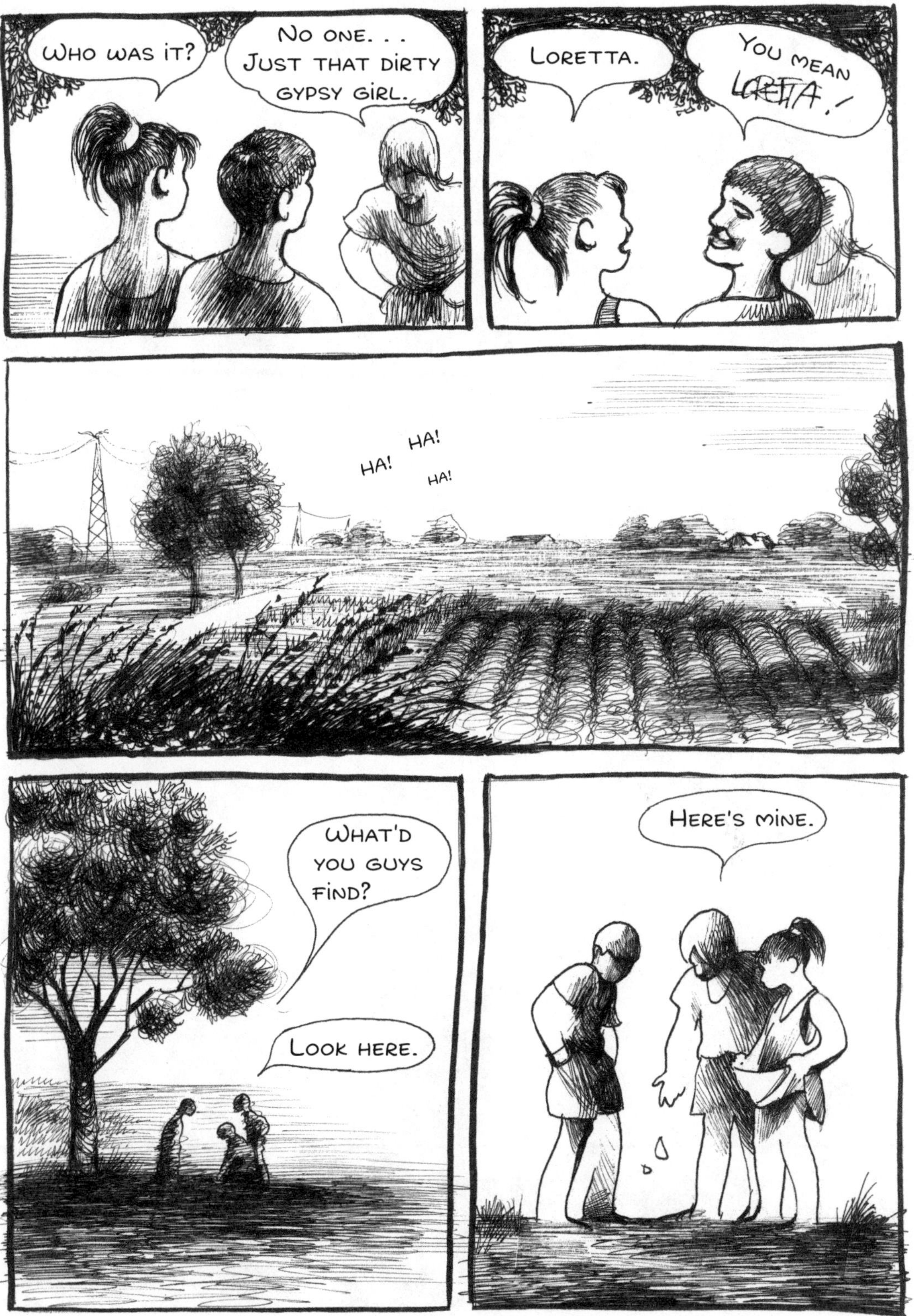
Who was it?
No one. . . Just that dirty gypsy girl.
Loretta.
You mean Loretta!
HA! HA! HA!
What'd you guys find?
Look here.
Here's mine.

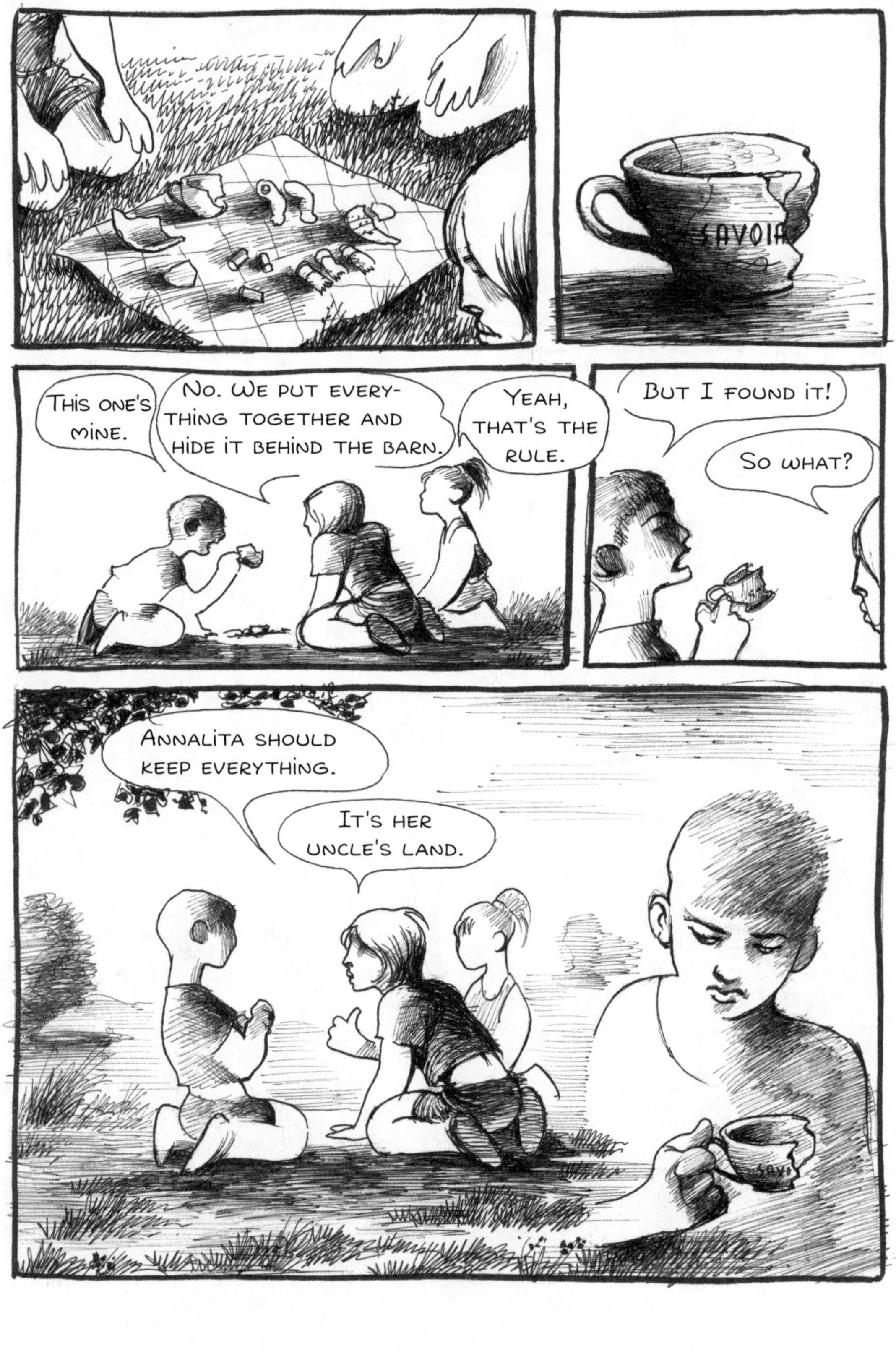
SAVOIA
This one's mine.
No. We put every-thing together and hide it behind the barn.
Yeah, that's the rule.
But I found it!
So what?
Annalita should keep everything.
It's her uncle's land.
SAVO

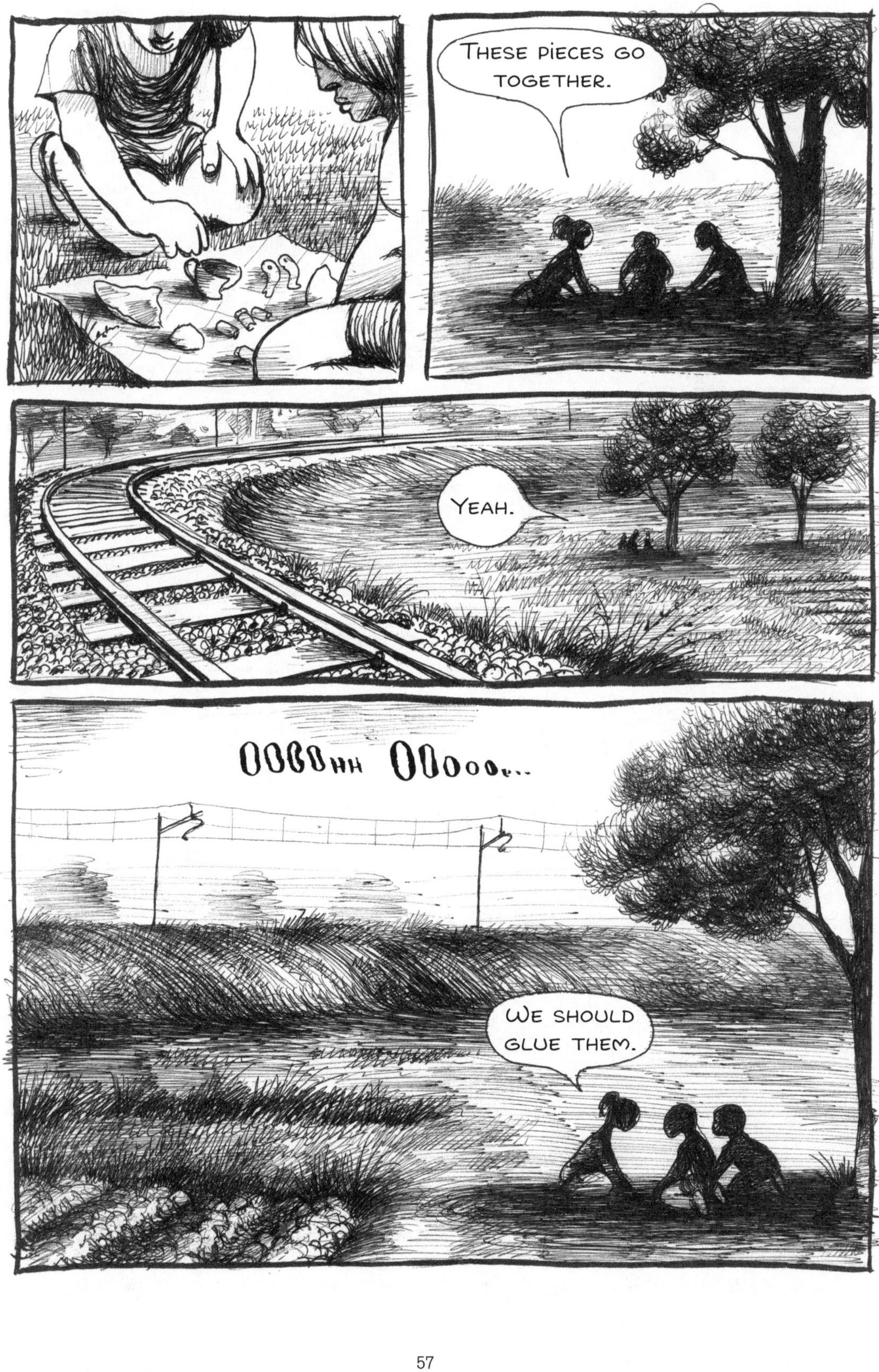
These pieces go together.
Yeah.
OOOOhh OOooo...
We should glue them.

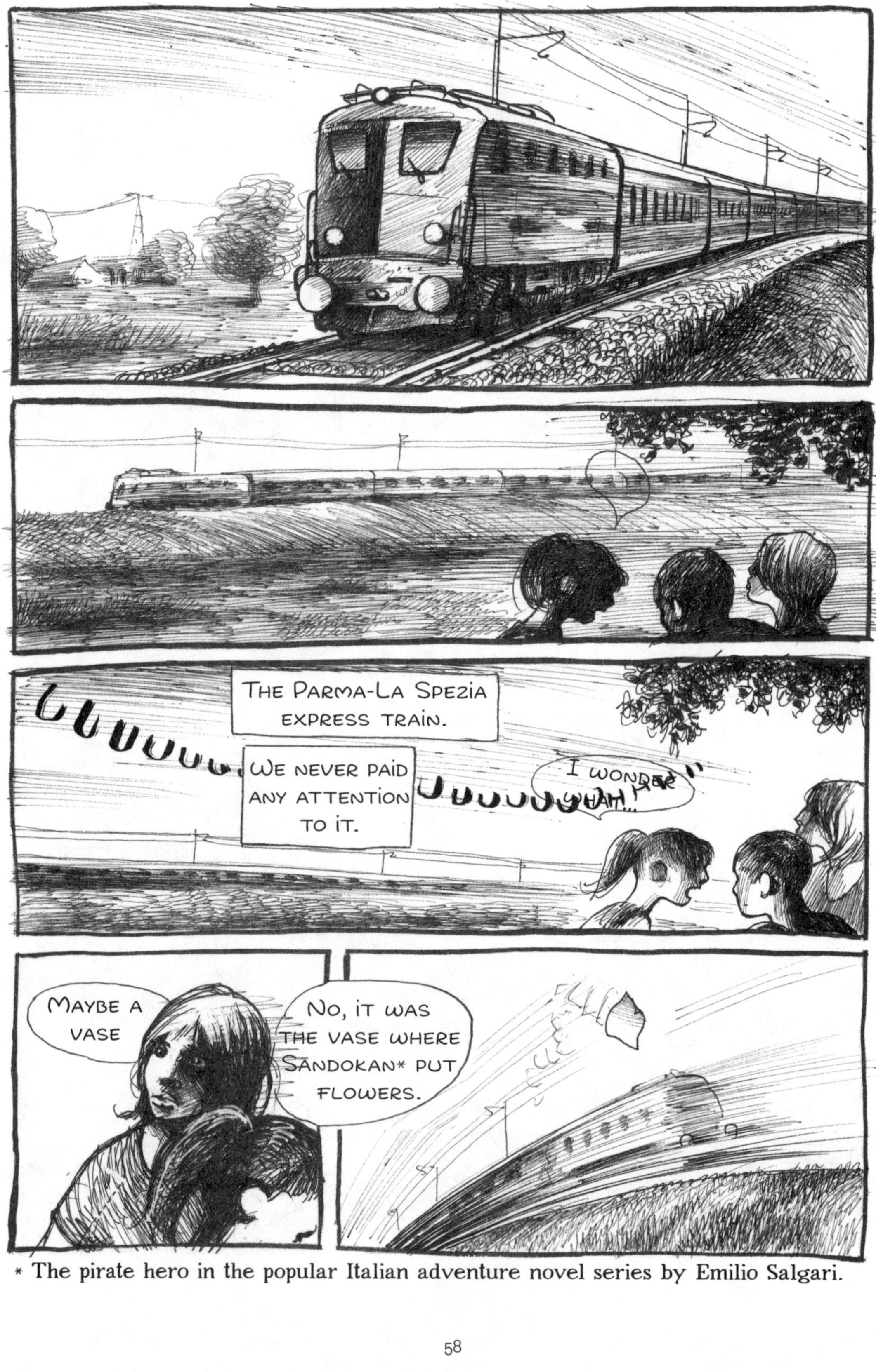

The Parma-La Spezia express train.
We never paid any attention to it.
I wonder what...
Maybe a vase
No, it was the vase where Sandokan* put flowers.

* The pirate hero in the popular Italian adventure novel series by Emilio Salgari.

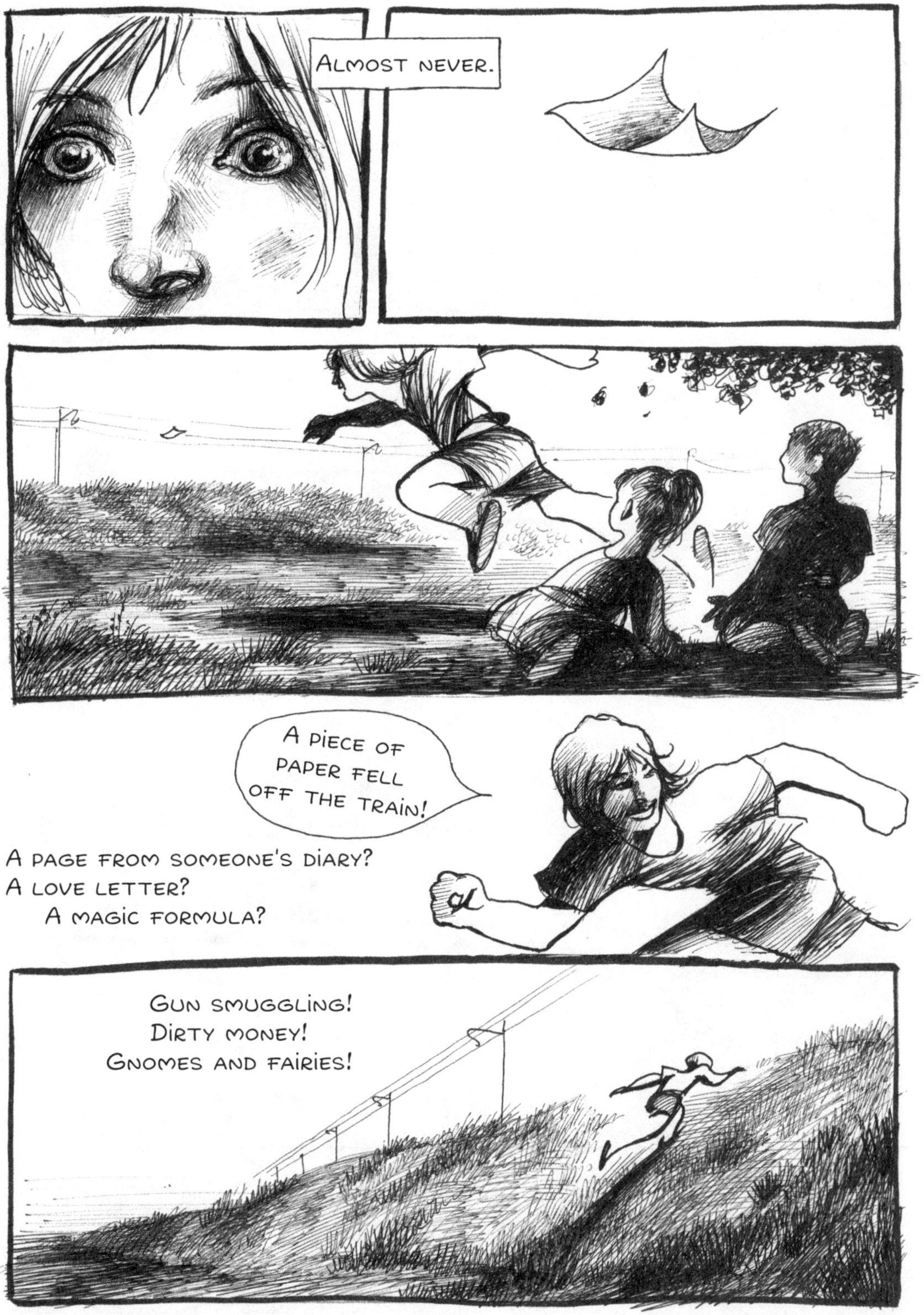
Almost never.
A piece of paper fell off the train!
A page from someone's diary?
A love letter?
A magic formula?
Gun smuggling!
Dirty money!
Gnomes and fairies!

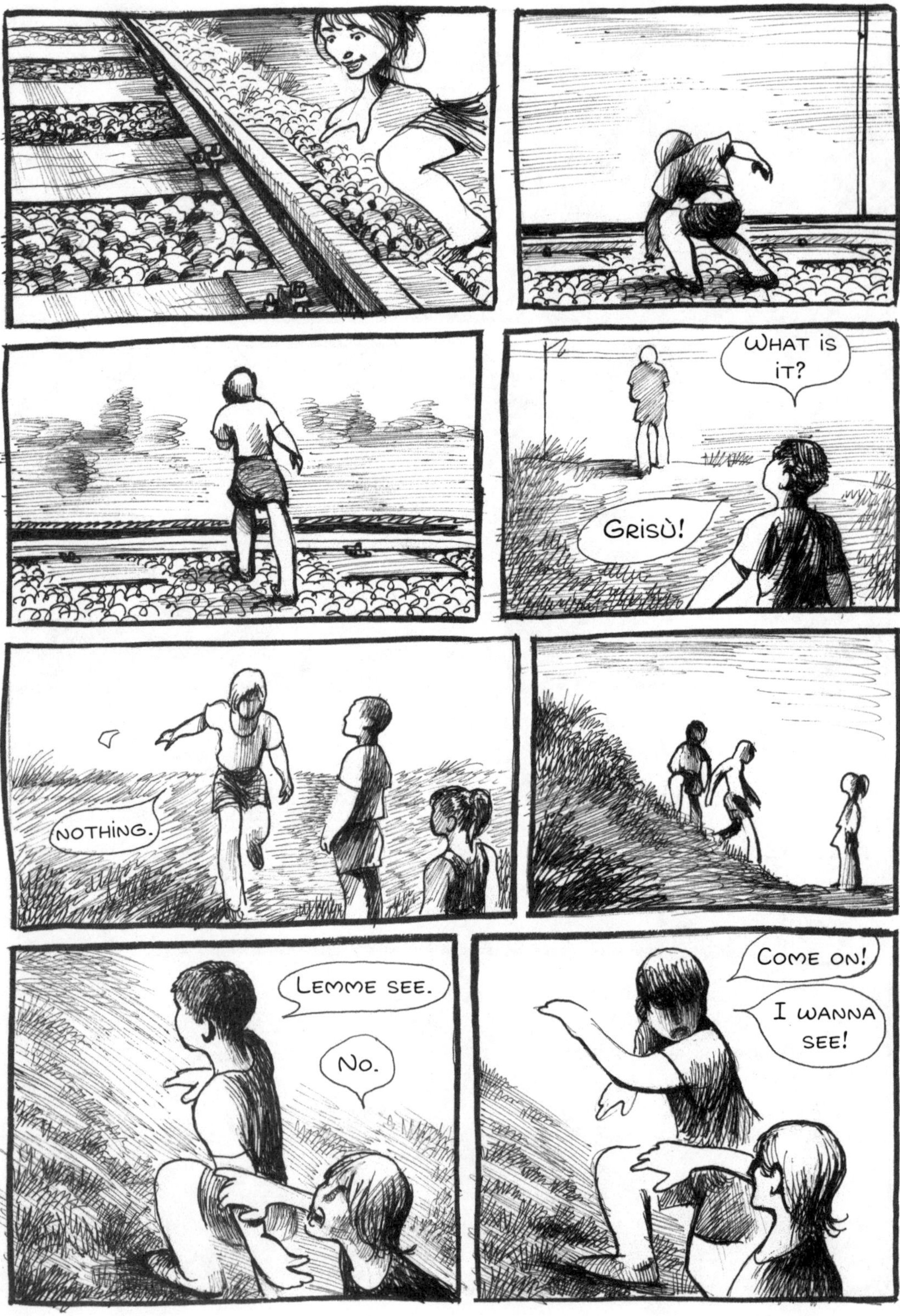
WHAT IS IT?
GRISÙ!
NOTHING.
LEMME SEE.
NO.
COME ON!
I WANNA SEE!

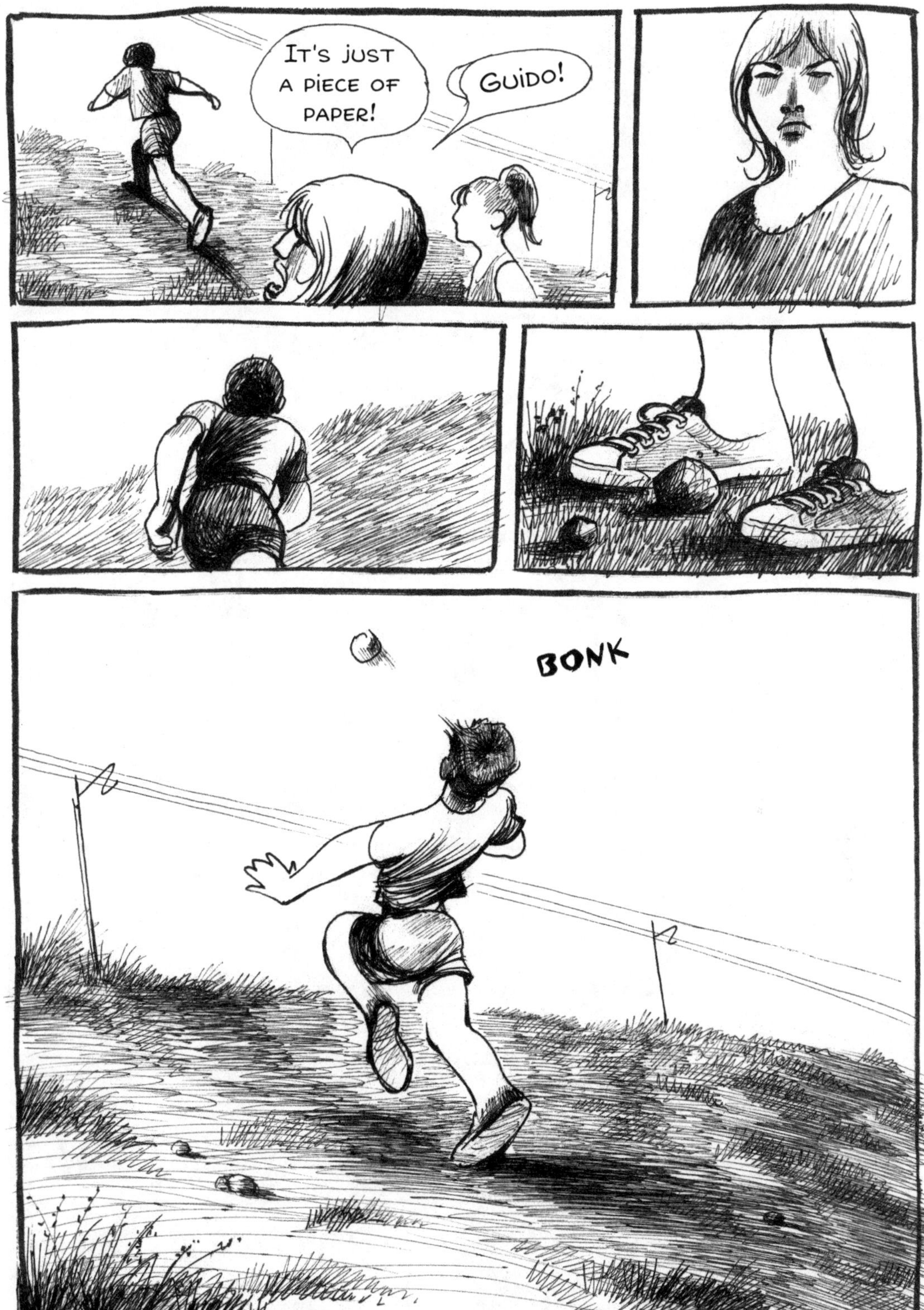
IT'S JUST A PIECE OF PAPER!
GUIDO!
BONK

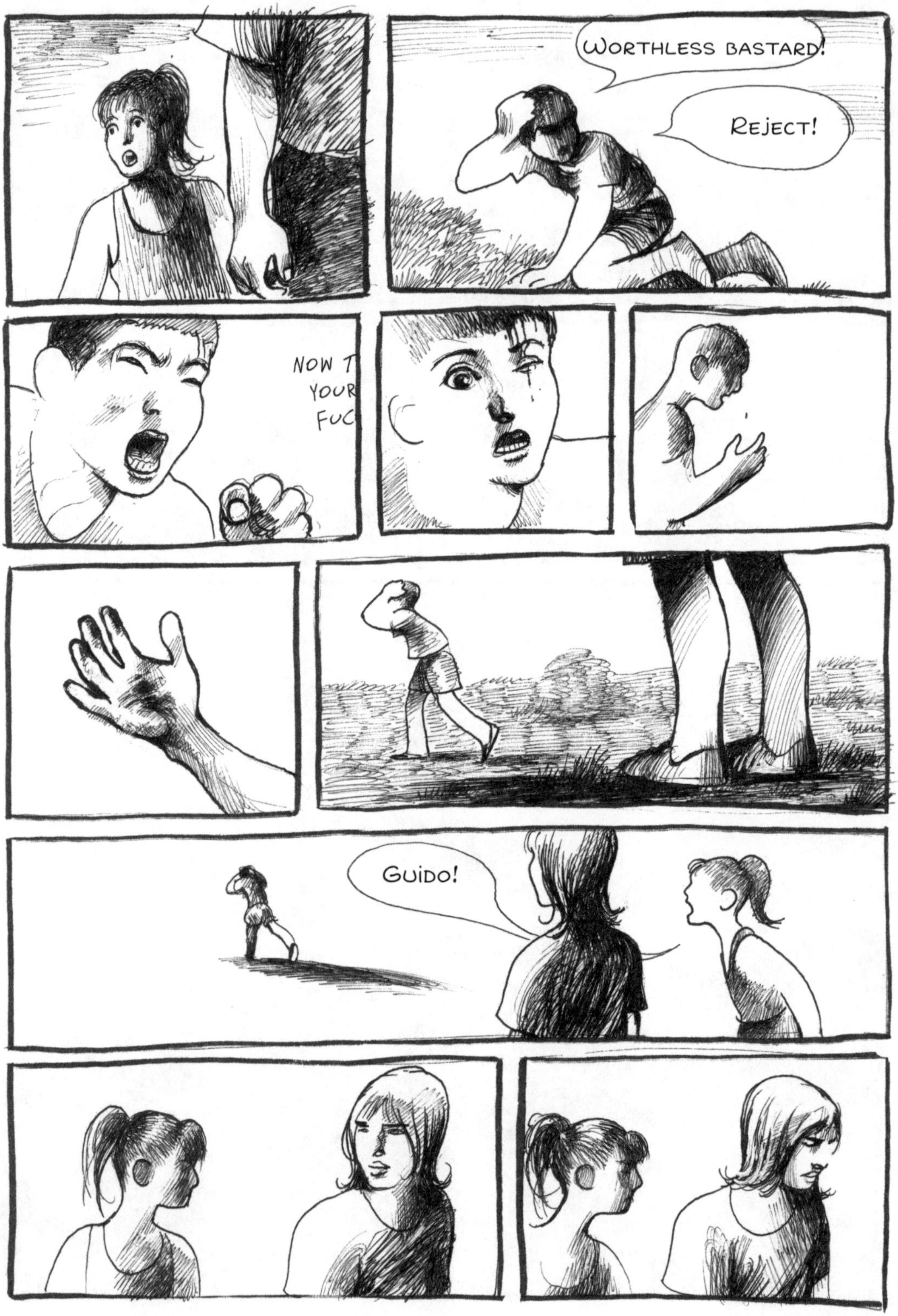
WORTHLESS BASTARD!
REJECT!
NOW T
YOUR
FUC
GUIDO!

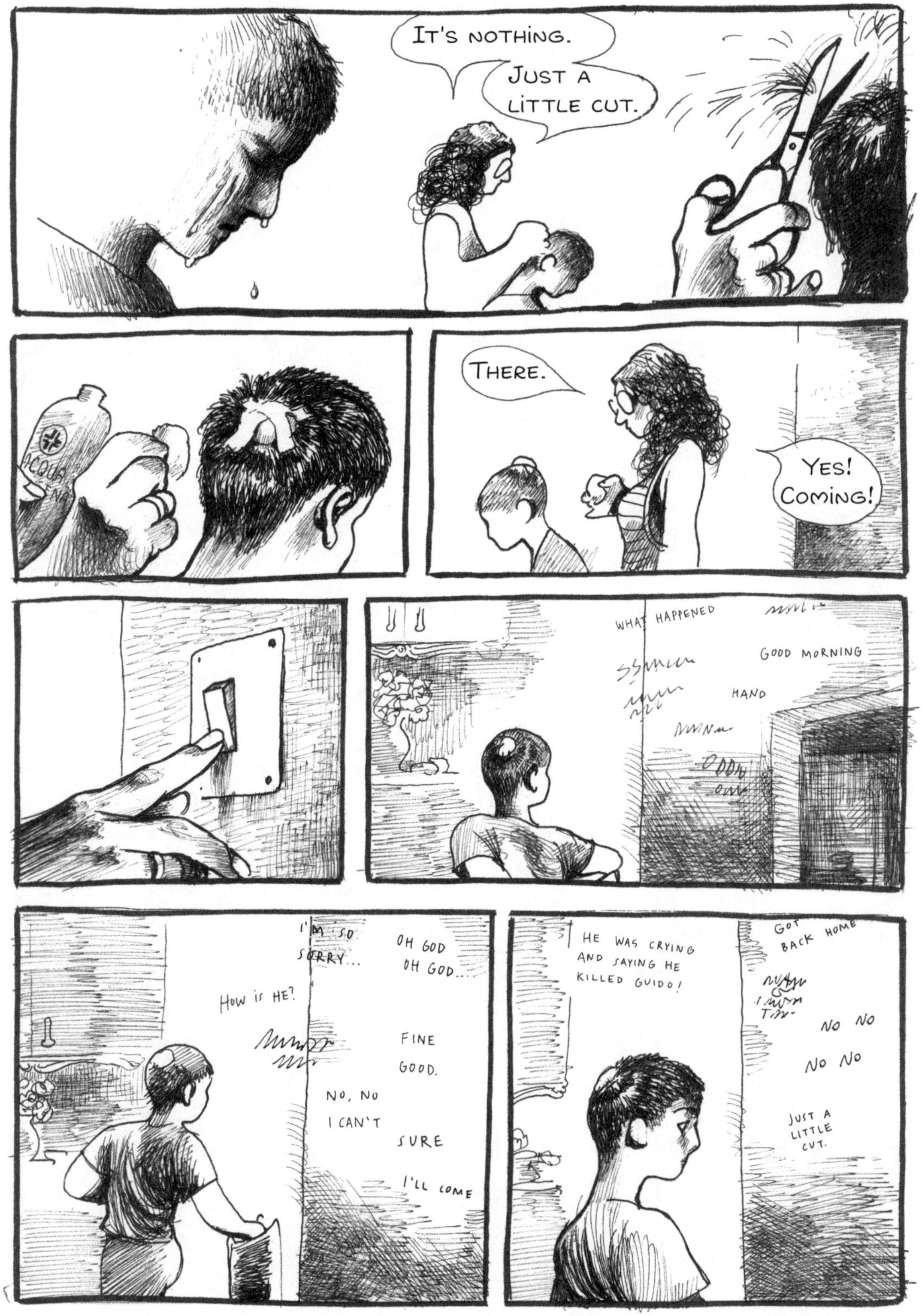
It's nothing.
Just a little cut.
There.
Yes! Coming!
What happened
Good morning
Hand
I'm so sorry...
Oh God oh God...
How is he?
Fine
Good.
No, no I can't
Sure
I'll come
He was crying and saying he killed Guido!
Got back home
No no
No no
Just a little cut.

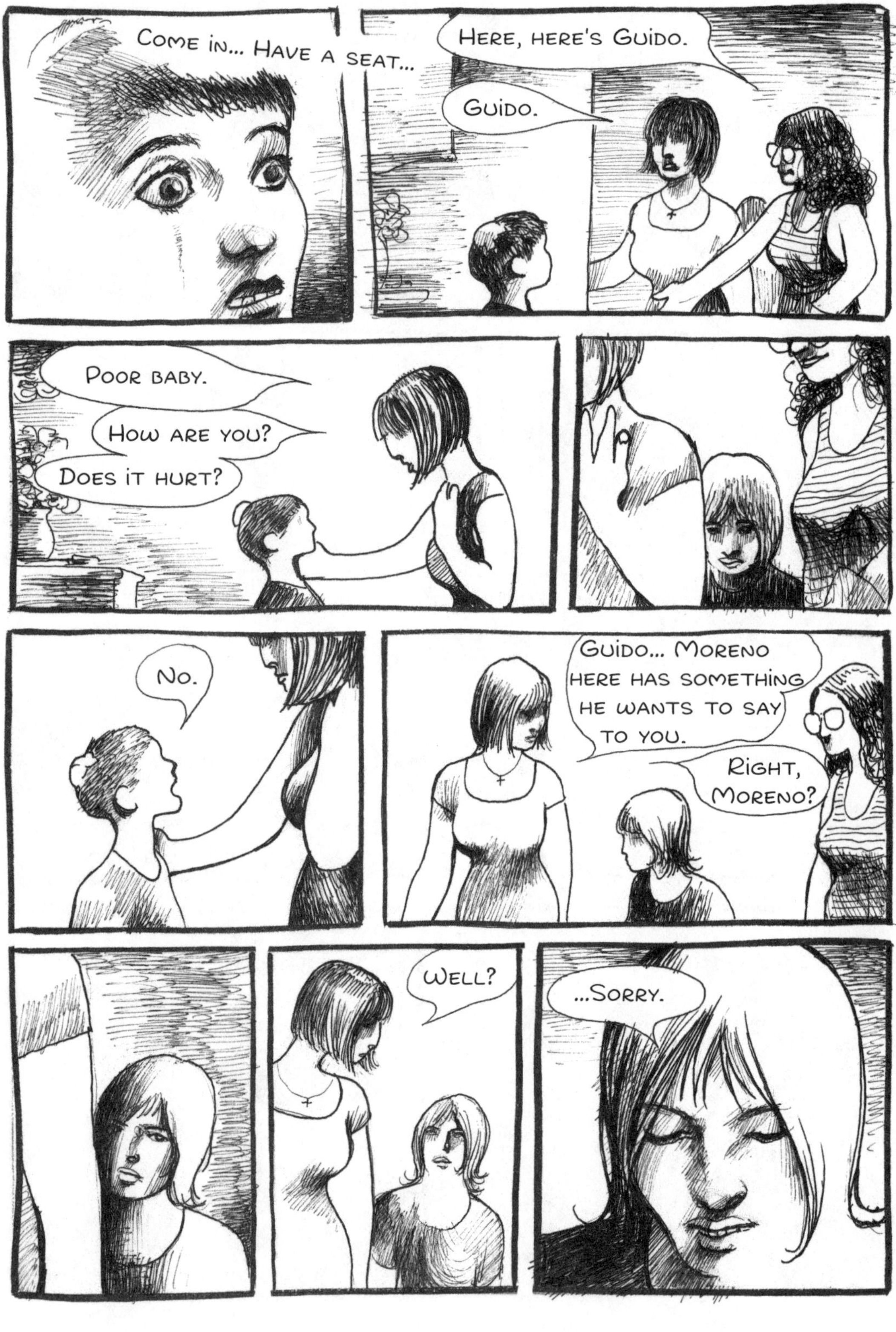
Come in... Have a seat...
Here, here's Guido.
Guido.
Poor baby.
How are you?
Does it hurt?
No.
Guido... Moreno here has something he wants to say to you.
Right, Moreno?
Well?
...Sorry.

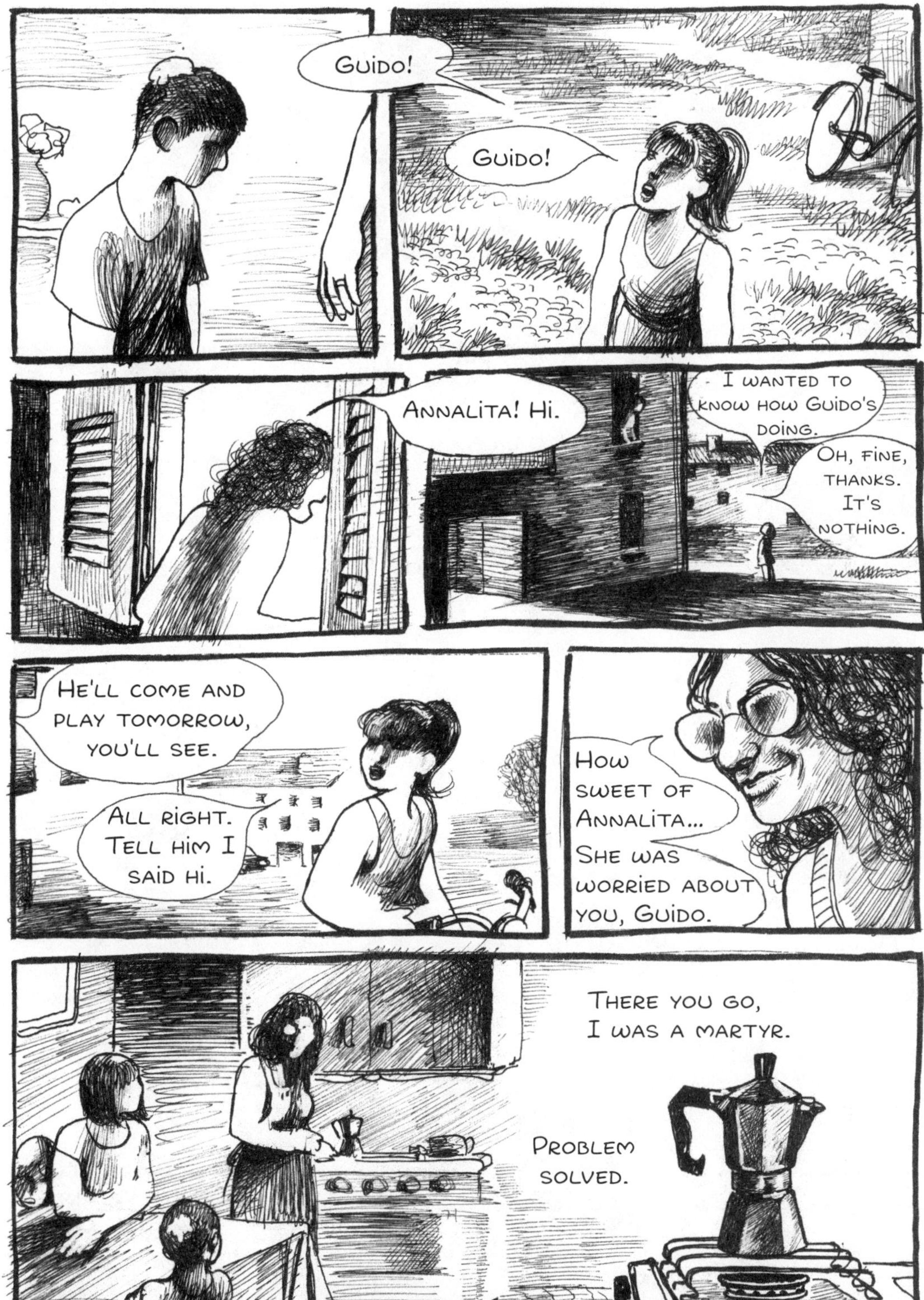
Guido!
Guido!
Annalita! Hi.
I wanted to know how Guido's doing.
Oh, fine, thanks. It's nothing.
He'll come and play tomorrow, you'll see.
All right. Tell him I said hi.
How sweet of Annalita... She was worried about you, Guido.
There you go, I was a martyr.
Problem solved.

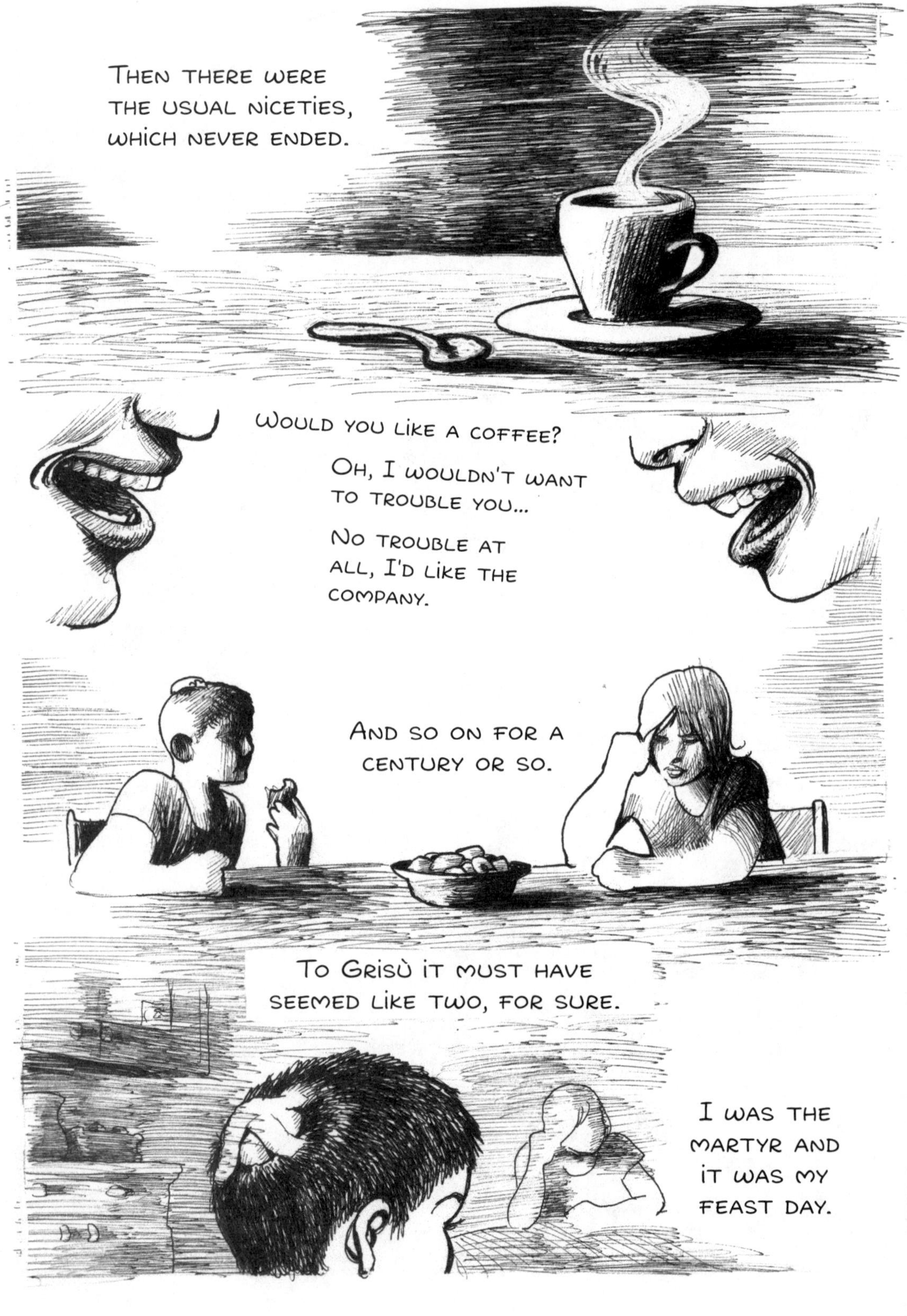
Then there were the usual niceties, which never ended.
Would you like a coffee?
Oh, I wouldn't want to trouble you...
No trouble at all, I'd like the company.
And so on for a century or so.
To Grisù it must have seemed like two, for sure.
I was the martyr and it was my feast day.

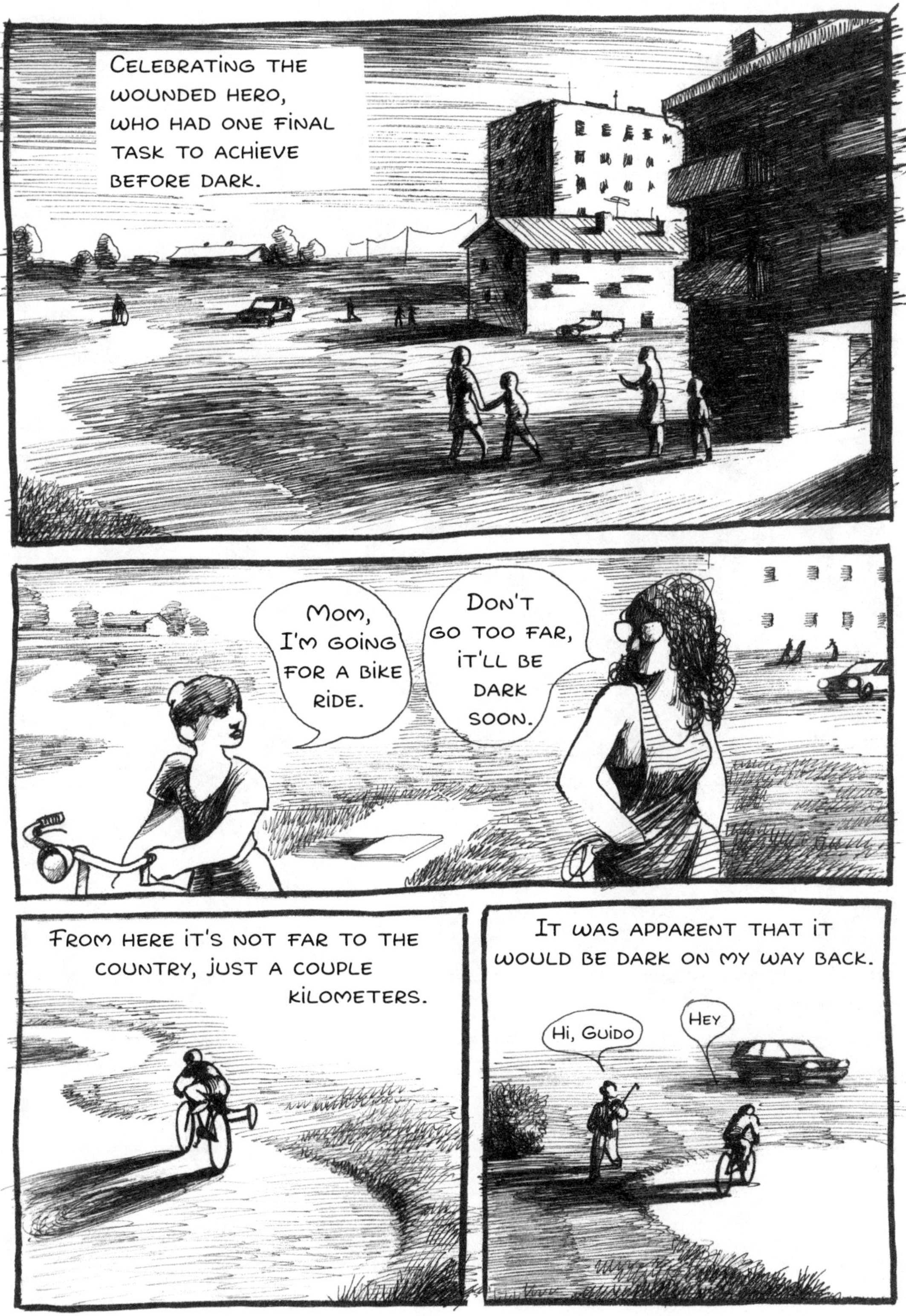

Celebrating the wounded hero, who had one final task to achieve before dark.
Mom, I'm going for a bike ride.
Don't go too far, it'll be dark soon.
From here it's not far to the country, just a couple kilometers.
It was apparent that it would be dark on my way back.
Hi, Guido
Hey

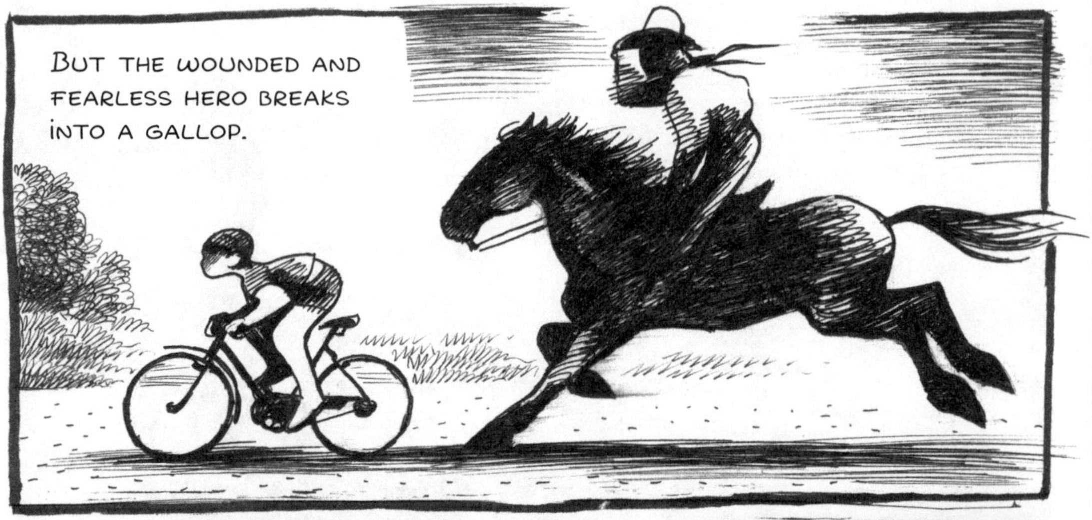
But the wounded and fearless hero breaks into a gallop.

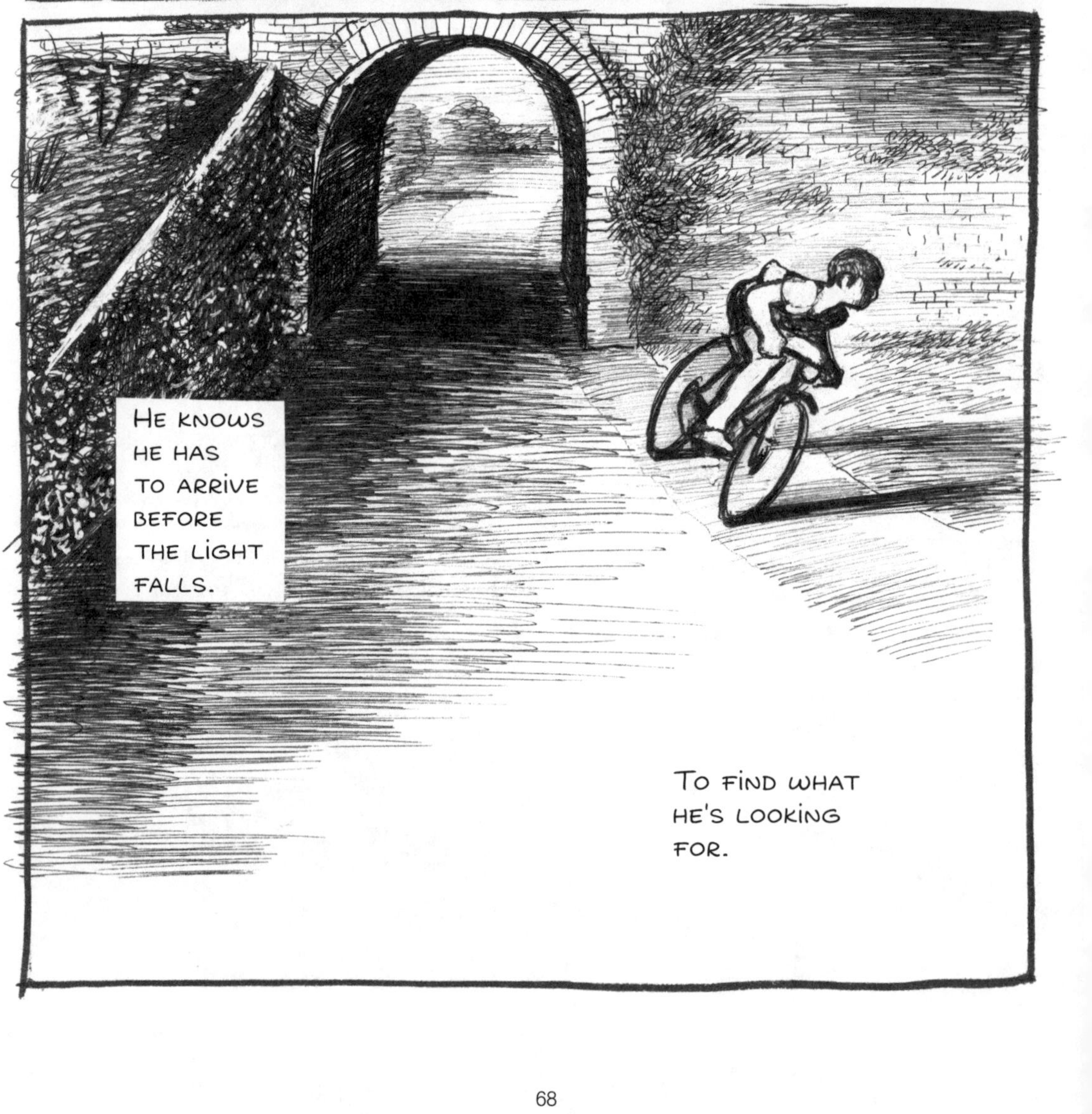
He knows he has to arrive before the light falls.
To find what he's looking for.

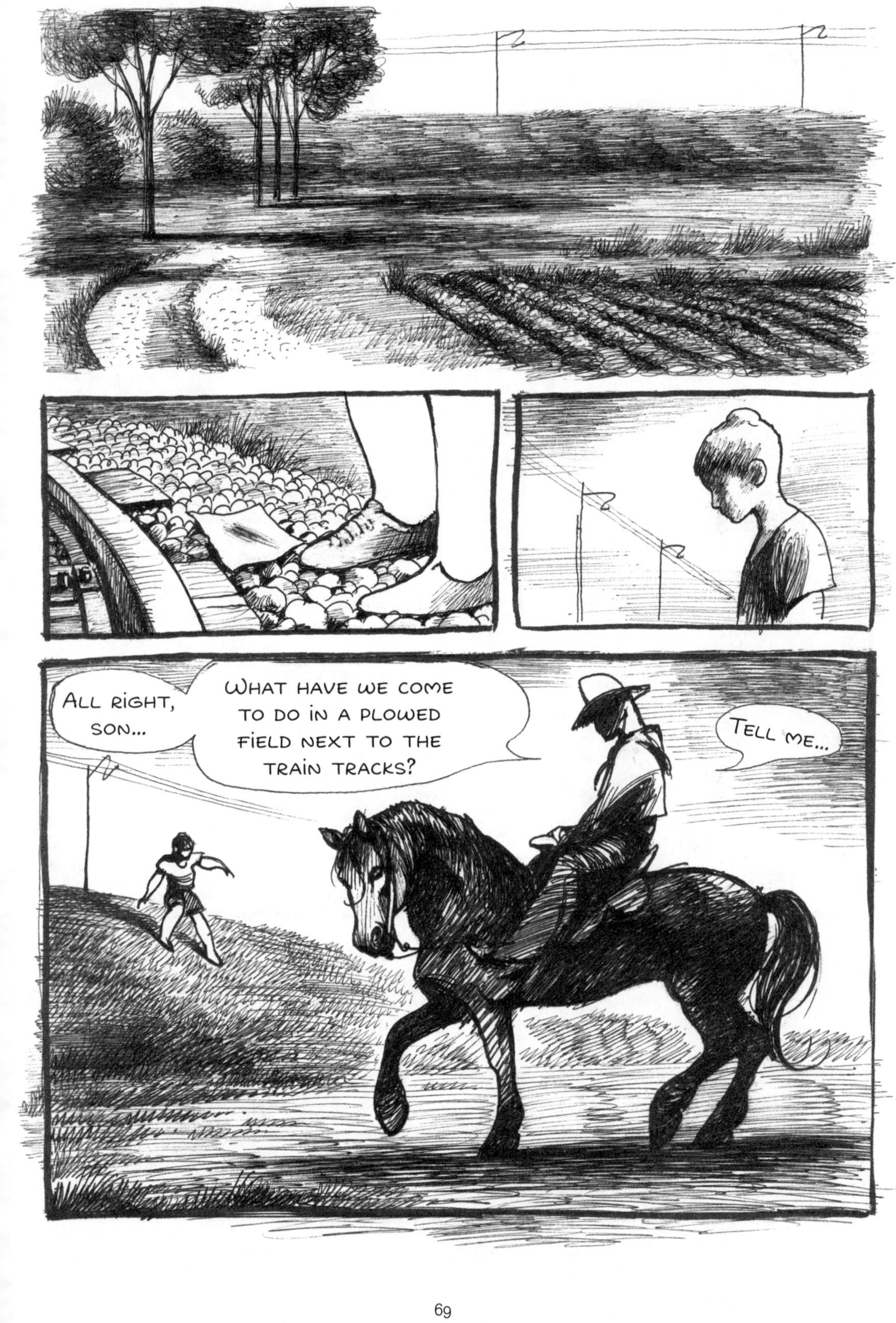
All right, son...
What have we come to do in a plowed field next to the train tracks?
Tell me...

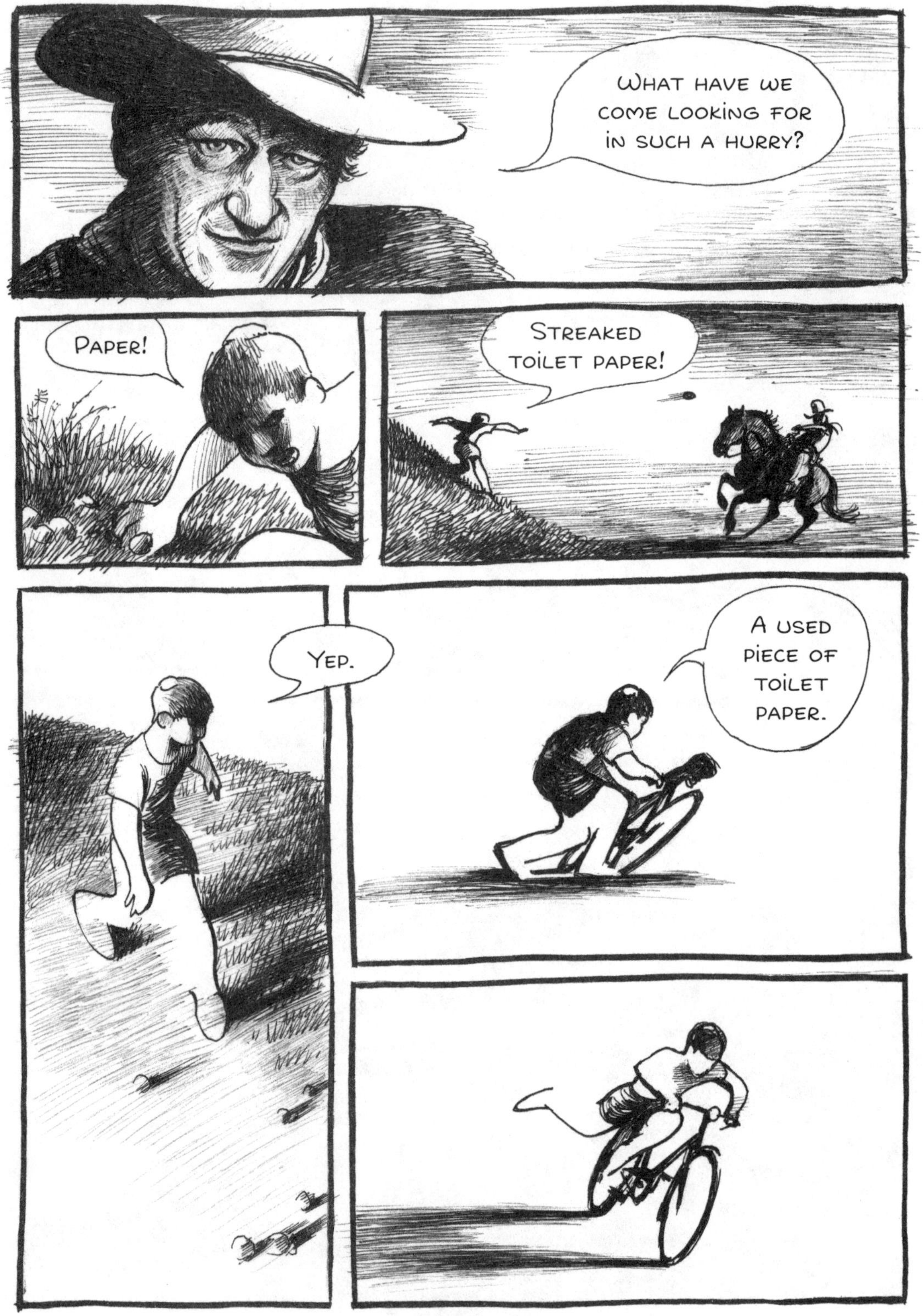
WHAT HAVE WE COME LOOKING FOR IN SUCH A HURRY?
PAPER!
STREAKED TOILET PAPER!
YEP.
A USED PIECE OF TOILET PAPER.

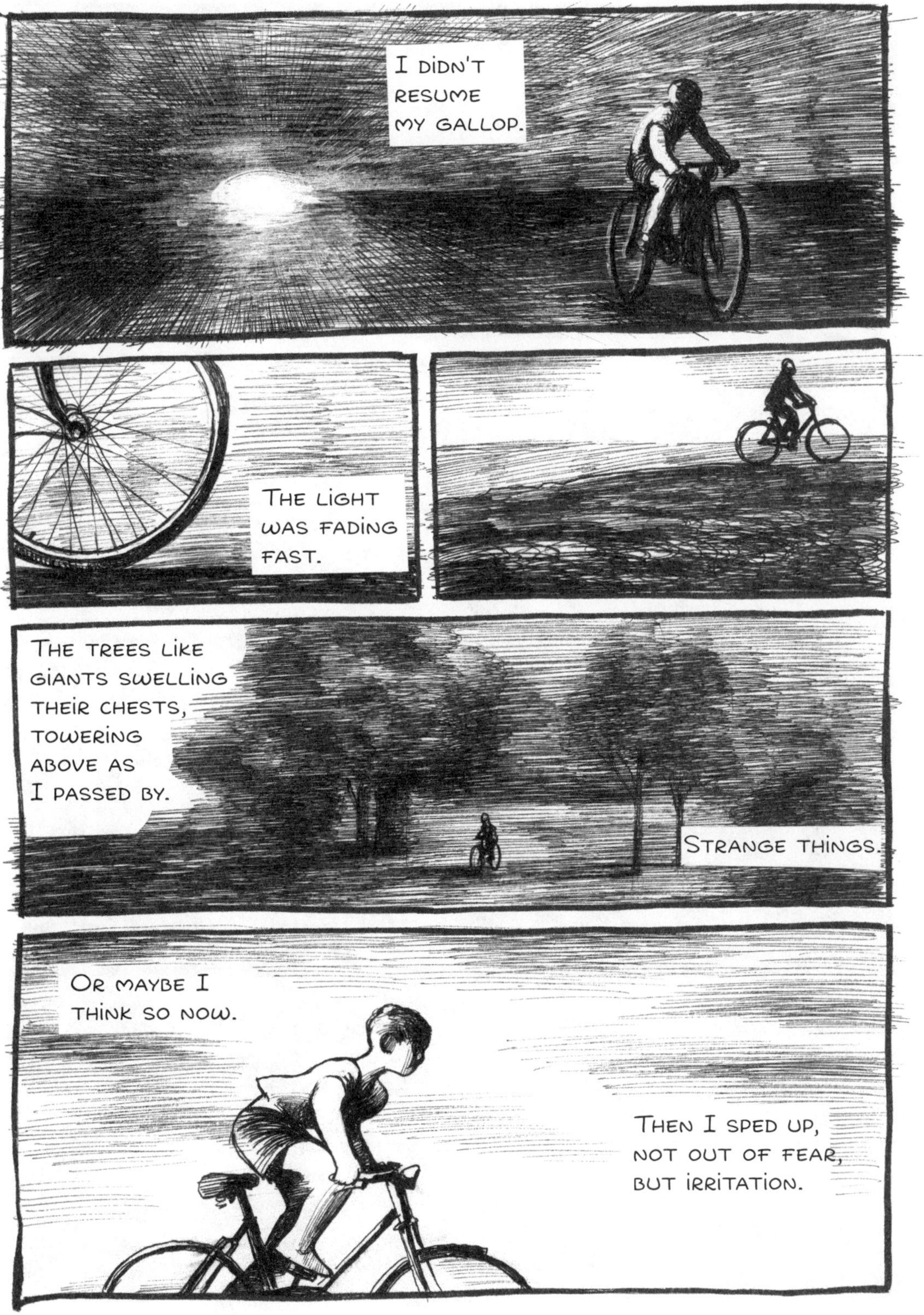
I DIDN'T RESUME MY GALLOP.
THE LIGHT WAS FADING FAST.
THE TREES LIKE GIANTS SWELLING THEIR CHESTS, TOWERING ABOVE AS I PASSED BY.
STRANGE THINGS.
OR MAYBE I THINK SO NOW.
THEN I SPED UP, NOT OUT OF FEAR, BUT IRRITATION.

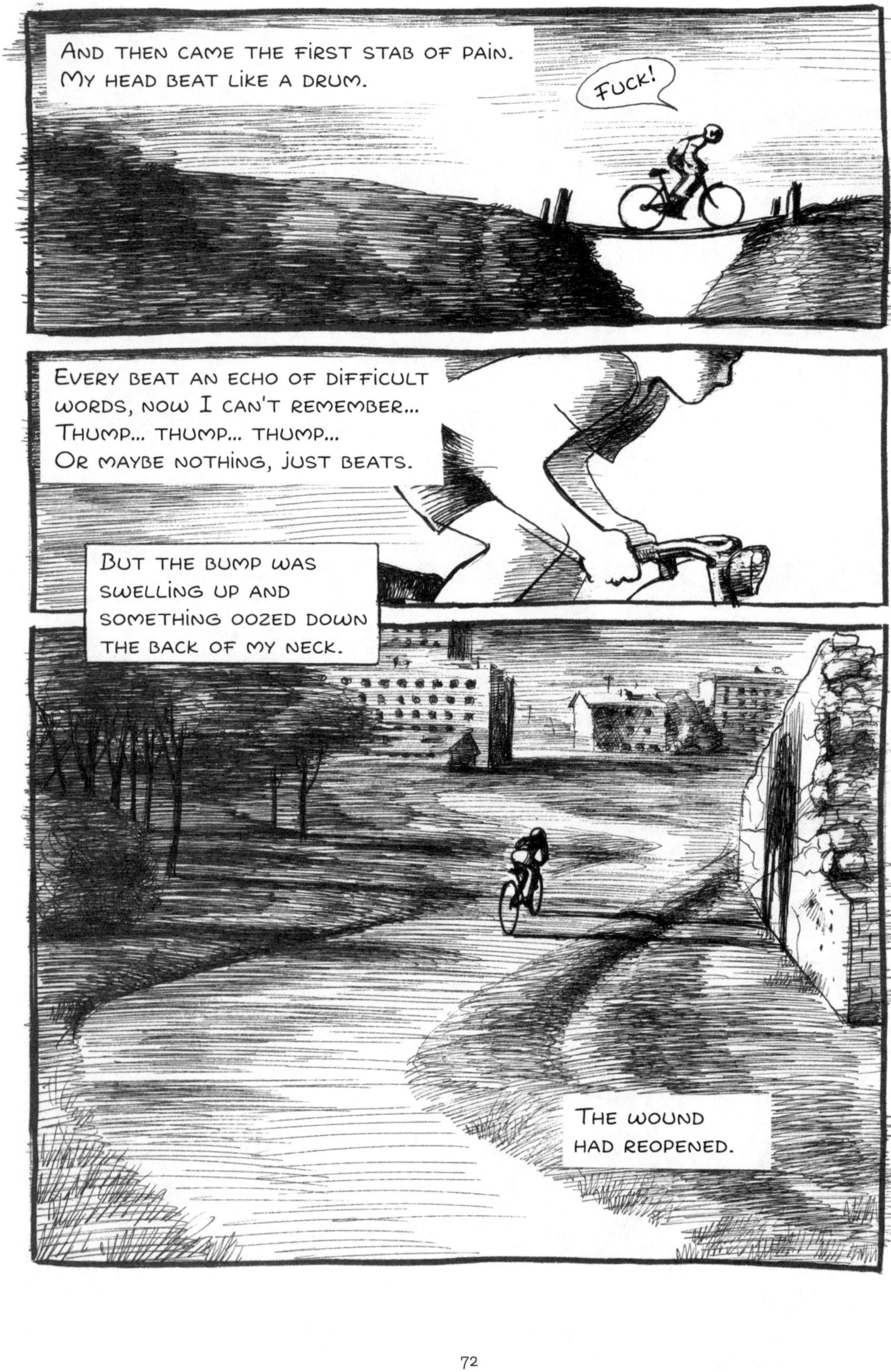
AND THEN CAME THE FIRST STAB OF PAIN. MY HEAD BEAT LIKE A DRUM.
FUCK!
EVERY BEAT AN ECHO OF DIFFICULT WORDS, NOW I CAN'T REMEMBER... THUMP... THUMP... THUMP... OR MAYBE NOTHING, JUST BEATS.
BUT THE BUMP WAS SWELLING UP AND SOMETHING OOZED DOWN THE BACK OF MY NECK.
THE WOUND HAD REOPENED.

III

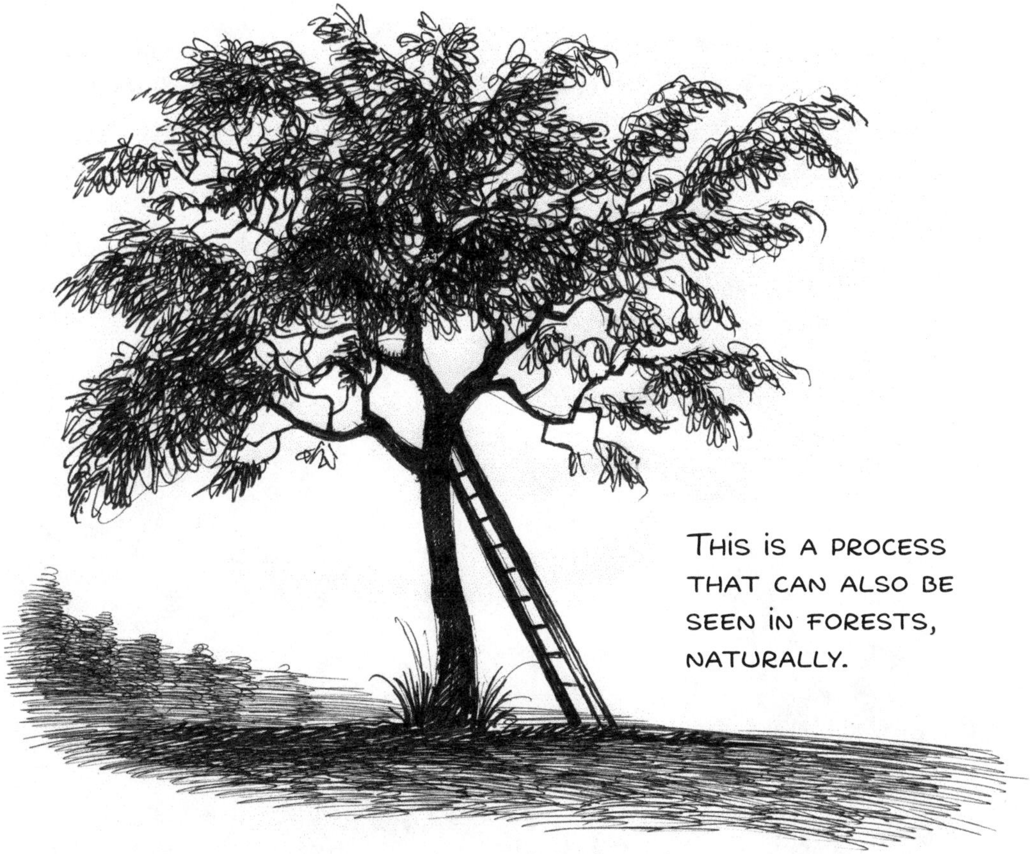

THIS IS A PROCESS THAT CAN ALSO BE SEEN IN FORESTS, NATURALLY.

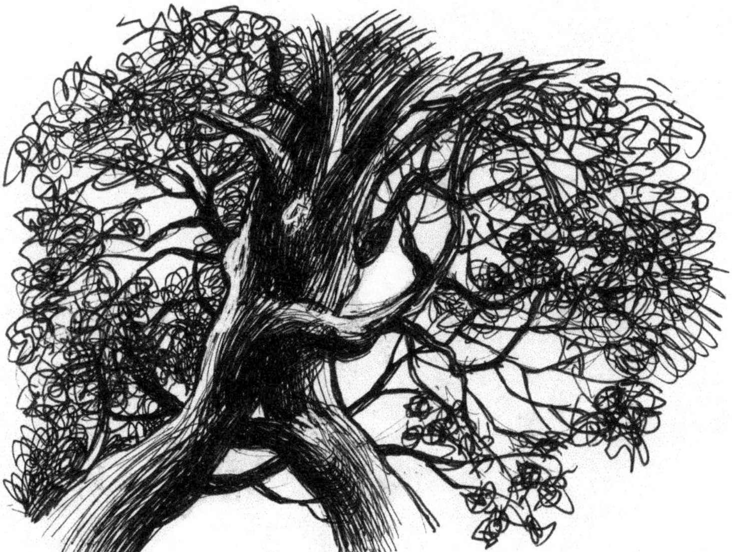

WHEN PARTS OF ONE PLANT COME INTO CONTACT WITH NEARBY TREES OF THE SAME SPECIES.

THEY LATCH ON, LITERALLY FUSE TOGETHER, AND CONTINUE GROWING AS A SINGLE PLANT.

OFTEN BECOMING A HARDIER, MORE PRODUCTIVE PLANT.

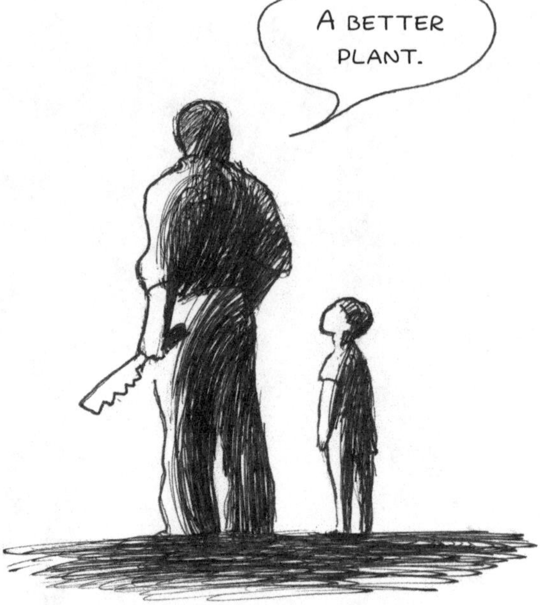
A BETTER PLANT.

THAT'S WHY YOU NEED TO GRAFT WHEN A TREE STOPS PRODUCING FRUIT, OR PRODUCES FRUIT OF VERY POOR QUALITY.

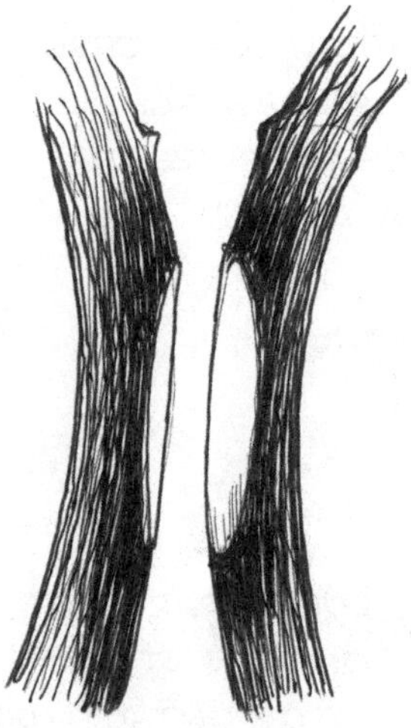

MY FATHER ALSO SAYS THAT THERE ARE CERTAIN RULES YOU HAVE TO FOLLOW FOR THE GRAFT TO SUCCEED.

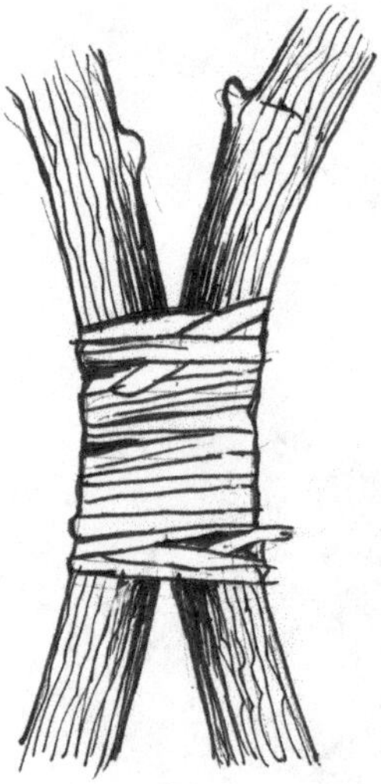

LIKE POLARITY, THE NATURAL ORIENTATION OF THE PLANT.

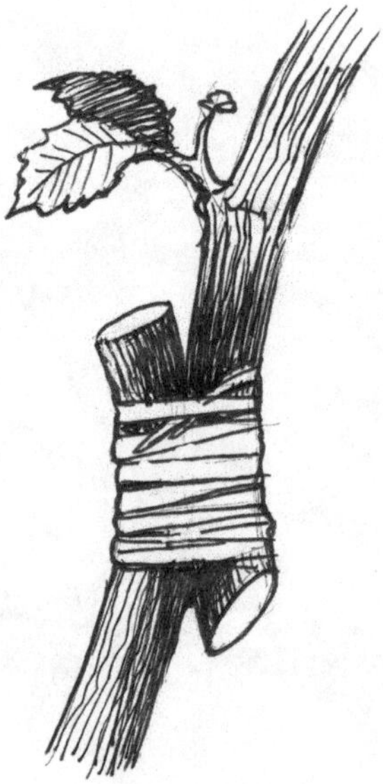

THE TIME OF YEAR.
THE PROPER CUT.

ESPECIALLY THE COMPATIBILITY OF THE PLANTS, WHICH MUST BELONG TO THE SAME FAMILY.

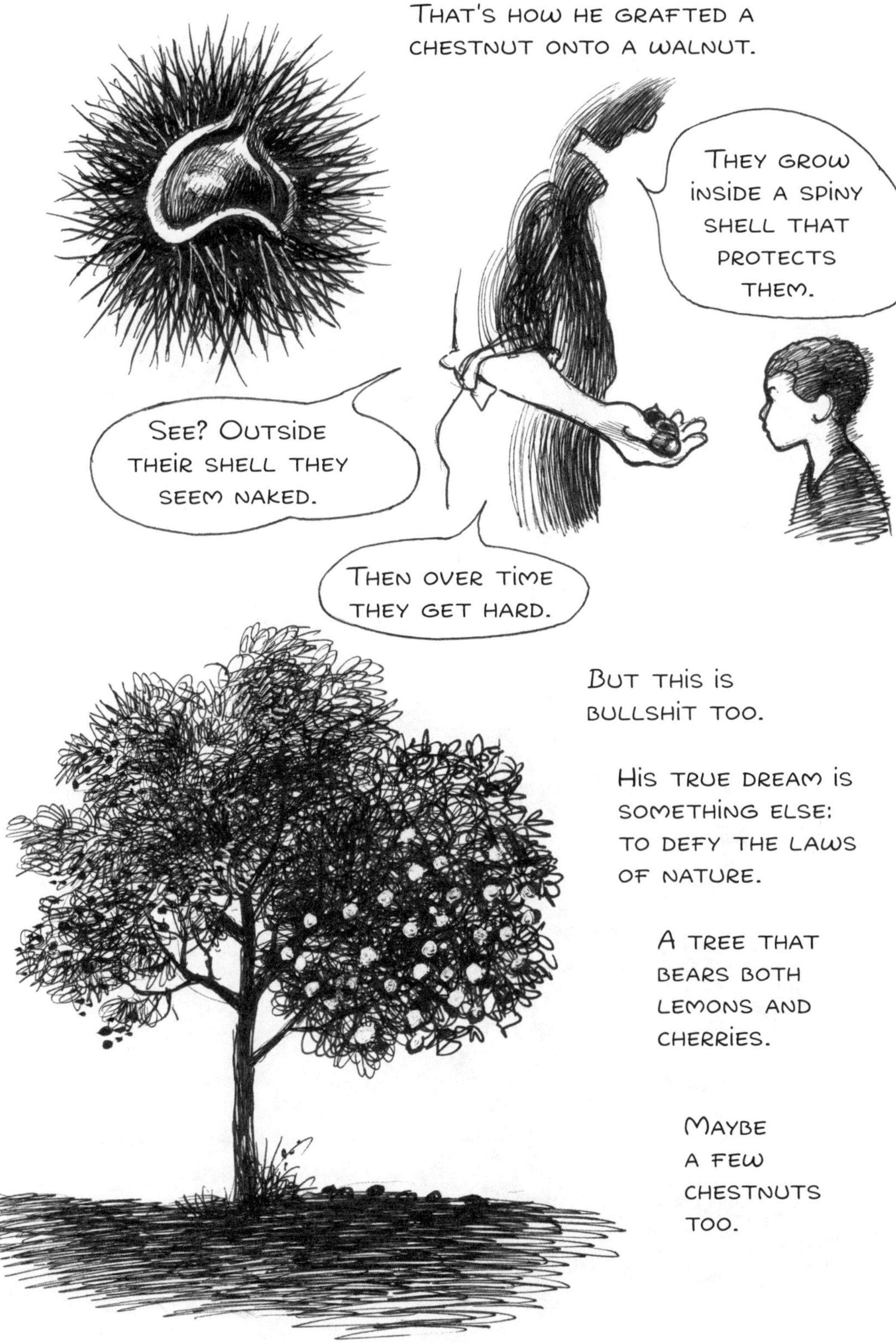
THAT'S HOW HE GRAFTED A CHESTNUT ONTO A WALNUT.
THEY GROW INSIDE A SPINY SHELL THAT PROTECTS THEM.
SEE? OUTSIDE THEIR SHELL THEY SEEM NAKED.
THEN OVER TIME THEY GET HARD.
BUT THIS IS BULLSHIT TOO.
HIS TRUE DREAM IS SOMETHING ELSE: TO DEFY THE LAWS OF NATURE.
A TREE THAT BEARS BOTH LEMONS AND CHERRIES.
MAYBE A FEW CHESTNUTS TOO.

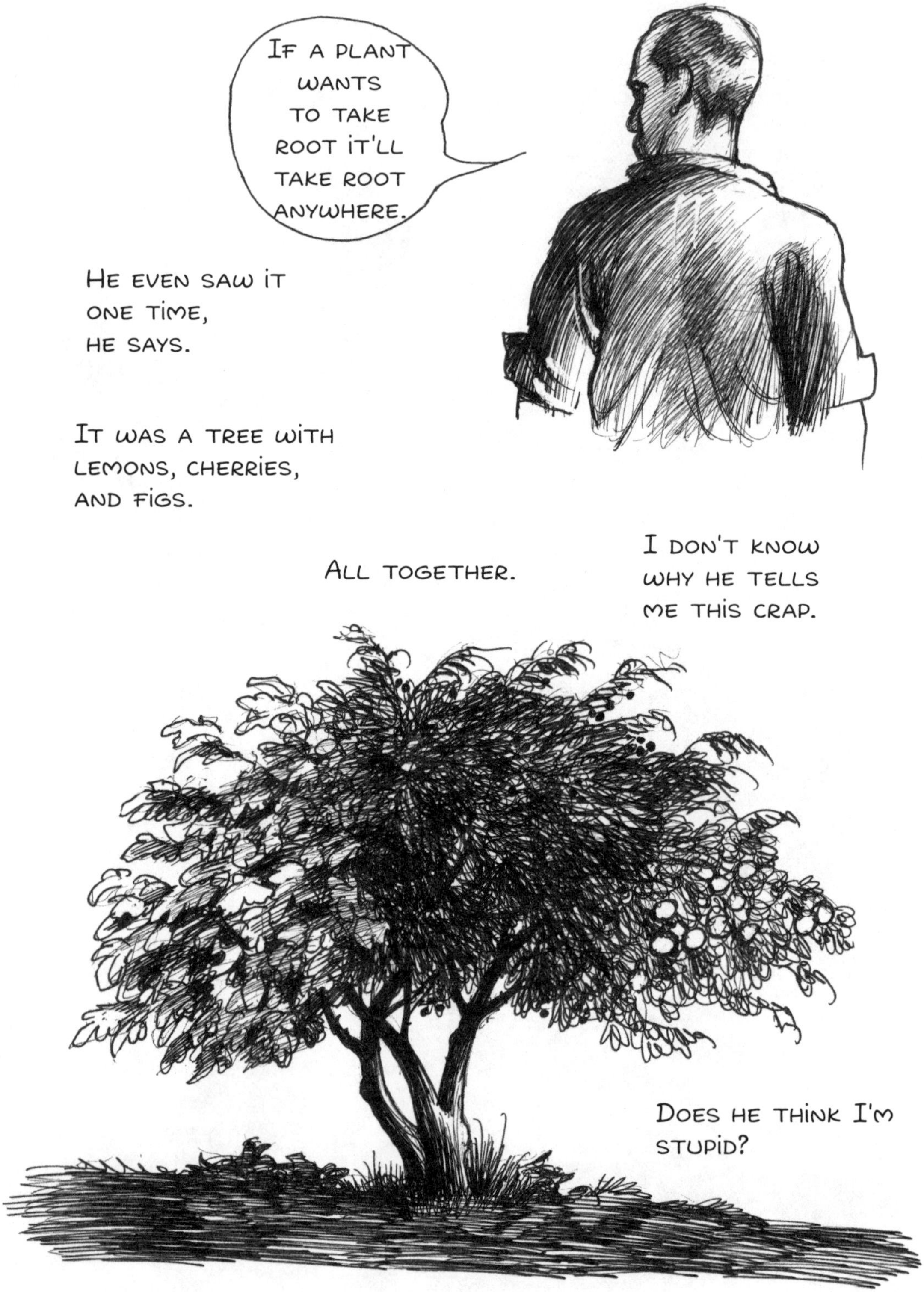
IF A PLANT WANTS TO TAKE ROOT IT'LL TAKE ROOT ANYWHERE.
HE EVEN SAW IT ONE TIME, HE SAYS.
IT WAS A TREE WITH LEMONS, CHERRIES, AND FIGS.
ALL TOGETHER.
I DON'T KNOW WHY HE TELLS ME THIS CRAP.
DOES HE THINK I'M STUPID?

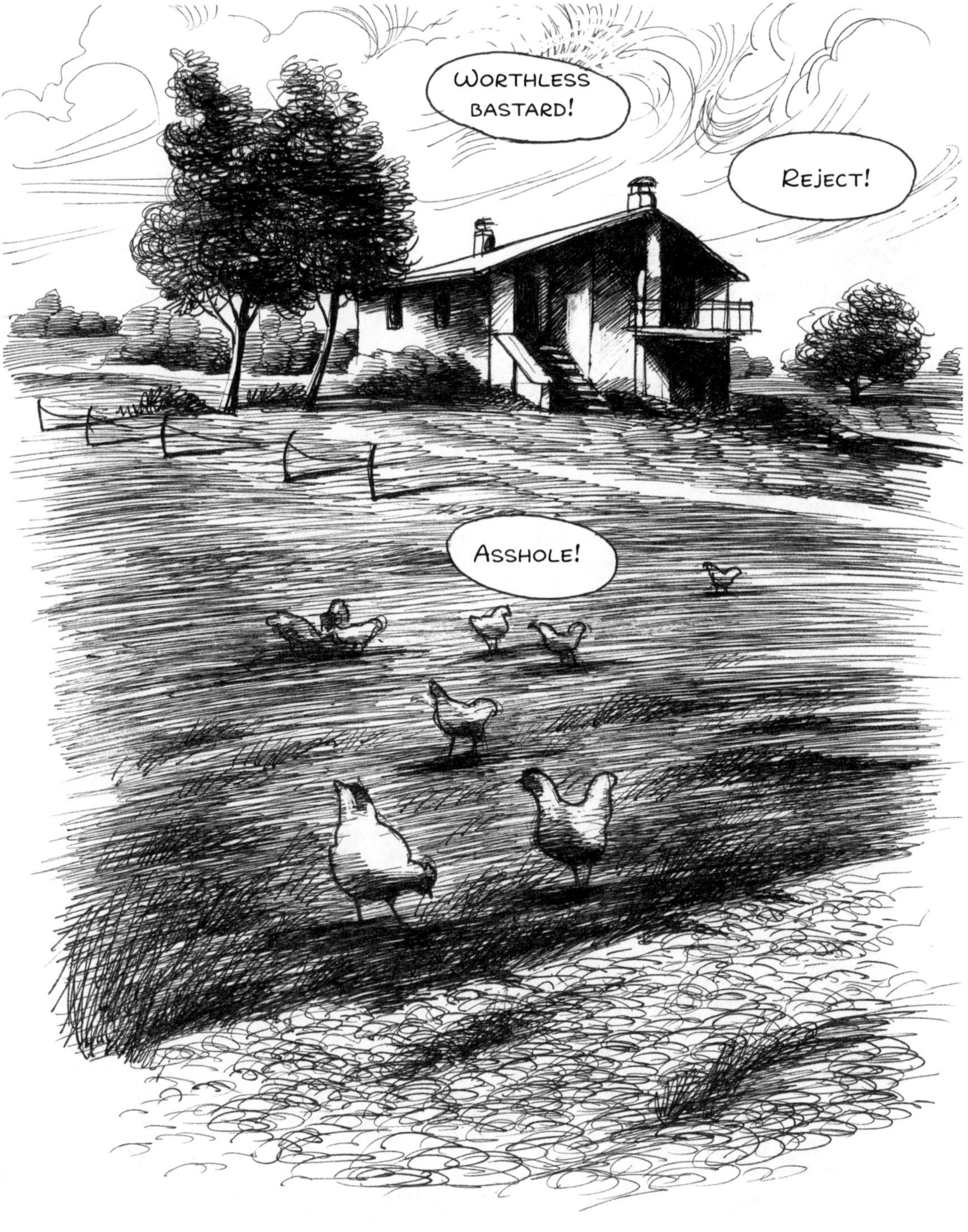
Worthless bastard!
Reject!
Asshole!

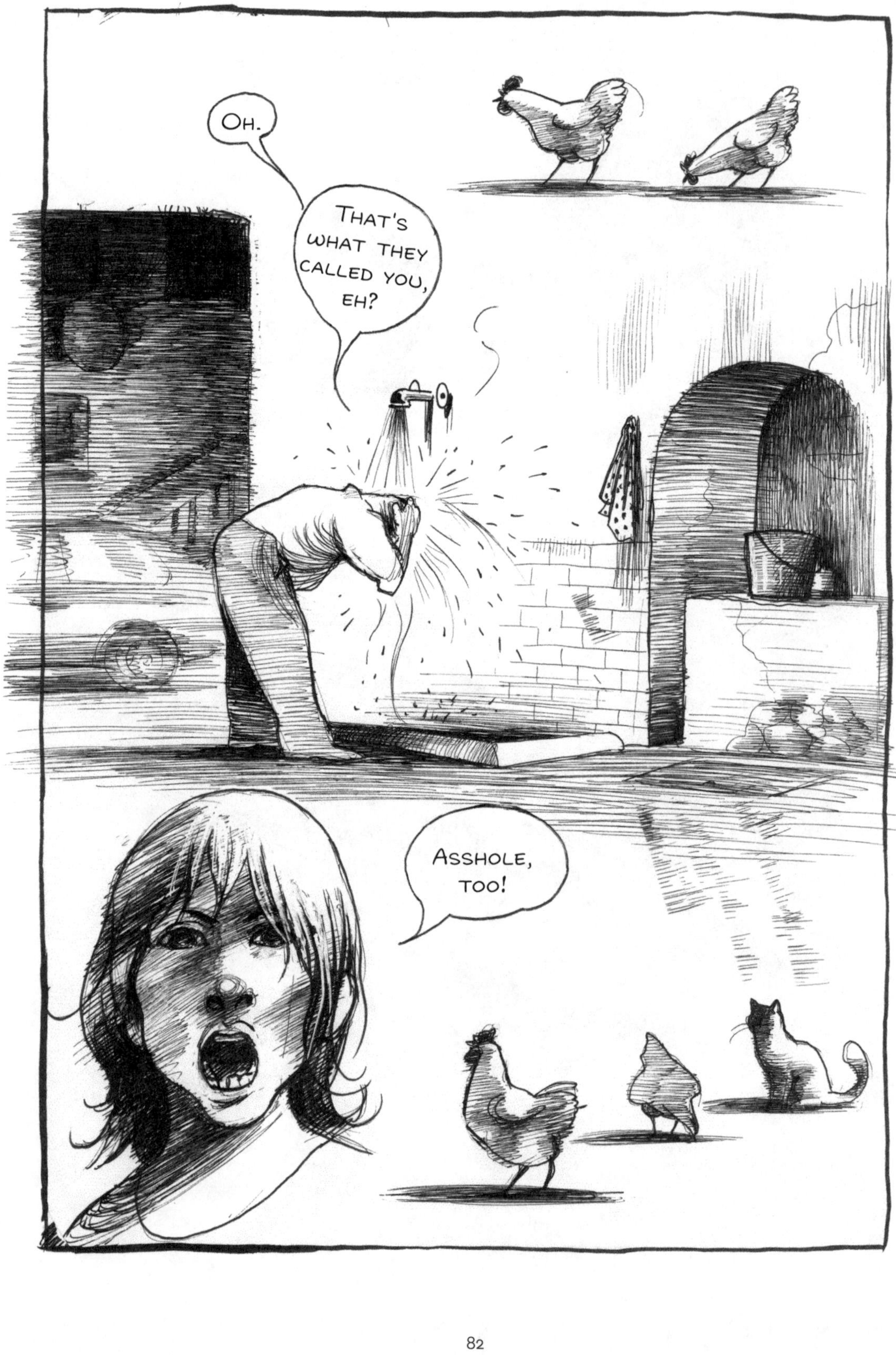
Oh.
That's what they called you, eh?
Asshole, too!

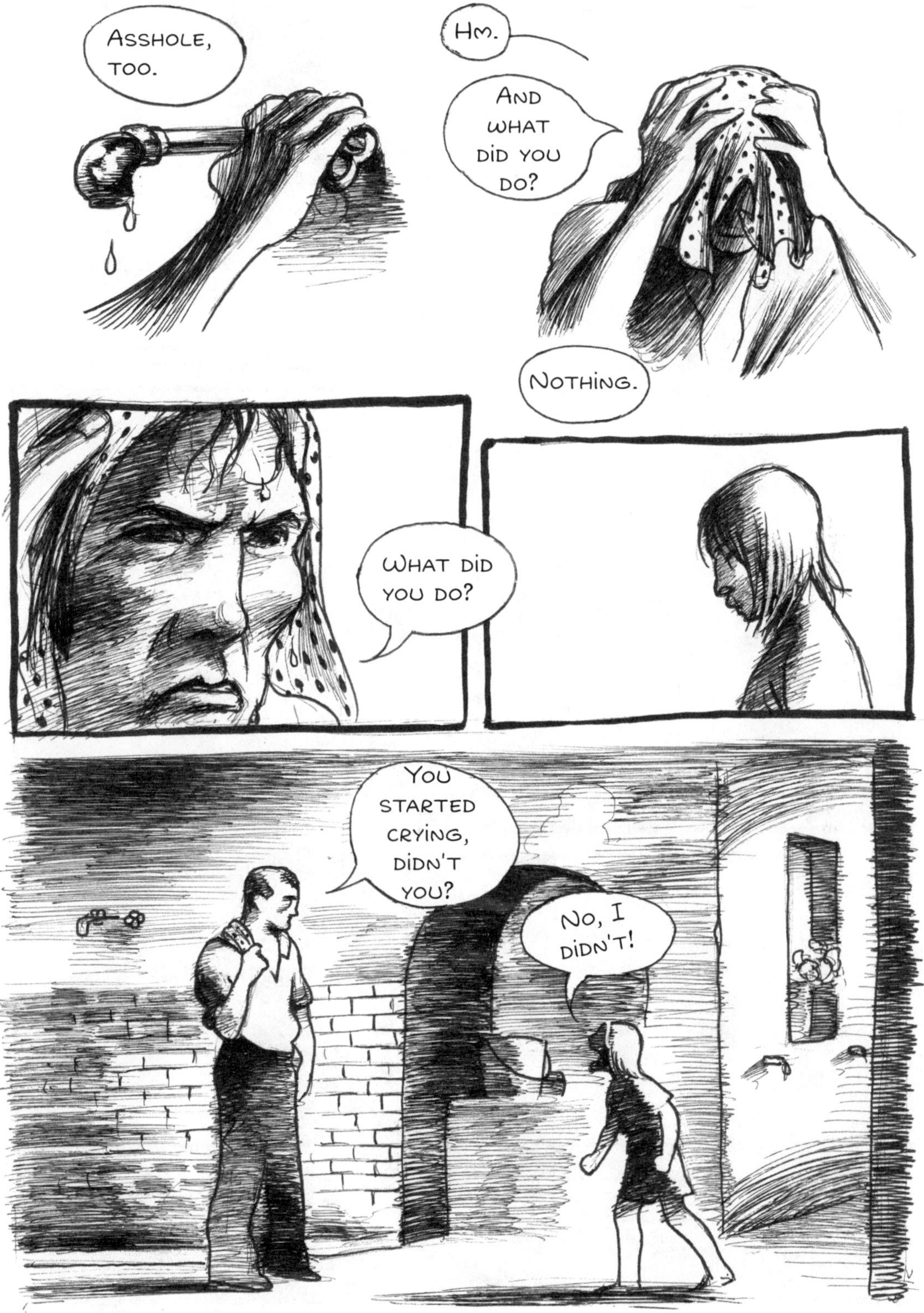
ASSHOLE, TOO.
HM.
AND WHAT DID YOU DO?
NOTHING.
WHAT DID YOU DO?
YOU STARTED CRYING, DIDN'T YOU?
NO, I DIDN'T!

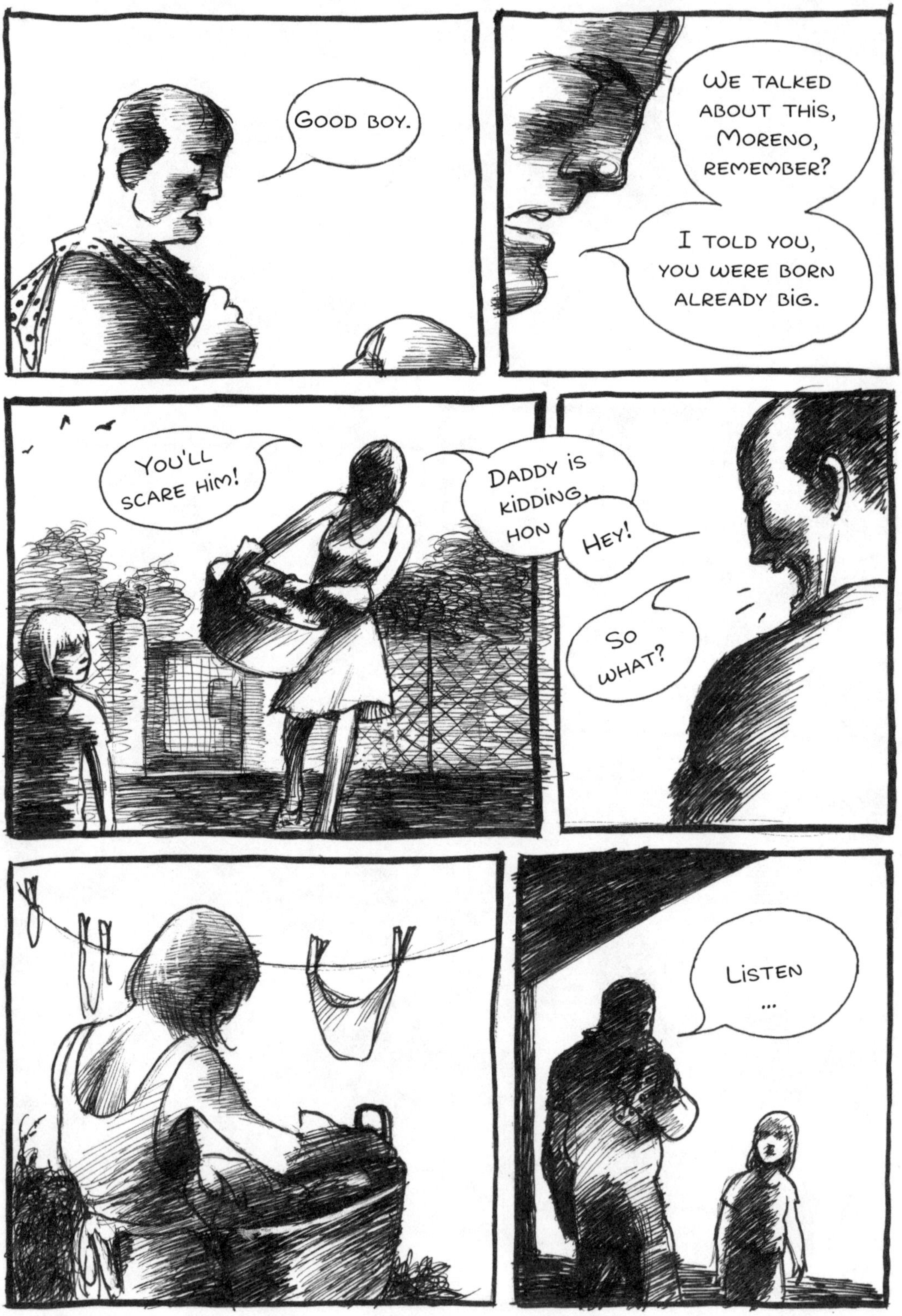
GOOD BOY.
WE TALKED ABOUT THIS, MORENO, REMEMBER?
I TOLD YOU, YOU WERE BORN ALREADY BIG.
YOU'LL SCARE HIM!
DADDY IS KIDDING, HON
HEY!
SO WHAT?
LISTEN ...

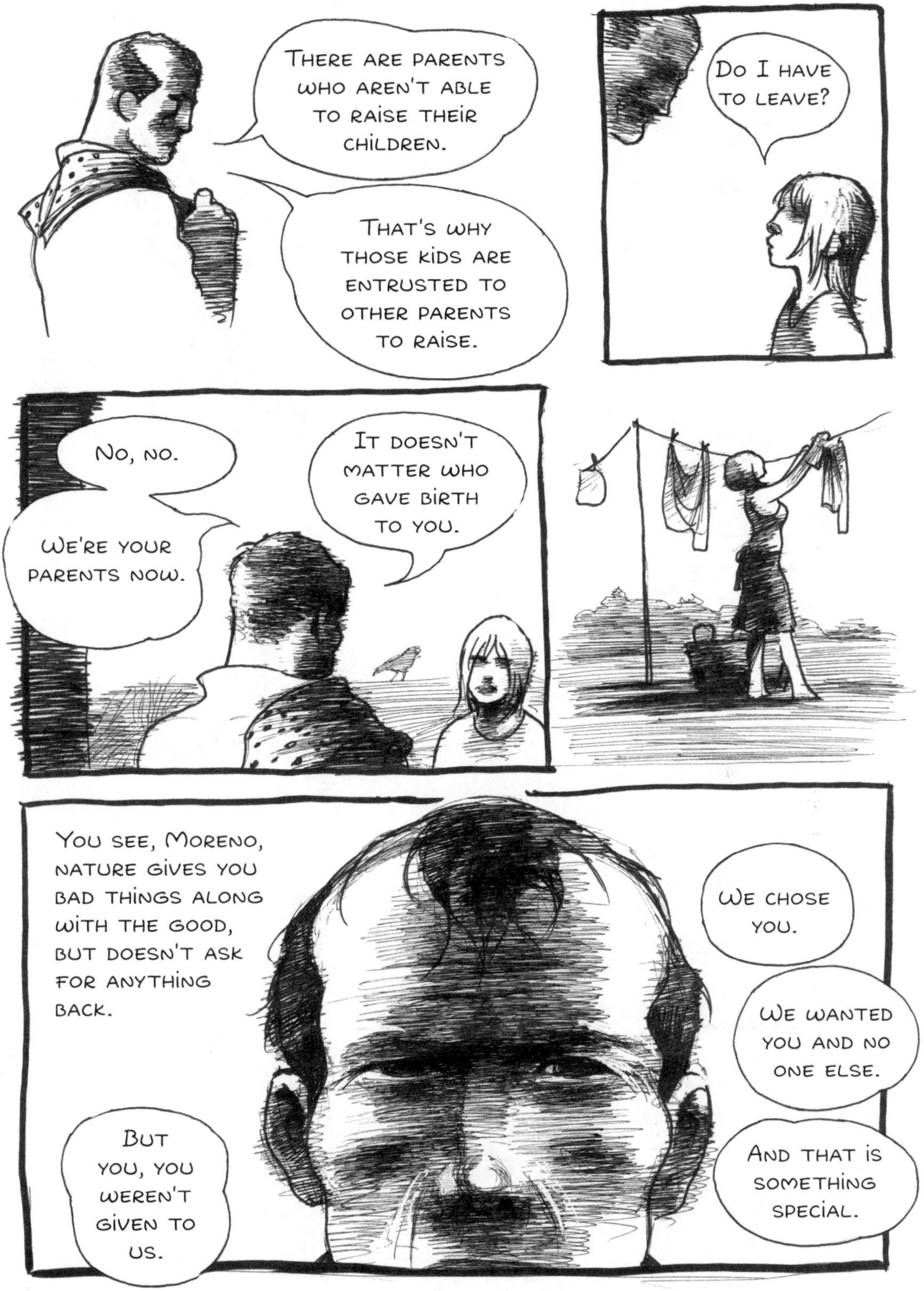
There are parents who aren't able to raise their children.
That's why those kids are entrusted to other parents to raise.
Do I have to leave?
No, no.
We're your parents now.
It doesn't matter who gave birth to you.
You see, Moreno, nature gives you bad things along with the good, but doesn't ask for anything back.
But you, you weren't given to us.
We chose you.
We wanted you and no one else.
And that is something special.

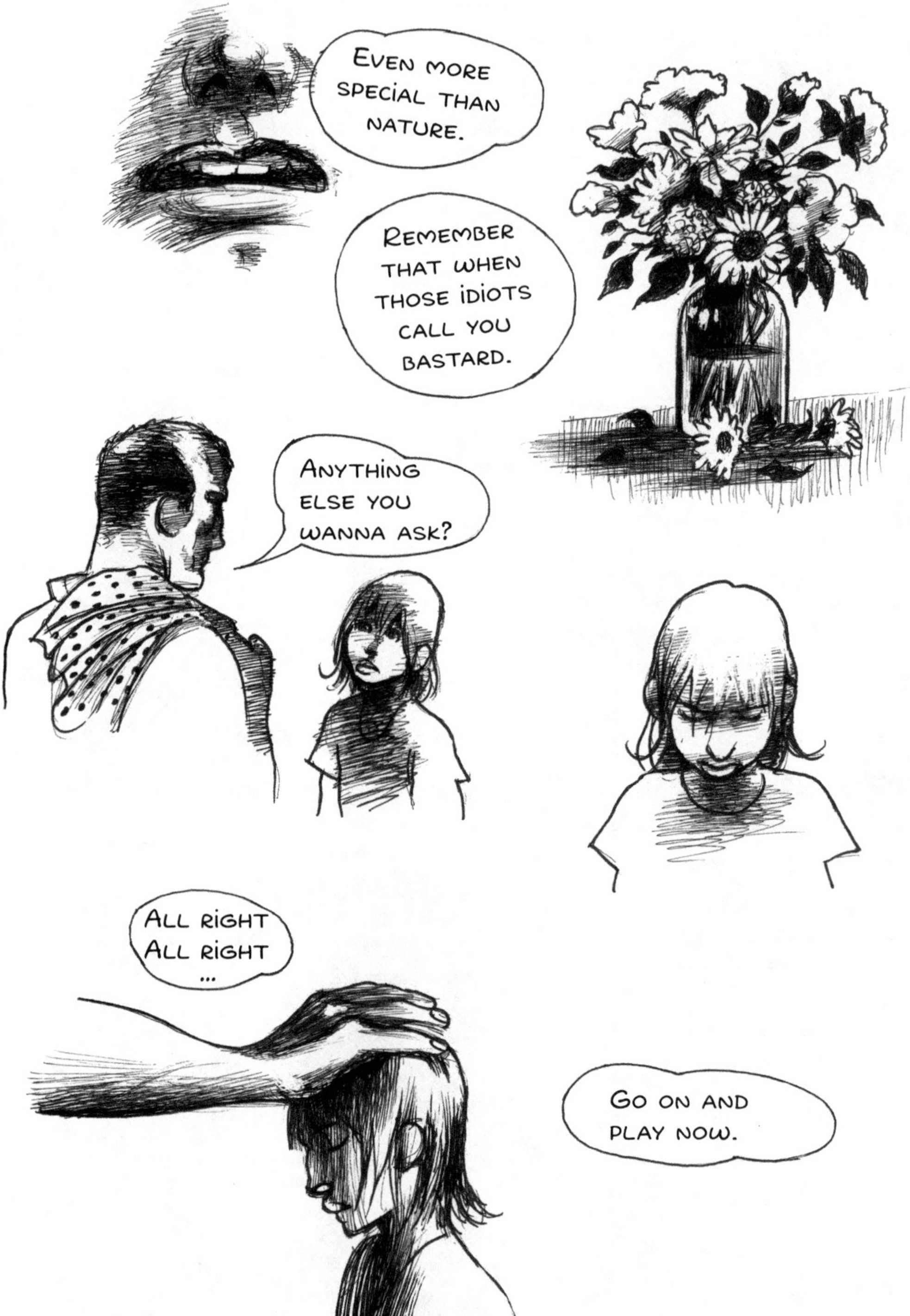

Even more special than nature.
Remember that when those idiots call you bastard.
Anything else you wanna ask?
All right All right ...
Go on and play now.

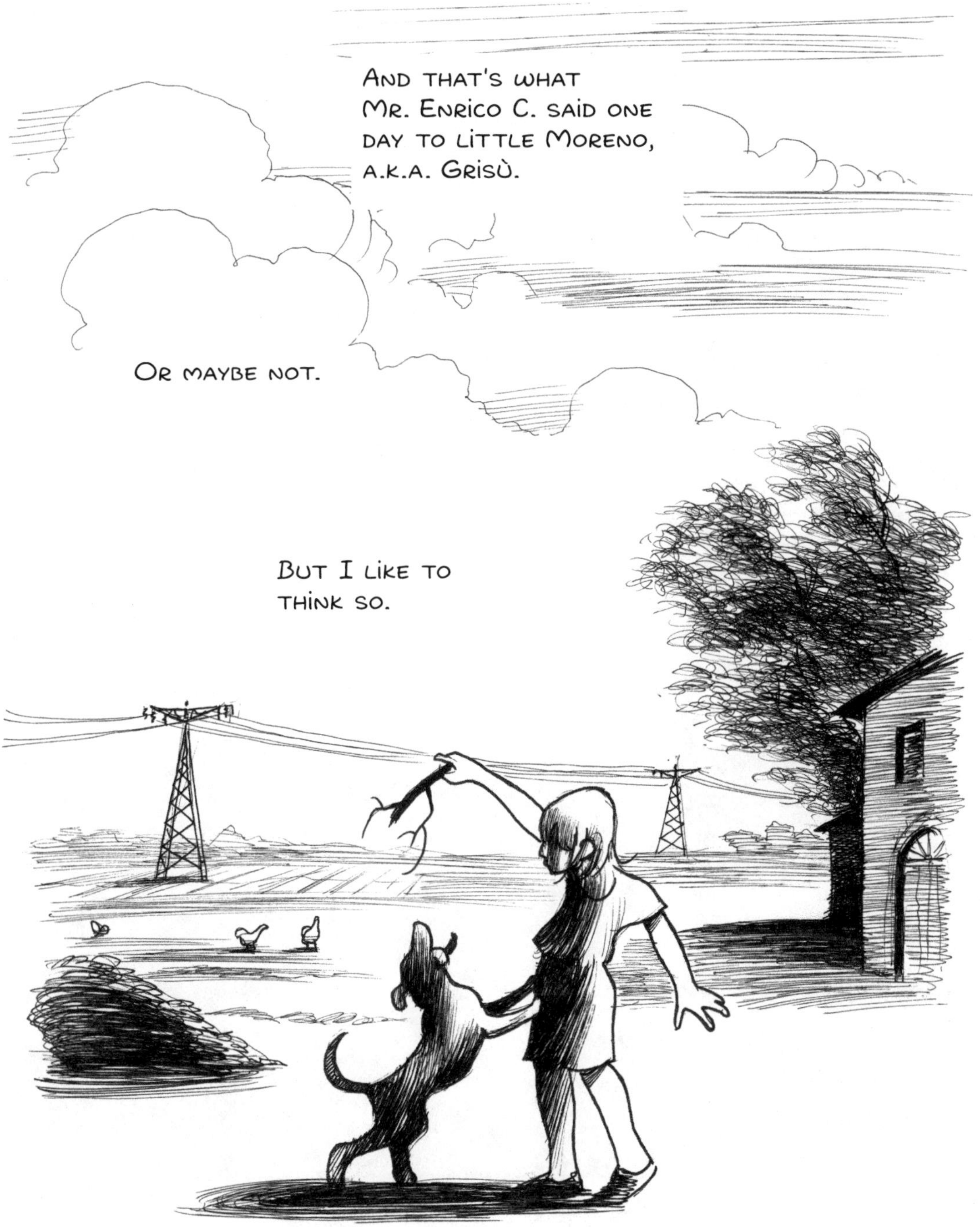
And that's what Mr. Enrico C. said one day to little Moreno, a.k.a. Grisù.
Or maybe not.
But I like to think so.

IV

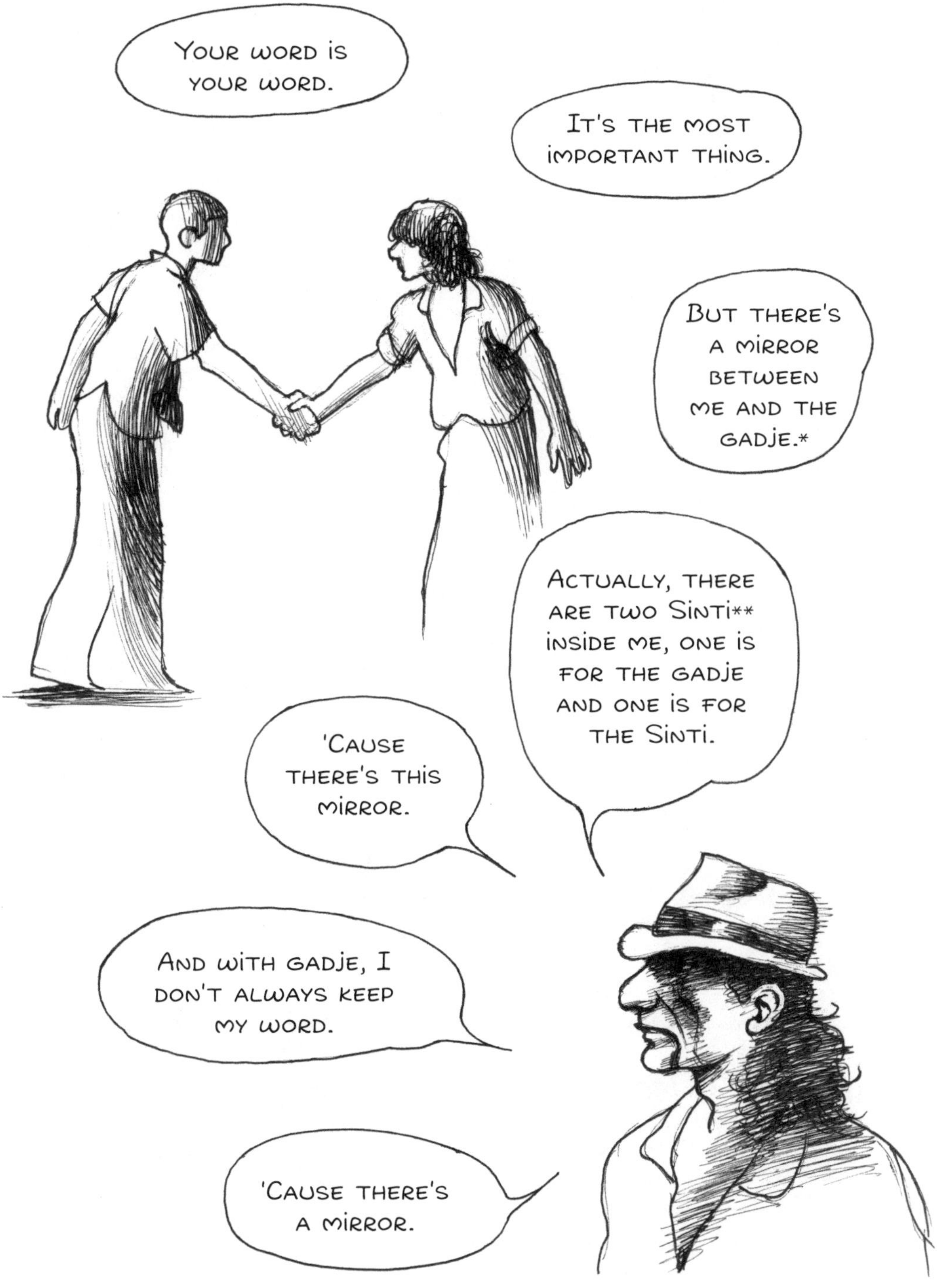
YOUR WORD IS YOUR WORD.
IT'S THE MOST IMPORTANT THING.
BUT THERE'S A MIRROR BETWEEN ME AND THE GADJE.*
ACTUALLY, THERE ARE TWO SINTI** INSIDE ME, ONE IS FOR THE GADJE AND ONE IS FOR THE SINTI.
'CAUSE THERE'S THIS MIRROR.
AND WITH GADJE, I DON'T ALWAYS KEEP MY WORD.
'CAUSE THERE'S A MIRROR.

* Term used by Romani ethnic groups to describe non-Roma.
** Romani from Western Europe.

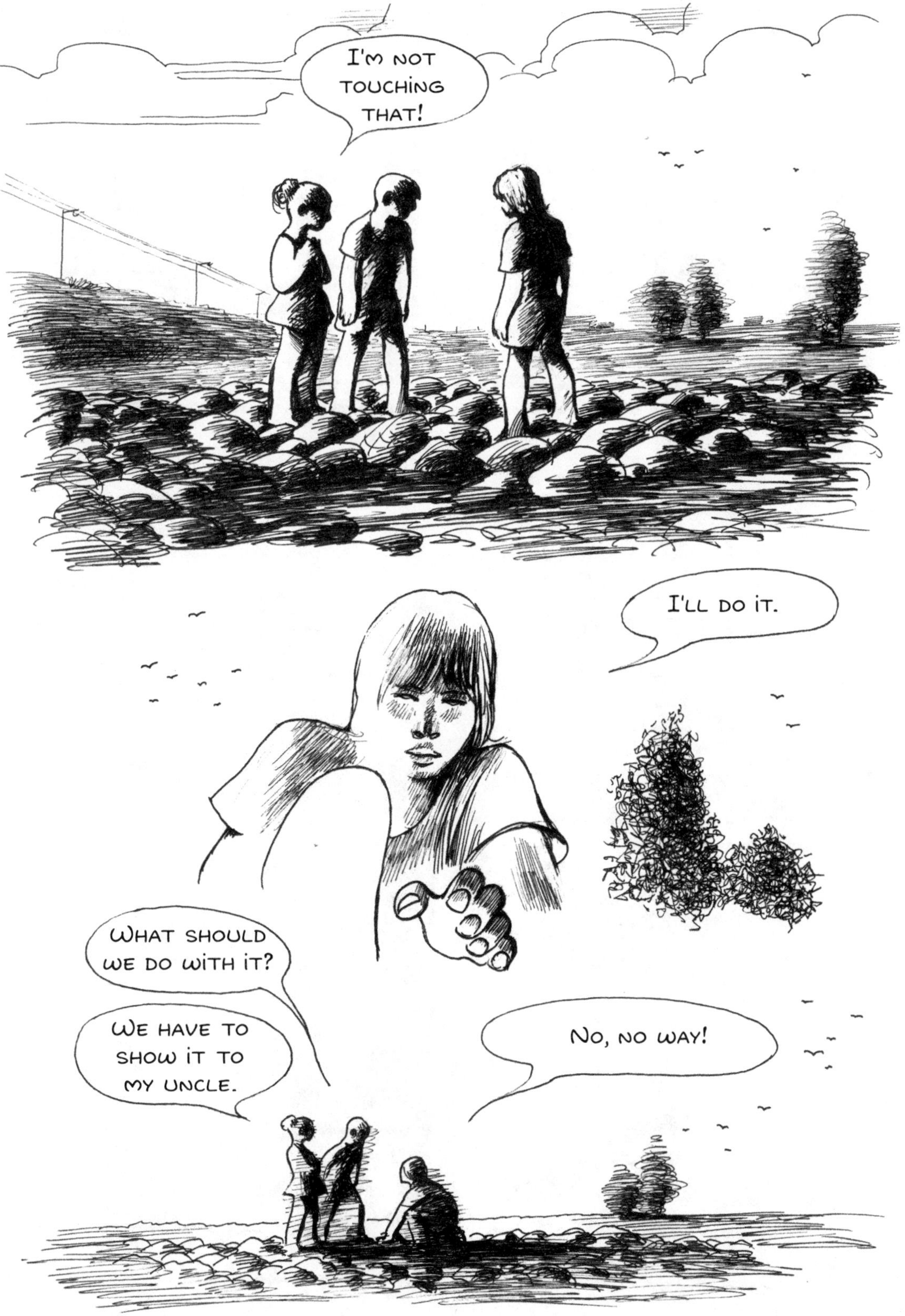
I'M NOT TOUCHING THAT!
I'LL DO IT.
WHAT SHOULD WE DO WITH IT?
WE HAVE TO SHOW IT TO MY UNCLE.
NO, NO WAY!

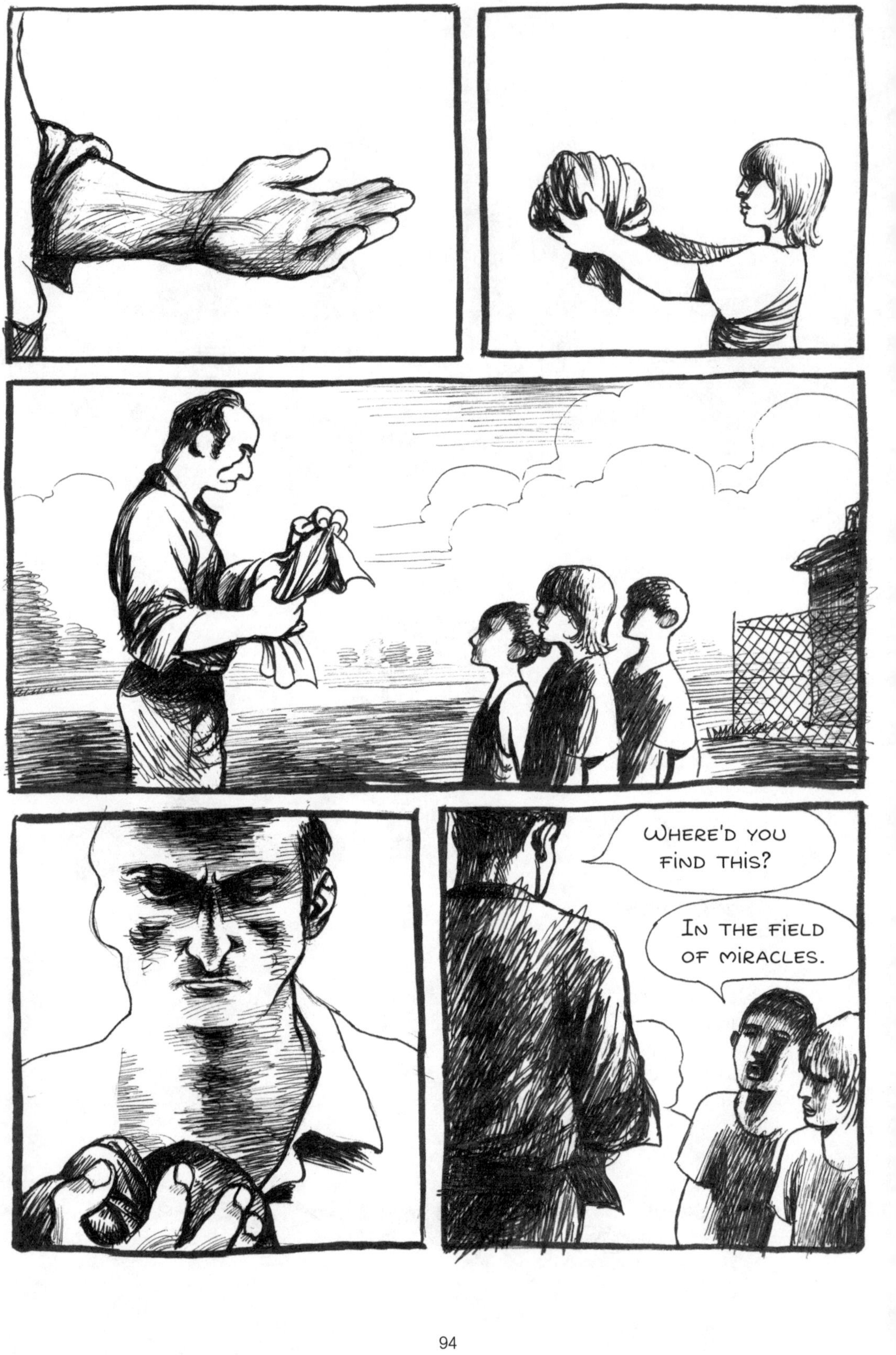
WHERE'D YOU FIND THIS?
IN THE FIELD OF MIRACLES.

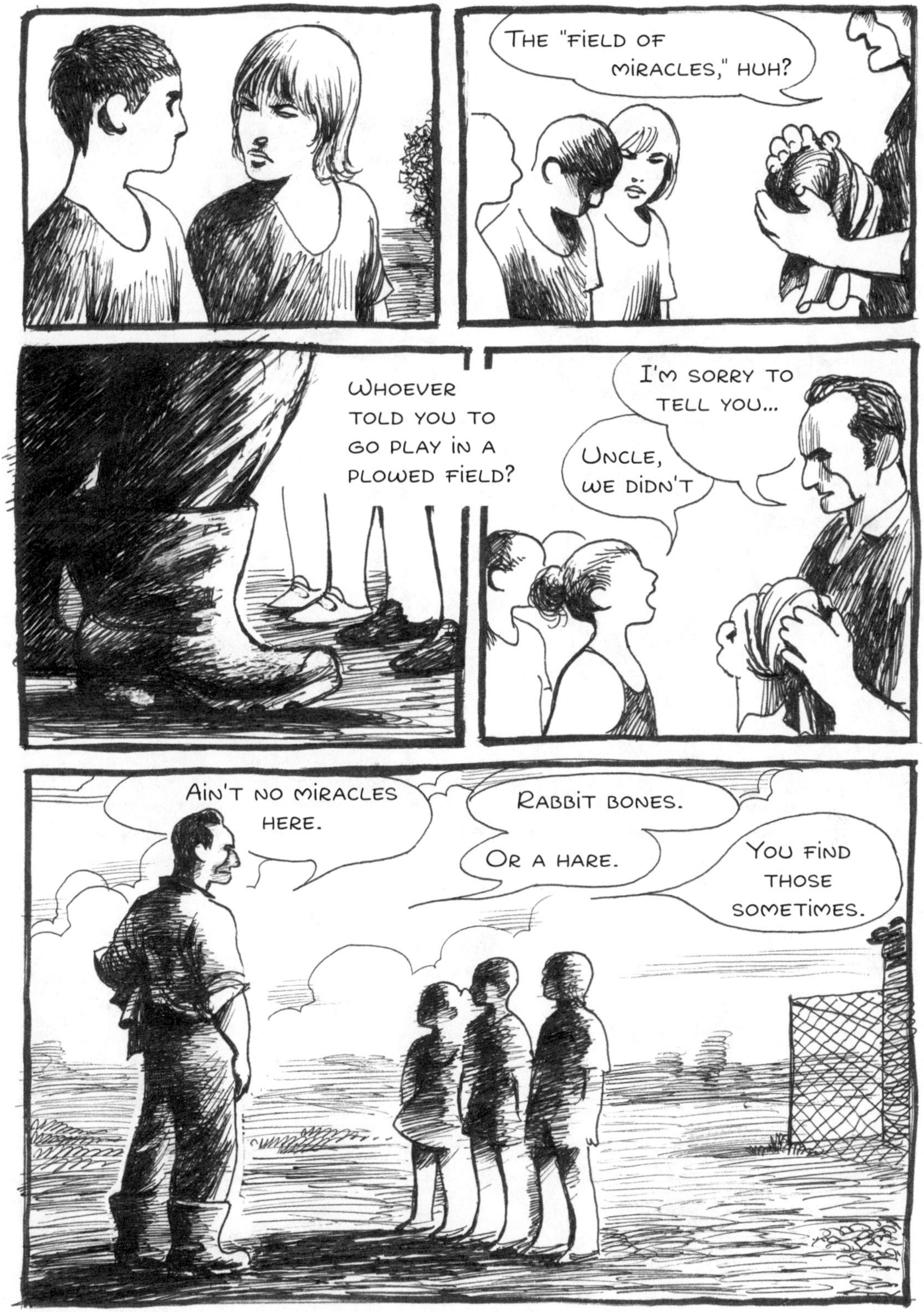
THE "FIELD OF MIRACLES," HUH?
WHOEVER TOLD YOU TO GO PLAY IN A PLOWED FIELD?
I'M SORRY TO TELL YOU...
UNCLE, WE DIDN'T
AIN'T NO MIRACLES HERE.
RABBIT BONES.
OR A HARE.
YOU FIND THOSE SOMETIMES.

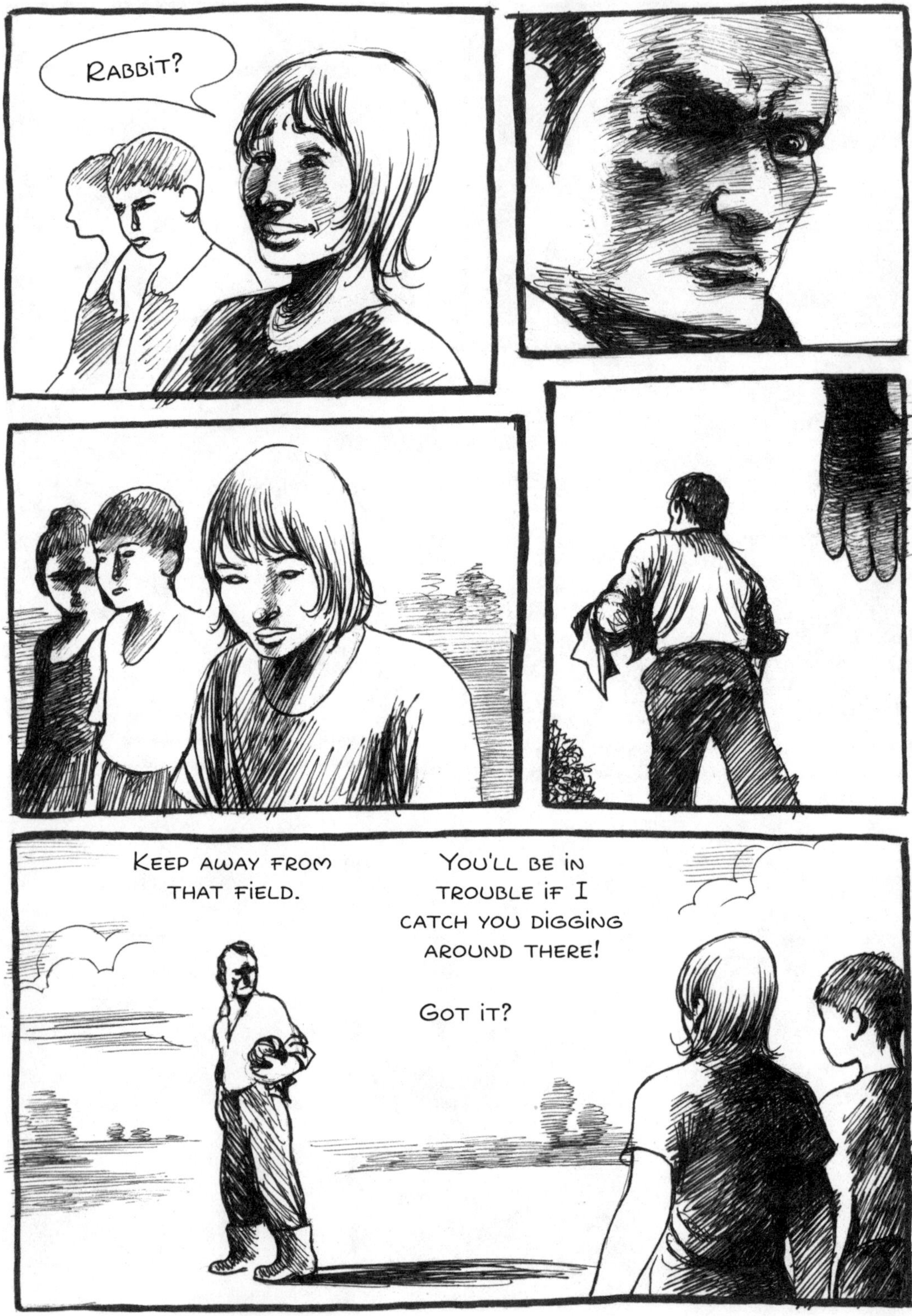
RABBIT?
KEEP AWAY FROM THAT FIELD.
YOU'LL BE IN TROUBLE IF I CATCH YOU DIGGING AROUND THERE!
GOT IT?

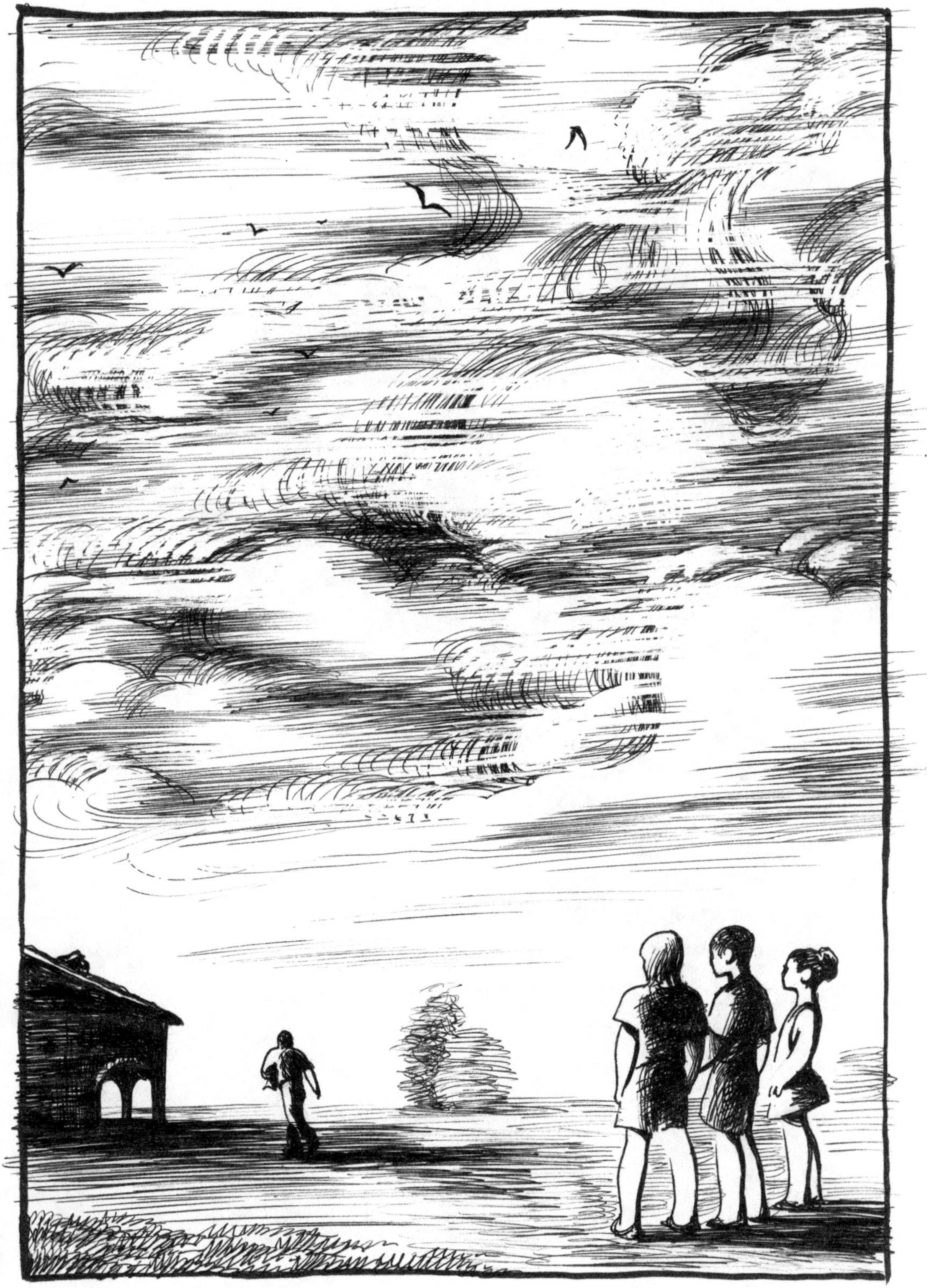

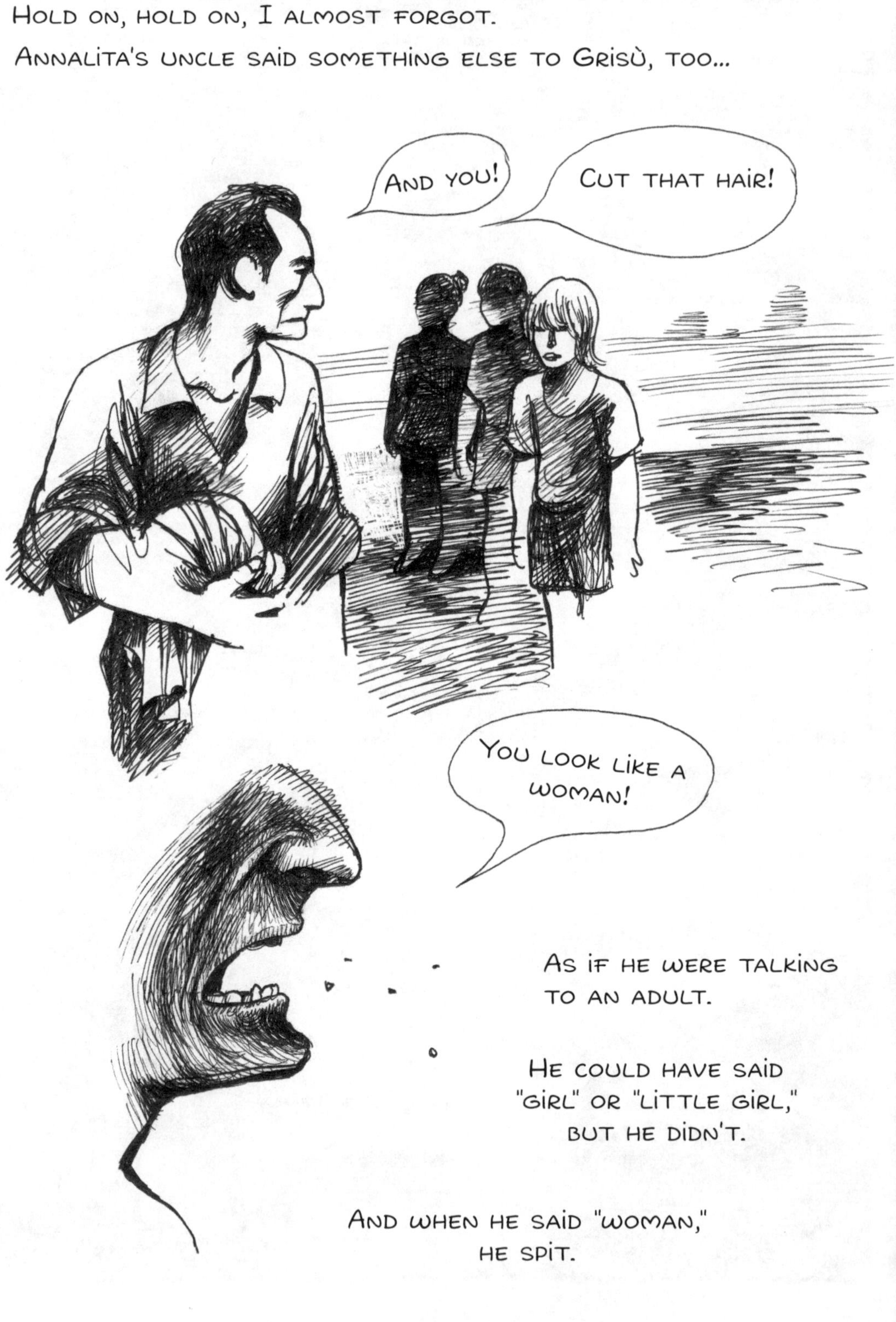
Hold on, hold on, I almost forgot.
Annalita's uncle said something else to Grisù, too...
And you!
Cut that hair!
You look like a woman!
As if he were talking to an adult.
He could have said "girl" or "little girl," but he didn't.
And when he said "woman," he spit.

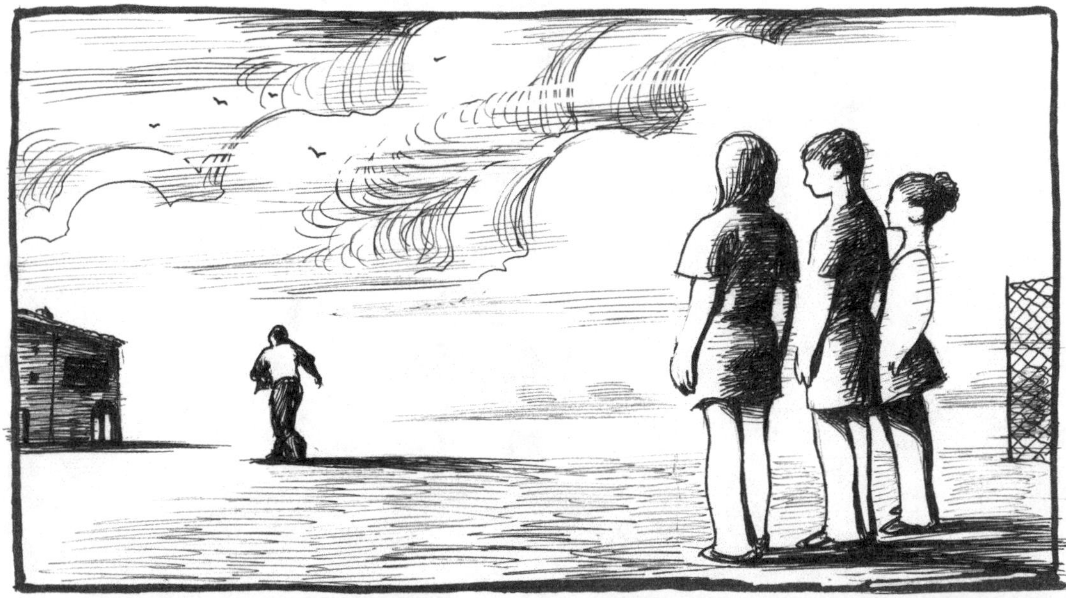

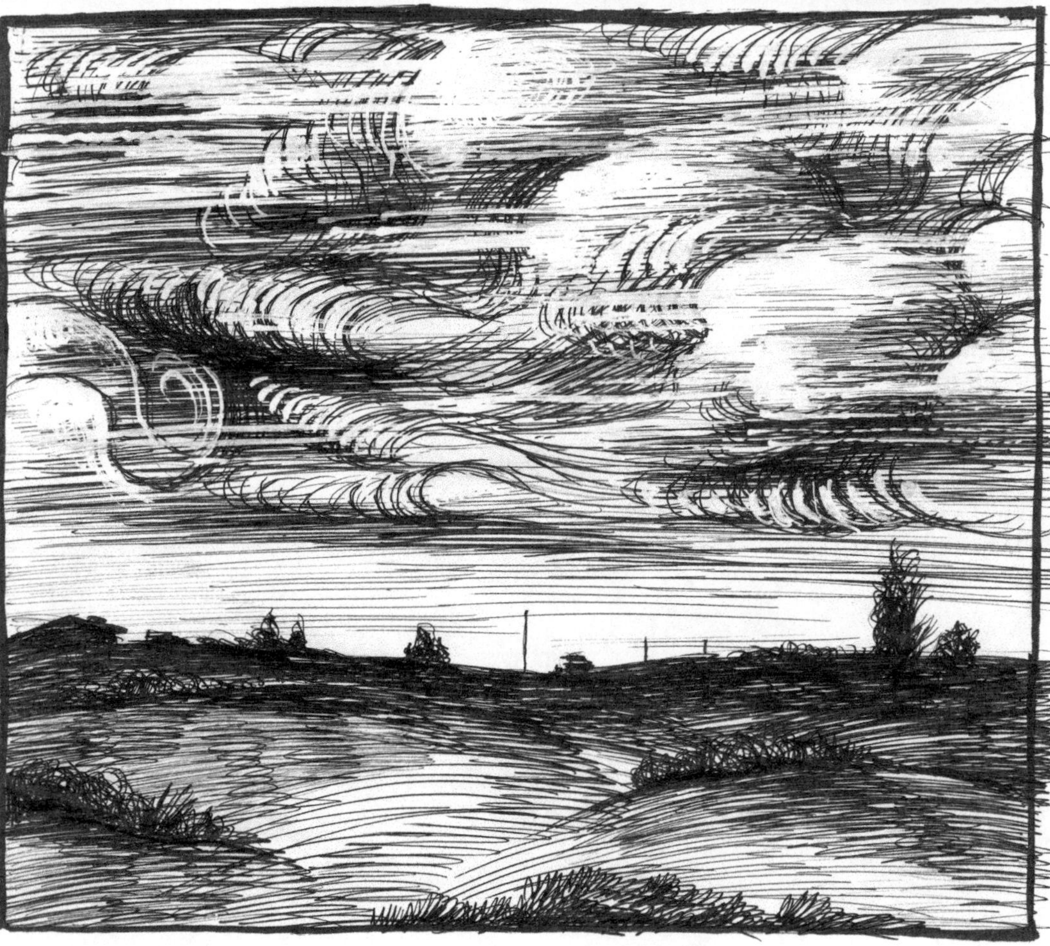

RABBIT SKULL.

*Oryctolagus
cuniculus.*

CAT SKULL.

Felis silvestris catus.

FOX SKULL.

Vulpes vulpes.

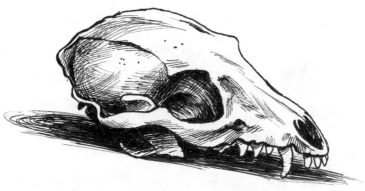

ADULT HUMAN SKULL.

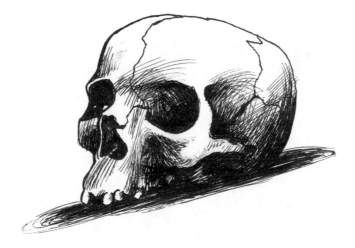

*Homo sapiens
    sapiens.*

CHILD'S SKULL.

Homo sapiens sapiens.

V

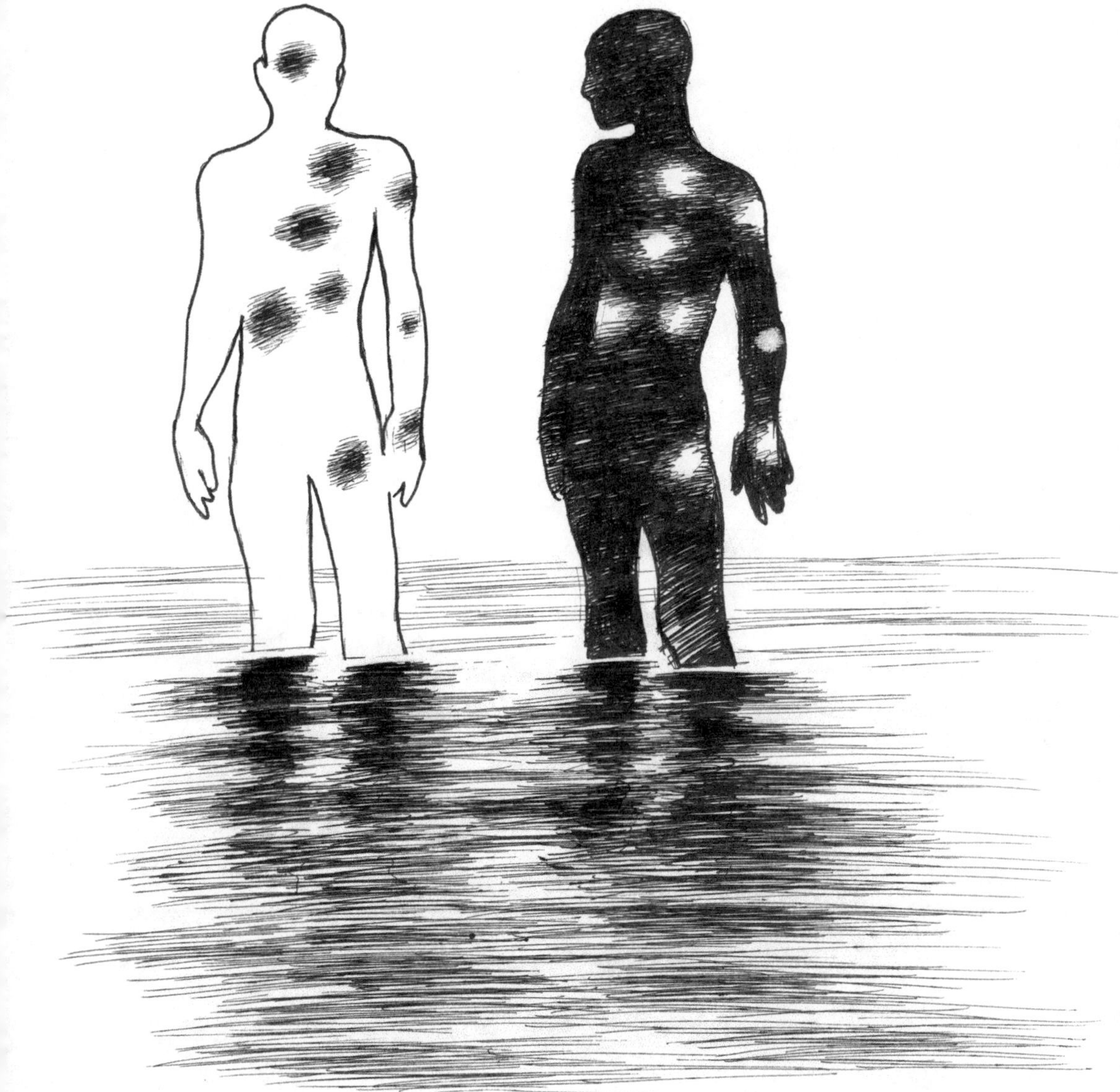

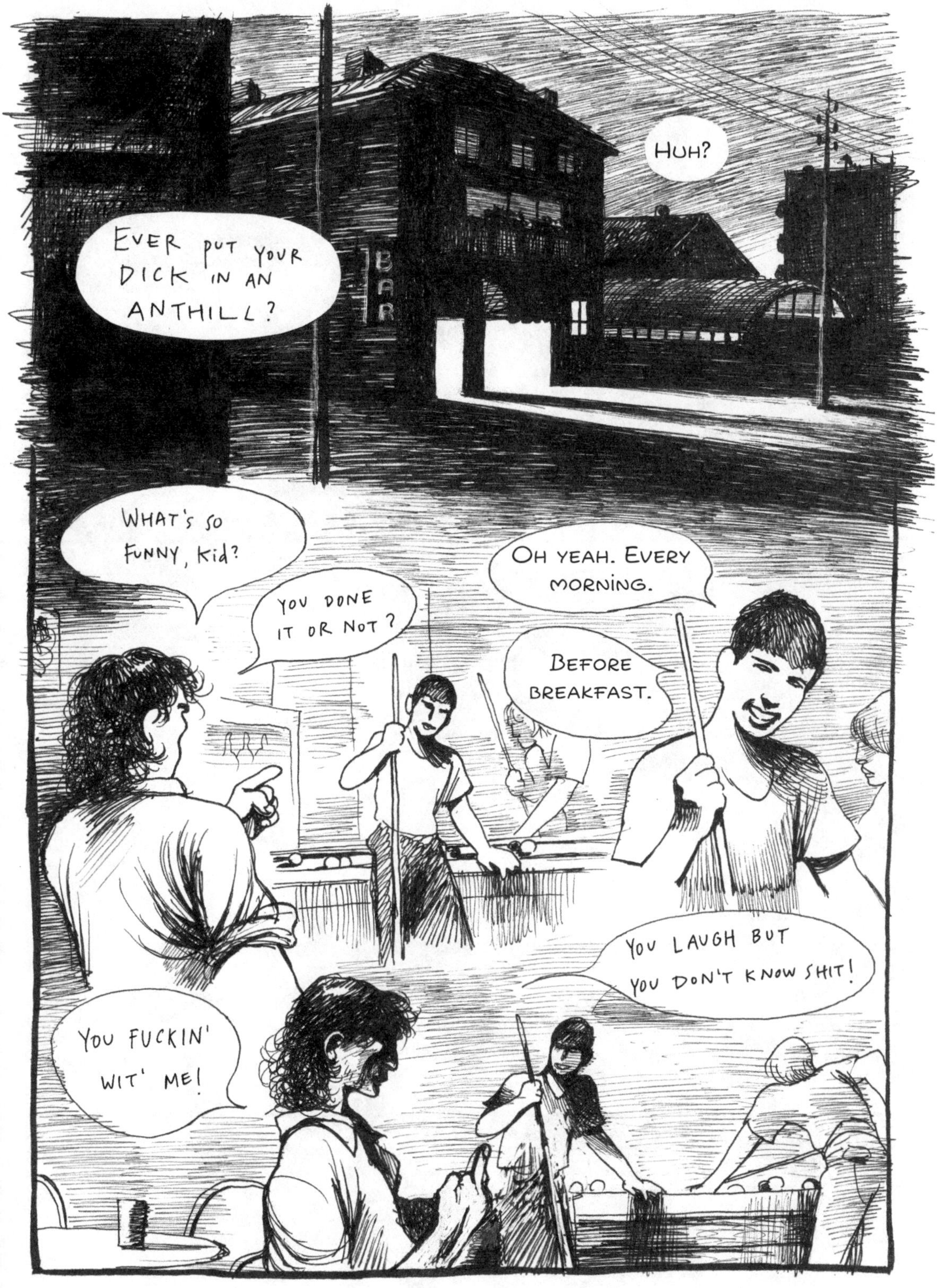
EVER PUT YOUR DICK IN AN ANTHILL?
HUH?
BAR
WHAT'S SO FUNNY, KID?
YOU DONE IT OR NOT?
OH YEAH. EVERY MORNING.
BEFORE BREAKFAST.
YOU LAUGH BUT YOU DON'T KNOW SHIT!
YOU FUCKIN' WIT' ME!

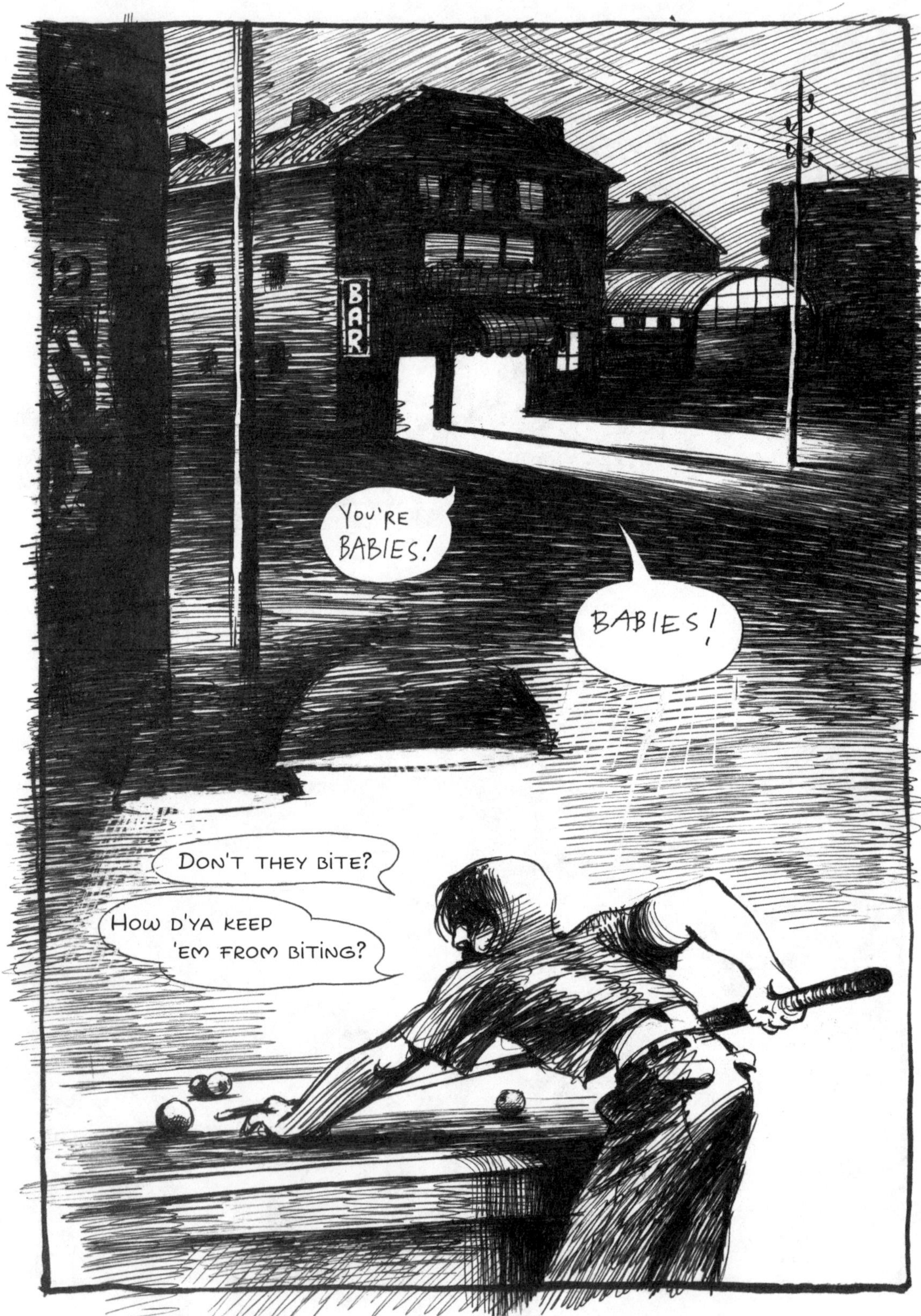
BAR
YOU'RE BABIES!
BABIES!
DON'T THEY BITE?
HOW D'YA KEEP 'EM FROM BITING?

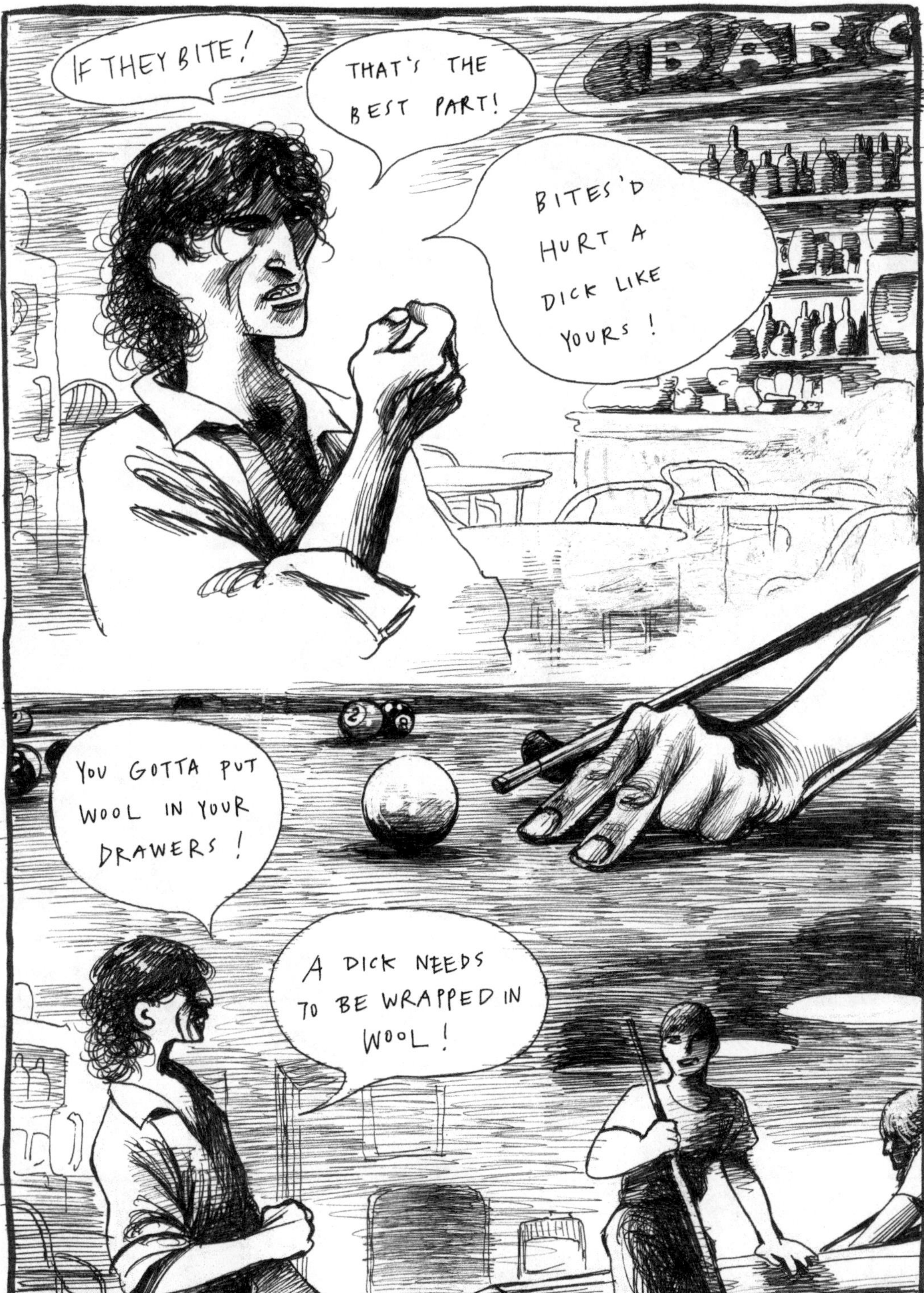
BAR
IF THEY BITE!
THAT'S THE BEST PART!
BITES'D HURT A DICK LIKE YOURS!
YOU GOTTA PUT WOOL IN YOUR DRAWERS!
A DICK NEEDS TO BE WRAPPED IN WOOL!

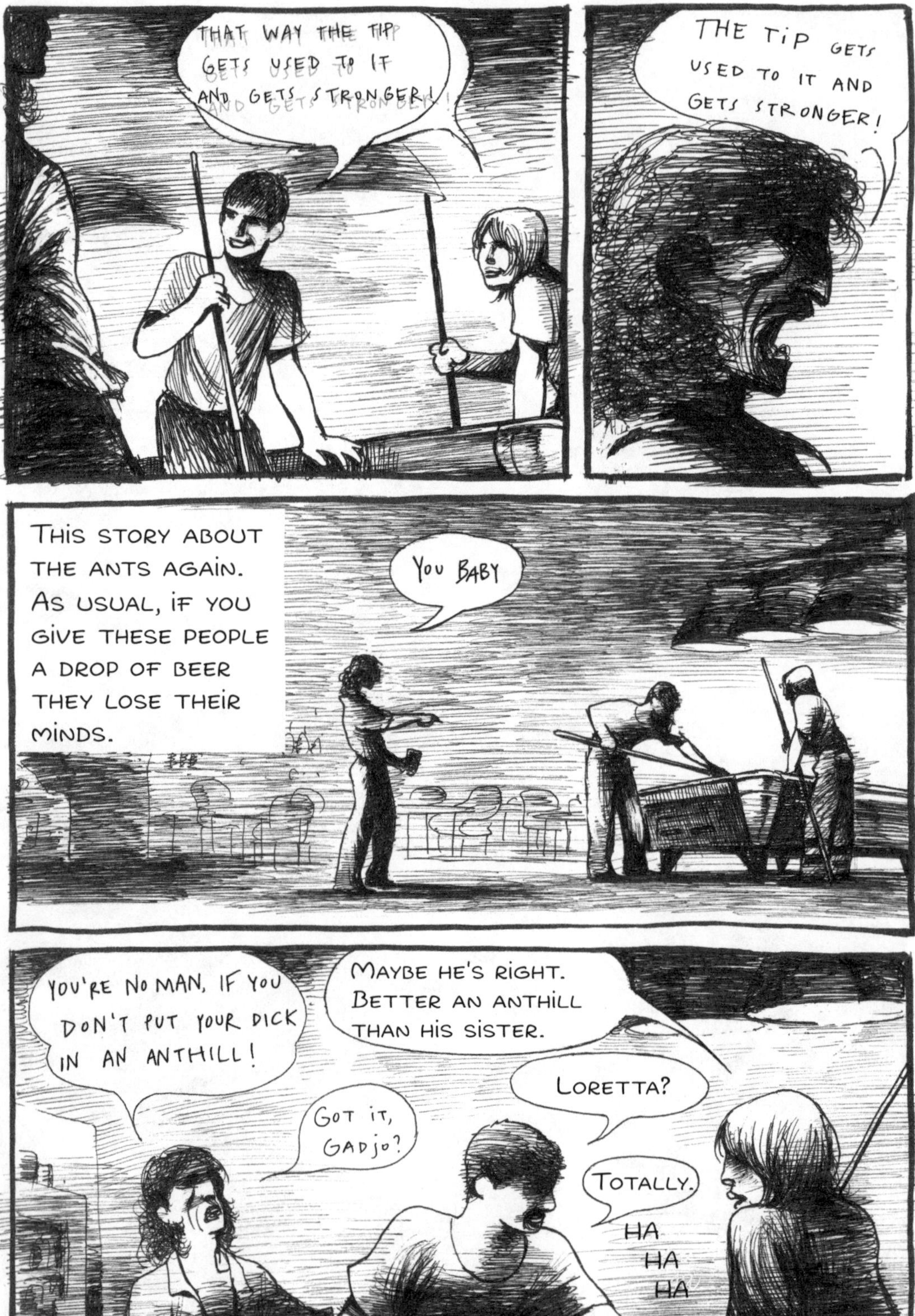
THAT WAY THE TIP GETS USED TO IT AND GETS STRONGER!
THE TIP GETS USED TO IT AND GETS STRONGER!
THIS STORY ABOUT THE ANTS AGAIN. AS USUAL, IF YOU GIVE THESE PEOPLE A DROP OF BEER THEY LOSE THEIR MINDS.
YOU BABY
YOU'RE NO MAN, IF YOU DON'T PUT YOUR DICK IN AN ANTHILL!
MAYBE HE'S RIGHT. BETTER AN ANTHILL THAN HIS SISTER.
LORETTA?
GOT IT, GADJO?
TOTALLY.
HA HA HA

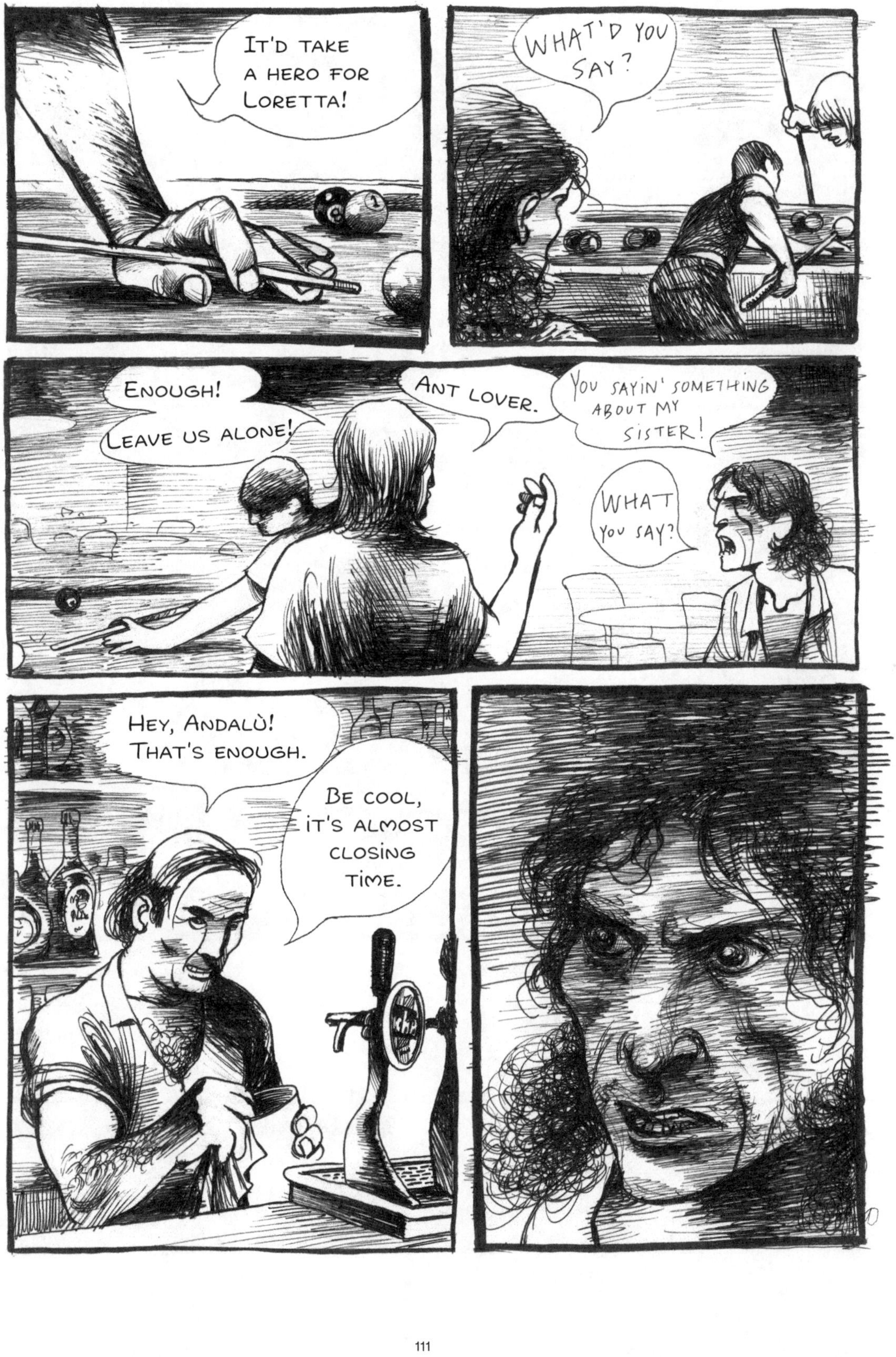
It'd take a hero for Loretta!
What'd you say?
Enough!
Leave us alone!
Ant lover.
You sayin' something about my sister!
What you say?
Hey, Andalù! That's enough.
Be cool, it's almost closing time.

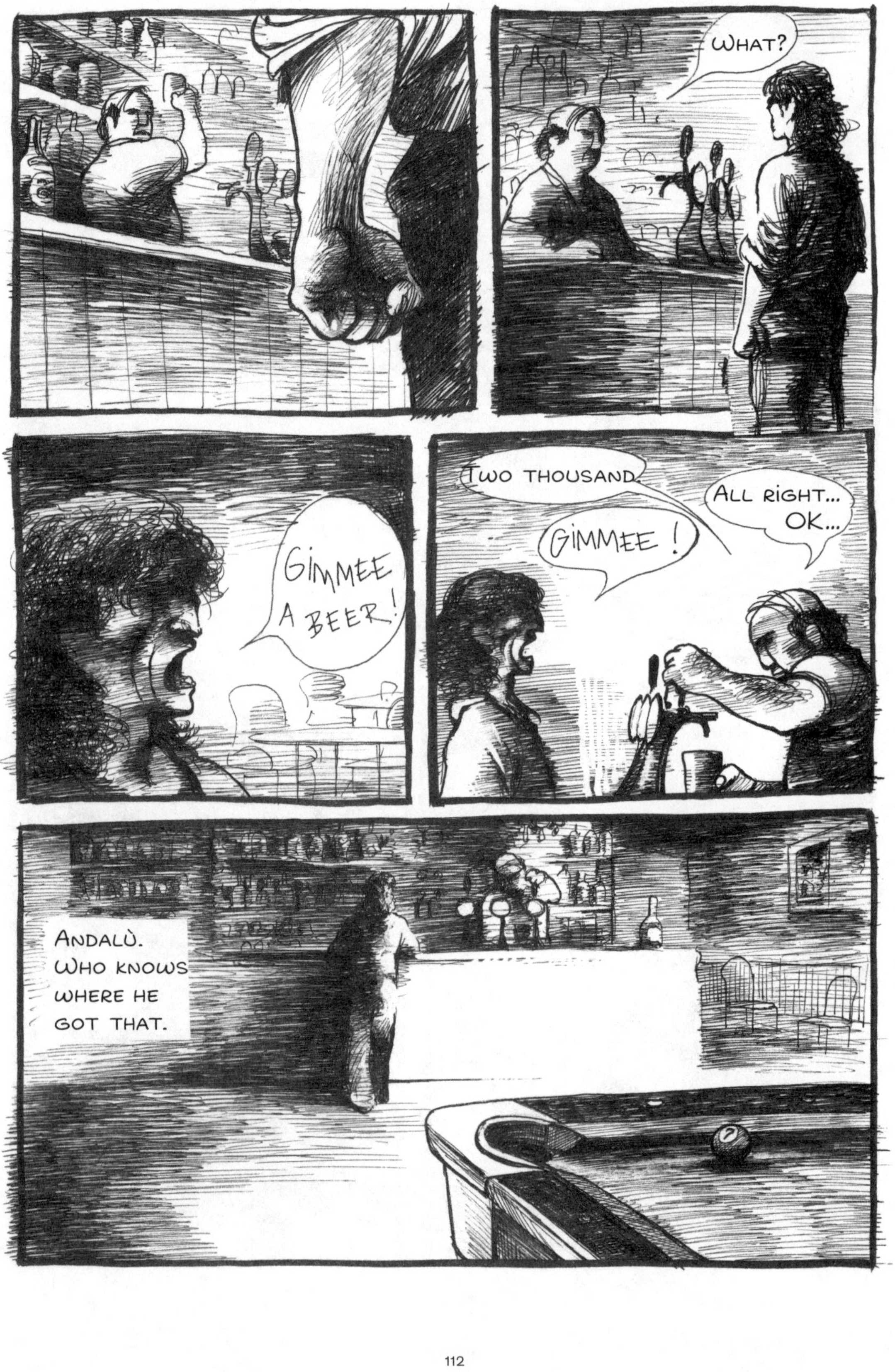
WHAT?
GIMMEE A BEER!
TWO THOUSAND
GIMMEE!
ALL RIGHT... OK...
ANDALÙ. WHO KNOWS WHERE HE GOT THAT.

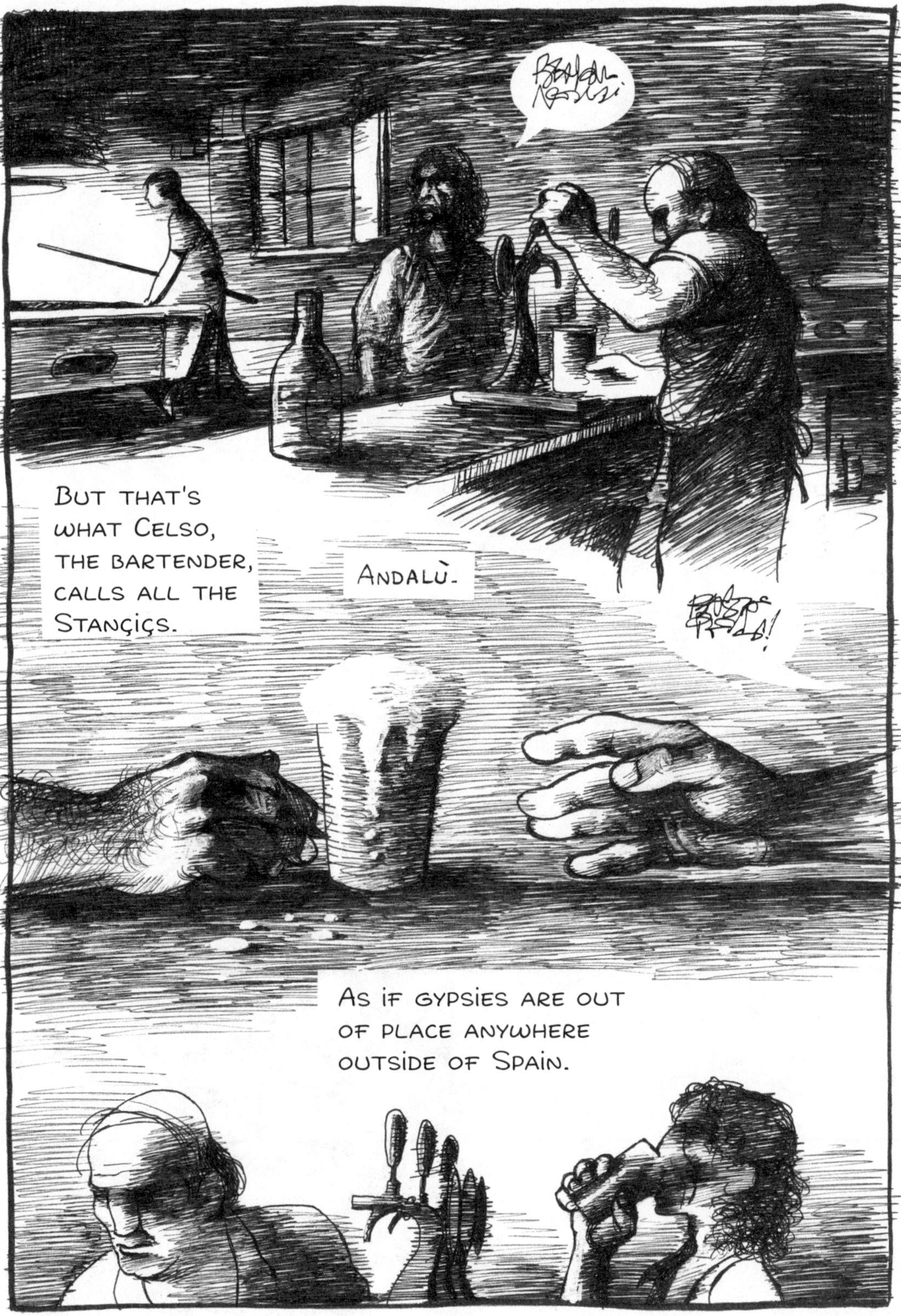

But that's what Celso, the bartender, calls all the Stançiçs.
Andalù.
As if gypsies are out of place anywhere outside of Spain.

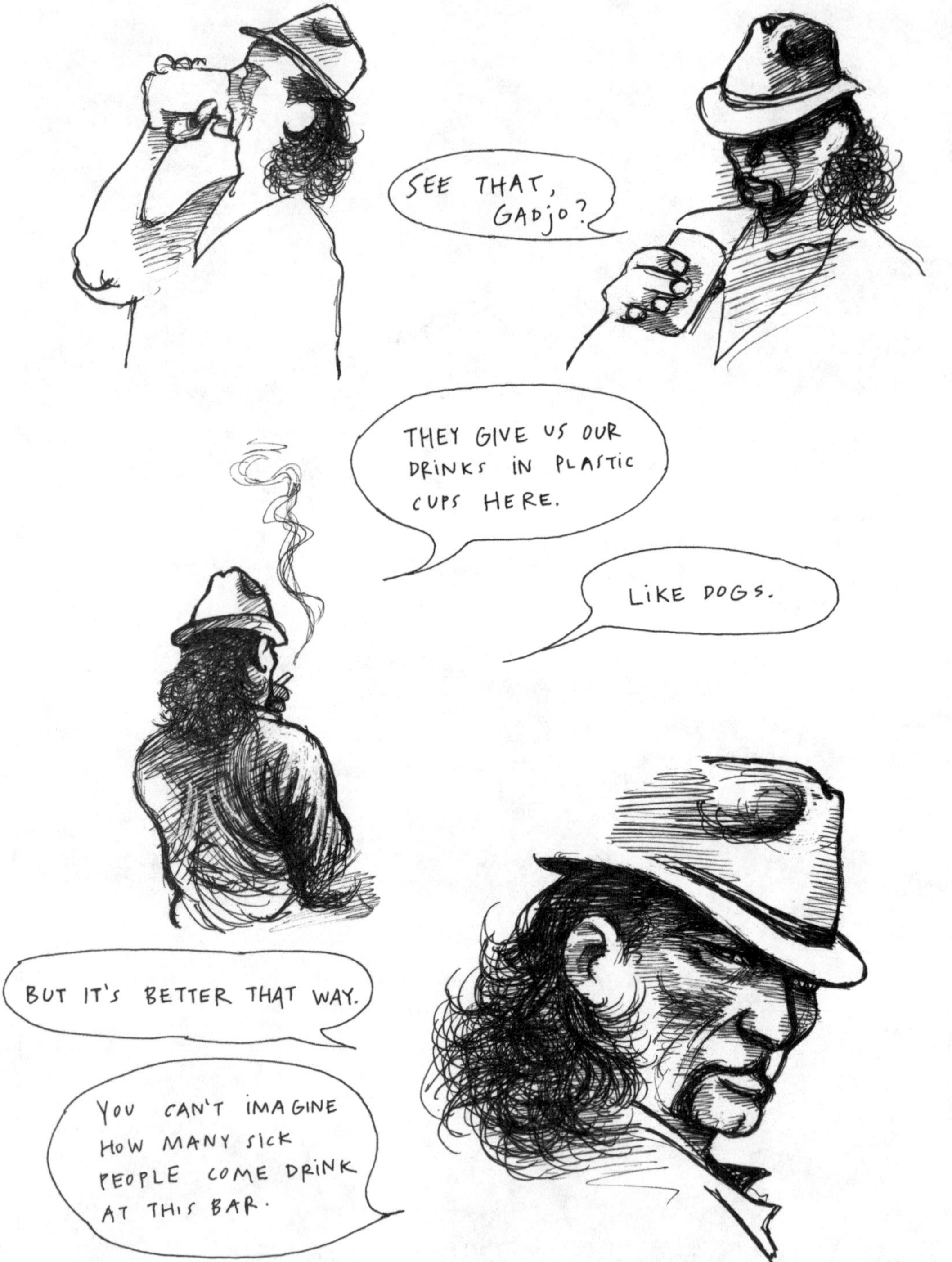

SEE THAT, GADJO?
THEY GIVE US OUR DRINKS IN PLASTIC CUPS HERE.
LIKE DOGS.
BUT IT'S BETTER THAT WAY.
YOU CAN'T IMAGINE HOW MANY SICK PEOPLE COME DRINK AT THIS BAR.

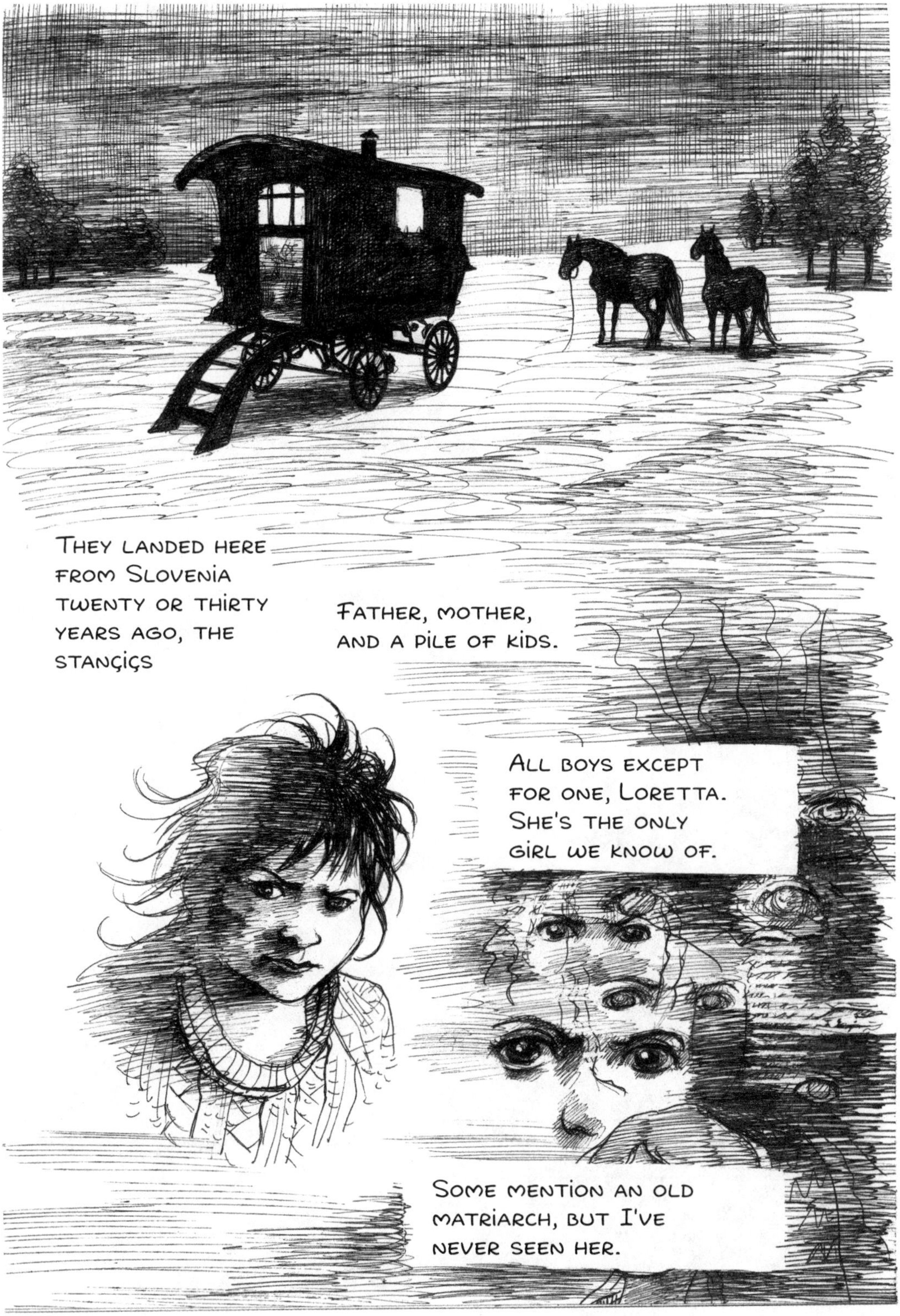

They landed here from Slovenia twenty or thirty years ago, the Stançiçs
Father, mother, and a pile of kids.
All boys except for one, Loretta. She's the only girl we know of.
Some mention an old matriarch, but I've never seen her.

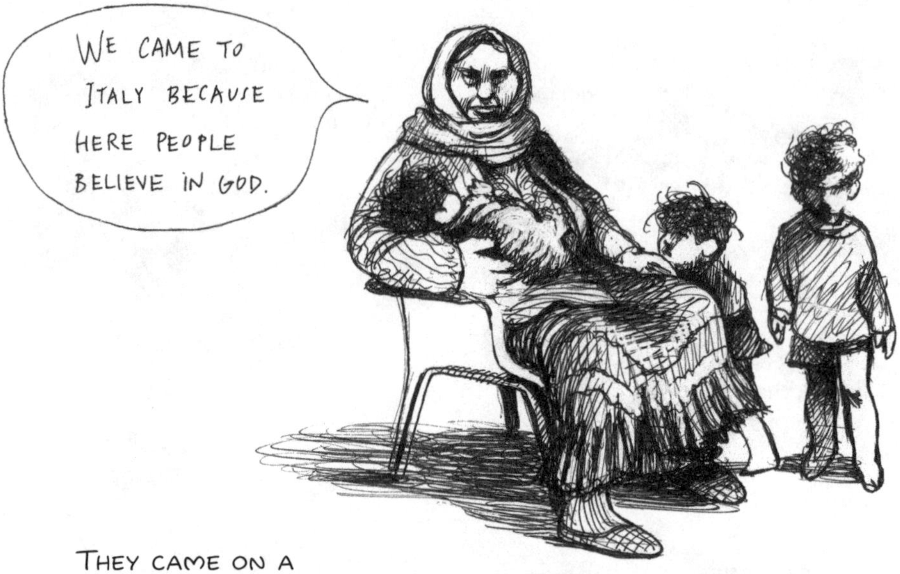
WE CAME TO ITALY BECAUSE HERE PEOPLE BELIEVE IN GOD.

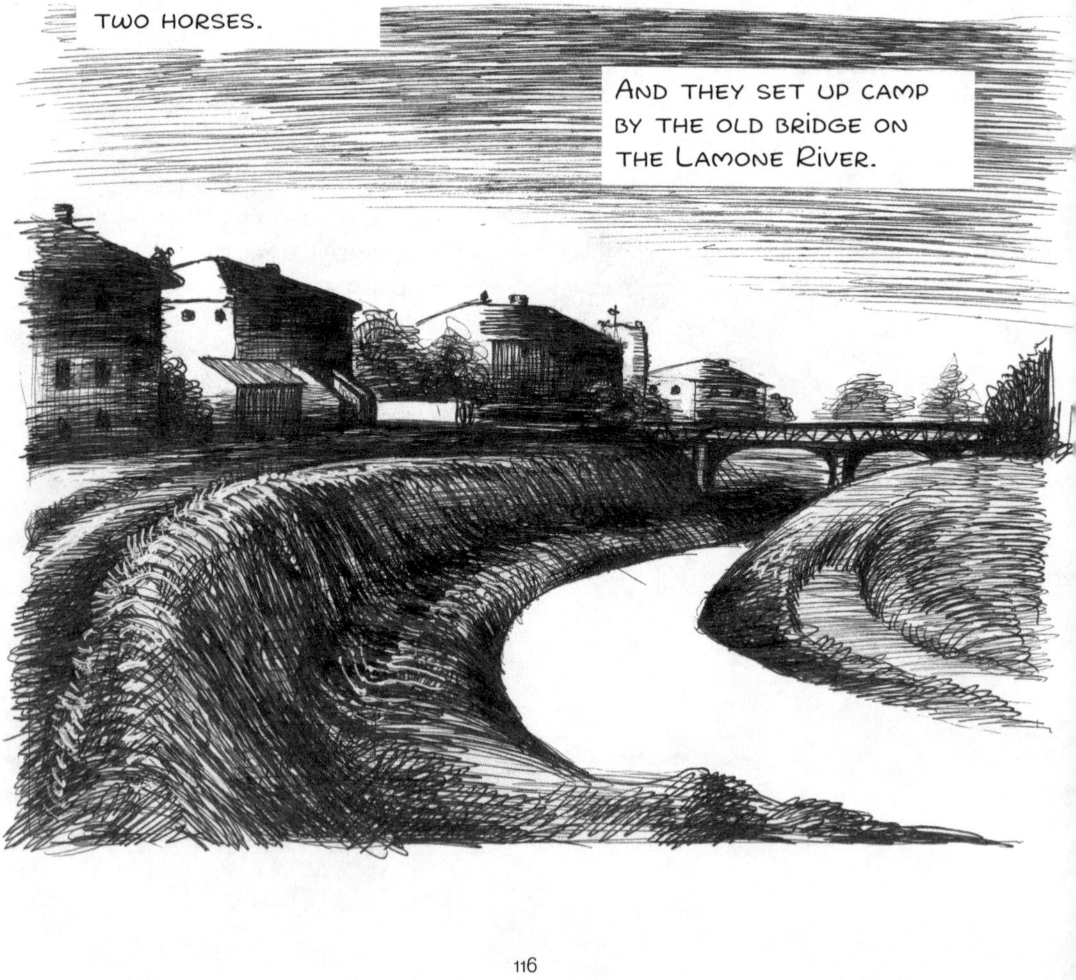
THEY CAME ON A WAGON PULLED BY TWO HORSES.
AND THEY SET UP CAMP BY THE OLD BRIDGE ON THE LAMONE RIVER.

THE CITY TRIED, ASSIGNED THEM AN APARTMENT IN TOWN, BUT IT WAS NO USE—THEY'RE NOT MADE TO LIVE IN HOUSES LIKE US.

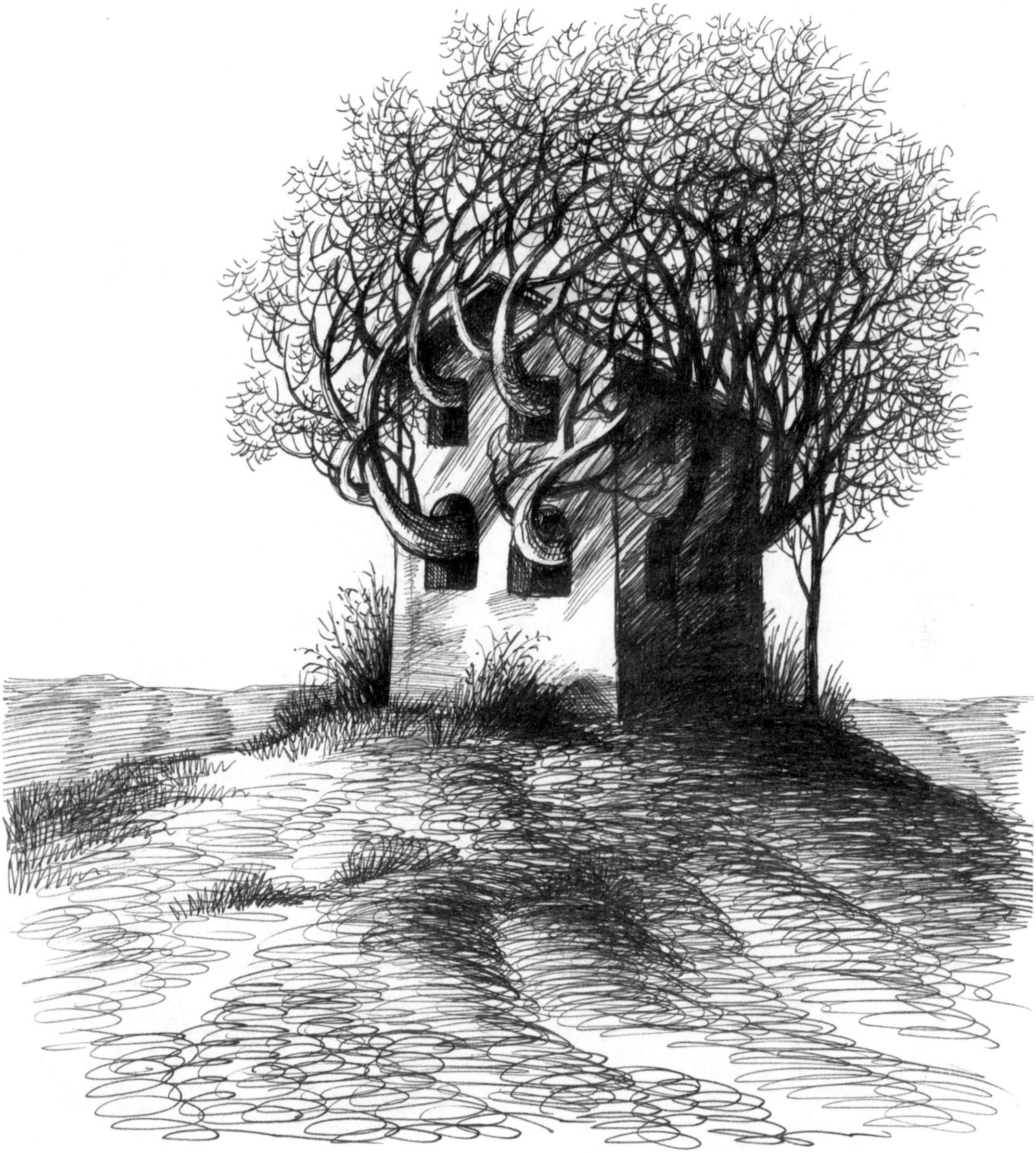

Within a few months, they'd left the apartment and settled into the abandoned farmhouse next to the train tracks.

An old dump owned by the city without electricity or water.

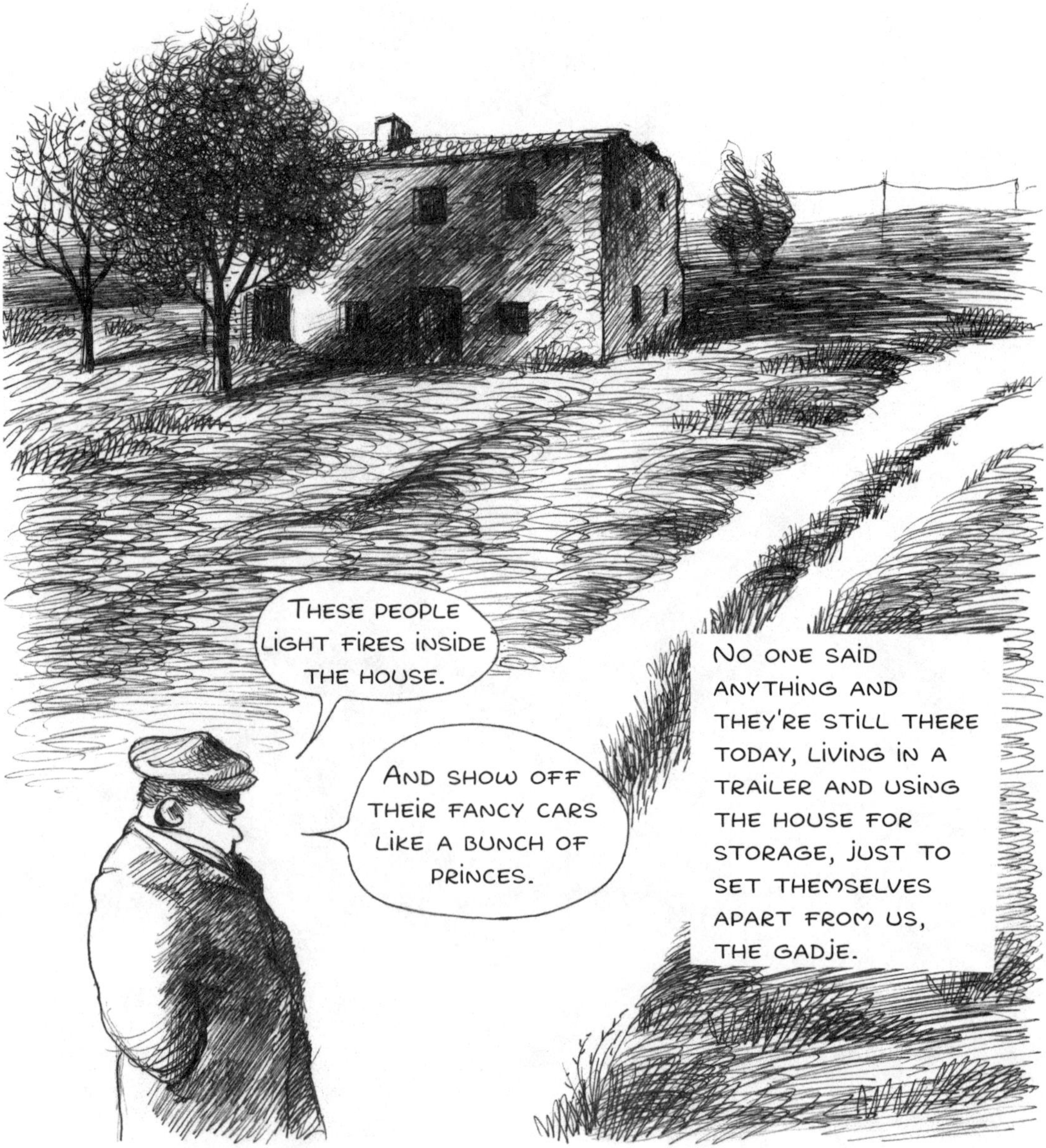
These people light fires inside the house.
And show off their fancy cars like a bunch of princes.
No one said anything and they're still there today, living in a trailer and using the house for storage, just to set themselves apart from us, the gadje.

THAT'S ALL I KNOW,
AND IT'S MORE THAN
ENOUGH.

BESIDES, WHO
GIVES A SHIT.

THEY'RE GYPSIES, WHAT
ELSE IS THERE TO KNOW?

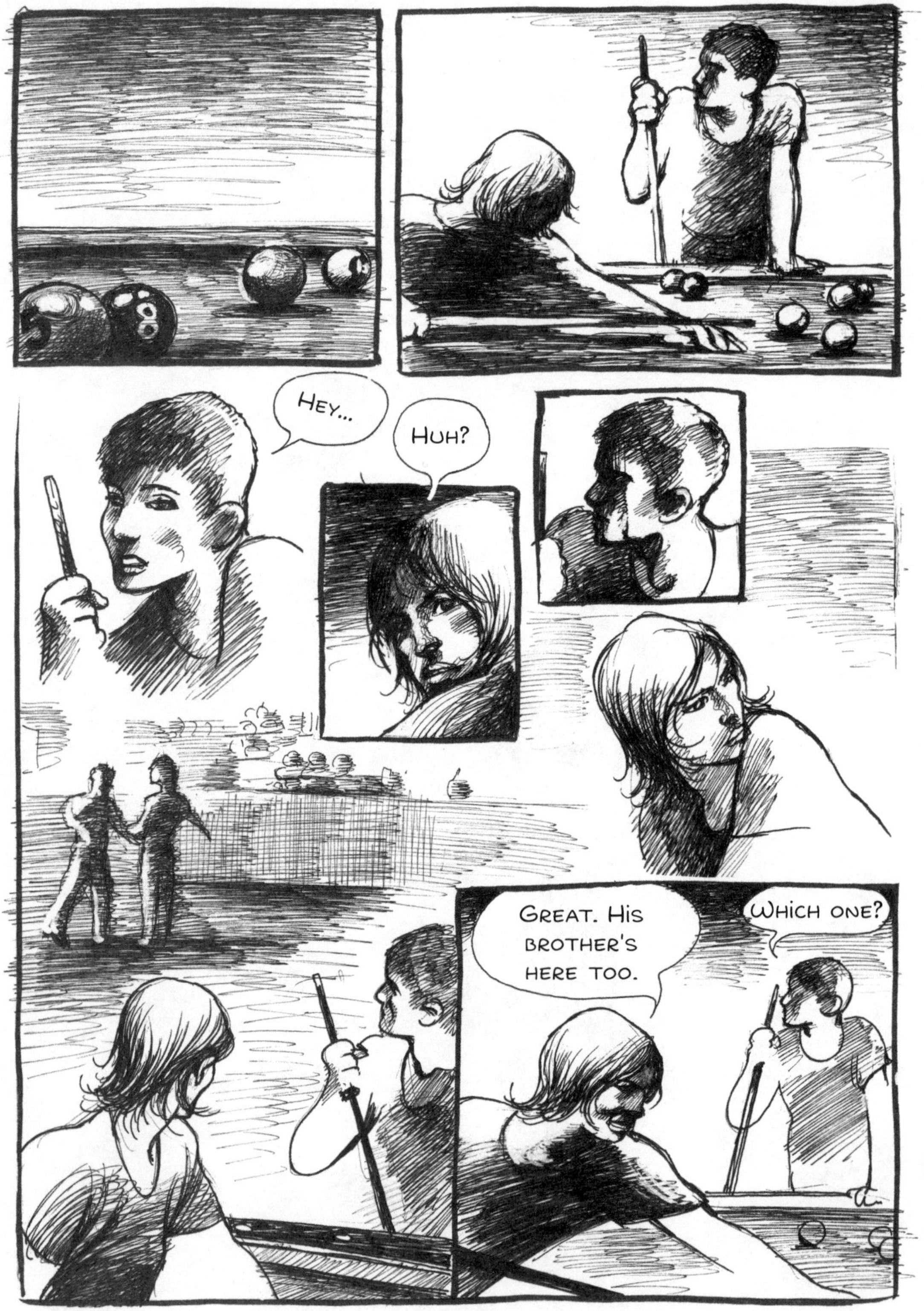
Hey...
Huh?
Great. His brother's here too.
Which one?

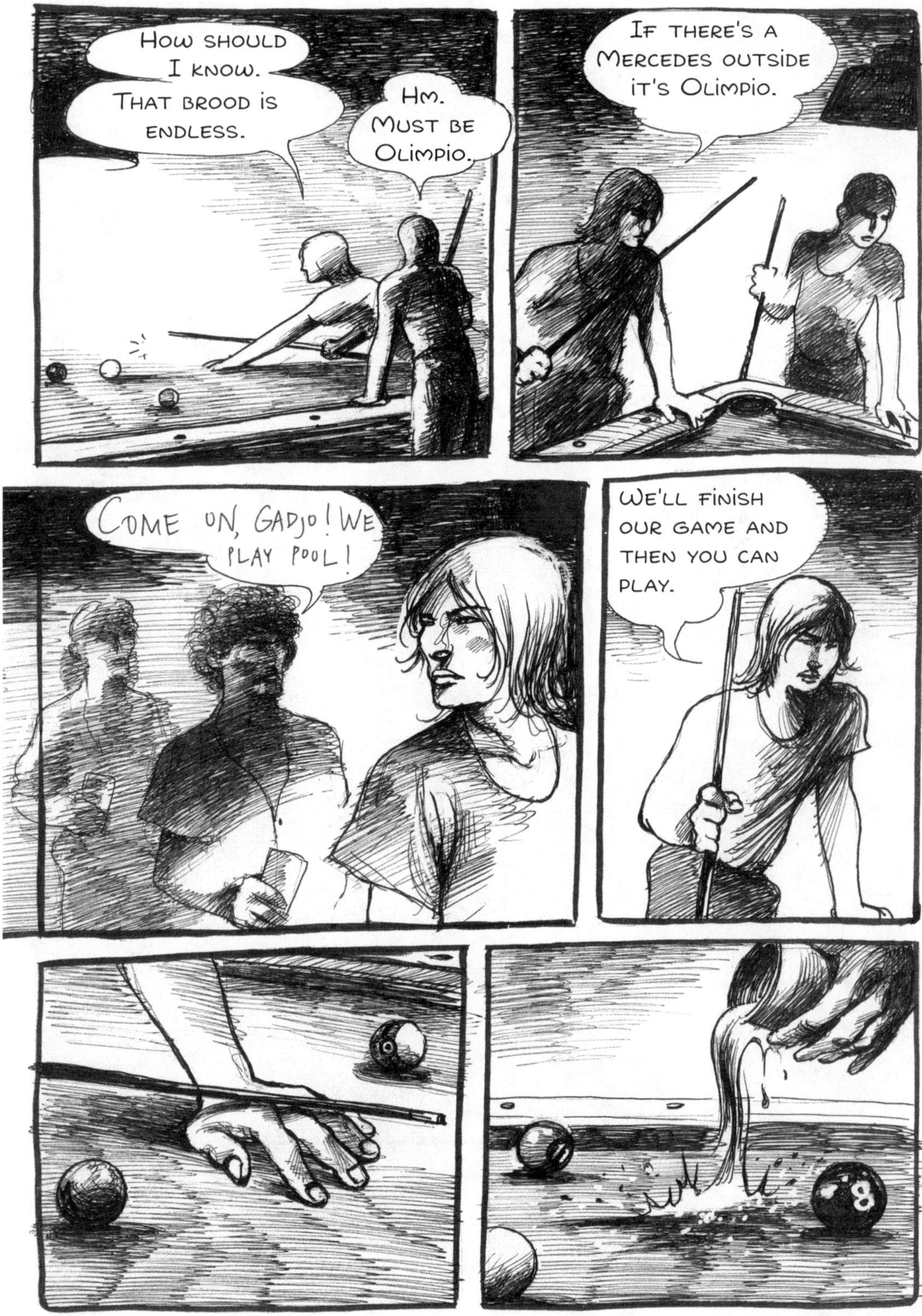
How should I know.
That brood is endless.
Hm. Must be Olimpio.
If there's a Mercedes outside it's Olimpio.
Come on, Gadjo! We play pool!
We'll finish our game and then you can play.

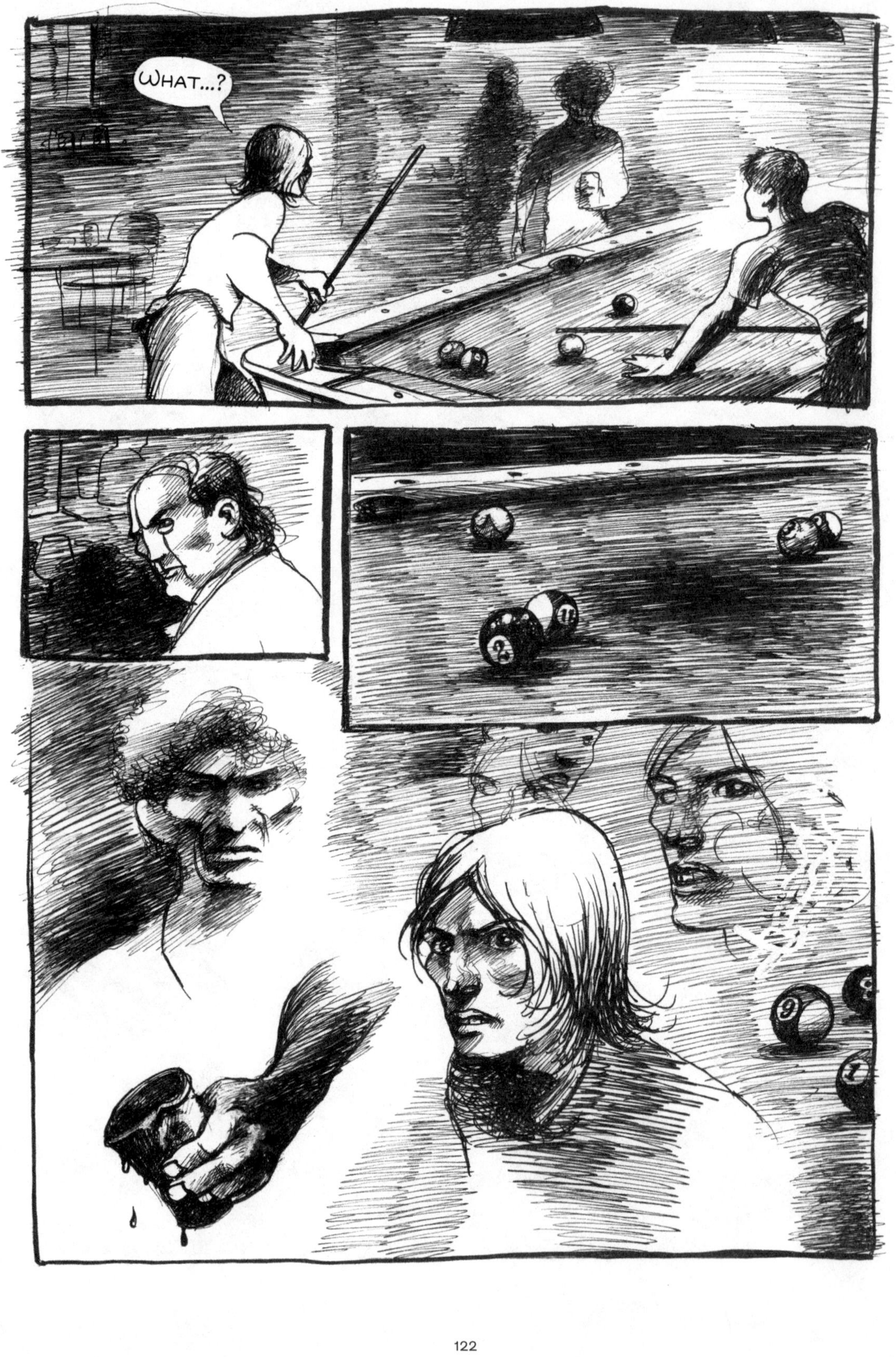
WHAT...?

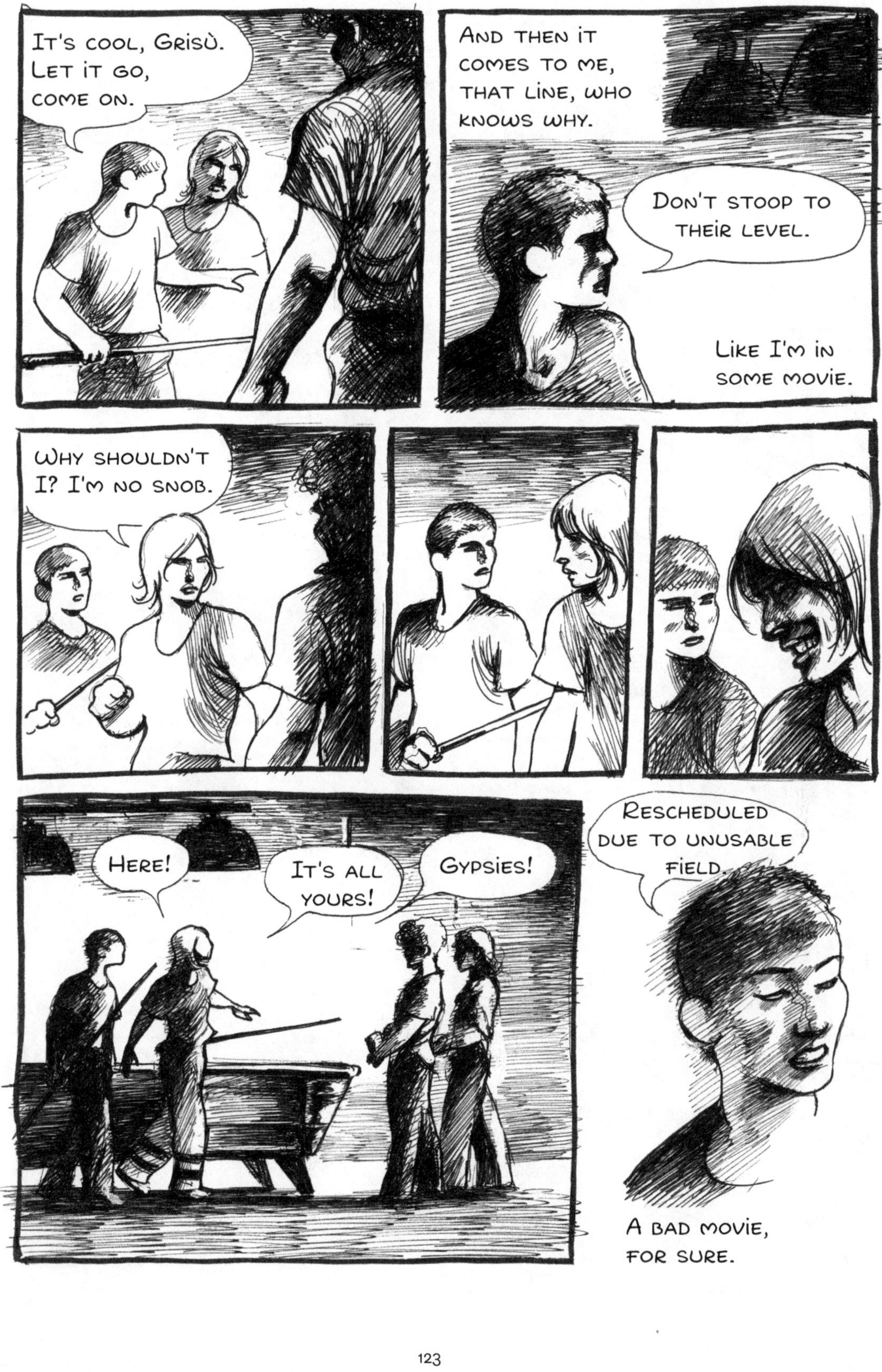
It's cool, Grisù. Let it go, come on.
And then it comes to me, that line, who knows why.
Don't stoop to their level.
Like I'm in some movie.
Why shouldn't I? I'm no snob.
Here!
It's all yours!
Gypsies!
Rescheduled due to unusable field.
A bad movie, for sure.

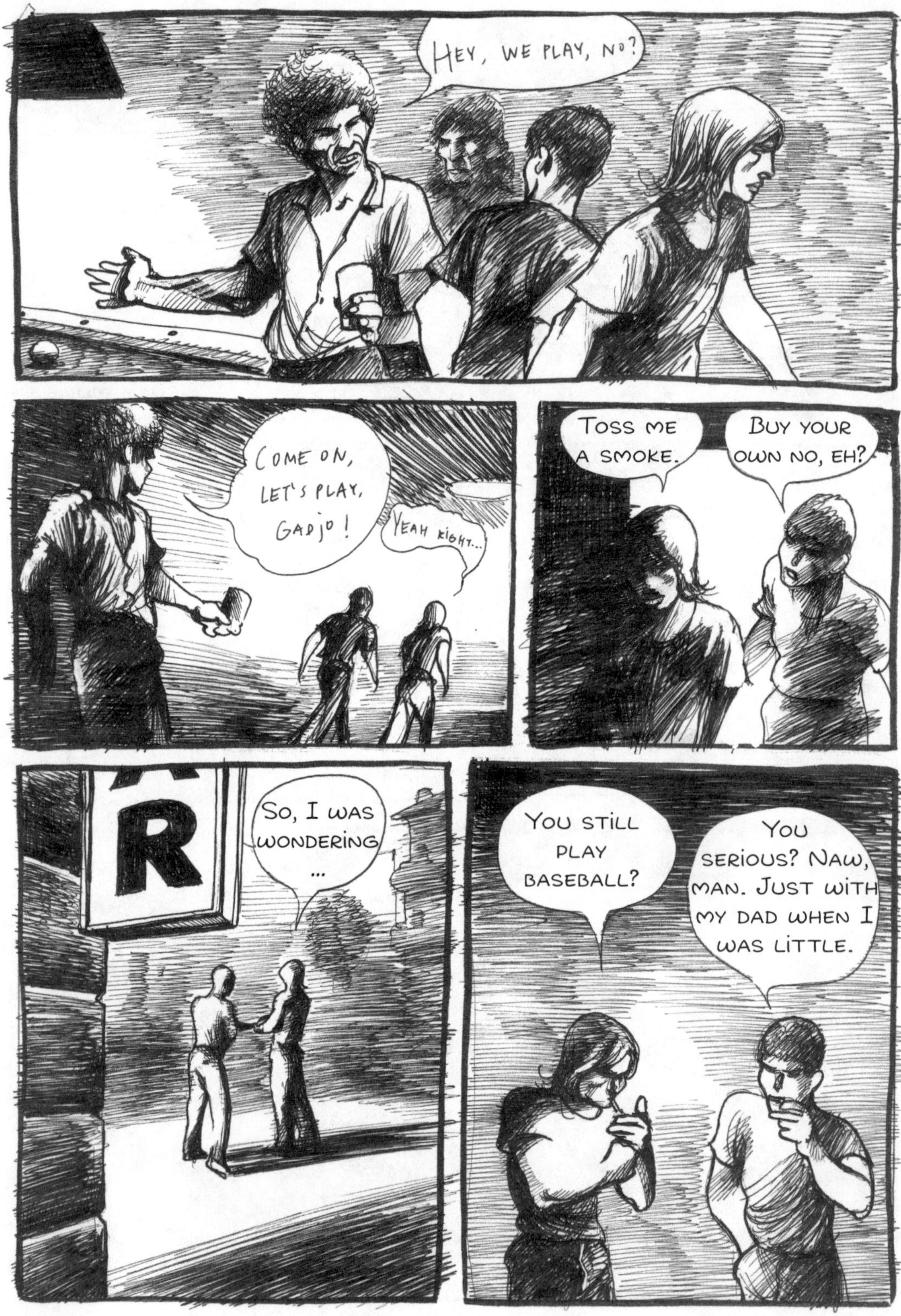
HEY, WE PLAY, NO?
COME ON, LET'S PLAY, GADJO!
YEAH RIGHT...
TOSS ME A SMOKE.
BUY YOUR OWN NO, EH?
SO, I WAS WONDERING ...
YOU STILL PLAY BASEBALL?
YOU SERIOUS? NAW, MAN. JUST WITH MY DAD WHEN I WAS LITTLE.

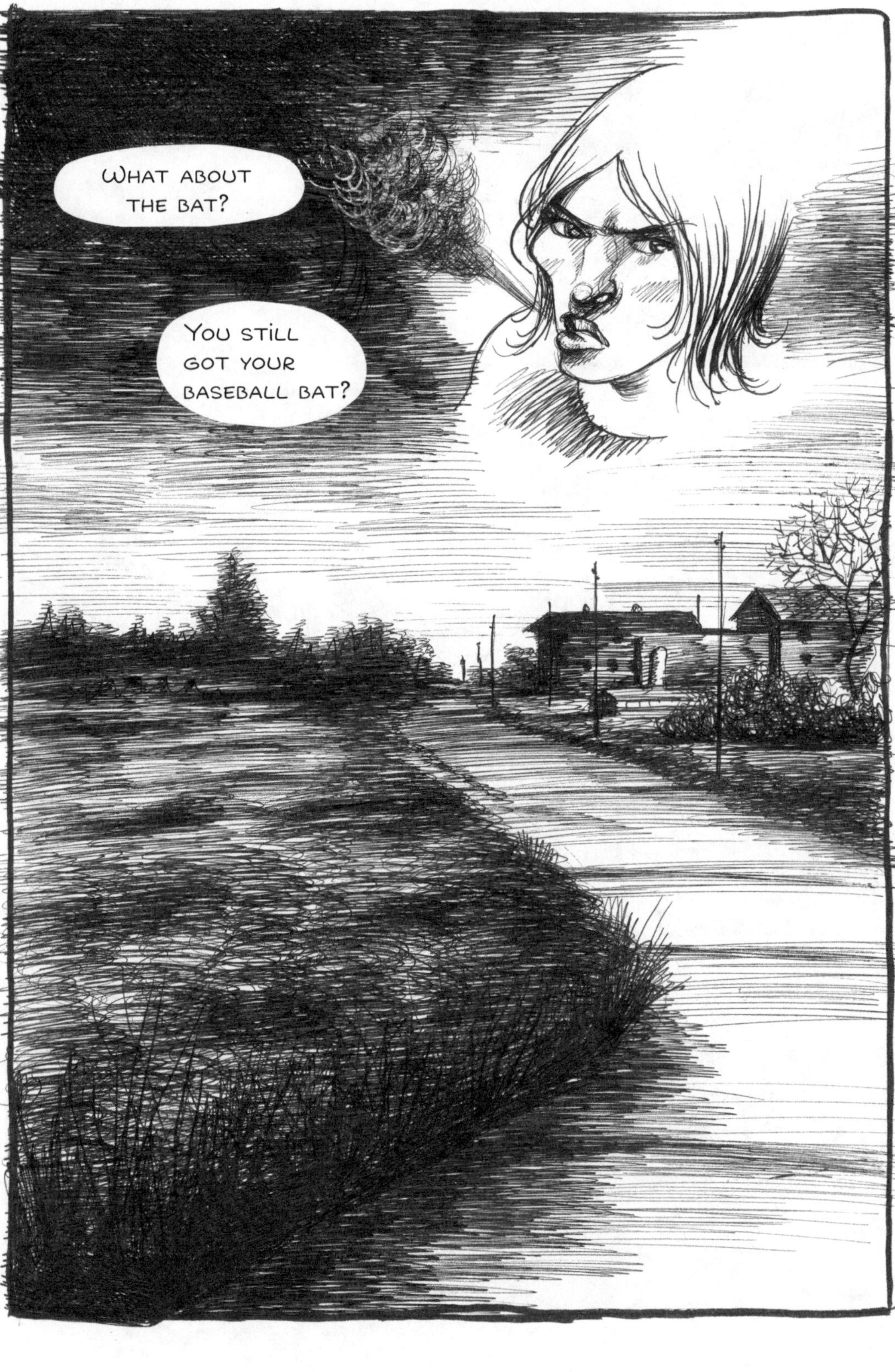
WHAT ABOUT THE BAT?
YOU STILL GOT YOUR BASEBALL BAT?

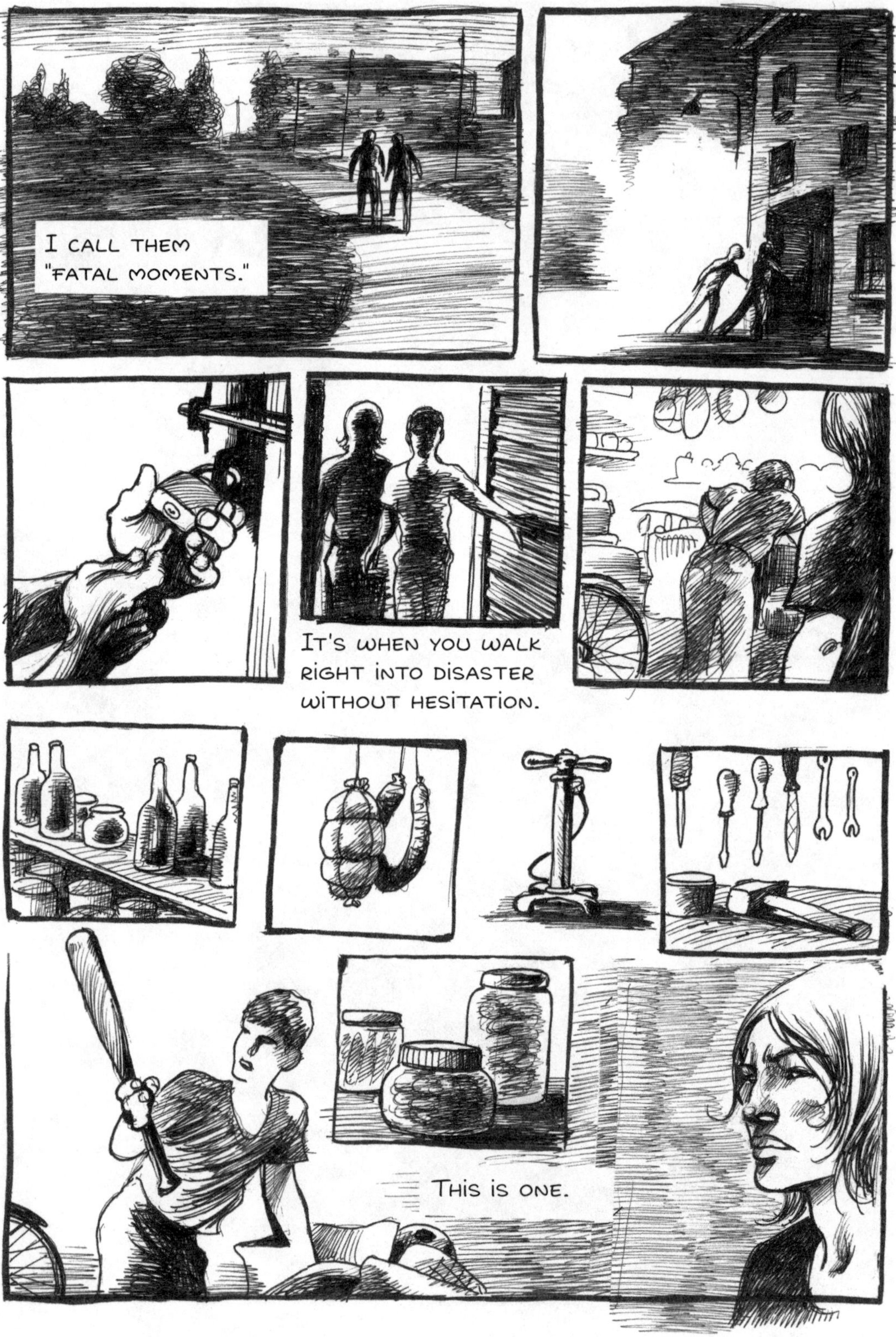
I CALL THEM "FATAL MOMENTS."
IT'S WHEN YOU WALK RIGHT INTO DISASTER WITHOUT HESITATION.
THIS IS ONE.

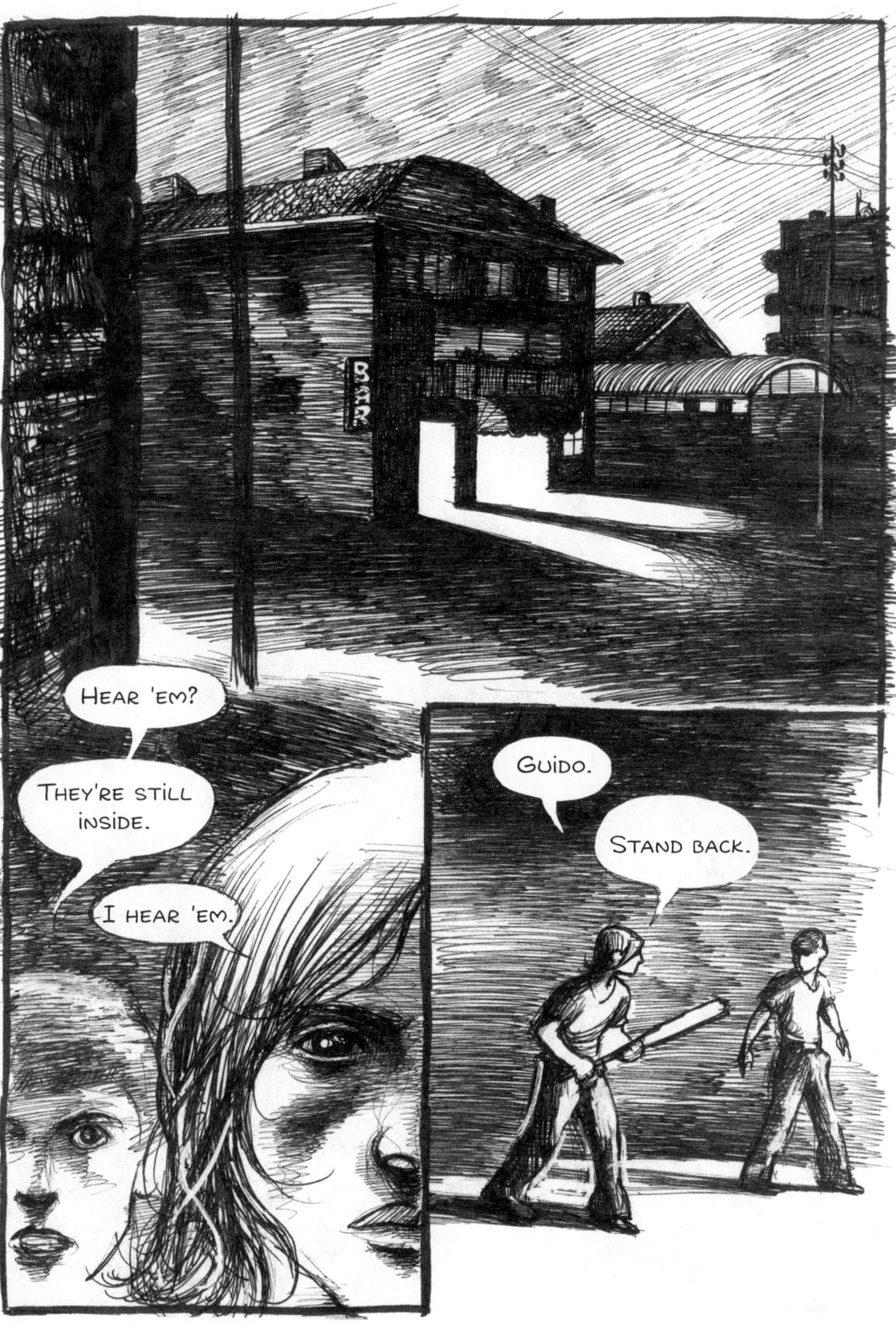
BAR
HEAR 'EM?
THEY'RE STILL INSIDE.
I HEAR 'EM.
GUIDO.
STAND BACK.

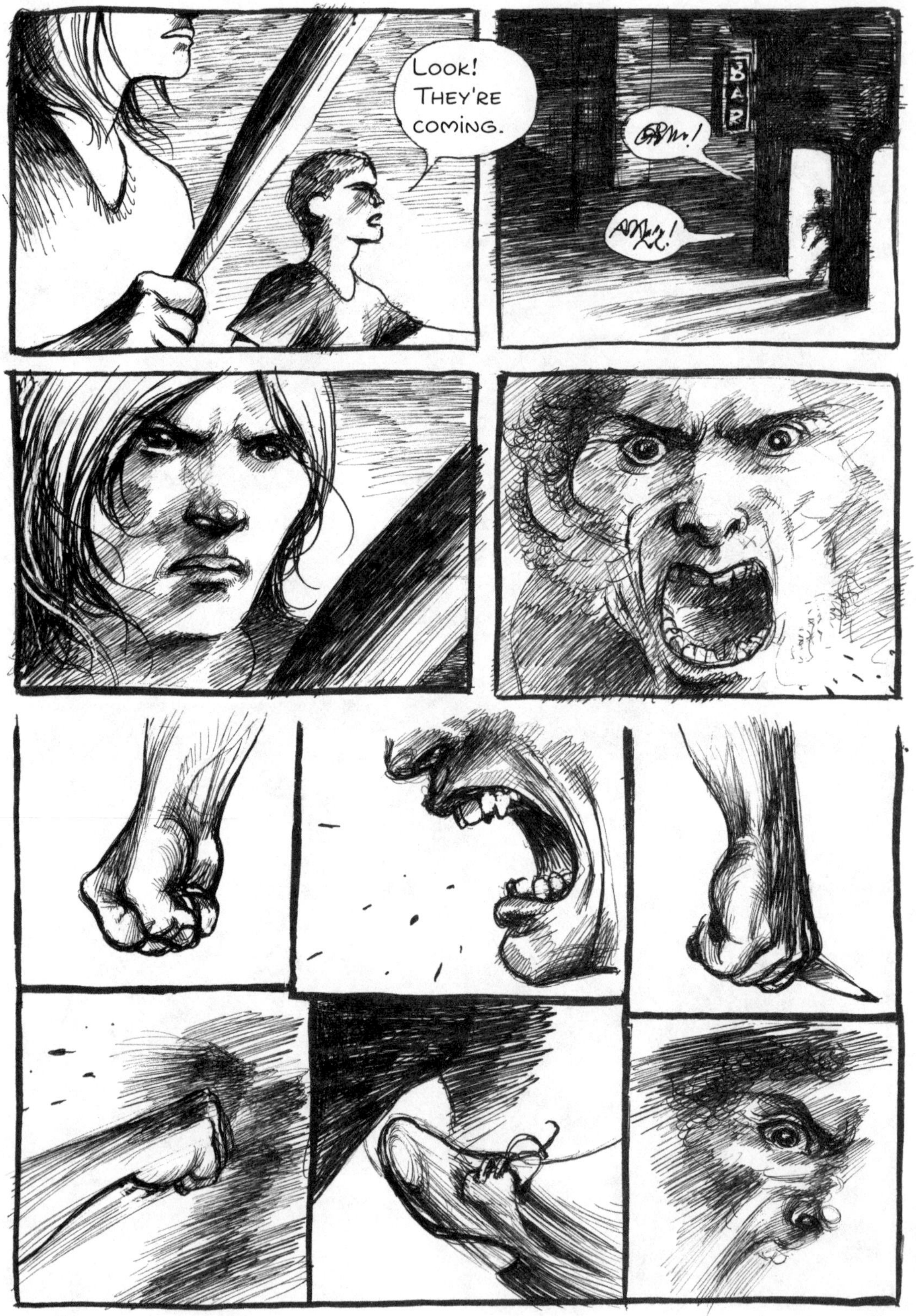
Look! They're coming.

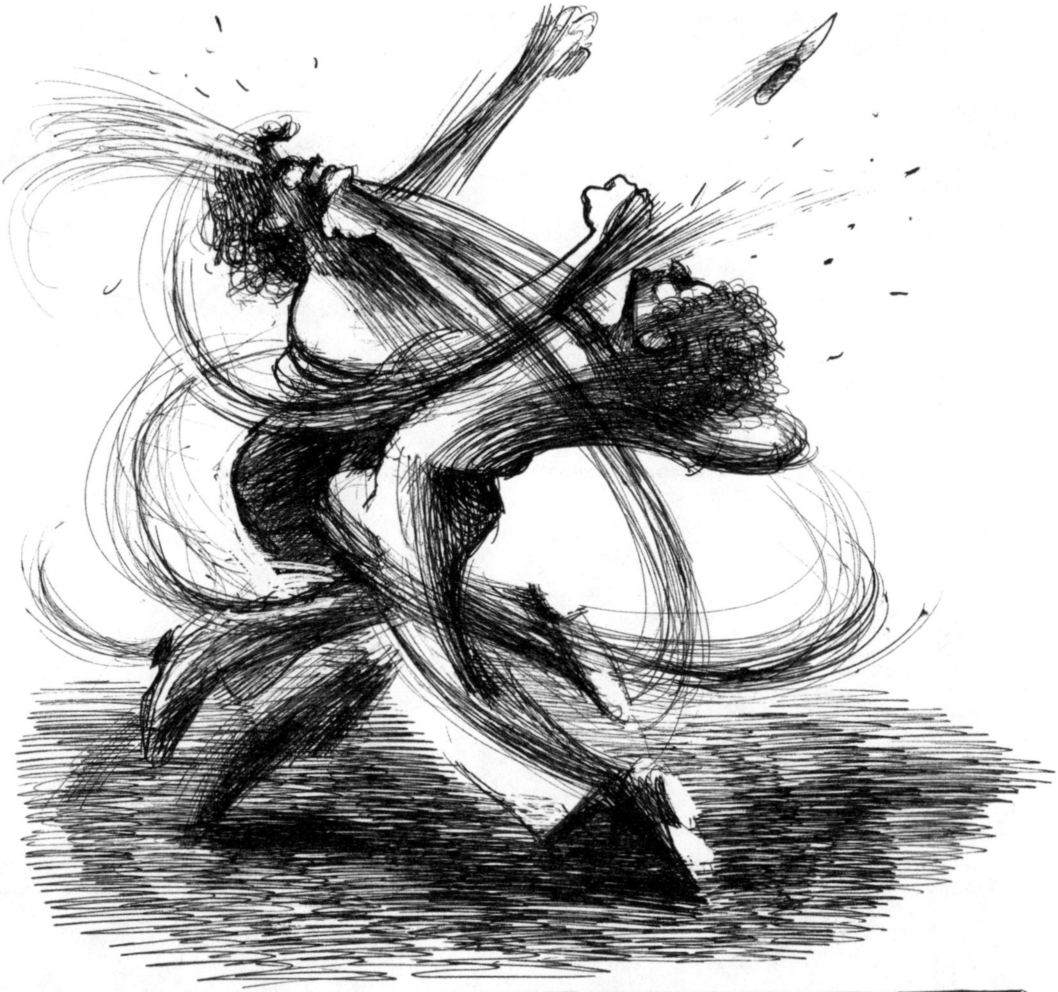

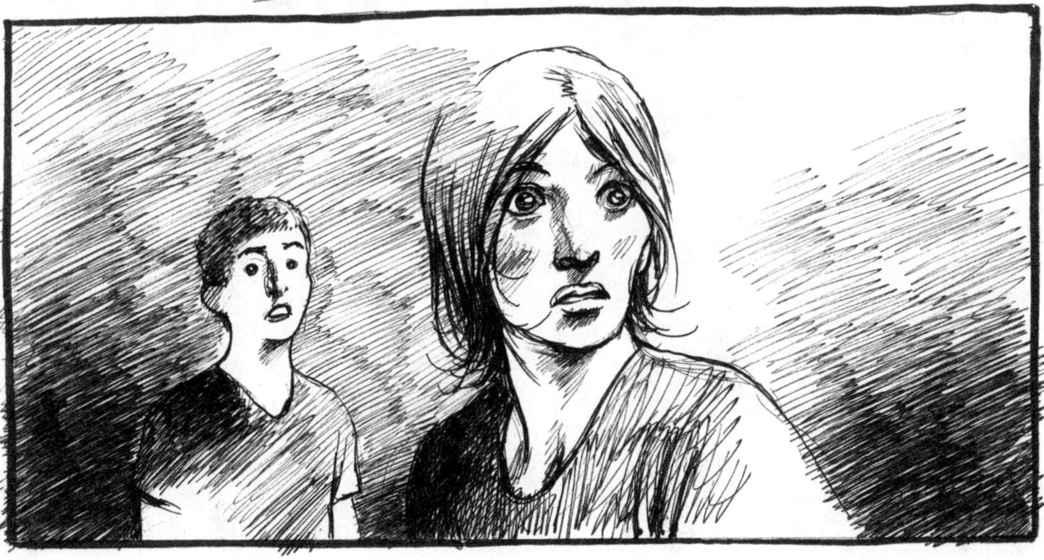

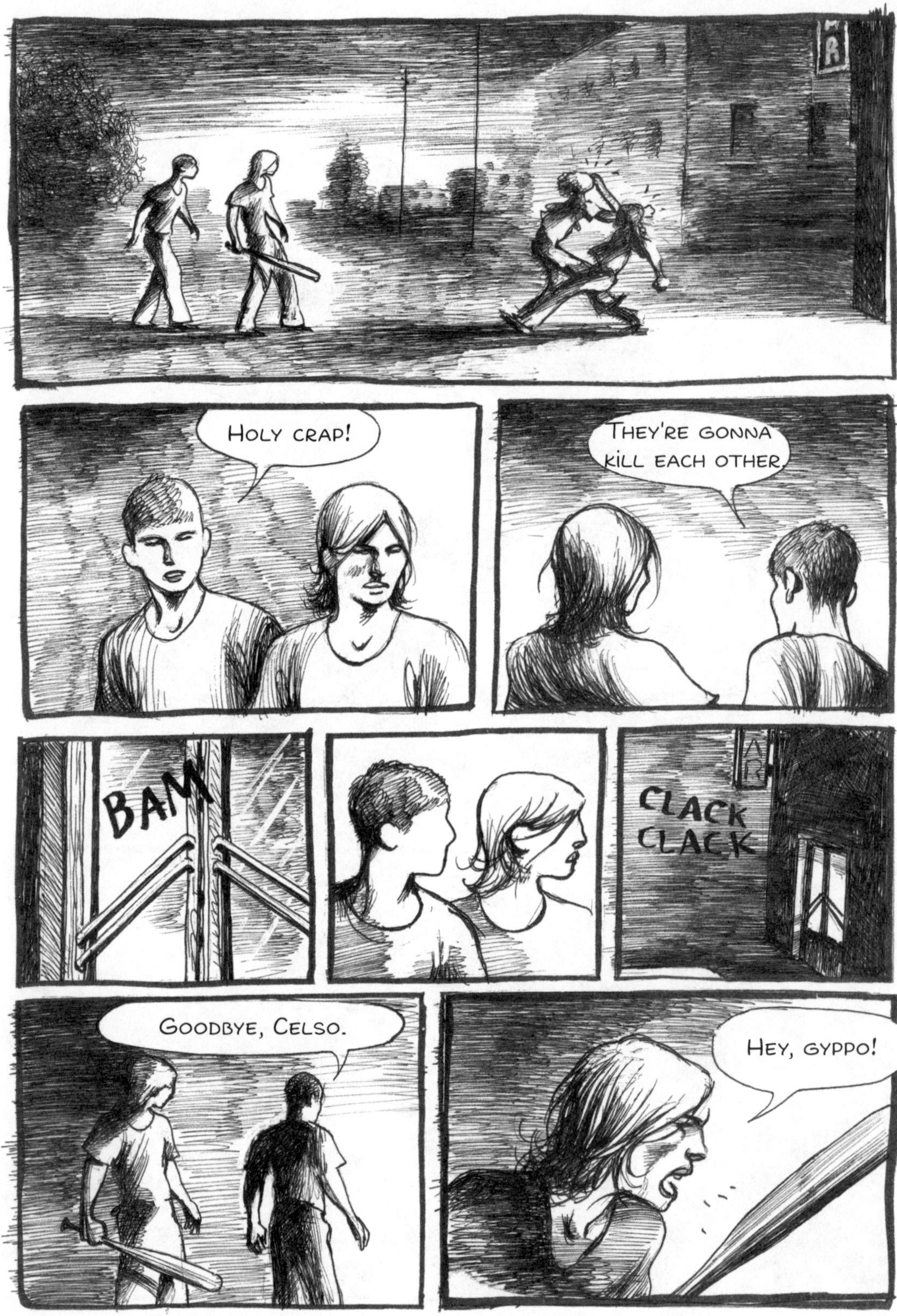
HOLY CRAP!
THEY'RE GONNA KILL EACH OTHER.
BAM
CLACK CLACK
GOODBYE, CELSO.
HEY, GYPPO!

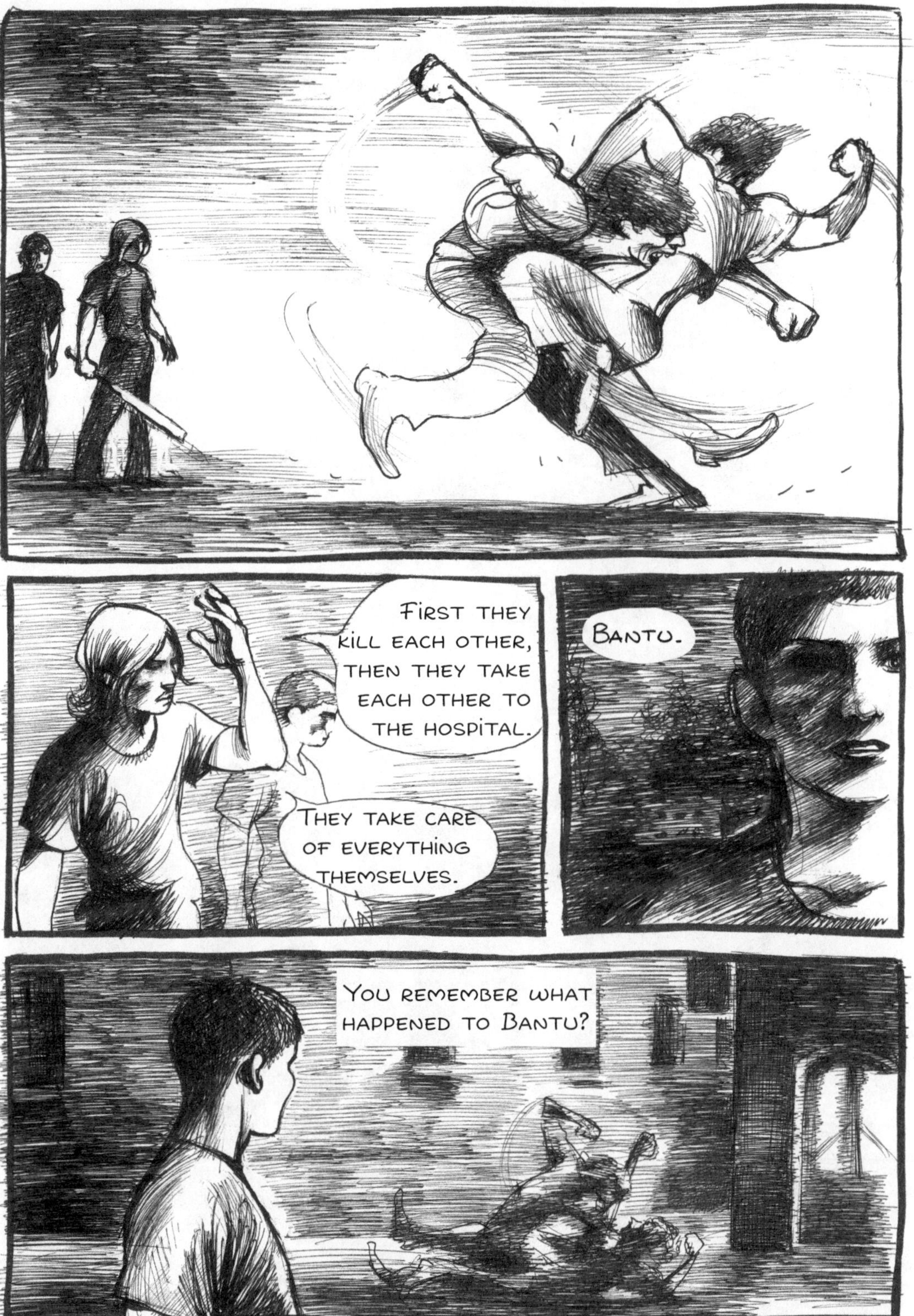
First they kill each other, then they take each other to the hospital.
They take care of everything themselves.
Bantu.
You remember what happened to Bantu?

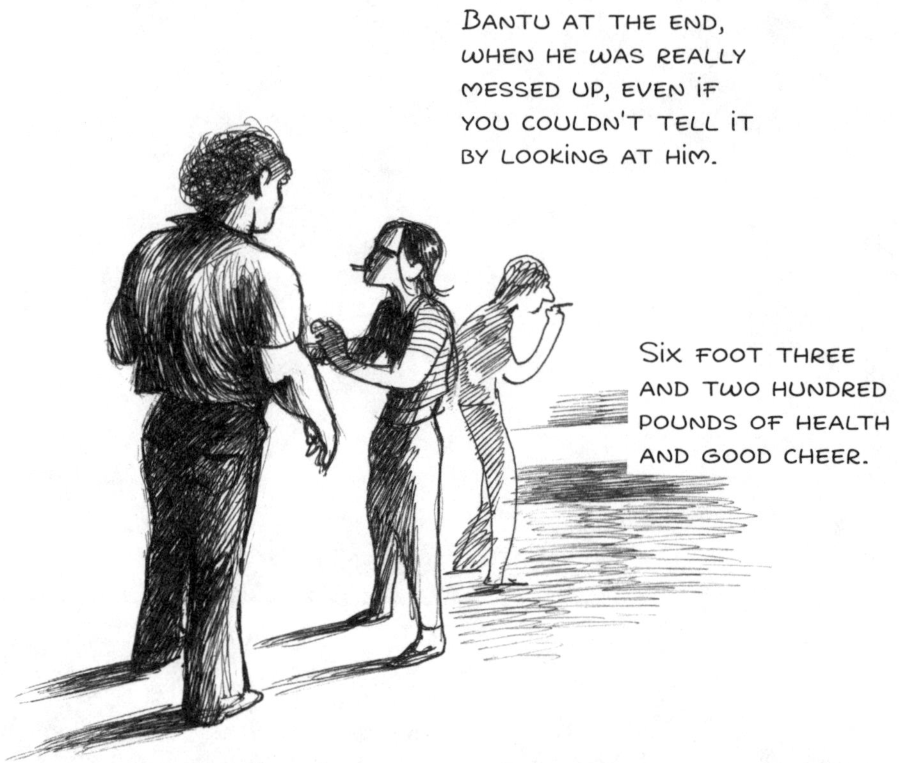
BANTU AT THE END, WHEN HE WAS REALLY MESSED UP, EVEN IF YOU COULDN'T TELL IT BY LOOKING AT HIM.
SIX FOOT THREE AND TWO HUNDRED POUNDS OF HEALTH AND GOOD CHEER.

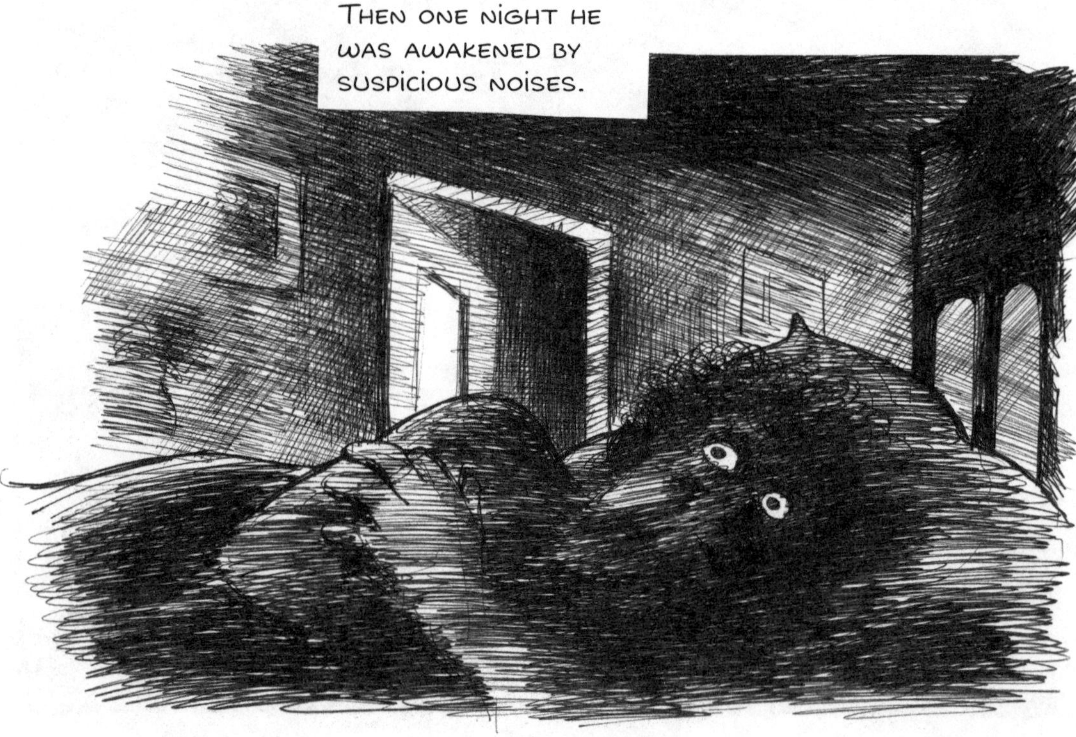
THEN ONE NIGHT HE WAS AWAKENED BY SUSPICIOUS NOISES.

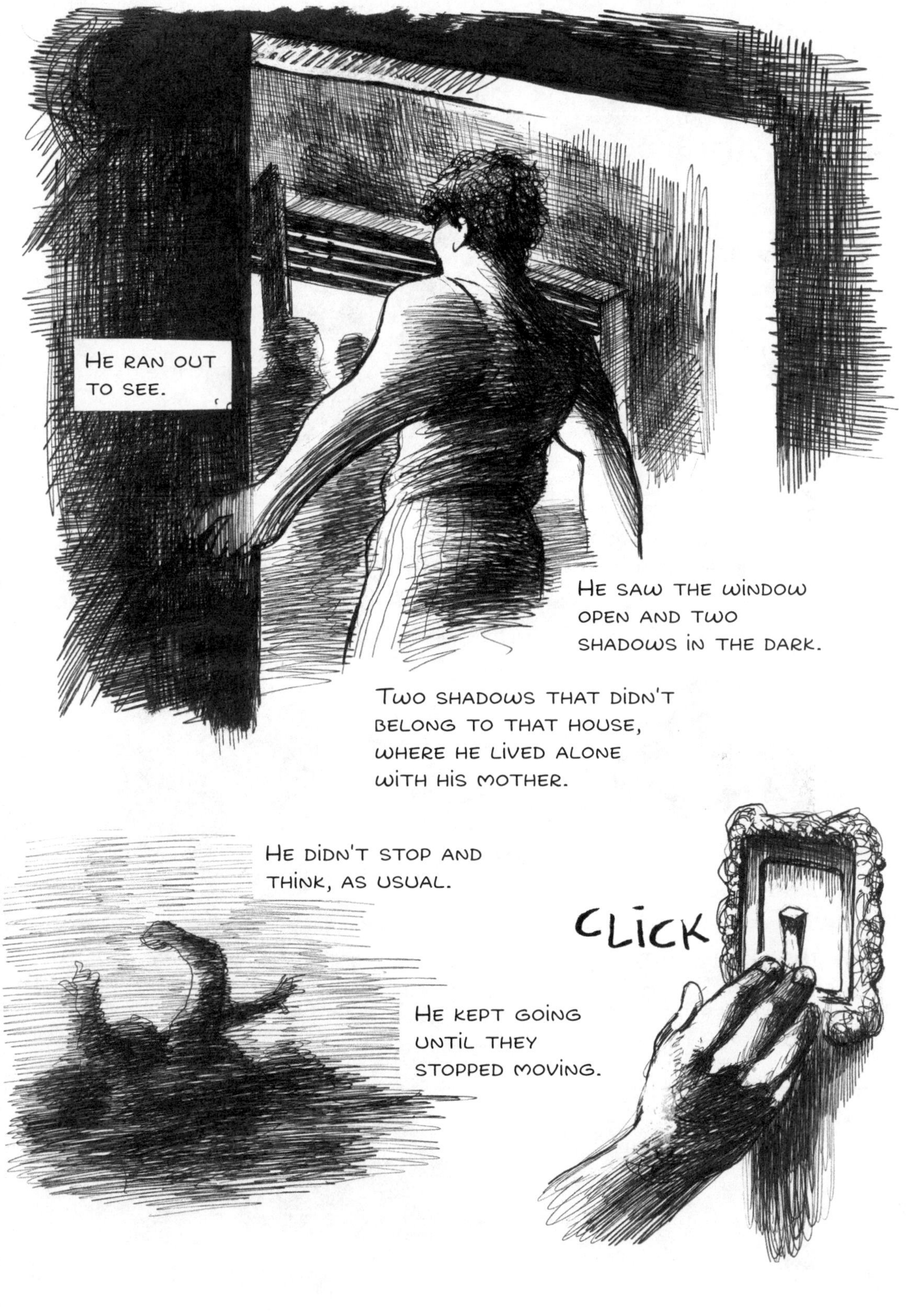
He ran out to see.
He saw the window open and two shadows in the dark.
Two shadows that didn't belong to that house, where he lived alone with his mother.
He didn't stop and think, as usual.
CLICK
He kept going until they stopped moving.

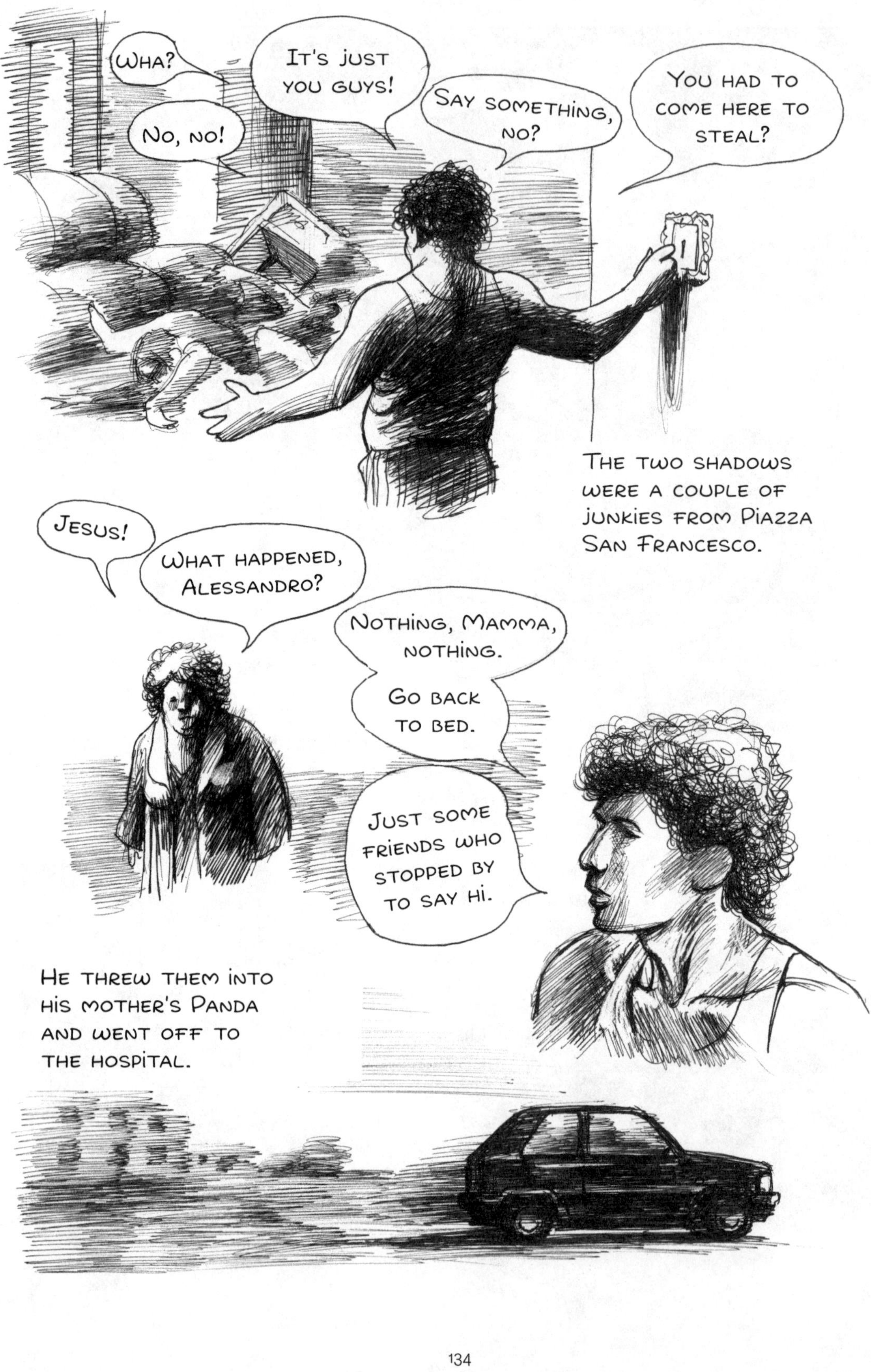
Wha?
No, no!
It's just you guys!
Say something, no?
You had to come here to steal?
The two shadows were a couple of junkies from Piazza San Francesco.
Jesus!
What happened, Alessandro?
Nothing, Mamma, nothing.
Go back to bed.
Just some friends who stopped by to say hi.
He threw them into his mother's Panda and went off to the hospital.

HOW THEY ALL FIT IS A
MYSTERY IN ITSELF.

BANTU ALONE, FOR
EXAMPLE, COULDN'T GET
OUT OF THAT CAR, HE
SLIPPED IT ON LIKE AN
UNDERSHIRT.

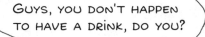

GUYS, YOU DON'T HAPPEN
TO HAVE A DRINK, DO YOU?

BEFORE LEAVING THEM AT THE EMERGENCY
ROOM HE WENT THROUGH THEIR POCKETS,
BUT THEY DIDN'T HAVE ANYTHING, JUST
A COUPLE PIECES OF PAKISTANI, WHICH HE
SMOKED ON THE WAY HOME.

THE TWO SHADOWS
GOT THEMSELVES
A MONTH OF CASTS
AND METHADONE
AT OSPEDALE
MAGGIORE.

EMERGENCY ✚ →

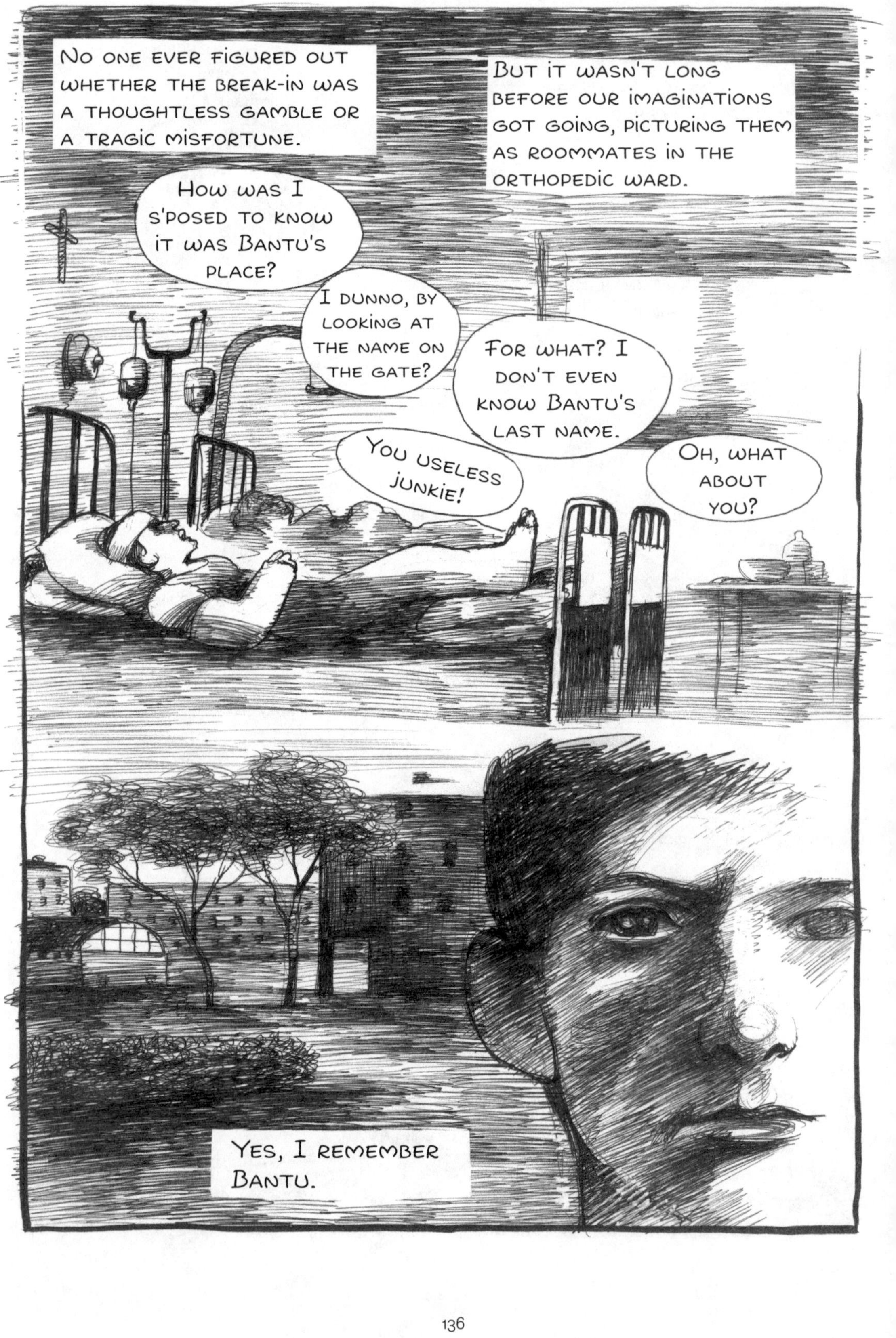
No one ever figured out whether the break-in was a thoughtless gamble or a tragic misfortune.
But it wasn't long before our imaginations got going, picturing them as roommates in the orthopedic ward.
How was I s'posed to know it was Bantu's place?
I dunno, by looking at the name on the gate?
For what? I don't even know Bantu's last name.
You useless junkie!
Oh, what about you?
Yes, I remember Bantu.

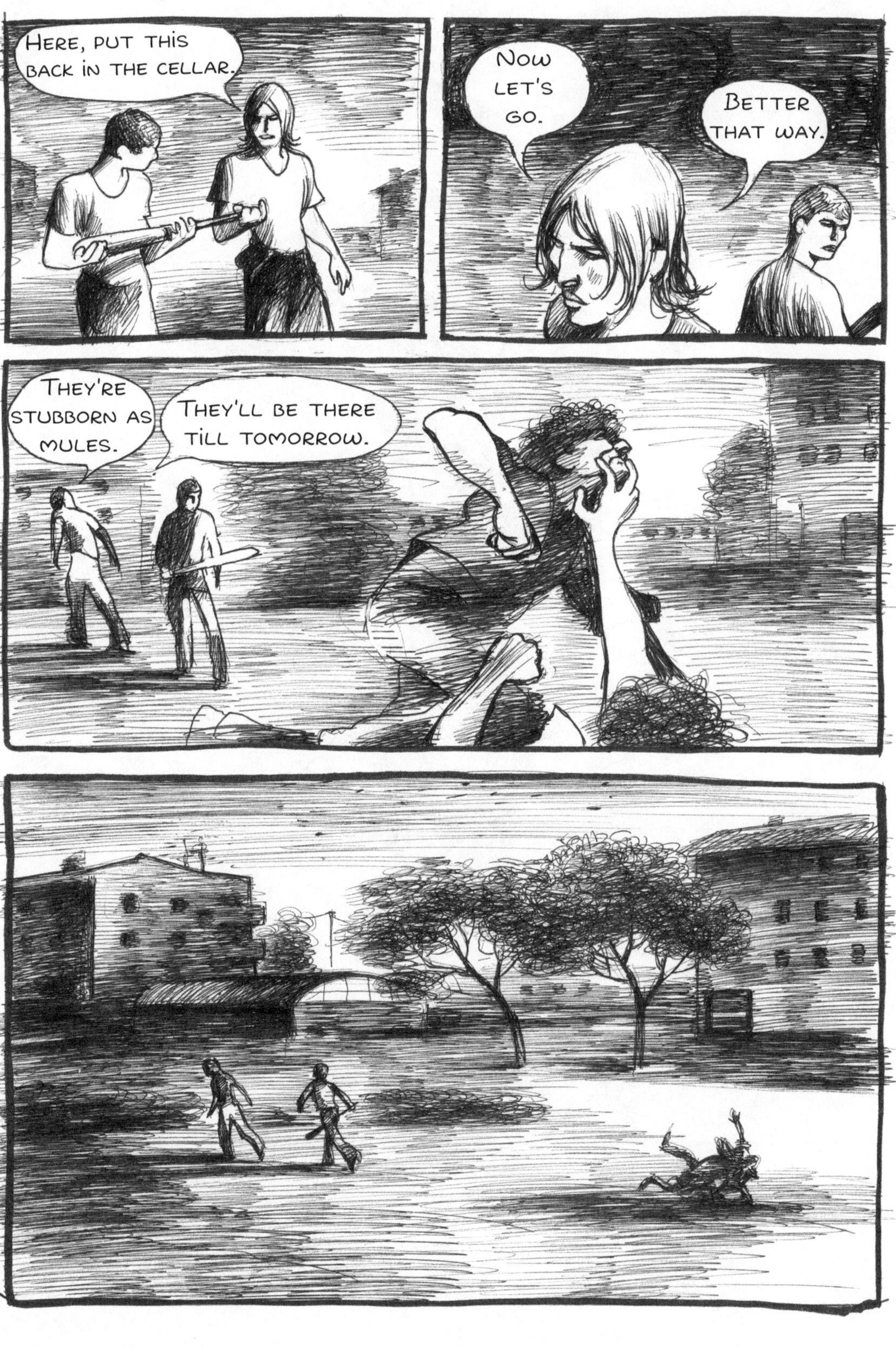
Here, put this back in the cellar.
Now let's go.
Better that way.
They're stubborn as mules.
They'll be there till tomorrow.

DON'T SINK TO THEIR LEVEL.

NO, JOHN WOULD NEVER SAY THAT.

DON'T DIRTY YOUR HANDS. IT'S NOT WORTH IT.

MAYBE THAT BEANPOLE ALAN LADD WOULD THOUGH.

YEAH, HE WOULD
SAY ANYTHING.

WITH THAT COOL
SNEER AND TOUSLED
HAIR HE'D SAY
ANYTHING.

ONLY GOOD
GYPSY'S A
DEAD GYPSY.

DON'T FORGET
IT, SON.

VI

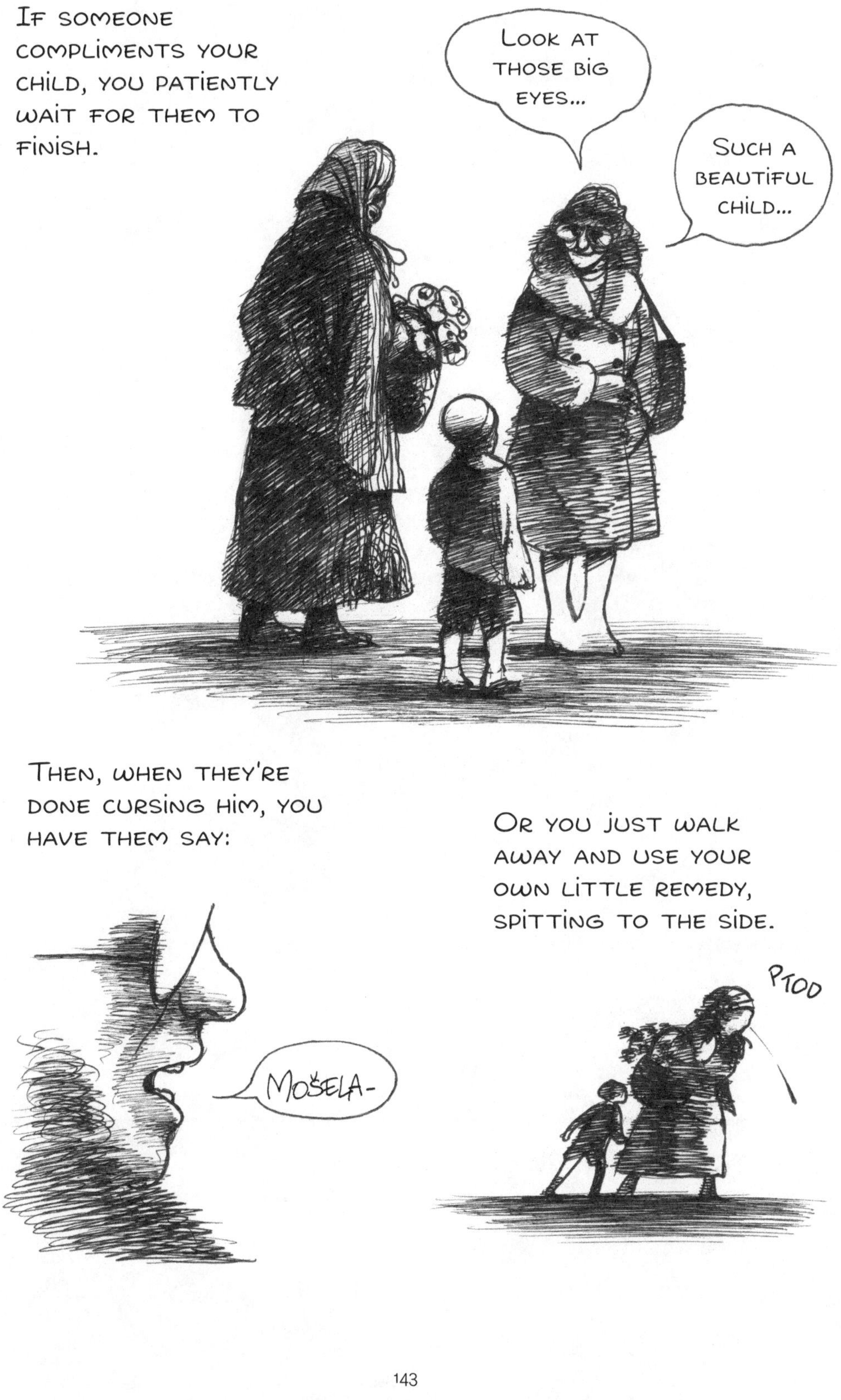
If someone compliments your child, you patiently wait for them to finish.
Look at those big eyes...
Such a beautiful child...
Then, when they're done cursing him, you have them say:
Or you just walk away and use your own little remedy, spitting to the side.
Mošela-
Ptoo

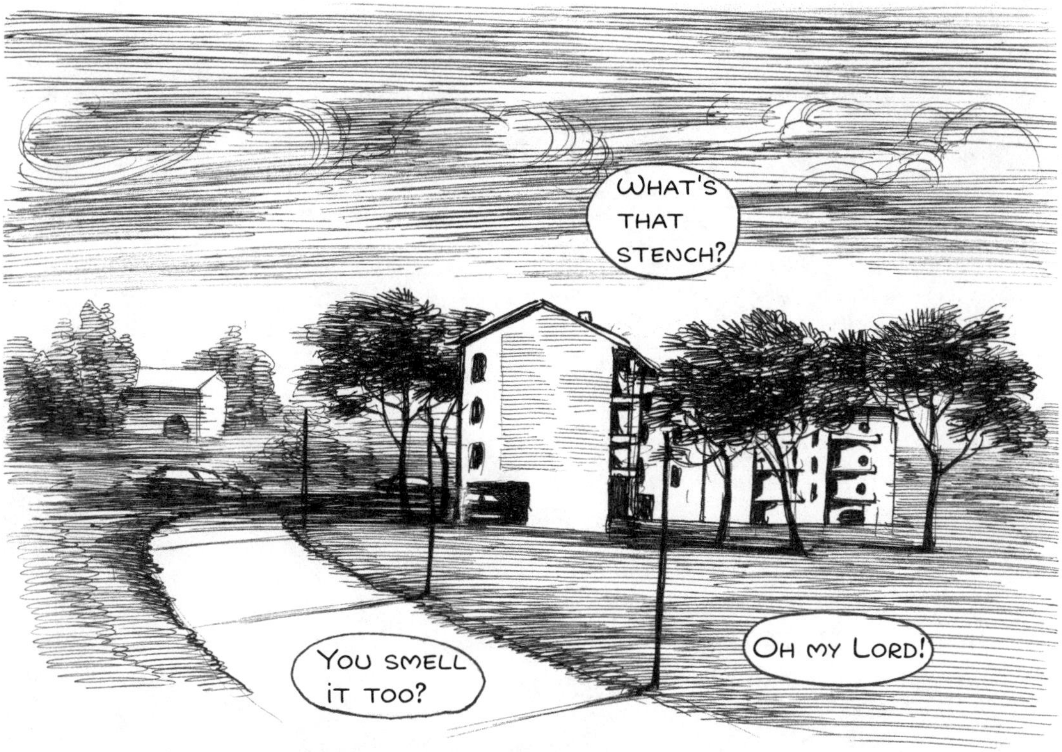
What's that stench?
You smell it too?
Oh my Lord!

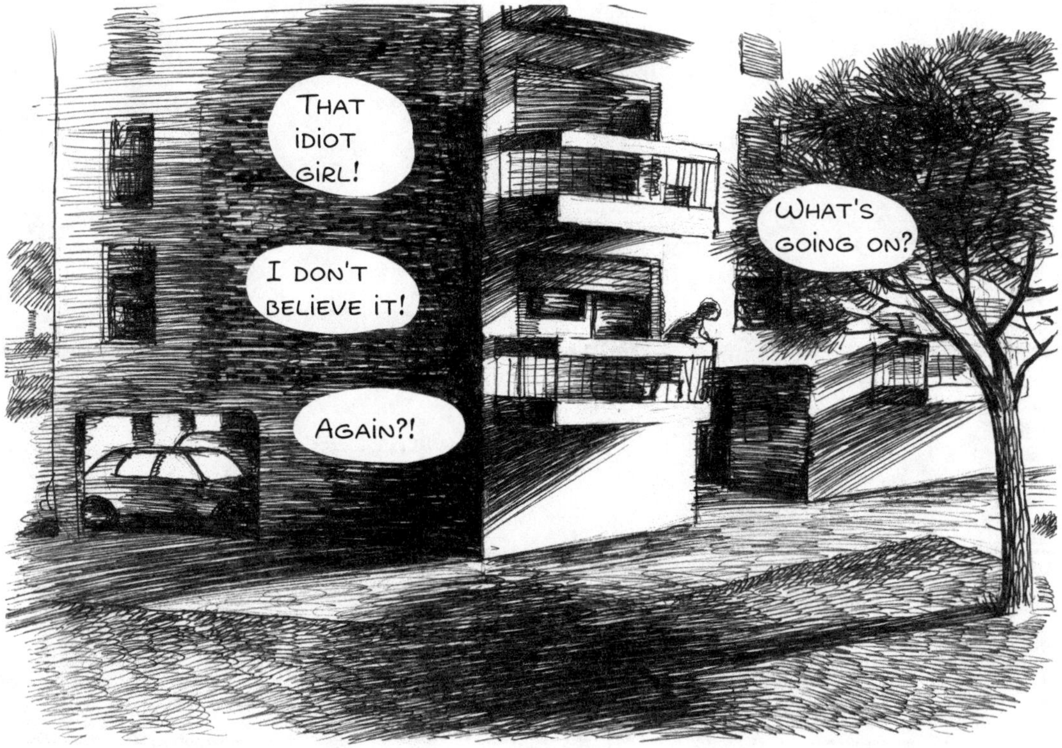
That idiot girl!
I don't believe it!
Again?!
What's going on?

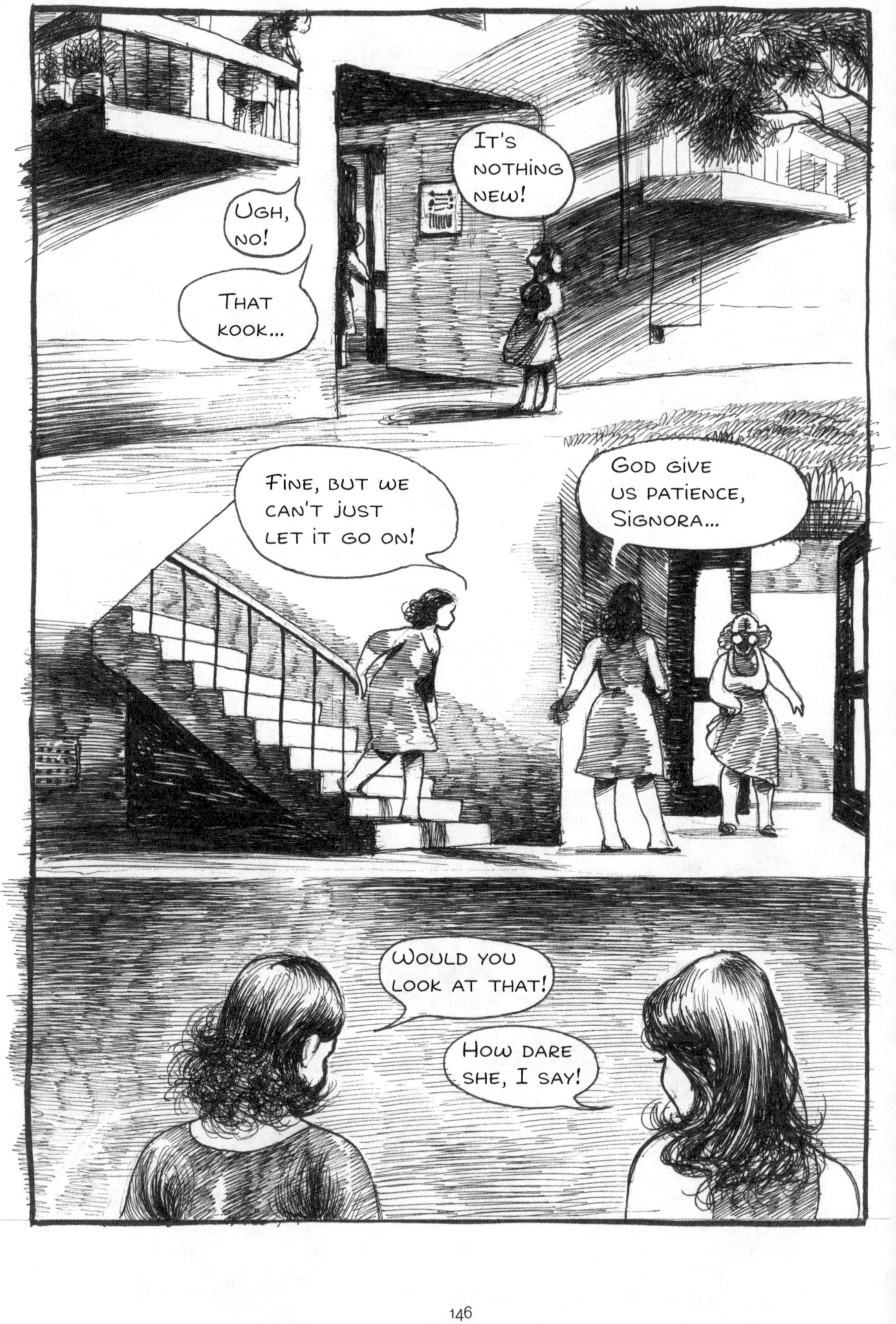
It's nothing new!
Ugh, no!
That kook...
Fine, but we can't just let it go on!
God give us patience, Signora...
Would you look at that!
How dare she, I say!

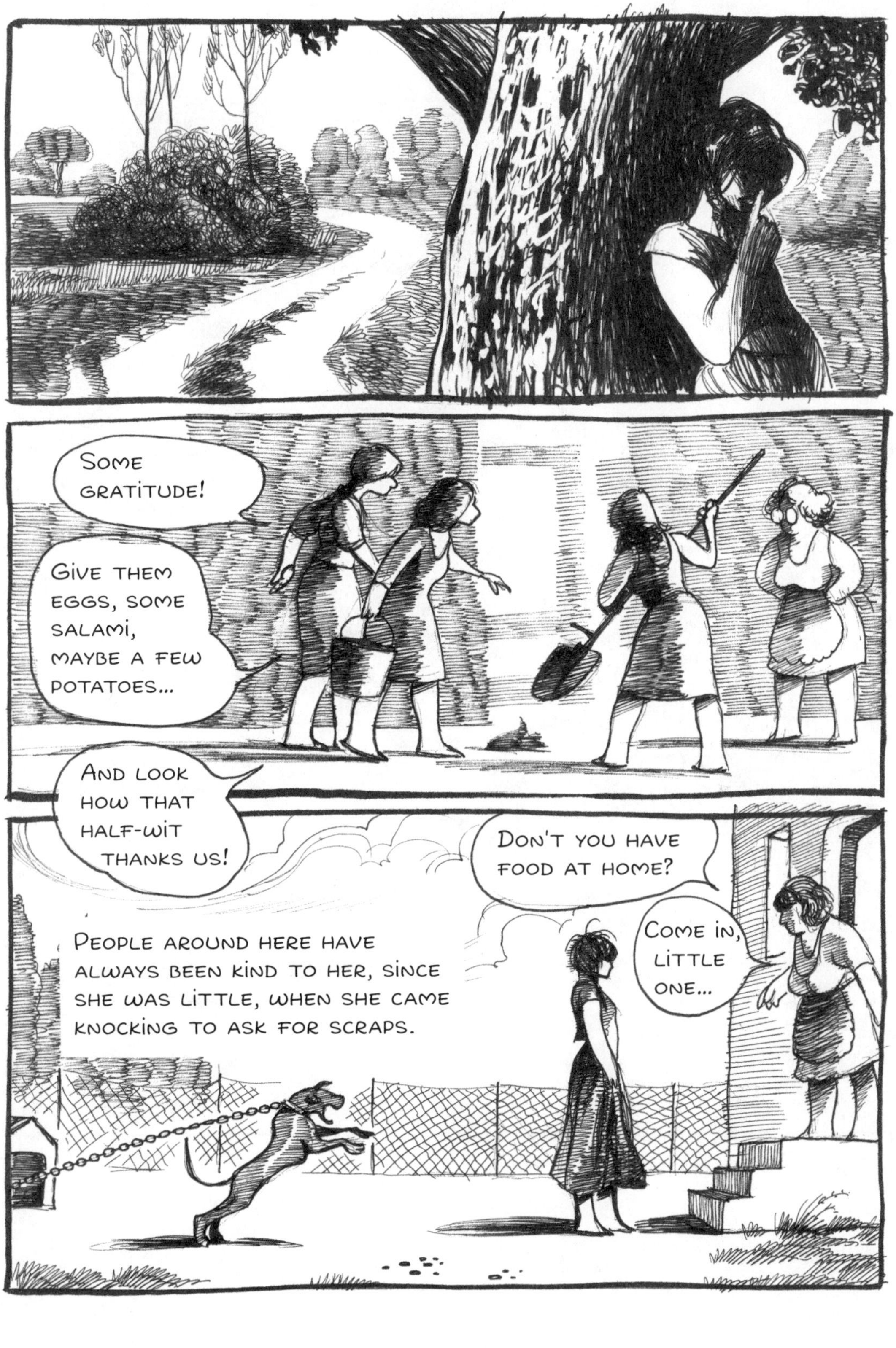
Some gratitude!
Give them eggs, some salami, maybe a few potatoes...
And look how that half-wit thanks us!
Don't you have food at home?
Come in, little one...
People around here have always been kind to her, since she was little, when she came knocking to ask for scraps.

WELL, "LITTLE" IN A MANNER OF SPEAKING.

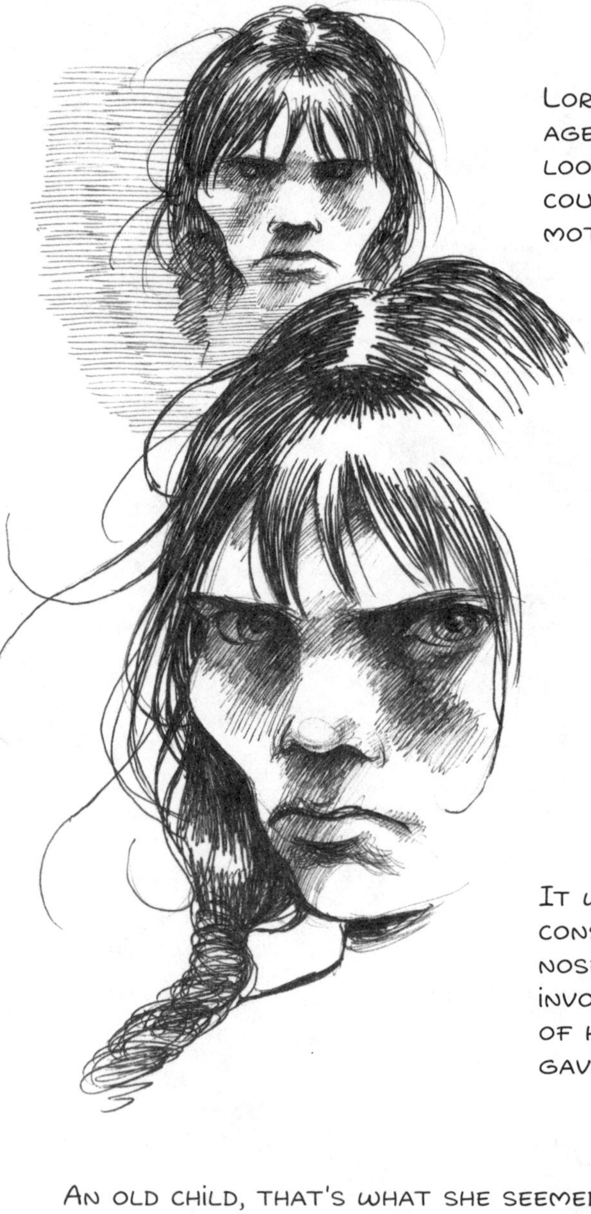

LORETTA IS THE SAME AGE AS US, BUT TO LOOK AT HER SHE COULD HAVE BEEN OUR MOTHER, EVEN THEN.

AND HER EYES: THEY STARED RIGHT AT YOU, BUT WITHOUT ANY CURIOSITY.

AS IF SHE EXPECTED NOTHING.

FROM YOU OR FROM ANYONE ELSE.

IT WAS ONLY THE CONSTANT RUNNY NOSE AND CERTAIN INVOLUNTARY GESTURES OF HER HANDS THAT GAVE AWAY HER AGE.

AN OLD CHILD, THAT'S WHAT SHE SEEMED.

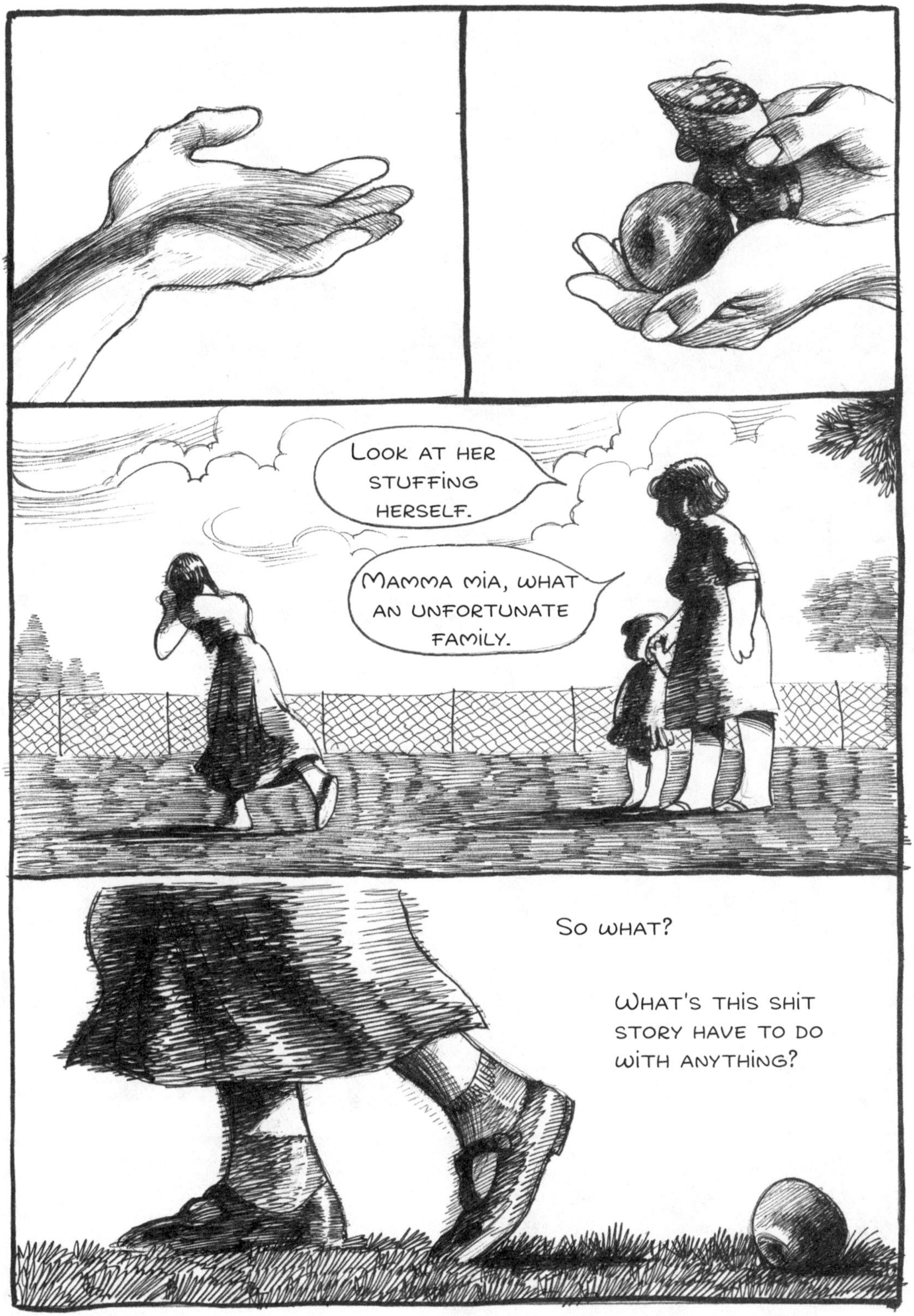
Look at her stuffing herself.
Mamma mia, what an unfortunate family.
So what?
What's this shit story have to do with anything?

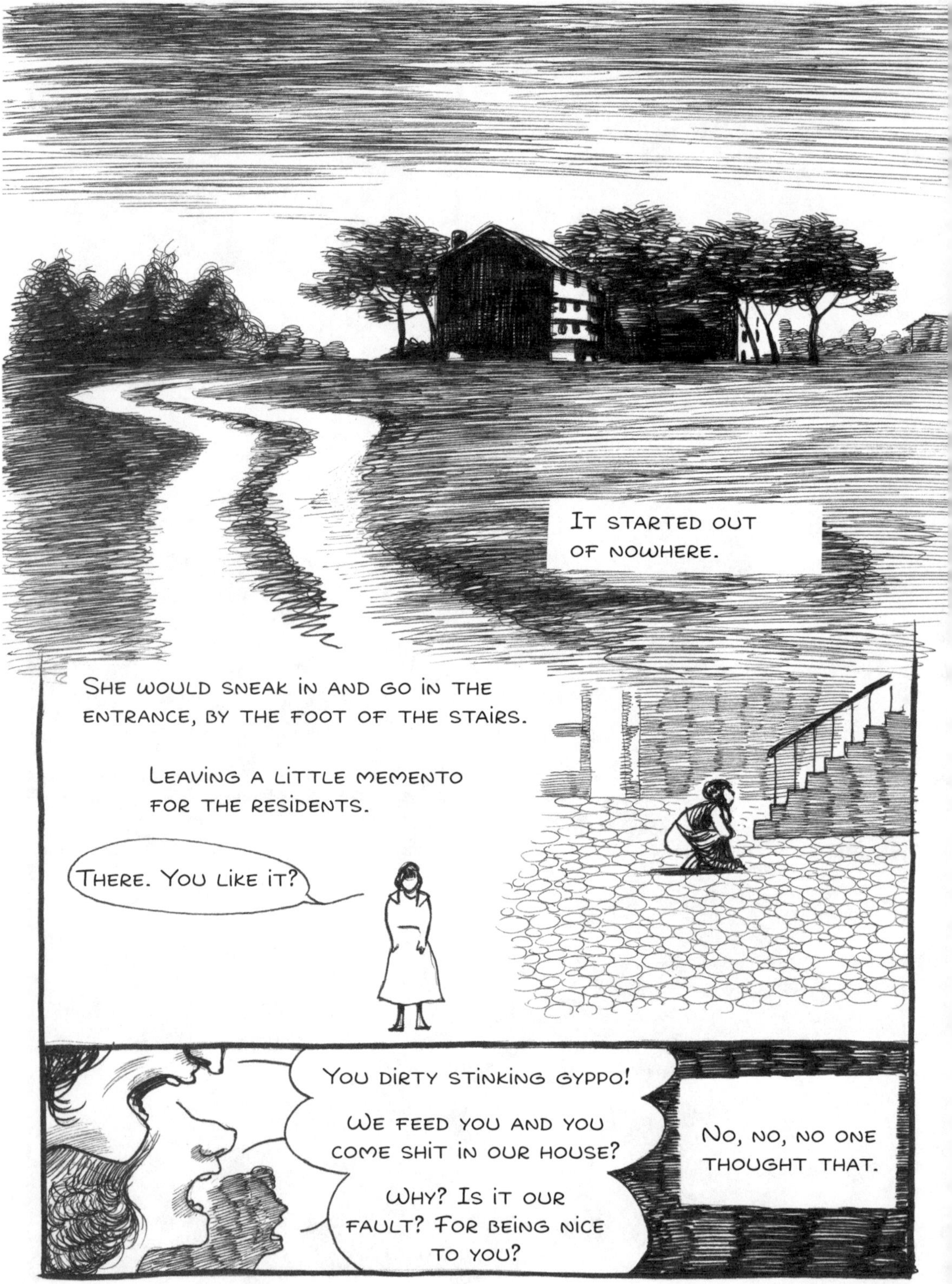

It started out of nowhere.
She would sneak in and go in the entrance, by the foot of the stairs.
Leaving a little memento for the residents.
There. You like it?
You dirty stinking gyppo!
We feed you and you come shit in our house?
Why? Is it our fault? For being nice to you?
No, no, no one thought that.

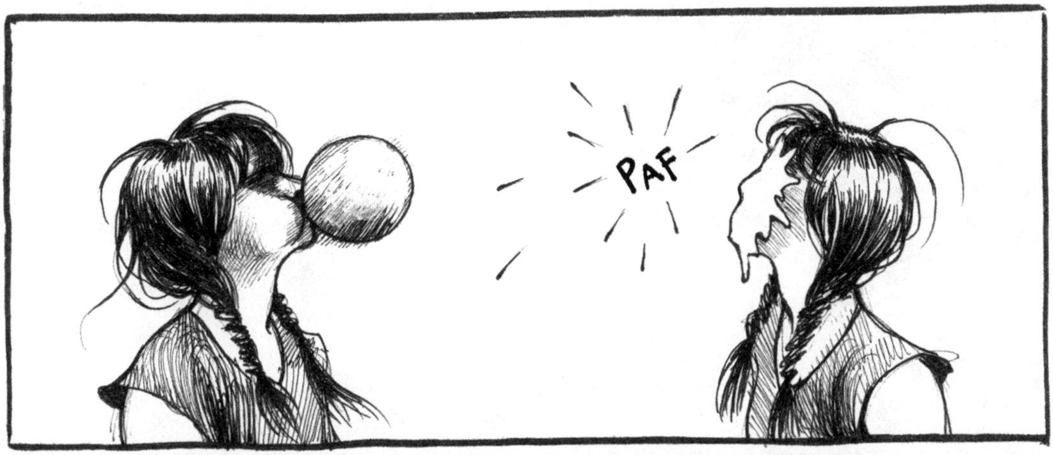
PAF

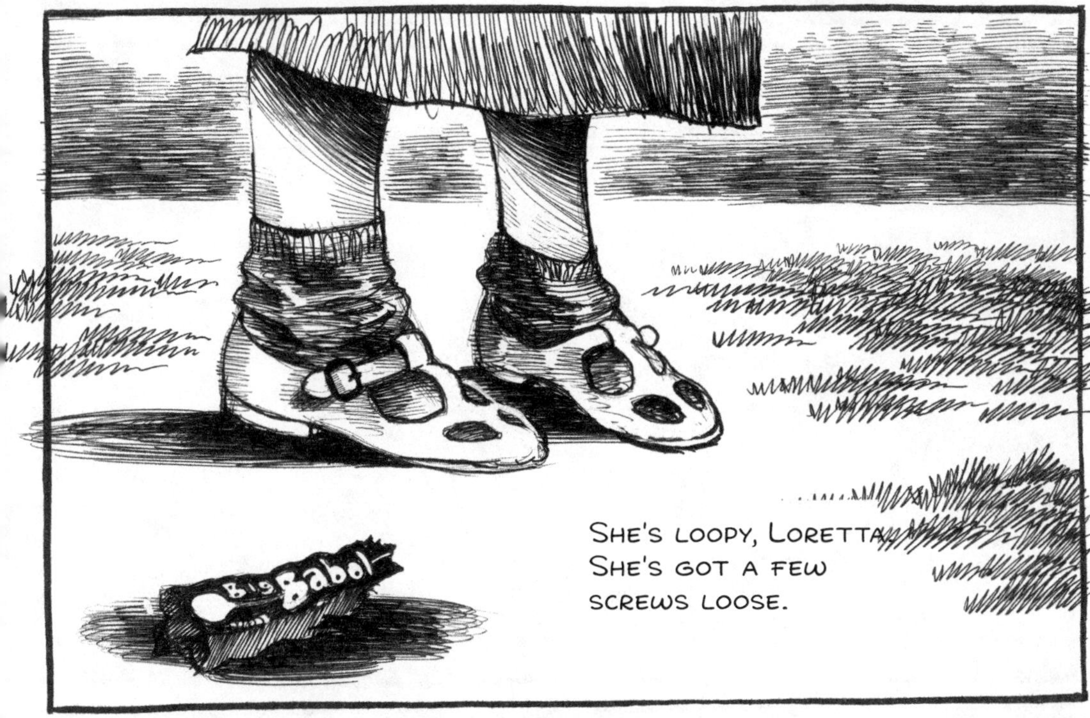
Big Babol
SHE'S LOOPY, LORETTA. SHE'S GOT A FEW SCREWS LOOSE.

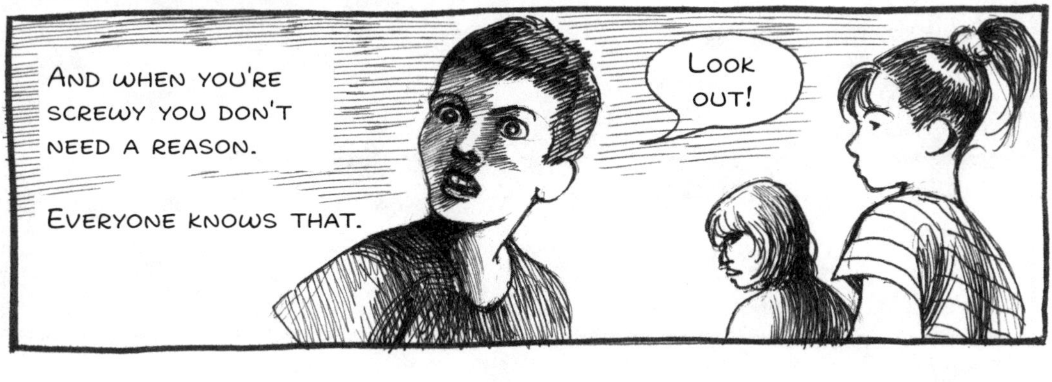
AND WHEN YOU'RE SCREWY YOU DON'T NEED A REASON.
EVERYONE KNOWS THAT.
LOOK OUT!

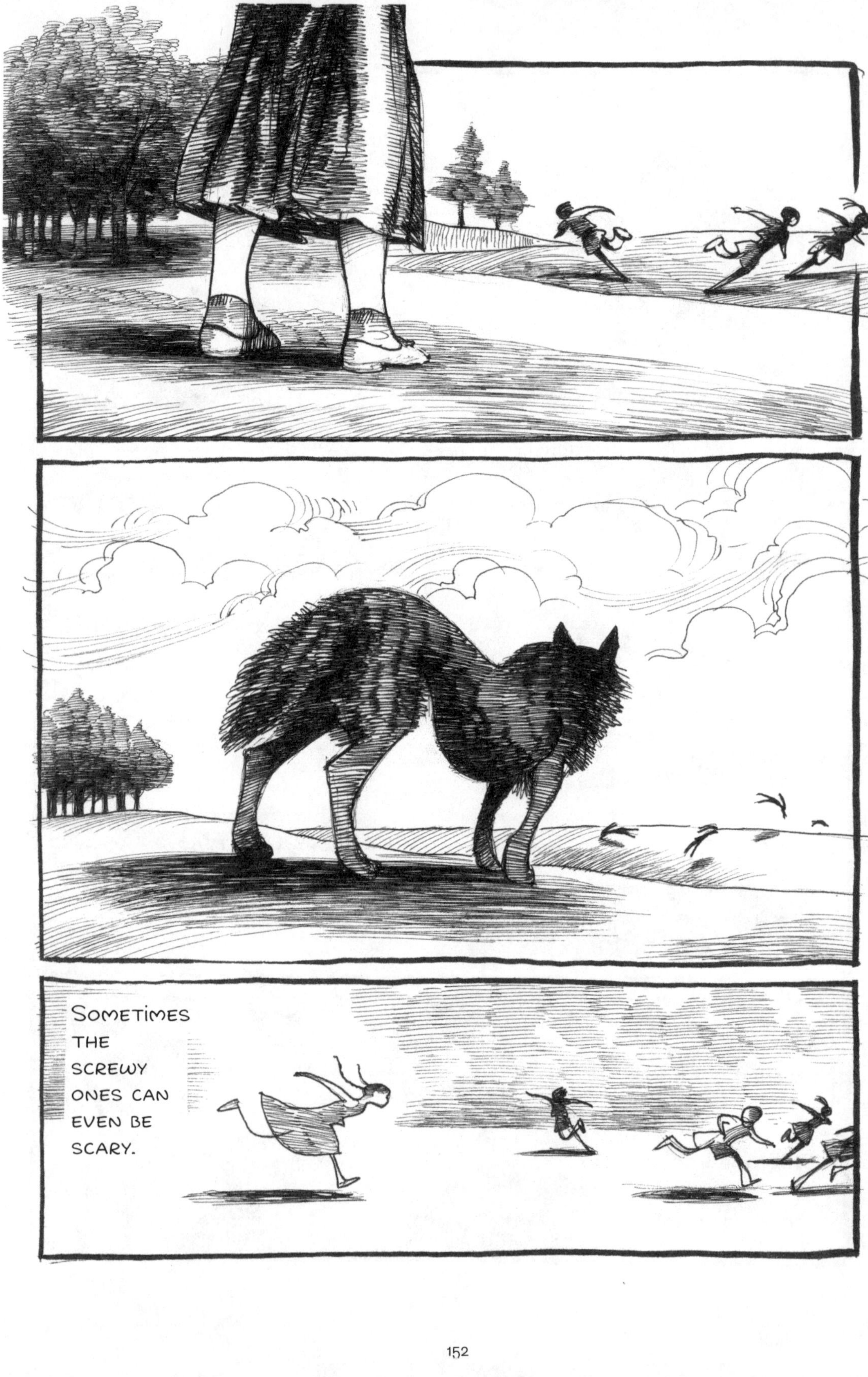
SOMETIMES THE SCREWY ONES CAN EVEN BE SCARY.

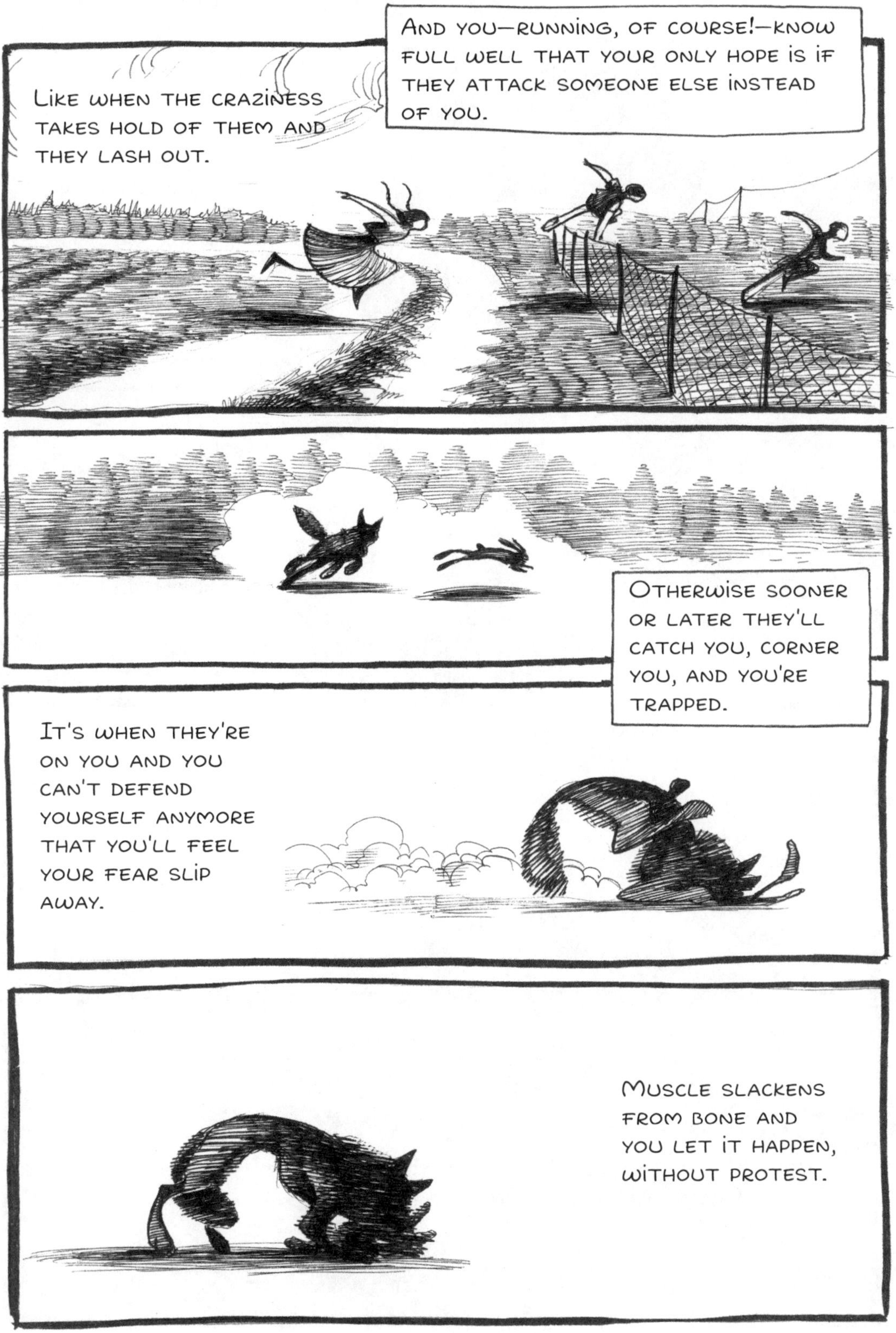
LIKE WHEN THE CRAZINESS TAKES HOLD OF THEM AND THEY LASH OUT.
AND YOU—RUNNING, OF COURSE!—KNOW FULL WELL THAT YOUR ONLY HOPE IS IF THEY ATTACK SOMEONE ELSE INSTEAD OF YOU.
OTHERWISE SOONER OR LATER THEY'LL CATCH YOU, CORNER YOU, AND YOU'RE TRAPPED.
IT'S WHEN THEY'RE ON YOU AND YOU CAN'T DEFEND YOURSELF ANYMORE THAT YOU'LL FEEL YOUR FEAR SLIP AWAY.
MUSCLE SLACKENS FROM BONE AND YOU LET IT HAPPEN, WITHOUT PROTEST.

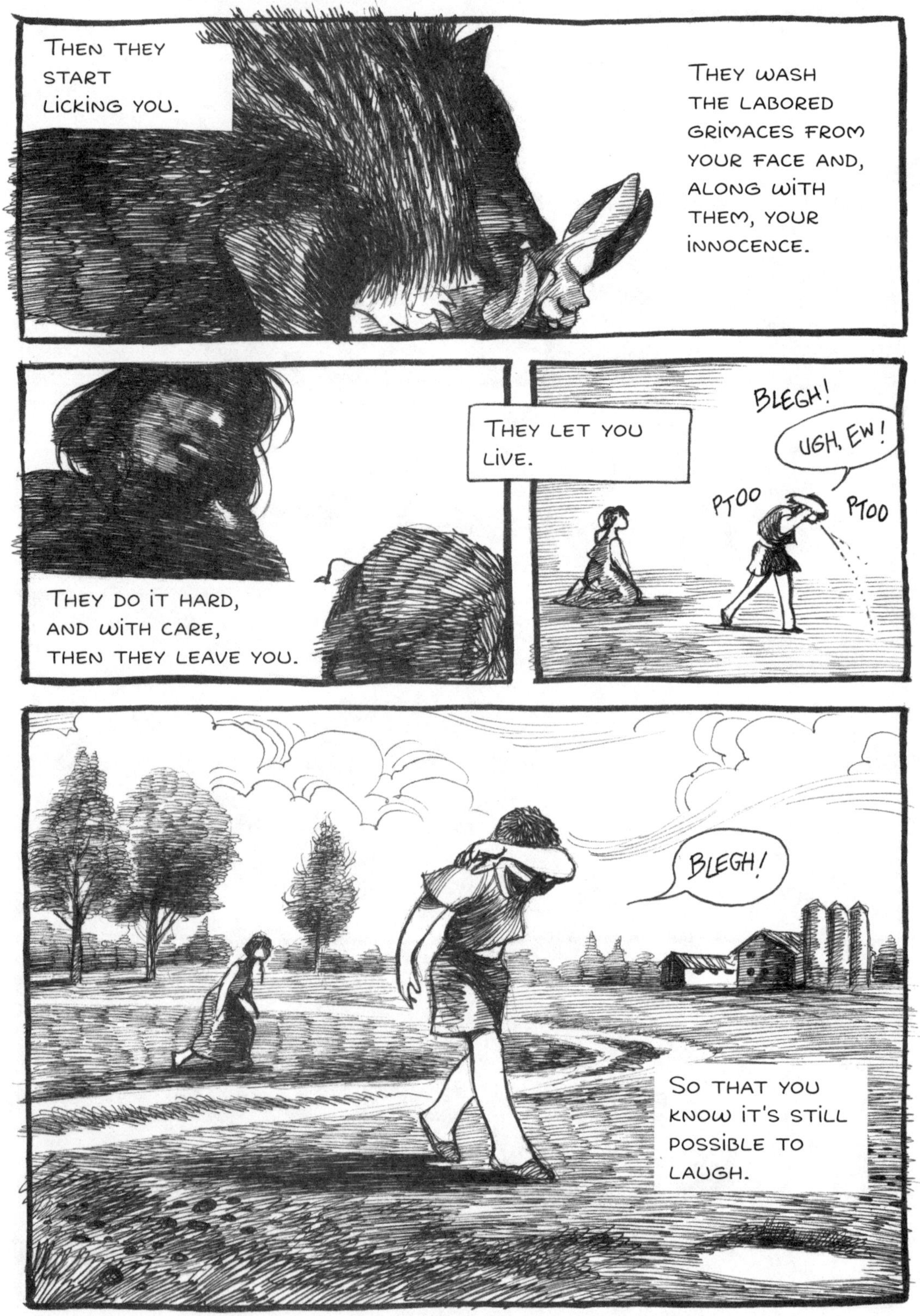
Then they start licking you.
They wash the labored grimaces from your face and, along with them, your innocence.
They do it hard, and with care, then they leave you.
They let you live.
BLEGH!
UGH, EW!
PTOO
PTOO
BLEGH!
So that you know it's still possible to laugh.

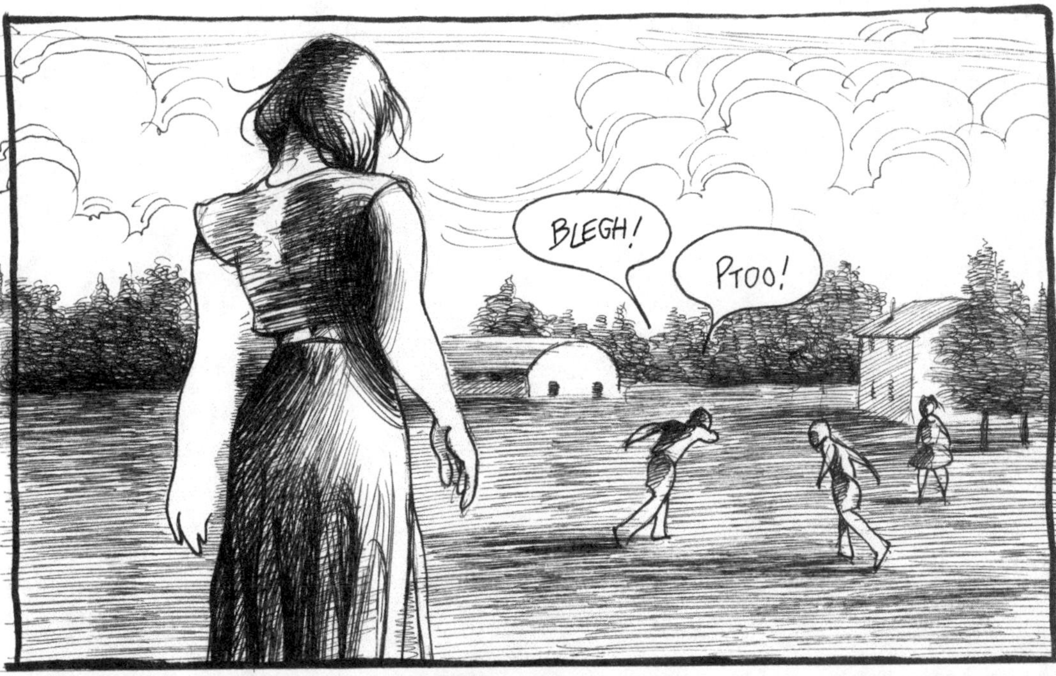
BLEGH!
PTOO!

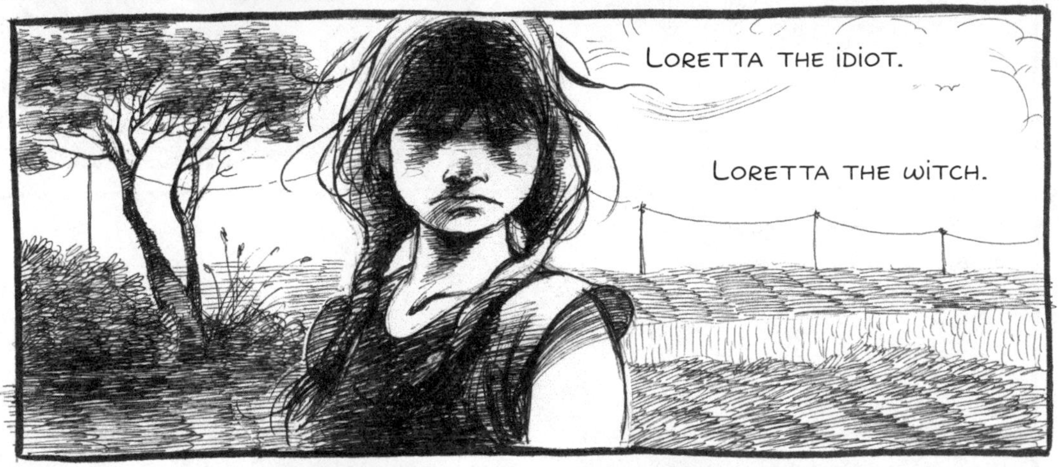
LORETTA THE IDIOT.
LORETTA THE WITCH.

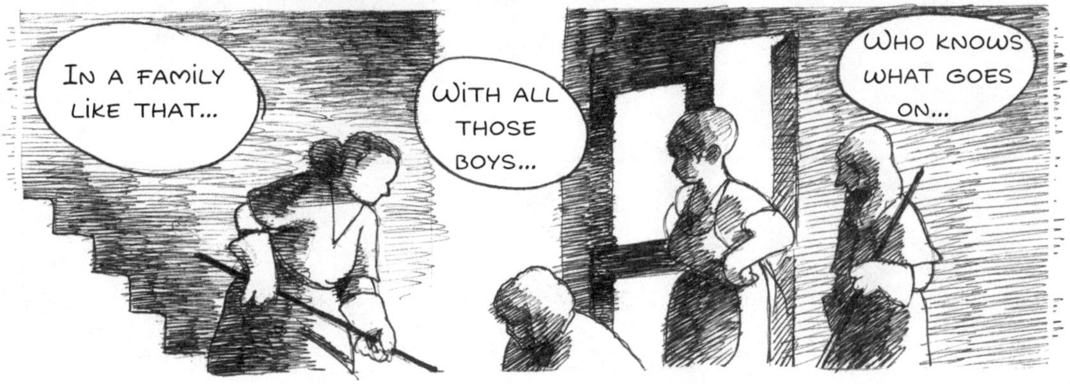
IN A FAMILY LIKE THAT...
WITH ALL THOSE BOYS...
WHO KNOWS WHAT GOES ON...

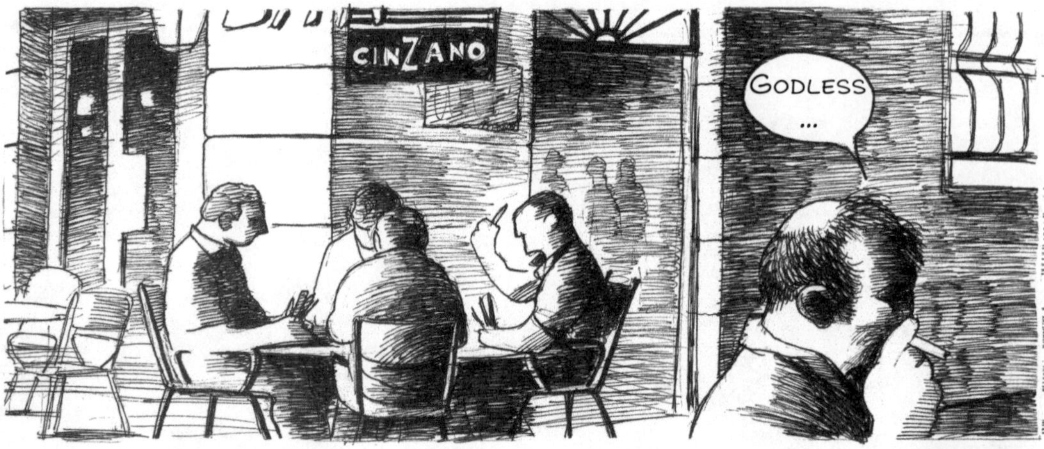
CINZANO
GODLESS ...

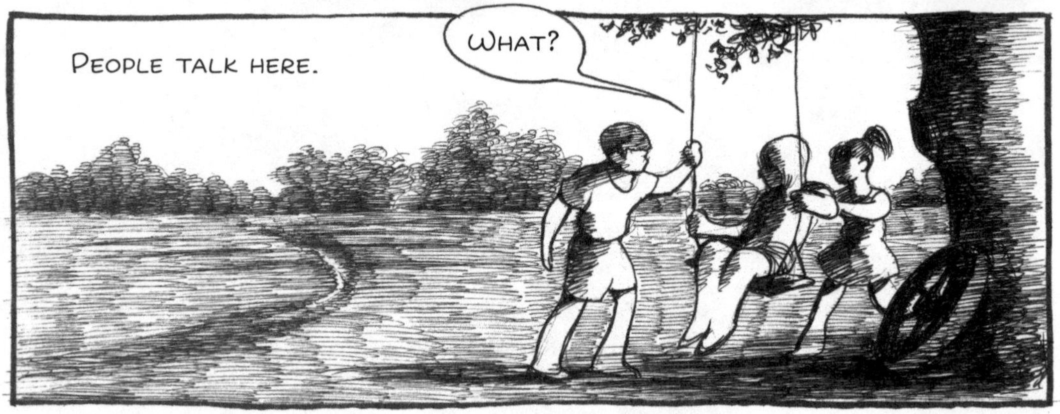
PEOPLE TALK HERE.
WHAT?

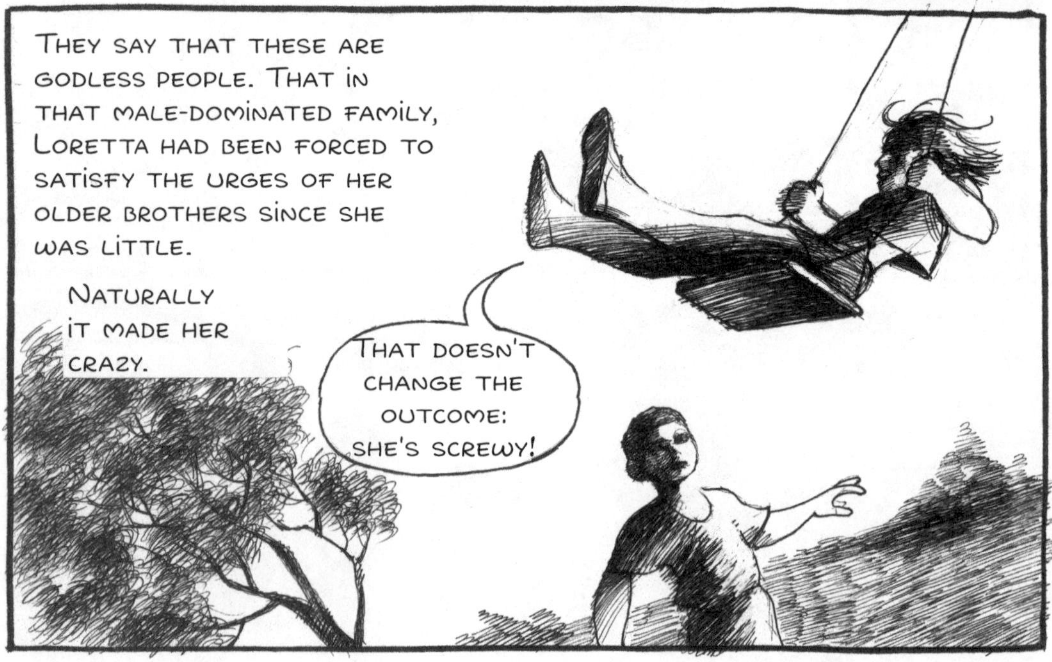
THEY SAY THAT THESE ARE GODLESS PEOPLE. THAT IN THAT MALE-DOMINATED FAMILY, LORETTA HAD BEEN FORCED TO SATISFY THE URGES OF HER OLDER BROTHERS SINCE SHE WAS LITTLE.
NATURALLY IT MADE HER CRAZY.
THAT DOESN'T CHANGE THE OUTCOME: SHE'S SCREWY!

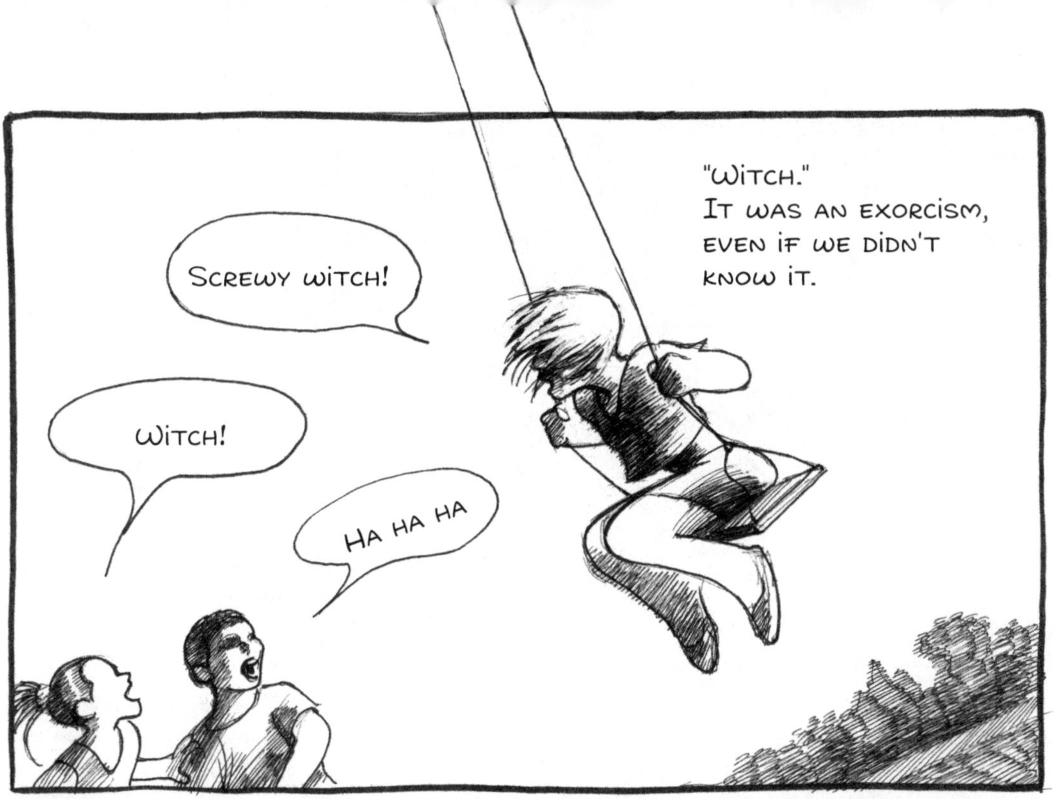
"Witch."
It was an exorcism, even if we didn't know it.
Screwy witch!
Witch!
Ha ha ha

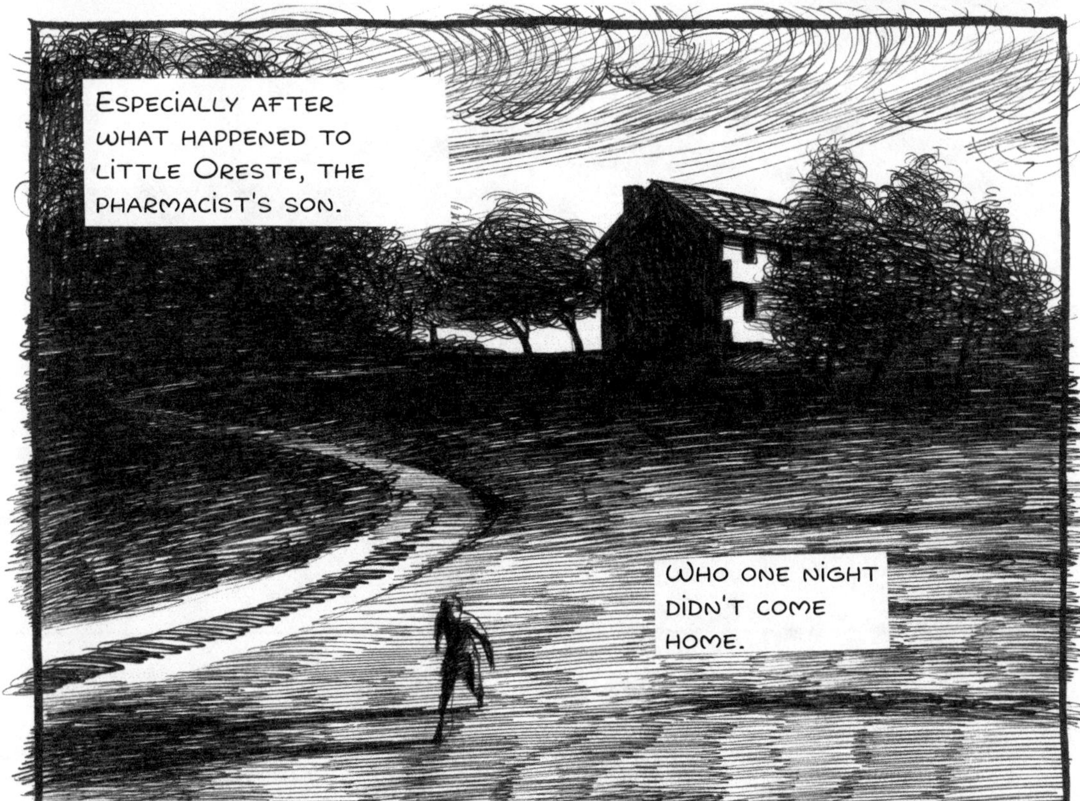
Especially after what happened to little Oreste, the pharmacist's son.
Who one night didn't come home.

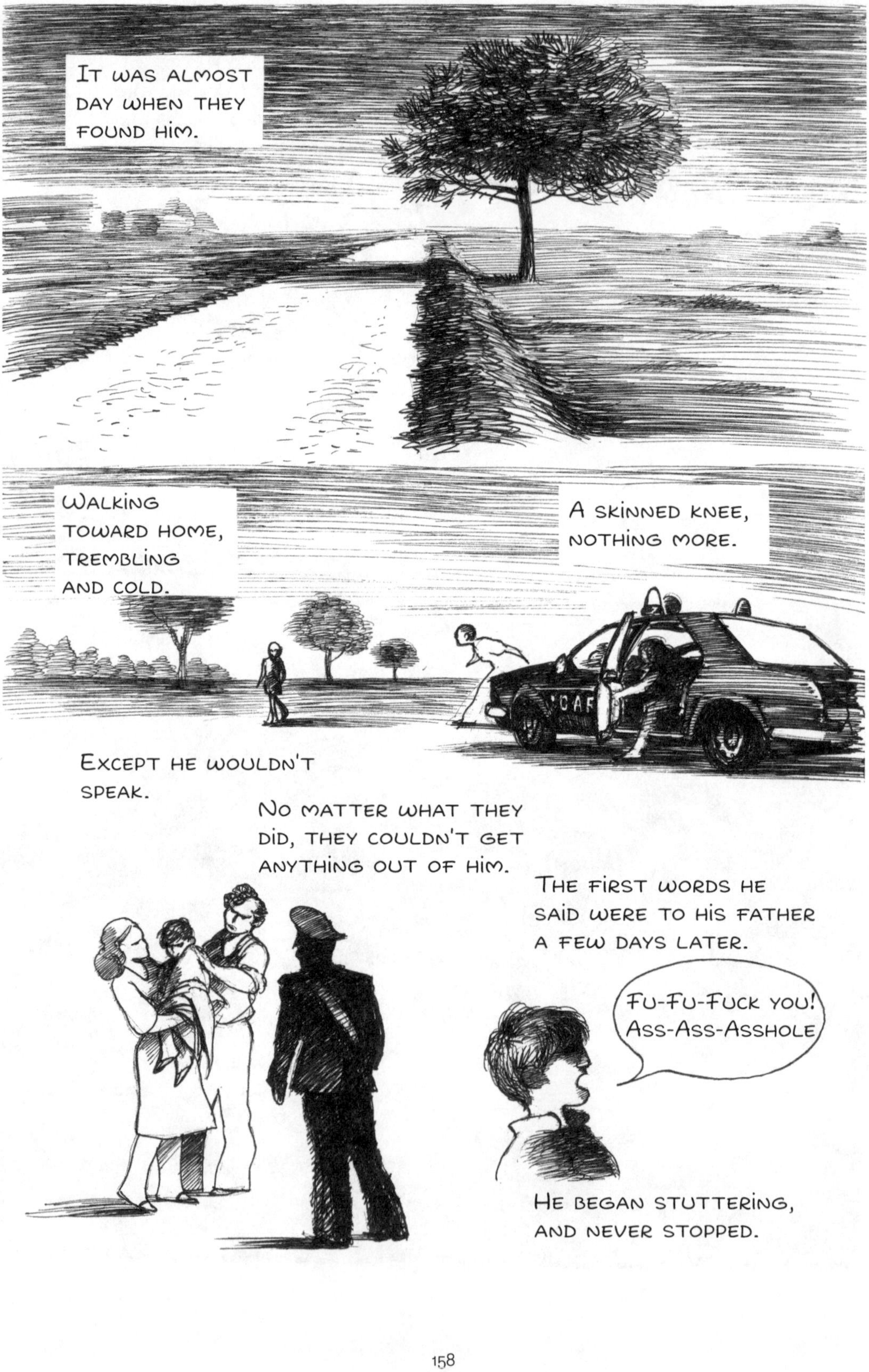
It was almost day when they found him.
Walking toward home, trembling and cold.
A skinned knee, nothing more.
Except he wouldn't speak.
No matter what they did, they couldn't get anything out of him.
The first words he said were to his father a few days later.
Fu-Fu-Fuck you! Ass-Ass-Asshole
He began stuttering, and never stopped.

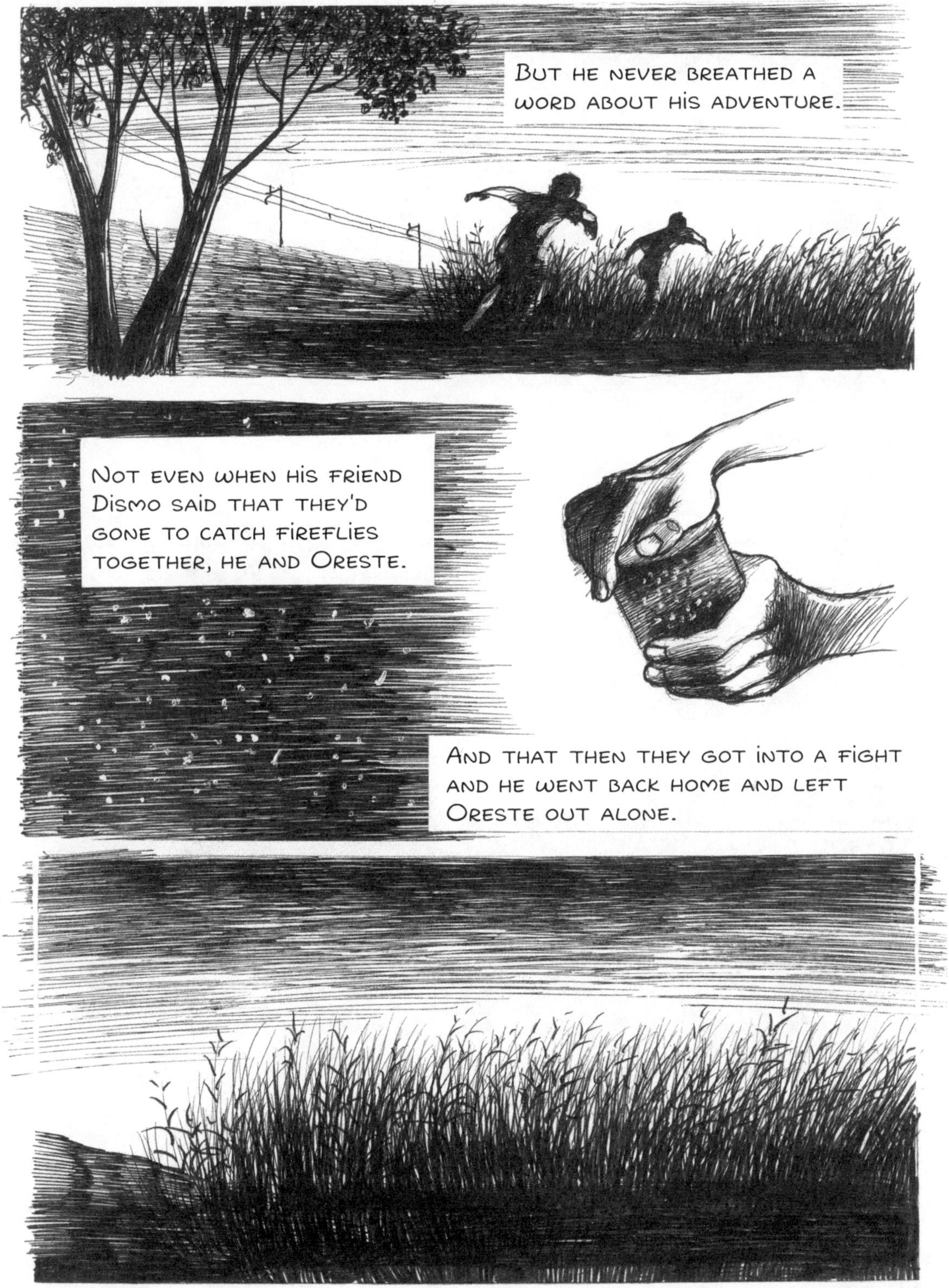
BUT HE NEVER BREATHED A WORD ABOUT HIS ADVENTURE.
NOT EVEN WHEN HIS FRIEND DISMO SAID THAT THEY'D GONE TO CATCH FIREFLIES TOGETHER, HE AND ORESTE.
AND THAT THEN THEY GOT INTO A FIGHT AND HE WENT BACK HOME AND LEFT ORESTE OUT ALONE.

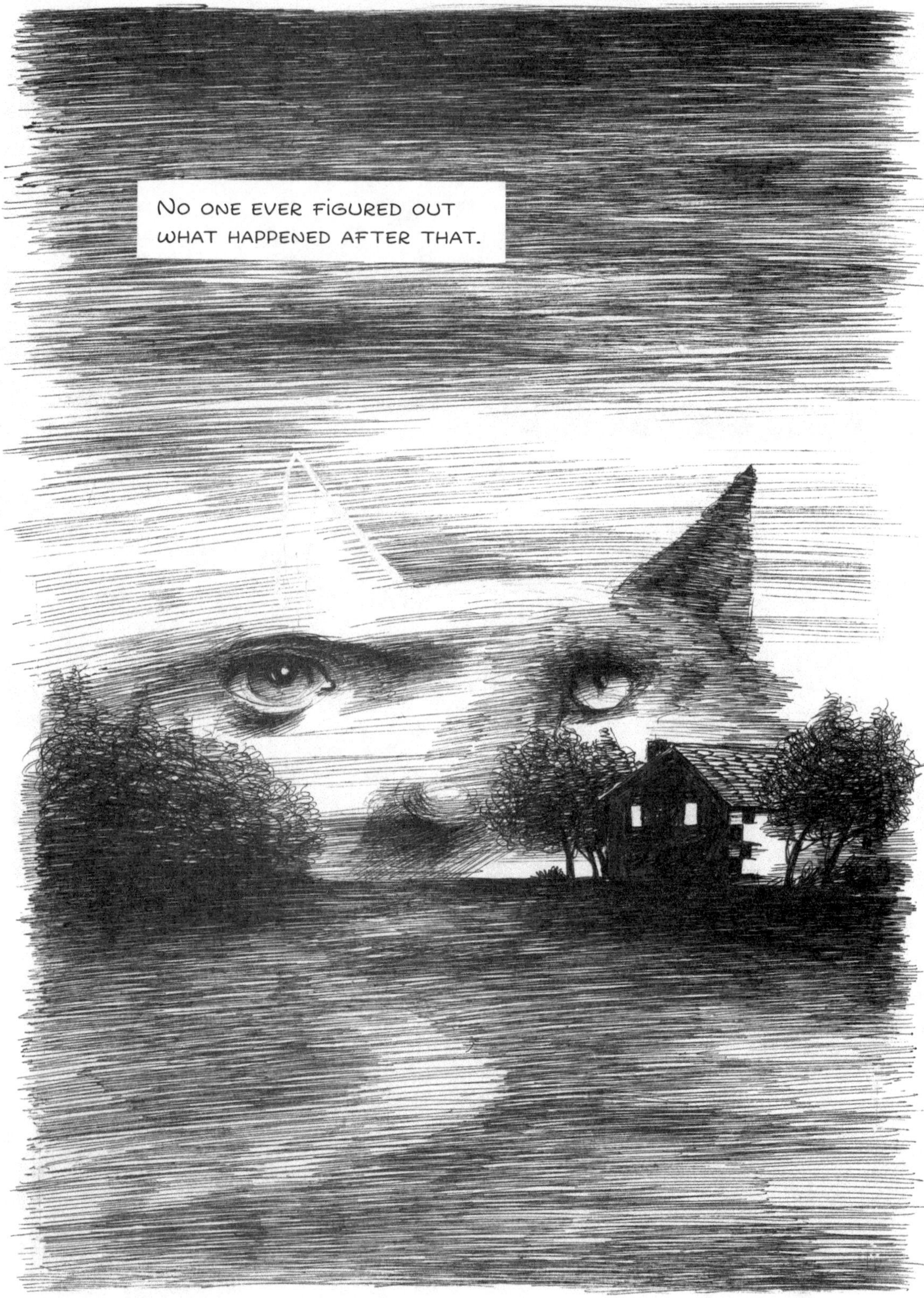
NO ONE EVER FIGURED OUT
WHAT HAPPENED AFTER THAT.

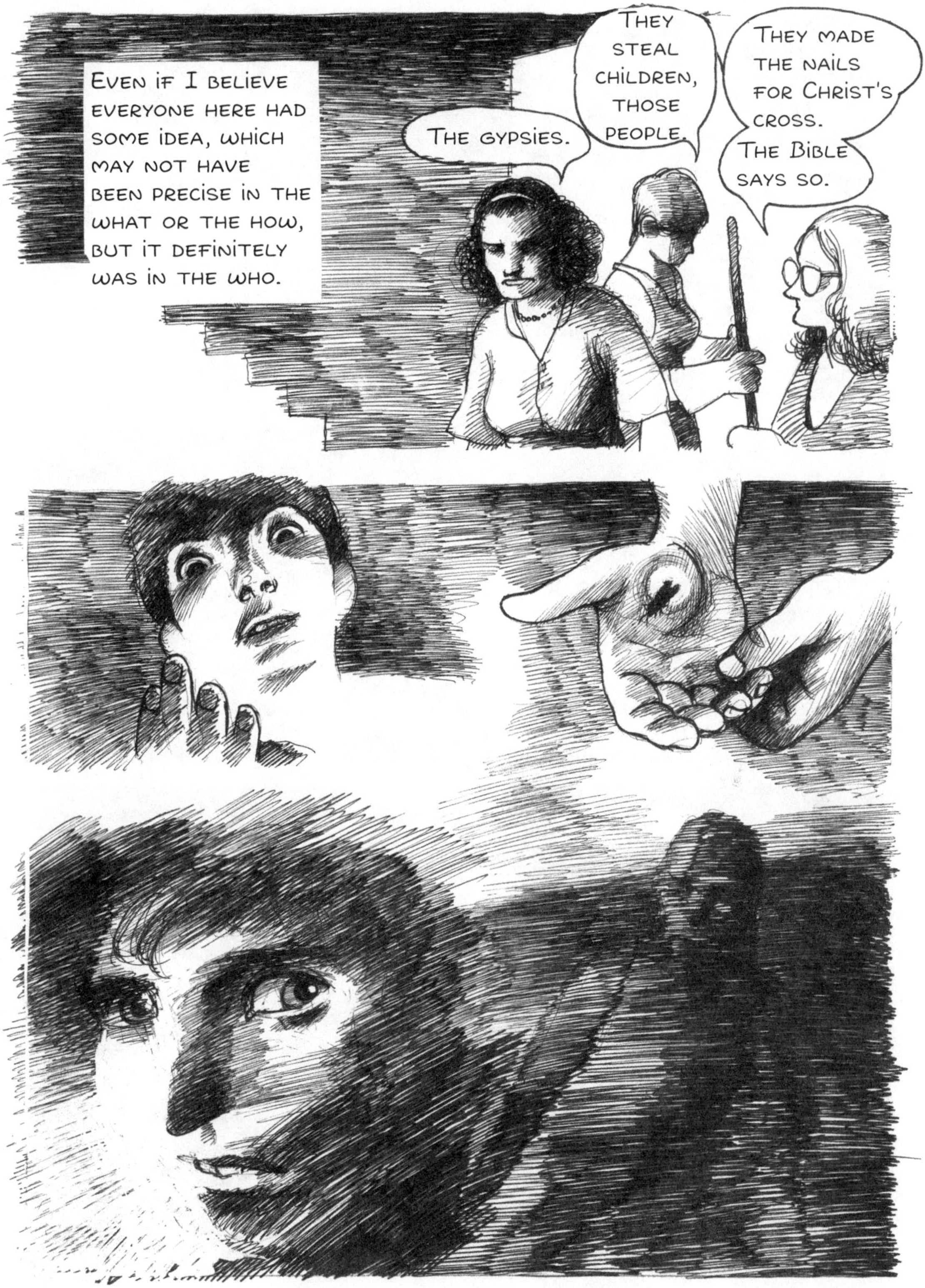
Even if I believe everyone here had some idea, which may not have been precise in the what or the how, but it definitely was in the who.
The gypsies.
They steal children, those people.
They made the nails for Christ's cross.
The Bible says so.

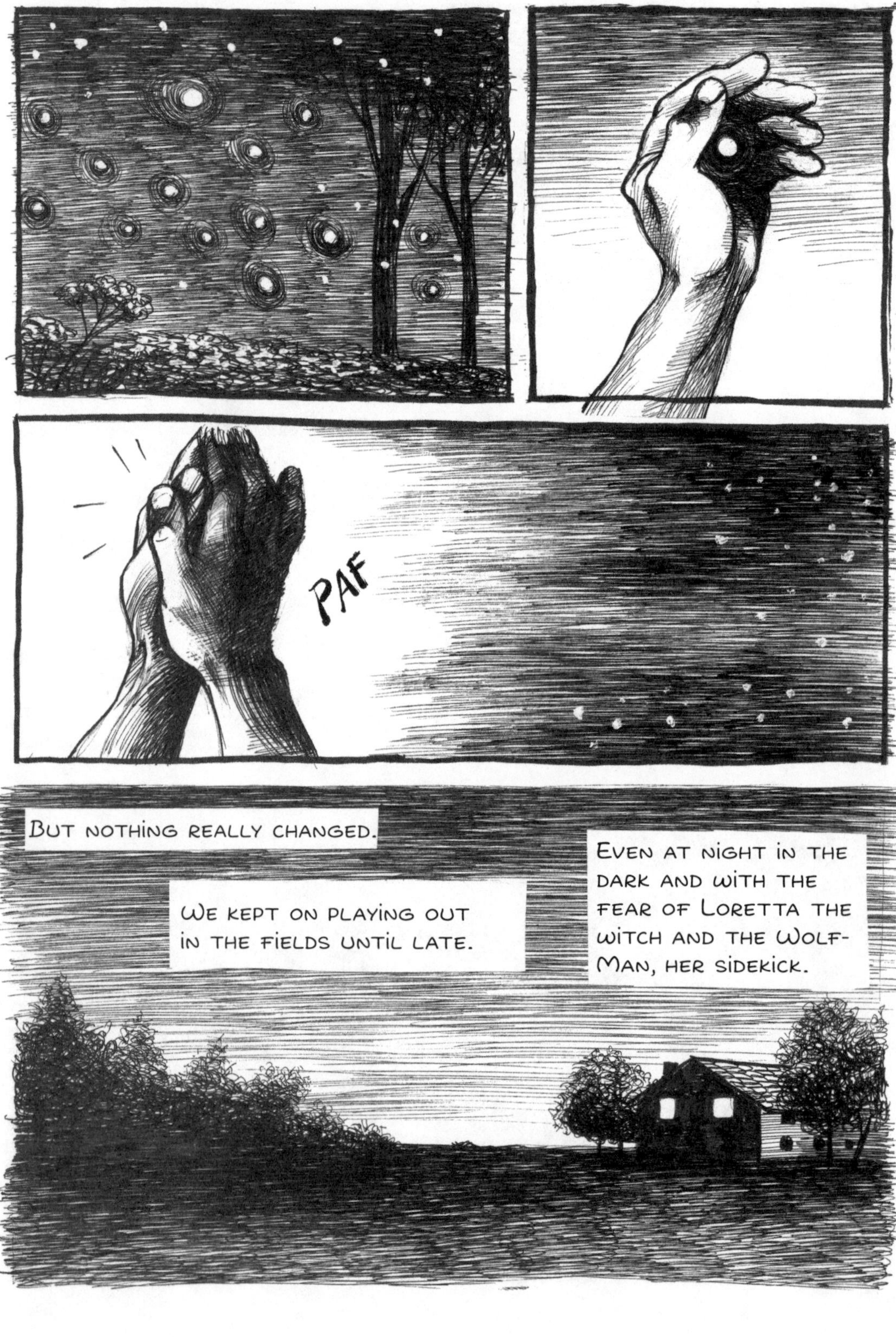
PAF
But nothing really changed.
We kept on playing out in the fields until late.
Even at night in the dark and with the fear of Loretta the witch and the Wolf-Man, her sidekick.

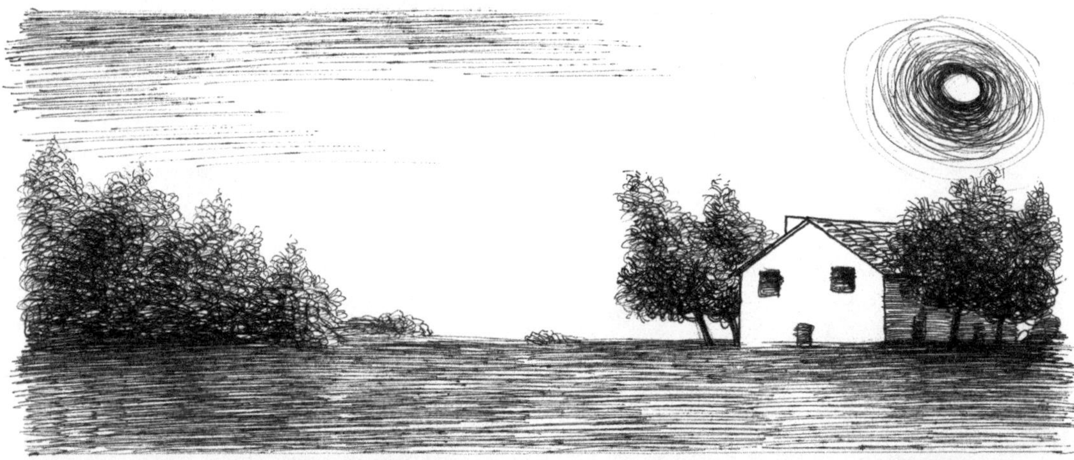

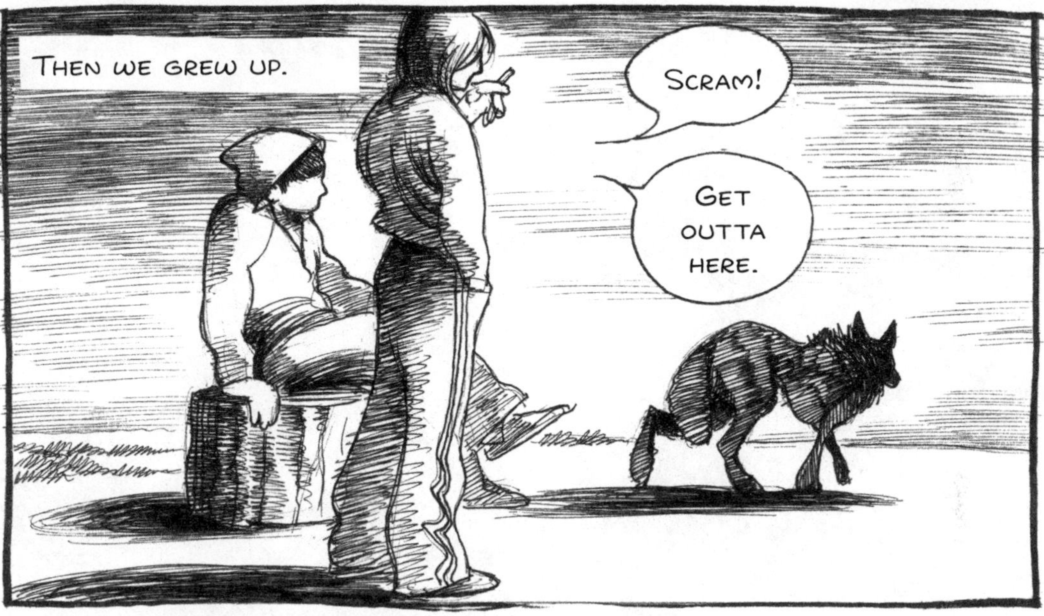
Then we grew up.
Scram!
Get outta here.

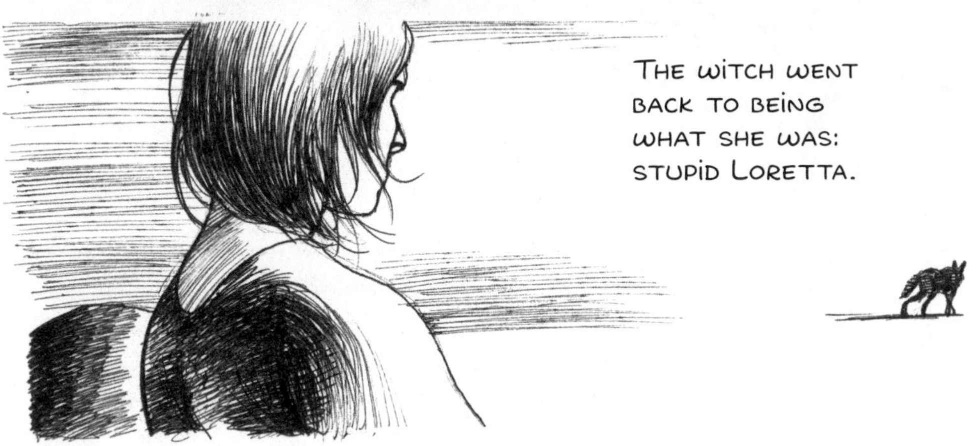
The witch went back to being what she was: stupid Loretta.

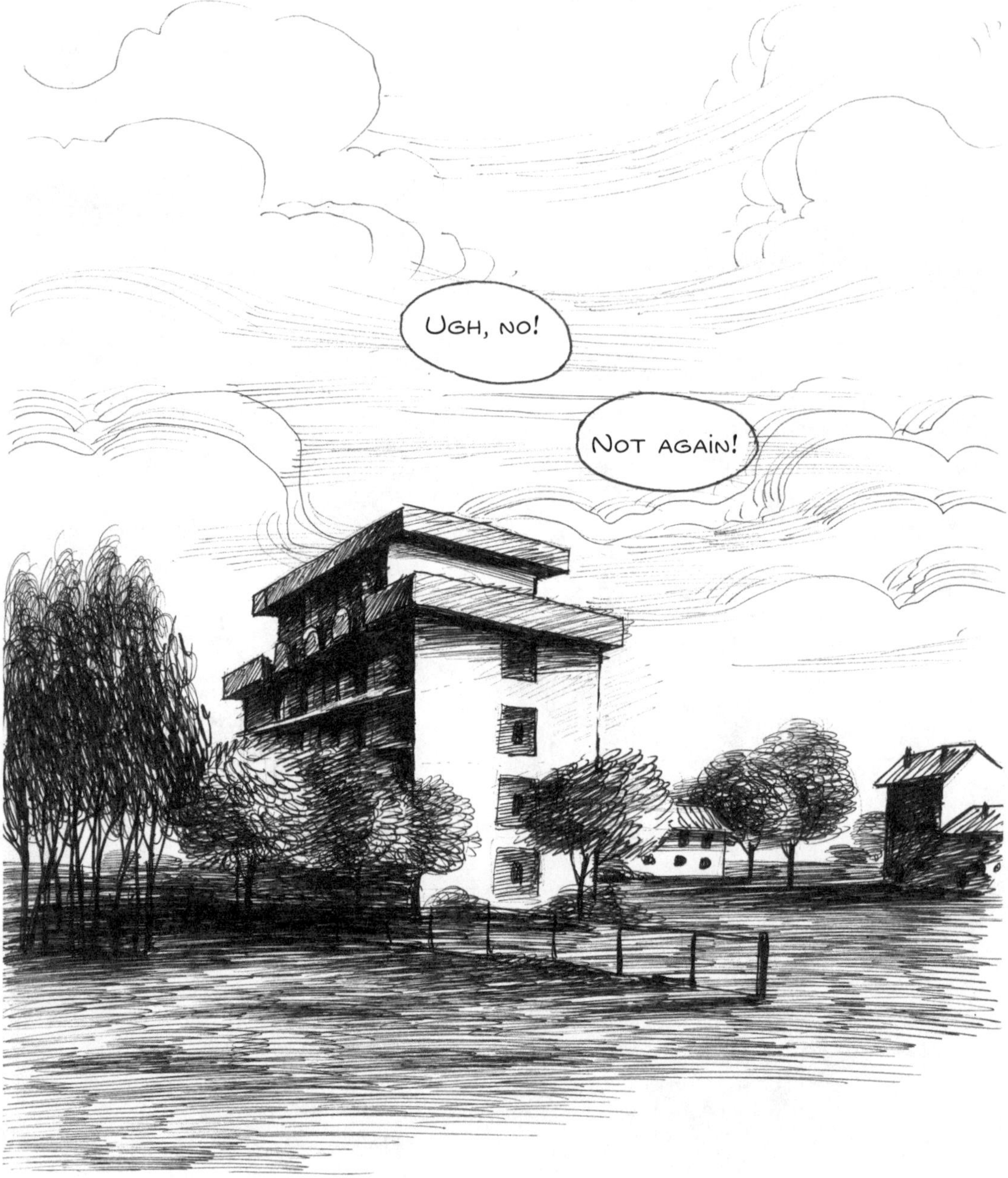
Ugh, no!
Not again!

VII

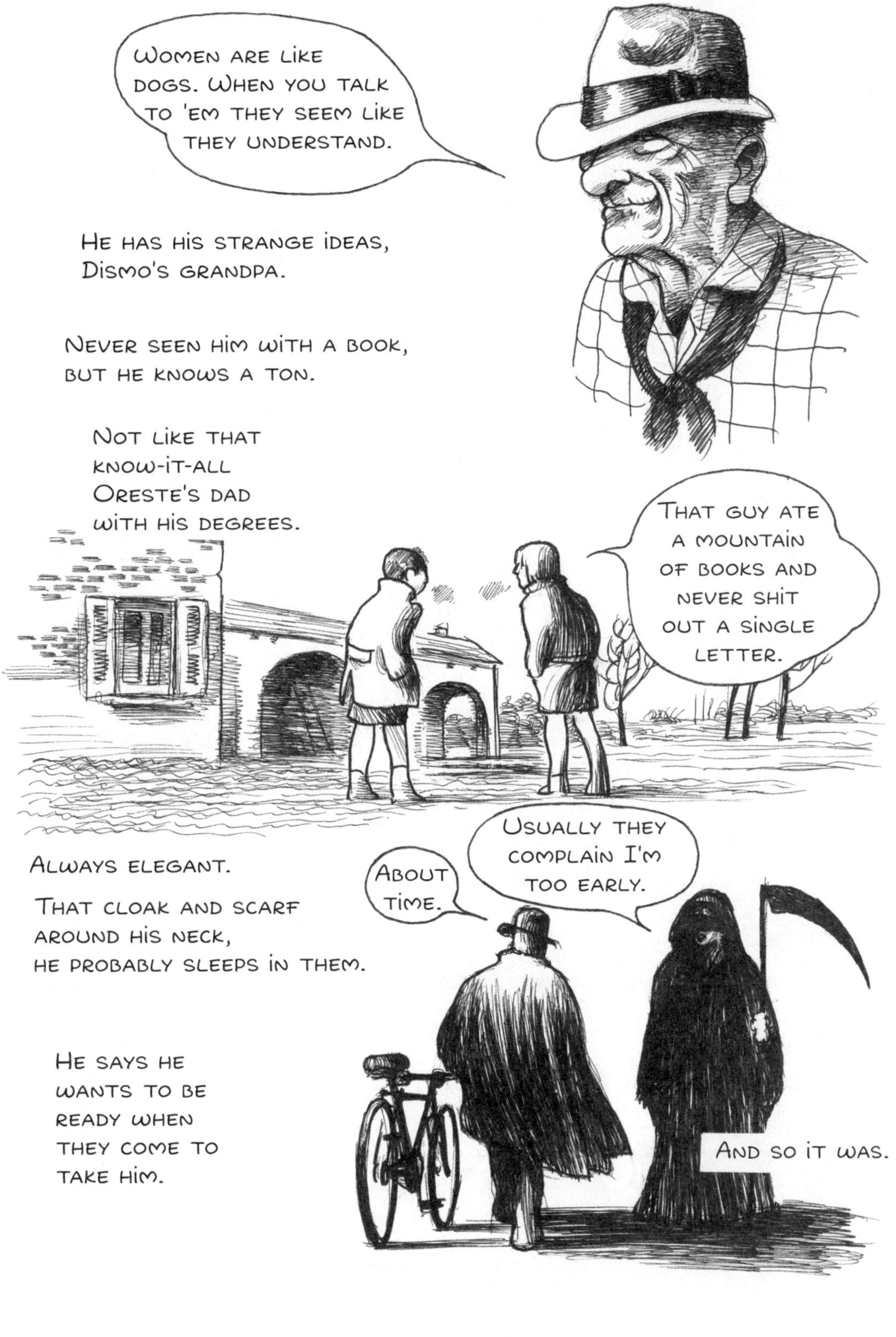
Women are like dogs. When you talk to 'em they seem like they understand.
He has his strange ideas, Dismo's grandpa.
Never seen him with a book, but he knows a ton.
Not like that know-it-all Oreste's dad with his degrees.
That guy ate a mountain of books and never shit out a single letter.
Always elegant.
That cloak and scarf around his neck, he probably sleeps in them.
About time.
Usually they complain I'm too early.
He says he wants to be ready when they come to take him.
And so it was.

ANNALITA'S UNCLE?

MAYBE DISMO'S GRANDPA.

WHO BUILT SLINGSHOTS FOR US TO SHOOT AT THE STANÇIÇS?

NO, I DON'T REMEMBER ANYMORE.

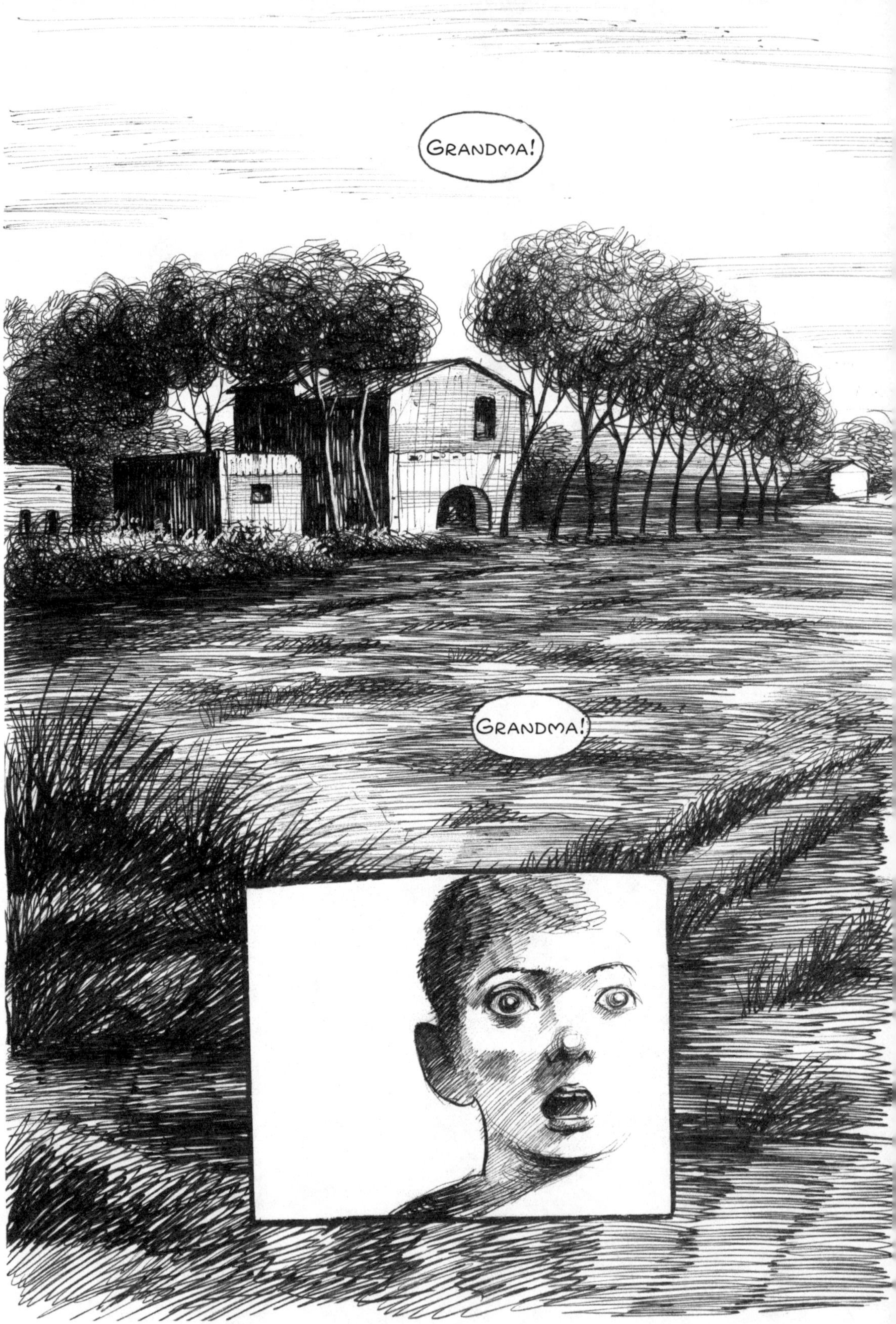
GRANDMA!
GRANDMA!

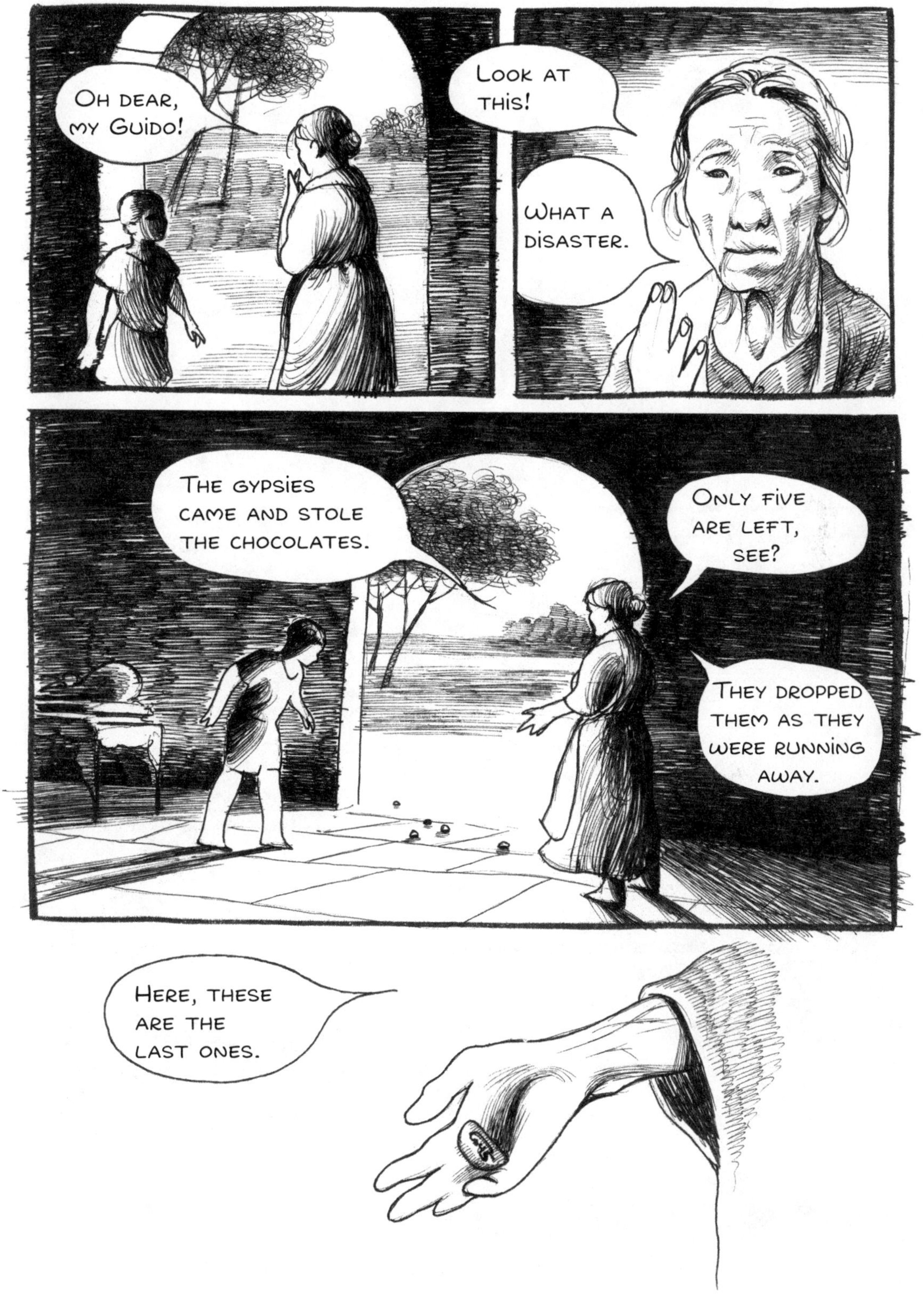
Oh dear, my Guido!
Look at this!
What a disaster.
The gypsies came and stole the chocolates.
Only five are left, see?
They dropped them as they were running away.
Here, these are the last ones.

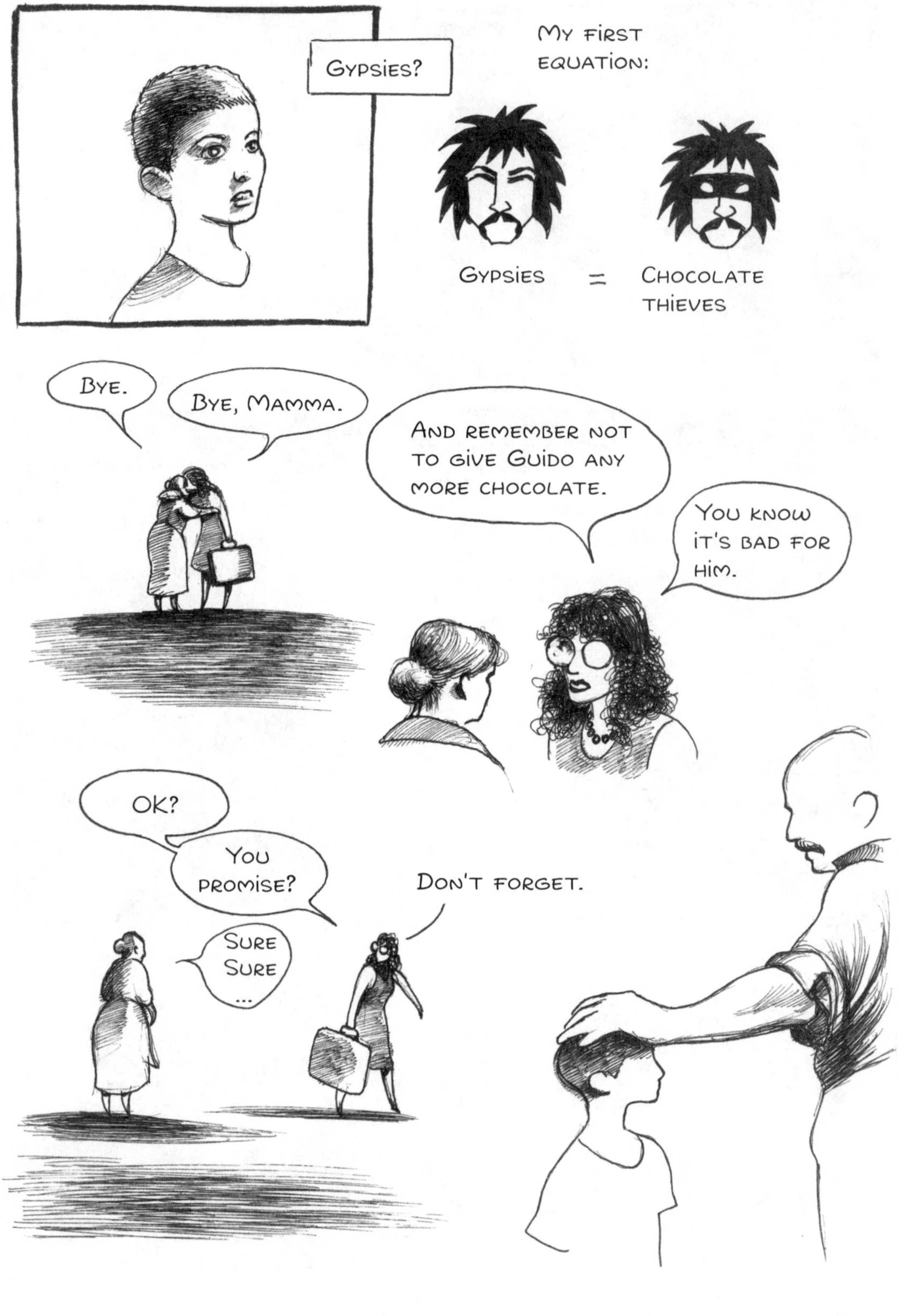
Gypsies?
My first equation:
Gypsies = Chocolate thieves
Bye.
Bye, Mamma.
And remember not to give Guido any more chocolate.
You know it's bad for him.
OK?
You promise?
Sure Sure ...
Don't forget.

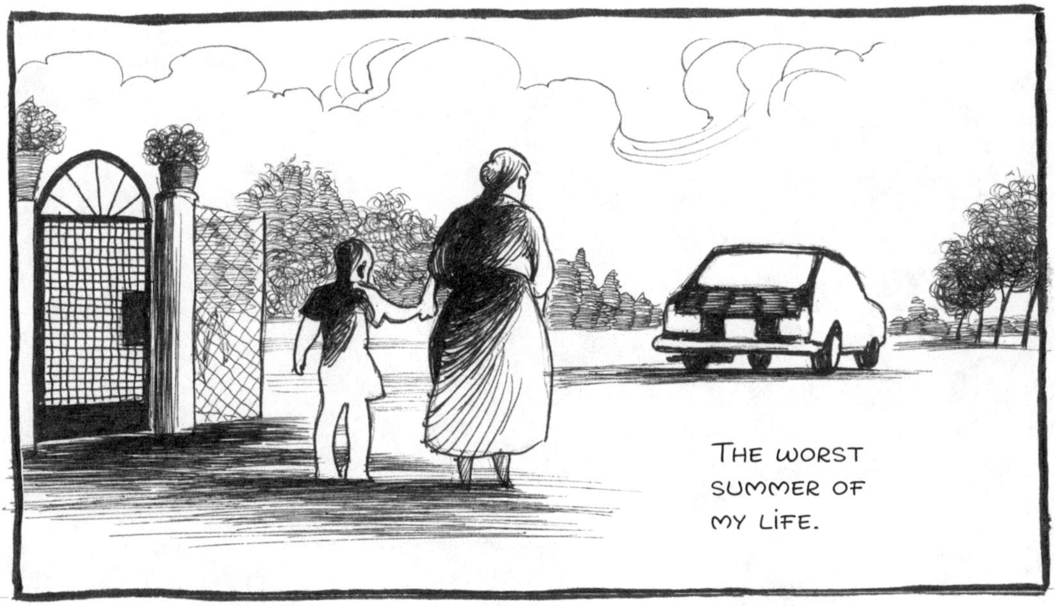
The worst summer of my life.

My folks went off and parked me at my nonna Ginevra's.

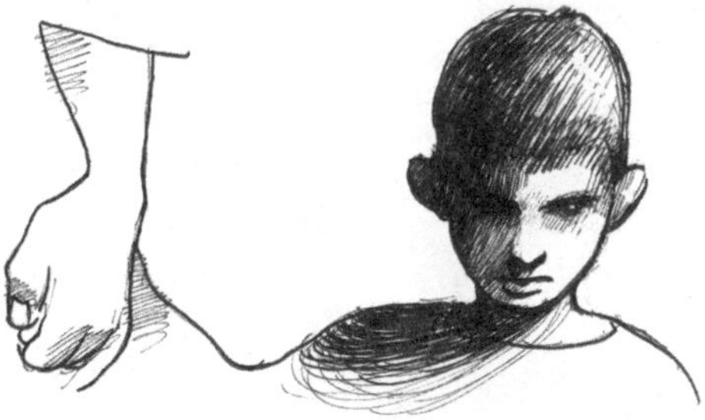

They were going to Parma. They said it was nothing big, my father had something to take care of and they would be back in a few days.

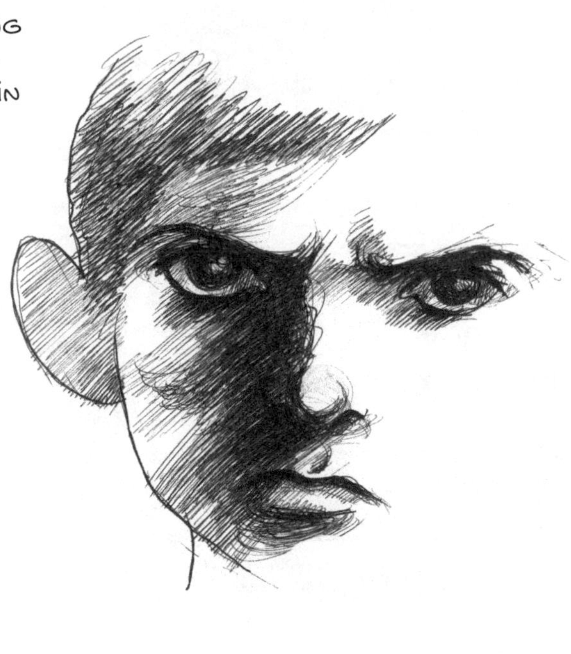

But I knew it wasn't true.

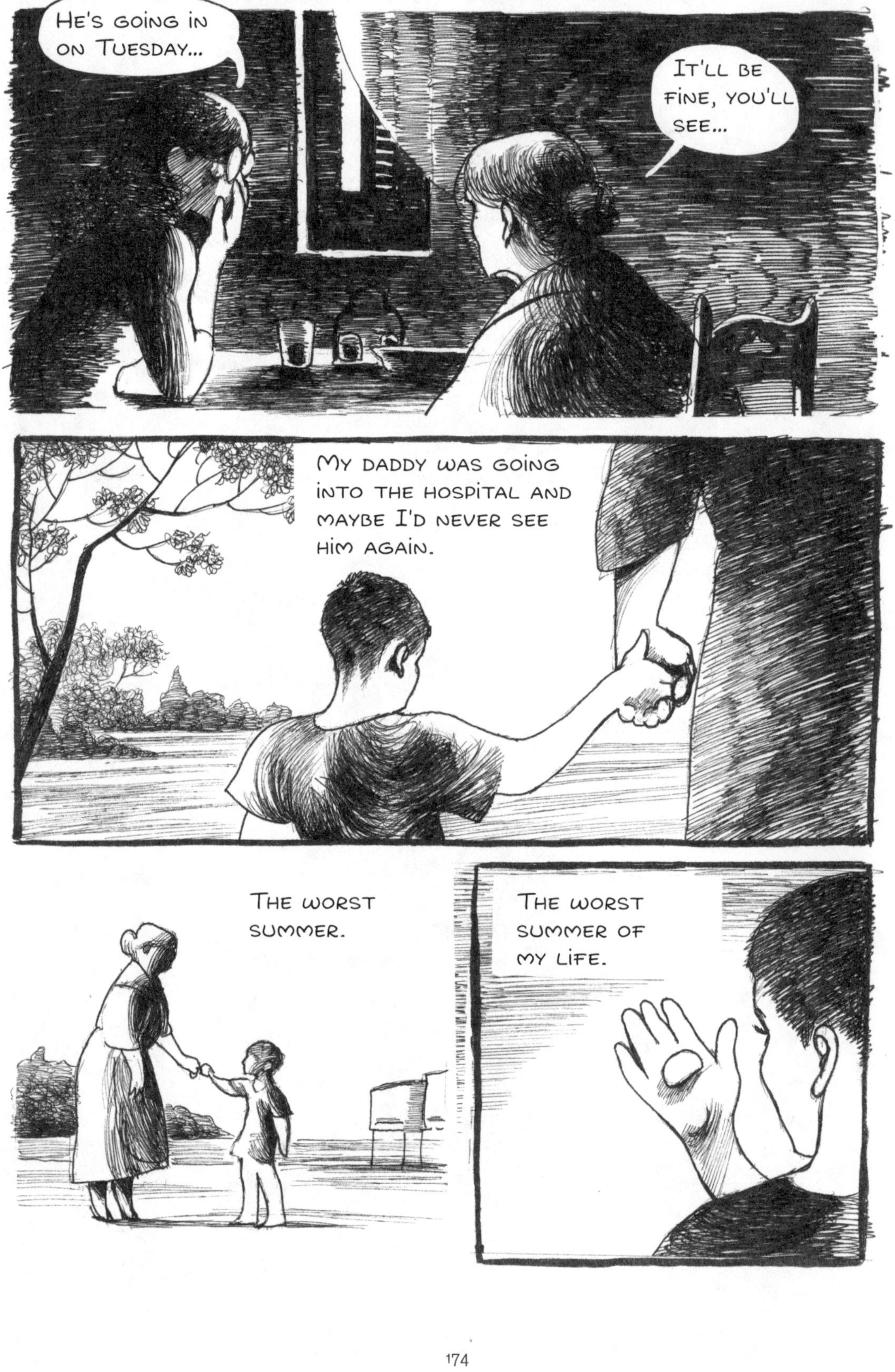
HE'S GOING IN ON TUESDAY...
IT'LL BE FINE, YOU'LL SEE...
MY DADDY WAS GOING INTO THE HOSPITAL AND MAYBE I'D NEVER SEE HIM AGAIN.
THE WORST SUMMER.
THE WORST SUMMER OF MY LIFE.

IF IT WASN'T FOR MORENO, A.K.A. GRISÙ.

GUIDO!

HEYO!

MORENO!

GRISÙ.

THE LITTLE DRAGON FROM THE CARTOONS. WHO WANTS TO BE A FIREFIGHTER BUT CAN'T STOP HIMSELF FROM SPEWING FIRE EVERYWHERE.

WHAT'S HIS NAME?

GRISÙ, LIKE THE GASOLINE.

OH, GRISÙ. I LIKE THAT.

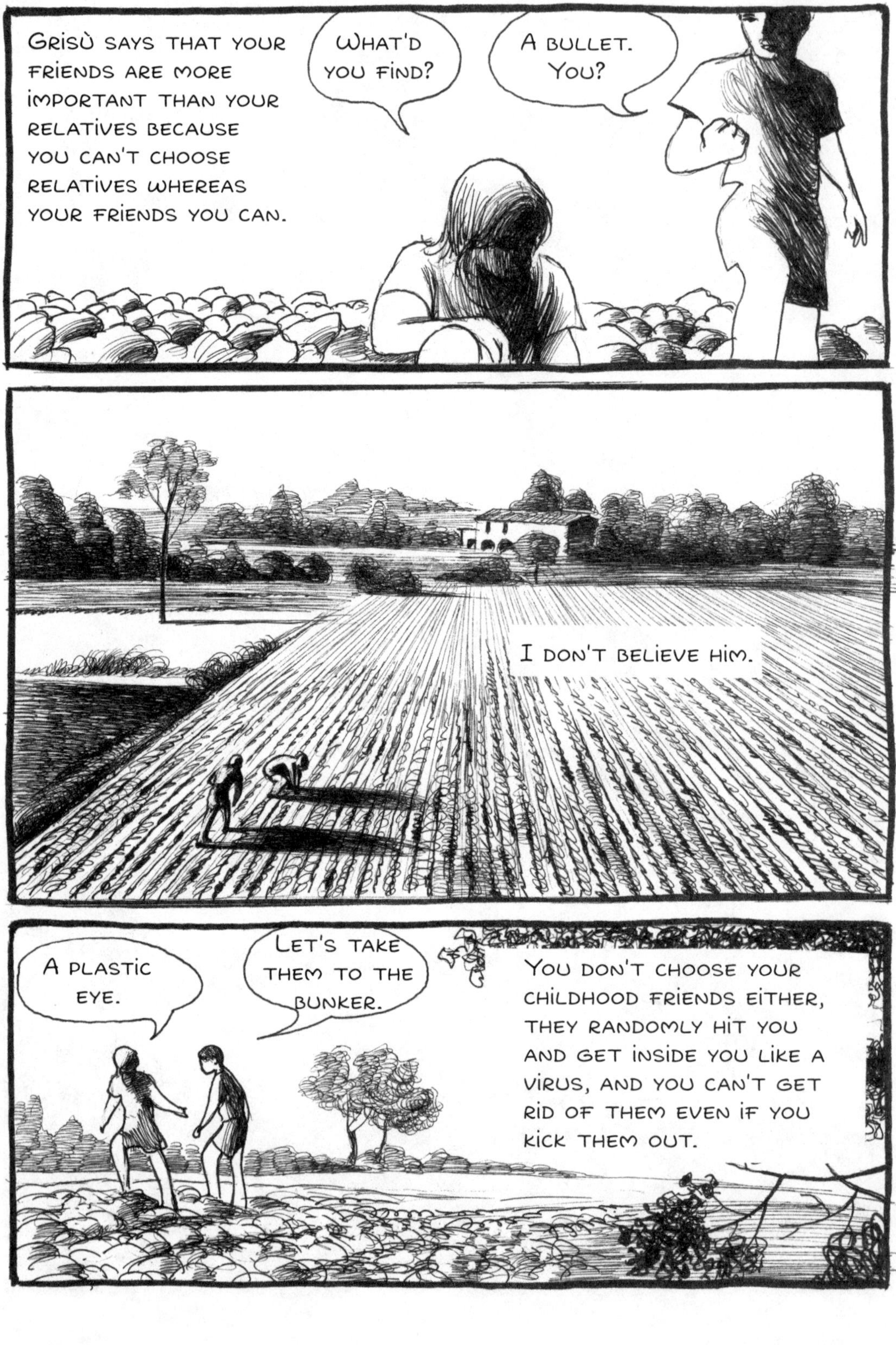
Grisù says that your friends are more important than your relatives because you can't choose relatives whereas your friends you can.
What'd you find?
A bullet. You?
I don't believe him.
A plastic eye.
Let's take them to the bunker.
You don't choose your childhood friends either, they randomly hit you and get inside you like a virus, and you can't get rid of them even if you kick them out.

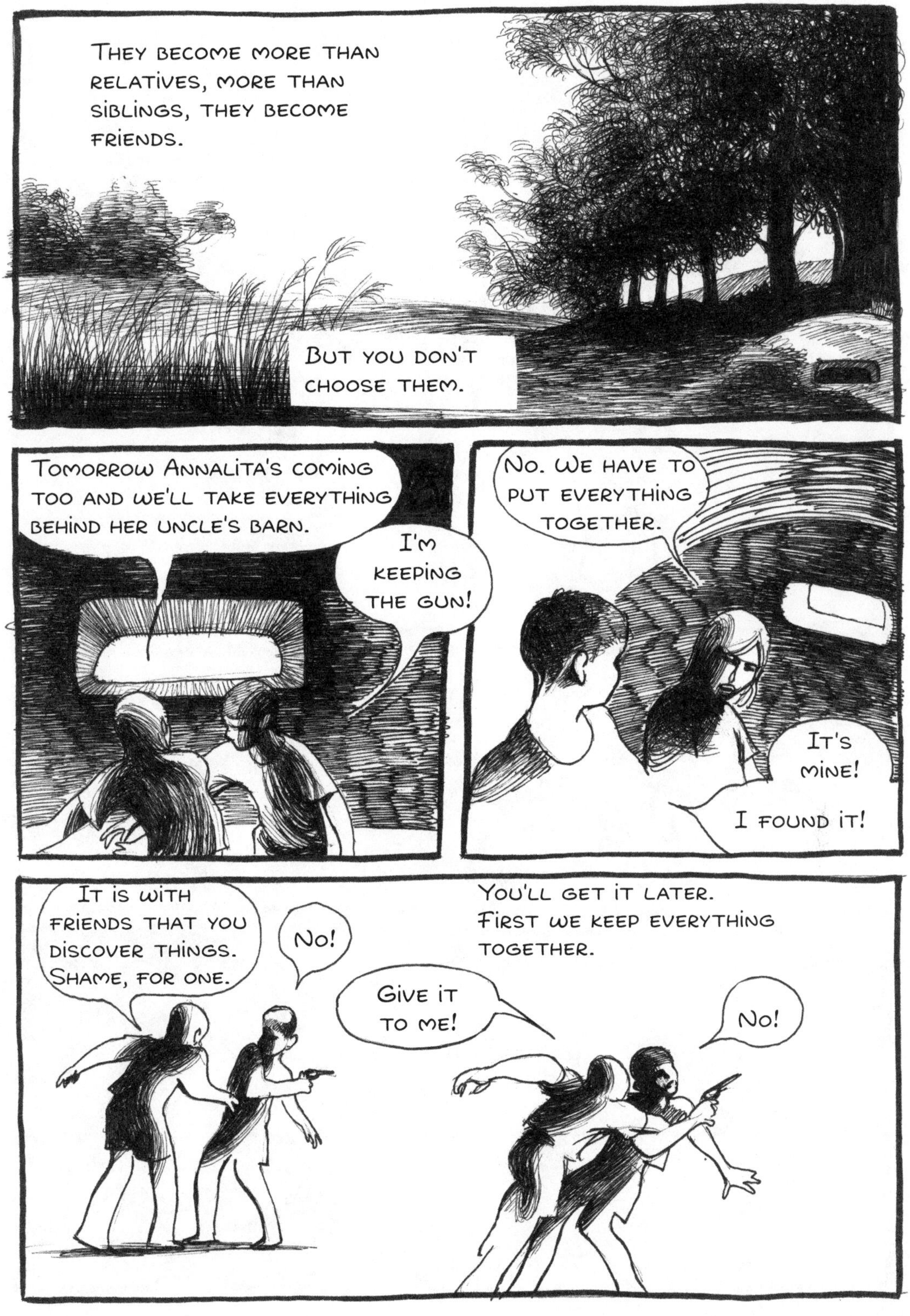
They become more than relatives, more than siblings, they become friends.
But you don't choose them.
Tomorrow Annalita's coming too and we'll take everything behind her uncle's barn.
I'm keeping the gun!
No. We have to put everything together.
It's mine!
I found it!
It is with friends that you discover things. Shame, for one.
No!
Give it to me!
You'll get it later. First we keep everything together.
No!

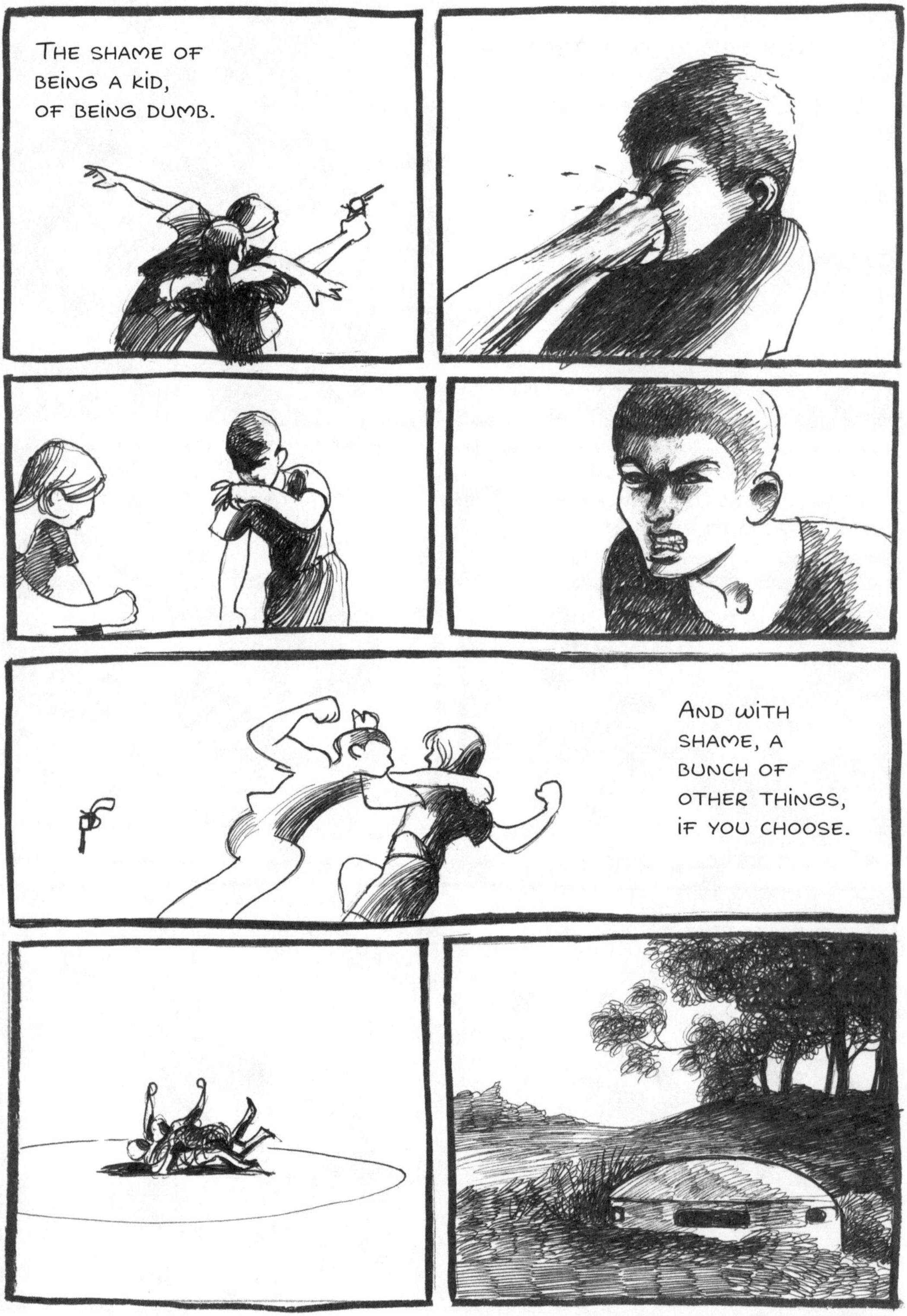
THE SHAME OF BEING A KID, OF BEING DUMB.
AND WITH SHAME, A BUNCH OF OTHER THINGS, IF YOU CHOOSE.

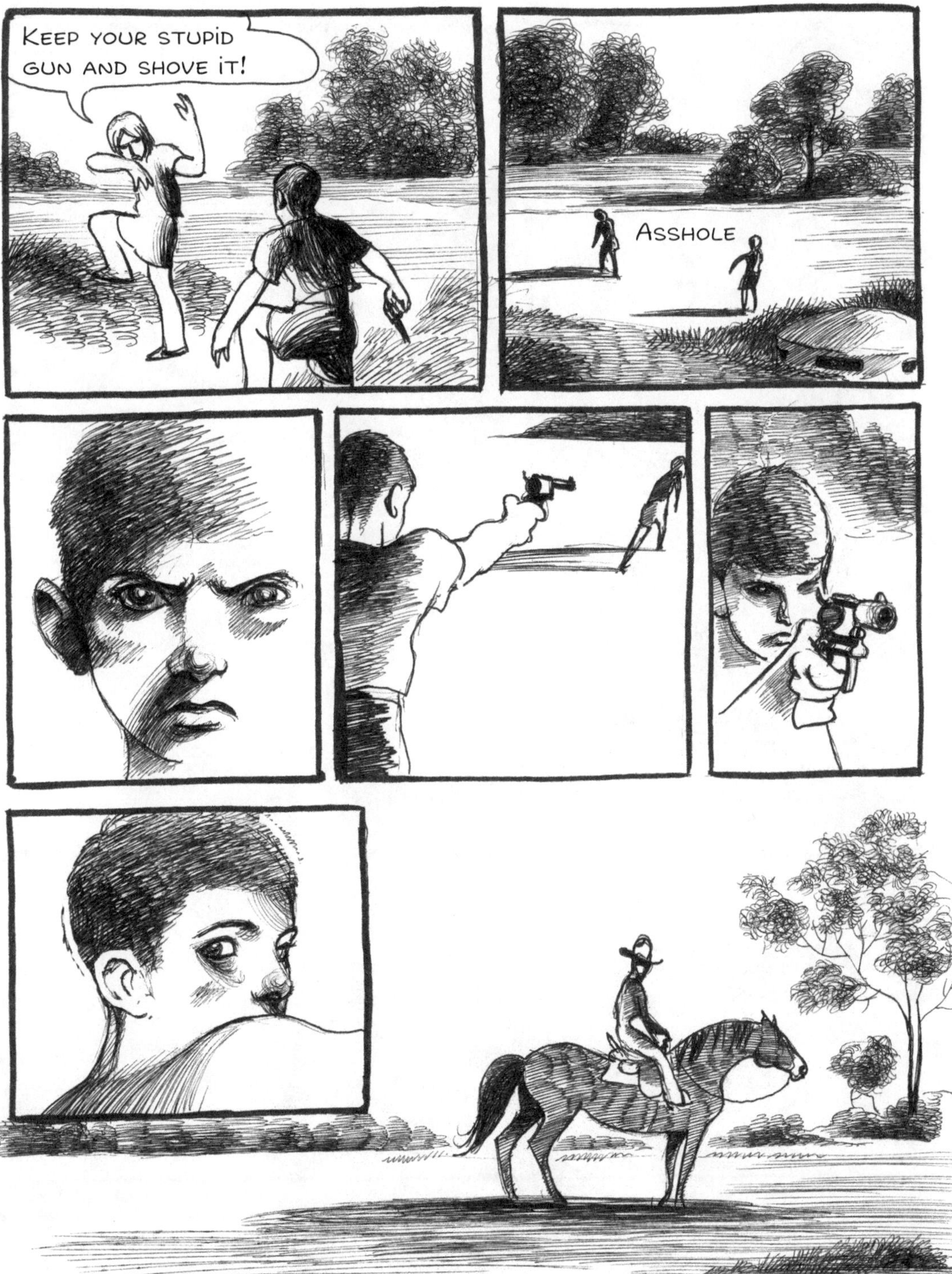
KEEP YOUR STUPID GUN AND SHOVE IT!
ASSHOLE

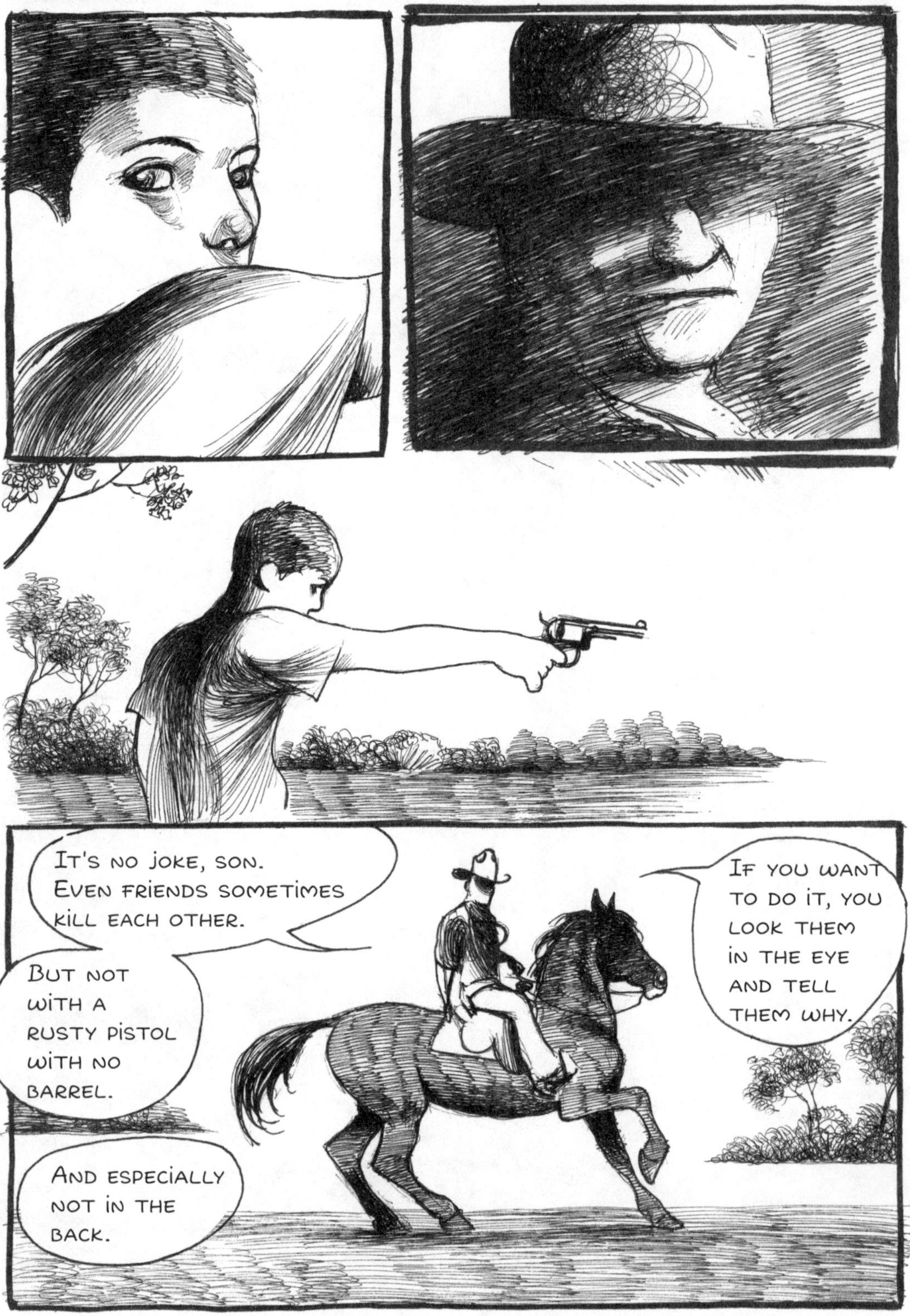
It's no joke, son. Even friends sometimes kill each other.
If you want to do it, you look them in the eye and tell them why.
But not with a rusty pistol with no barrel.
And especially not in the back.

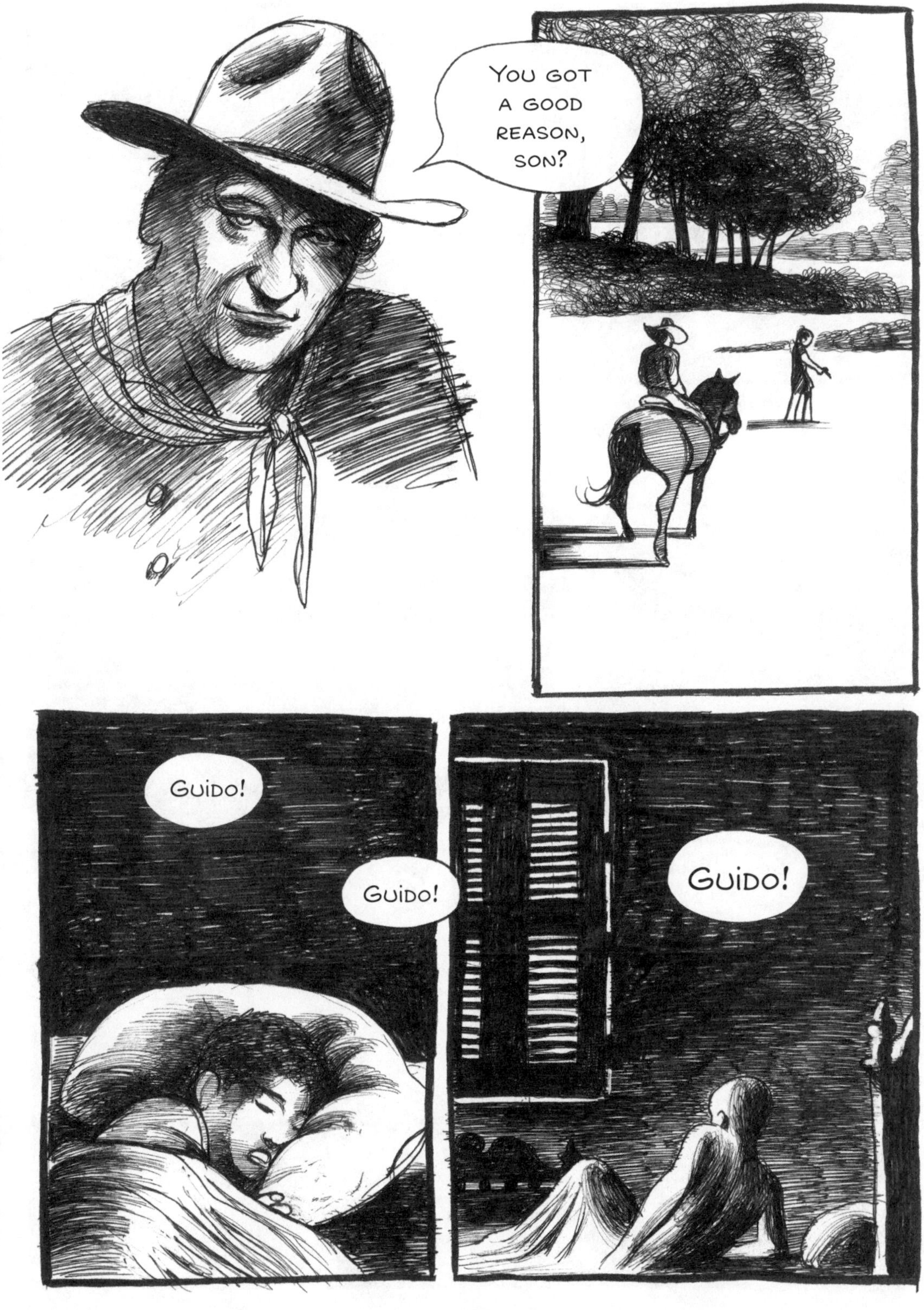
YOU GOT A GOOD REASON, SON?
GUIDO!
GUIDO!
GUIDO!

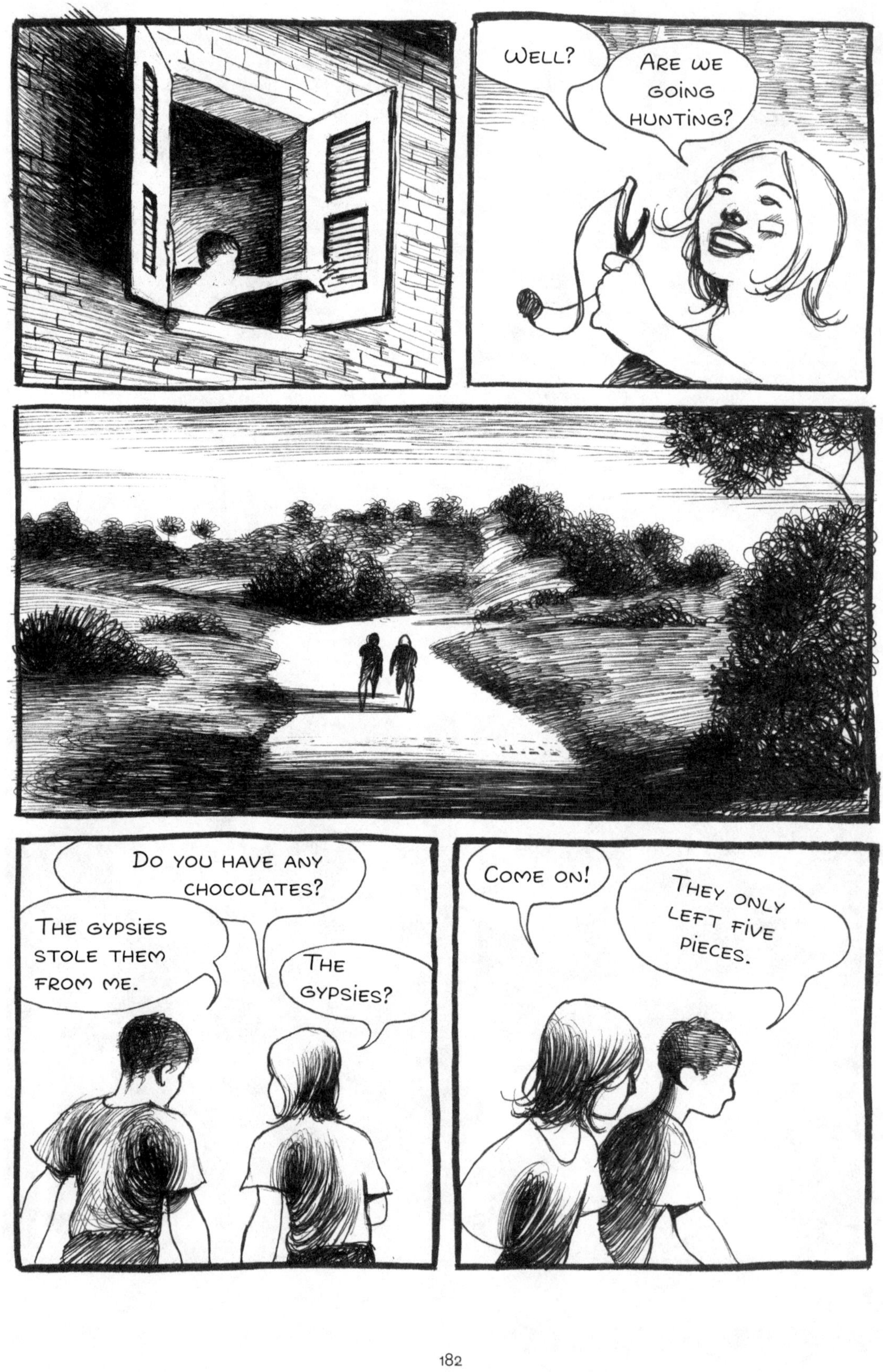
WELL?
ARE WE GOING HUNTING?
DO YOU HAVE ANY CHOCOLATES?
THE GYPSIES STOLE THEM FROM ME.
THE GYPSIES?
COME ON!
THEY ONLY LEFT FIVE PIECES.

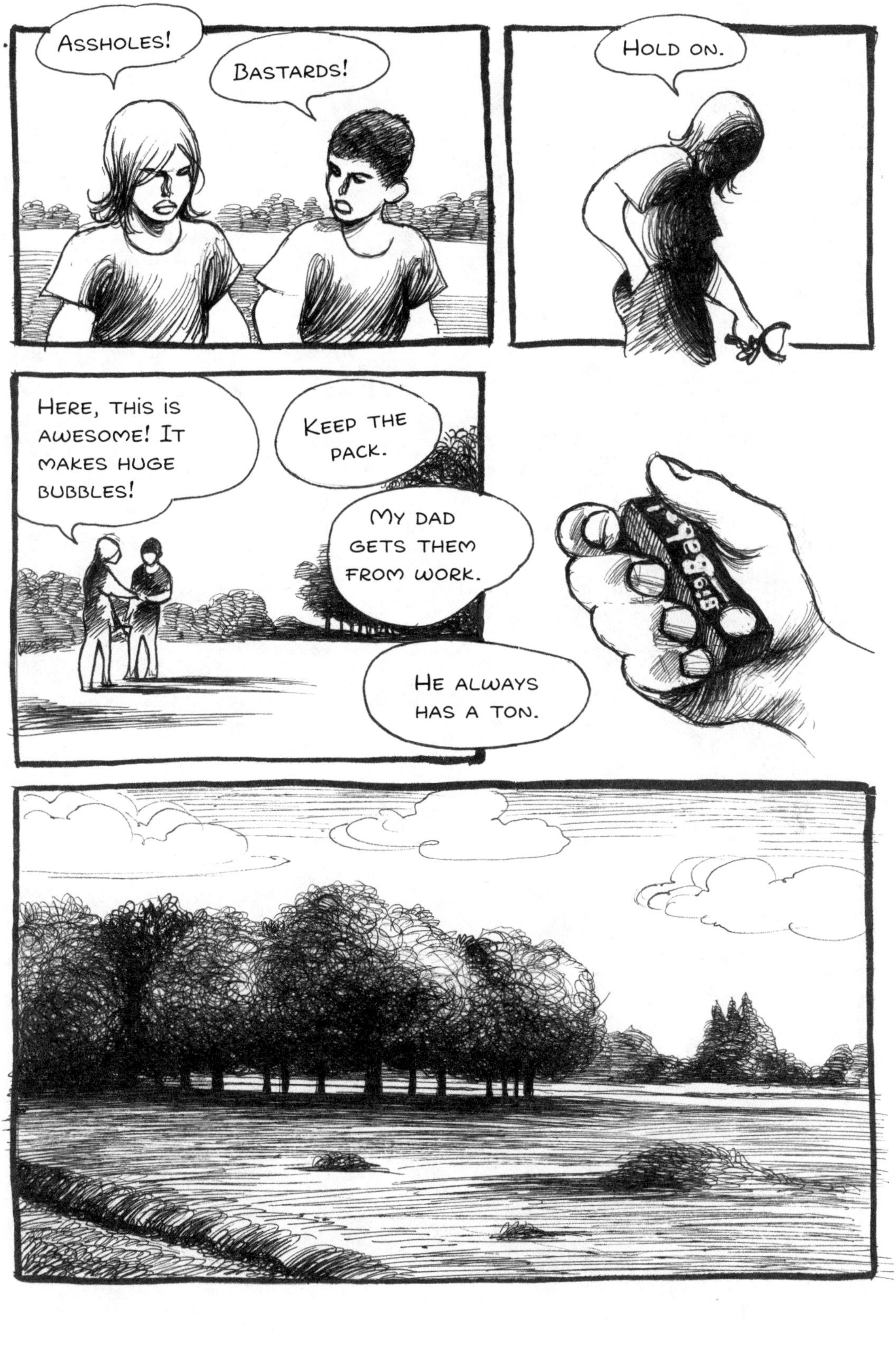
Assholes!
Bastards!
Hold on.
Here, this is awesome! It makes huge bubbles!
Keep the pack.
My dad gets them from work.
He always has a ton.

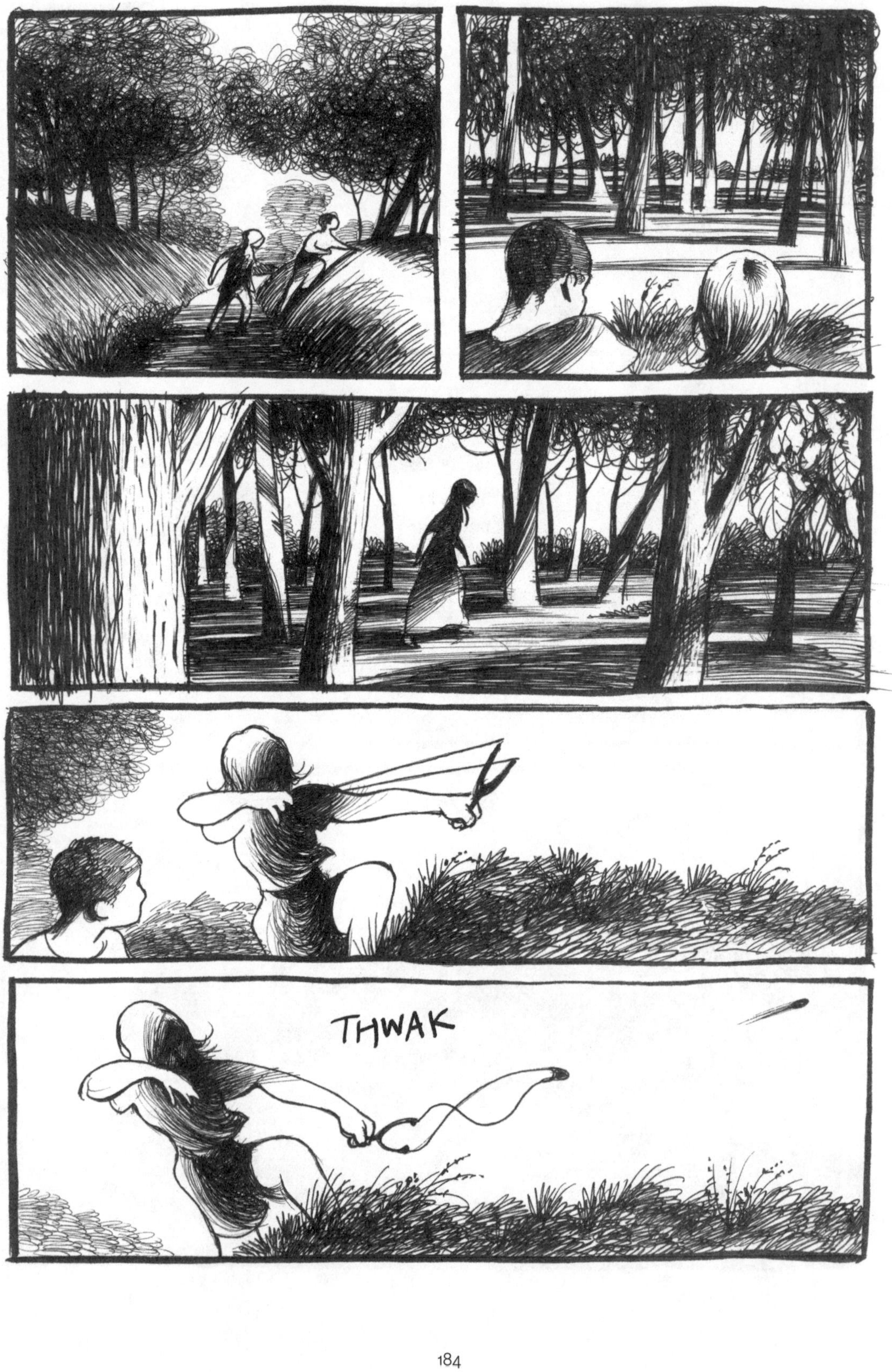
THWAK

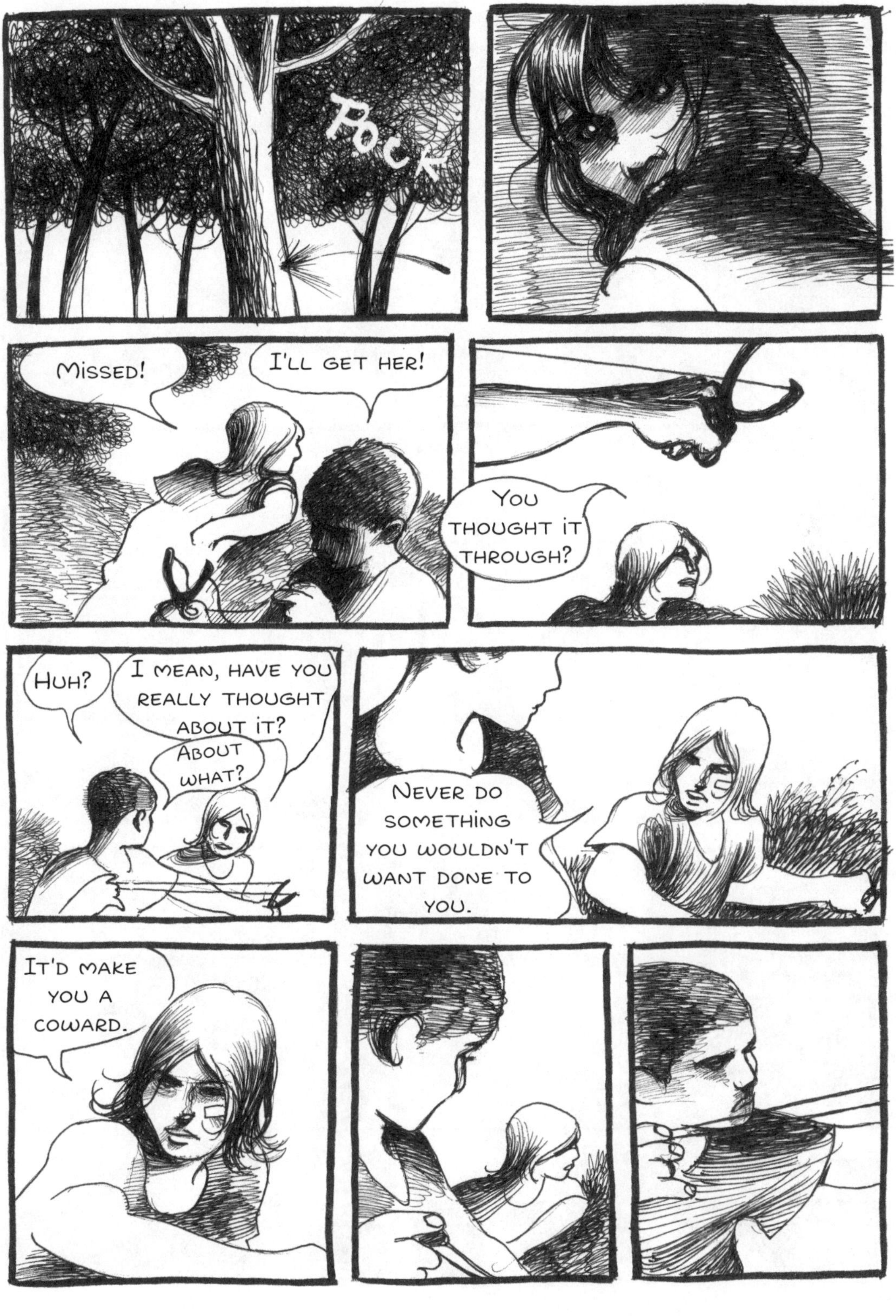
POCK
Missed!
I'll get her!
You thought it through?
Huh?
I mean, have you really thought about it?
About what?
Never do something you wouldn't want done to you.
It'd make you a coward.

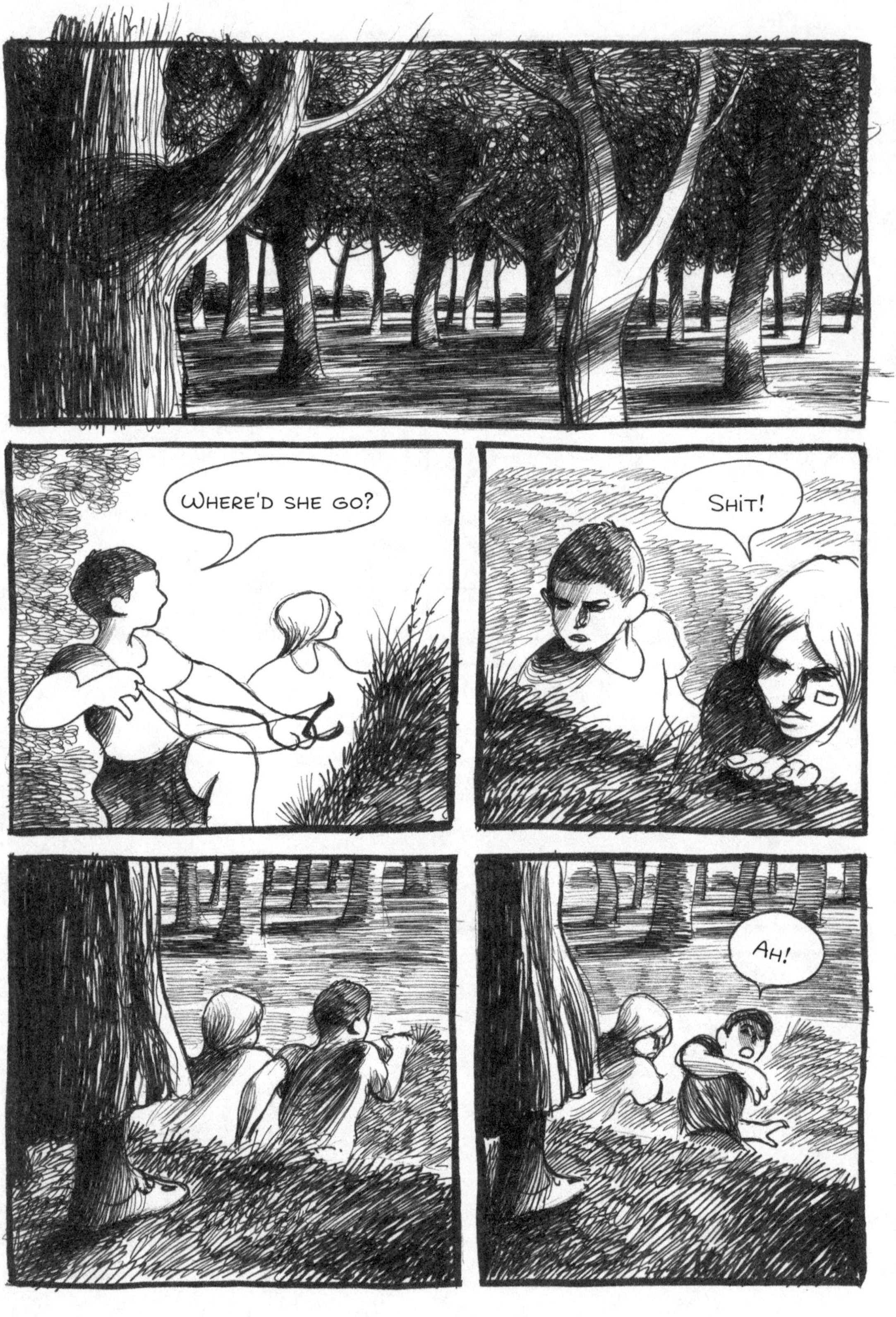

Where'd she go?
Shit!
Ah!

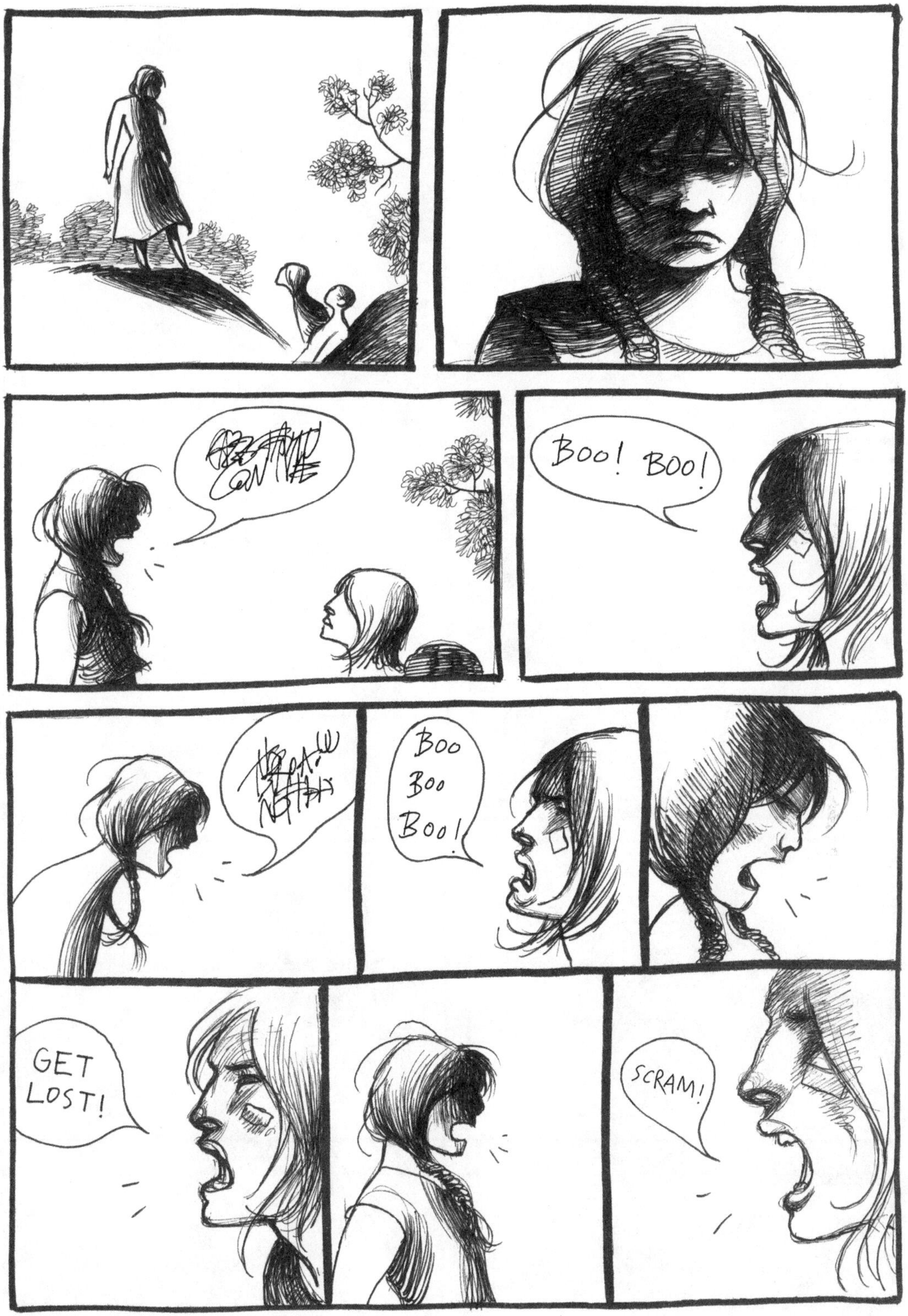
BOO! BOO!
BOO BOO BOO!
GET LOST!
SCRAM!

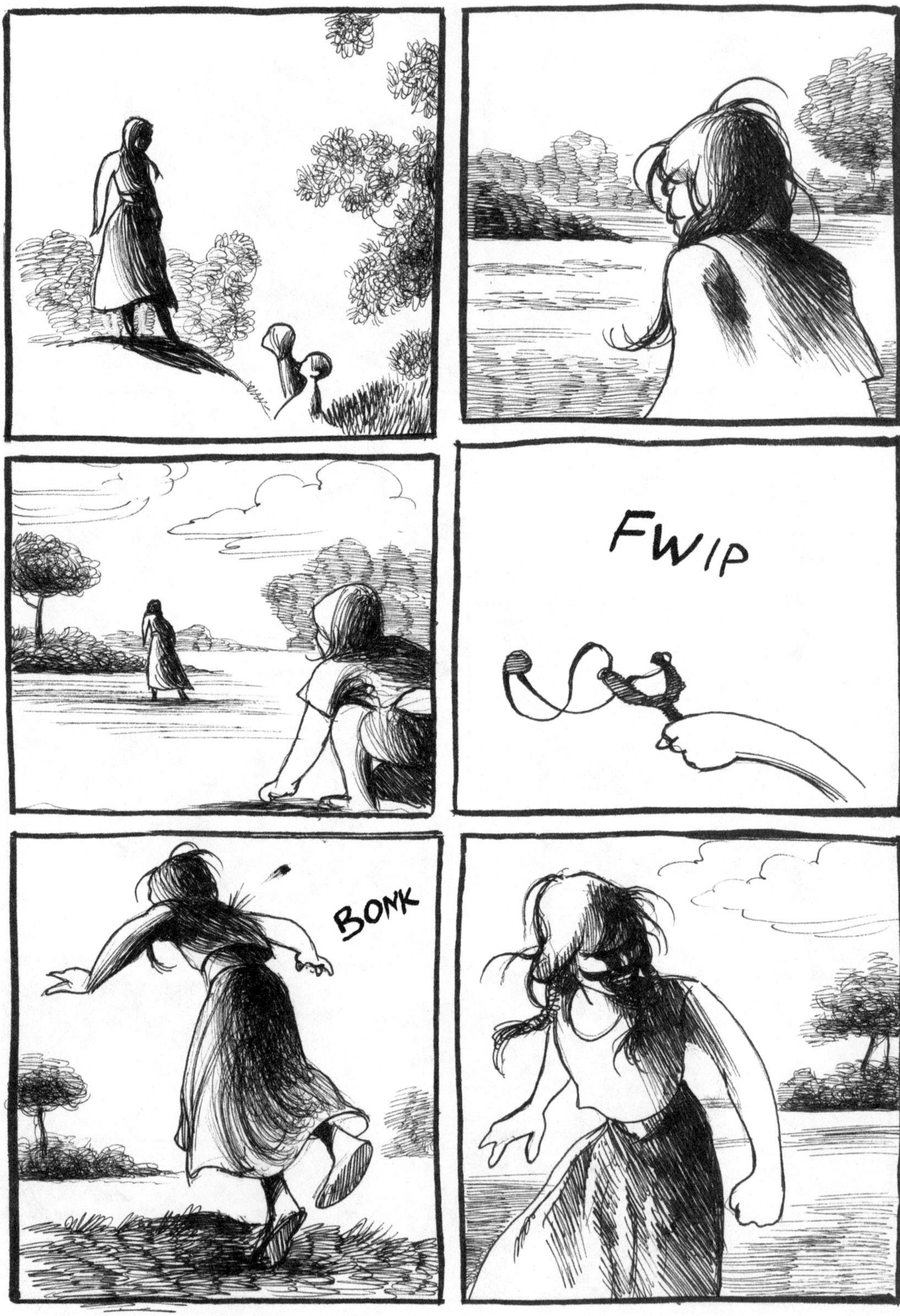
FWIP
BONK

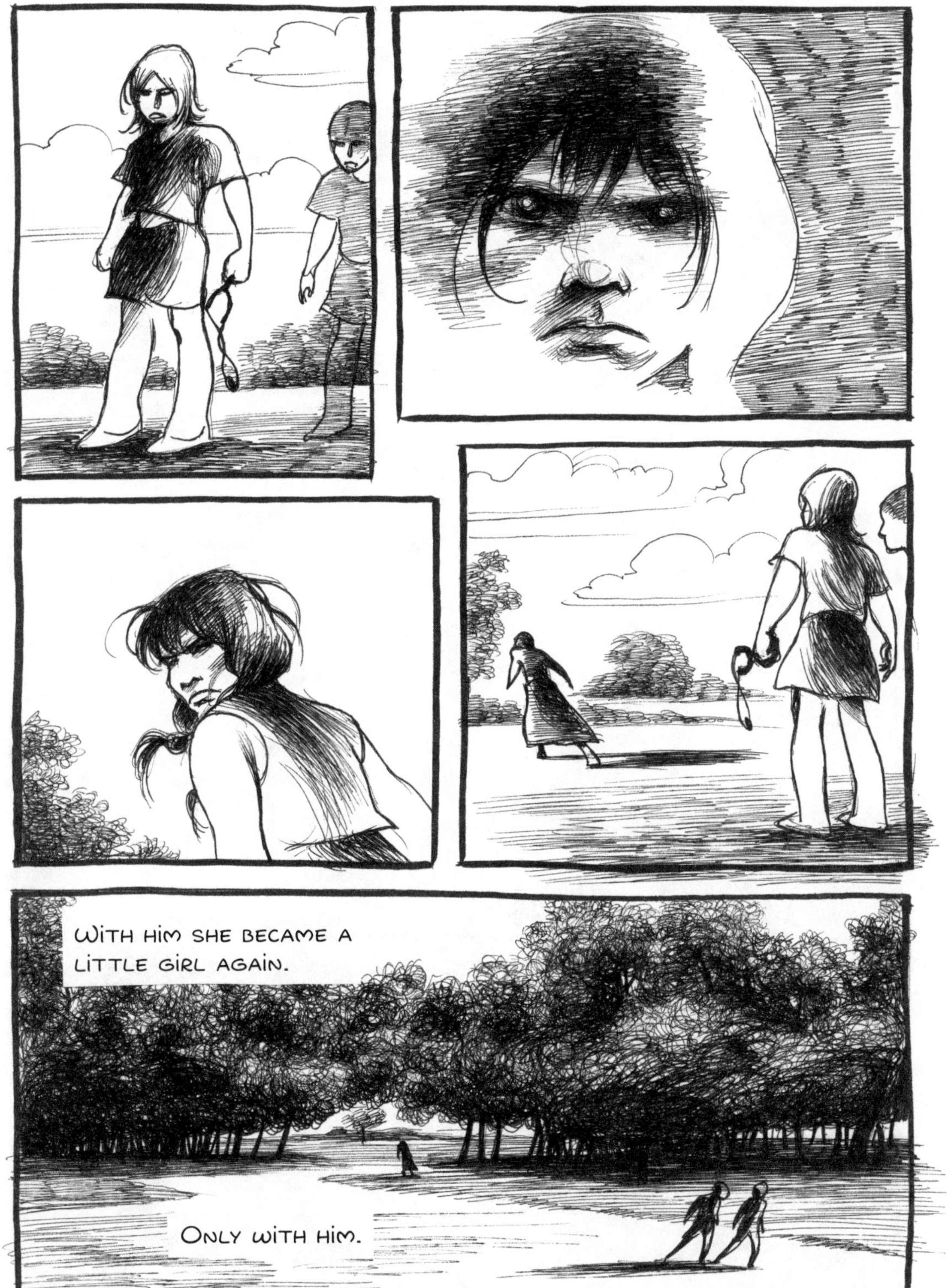
With him she became a little girl again.
Only with him.

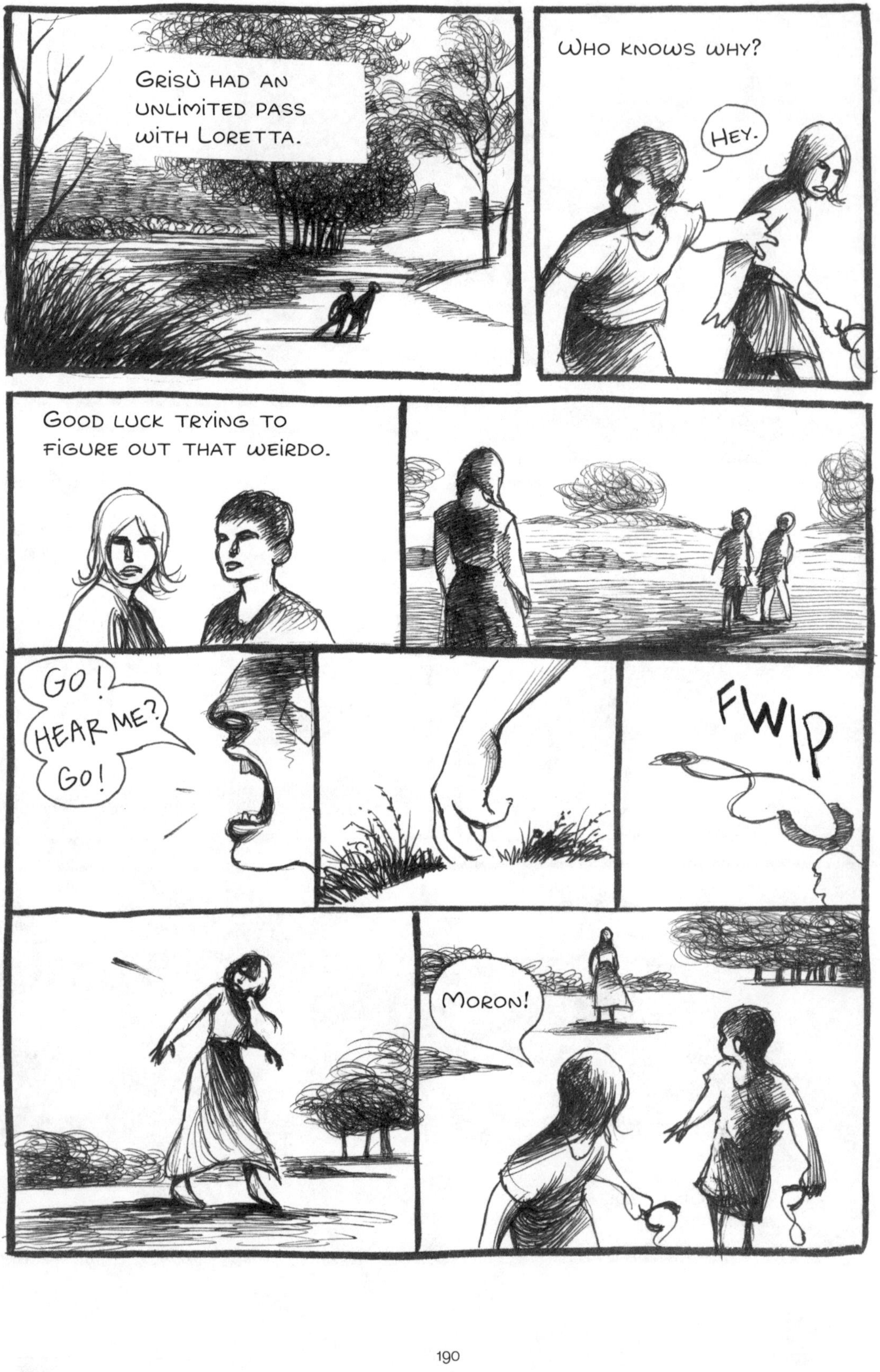
Grisù had an unlimited pass with Loretta.
Who knows why?
Hey.
Good luck trying to figure out that weirdo.
Go! Hear me? Go!
FWIP
Moron!

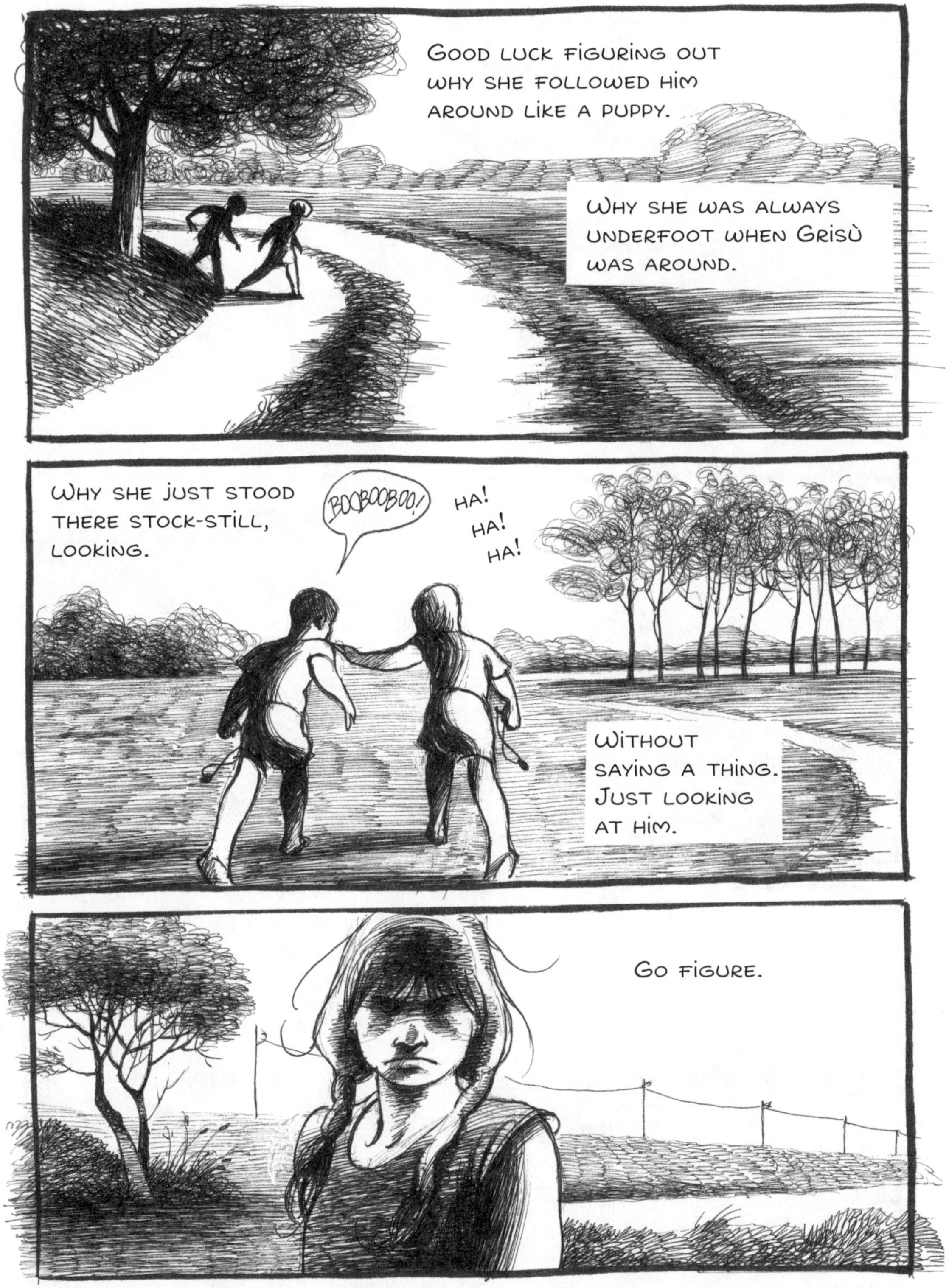
GOOD LUCK FIGURING OUT WHY SHE FOLLOWED HIM AROUND LIKE A PUPPY.
WHY SHE WAS ALWAYS UNDERFOOT WHEN GRISÙ WAS AROUND.
WHY SHE JUST STOOD THERE STOCK-STILL, LOOKING.
BOOBOOBOO!
HA! HA! HA!
WITHOUT SAYING A THING. JUST LOOKING AT HIM.
GO FIGURE.

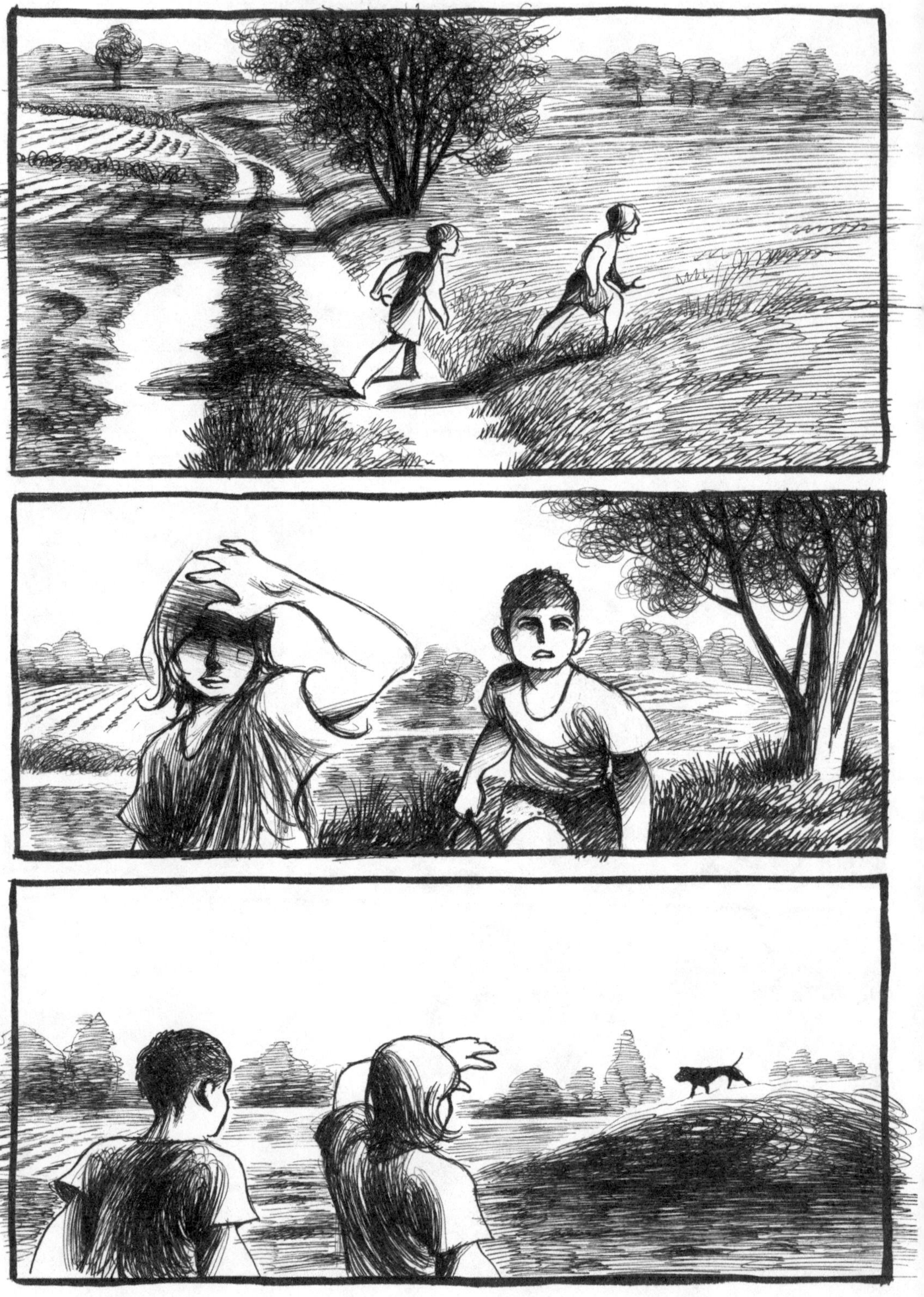

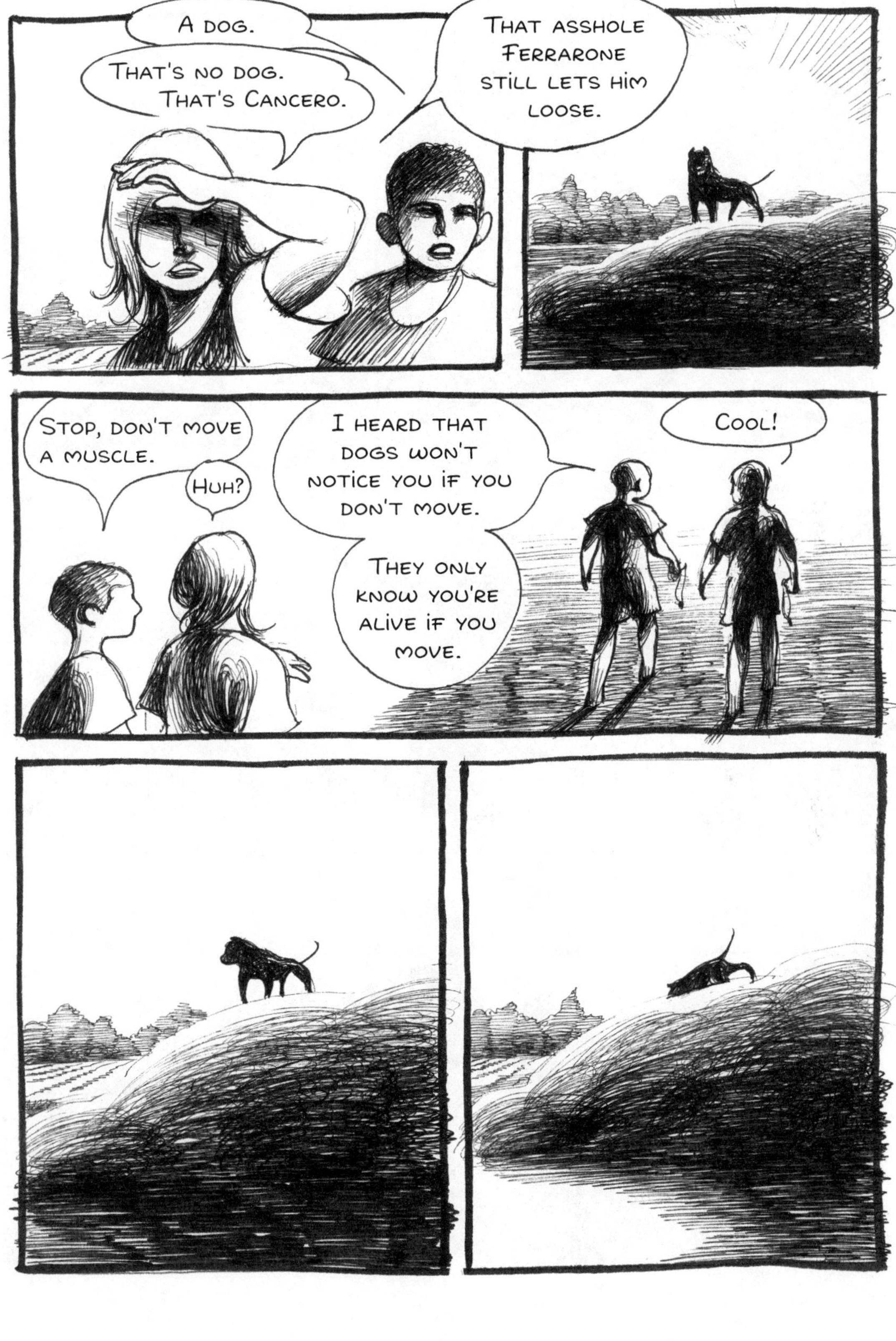
A dog.
That's no dog. That's Cancero.
That asshole Ferrarone still lets him loose.
Stop, don't move a muscle.
Huh?
I heard that dogs won't notice you if you don't move.
They only know you're alive if you move.
Cool!

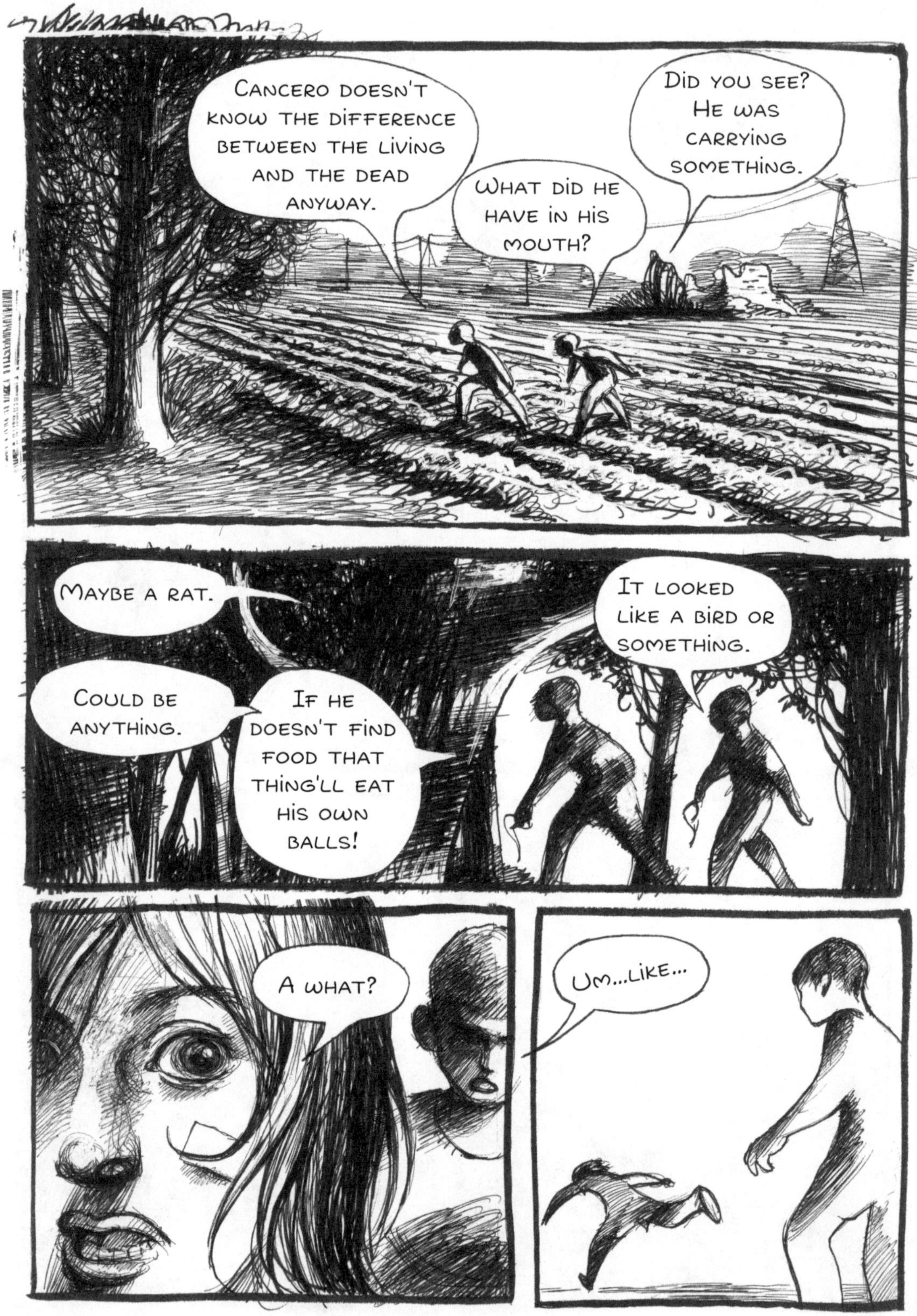
Cancero doesn't know the difference between the living and the dead anyway.
What did he have in his mouth?
Did you see? He was carrying something.
Maybe a rat.
It looked like a bird or something.
Could be anything.
If he doesn't find food that thing'll eat his own balls!
A what?
Um...like...

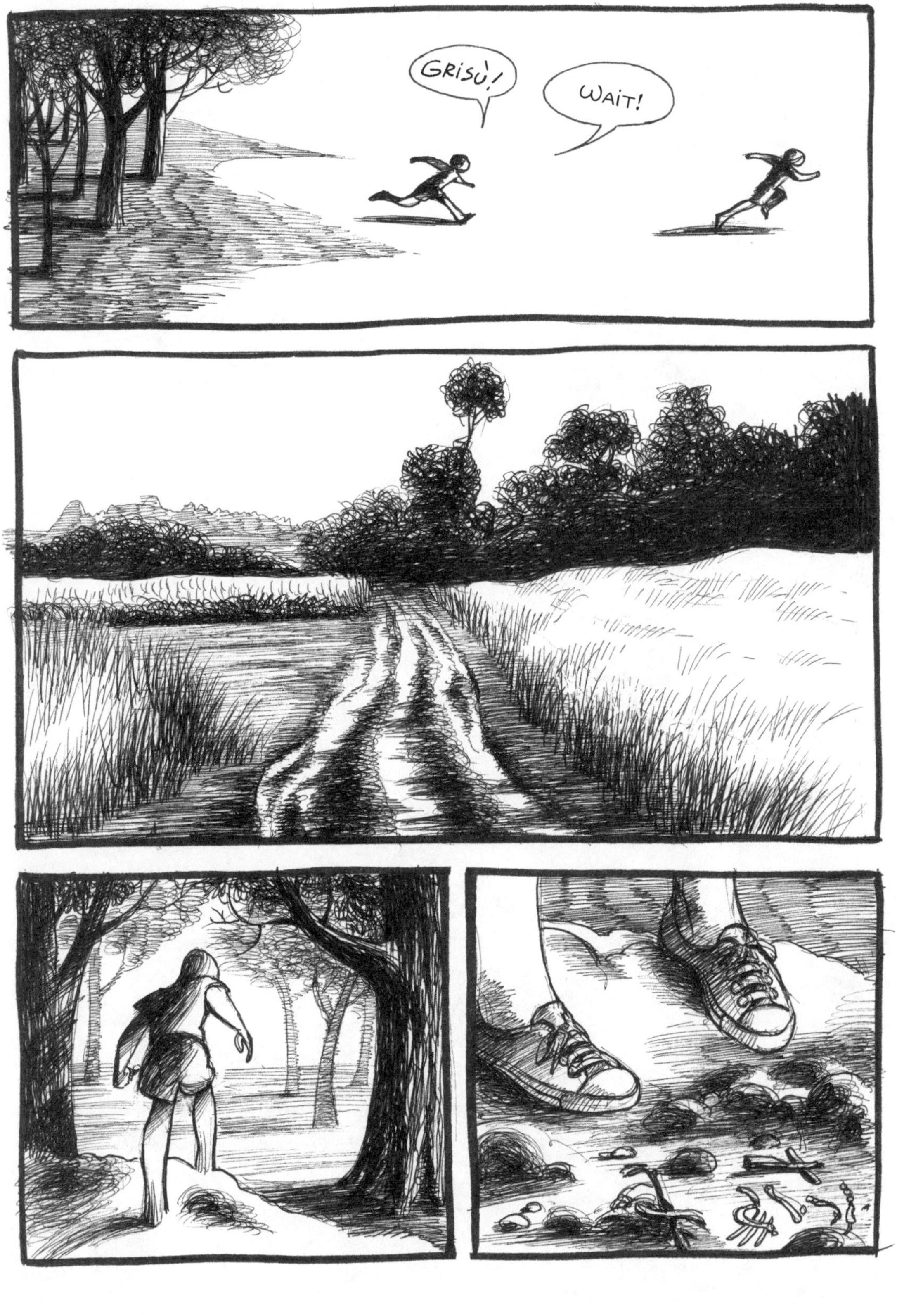
GRISÙ!
WAIT!

THE FIRST TIME HE
TOOK ONE FROM THE
MOUTH OF FRIS, THE
FAMILY DOG.

HE BURIED IT IN
SECRET SO THE
DOG WOULDN'T GET
IN TROUBLE.

THEN THERE WERE
OTHERS.

NANI, CRUSHED TO DEATH
SOMEHOW.
FLICK AND FLOCK, FOUND
DEAD IN THE HENHOUSE
ONE MORNING.

HE BURIED THEM
TOGETHER AND GAVE
EACH ONE A NAME.

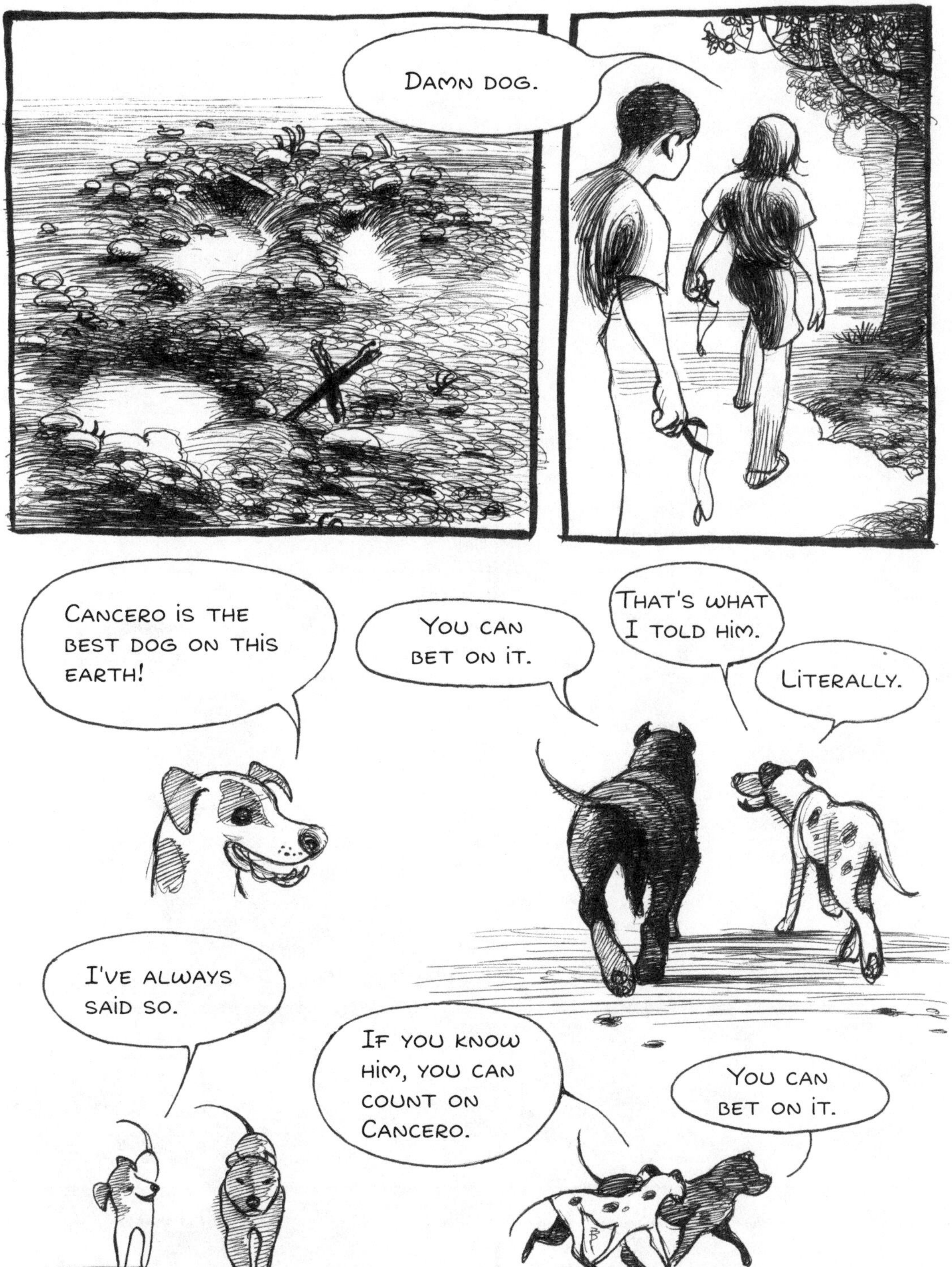
DAMN DOG.
CANCERO IS THE BEST DOG ON THIS EARTH!
YOU CAN BET ON IT.
THAT'S WHAT I TOLD HIM.
LITERALLY.
I'VE ALWAYS SAID SO.
IF YOU KNOW HIM, YOU CAN COUNT ON CANCERO.
YOU CAN BET ON IT.

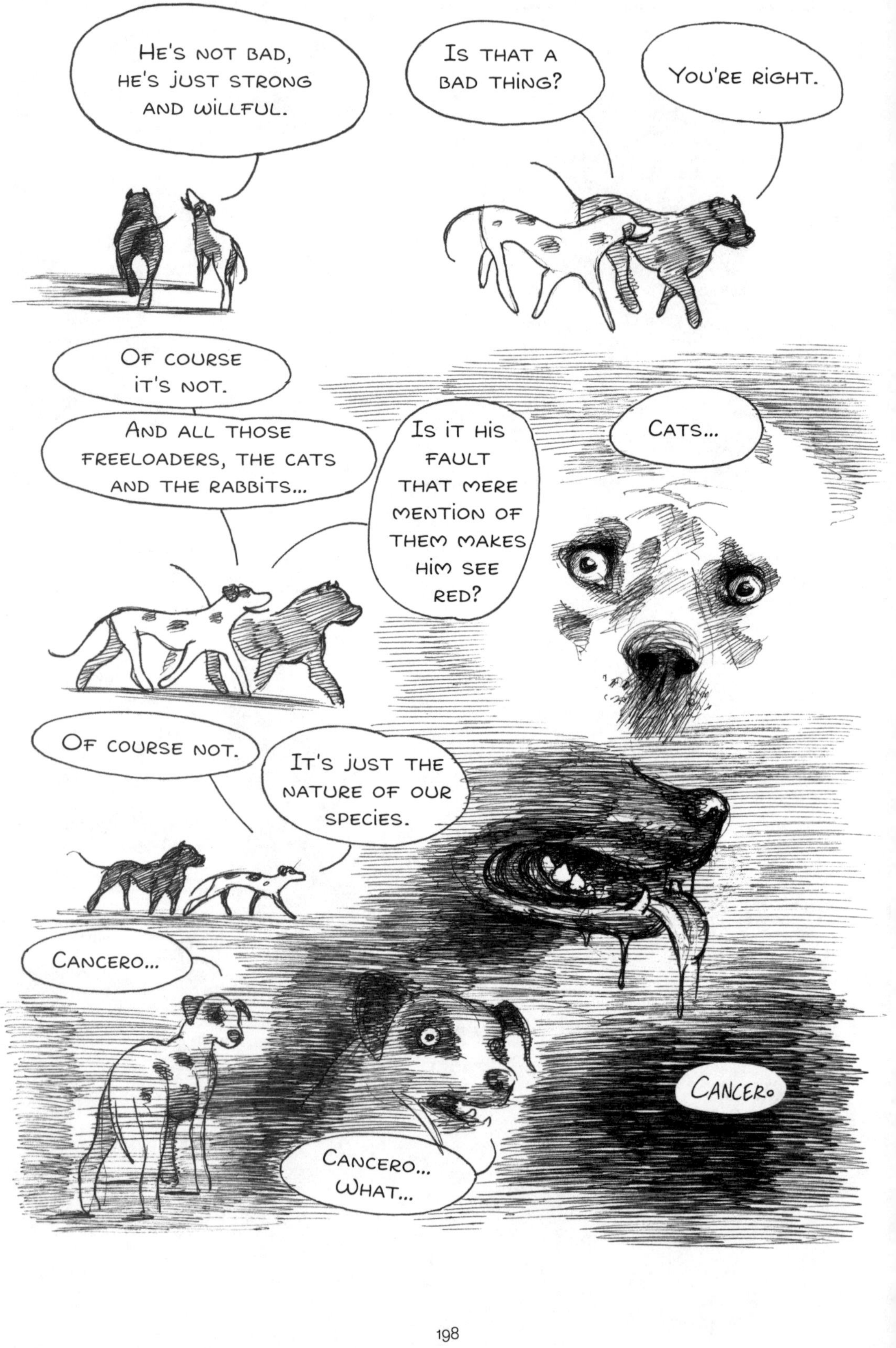
He's not bad, he's just strong and willful.
Is that a bad thing?
You're right.
Of course it's not.
And all those freeloaders, the cats and the rabbits...
Is it his fault that mere mention of them makes him see red?
Cats...
Of course not.
It's just the nature of our species.
Cancero...
Cancero
Cancero... What...

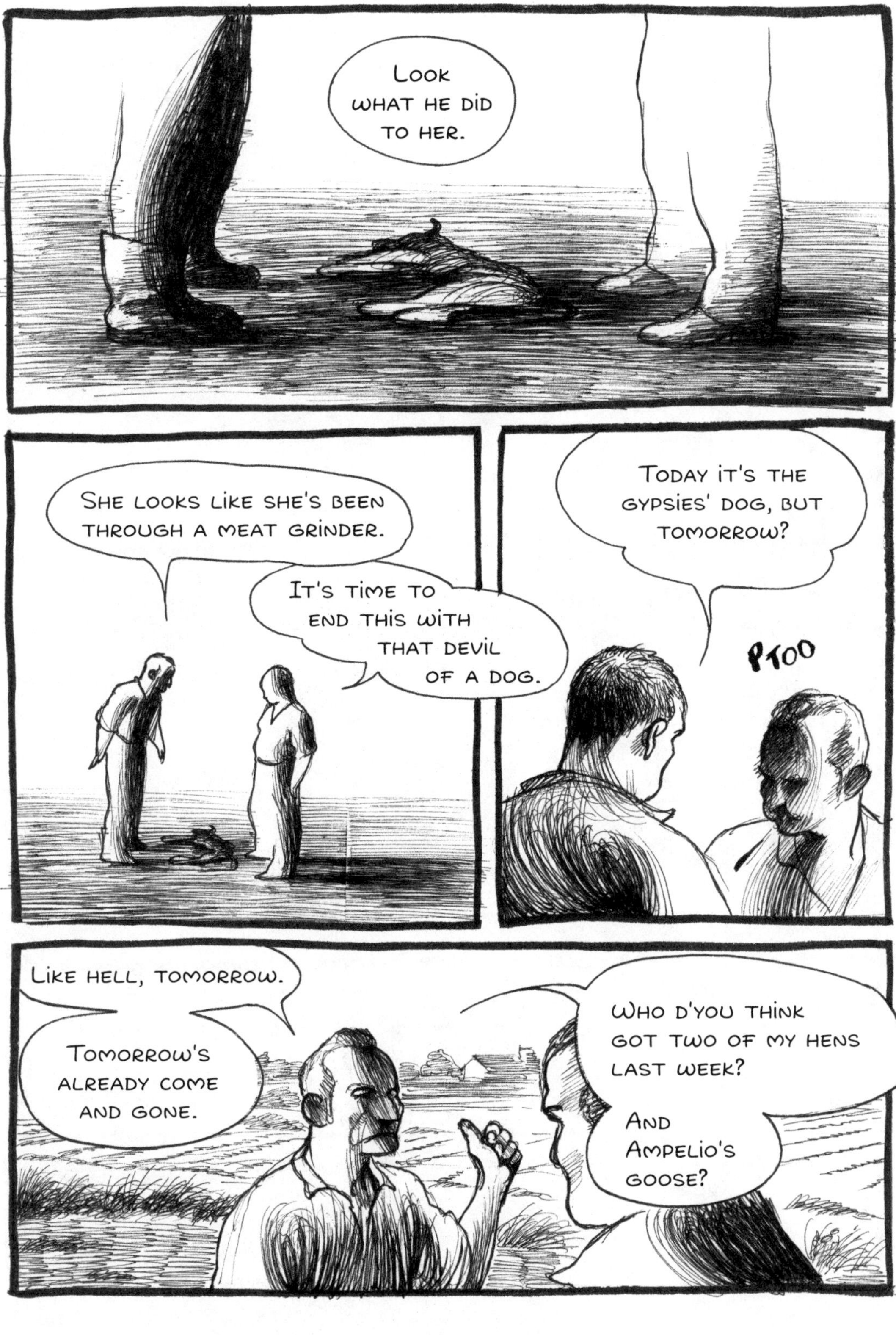

Look what he did to her.
She looks like she's been through a meat grinder.
It's time to end this with that devil of a dog.
Today it's the gypsies' dog, but tomorrow?
PTOO
Like hell, tomorrow.
Tomorrow's already come and gone.
Who d'you think got two of my hens last week?
And Ampelio's goose?

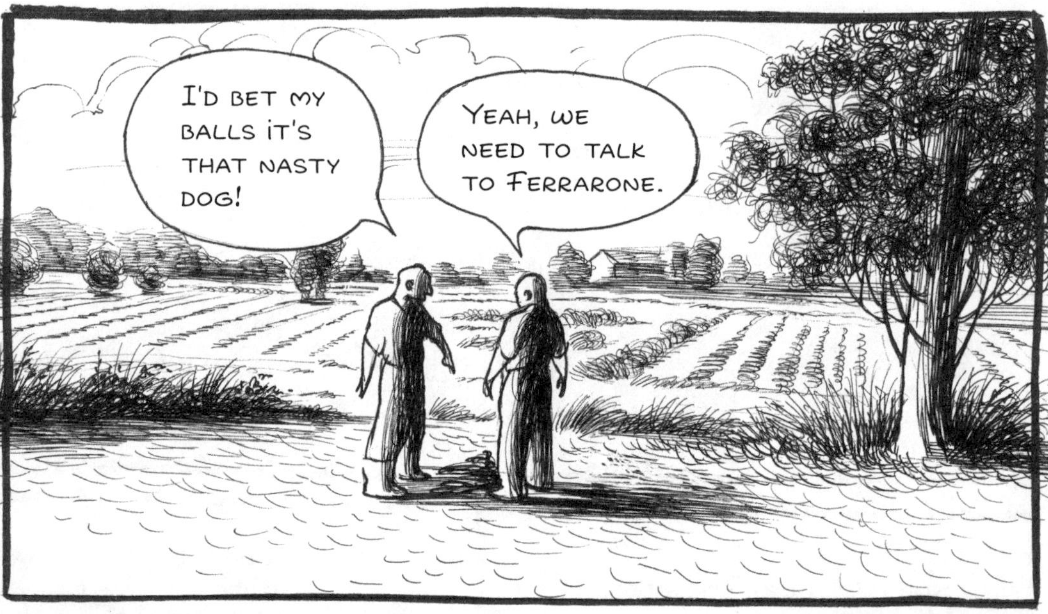
I'd bet my balls it's that nasty dog!
Yeah, we need to talk to Ferrarone.

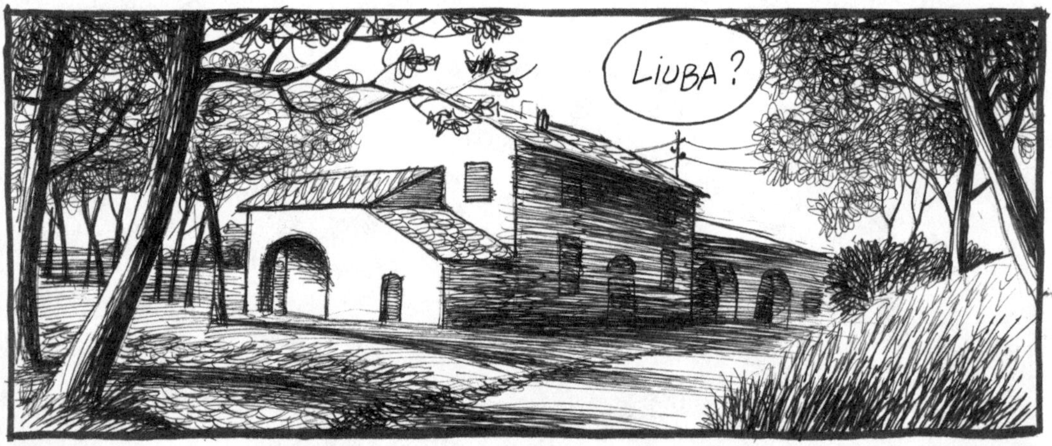
Liuba?

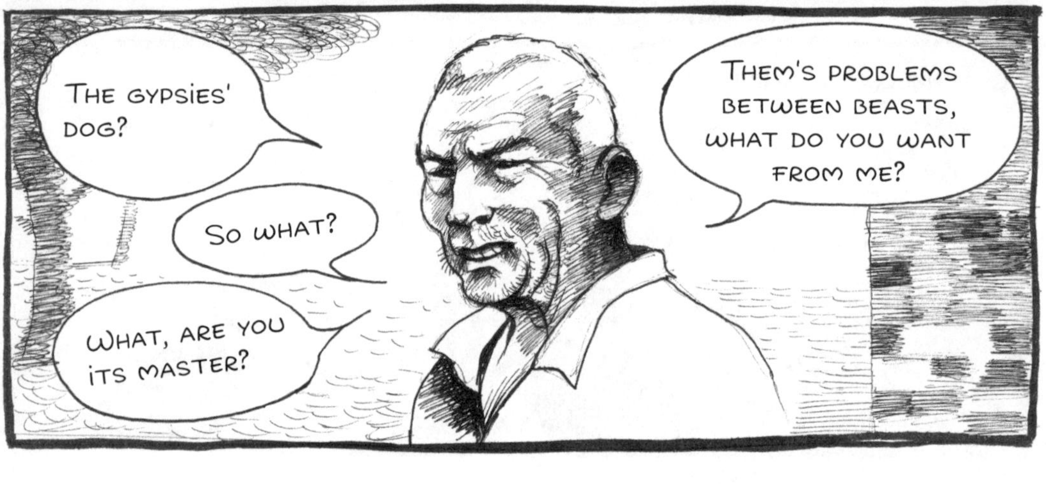
The gypsies' dog?
So what?
What, are you its master?
Them's problems between beasts, what do you want from me?

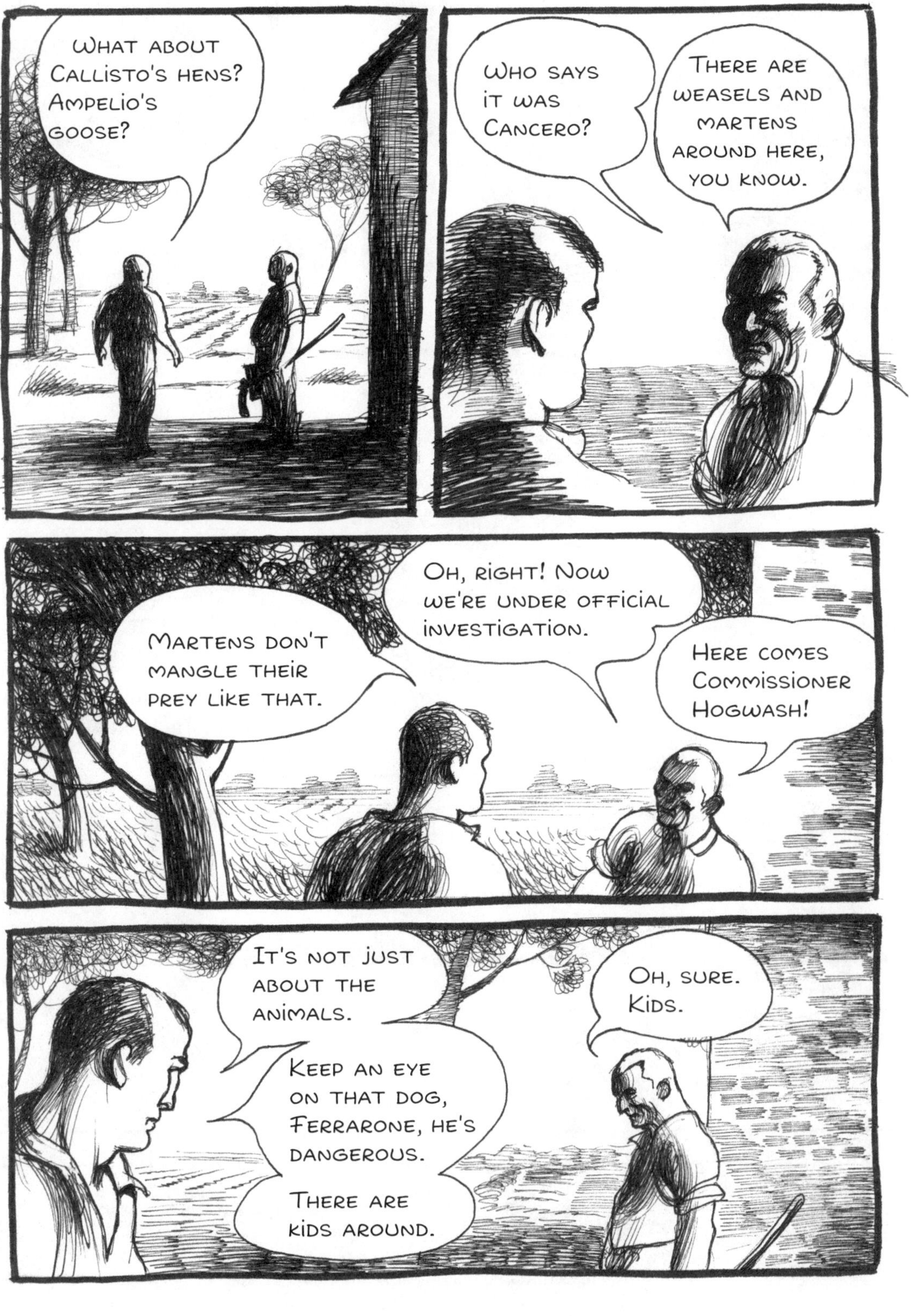
What about Callisto's hens? Ampelio's goose?
Who says it was Cancero?
There are weasels and martens around here, you know.
Martens don't mangle their prey like that.
Oh, right! Now we're under official investigation.
Here comes Commissioner Hogwash!
It's not just about the animals.
Keep an eye on that dog, Ferrarone, he's dangerous.
There are kids around.
Oh, sure. Kids.

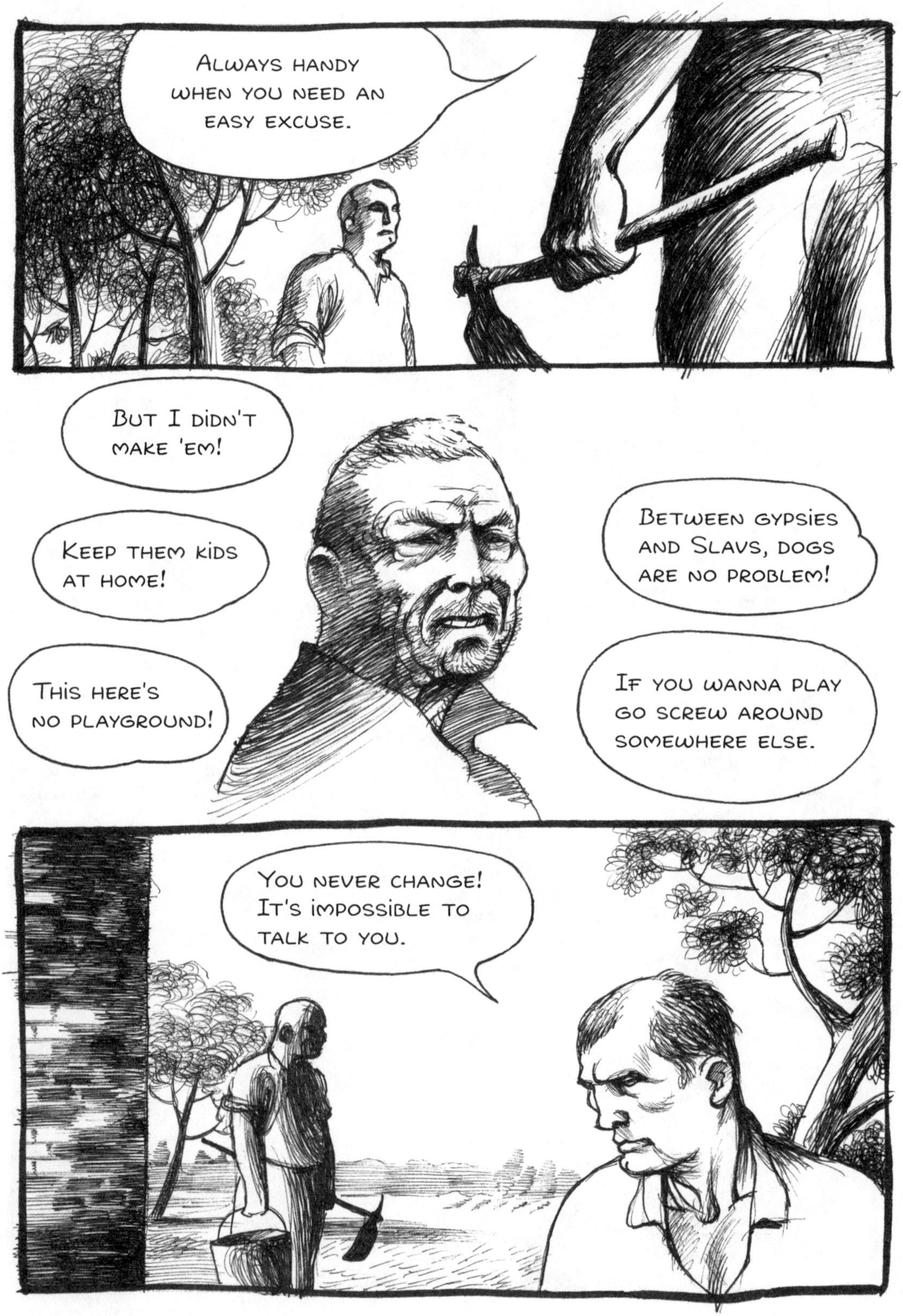
Always handy when you need an easy excuse.
But I didn't make 'em!
Keep them kids at home!
This here's no playground!
Between gypsies and Slavs, dogs are no problem!
If you wanna play go screw around somewhere else.
You never change! It's impossible to talk to you.

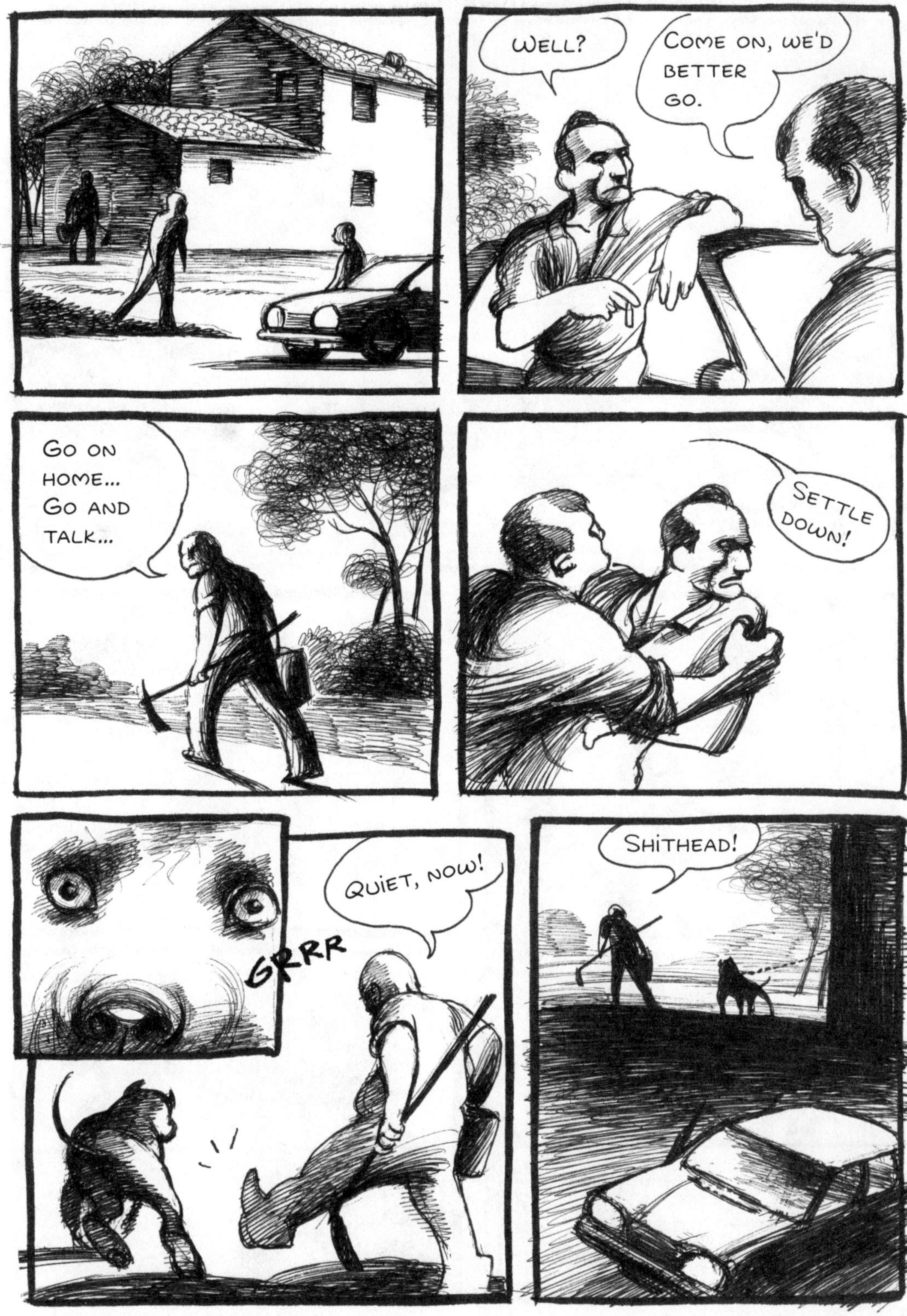
Well?
Come on, we'd better go.
Go on home... Go and talk...
Settle down!
GRRR
Quiet, now!
Shithead!

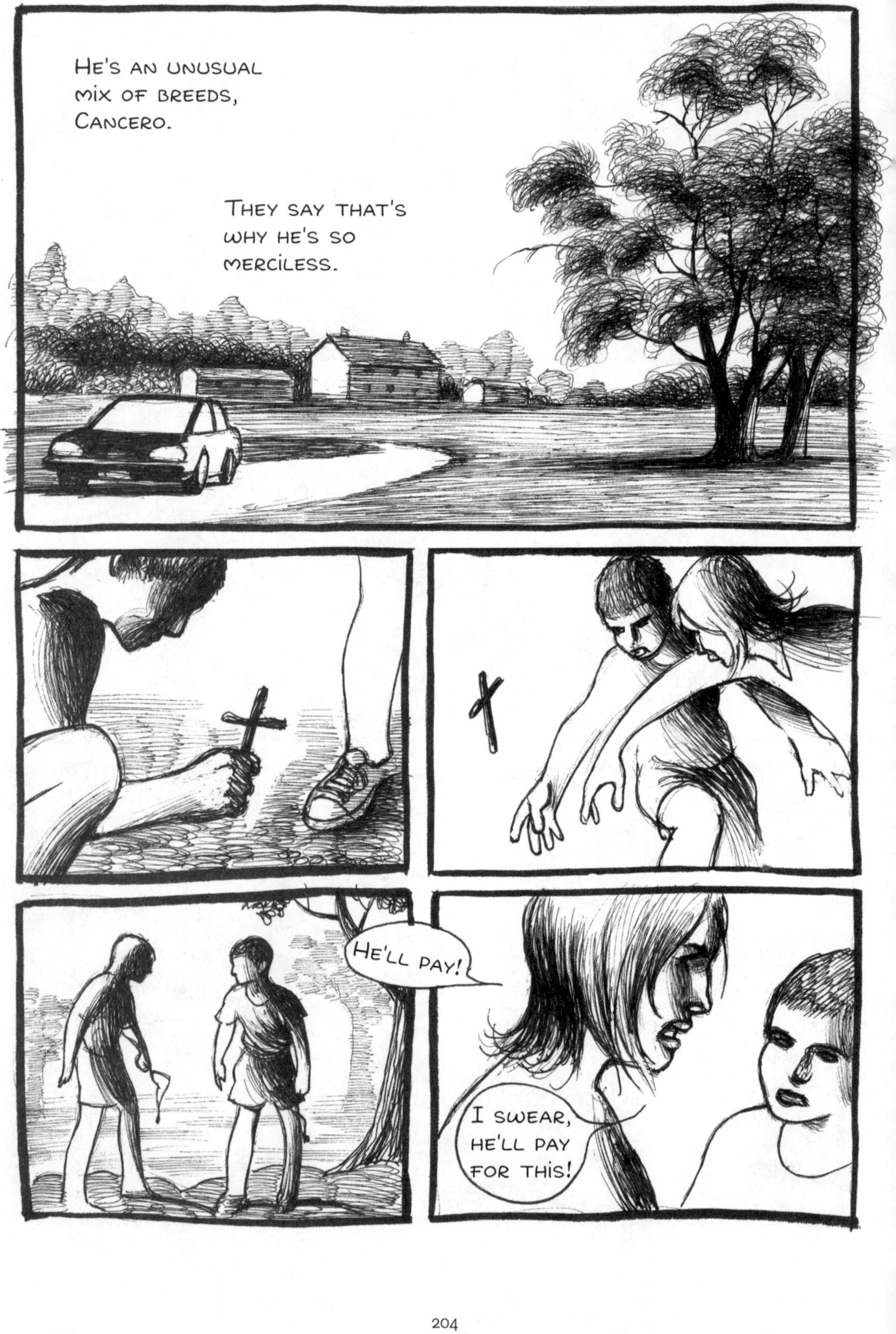
He's an unusual mix of breeds, Cancero.
They say that's why he's so merciless.
He'll pay!
I swear, he'll pay for this!

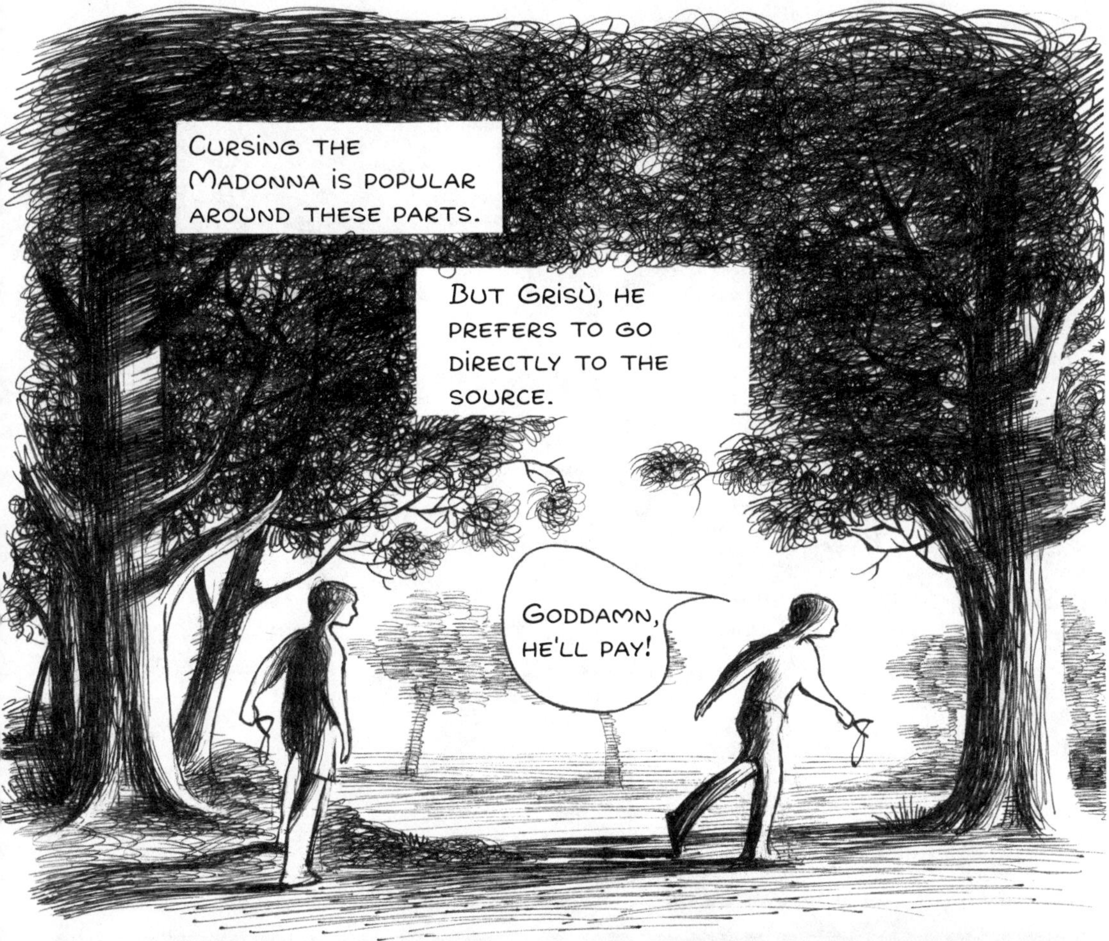
Cursing the Madonna is popular around these parts.
But Grisù, he prefers to go directly to the source.
Goddamn, he'll pay!

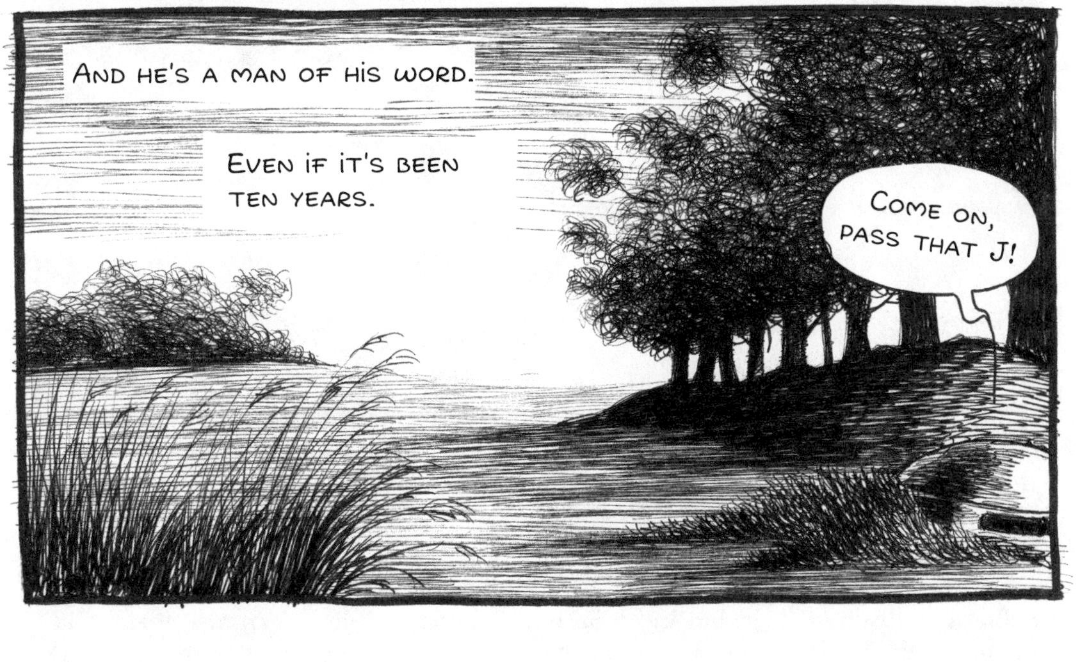
And he's a man of his word.
Even if it's been ten years.
Come on, pass that J!

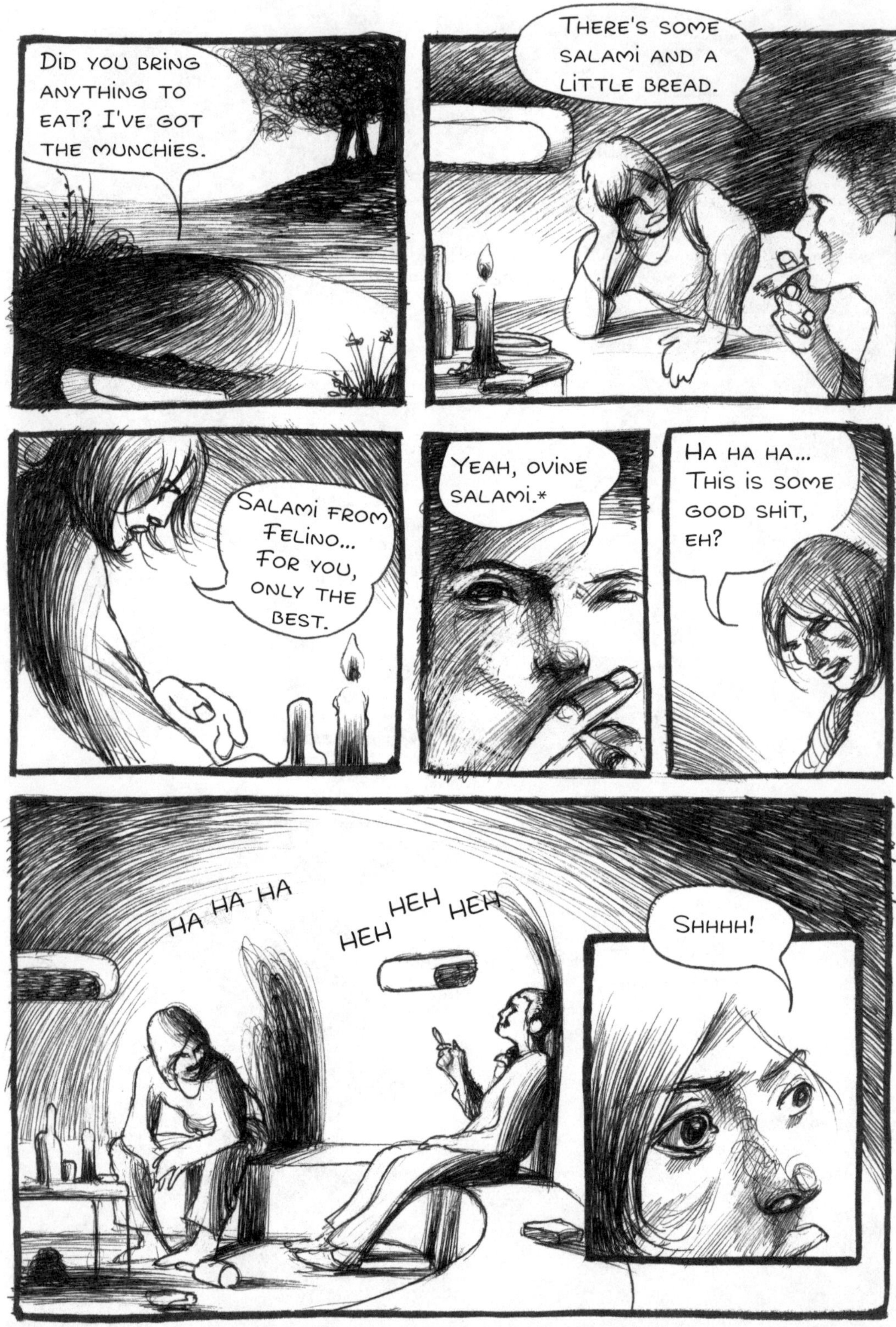
DID YOU BRING ANYTHING TO EAT? I'VE GOT THE MUNCHIES.
THERE'S SOME SALAMI AND A LITTLE BREAD.
SALAMI FROM FELINO... FOR YOU, ONLY THE BEST.
YEAH, OVINE SALAMI.*
HA HA HA... THIS IS SOME GOOD SHIT, EH?
HA HA HA
HEH HEH HEH
SHHHH!

* Felino is a town in Italy, but the original, "Salame di felino," can also mean "cat salami." Guido is riffing on this double meaning when he responds, joking, "Yeah, ovine salami."

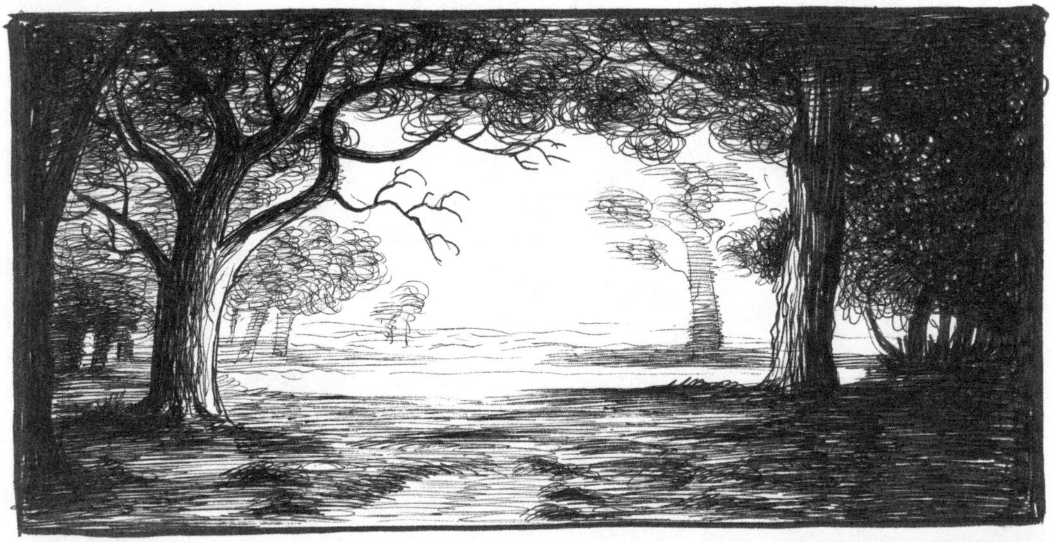
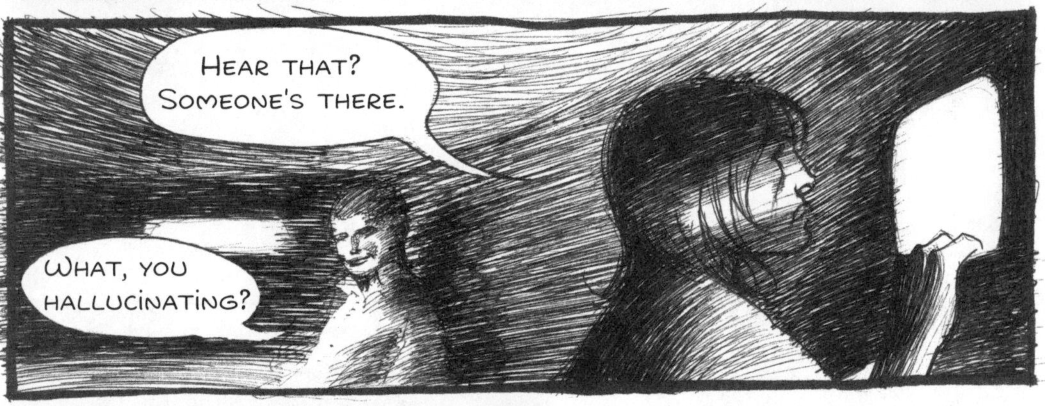
Hear that? Someone's there.
What, you hallucinating?
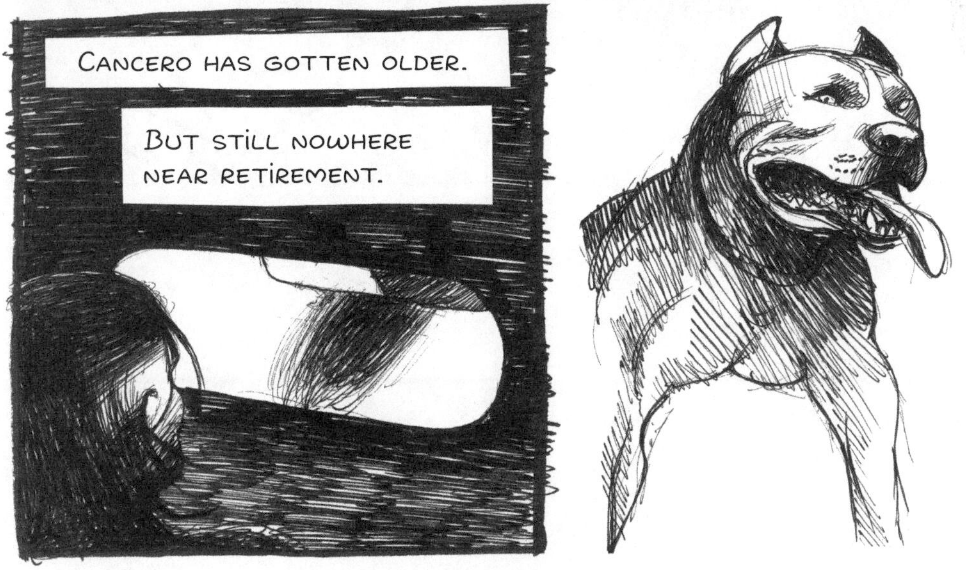
Cancero has gotten older.
But still nowhere near retirement.

CUT THE END
OF THE SALAMI.

MAKE THE STRING
LONGER WITH SOME
STURDY TWINE.

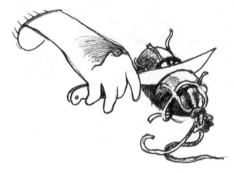

WRAP IT TIGHT
AROUND THE
SALAMI.

MAKE IT SO IT'S HARD
TO TEAR, EVEN BY THE
TEETH OF A DEMON
LIKE CANCERO.

NOW YOU'RE READY.

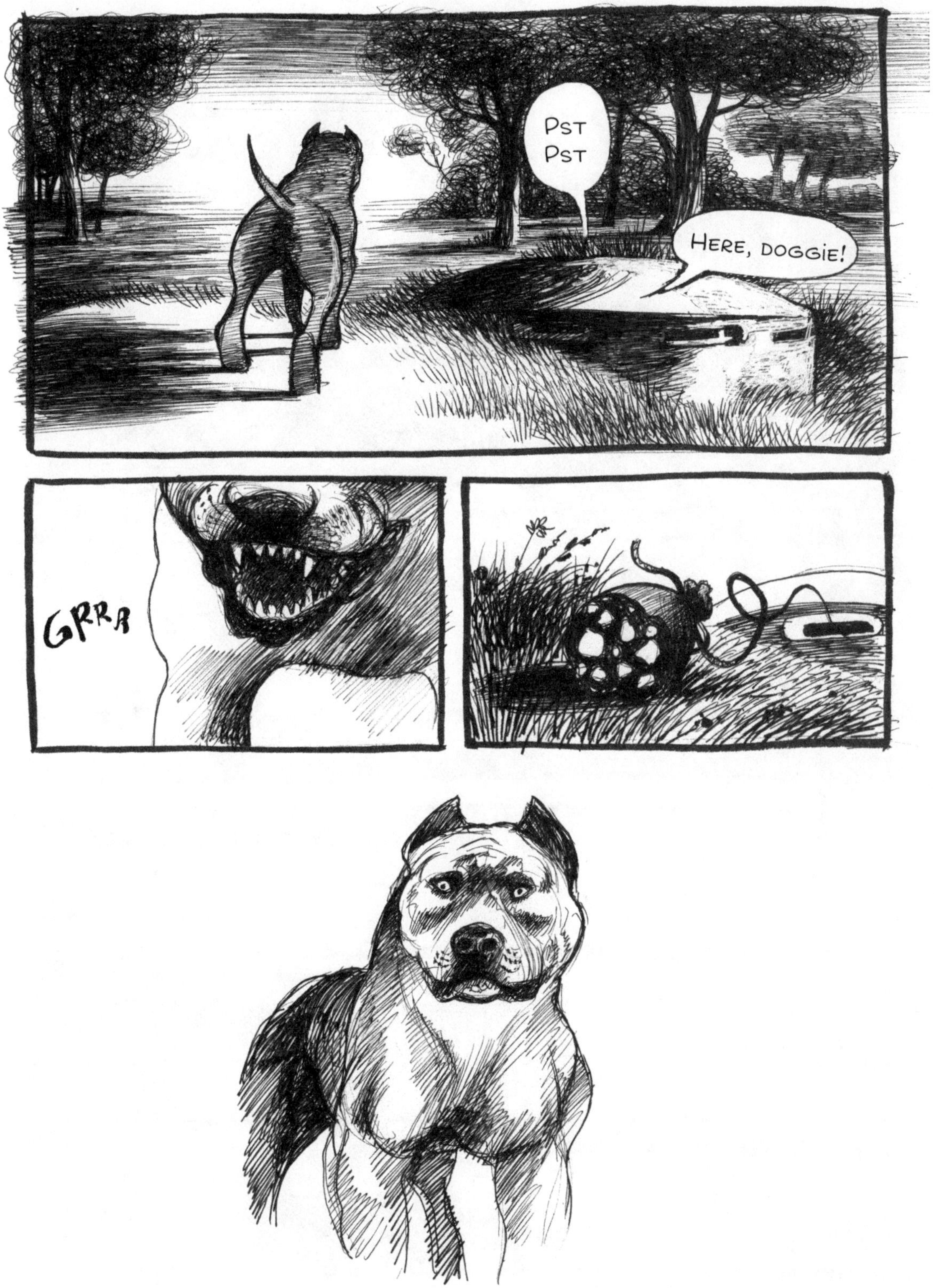
Pst
Pst
Here, doggie!
GRRR

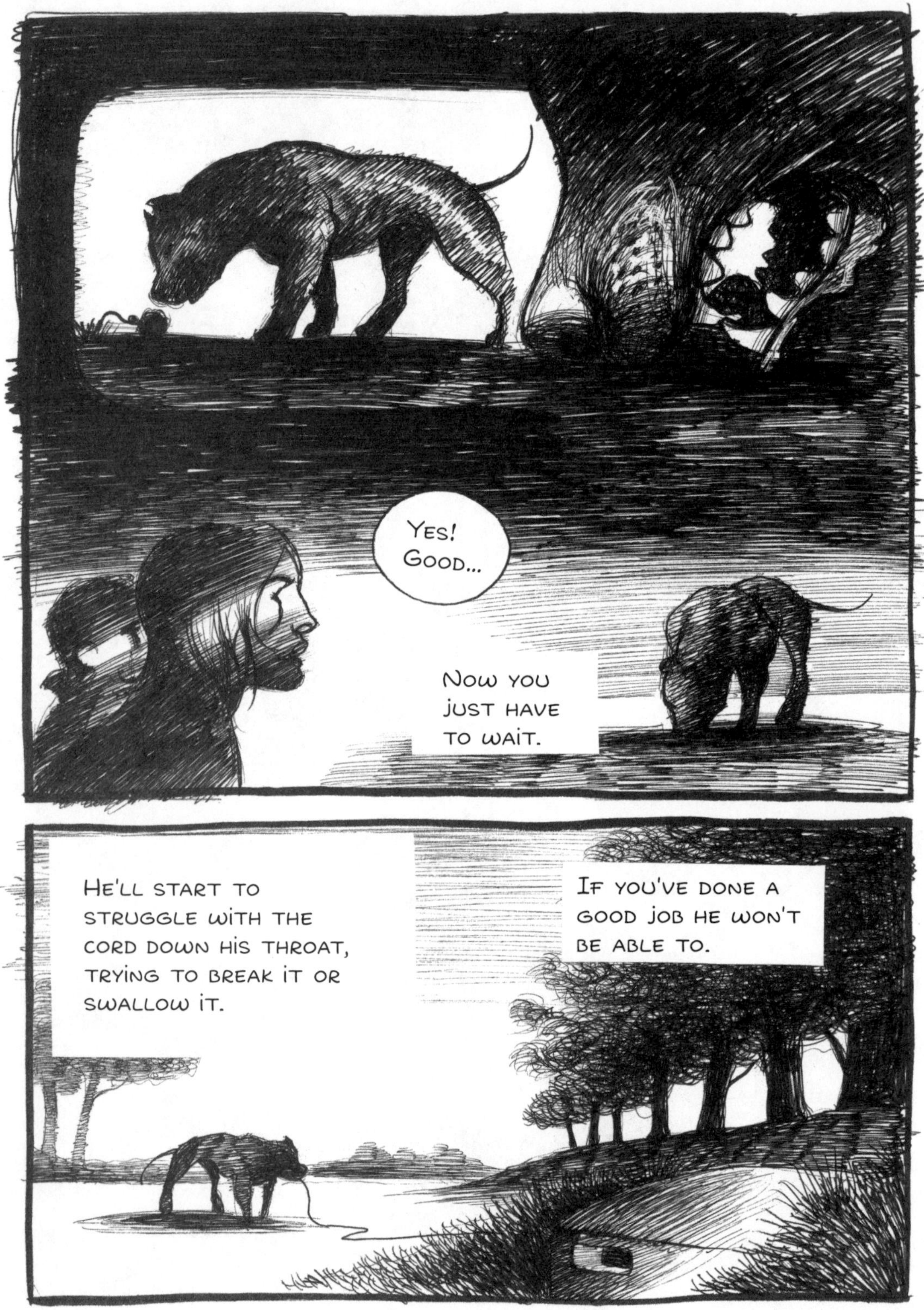
YES! GOOD...
NOW YOU JUST HAVE TO WAIT.
HE'LL START TO STRUGGLE WITH THE CORD DOWN HIS THROAT, TRYING TO BREAK IT OR SWALLOW IT.
IF YOU'VE DONE A GOOD JOB HE WON'T BE ABLE TO.

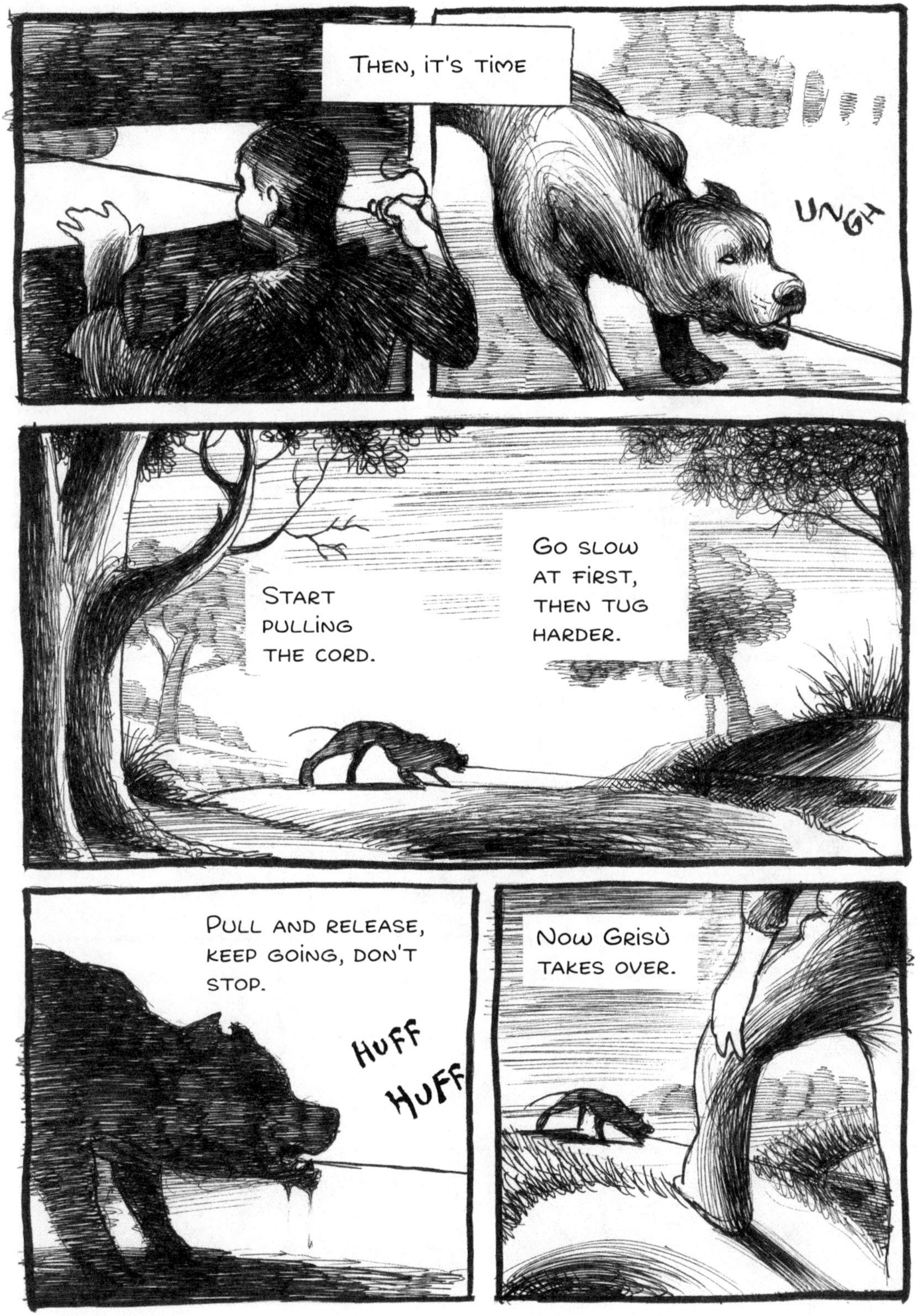
Then, it's time
UNGH
Start pulling the cord.
Go slow at first, then tug harder.
Pull and release, keep going, don't stop.
HUFF
HUFF
Now Grisù takes over.

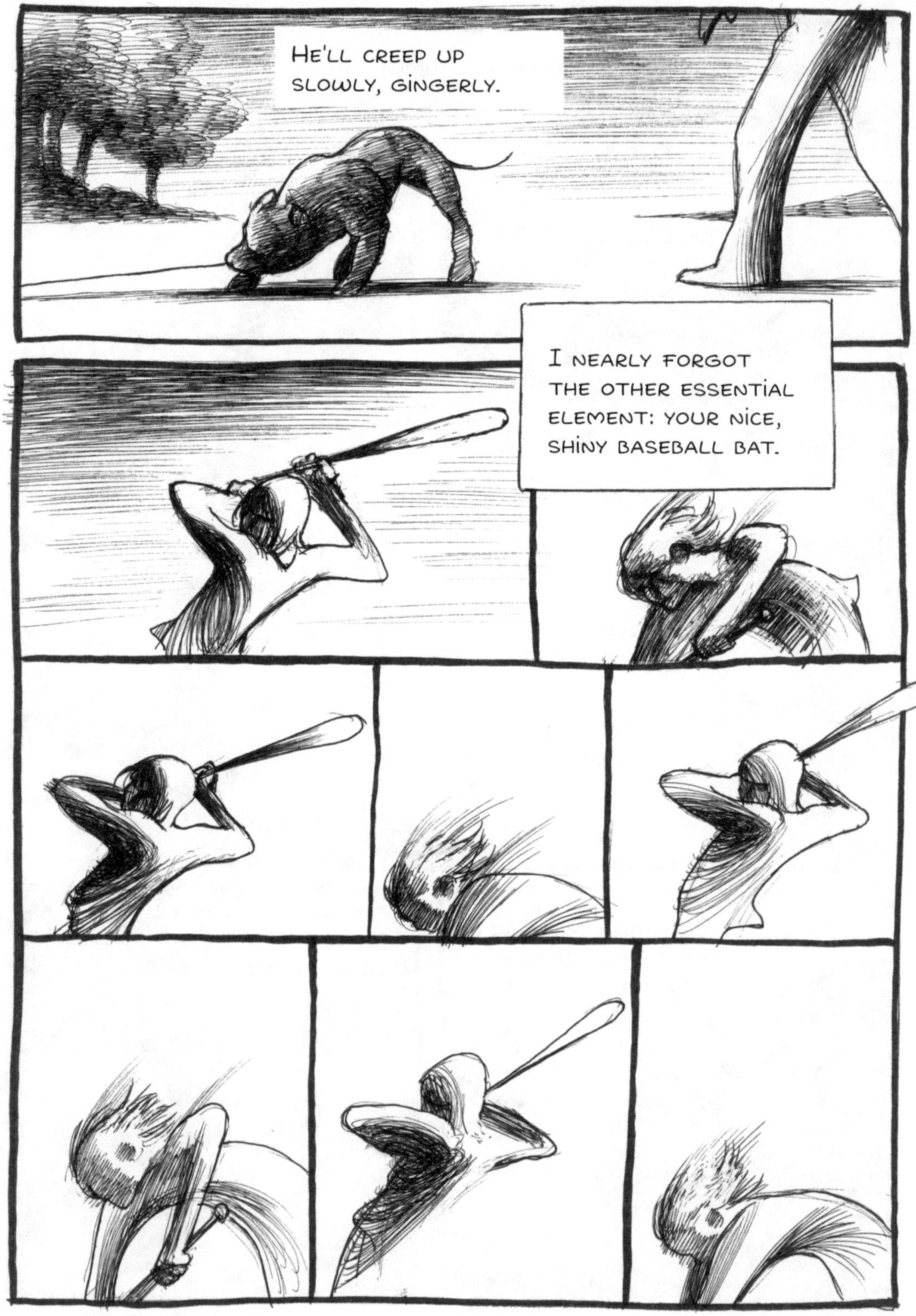
He'll creep up slowly, gingerly.
I nearly forgot the other essential element: your nice, shiny baseball bat.

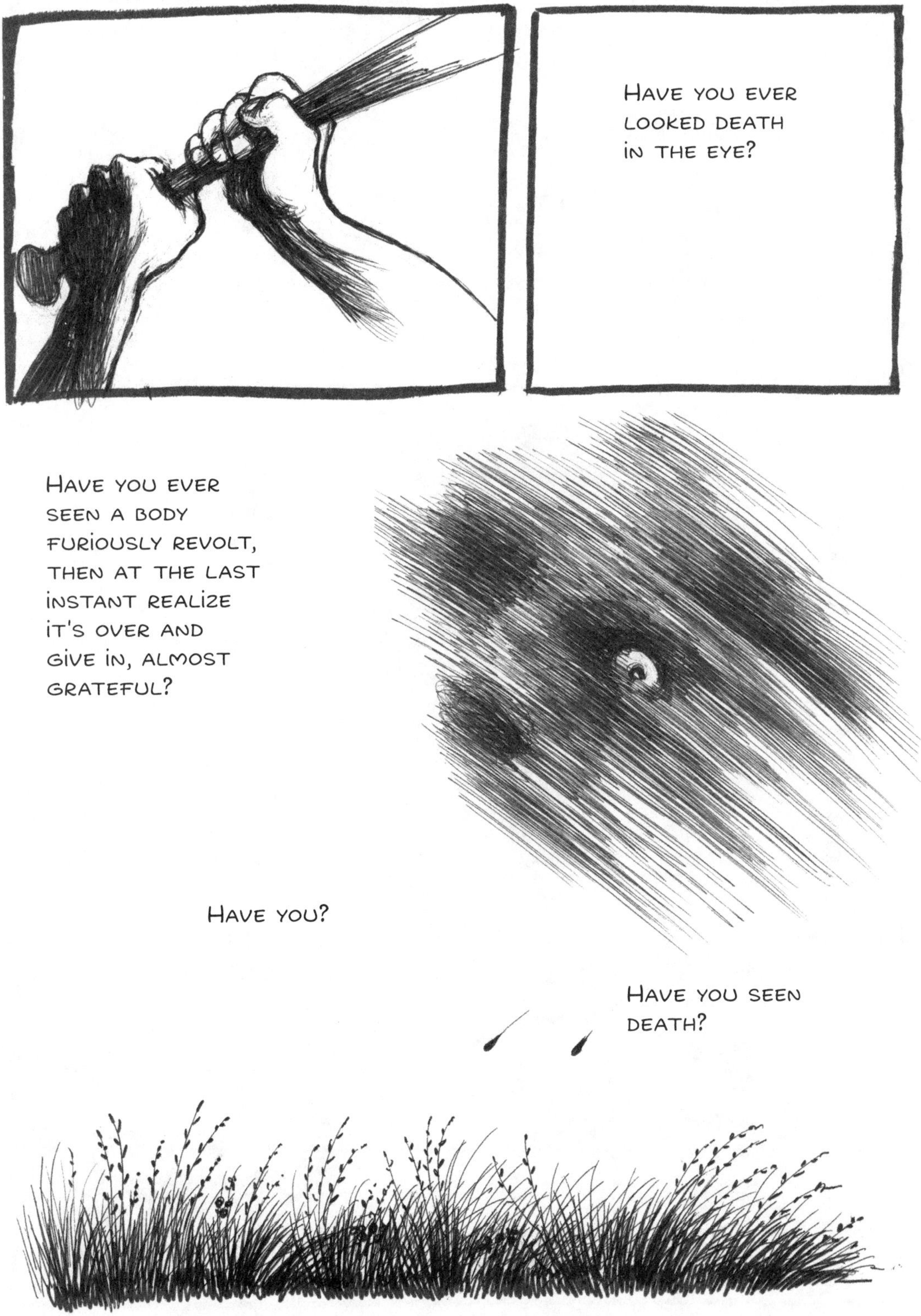
Have you ever looked death in the eye?
Have you ever seen a body furiously revolt, then at the last instant realize it's over and give in, almost grateful?
Have you?
Have you seen death?

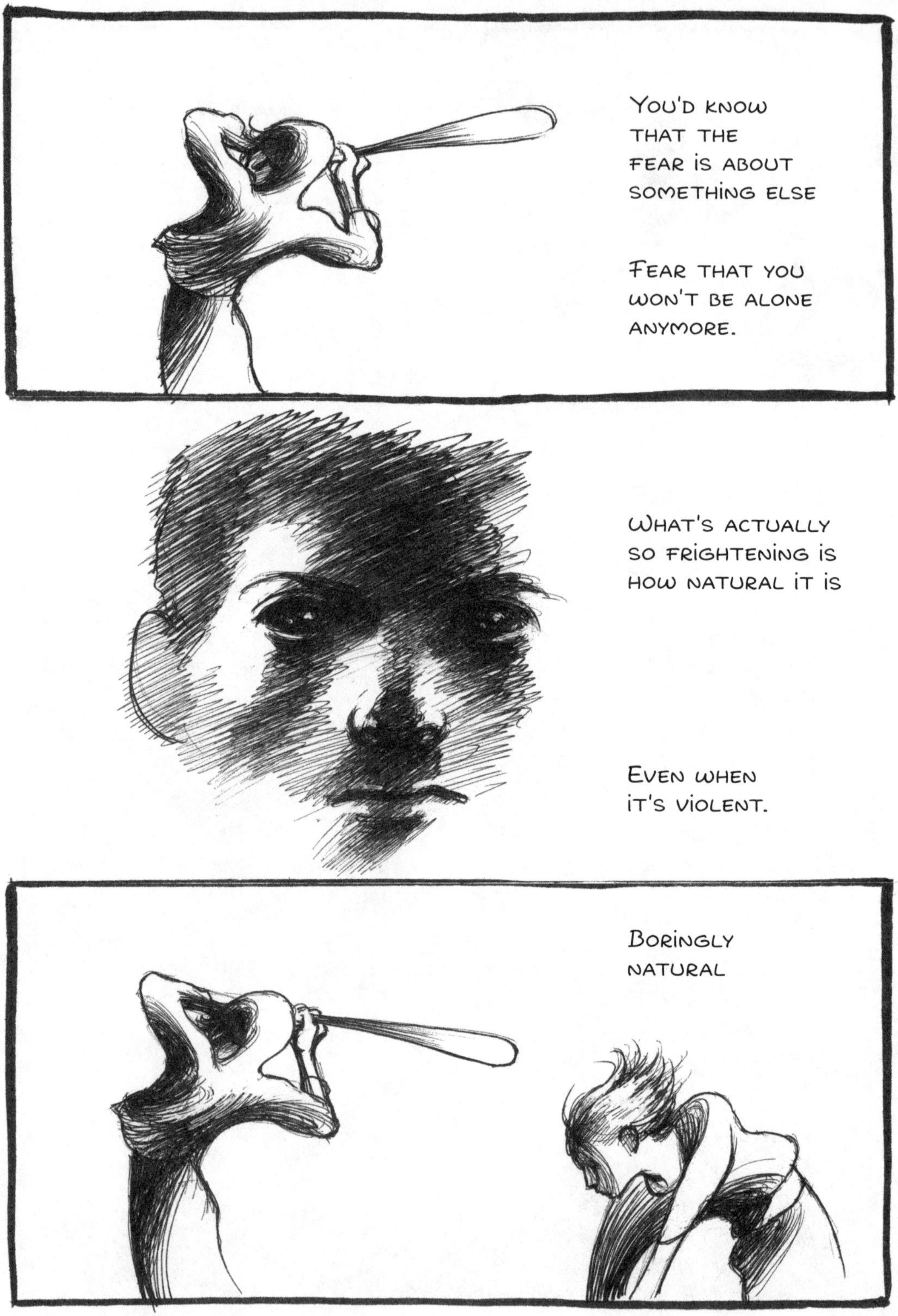
You'd know that the fear is about something else
Fear that you won't be alone anymore.
What's actually so frightening is how natural it is
Even when it's violent.
Boringly natural

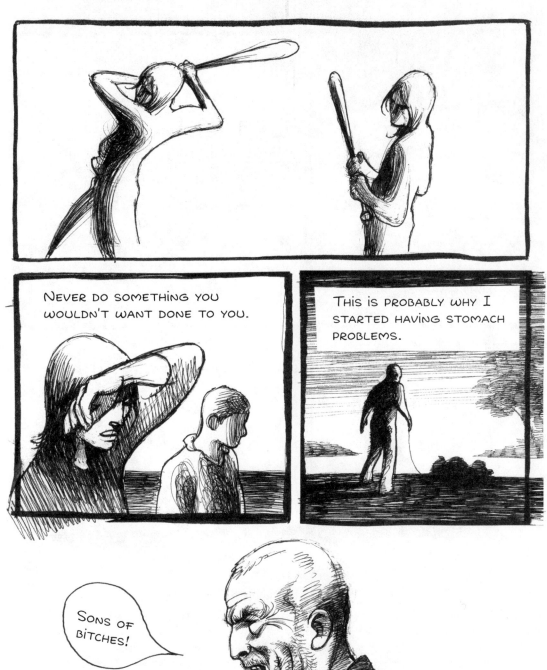

NEVER DO SOMETHING YOU WOULDN'T WANT DONE TO YOU.

THIS IS PROBABLY WHY I STARTED HAVING STOMACH PROBLEMS.

SONS OF BITCHES!

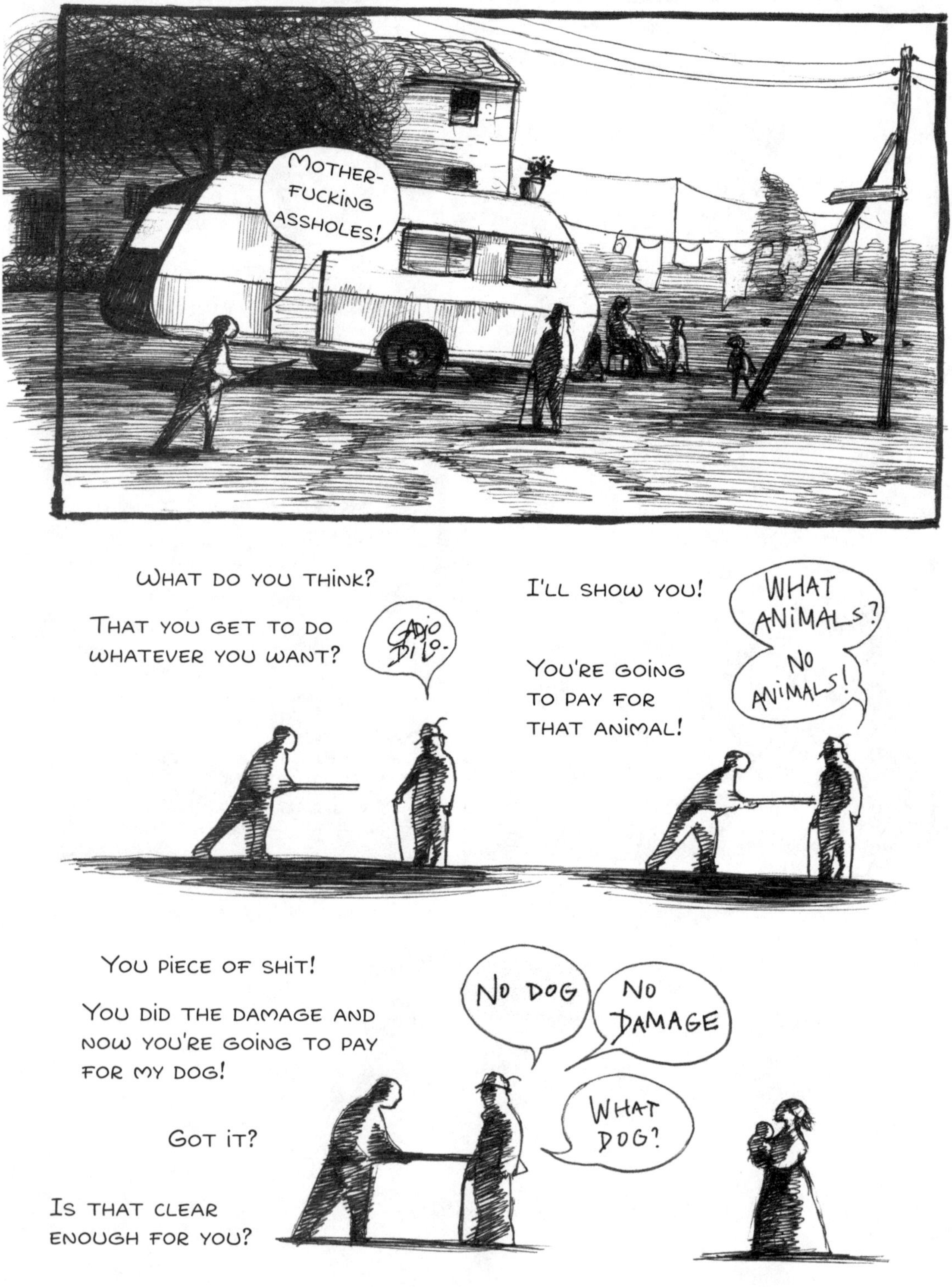
MOTHER-FUCKING ASSHOLES!
WHAT DO YOU THINK?
THAT YOU GET TO DO WHATEVER YOU WANT?
GADJO DILO.
I'LL SHOW YOU!
WHAT ANIMALS?
NO ANIMALS!
YOU'RE GOING TO PAY FOR THAT ANIMAL!
YOU PIECE OF SHIT!
YOU DID THE DAMAGE AND NOW YOU'RE GOING TO PAY FOR MY DOG!
NO DOG
NO DAMAGE
WHAT DOG?
GOT IT?
IS THAT CLEAR ENOUGH FOR YOU?

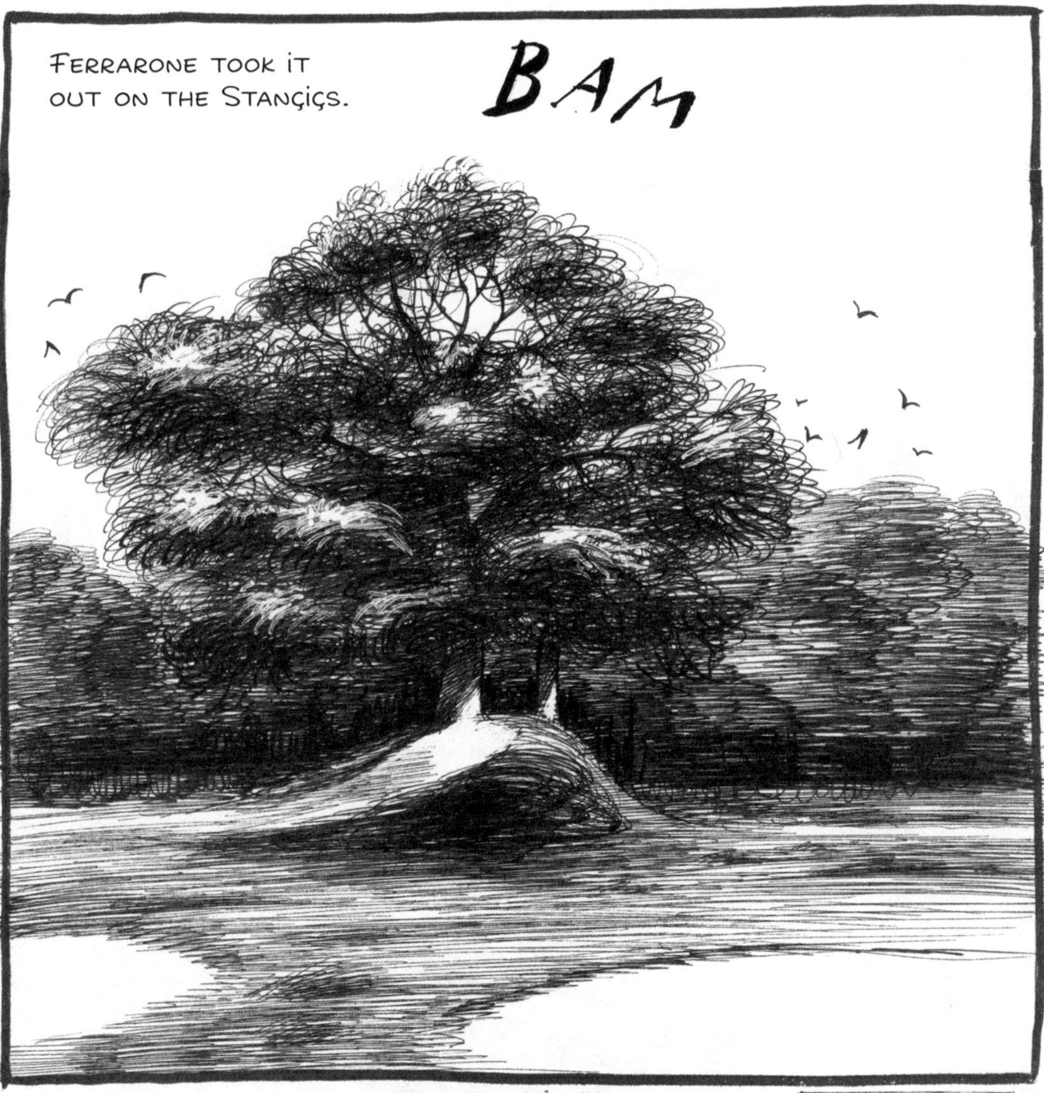
Ferrarone took it out on the Stançiçs.
BAM

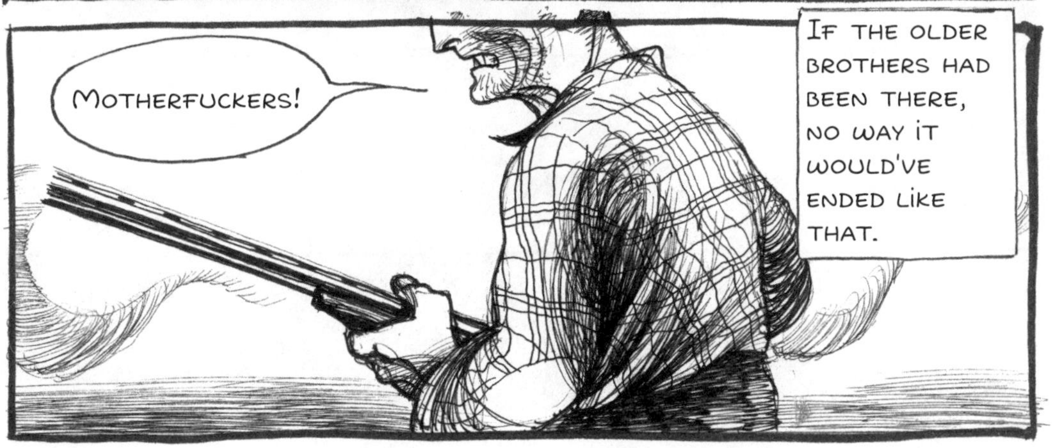
Motherfuckers!
If the older brothers had been there, no way it would've ended like that.

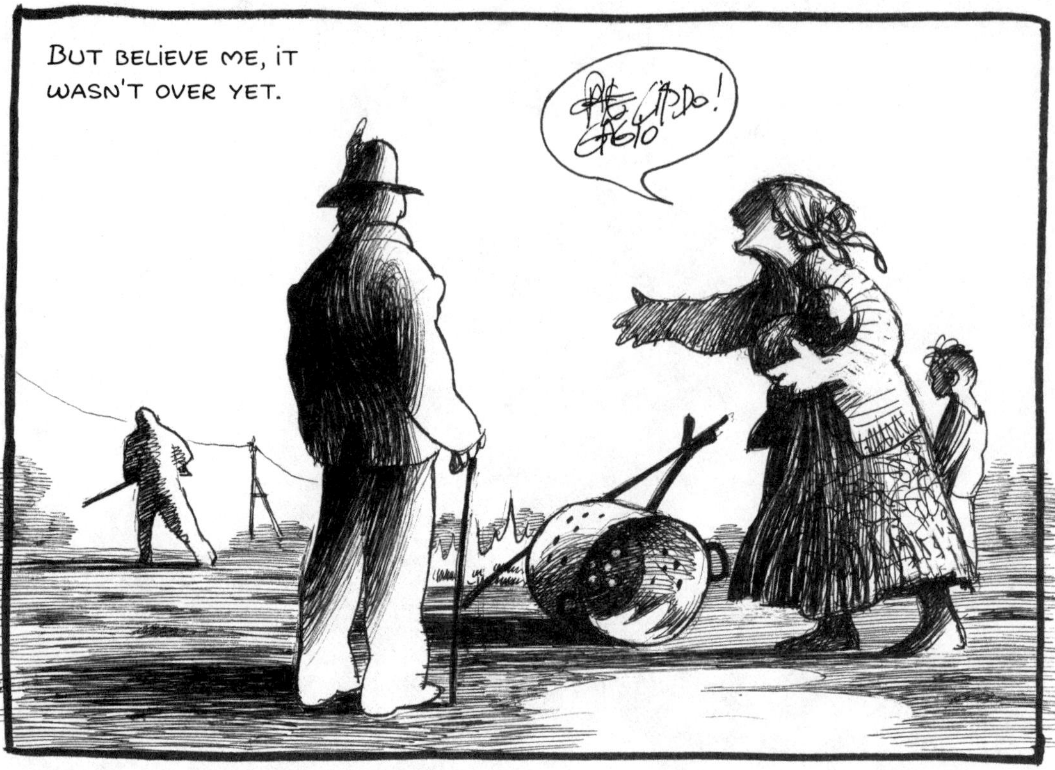
BUT BELIEVE ME, IT WASN'T OVER YET.

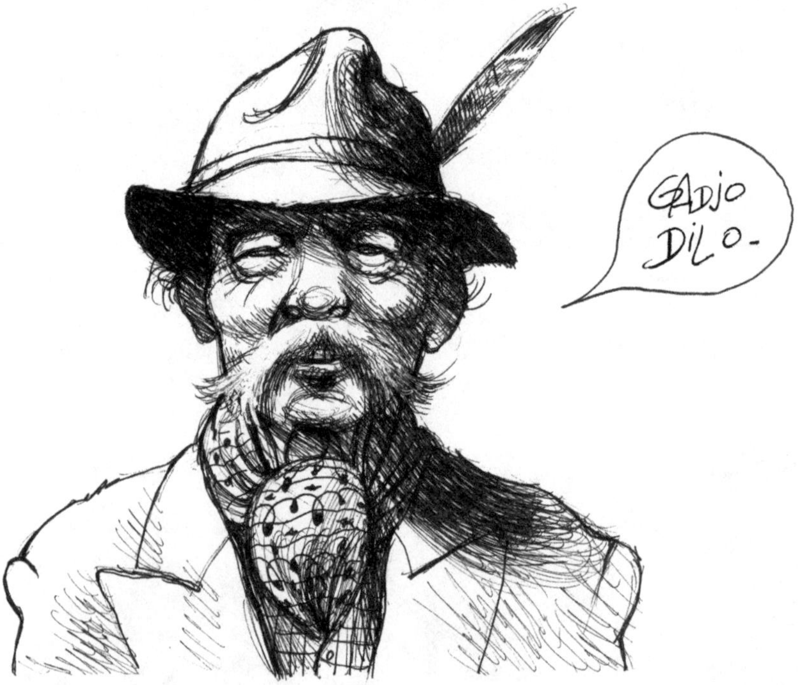
GADJO DILO.

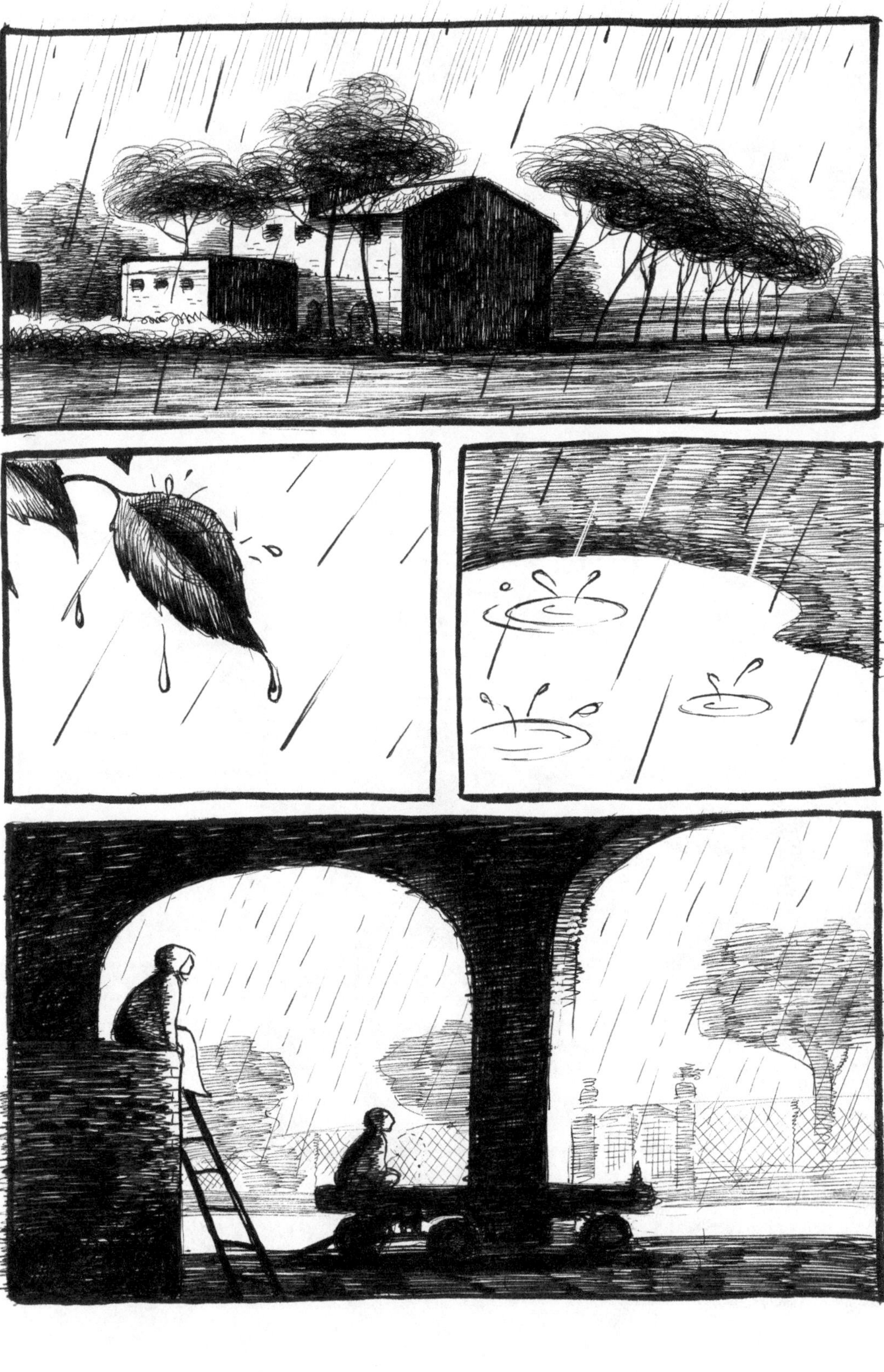

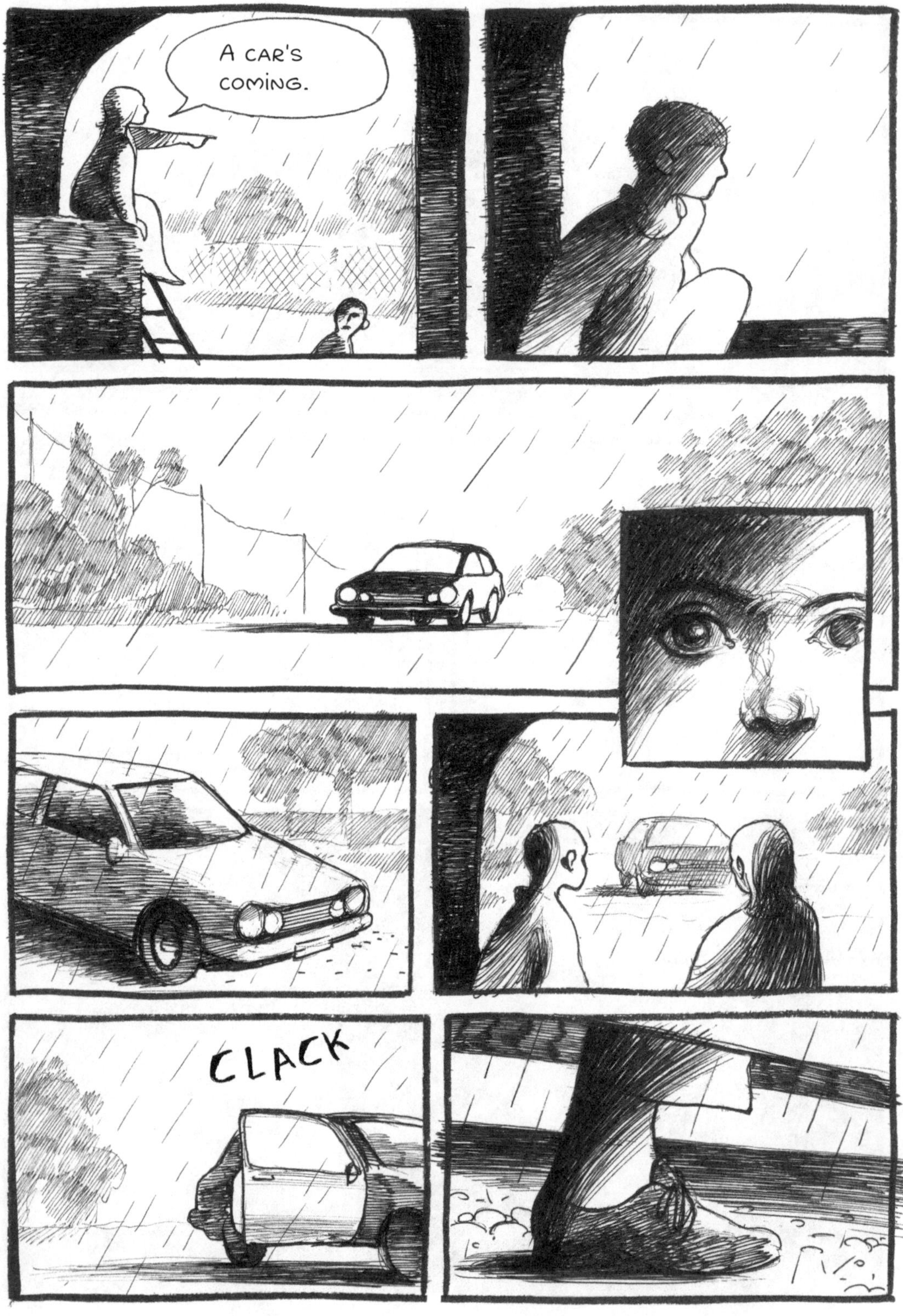
A car's coming.
CLACK

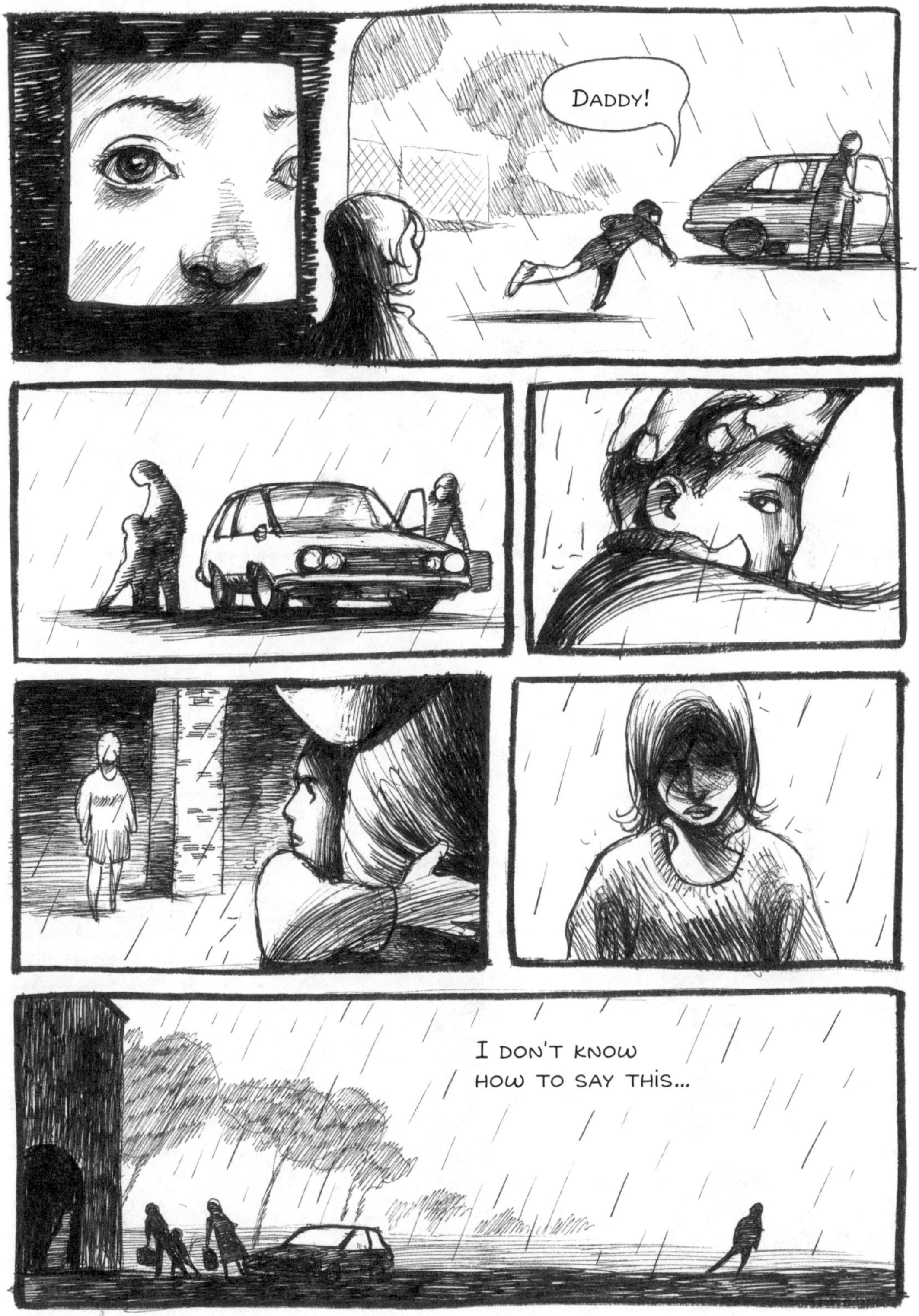
DADDY!
I DON'T KNOW
HOW TO SAY THIS...

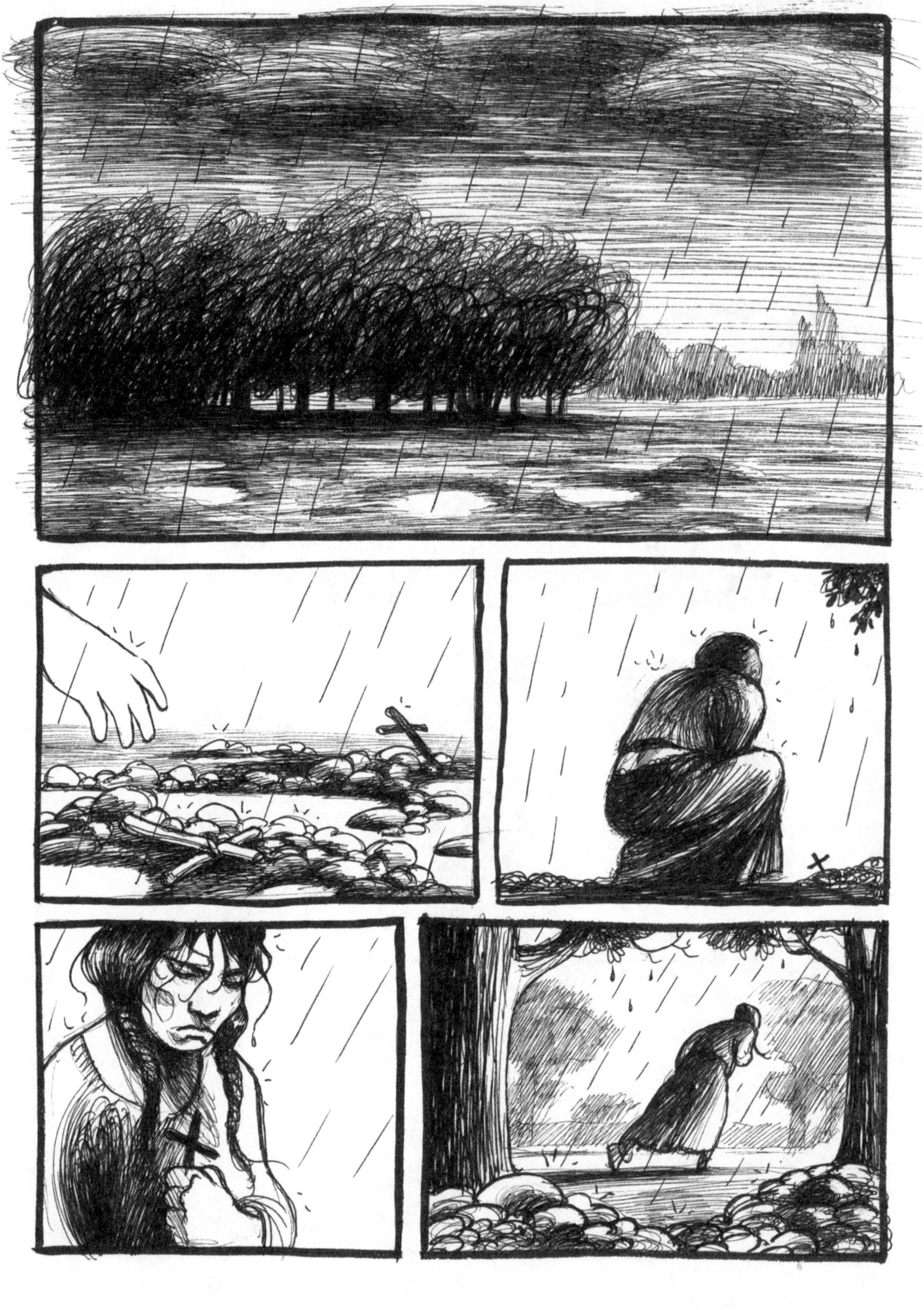

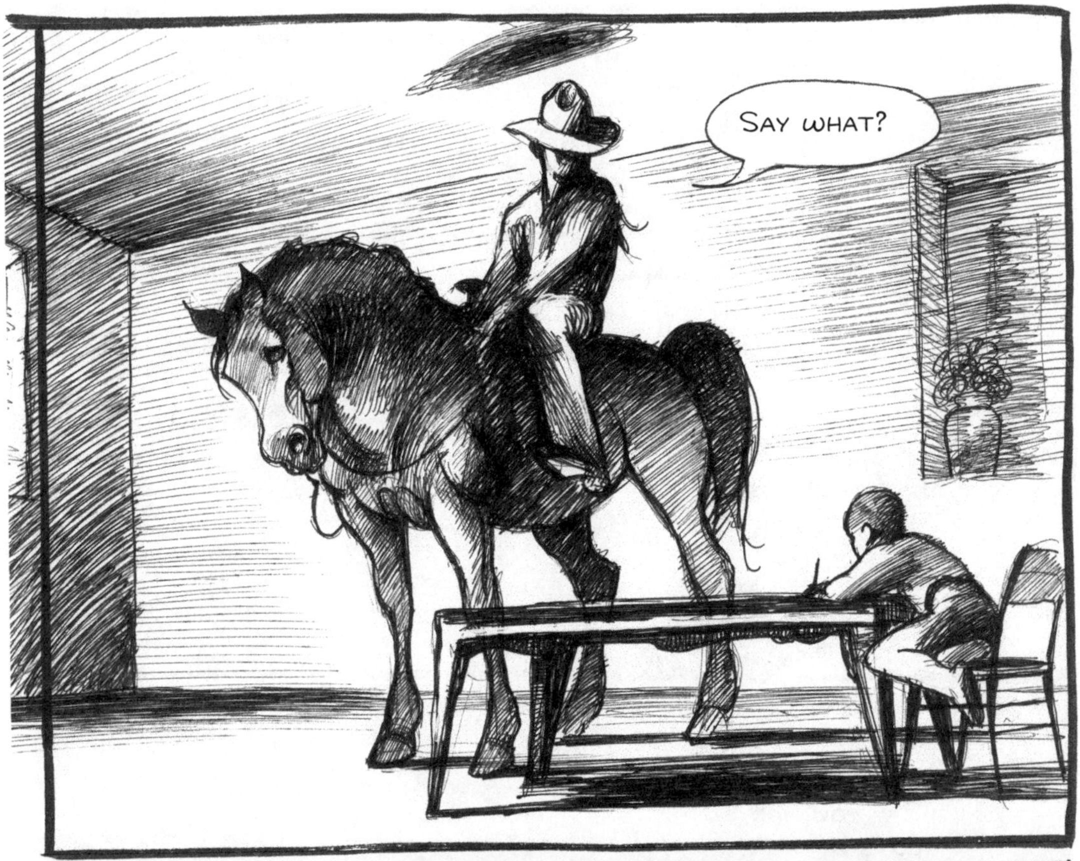
SAY WHAT?

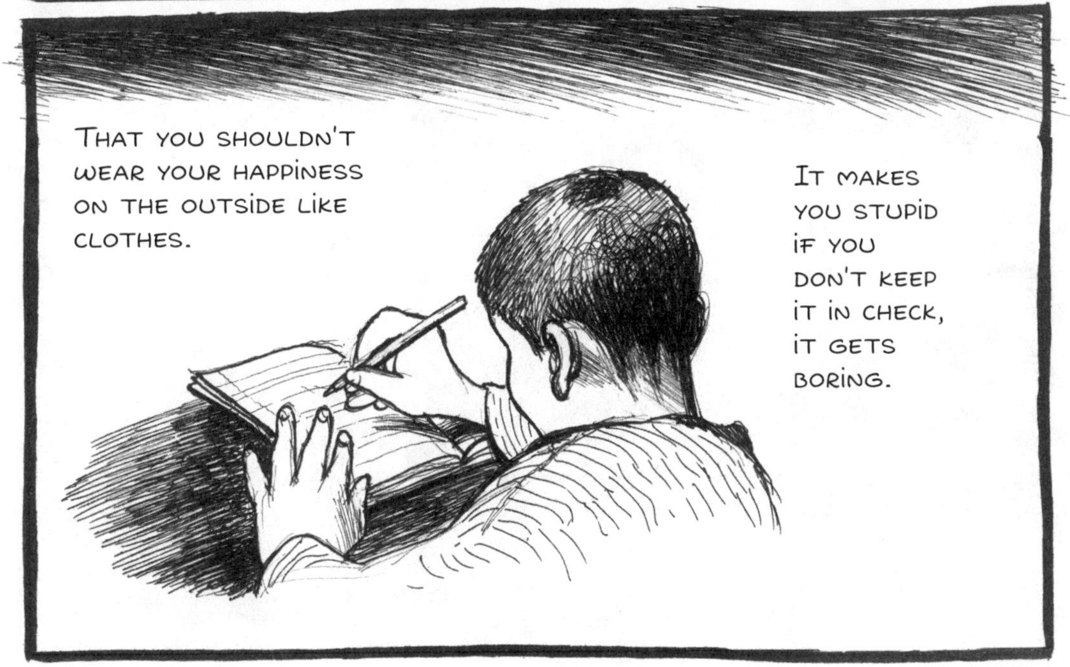
THAT YOU SHOULDN'T WEAR YOUR HAPPINESS ON THE OUTSIDE LIKE CLOTHES.
IT MAKES YOU STUPID IF YOU DON'T KEEP IT IN CHECK, IT GETS BORING.

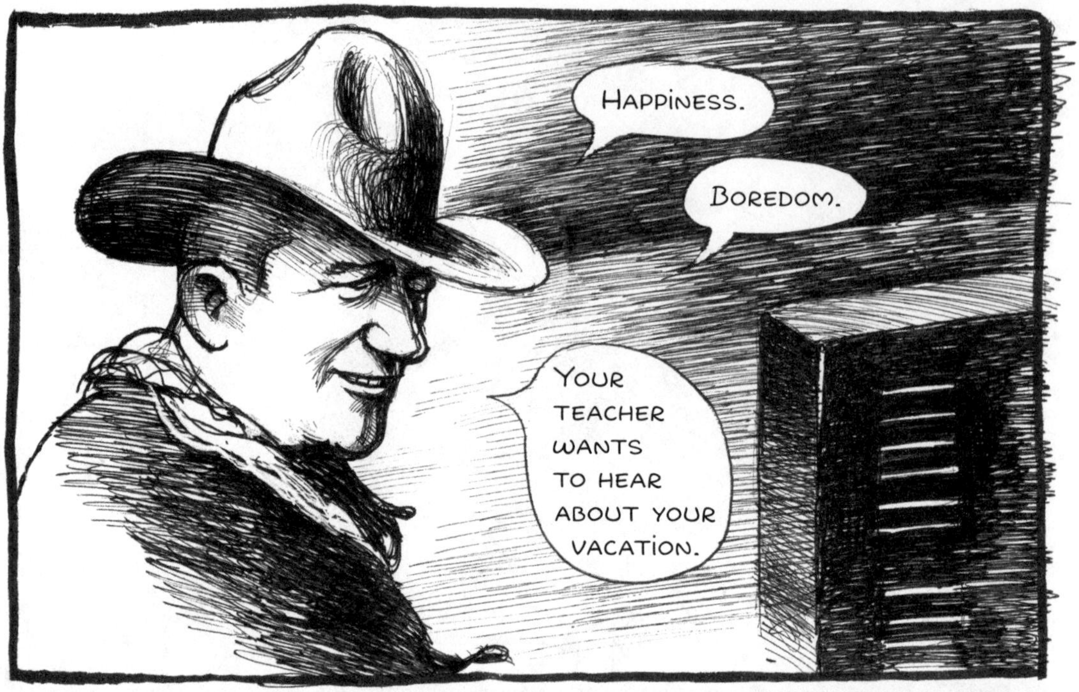
Happiness.
Boredom.
Your teacher wants to hear about your vacation.

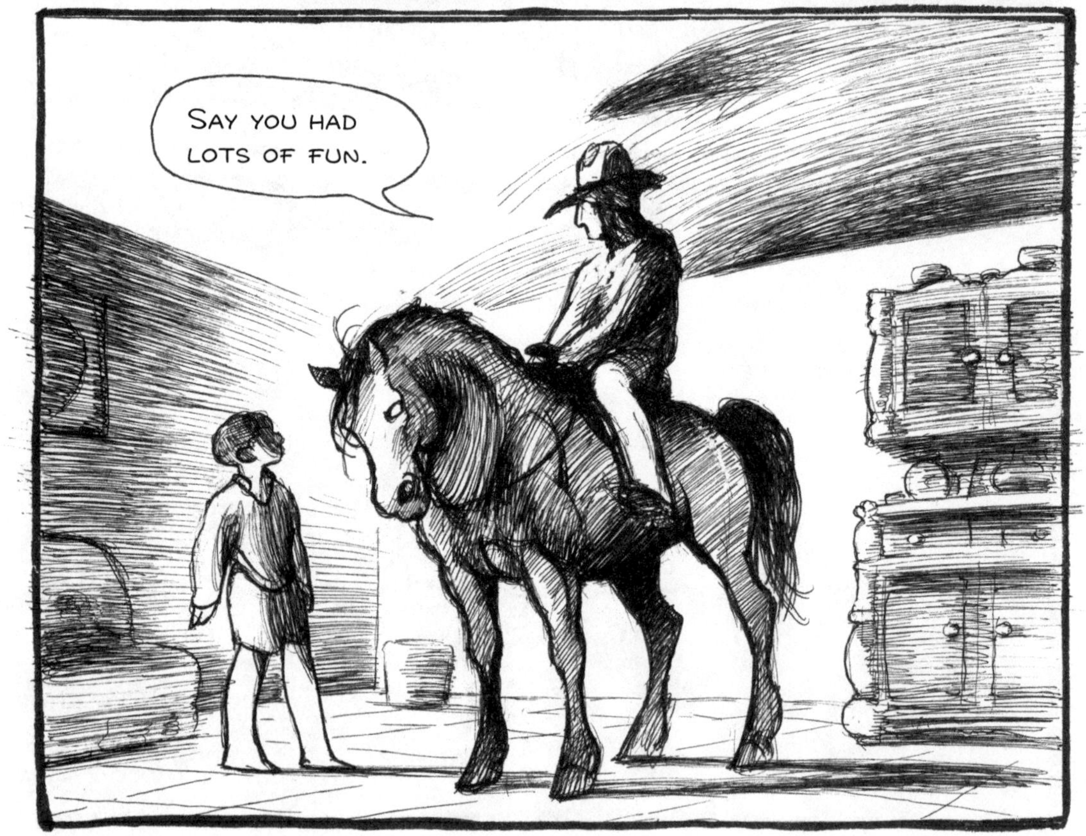
Say you had lots of fun.

VIII

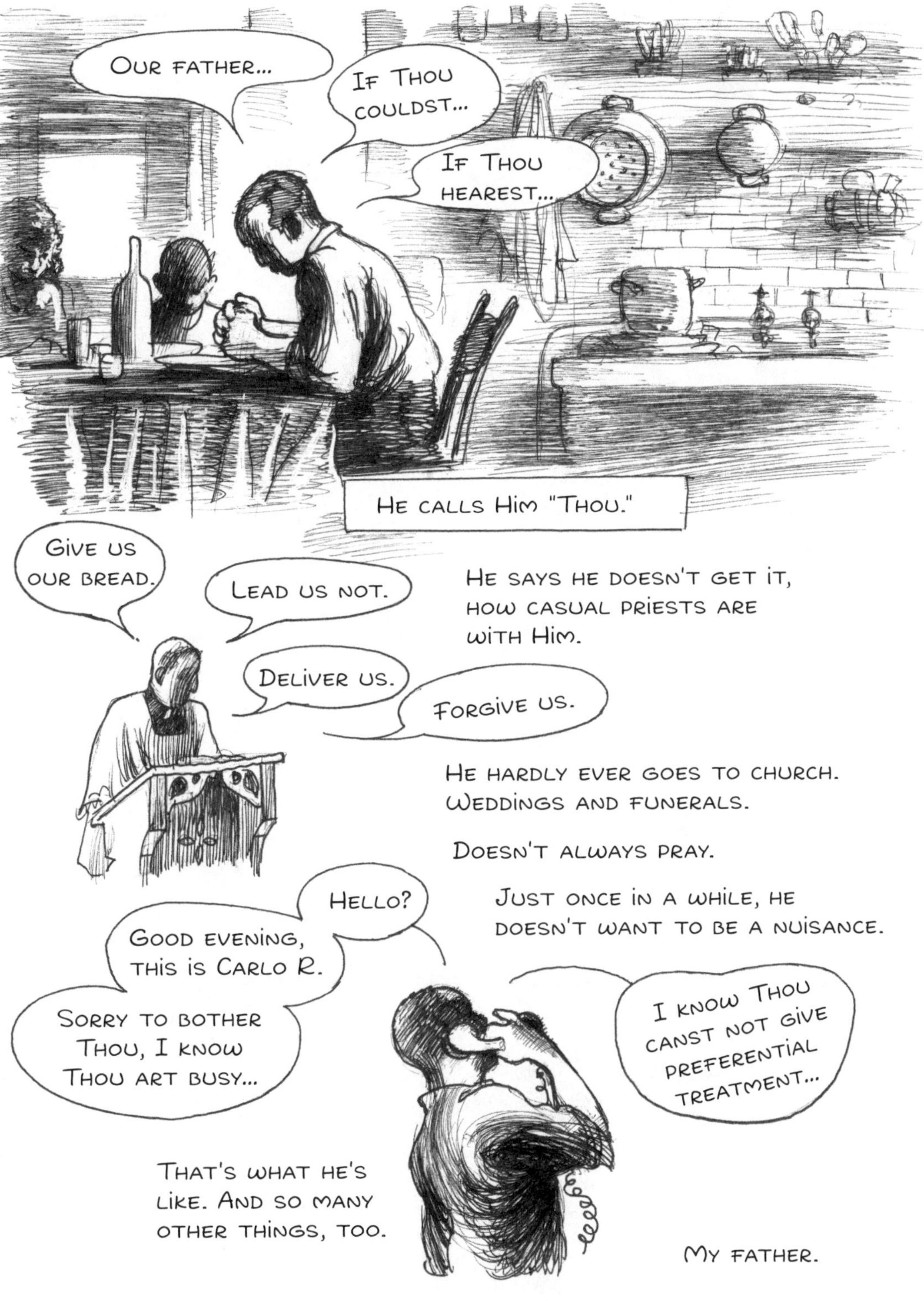
Our father...
If Thou couldst...
If Thou hearest...
He calls Him "Thou."
Give us our bread.
Lead us not.
He says he doesn't get it, how casual priests are with Him.
Deliver us.
Forgive us.
He hardly ever goes to church. Weddings and funerals.
Doesn't always pray.
Just once in a while, he doesn't want to be a nuisance.
Hello?
Good evening, this is Carlo R.
Sorry to bother Thou, I know Thou art busy...
I know Thou canst not give preferential treatment...
That's what he's like. And so many other things, too.
My father.

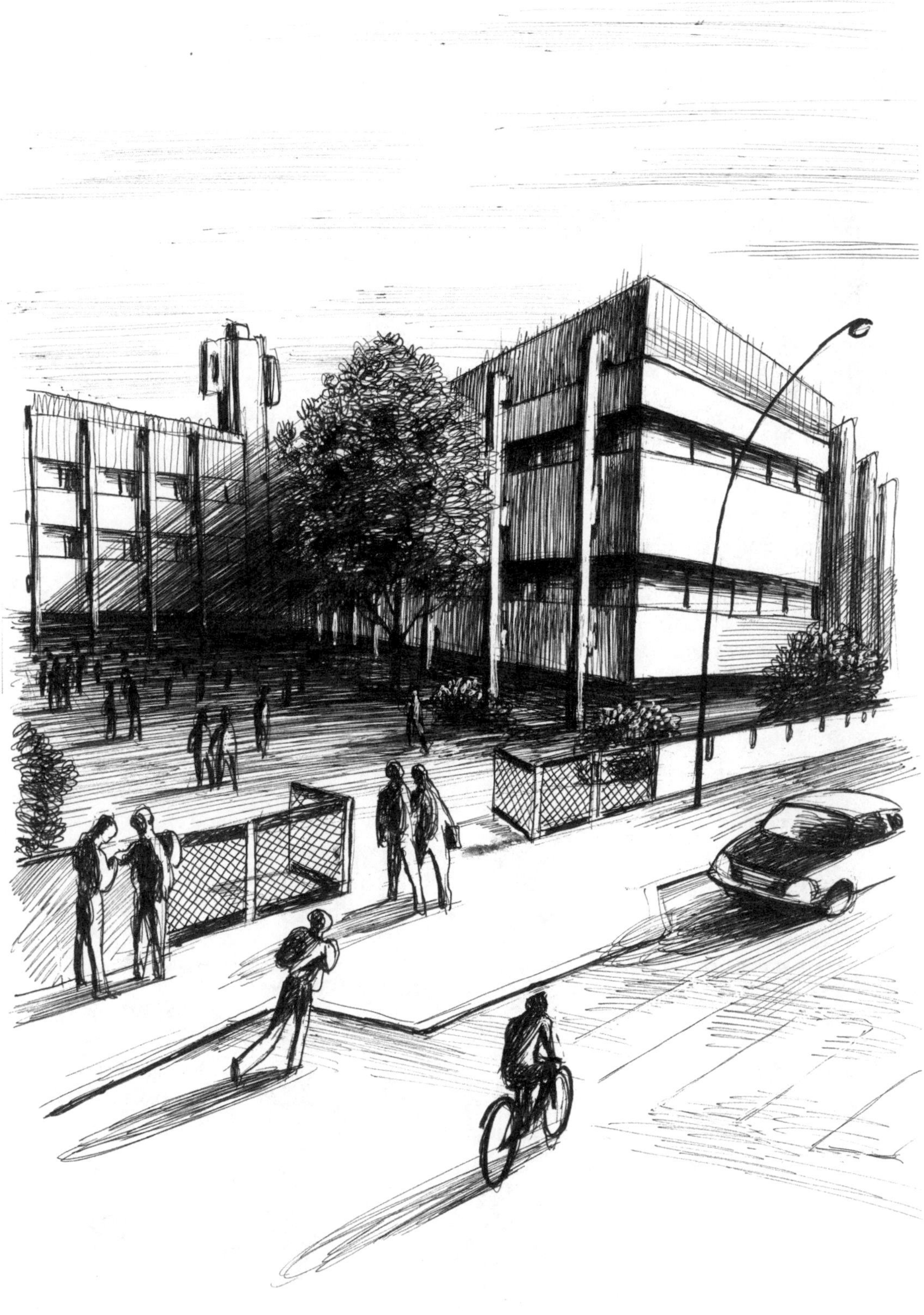

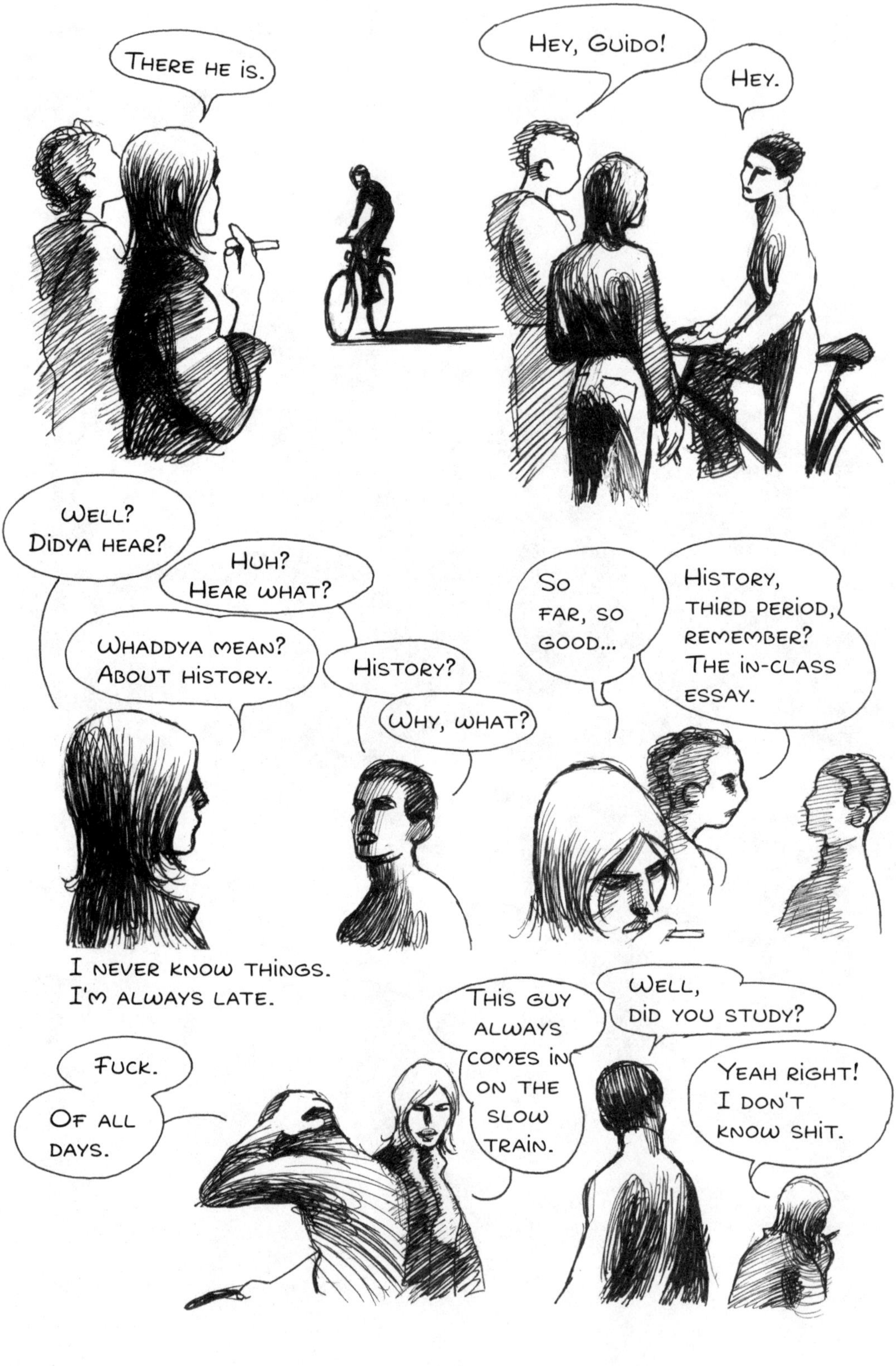
THERE HE IS.
HEY, GUIDO!
HEY.
WELL? DIDYA HEAR?
HUH? HEAR WHAT?
WHADDYA MEAN? ABOUT HISTORY.
HISTORY?
WHY, WHAT?
SO FAR, SO GOOD...
HISTORY, THIRD PERIOD, REMEMBER? THE IN-CLASS ESSAY.
I NEVER KNOW THINGS. I'M ALWAYS LATE.
FUCK.
OF ALL DAYS.
THIS GUY ALWAYS COMES IN ON THE SLOW TRAIN.
WELL, DID YOU STUDY?
YEAH RIGHT! I DON'T KNOW SHIT.

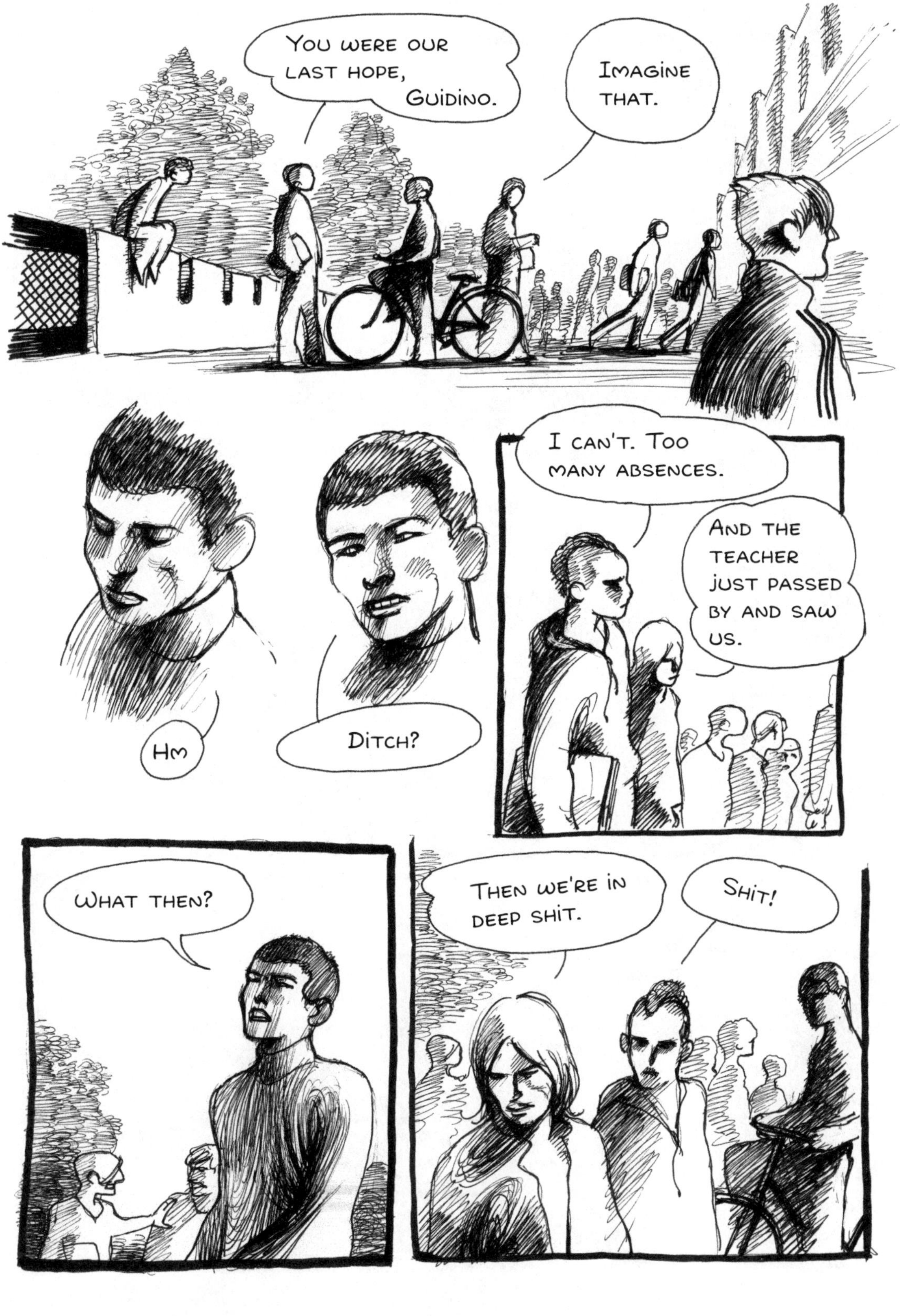
You were our last hope, Guidino.
Imagine that.
Hm
Ditch?
I can't. Too many absences.
And the teacher just passed by and saw us.
What then?
Then we're in deep shit.
Shit!

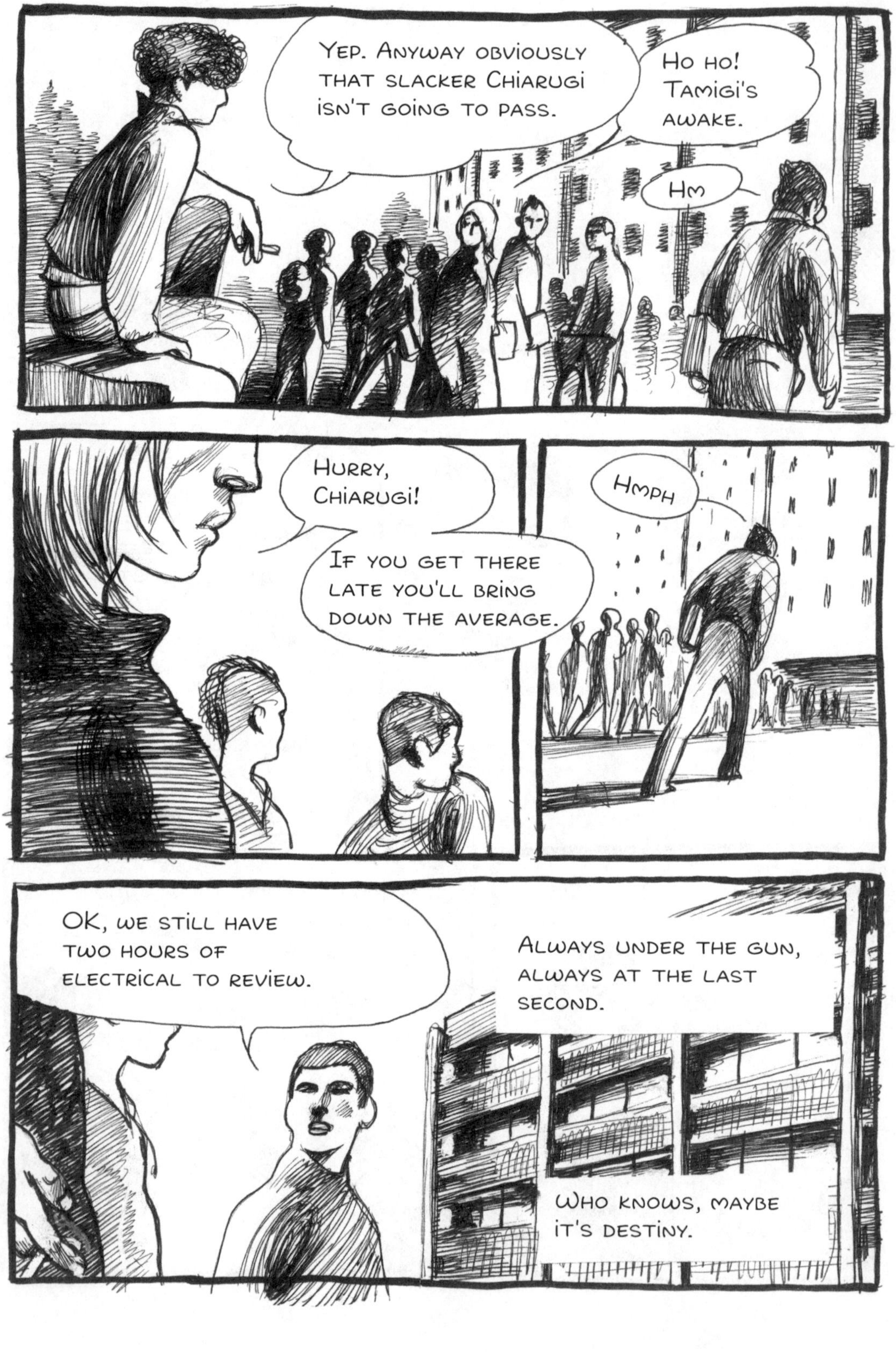
Yep. Anyway obviously that slacker Chiarugi isn't going to pass.
Ho ho! Tamigi's awake.
Hm
Hurry, Chiarugi!
If you get there late you'll bring down the average.
Hmph
OK, we still have two hours of electrical to review.
Always under the gun, always at the last second.
Who knows, maybe it's destiny.

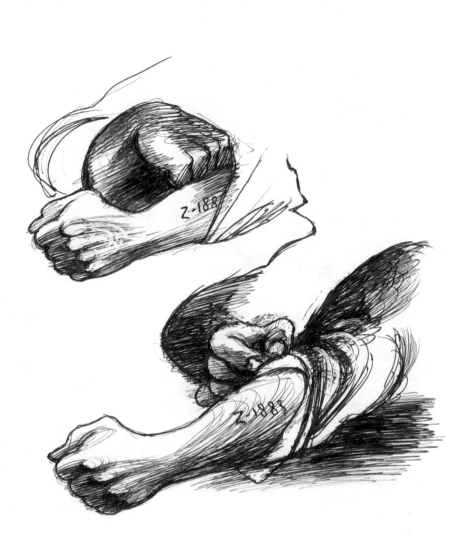

OUR NUMBERS WERE PRECEDED
BY A Z.

IT STOOD FOR "ZIGEUNER."

GYPSY.

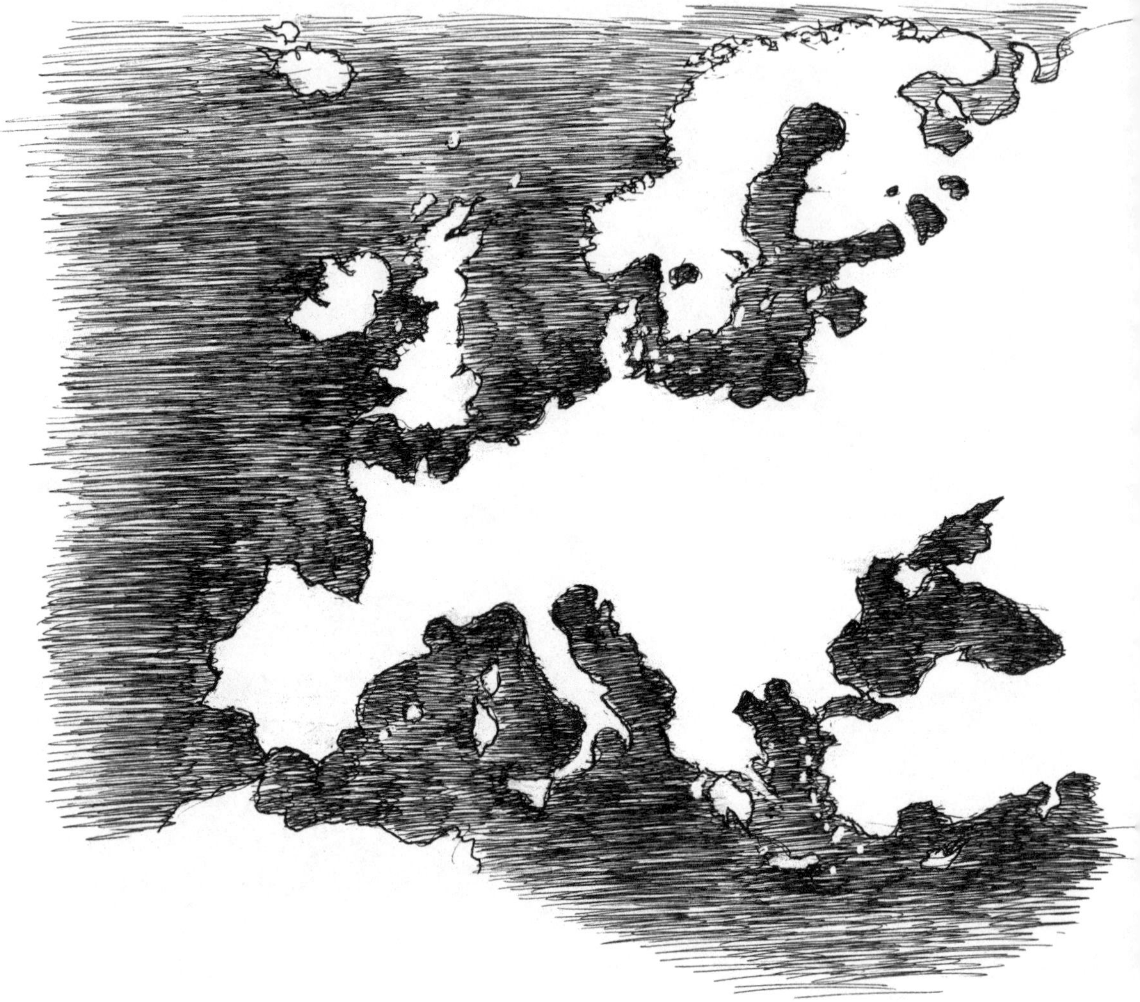

THE EUROPEANS, FROM THE SIXTEENTH CENTURY ON, SUDDENLY SEEMED LIKE AMATEURS.

FORCED SETTLEMENT, LEGALIZED HOMICIDE, SLAVERY, TORTURE...

ALL CHILD'S PLAY.

HE HAD A MORE RADICAL PROJECT: END IT ONCE AND FOR ALL, FOREVER WIPE GYPSIES FROM THE FACE OF THE EARTH.

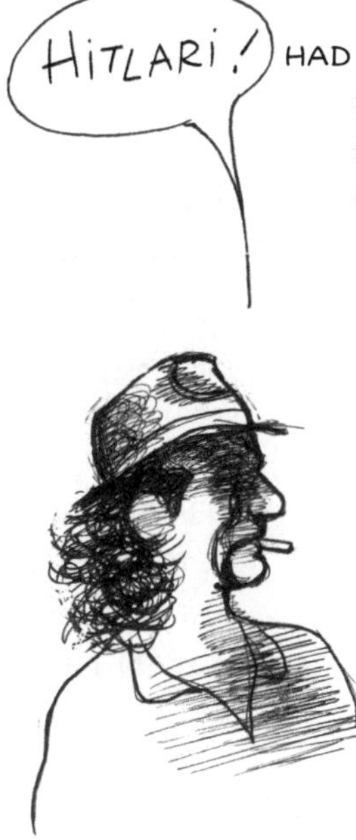
HITLARI!

IT WAS A MATTER OF "RACIAL HYGIENE." THEY WERE VAGABONDS, "ASOCIAL," SUBHUMAN, MEMBERS OF A LESSER RACE.

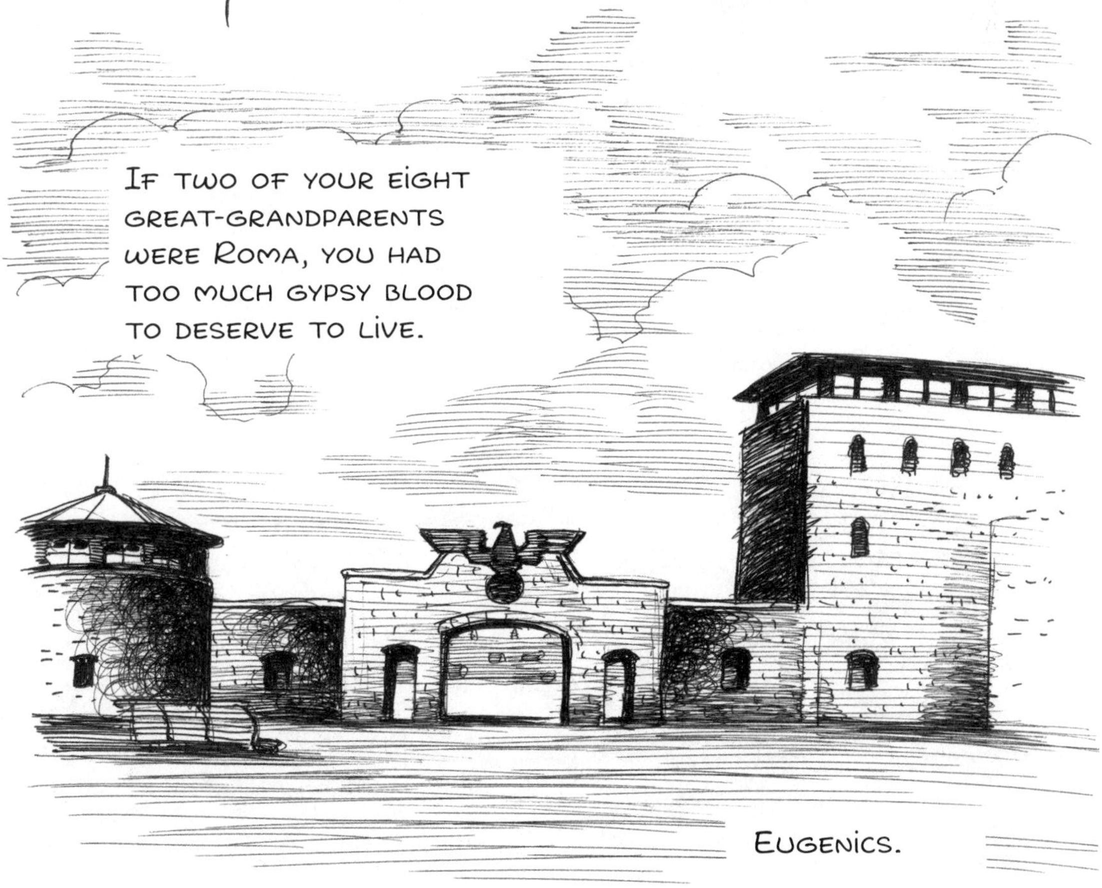
IF TWO OF YOUR EIGHT GREAT-GRANDPARENTS WERE ROMA, YOU HAD TOO MUCH GYPSY BLOOD TO DESERVE TO LIVE.
EUGENICS.

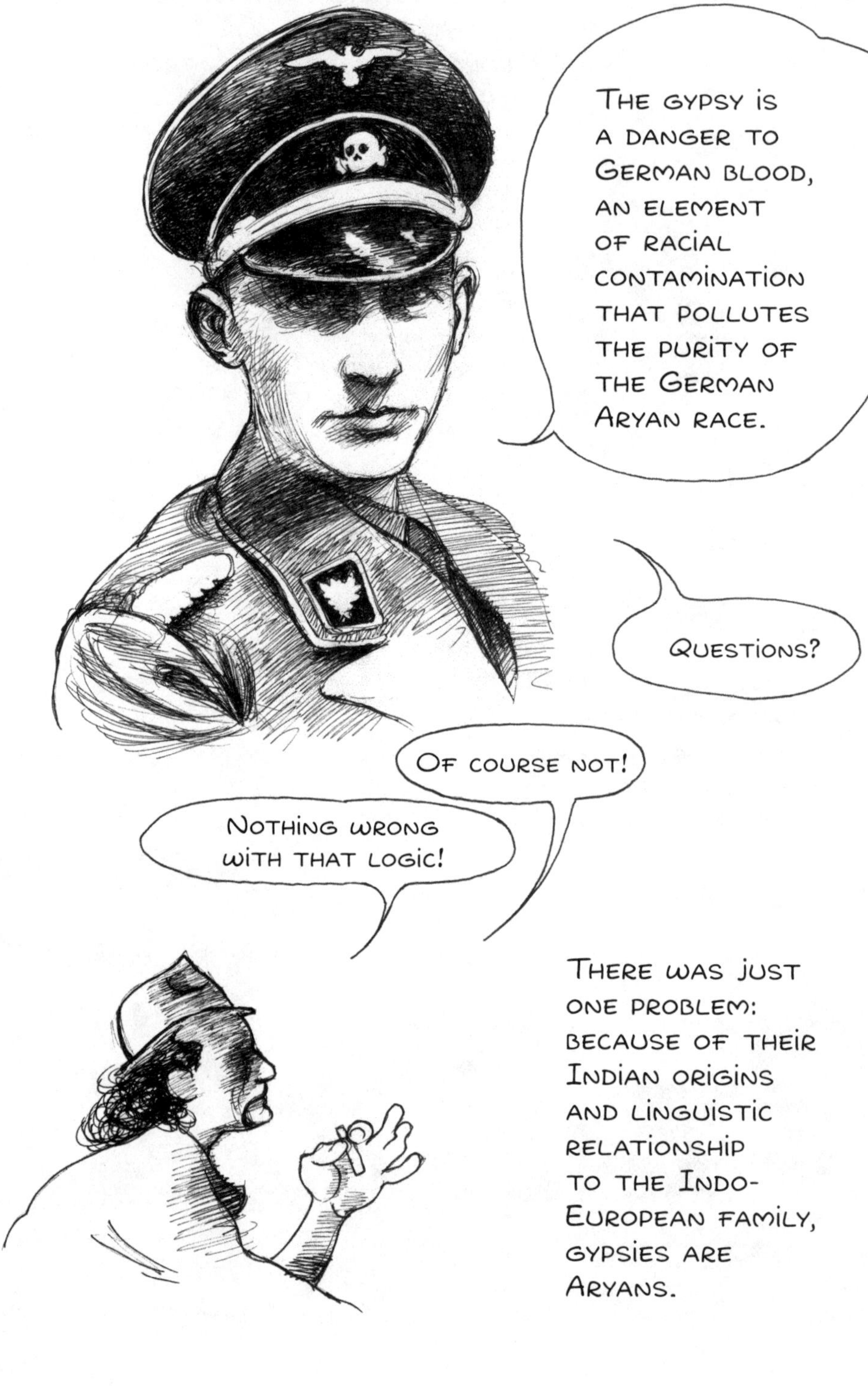
The gypsy is a danger to German blood, an element of racial contamination that pollutes the purity of the German Aryan race.
Questions?
Of course not!
Nothing wrong with that logic!
There was just one problem: because of their Indian origins and linguistic relationship to the Indo-European family, gypsies are Aryans.

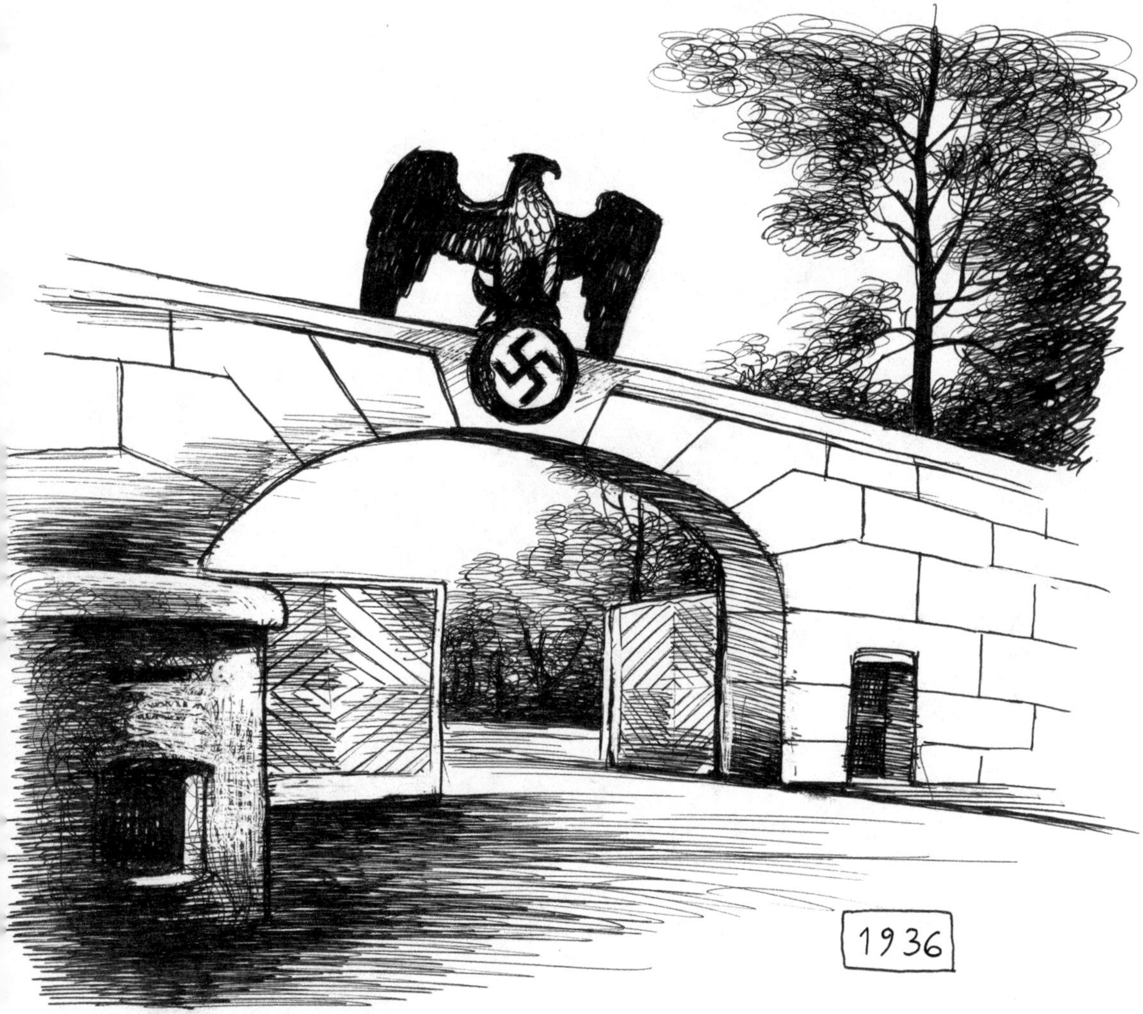
1936

AT THE CENTER FOR RESEARCH ON RACIAL HYGIENE AND DEMOGRAPHIC BIOLOGY IN BERLIN, STUDIES ARE CONDUCTED TO DETERMINE THE EXACT ORIGINS OF THE GYPSIES.

AS IT TURNS OUT, THE ONLY "TRUE ARYANS," THE PURE RACE SO IMPORTANT TO THE NAZIS, ARE PURE GYPSIES.

WHAT OF THE DOGMA OF *Blut und Boden* (BLOOD AND SOIL)? THE MYTH OF THE RACIAL PURITY AND GENETIC SUPERIORITY OF THE GERMANIC PEOPLE?

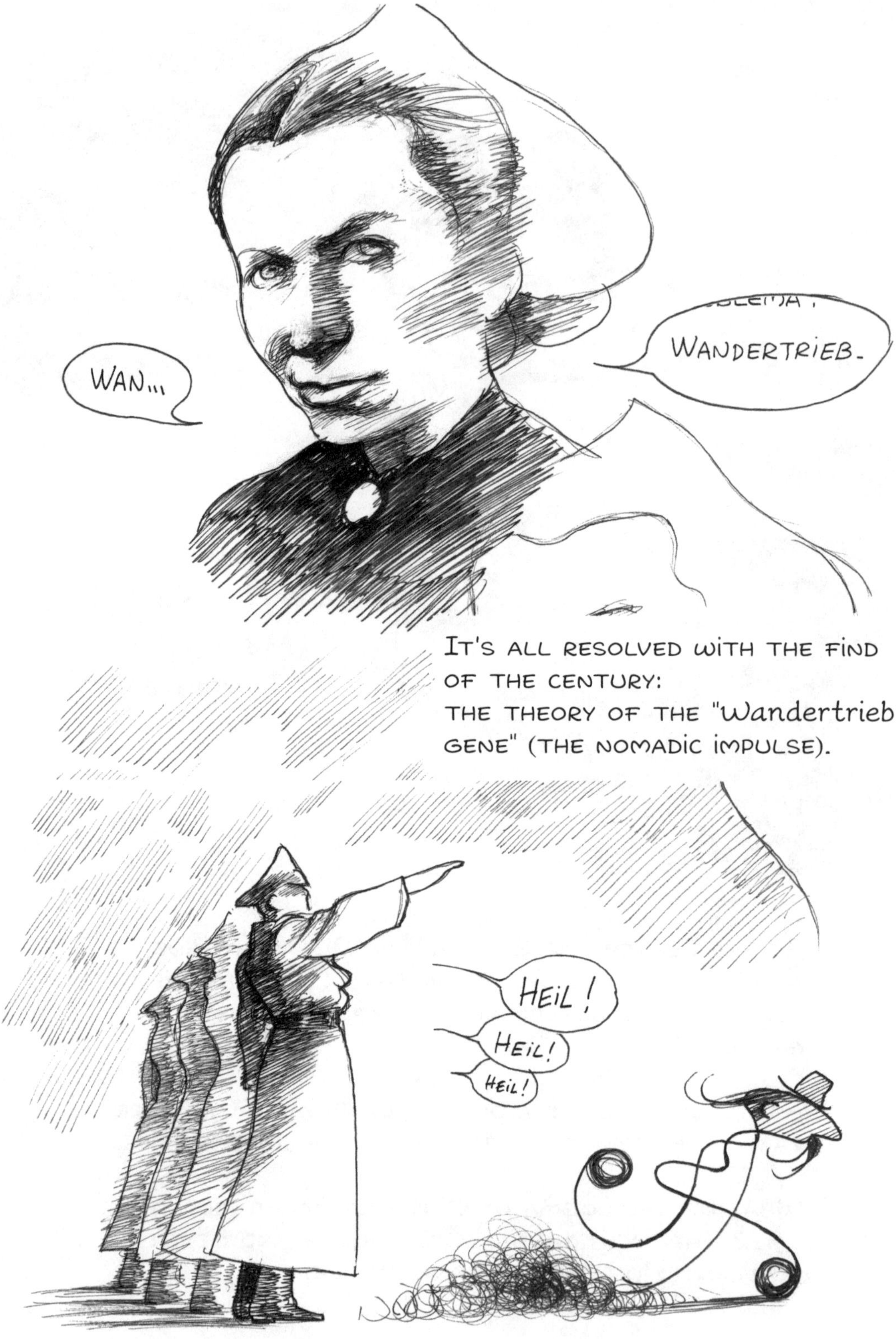
WAN...
WANDERTRIEB.
IT'S ALL RESOLVED WITH THE FIND OF THE CENTURY:
THE THEORY OF THE "Wandertrieb GENE" (THE NOMADIC IMPULSE).
HEIL!
HEIL!
HEIL!

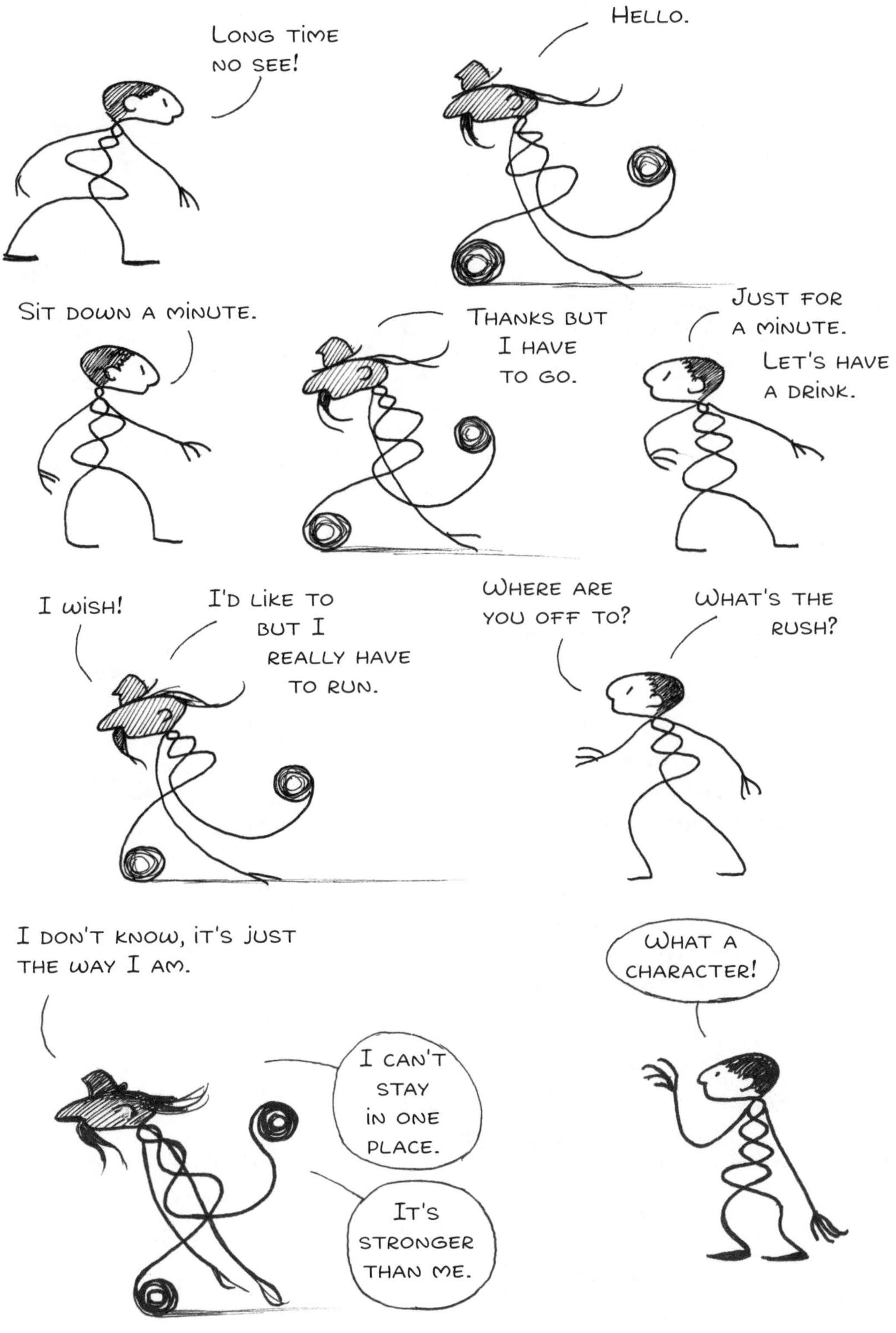

LONG TIME NO SEE!
HELLO.
SIT DOWN A MINUTE.
THANKS BUT I HAVE TO GO.
JUST FOR A MINUTE.
LET'S HAVE A DRINK.
I WISH!
I'D LIKE TO BUT I REALLY HAVE TO RUN.
WHERE ARE YOU OFF TO?
WHAT'S THE RUSH?
I DON'T KNOW, IT'S JUST THE WAY I AM.
I CAN'T STAY IN ONE PLACE.
IT'S STRONGER THAN ME.
WHAT A CHARACTER!

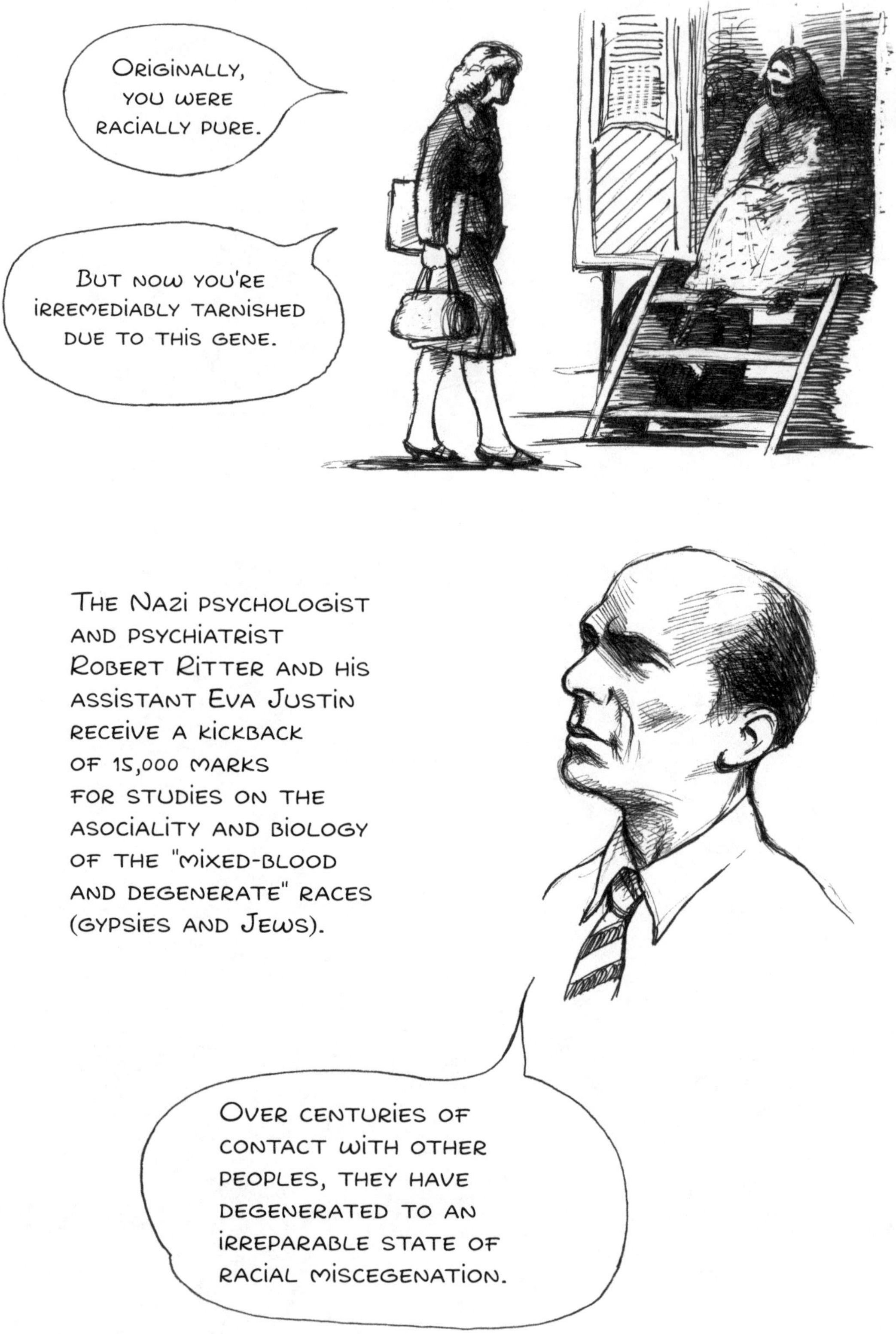
ORIGINALLY, YOU WERE RACIALLY PURE.
BUT NOW YOU'RE IRREMEDIABLY TARNISHED DUE TO THIS GENE.
THE NAZI PSYCHOLOGIST AND PSYCHIATRIST ROBERT RITTER AND HIS ASSISTANT EVA JUSTIN RECEIVE A KICKBACK OF 15,000 MARKS FOR STUDIES ON THE ASOCIALITY AND BIOLOGY OF THE "MIXED-BLOOD AND DEGENERATE" RACES (GYPSIES AND JEWS).
OVER CENTURIES OF CONTACT WITH OTHER PEOPLES, THEY HAVE DEGENERATED TO AN IRREPARABLE STATE OF RACIAL MISCEGENATION.

"FURTHERMORE, THE RESULTS OF OUR INVESTIGATIONS
HAVE ALLOWED US TO CHARACTERIZE THE GYPSIES AS
BEING A PEOPLE OF ENTIRELY PRIMITIVE ETHNOLOGICAL
ORIGINS, WHOSE MENTAL BACKWARDNESS MAKES THEM
INCAPABLE OF REAL SOCIAL ADAPTATION."

"THE GYPSY QUESTION CAN ONLY BE SOLVED WHEN
THE MAIN BODY OF ASOCIAL AND WORTHLESS
GYPSY INDIVIDUALS OF MIXED BLOOD IS COLLECTED
TOGETHER IN LARGE LABOR CAMPS AND KEPT
WORKING THERE, AND WHEN THE FURTHER
BREEDING OF THIS POPULATION OF MIXED BLOOD IS
PERMANENTLY STOPPED."

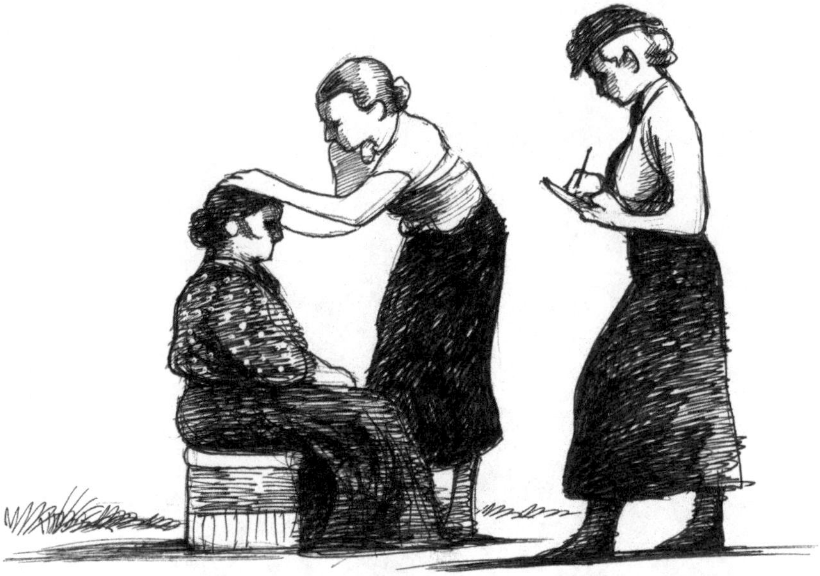

"THUS THERE IS NO LONGER ANY IMPEDIMENT TO IMPLEMENTING RACIAL HYGIENE MEASURES."

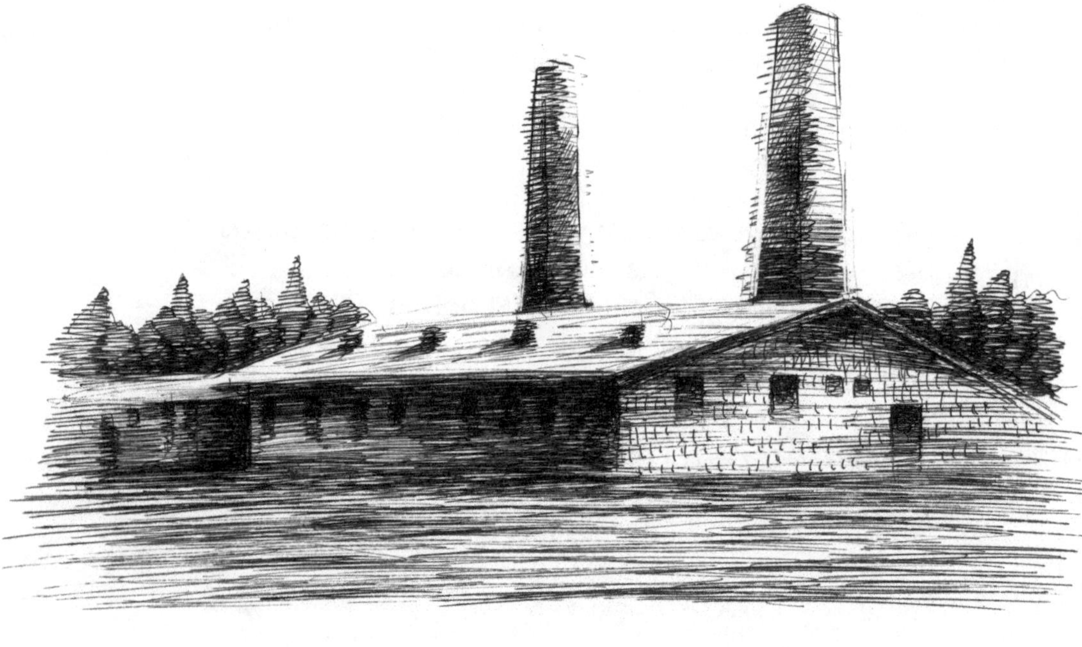

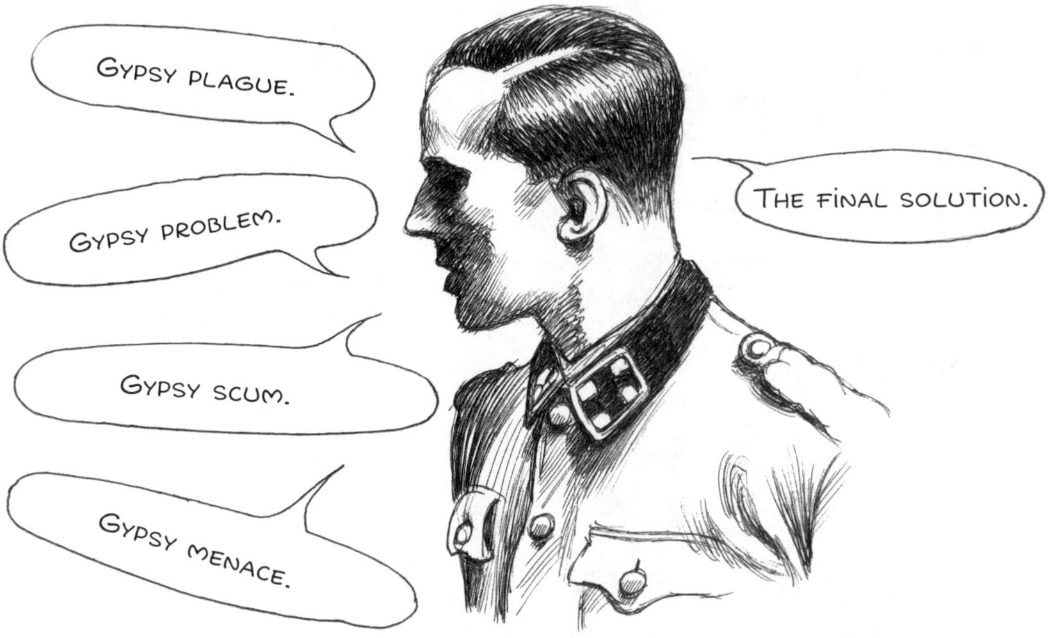
GYPSY PLAGUE.
GYPSY PROBLEM.
GYPSY SCUM.
GYPSY MENACE.
THE FINAL SOLUTION.

THE FIRST TWO PHASES OF THE "FINAL SOLUTION"—EXTERMINATION BY GUNFIRE AND IN GAS VANS—PROVED TO BE INEFFICIENT.

THEY COULDN'T HANDLE LARGE NUMBERS AND IT WAS DISTURBING FOR THE WORKERS.

IN ADDITION, CLEARING THE VANS AFTER AN EXECUTION TOOK TOO LONG AND THE CLEANUP WAS DISGUSTING AND UNSANITARY.

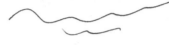

PHASE THREE BEGAN WITH THE USE OF STATIONARY GAS CHAMBERS IN MARCH 1942.

GIFTGAS
ZYKLON

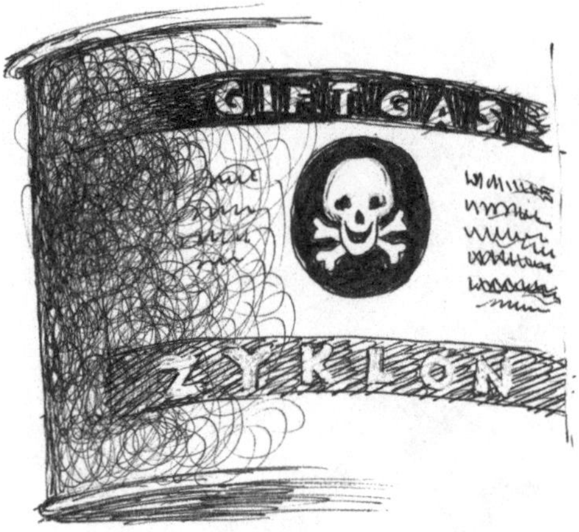

AUSCHWITZ-BIRKENAU-

TREBLINKA-

GIFTGAS
ZYKLON

BELZEC-

SOBIBOR-

MAJDANEK-

CHELMNO-

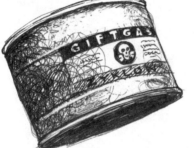

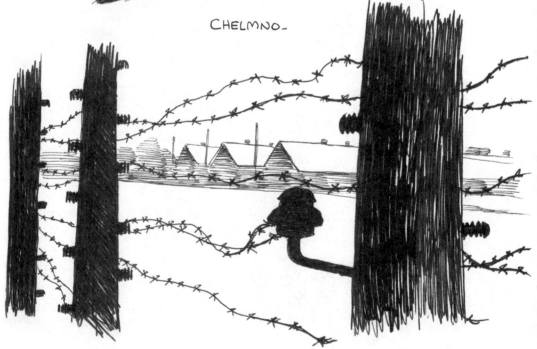

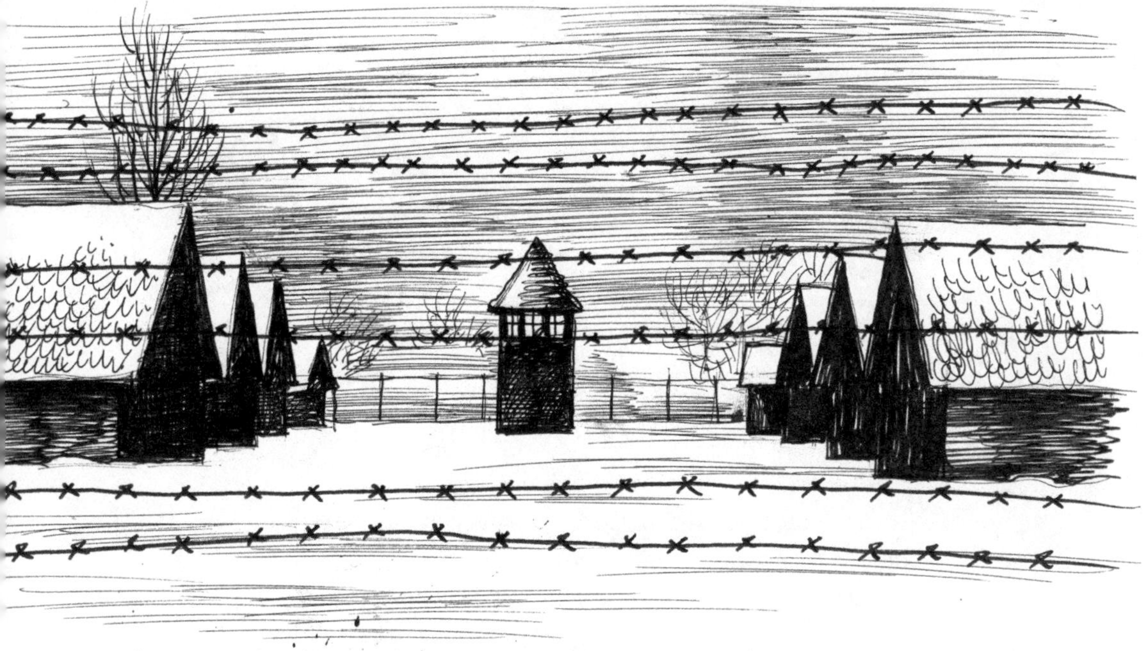

FIVE HUNDRED THOUSAND.

SOME SPEAK OF EIGHT HUNDRED THOUSAND OR A MILLION.

OTHERS SAY NO,
IT WAS "ONLY"
THIRTY OR FORTY THOUSAND.

FIVE HUNDRED THOUSAND IS THE AGREED-UPON NUMBER, BUT THERE WERE NO VITAL RECORDS FOR GYPSIES IN EUROPE, AND THE EXACT NUMBER OF SINTI AND ROMA EXTERMINATED WILL NEVER BE KNOWN.

THEY CALL IT
THE PORRAJMOS,
WHICH IN
THE ROMANI
LANGUAGE
MEANS
"DEVOURING."

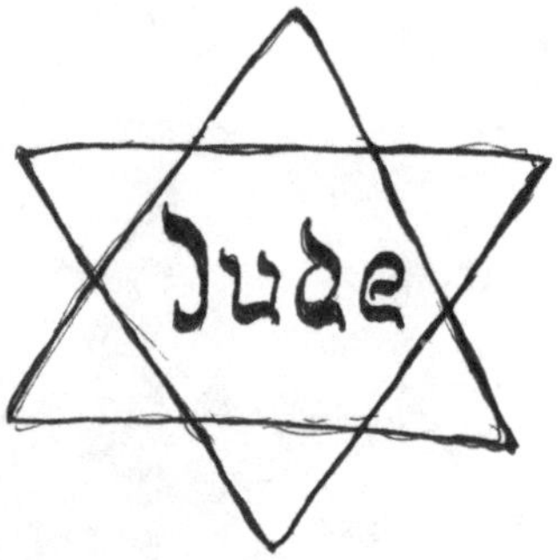
Jude

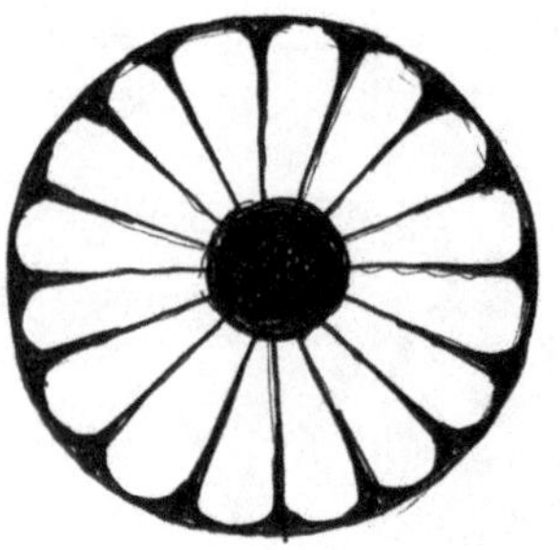

ALONG WITH THE JEWS, THE GYPSIES WERE THE ONLY ONES PERSECUTED EXCLUSIVELY FOR RACIAL REASONS.

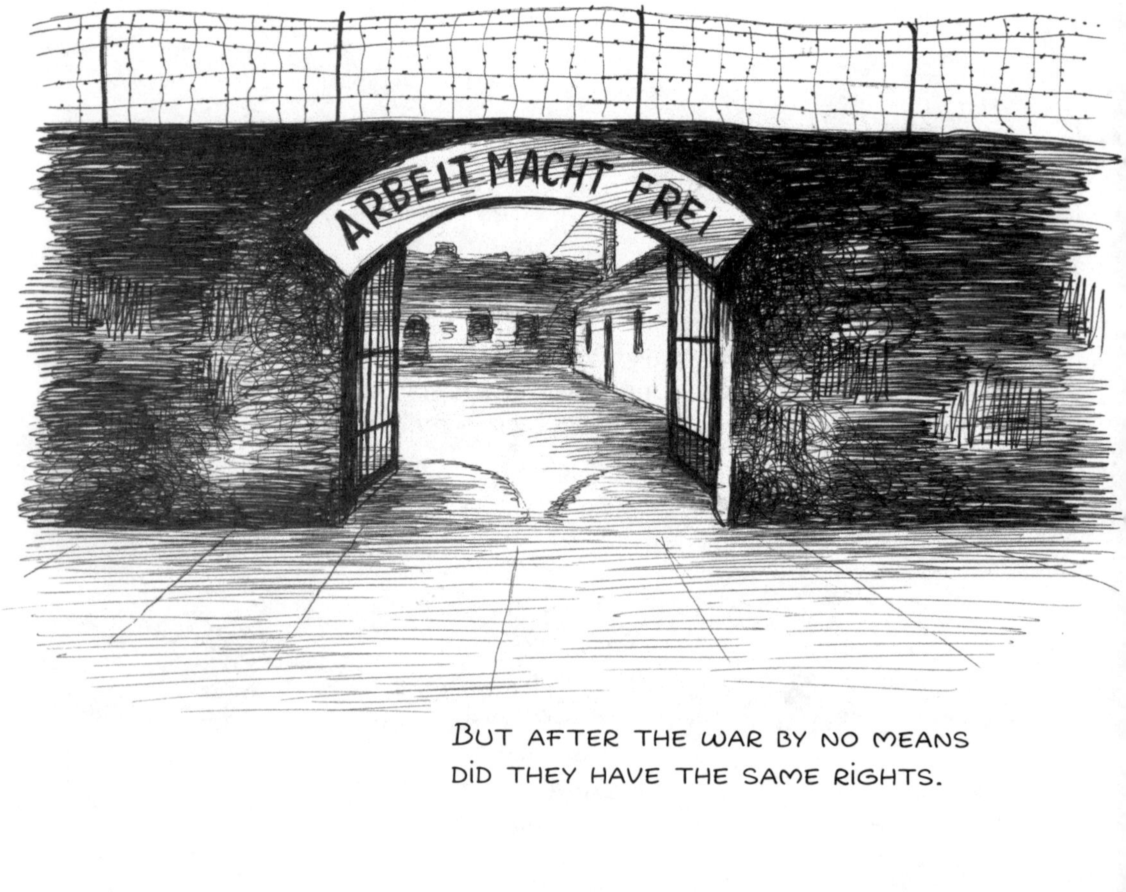
ARBEIT MACHT FREI

BUT AFTER THE WAR BY NO MEANS DID THEY HAVE THE SAME RIGHTS.

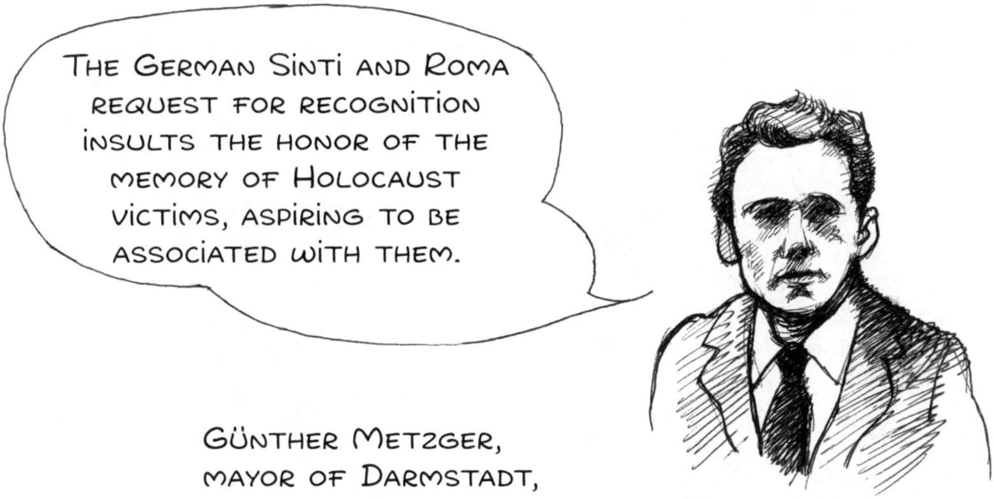
THE GERMAN SINTI AND ROMA REQUEST FOR RECOGNITION INSULTS THE HONOR OF THE MEMORY OF HOLOCAUST VICTIMS, ASPIRING TO BE ASSOCIATED WITH THEM.

GÜNTHER METZGER, MAYOR OF DARMSTADT, 1985.

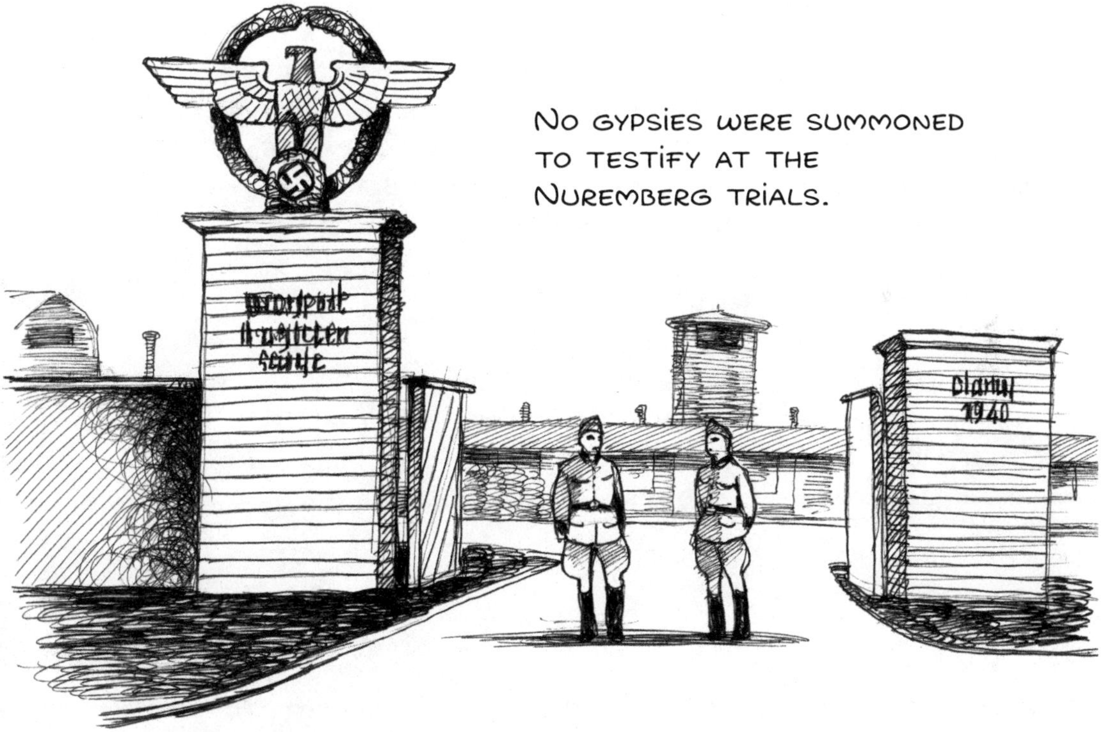

NO GYPSIES WERE SUMMONED TO TESTIFY AT THE NUREMBERG TRIALS.

NOR AT SUBSEQUENT NAZI TRIALS FOR CRIMES AGAINST HUMANITY.

No one was convicted on charges related to the extermination of the gypsies, except one low-ranking soldier.

Many scientists in the Reich—most of them—returned to their regular academic positions or continued to conduct their research undisturbed.

Ritter recommended detention and forced labor, as well as the preventative sterilization of all Roma and Sinti individuals, especially children over twelve. On almost all the files of his study subjects he wrote the word "evak" (evacuate).

After the war, Ritter was employed as a psychologist at the Frankfurt Public Health Office.

Eva Justin worked in social services.

Hans Heinze, supervisor of the child euthanasia program, became director of juvenile psychiatry at Wunstdorf Hospital.

Professor Wolfgang Abel, head of Ethnography at the Kaiser Wilhelm Institute of Anthropology, Human Heredity, and Eugenics, says in an interview about the gypsy "final solution":

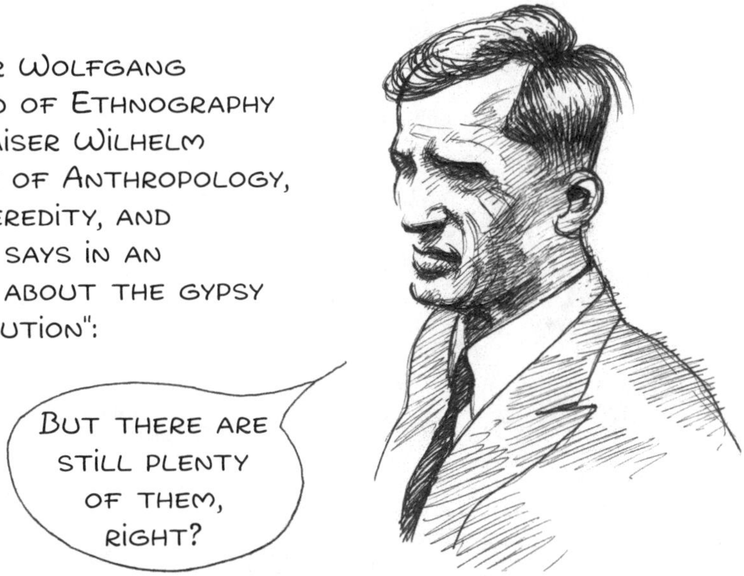
But there are still plenty of them, right?

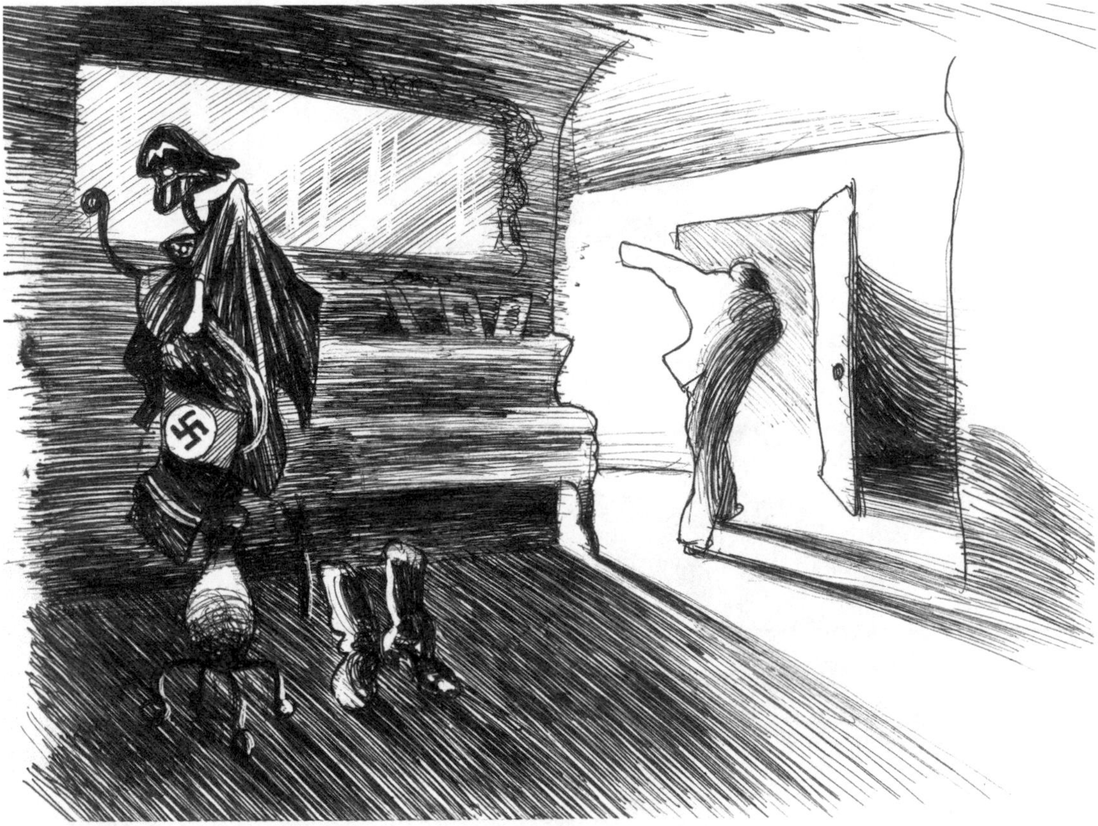

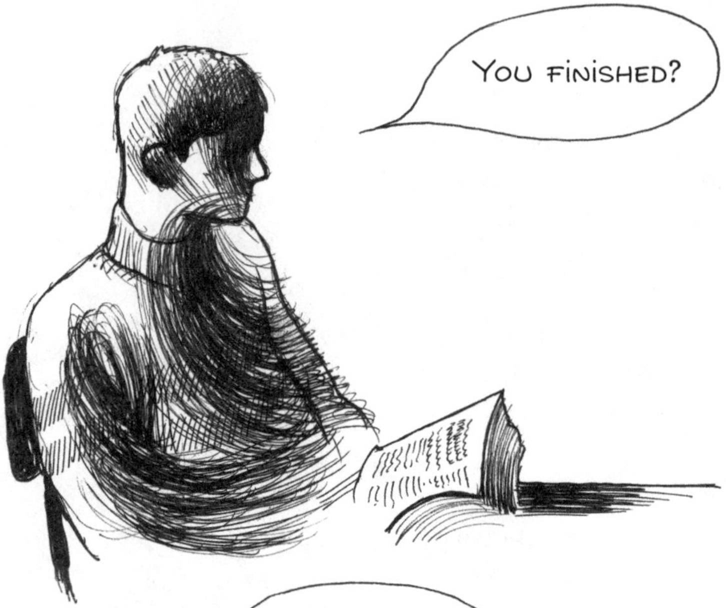
You finished?

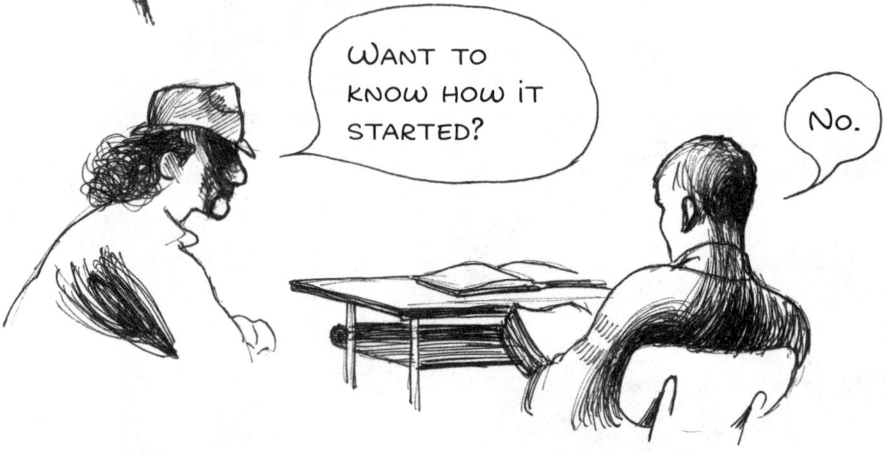
Want to know how it started?
No.

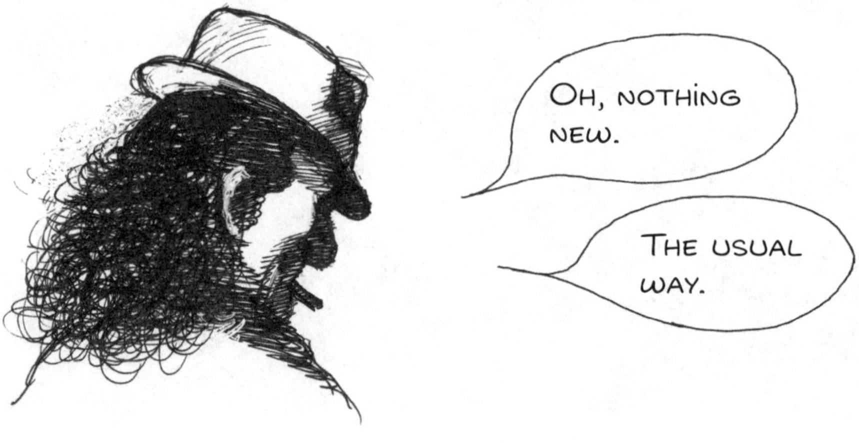
Oh, nothing new.
The usual way.

REGISTRATION.

FINGERPRINTING.

RACIAL CERTIFICATES.

FORCED SETTLEMENT.
RELOCATION PROHIBITED.

ALREADY—SINCE 1929—THEY COULDN'T GO ANYWHERE WITHOUT POLICE PERMISSION.

COMPULSORY STERILIZATION AND CASTRATION.

STARTING IN 1938, A LAW TARGETED EXCLUSIVELY AT GYPSIES REQUIRED THEM TO CHOOSE: STERILIZATION OR INTERNMENT.

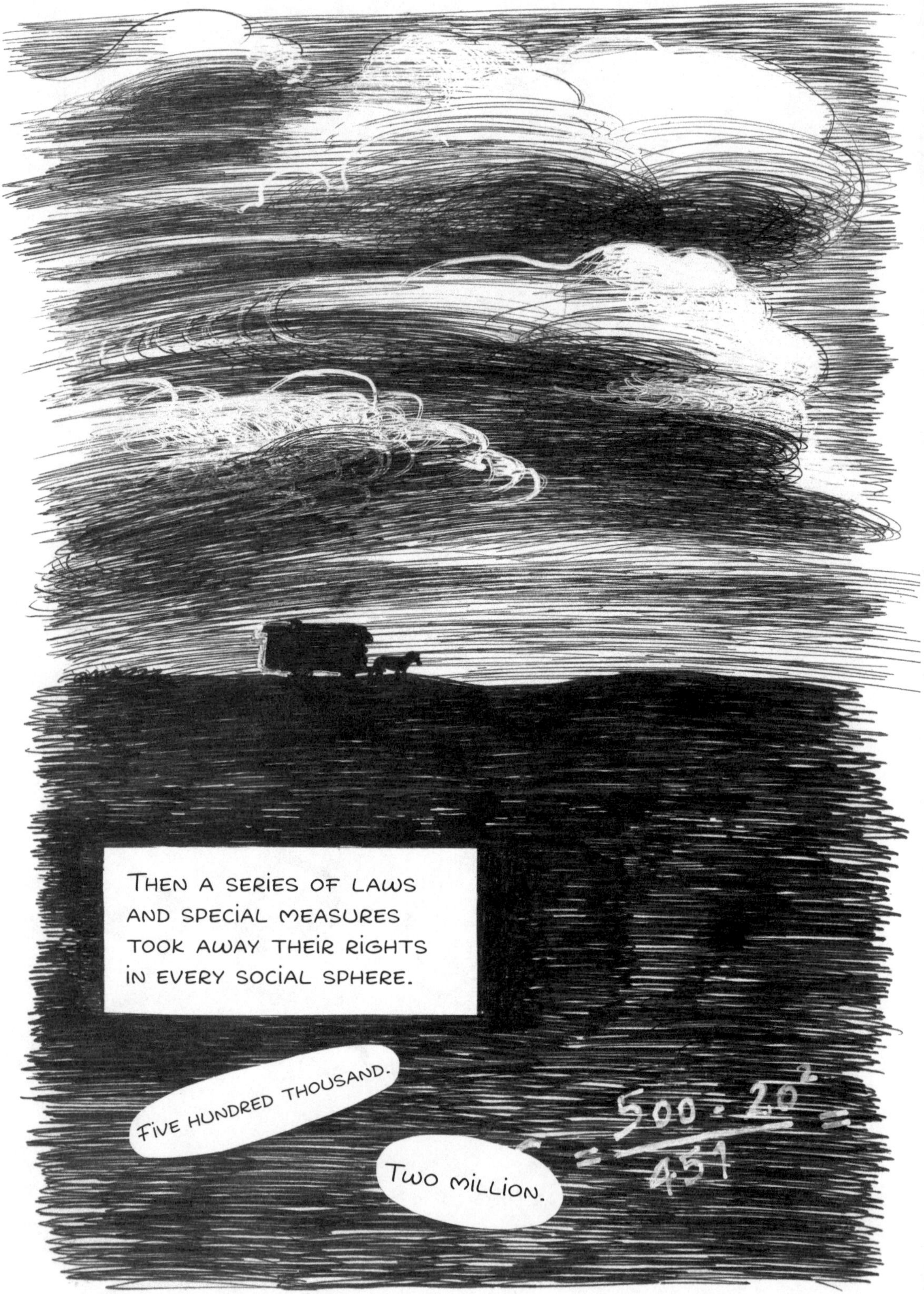
Then a series of laws and special measures took away their rights in every social sphere.
Five hundred thousand.
Two million.
= 500 · 20² / 451 =

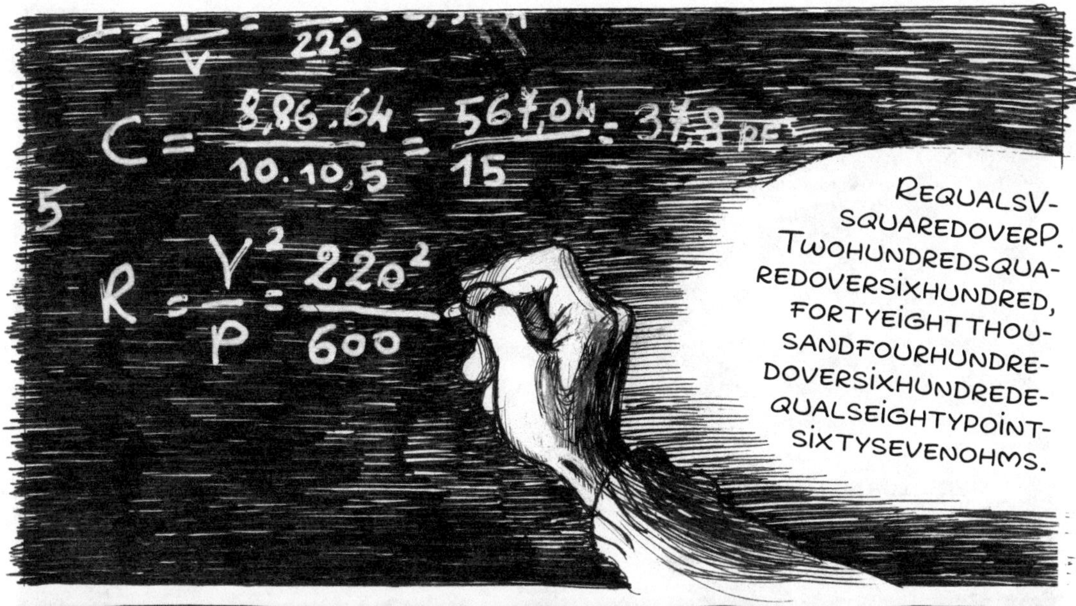
REQUALSV-
SQUAREDOVERP.
TWOHUNDREDSQUA-
REDOVERSIXHUNDRED,
FORTYEIGHTTHOU-
SANDFOURHUNDRE-
DOVERSIXHUNDREDE-
QUALSEIGHTYPOINT-
SIXTYSEVENOHMS.

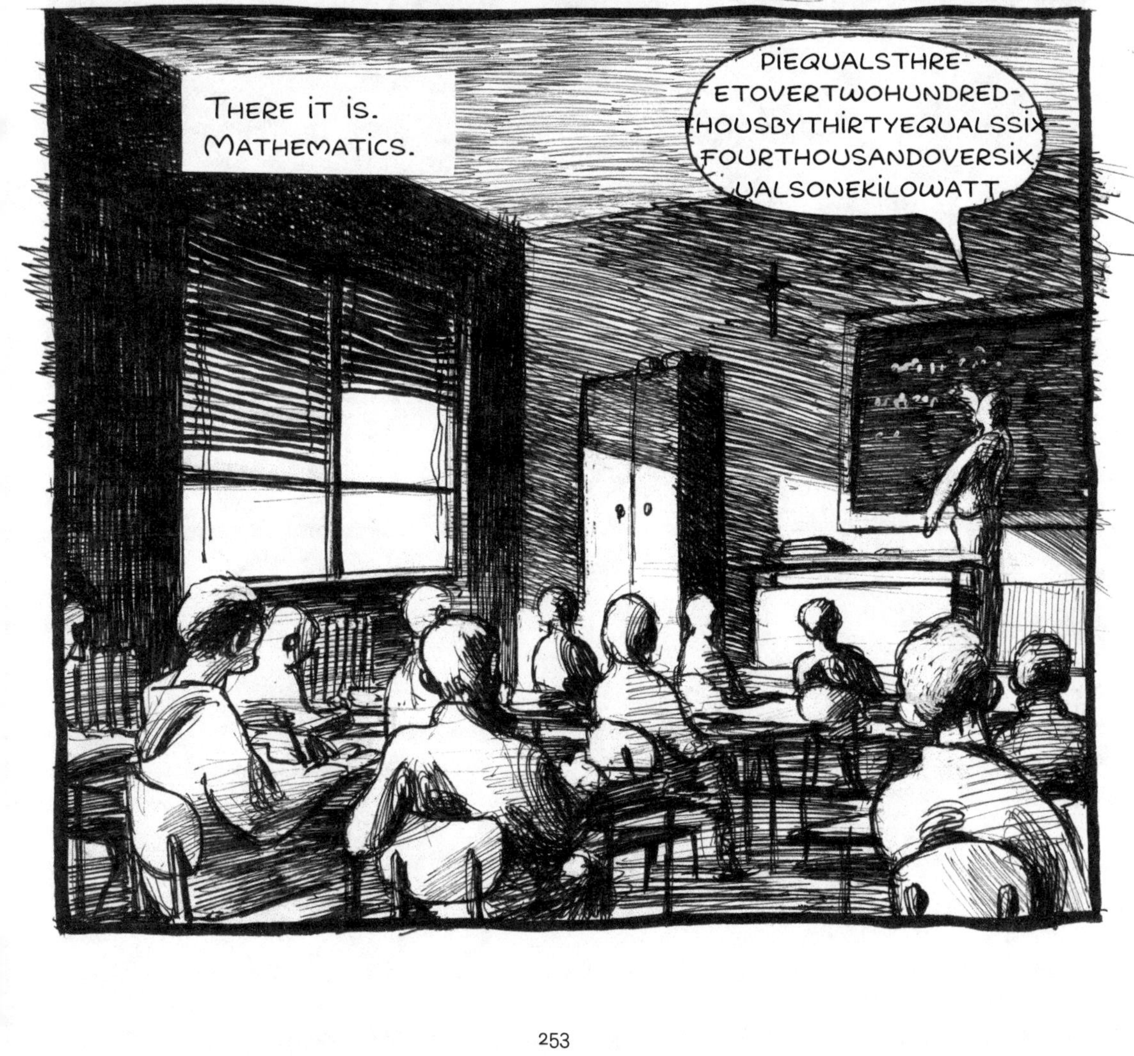
THERE IT IS.
MATHEMATICS.
PIEQUALSTHRE-
ETOVERTWOHUNDRED-
THOUSBYTHIRTYEQUALSSIX
FOURTHOUSANDOVERSIX
UALSONEKILOWATT

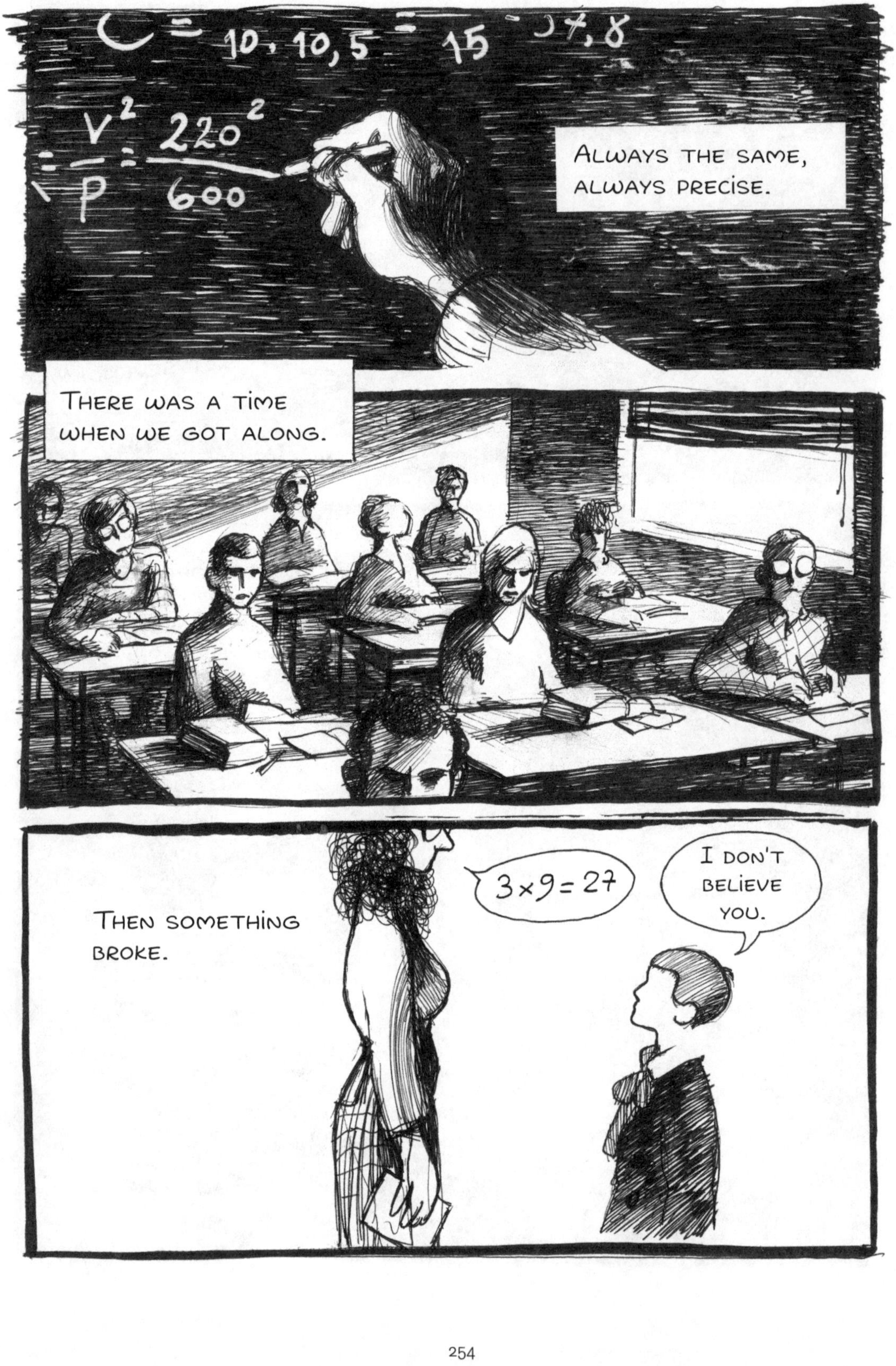
Always the same,
always precise.
There was a time
when we got along.
Then something
broke.
3×9=27
I don't
believe
you.

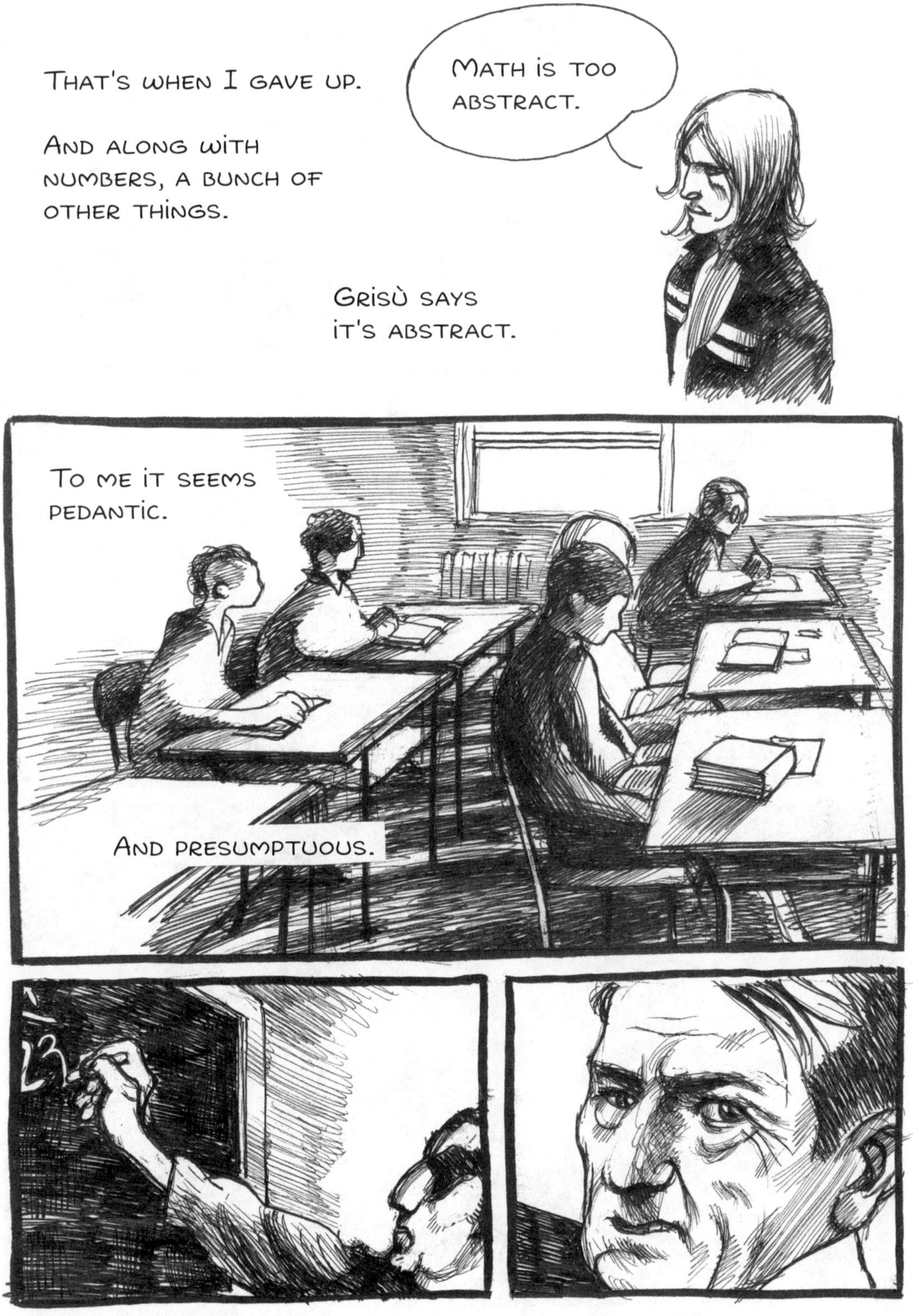
THAT'S WHEN I GAVE UP.
AND ALONG WITH NUMBERS, A BUNCH OF OTHER THINGS.
MATH IS TOO ABSTRACT.
GRISÙ SAYS IT'S ABSTRACT.
TO ME IT SEEMS PEDANTIC.
AND PRESUMPTUOUS.

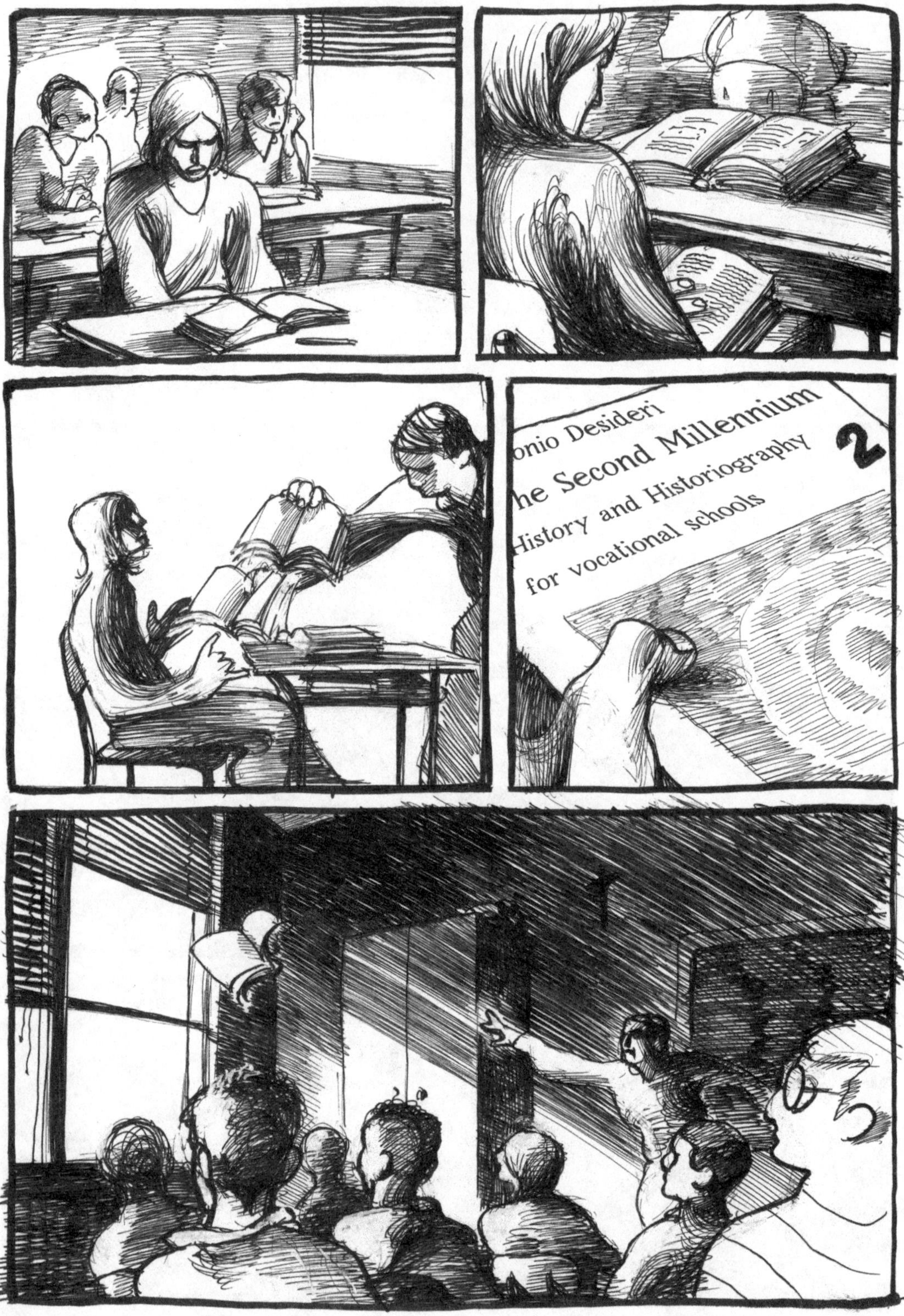
onio Desideri
he Second Millennium
History and Historiography
for vocational schools
2

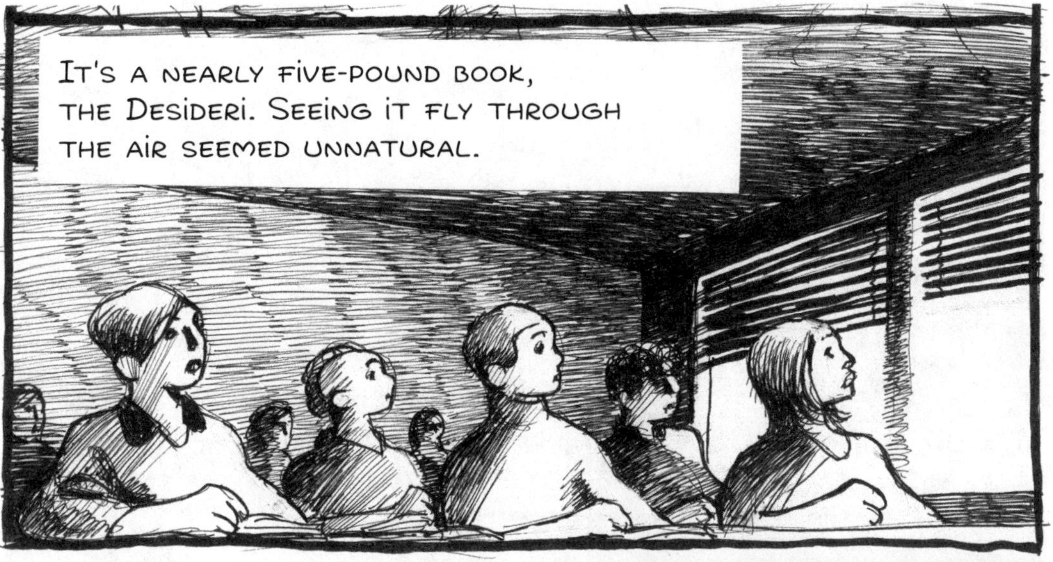
It's a nearly five-pound book, the Desideri. Seeing it fly through the air seemed unnatural.

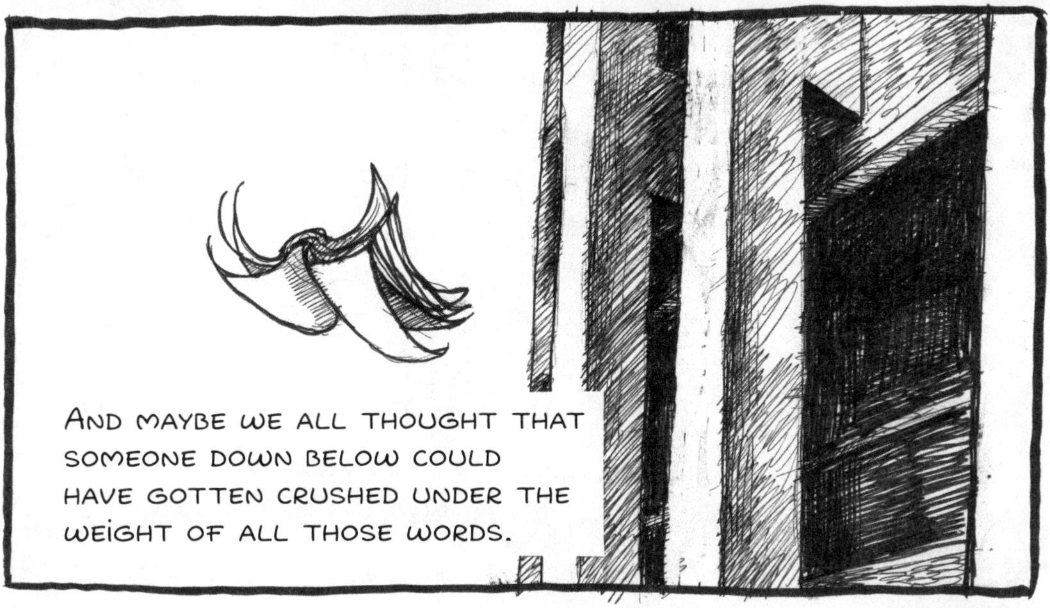
And maybe we all thought that someone down below could have gotten crushed under the weight of all those words.

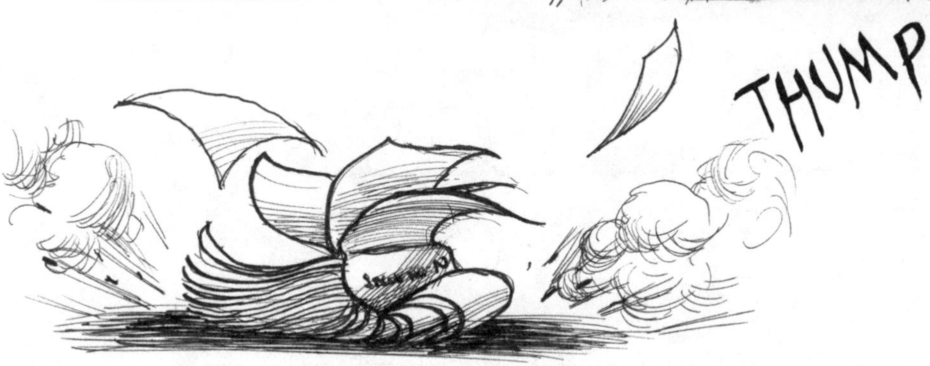
THUMP

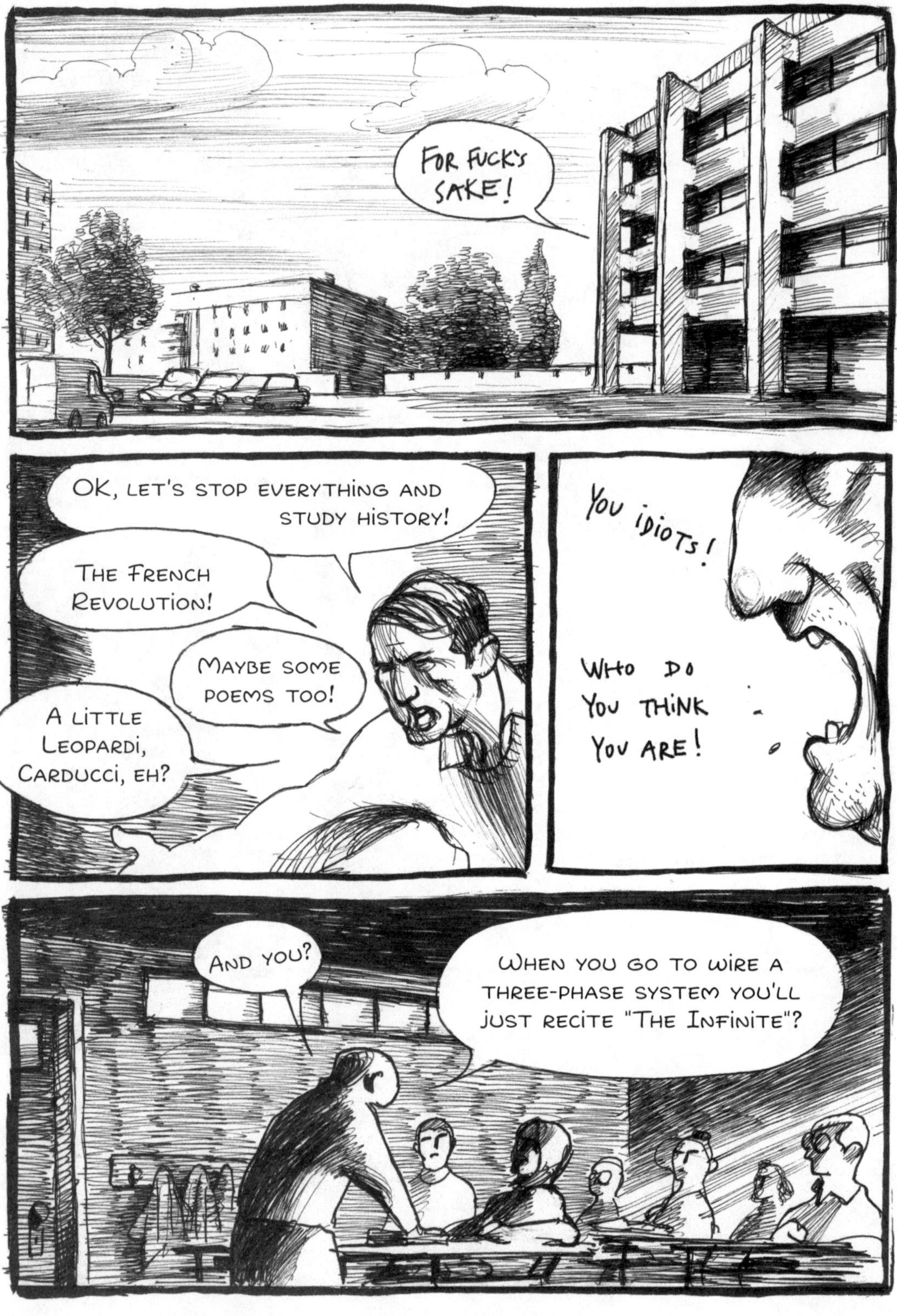
FOR FUCK'S SAKE!
OK, LET'S STOP EVERYTHING AND STUDY HISTORY!
THE FRENCH REVOLUTION!
MAYBE SOME POEMS TOO!
A LITTLE LEOPARDI, CARDUCCI, EH?
YOU IDIOTS!
WHO DO YOU THINK YOU ARE!
AND YOU?
WHEN YOU GO TO WIRE A THREE-PHASE SYSTEM YOU'LL JUST RECITE "THE INFINITE"?

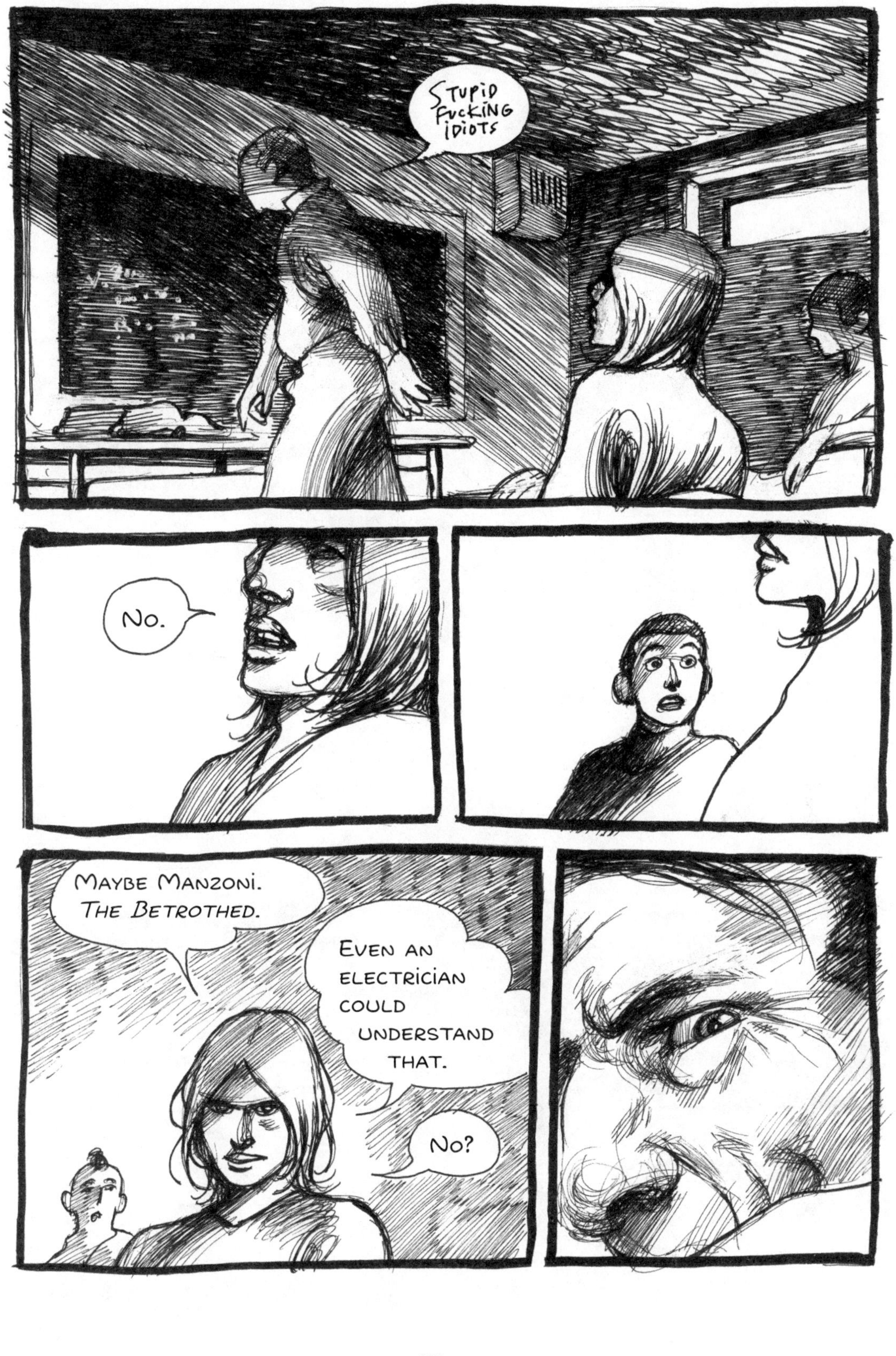
Stupid fucking idiots
No.
Maybe Manzoni. The Betrothed.
Even an electrician could understand that.
No?

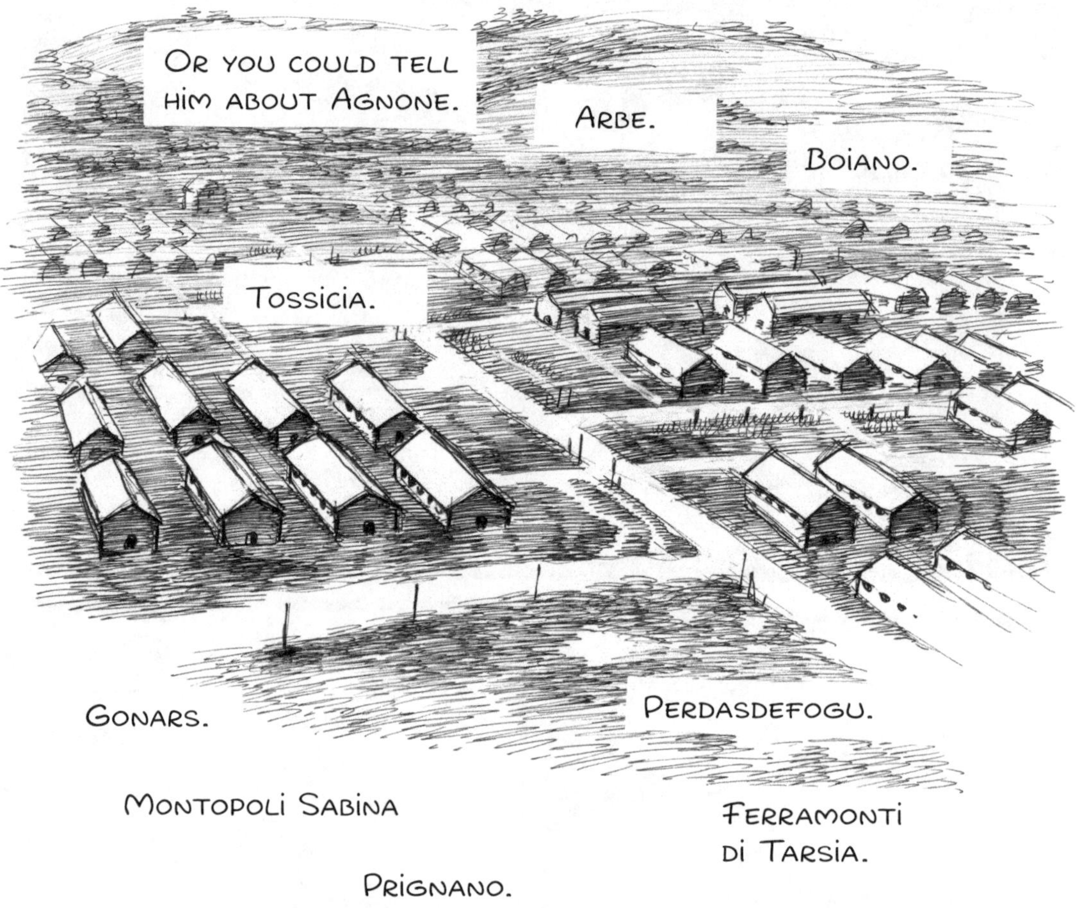
OR YOU COULD TELL HIM ABOUT AGNONE.
ARBE.
BOIANO.
TOSSICIA.
GONARS.
PERDASDEFOGU.
MONTOPOLI SABINA
FERRAMONTI DI TARSIA.
PRIGNANO.

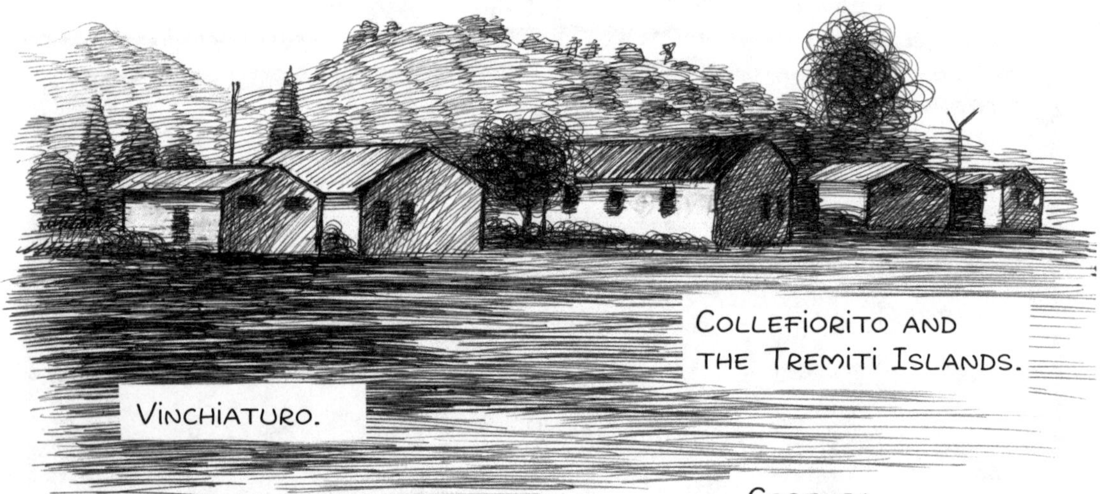
COLLEFIORITO AND THE TREMITI ISLANDS.
VINCHIATURO.
COSENZA.

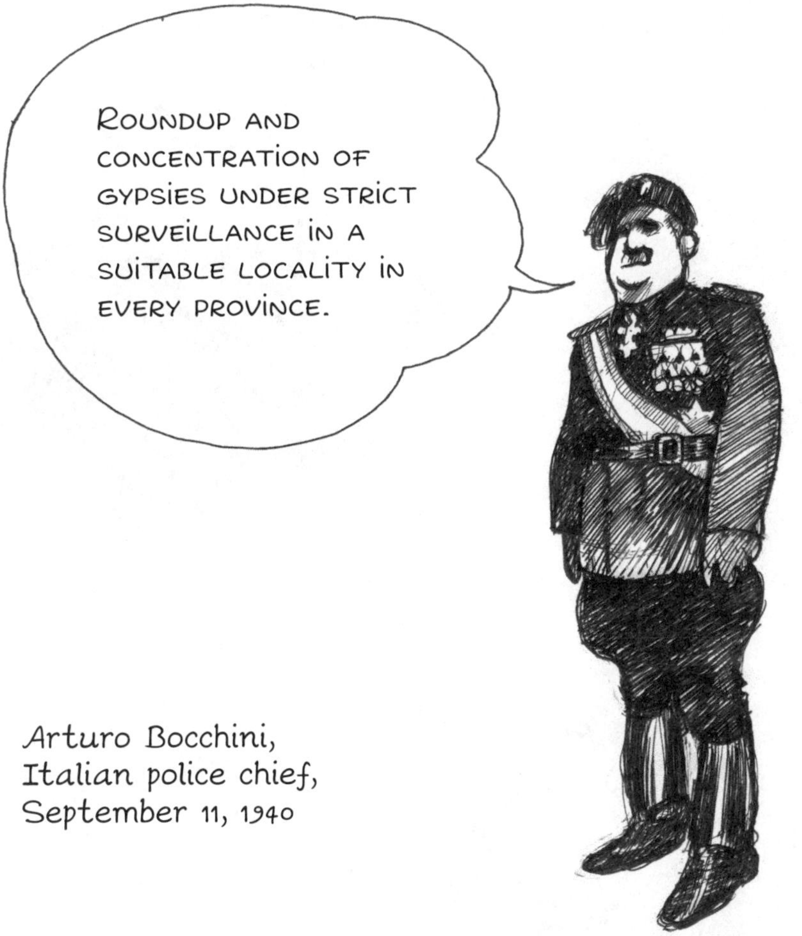
Roundup and concentration of gypsies under strict surveillance in a suitable locality in every province.
Arturo Bocchini, Italian police chief, September 11, 1940

Of course, besides the Risiera di San Sabba in Trieste, where they burned three or four thousand people in the ovens, the rest of the Italian camps were nothing compared to the efficient Nazi ones

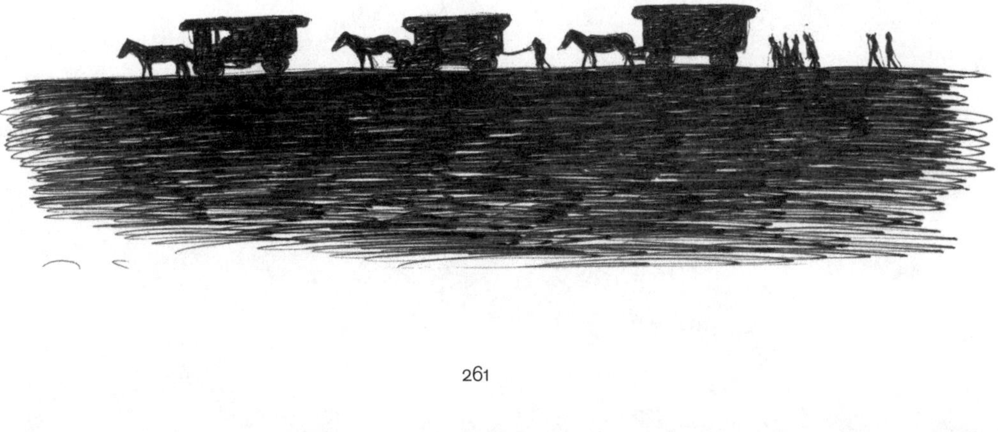

They used other methods

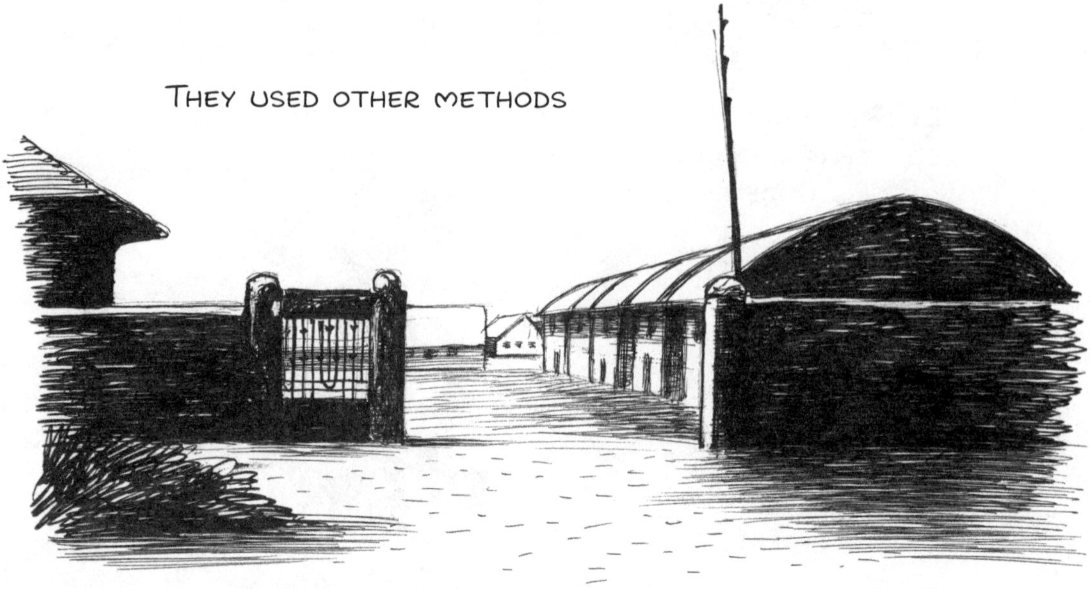

Cold.

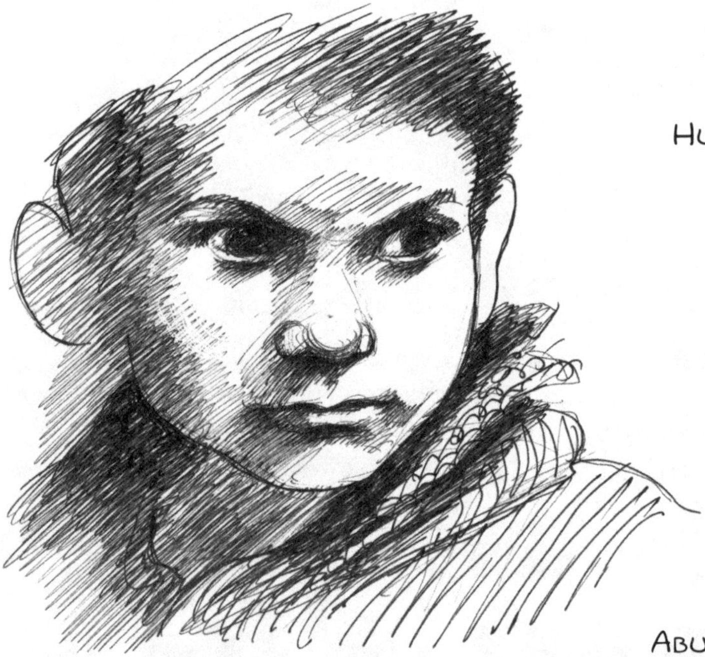

Hunger.

Toxic sanitary conditions.

Abuse and torture.

At Arbe the average was twelve deaths a day. Mostly children and the elderly.

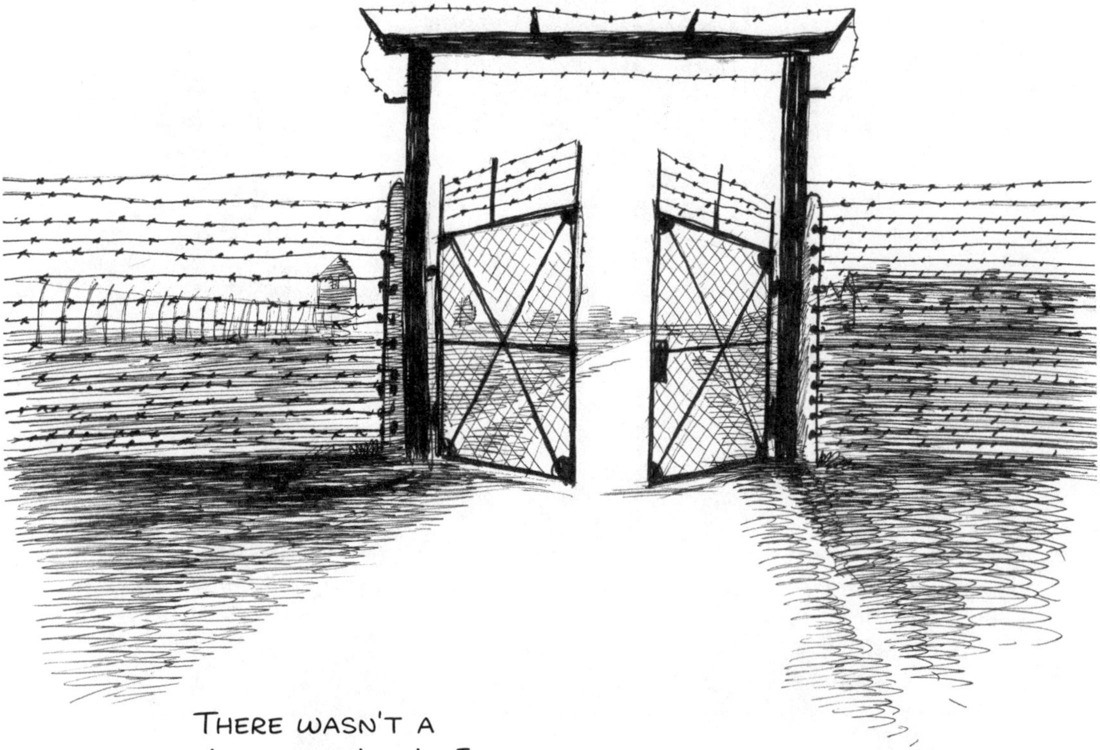

There wasn't a single region in Italy without at least one concentration camp.

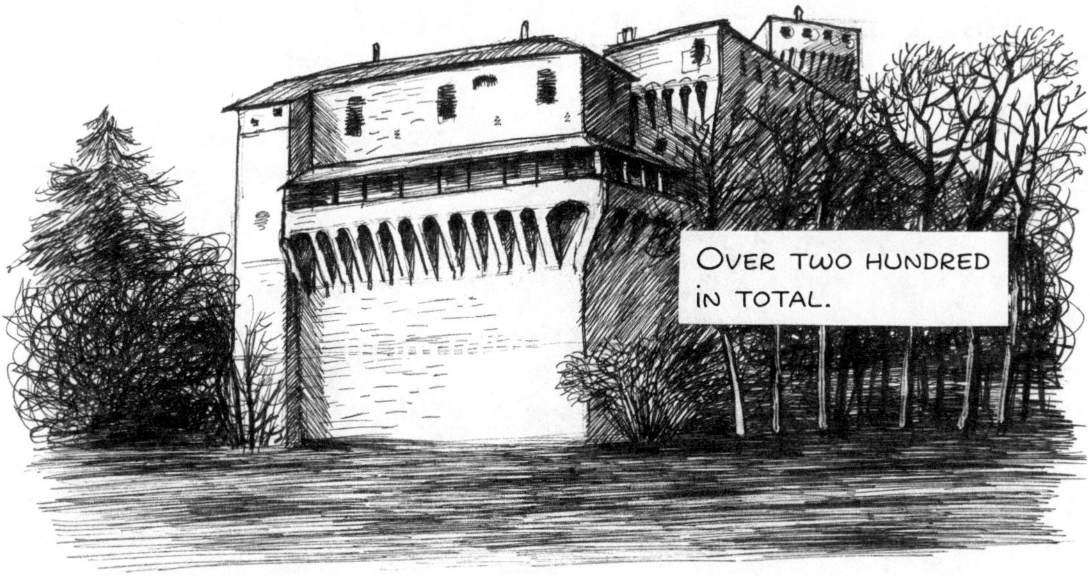
Over two hundred in total.

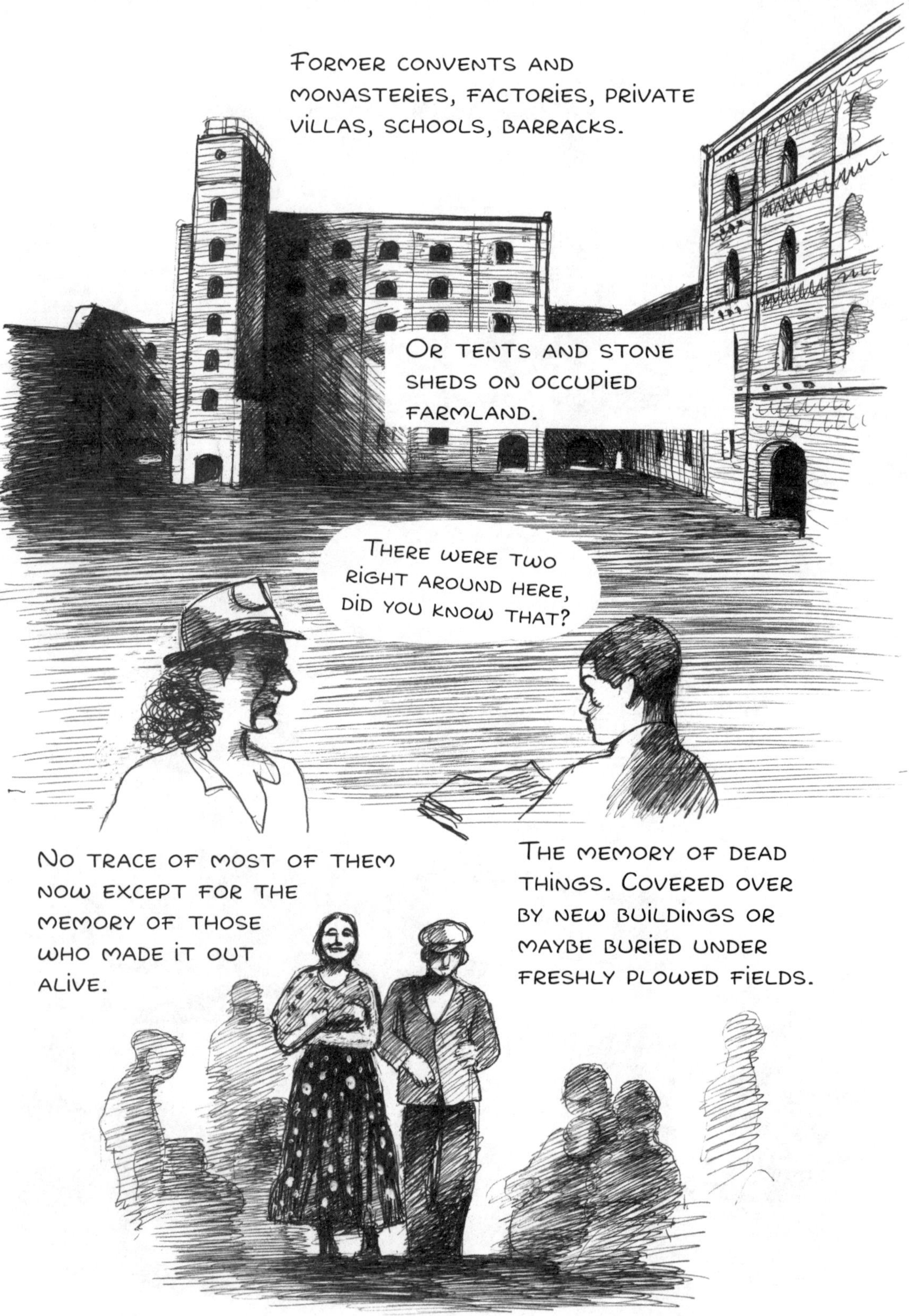
FORMER CONVENTS AND MONASTERIES, FACTORIES, PRIVATE VILLAS, SCHOOLS, BARRACKS.
OR TENTS AND STONE SHEDS ON OCCUPIED FARMLAND.
THERE WERE TWO RIGHT AROUND HERE, DID YOU KNOW THAT?
NO TRACE OF MOST OF THEM NOW EXCEPT FOR THE MEMORY OF THOSE WHO MADE IT OUT ALIVE.
THE MEMORY OF DEAD THINGS. COVERED OVER BY NEW BUILDINGS OR MAYBE BURIED UNDER FRESHLY PLOWED FIELDS.

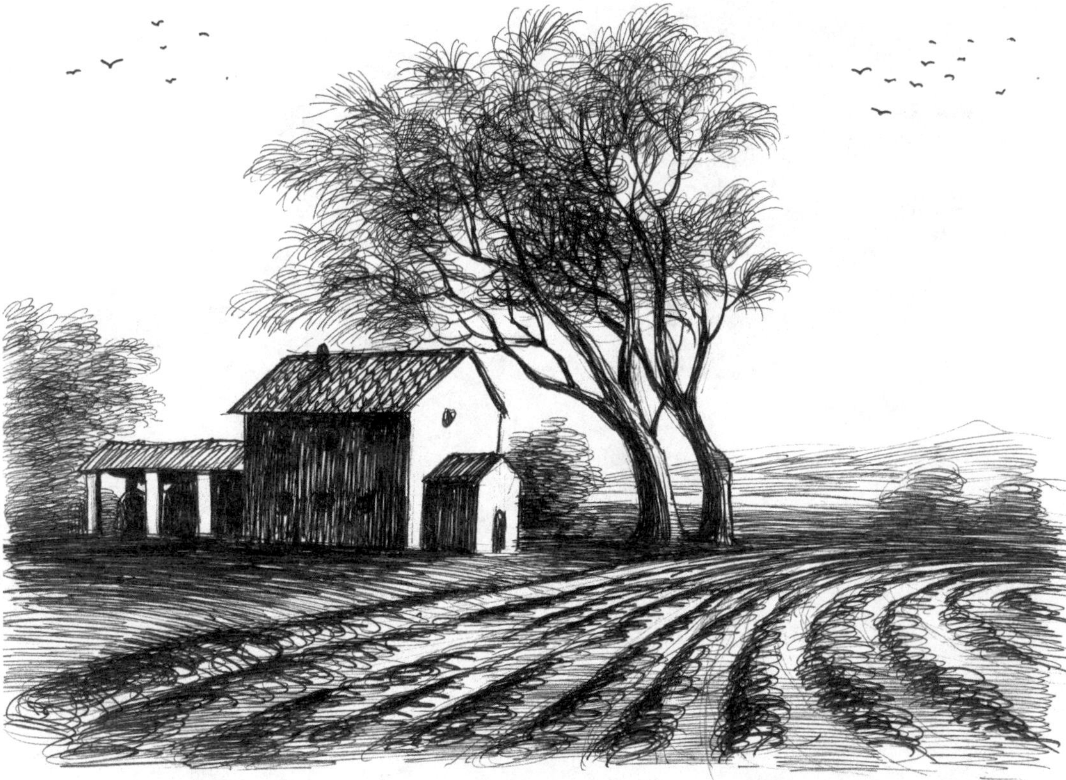

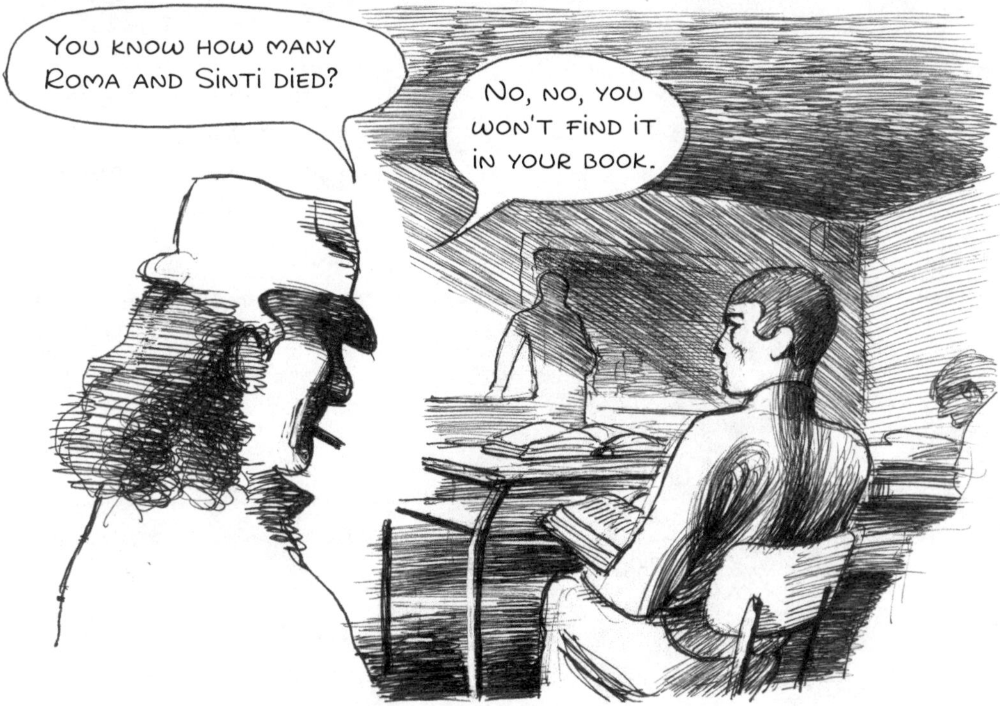
You know how many Roma and Sinti died?
No, no, you won't find it in your book.

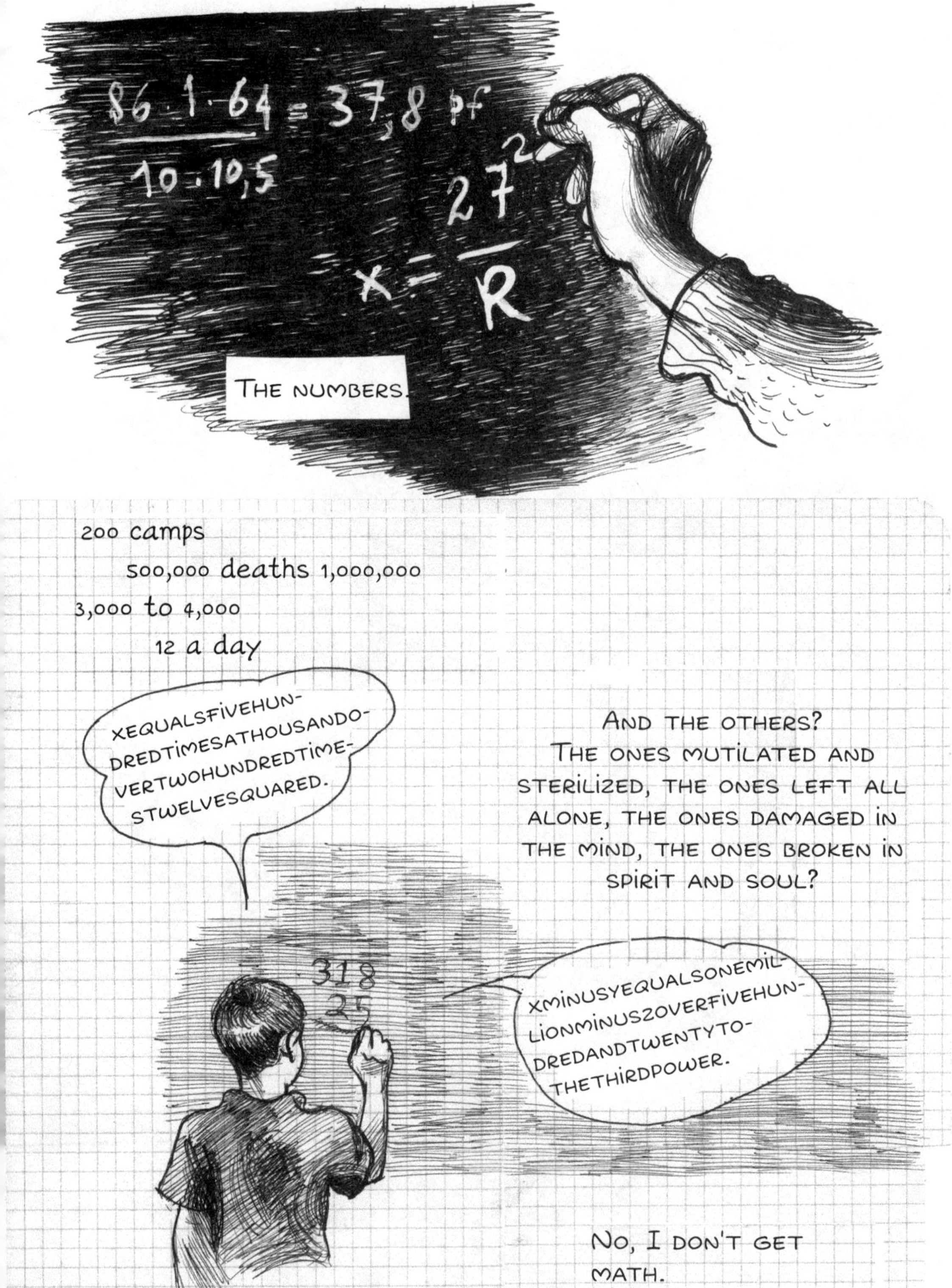
86·1·64 = 37,8 pf
10·10,5
x = 27²/R
THE NUMBERS.
200 camps
500,000 deaths 1,000,000
3,000 to 4,000
12 a day
XEQUALSFIVEHUNDREDTIMESATHOUSANDOVERTWOHUNDREDTIMESTWELVESQUARED.
AND THE OTHERS? THE ONES MUTILATED AND STERILIZED, THE ONES LEFT ALL ALONE, THE ONES DAMAGED IN THE MIND, THE ONES BROKEN IN SPIRIT AND SOUL?
318
25
XMINUSYEQUALSONEMILLIONMINUSZOVERFIVEHUNDREDANDTWENTYTOTHETHIRDPOWER.
NO, I DON'T GET MATH.

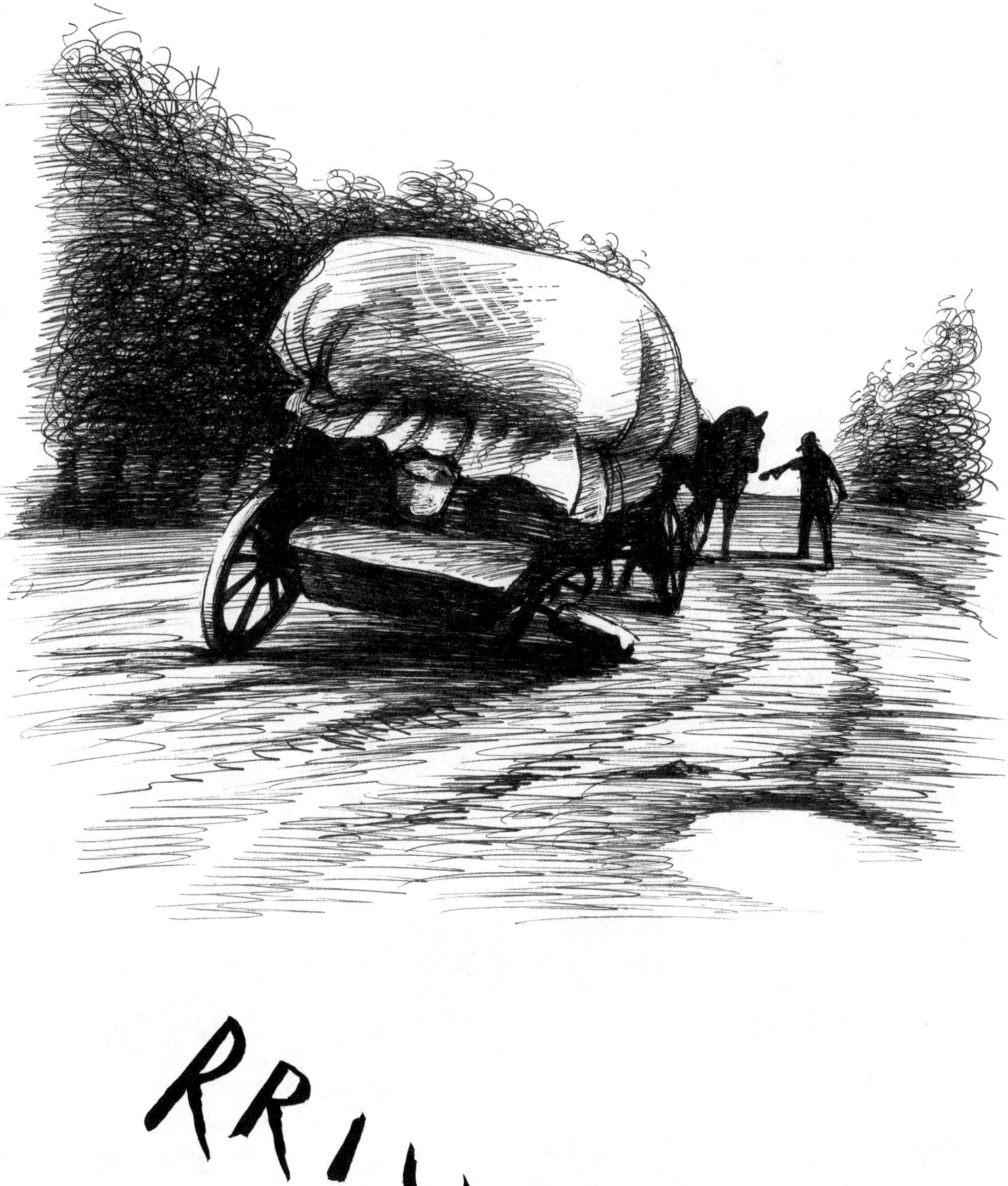
RRIIIIIIII...

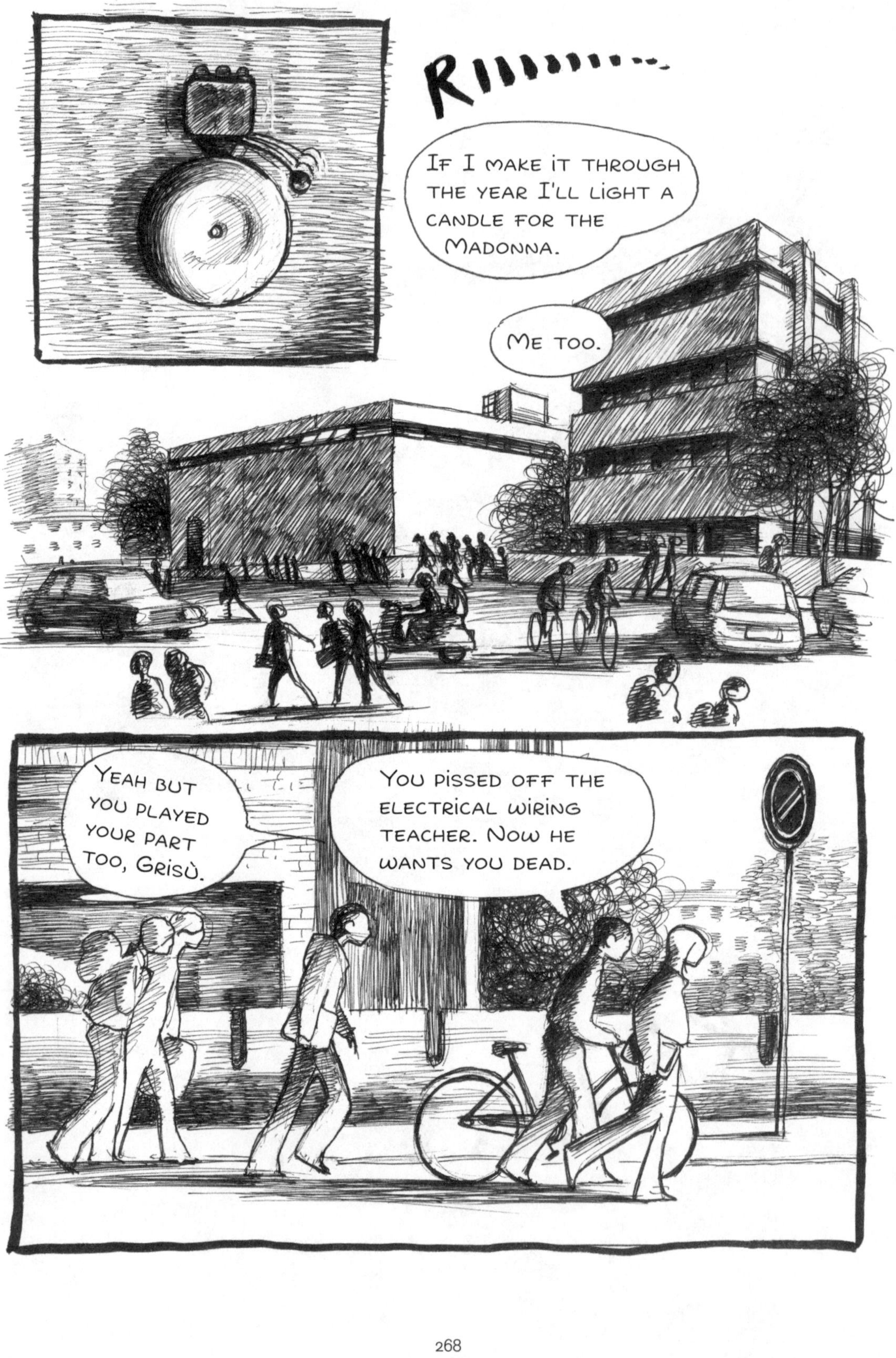
Riiiiiiii...
If I make it through the year I'll light a candle for the Madonna.
Me too.
Yeah but you played your part too, Grisù.
You pissed off the electrical wiring teacher. Now he wants you dead.

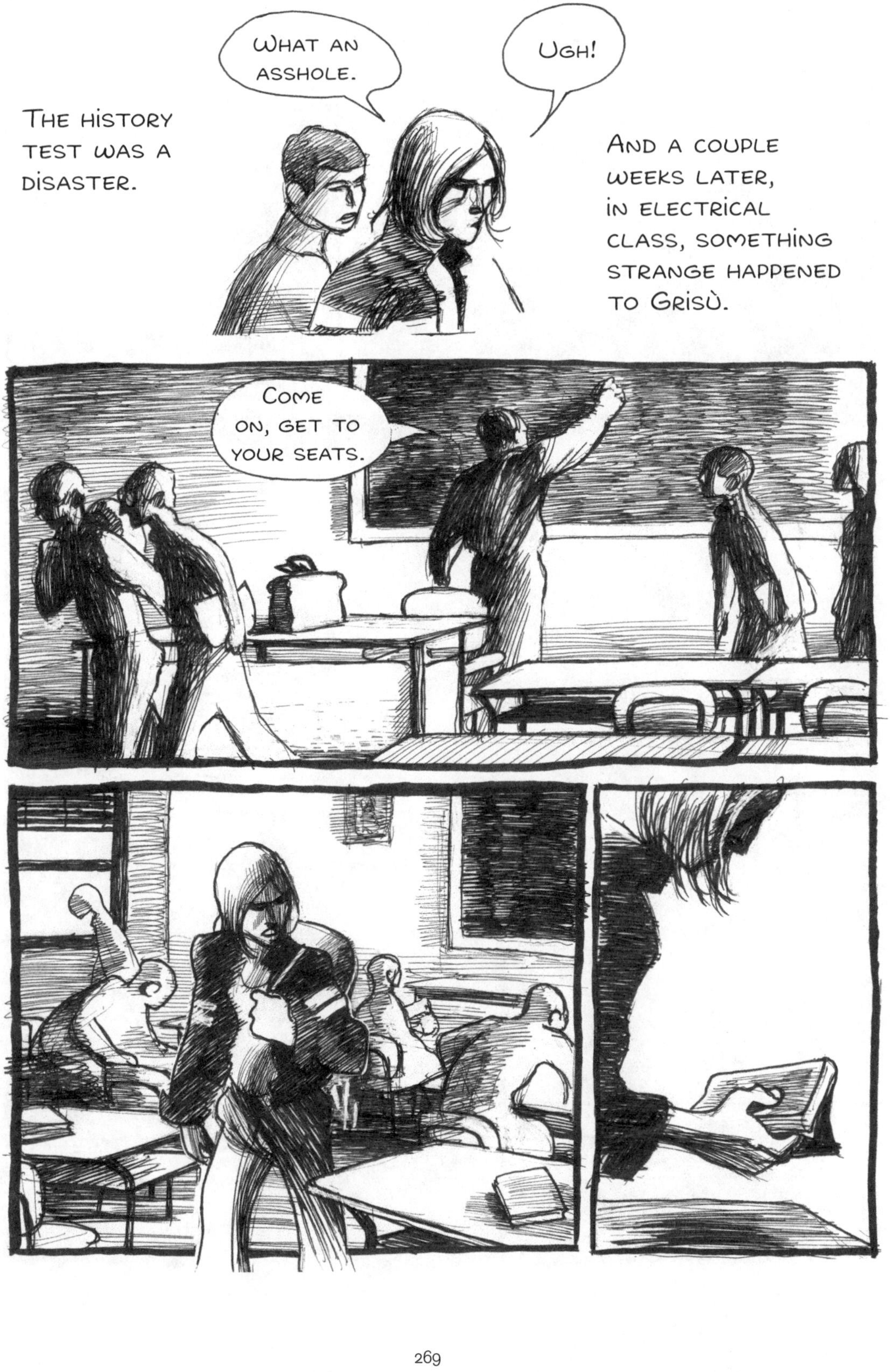
The history test was a disaster.
What an asshole.
Ugh!
And a couple weeks later, in electrical class, something strange happened to Grisù.
Come on, get to your seats.

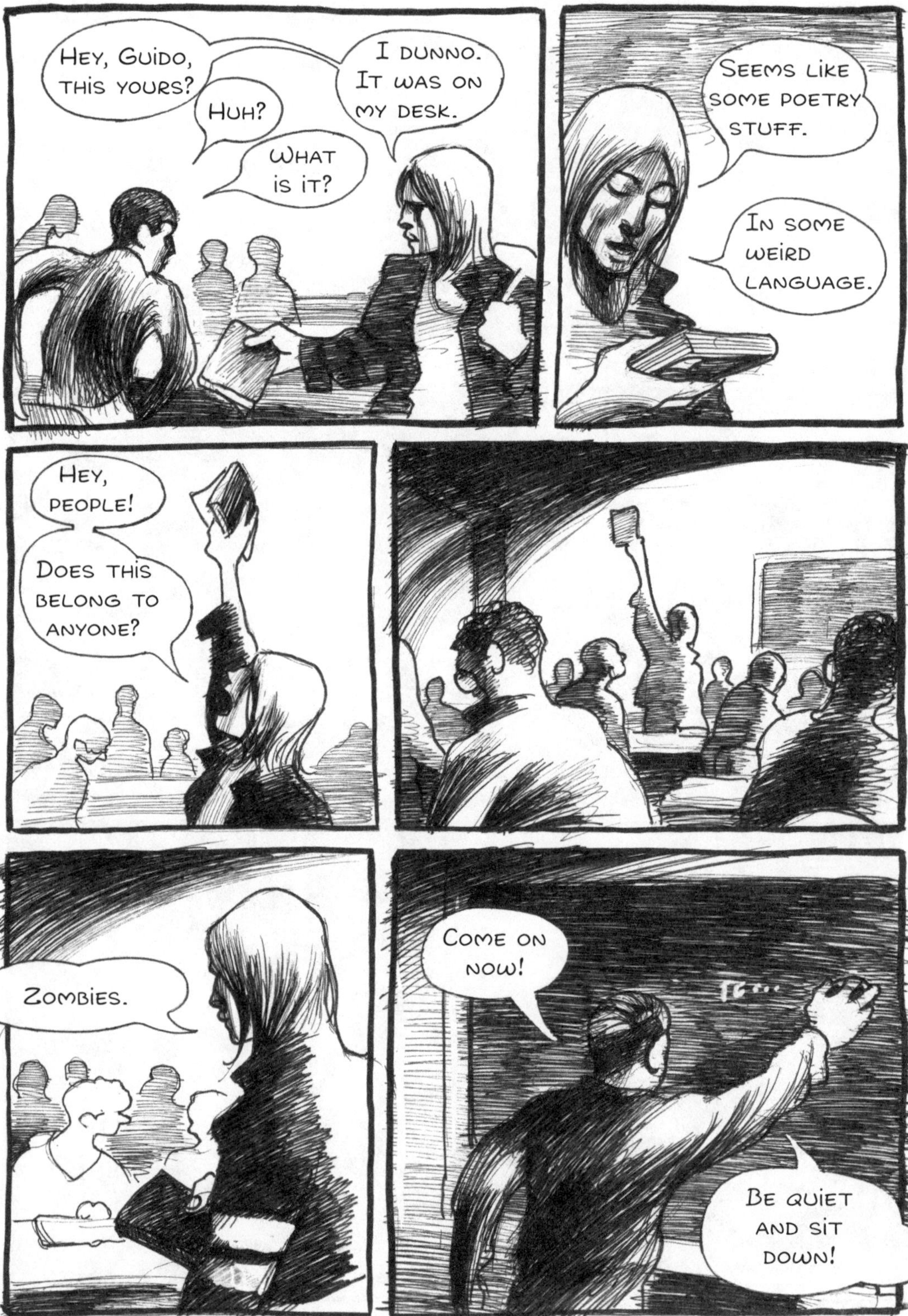
Hey, Guido, this yours?
Huh?
What is it?
I dunno. It was on my desk.
Seems like some poetry stuff.
In some weird language.
Hey, people!
Does this belong to anyone?
Zombies.
Come on now!
Be quiet and sit down!

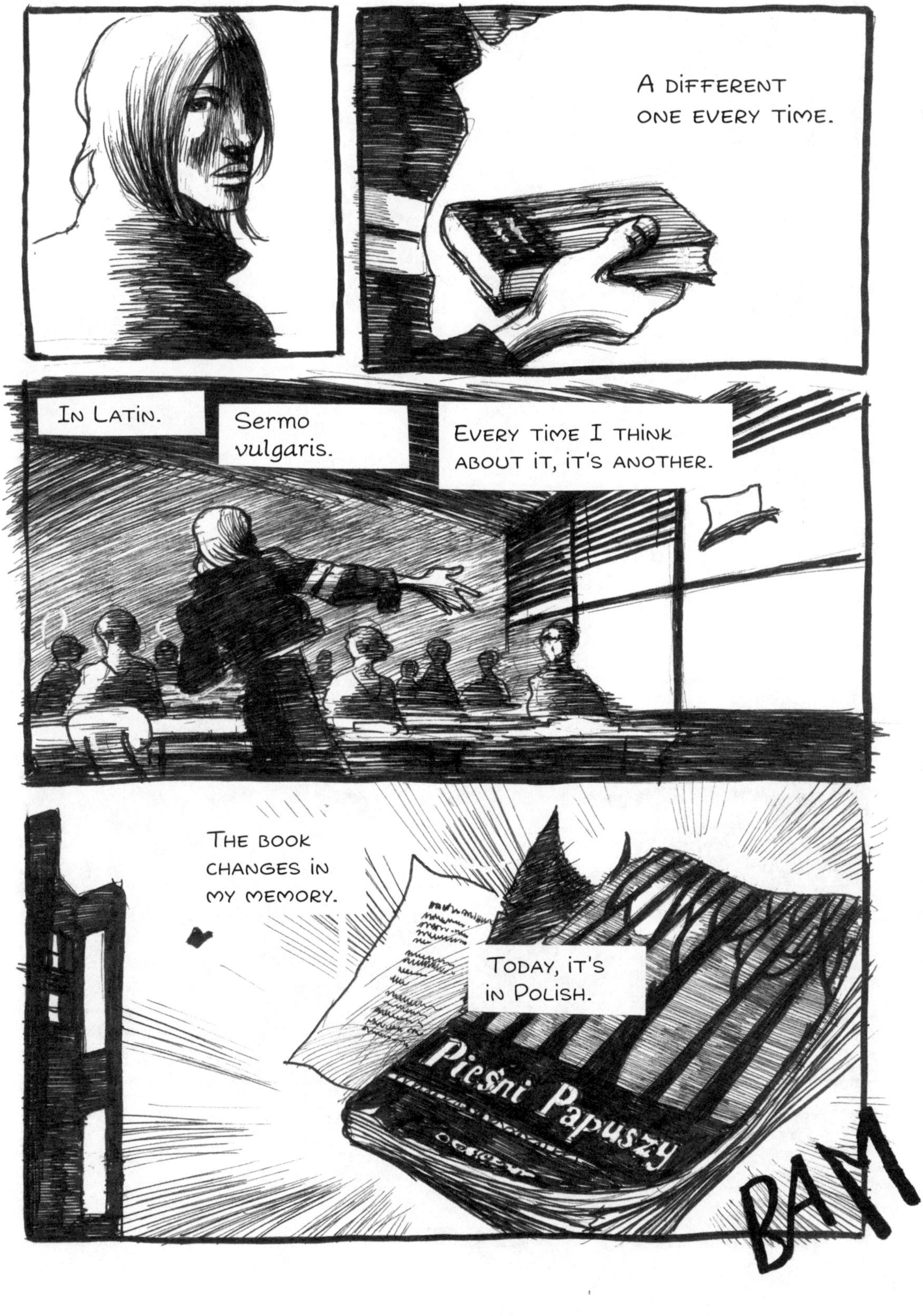
A DIFFERENT ONE EVERY TIME.
IN LATIN.
Sermo vulgaris.
EVERY TIME I THINK ABOUT IT, IT'S ANOTHER.
THE BOOK CHANGES IN MY MEMORY.
TODAY, IT'S IN POLISH.
Pieśni Papuszy
BAM

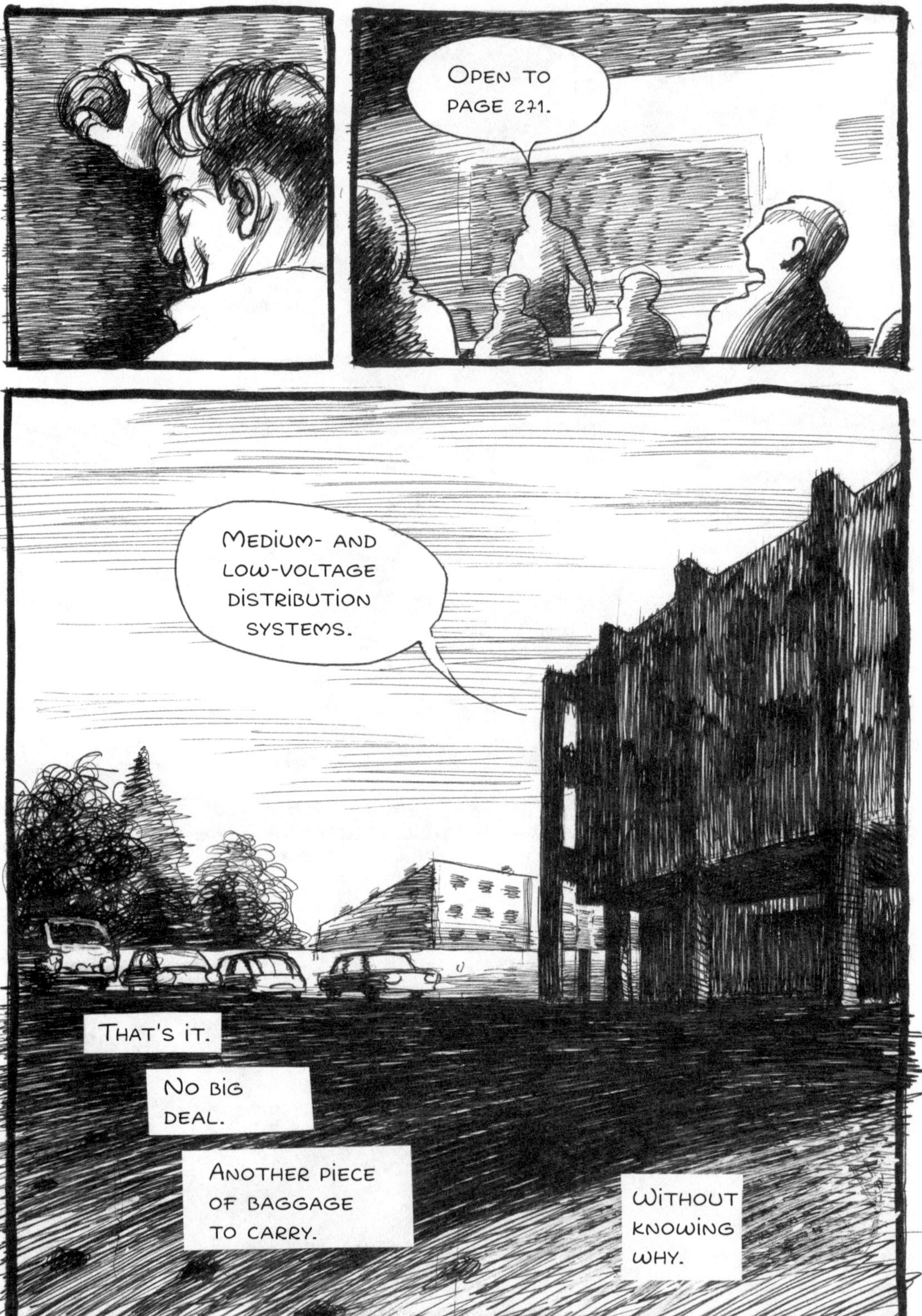
Open to page 271.
Medium- and low-voltage distribution systems.
That's it.
No big deal.
Another piece of baggage to carry.
Without knowing why.

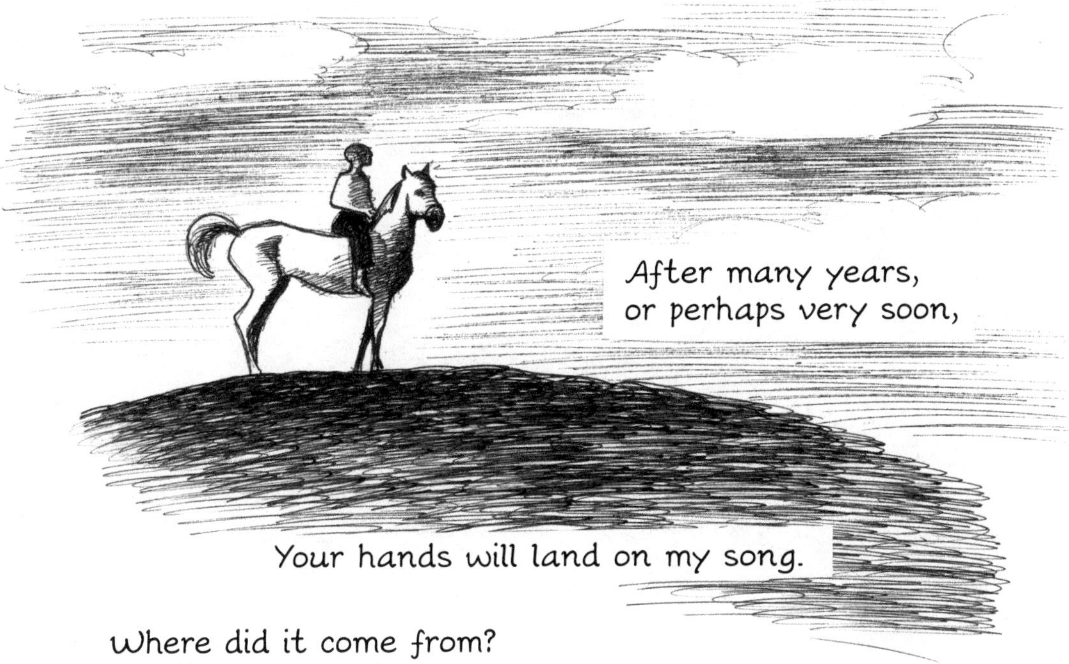
After many years,
or perhaps very soon,
Your hands will land on my song.

Where did it come from?
Daytime or sleep?

Then you'll remember me and think-
Truth or legend?

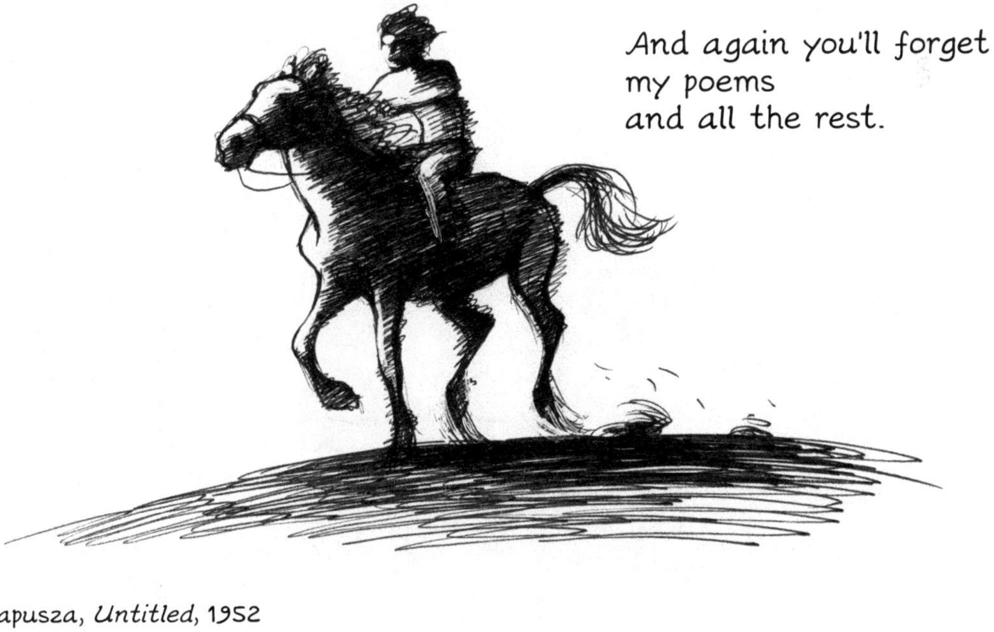
And again you'll forget
my poems
and all the rest.

*Papusza, *Untitled*, 1952

IX

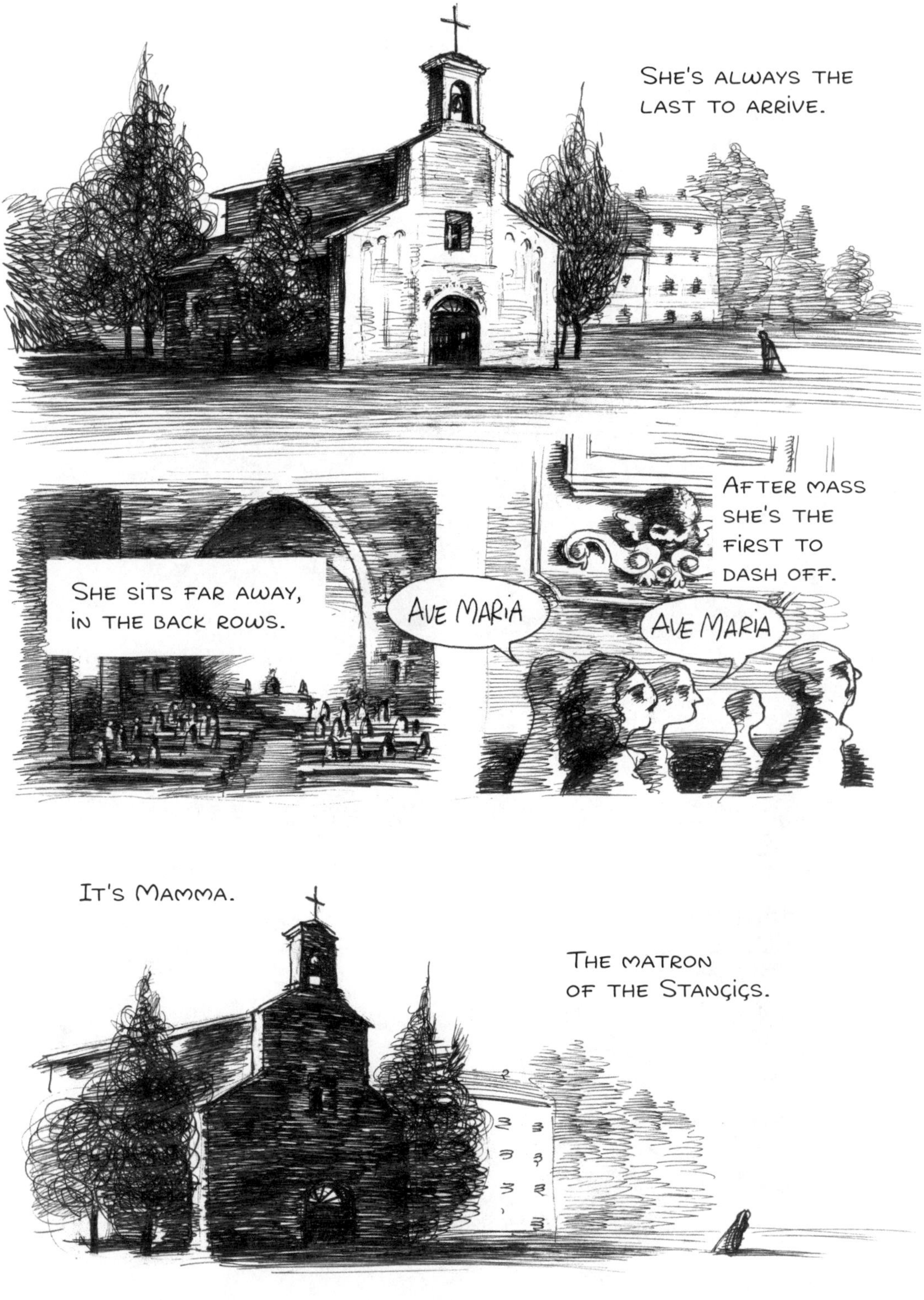

She's always the last to arrive.
She sits far away, in the back rows.
Ave Maria
After mass she's the first to dash off.
Ave Maria
It's Mamma.
The matron of the Stançiçs.

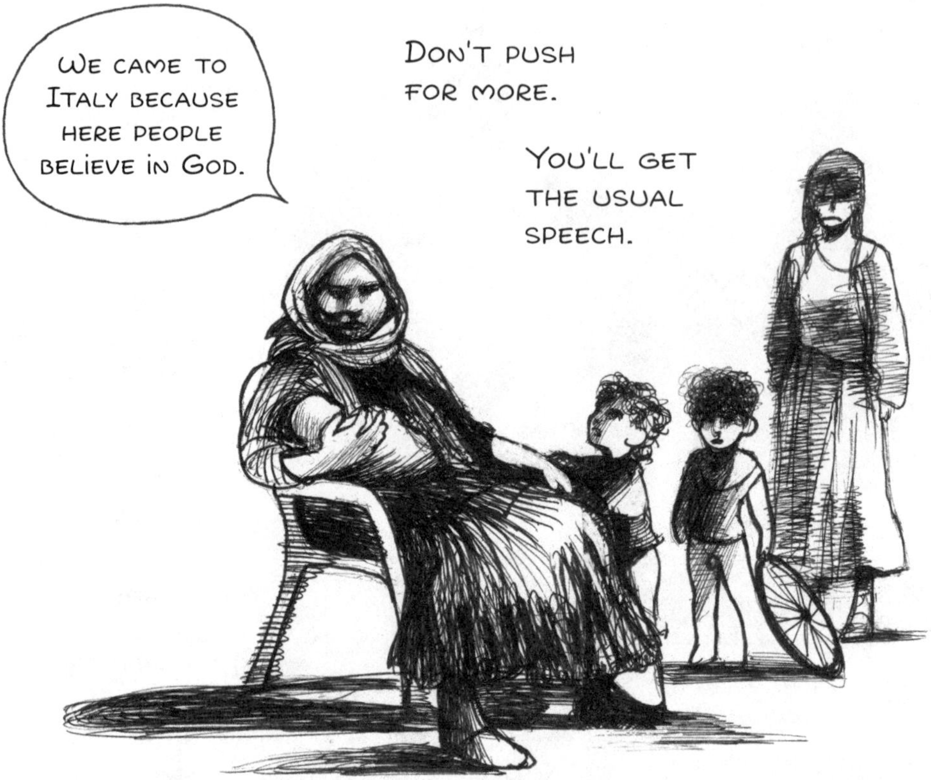
WE CAME TO ITALY BECAUSE HERE PEOPLE BELIEVE IN GOD.
DON'T PUSH FOR MORE.
YOU'LL GET THE USUAL SPEECH.

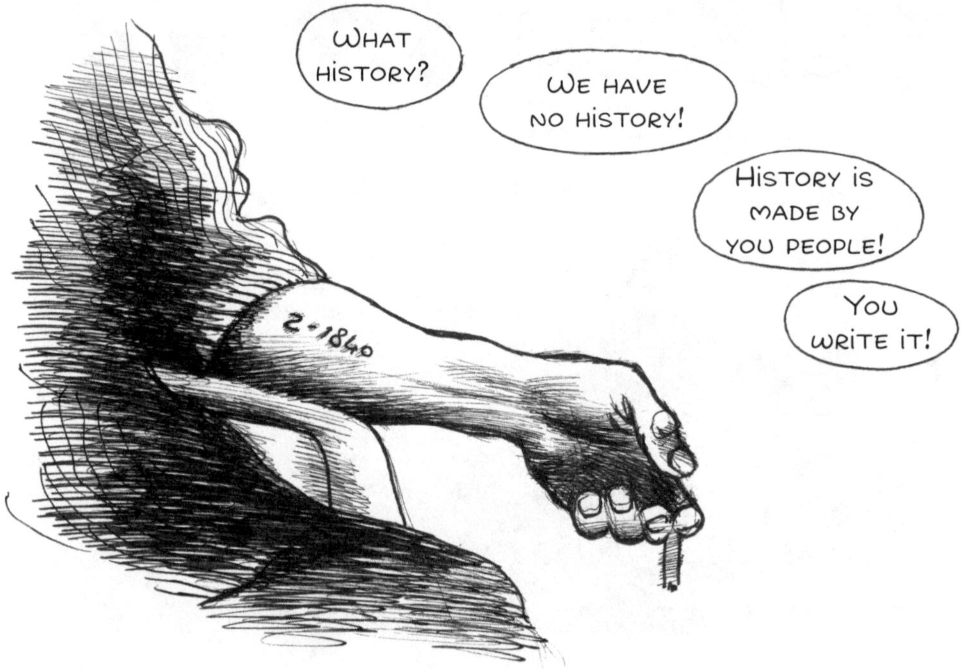
WHAT HISTORY?
WE HAVE NO HISTORY!
HISTORY IS MADE BY YOU PEOPLE!
YOU WRITE IT!
Z-1840

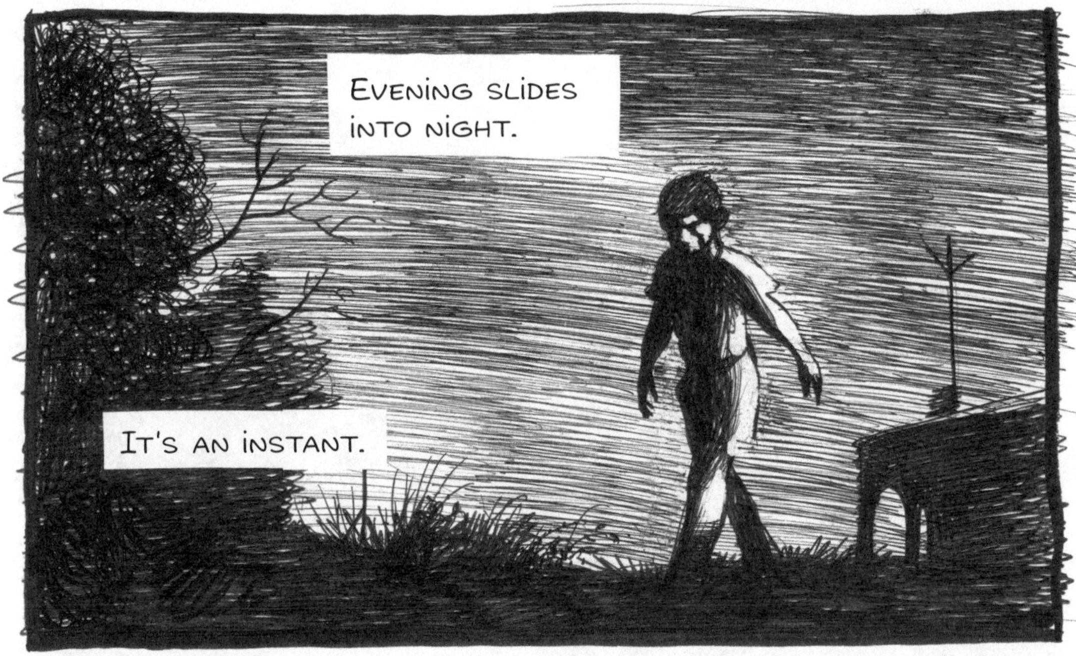
Evening slides into night.
It's an instant.

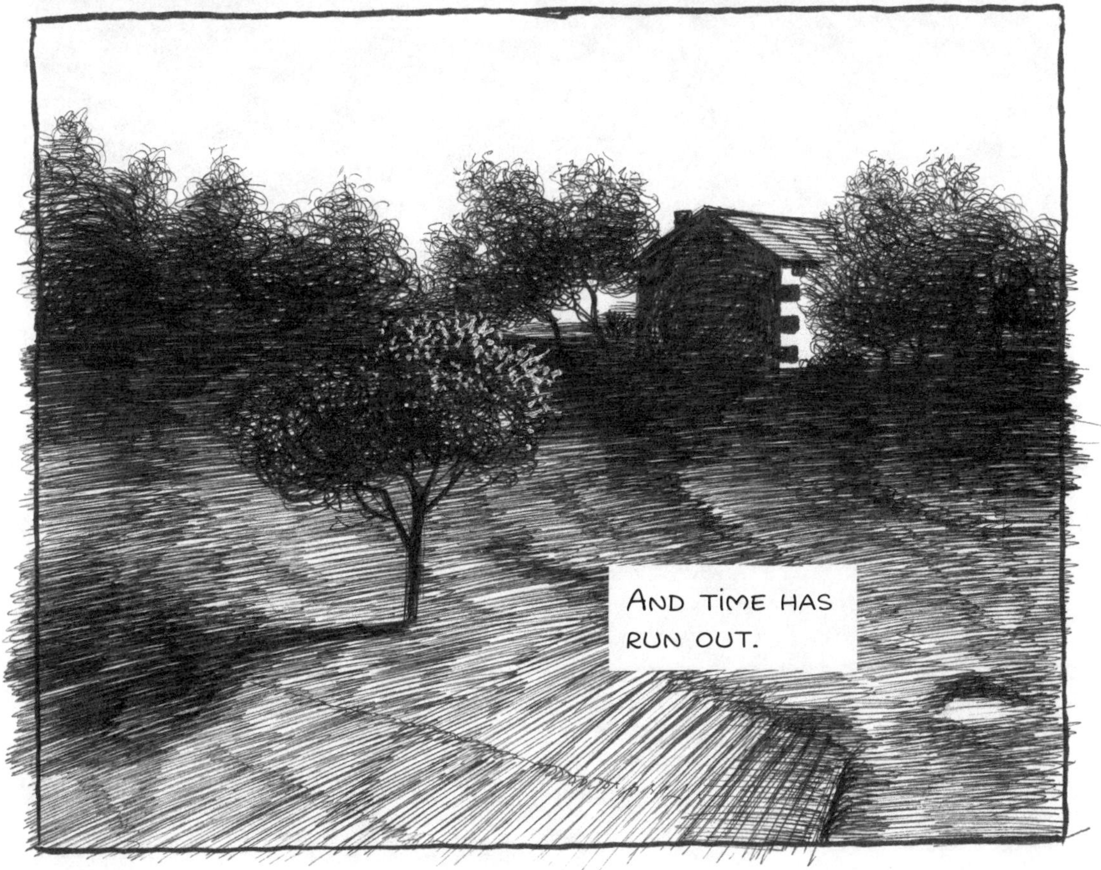
And time has run out.

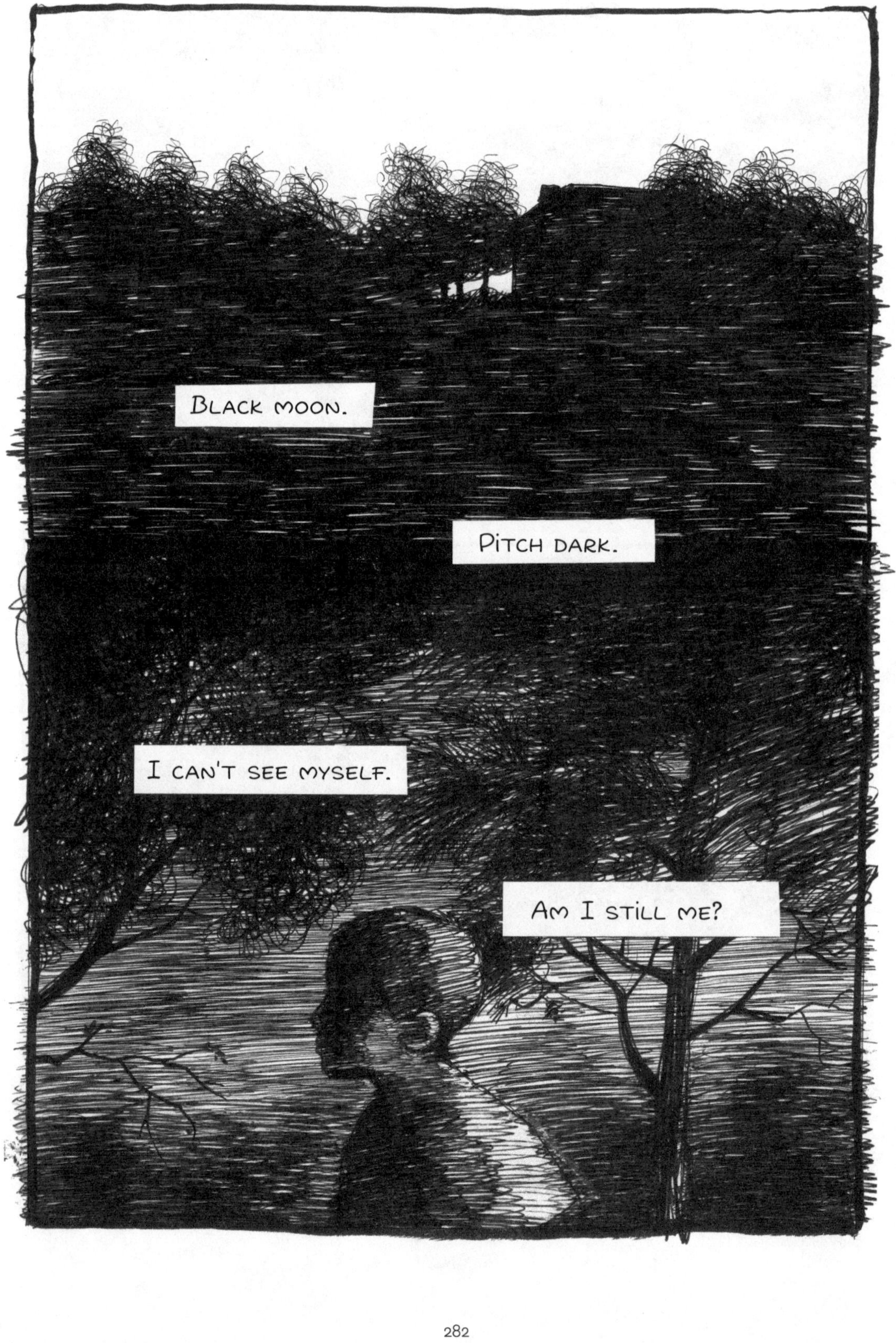
Black moon.
Pitch dark.
I can't see myself.
Am I still me?

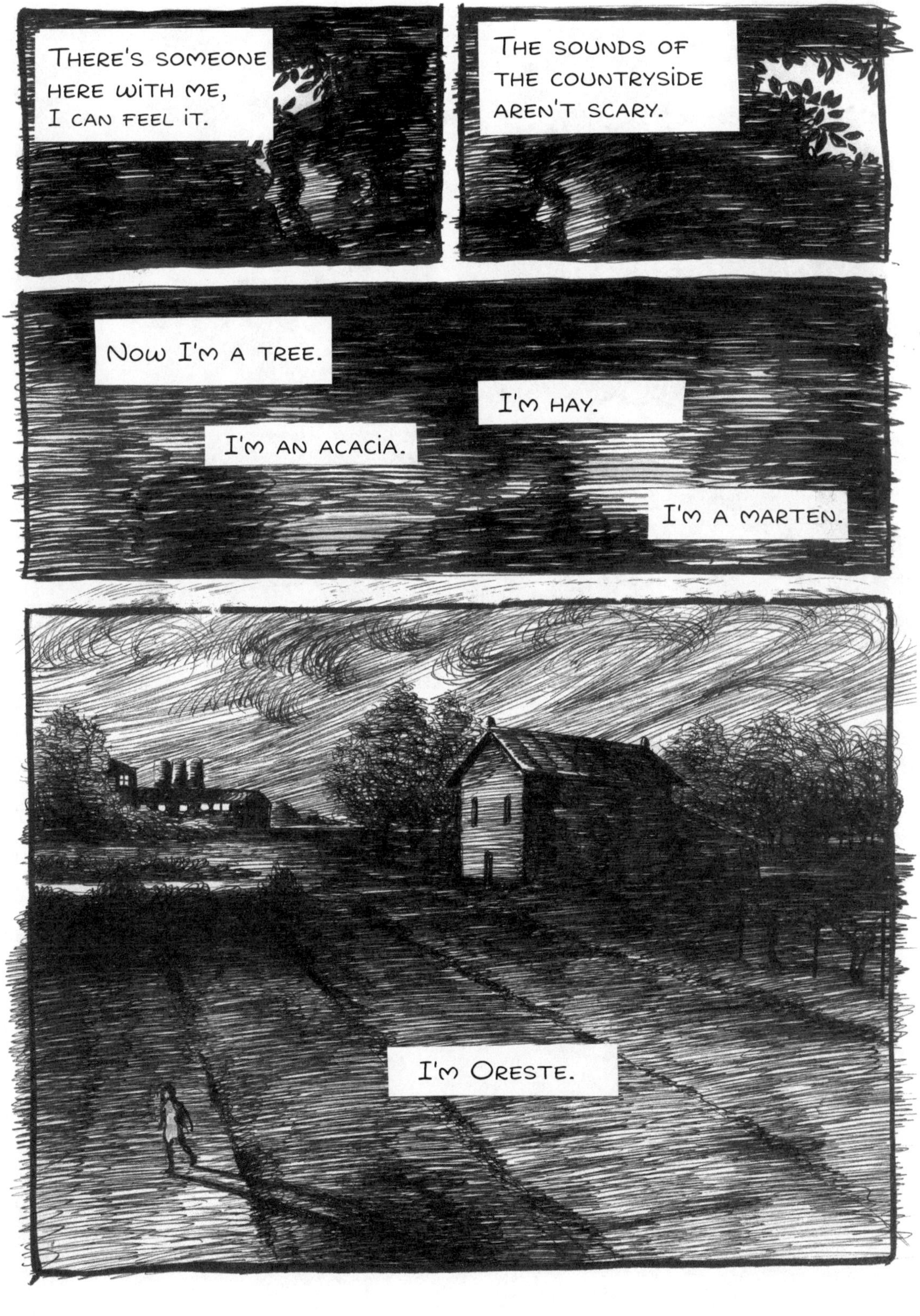
There's someone here with me, I can feel it.
The sounds of the countryside aren't scary.
Now I'm a tree.
I'm hay.
I'm an acacia.
I'm a marten.
I'm Oreste.

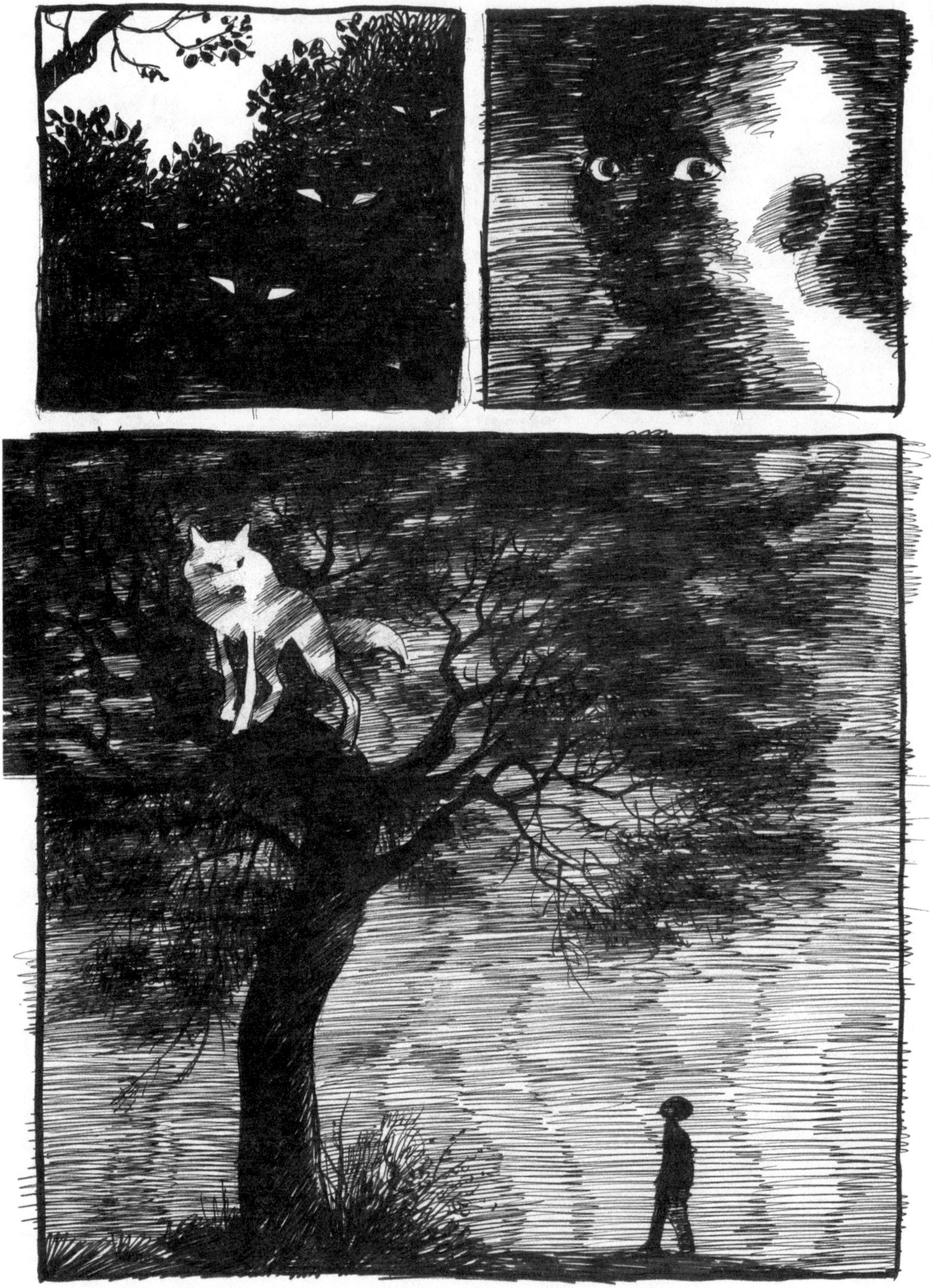

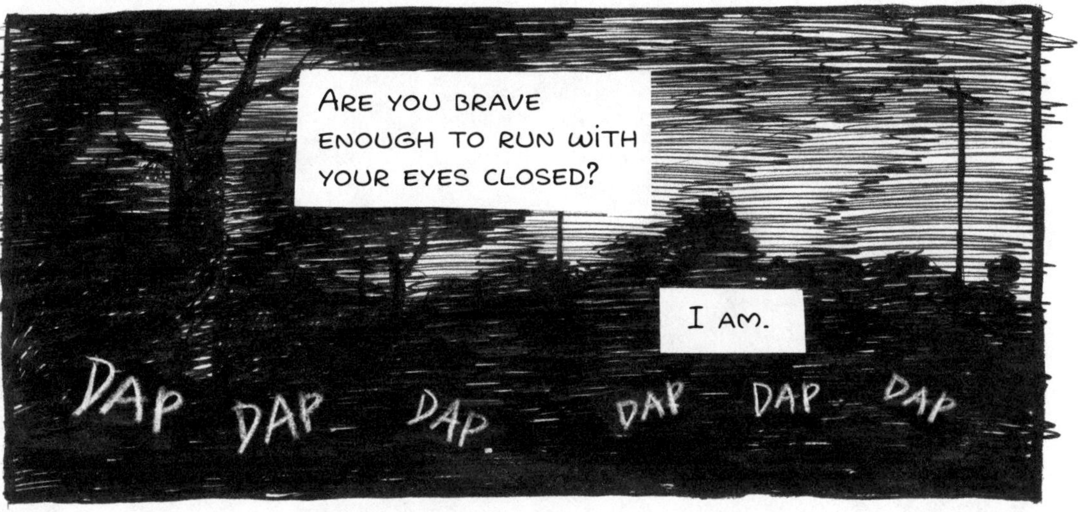
ARE YOU BRAVE ENOUGH TO RUN WITH YOUR EYES CLOSED?
I AM.
DAP DAP DAP DAP DAP DAP

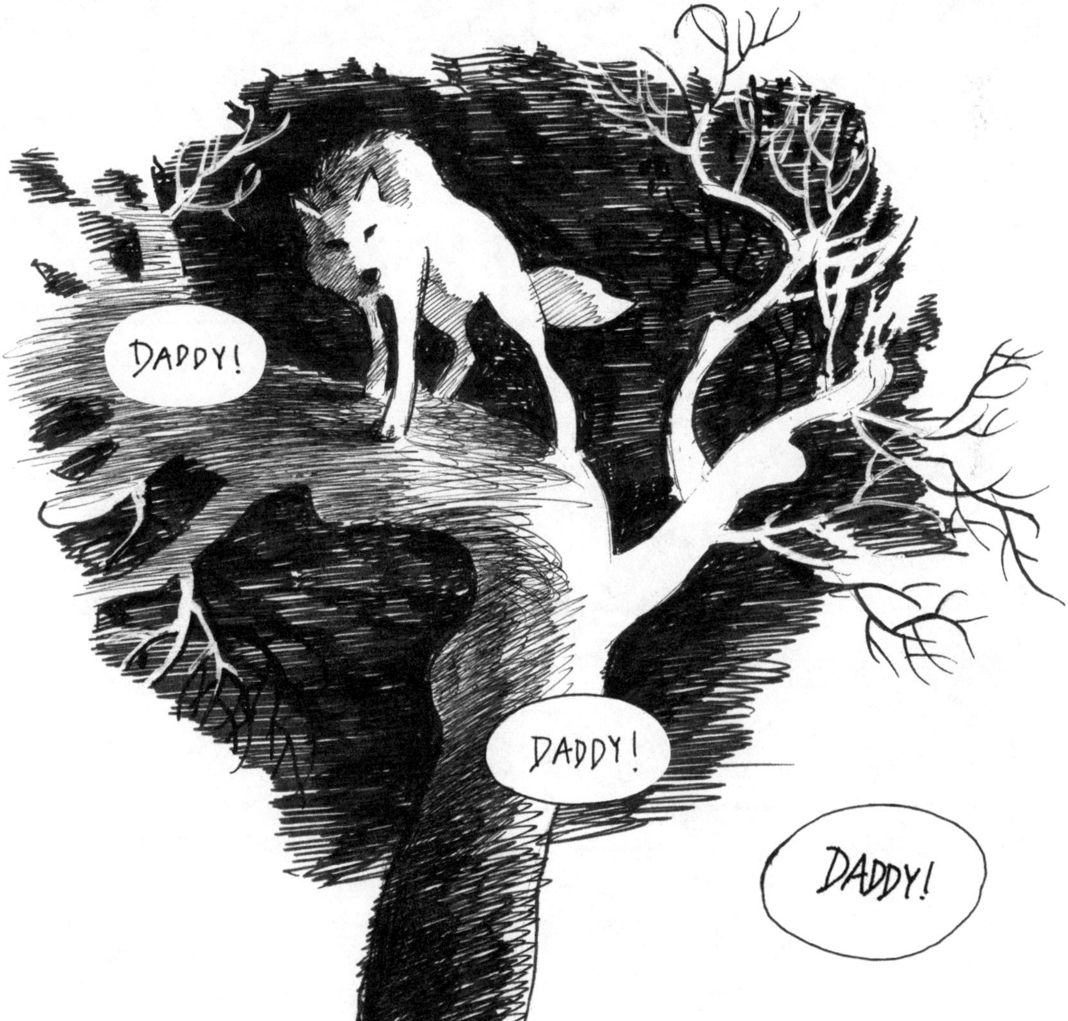
DADDY!
DADDY!
DADDY!

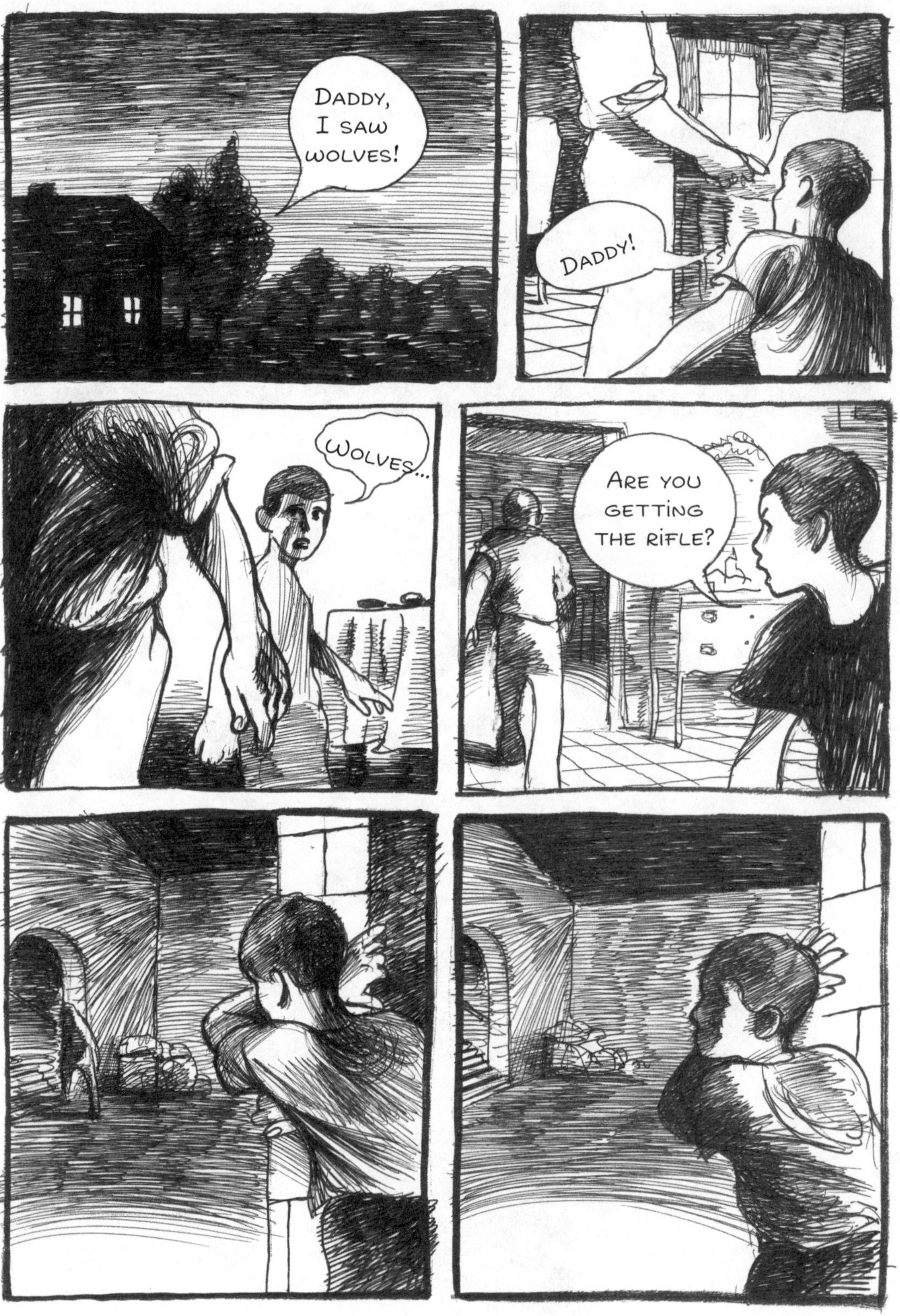
DADDY, I SAW WOLVES!
DADDY!
WOLVES...
ARE YOU GETTING THE RIFLE?

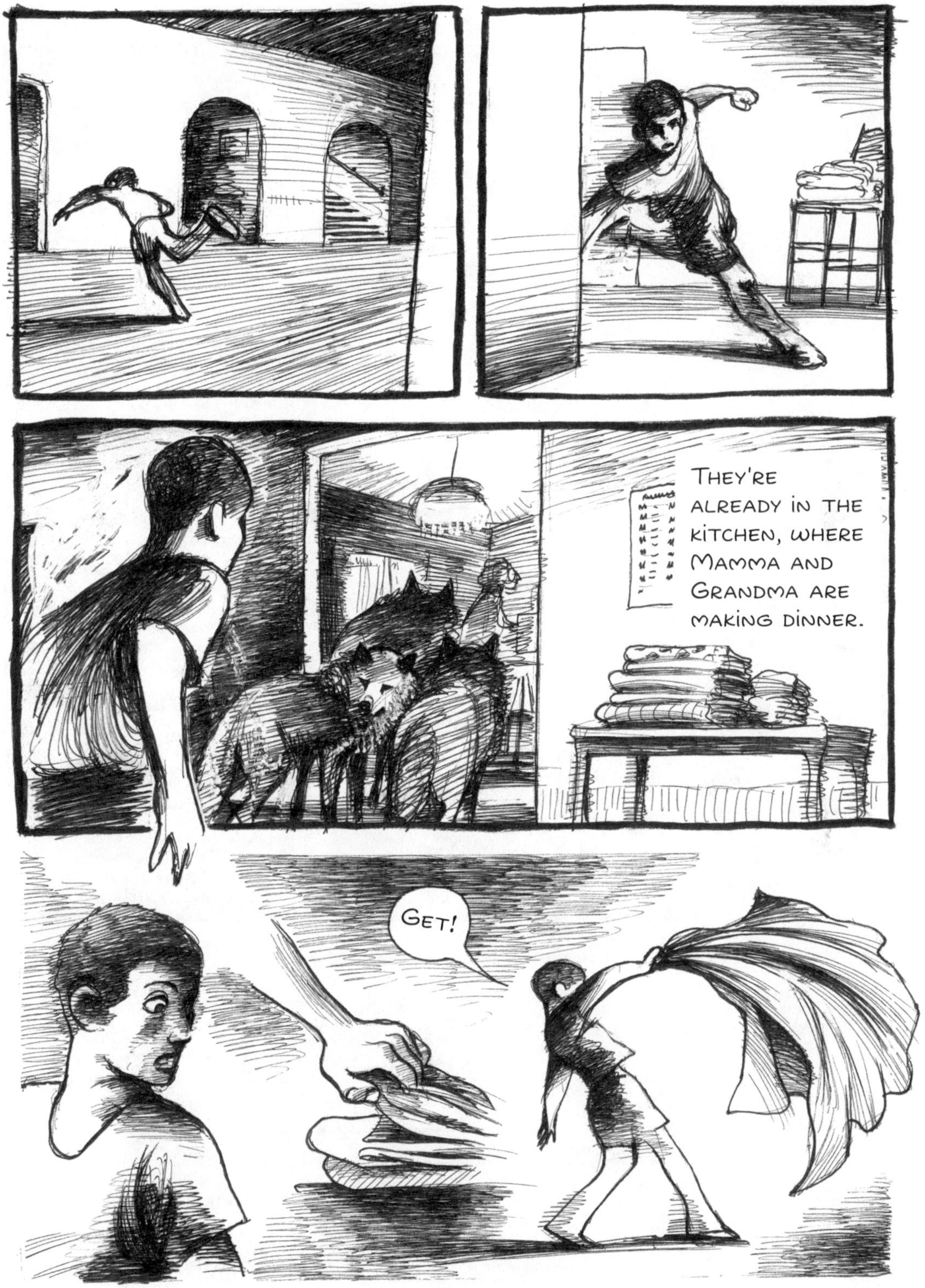
They're already in the kitchen, where Mamma and Grandma are making dinner.
Get!

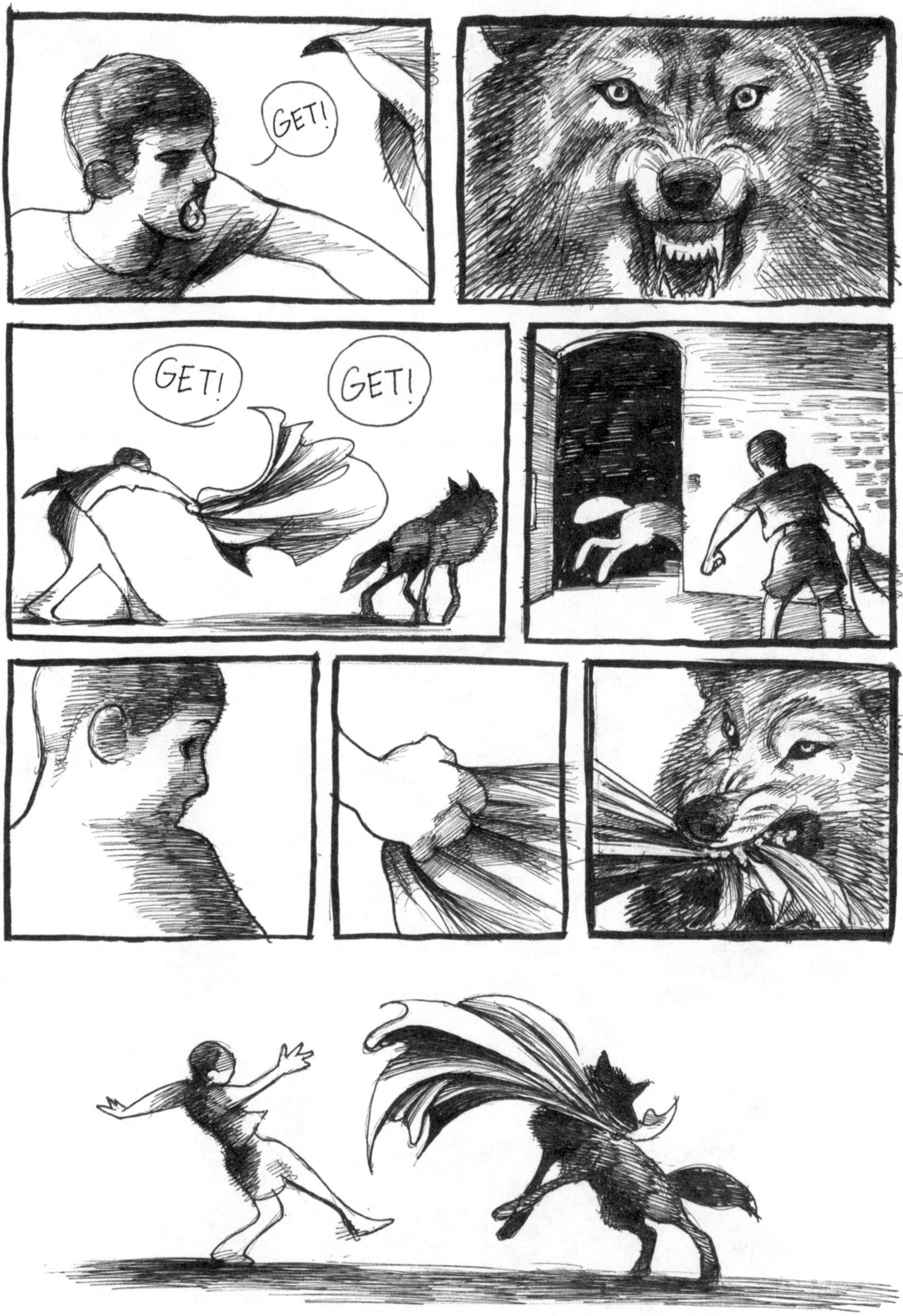
GET!
GET!
GET!

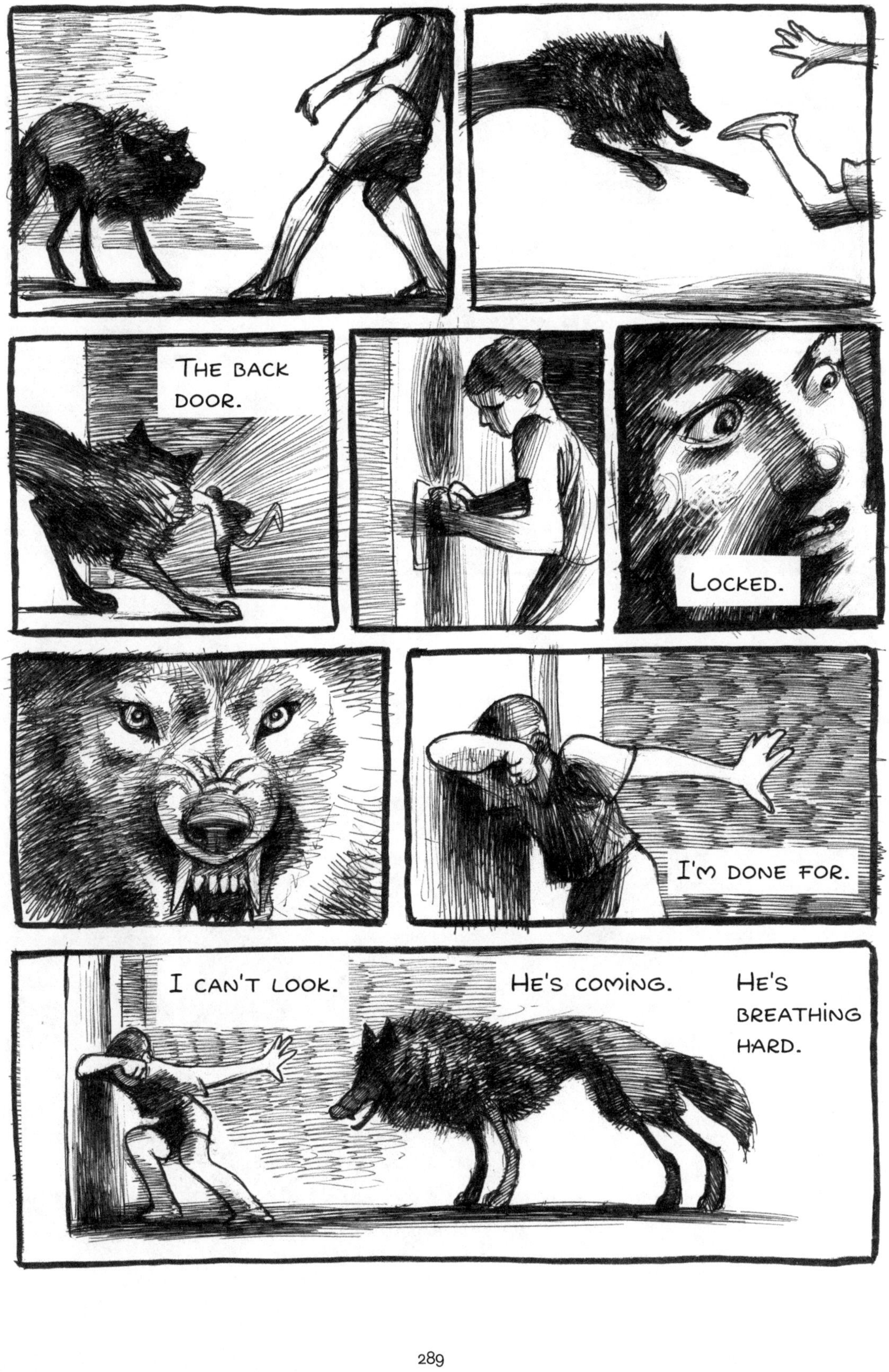
The back door.
Locked.
I'm done for.
I can't look.
He's coming.
He's breathing hard.

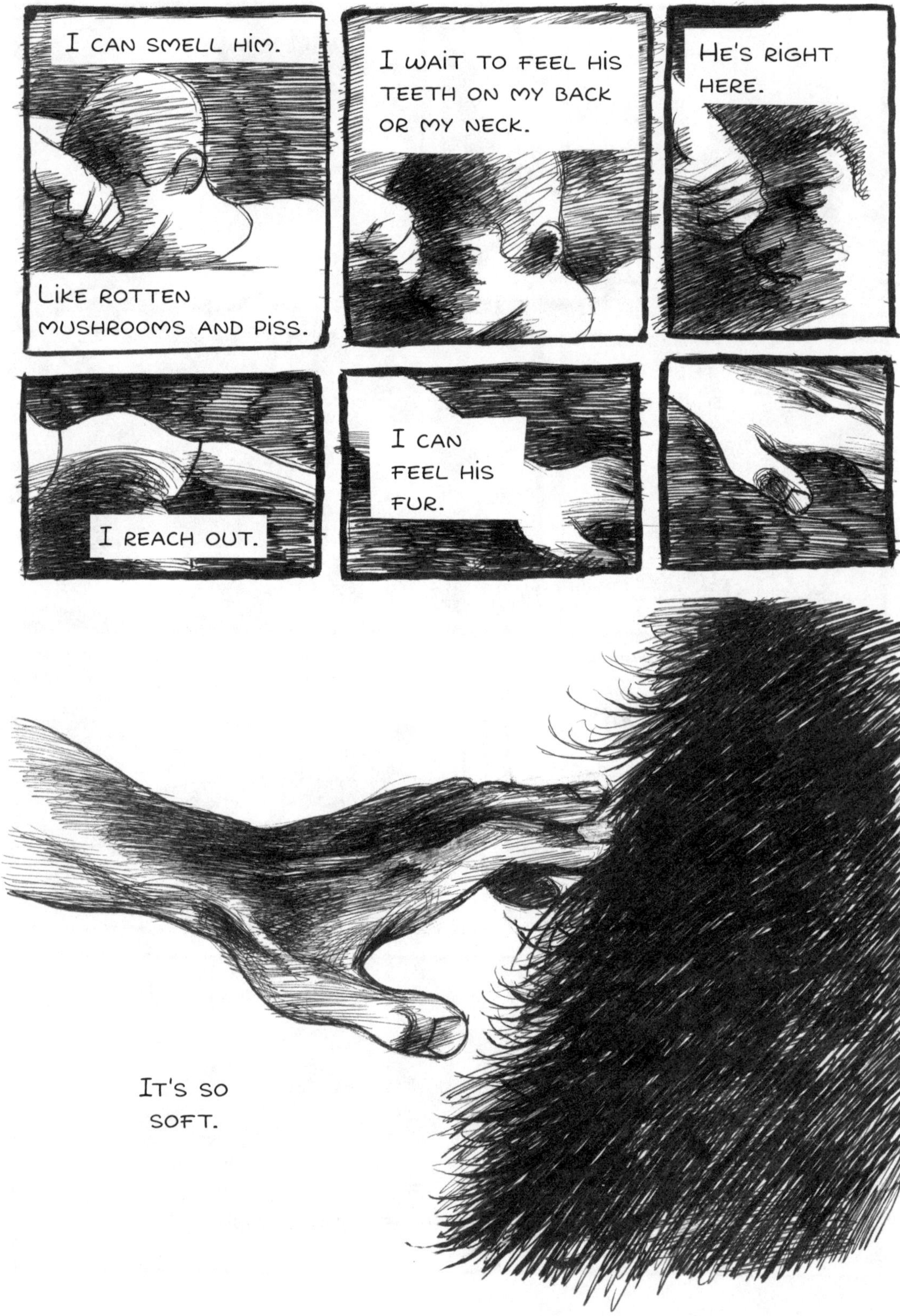
I can smell him.
Like rotten mushrooms and piss.
I wait to feel his teeth on my back or my neck.
He's right here.
I reach out.
I can feel his fur.
It's so soft.

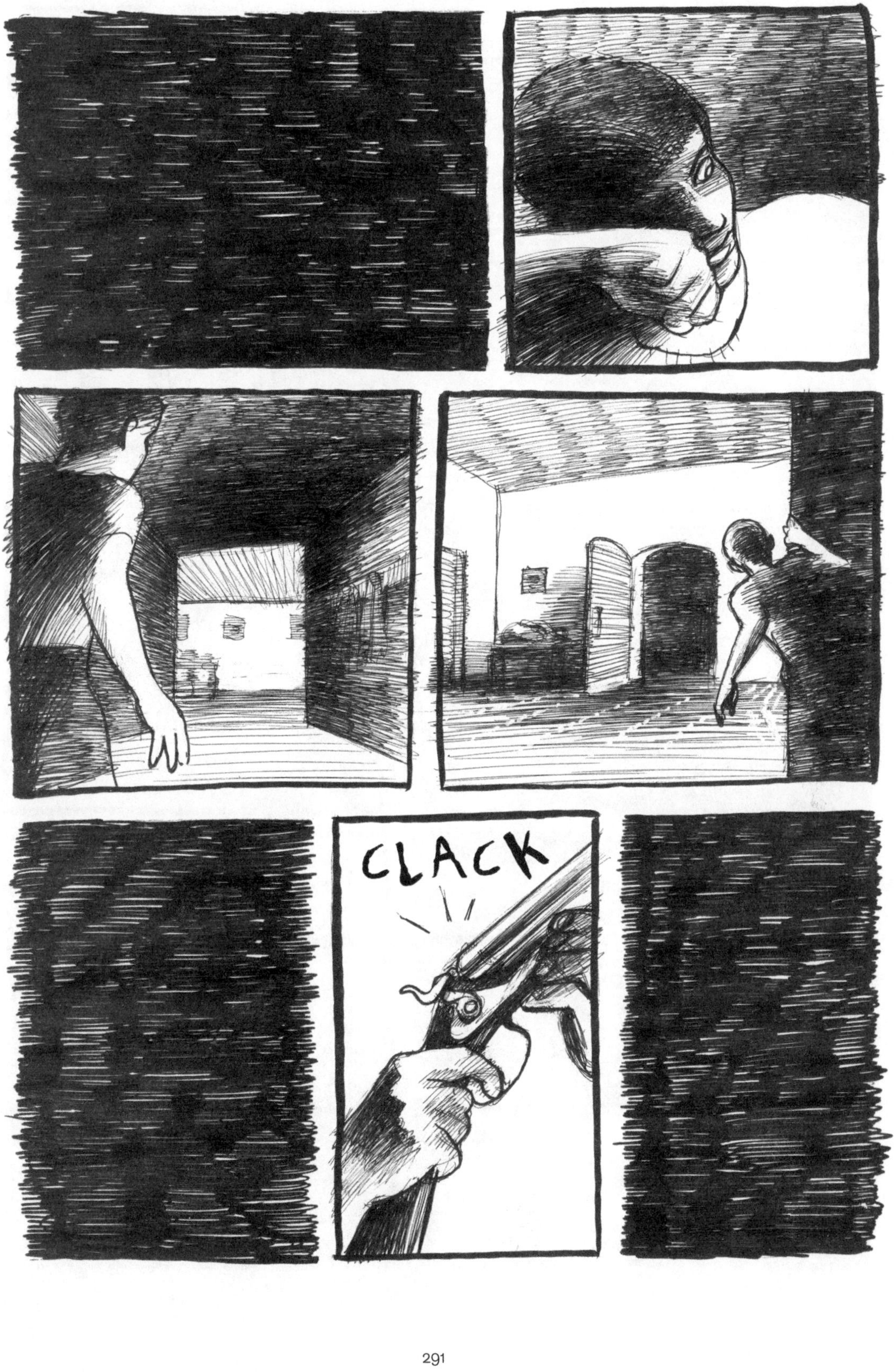
CLACK

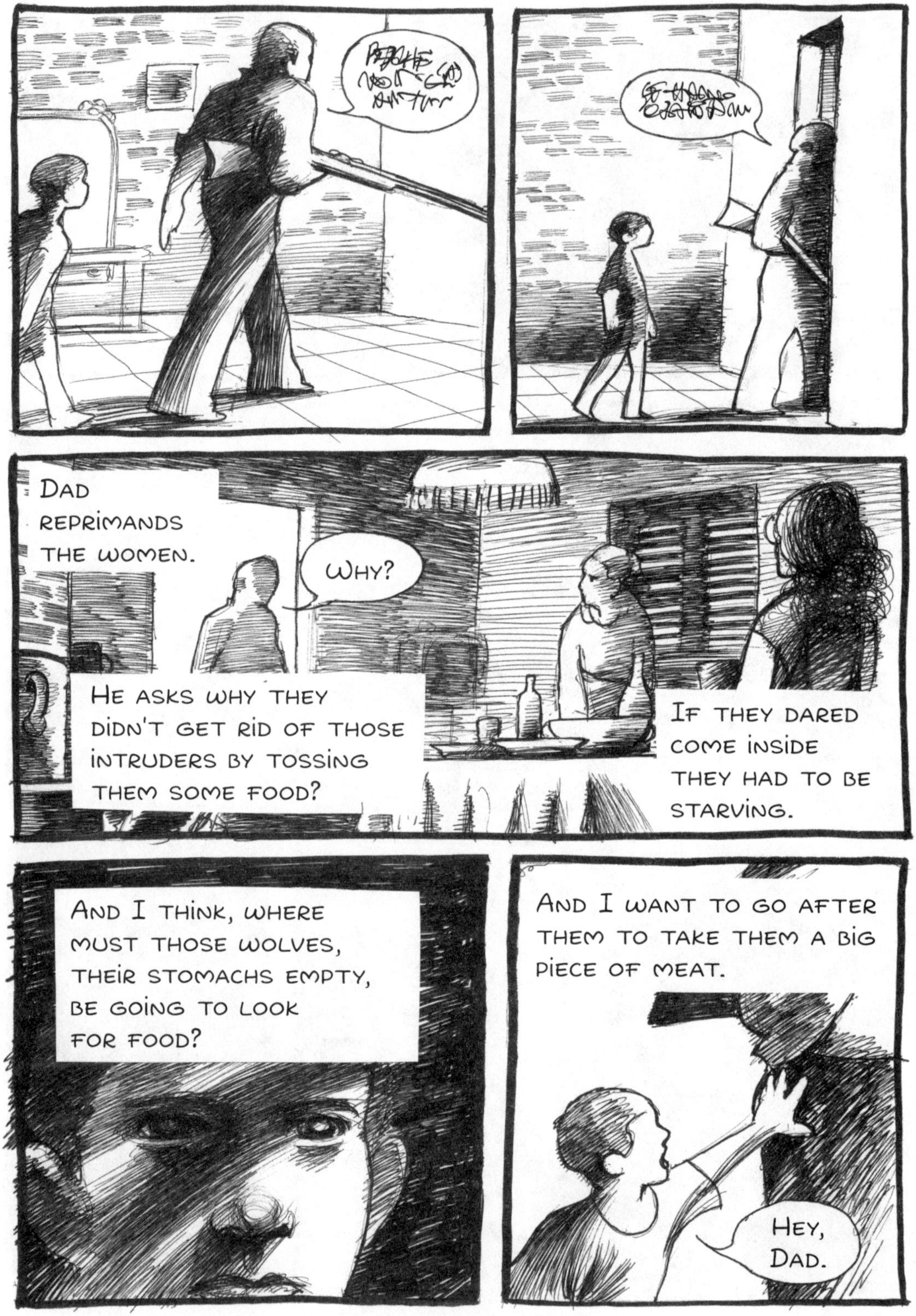
Dad reprimands the women.
Why?
He asks why they didn't get rid of those intruders by tossing them some food?
If they dared come inside they had to be starving.
And I think, where must those wolves, their stomachs empty, be going to look for food?
And I want to go after them to take them a big piece of meat.
Hey, Dad.

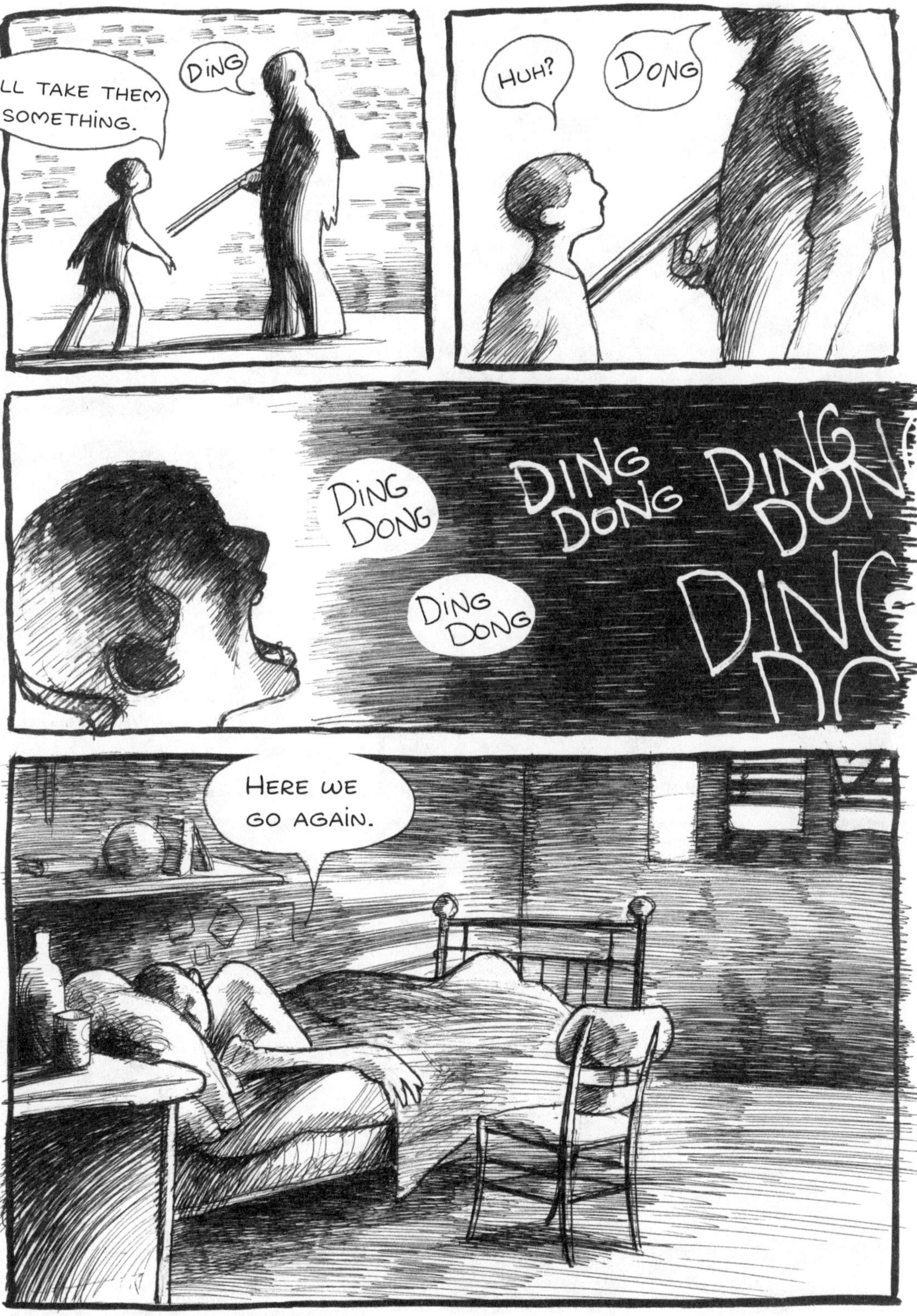
I'LL TAKE THEM SOMETHING.
DING
HUH?
DONG
DING DONG
DING DONG
DING DONG
HERE WE GO AGAIN.

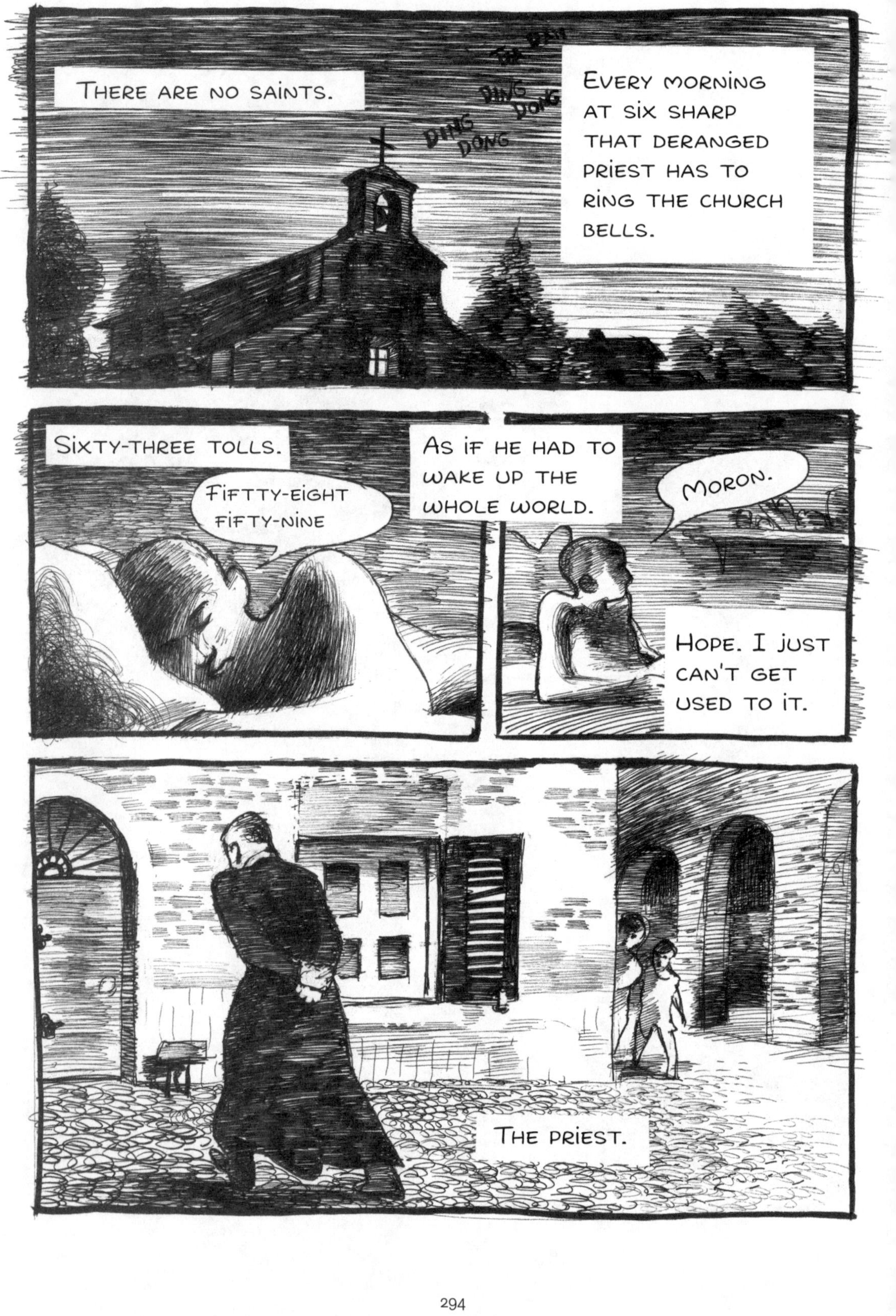
There are no saints.
DING DONG
DING DONG
Every morning at six sharp that deranged priest has to ring the church bells.
Sixty-three tolls.
Fiftty-eight fifty-nine
As if he had to wake up the whole world.
Moron.
Hope. I just can't get used to it.
The priest.

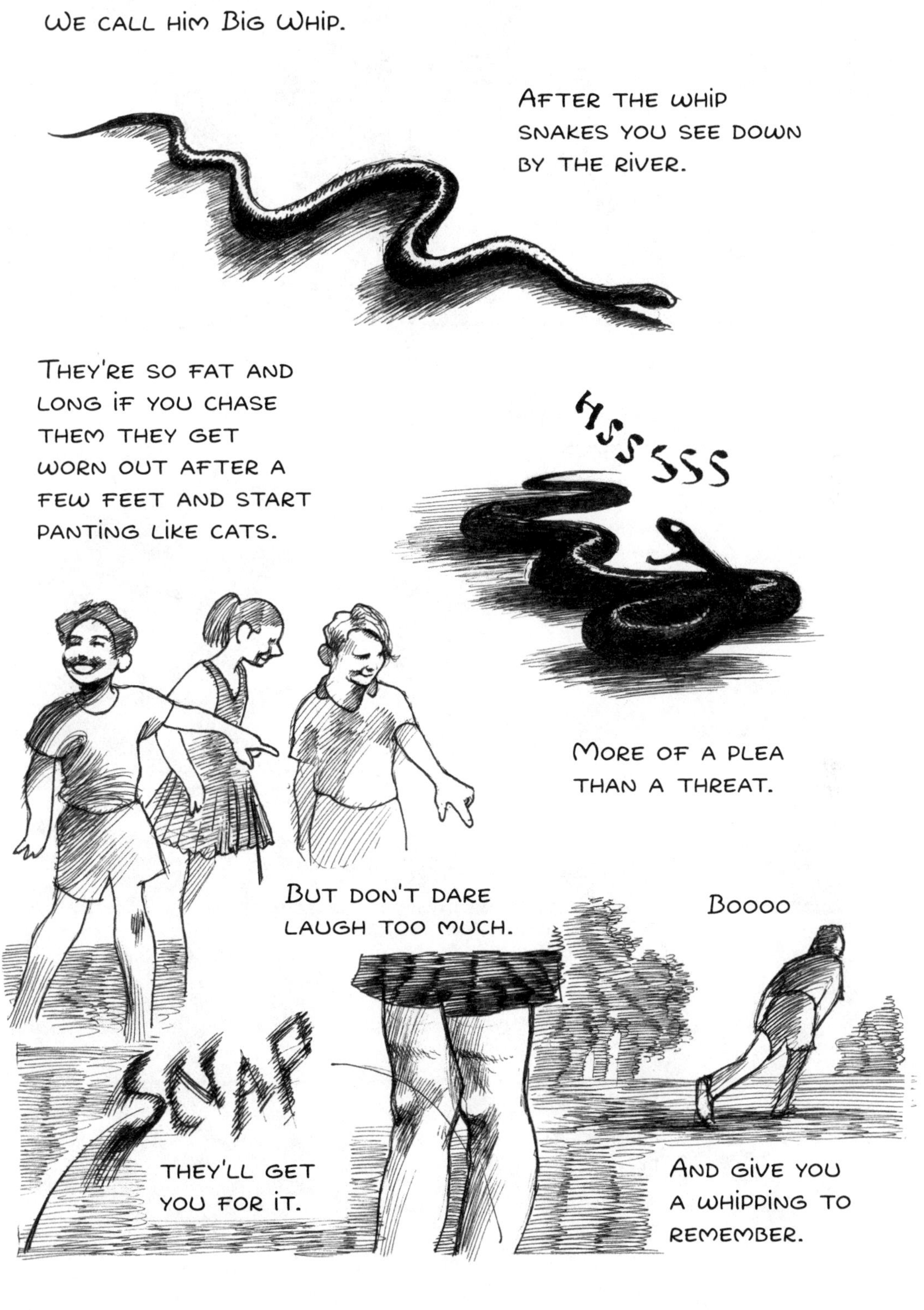
WE CALL HIM BIG WHIP.
AFTER THE WHIP SNAKES YOU SEE DOWN BY THE RIVER.
THEY'RE SO FAT AND LONG IF YOU CHASE THEM THEY GET WORN OUT AFTER A FEW FEET AND START PANTING LIKE CATS.
HSSSSS
MORE OF A PLEA THAN A THREAT.
BUT DON'T DARE LAUGH TOO MUCH.
BOOOO
SNAP
THEY'LL GET YOU FOR IT.
AND GIVE YOU A WHIPPING TO REMEMBER.

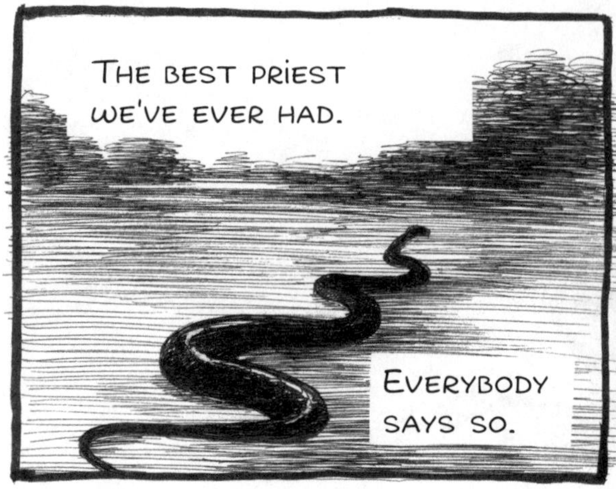
The best priest we've ever had.
Everybody says so.

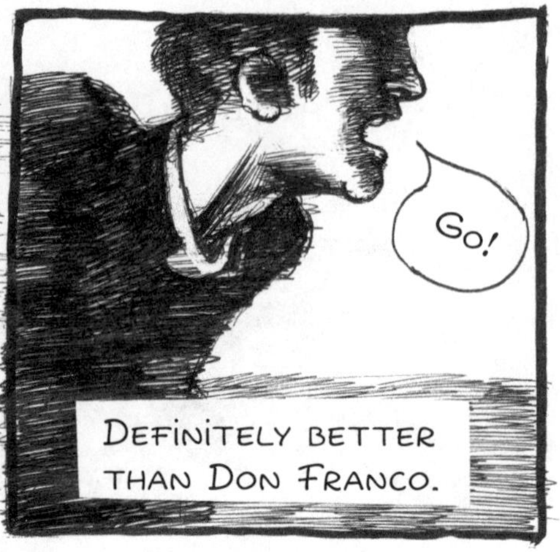
Go!
Definitely better than Don Franco.

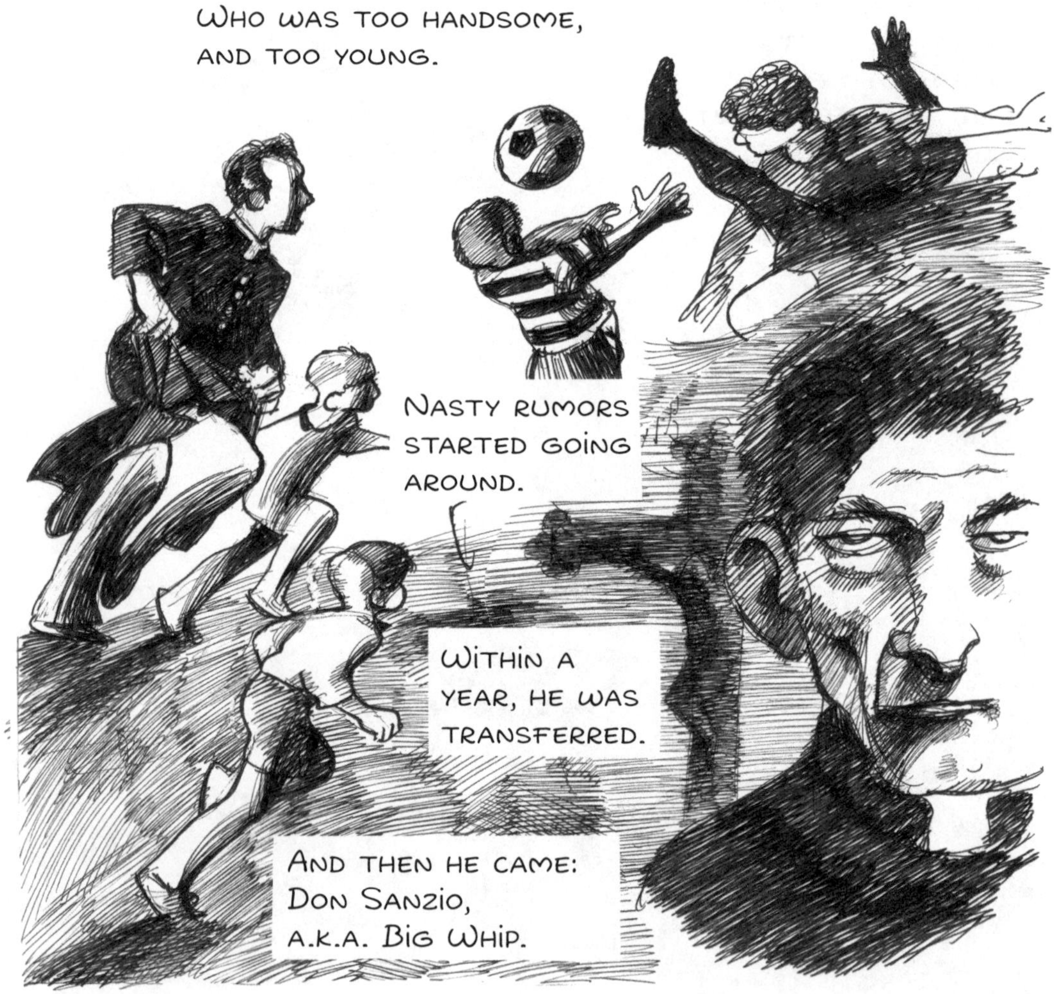
Who was too handsome, and too young.
Nasty rumors started going around.
Within a year, he was transferred.
And then he came: Don Sanzio, a.k.a. Big Whip.

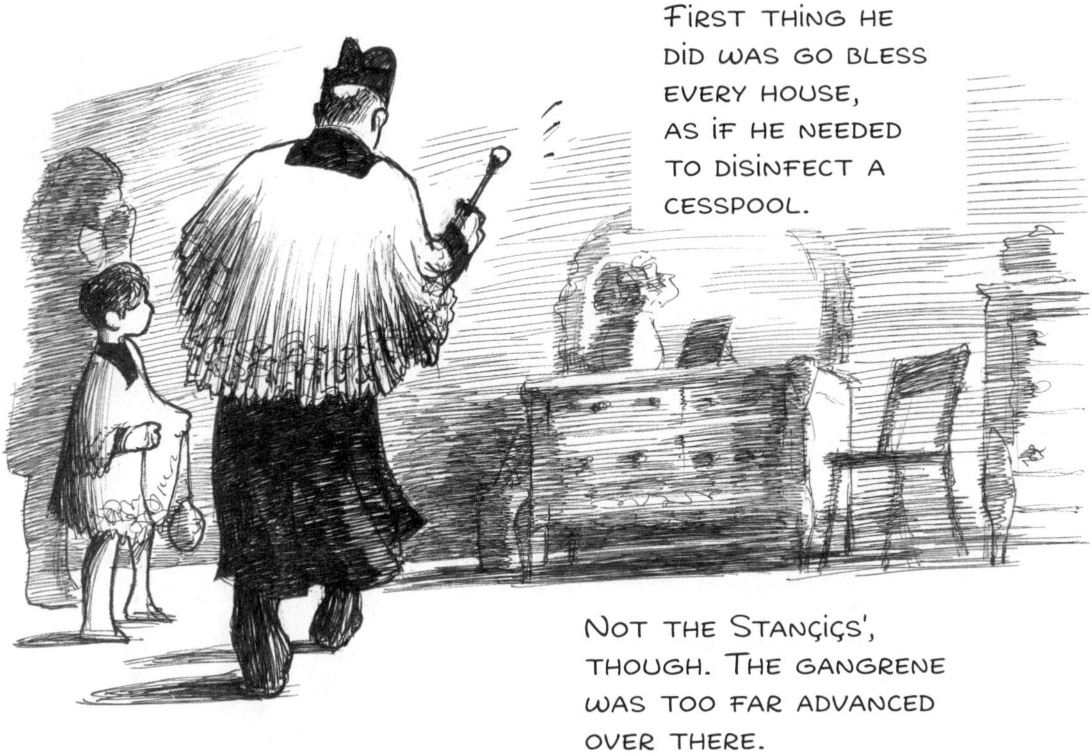
FIRST THING HE DID WAS GO BLESS EVERY HOUSE, AS IF HE NEEDED TO DISINFECT A CESSPOOL.
NOT THE STANÇIÇS', THOUGH. THE GANGRENE WAS TOO FAR ADVANCED OVER THERE.

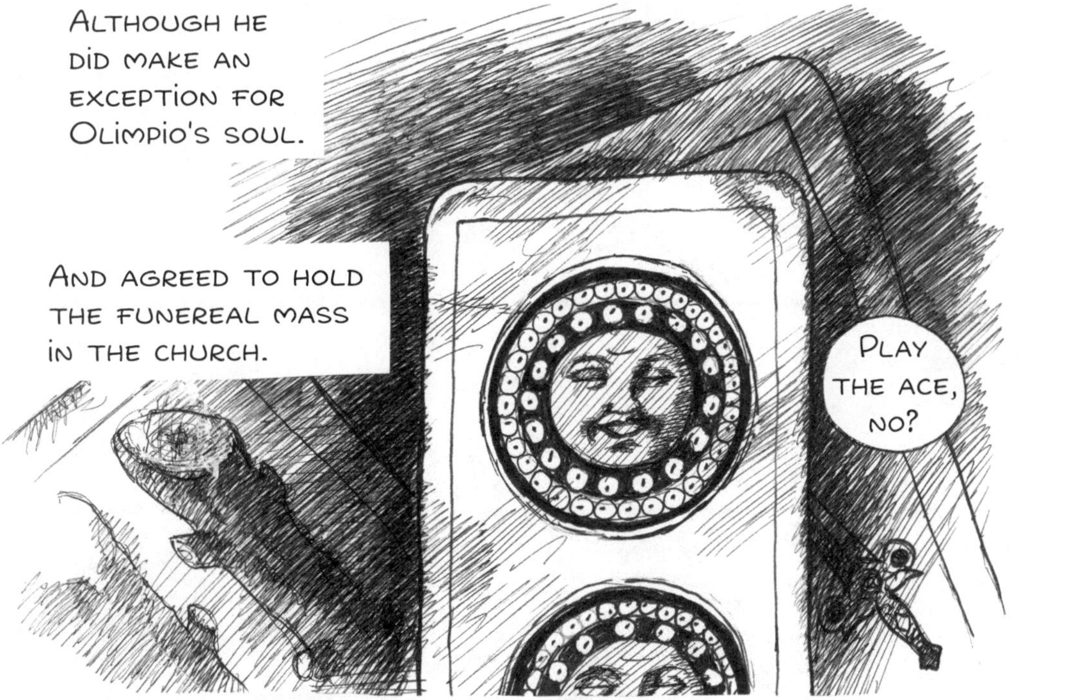
ALTHOUGH HE DID MAKE AN EXCEPTION FOR OLIMPIO'S SOUL.
AND AGREED TO HOLD THE FUNEREAL MASS IN THE CHURCH.
PLAY THE ACE, NO?

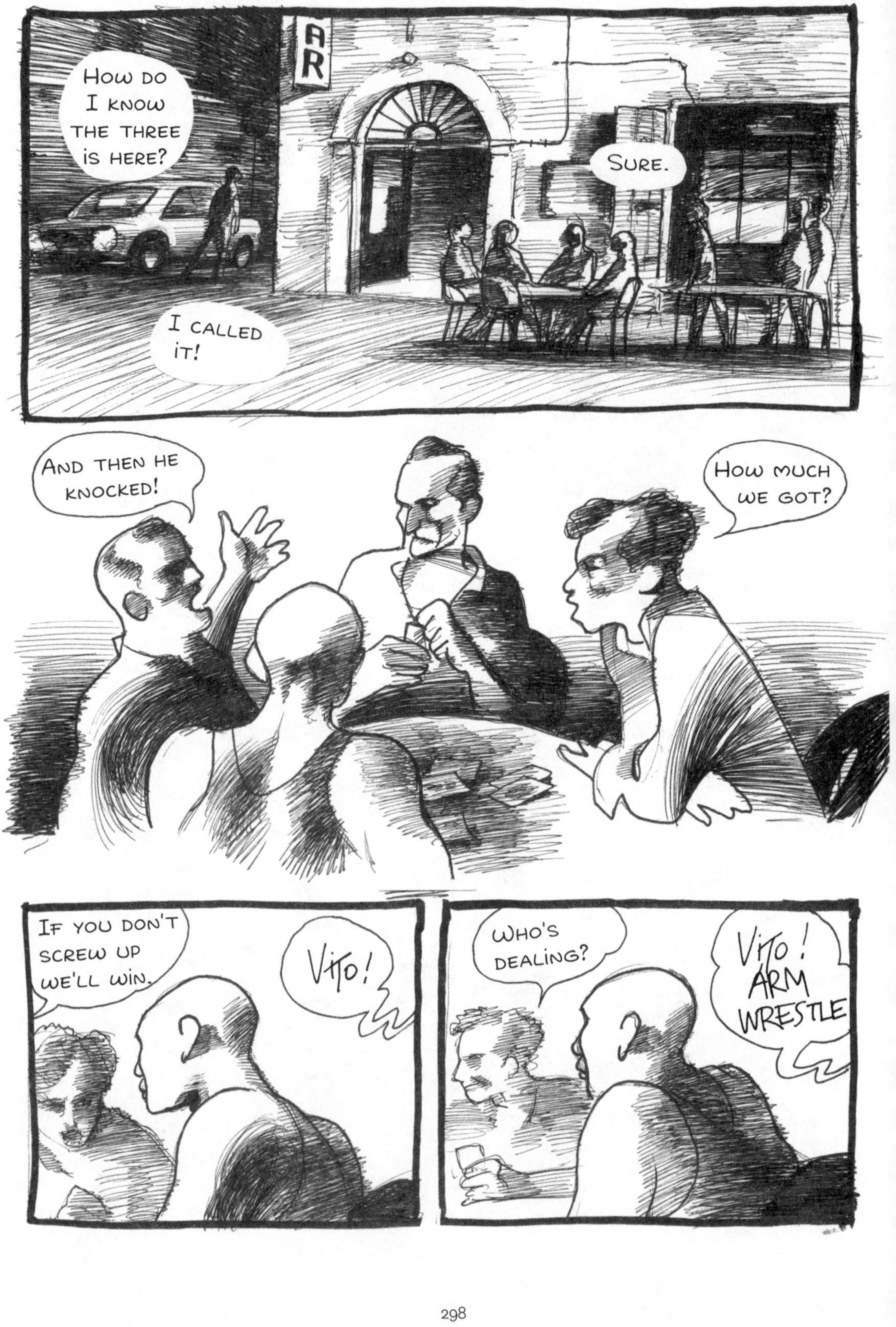
How do I know the three is here?
Sure.
I called it!
And then he knocked!
How much we got?
If you don't screw up we'll win.
Vito!
Who's dealing?
Vito! Arm wrestle

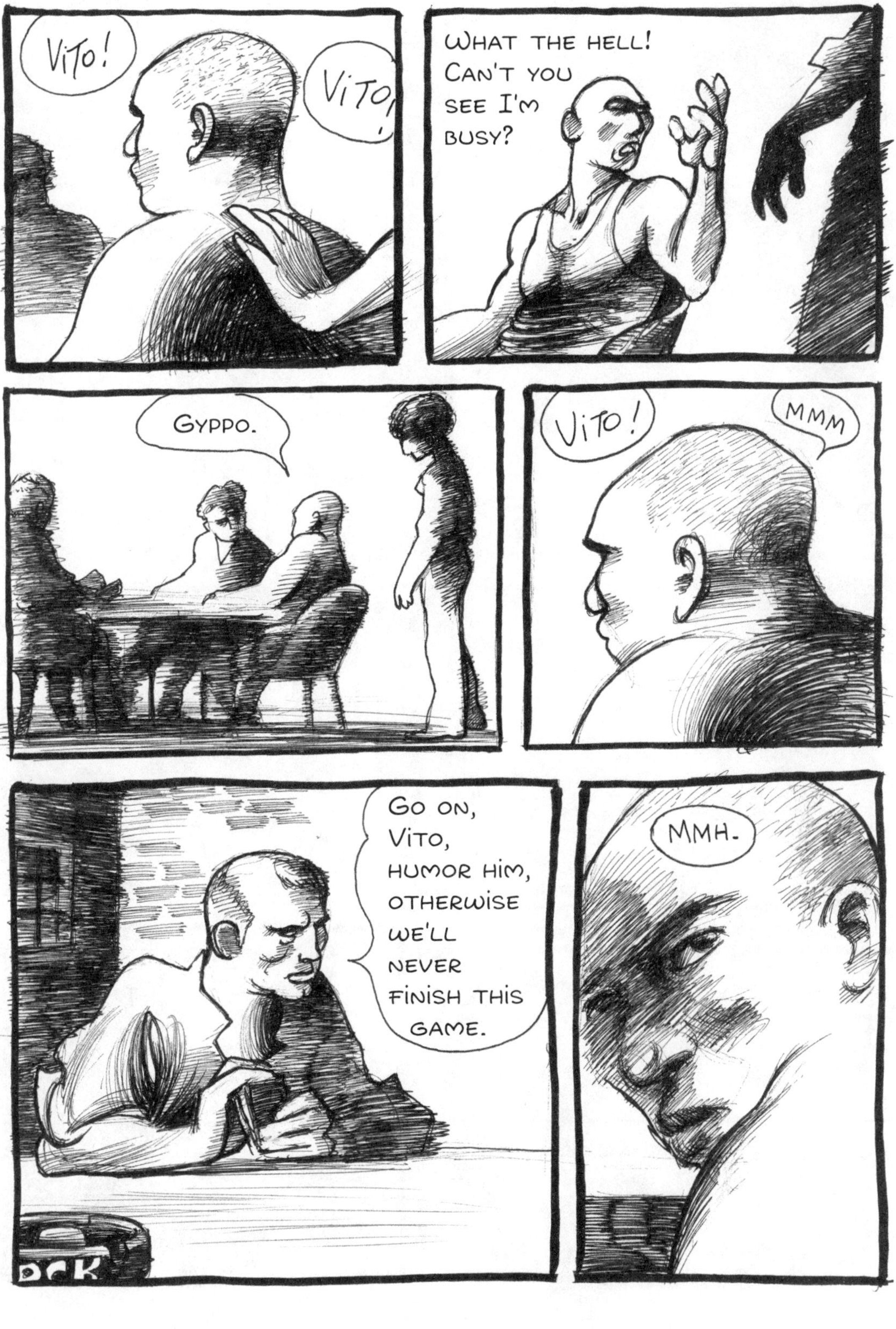
VITO!
VITO!
WHAT THE HELL! CAN'T YOU SEE I'M BUSY?
GYPPO.
VITO!
MMM
GO ON, VITO, HUMOR HIM, OTHERWISE WE'LL NEVER FINISH THIS GAME.
MMH.
DCK

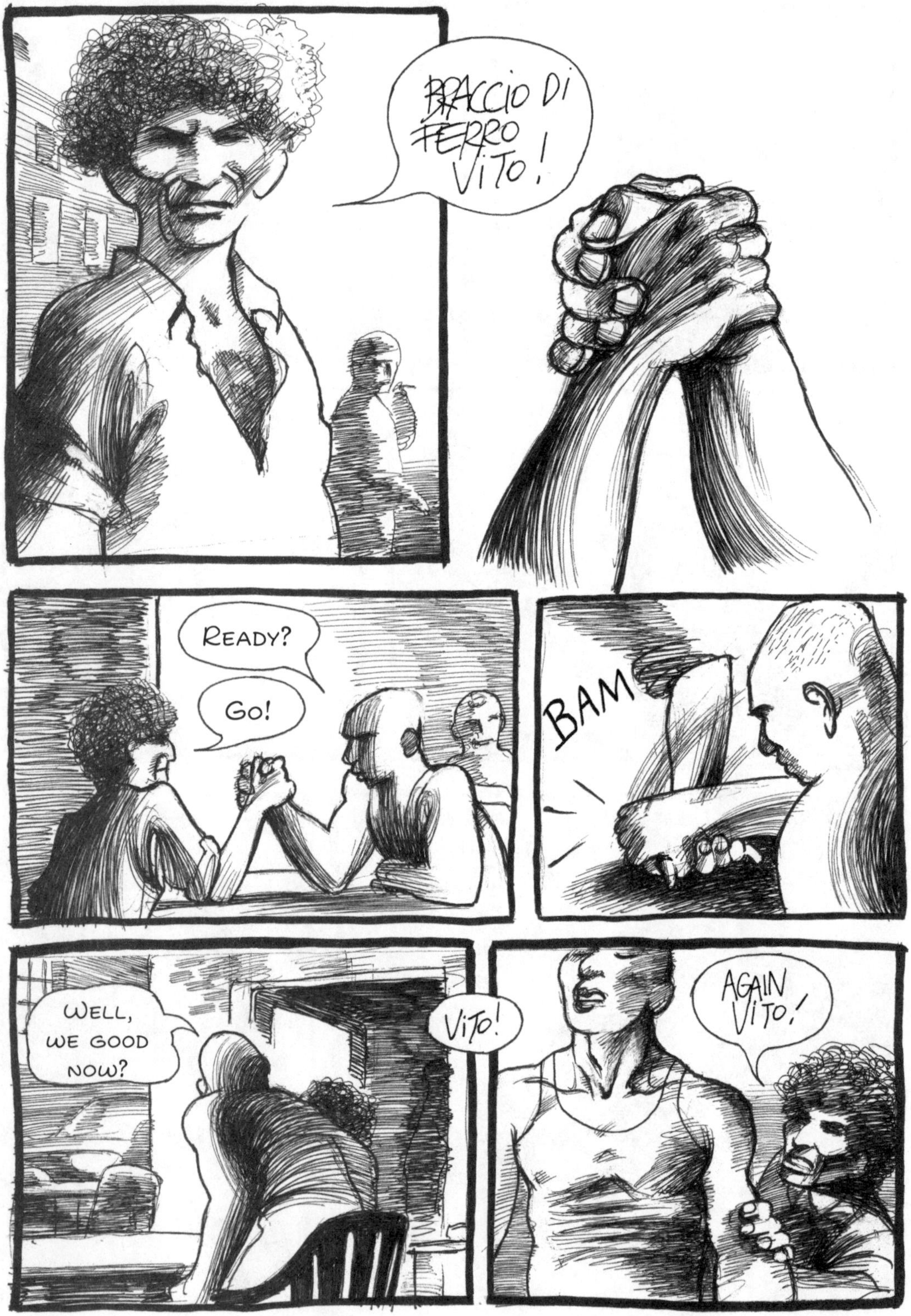
BRACCIO DI FERRO VITO!
READY?
GO!
BAM
WELL, WE GOOD NOW?
VITO!
AGAIN VITO!

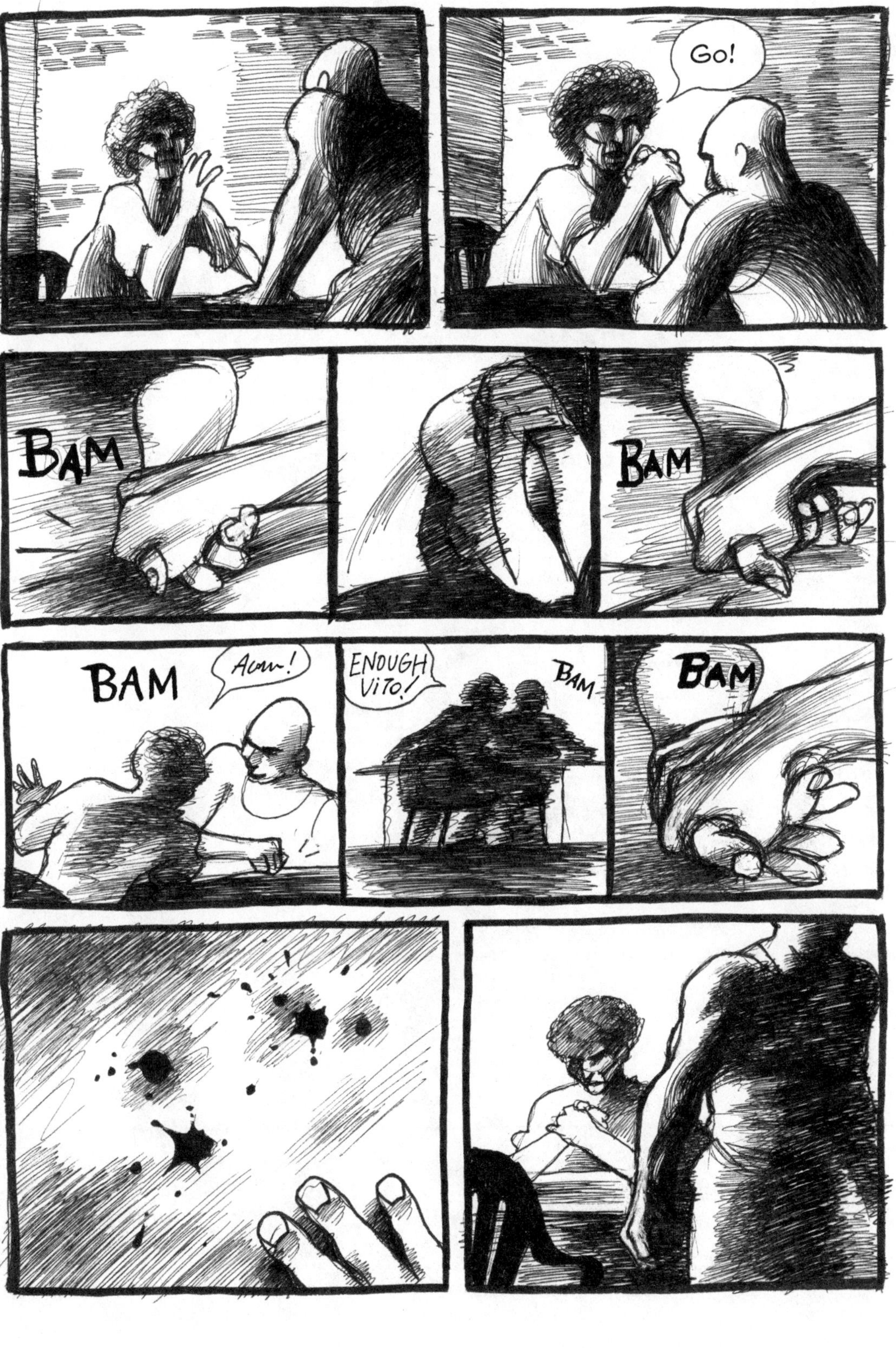
Go!
BAM
BAM
BAM
ENOUGH VITO!
BAM
BAM

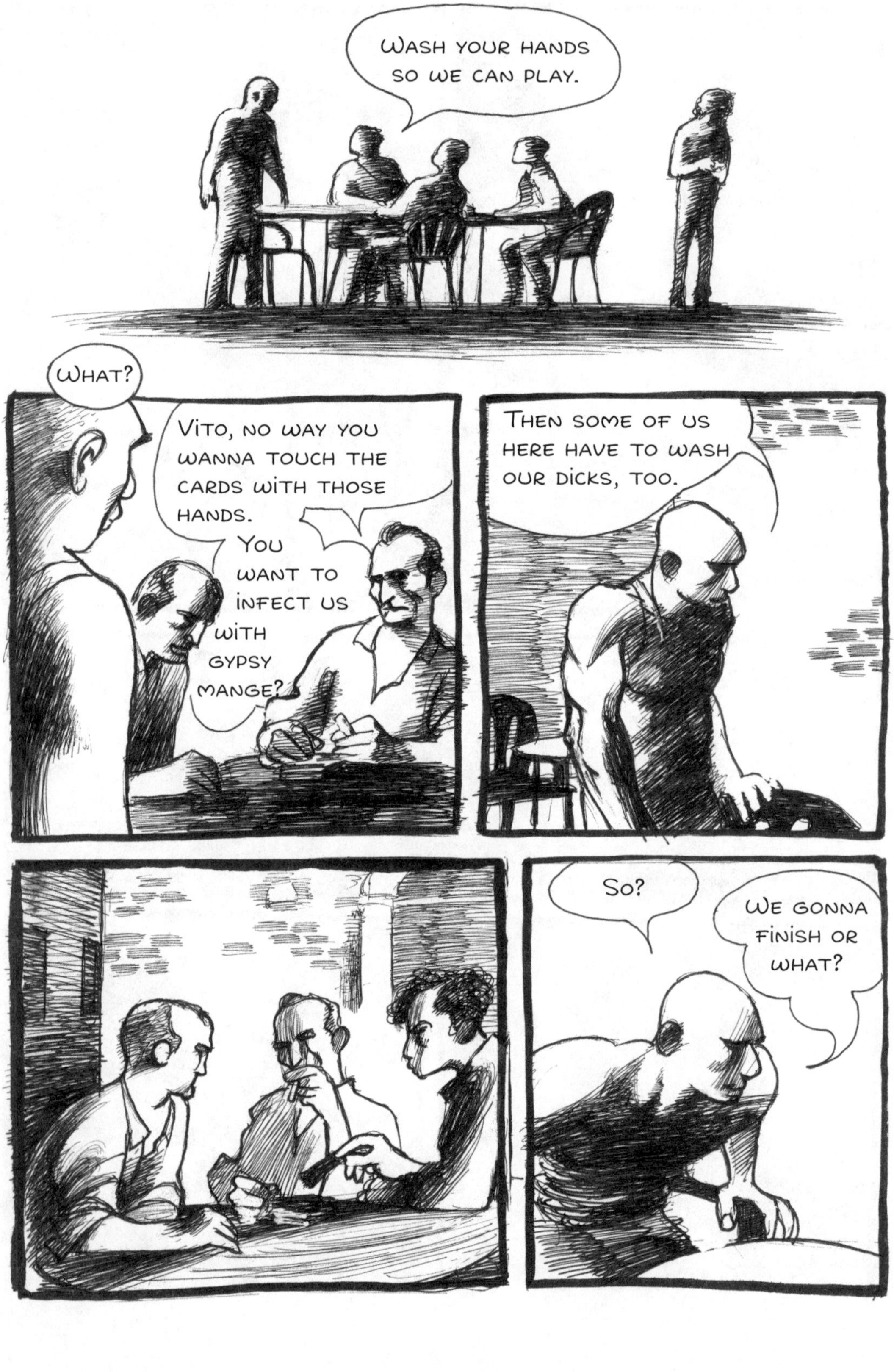
Wash your hands so we can play.
What?
Vito, no way you wanna touch the cards with those hands.
You want to infect us with gypsy mange?
Then some of us here have to wash our dicks, too.
So?
We gonna finish or what?

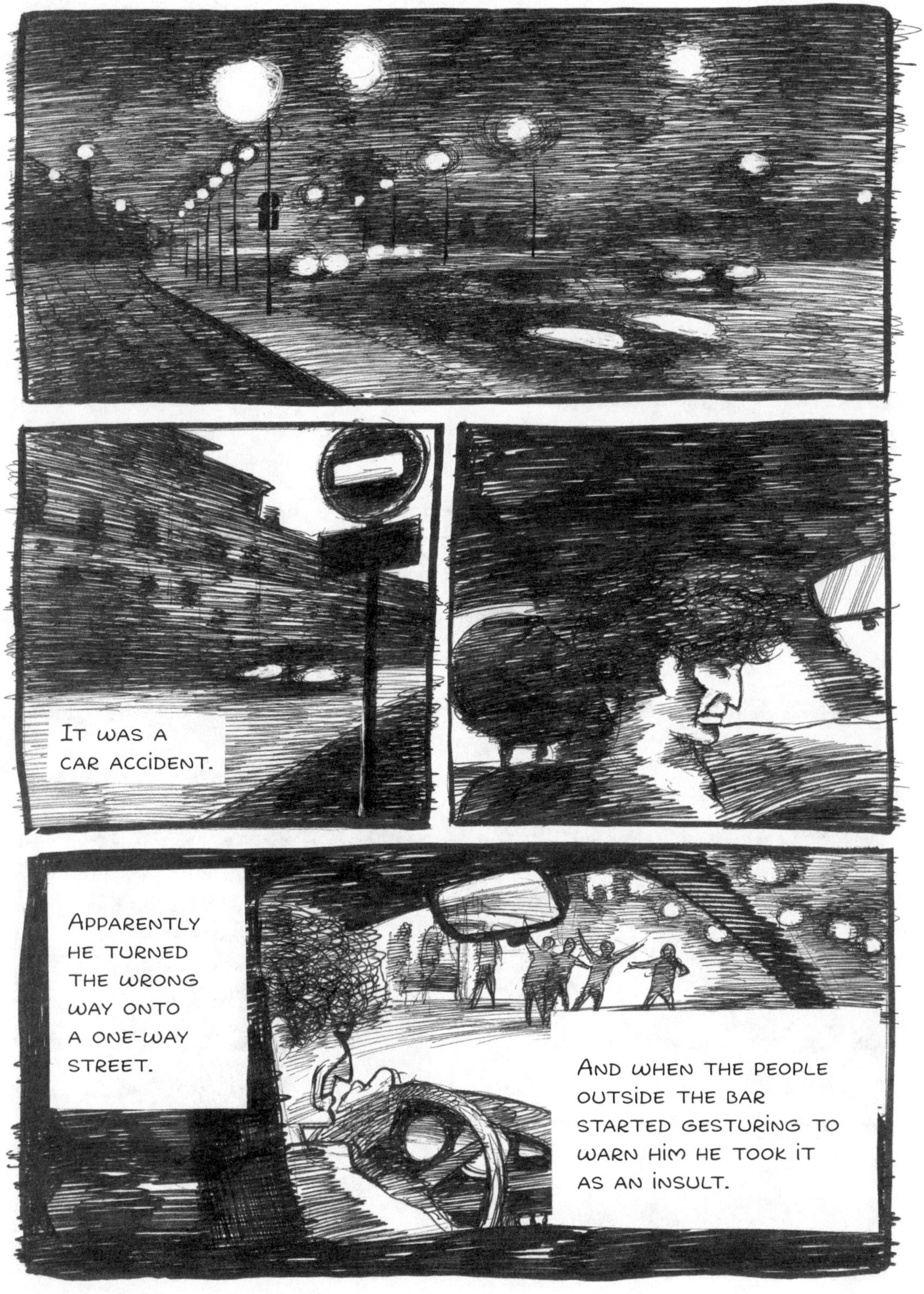
It was a car accident.
Apparently he turned the wrong way onto a one-way street.
And when the people outside the bar started gesturing to warn him he took it as an insult.

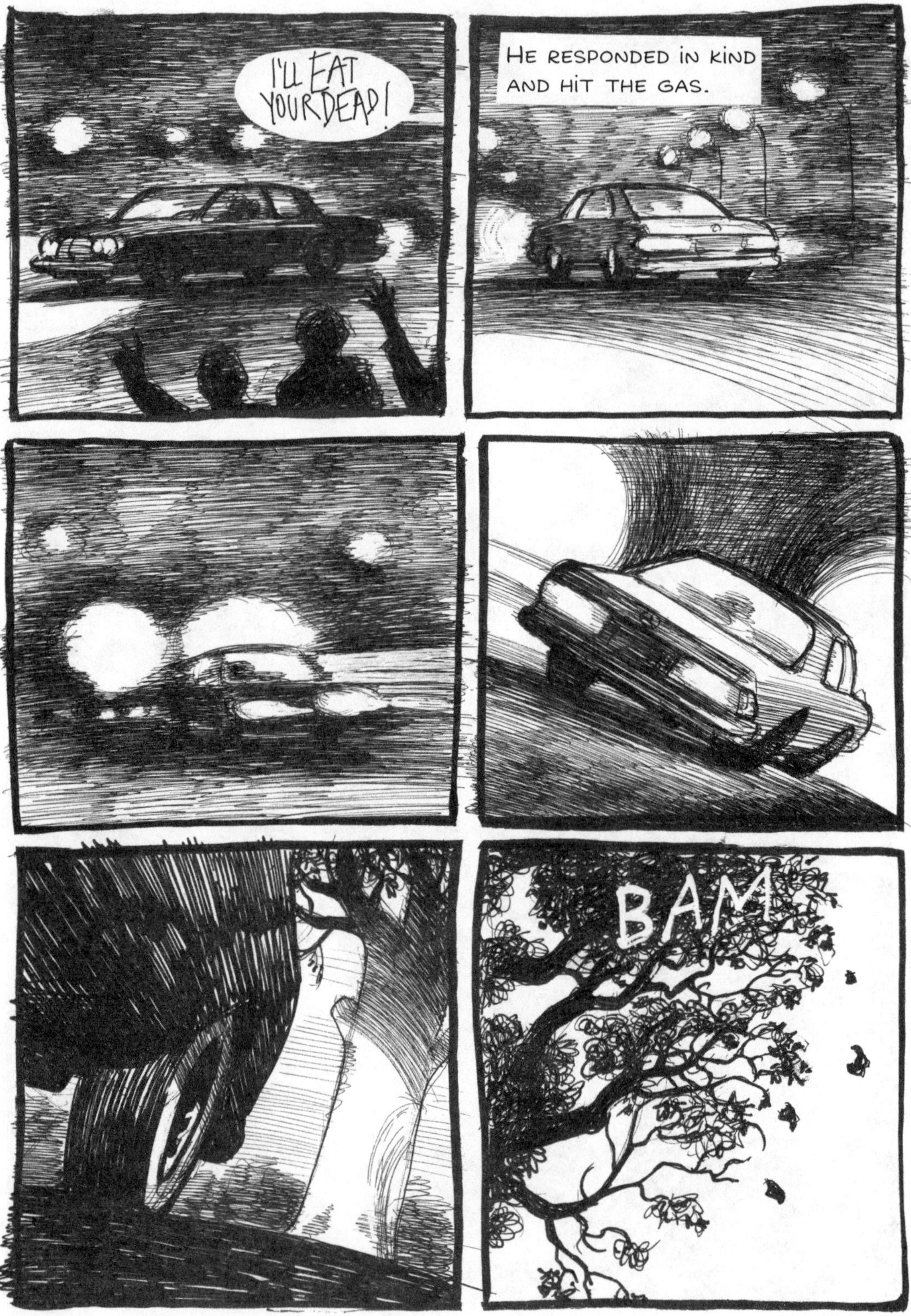
I'LL EAT YOUR DEAD!
HE RESPONDED IN KIND AND HIT THE GAS.
BAM

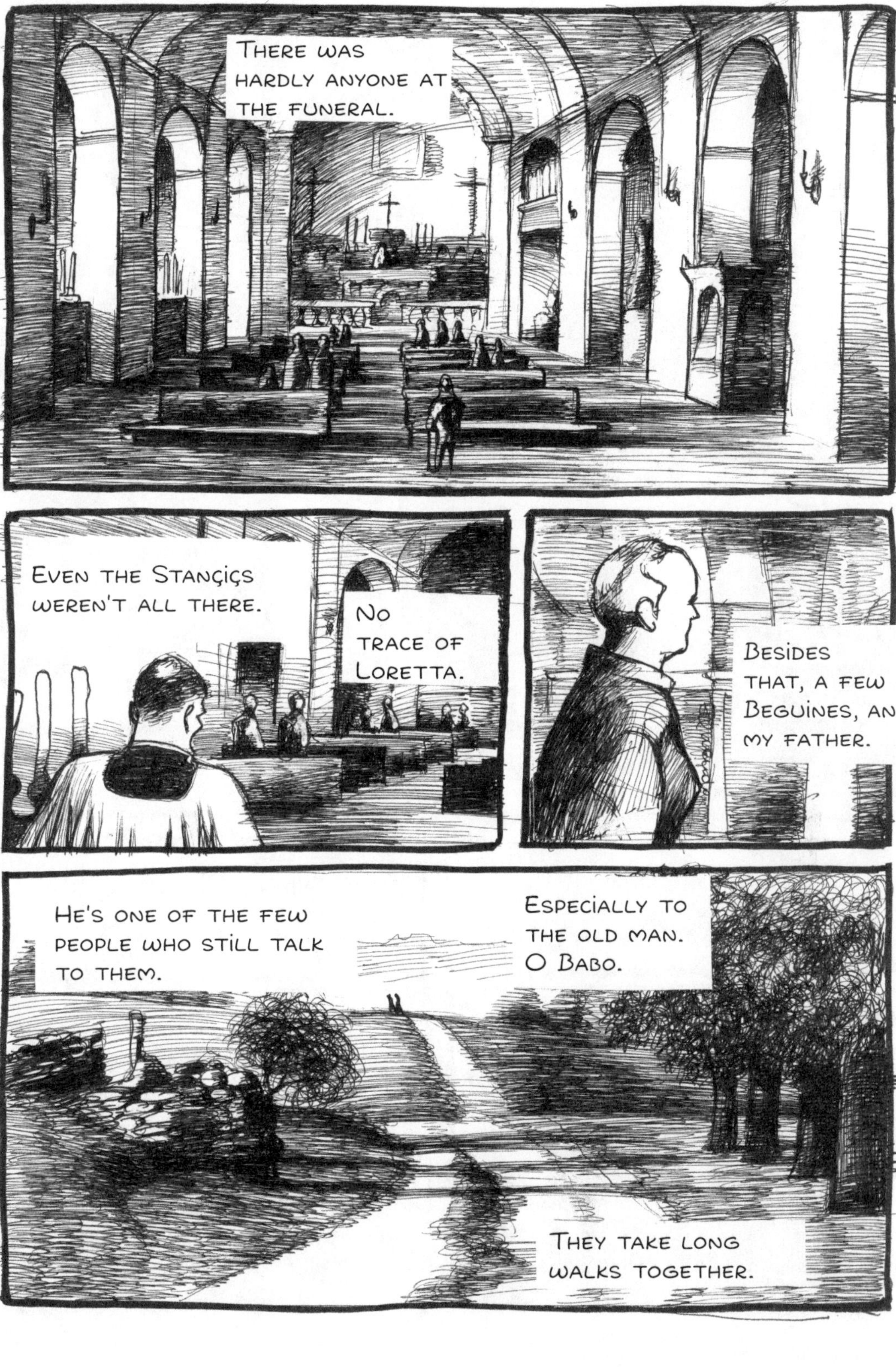
There was hardly anyone at the funeral.
Even the Stançiçs weren't all there.
No trace of Loretta.
Besides that, a few Beguines, and my father.
He's one of the few people who still talk to them.
Especially to the old man. O Babo.
They take long walks together.

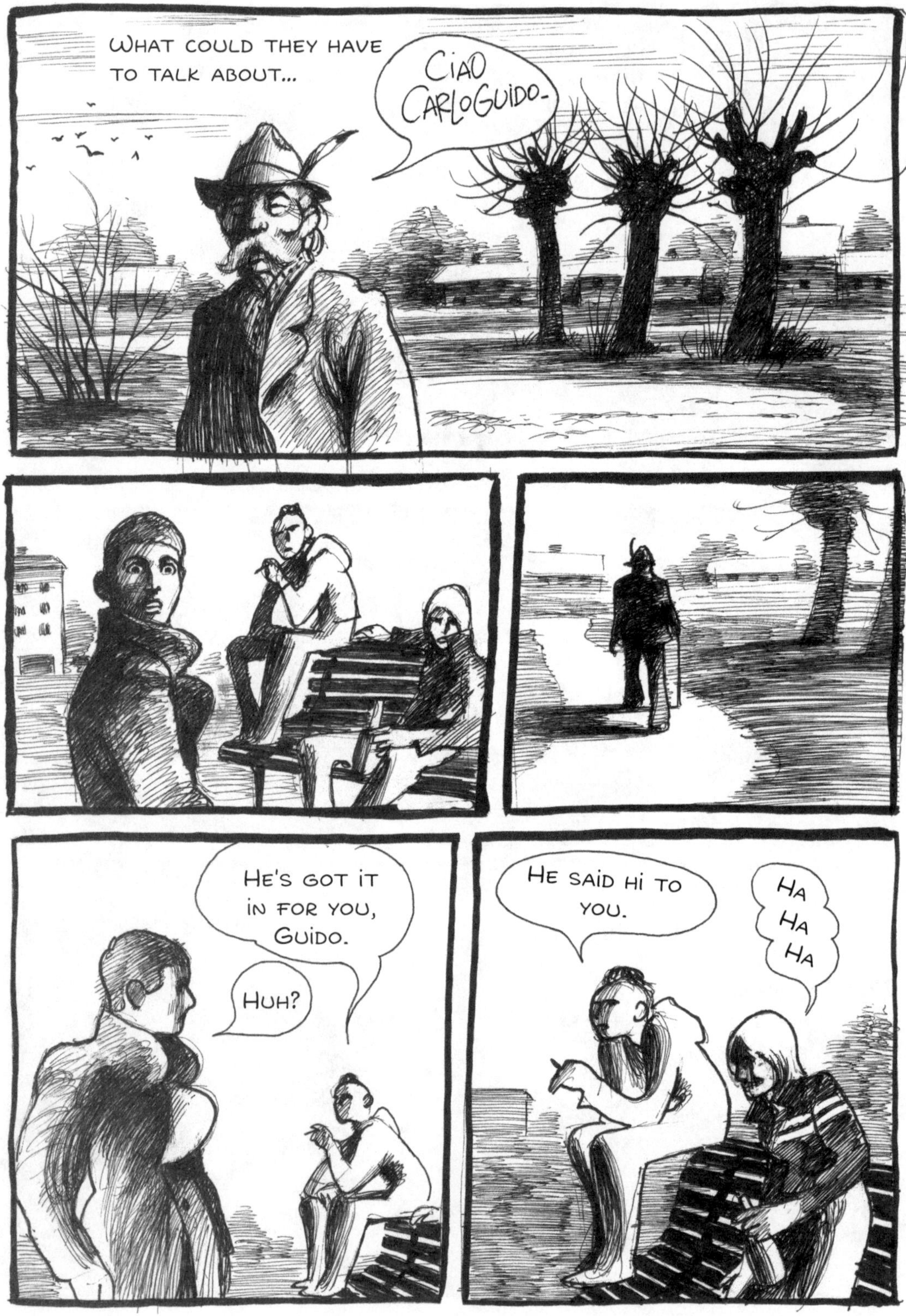
WHAT COULD THEY HAVE TO TALK ABOUT...
CIAO CARLOGUIDO_
HE'S GOT IT IN FOR YOU, GUIDO.
HUH?
HE SAID HI TO YOU.
HA HA HA

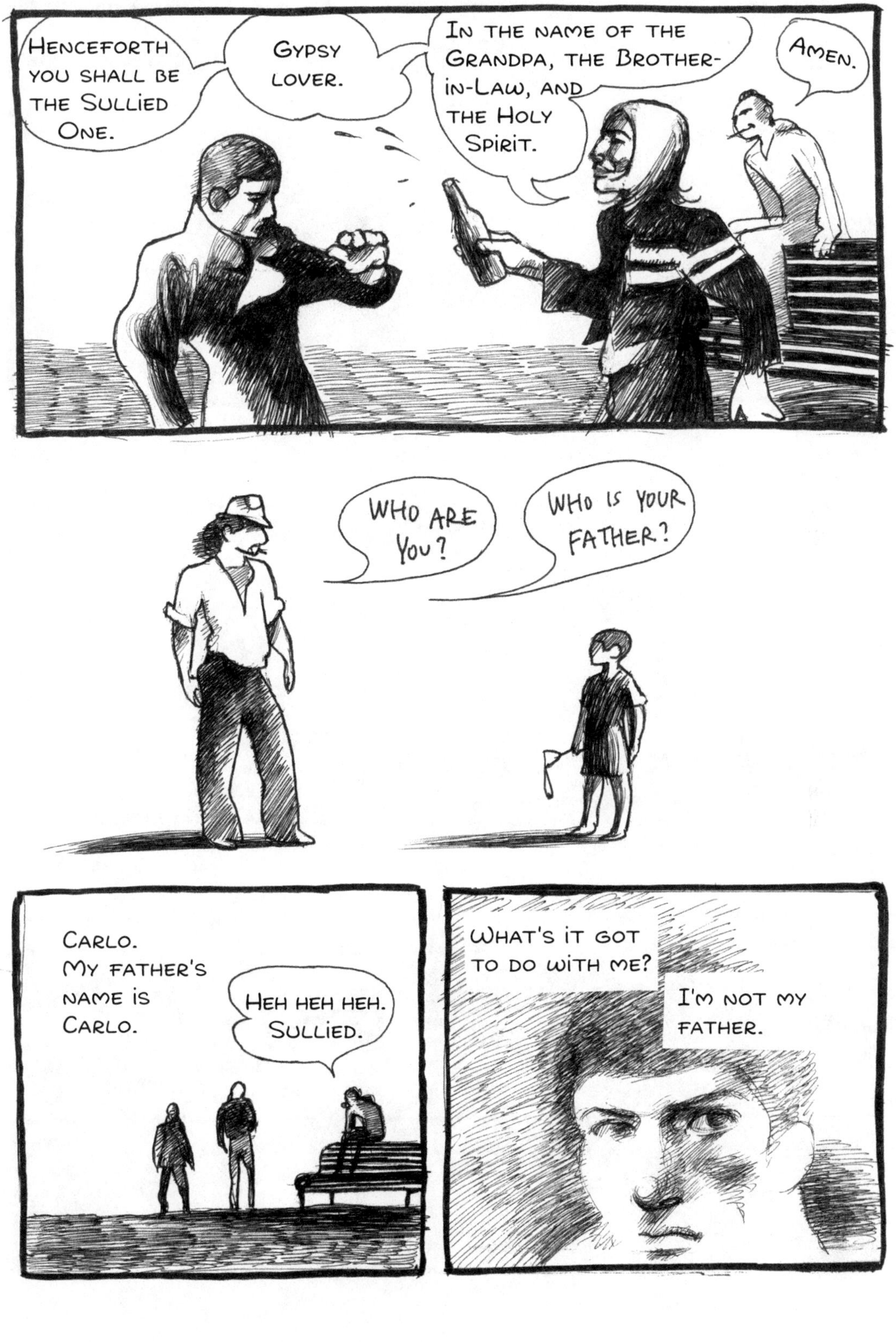
HENCEFORTH YOU SHALL BE THE SULLIED ONE.
GYPSY LOVER.
IN THE NAME OF THE GRANDPA, THE BROTHER-IN-LAW, AND THE HOLY SPIRIT.
AMEN.
WHO ARE YOU?
WHO IS YOUR FATHER?
CARLO. MY FATHER'S NAME IS CARLO.
HEH HEH HEH. SULLIED.
WHAT'S IT GOT TO DO WITH ME?
I'M NOT MY FATHER.

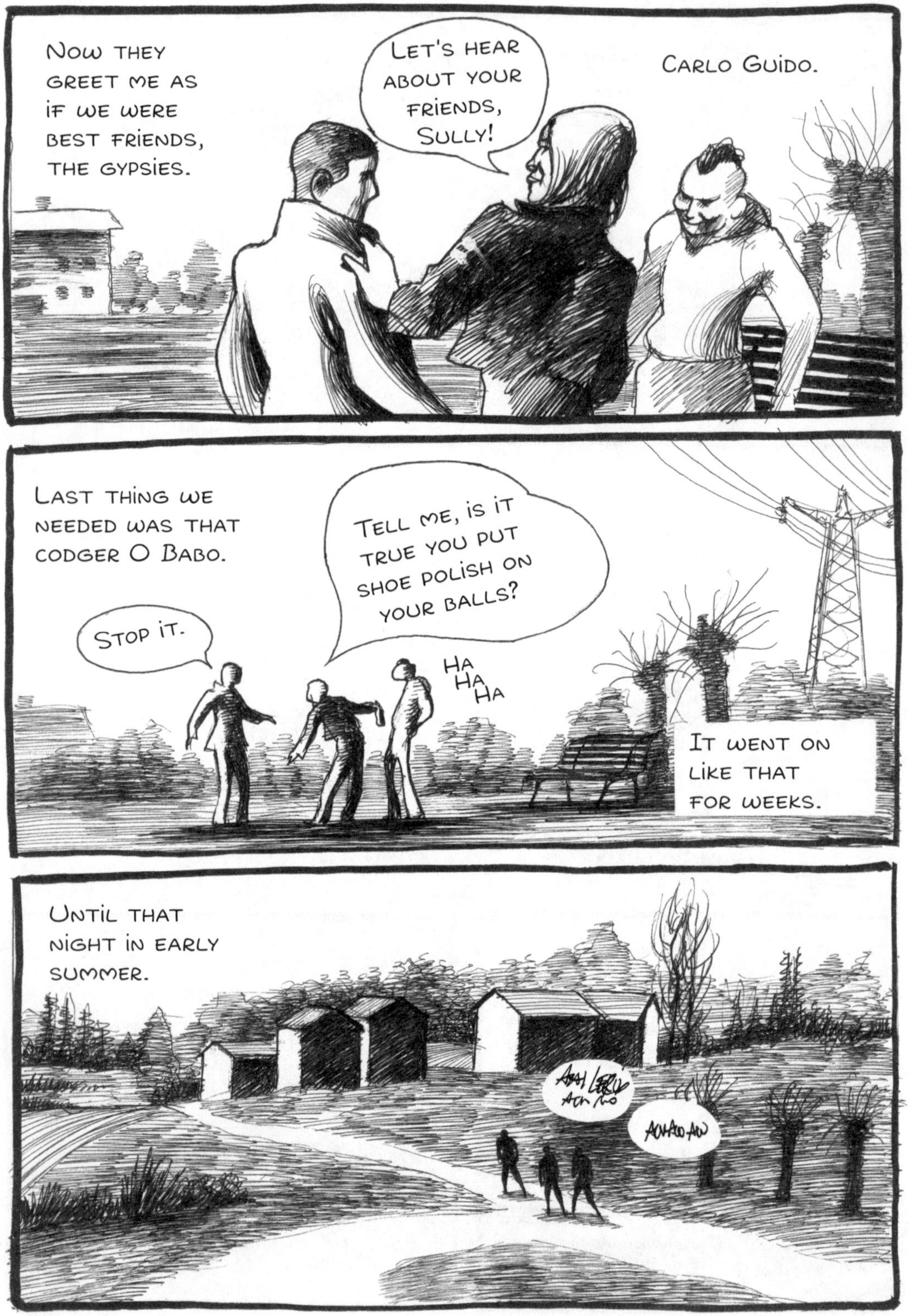
Now they greet me as if we were best friends, the gypsies.
Let's hear about your friends, Sully!
Carlo Guido.
Last thing we needed was that codger O Babo.
Tell me, is it true you put shoe polish on your balls?
Stop it.
Ha Ha Ha
It went on like that for weeks.
Until that night in early summer.

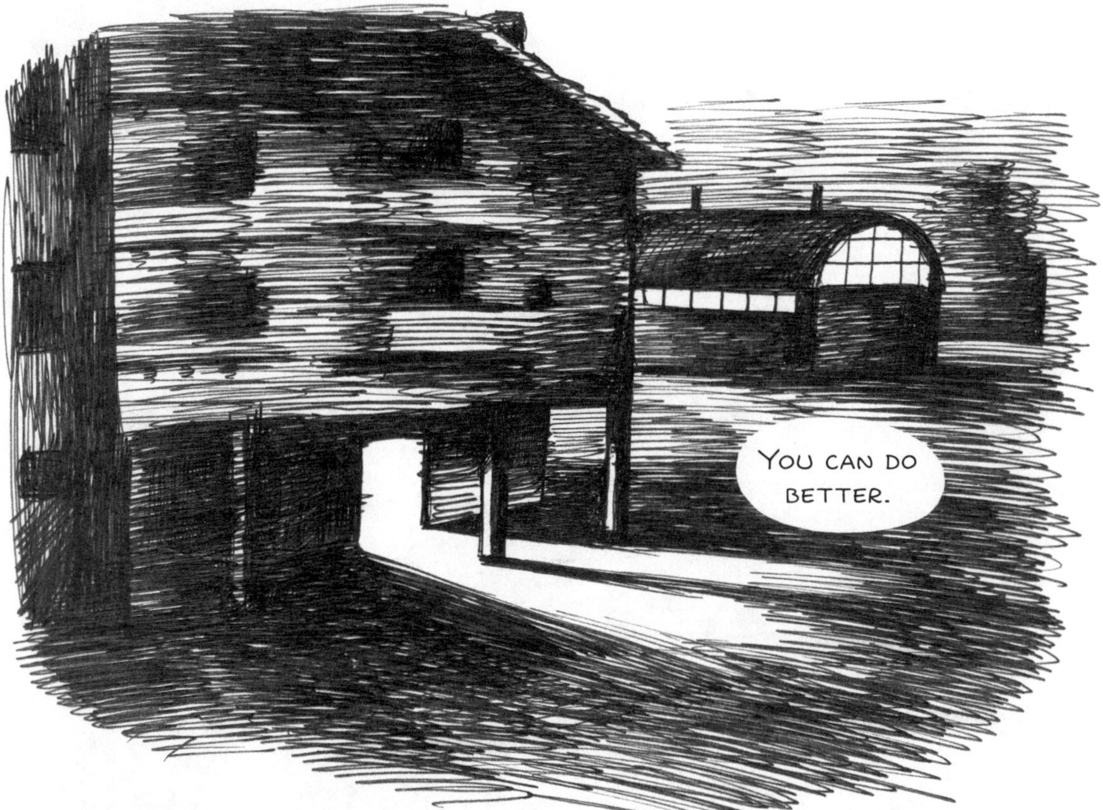
You can do better.

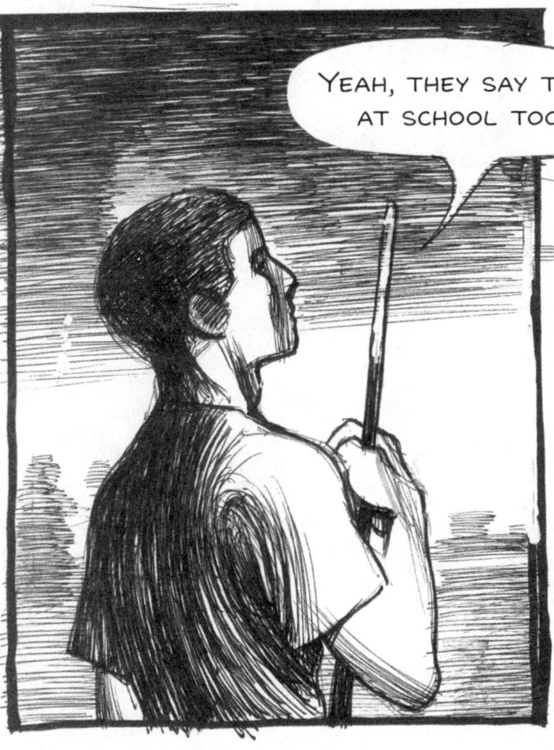
Yeah, they say that at school too.

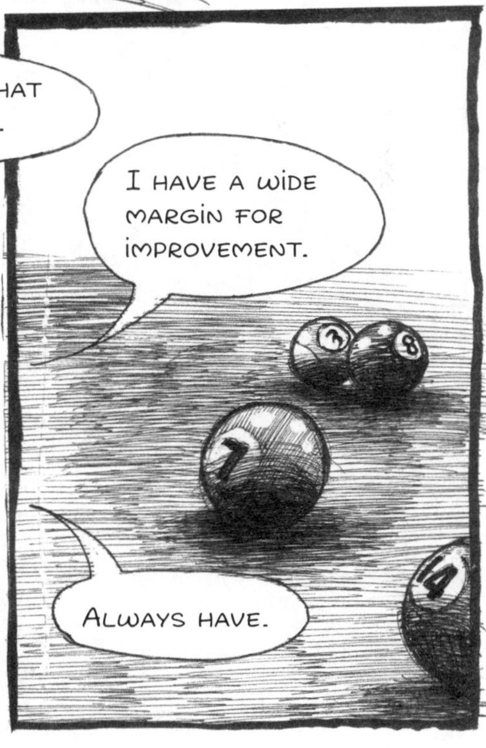
I have a wide margin for improvement.
Always have.

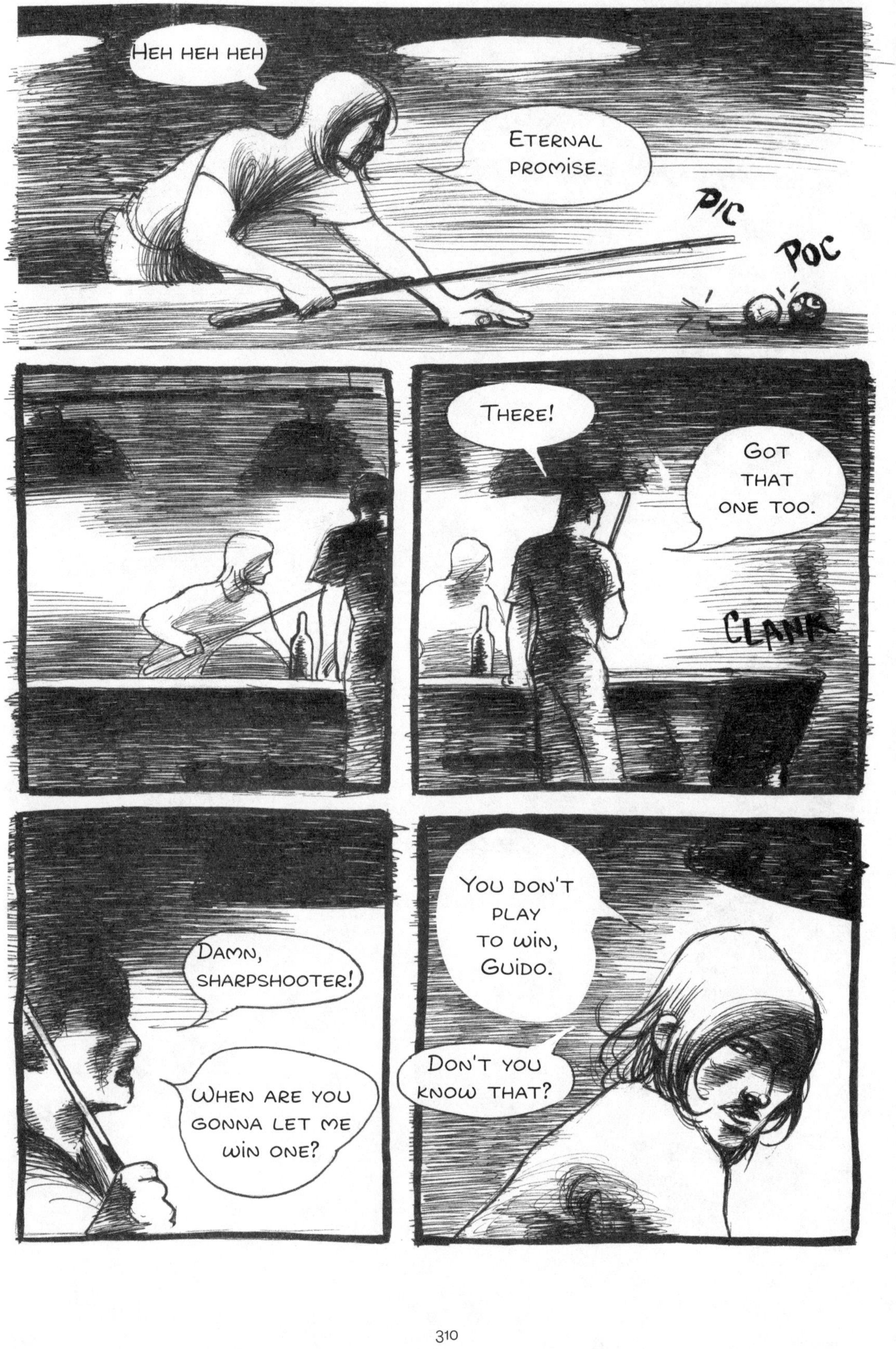
Heh heh heh
Eternal promise.
PIC
POC
There!
Got that one too.
CLANK
Damn, sharpshooter!
When are you gonna let me win one?
You don't play to win, Guido.
Don't you know that?

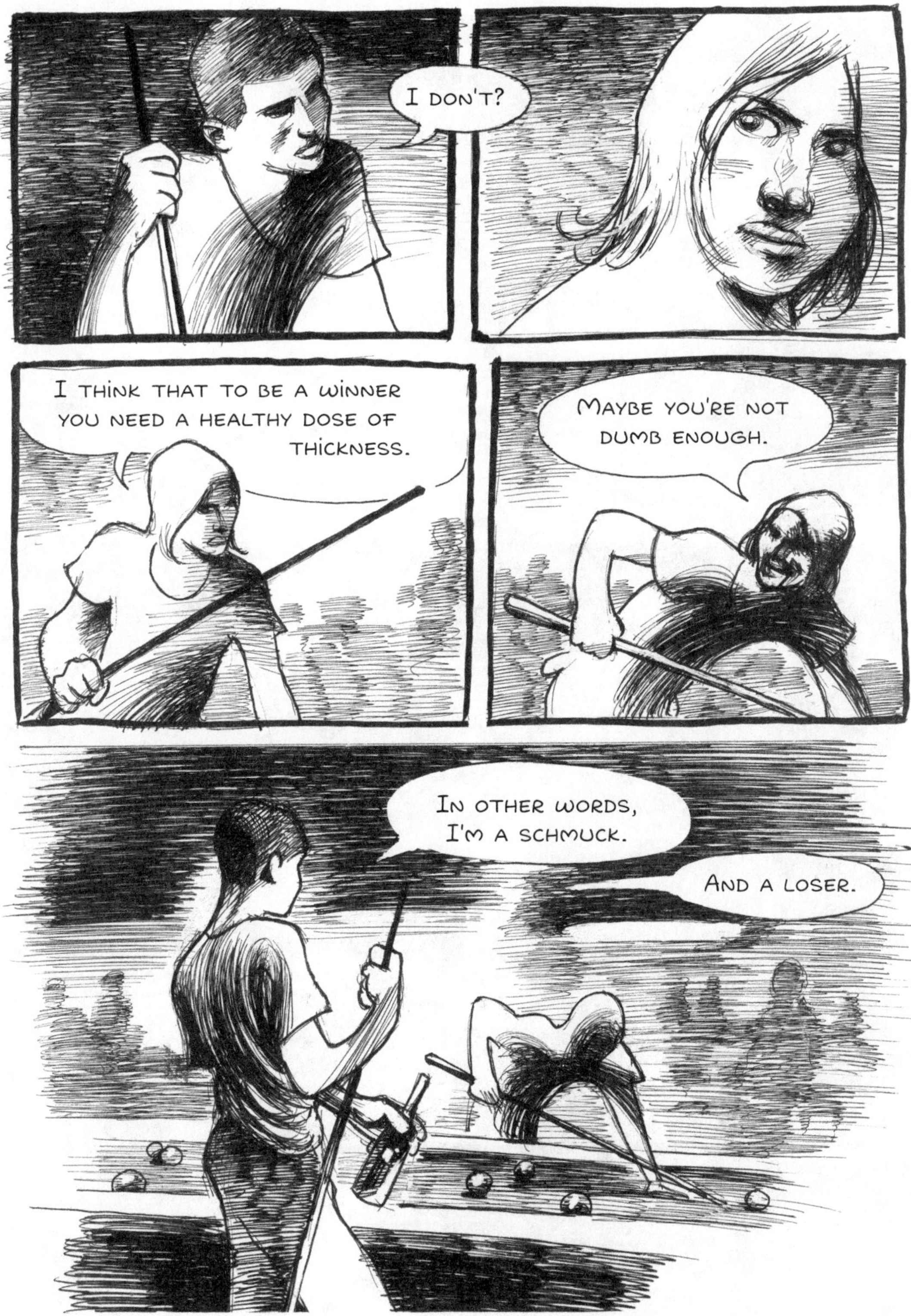
I DON'T?
I THINK THAT TO BE A WINNER YOU NEED A HEALTHY DOSE OF THICKNESS.
MAYBE YOU'RE NOT DUMB ENOUGH.
IN OTHER WORDS, I'M A SCHMUCK.
AND A LOSER.

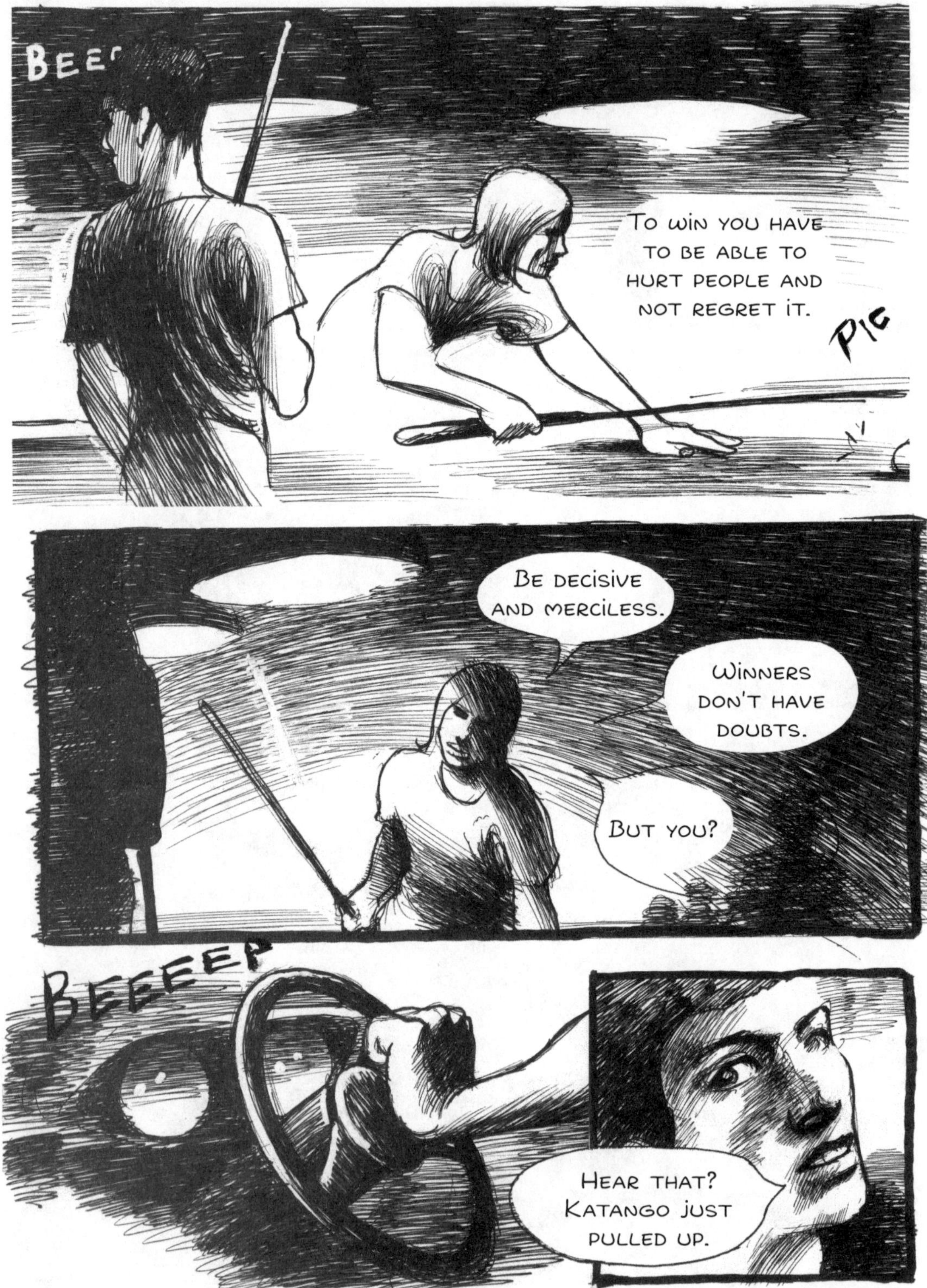
BEE
To win you have to be able to hurt people and not regret it.
PIC
Be decisive and merciless.
Winners don't have doubts.
But you?
BEEEEP
Hear that? Katango just pulled up.

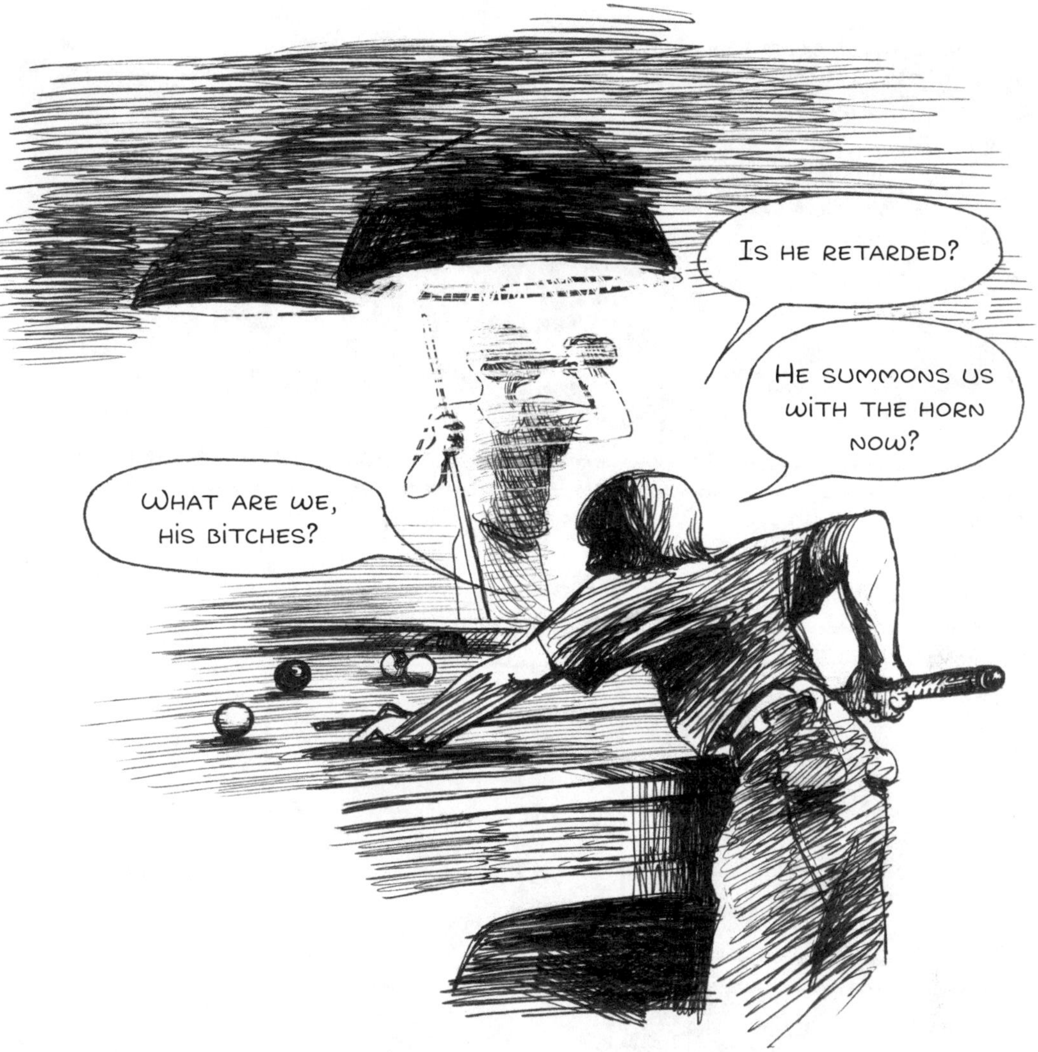
Is he retarded?
He summons us with the horn now?
What are we, his bitches?

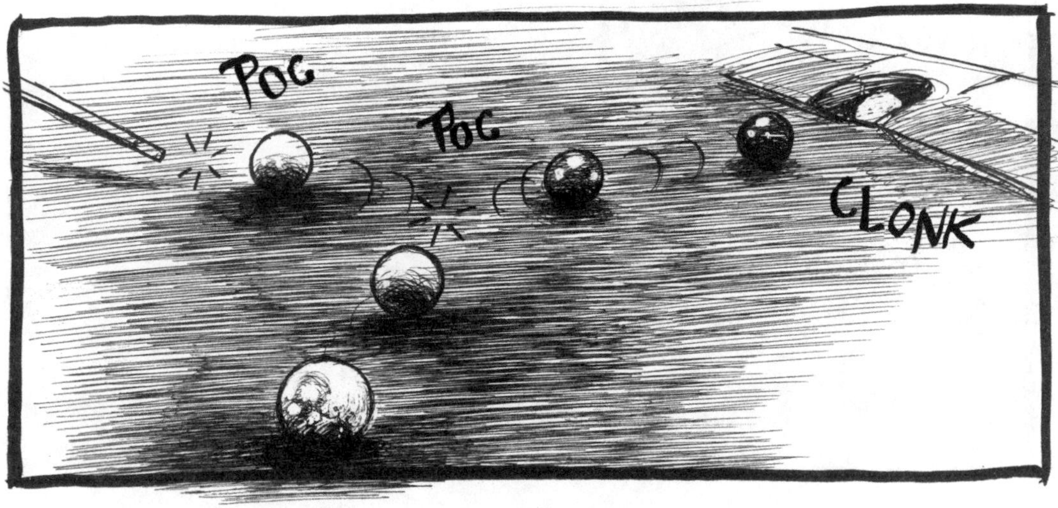
POC
POC
CLONK

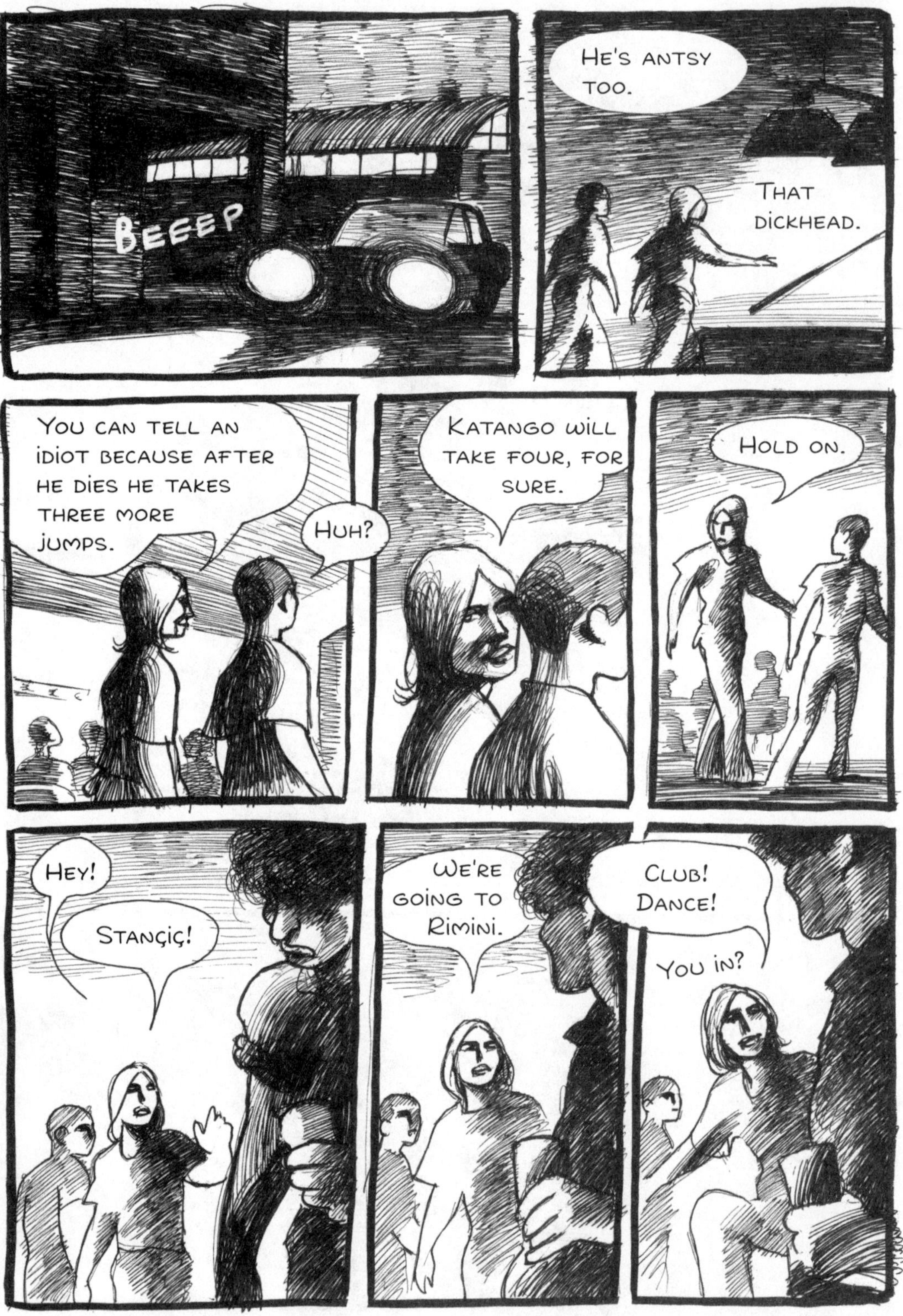
BEEEP
He's antsy too.
That dickhead.
You can tell an idiot because after he dies he takes three more jumps.
Huh?
Katango will take four, for sure.
Hold on.
Hey!
Stançiç!
We're going to Rimini.
Club! Dance!
You in?

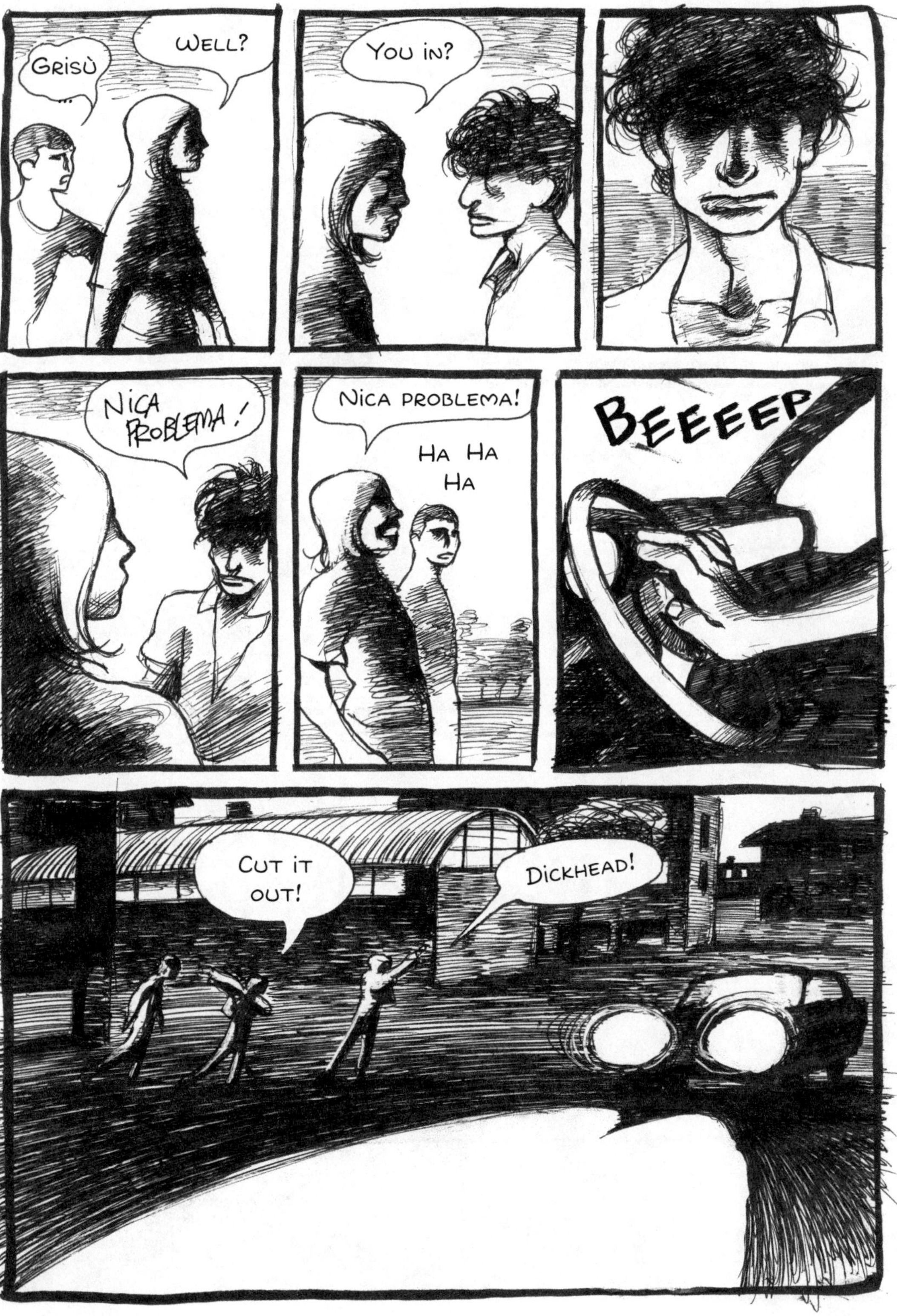
Grisù
...
Well?
You in?
Nica problema!
Nica problema!
Ha Ha Ha
Beeeep
Cut it out!
Dickhead!

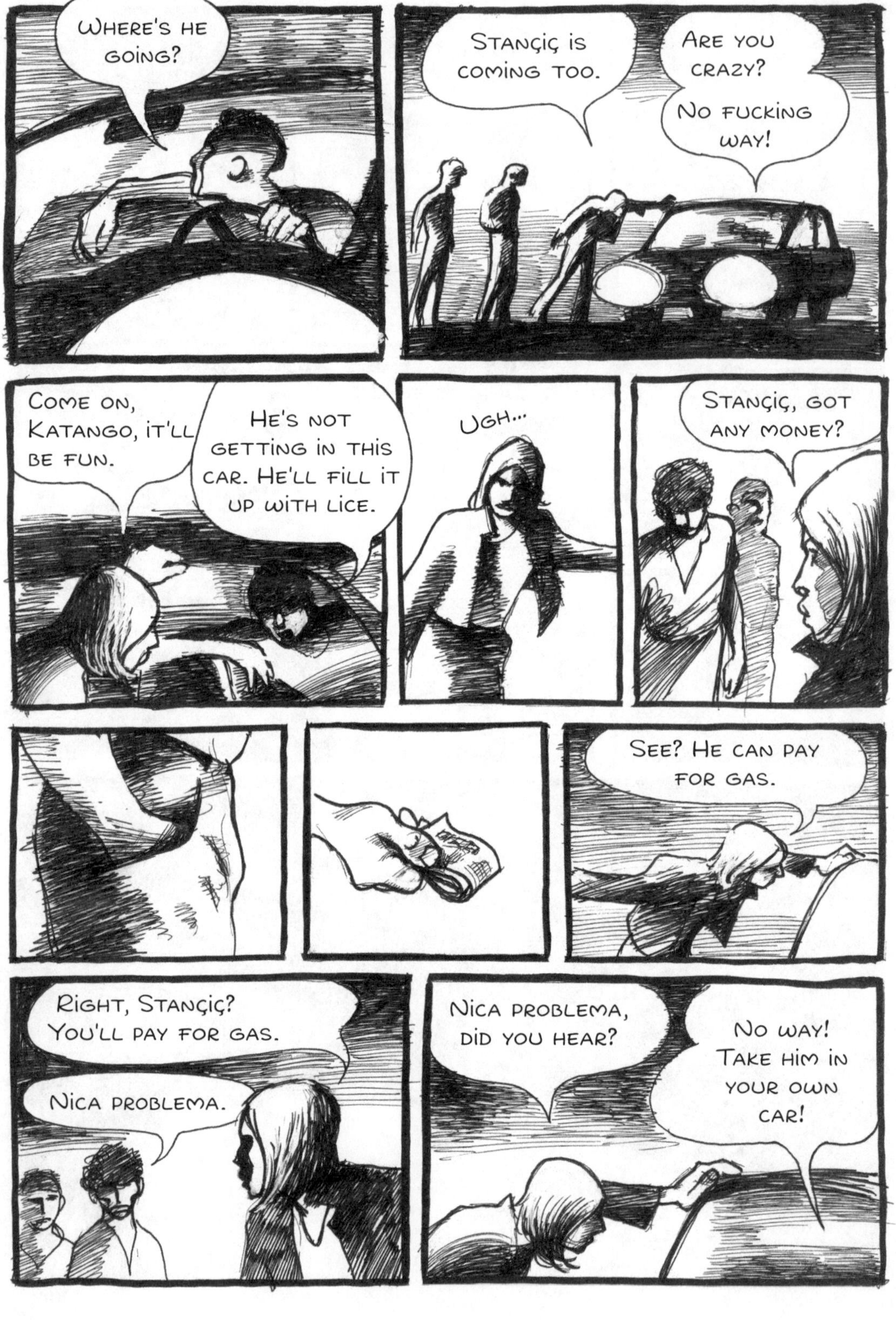
Where's he going?
Stançiç is coming too.
Are you crazy?
No fucking way!
Come on, Katango, it'll be fun.
He's not getting in this car. He'll fill it up with lice.
Ugh...
Stançiç, got any money?
See? He can pay for gas.
Right, Stançiç? You'll pay for gas.
Nica problema.
Nica problema, did you hear?
No way! Take him in your own car!

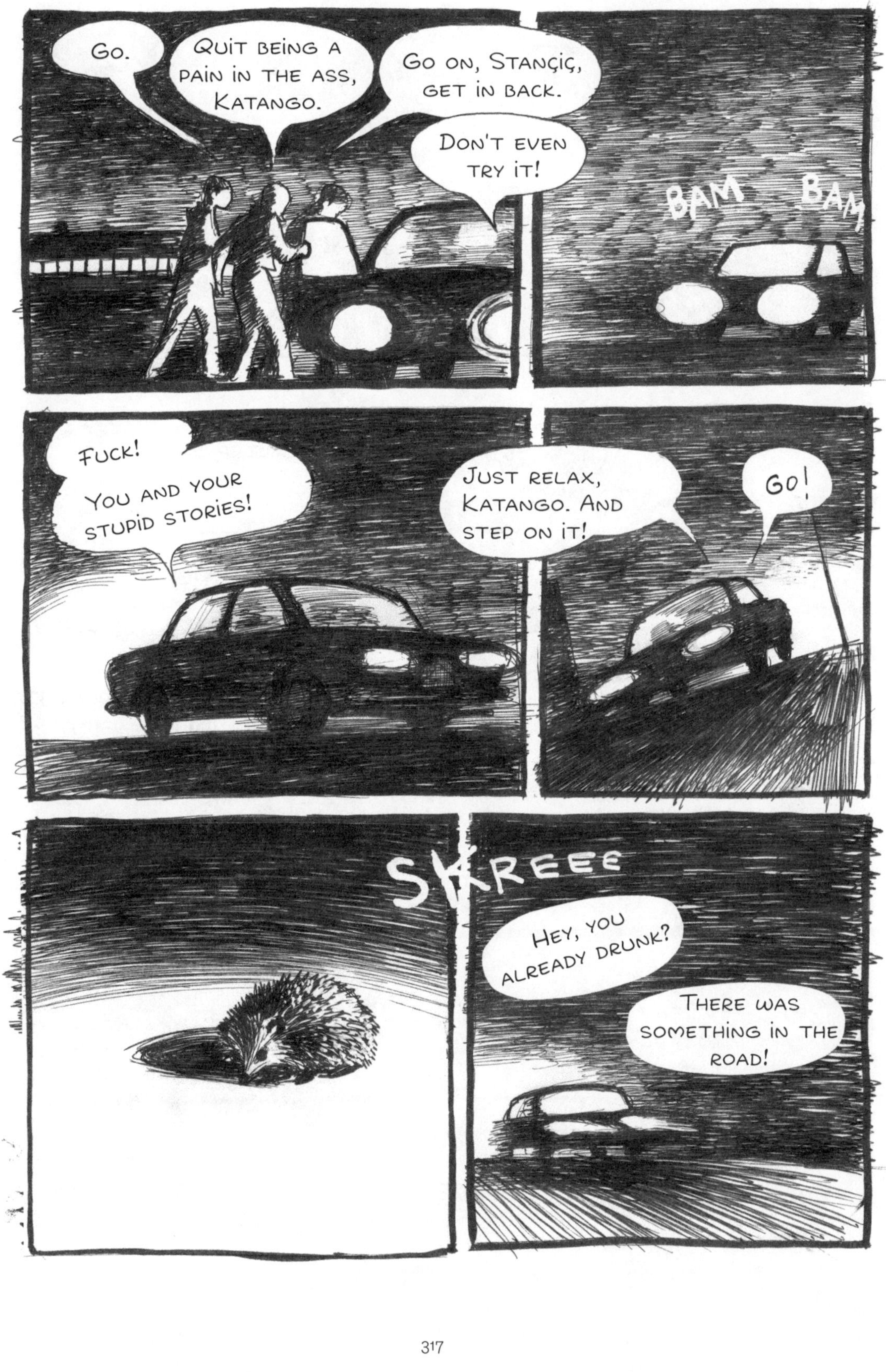
Go.
Quit being a pain in the ass, Katango.
Go on, Stançiç, get in back.
Don't even try it!
BAM BAM
Fuck!
You and your stupid stories!
Just relax, Katango. And step on it!
Go!
SKREEE
Hey, you already drunk?
There was something in the road!

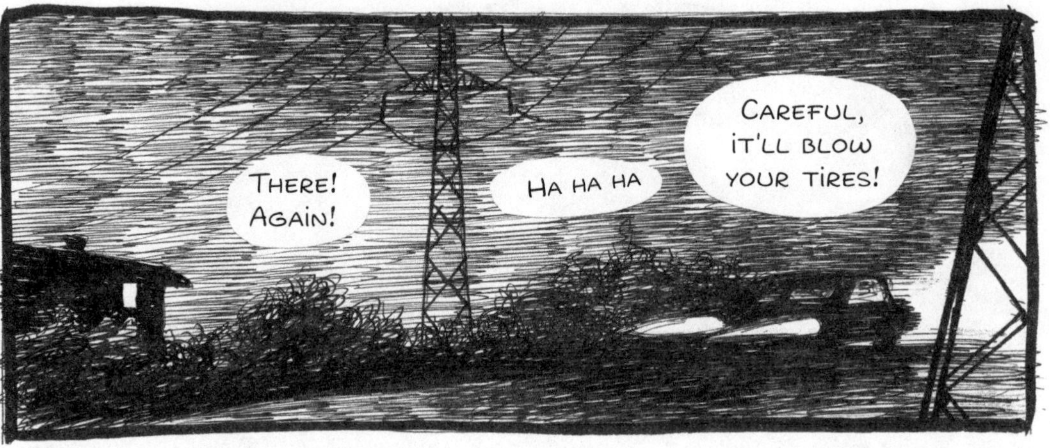
There! Again!
Ha ha ha
Careful, it'll blow your tires!

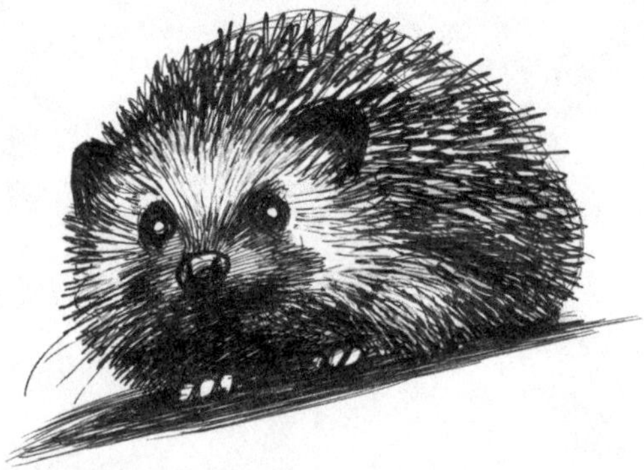

We stew them in winter when they fatten up.

Aspic with fragrant herbs—garlic, bay leaf, thyme, red pepper—in summer, when it runs all night and its meat is warm and pungent.

You never hunt a female who's pregnant or found with her young.

You only hunt them to eat right away.

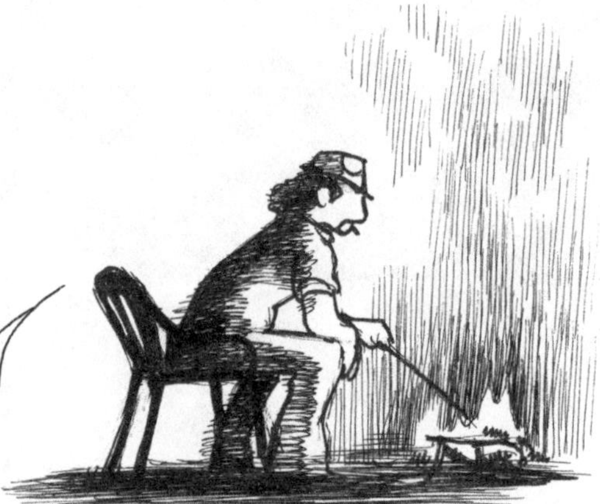
You have to set limits, control your impulses.
That mastery is what makes a good Sinto.

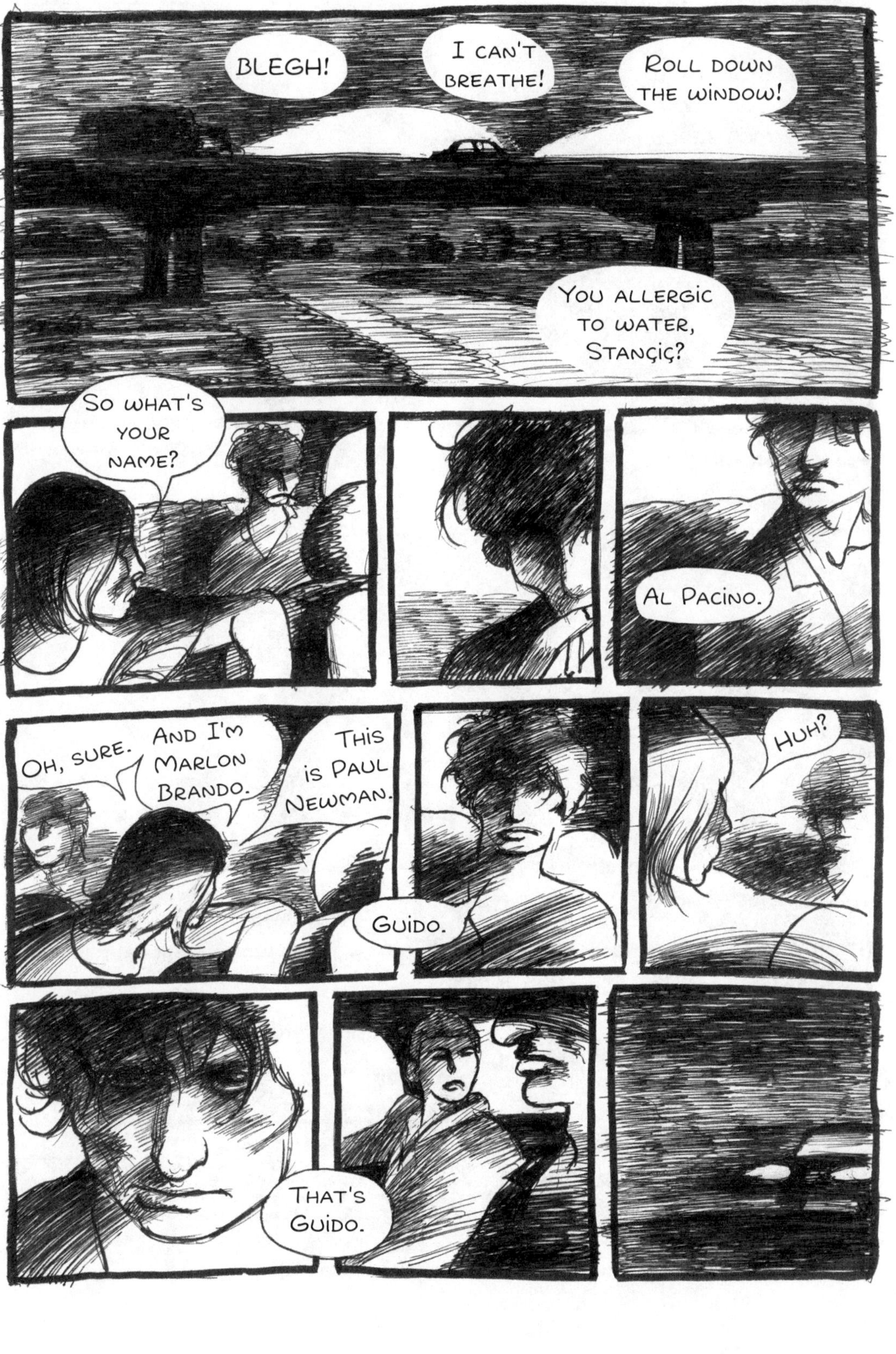
BLEGH!
I CAN'T BREATHE!
ROLL DOWN THE WINDOW!
YOU ALLERGIC TO WATER, STANÇIÇ?
SO WHAT'S YOUR NAME?
AL PACINO.
OH, SURE.
AND I'M MARLON BRANDO.
THIS IS PAUL NEWMAN.
GUIDO.
HUH?
THAT'S GUIDO.

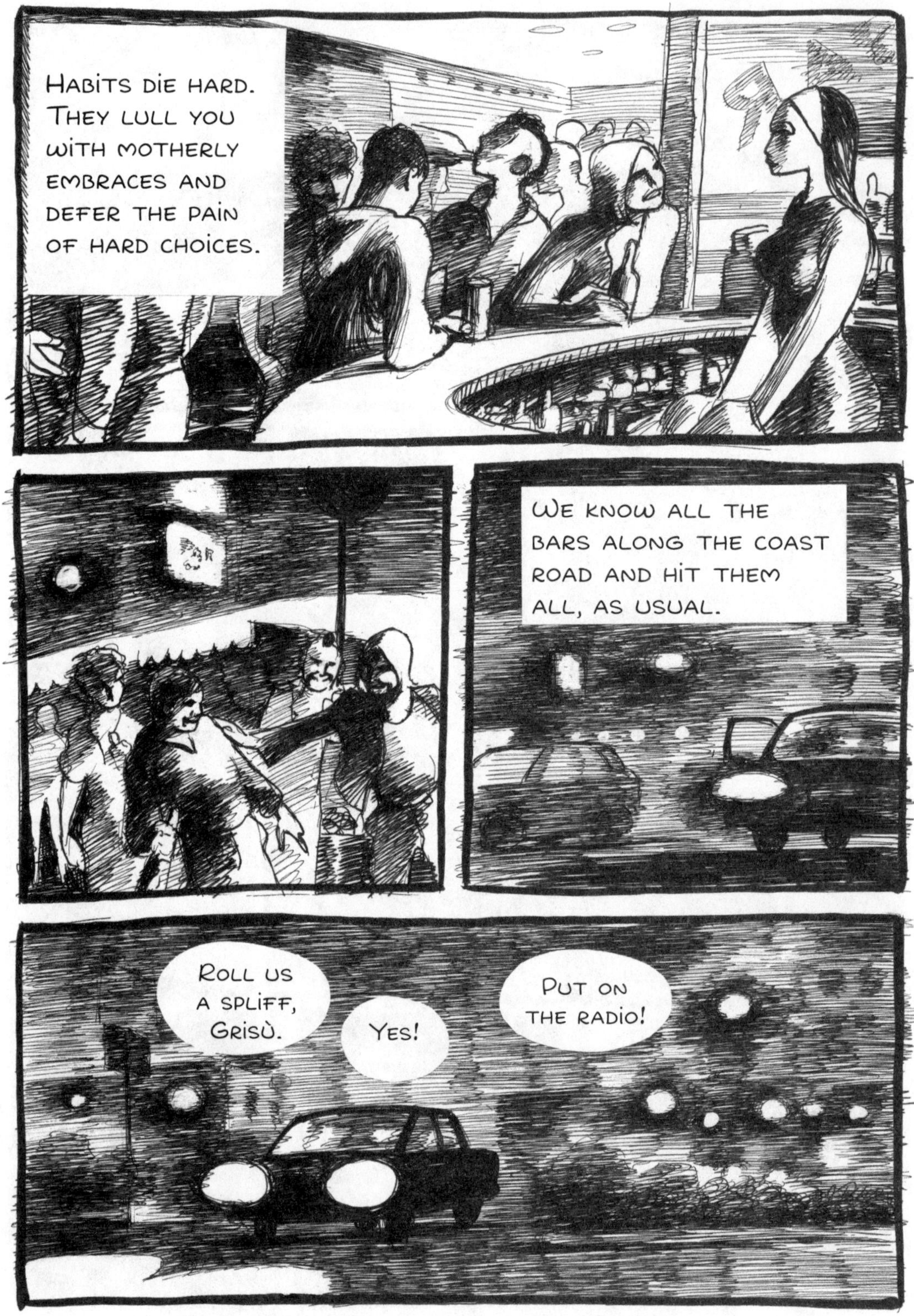
Habits die hard. They lull you with motherly embraces and defer the pain of hard choices.
We know all the bars along the coast road and hit them all, as usual.
Roll us a spliff, Grisù.
Yes!
Put on the radio!

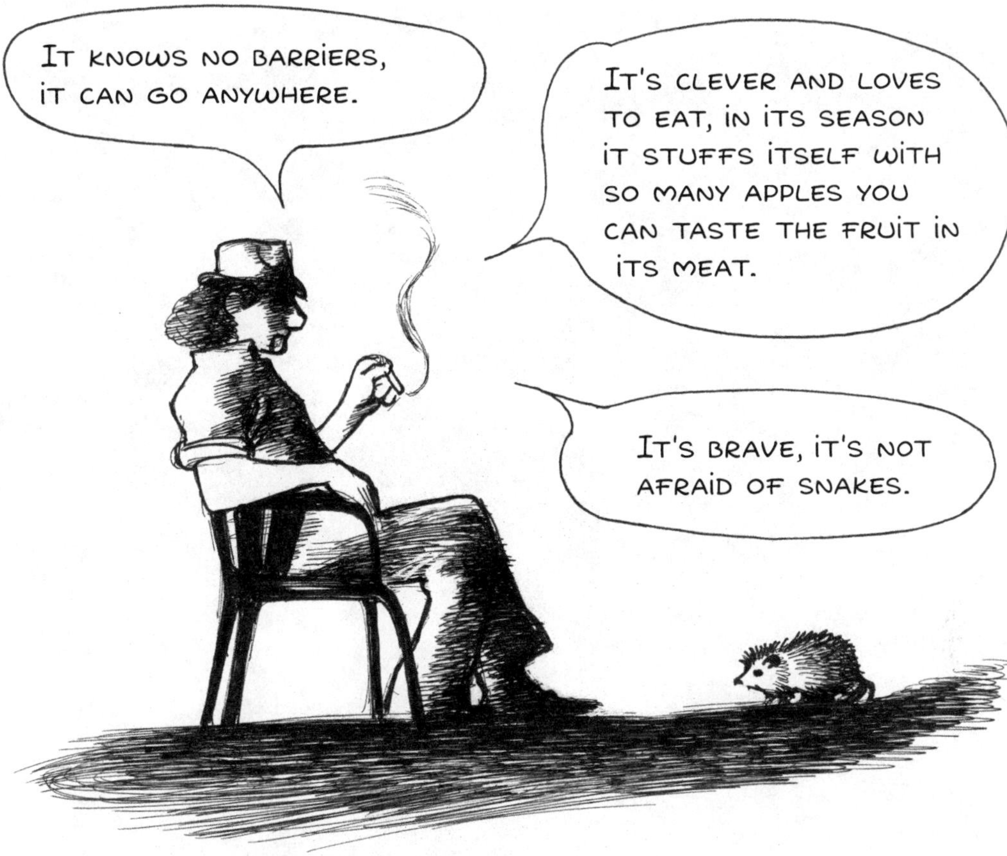
IT KNOWS NO BARRIERS, IT CAN GO ANYWHERE.
IT'S CLEVER AND LOVES TO EAT, IN ITS SEASON IT STUFFS ITSELF WITH SO MANY APPLES YOU CAN TASTE THE FRUIT IN ITS MEAT.
IT'S BRAVE, IT'S NOT AFRAID OF SNAKES.

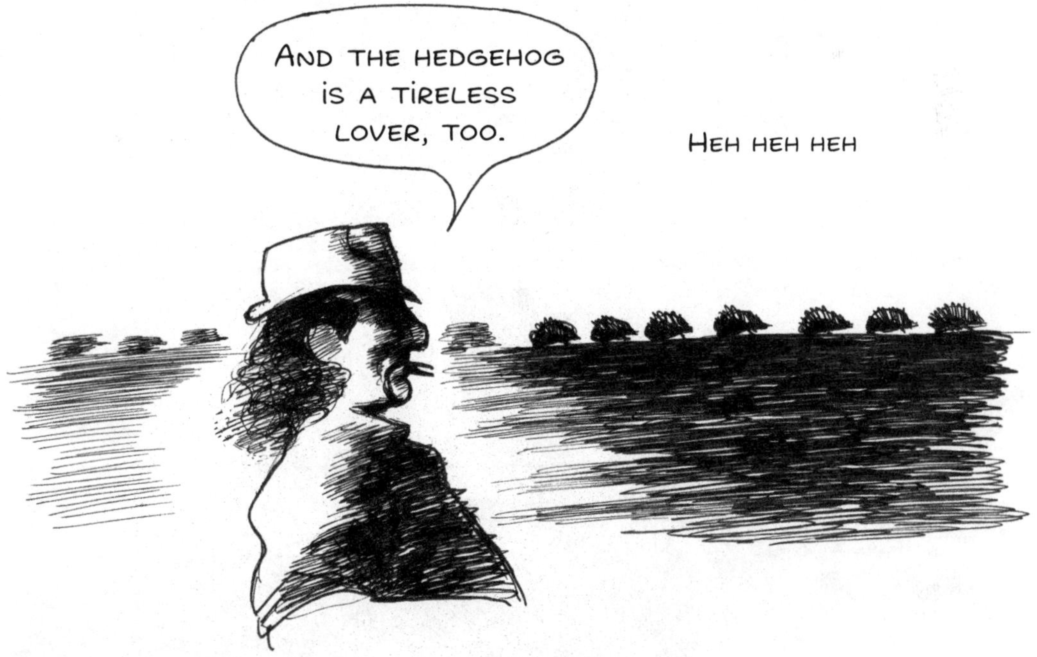
AND THE HEDGEHOG IS A TIRELESS LOVER, TOO.
HEH HEH HEH

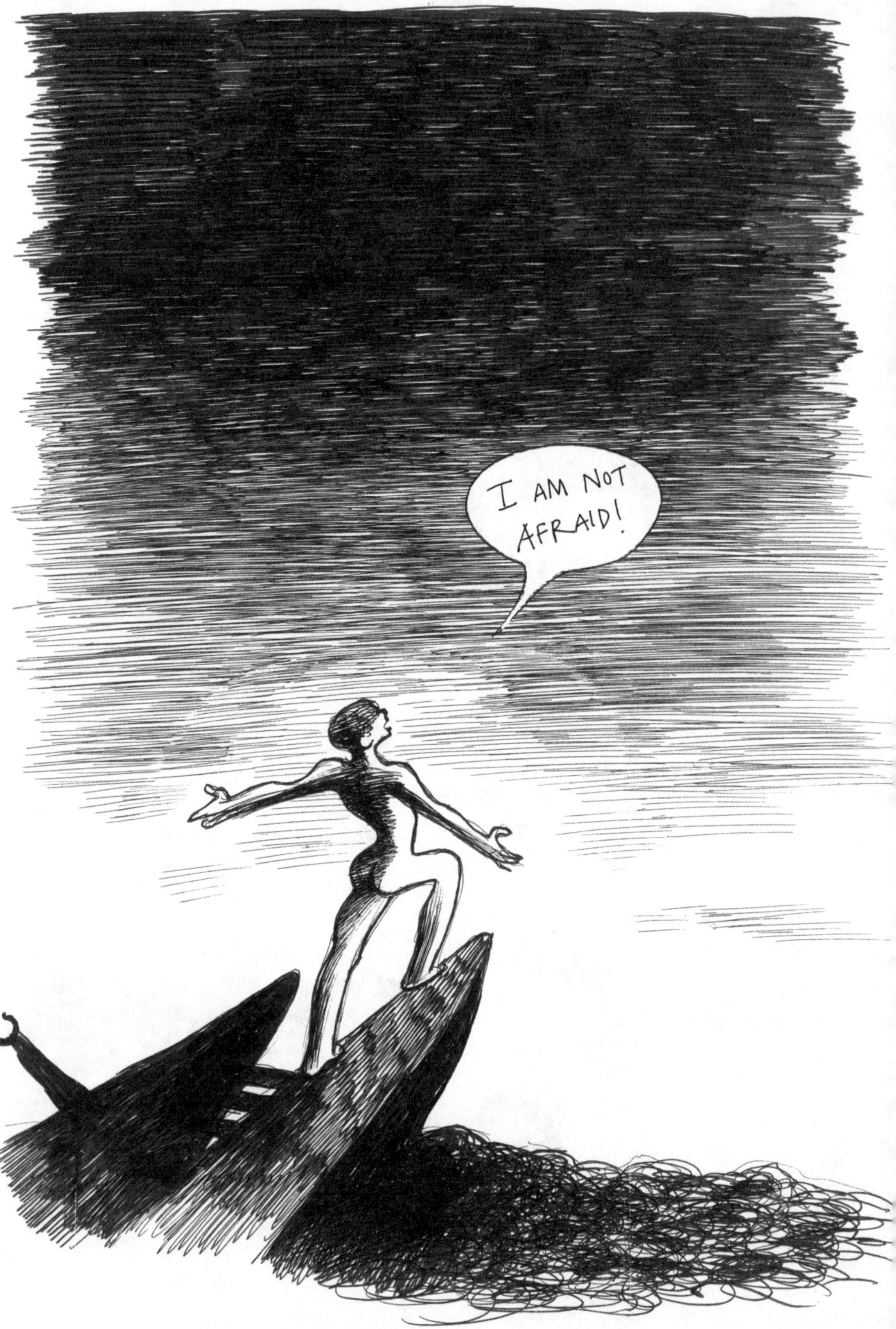
I AM NOT AFRAID!

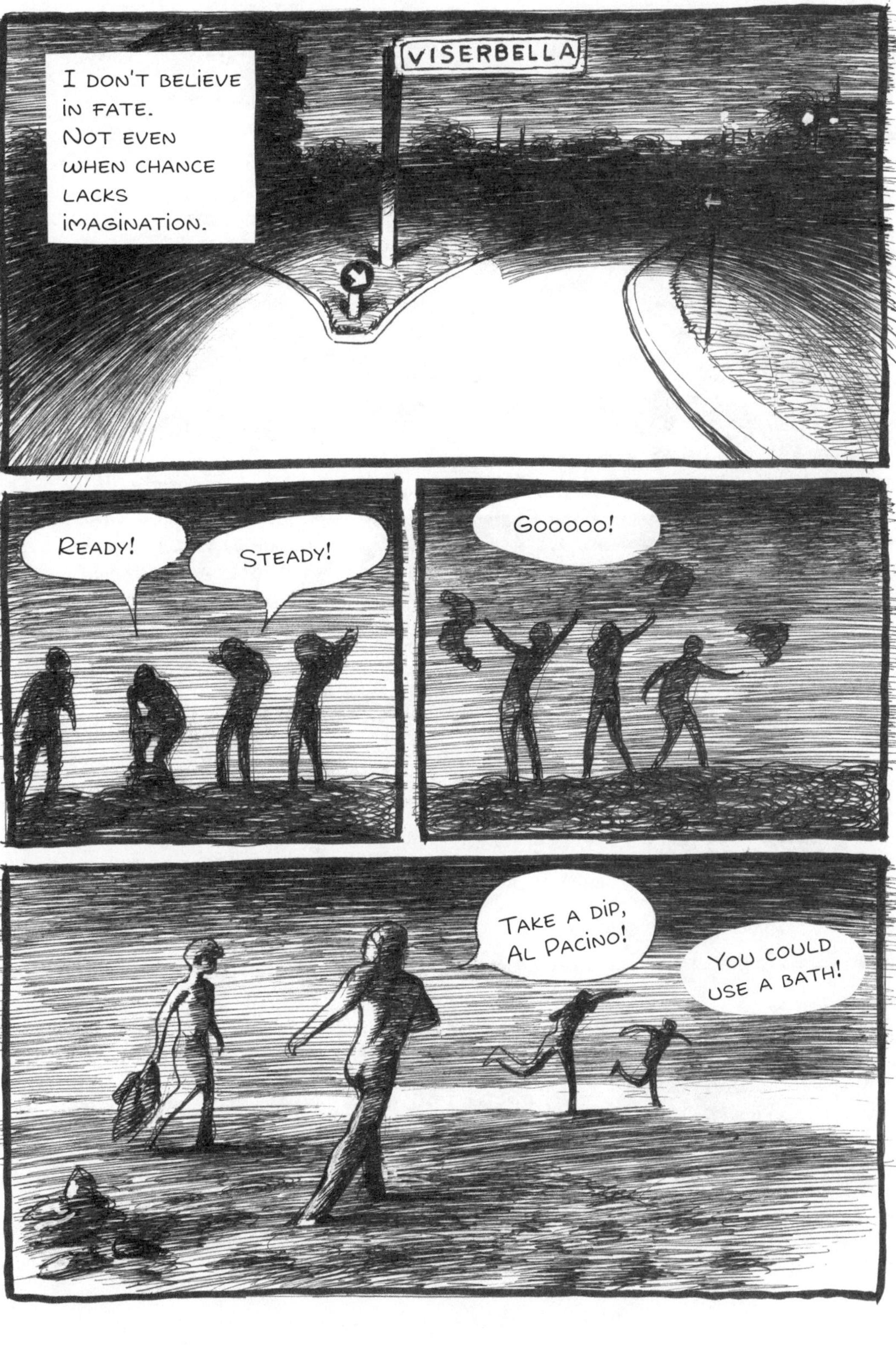
VISERBELLA
I don't believe in fate. Not even when chance lacks imagination.
Ready!
Steady!
Gooooo!
Take a dip, Al Pacino!
You could use a bath!

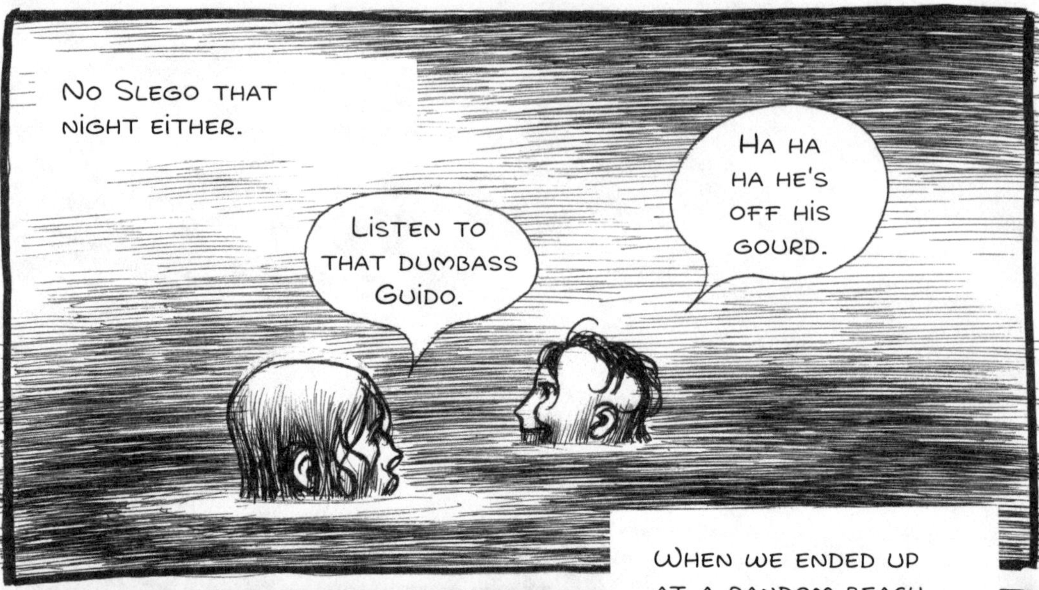
No Slego that night either.
Listen to that dumbass Guido.
Ha ha ha he's off his gourd.

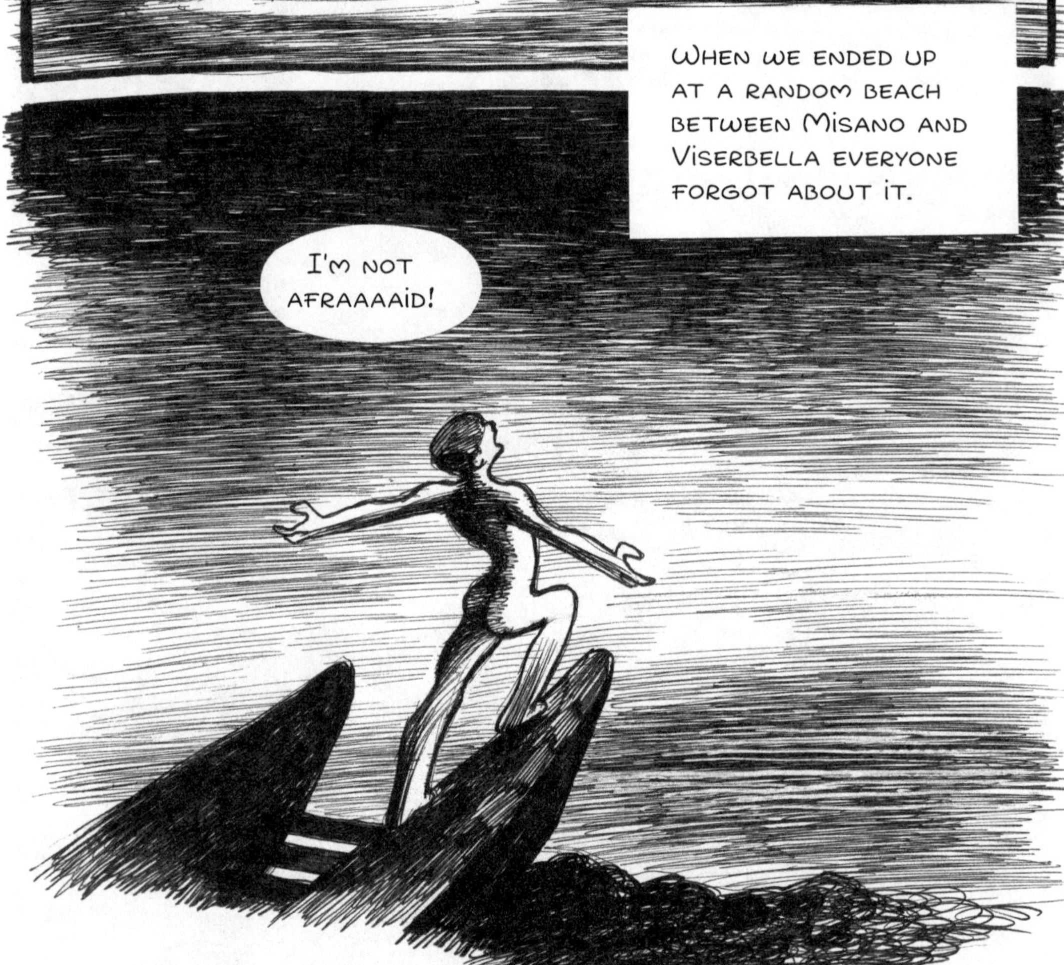
When we ended up at a random beach between Misano and Viserbella everyone forgot about it.
I'm not afraaaaid!

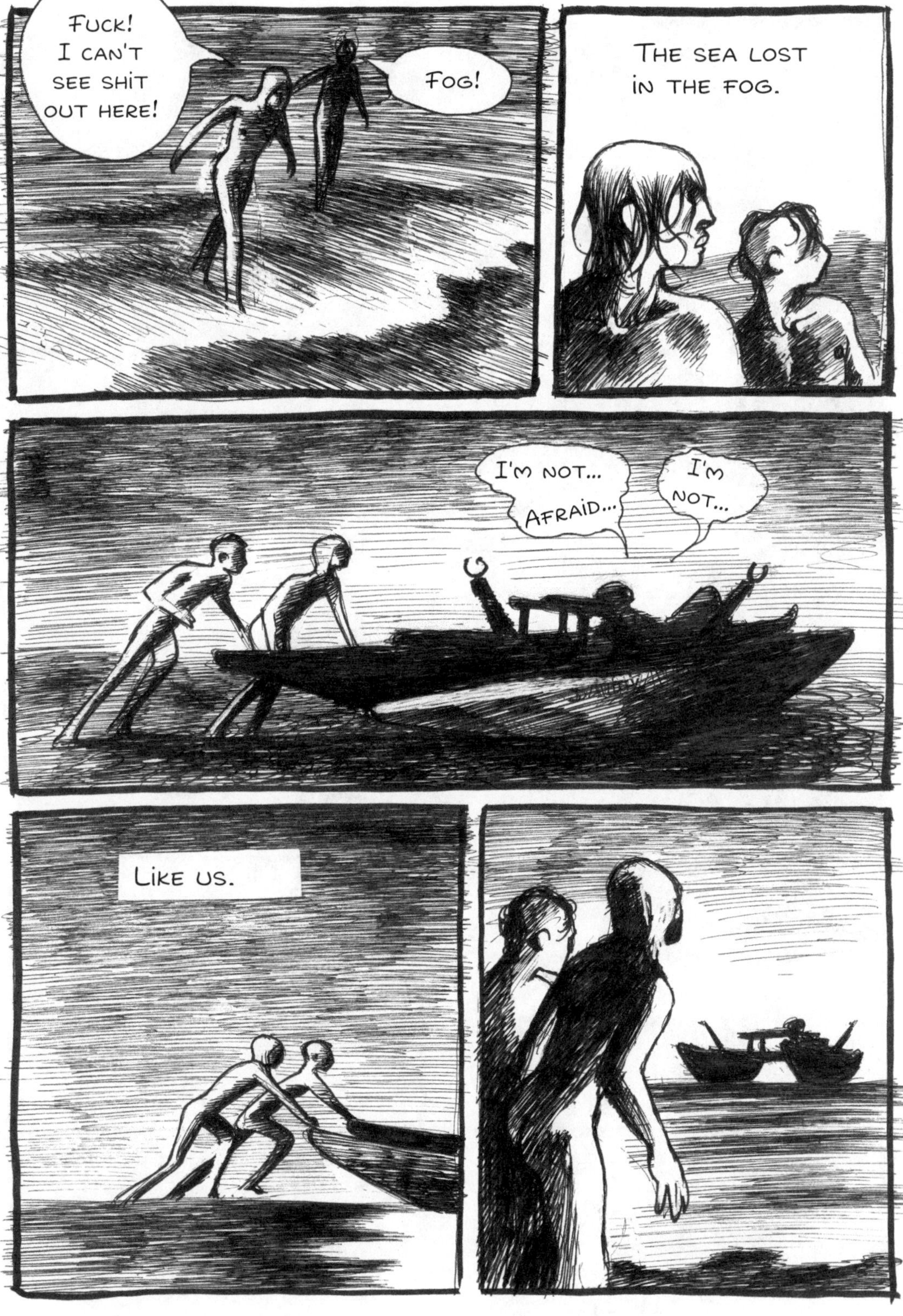
Fuck!
I can't
see shit
out here!
Fog!
The sea lost
in the fog.
I'm not...
Afraid...
I'm
not...
Like us.

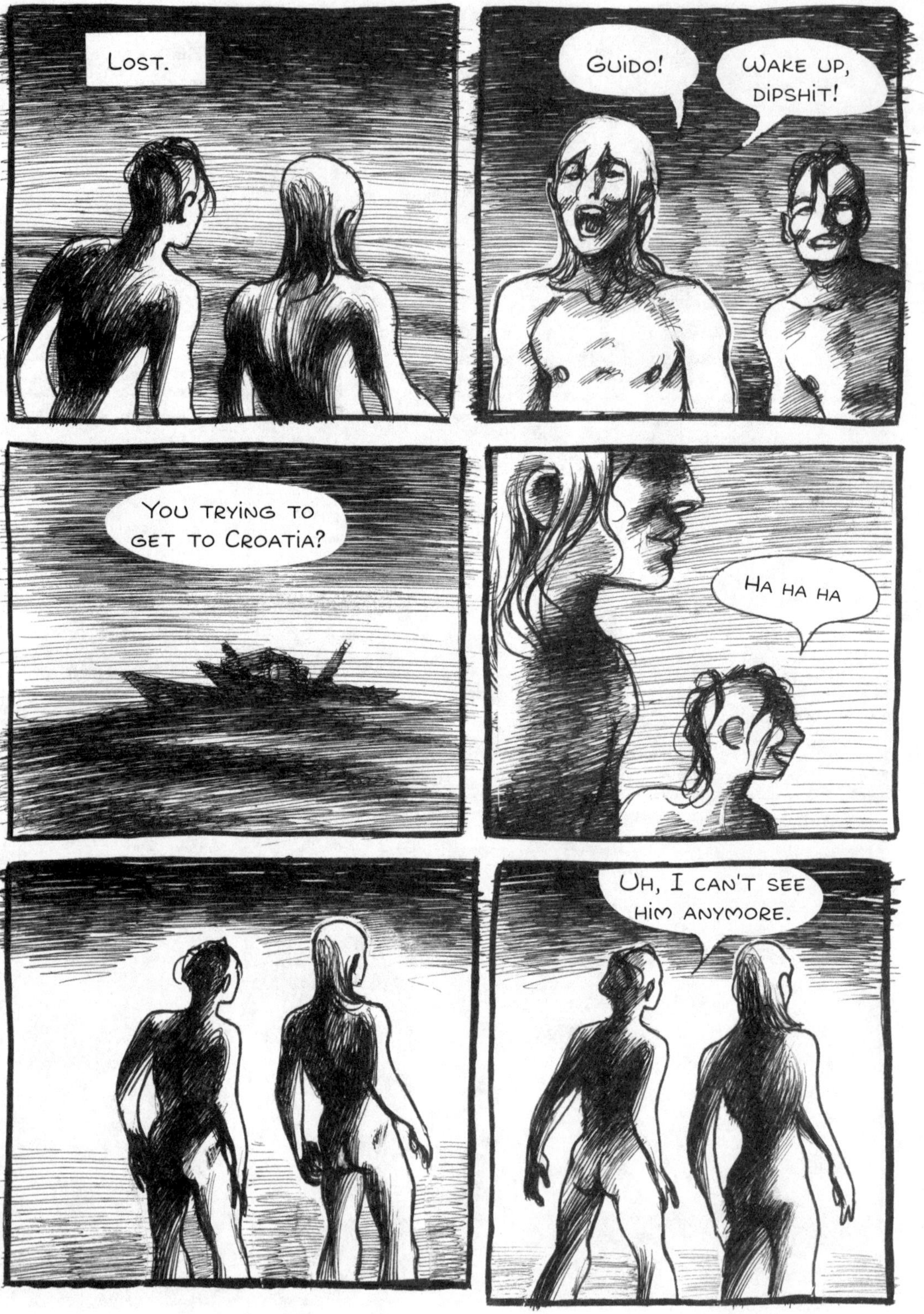
Lost.
Guido!
Wake up, dipshit!
You trying to get to Croatia?
Ha ha ha
Uh, I can't see him anymore.

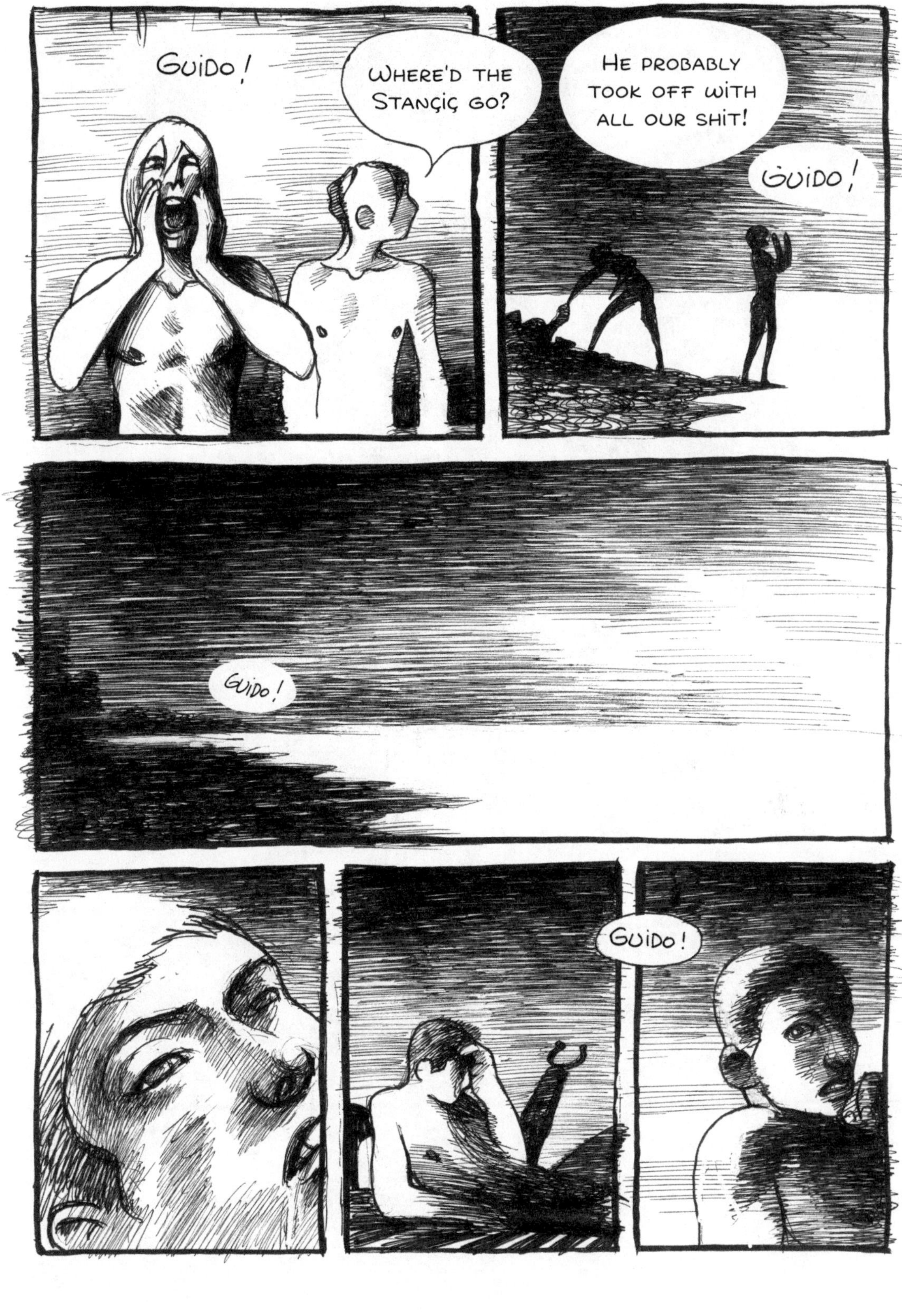
GUIDO!
WHERE'D THE STANÇIÇ GO?
HE PROBABLY TOOK OFF WITH ALL OUR SHIT!
GUIDO!
GUIDO!
GUIDO!

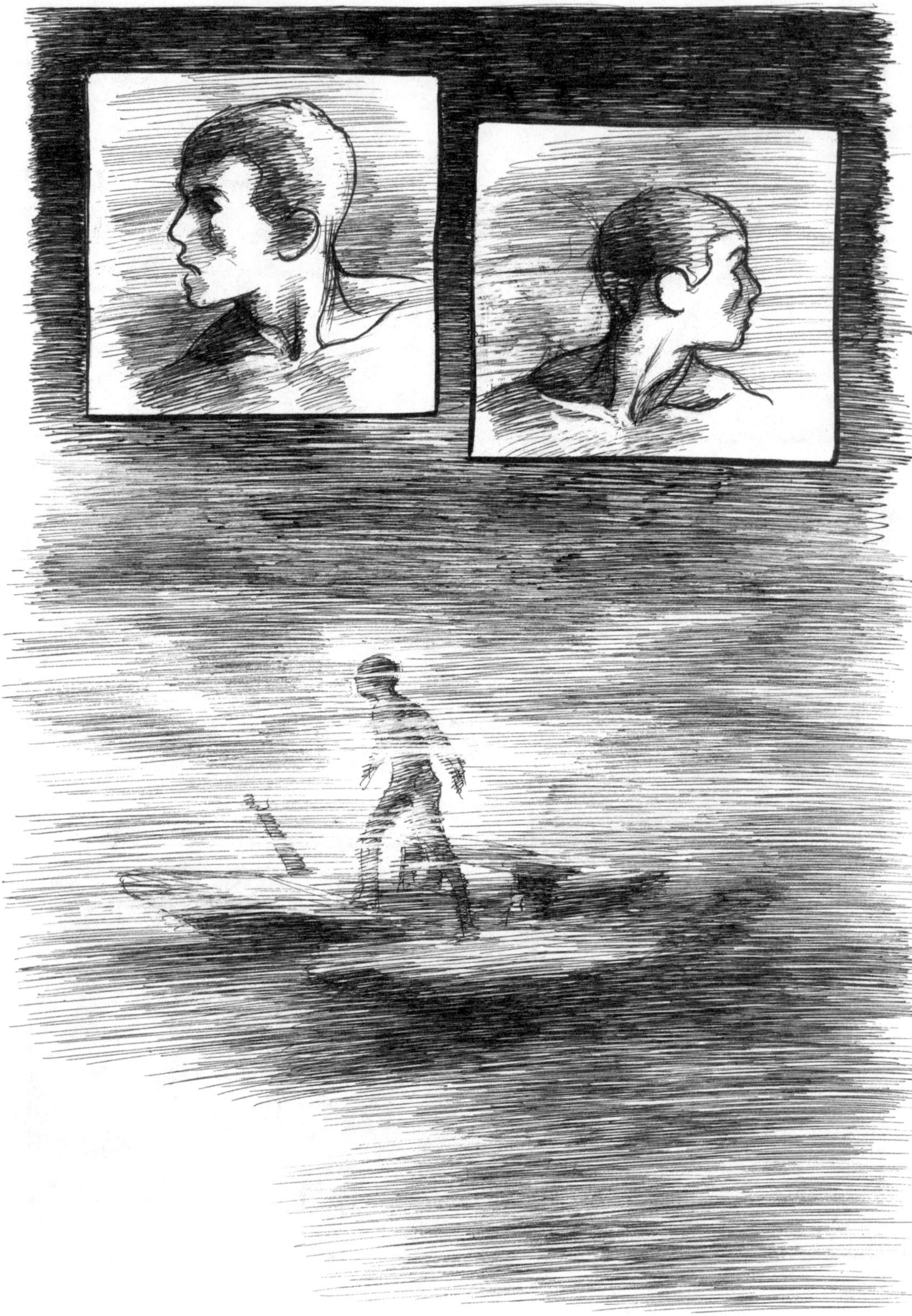

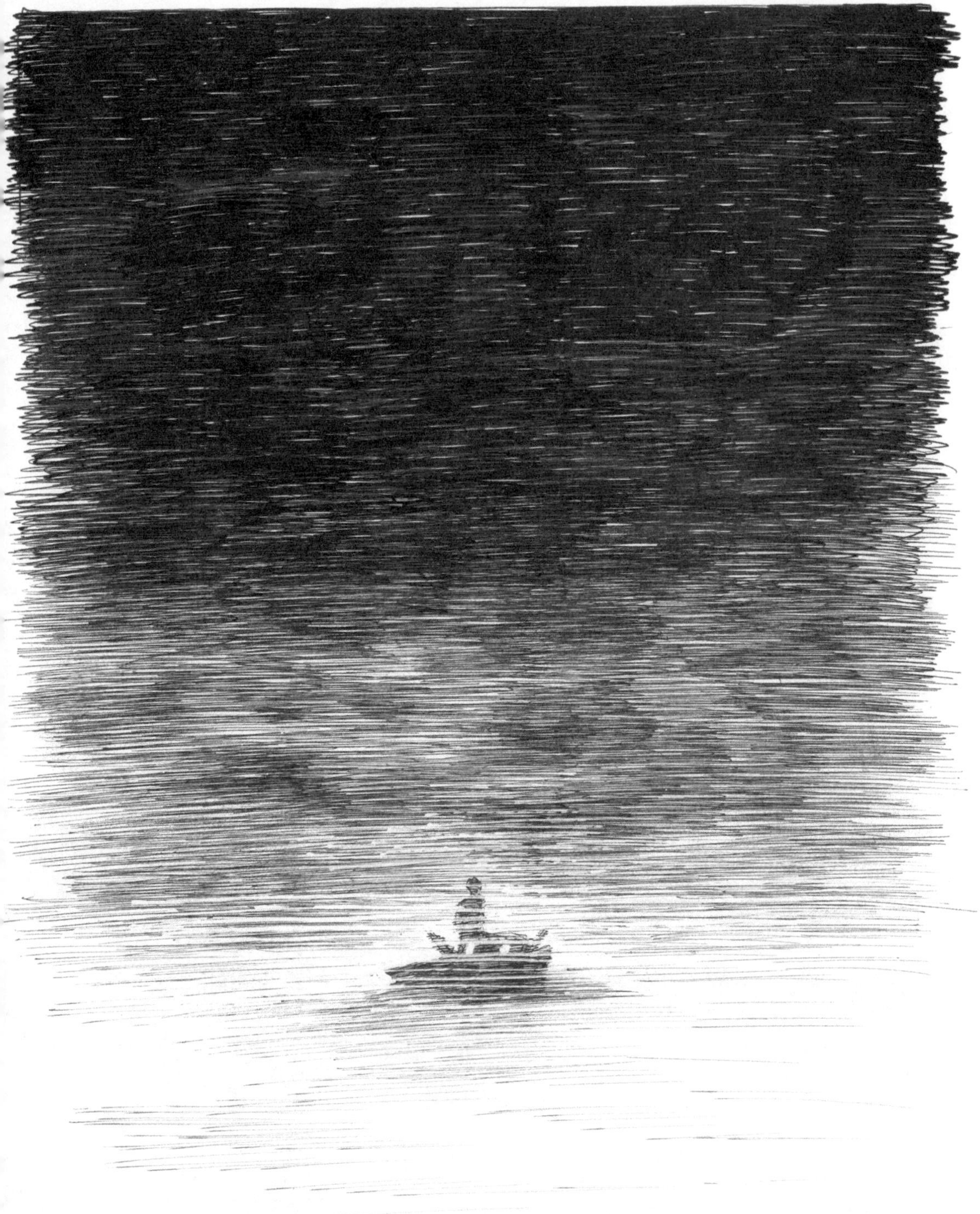

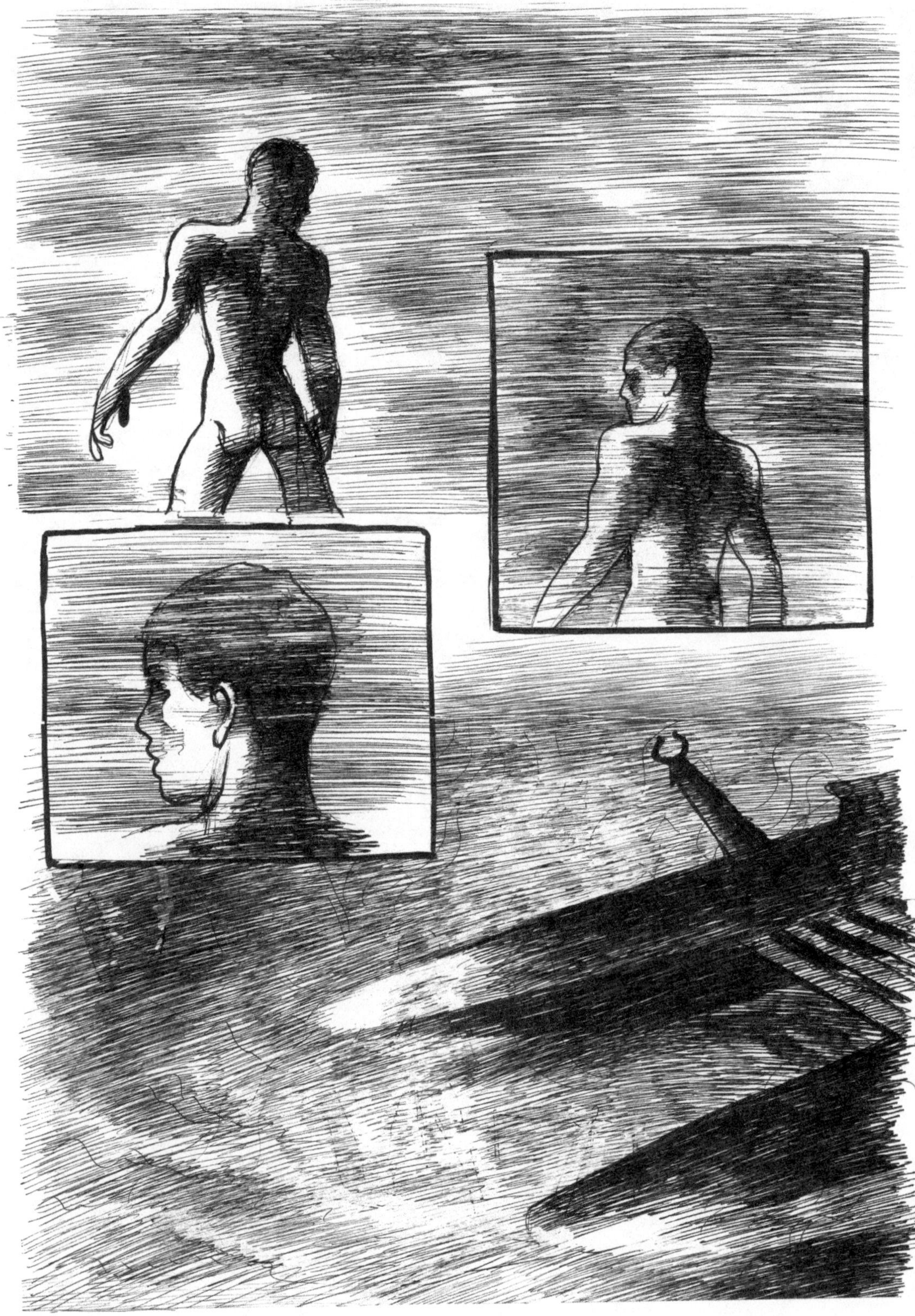

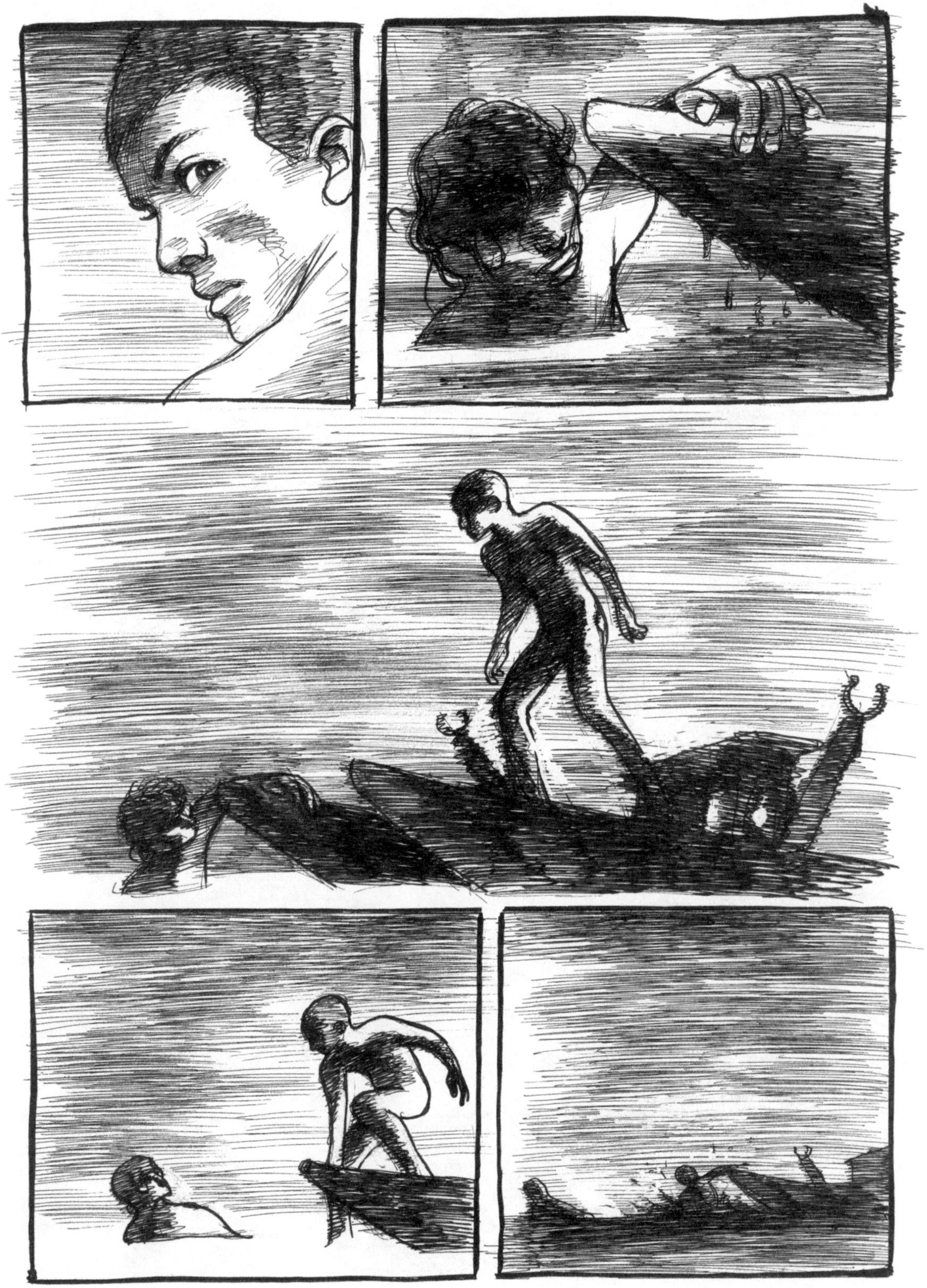

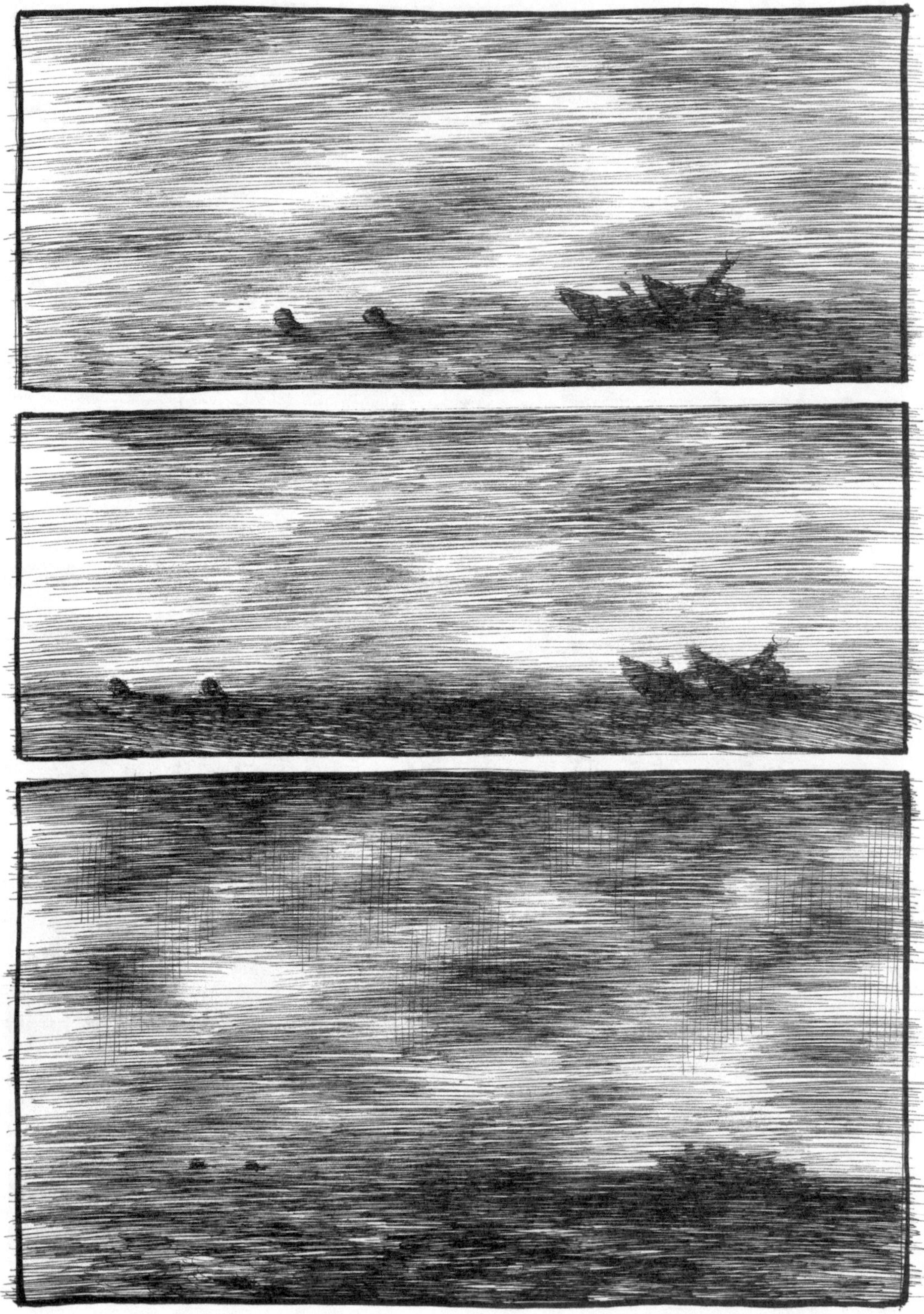

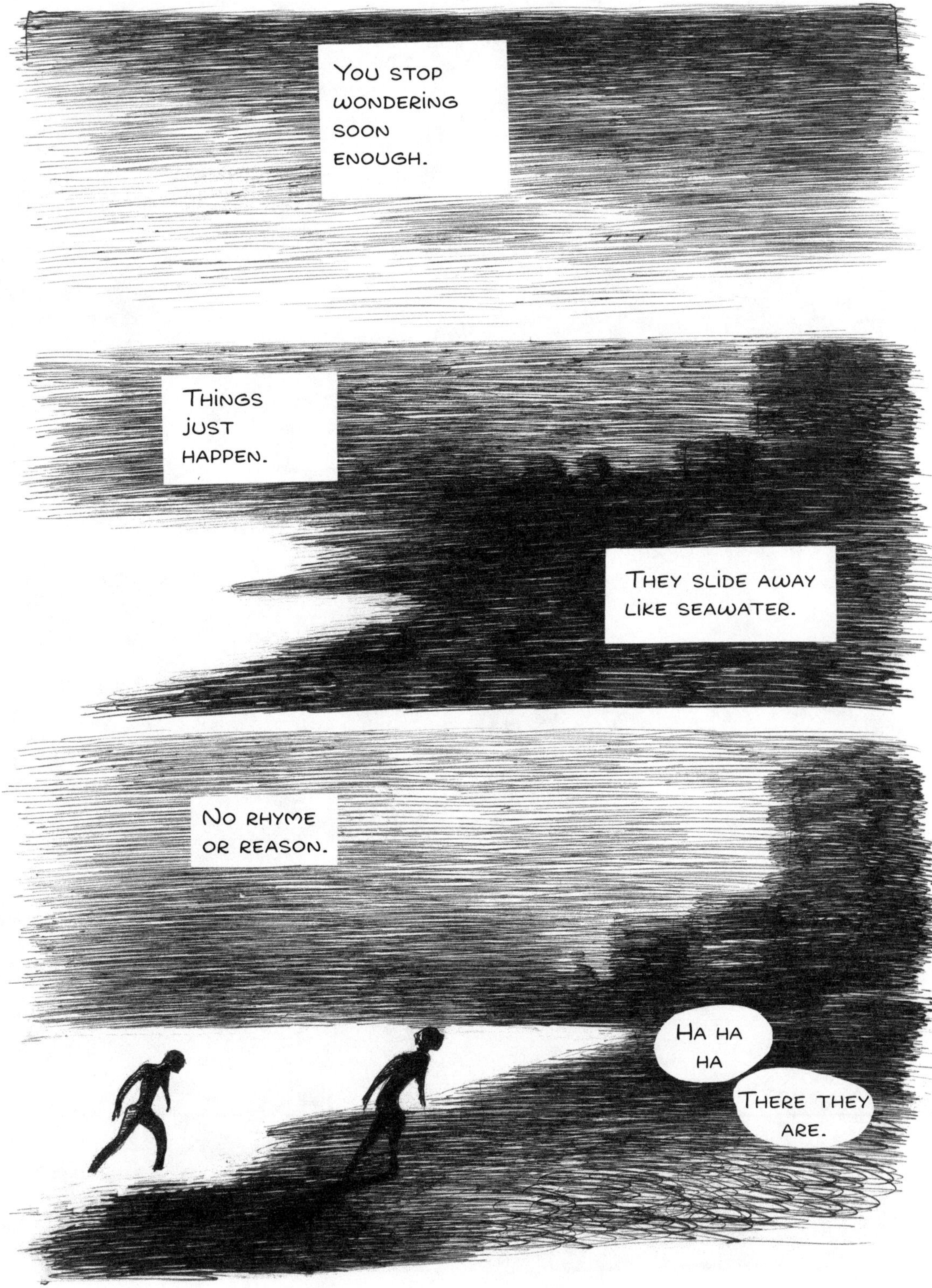
You stop wondering soon enough.
Things just happen.
They slide away like seawater.
No rhyme or reason.
Ha ha ha
There they are.

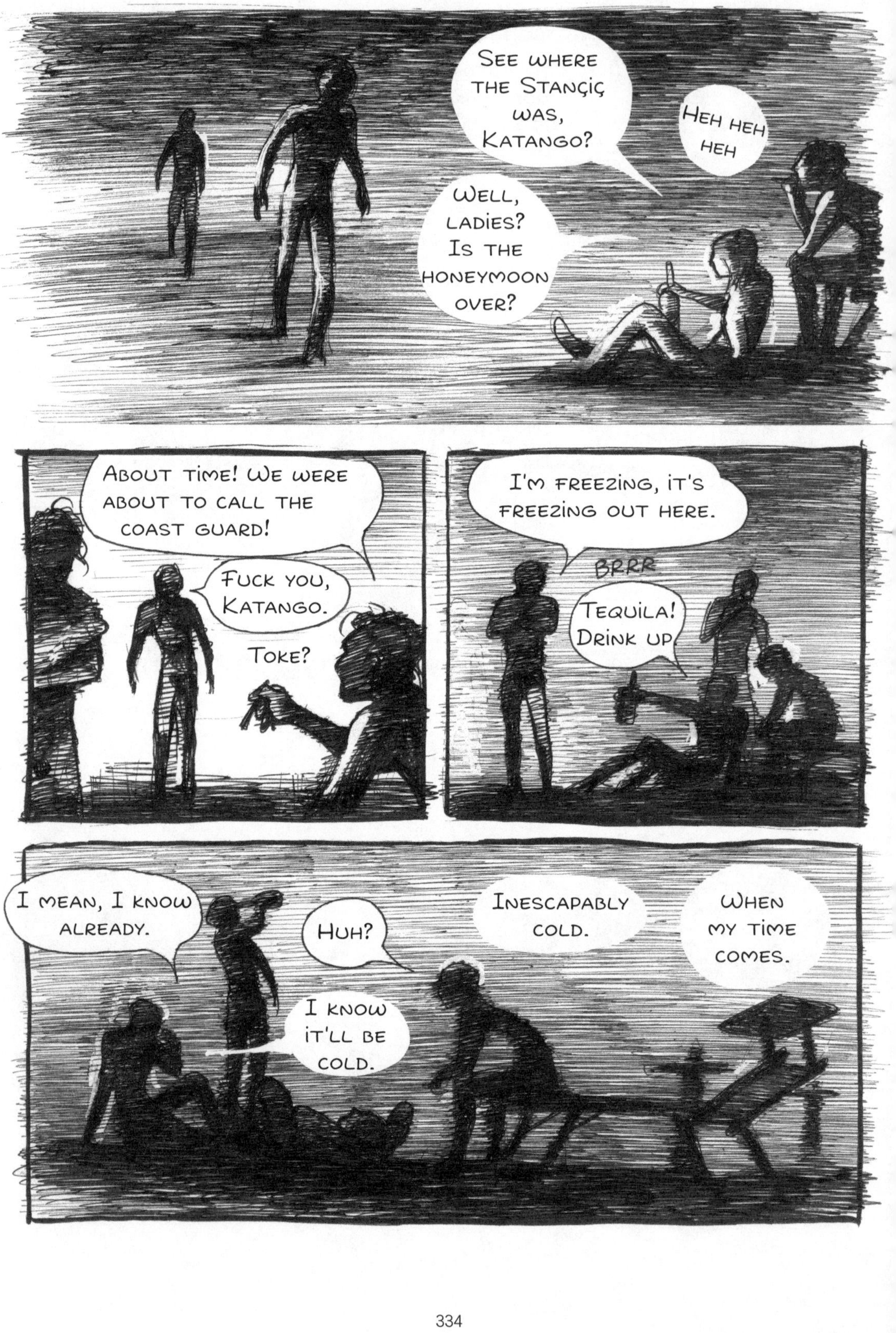

See where the Stançiç was, Katango?
Heh heh heh
Well, ladies? Is the honeymoon over?
About time! We were about to call the coast guard!
Fuck you, Katango.
Toke?
I'm freezing, it's freezing out here.
BRRR
Tequila! Drink up
I mean, I know already.
Huh?
I know it'll be cold.
Inescapably cold.
When my time comes.

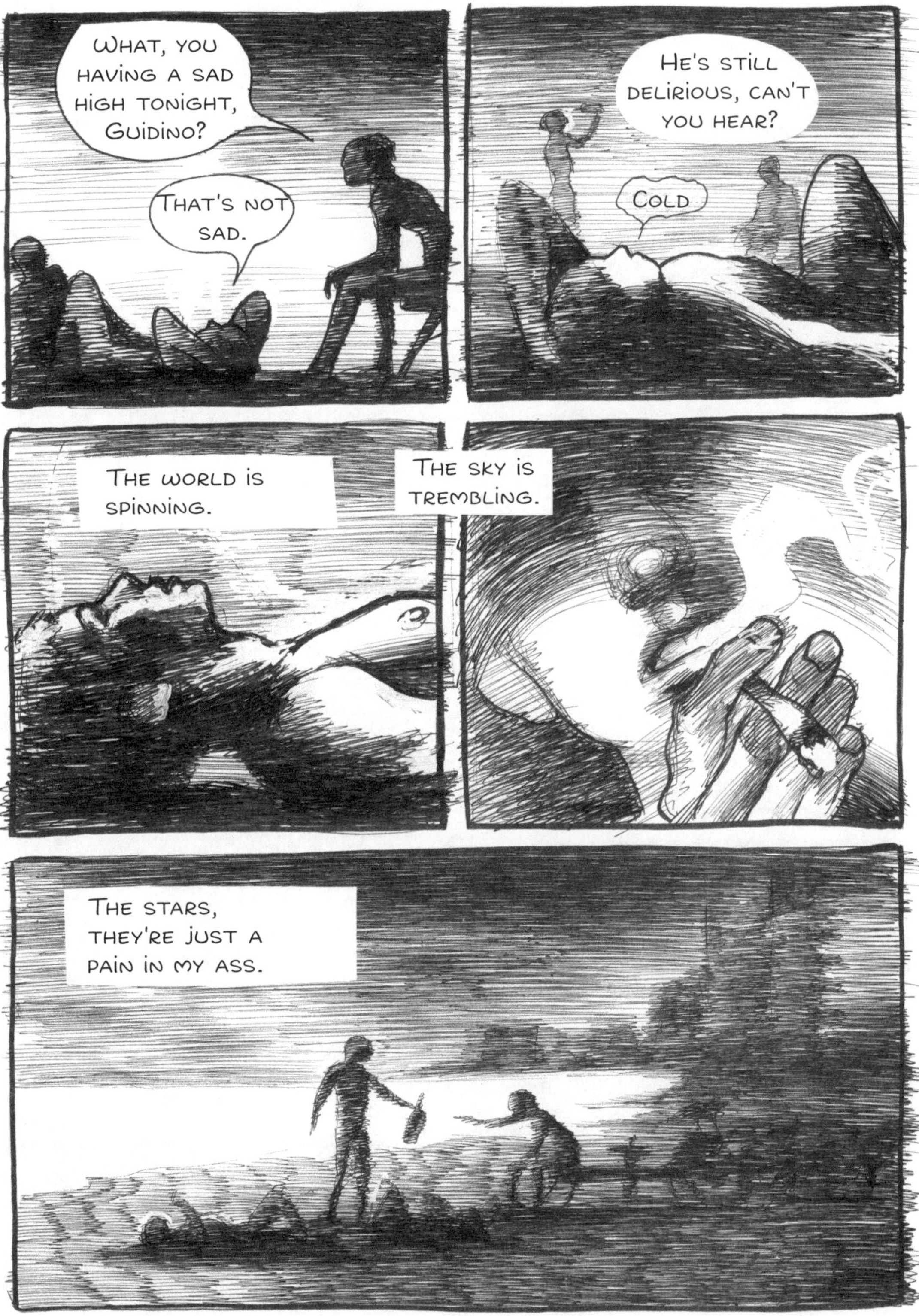
WHAT, YOU HAVING A SAD HIGH TONIGHT, GUIDINO?
THAT'S NOT SAD.
HE'S STILL DELIRIOUS, CAN'T YOU HEAR?
COLD
THE WORLD IS SPINNING.
THE SKY IS TREMBLING.
THE STARS, THEY'RE JUST A PAIN IN MY ASS.

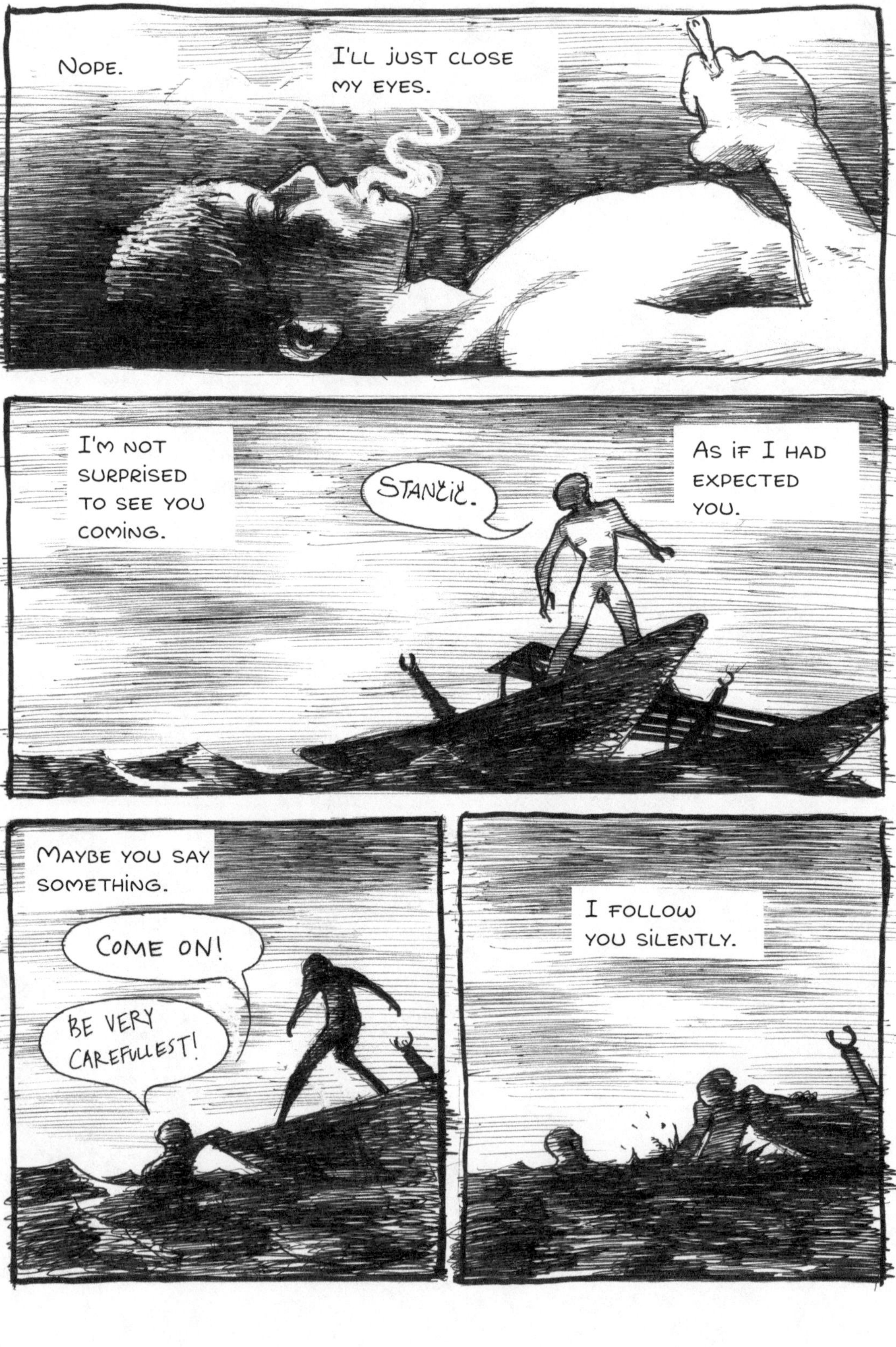
Nope.
I'll just close my eyes.
I'm not surprised to see you coming.
Stančič.
As if I had expected you.
Maybe you say something.
Come on!
Be very carefullest!
I follow you silently.

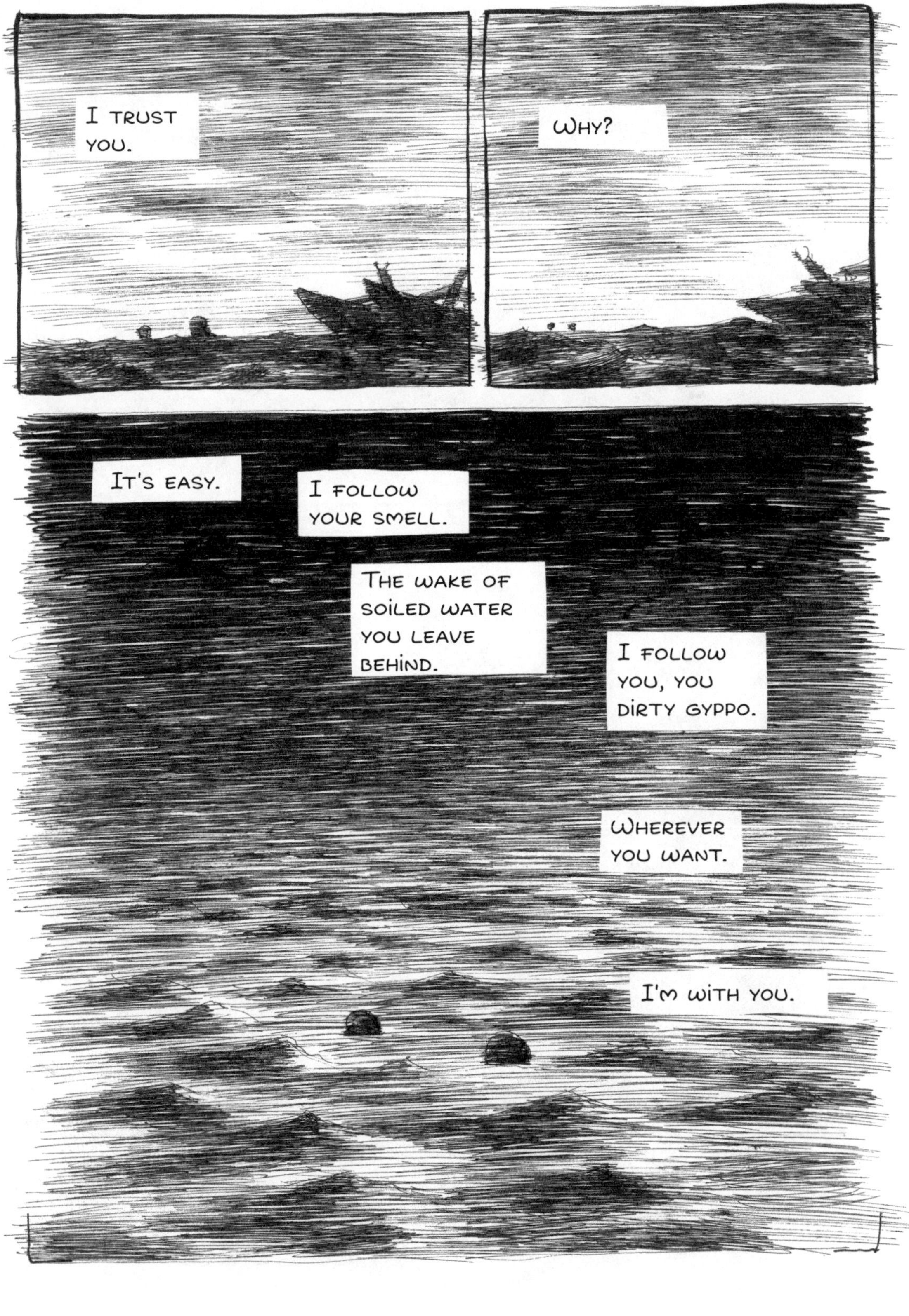
I TRUST YOU.
WHY?
IT'S EASY.
I FOLLOW YOUR SMELL.
THE WAKE OF SOILED WATER YOU LEAVE BEHIND.
I FOLLOW YOU, YOU DIRTY GYPPO.
WHEREVER YOU WANT.
I'M WITH YOU.

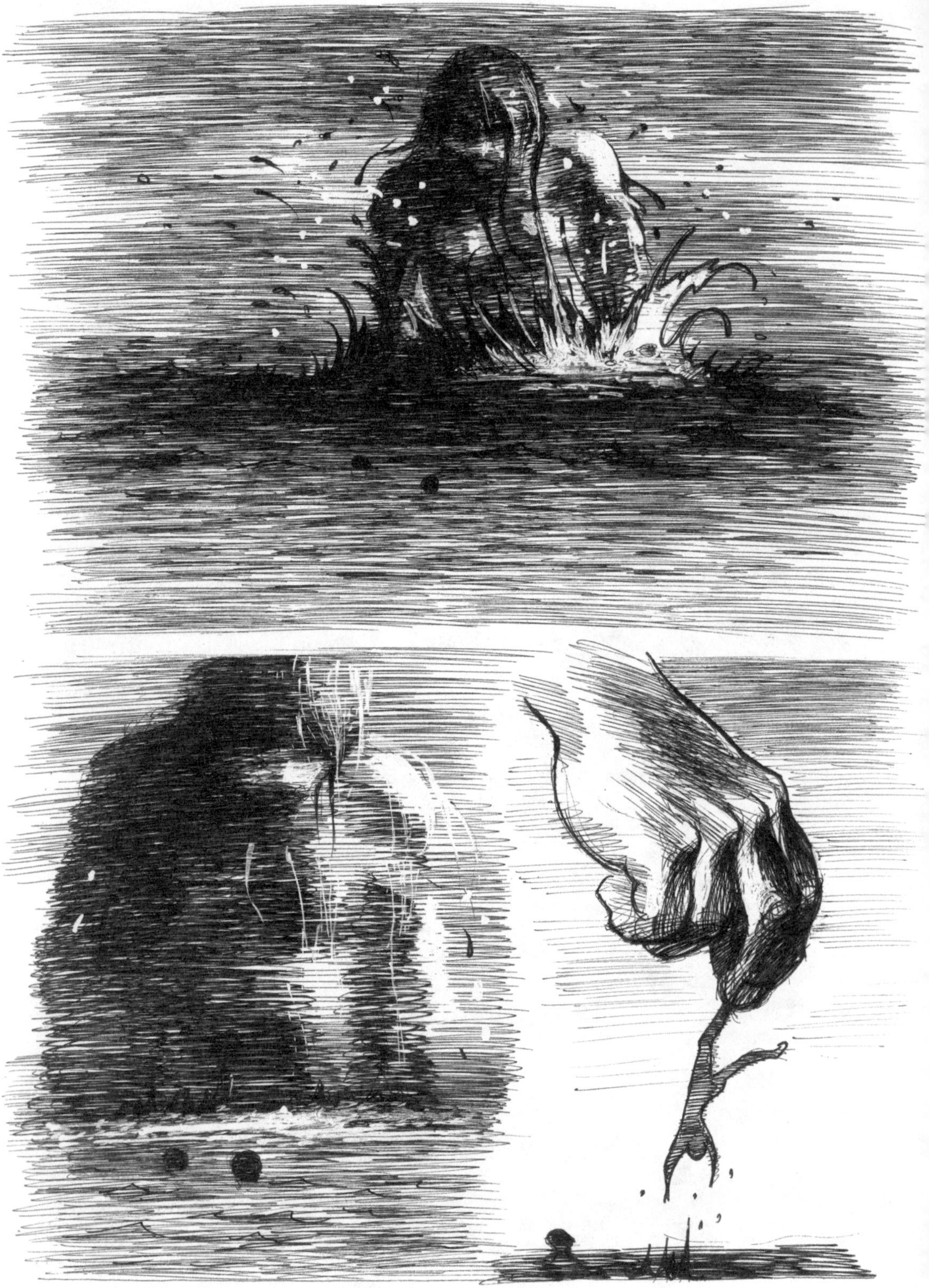

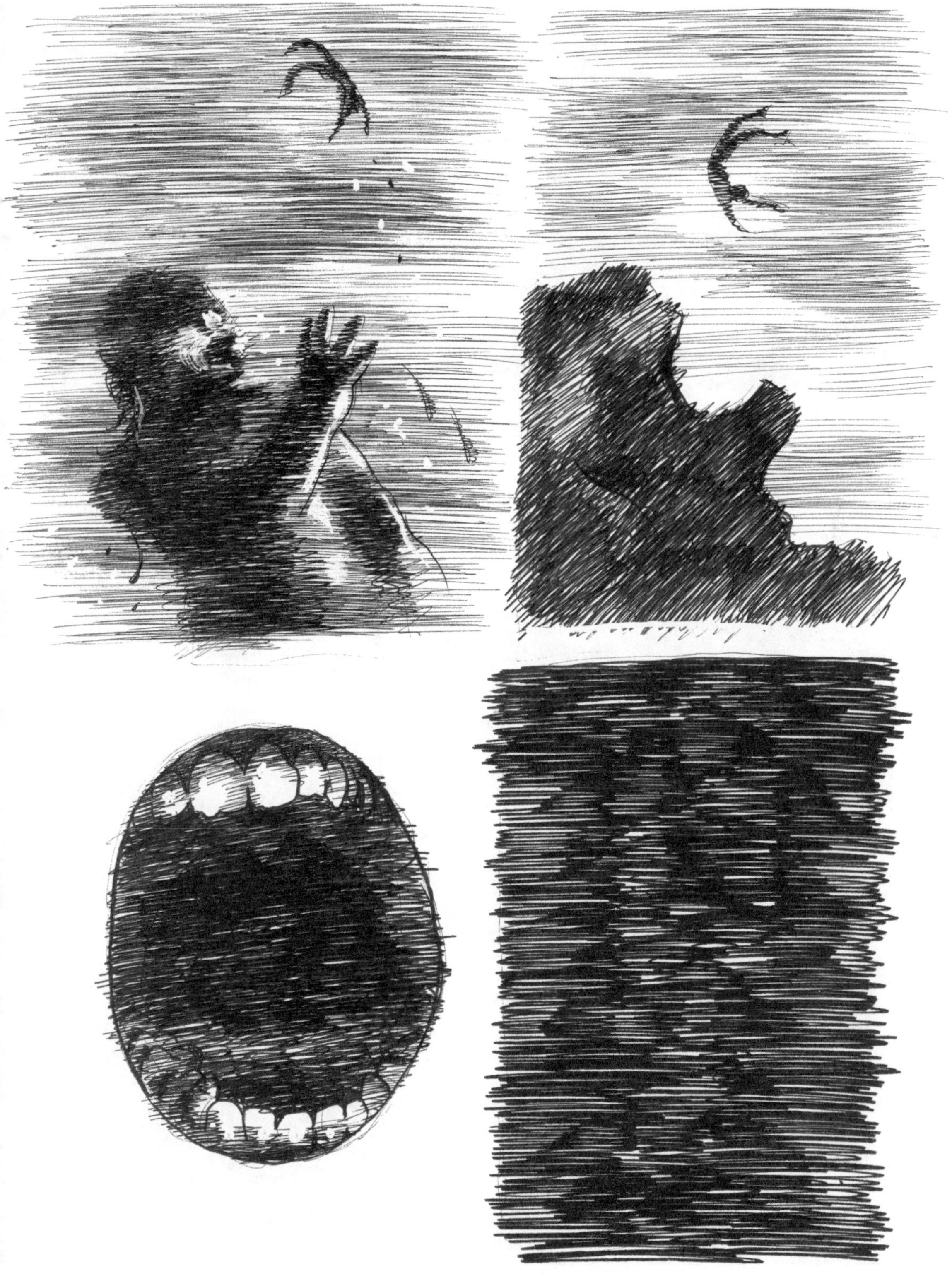

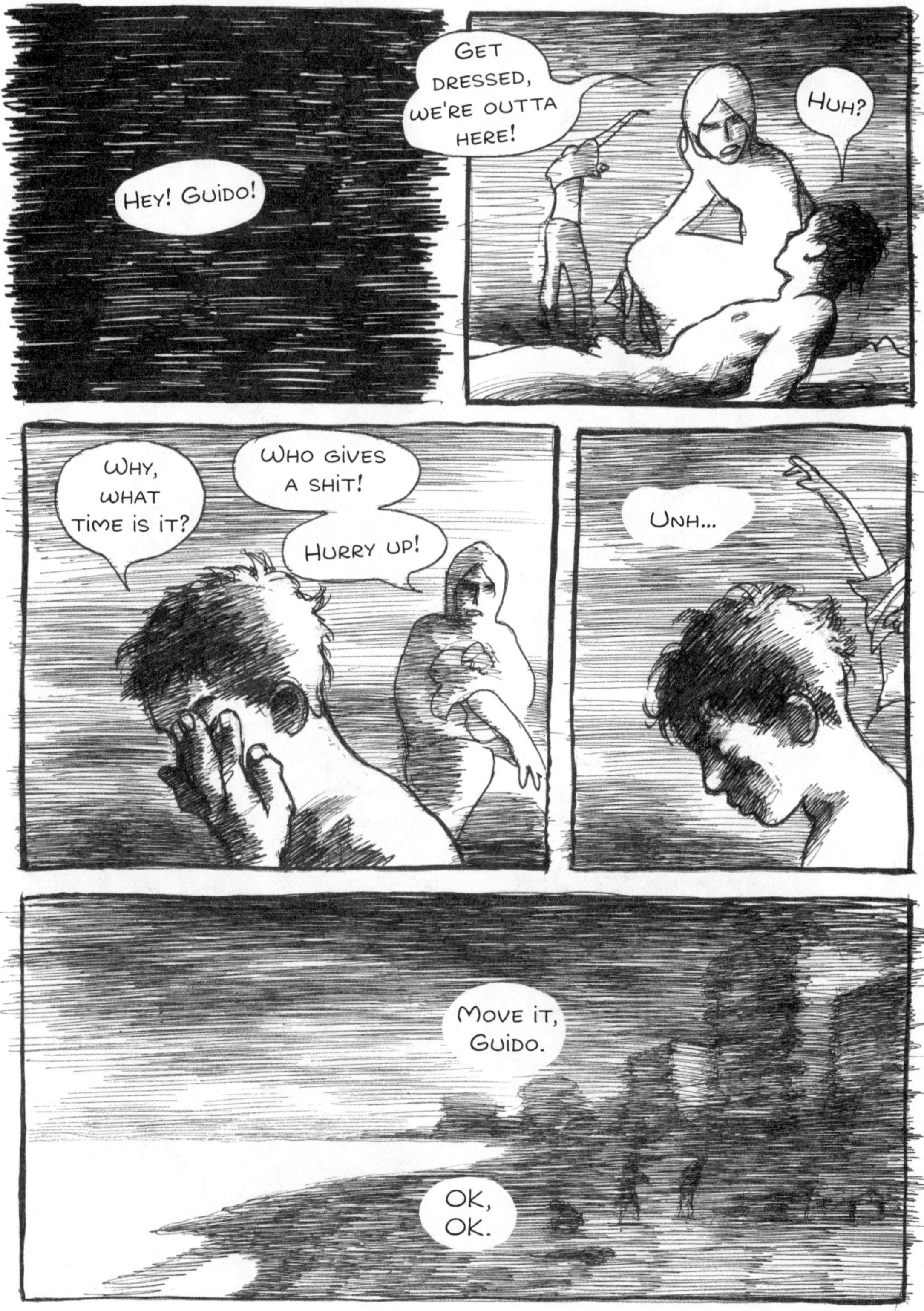
Hey! Guido!
Get dressed, we're outta here!
Huh?
Why, what time is it?
Who gives a shit!
Hurry up!
Unh...
Move it, Guido.
OK, OK.

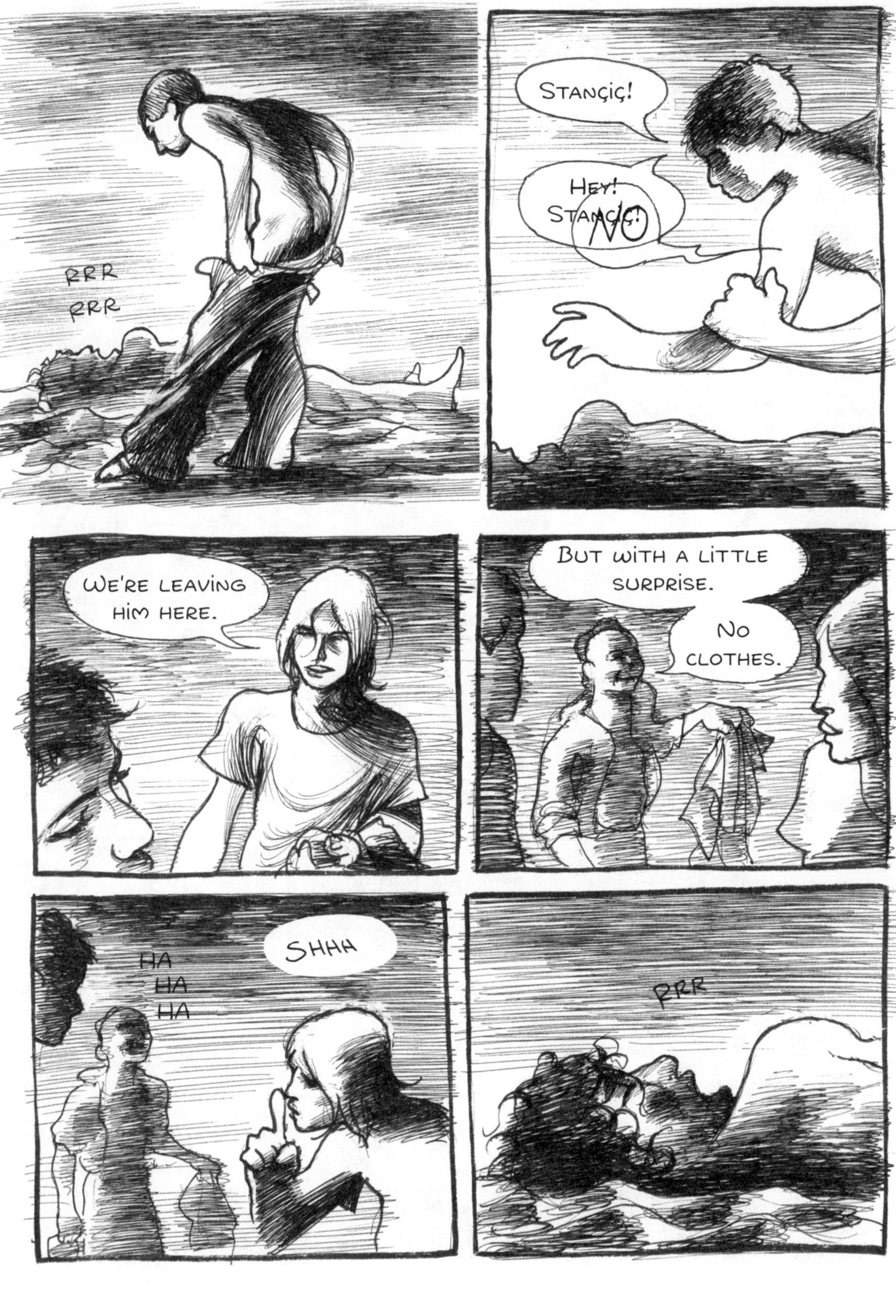
RRR
RRR
Stançiç!
Hey! Stançiç!
NO
We're leaving him here.
But with a little surprise.
No clothes.
HA
HA
HA
SHHH
RRR

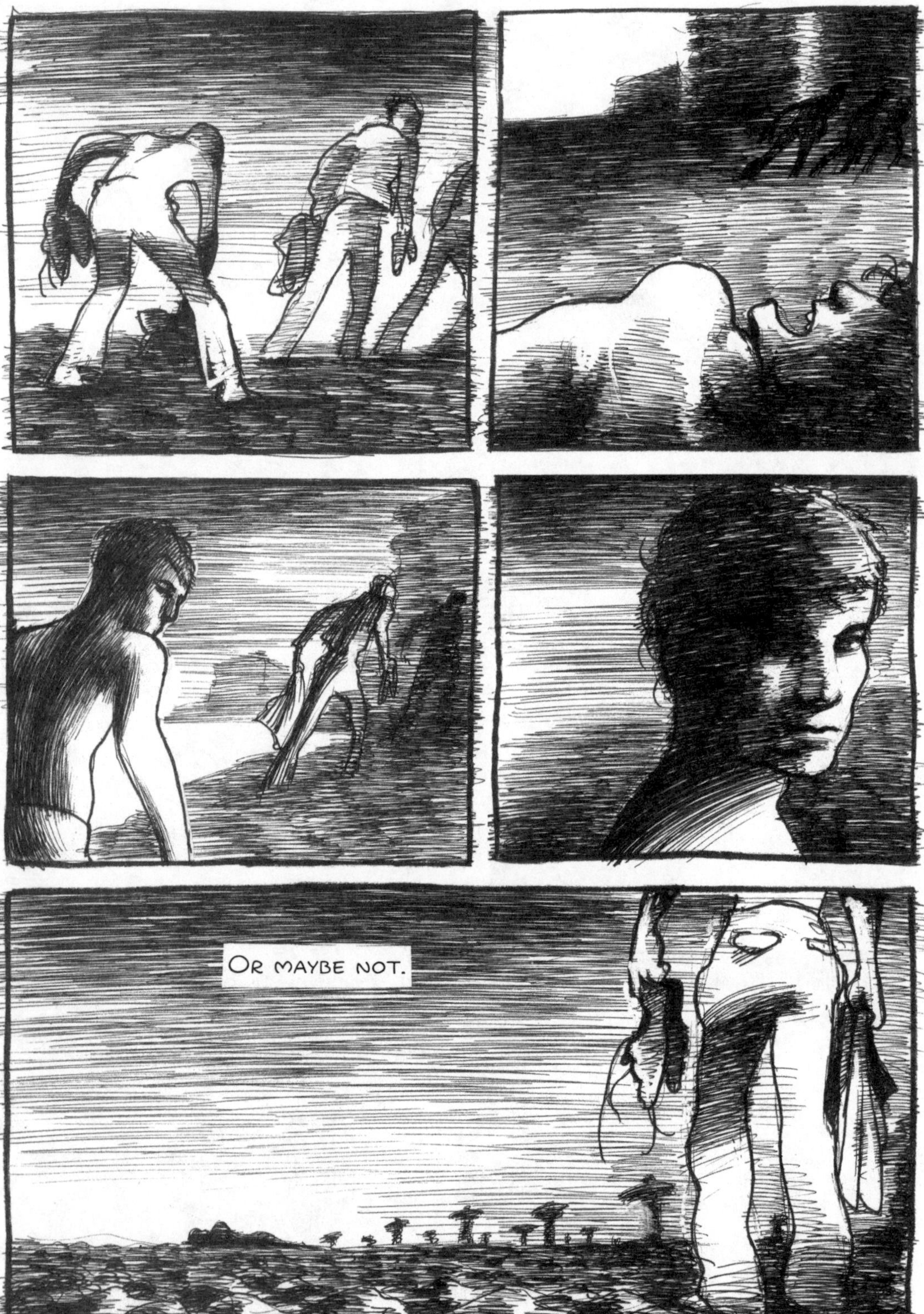
OR MAYBE NOT.

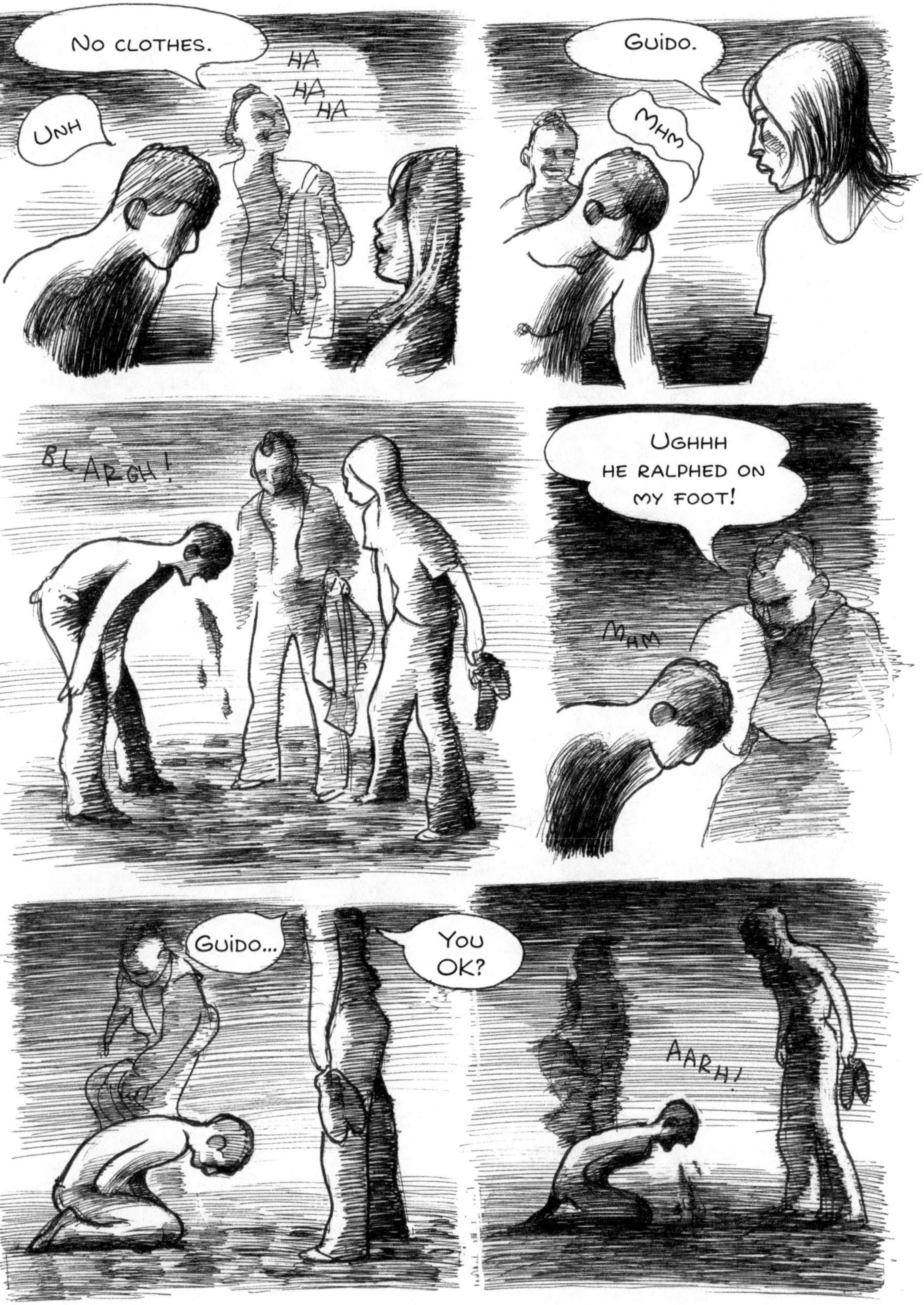
No clothes.
HA HA HA
Unh
Guido.
Mhm
BLARGH!
Ughhh he ralphed on my foot!
Mhm
Guido...
You OK?
AARH!

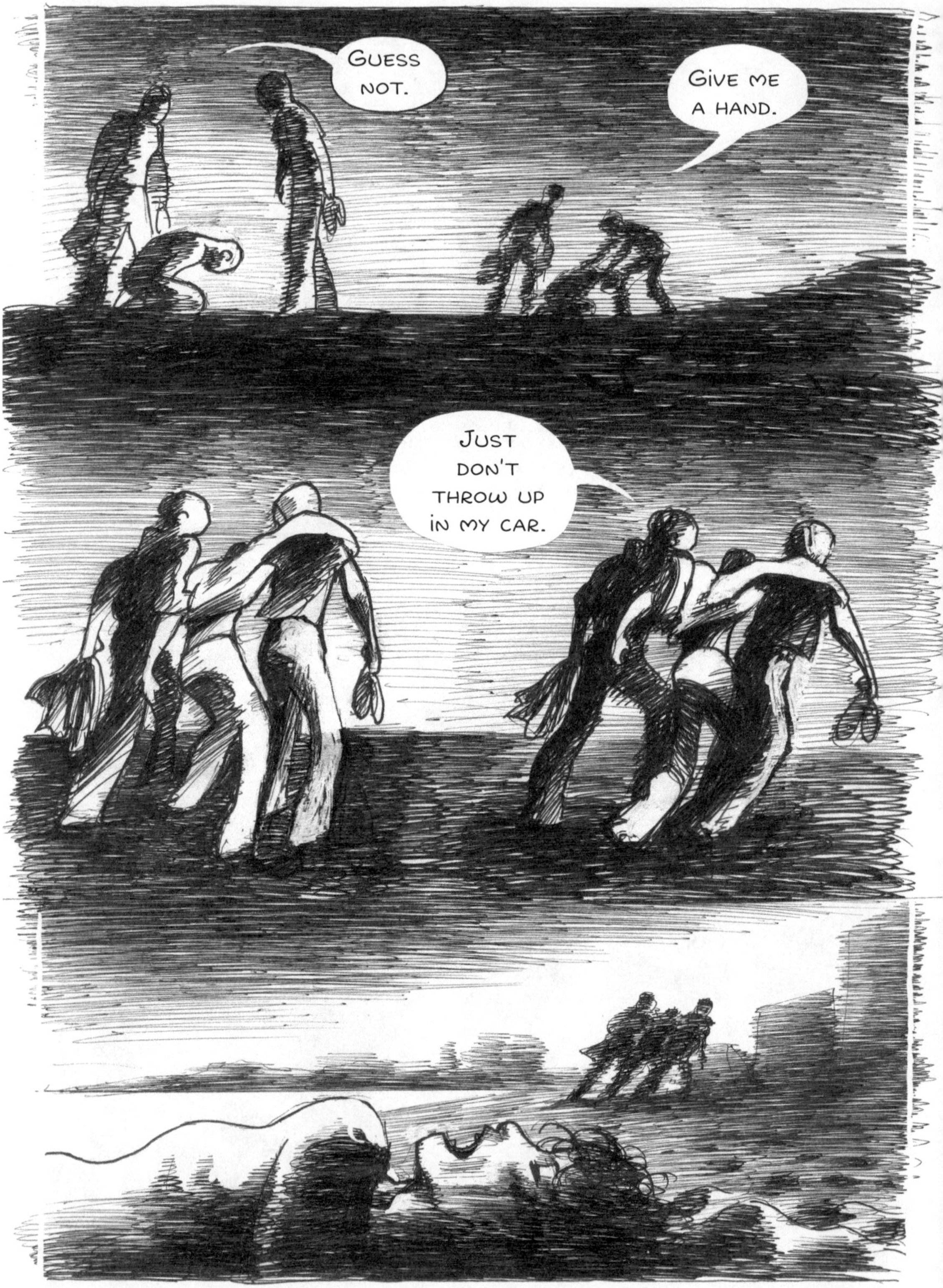
GUESS NOT.
GIVE ME A HAND.
JUST DON'T THROW UP IN MY CAR.

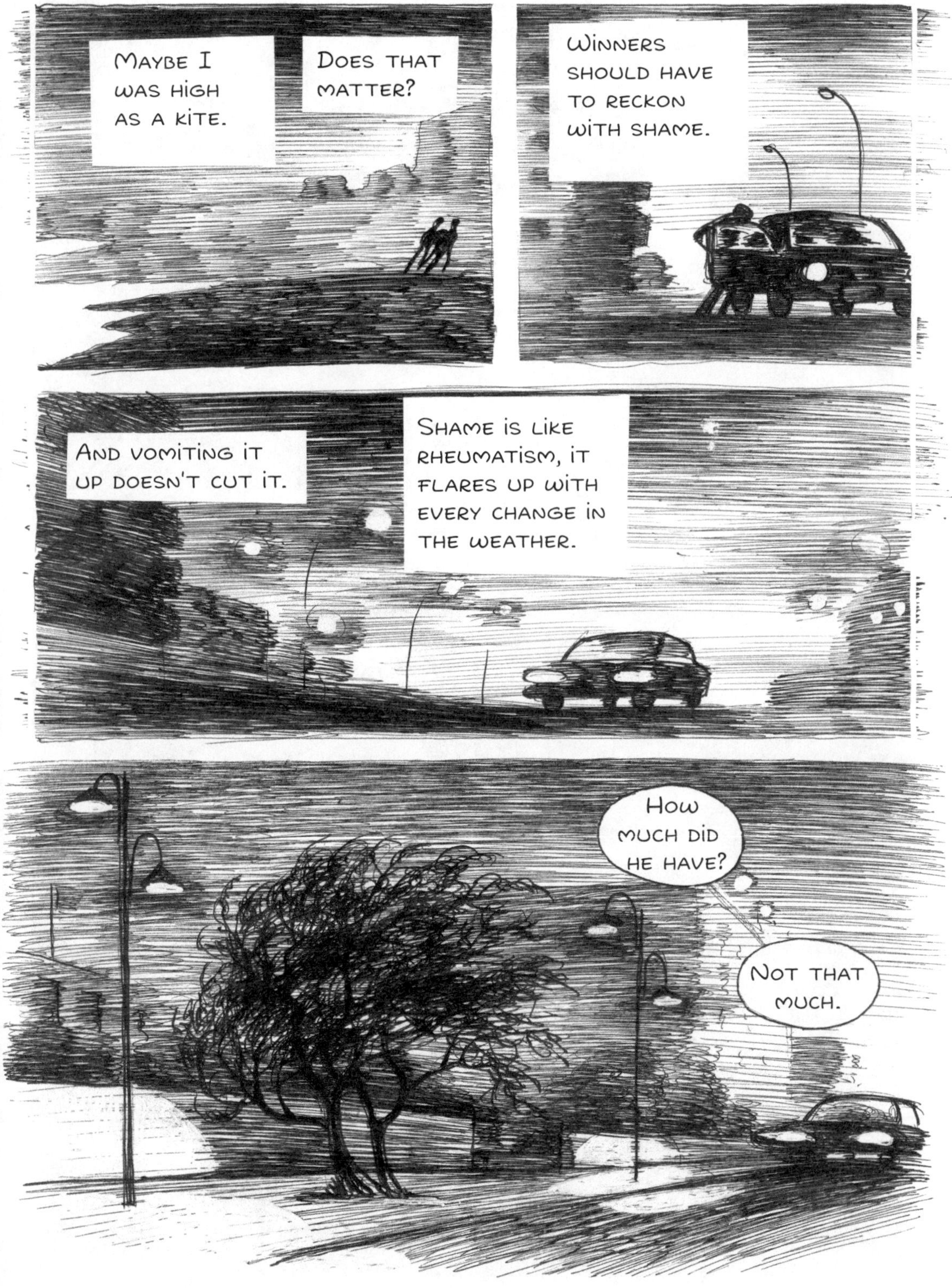

MAYBE I WAS HIGH AS A KITE.
DOES THAT MATTER?
WINNERS SHOULD HAVE TO RECKON WITH SHAME.
AND VOMITING IT UP DOESN'T CUT IT.
SHAME IS LIKE RHEUMATISM, IT FLARES UP WITH EVERY CHANGE IN THE WEATHER.
HOW MUCH DID HE HAVE?
NOT THAT MUCH.

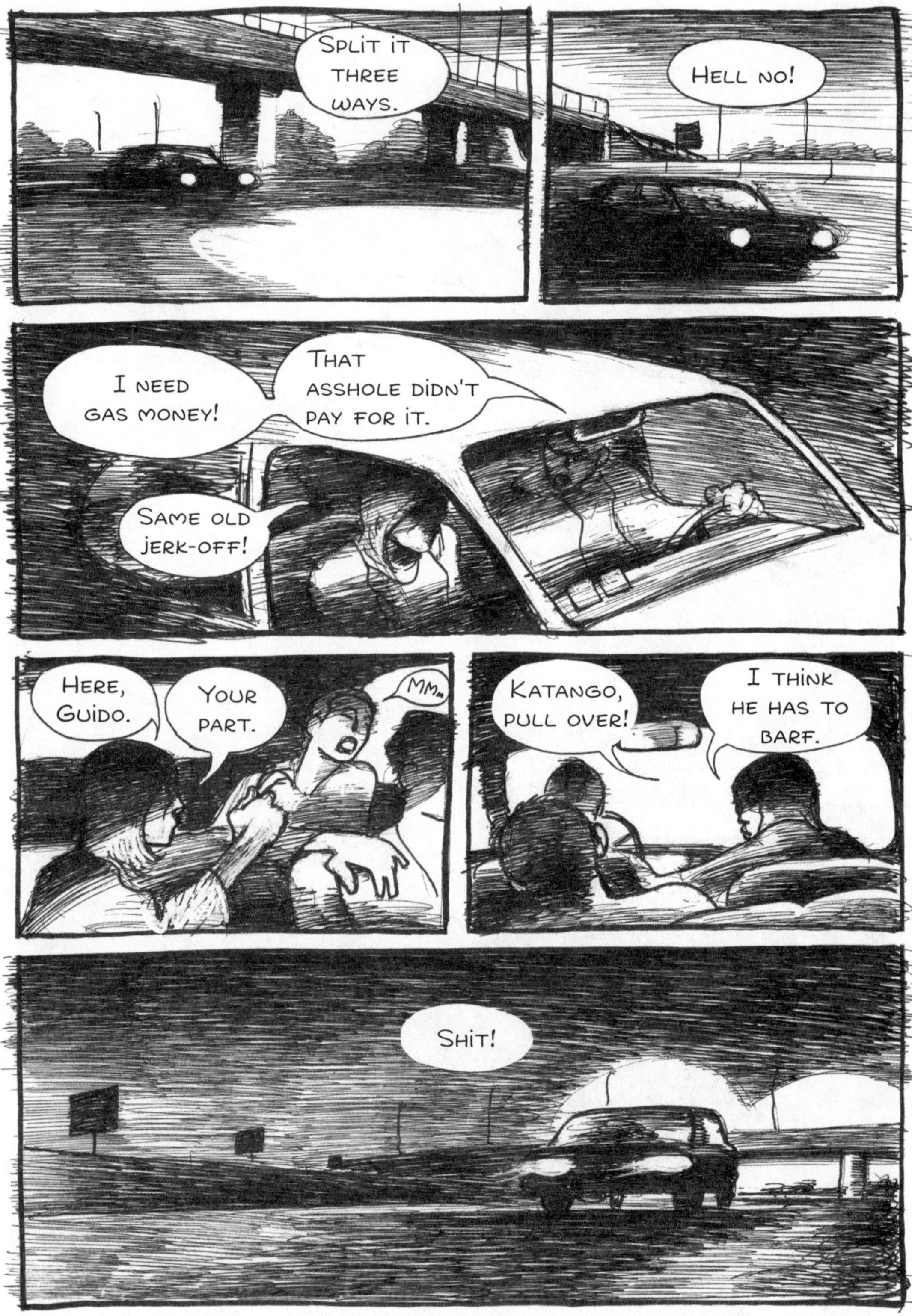
Split it three ways.
Hell no!
I need gas money!
That asshole didn't pay for it.
Same old jerk-off!
Here, Guido.
Your part.
Mm
Katango, pull over!
I think he has to barf.
Shit!

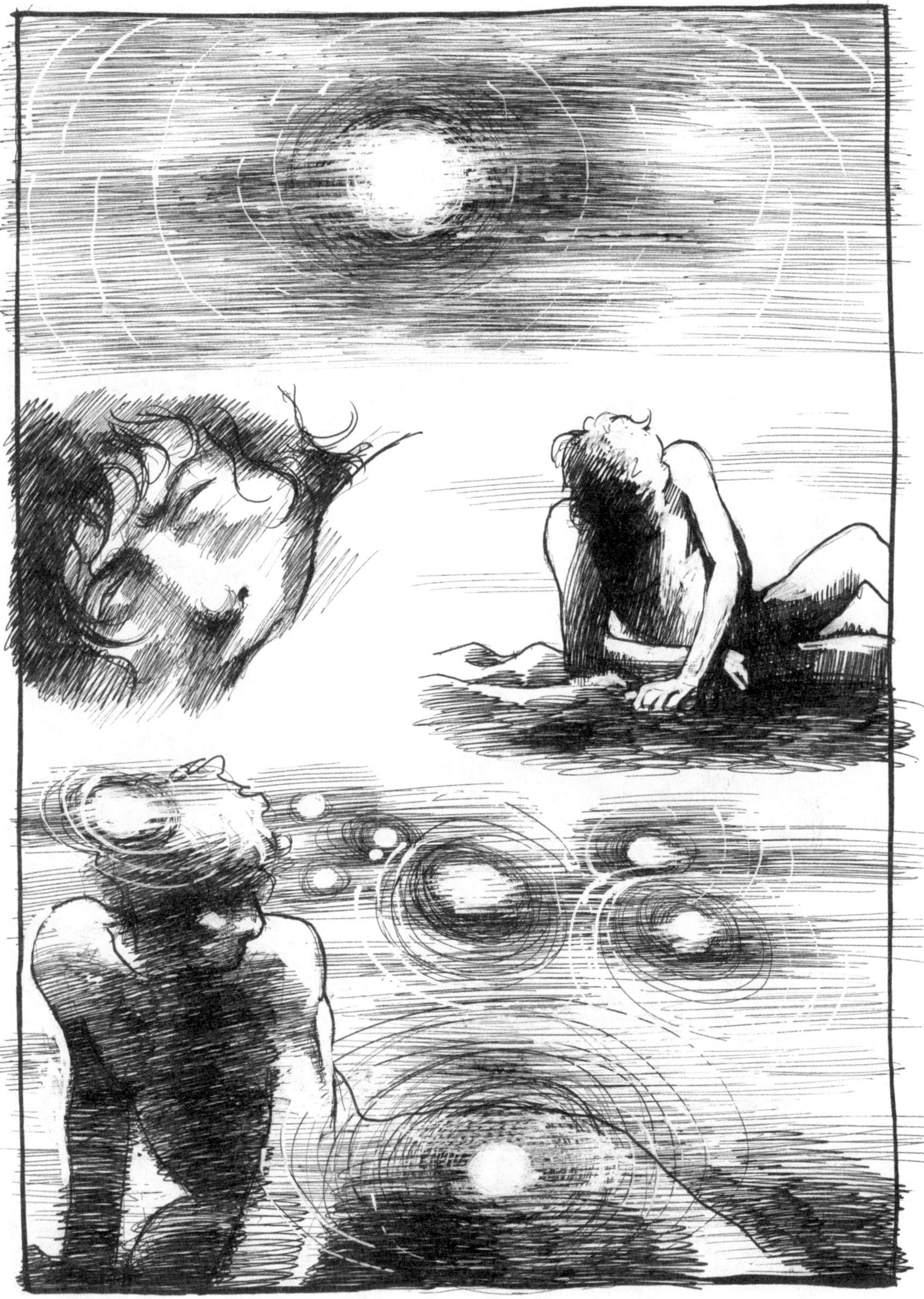

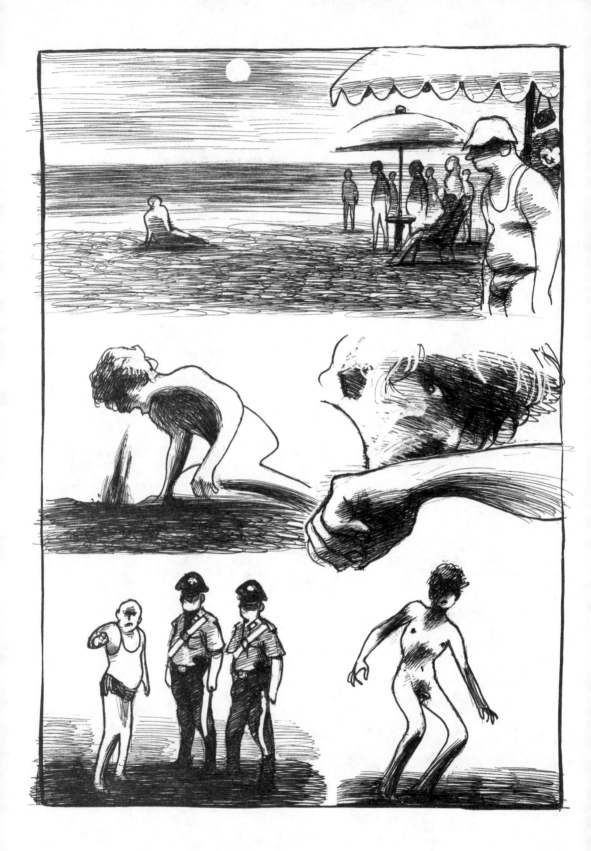

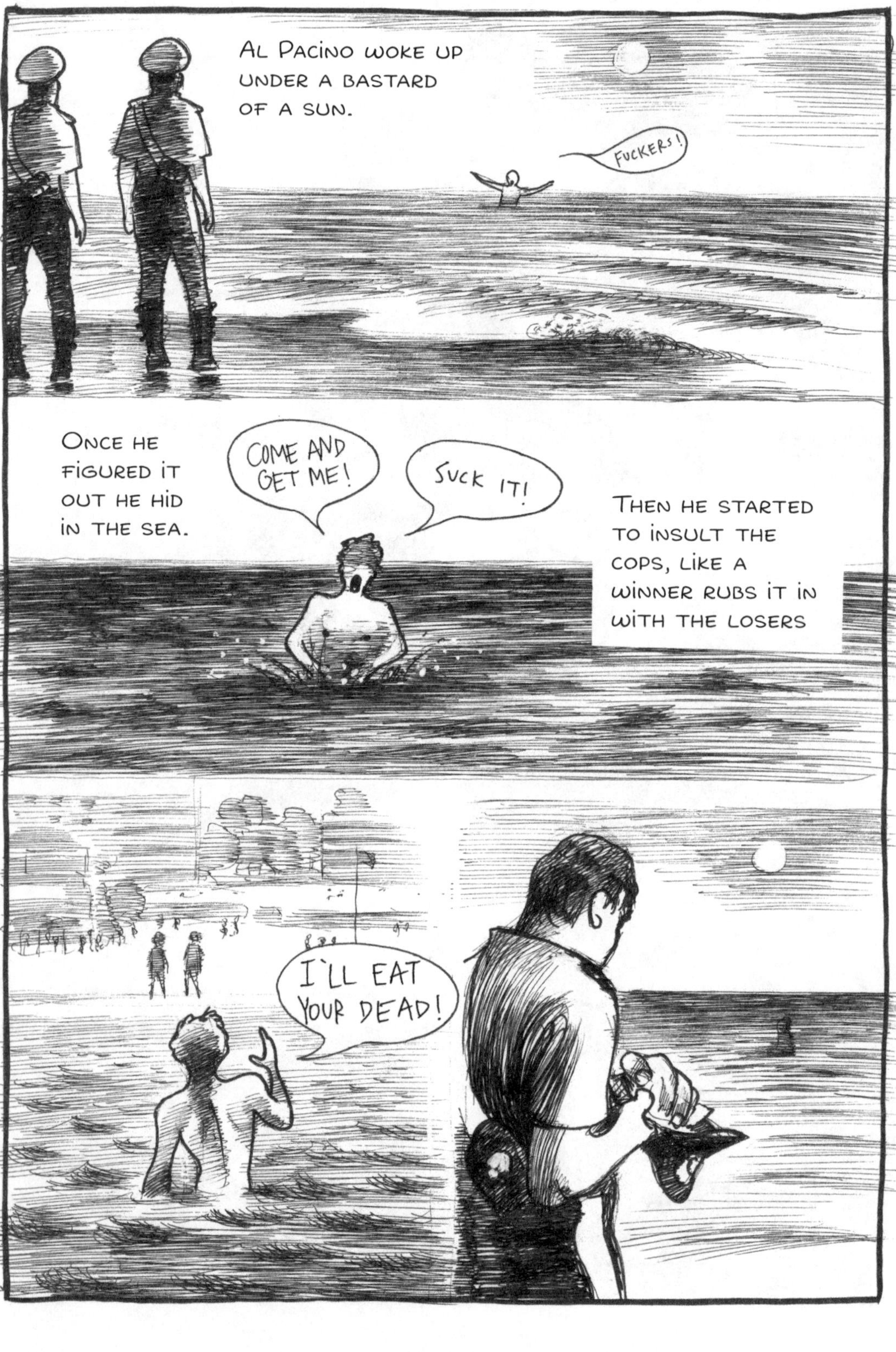
AL PACINO WOKE UP UNDER A BASTARD OF A SUN.
FUCKERS!
ONCE HE FIGURED IT OUT HE HID IN THE SEA.
COME AND GET ME!
SUCK IT!
THEN HE STARTED TO INSULT THE COPS, LIKE A WINNER RUBS IT IN WITH THE LOSERS
I`LL EAT YOUR DEAD!

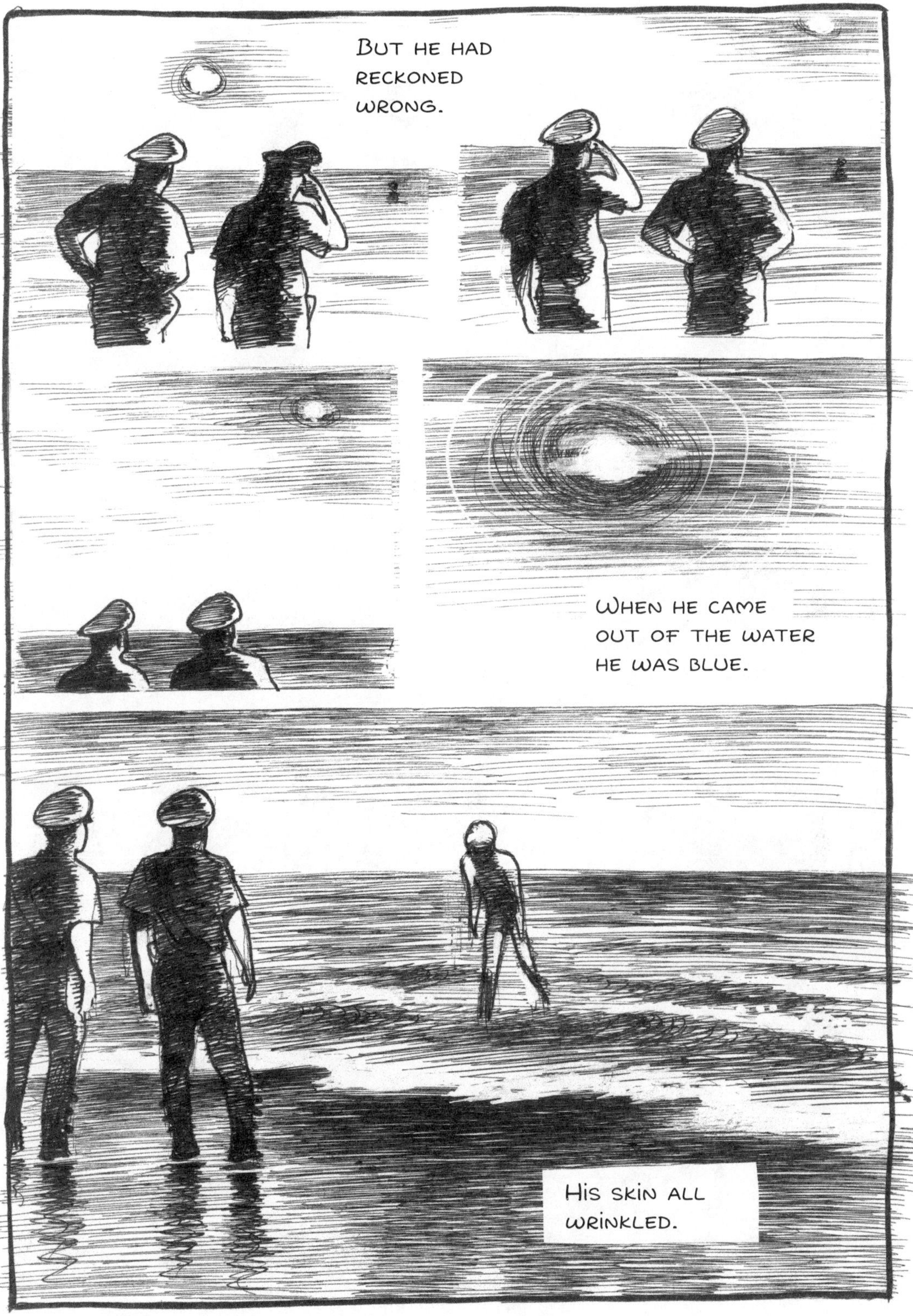
But he had reckoned wrong.
When he came out of the water he was blue.
His skin all wrinkled.

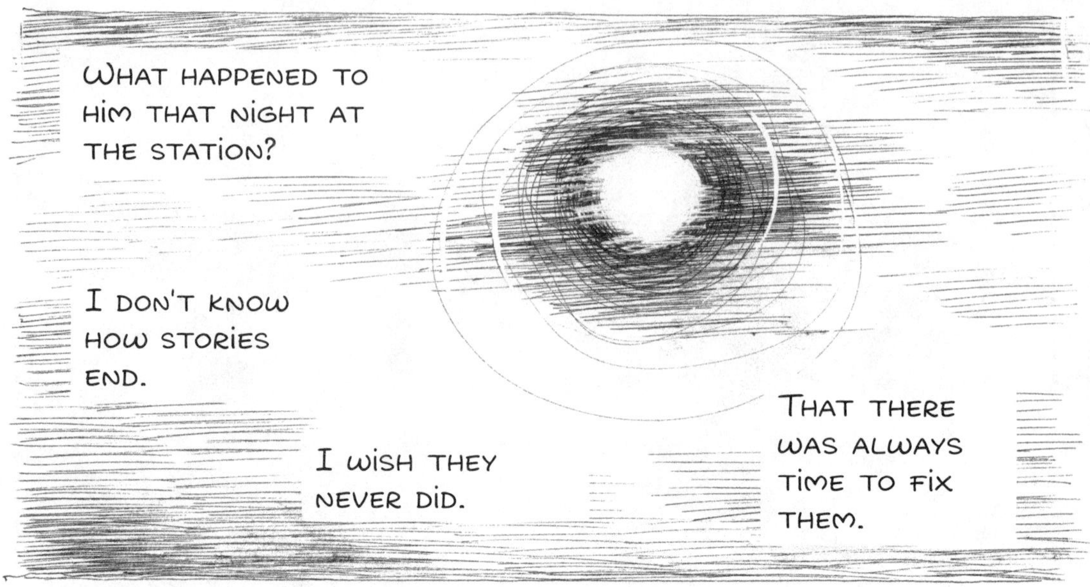
WHAT HAPPENED TO HIM THAT NIGHT AT THE STATION?
I DON'T KNOW HOW STORIES END.
I WISH THEY NEVER DID.
THAT THERE WAS ALWAYS TIME TO FIX THEM.

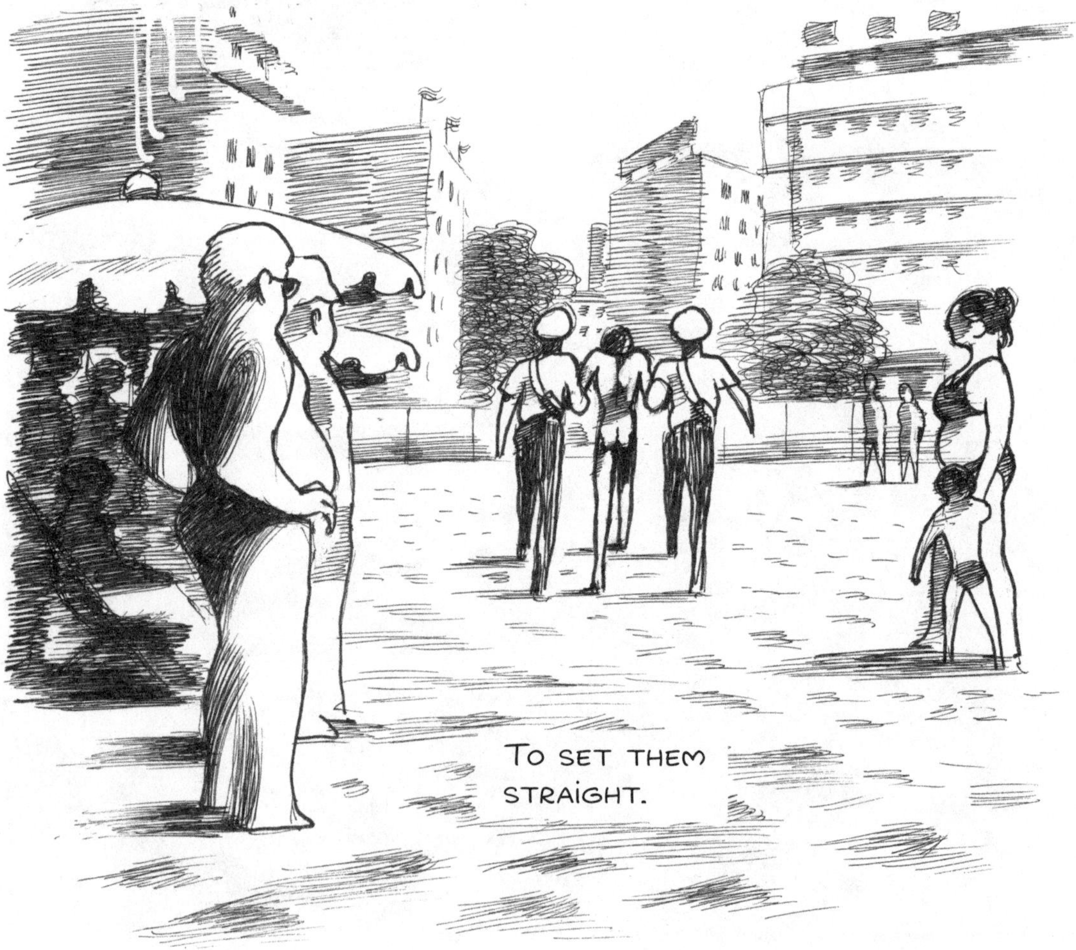
TO SET THEM STRAIGHT.

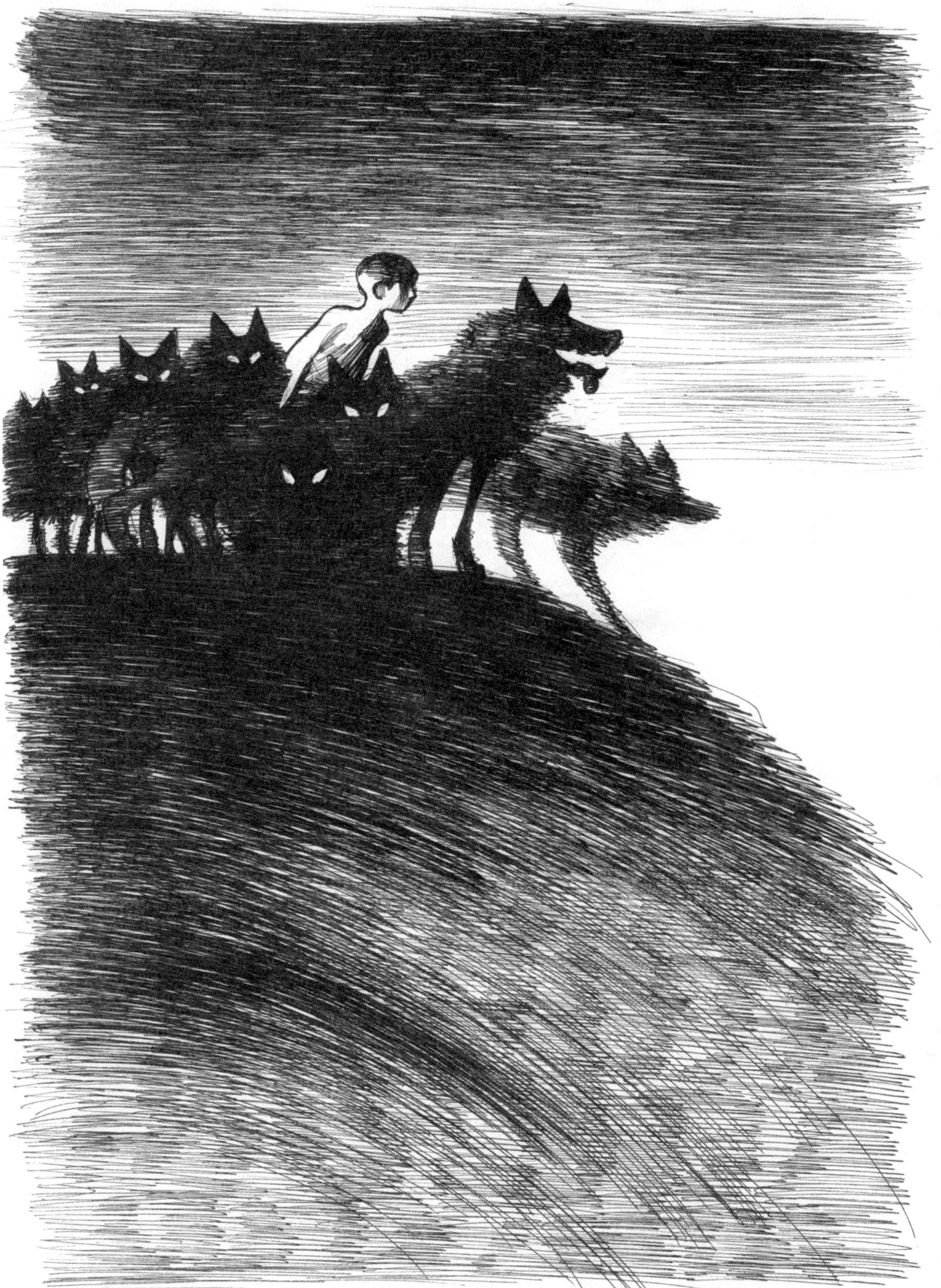

X

DREAMING OF
A HOUSE, AN
ENCLOSED SPACE,
MEANS DEATH.

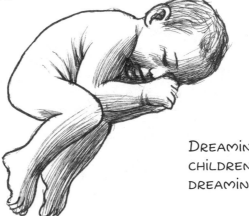

DREAMING OF
CHILDREN IS LIKE
DREAMING OF DEVILS.

IT'S NOT
GOOD.

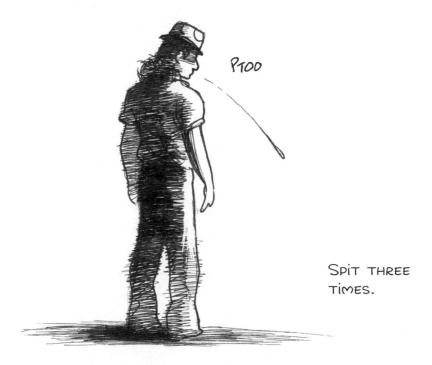

PTOO

SPIT THREE
TIMES.

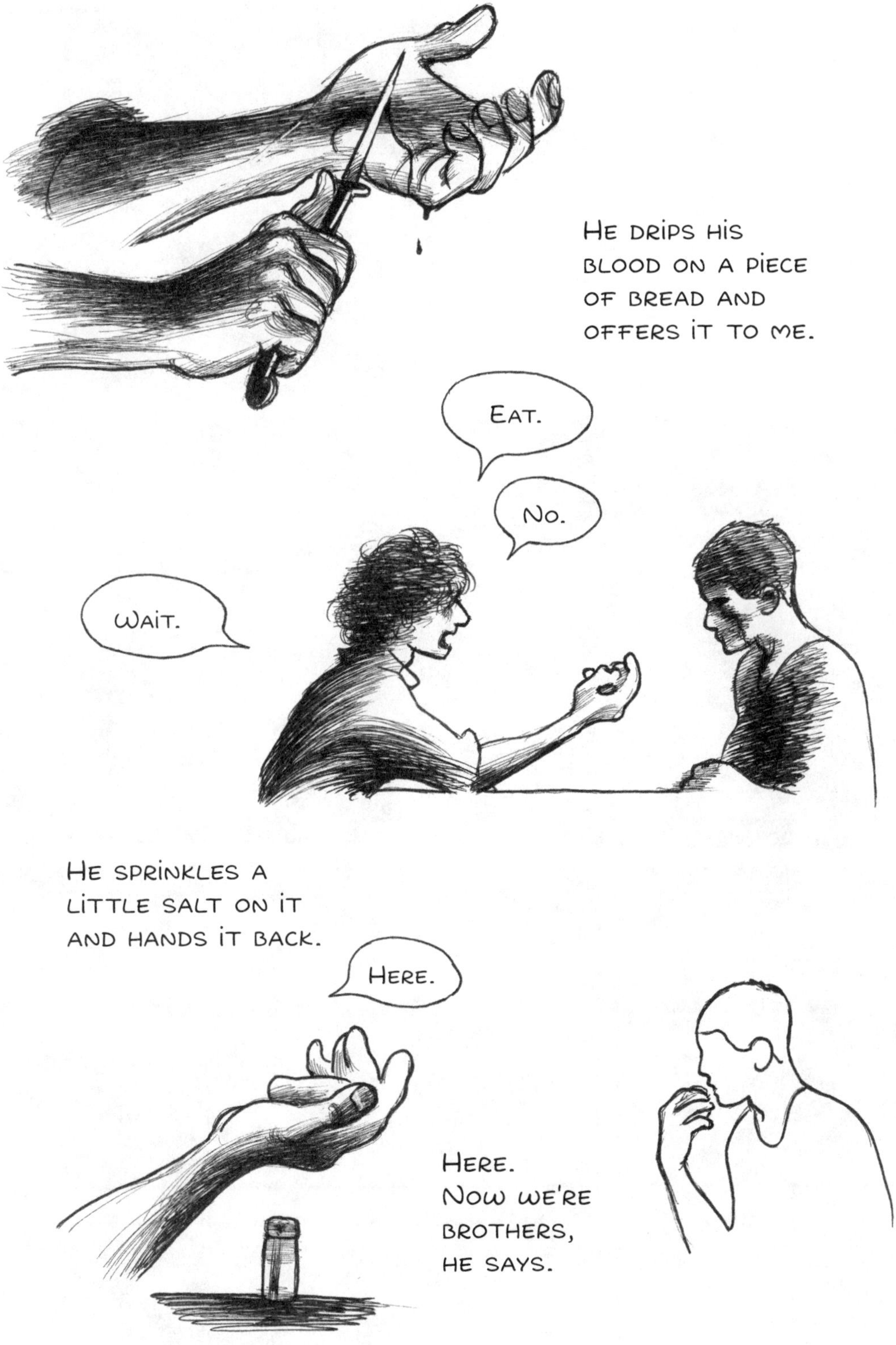
He drips his blood on a piece of bread and offers it to me.
Eat.
No.
Wait.
He sprinkles a little salt on it and hands it back.
Here.
Here. Now we're brothers, he says.

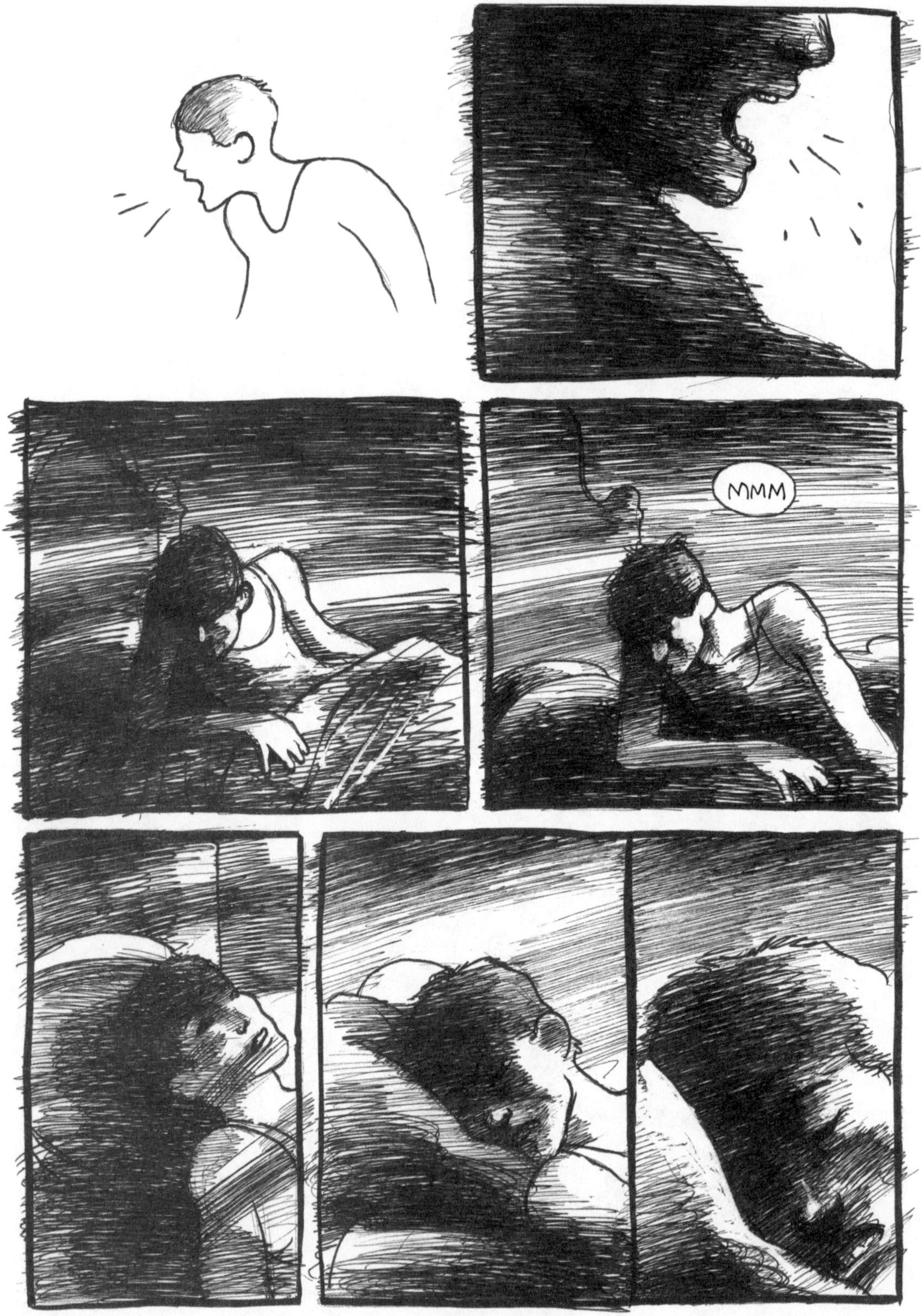
MMM

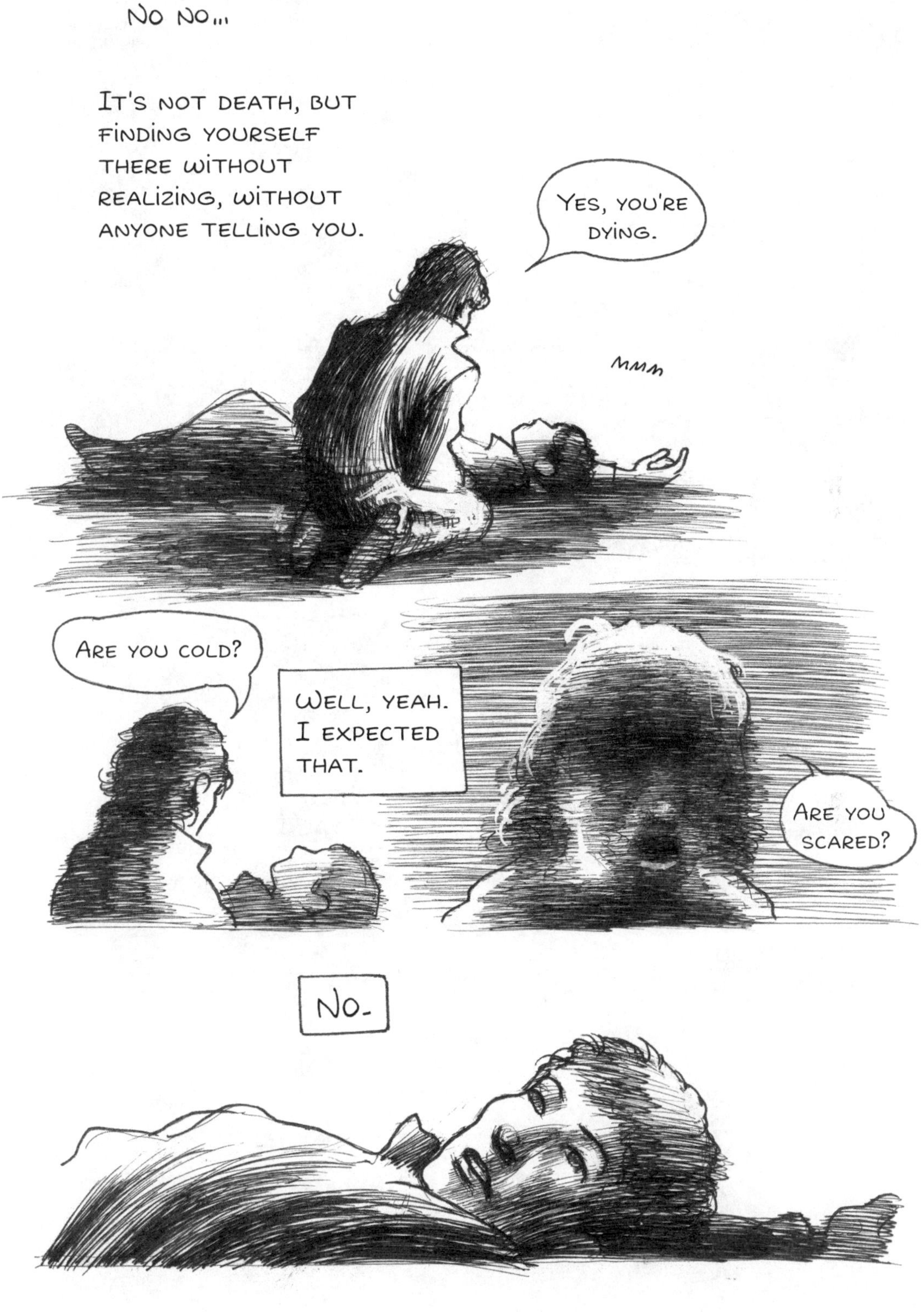
No no...
It's not death, but finding yourself there without realizing, without anyone telling you.
Yes, you're dying.
Mmm
Are you cold?
Well, yeah. I expected that.
Are you scared?
No.

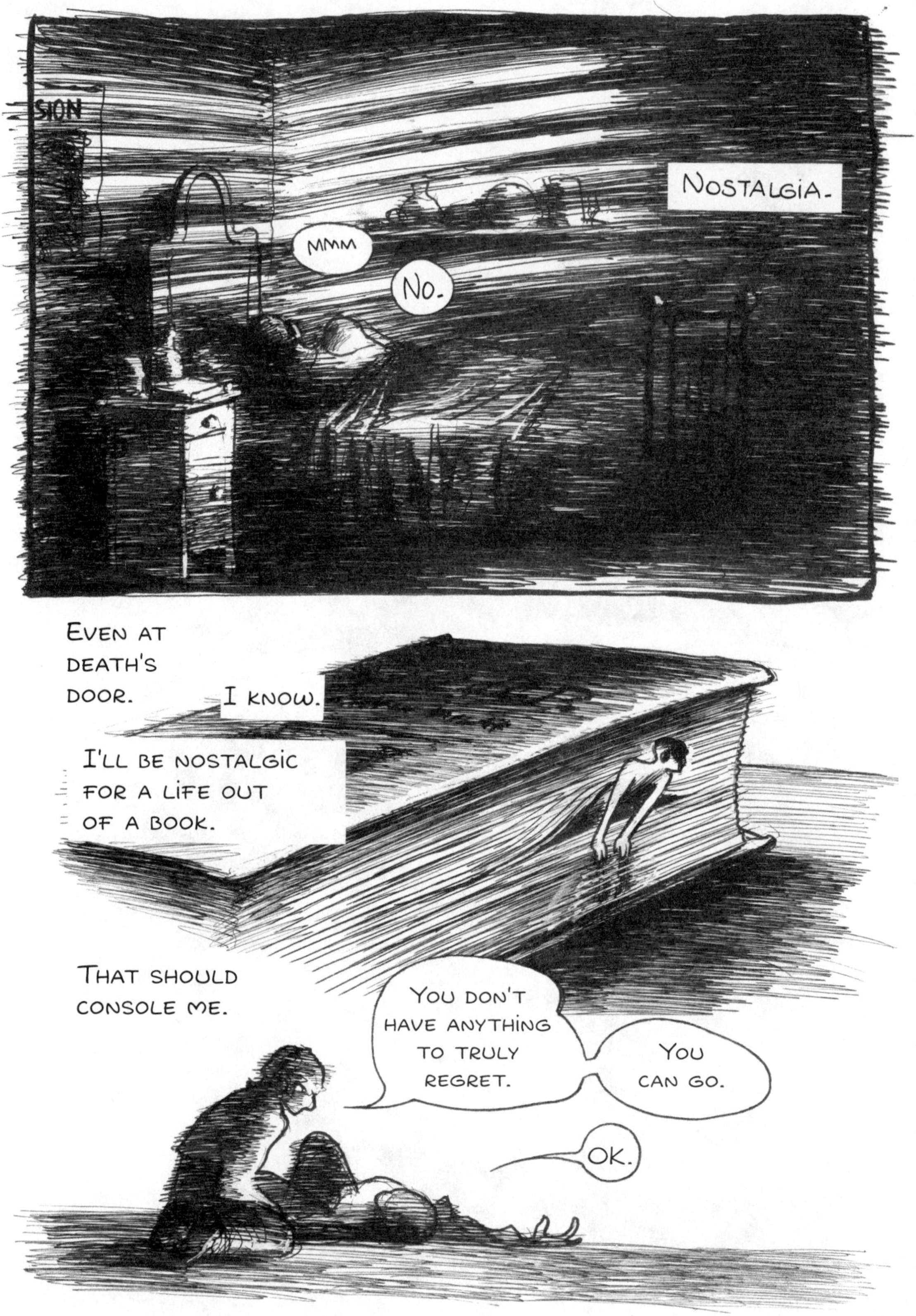
Nostalgia.
MMM
No.
Even at death's door.
I know.
I'll be nostalgic for a life out of a book.
That should console me.
You don't have anything to truly regret.
You can go.
OK.

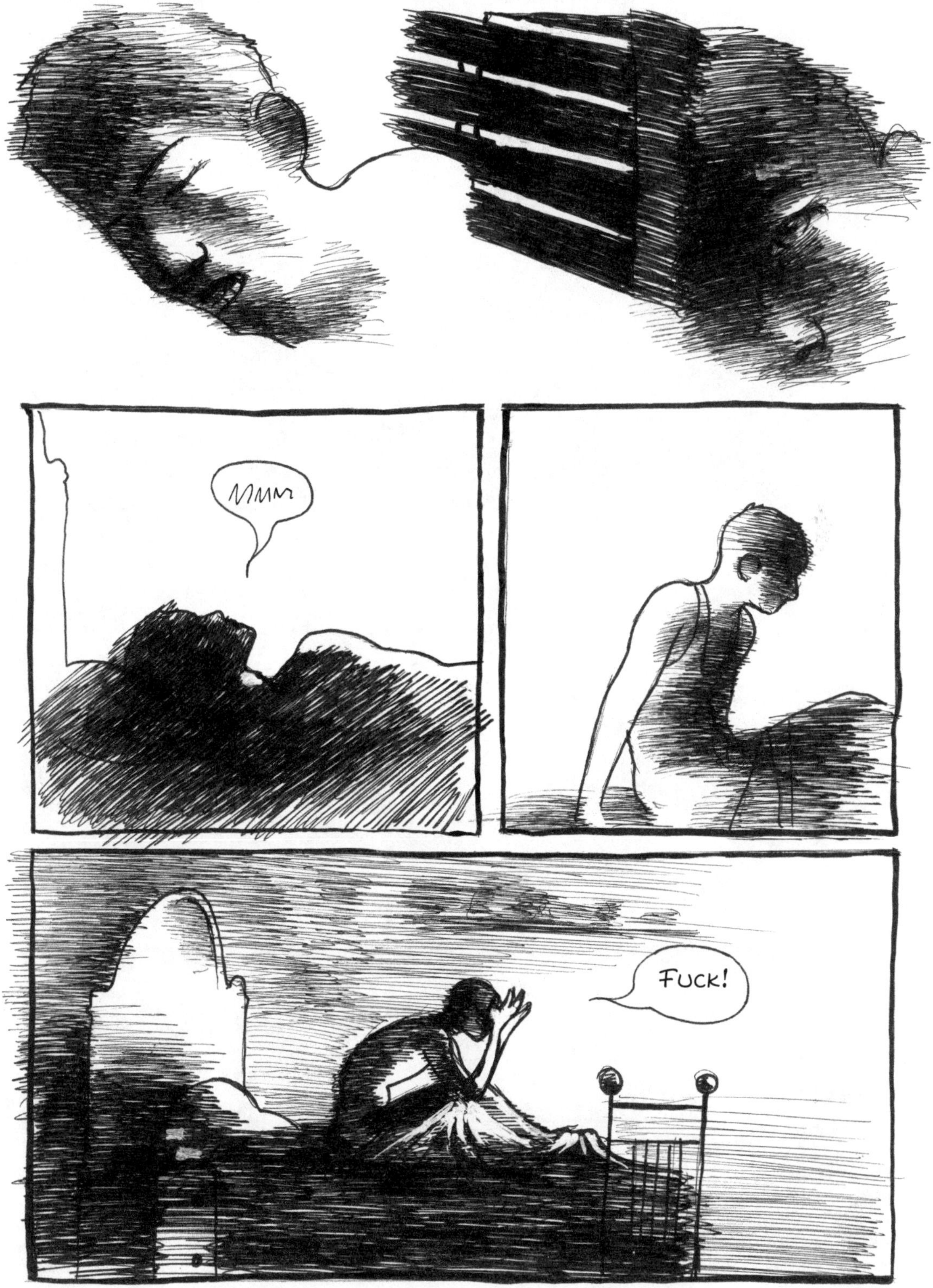
MMM
FUCK!

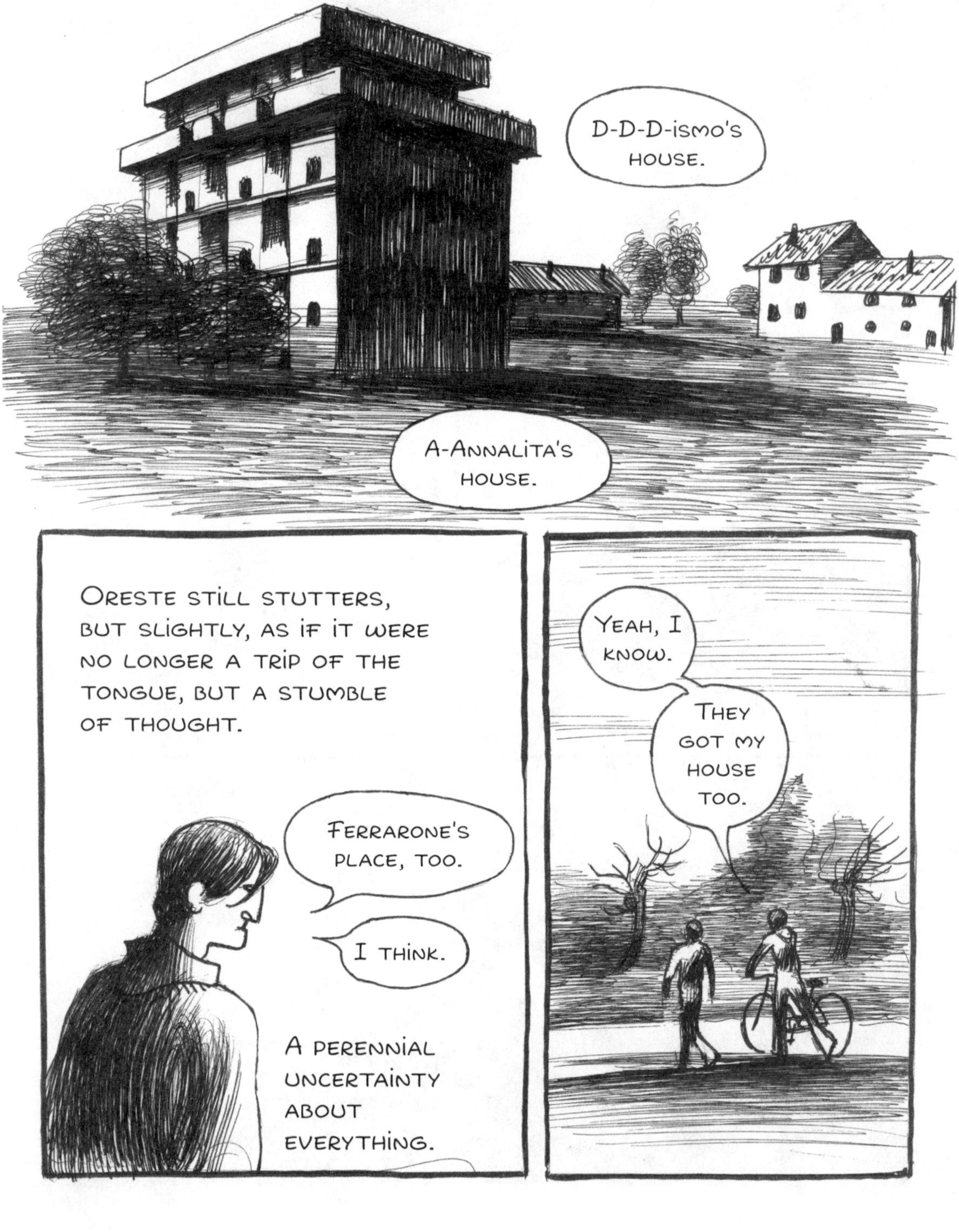
D-D-D-ismo's house.
A-Annalita's house.
Oreste still stutters, but slightly, as if it were no longer a trip of the tongue, but a stumble of thought.
Ferrarone's place, too.
I think.
A perennial uncertainty about everything.
Yeah, I know.
They got my house too.

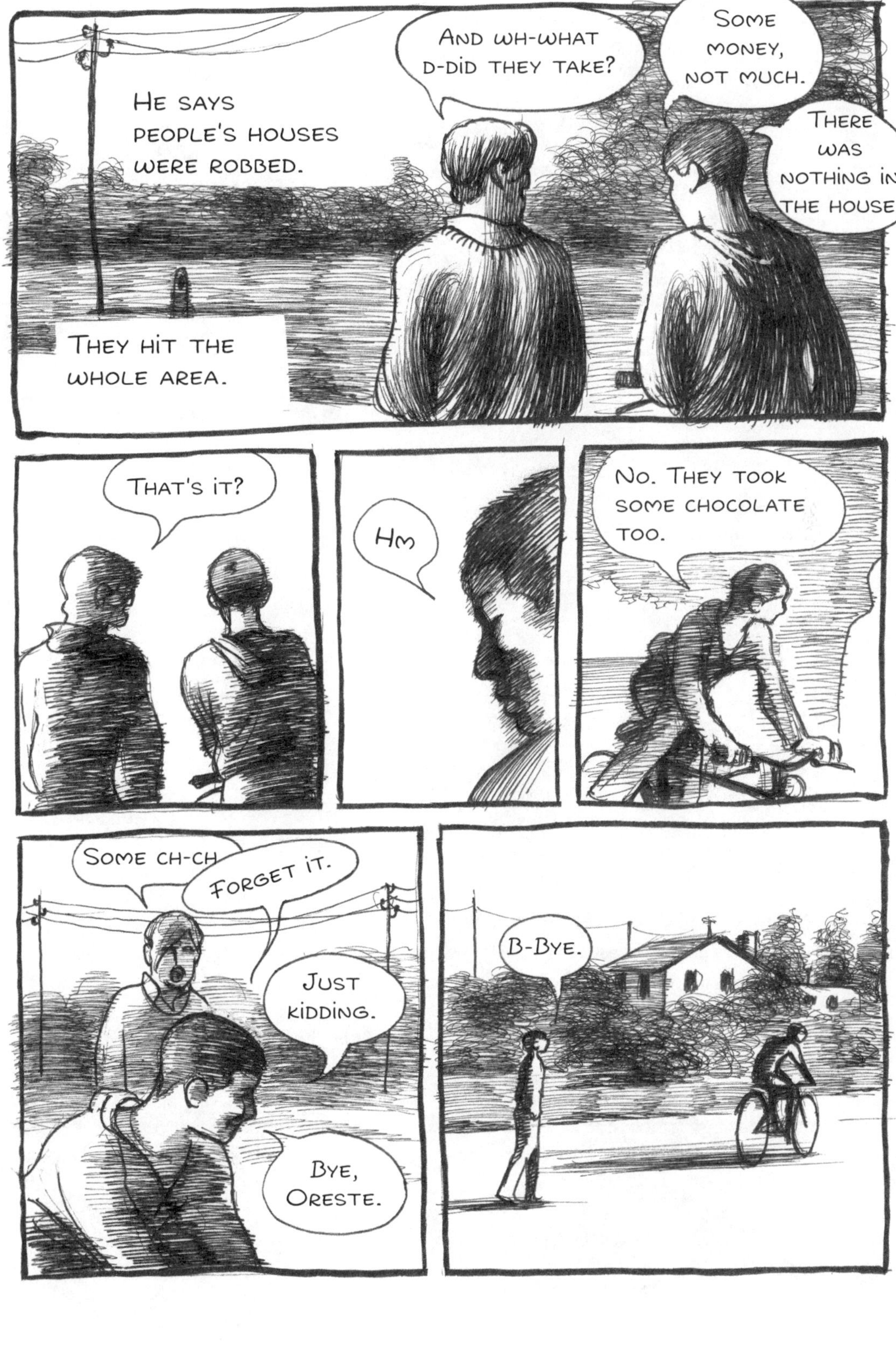
HE SAYS PEOPLE'S HOUSES WERE ROBBED.
THEY HIT THE WHOLE AREA.
AND WH-WHAT D-DID THEY TAKE?
SOME MONEY, NOT MUCH.
THERE WAS NOTHING IN THE HOUSE.
THAT'S IT?
HM
NO. THEY TOOK SOME CHOCOLATE TOO.
SOME CH-CH
FORGET IT.
JUST KIDDING.
BYE, ORESTE.
B-BYE.

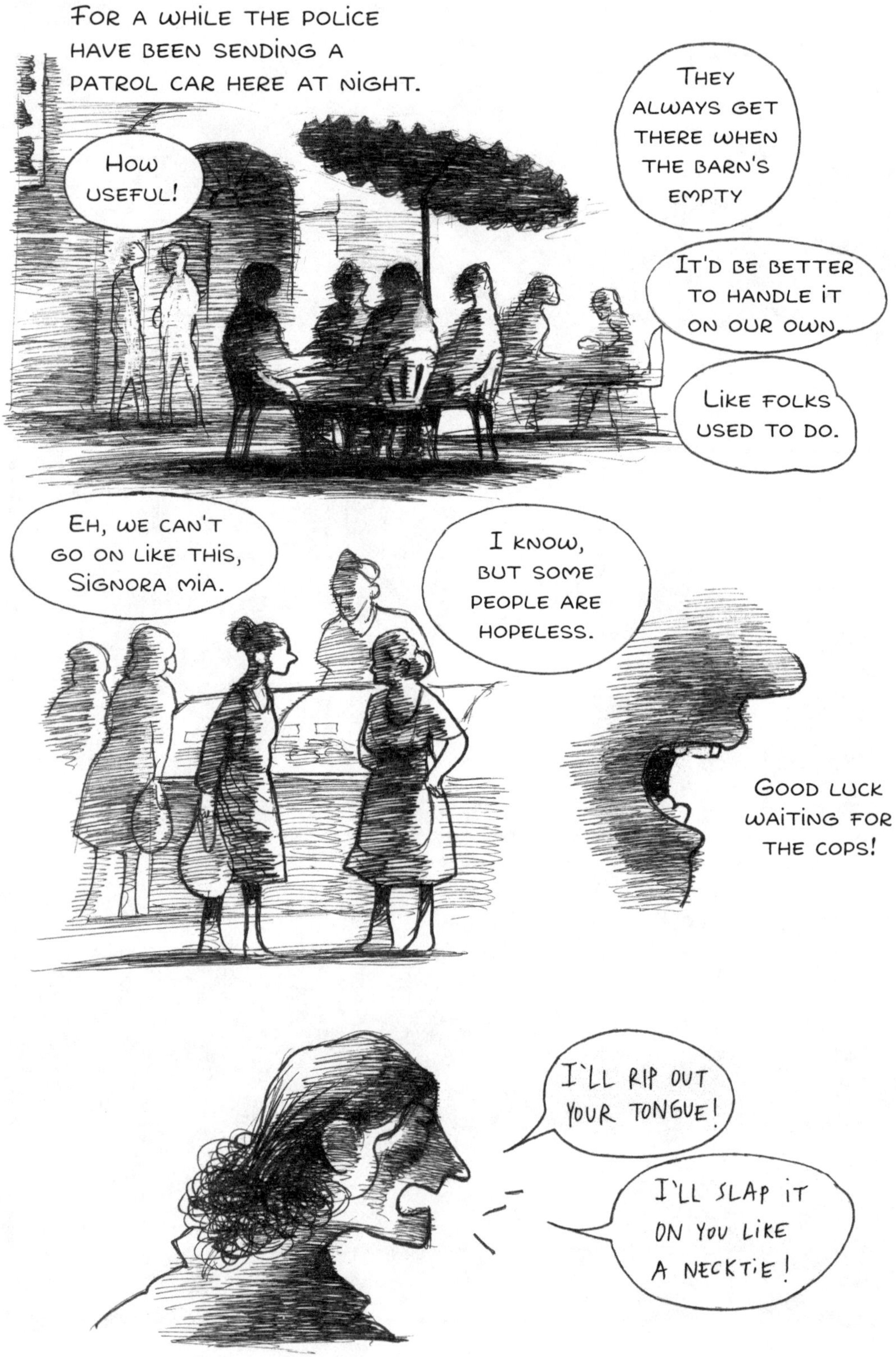
FOR A WHILE THE POLICE HAVE BEEN SENDING A PATROL CAR HERE AT NIGHT.
HOW USEFUL!
THEY ALWAYS GET THERE WHEN THE BARN'S EMPTY
IT'D BE BETTER TO HANDLE IT ON OUR OWN.
LIKE FOLKS USED TO DO.
EH, WE CAN'T GO ON LIKE THIS, SIGNORA MIA.
I KNOW, BUT SOME PEOPLE ARE HOPELESS.
GOOD LUCK WAITING FOR THE COPS!
I'LL RIP OUT YOUR TONGUE!
I'LL SLAP IT ON YOU LIKE A NECKTIE!

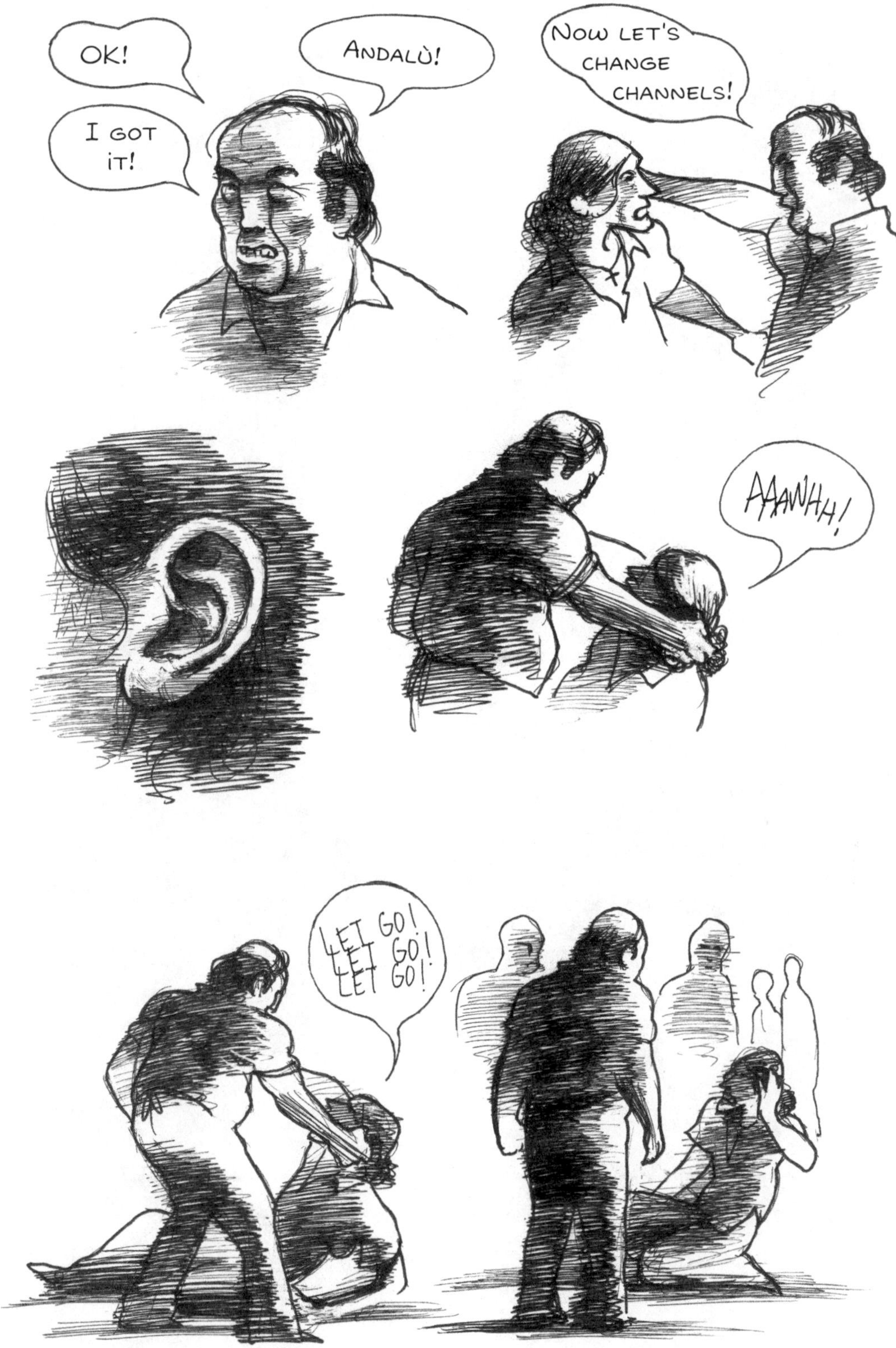
OK!
I GOT IT!
ANDALÙ!
NOW LET'S CHANGE CHANNELS!
AAAWHH!
LET GO! LET GO! LET GO!

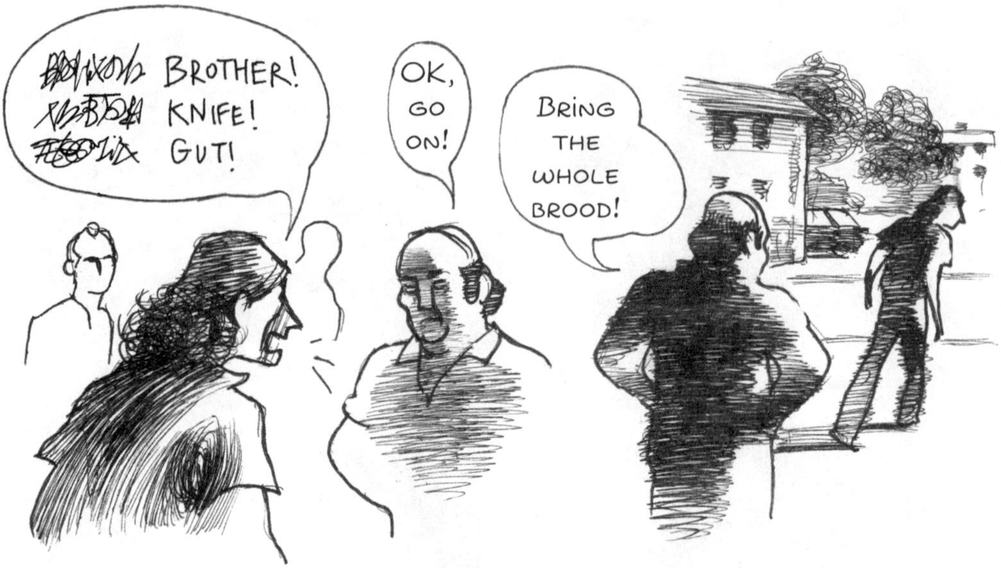
BROTHER! KNIFE! GUT!
OK, GO ON!
BRING THE WHOLE BROOD!

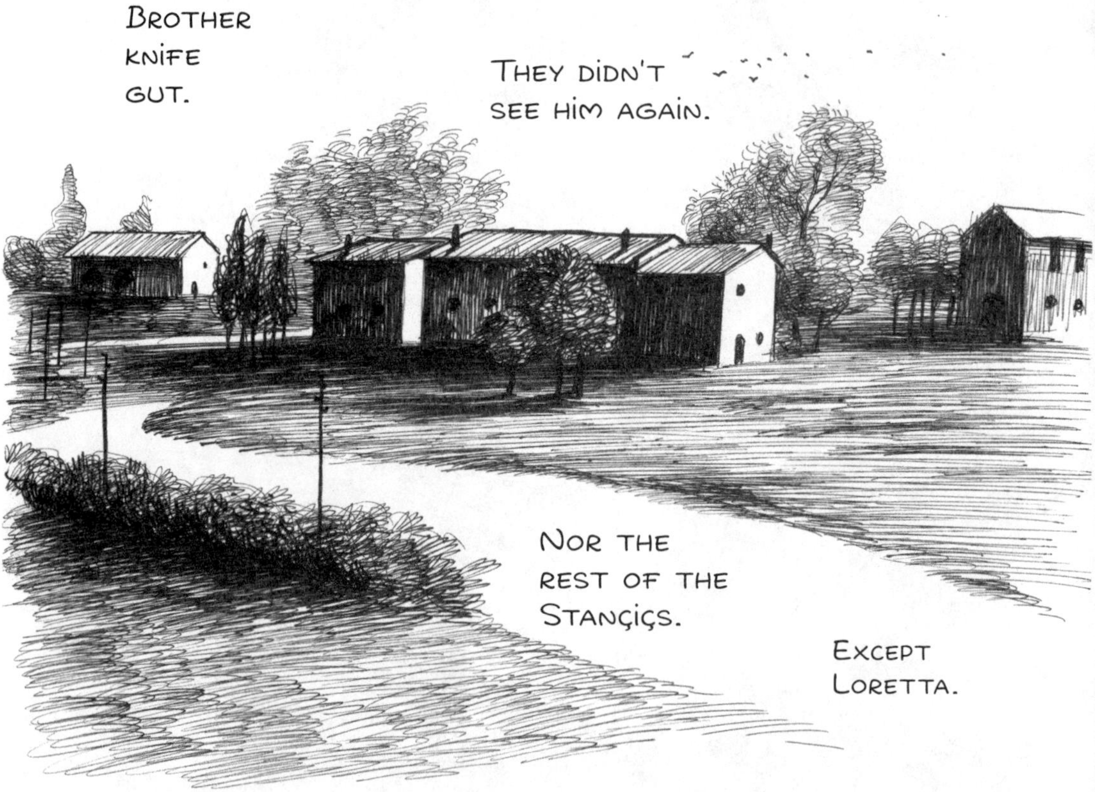
BROTHER KNIFE GUT.
THEY DIDN'T SEE HIM AGAIN.
NOR THE REST OF THE STANÇIÇS.
EXCEPT LORETTA.

SHE'D BEEN GONE
FOR A WHILE.
BUT THAT WAS NORMAL.

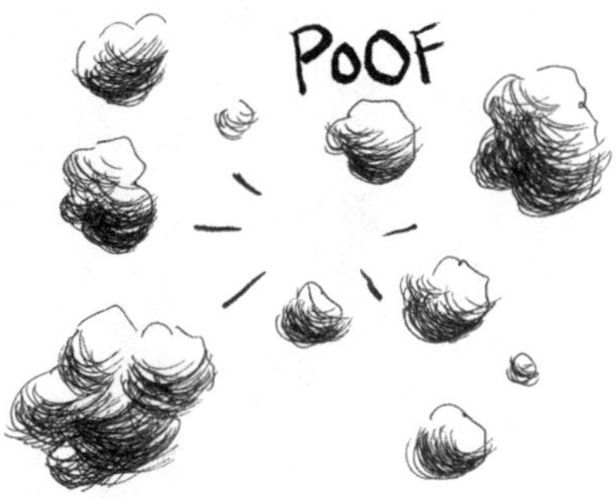
POOF

SINCE SHE
WAS LITTLE.

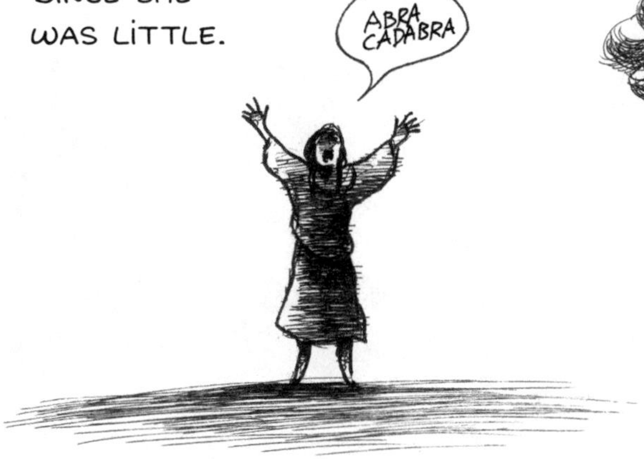
ABRA CADABRA

SHE WOULD
DISAPPEAR.

AFTER FIVE OR
SIX MONTHS,
WHEN YOU'D
NEARLY
FORGOTTEN
WHAT SHE
LOOKED LIKE...

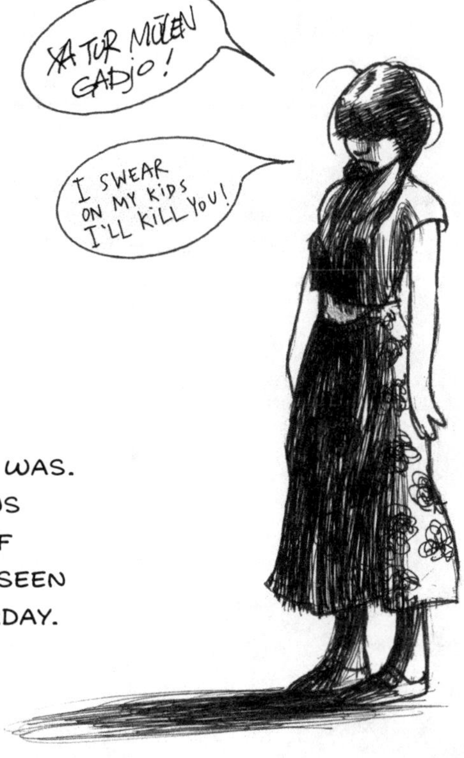
XATUR MULEN GADJO!
I SWEAR ON MY KIDS I'LL KILL YOU!

THERE SHE WAS.
BUGGING US
AGAIN, AS IF
WE'D JUST SEEN
HER YESTERDAY.

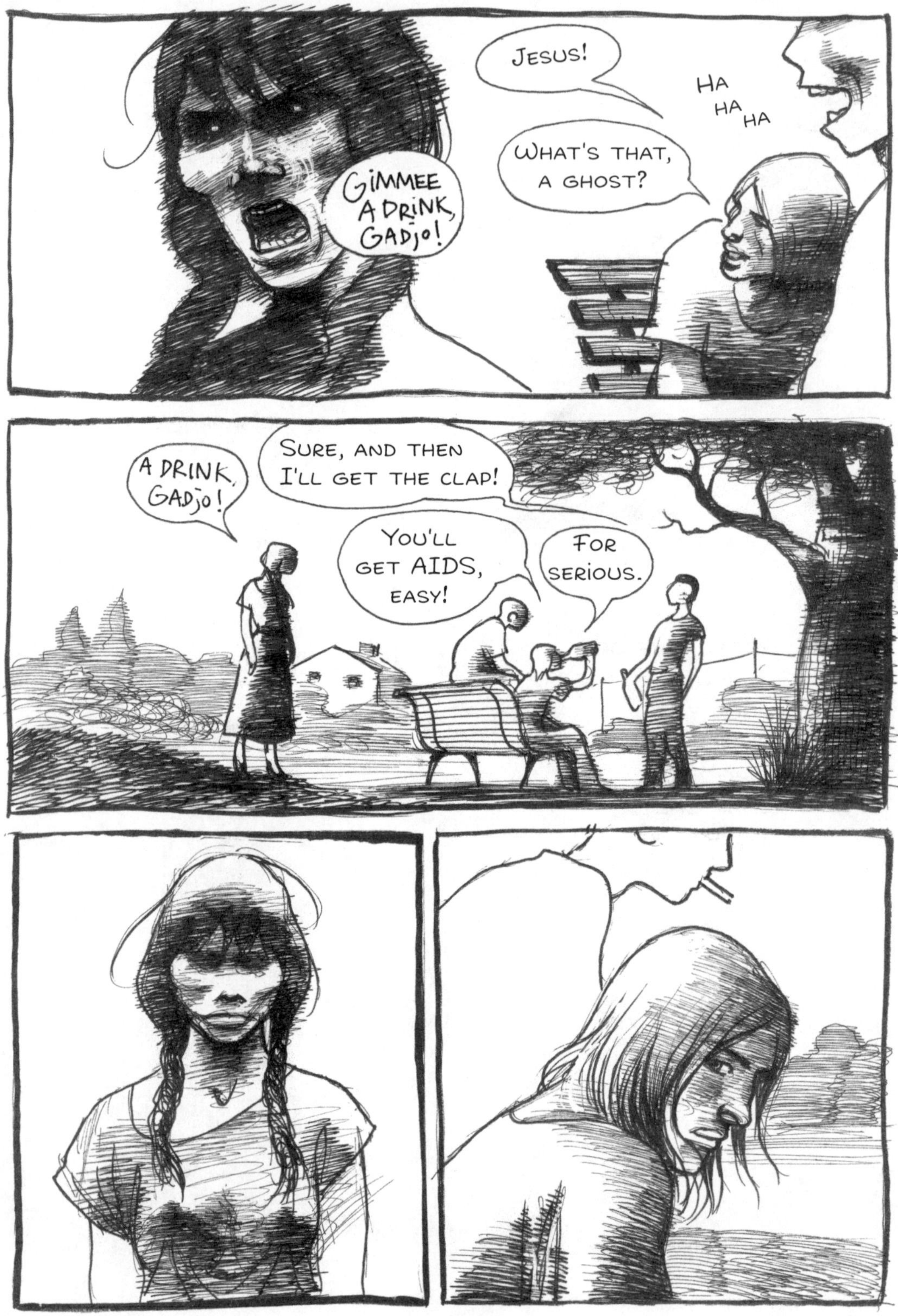
Gimmee a drink, Gadjo!
Jesus!
Ha ha ha
What's that, a ghost?
A drink, Gadjo!
Sure, and then I'll get the clap!
You'll get AIDS, easy!
For serious.

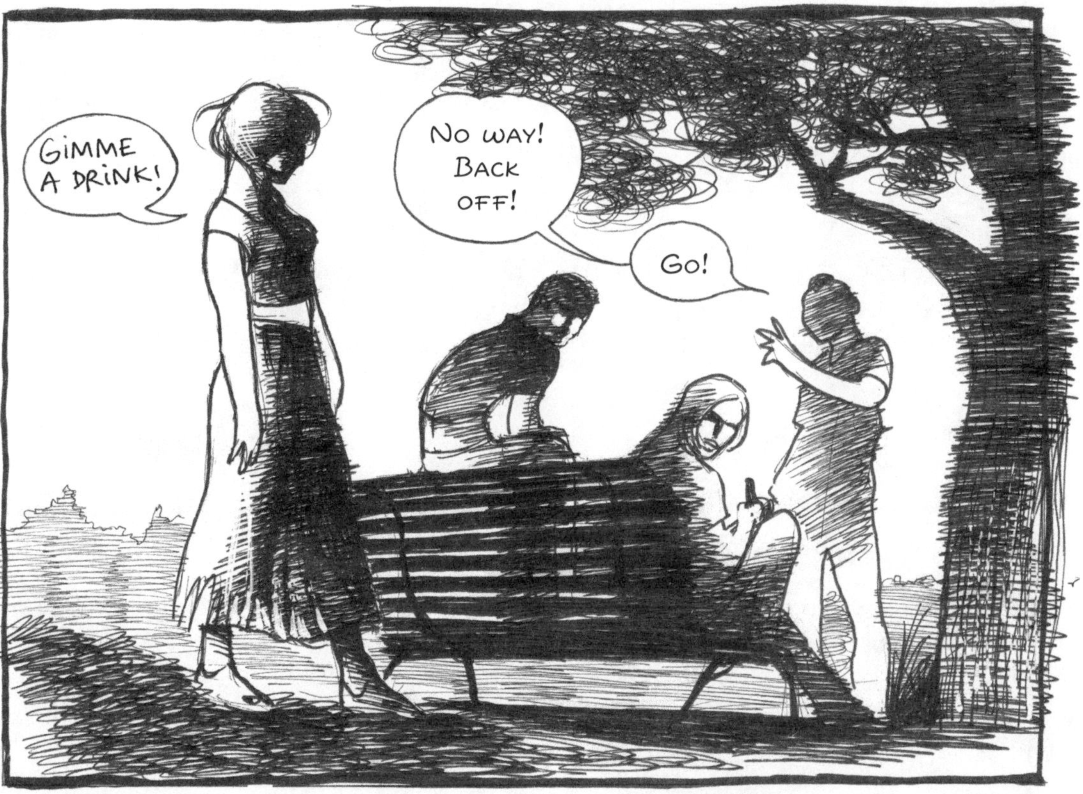
GIMME A DRINK!
NO WAY! BACK OFF!
GO!

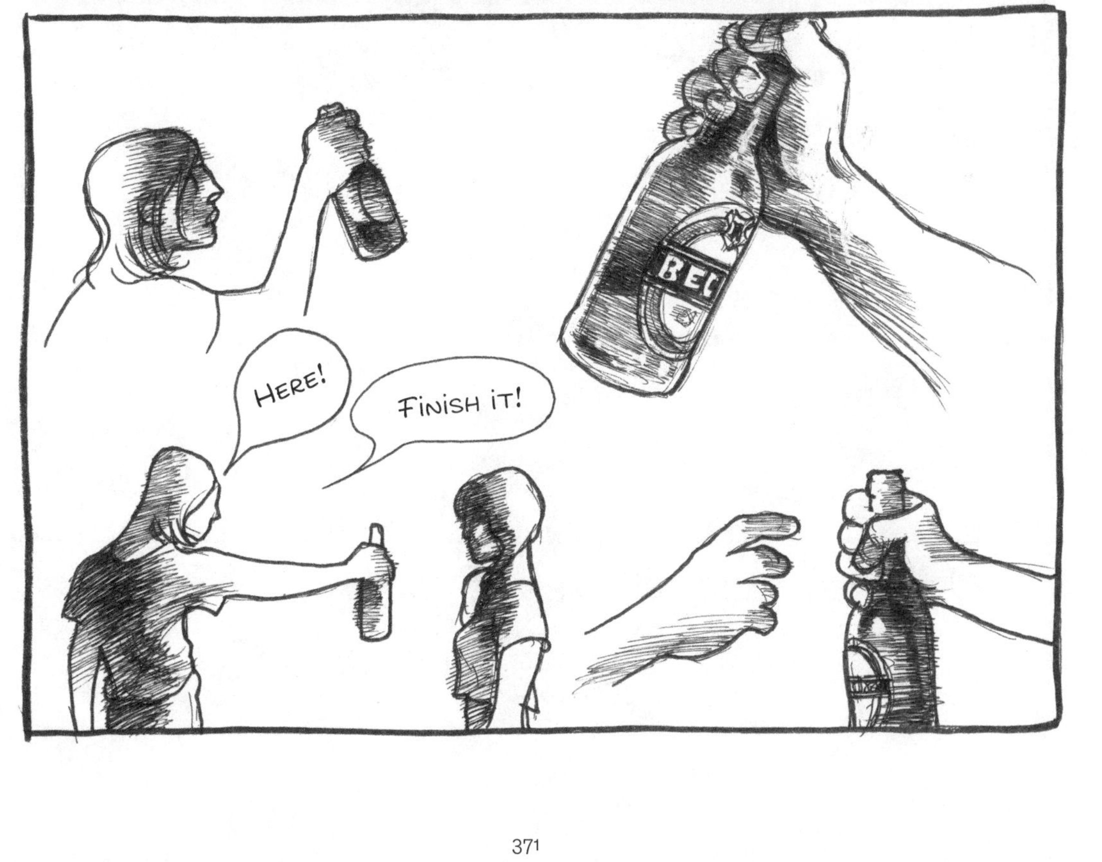
HERE!
FINISH IT!

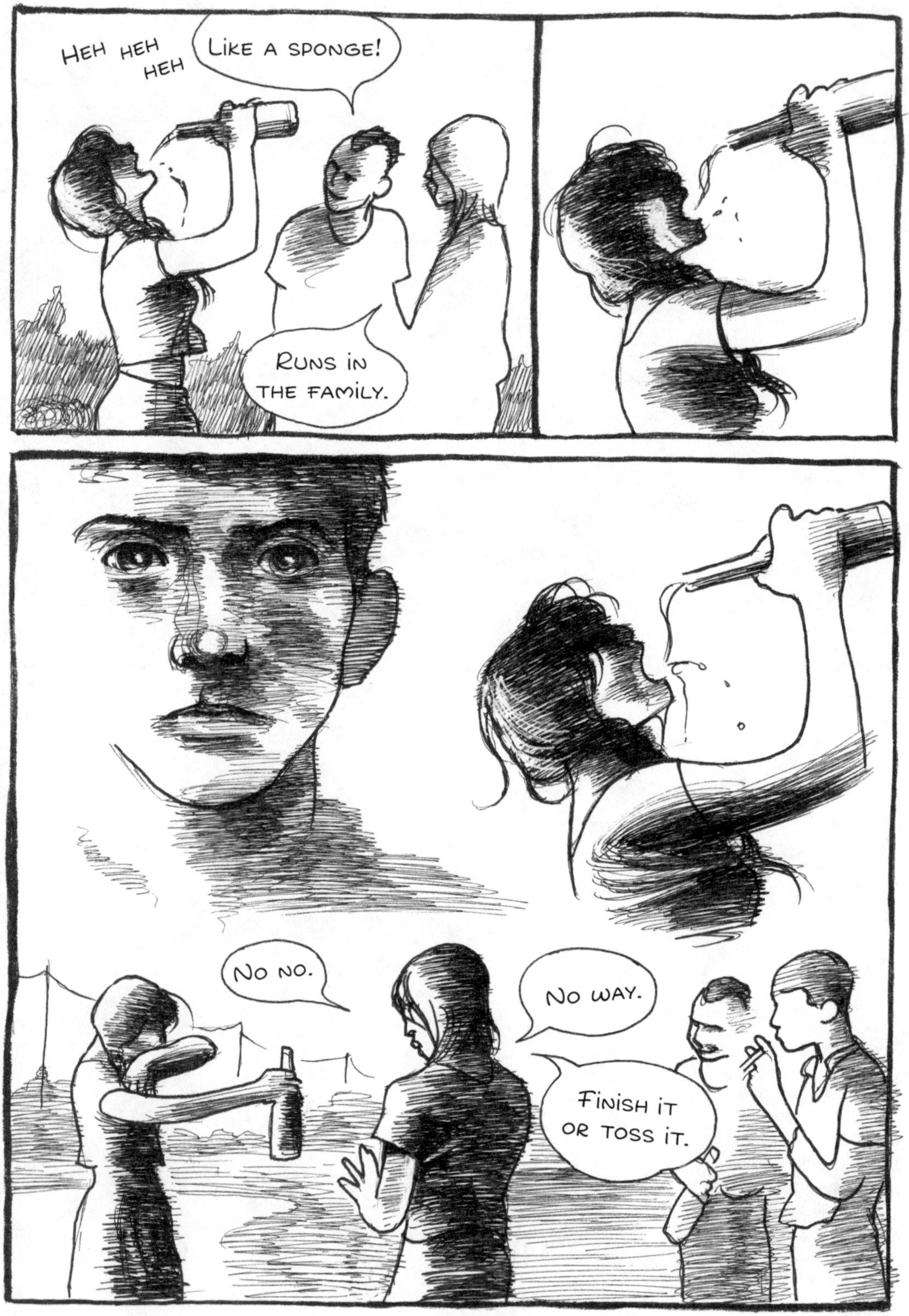
HEH HEH
HEH
LIKE A SPONGE!
RUNS IN THE FAMILY.
NO NO.
NO WAY.
FINISH IT OR TOSS IT.

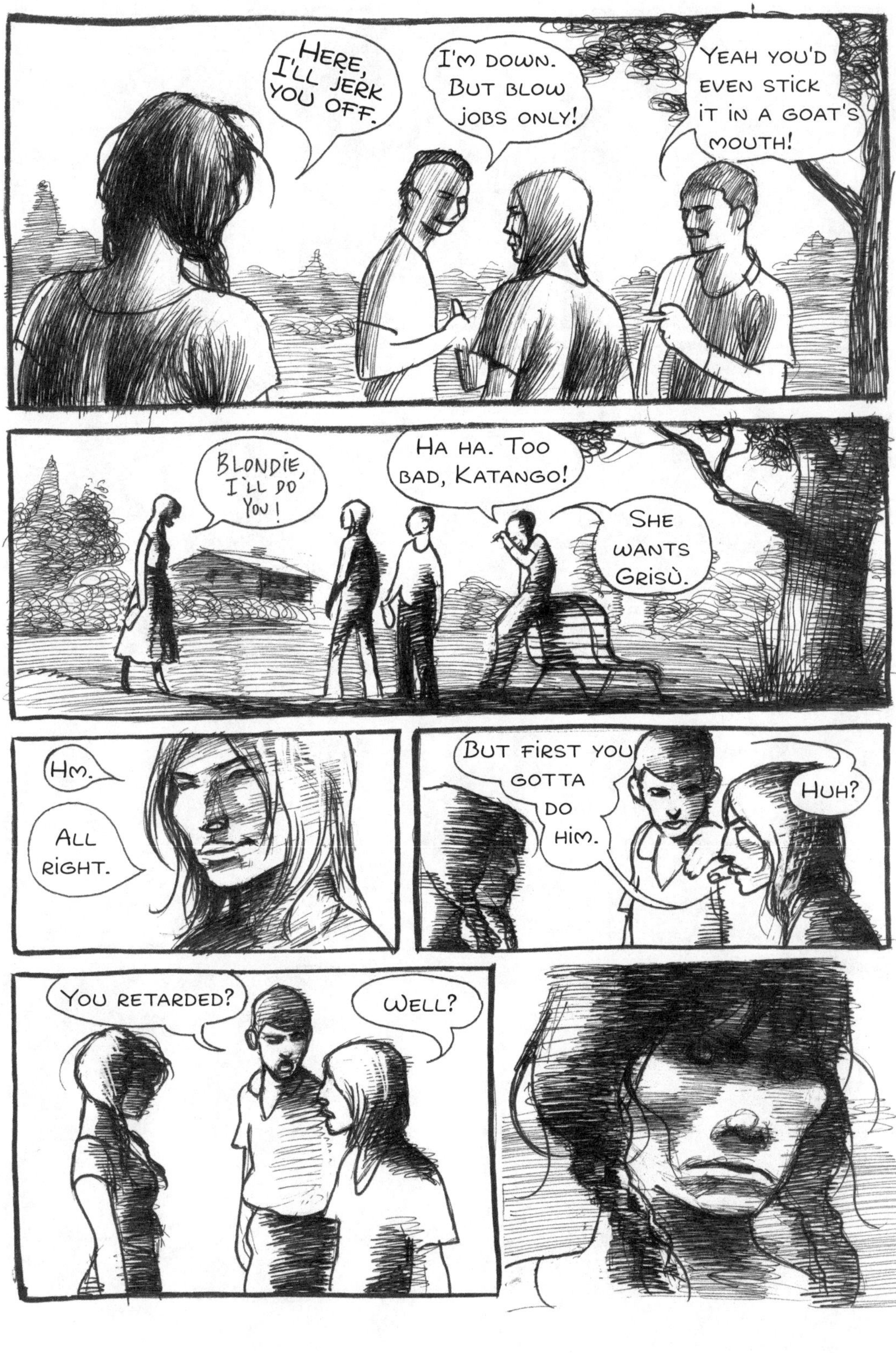

Here, I'll jerk you off.
I'm down. But blow jobs only!
Yeah you'd even stick it in a goat's mouth!
Blondie, I'll do you!
Ha ha. Too bad, Katango!
She wants Grisù.
Hm.
All right.
But first you gotta do him.
Huh?
You retarded?
Well?

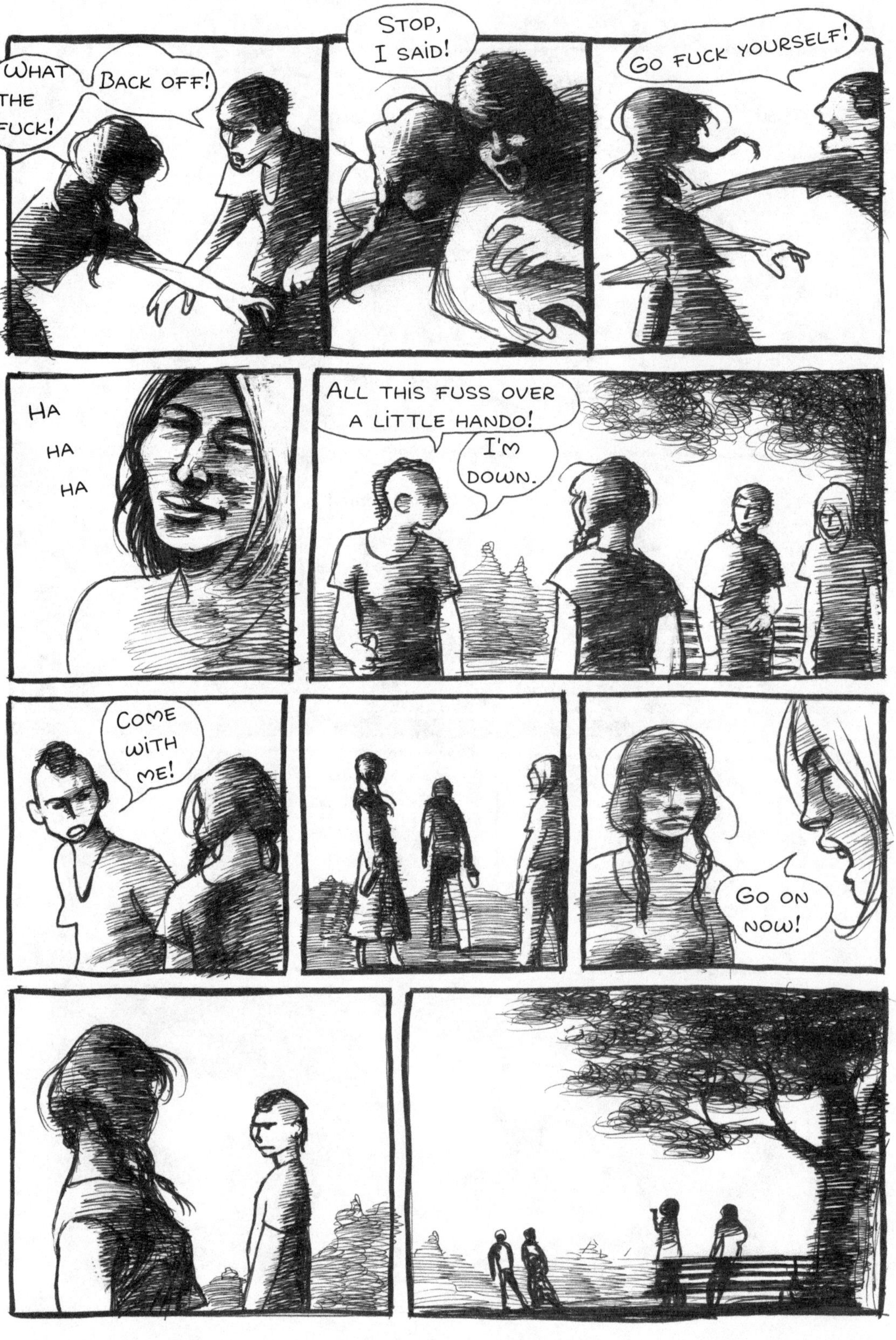
WHAT THE FUCK!
BACK OFF!
STOP, I SAID!
GO FUCK YOURSELF!
HA
HA
HA
ALL THIS FUSS OVER A LITTLE HANDO!
I'M DOWN.
COME WITH ME!
GO ON NOW!

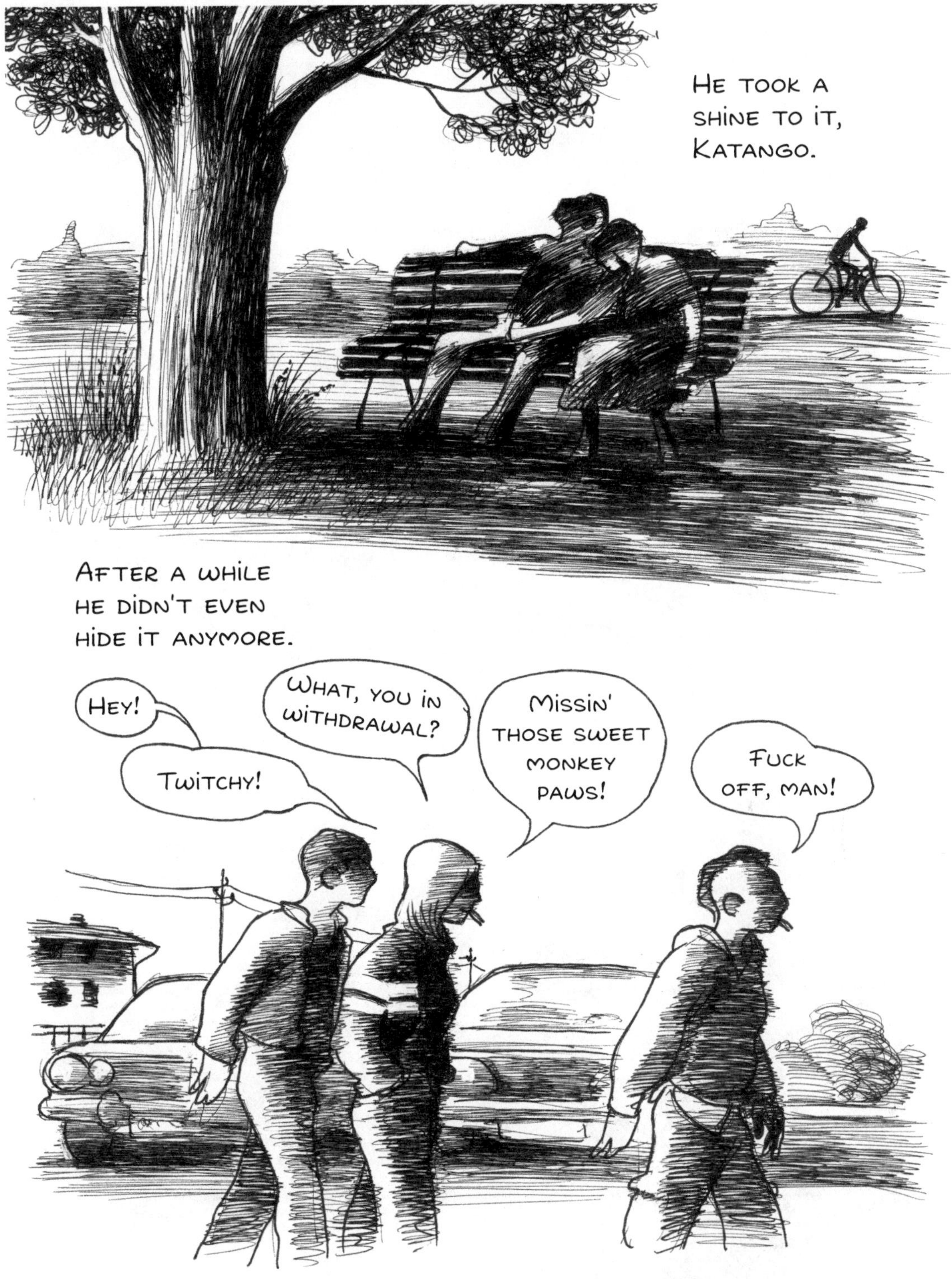
HE TOOK A SHINE TO IT, KATANGO.
AFTER A WHILE HE DIDN'T EVEN HIDE IT ANYMORE.
HEY!
TWITCHY!
WHAT, YOU IN WITHDRAWAL?
MISSIN' THOSE SWEET MONKEY PAWS!
FUCK OFF, MAN!

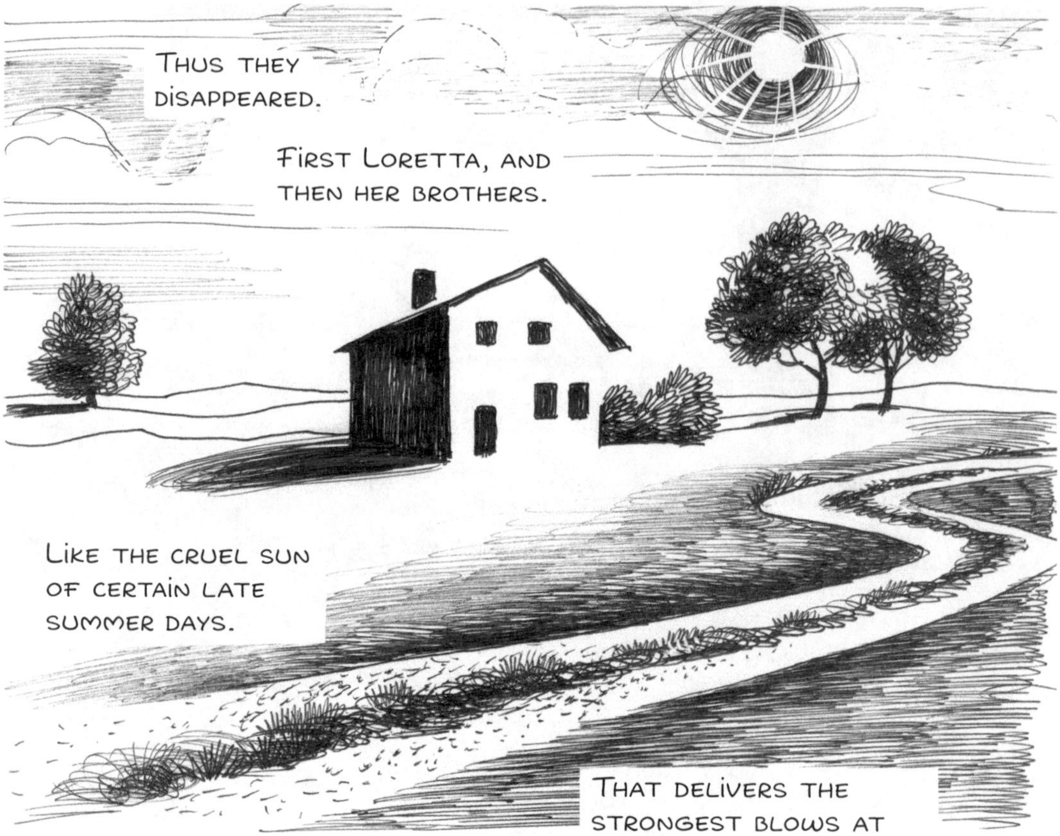

Thus they disappeared.
First Loretta, and then her brothers.
Like the cruel sun of certain late summer days.

That delivers the strongest blows at the end, right before cutting out.

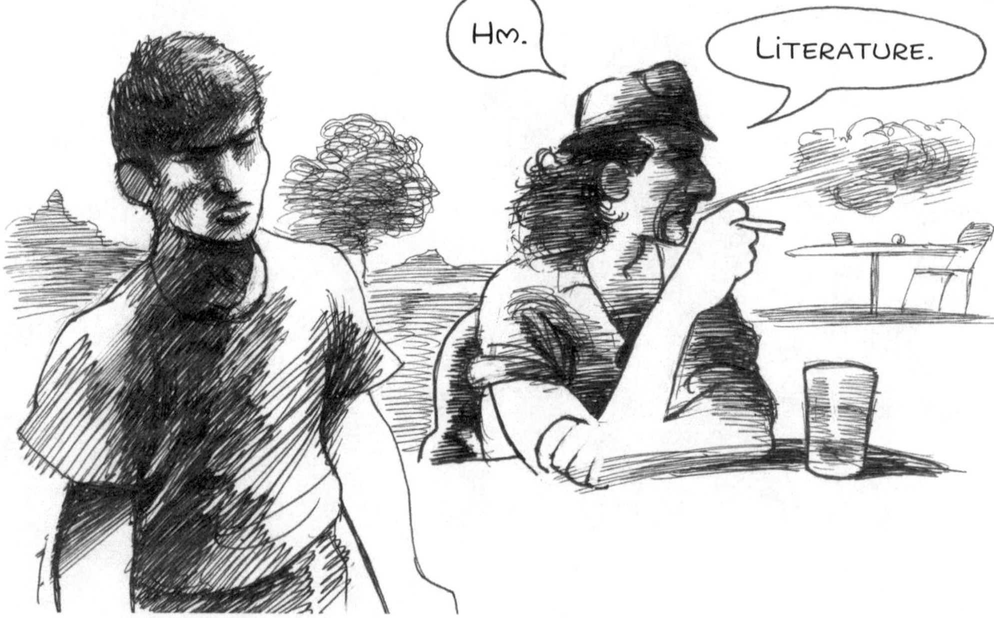

Hm.
Literature.

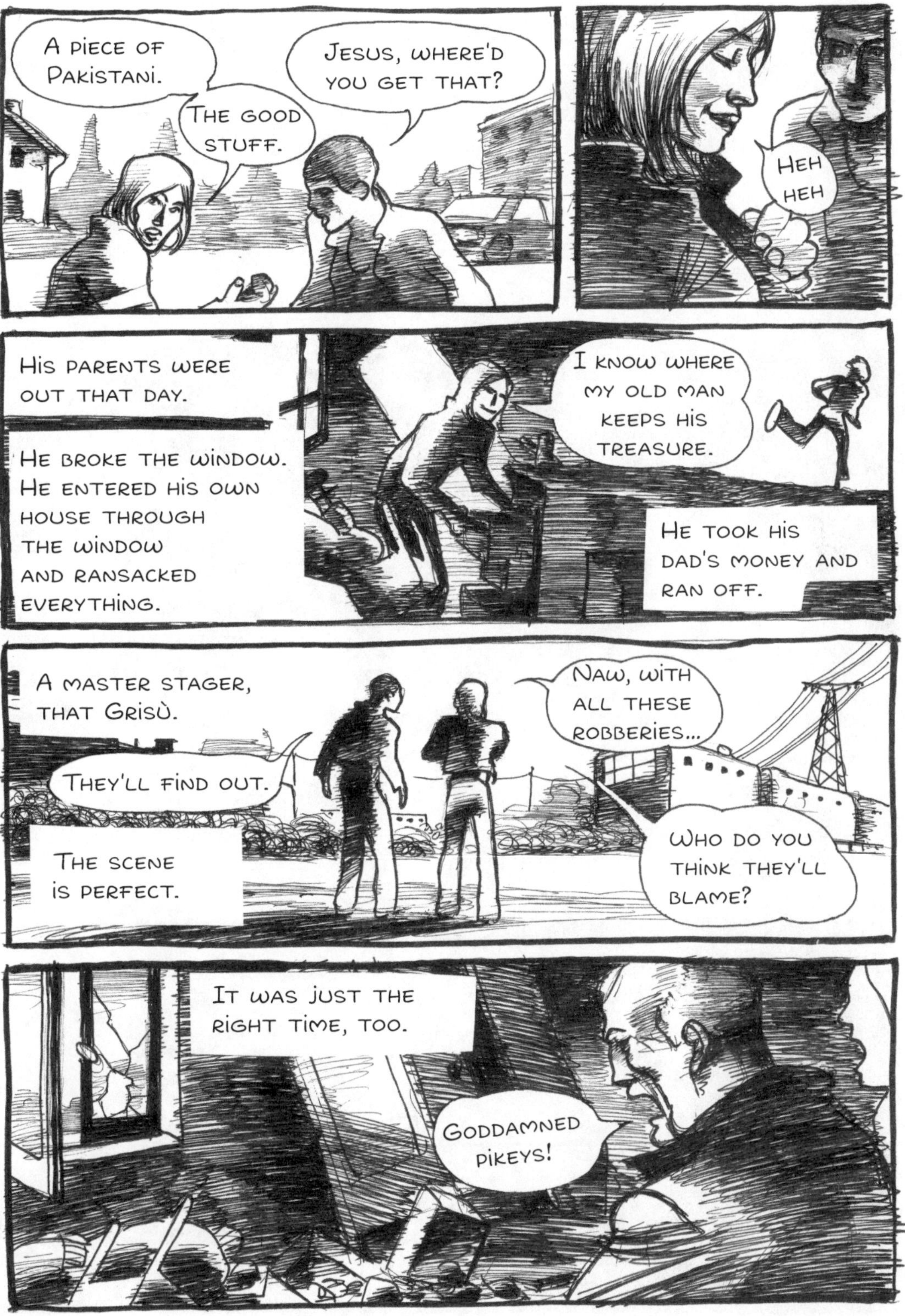
A piece of Pakistani.
The good stuff.
Jesus, where'd you get that?
Heh heh
His parents were out that day.
He broke the window. He entered his own house through the window and ransacked everything.
I know where my old man keeps his treasure.
He took his dad's money and ran off.
A master stager, that Grisù.
They'll find out.
Naw, with all these robberies...
The scene is perfect.
Who do you think they'll blame?
It was just the right time, too.
Goddamned pikeys!

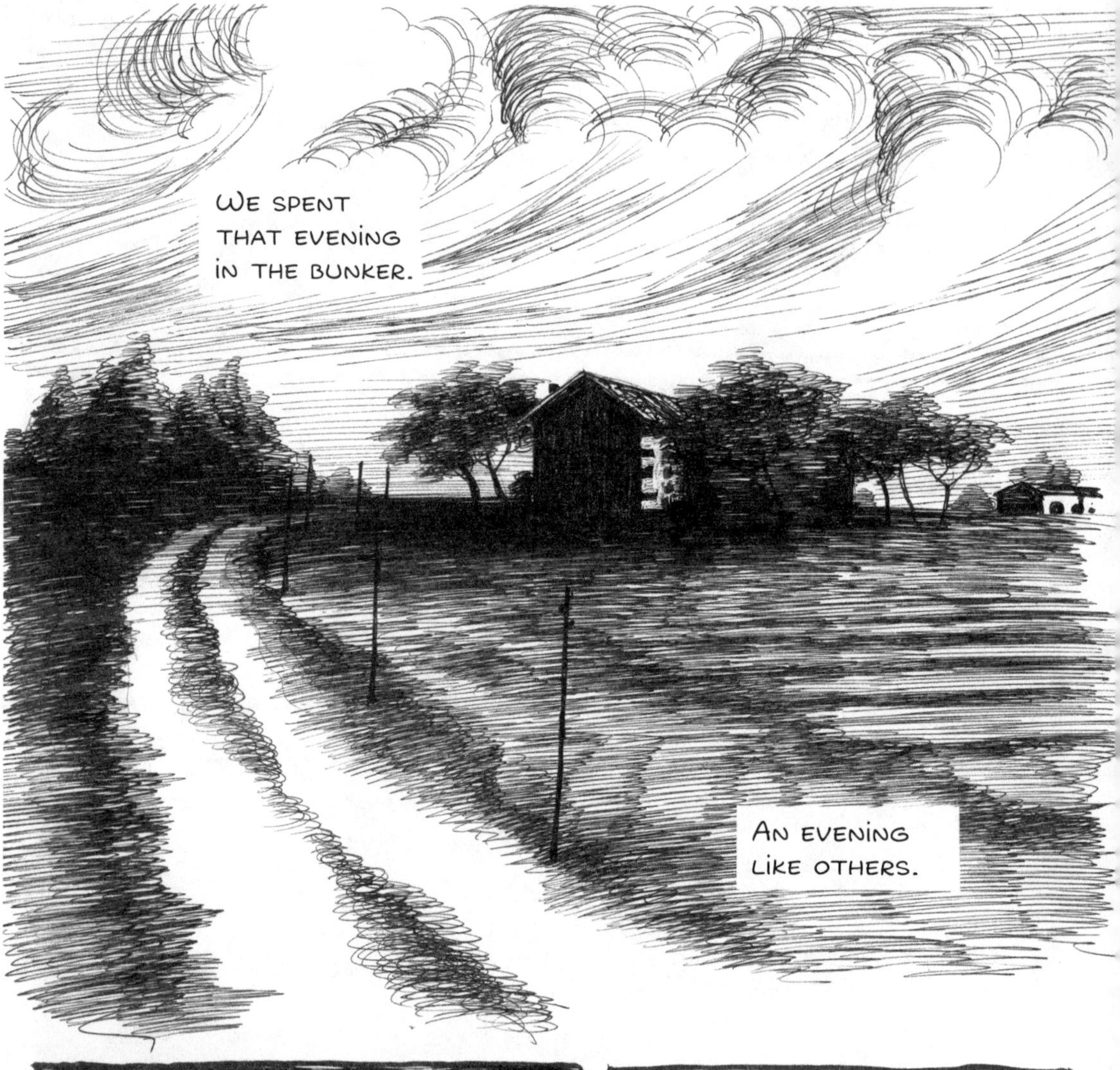
WE SPENT THAT EVENING IN THE BUNKER.
AN EVENING LIKE OTHERS.

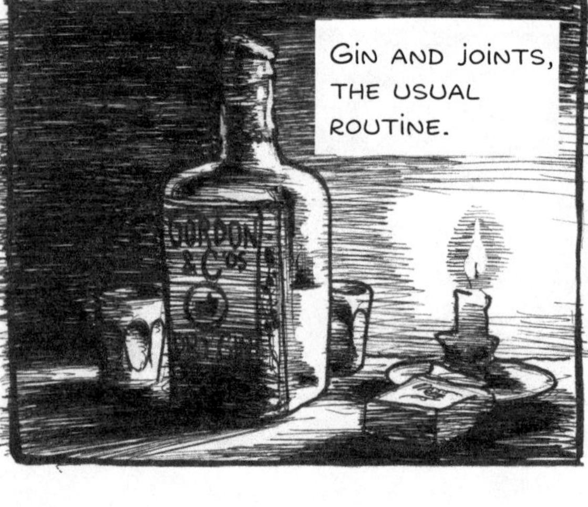
GIN AND JOINTS, THE USUAL ROUTINE.

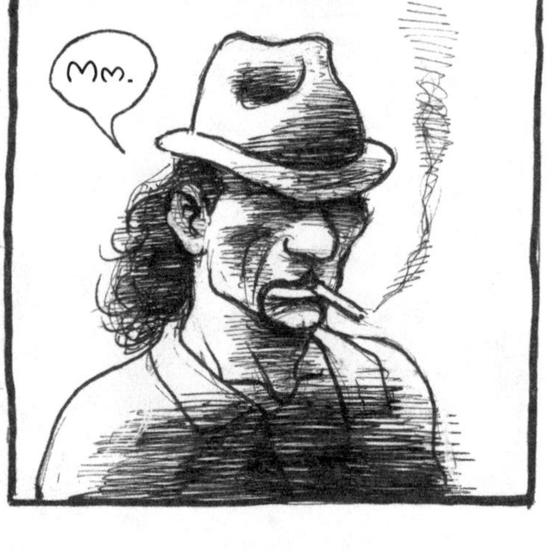
Mm.

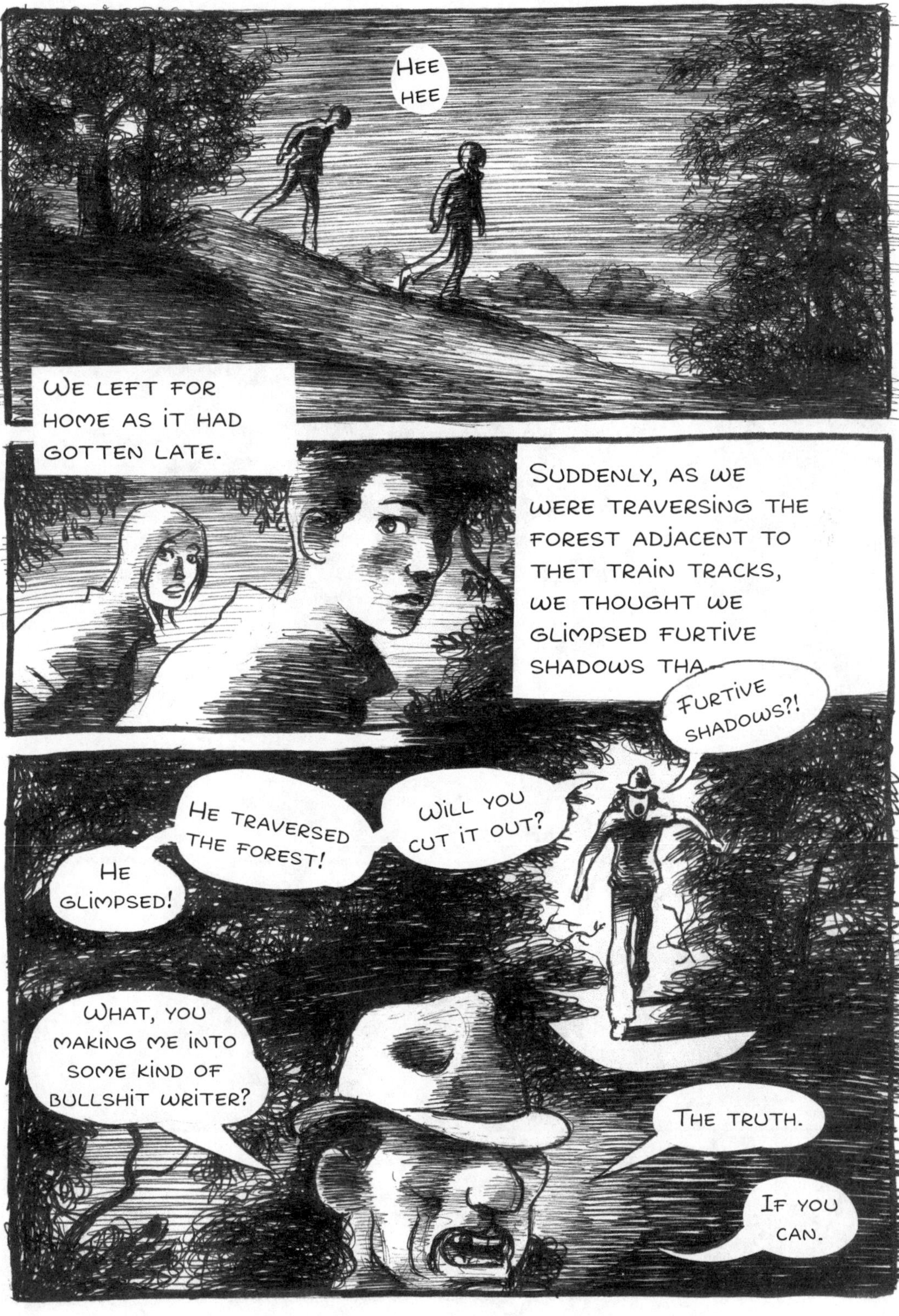
HEE HEE
WE LEFT FOR HOME AS IT HAD GOTTEN LATE.
SUDDENLY, AS WE WERE TRAVERSING THE FOREST ADJACENT TO THET TRAIN TRACKS, WE THOUGHT WE GLIMPSED FURTIVE SHADOWS THA—
FURTIVE SHADOWS?!
WILL YOU CUT IT OUT?
HE TRAVERSED THE FOREST!
HE GLIMPSED!
WHAT, YOU MAKING ME INTO SOME KIND OF BULLSHIT WRITER?
THE TRUTH.
IF YOU CAN.

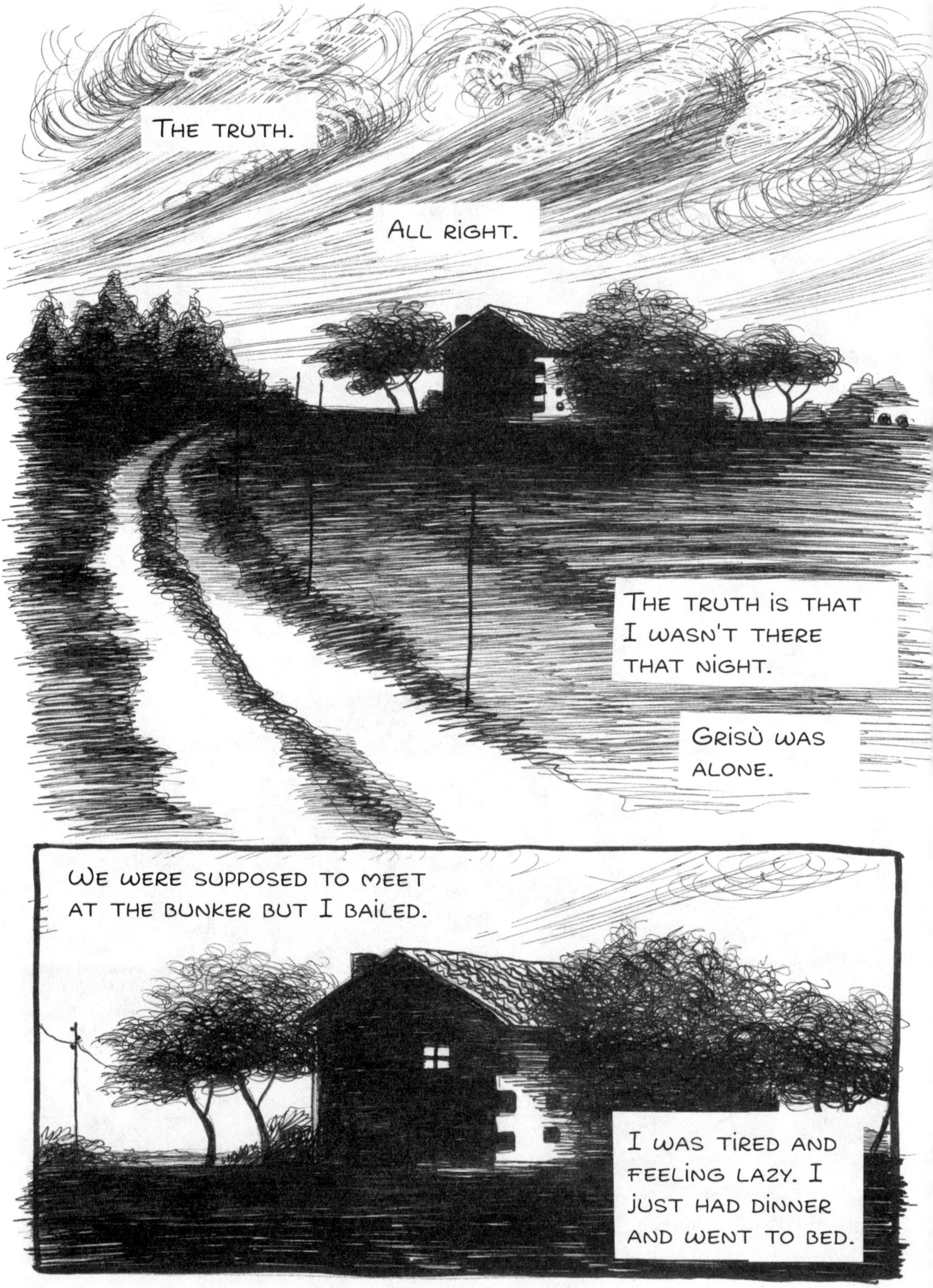
THE TRUTH.
ALL RIGHT.
THE TRUTH IS THAT I WASN'T THERE THAT NIGHT.
GRISÙ WAS ALONE.
WE WERE SUPPOSED TO MEET AT THE BUNKER BUT I BAILED.
I WAS TIRED AND FEELING LAZY. I JUST HAD DINNER AND WENT TO BED.

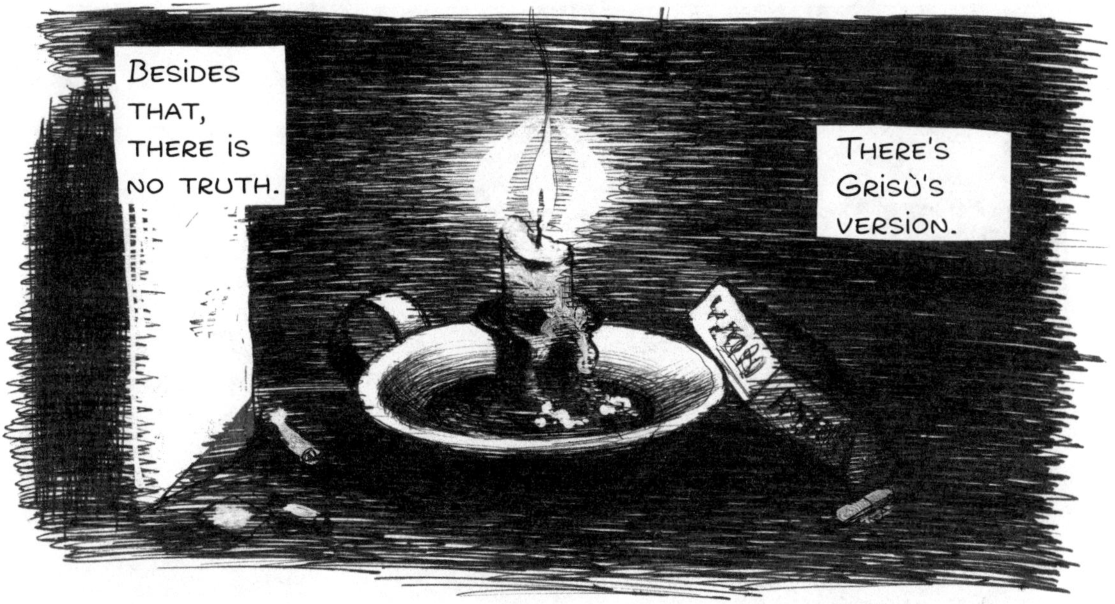
Besides that, there is no truth.
There's Grisù's version.

While he was waiting for me he started smoking the Pakistani stuff he'd picked up in the city that afternoon and topped it off with a little gin.

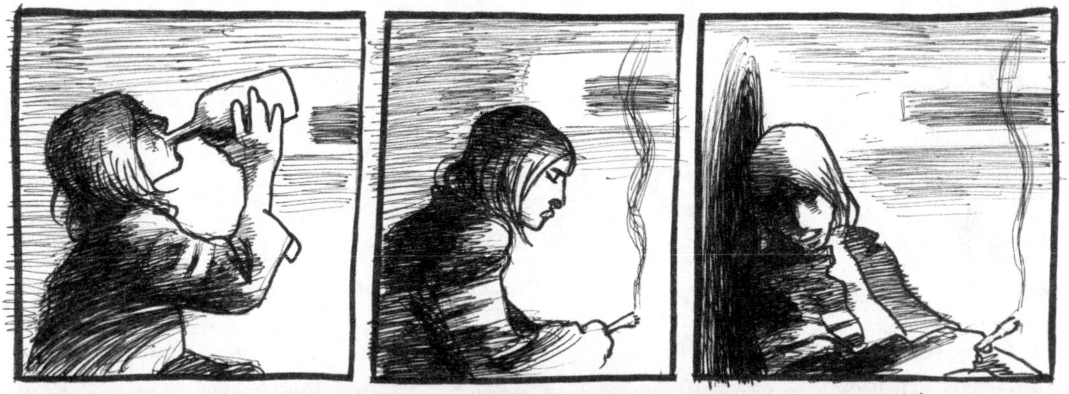

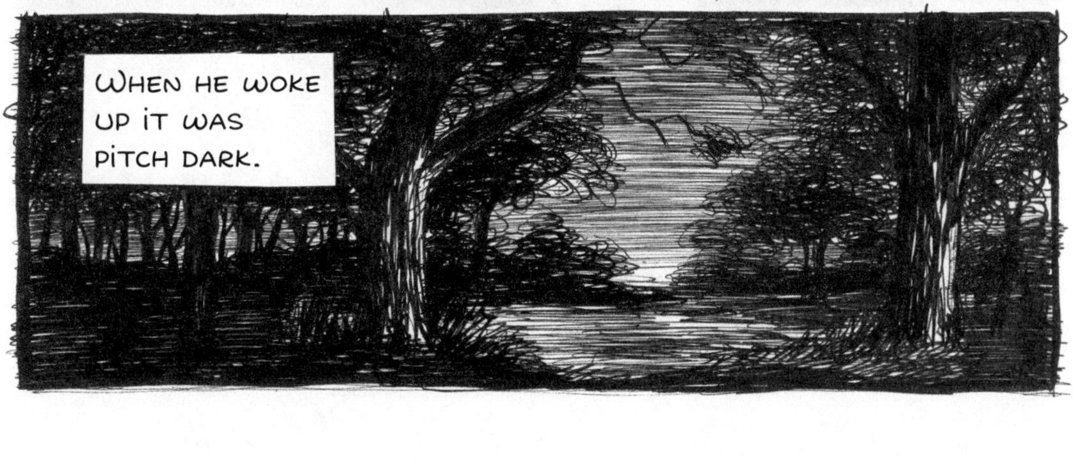
When he woke up it was pitch dark.

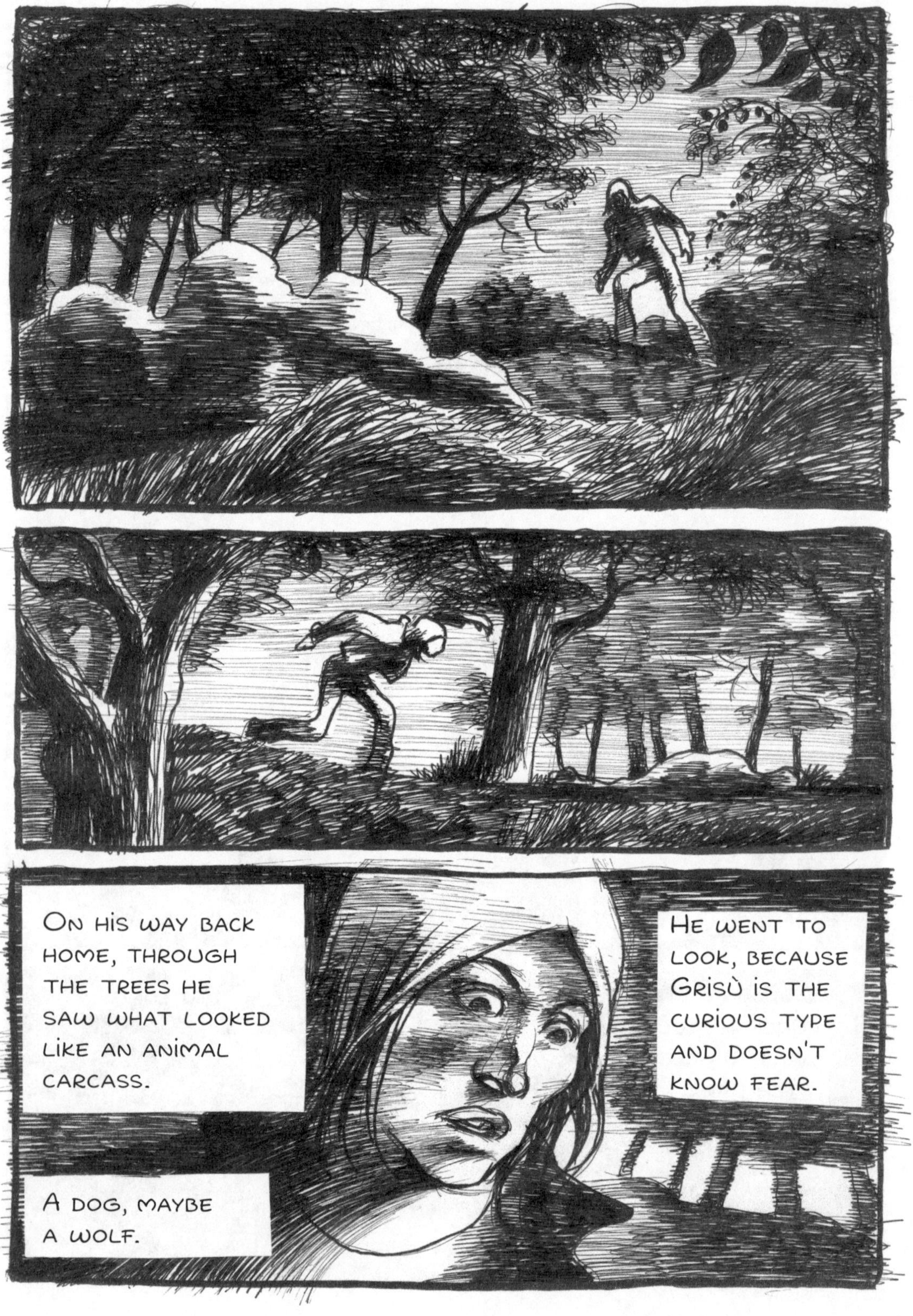
On his way back home, through the trees he saw what looked like an animal carcass.
He went to look, because Grisù is the curious type and doesn't know fear.
A dog, maybe a wolf.

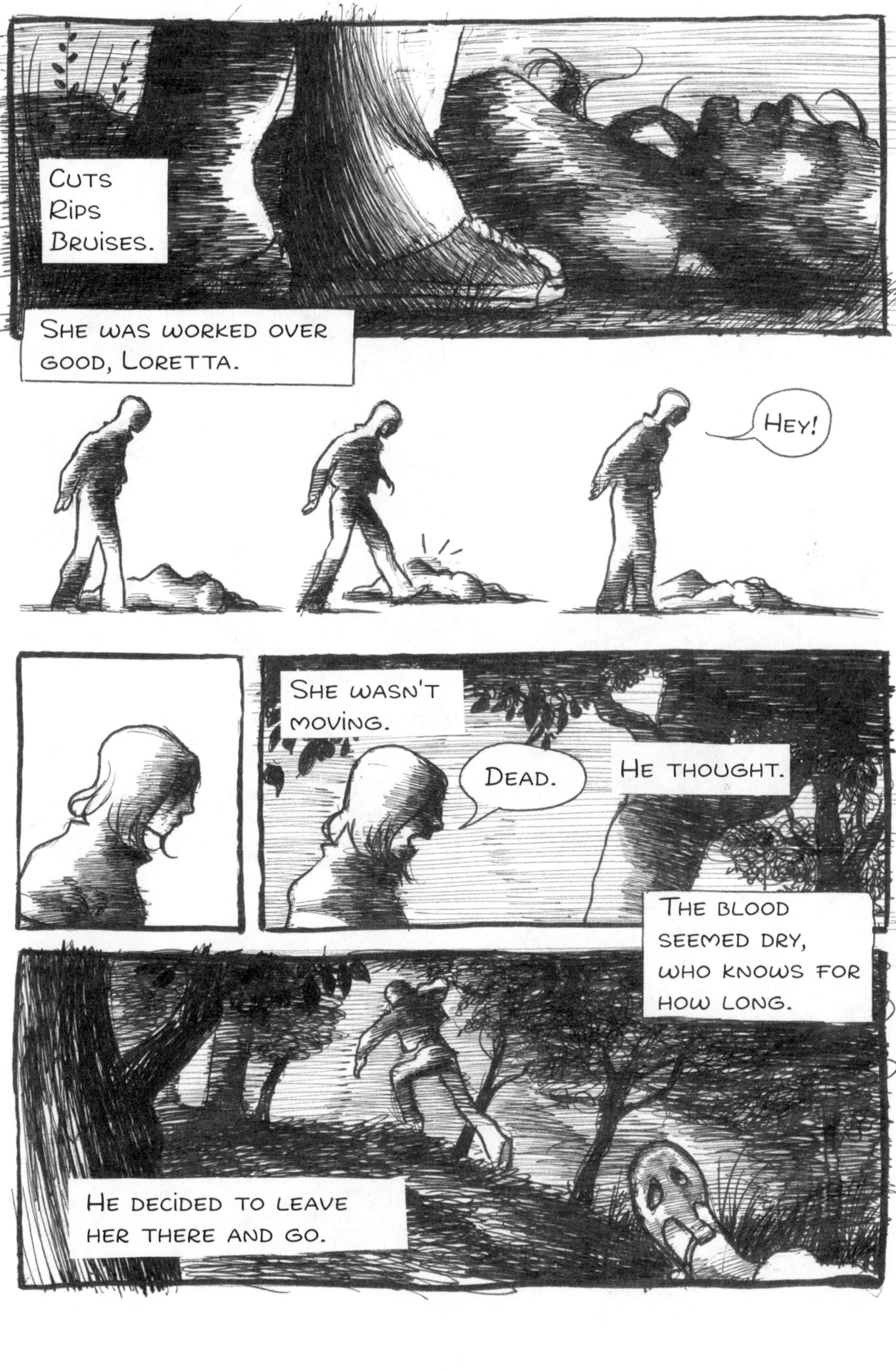
CUTS
RIPS
BRUISES.
SHE WAS WORKED OVER GOOD, LORETTA.
HEY!
SHE WASN'T MOVING.
DEAD.
HE THOUGHT.
THE BLOOD SEEMED DRY, WHO KNOWS FOR HOW LONG.
HE DECIDED TO LEAVE HER THERE AND GO.

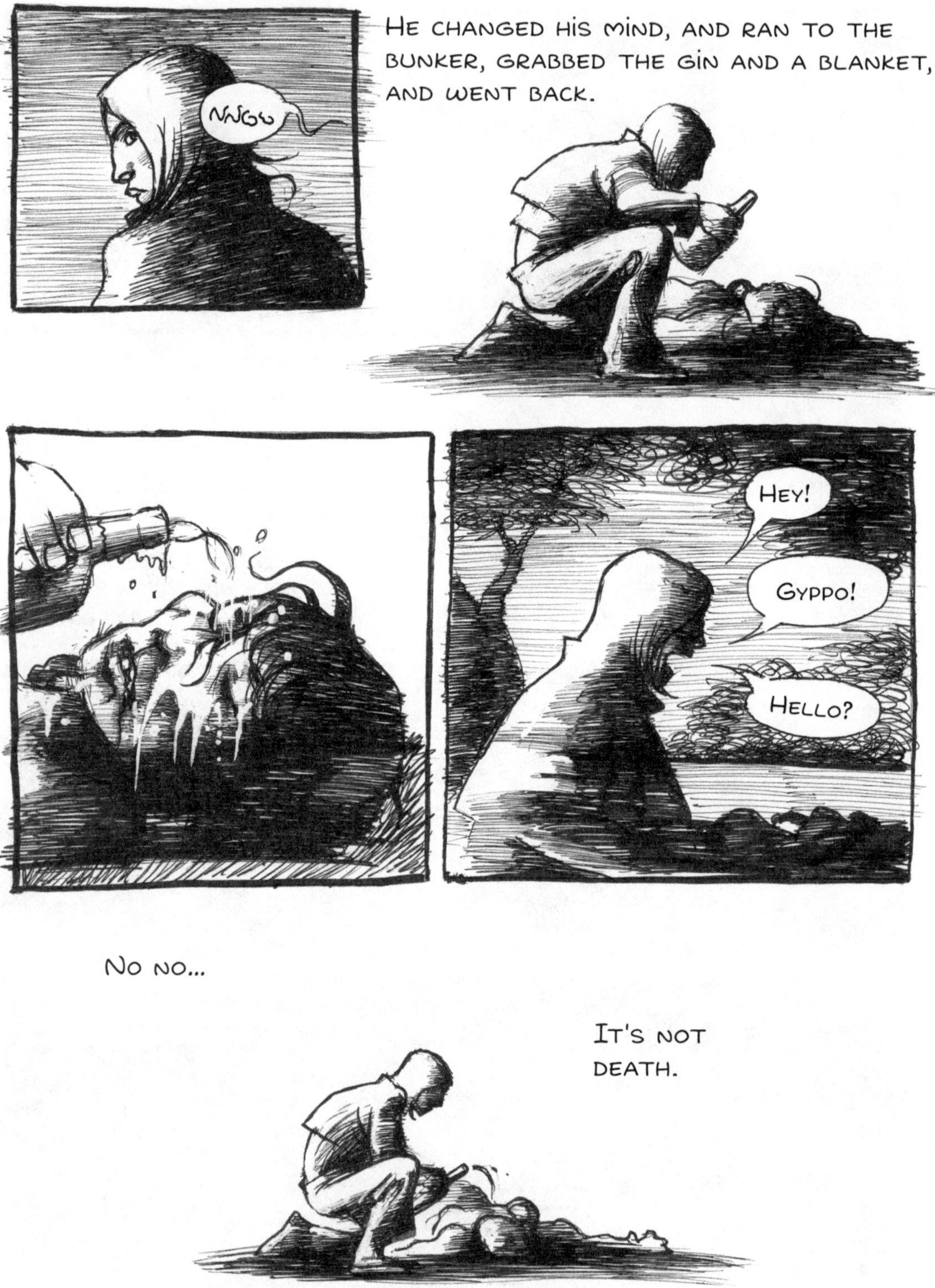
HE CHANGED HIS MIND, AND RAN TO THE BUNKER, GRABBED THE GIN AND A BLANKET, AND WENT BACK.
NNGU
HEY!
GYPPO!
HELLO?
NO NO...
IT'S NOT DEATH.

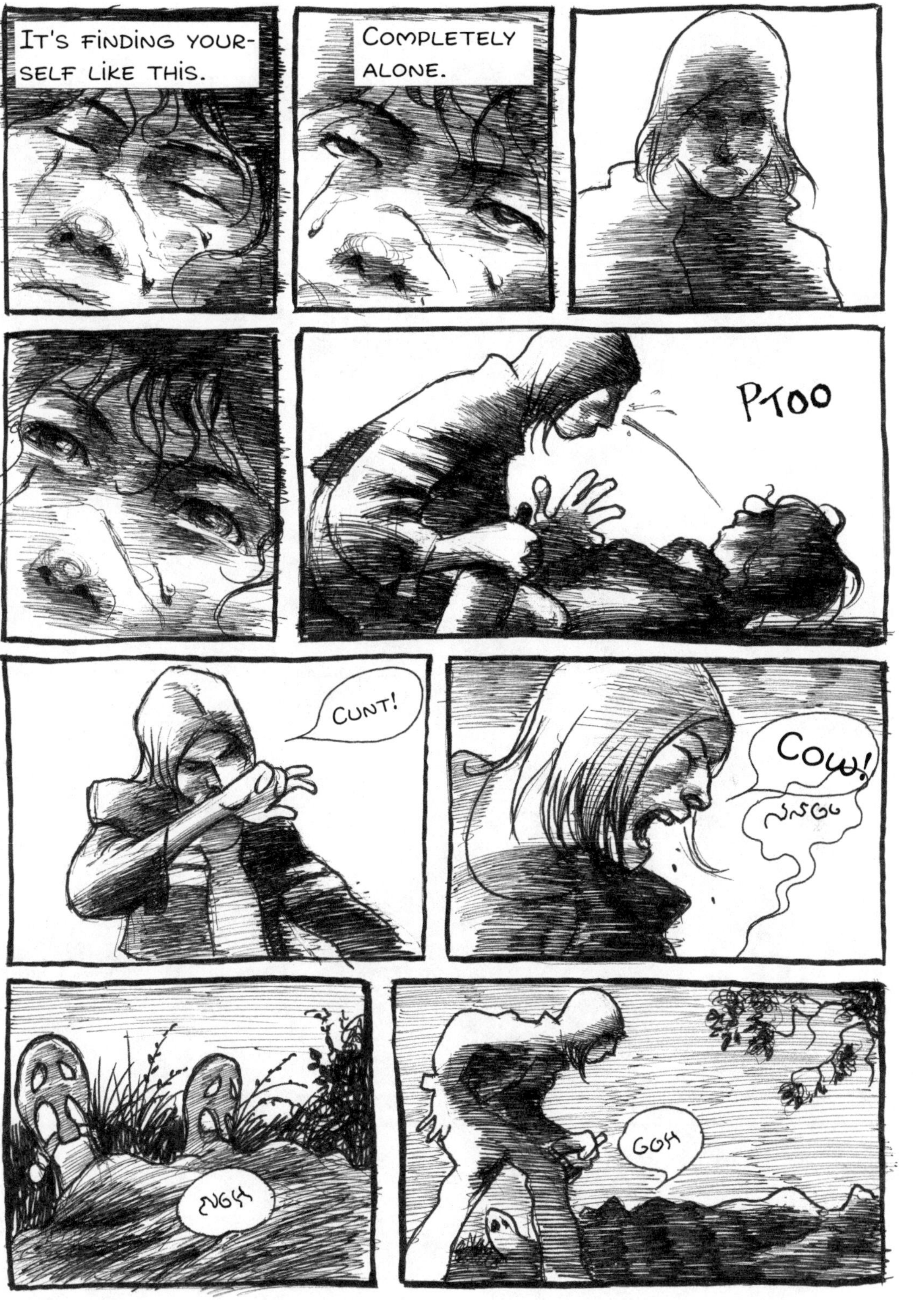

IT'S FINDING YOURSELF LIKE THIS.
COMPLETELY ALONE.
P-TOO
CUNT!
COW!
GOH

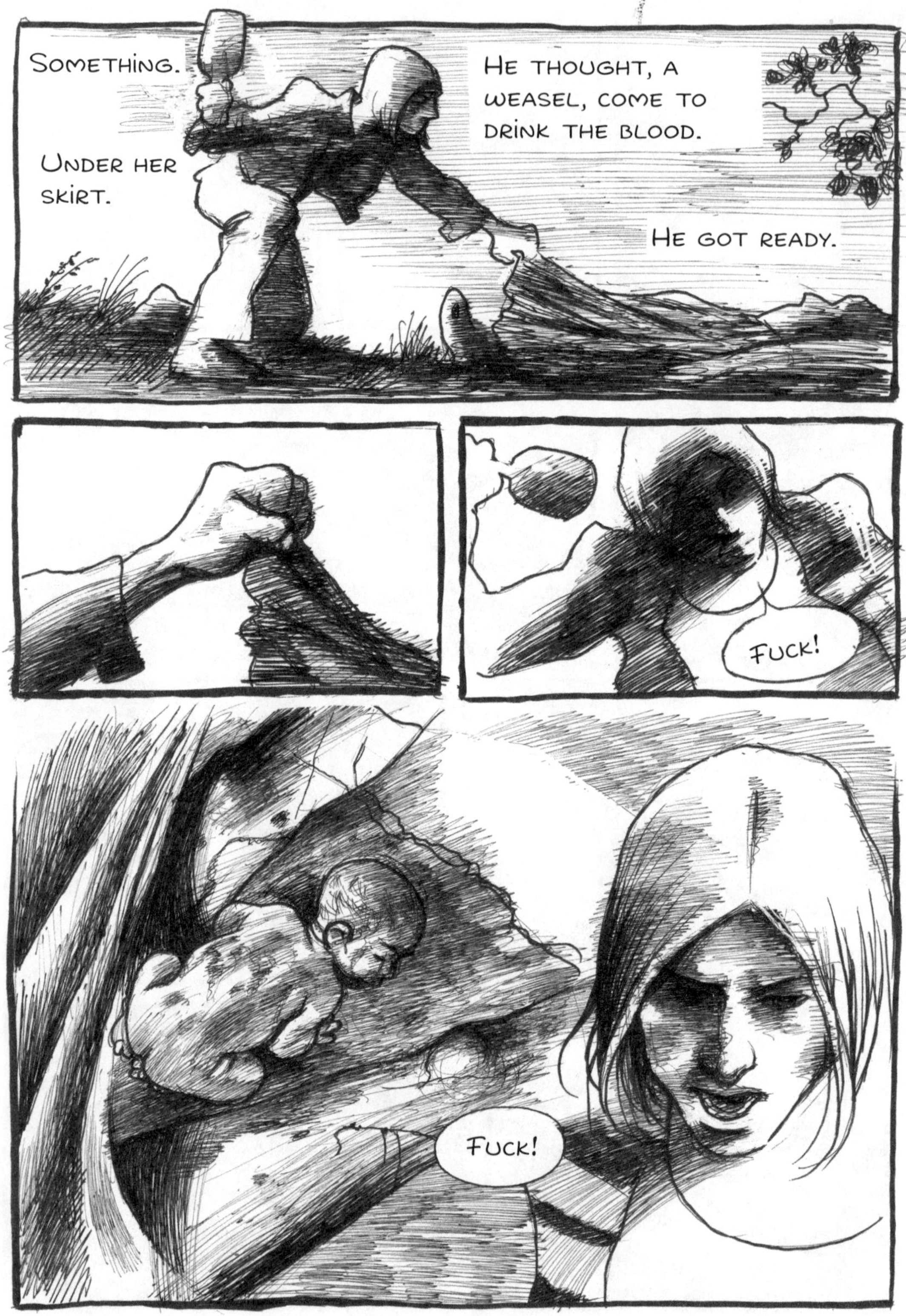
Something.
Under her skirt.
He thought, a weasel, come to drink the blood.
He got ready.
Fuck!
Fuck!

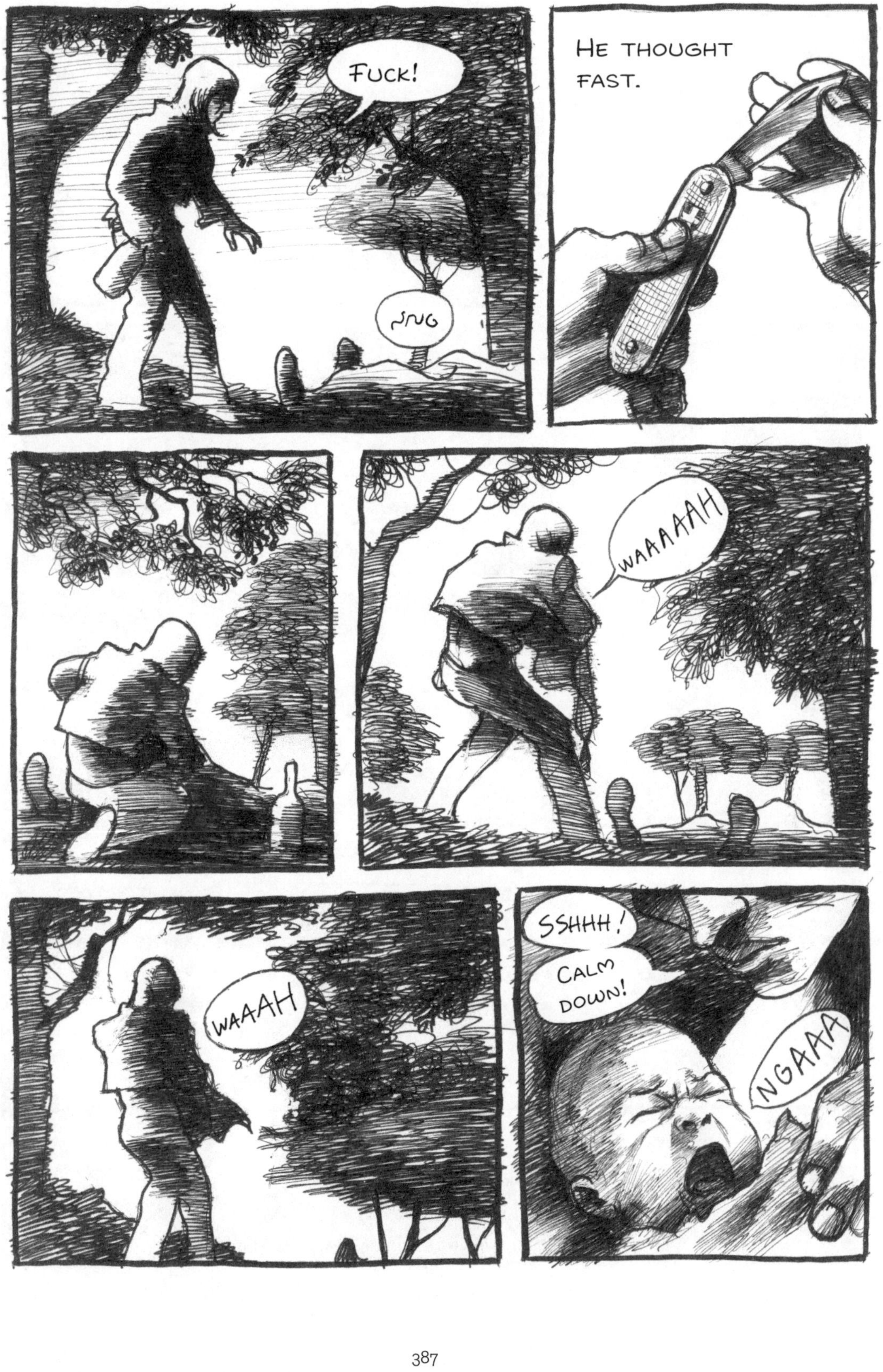
FUCK!
NNG
HE THOUGHT FAST.
WAAAAAH
WAAAH
SSHHH!
CALM DOWN!
NGAAA

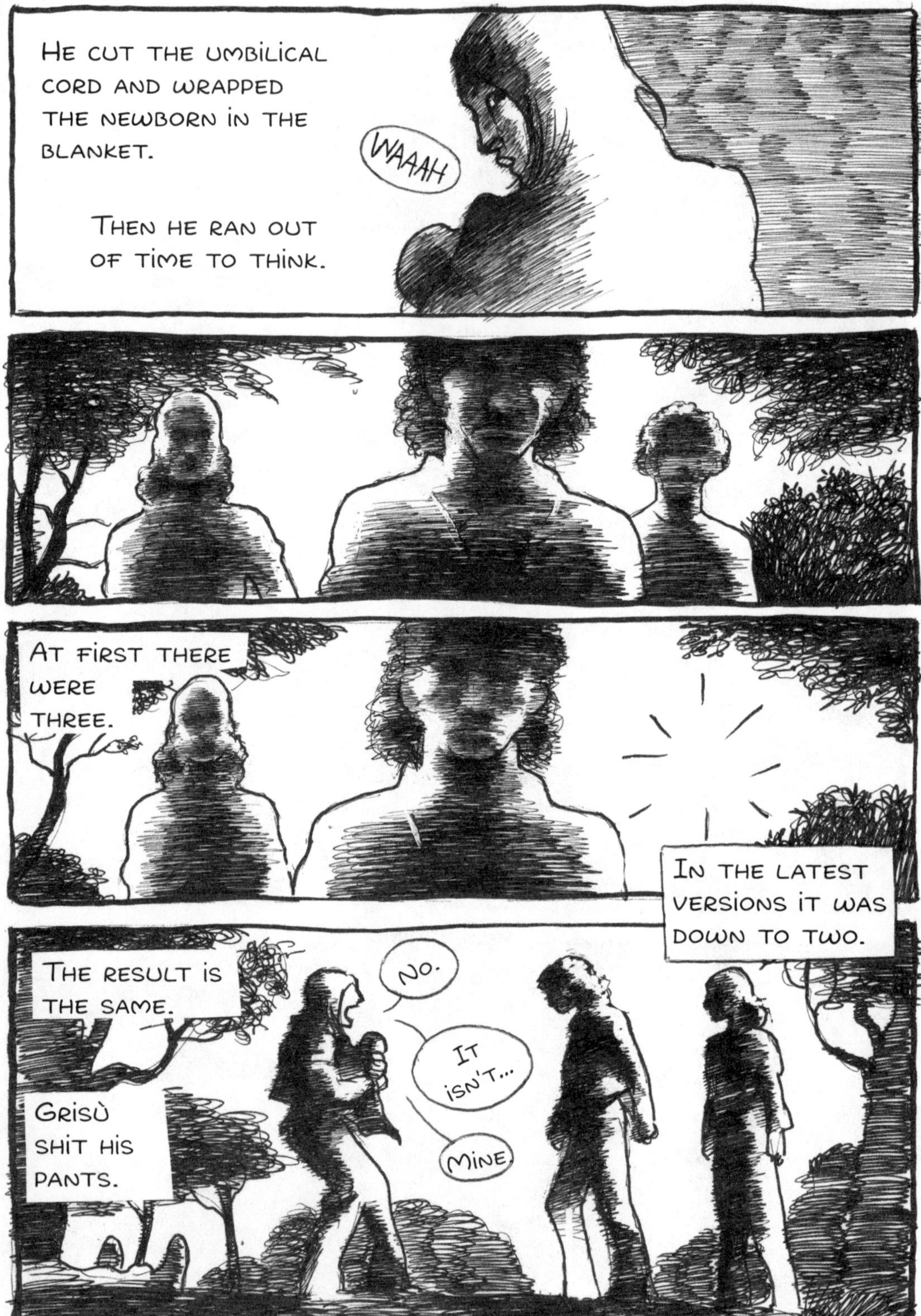
He cut the umbilical cord and wrapped the newborn in the blanket.
WAAAH
Then he ran out of time to think.
At first there were three.
In the latest versions it was down to two.
The result is the same.
No.
It isn't...
Mine.
Grisù shit his pants.

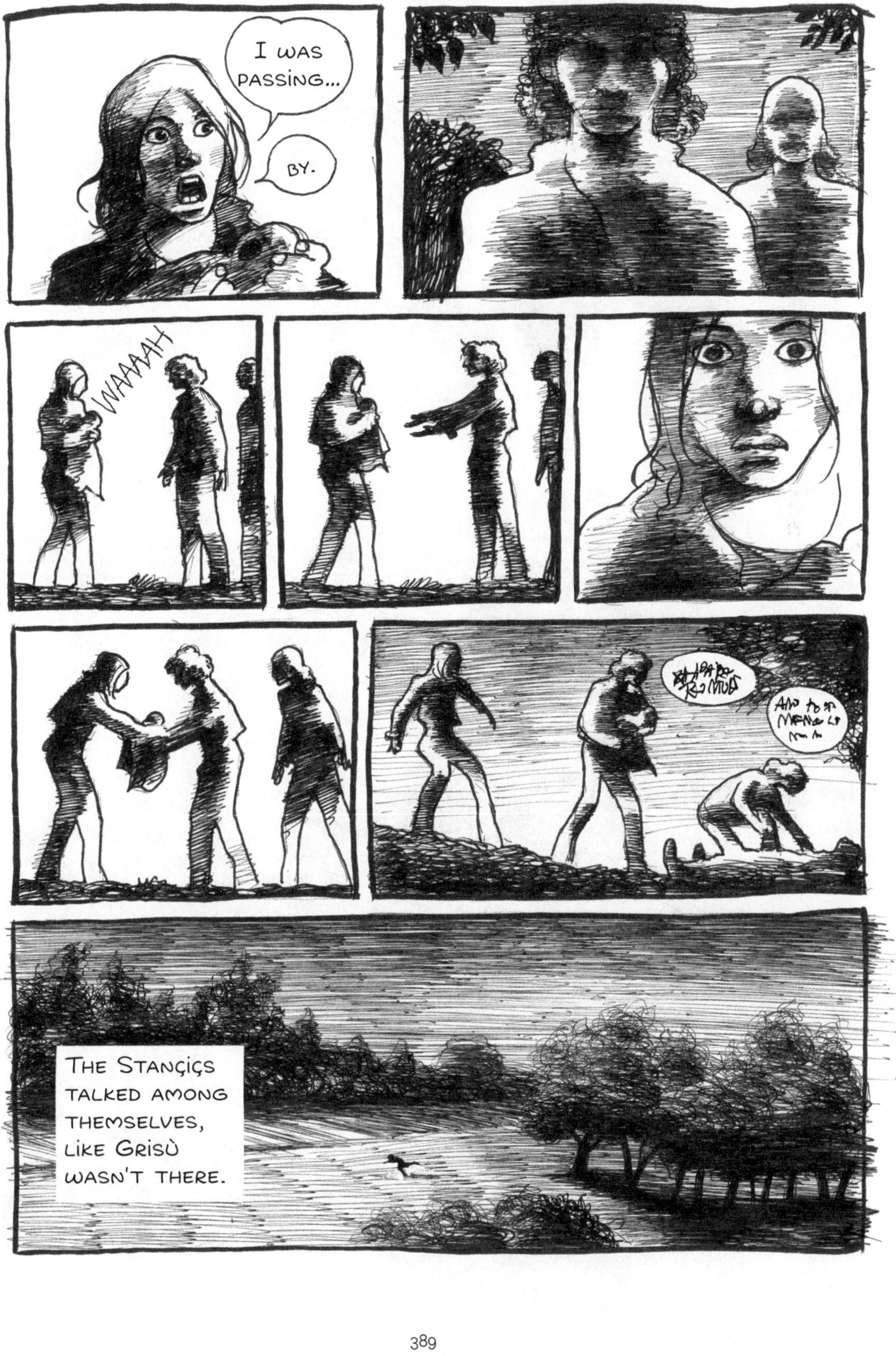
I WAS PASSING...
BY.
WAAAAH
THE STANÇIÇS TALKED AMONG THEMSELVES, LIKE GRISÙ WASN'T THERE.

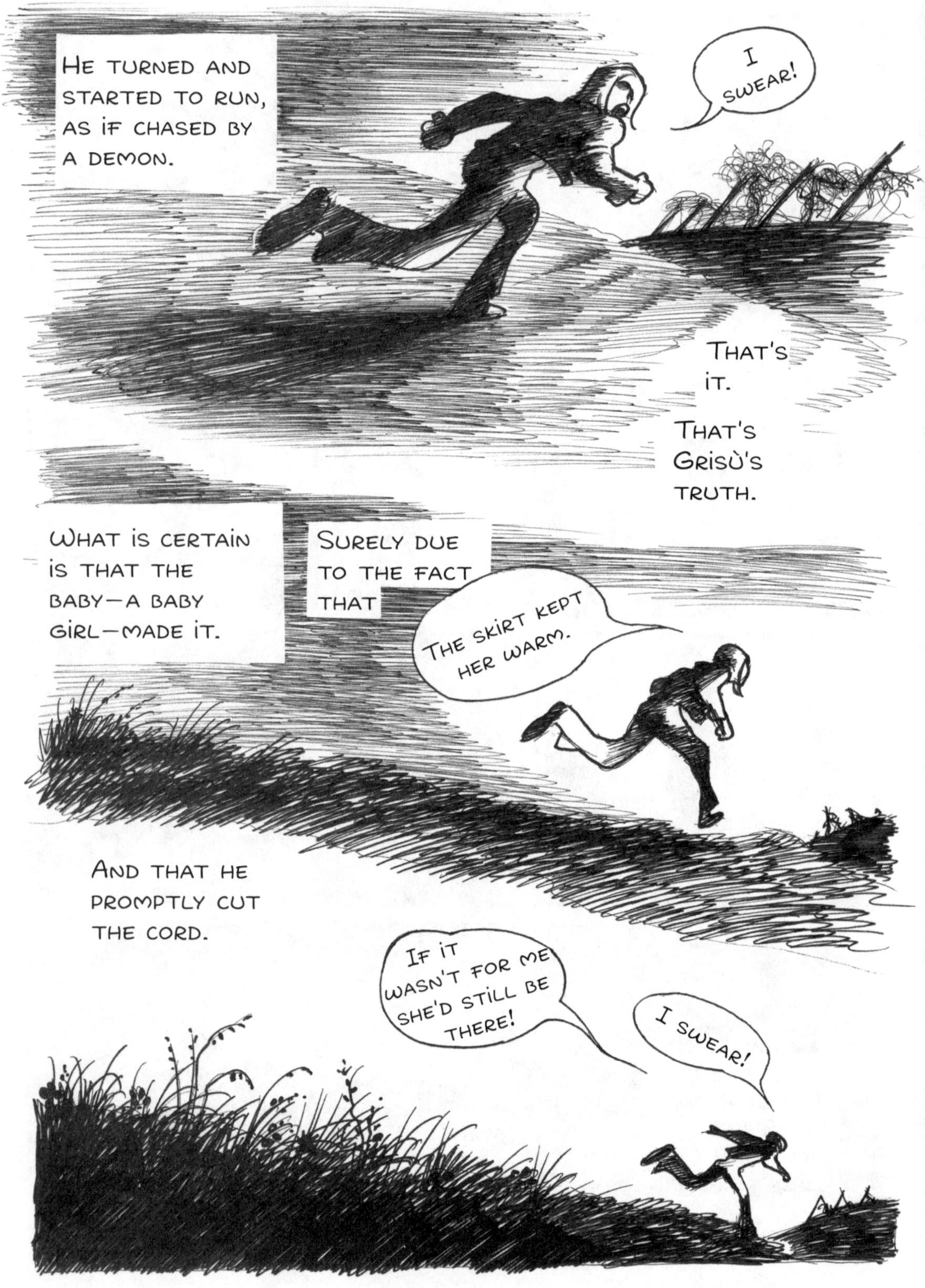
He turned and started to run, as if chased by a demon.
I swear!
That's it.
That's Grisù's truth.
What is certain is that the baby—a baby girl—made it.
Surely due to the fact that
The skirt kept her warm.
And that he promptly cut the cord.
If it wasn't for me she'd still be there!
I swear!

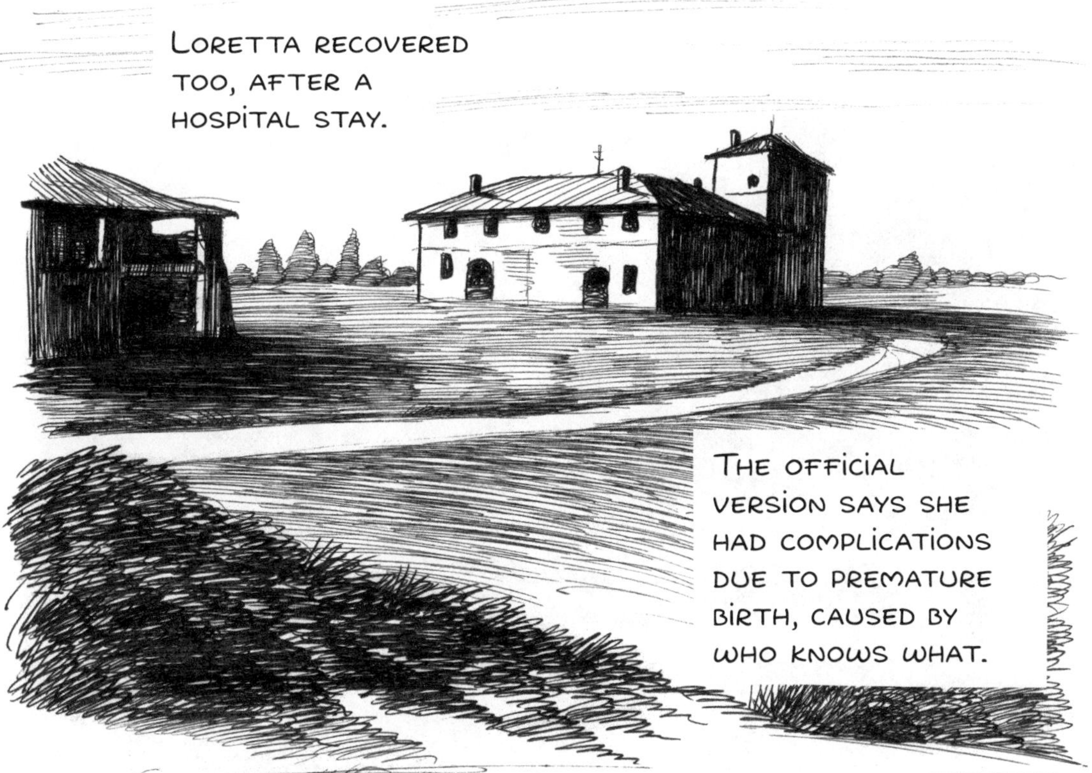
LORETTA RECOVERED TOO, AFTER A HOSPITAL STAY.
THE OFFICIAL VERSION SAYS SHE HAD COMPLICATIONS DUE TO PREMATURE BIRTH, CAUSED BY WHO KNOWS WHAT.

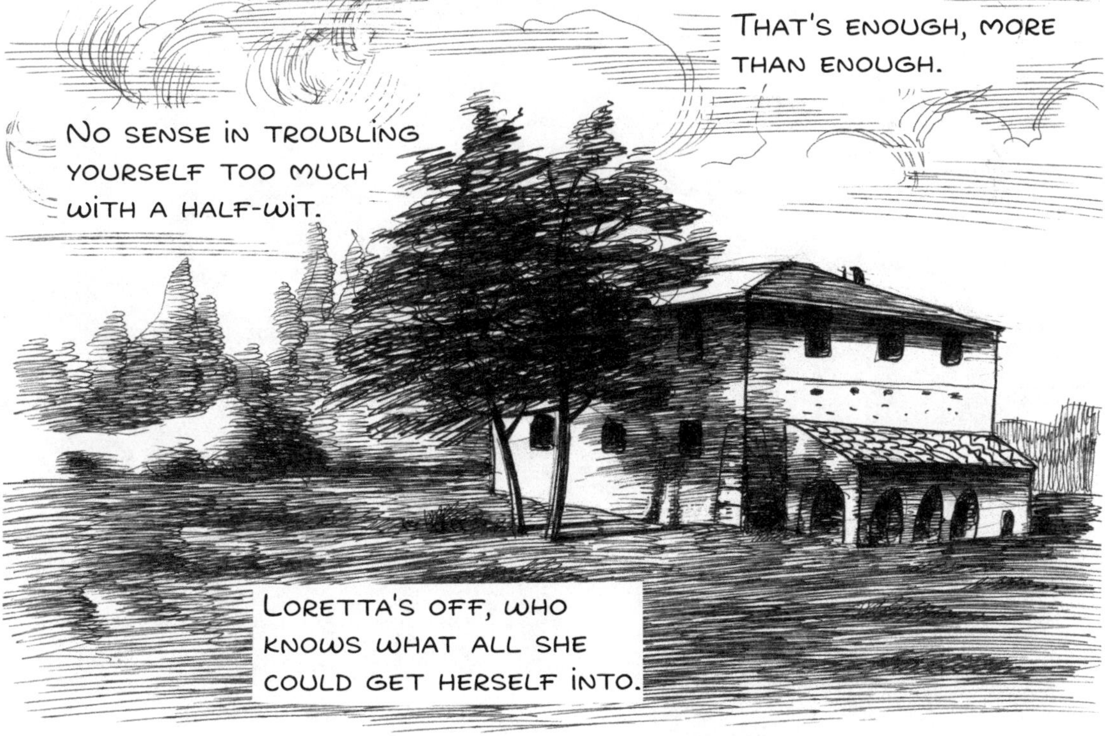
THAT'S ENOUGH, MORE THAN ENOUGH.
NO SENSE IN TROUBLING YOURSELF TOO MUCH WITH A HALF-WIT.
LORETTA'S OFF, WHO KNOWS WHAT ALL SHE COULD GET HERSELF INTO.

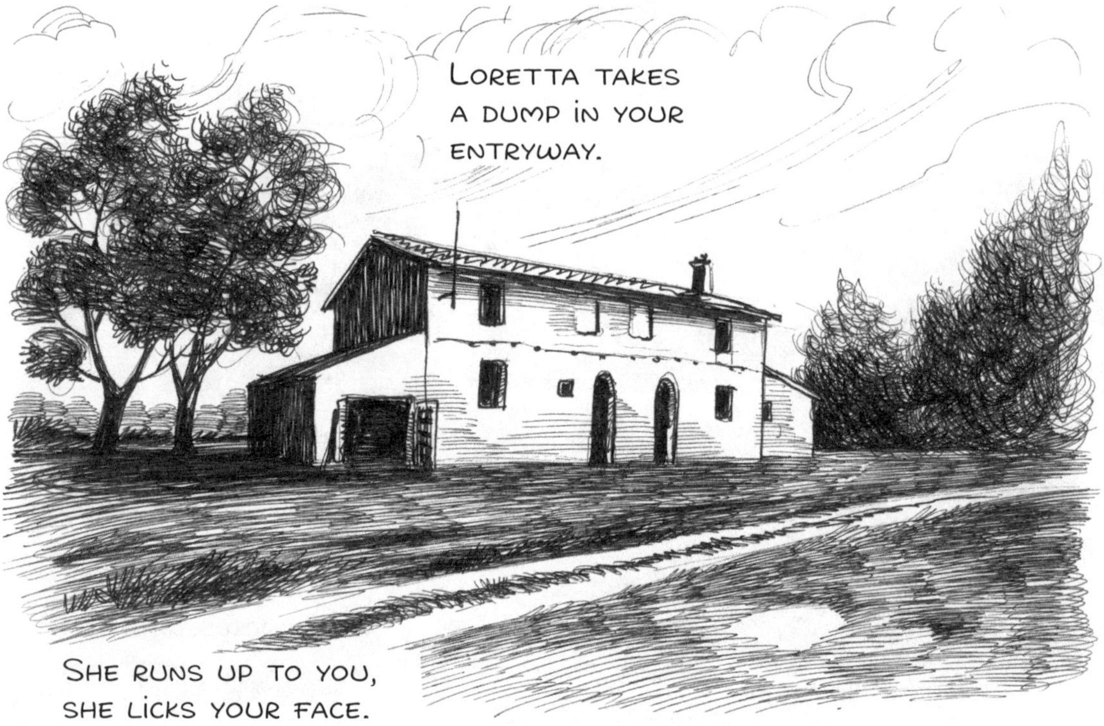
LORETTA TAKES
A DUMP IN YOUR
ENTRYWAY.
SHE RUNS UP TO YOU,
SHE LICKS YOUR FACE.

SHE HITS YOU.

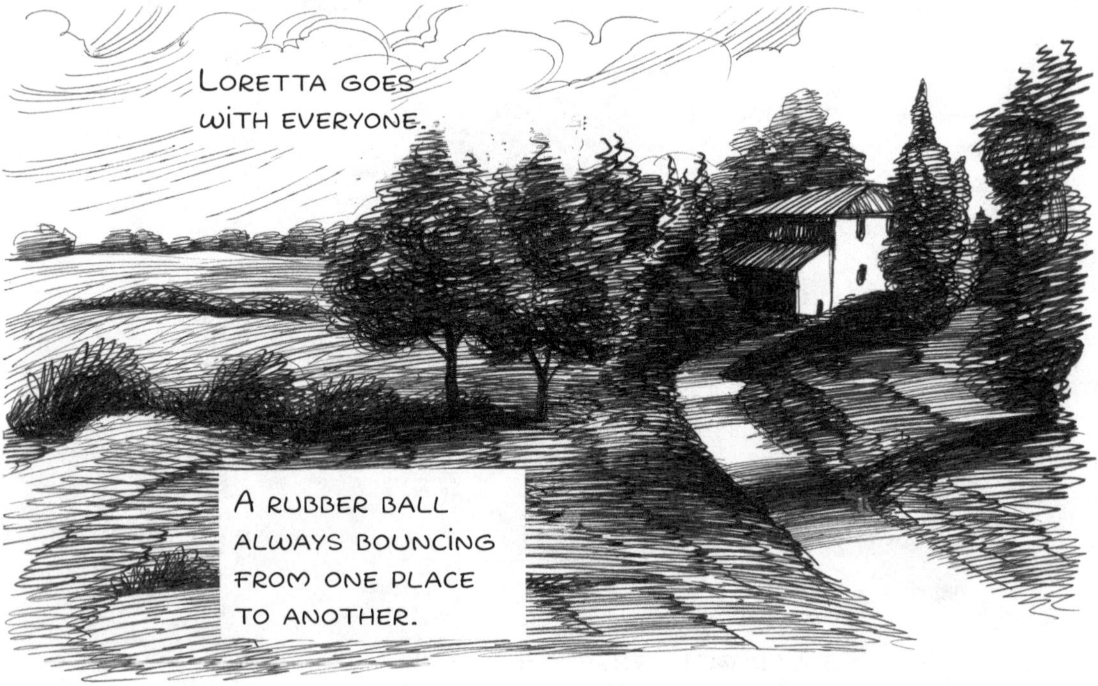
LORETTA GOES
WITH EVERYONE.
A RUBBER BALL
ALWAYS BOUNCING
FROM ONE PLACE
TO ANOTHER.

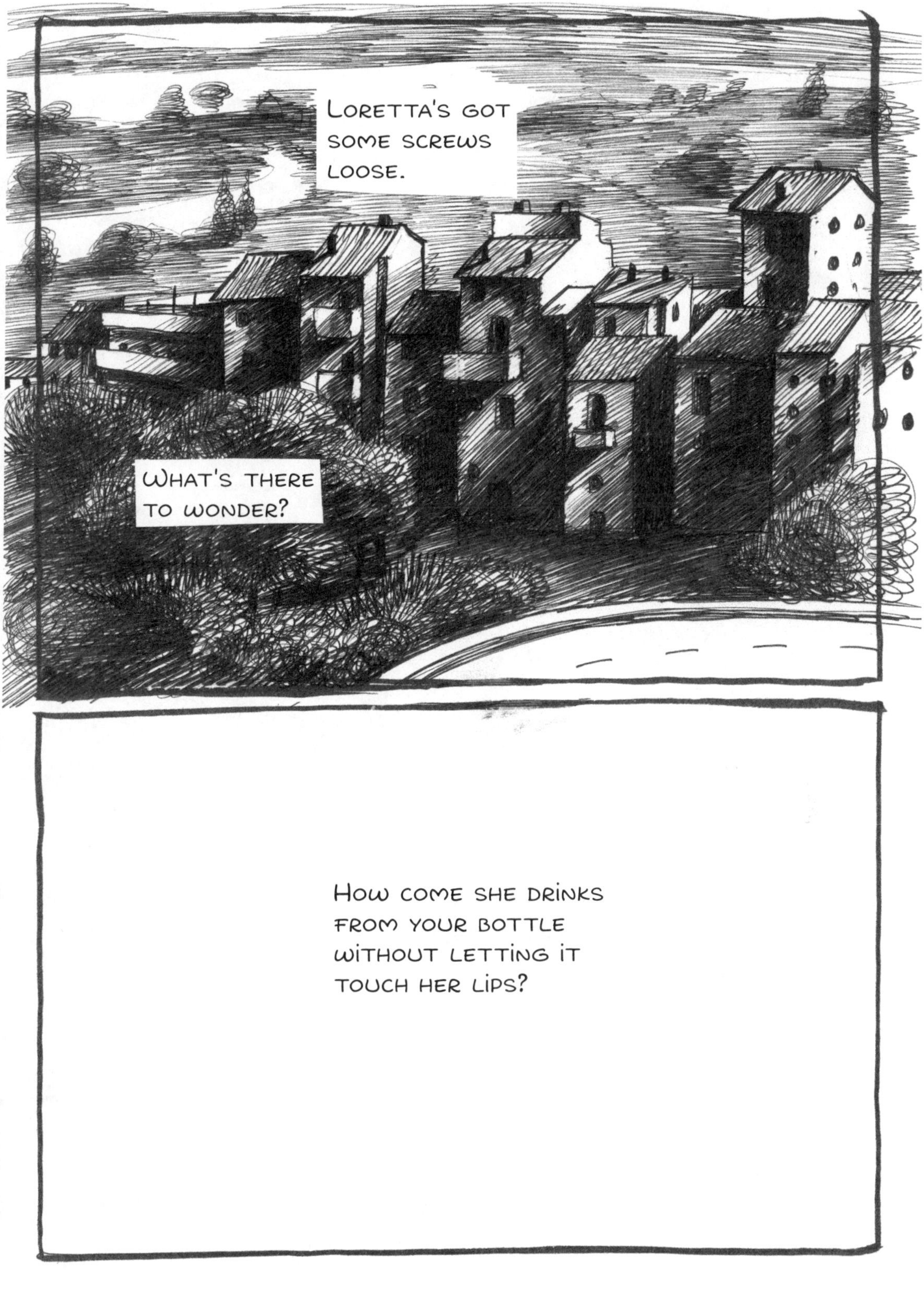
LORETTA'S GOT SOME SCREWS LOOSE.
WHAT'S THERE TO WONDER?
HOW COME SHE DRINKS FROM YOUR BOTTLE WITHOUT LETTING IT TOUCH HER LIPS?

XI

RICH PEOPLE LOOK THROUGH YOU.

LIKE YOU'RE TRANSPARENT.

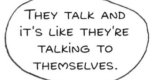
THEY TALK AND IT'S LIKE THEY'RE TALKING TO THEMSELVES.

KATANGO, FOR EXAMPLE, ALWAYS SEEMED LIKE HE WAS JUST THERE BY CHANCE, AND DIDN'T REALLY WANT TO BE.

AND NOW HE TELLS ME ABOUT HIS CHILDHOOD PROBLEMS. HOW HE SUFFERED FEELING DIFFERENT FROM US.

HIS GUILT OVER HIS LUXURY AND COMFORTS. HOW HE WANTED TO BE ONE OF US, A TRUE MEMBER OF THE GROUP.

YOU HAVE NO IDEA...

HE TELLS ME WEARING REGULAR SWEATS, LIKE MINE.

AS HE LOOKS THROUGH ME.

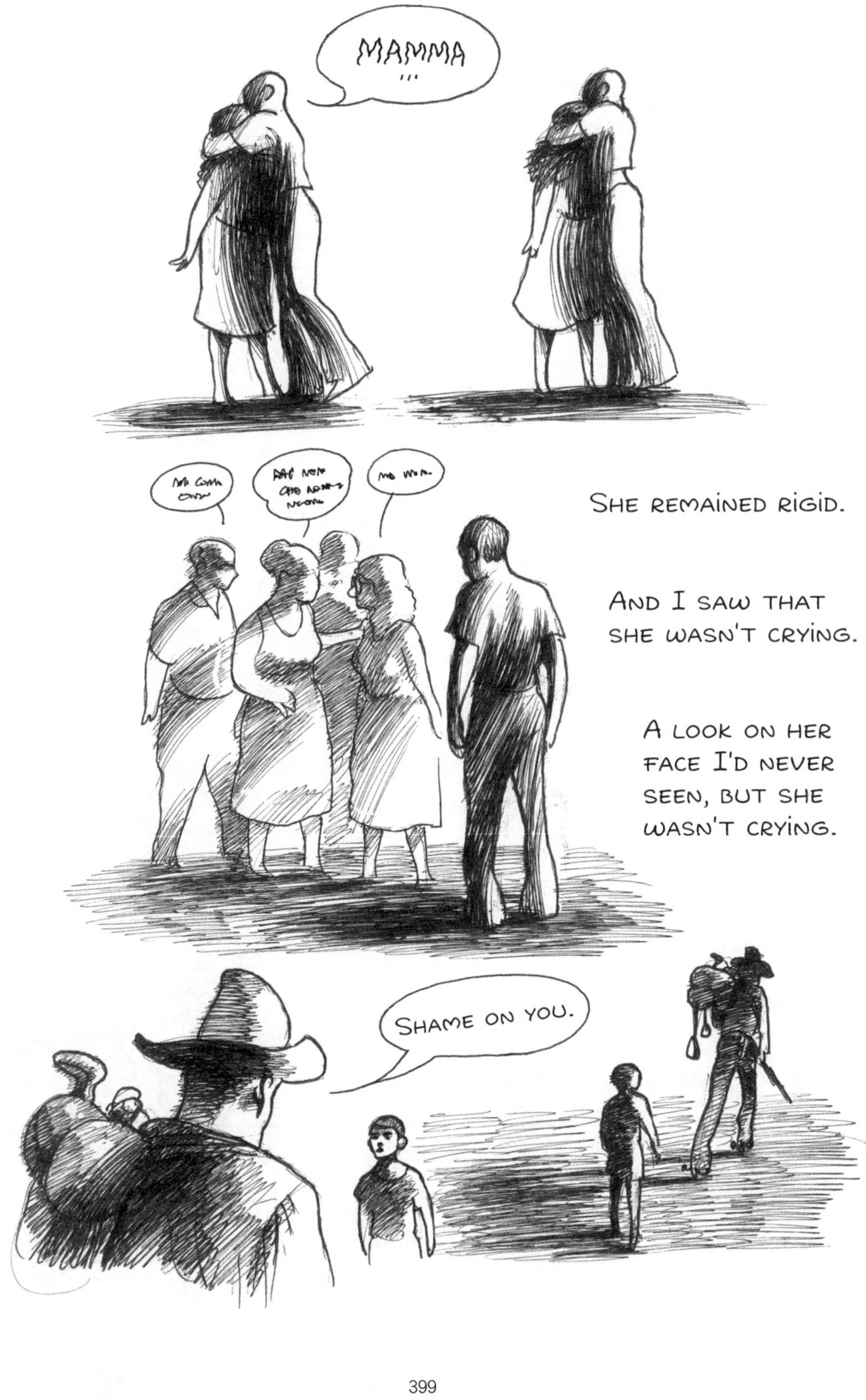
MAMMA
...
SHE REMAINED RIGID.
AND I SAW THAT SHE WASN'T CRYING.
A LOOK ON HER FACE I'D NEVER SEEN, BUT SHE WASN'T CRYING.
SHAME ON YOU.

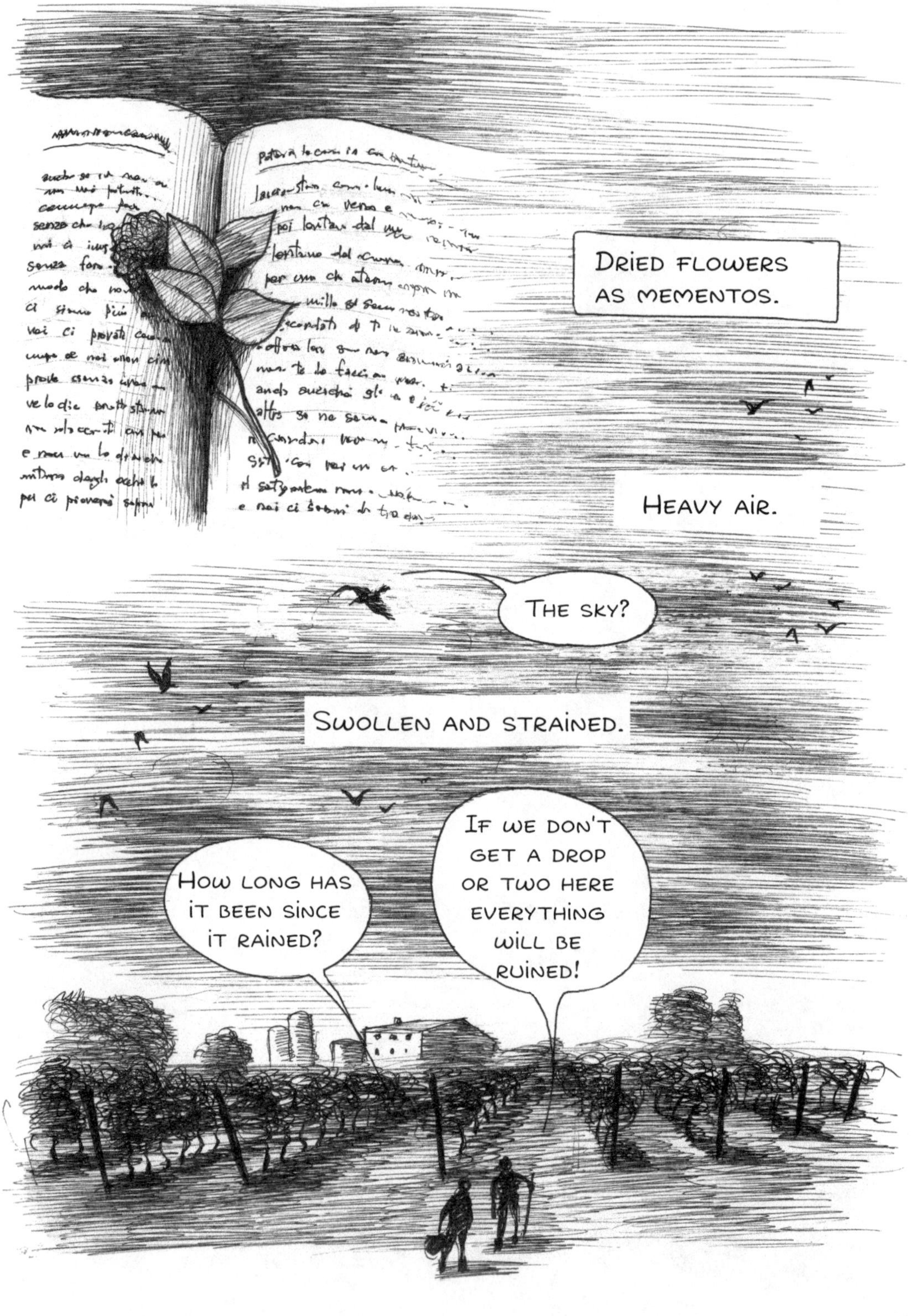
Dried flowers as mementos.
Heavy air.
The sky?
Swollen and strained.
How long has it been since it rained?
If we don't get a drop or two here everything will be ruined!

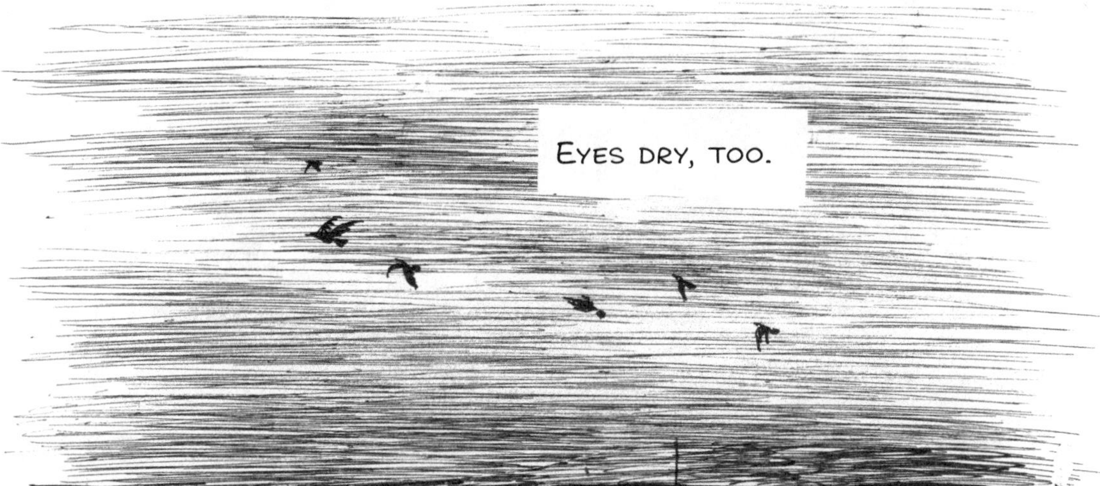
EYES DRY, TOO.

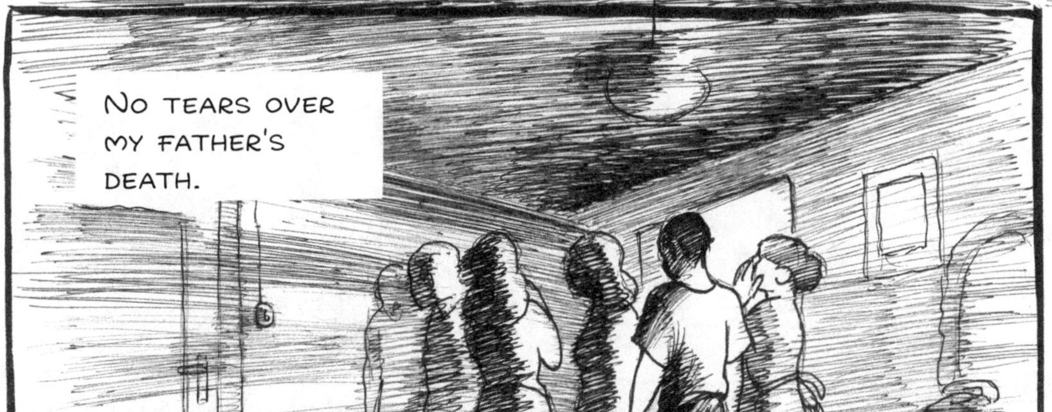
NO TEARS OVER
MY FATHER'S
DEATH.

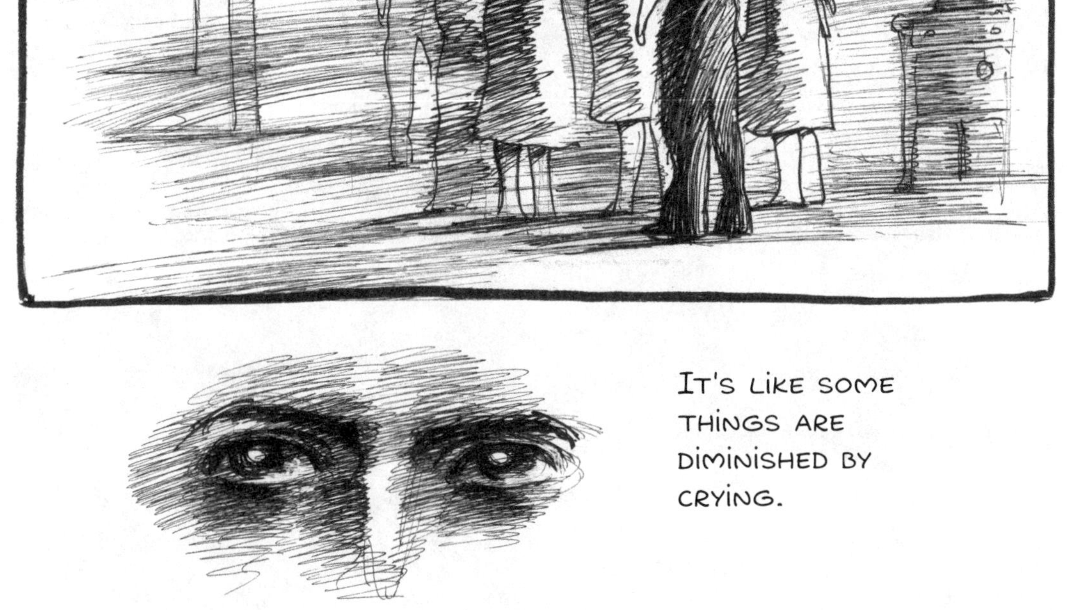

IT'S LIKE SOME
THINGS ARE
DIMINISHED BY
CRYING.

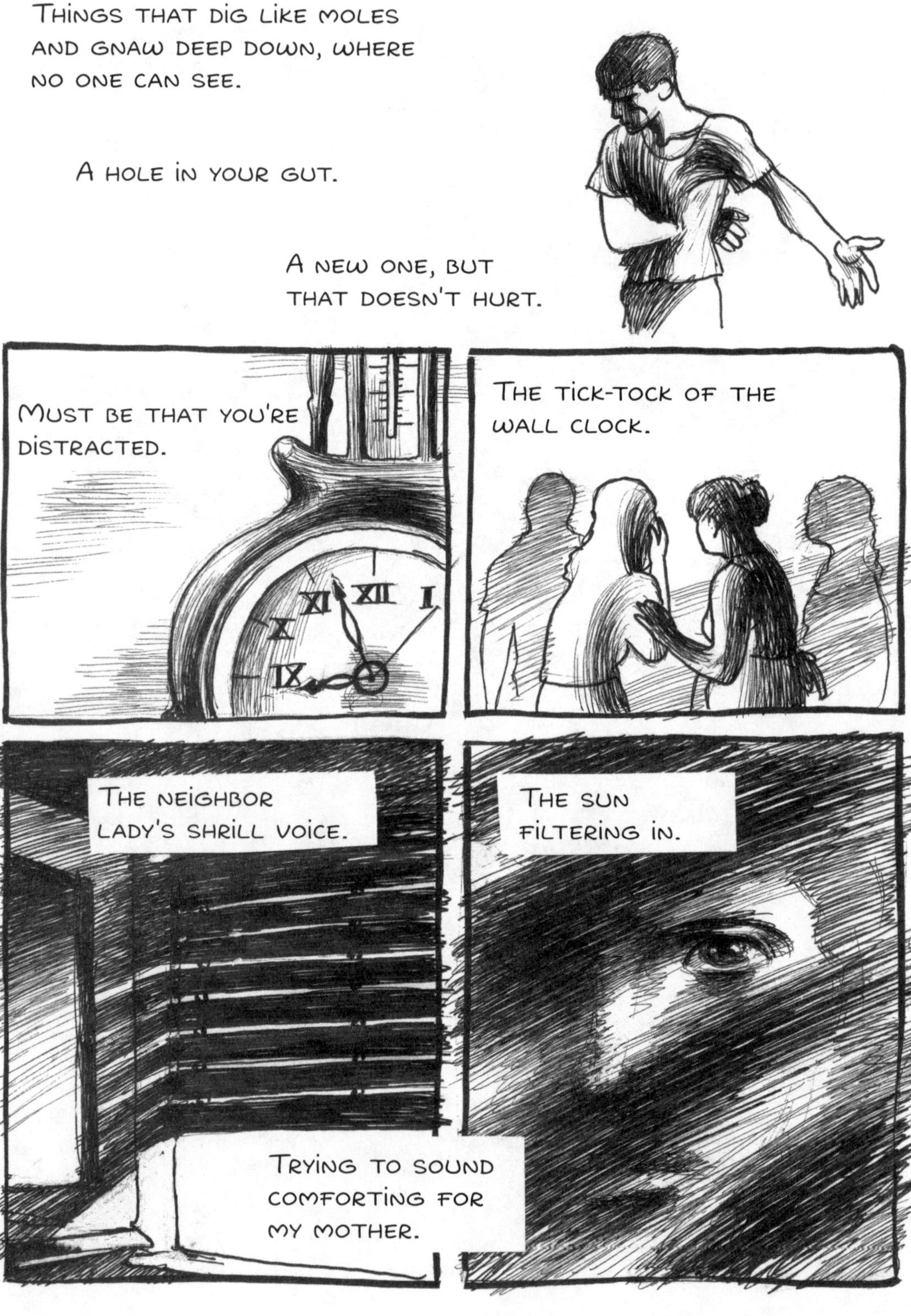
THINGS THAT DIG LIKE MOLES AND GNAW DEEP DOWN, WHERE NO ONE CAN SEE.
A HOLE IN YOUR GUT.
A NEW ONE, BUT THAT DOESN'T HURT.
MUST BE THAT YOU'RE DISTRACTED.
THE TICK-TOCK OF THE WALL CLOCK.
THE NEIGHBOR LADY'S SHRILL VOICE.
THE SUN FILTERING IN.
TRYING TO SOUND COMFORTING FOR MY MOTHER.

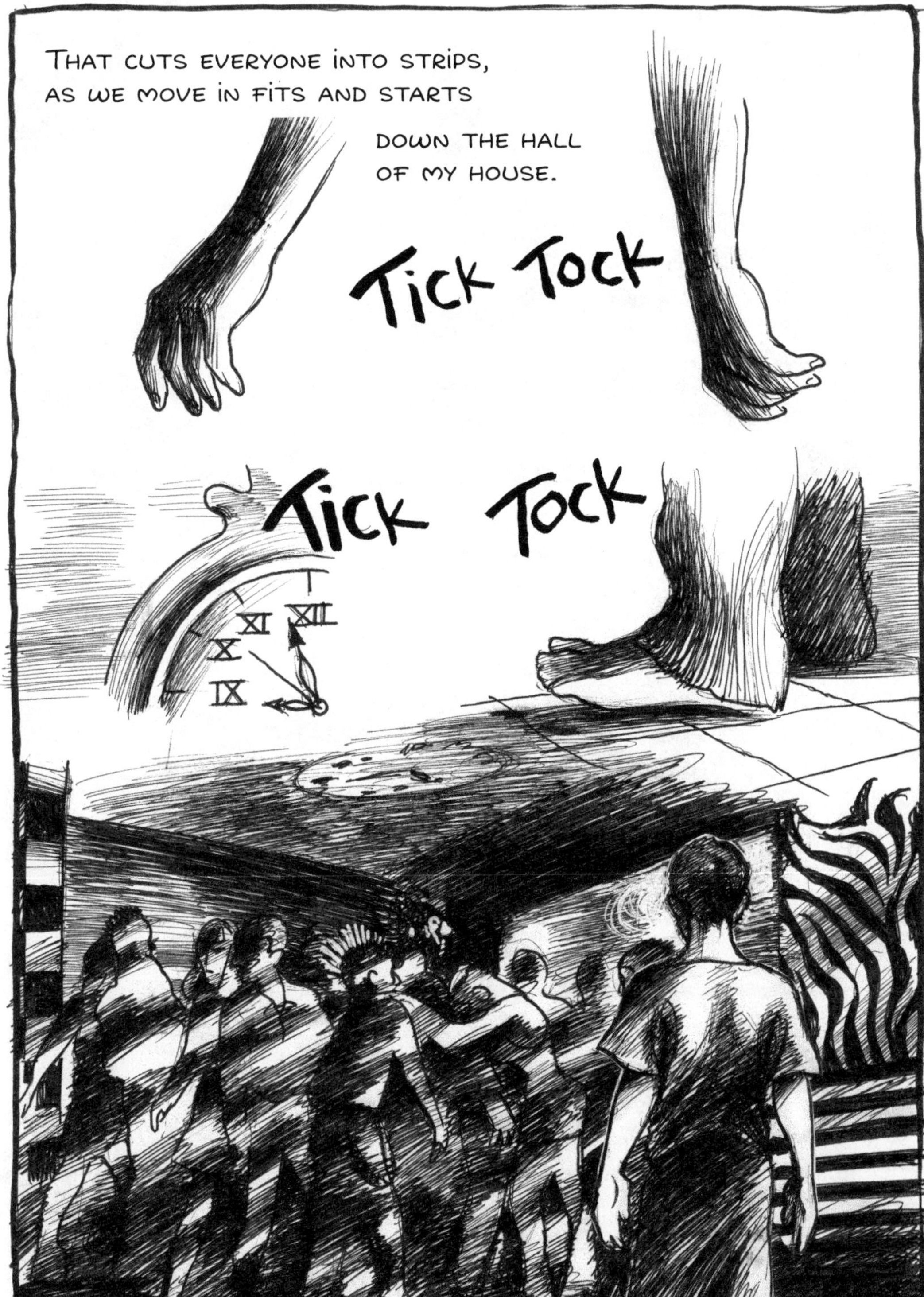

THAT CUTS EVERYONE INTO STRIPS,
AS WE MOVE IN FITS AND STARTS
DOWN THE HALL
OF MY HOUSE.
TICK TOCK
TICK TOCK

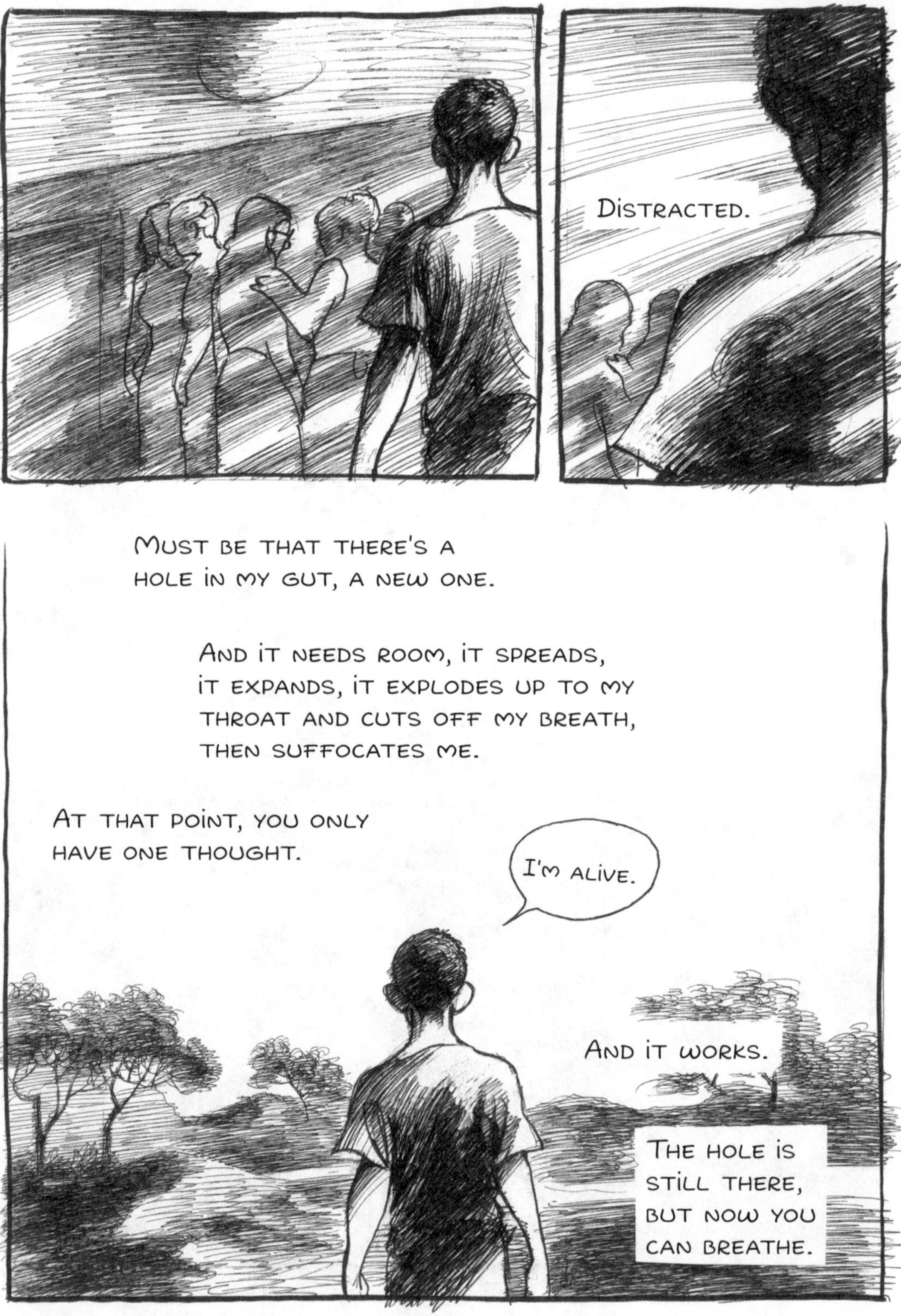
Distracted.
Must be that there's a hole in my gut, a new one.
And it needs room, it spreads, it expands, it explodes up to my throat and cuts off my breath, then suffocates me.
At that point, you only have one thought.
I'm alive.
And it works.
The hole is still there, but now you can breathe.

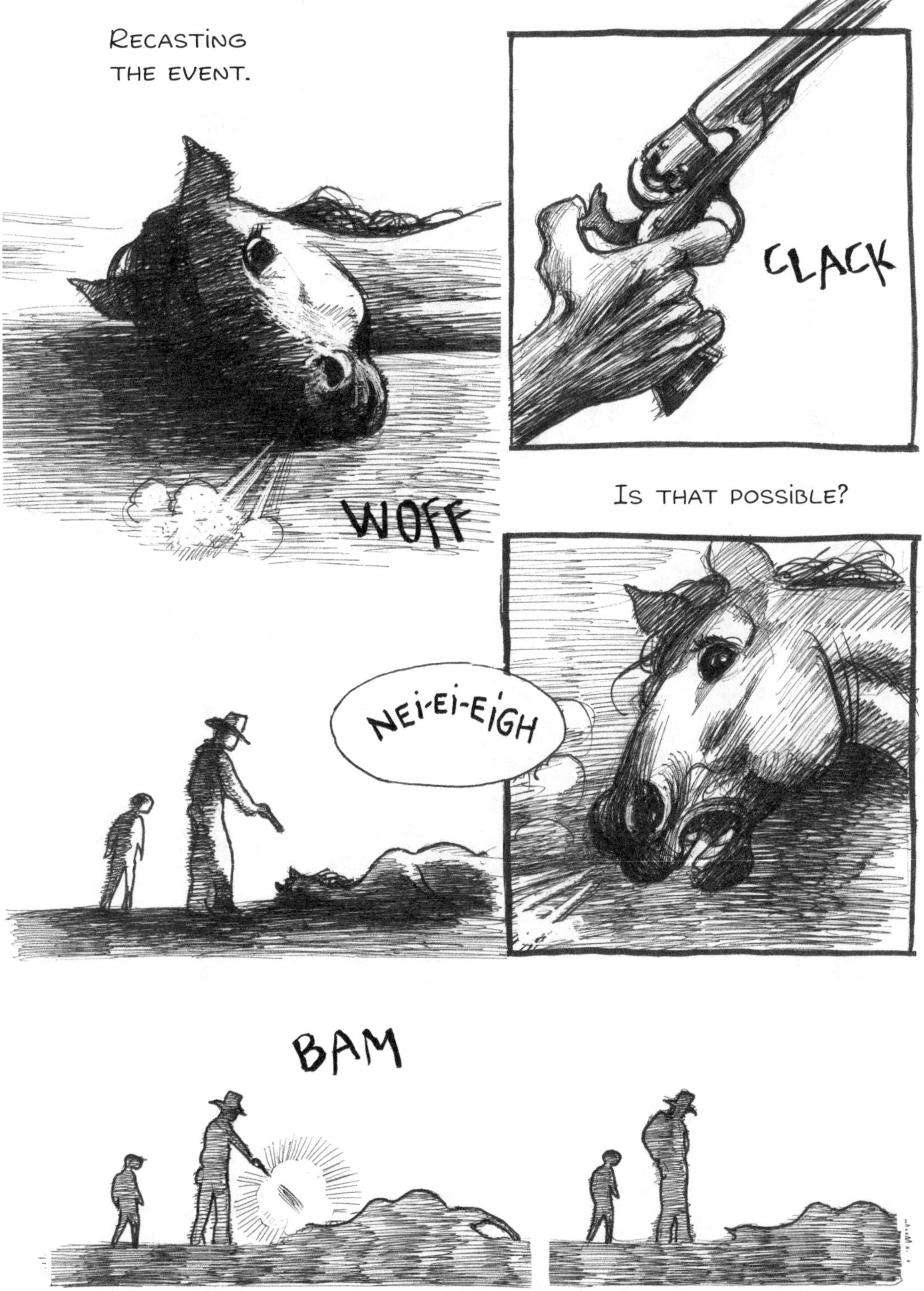
Recasting the event.
WOFF
CLACK
Is that possible?
NEI-EI-EIGH
BAM

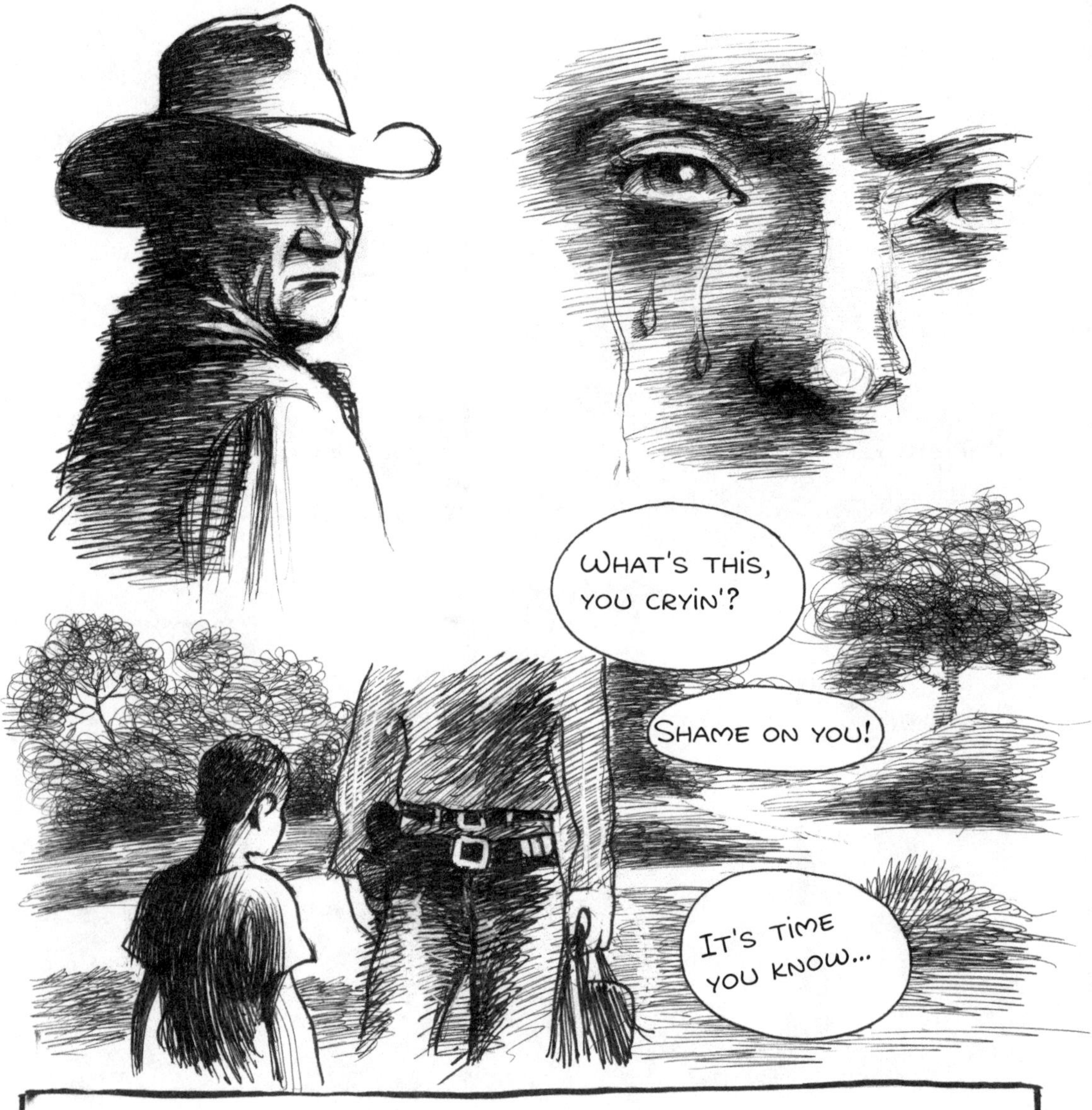
WHAT'S THIS, YOU CRYIN'?
SHAME ON YOU!
IT'S TIME YOU KNOW...

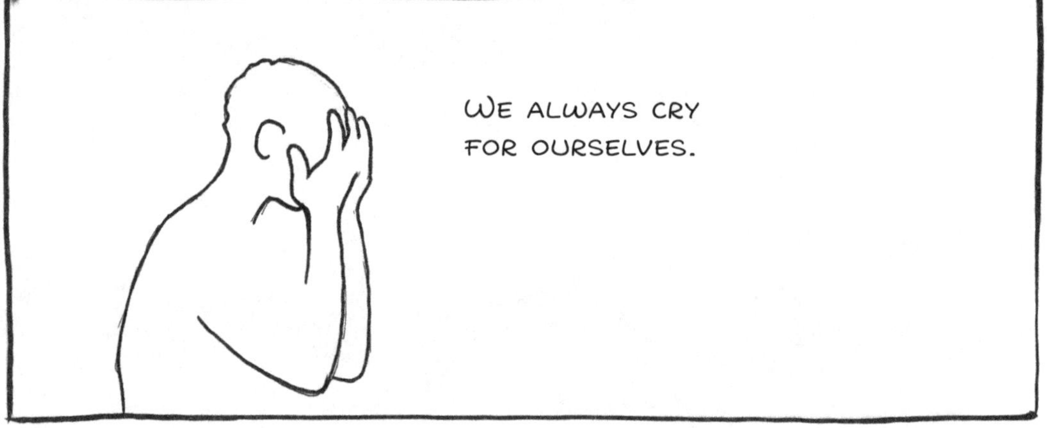
WE ALWAYS CRY FOR OURSELVES.

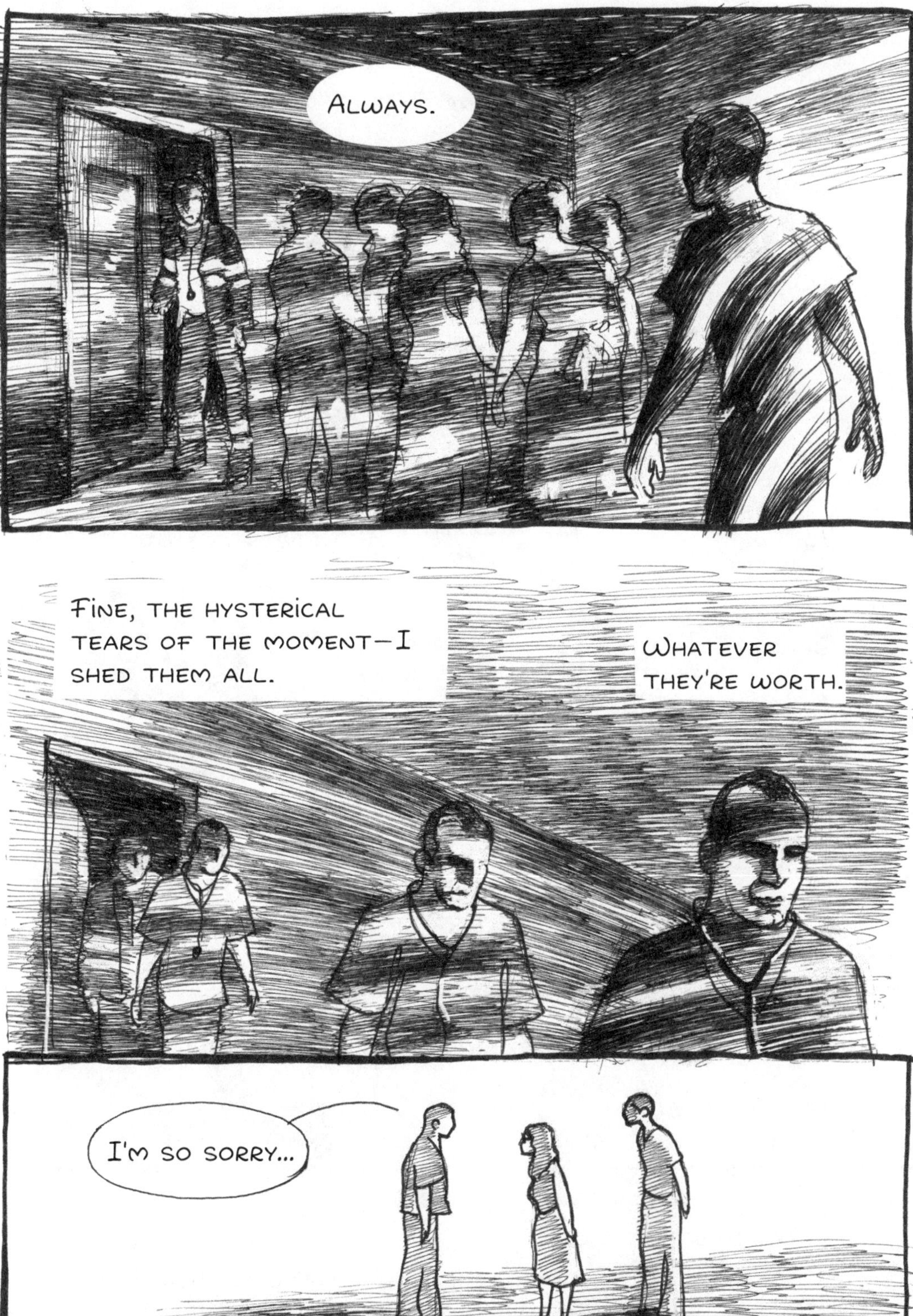
Always.
Fine, the hysterical tears of the moment—I shed them all.
Whatever they're worth.
I'm so sorry...

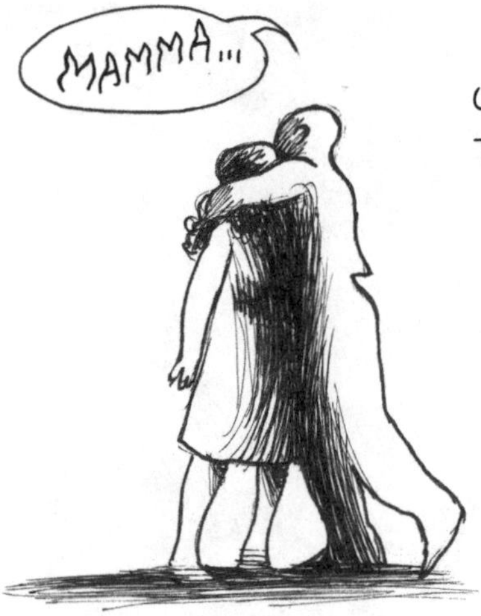
MAMMA...

WHATEVER THEY'RE WORTH.

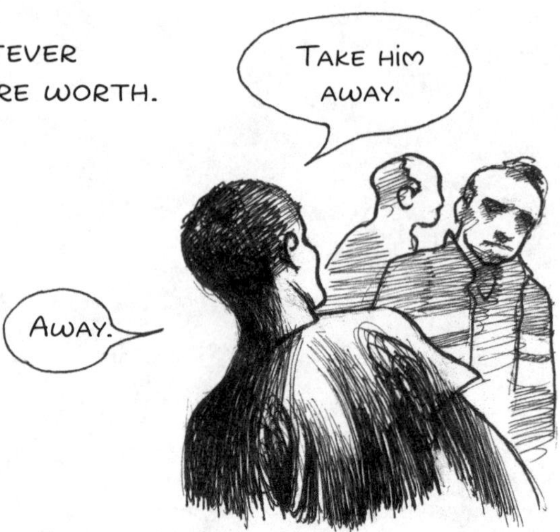
TAKE HIM AWAY.
AWAY.

IS THIS WHY PEOPLE BURN THE BELONGINGS OF THE DEAD?

TO FORGET THE SHAME?

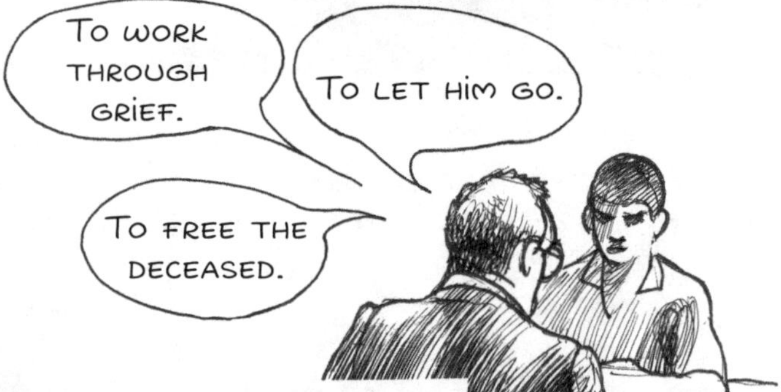
TO WORK THROUGH GRIEF.
TO LET HIM GO.
TO FREE THE DECEASED.

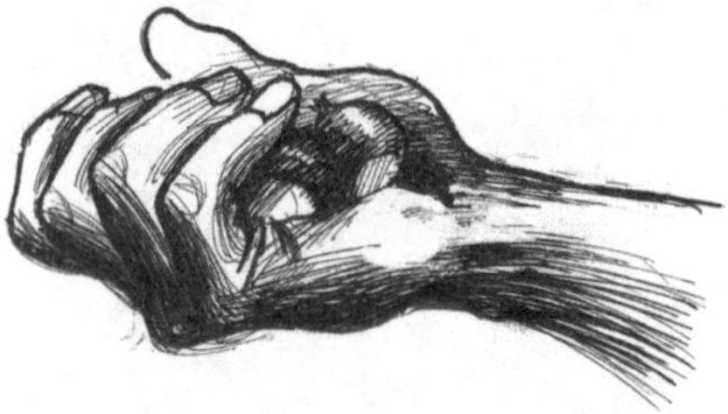

BULLSHIT.

IT'S TO FREE OURSELVES.

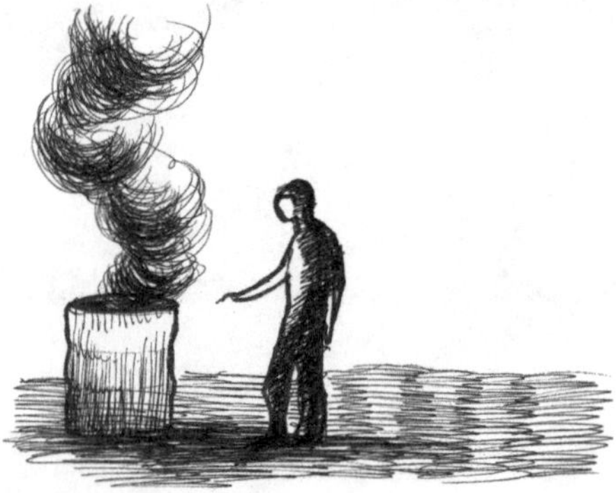

BURN EVERYTHING, TO BE ABLE TO RETURN TO ONESELF.

NO MORE AWKWARD EMBRACES, NO HYSTERICS OR FRANTIC TEARS.

NO MORE DRIED CHESTNUTS, KEPT IN POCKETS LIKE AMULETS.

I BURN MY FATHER.
TO FILL THE HOLE.
AND GO BACK TO BEING
THE SAME OLD DUMBASS.

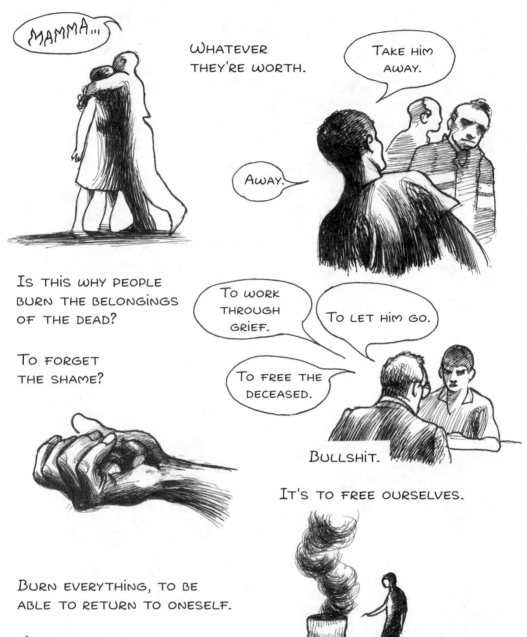

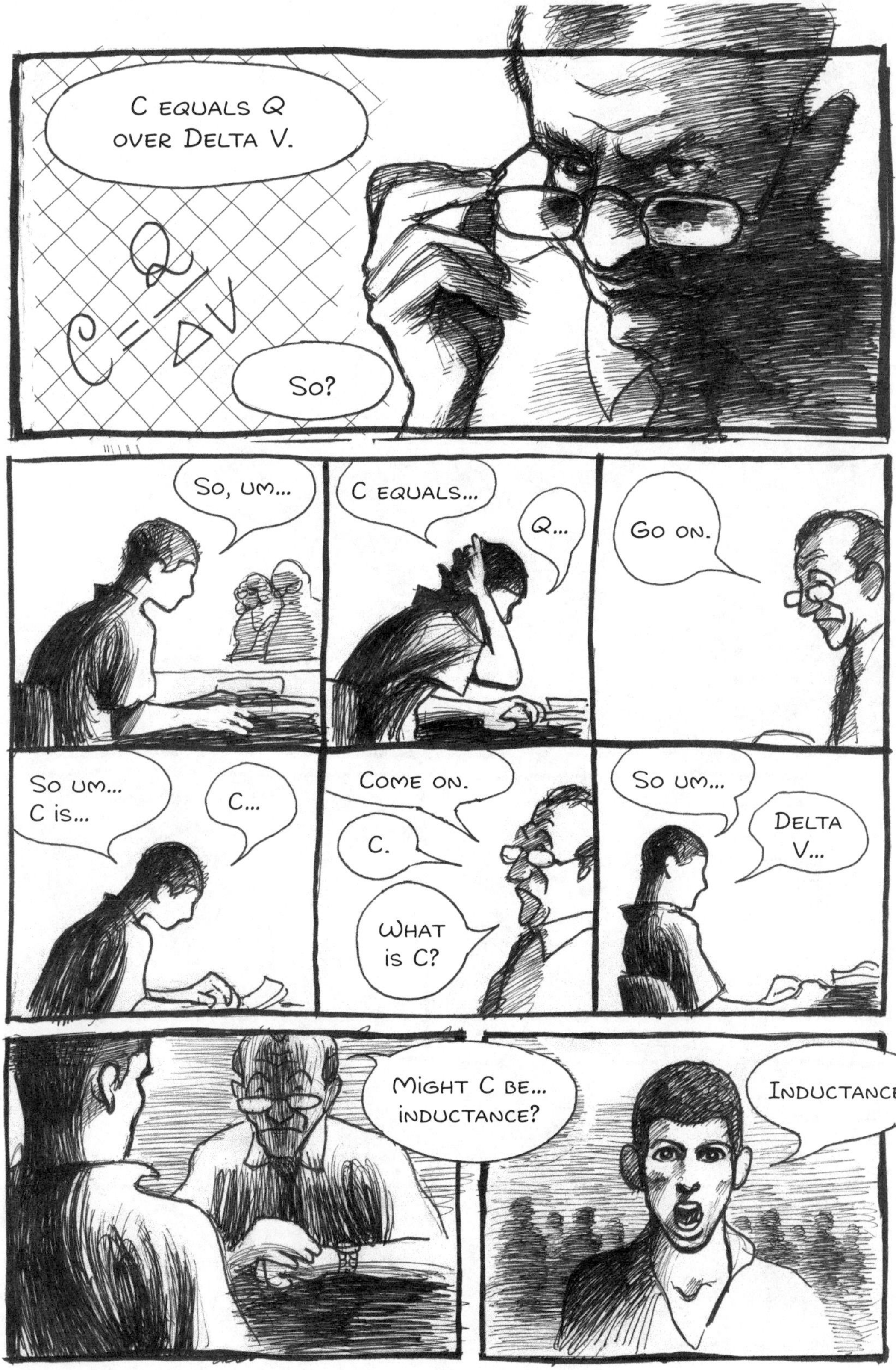
C equals Q over Delta V.
C = Q/ΔV
So?
So, um...
C equals...
Q...
Go on.
So um... C is...
C...
Come on.
C.
What is C?
So um...
Delta V...
Might C be... inductance?
Inductance!

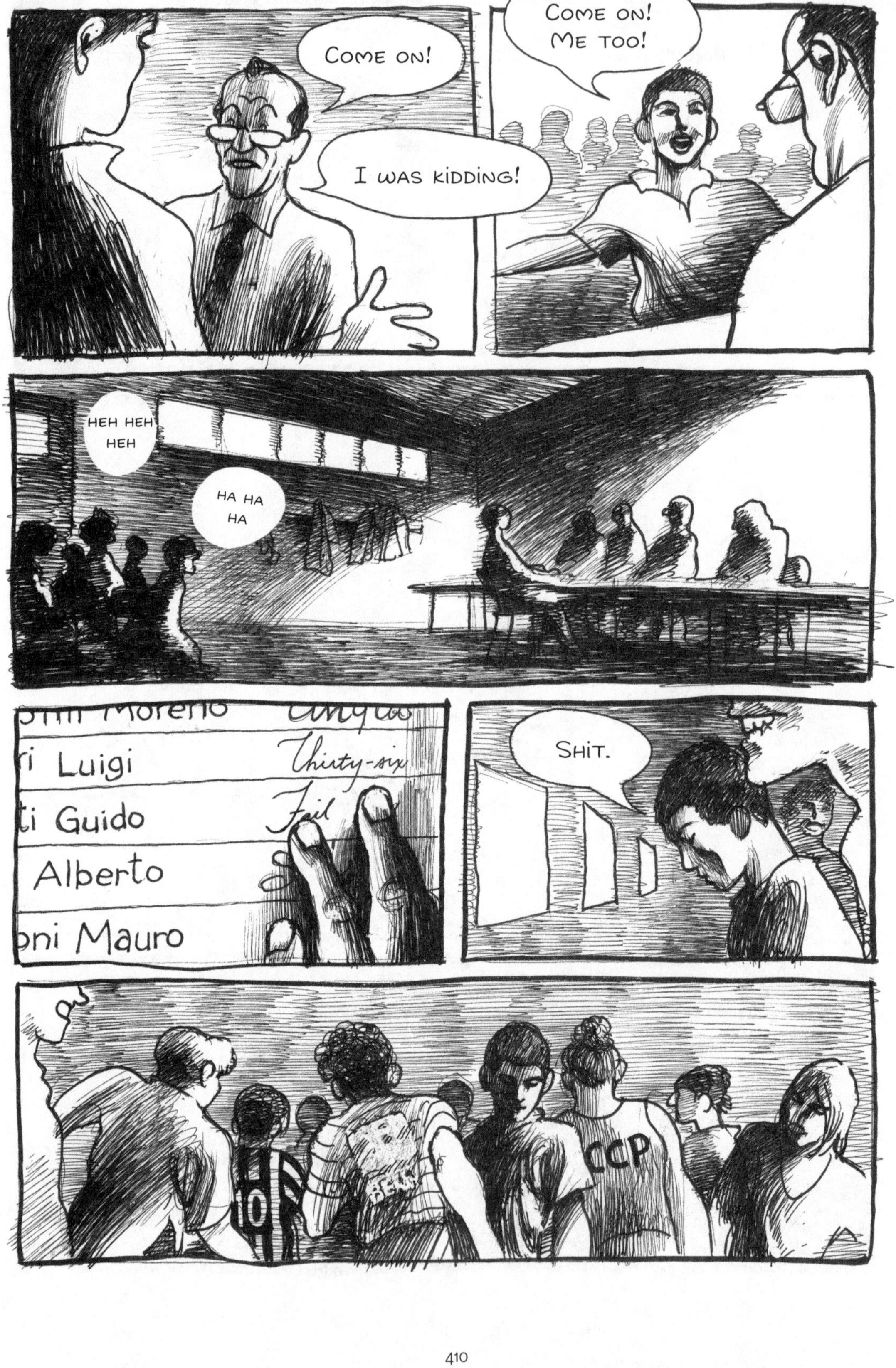
COME ON!
I WAS KIDDING!
COME ON! ME TOO!
HEH HEH HEH
HA HA HA
Luigi
Thirty-six
Guido
Fail
Alberto
Mauro
SHIT.

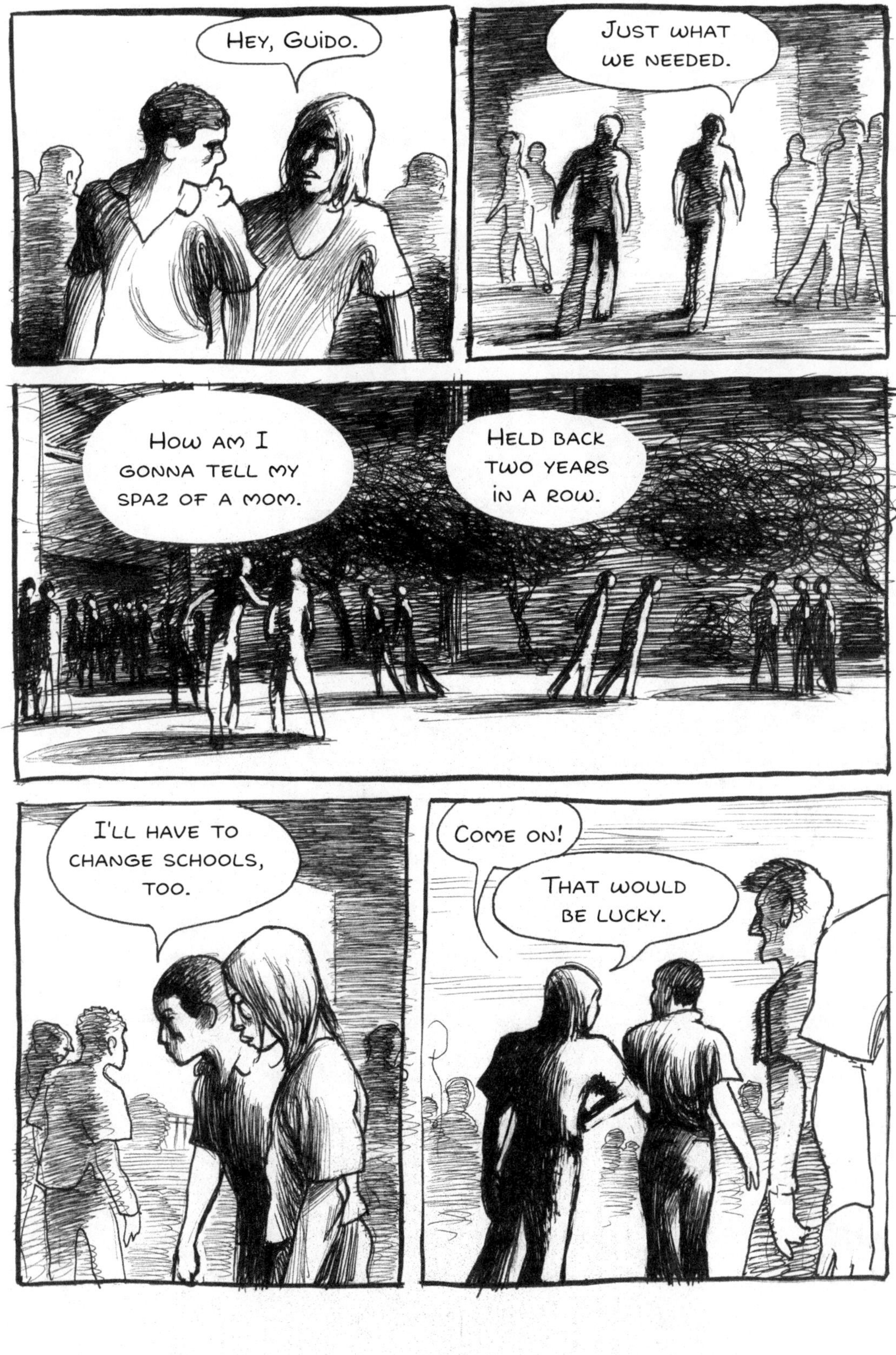
HEY, GUIDO.
JUST WHAT WE NEEDED.
HOW AM I GONNA TELL MY SPAZ OF A MOM.
HELD BACK TWO YEARS IN A ROW.
I'LL HAVE TO CHANGE SCHOOLS, TOO.
COME ON!
THAT WOULD BE LUCKY.

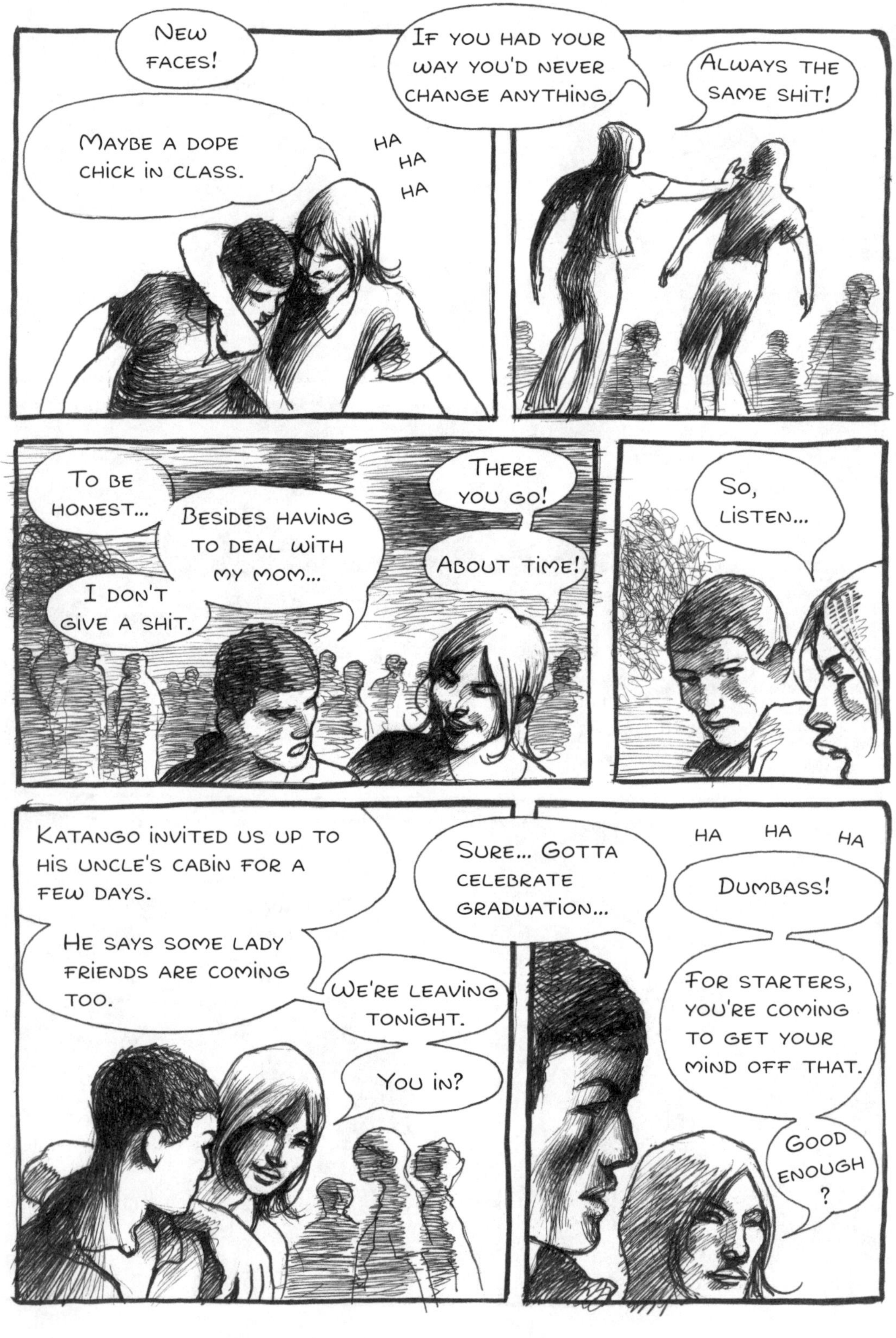
New faces!
Maybe a dope chick in class.
Ha ha ha
If you had your way you'd never change anything.
Always the same shit!
To be honest...
Besides having to deal with my mom...
I don't give a shit.
There you go!
About time!
So, listen...
Katango invited us up to his uncle's cabin for a few days.
He says some lady friends are coming too.
We're leaving tonight.
You in?
Sure... Gotta celebrate graduation...
Ha ha ha
Dumbass!
For starters, you're coming to get your mind off that.
Good enough?

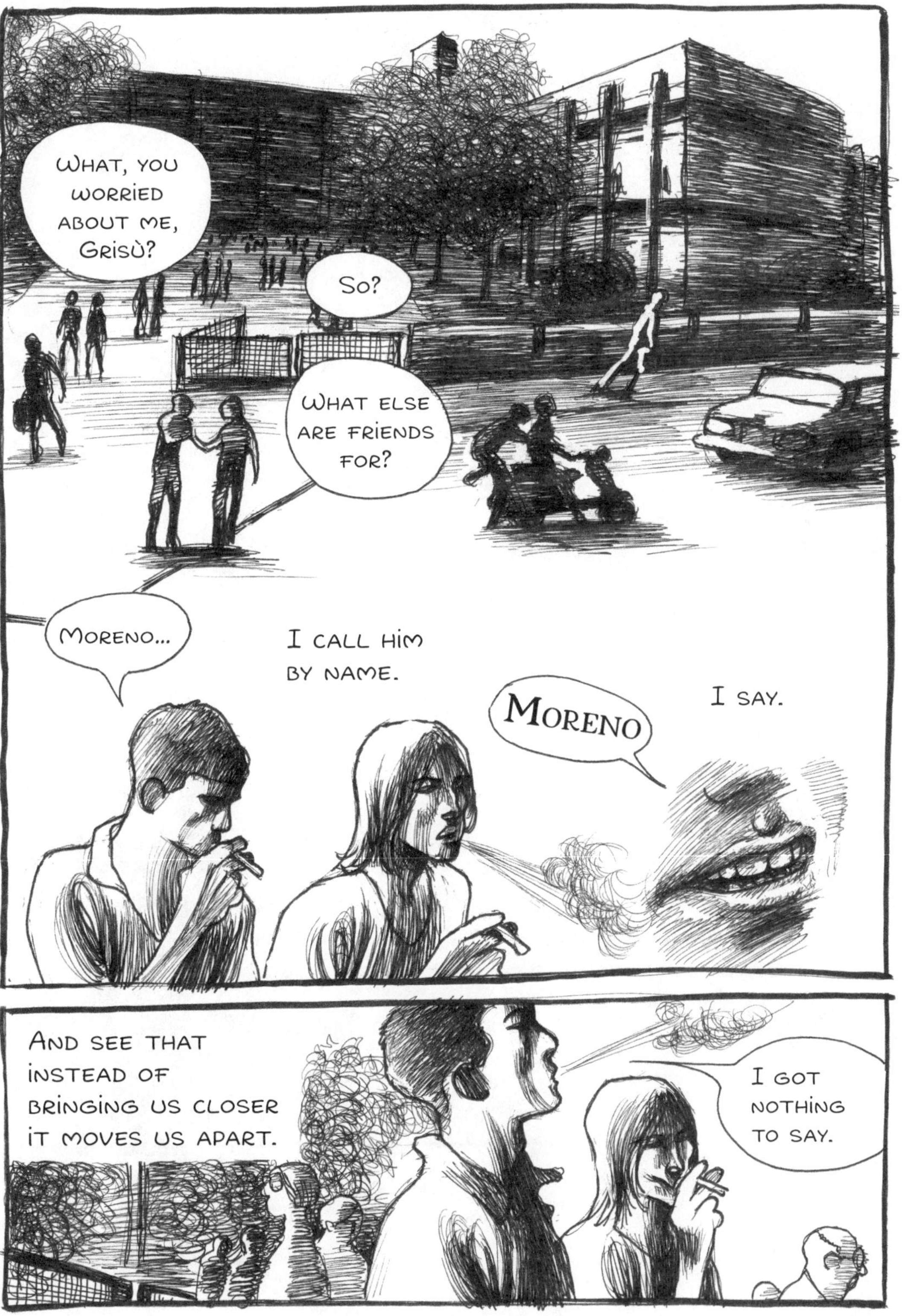
What, you worried about me, Grisù?
So?
What else are friends for?
Moreno...
I call him by name.
Moreno
I say.
And see that instead of bringing us closer it moves us apart.
I got nothing to say.

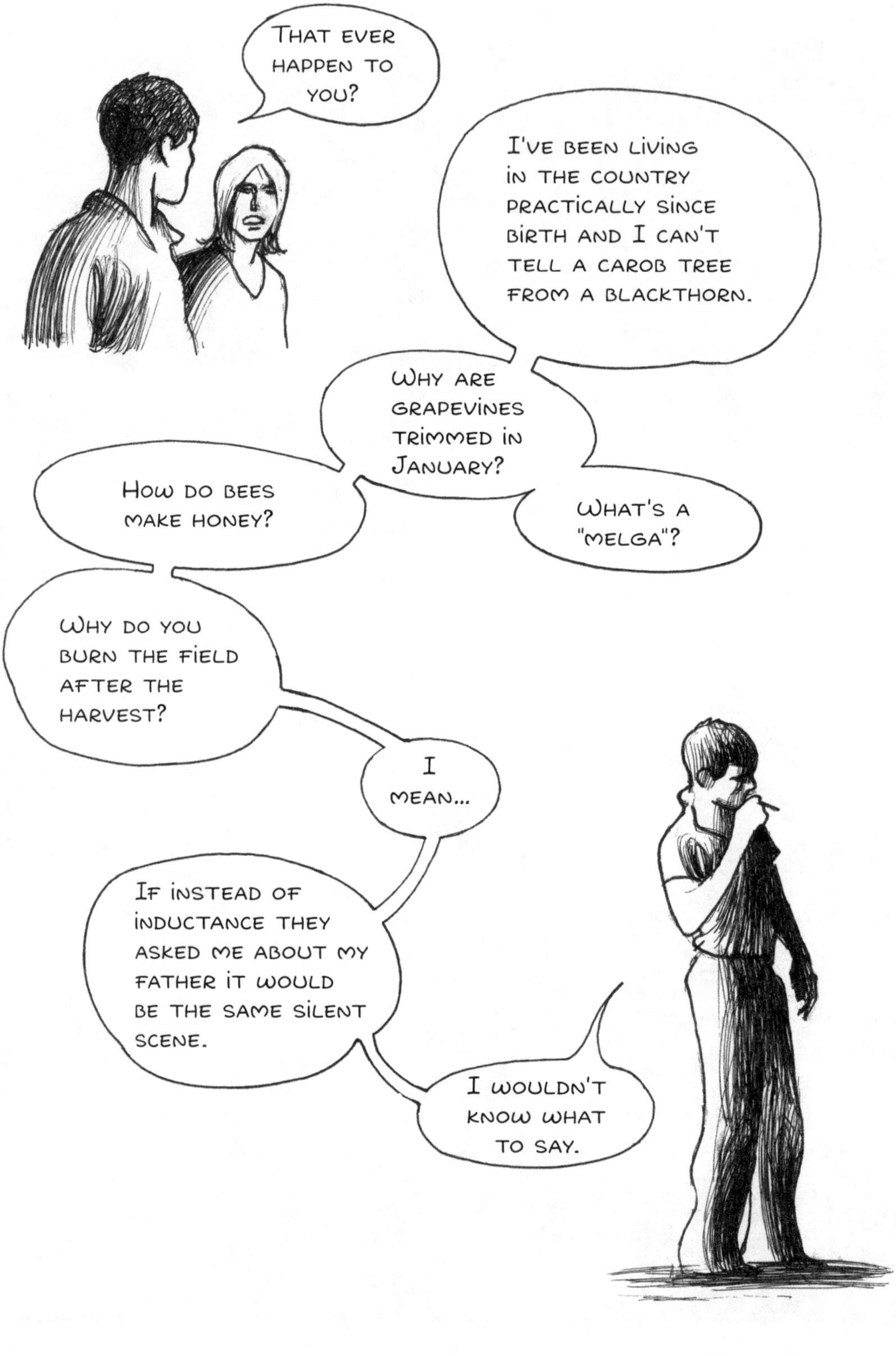
THAT EVER HAPPEN TO YOU?
I'VE BEEN LIVING IN THE COUNTRY PRACTICALLY SINCE BIRTH AND I CAN'T TELL A CAROB TREE FROM A BLACKTHORN.
WHY ARE GRAPEVINES TRIMMED IN JANUARY?
HOW DO BEES MAKE HONEY?
WHAT'S A "MELGA"?
WHY DO YOU BURN THE FIELD AFTER THE HARVEST?
I MEAN...
IF INSTEAD OF INDUCTANCE THEY ASKED ME ABOUT MY FATHER IT WOULD BE THE SAME SILENT SCENE.
I WOULDN'T KNOW WHAT TO SAY.

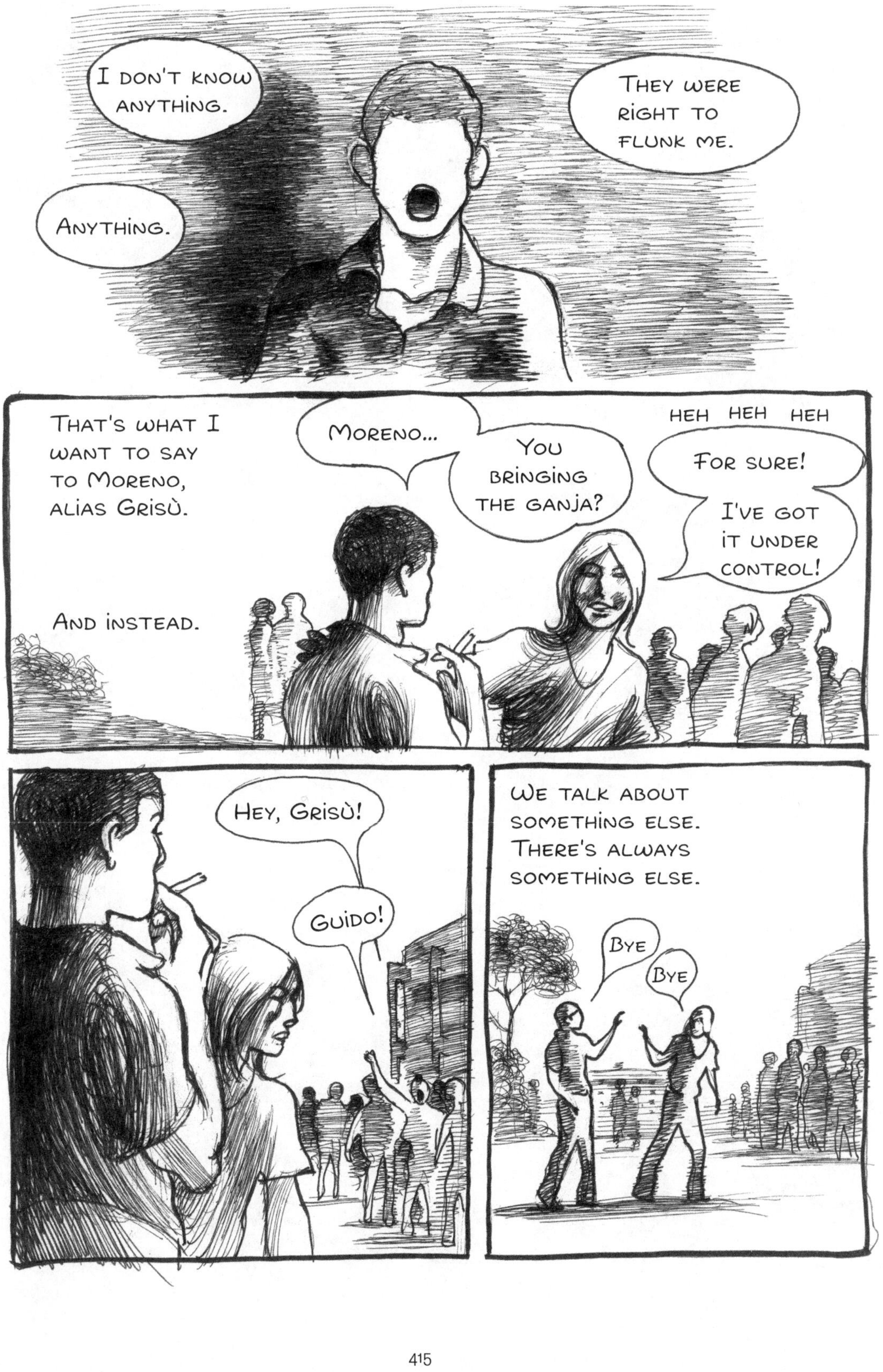
I don't know anything.
They were right to flunk me.
Anything.
That's what I want to say to Moreno, alias Grisù.
Moreno...
You bringing the ganja?
HEH HEH HEH
For sure!
I've got it under control!
And instead.
Hey, Grisù!
Guido!
We talk about something else. There's always something else.
Bye
Bye

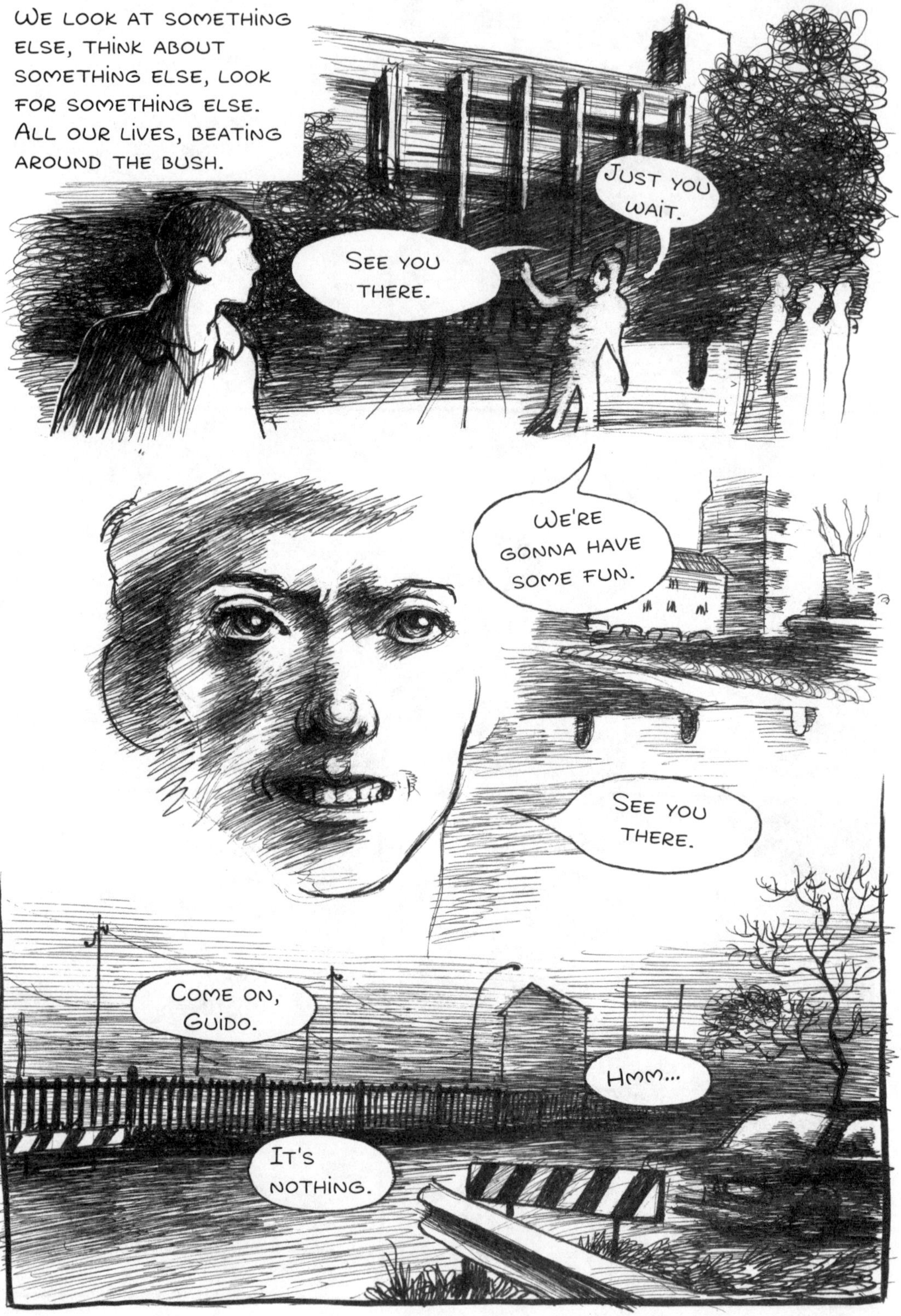
WE LOOK AT SOMETHING ELSE, THINK ABOUT SOMETHING ELSE, LOOK FOR SOMETHING ELSE. ALL OUR LIVES, BEATING AROUND THE BUSH.
SEE YOU THERE.
JUST YOU WAIT.
WE'RE GONNA HAVE SOME FUN.
SEE YOU THERE.
COME ON, GUIDO.
HMM...
IT'S NOTHING.

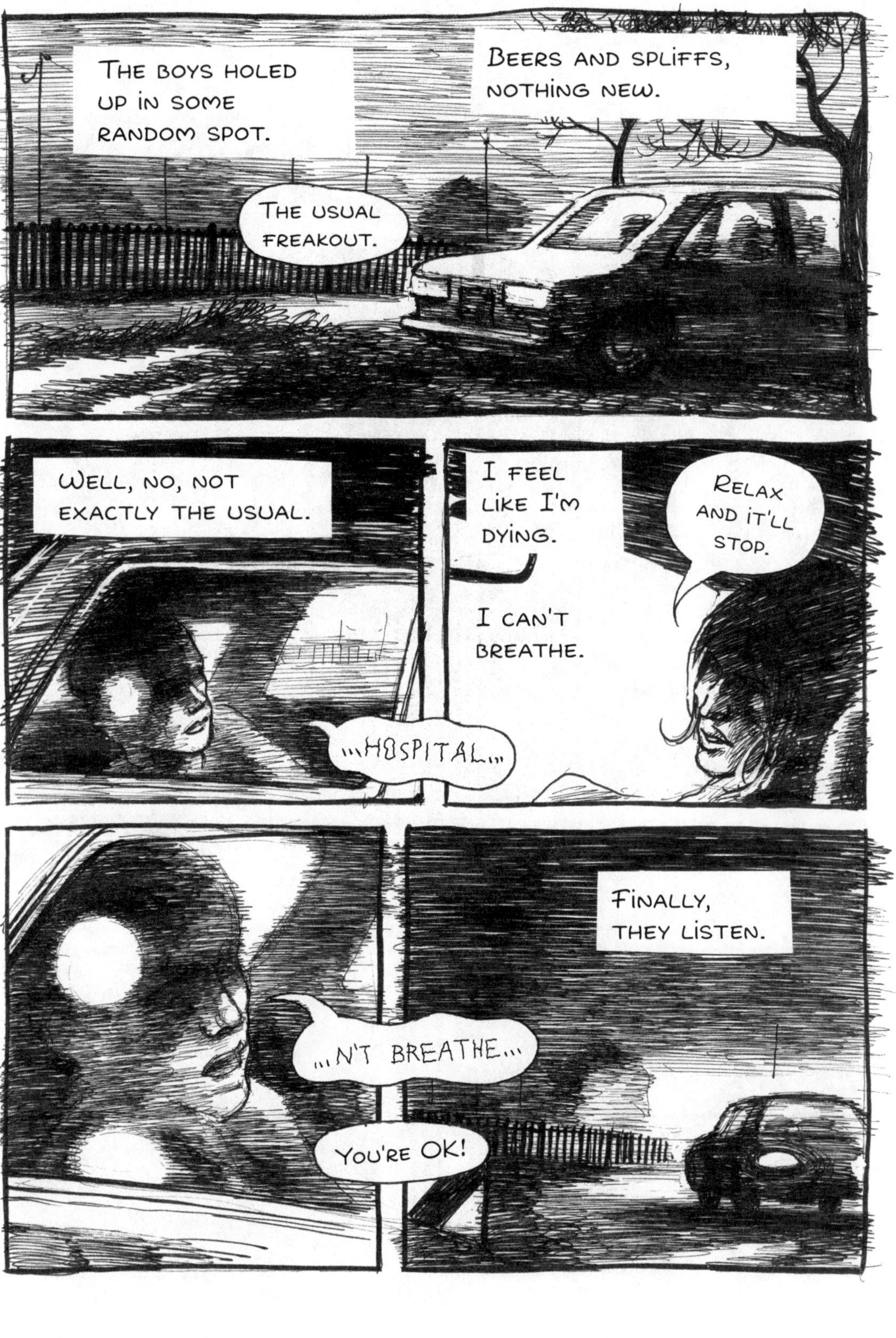

The boys holed up in some random spot.
Beers and spliffs, nothing new.
The usual freakout.
Well, no, not exactly the usual.
I feel like I'm dying.
I can't breathe.
Relax and it'll stop.
...hospital...
...n't breathe...
You're OK!
Finally, they listen.

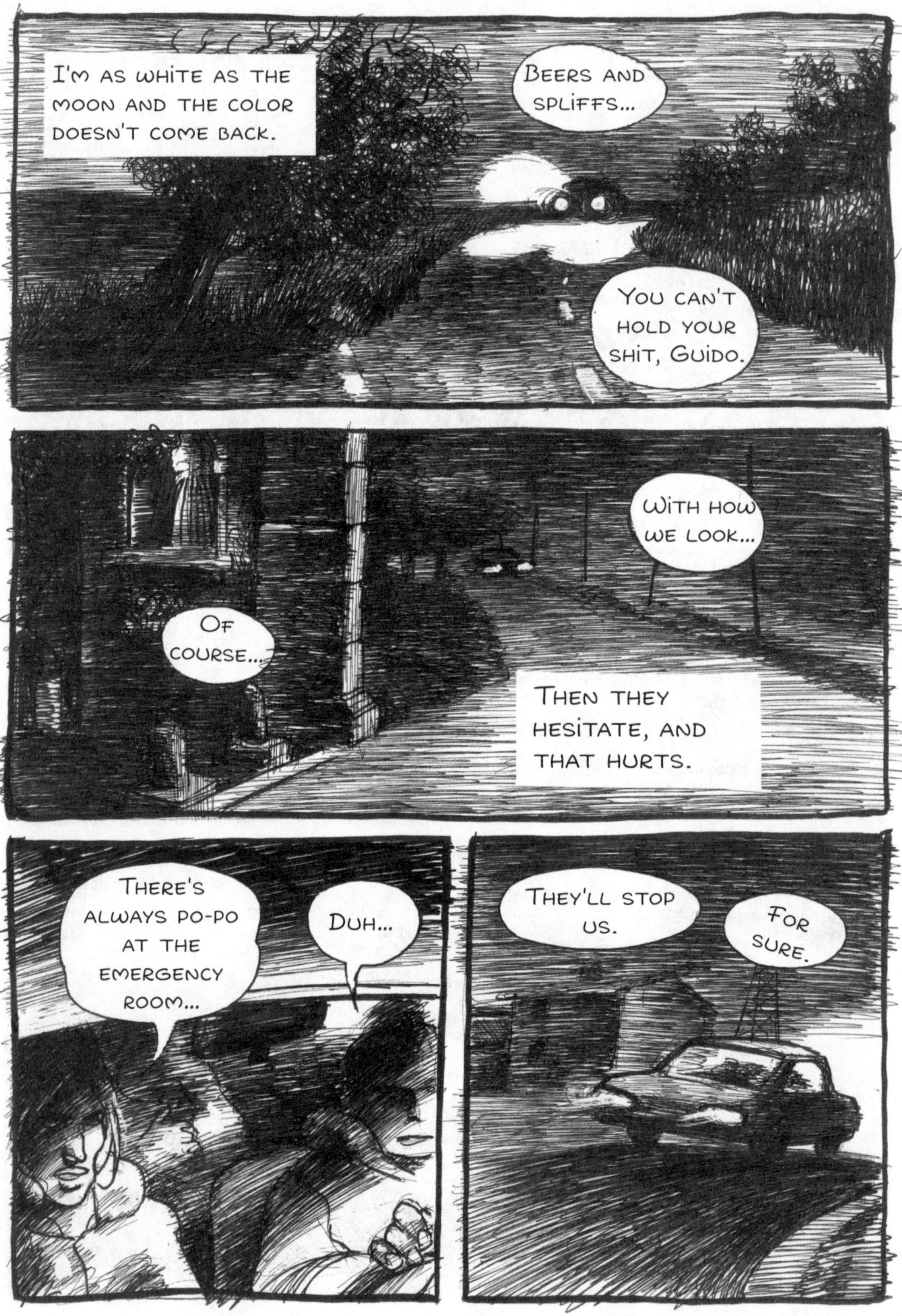
I'M AS WHITE AS THE MOON AND THE COLOR DOESN'T COME BACK.
BEERS AND SPLIFFS...
YOU CAN'T HOLD YOUR SHIT, GUIDO.
WITH HOW WE LOOK...
OF COURSE...
THEN THEY HESITATE, AND THAT HURTS.
THERE'S ALWAYS PO-PO AT THE EMERGENCY ROOM...
DUH...
THEY'LL STOP US.
FOR SURE.

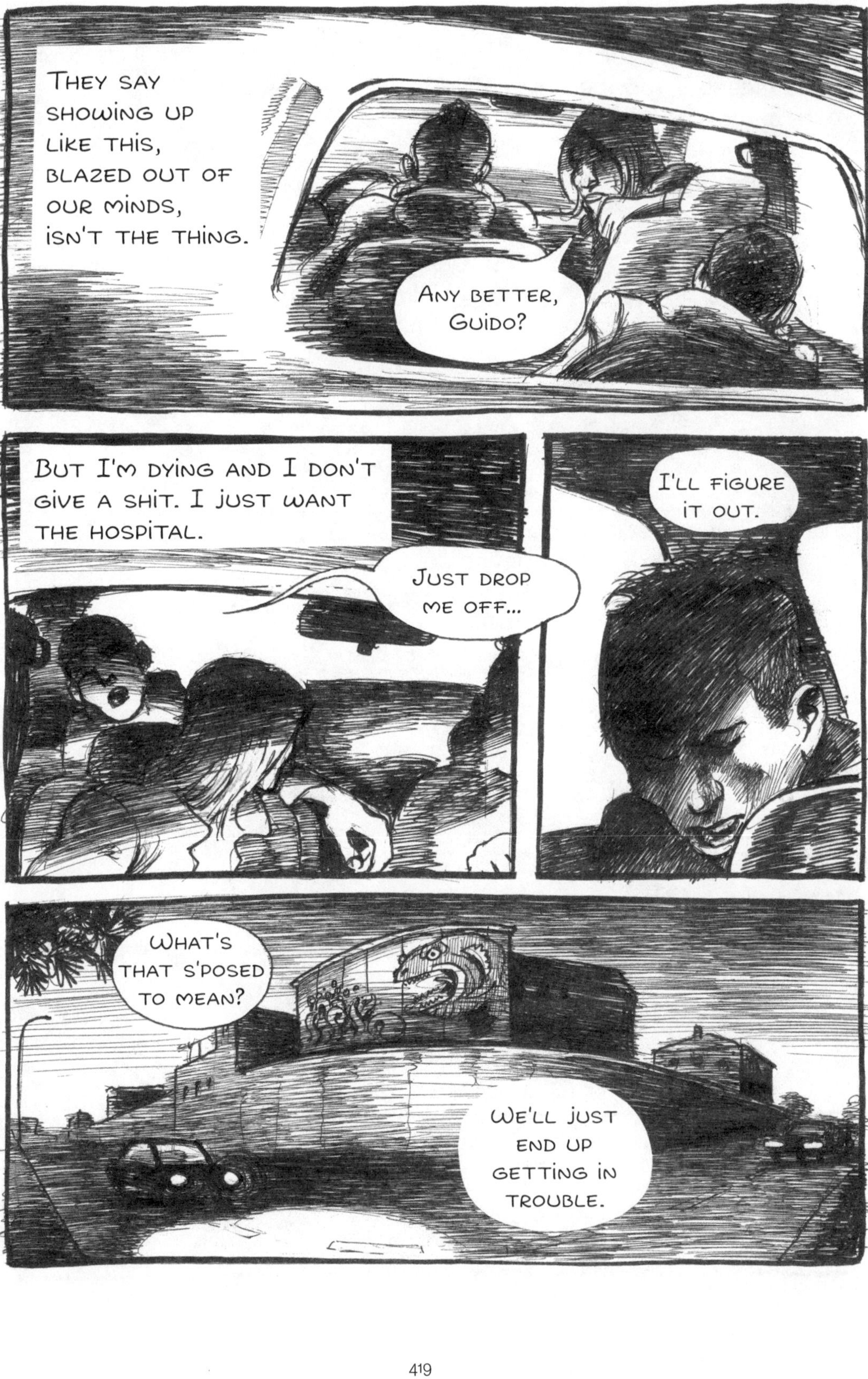

THEY SAY SHOWING UP LIKE THIS, BLAZED OUT OF OUR MINDS, ISN'T THE THING.
ANY BETTER, GUIDO?
BUT I'M DYING AND I DON'T GIVE A SHIT. I JUST WANT THE HOSPITAL.
JUST DROP ME OFF...
I'LL FIGURE IT OUT.
WHAT'S THAT S'POSED TO MEAN?
WE'LL JUST END UP GETTING IN TROUBLE.

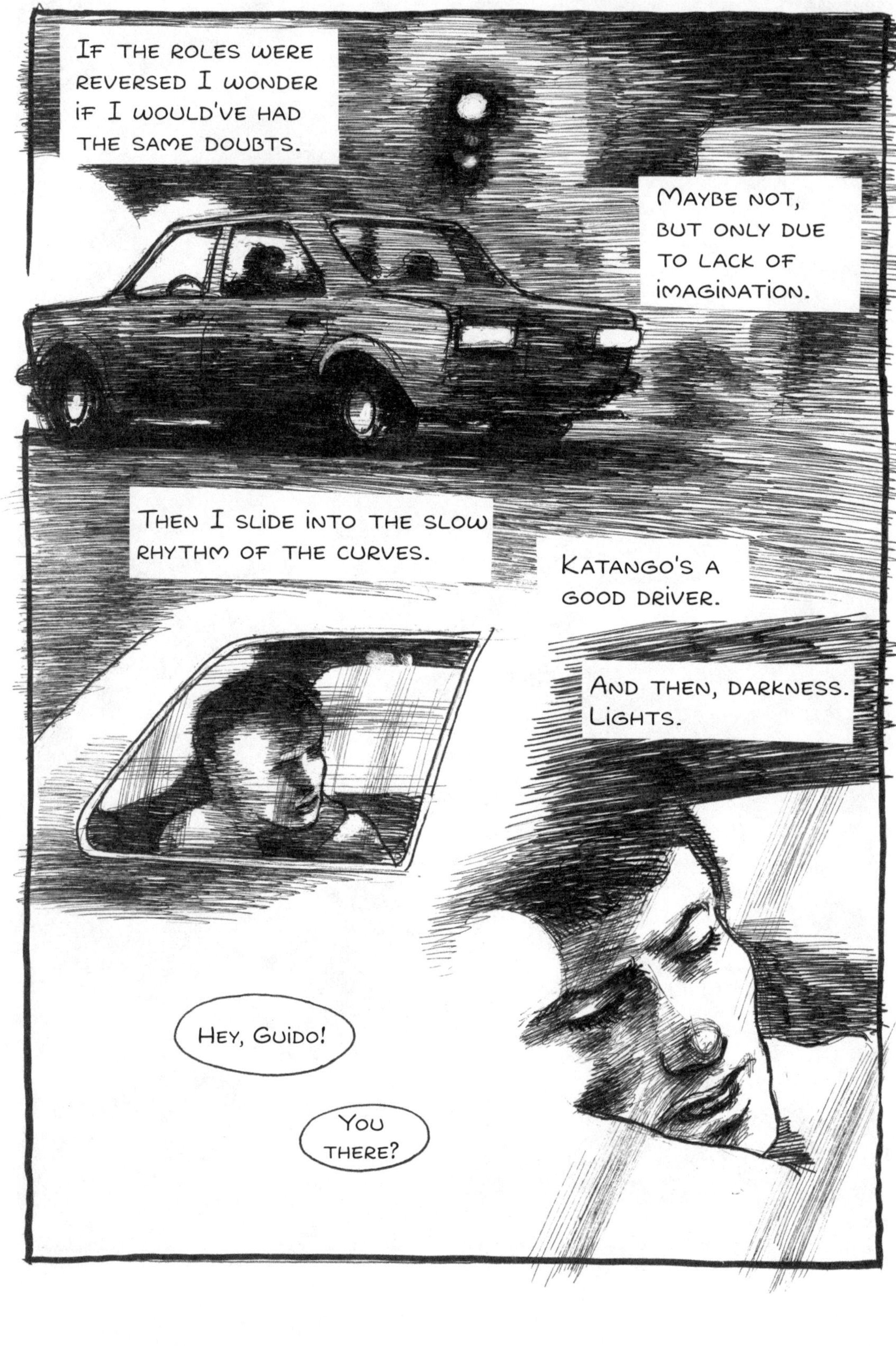
If the roles were reversed I wonder if I would've had the same doubts.
Maybe not, but only due to lack of imagination.
Then I slide into the slow rhythm of the curves.
Katango's a good driver.
And then, darkness. Lights.
Hey, Guido!
You there?

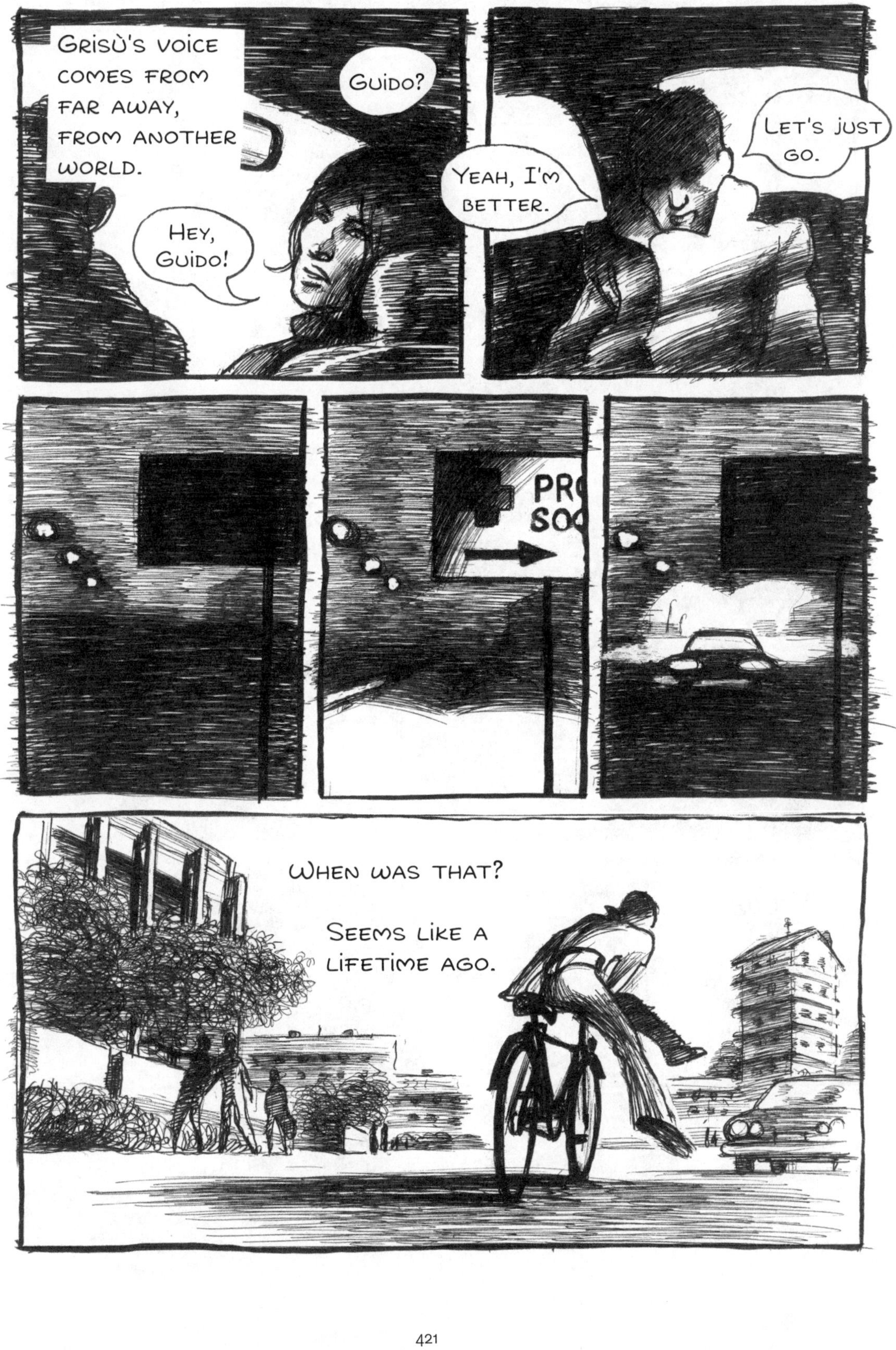
Grisù's voice comes from far away, from another world.
Guido?
Hey, Guido!
Yeah, I'm better.
Let's just go.
When was that?
Seems like a lifetime ago.

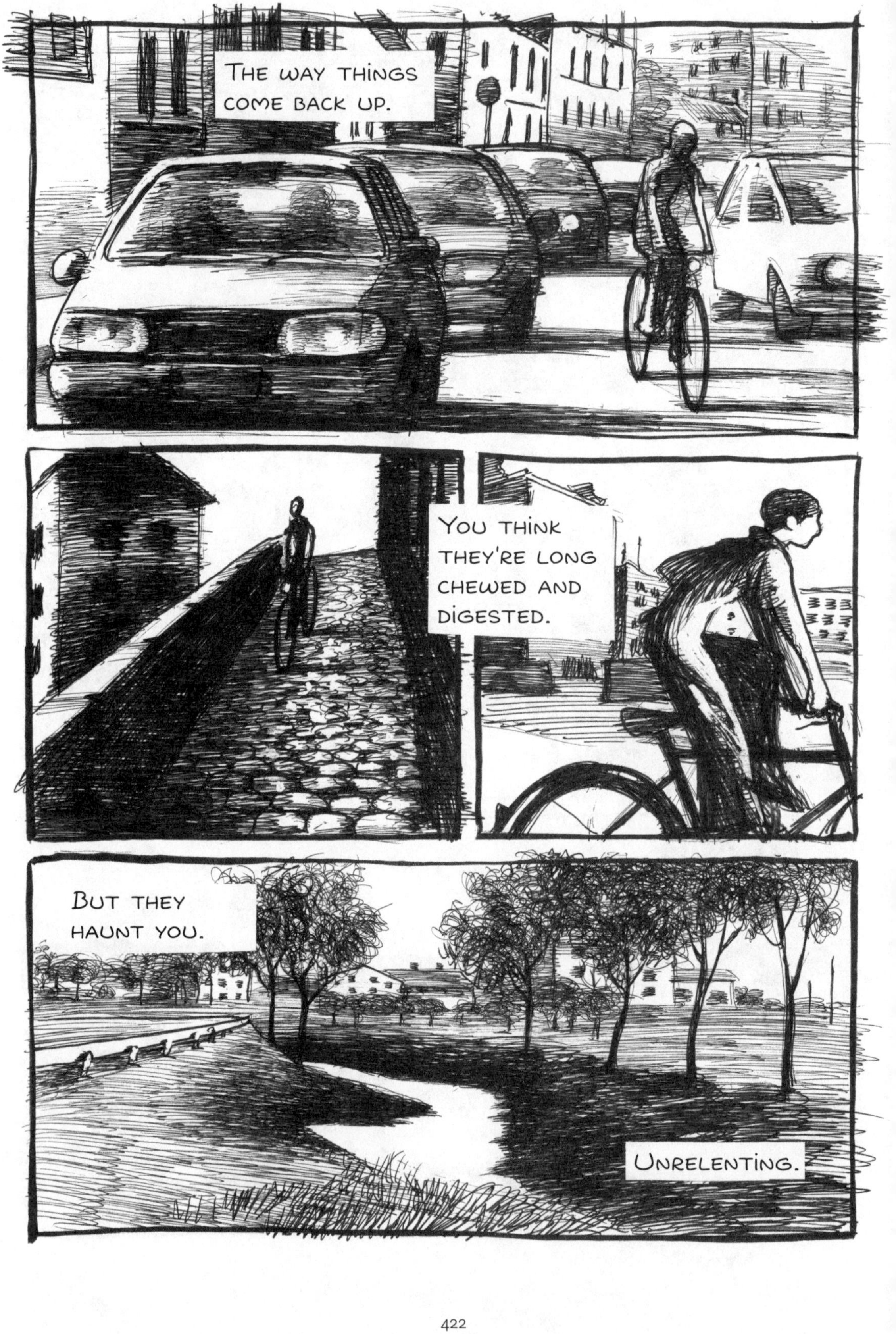
THE WAY THINGS COME BACK UP.
YOU THINK THEY'RE LONG CHEWED AND DIGESTED.
BUT THEY HAUNT YOU.
UNRELENTING.

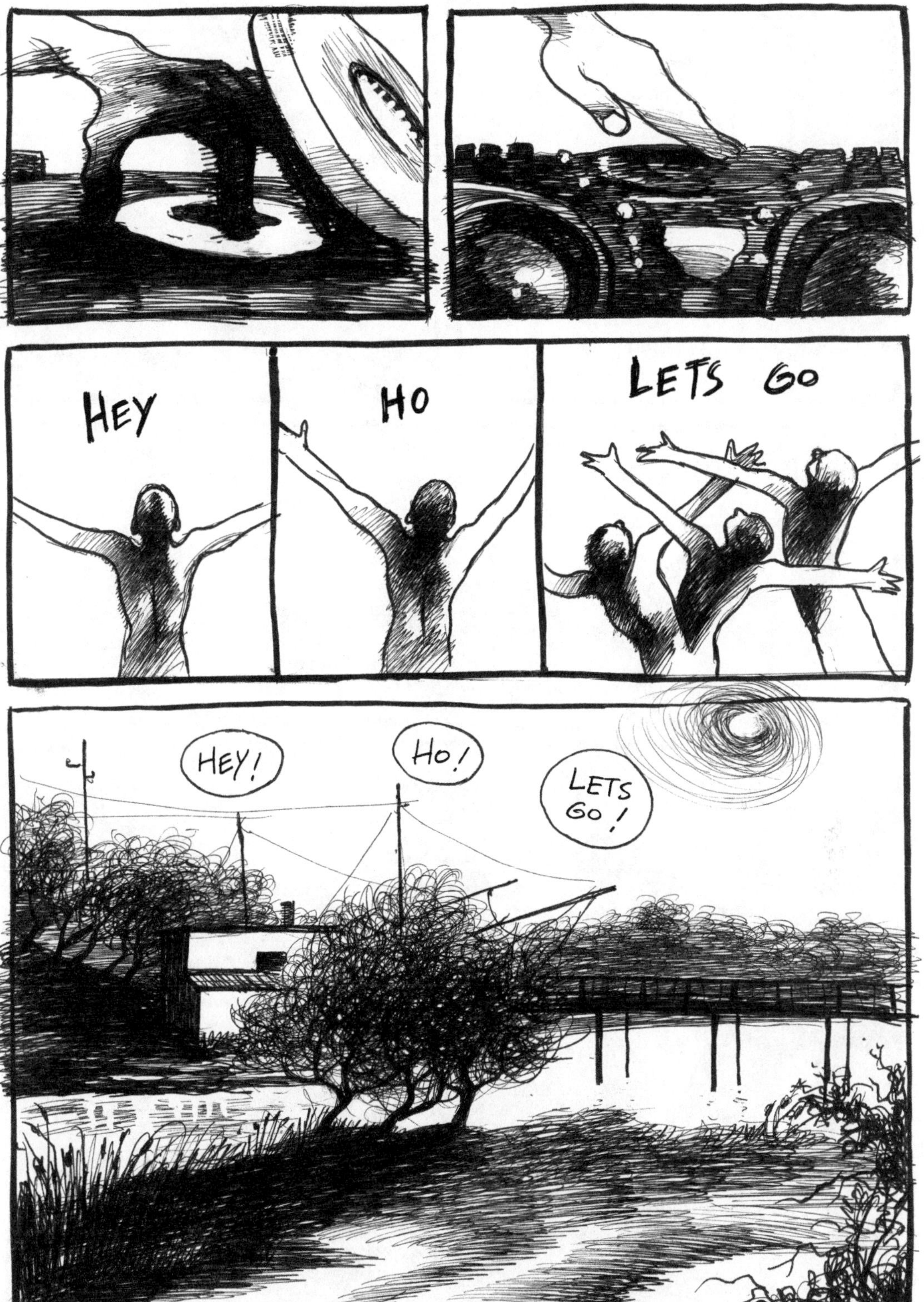
HEY
HO
LETS GO
HEY!
HO!
LETS GO!

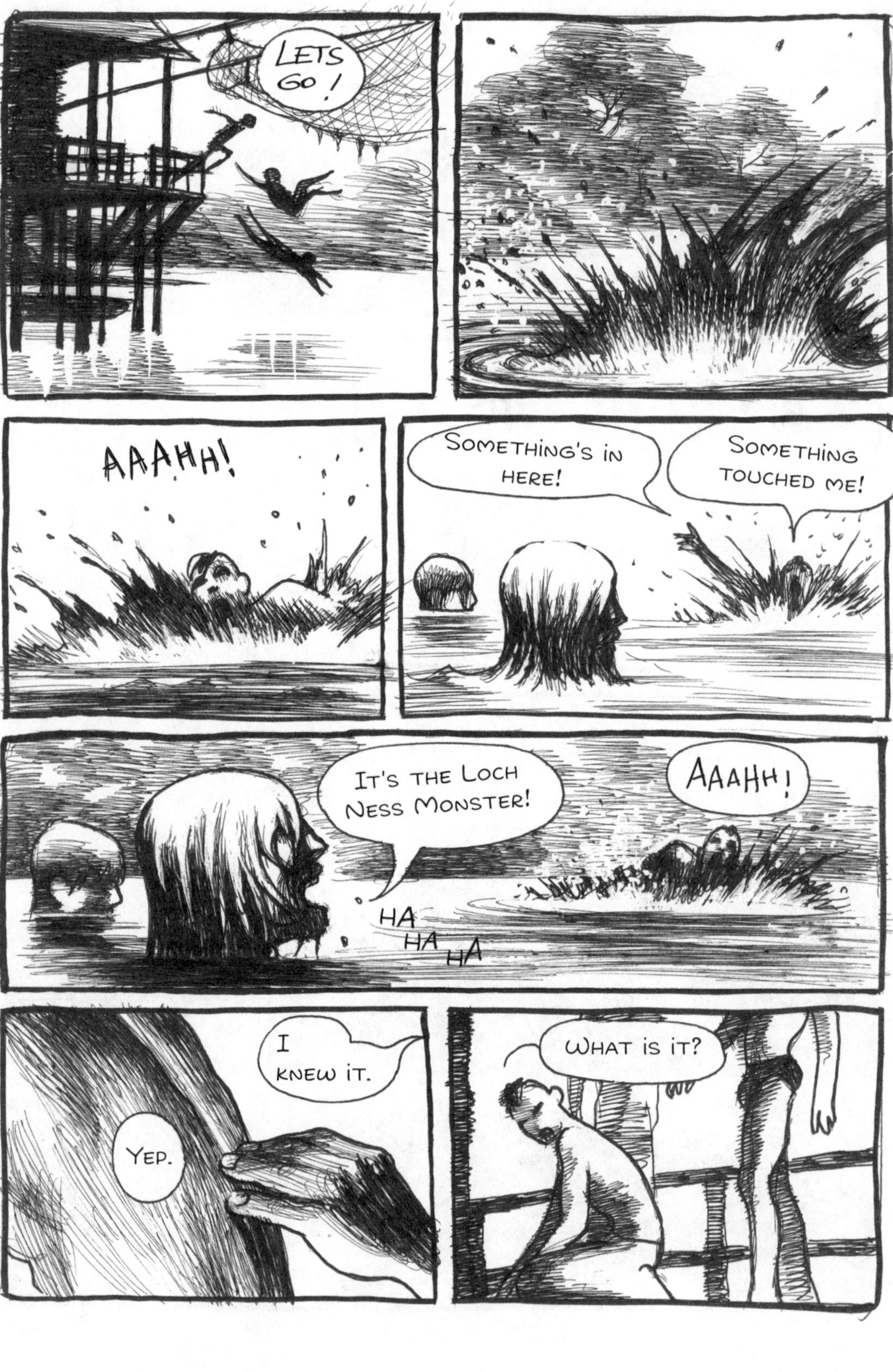

LETS GO!
AAAHH!
SOMETHING'S IN HERE!
SOMETHING TOUCHED ME!
IT'S THE LOCH NESS MONSTER!
AAAHH!
HA HA HA
I KNEW IT.
YEP.
WHAT IS IT?

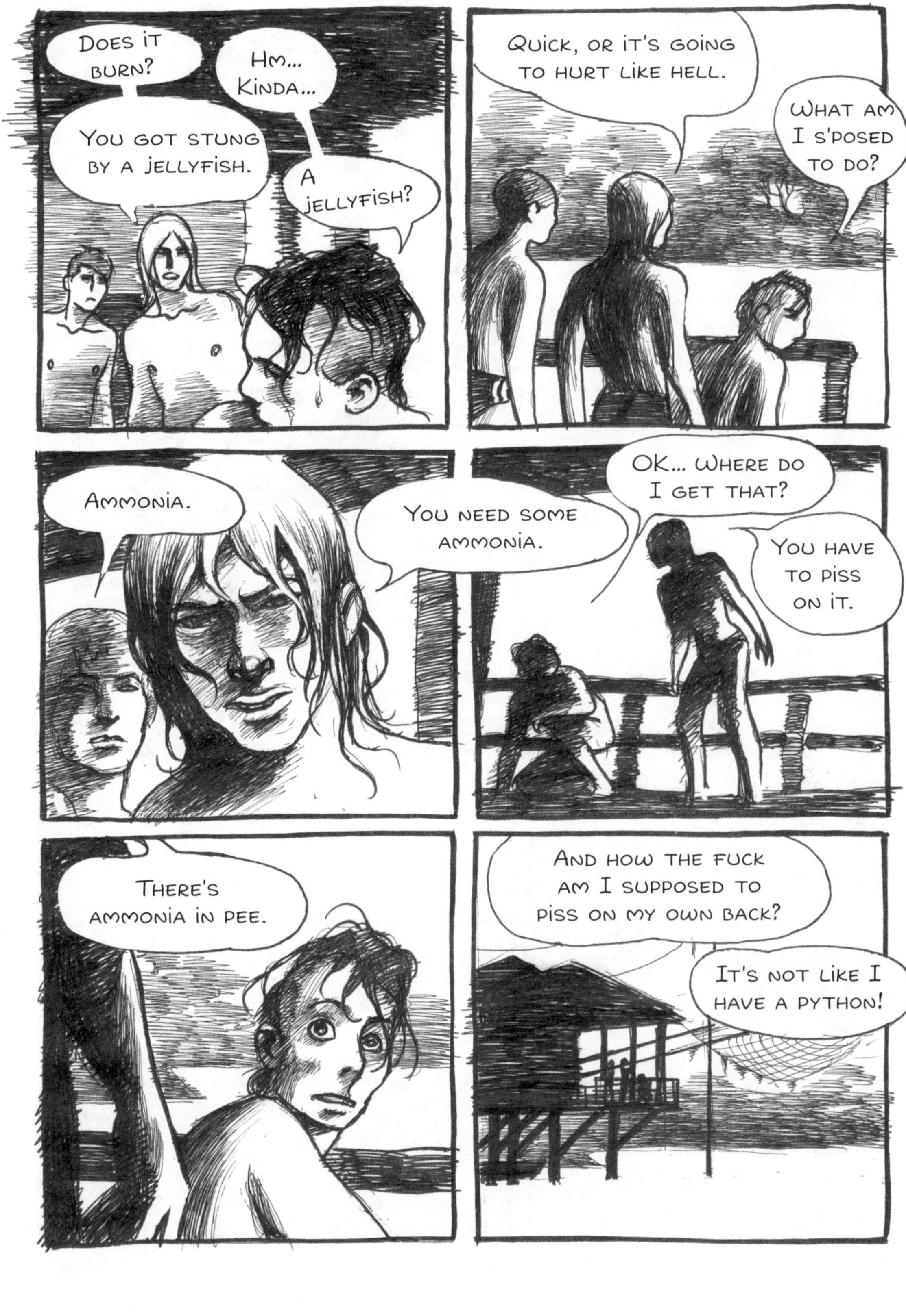

Does it burn?
Hm... Kinda...
You got stung by a jellyfish.
A jellyfish?
Quick, or it's going to hurt like hell.
What am I s'posed to do?
Ammonia.
You need some ammonia.
OK... Where do I get that?
You have to piss on it.
There's ammonia in pee.
And how the fuck am I supposed to piss on my own back?
It's not like I have a python!

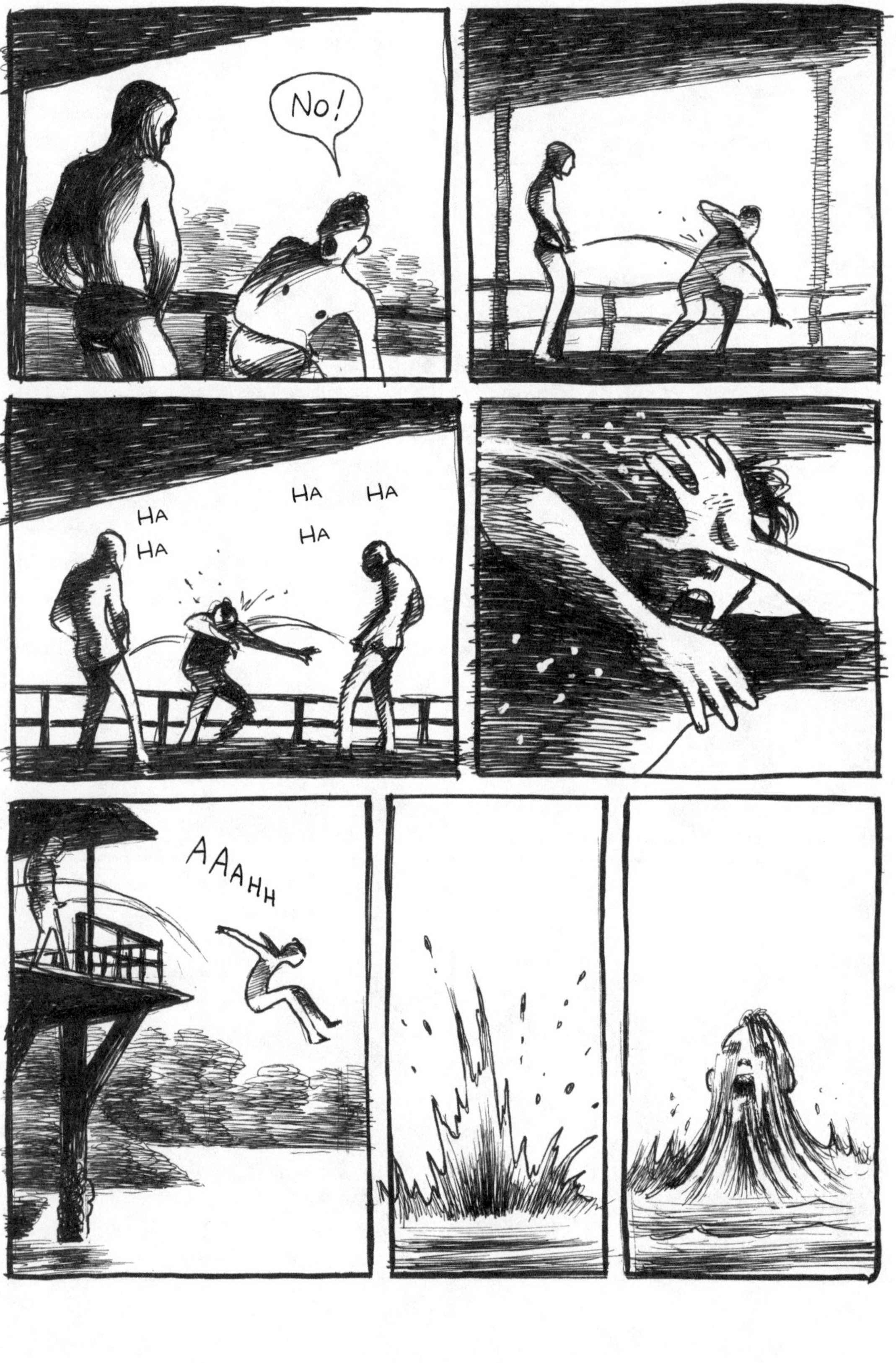
No!
HA
HA
HA
HA
HA
AAAHH

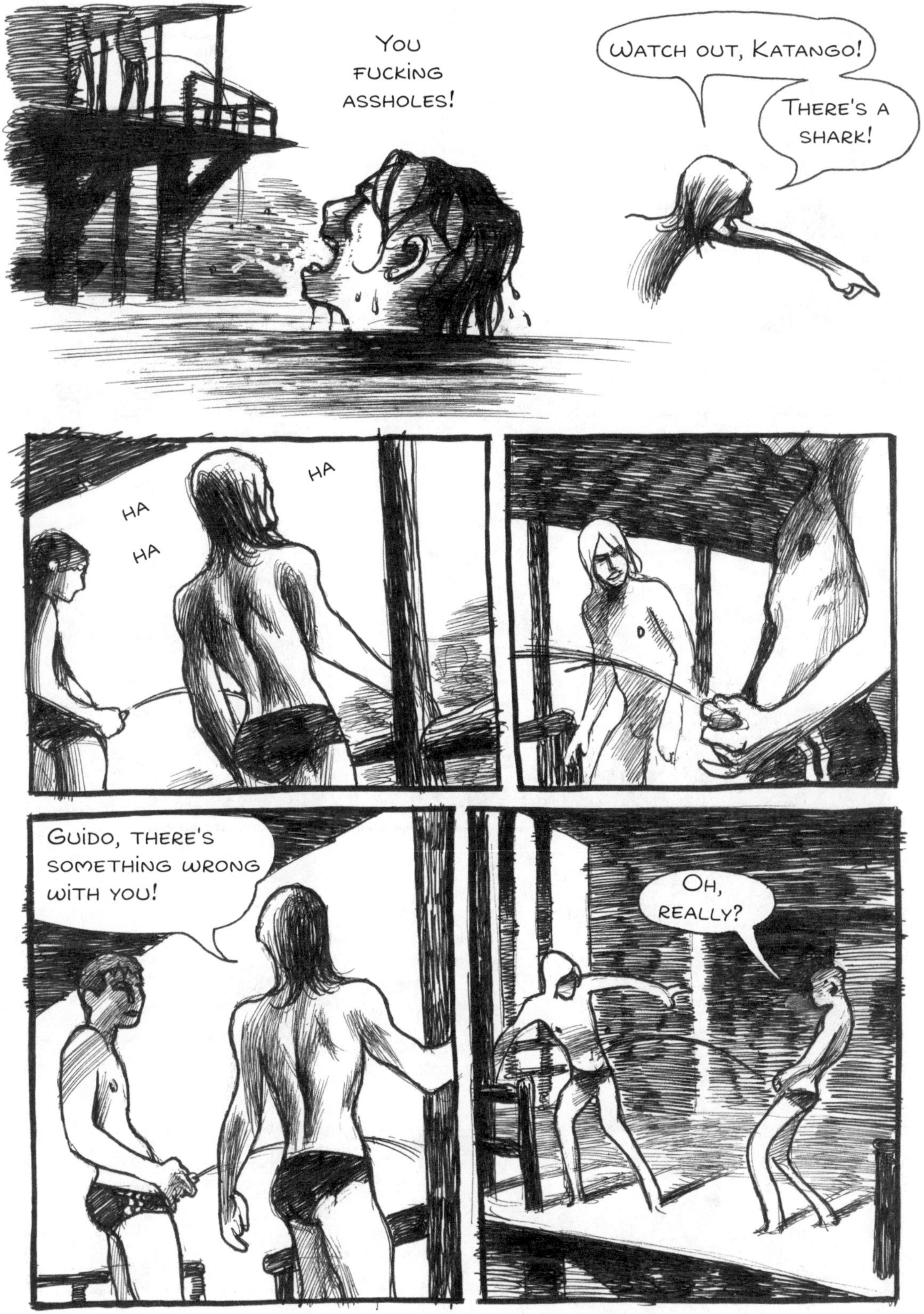
You fucking assholes!
Watch out, Katango!
There's a shark!
HA
HA
HA
Guido, there's something wrong with you!
Oh, really?

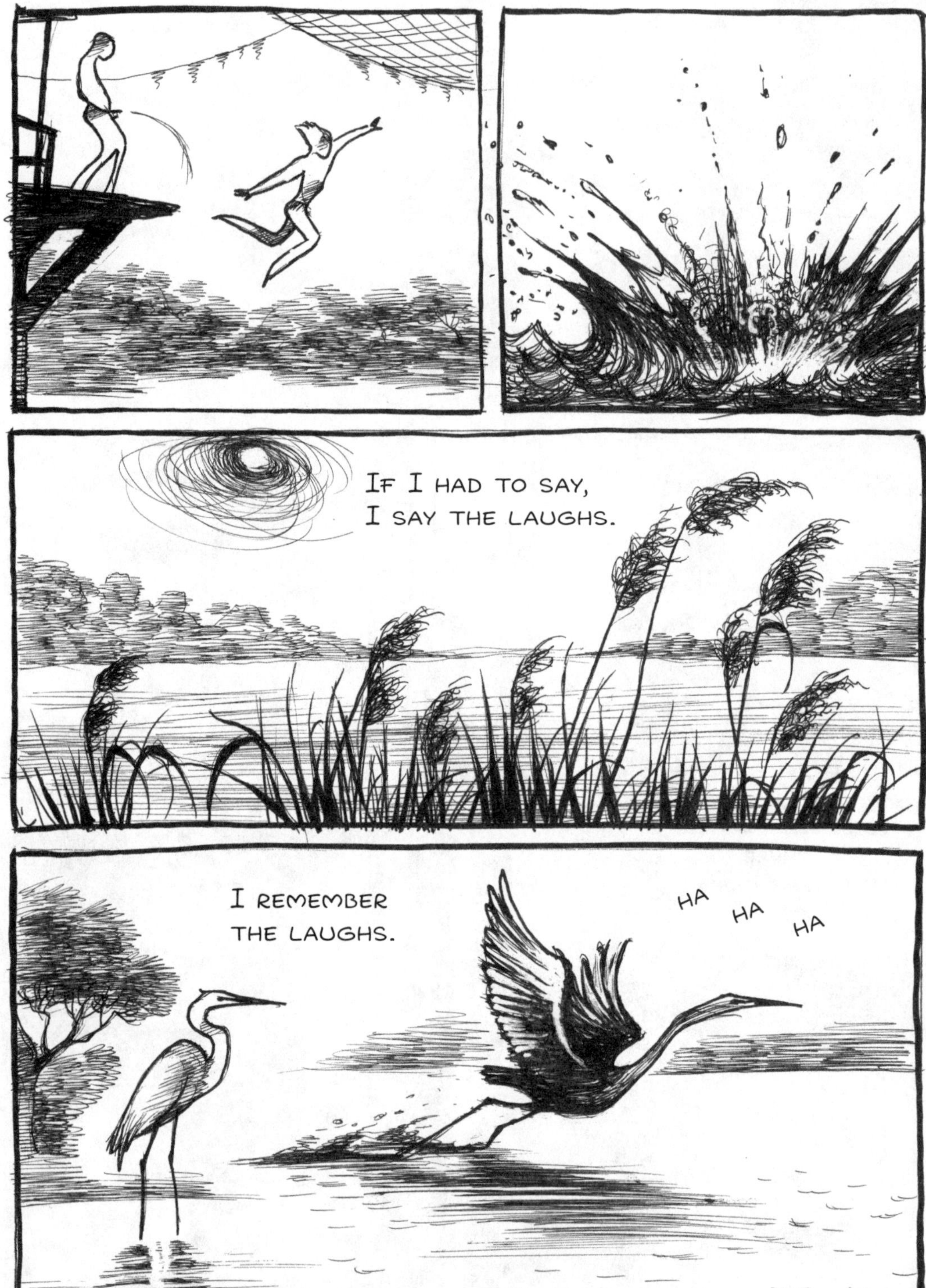
If I had to say,
I say the laughs.
I remember
the laughs.
HA
HA
HA

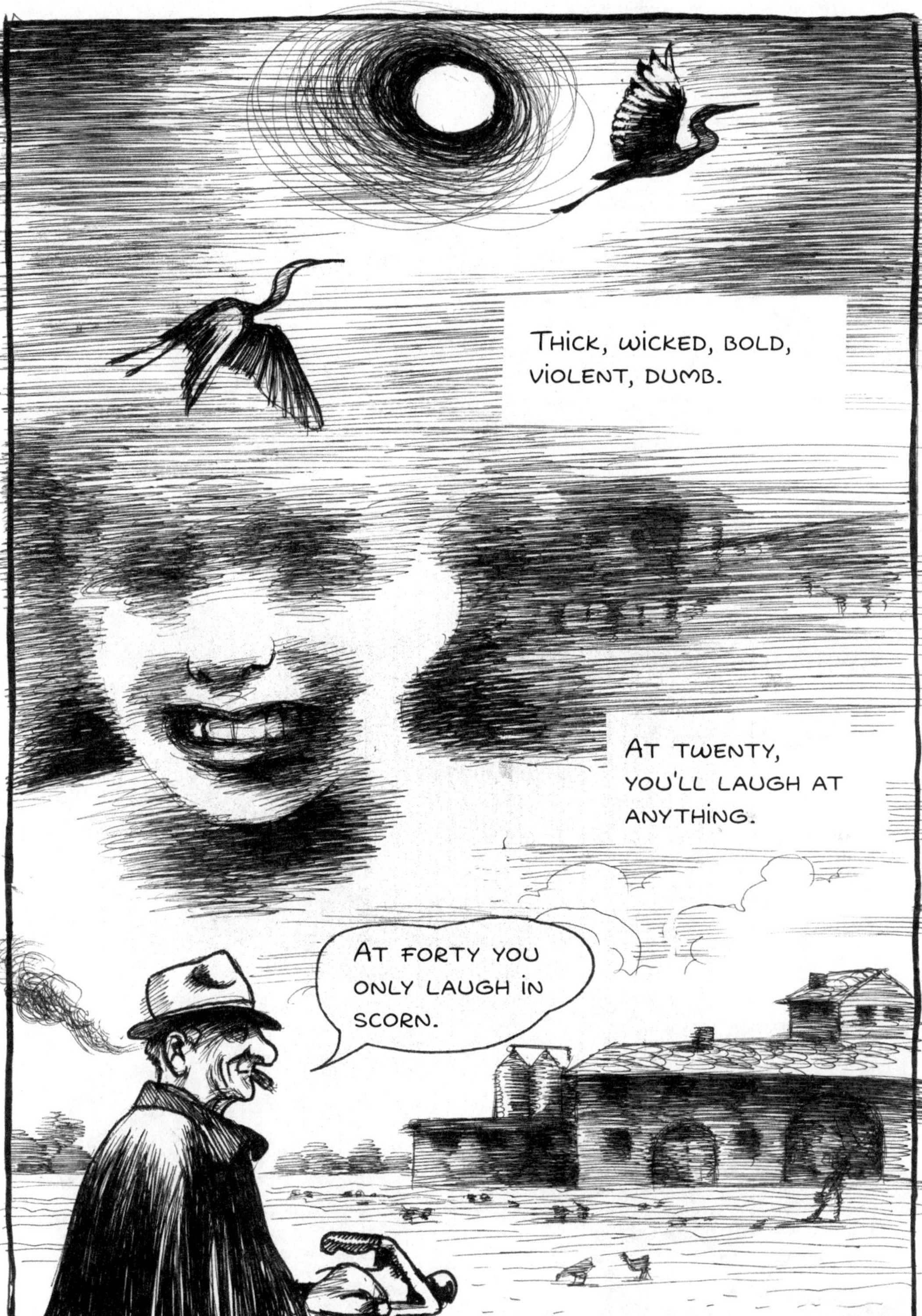
THICK, WICKED, BOLD, VIOLENT, DUMB.
AT TWENTY, YOU'LL LAUGH AT ANYTHING.
AT FORTY YOU ONLY LAUGH IN SCORN.

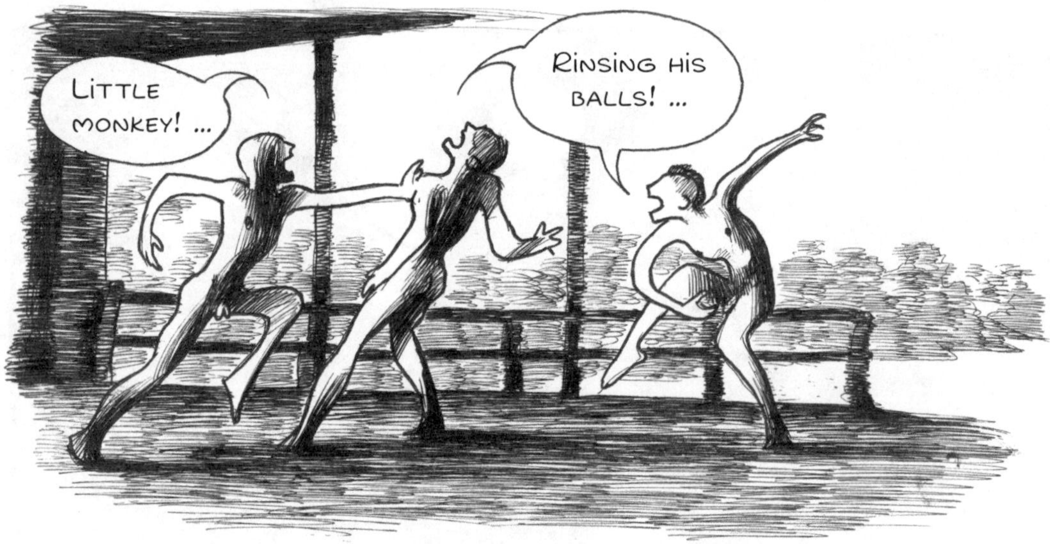
LITTLE MONKEY! ...
RINSING HIS BALLS! ...

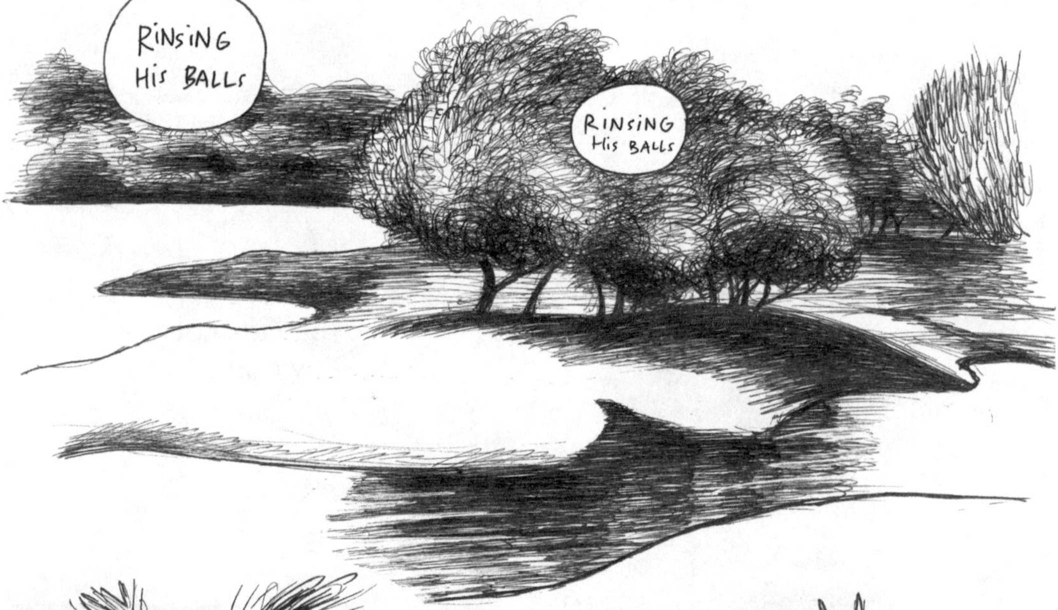
RINSING HIS BALLS
RINSING HIS BALLS

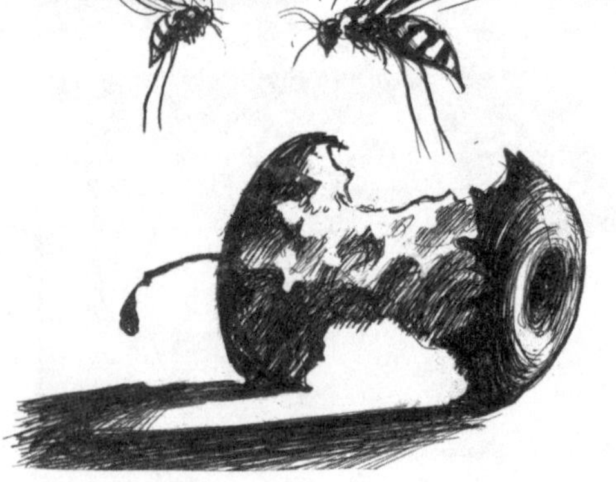

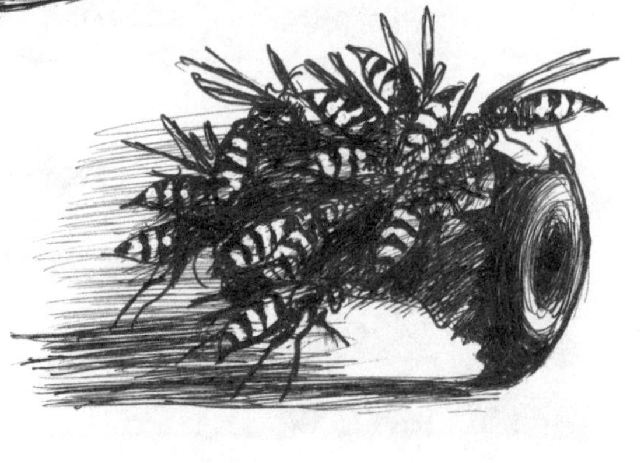

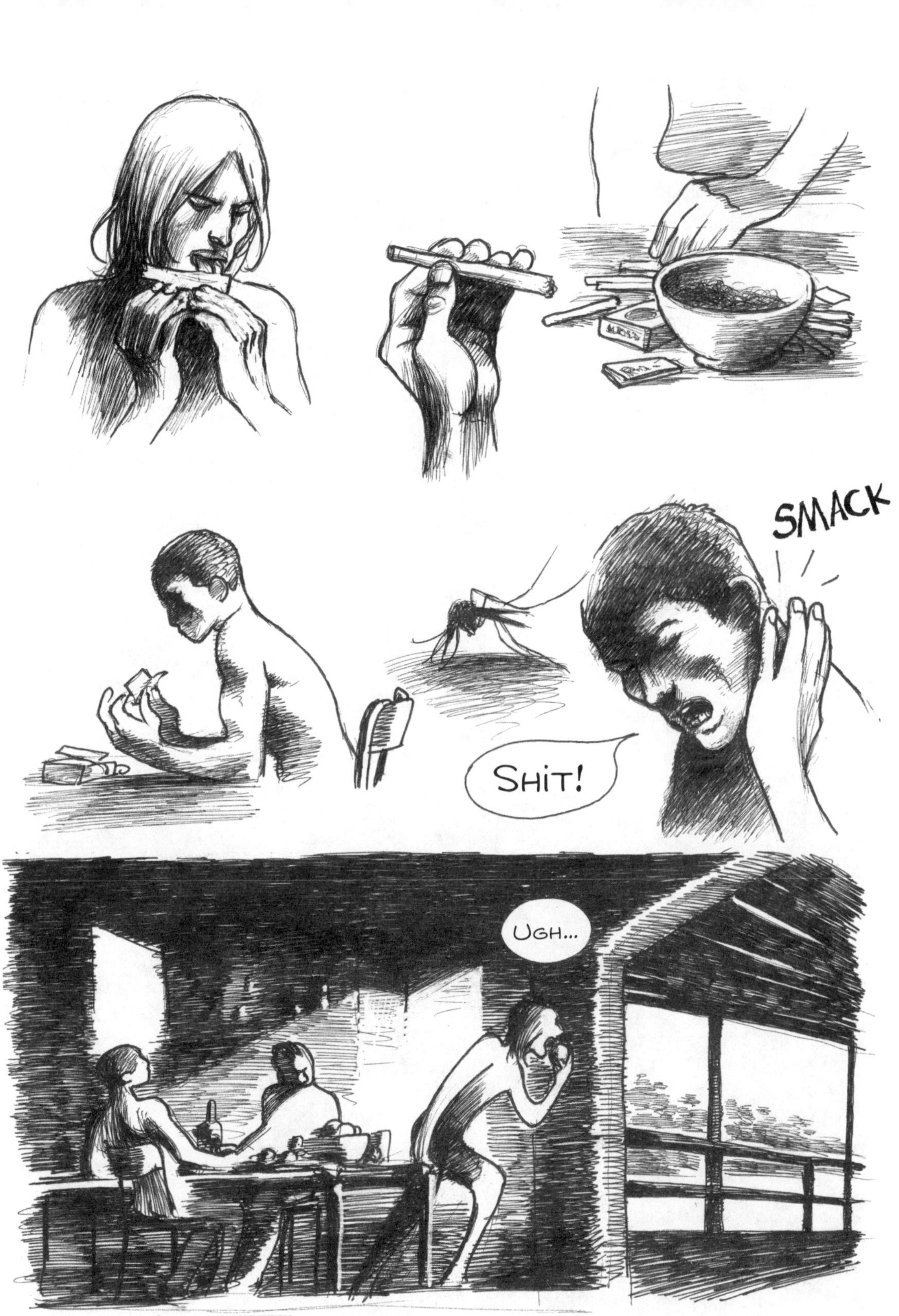
SMACK
SHIT!
UGH...

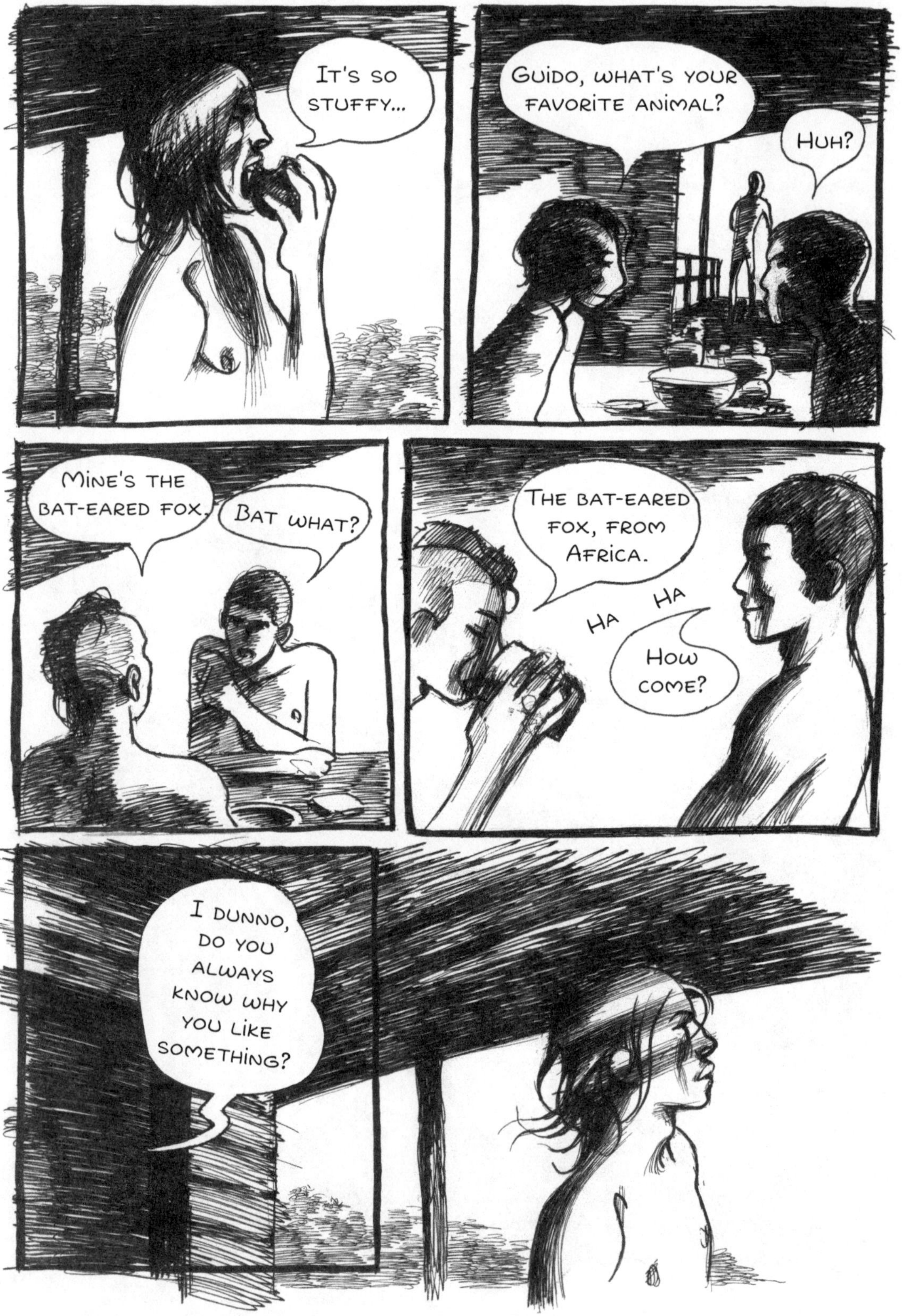
It's so stuffy...
Guido, what's your favorite animal?
Huh?
Mine's the bat-eared fox.
Bat what?
The bat-eared fox, from Africa.
Ha Ha
How come?
I dunno, do you always know why you like something?

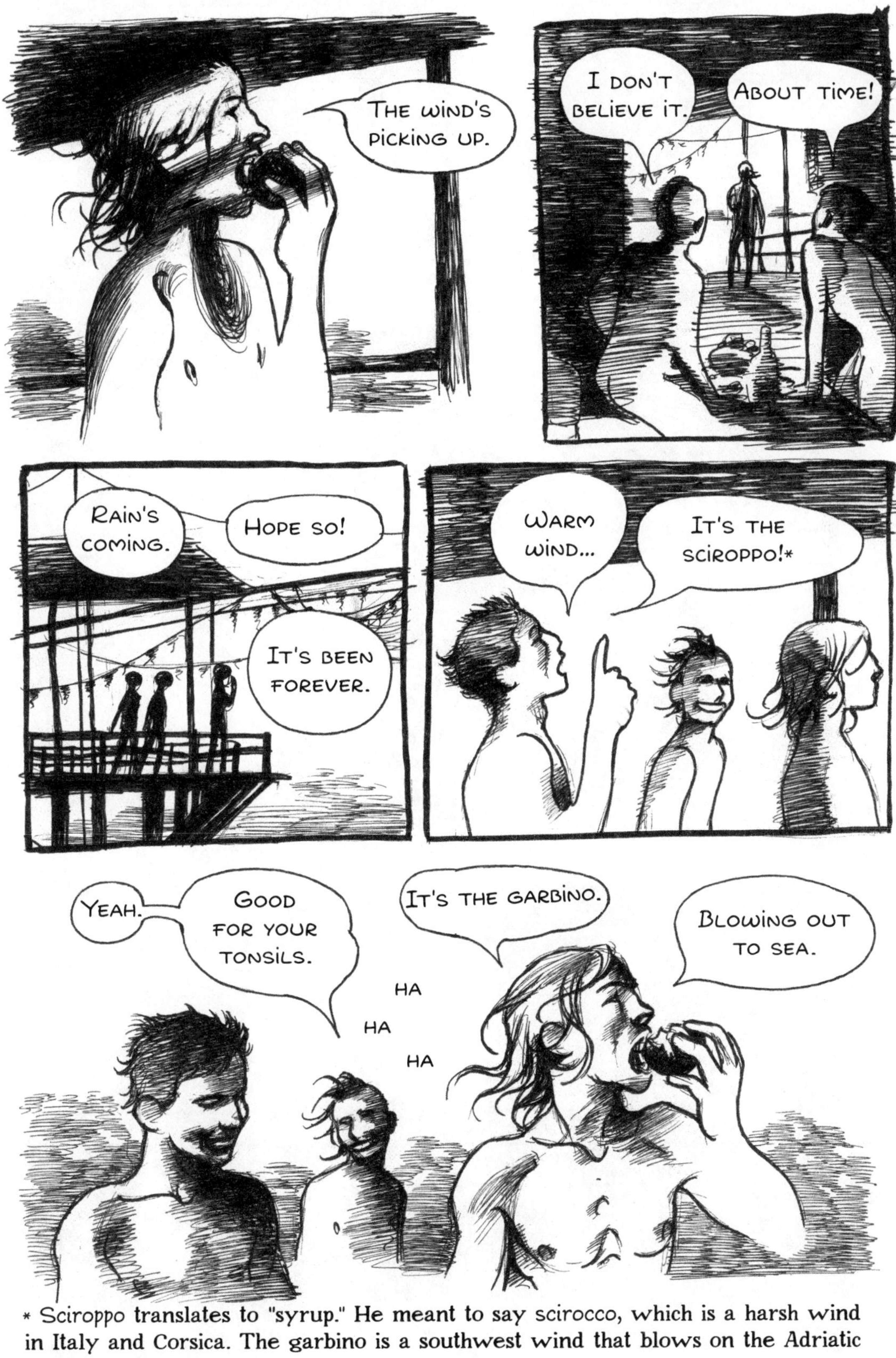
The wind's picking up.
I don't believe it.
About time!
Rain's coming.
Hope so!
It's been forever.
Warm wind...
It's the sciroppo!*
Yeah.
Good for your tonsils.
HA
HA
HA
It's the garbino.
Blowing out to sea.

* *Sciroppo* translates to "syrup." He meant to say *scirocco*, which is a harsh wind in Italy and Corsica. The *garbino* is a southwest wind that blows on the Adriatic coasts.

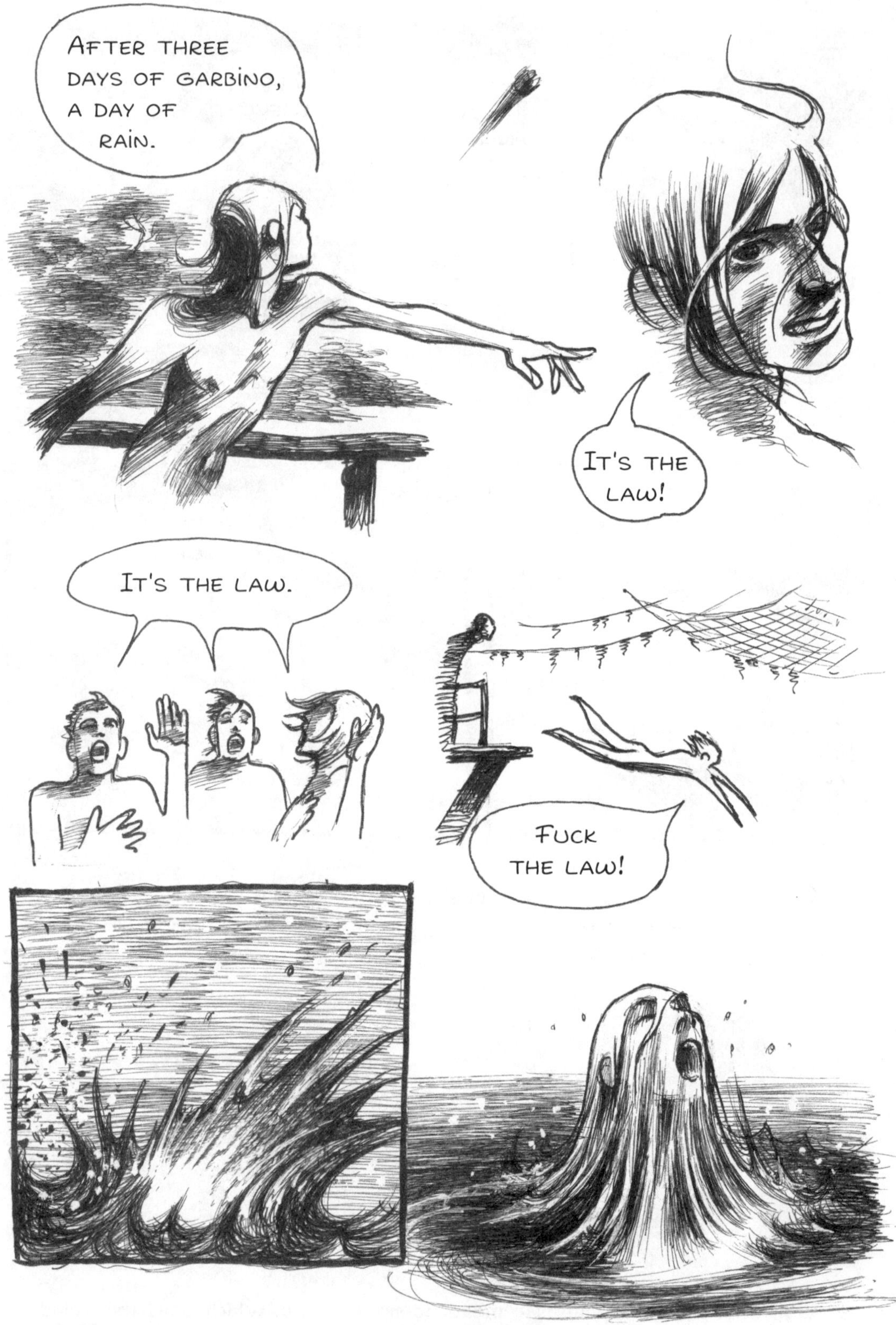
After three days of garbino, a day of rain.
It's the law!
It's the law.
Fuck the law!

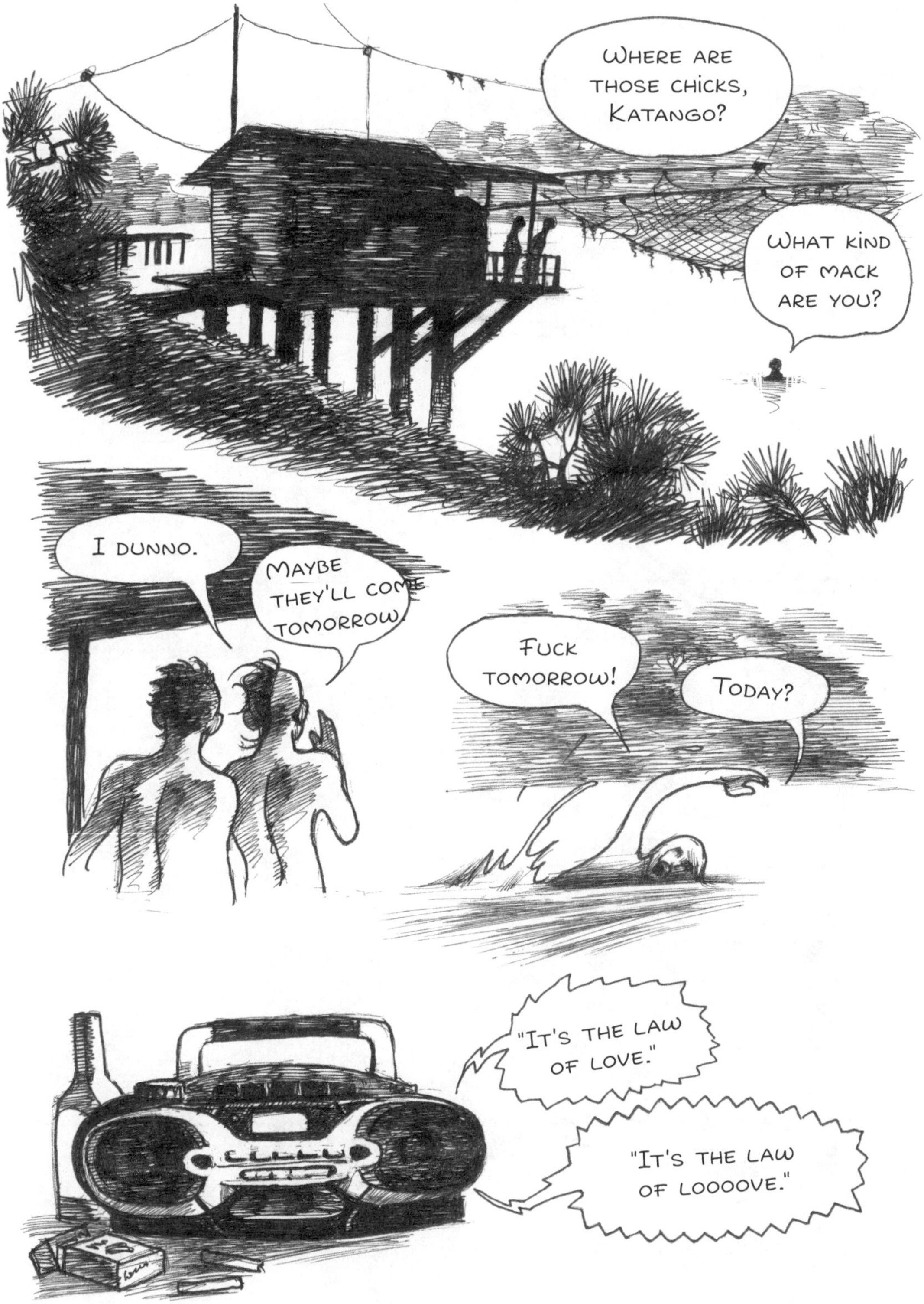
Where are those chicks, Katango?
What kind of mack are you?
I dunno.
Maybe they'll come tomorrow.
Fuck tomorrow!
Today?
"It's the law of love."
"It's the law of loooove."

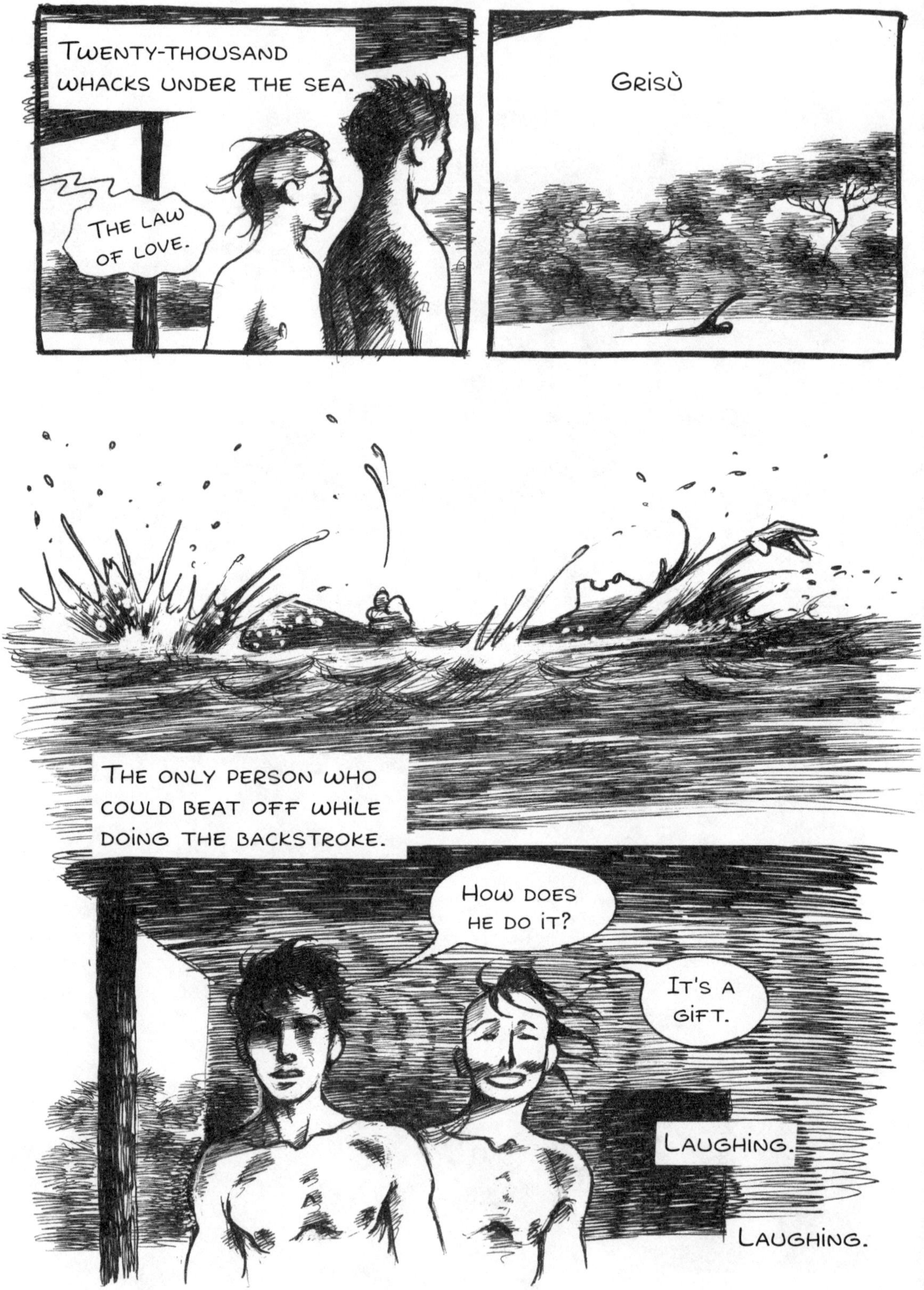

Twenty-thousand whacks under the sea.
The law of love.
Grisù
The only person who could beat off while doing the backstroke.
How does he do it?
It's a gift.
Laughing.
Laughing.

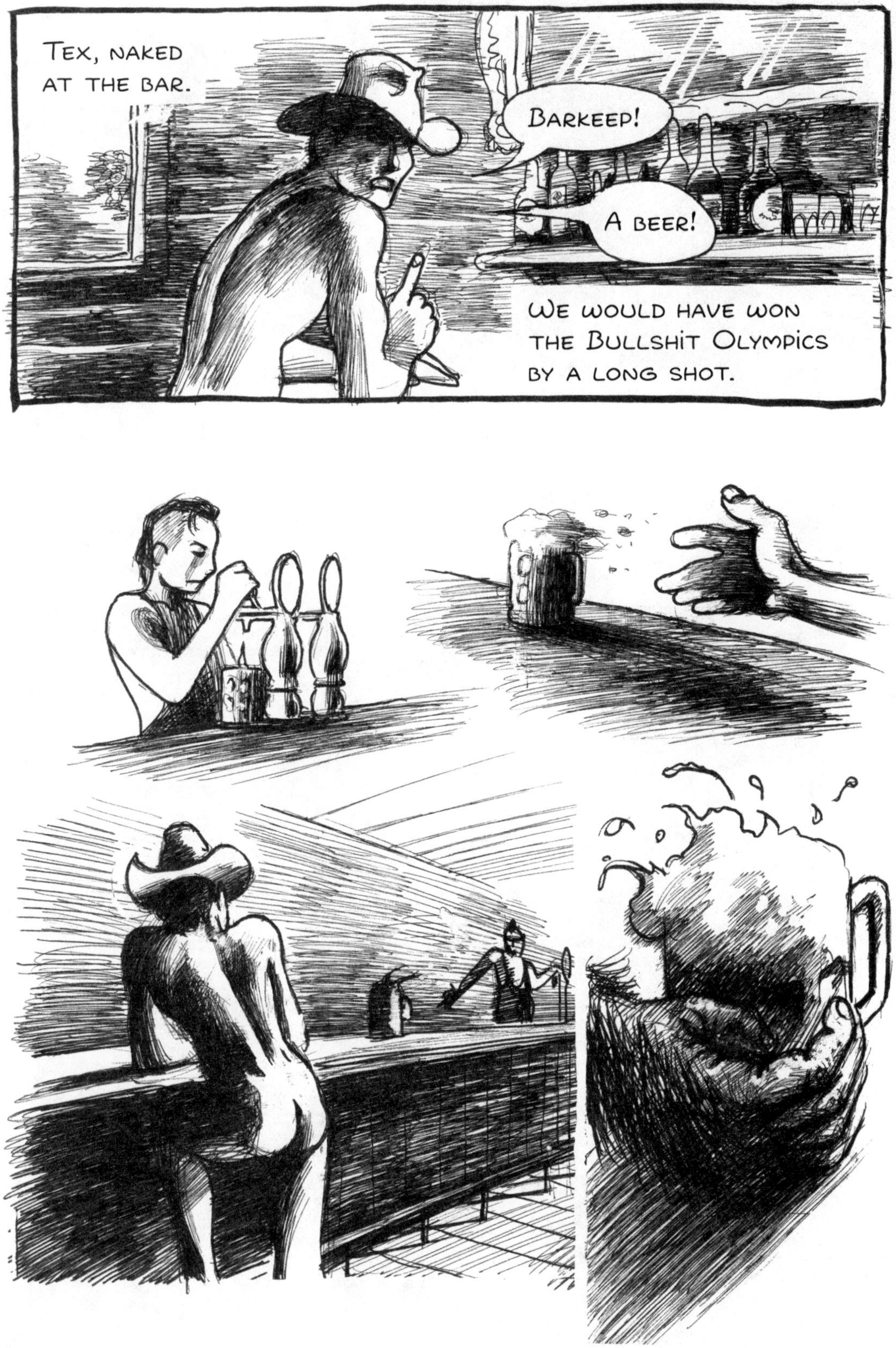
Tex, naked at the bar.
Barkeep!
A beer!
We would have won the Bullshit Olympics by a long shot.

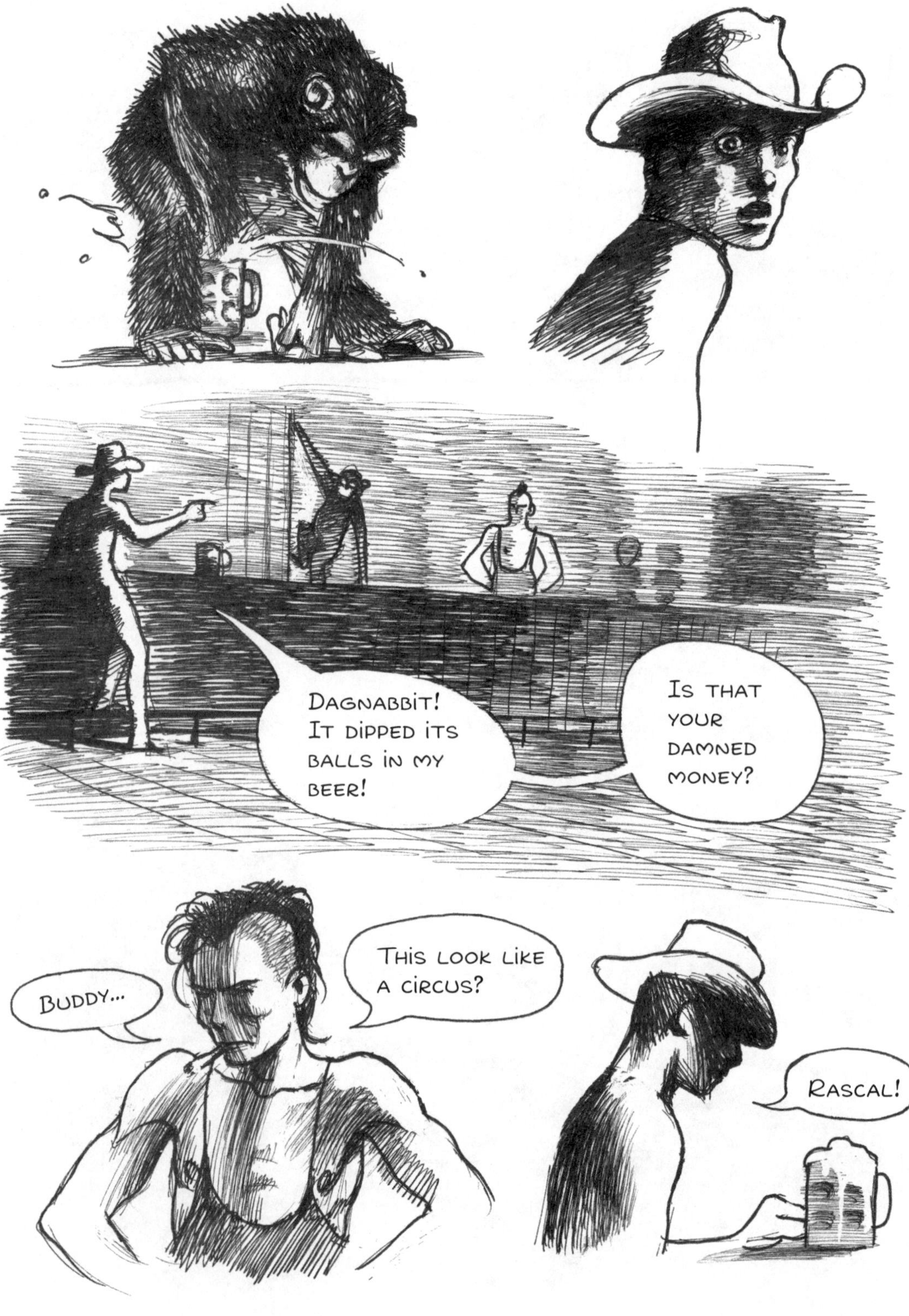

DAGNABBIT! IT DIPPED ITS BALLS IN MY BEER!
IS THAT YOUR DAMNED MONEY?
BUDDY...
THIS LOOK LIKE A CIRCUS?
RASCAL!

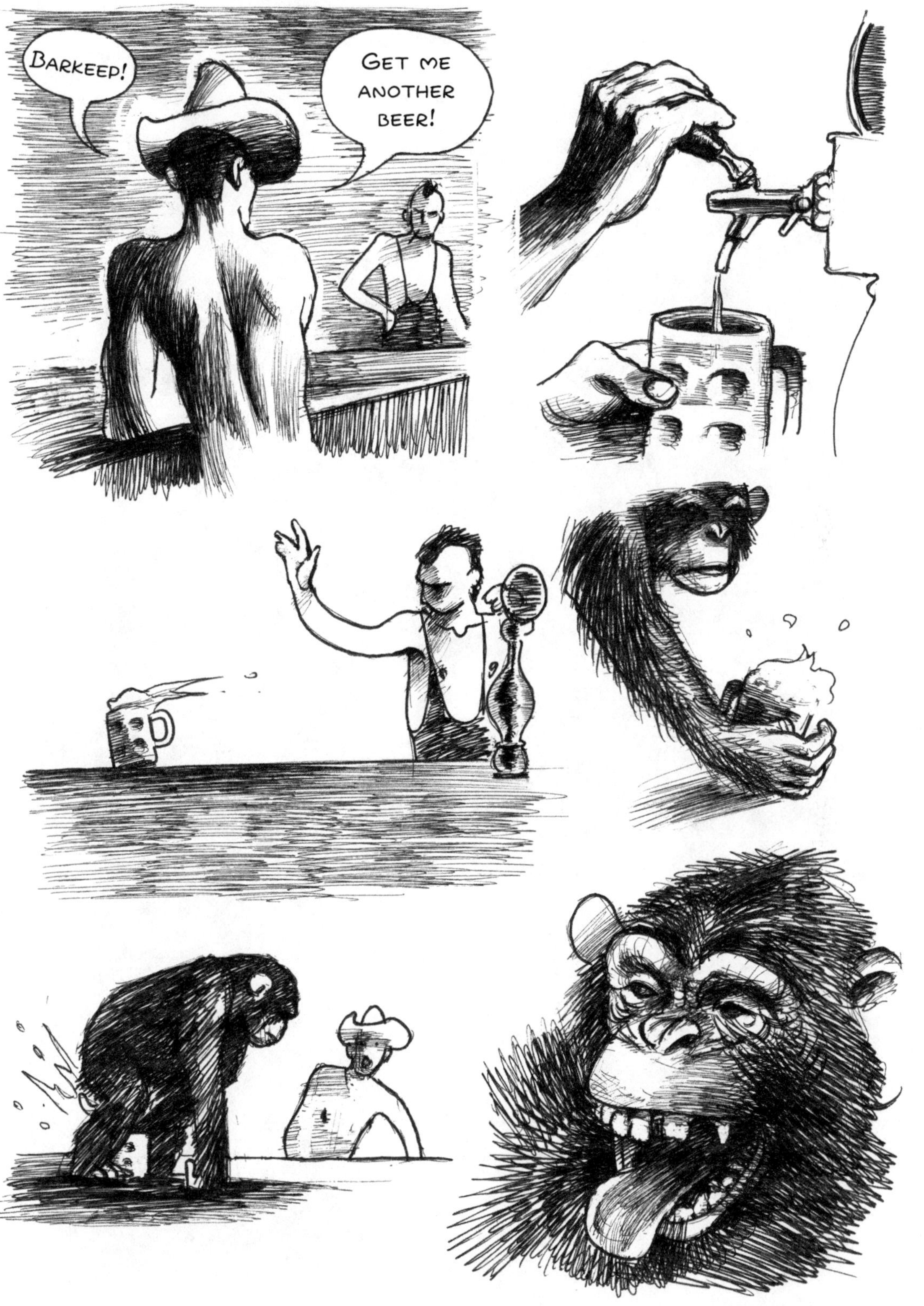
Barkeep!
Get me another beer!

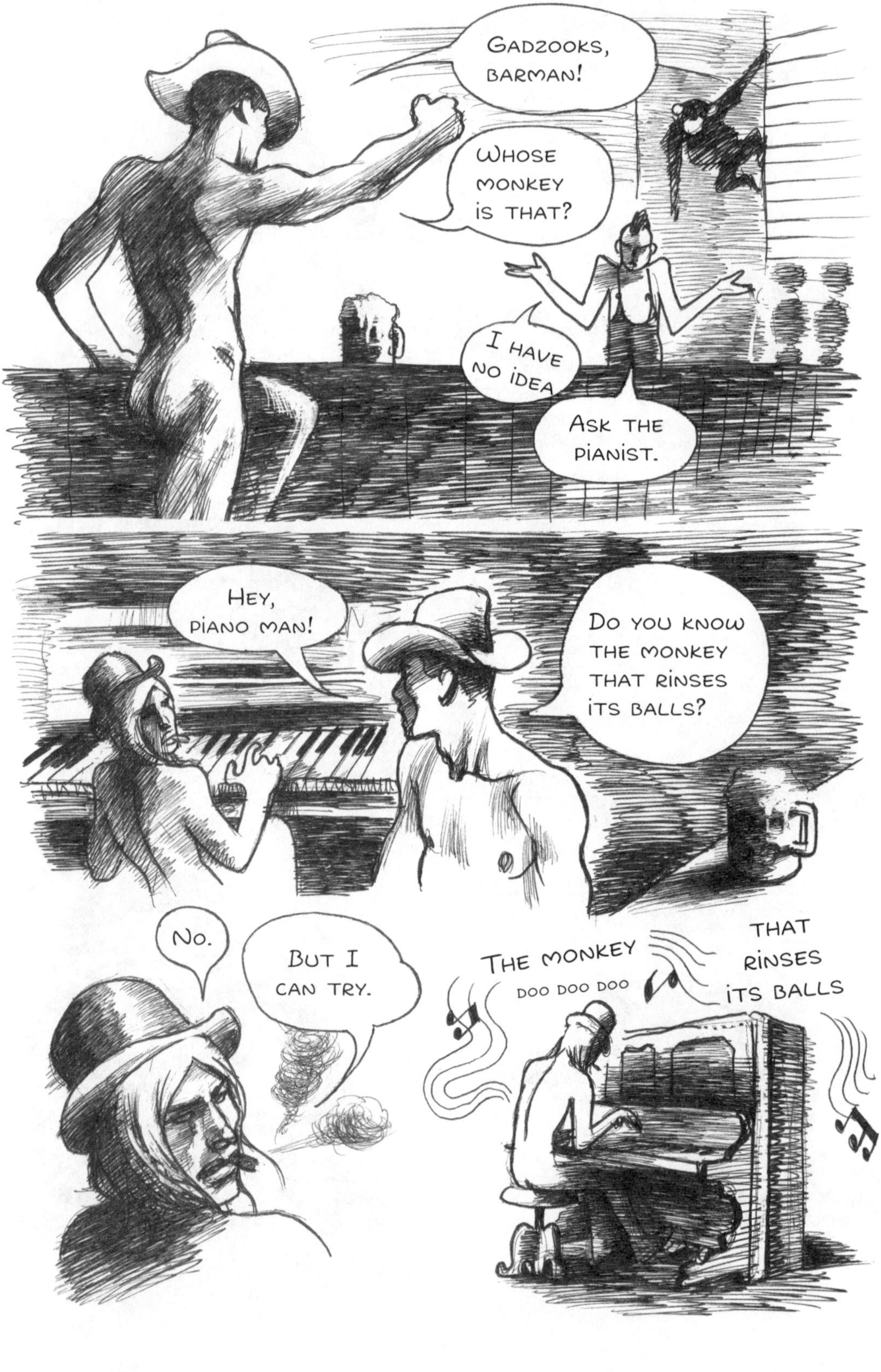
GADZOOKS, BARMAN!
WHOSE MONKEY IS THAT?
I HAVE NO IDEA
ASK THE PIANIST.
HEY, PIANO MAN!
DO YOU KNOW THE MONKEY THAT RINSES ITS BALLS?
NO.
BUT I CAN TRY.
THE MONKEY
DOO DOO DOO
THAT RINSES ITS BALLS

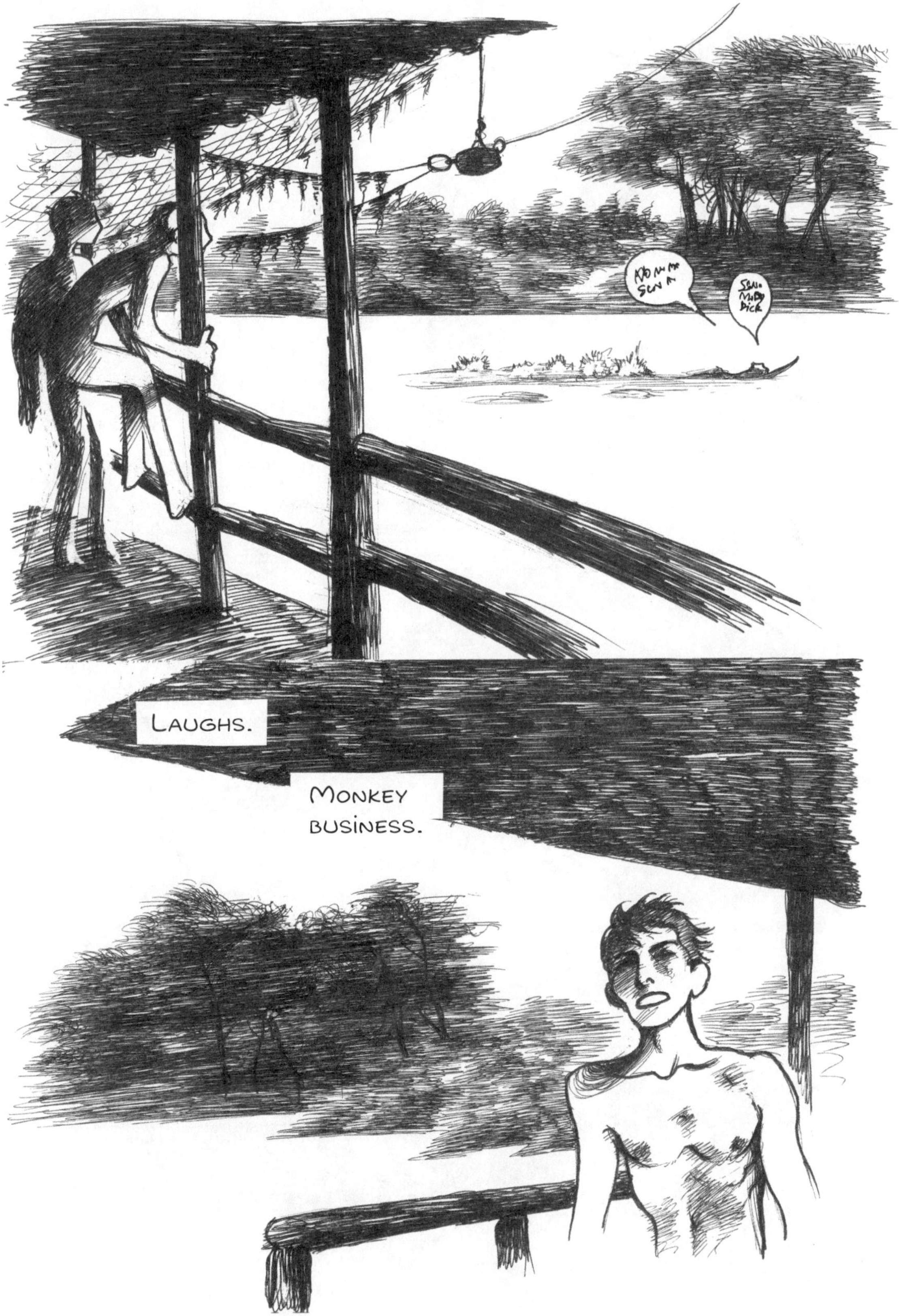
Laughs.
Monkey business.

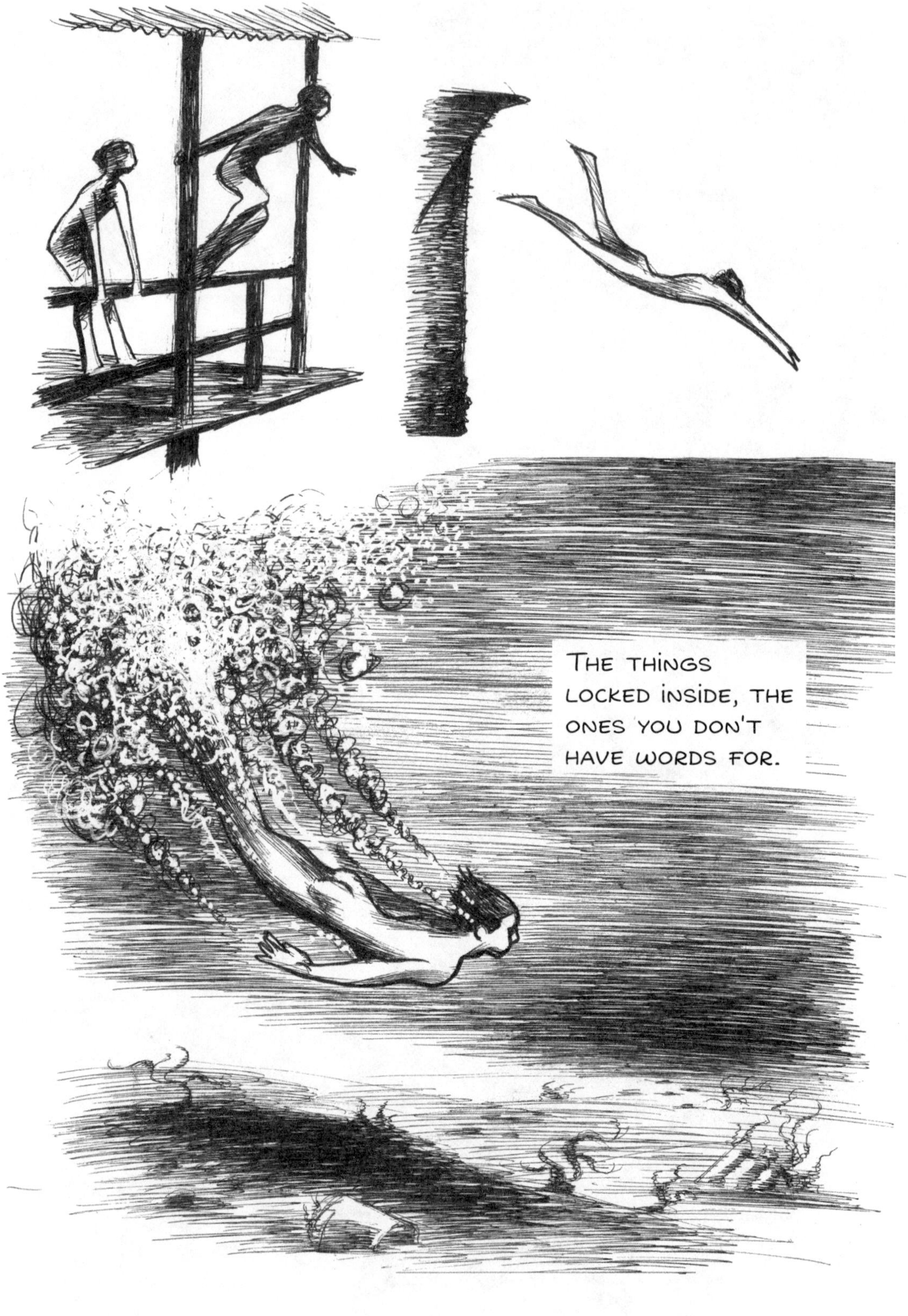
THE THINGS LOCKED INSIDE, THE ONES YOU DON'T HAVE WORDS FOR.

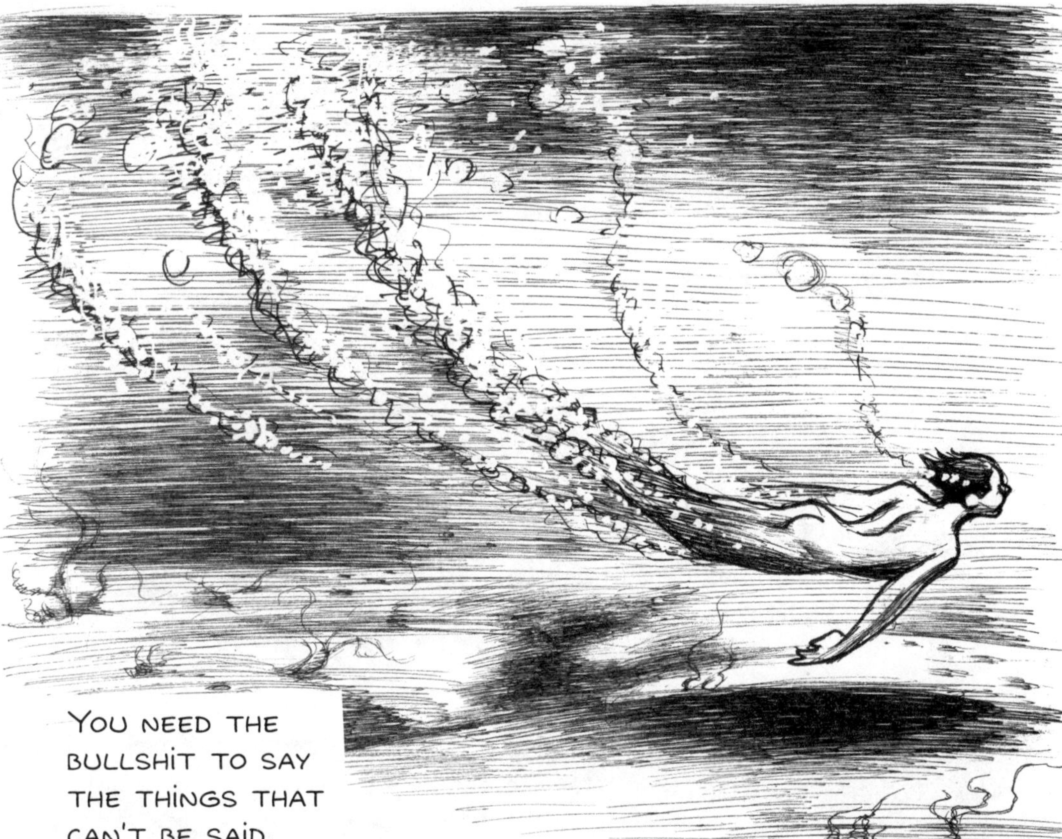
YOU NEED THE BULLSHIT TO SAY THE THINGS THAT CAN'T BE SAID.

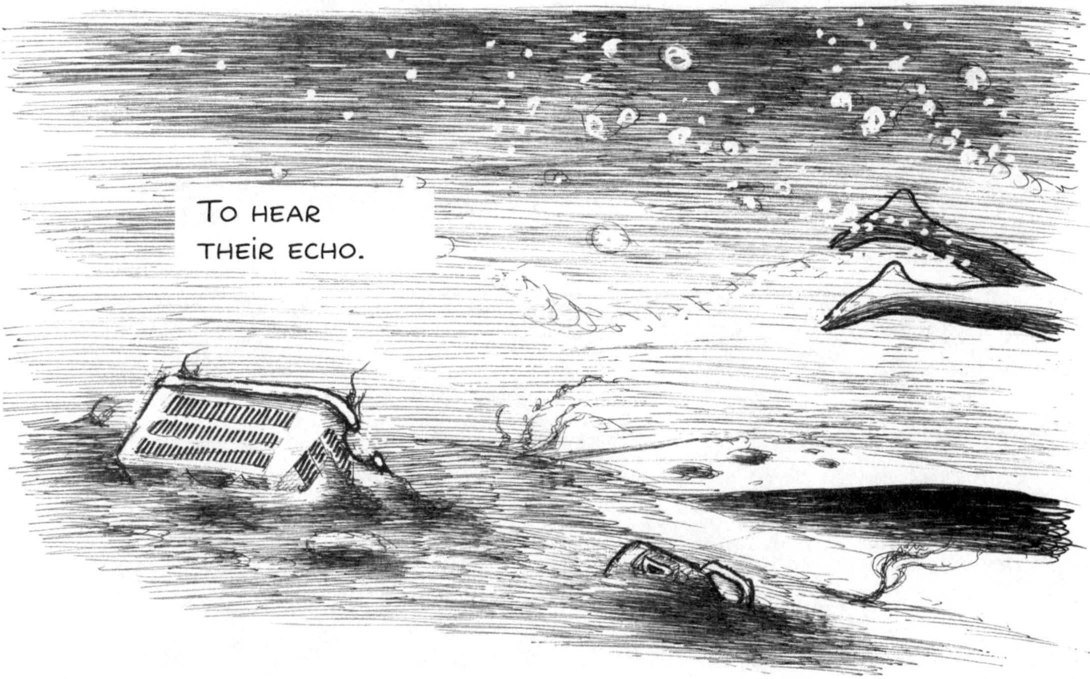
TO HEAR THEIR ECHO.

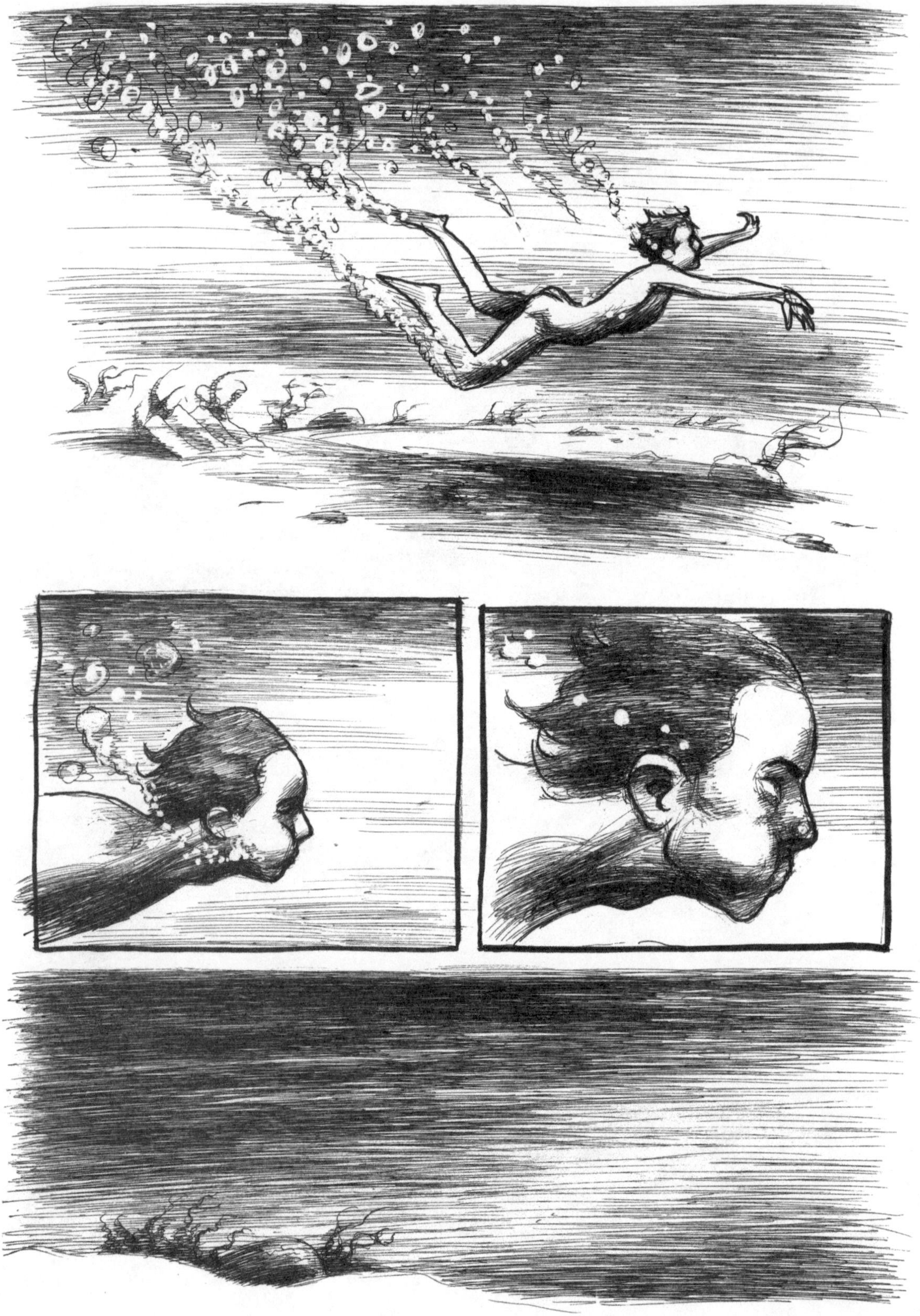

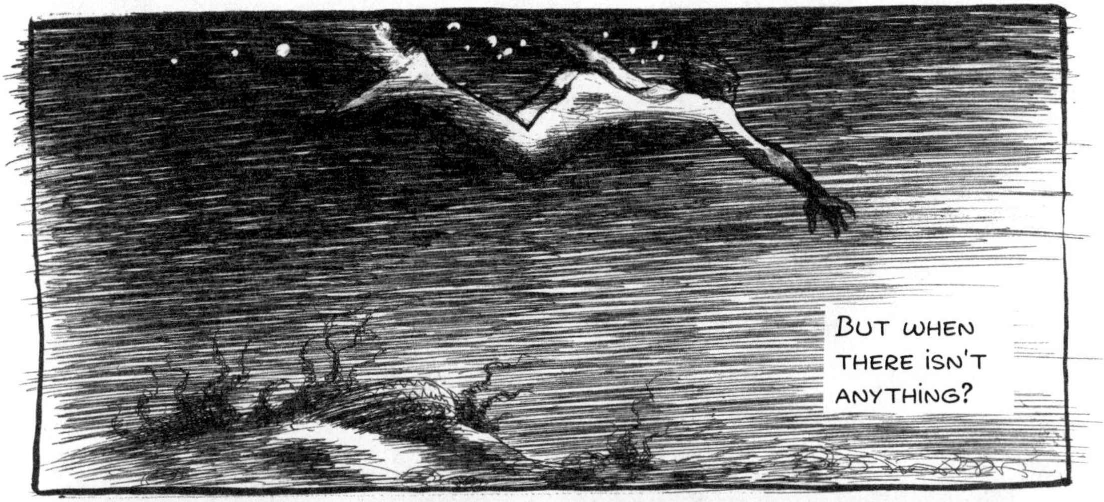
But when
there isn't
anything?

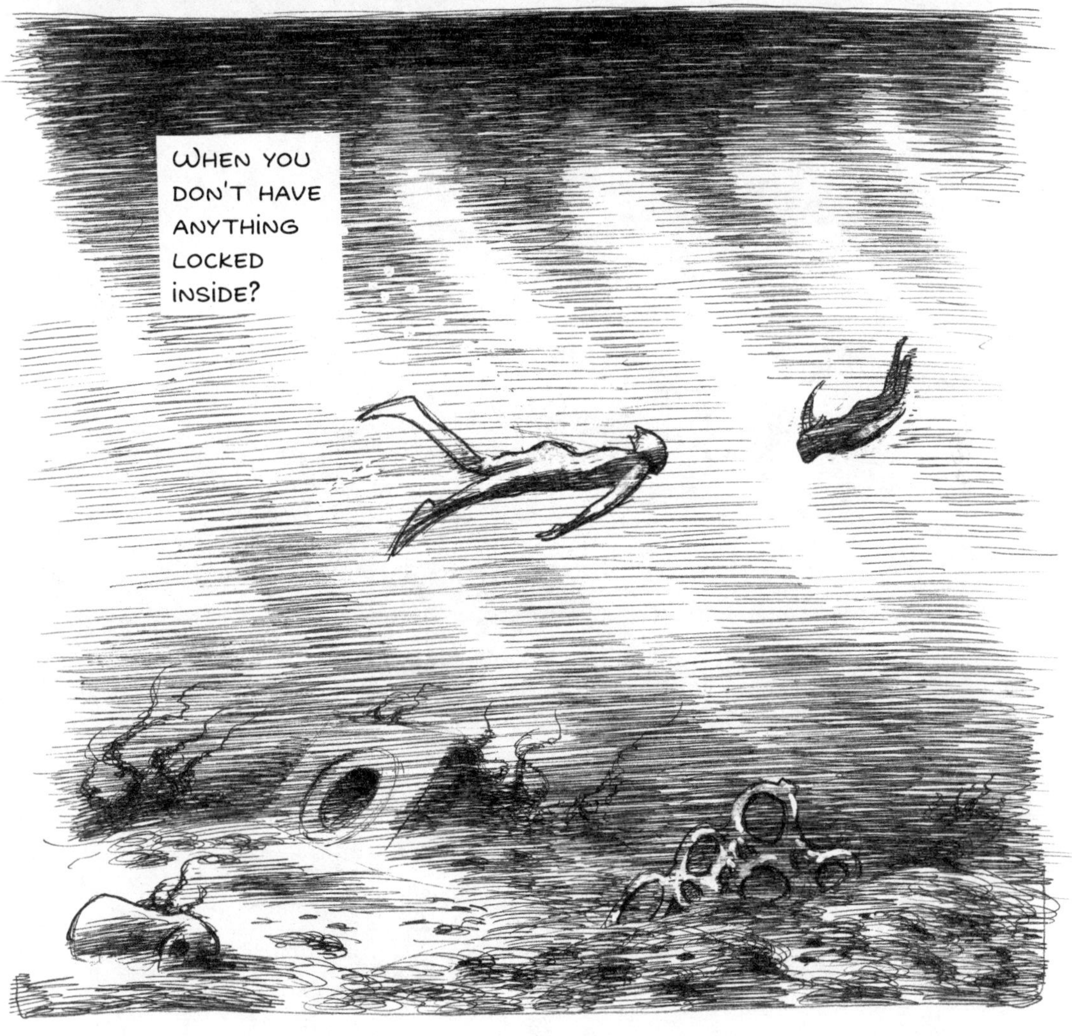
When you
don't have
anything
locked
inside?

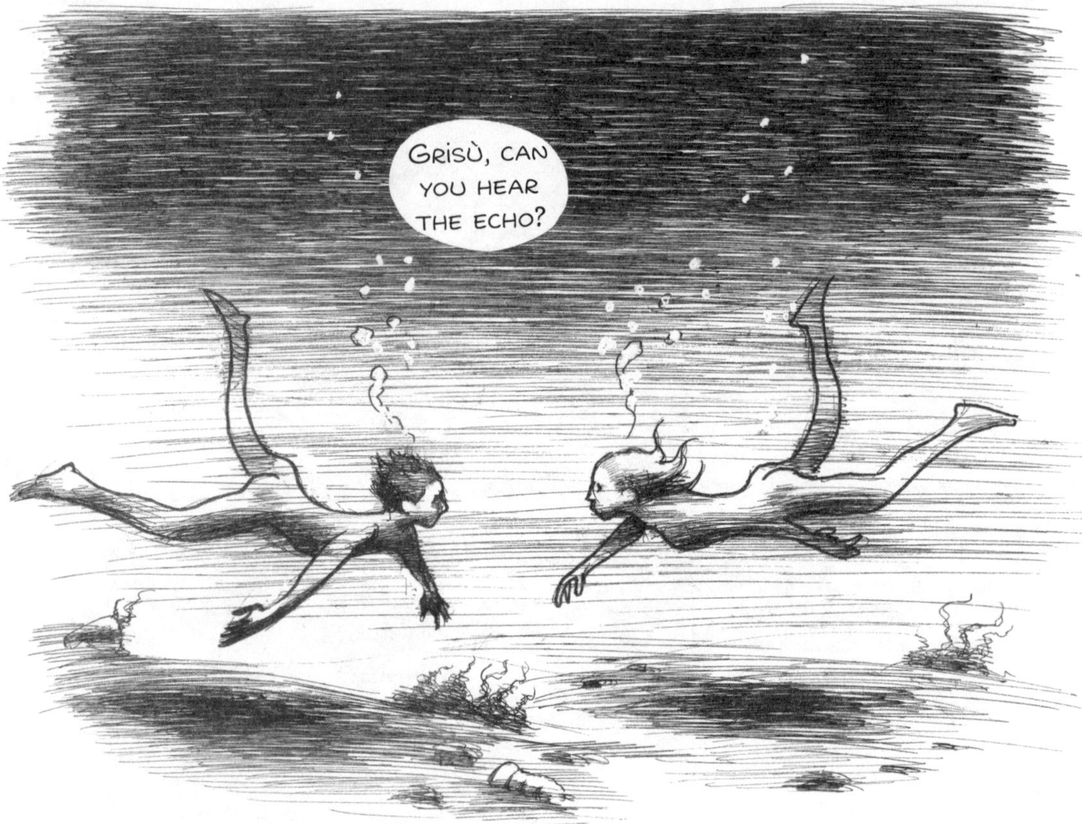
GRISÙ, CAN YOU HEAR THE ECHO?

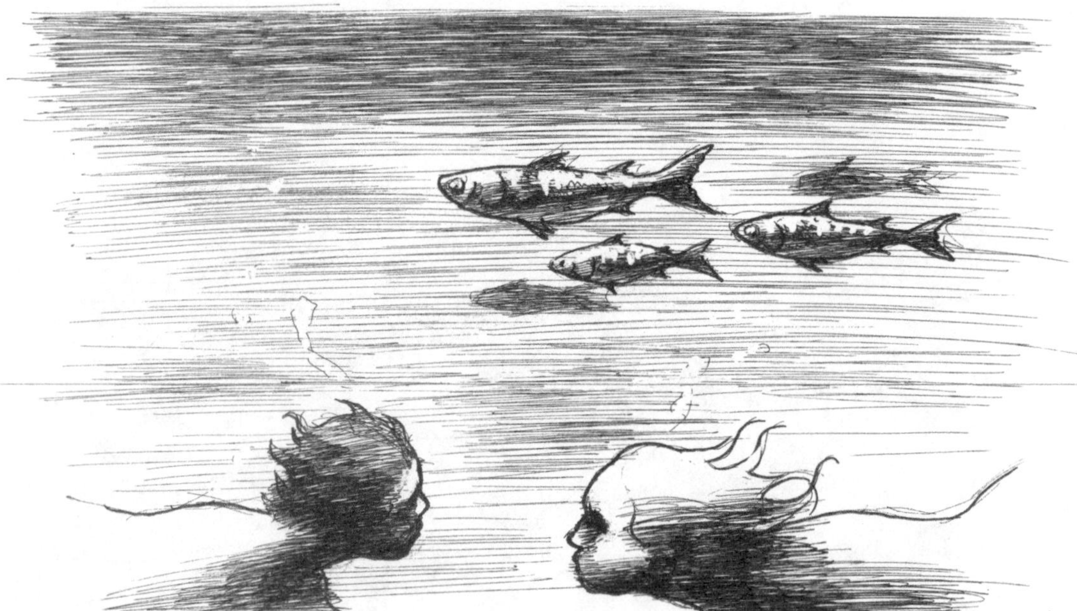

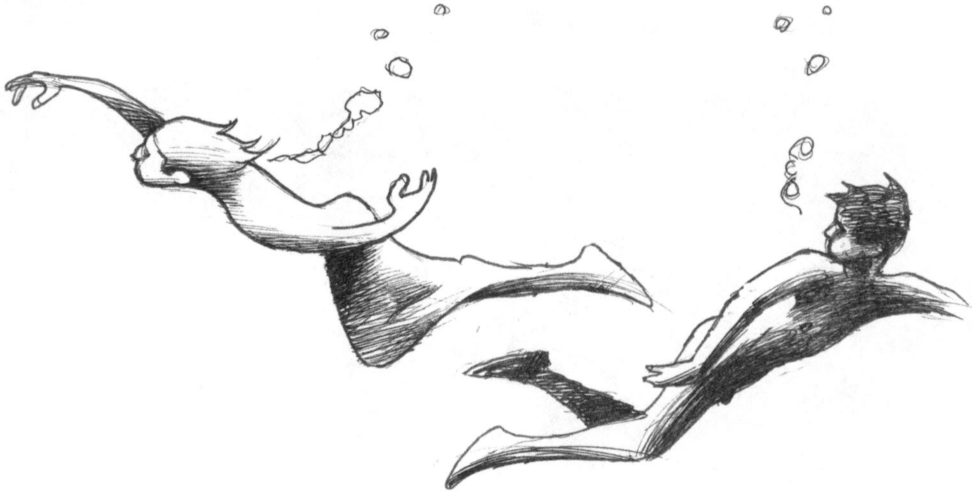

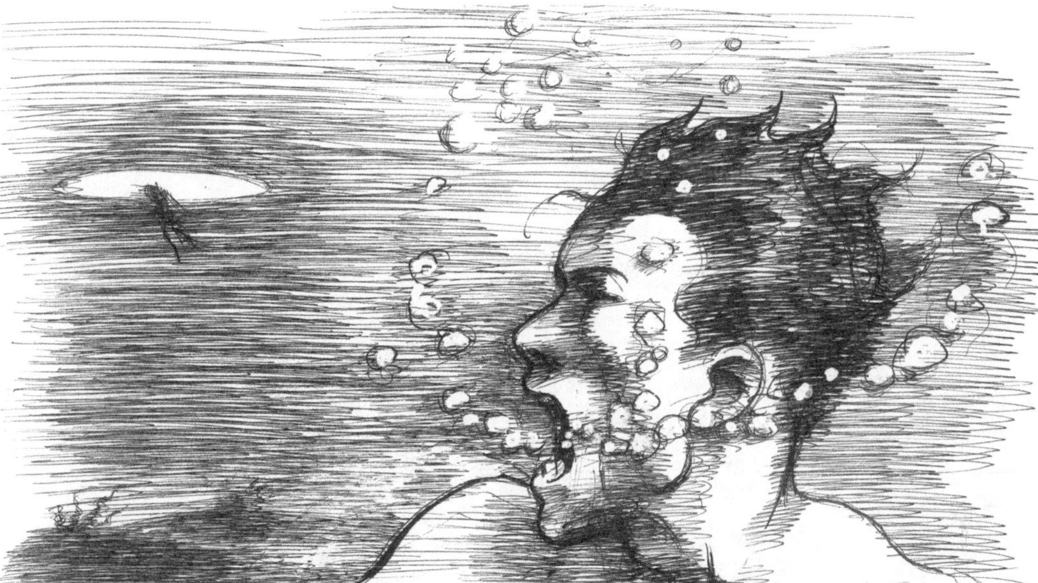

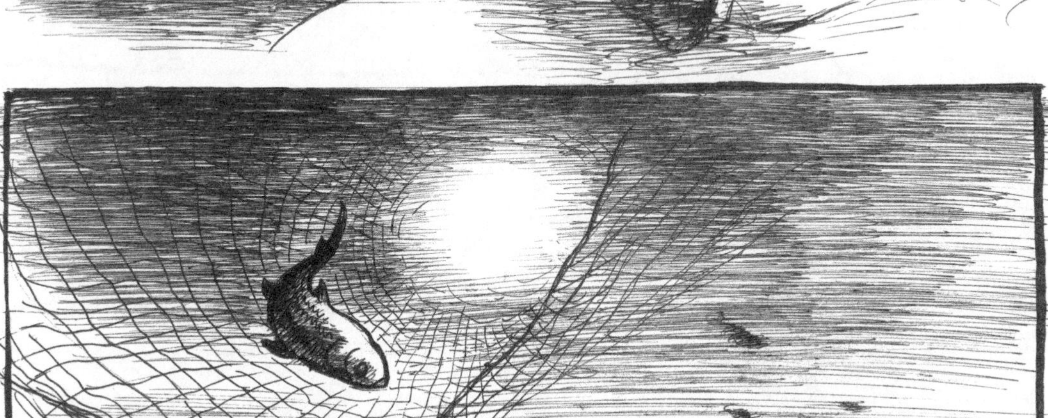

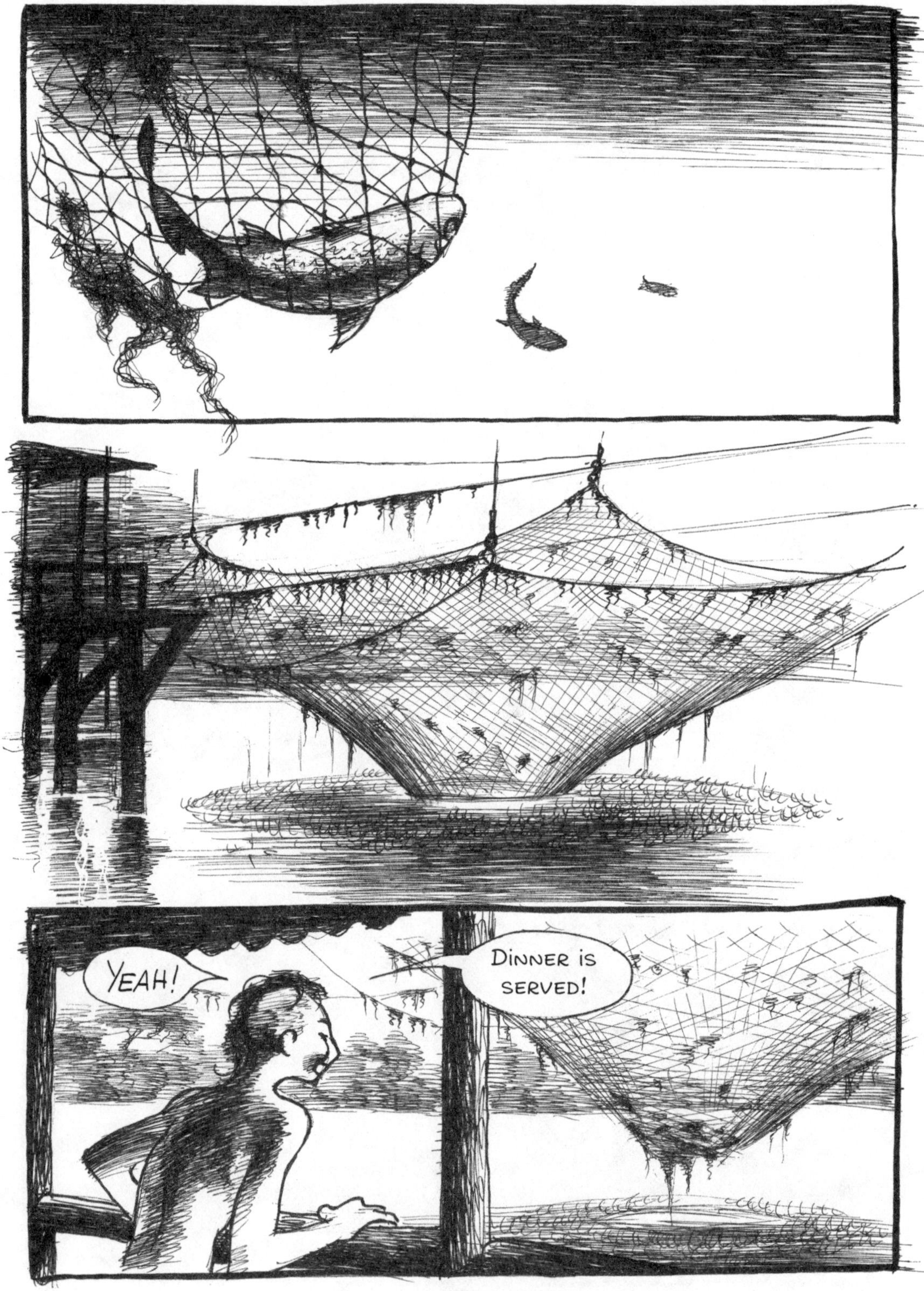

YEAH!
DINNER IS SERVED!

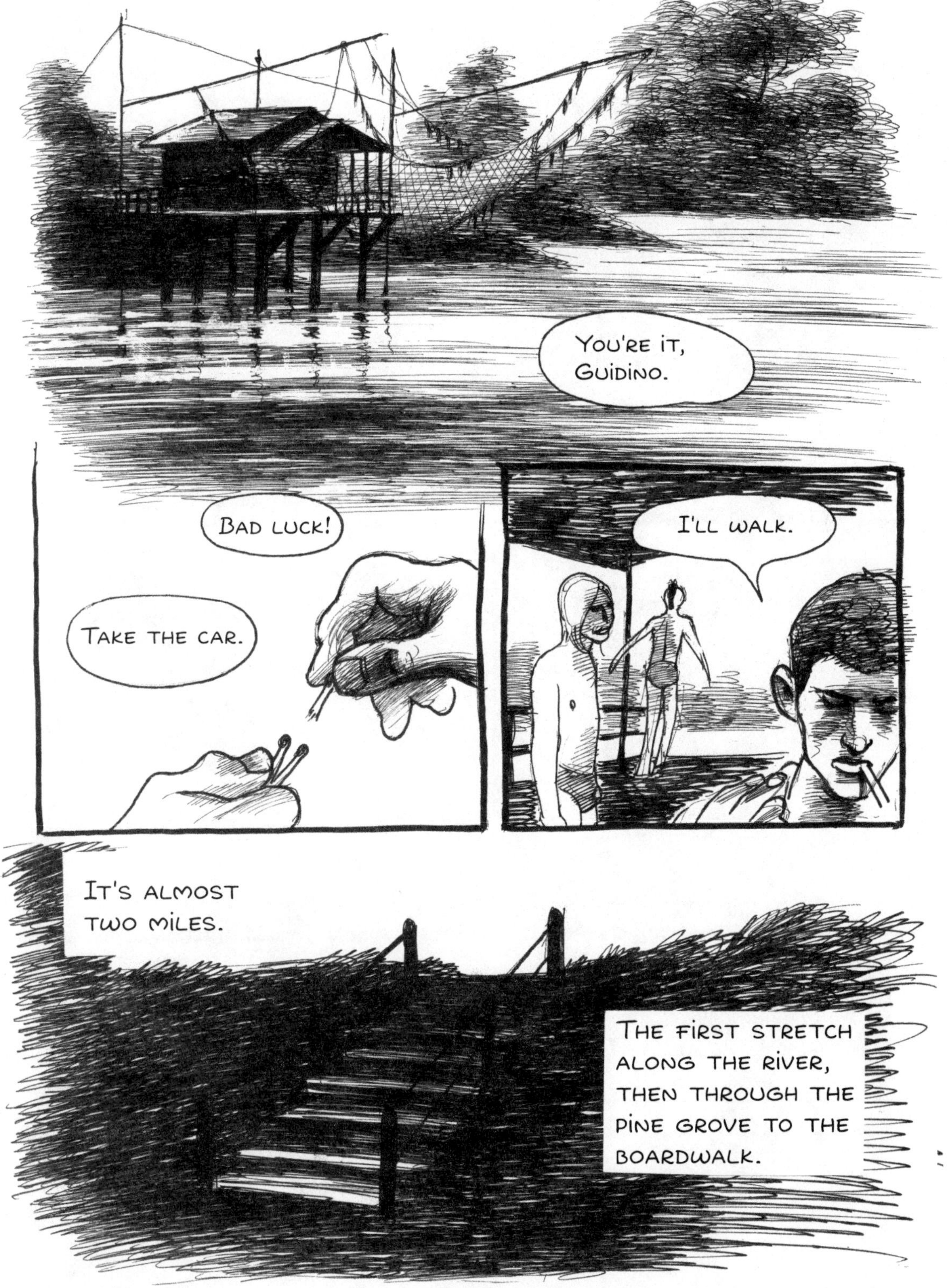
You're it, Guidino.
Bad luck!
Take the car.
I'll walk.
It's almost two miles.
The first stretch along the river, then through the pine grove to the boardwalk.

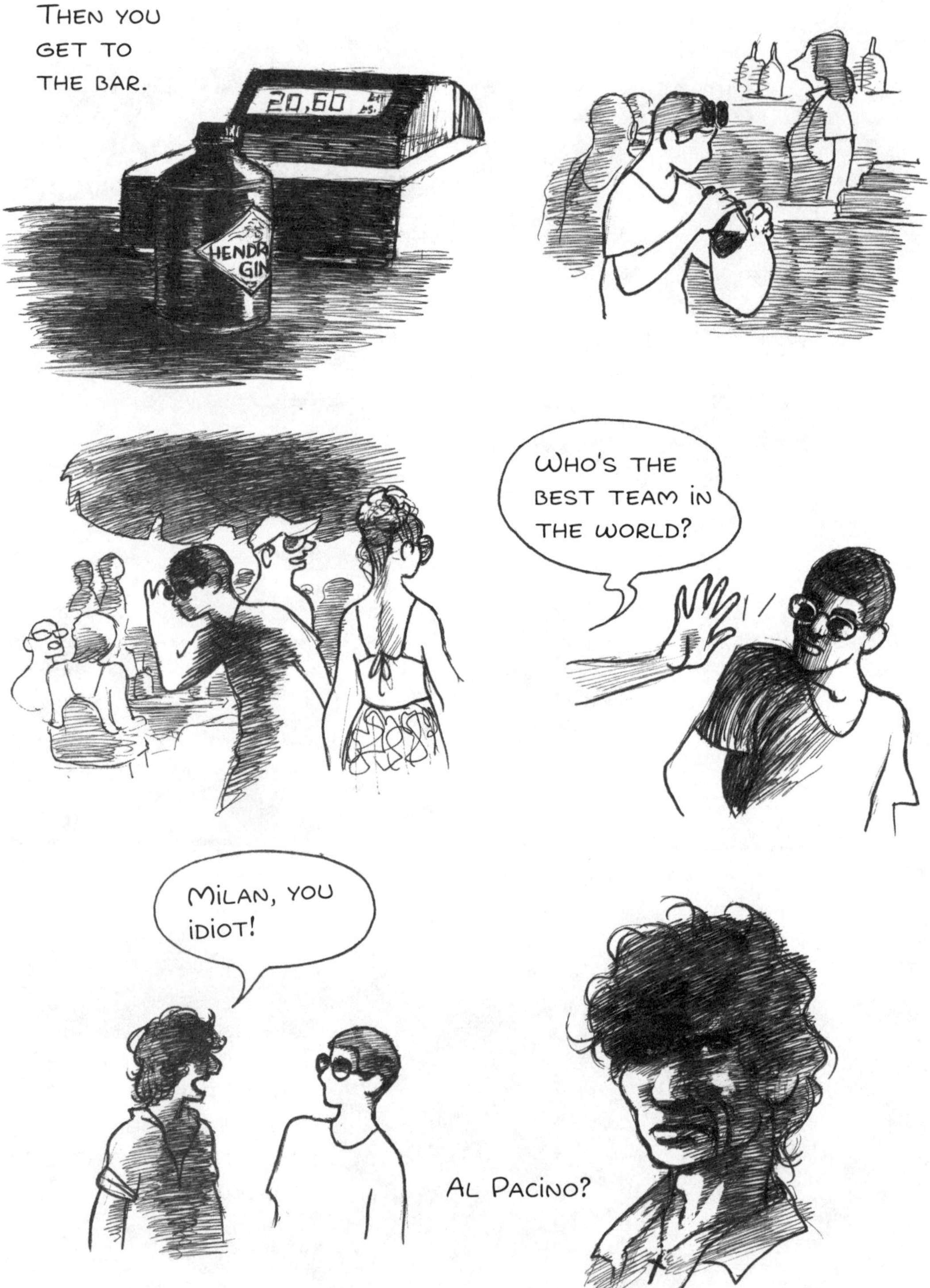
Then you get to the bar.
20,60
Who's the best team in the world?
Milan, you idiot!
Al Pacino?

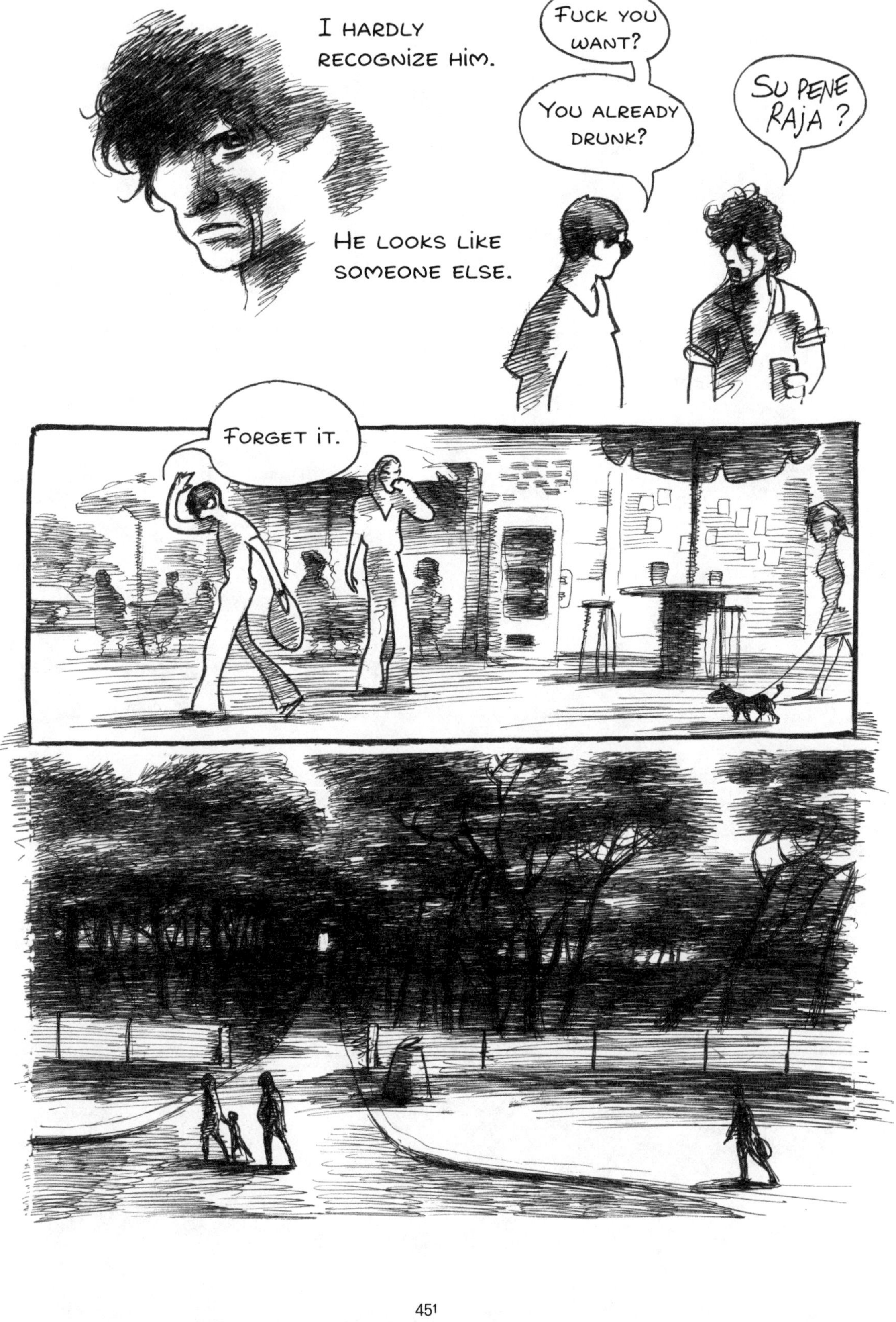
I HARDLY RECOGNIZE HIM.
HE LOOKS LIKE SOMEONE ELSE.
FUCK YOU WANT?
YOU ALREADY DRUNK?
SU PENE RAJA ?
FORGET IT.

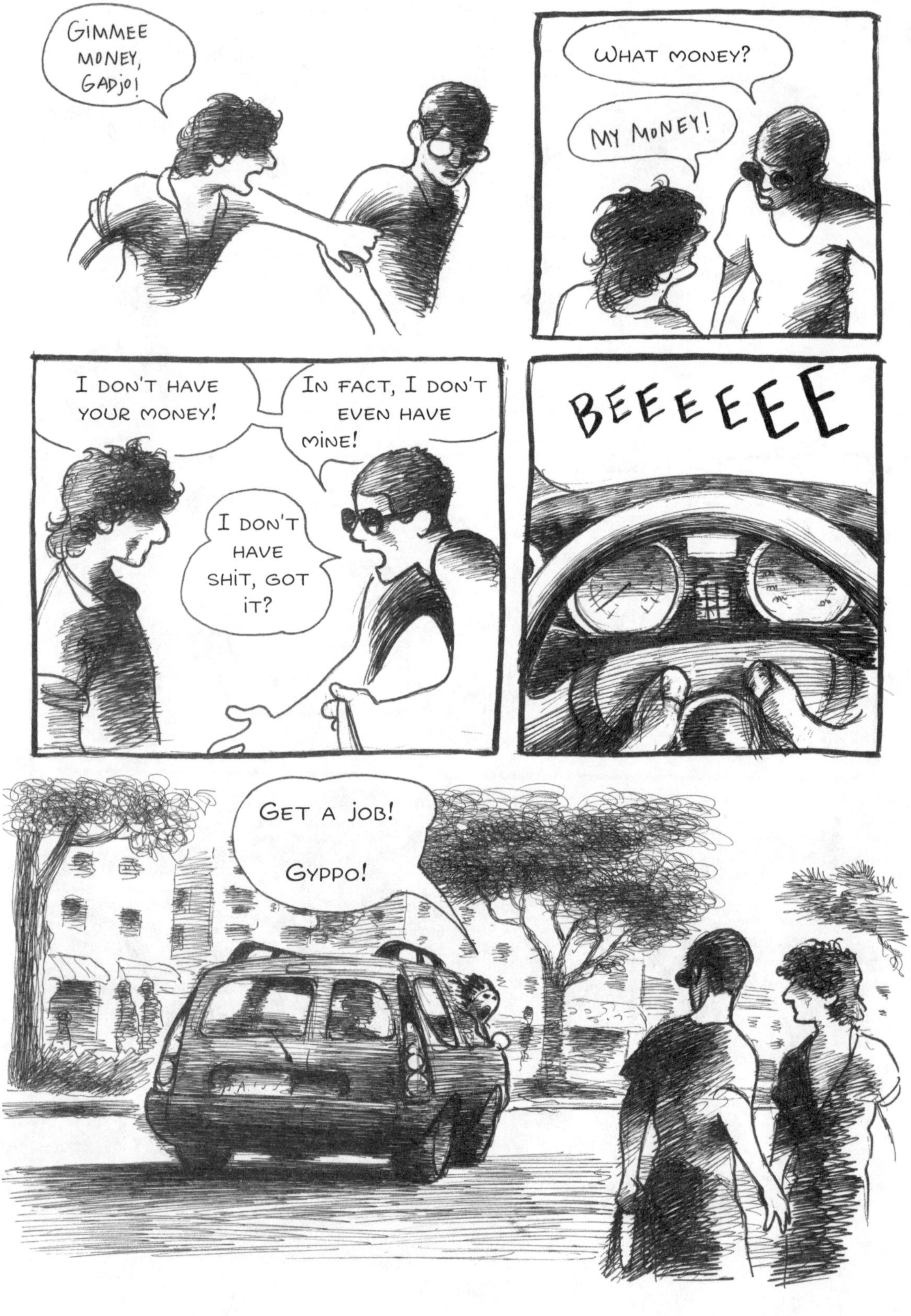
GIMMEE MONEY, GADJO!
WHAT MONEY?
MY MONEY!
I DON'T HAVE YOUR MONEY!
IN FACT, I DON'T EVEN HAVE MINE!
I DON'T HAVE SHIT, GOT IT?
BEEEEEE
GET A JOB!
GYPPO!

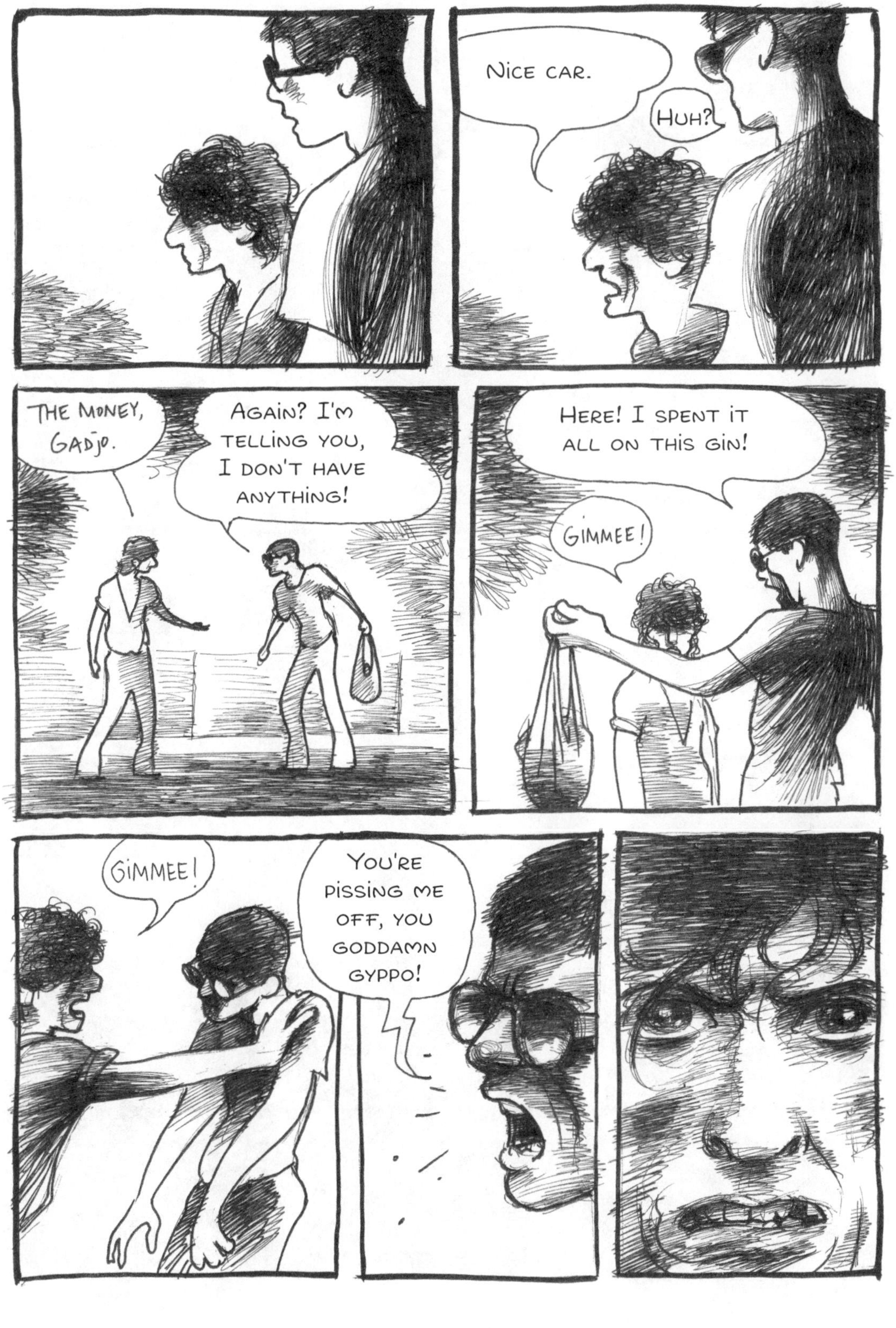
Nice car.
Huh?
The money, Gadjo.
Again? I'm telling you, I don't have anything!
Here! I spent it all on this gin!
Gimmee!
Gimmee!
You're pissing me off, you goddamn gyppo!

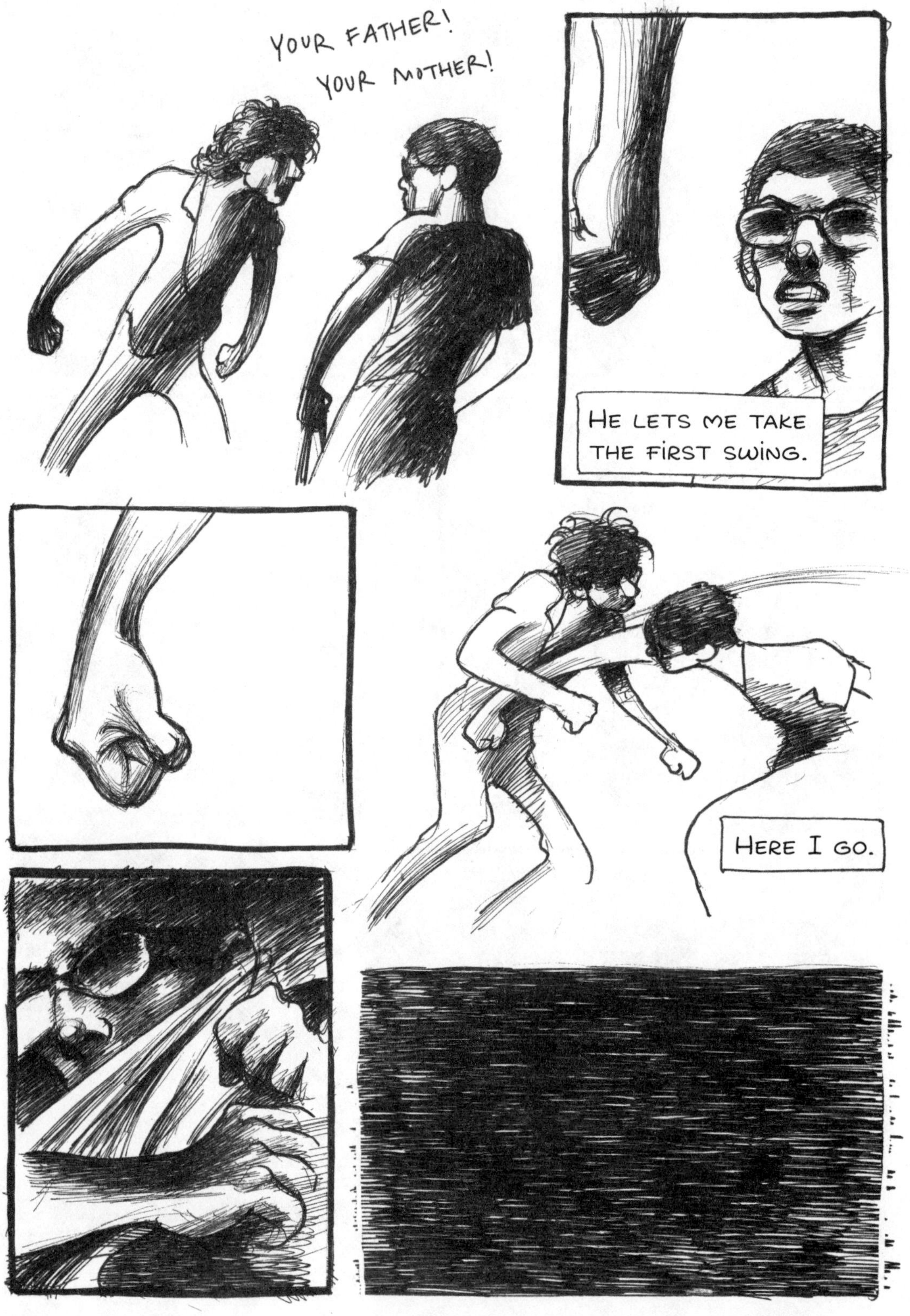
YOUR FATHER!
YOUR MOTHER!
HE LETS ME TAKE THE FIRST SWING.
HERE I GO.

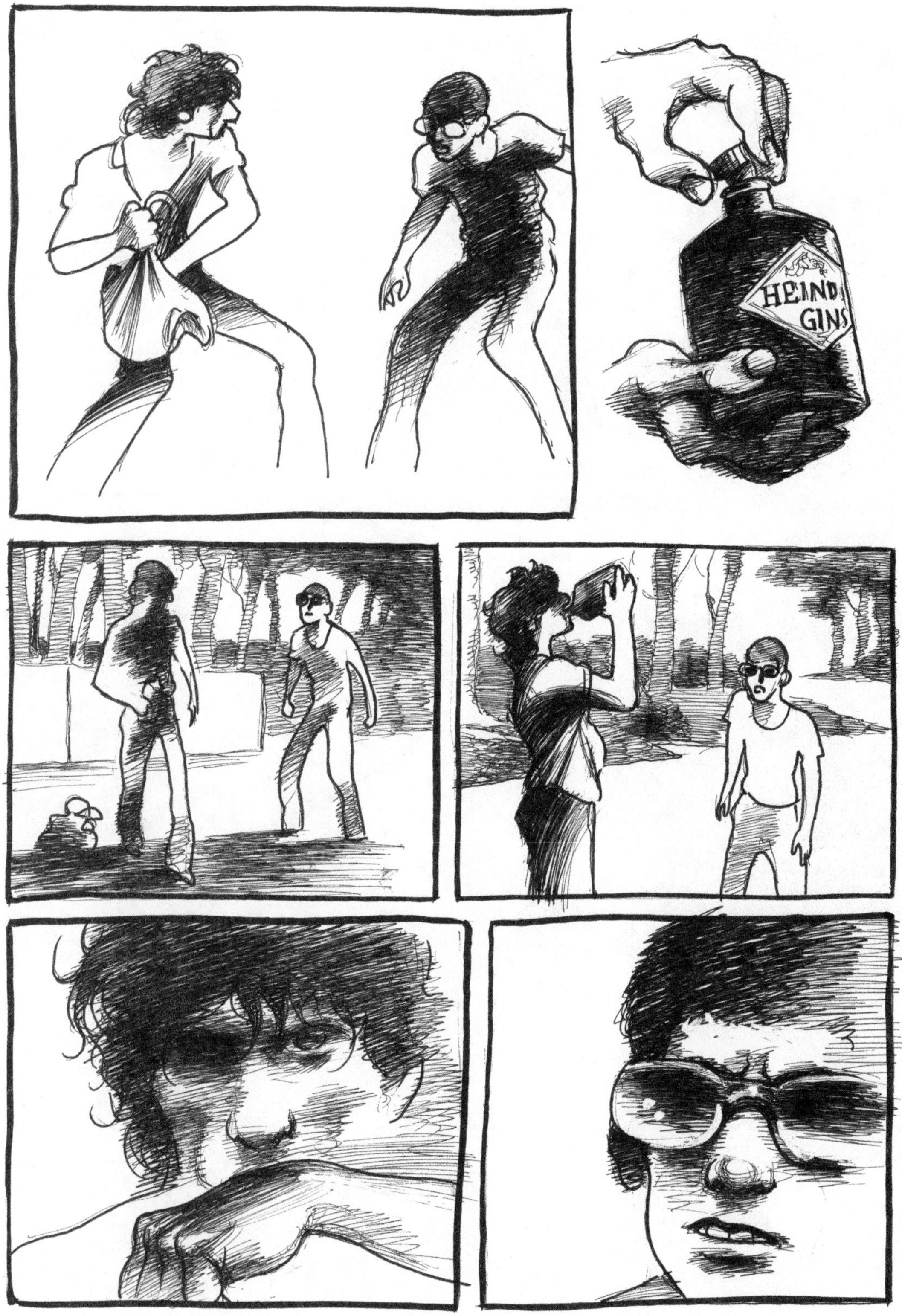
HEIND
GINS

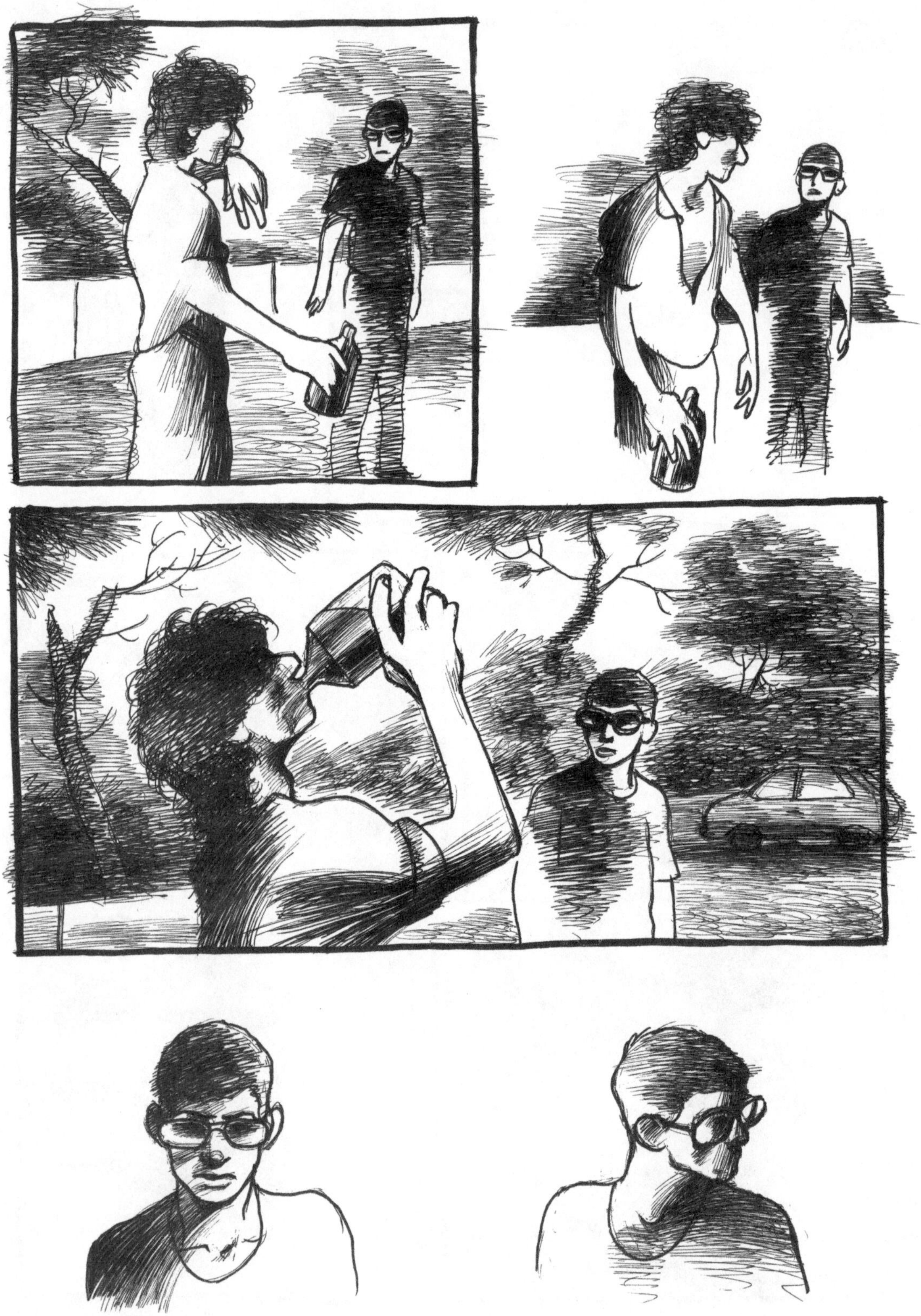

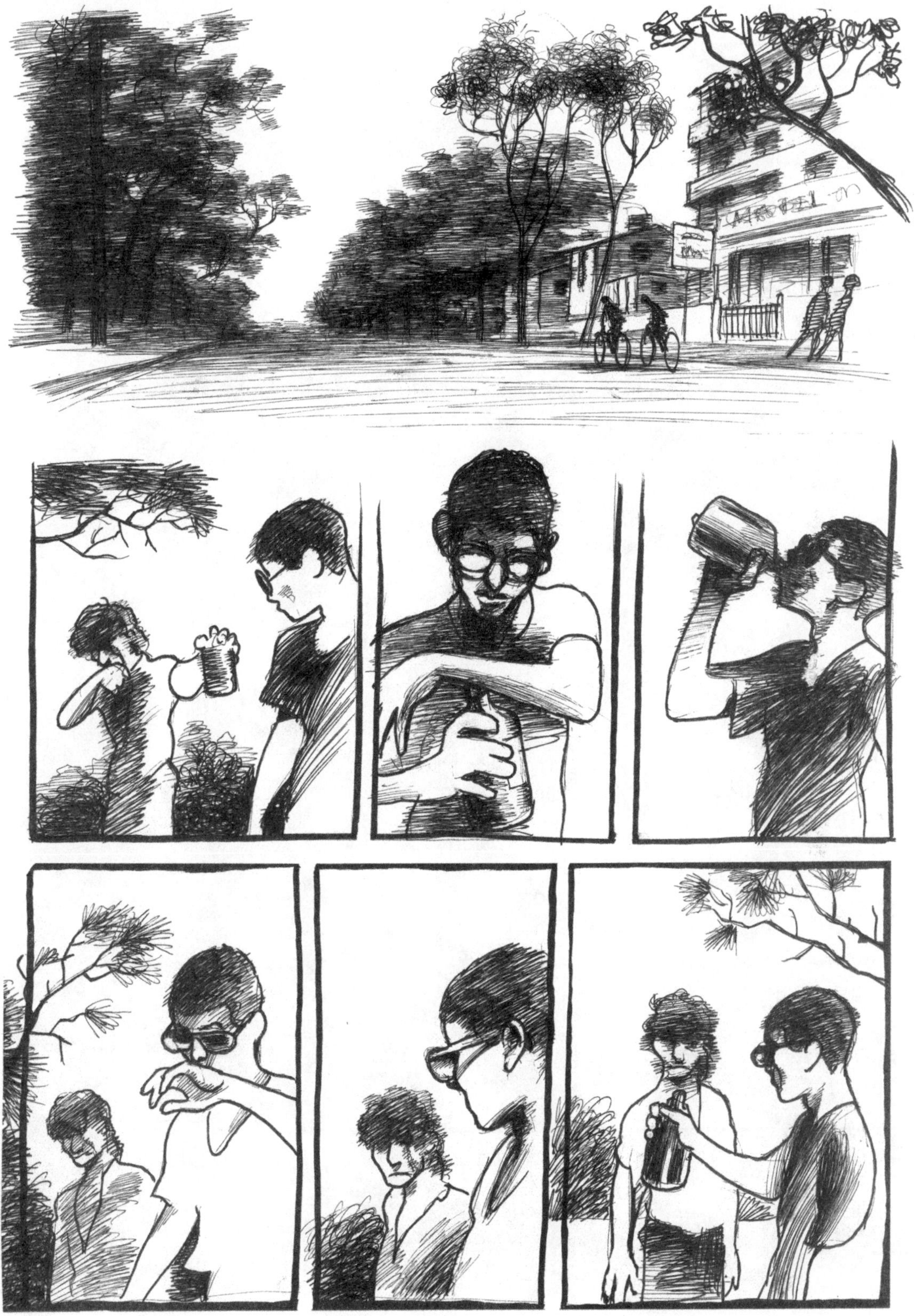

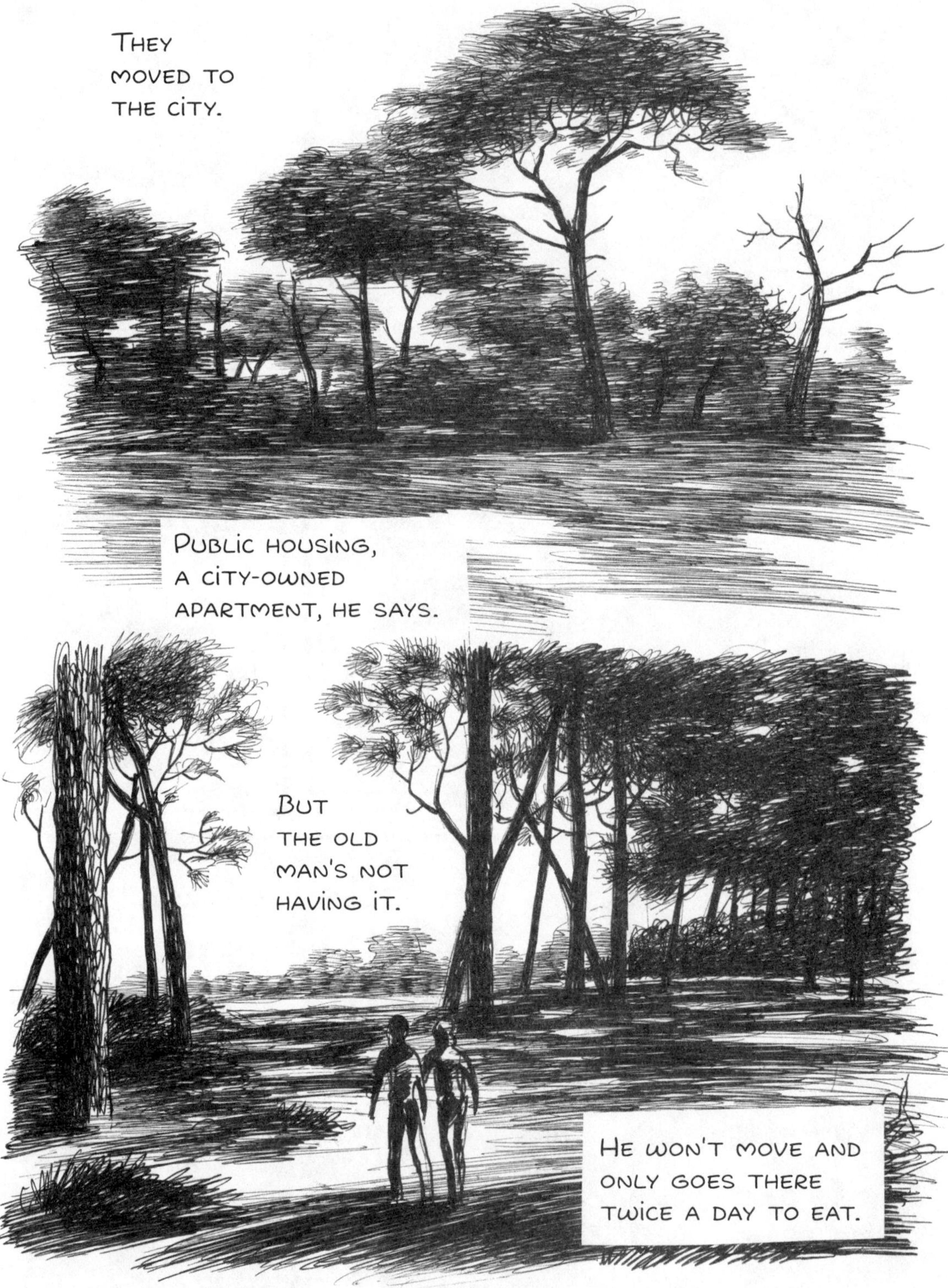
They moved to the city.
Public housing, a city-owned apartment, he says.
But the old man's not having it.
He won't move and only goes there twice a day to eat.

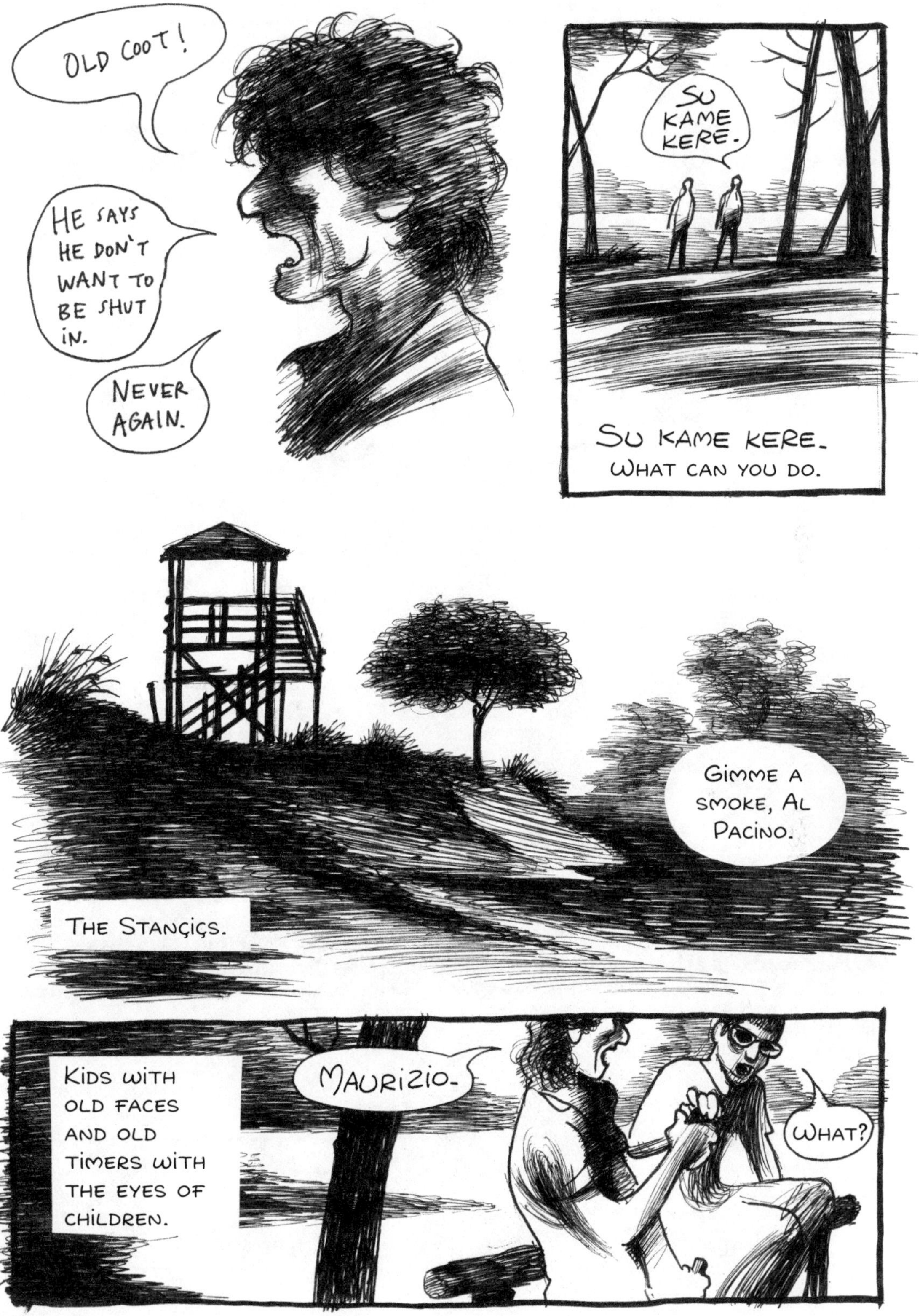
OLD COOT!
HE SAYS HE DON'T WANT TO BE SHUT IN.
NEVER AGAIN.
SU KAME KERE.
SU KAME KERE.
WHAT CAN YOU DO.
GIMME A SMOKE, AL PACINO.
THE STANÇIÇS.
KIDS WITH OLD FACES AND OLD TIMERS WITH THE EYES OF CHILDREN.
MAURIZIO.
WHAT?

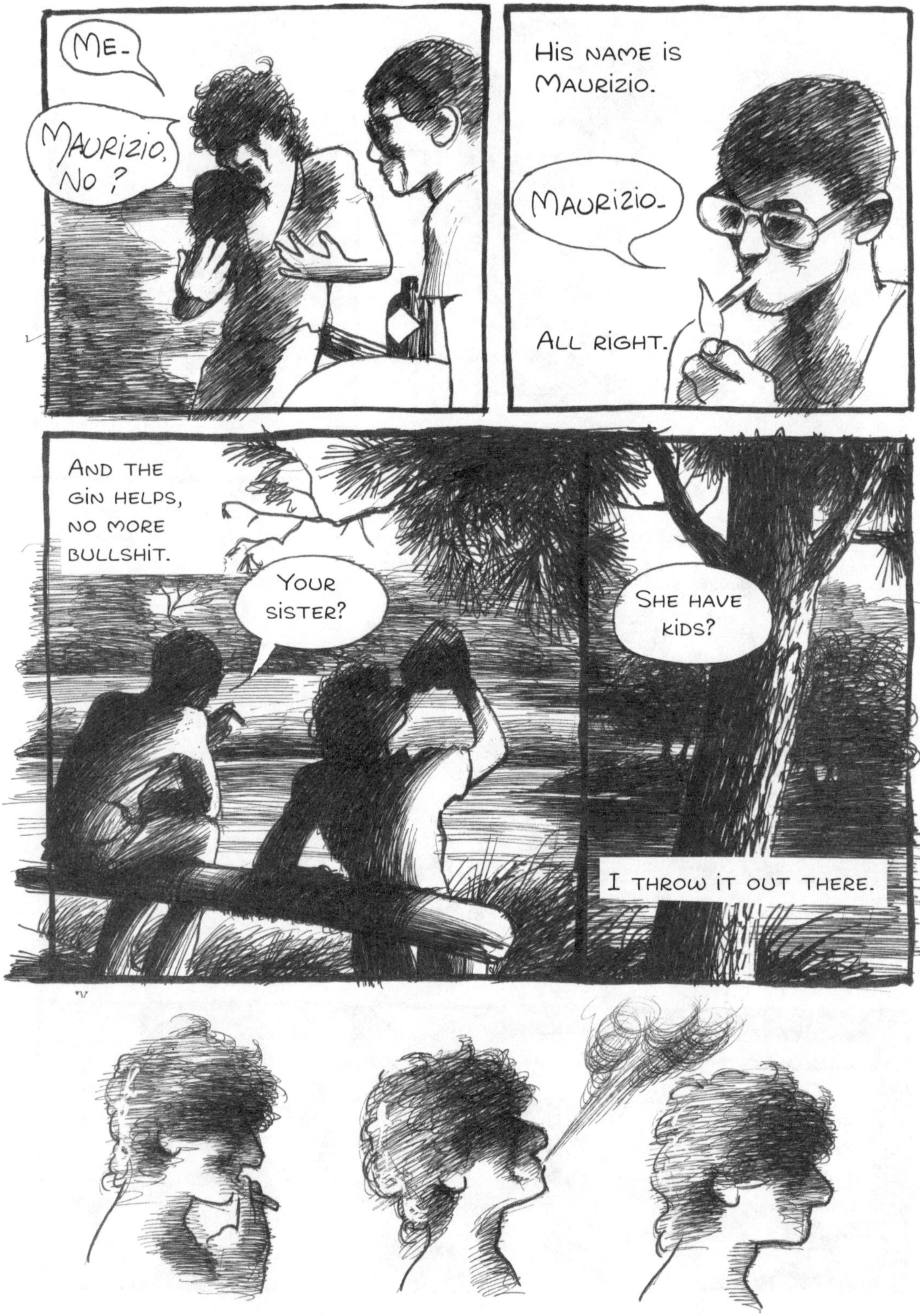
Me-
Maurizio, No ?
His name is Maurizio.
Maurizio-
All right.
And the gin helps, no more bullshit.
Your sister?
She have kids?
I throw it out there.

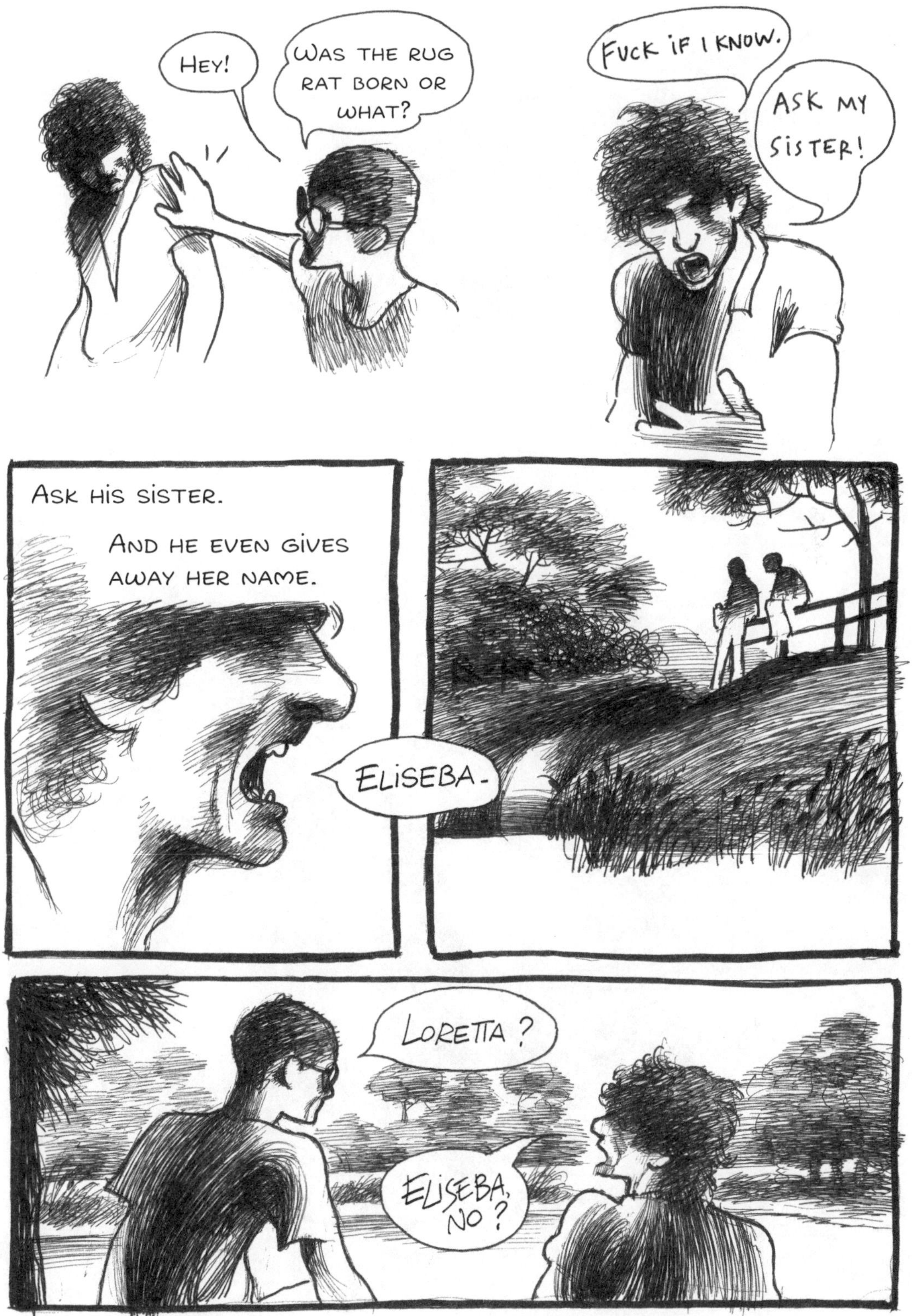
HEY!
WAS THE RUG RAT BORN OR WHAT?
FUCK IF I KNOW.
ASK MY SISTER!
ASK HIS SISTER.
AND HE EVEN GIVES AWAY HER NAME.
ELISEBA.
LORETTA?
ELISEBA, NO?

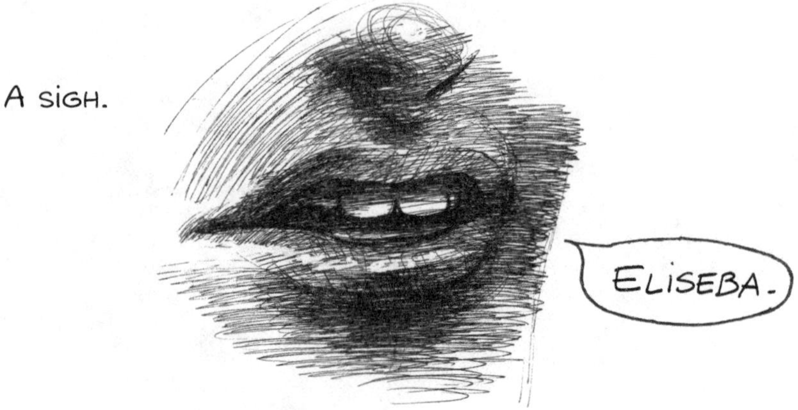
A SIGH.
ELISEBA.

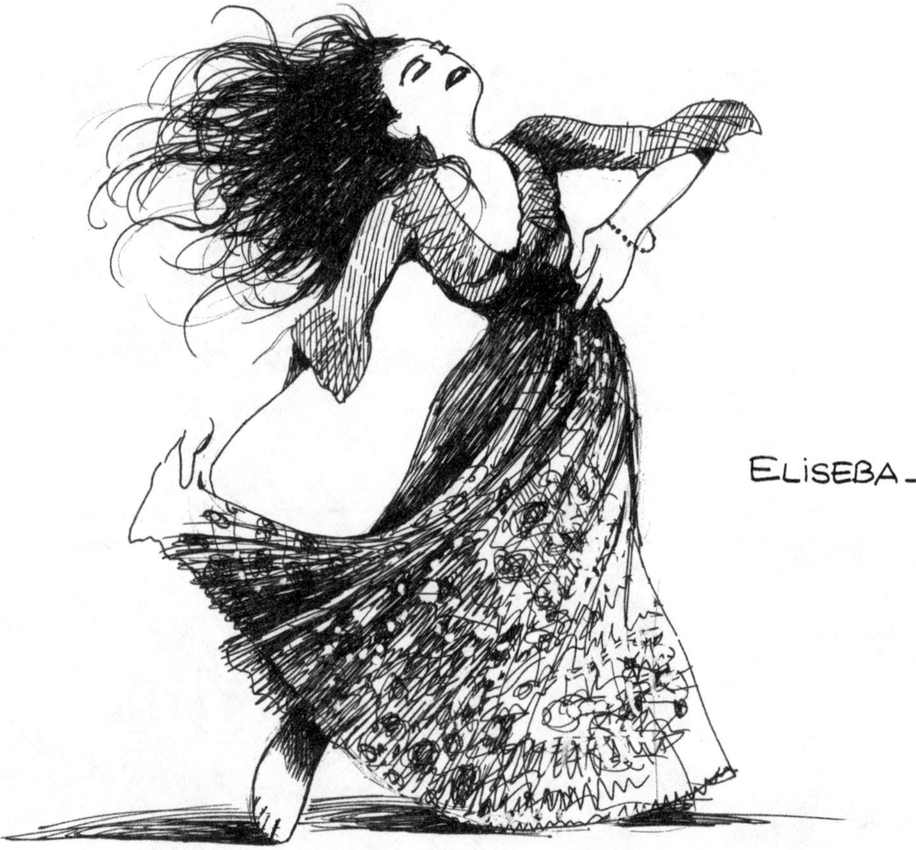
ELISEBA.

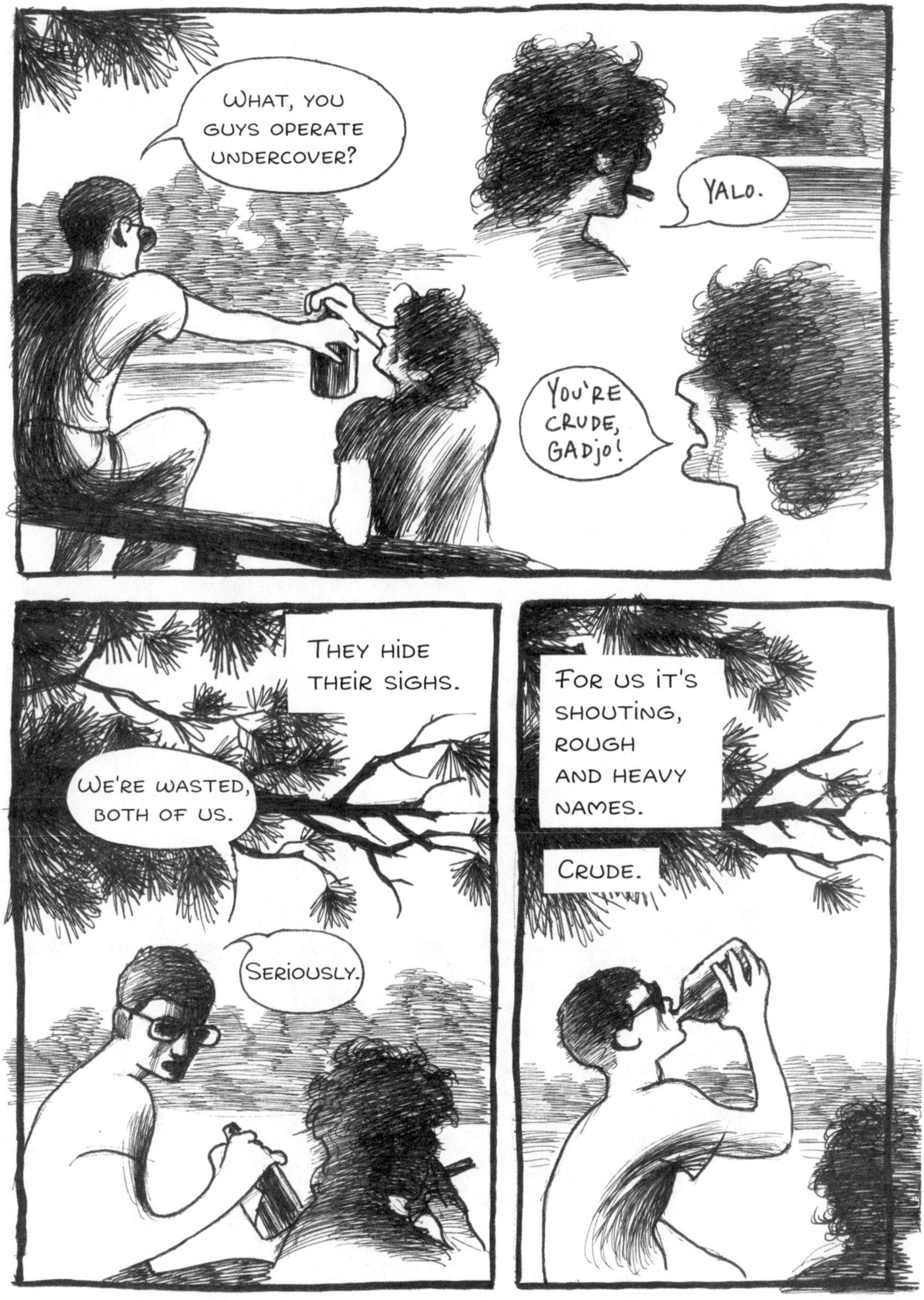
WHAT, YOU GUYS OPERATE UNDERCOVER?
YALO.
YOU'RE CRUDE, GADjo!
THEY HIDE THEIR SIGHS.
WE'RE WASTED, BOTH OF US.
SERIOUSLY.
FOR US IT'S SHOUTING, ROUGH AND HEAVY NAMES.
CRUDE.

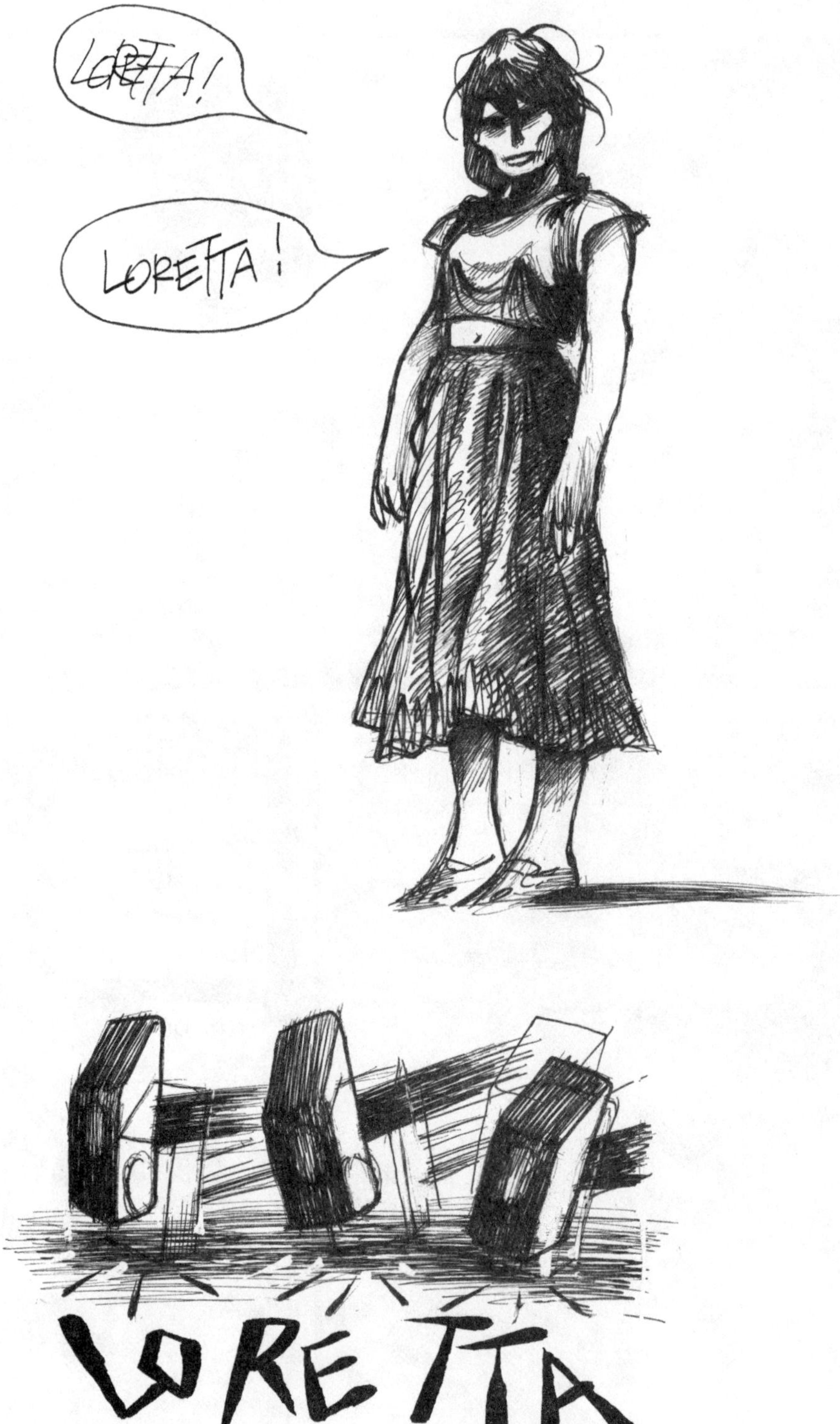
LORETTA!
LORETTA!
LORETTA

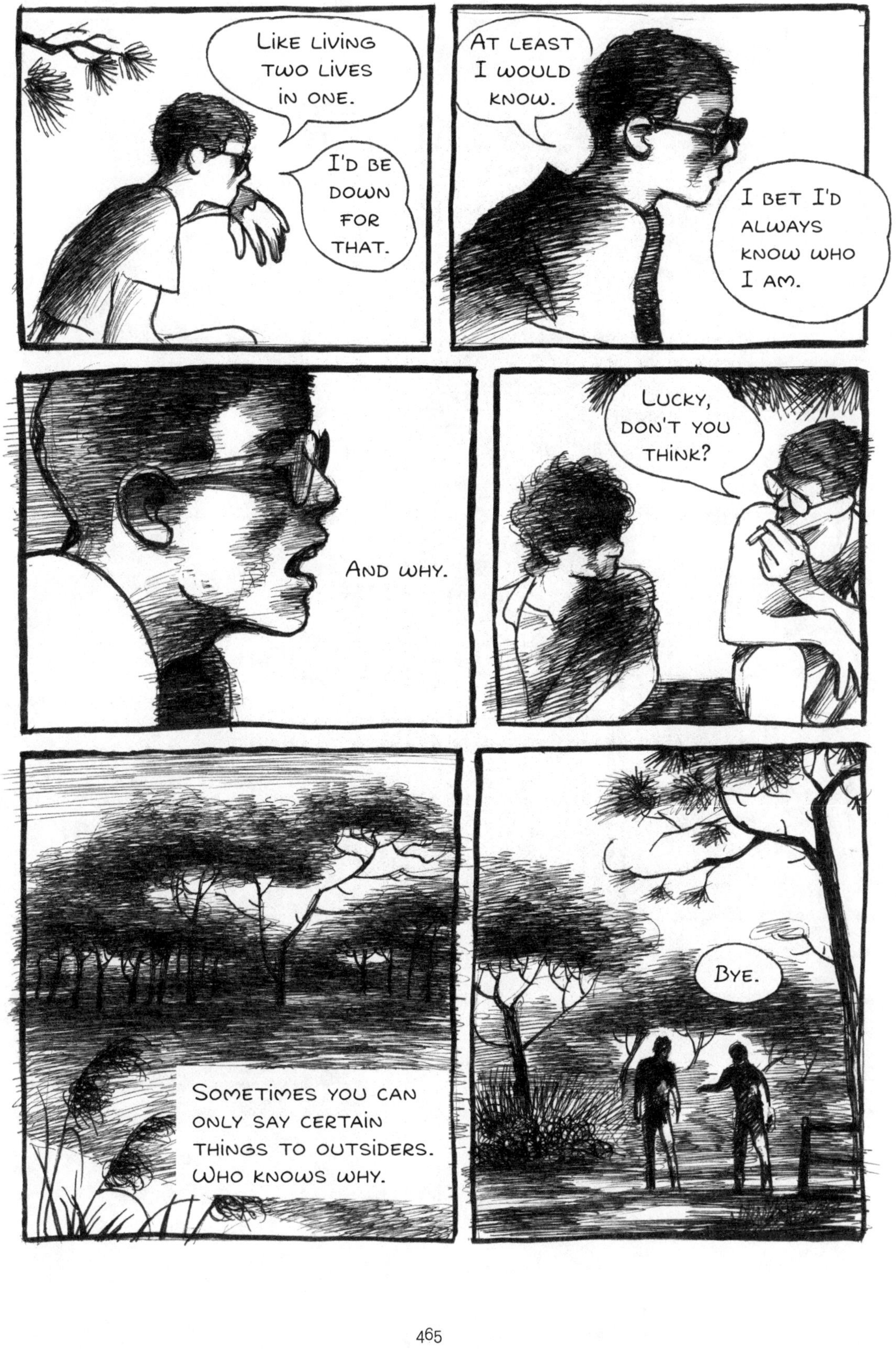
Like living two lives in one.
I'd be down for that.
At least I would know.
I bet I'd always know who I am.
And why.
Lucky, don't you think?
Sometimes you can only say certain things to outsiders. Who knows why.
Bye.

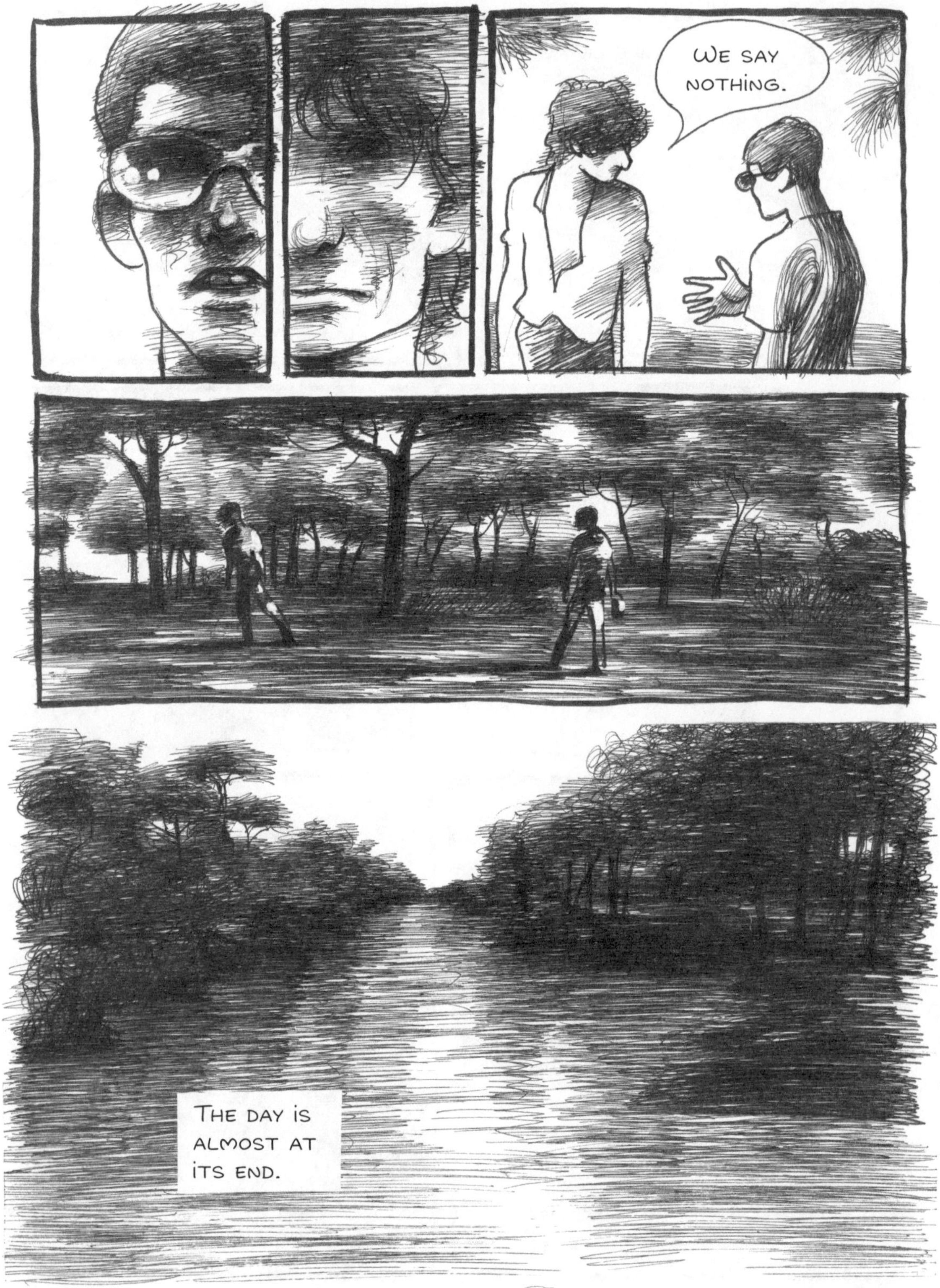
WE SAY
NOTHING.
THE DAY IS
ALMOST AT
ITS END.

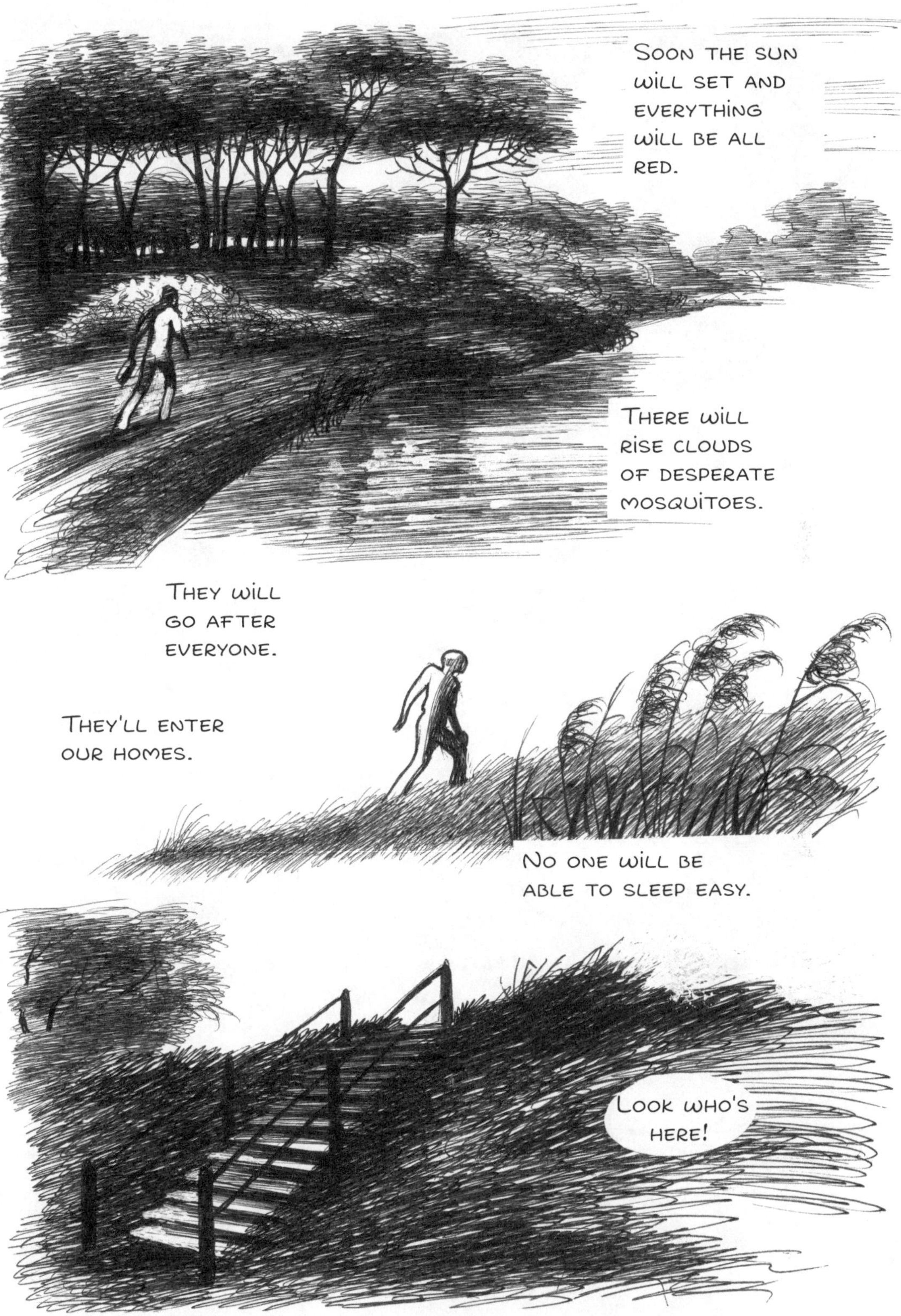
Soon the sun will set and everything will be all red.
There will rise clouds of desperate mosquitoes.
They will go after everyone.
They'll enter our homes.
No one will be able to sleep easy.
Look who's here!

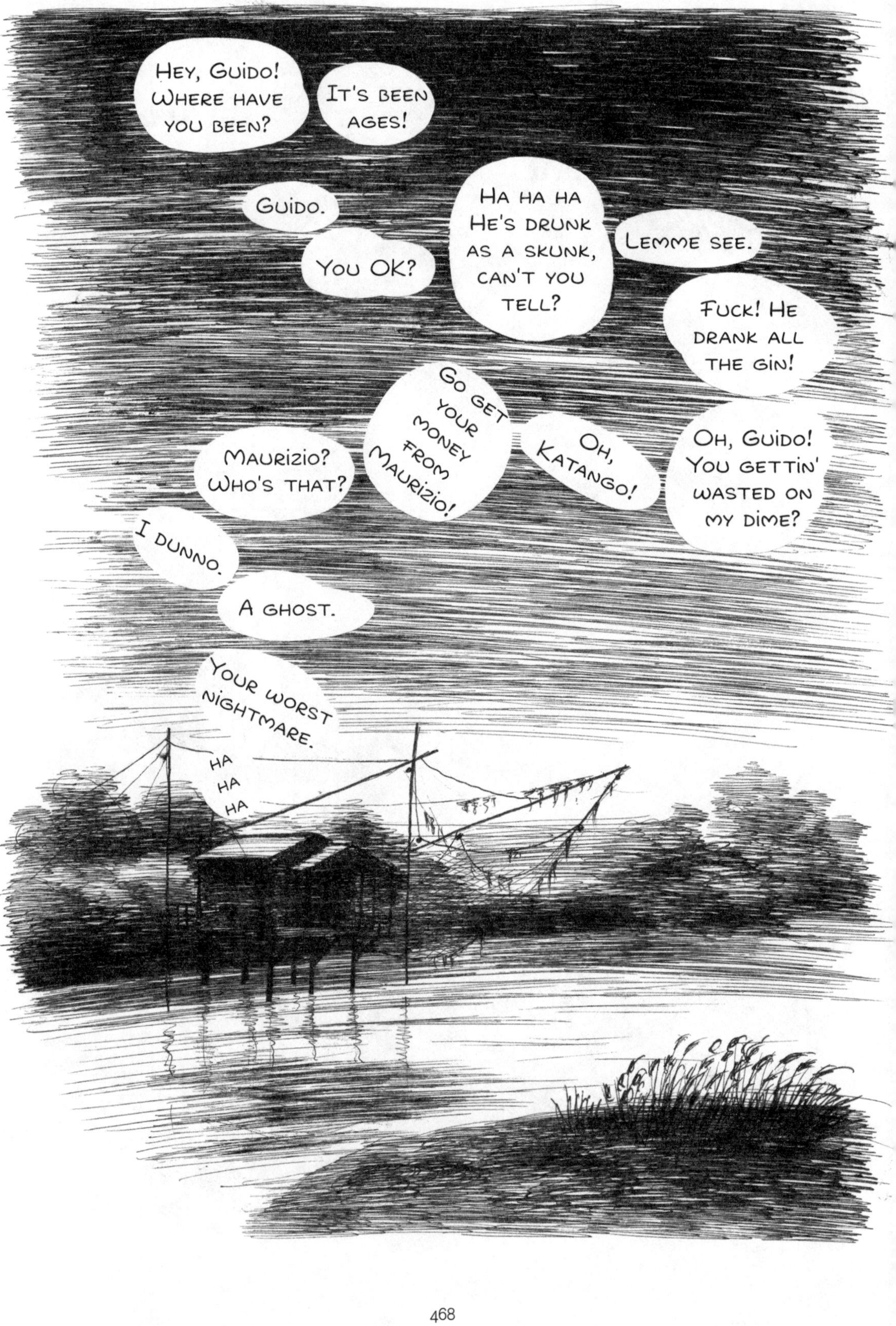

Hey, Guido! Where have you been?
It's been ages!
Guido.
You OK?
Ha ha ha He's drunk as a skunk, can't you tell?
Lemme see.
Fuck! He drank all the gin!
Go get your money from Maurizio!
Maurizio? Who's that?
Oh, Katango!
Oh, Guido! You gettin' wasted on my dime?
I dunno.
A ghost.
Your worst nightmare.
Ha ha ha

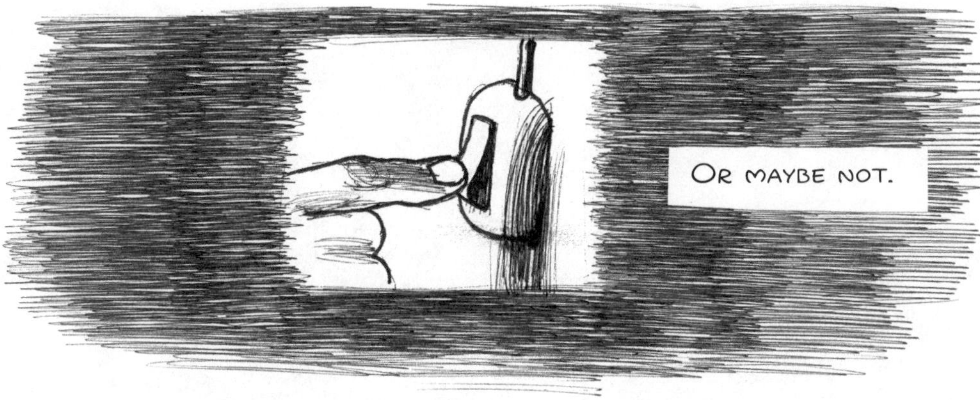
Or maybe not.

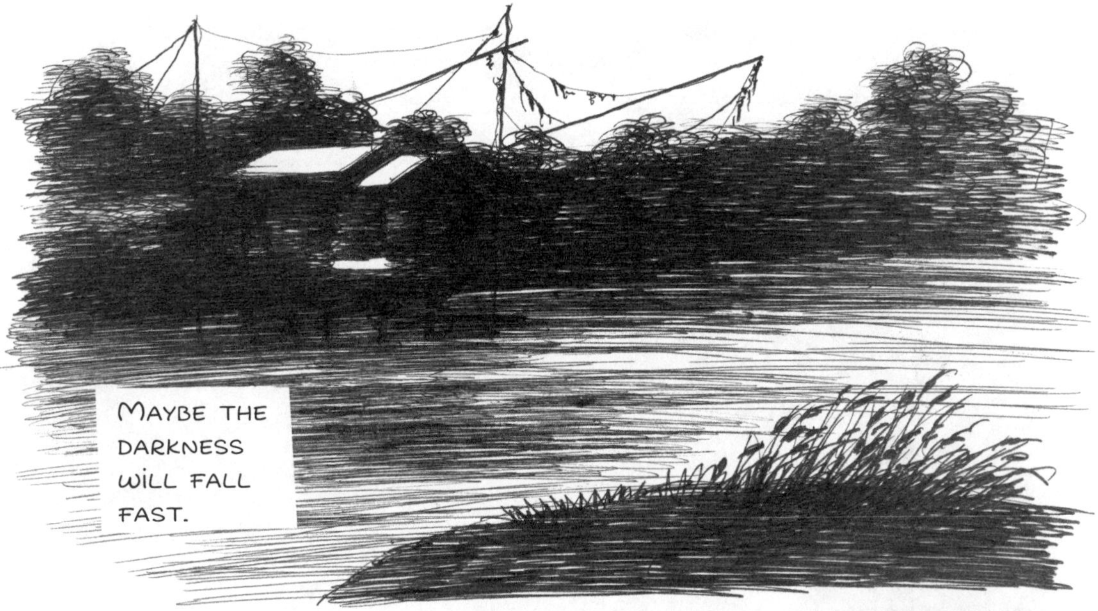
Maybe the darkness will fall fast.

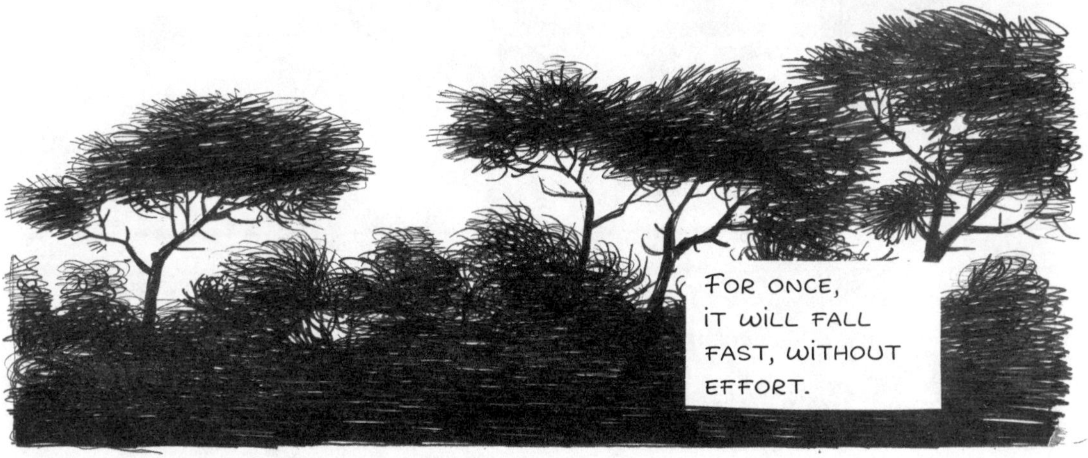
For once, it will fall fast, without effort.

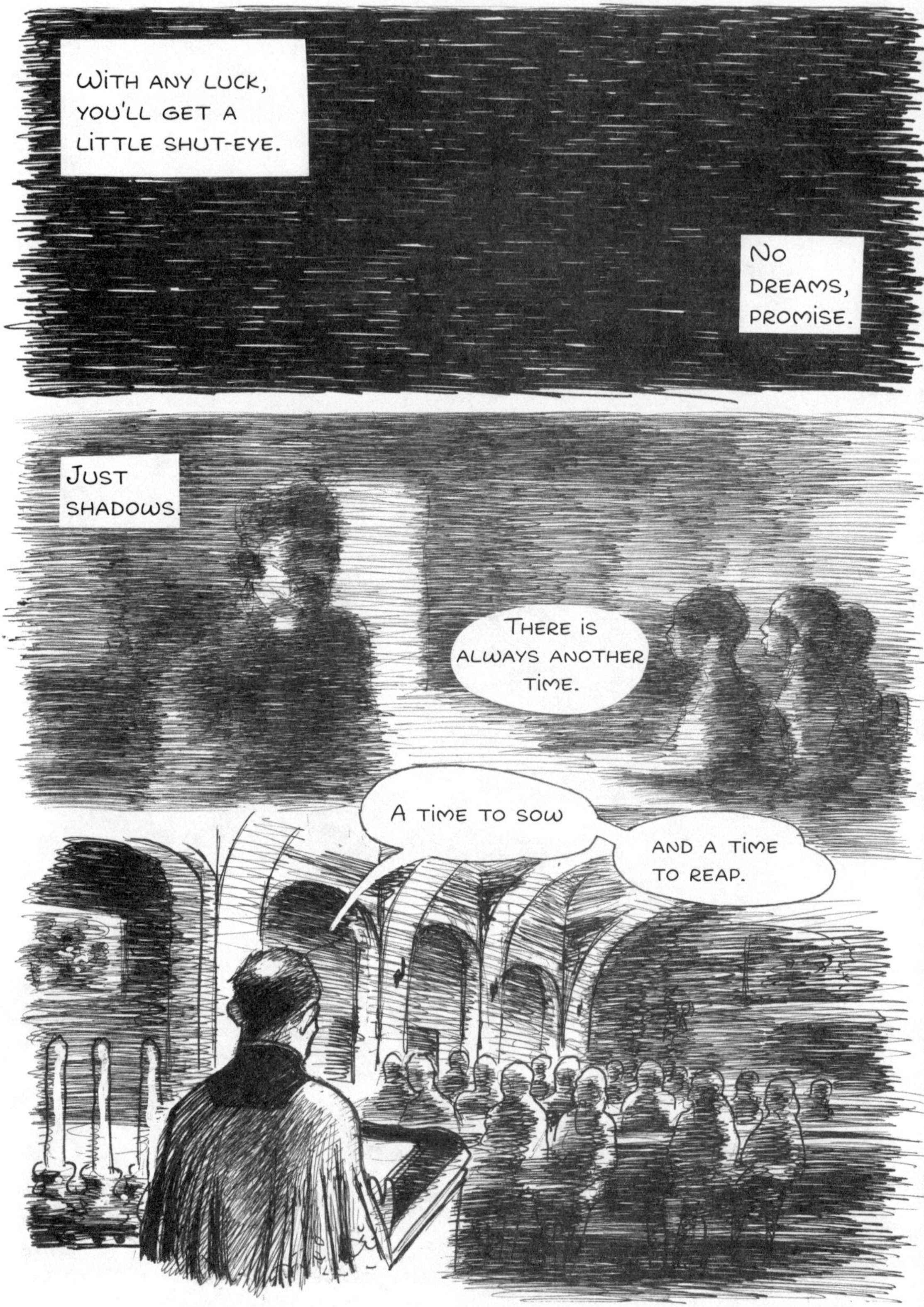
WITH ANY LUCK, YOU'LL GET A LITTLE SHUT-EYE.
NO DREAMS, PROMISE.
JUST SHADOWS.
THERE IS ALWAYS ANOTHER TIME.
A TIME TO SOW
AND A TIME TO REAP.

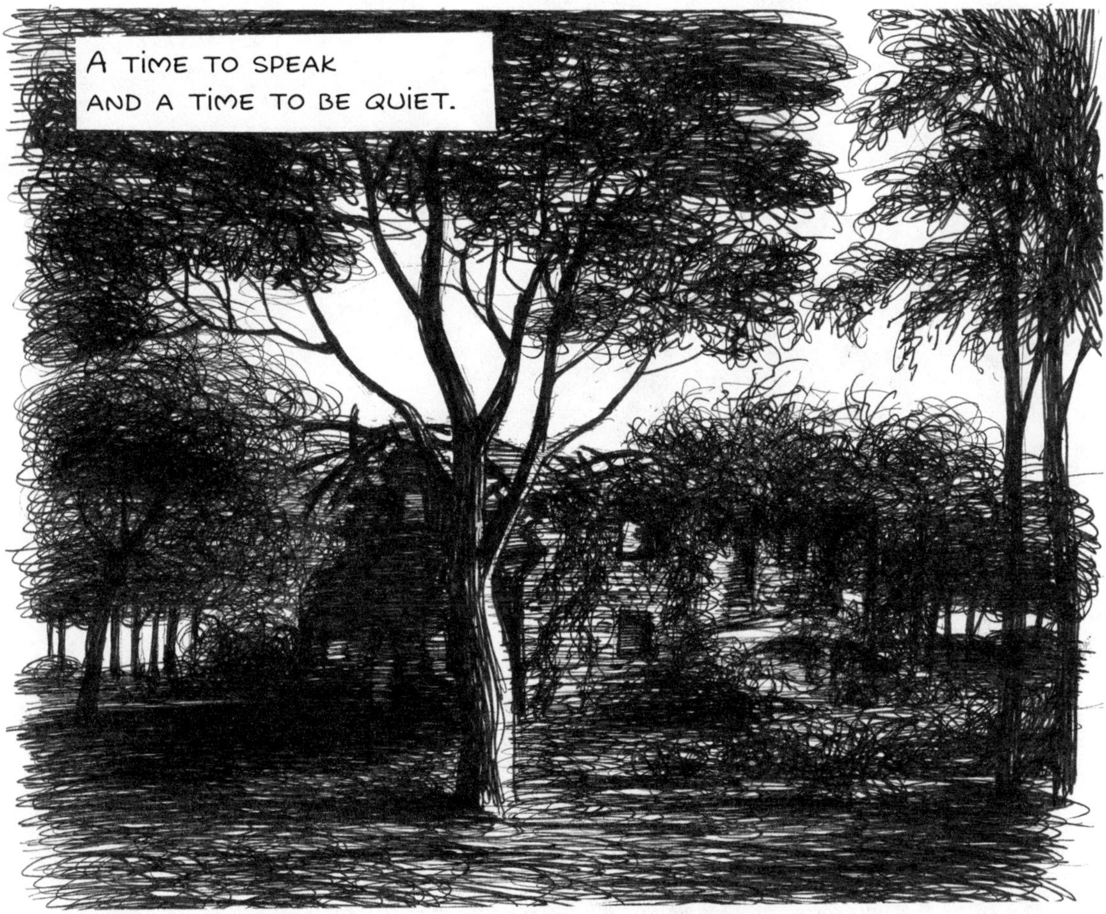
A time to speak
and a time to be quiet.

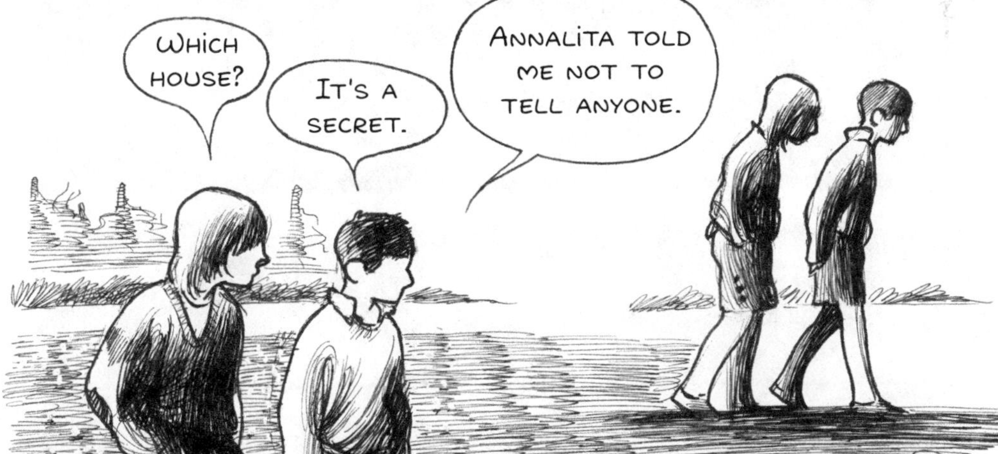
Which house?
It's a secret.
Annalita told me not to tell anyone.

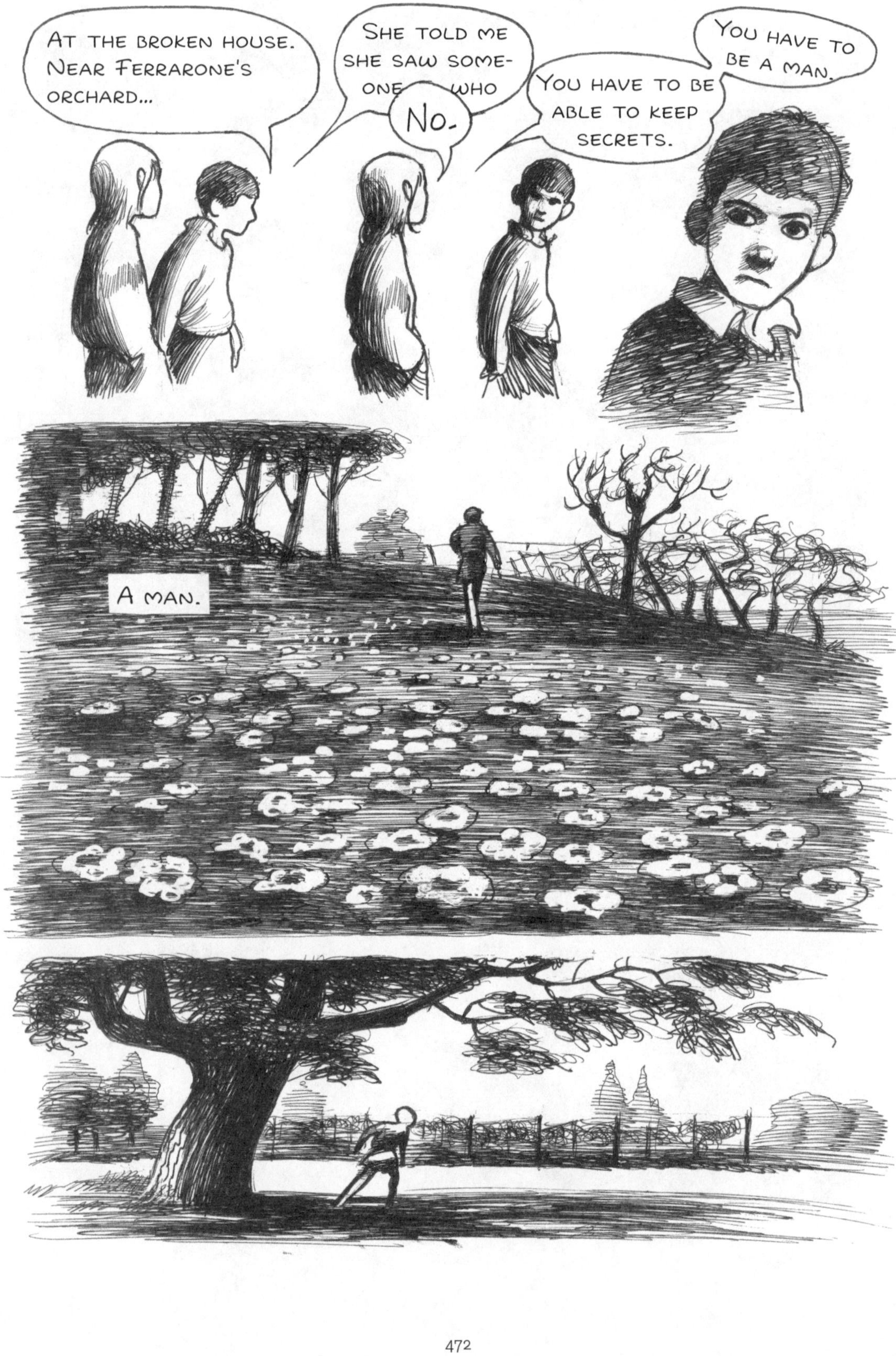
At the broken house. Near Ferrarone's orchard...
She told me she saw some-one who
No-
You have to be able to keep secrets.
You have to be a man.
A man.

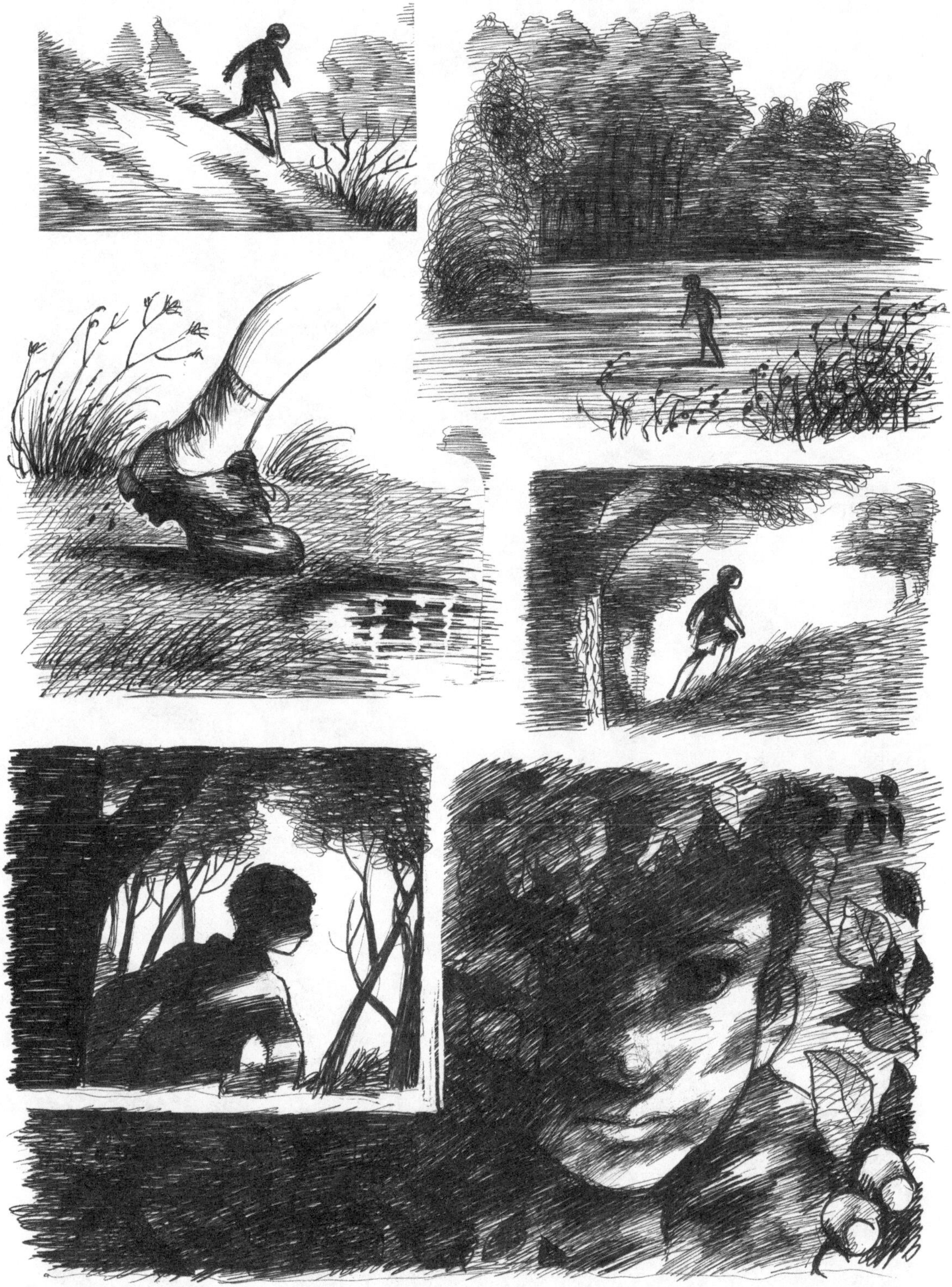

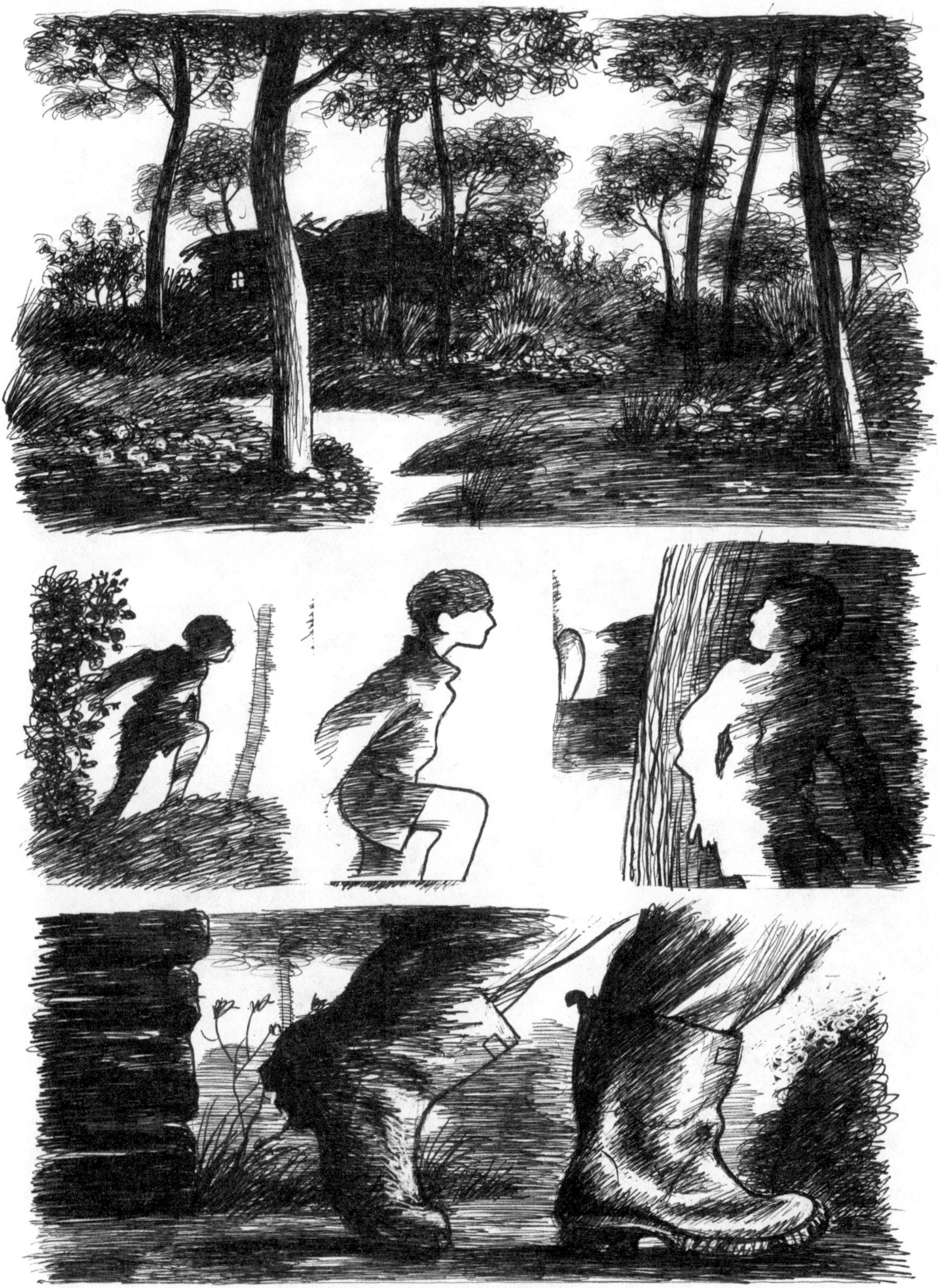

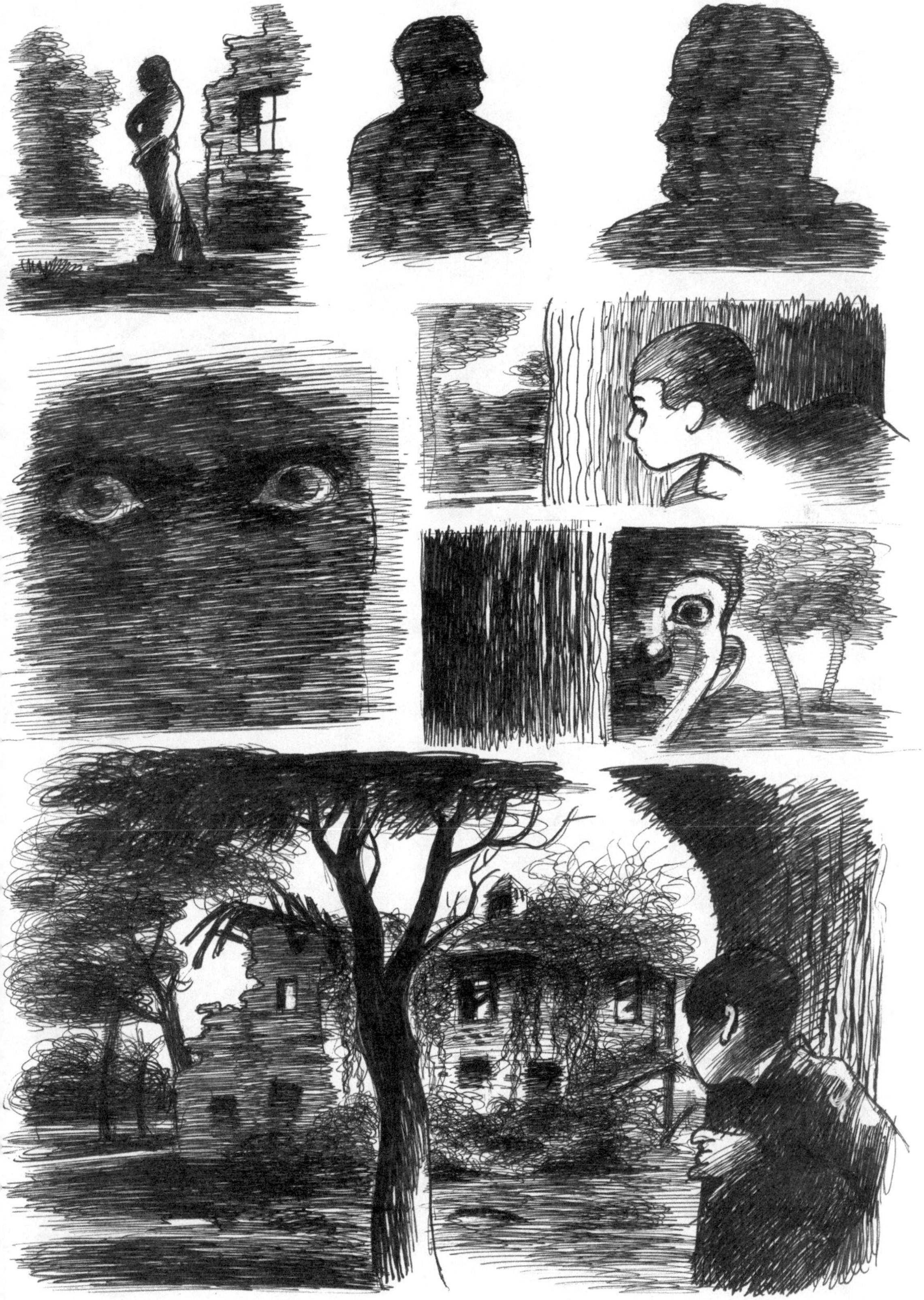

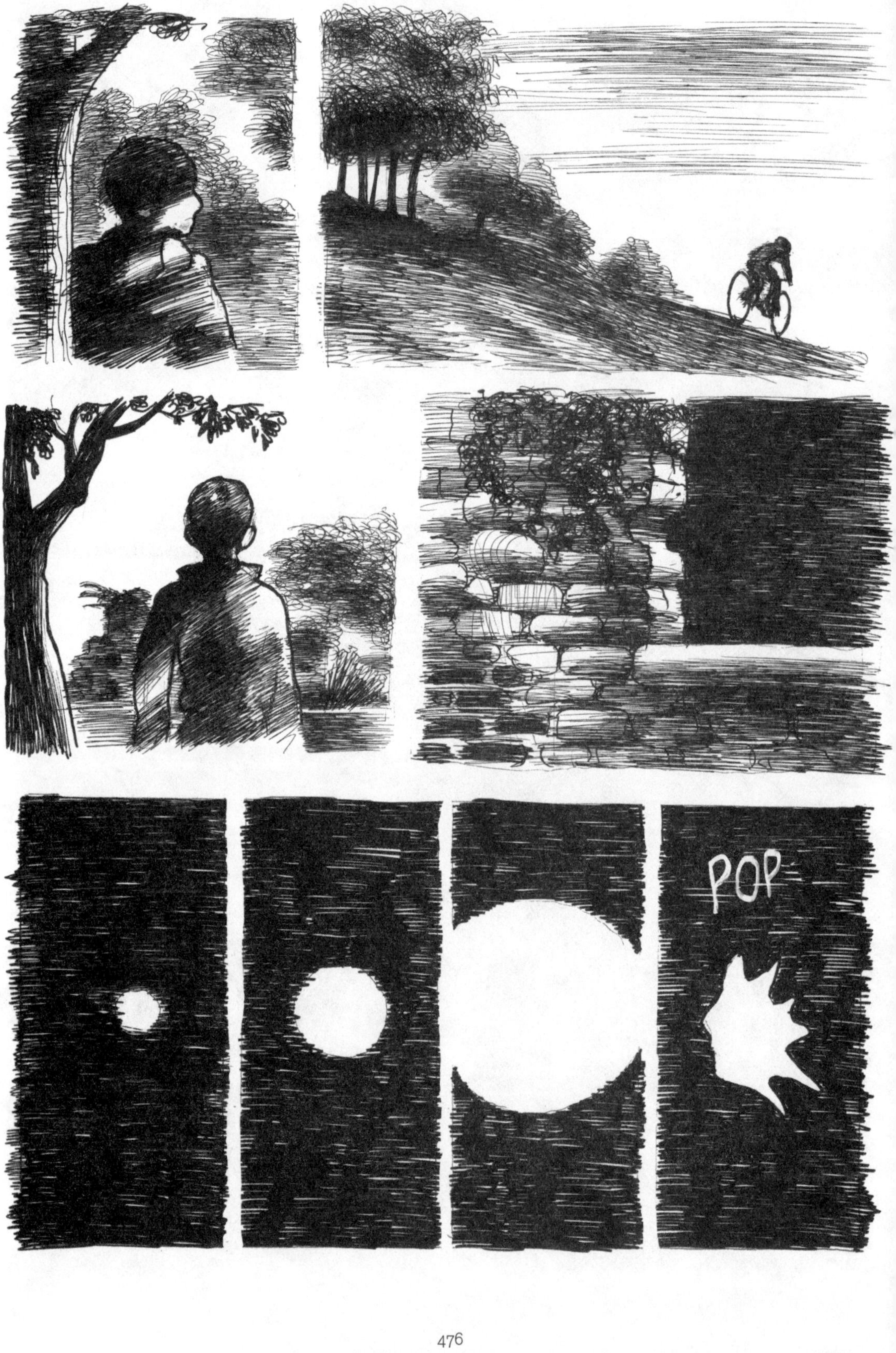
POP

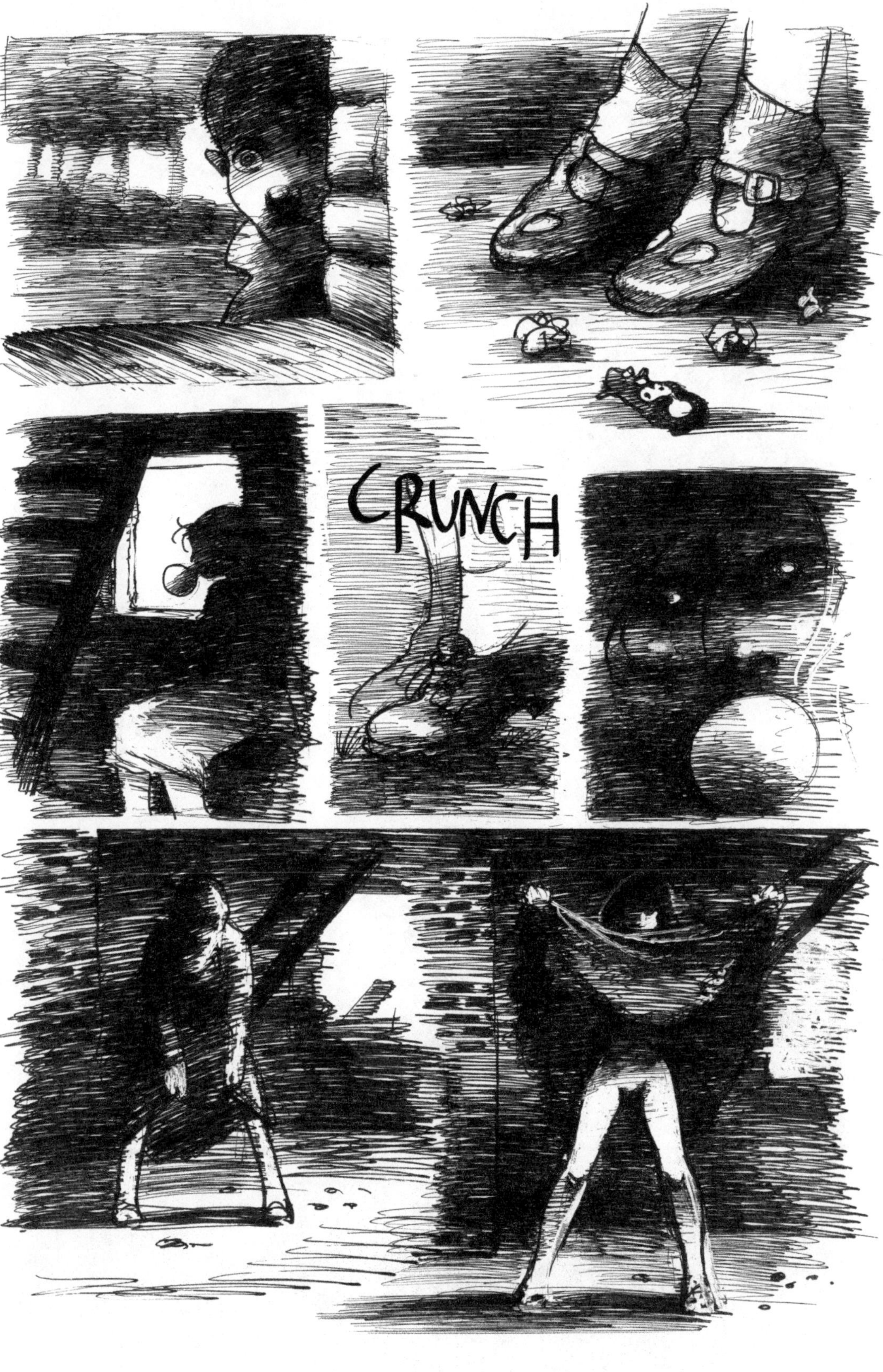
CRUNCH

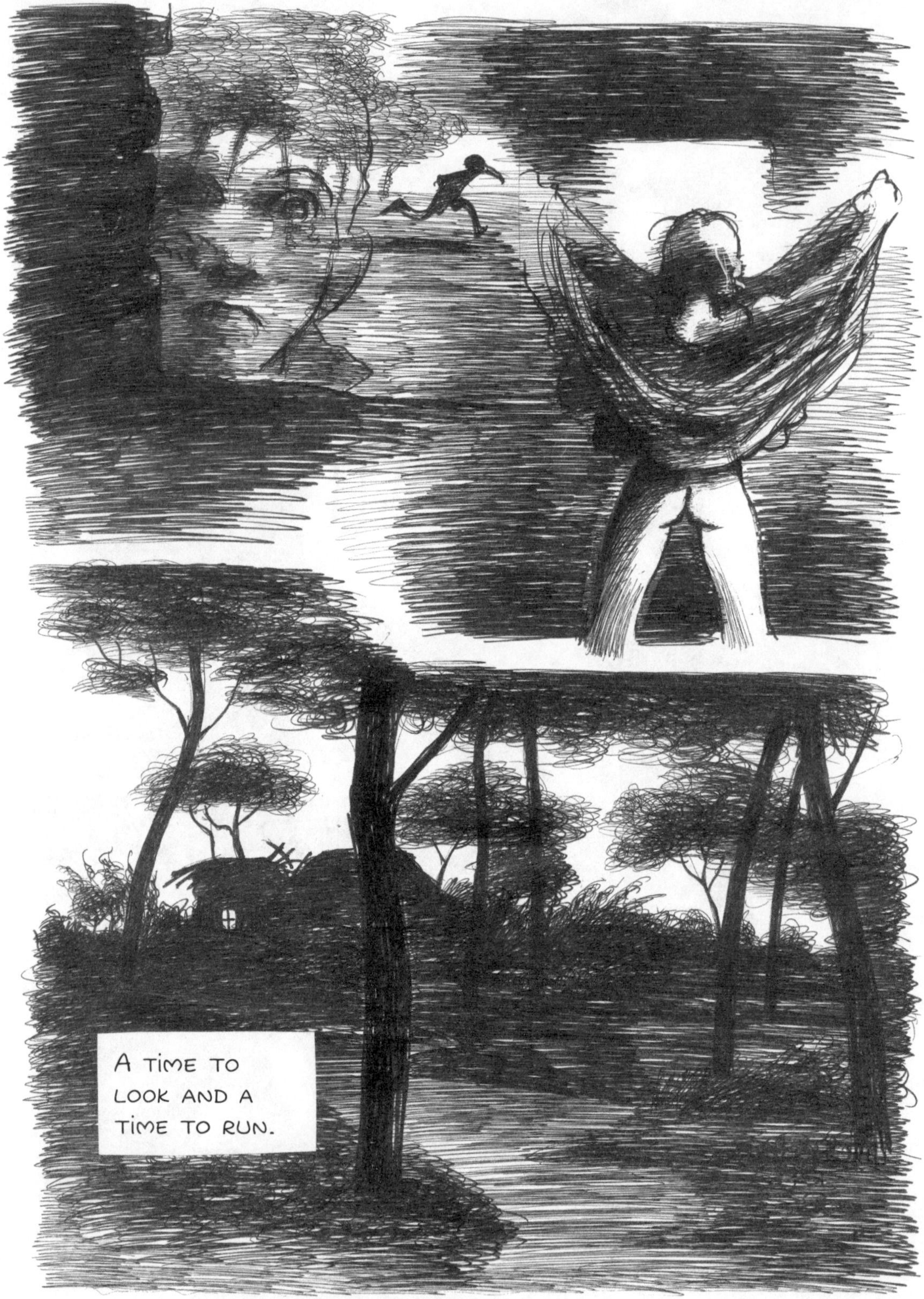
A TIME TO
LOOK AND A
TIME TO RUN.

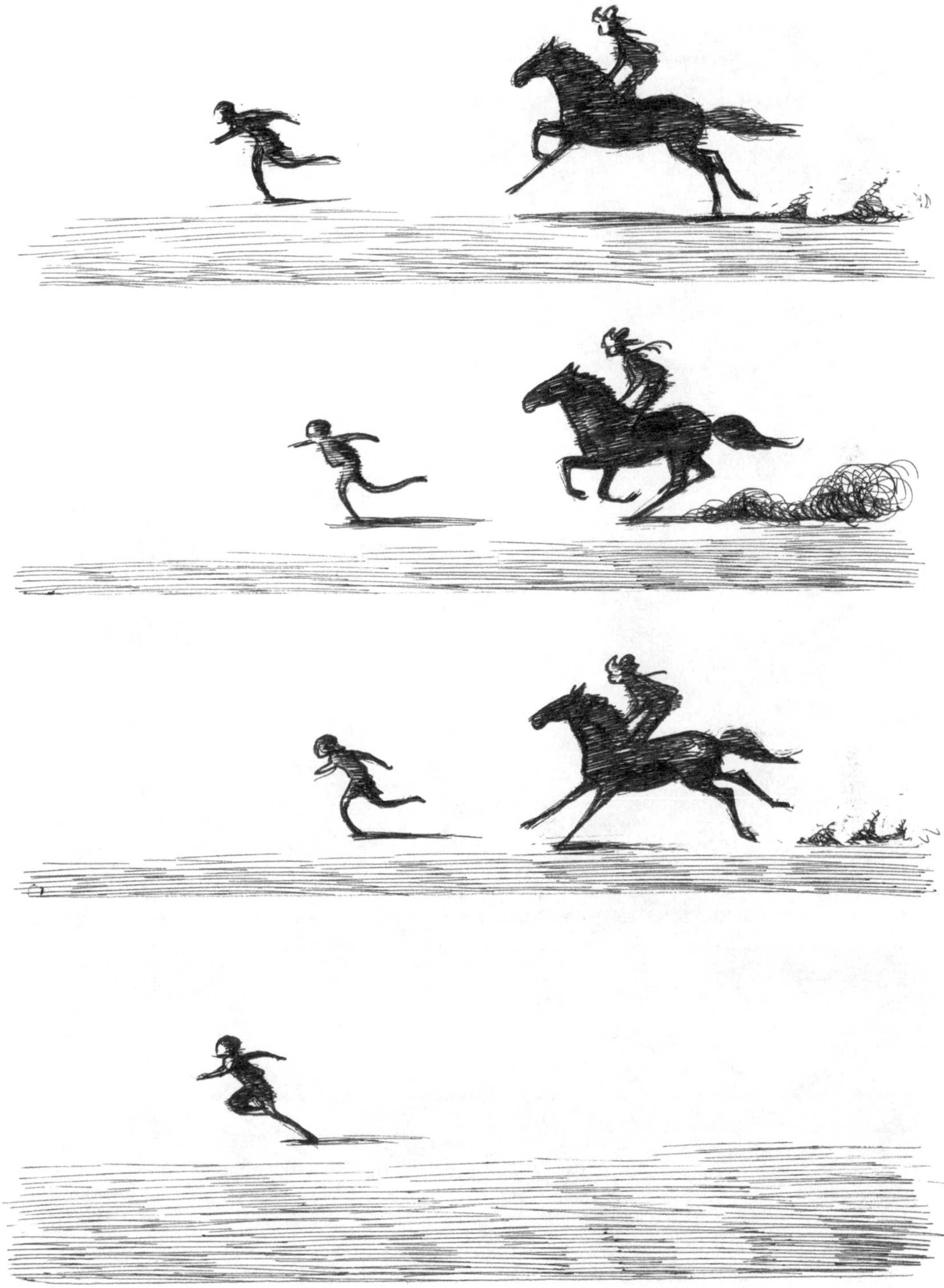

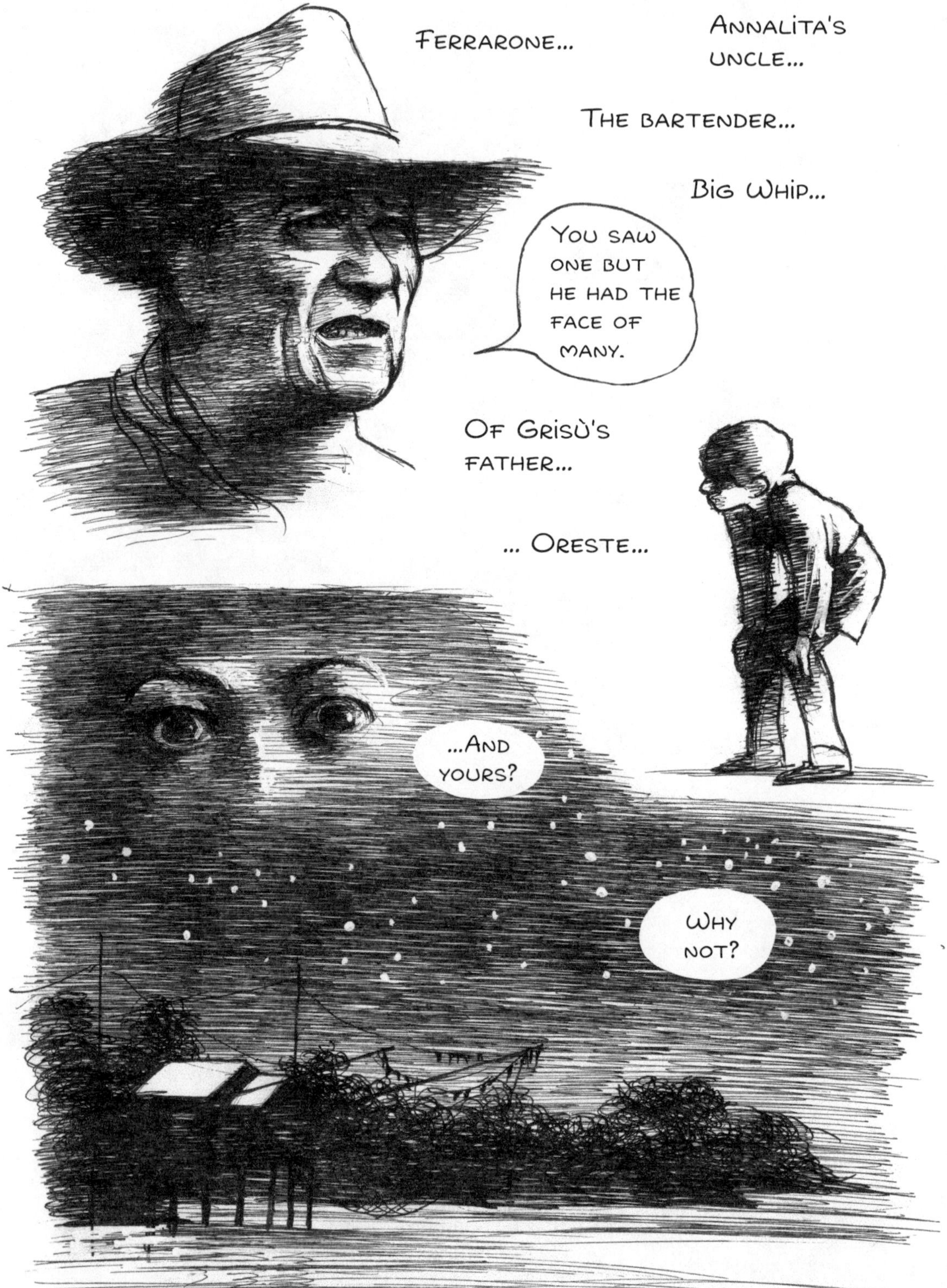
Ferrarone...
Annalita's uncle...
The bartender...
Big Whip...
You saw one but he had the face of many.
Of Grisù's father...
... Oreste...
...And yours?
Why not?

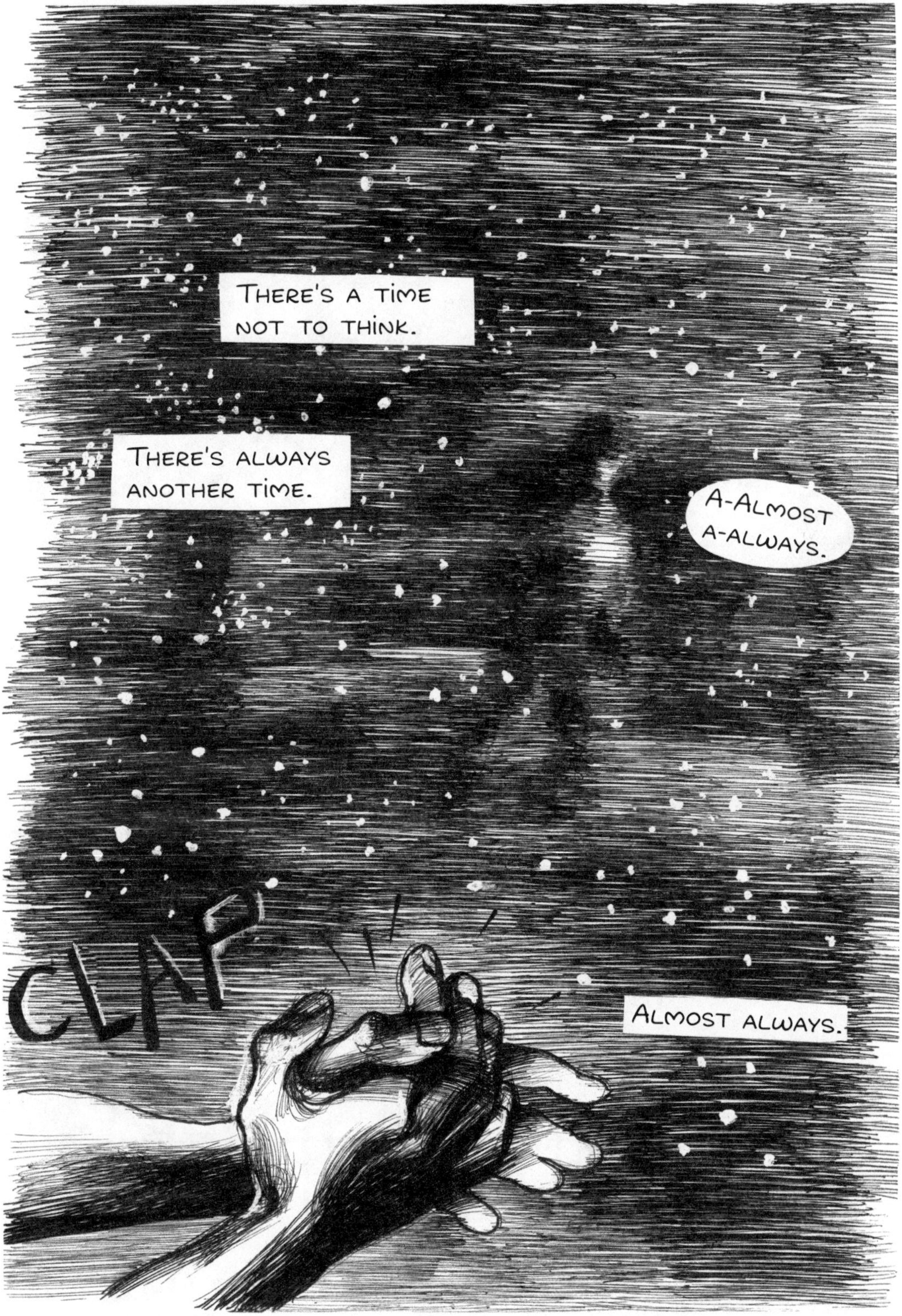
There's a time not to think.
There's always another time.
A-almost a-always.
CLAP
Almost always.

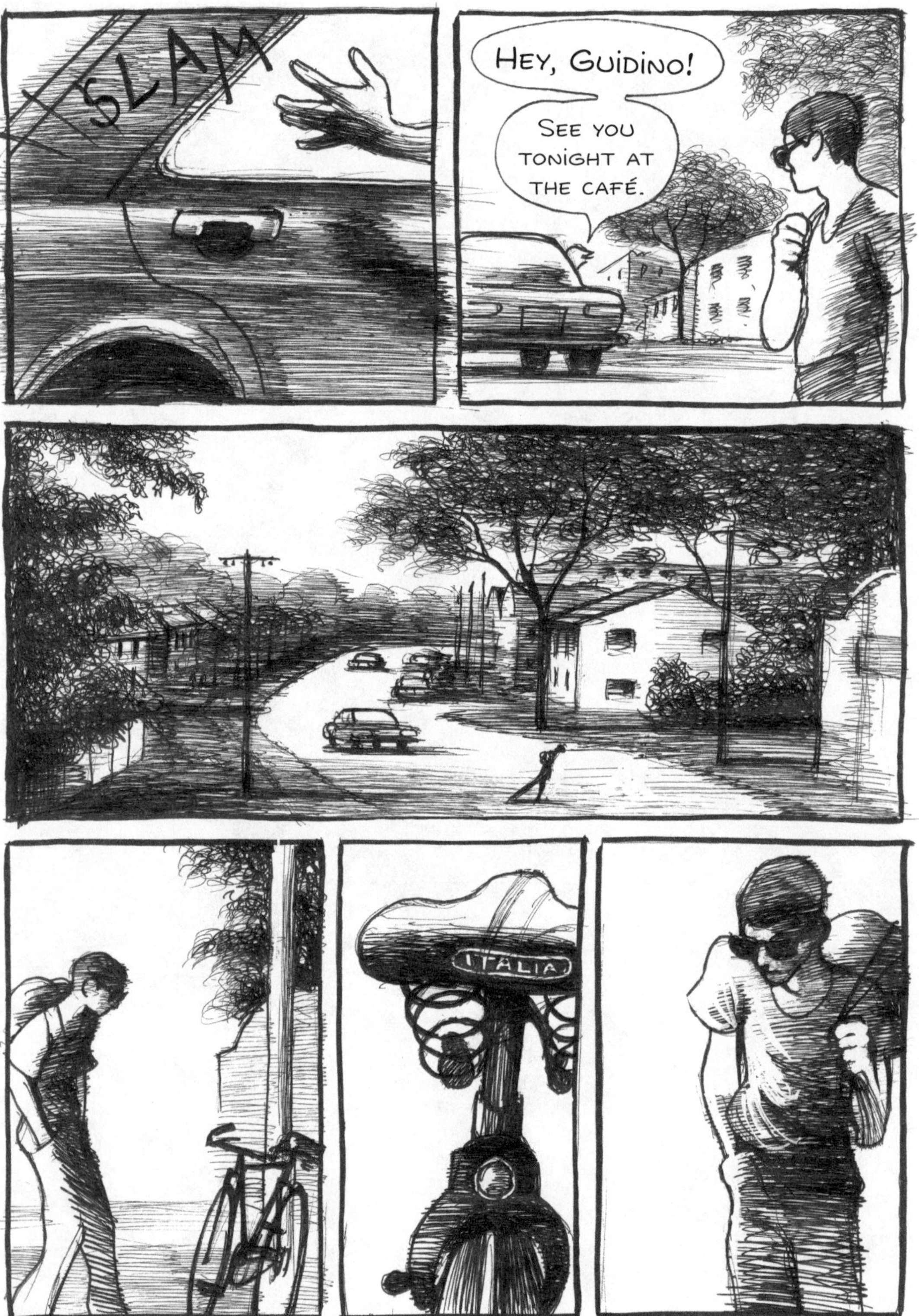
SLAM
Hey, Guidino!
See you tonight at the café.
ITALIA

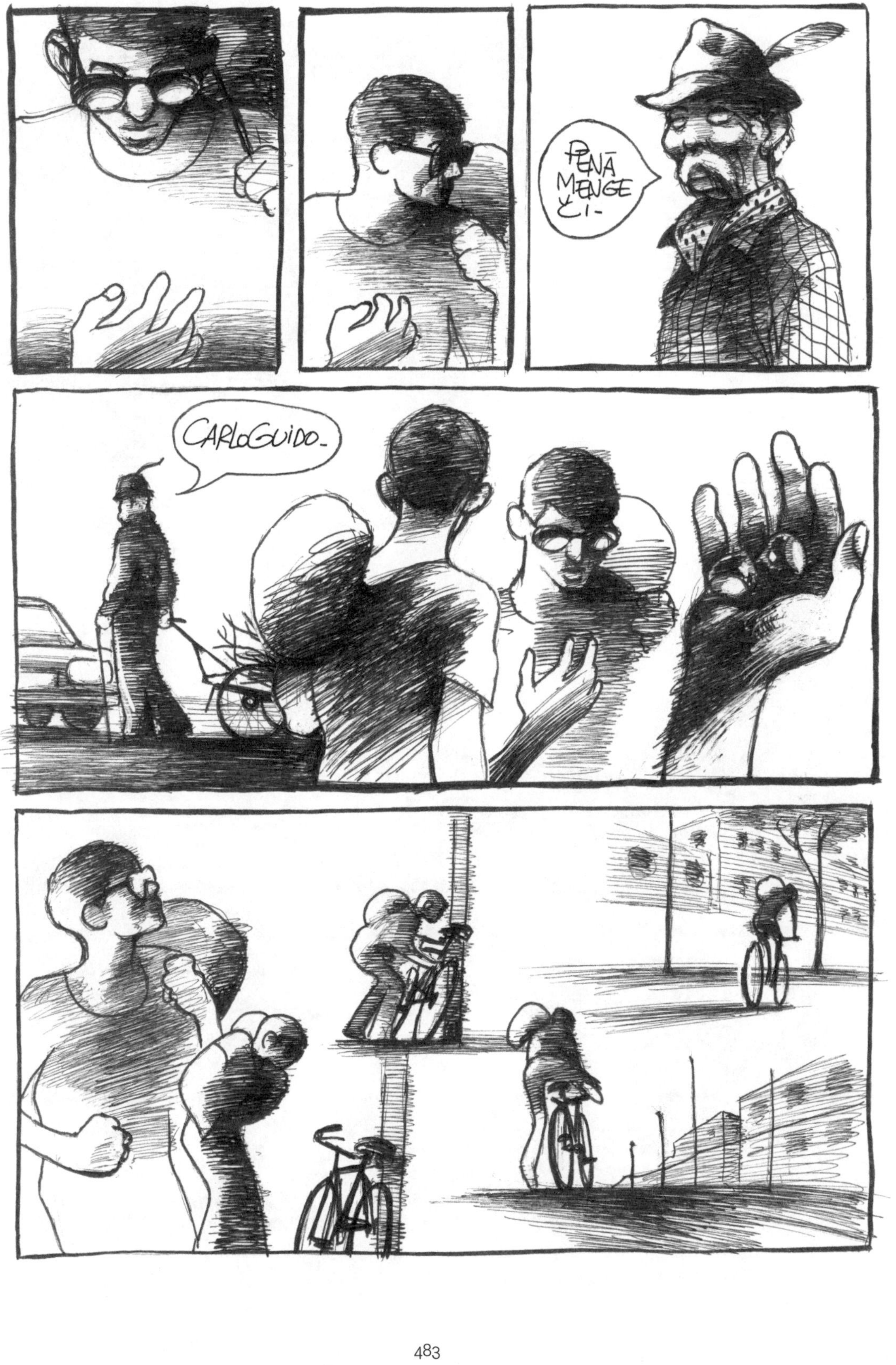
PENĀ MENGE ČI-
CARLOGUIDO-

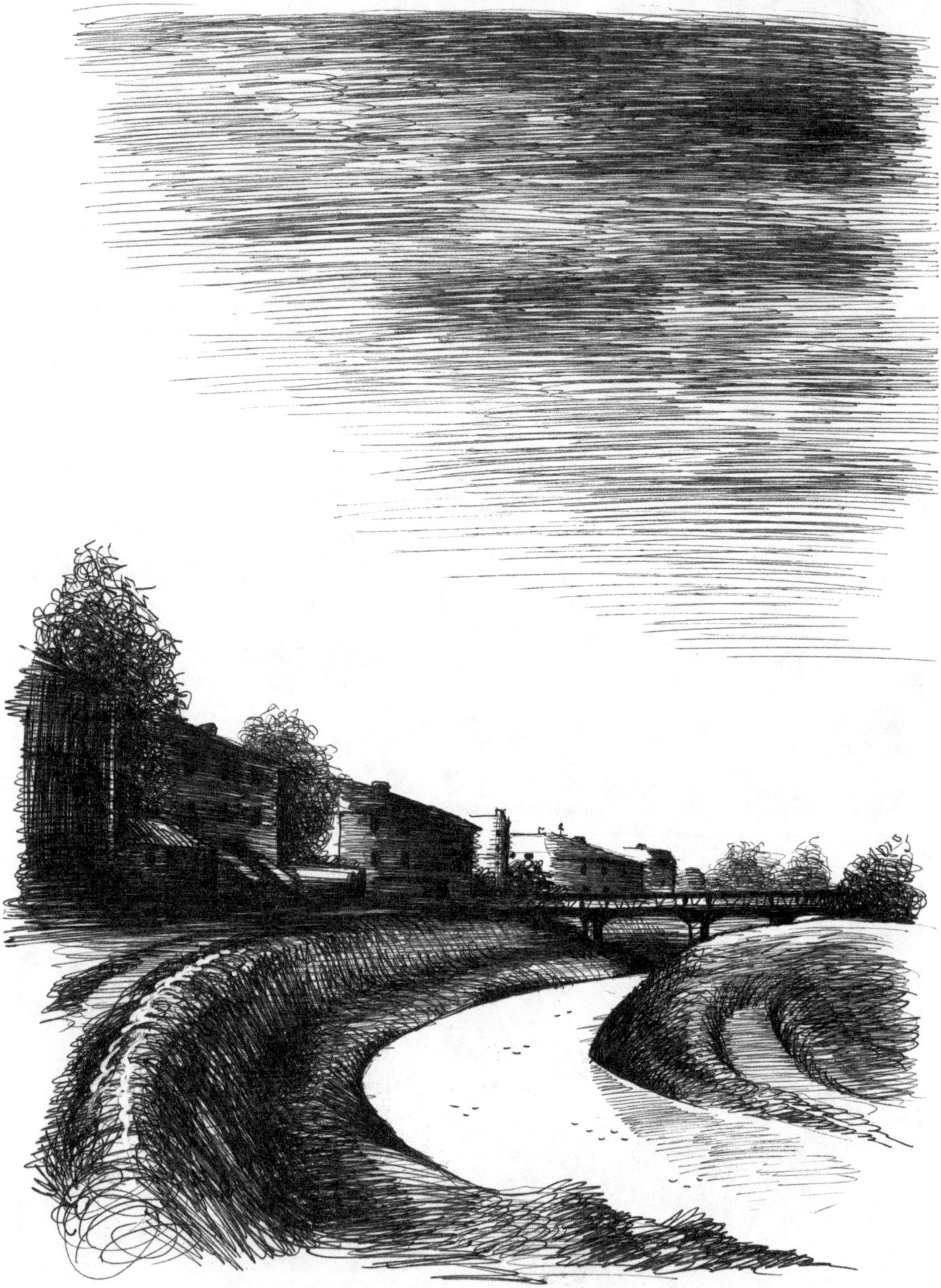

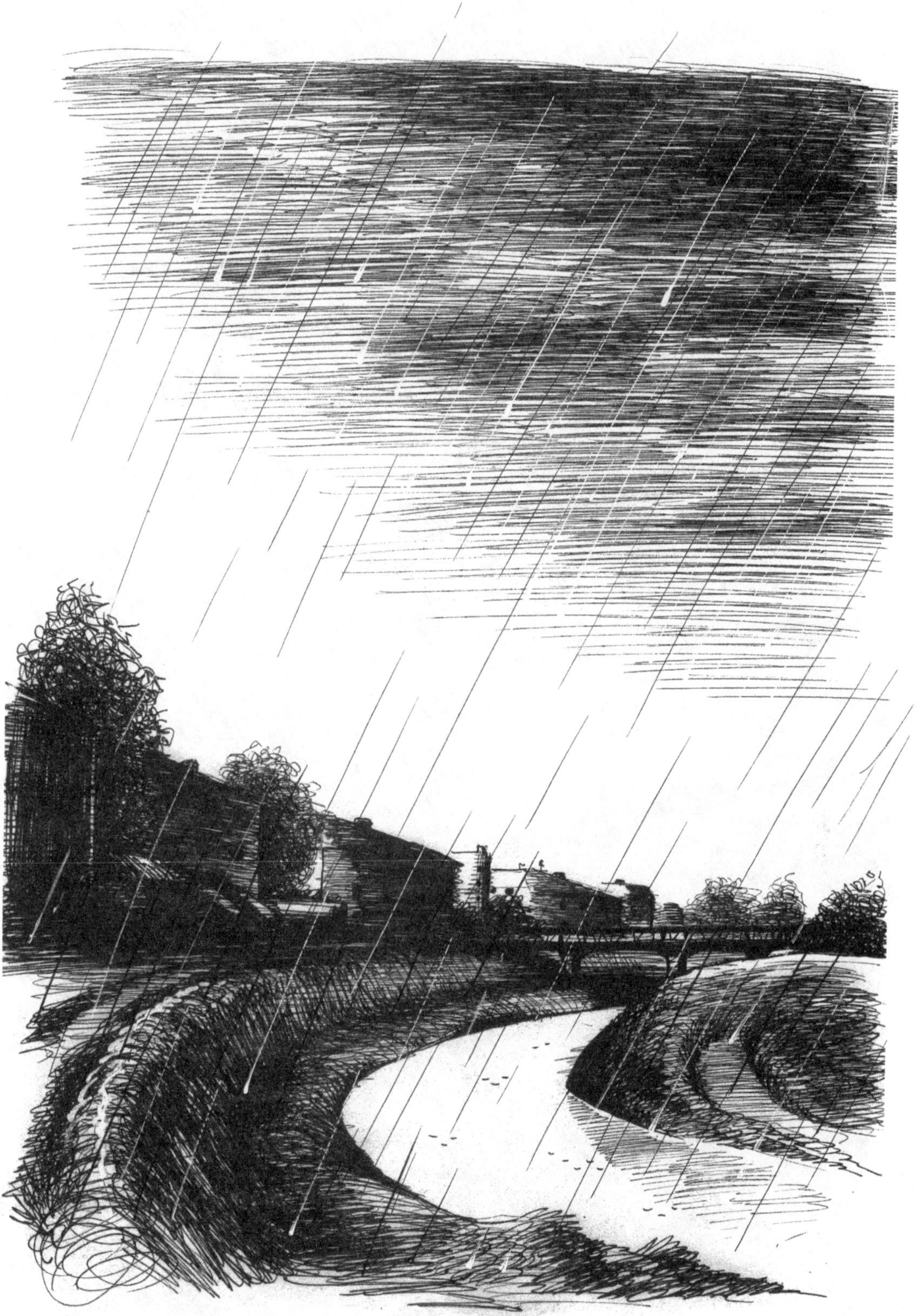

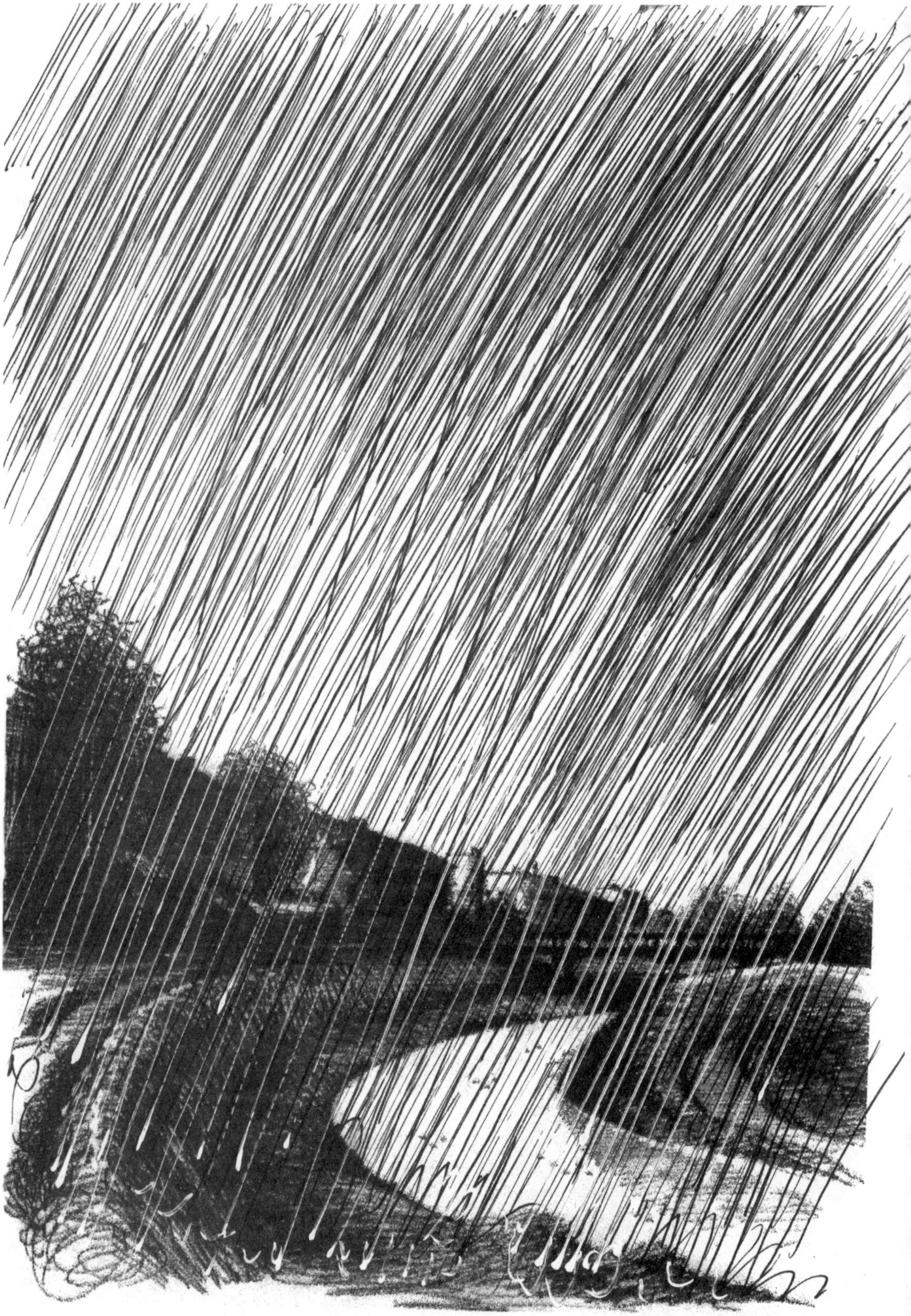

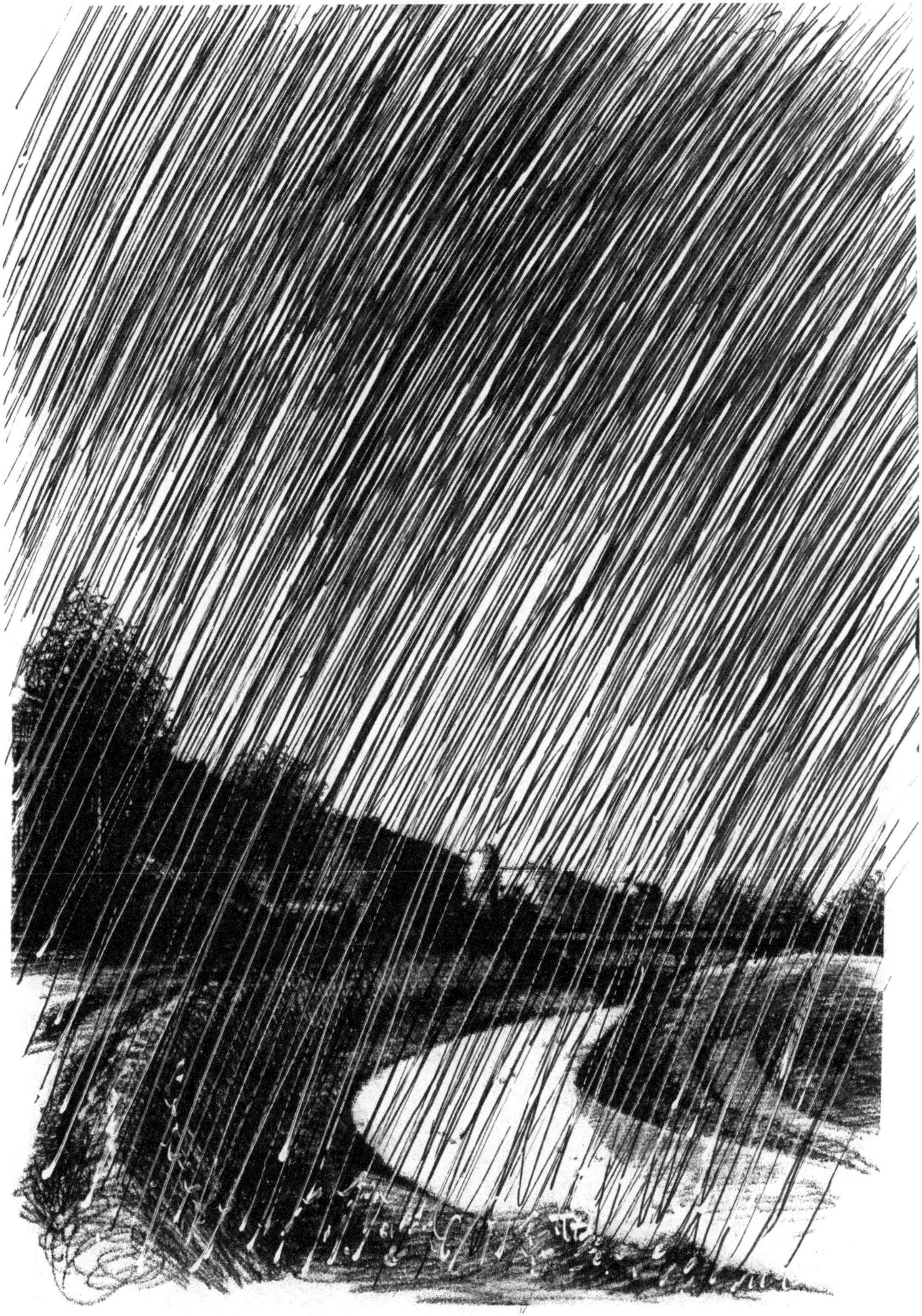

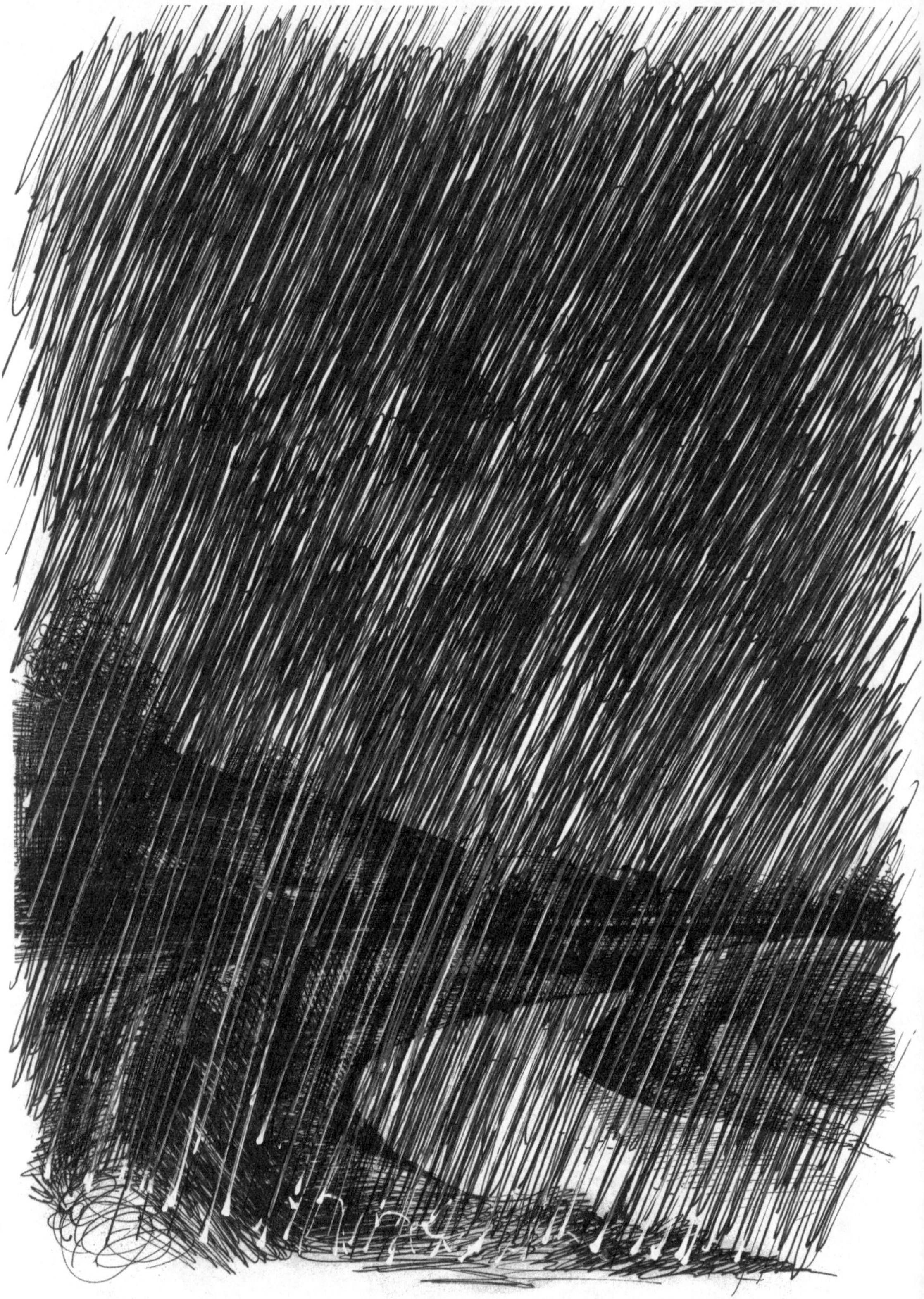

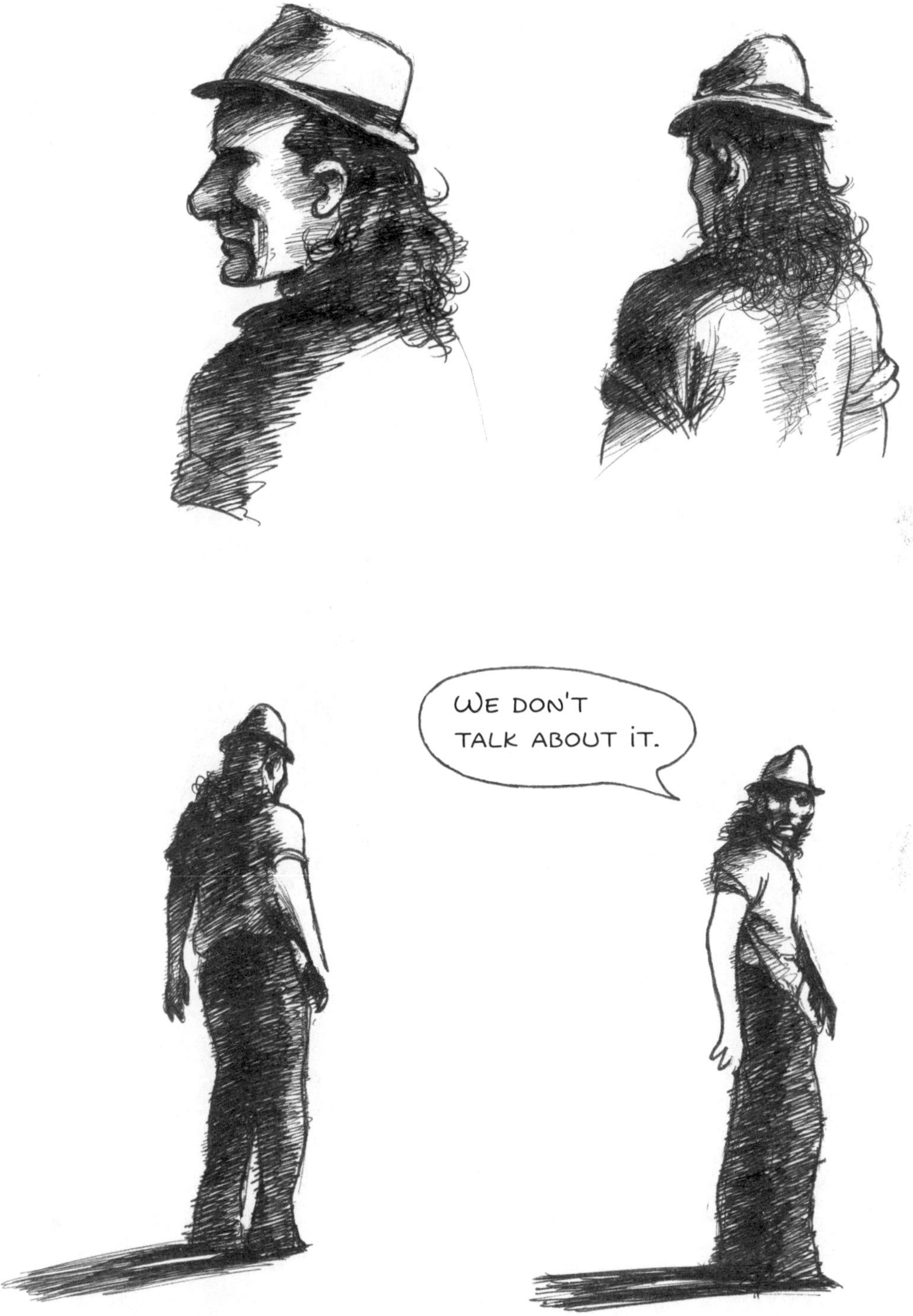
WE DON'T TALK ABOUT IT.

It'd be like
stepping in the
footsteps of
the dead.

So perfectly
that they
aren't changed
in the least.

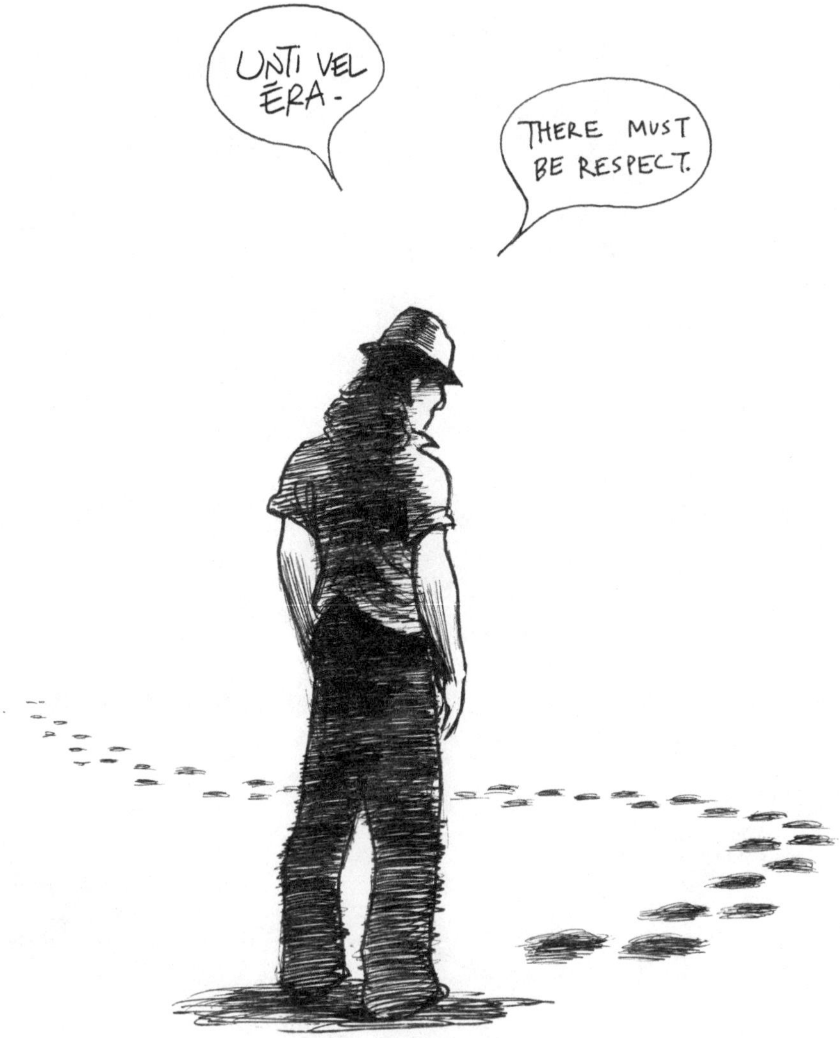
UNTI VEL ÉRA-
THERE MUST BE RESPECT.

XII

SAYING THAT A CHILD IS GOOD IS LIKE PUTTING A CURSE ON HIM.

BETTER JUST TO SAY THAT HE'S BAD.

OR NOT SAY ANYTHING.

SILENCE IS PRAISE.

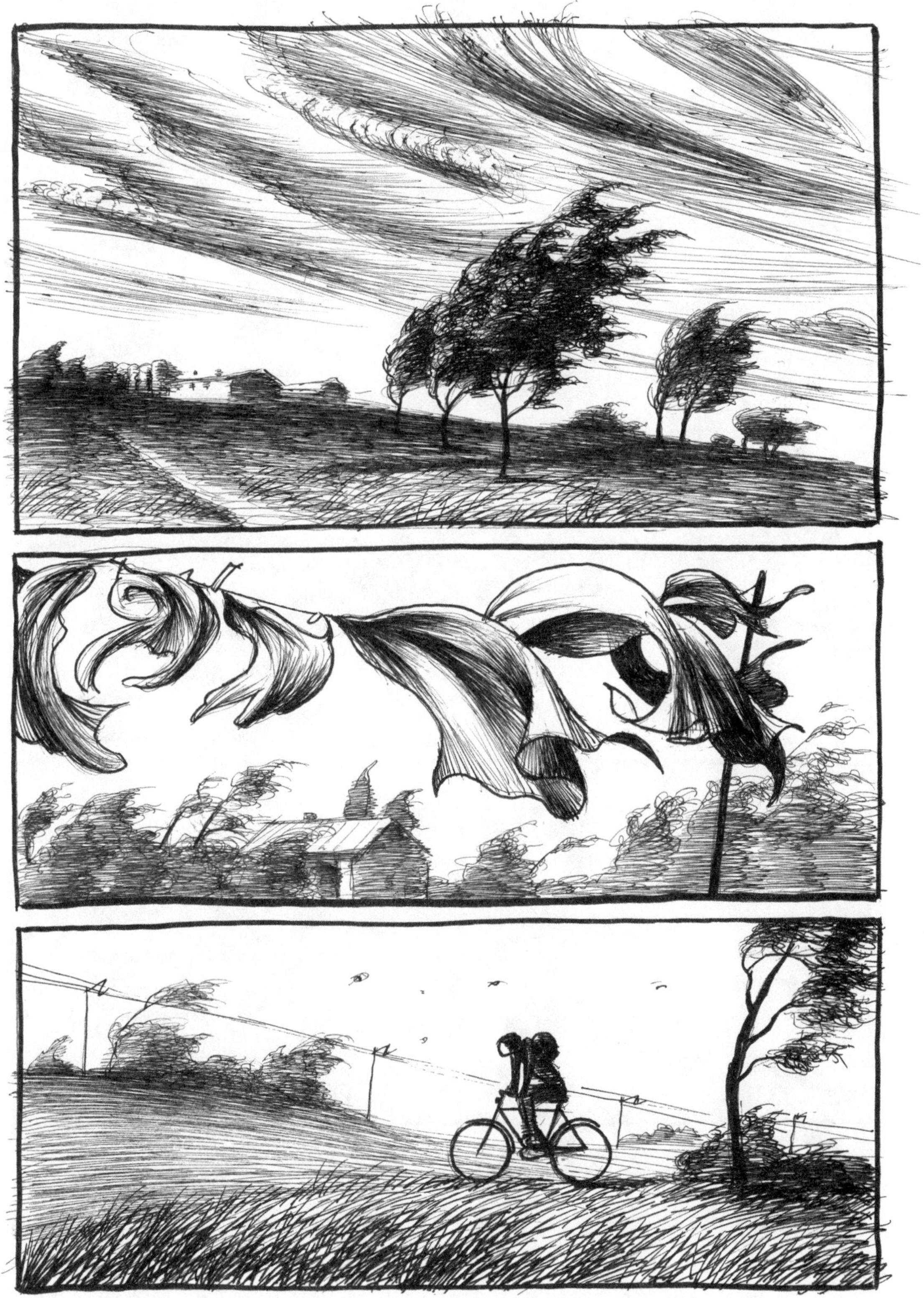

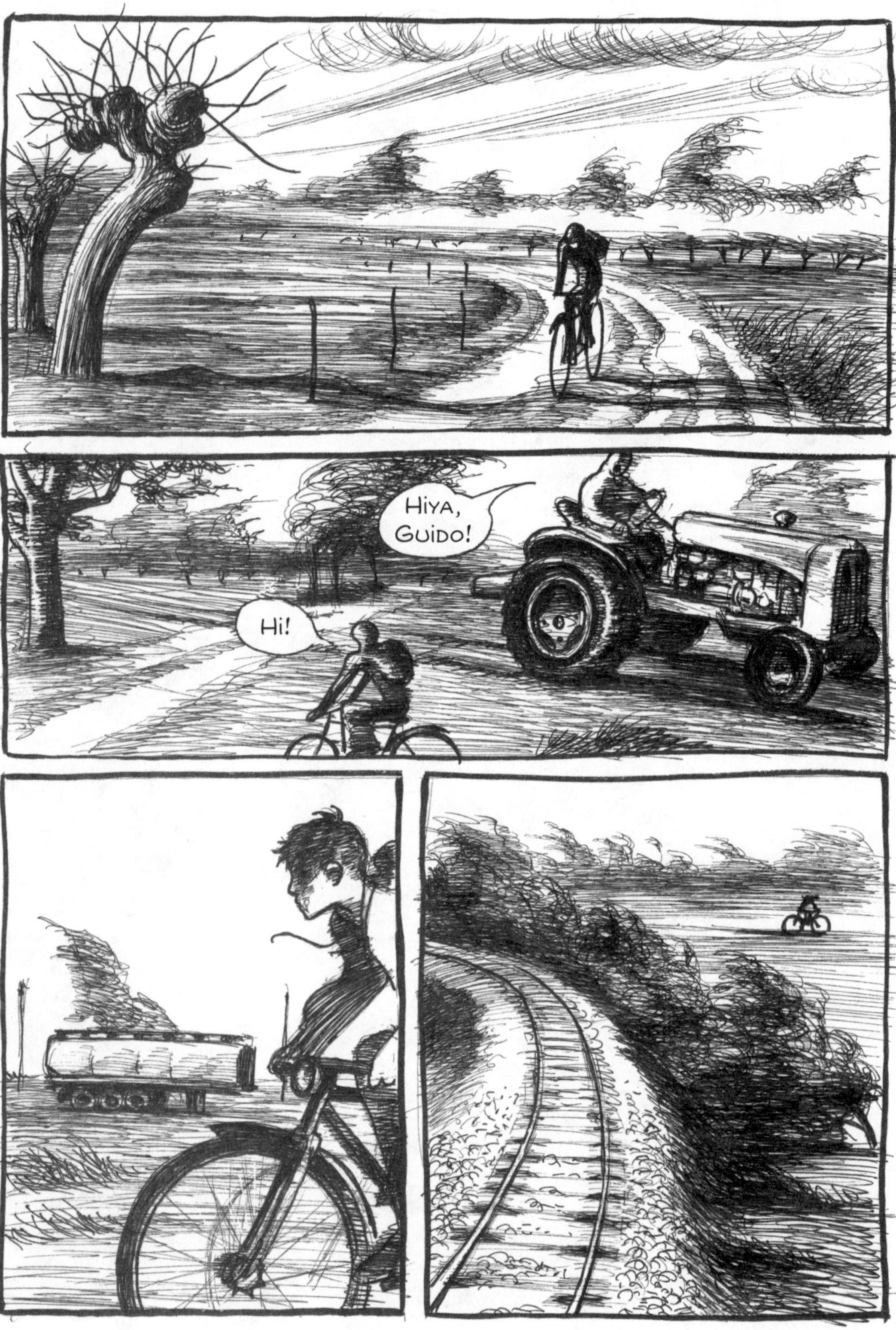
HIYA, GUIDO!
Hi!

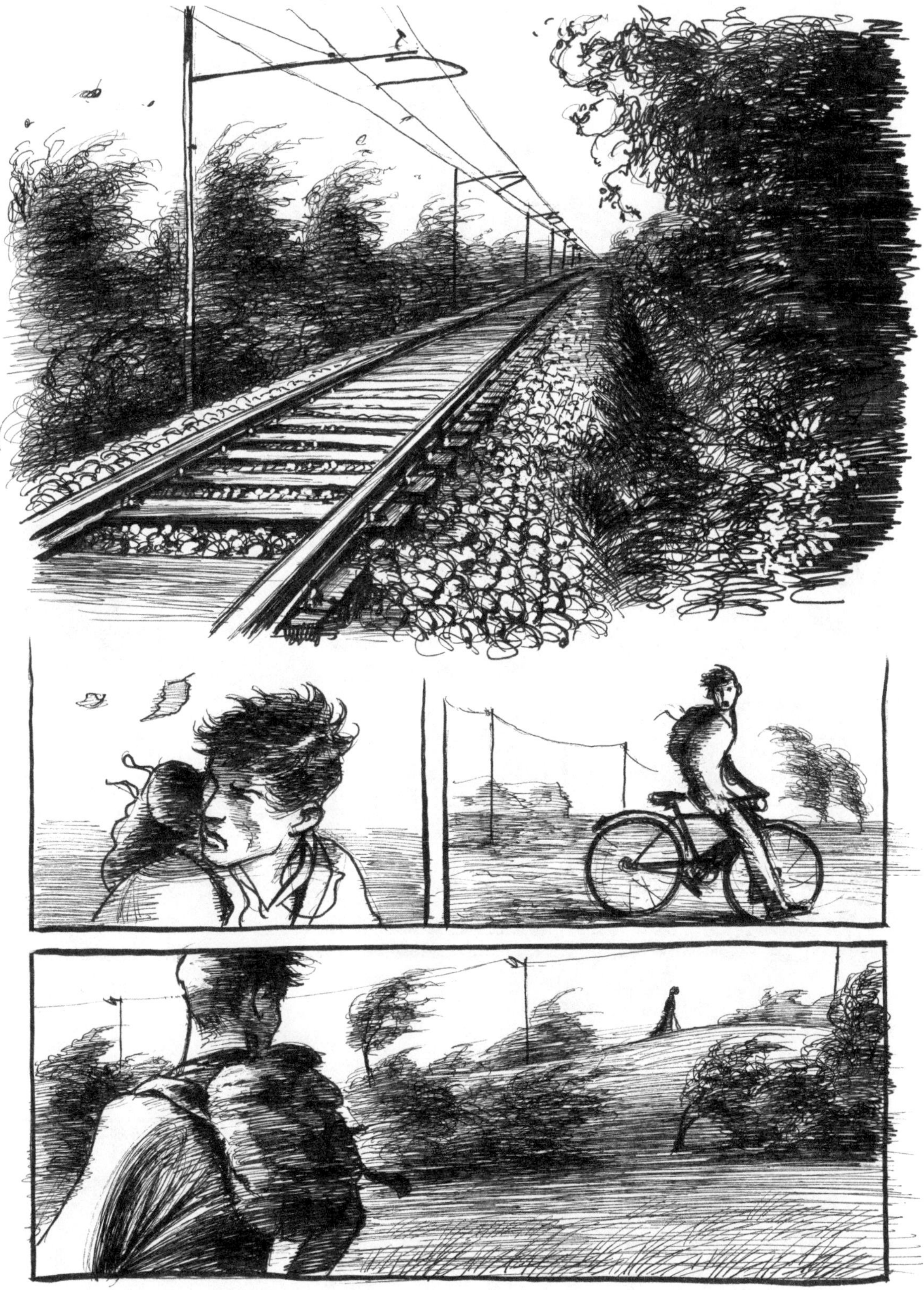

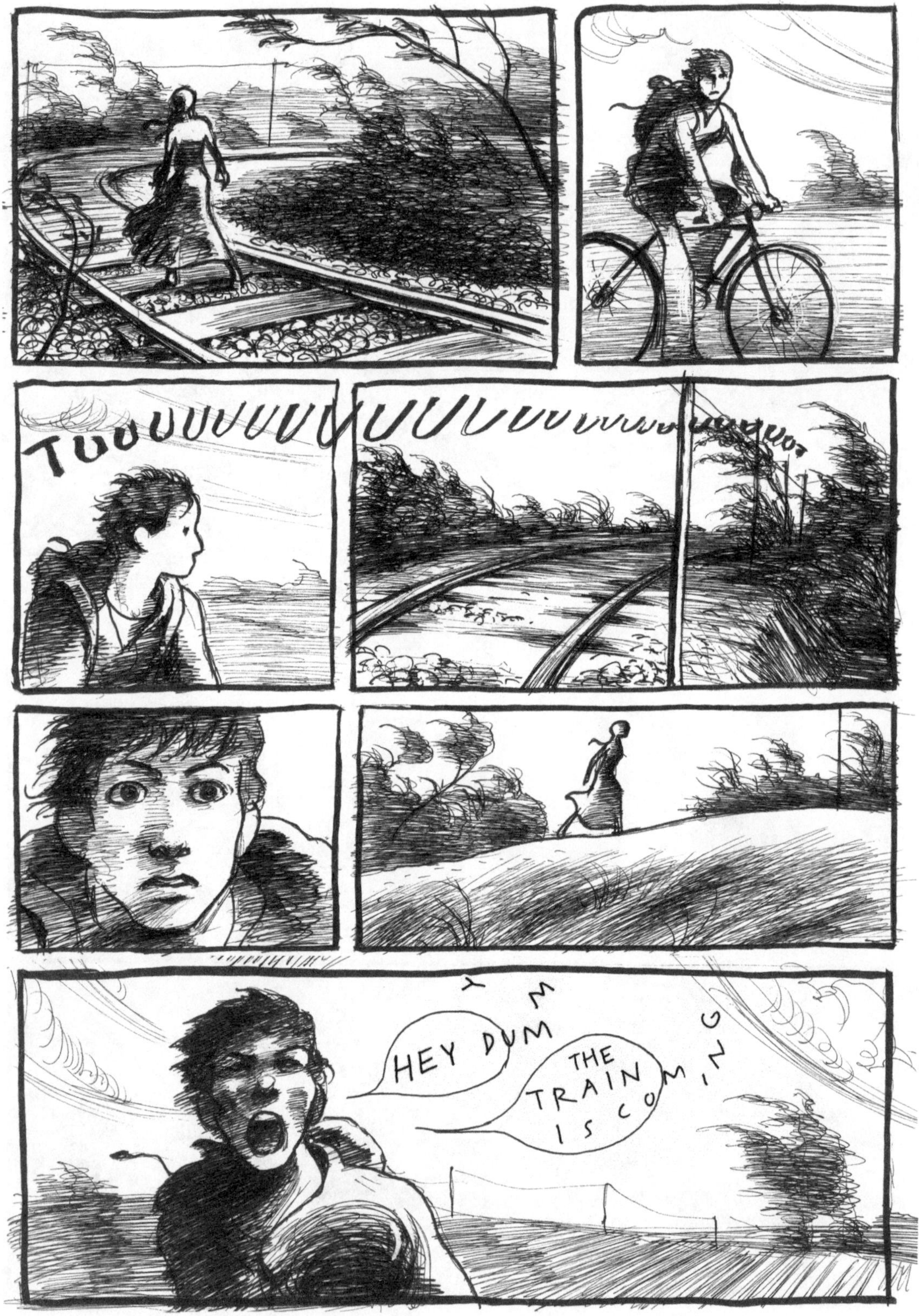
TUUUUUUUUUUUUUUUUUUUUUUUUU
HEY DUMMY
THE TRAIN IS COMING

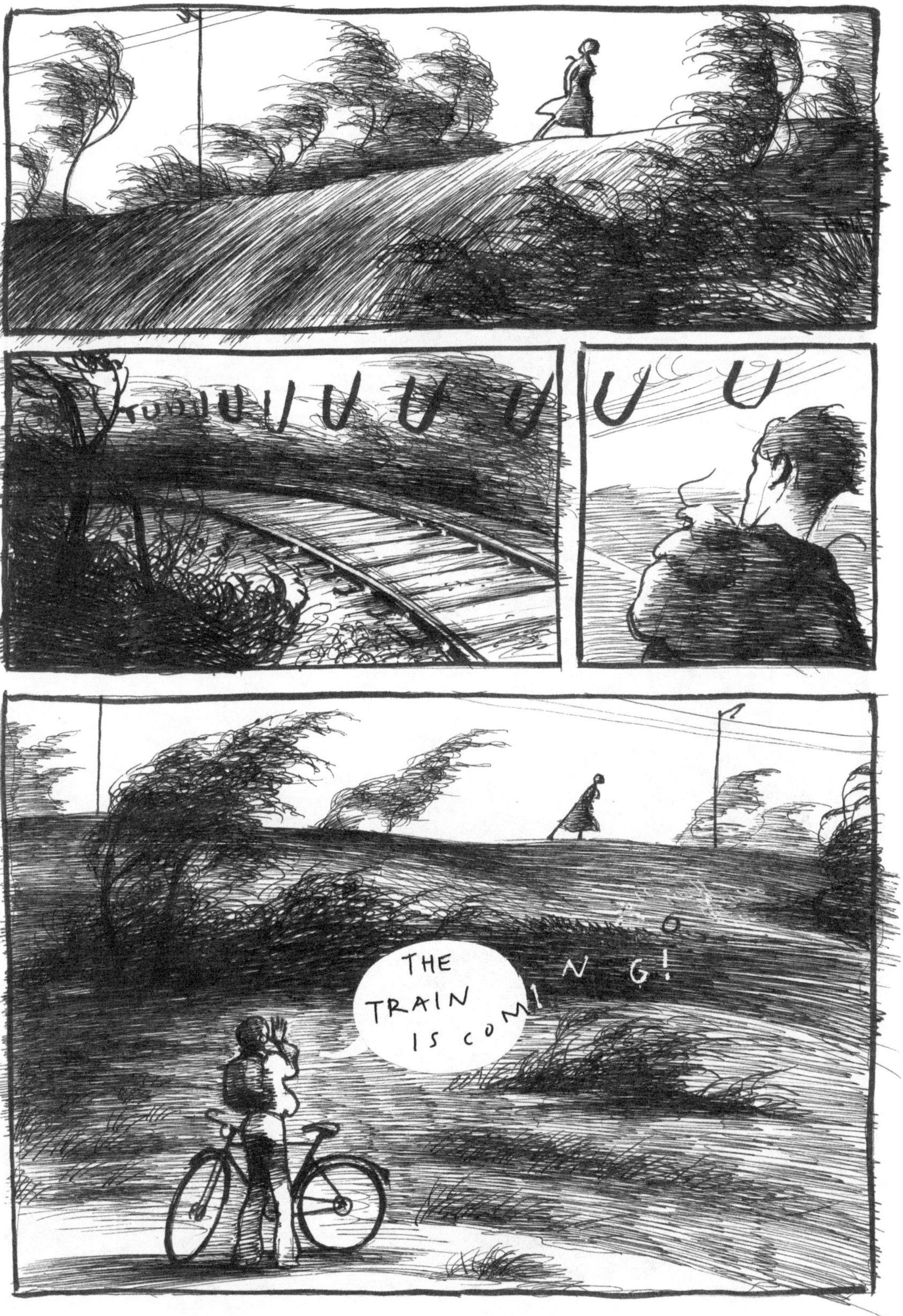
THE TRAIN IS COMING!

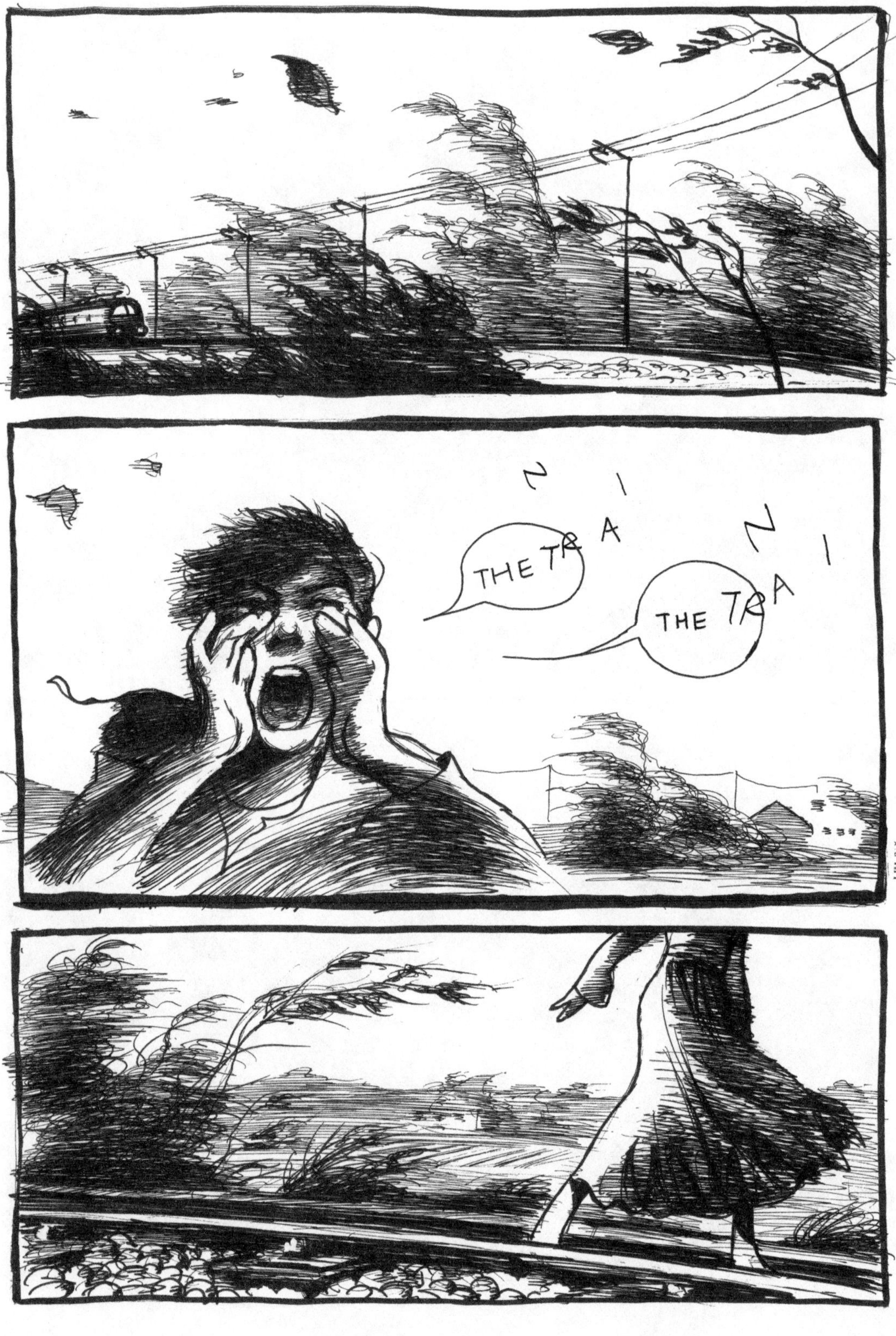
THE TRA I N
THE TRA I N

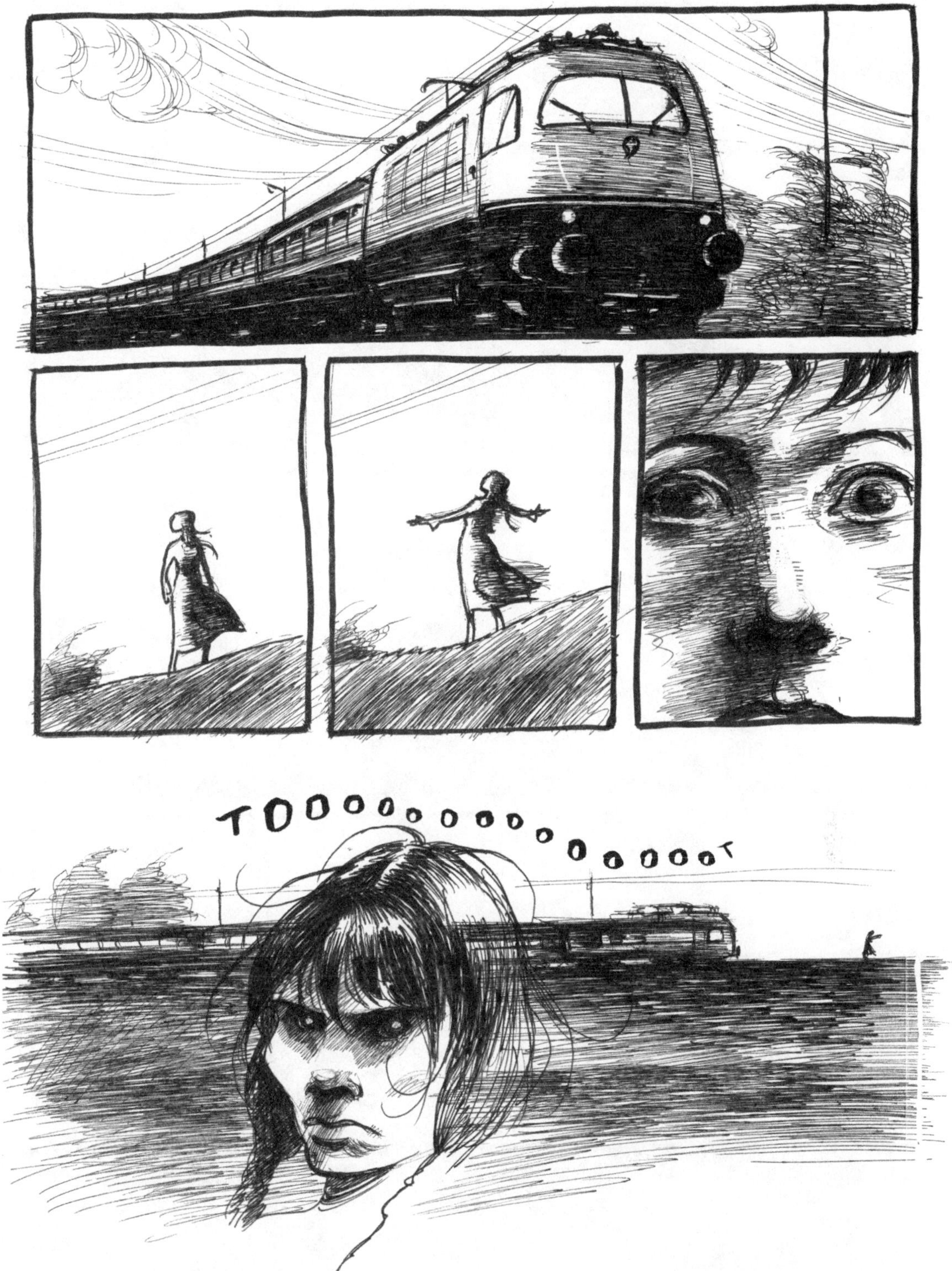
TOOoooooooooooooooT

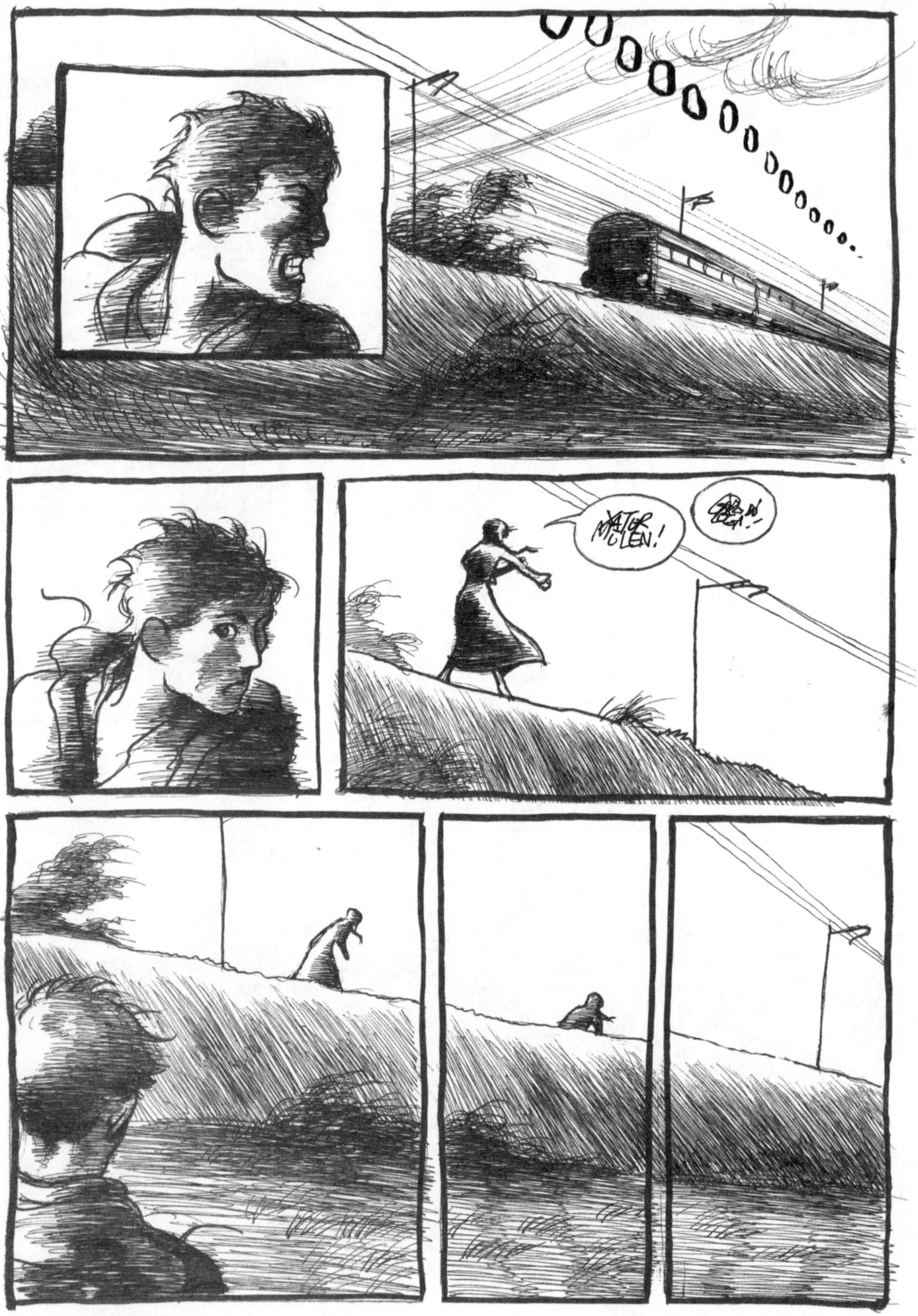
OOOOOOOOOOOOO...
MAJOR MULEN!

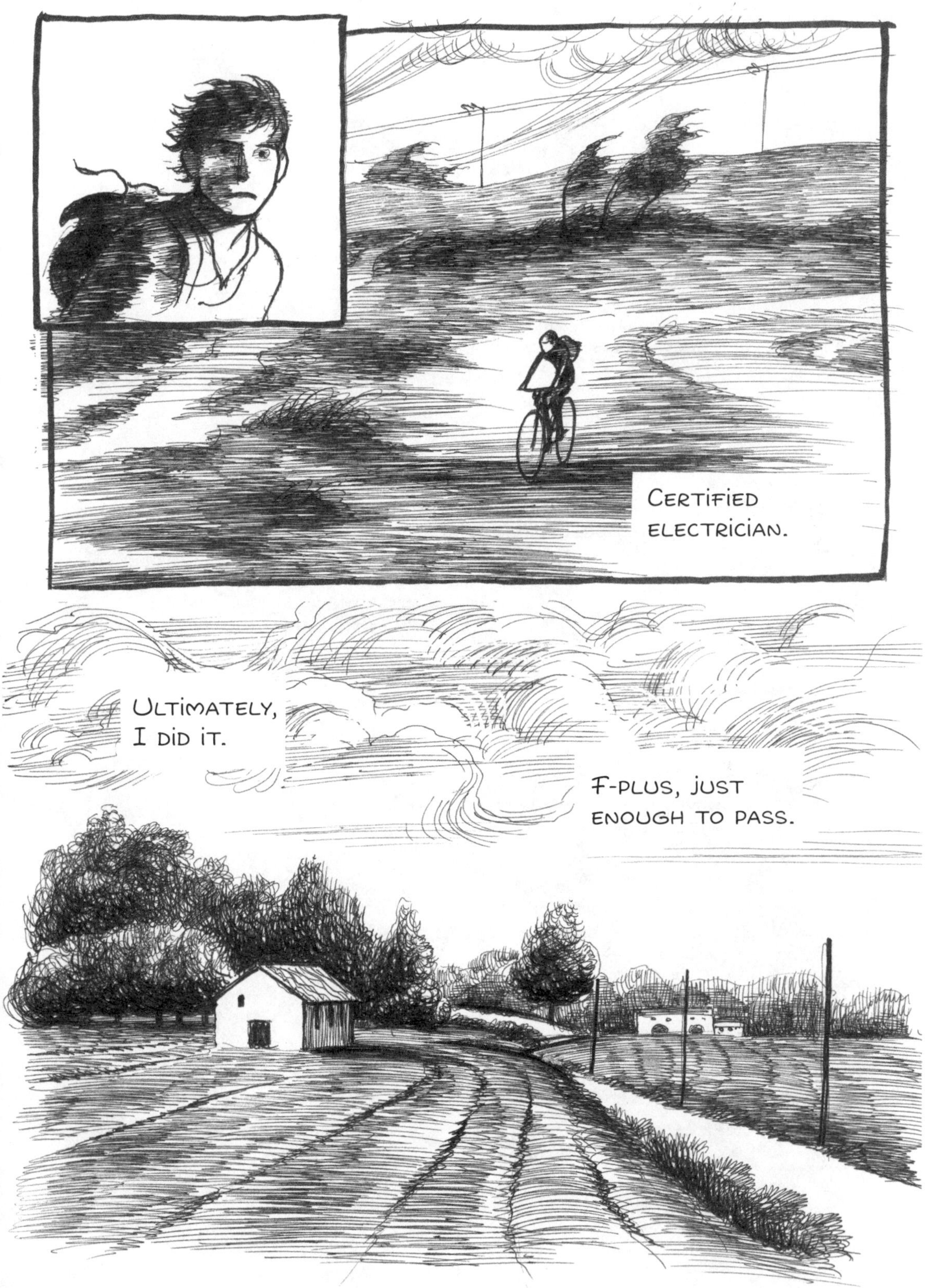
Certified electrician.
Ultimately, I did it.
F-plus, just enough to pass.

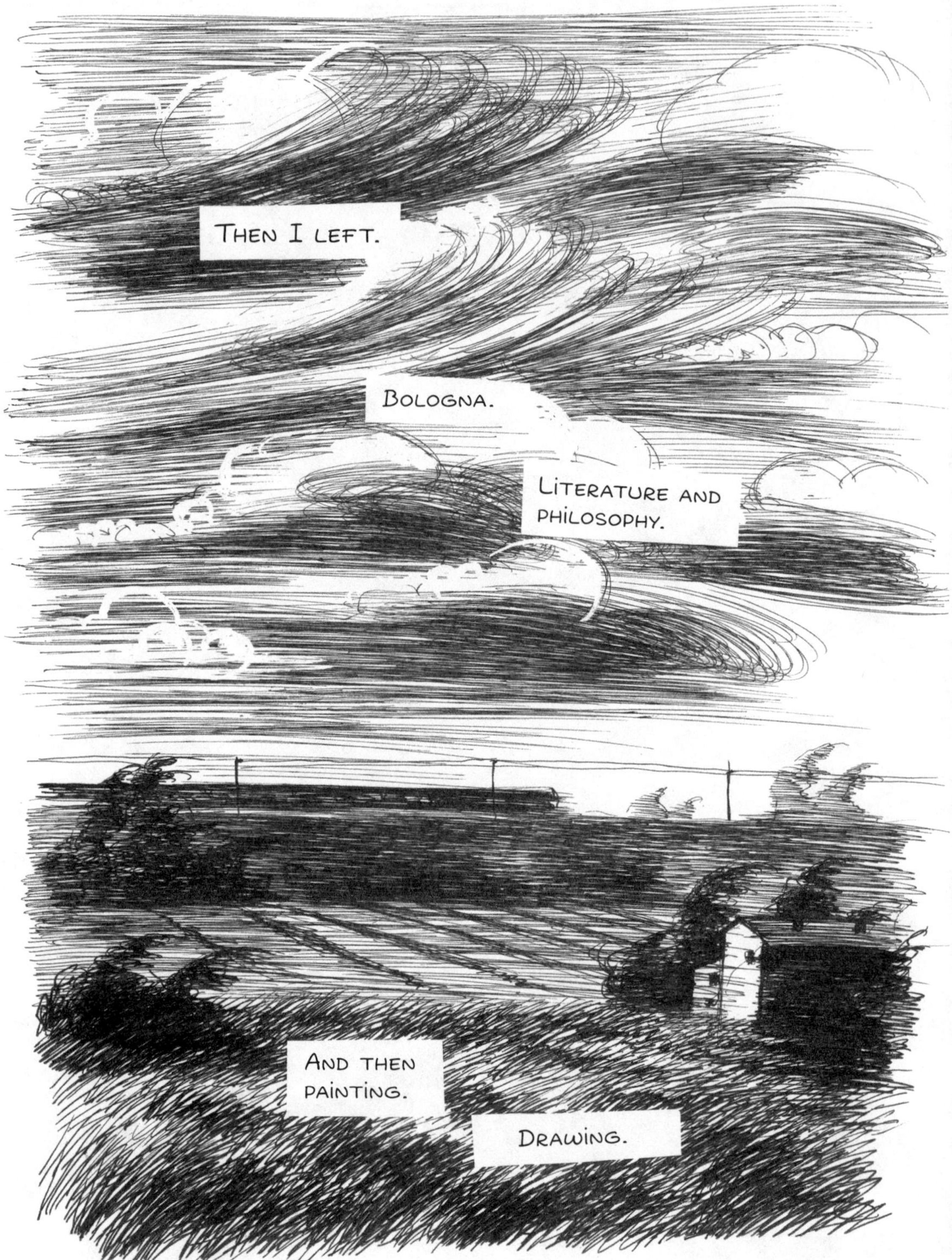
Then I left.
Bologna.
Literature and philosophy.
And then painting.
Drawing.

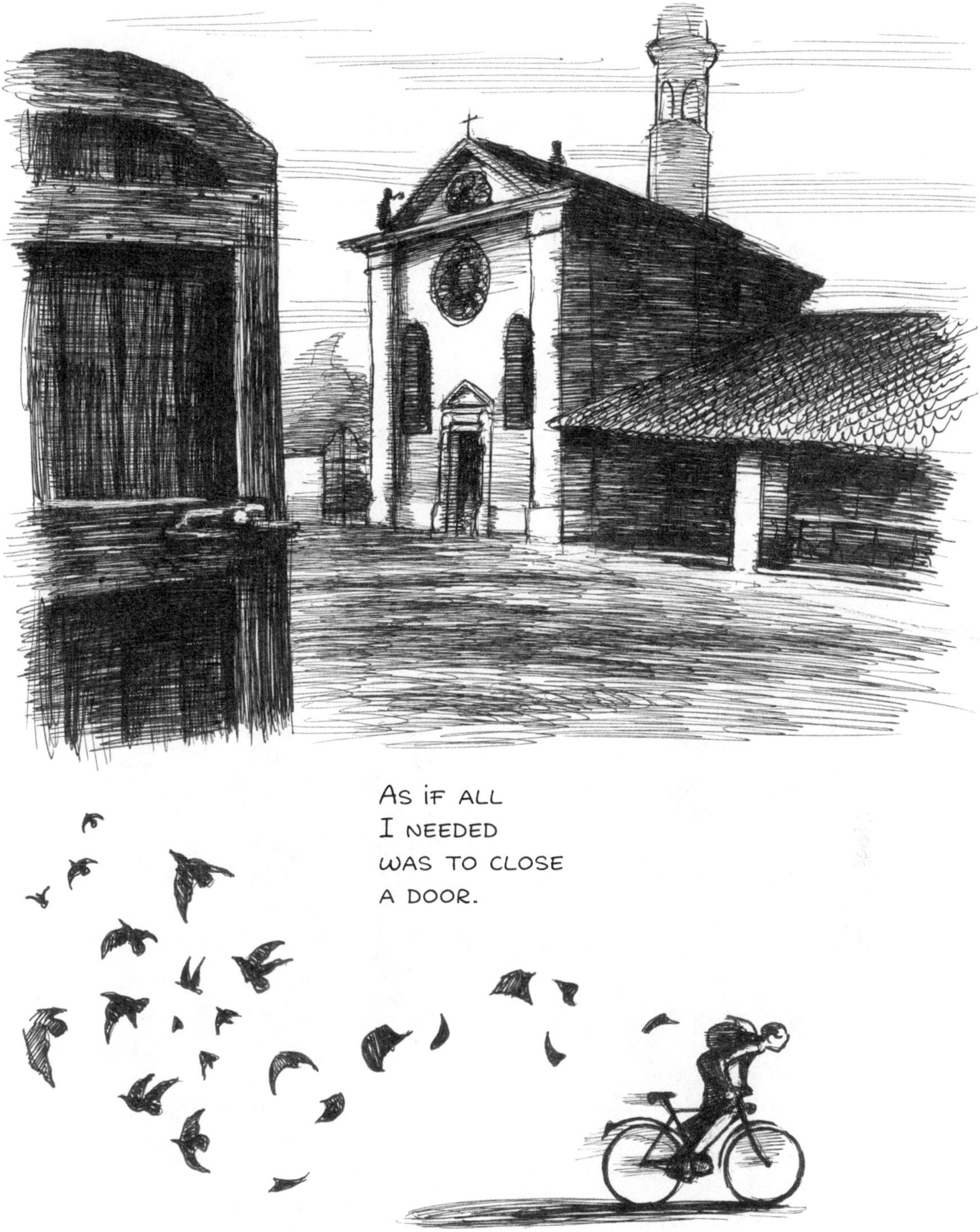
As if all
I needed
was to close
a door.

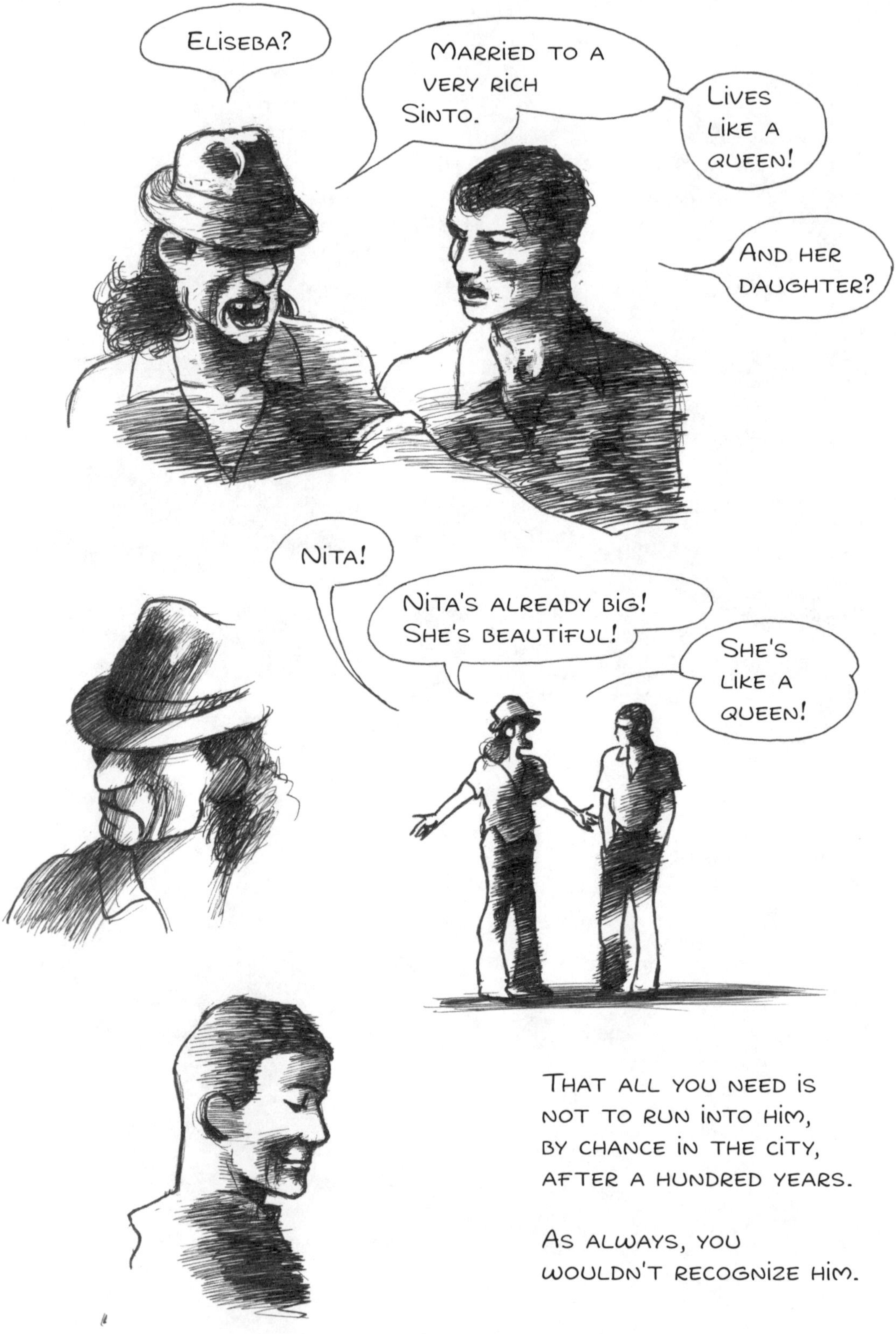
Eliseba?
Married to a very rich Sinto.
Lives like a queen!
And her daughter?
Nita!
Nita's already big! She's beautiful!
She's like a queen!
That all you need is not to run into him, by chance in the city, after a hundred years.
As always, you wouldn't recognize him.

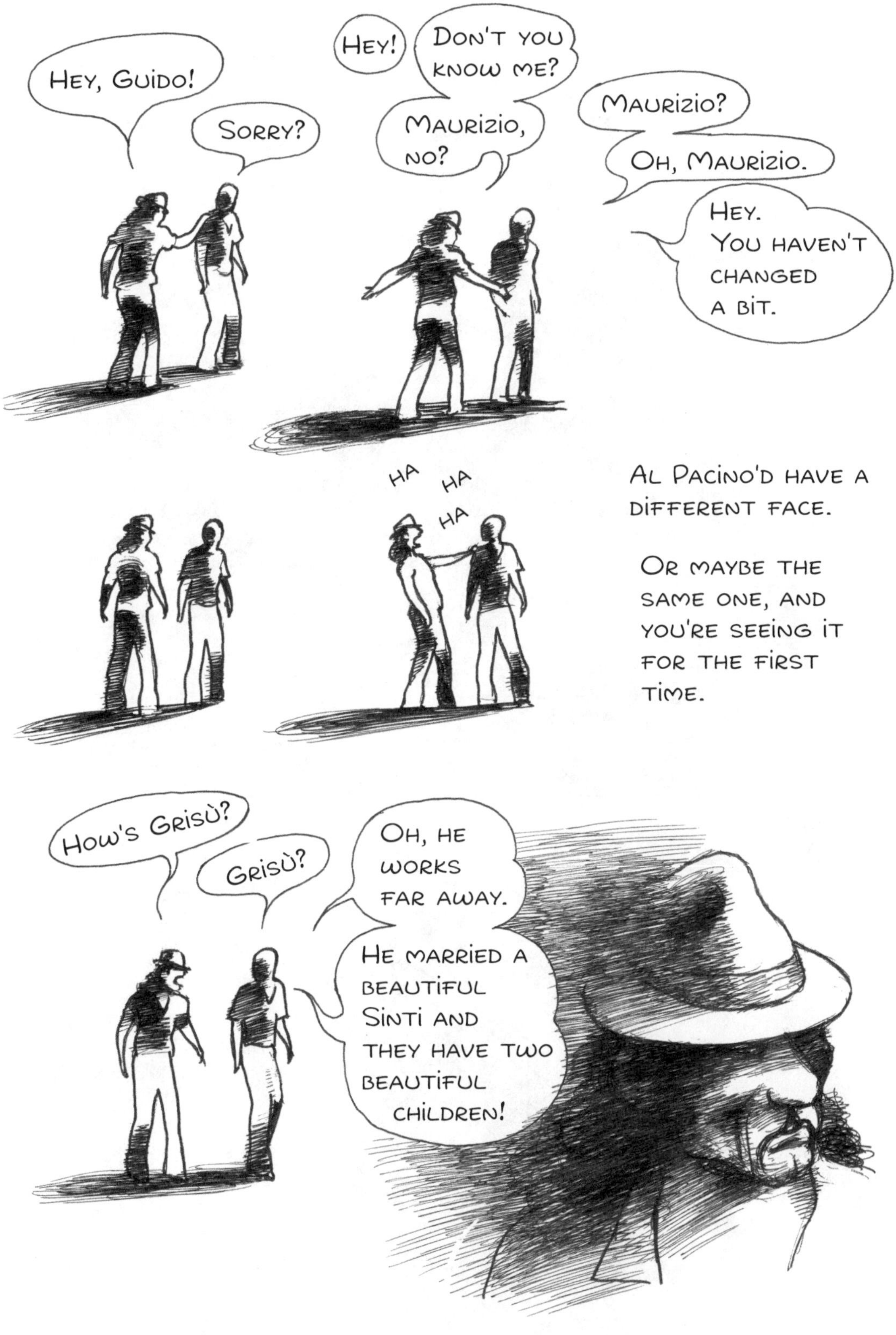
Hey, Guido!
Sorry?
Hey!
Don't you know me?
Maurizio, no?
Maurizio?
Oh, Maurizio.
Hey. You haven't changed a bit.
HA HA HA
Al Pacino'd have a different face.
Or maybe the same one, and you're seeing it for the first time.
How's Grisù?
Grisù?
Oh, he works far away.
He married a beautiful Sinti and they have two beautiful children!

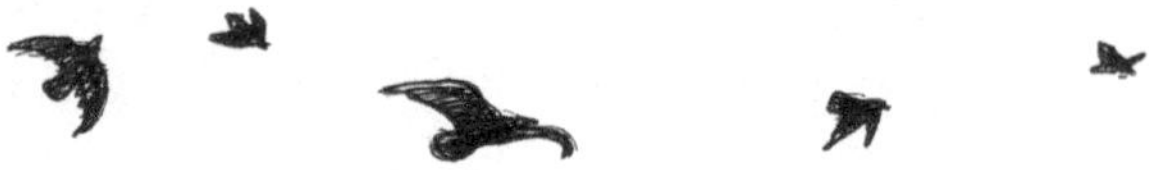

Well, sort of.

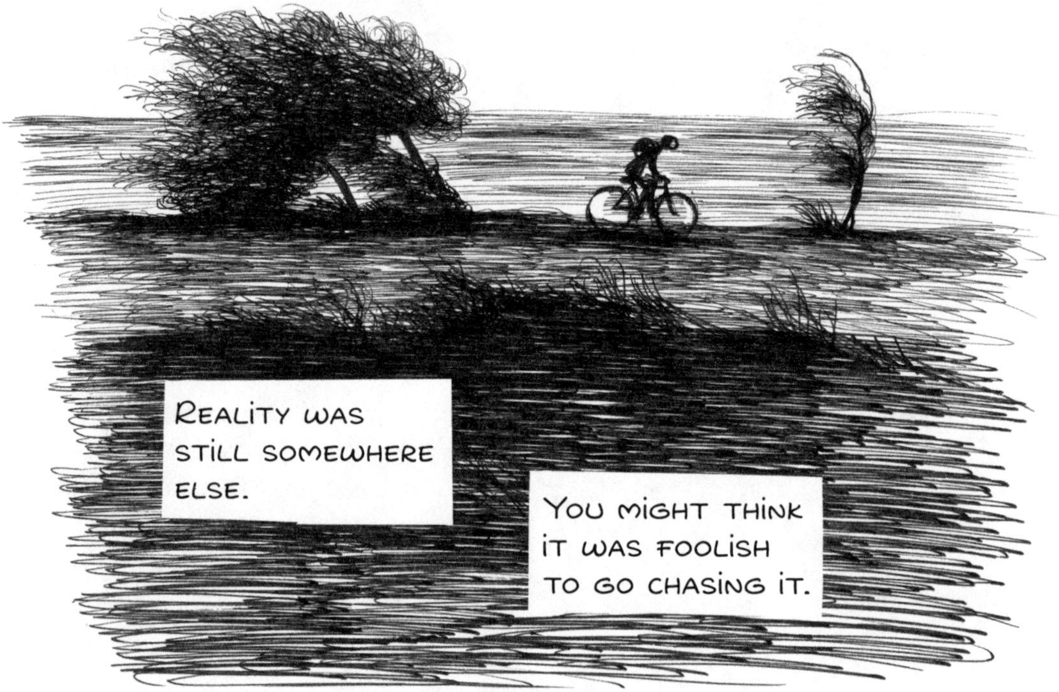

Reality was still somewhere else.
You might think it was foolish to go chasing it.

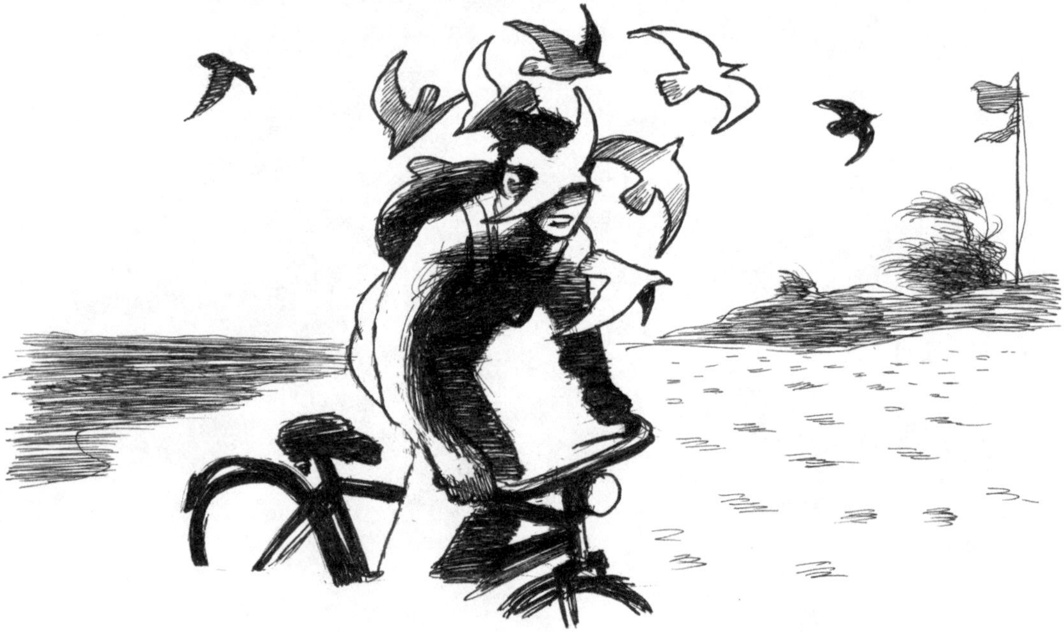

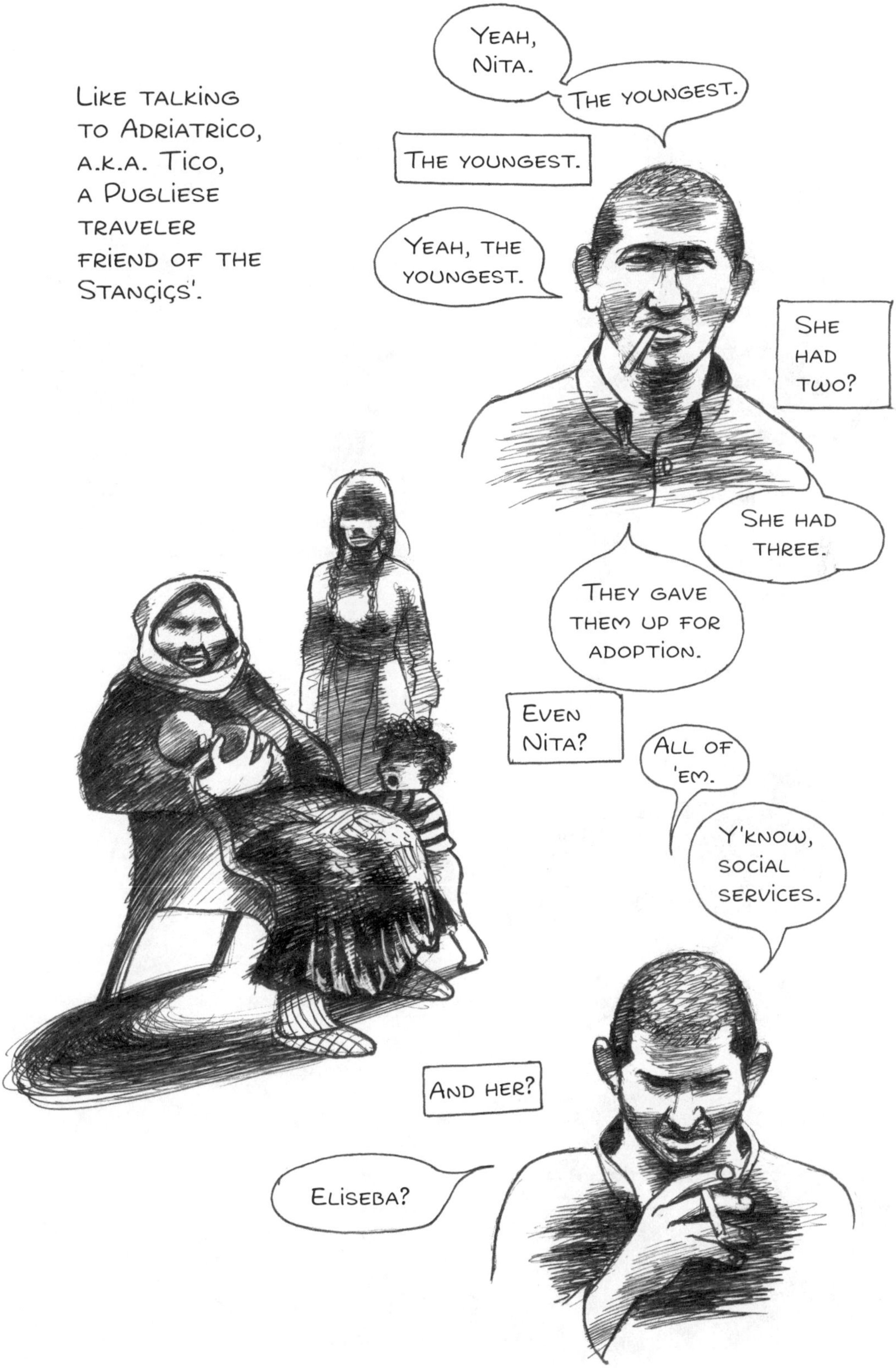
Like talking to Adriatrico, a.k.a. Tico, a Pugliese traveler friend of the Stançiçs'.
Yeah, Nita.
The youngest.
The youngest.
Yeah, the youngest.
She had two?
She had three.
They gave them up for adoption.
Even Nita?
All of 'em.
Y'know, social services.
And her?
Eliseba?

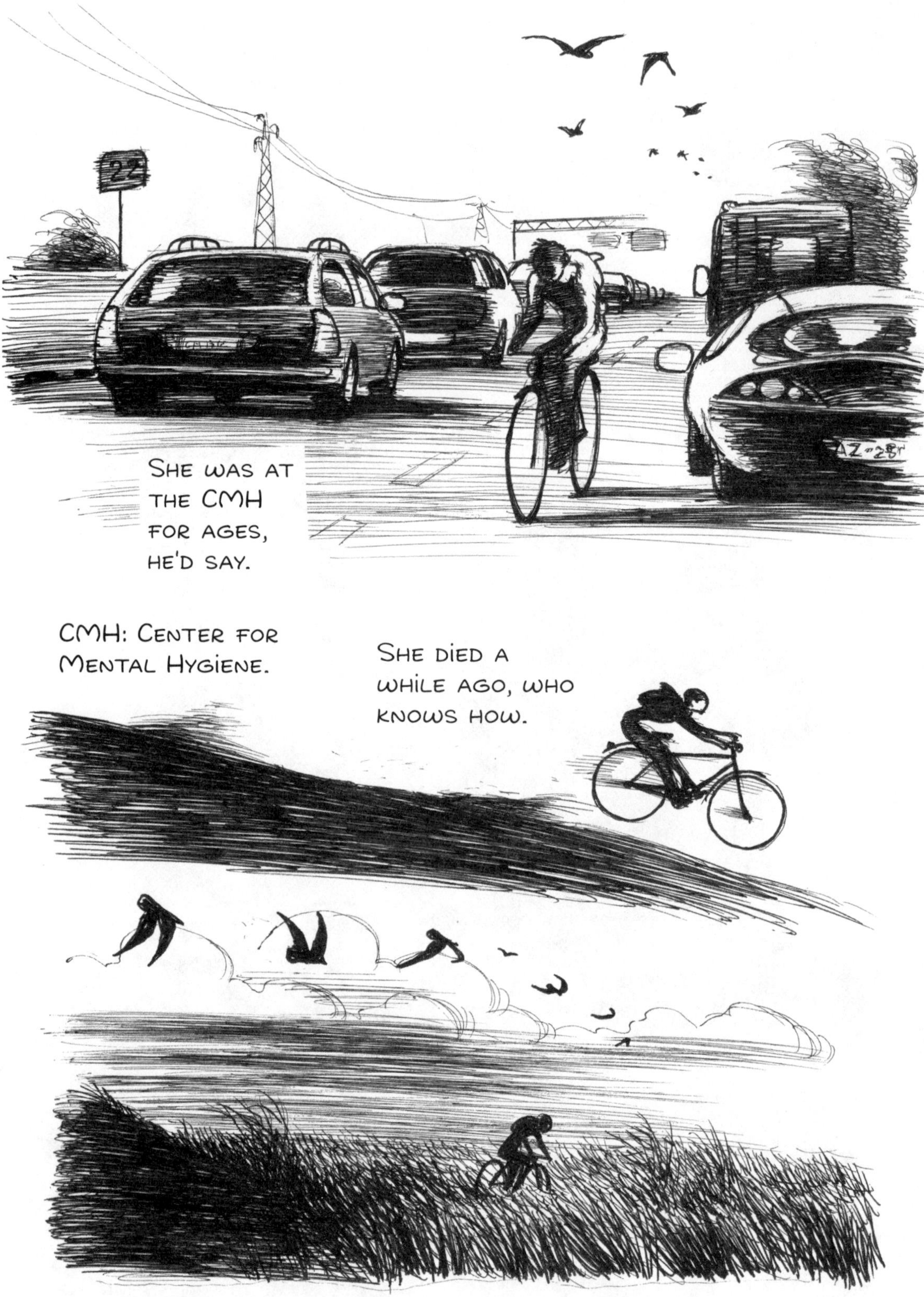
SHE WAS AT THE CMH FOR AGES, HE'D SAY.
CMH: CENTER FOR MENTAL HYGIENE.
SHE DIED A WHILE AGO, WHO KNOWS HOW.

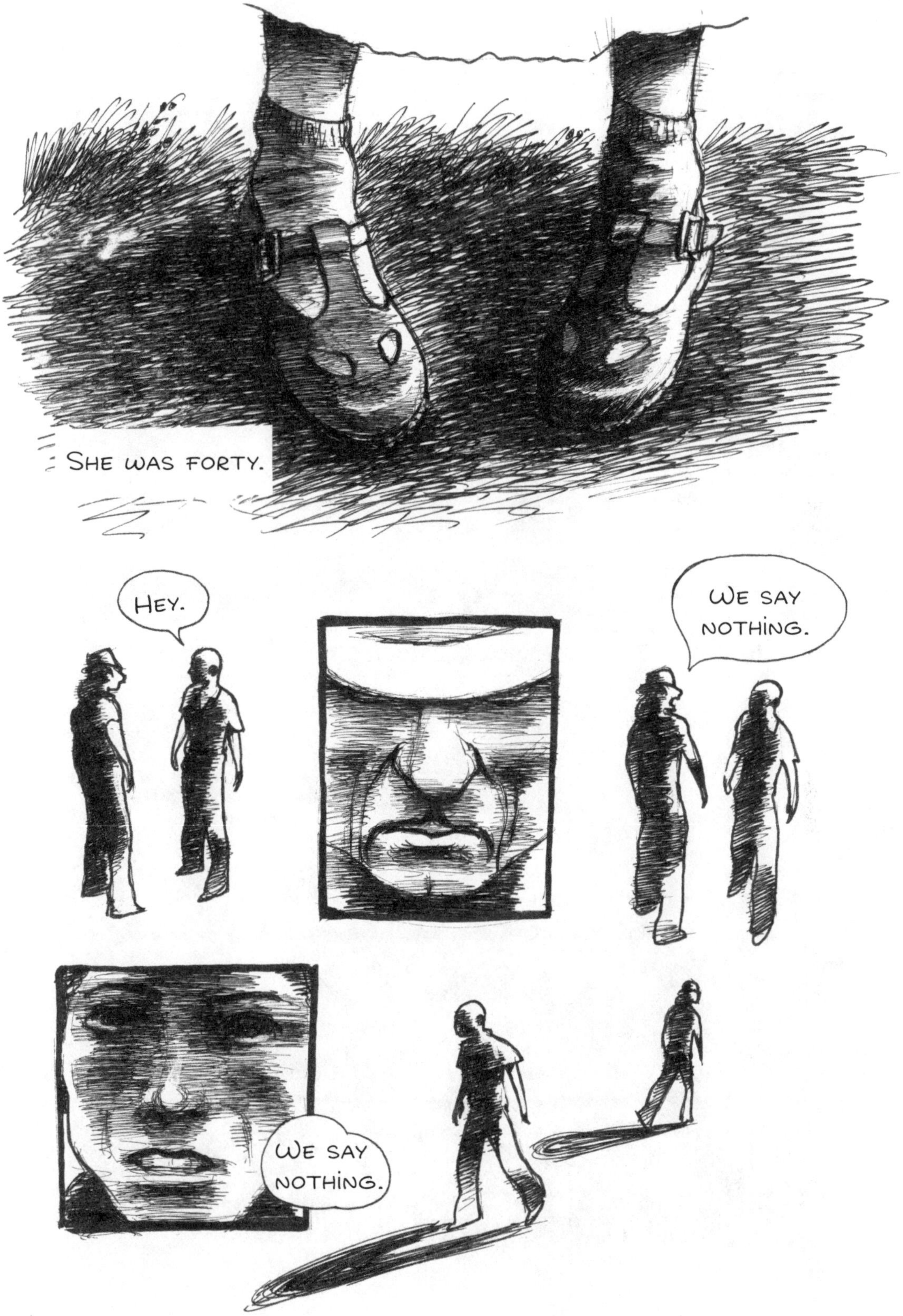
SHE WAS FORTY.
HEY.
WE SAY NOTHING.
WE SAY NOTHING.

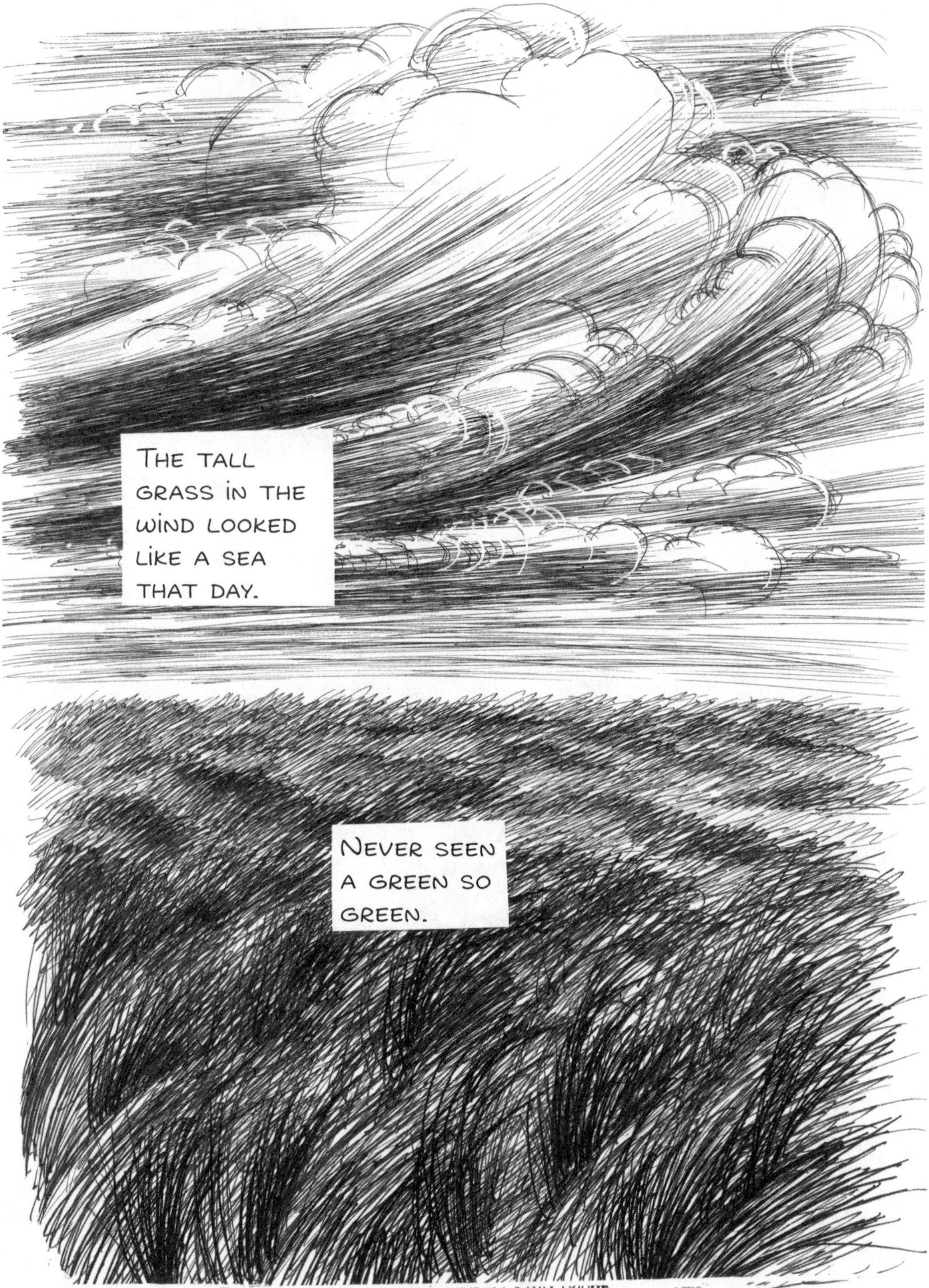
THE TALL GRASS IN THE WIND LOOKED LIKE A SEA THAT DAY.
NEVER SEEN A GREEN SO GREEN.

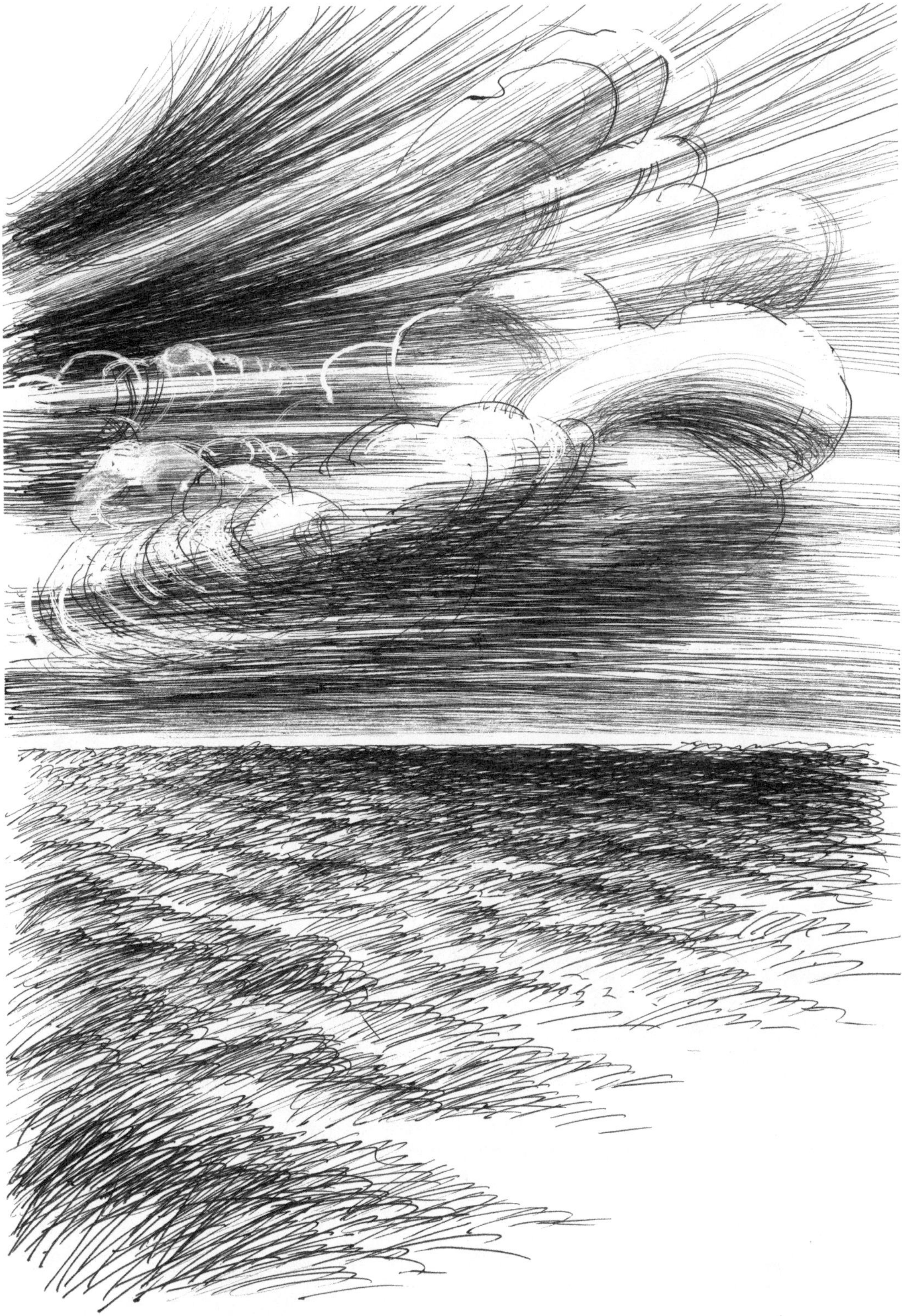

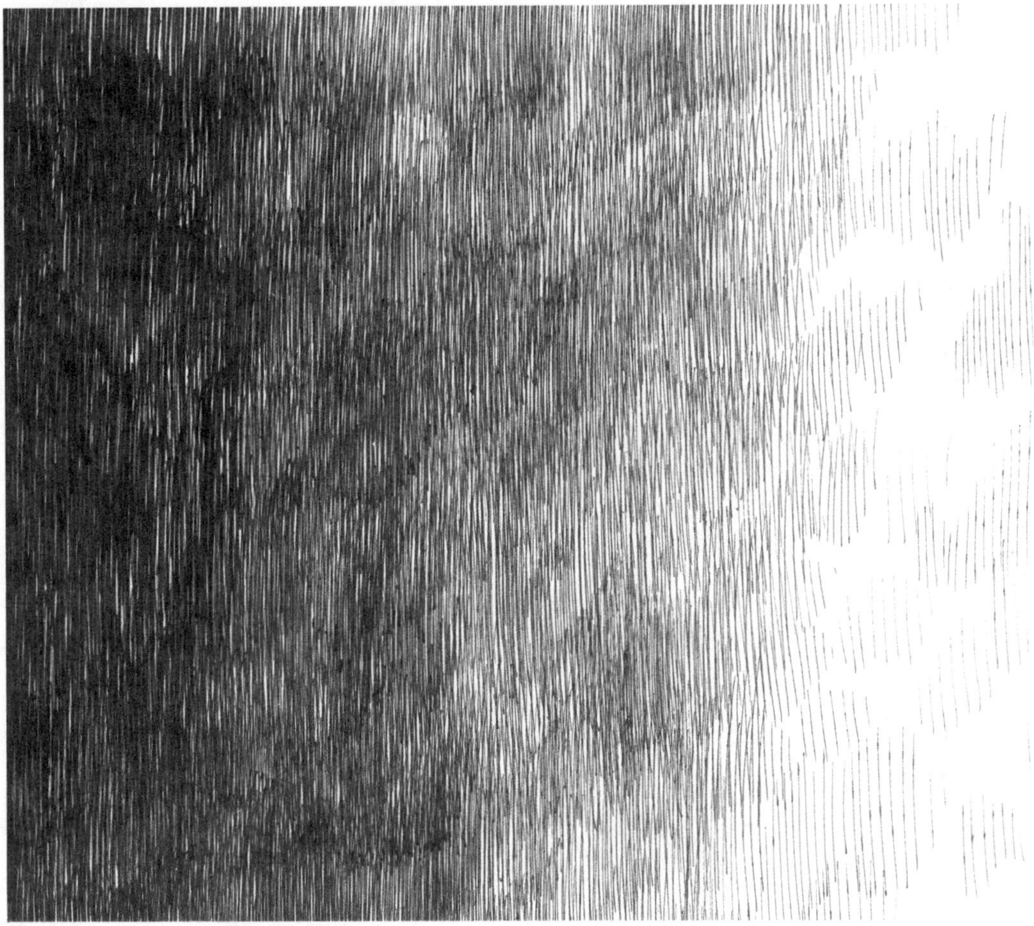

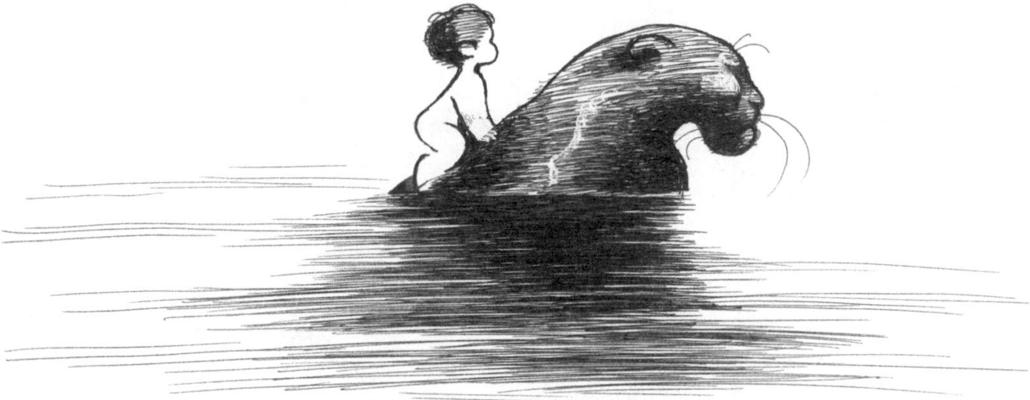

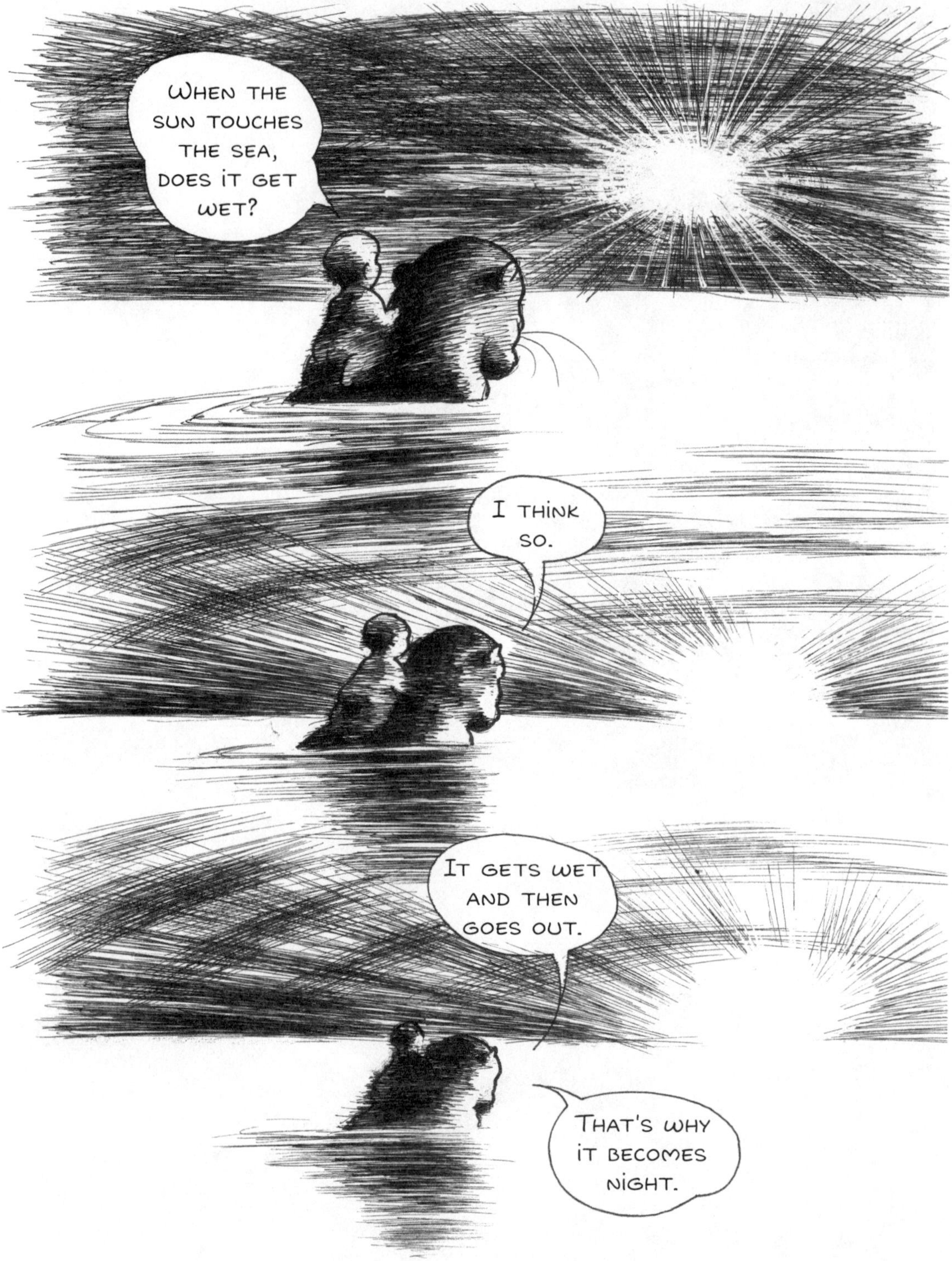
WHEN THE SUN TOUCHES THE SEA, DOES IT GET WET?
I THINK SO.
IT GETS WET AND THEN GOES OUT.
THAT'S WHY IT BECOMES NIGHT.

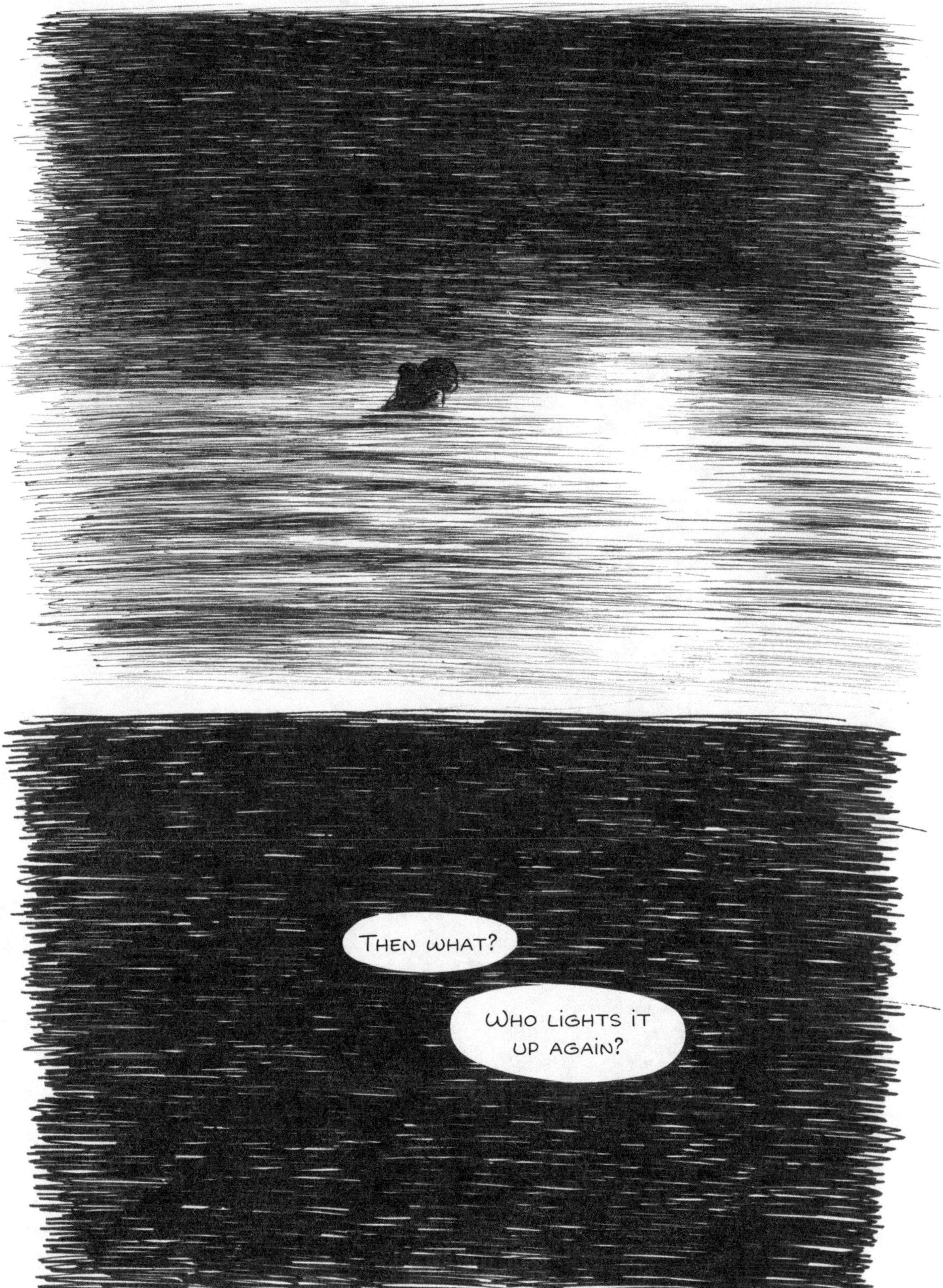
Then what?
Who lights it up again?

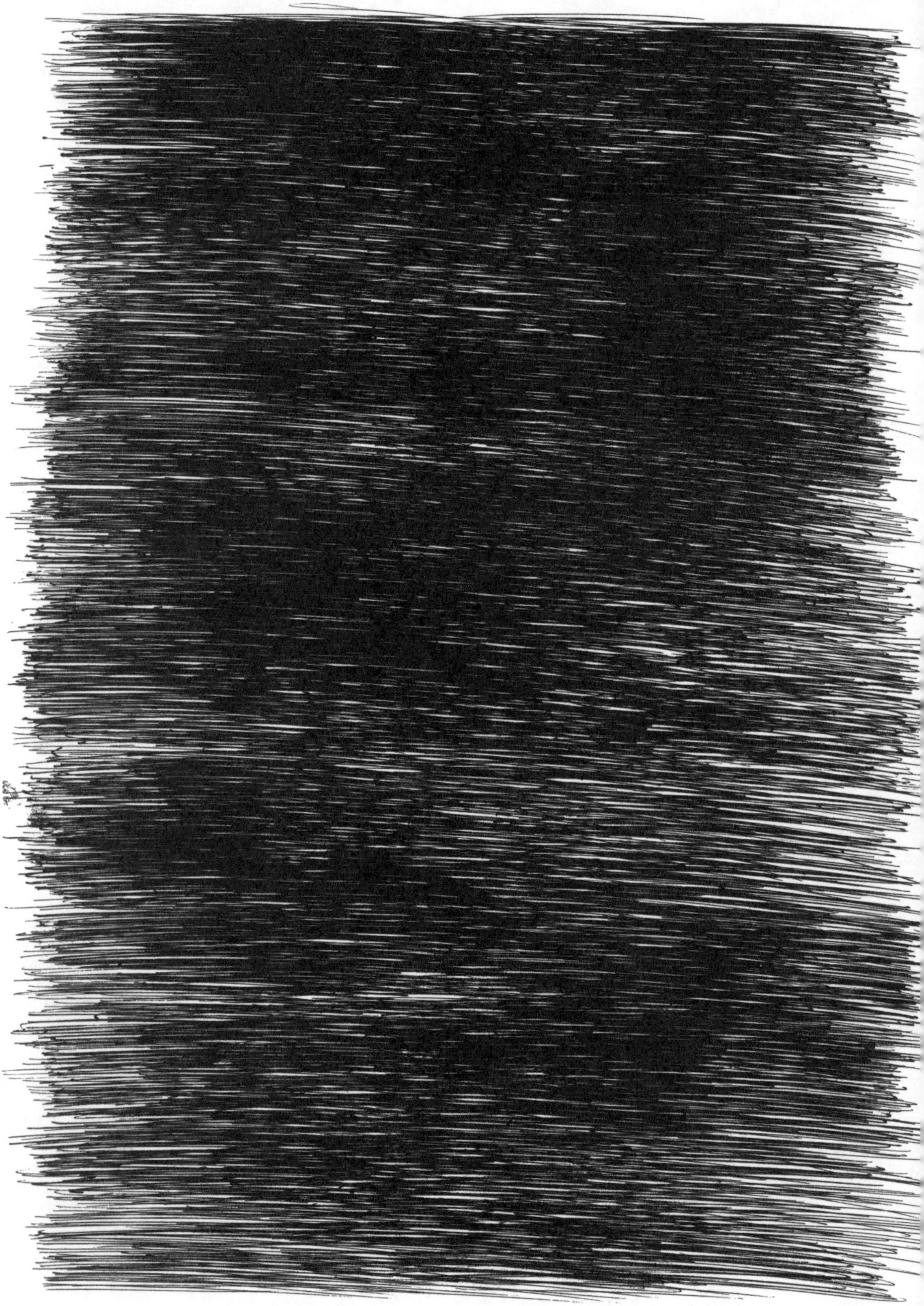

to Otello and Dina

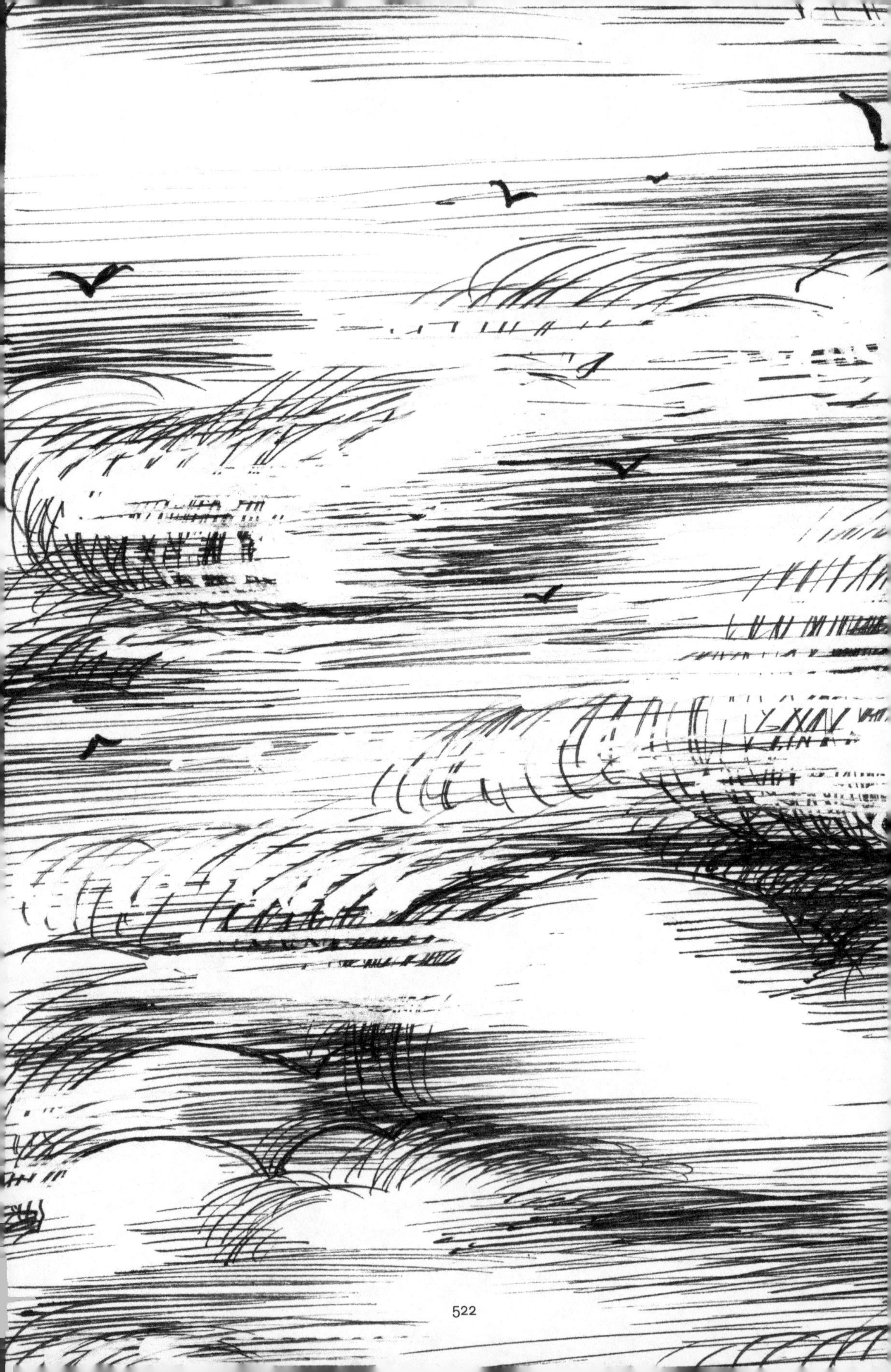

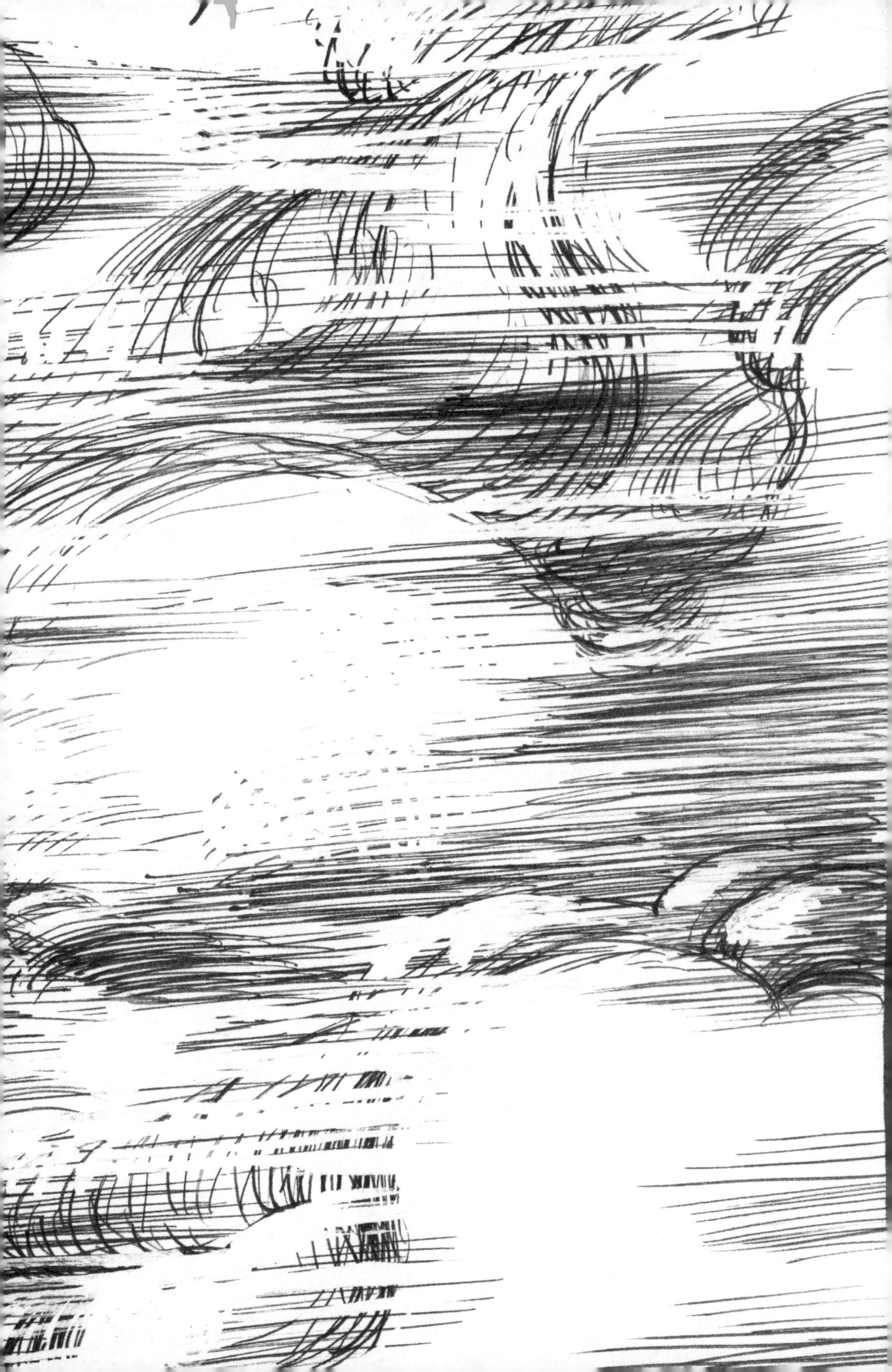

P.S.

Stories don't end, they go on between talk and hearsay, sometimes going back in time.

The following is one of the first things I drew and one of the last I finished.

It comes from far away. It's about rediscovering a doll.

THE STORY OF PAPUSZA

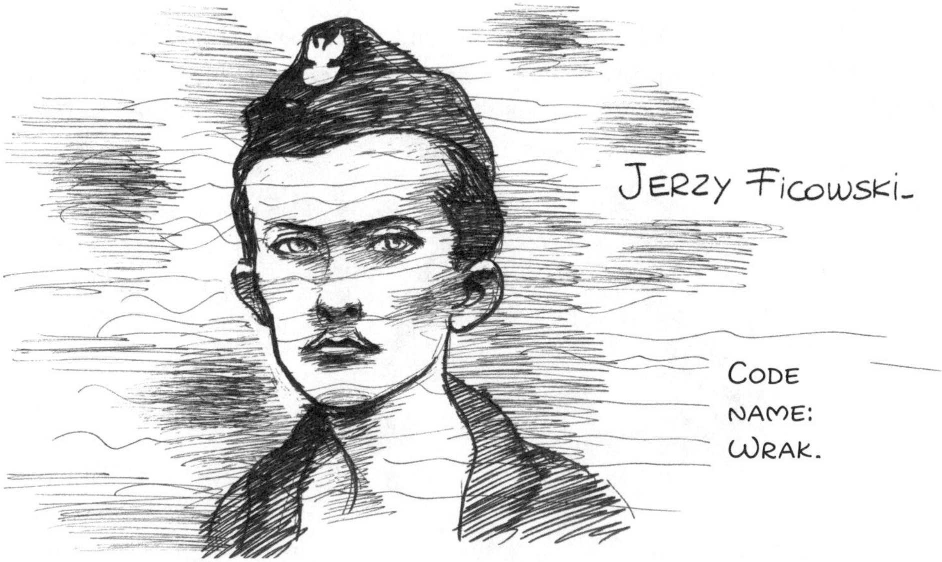
Jerzy Ficowski.
Code name: Wrak.

In his youth, he fights in the Polish resistance against Nazi occupation in the AK (Armia Krajowa, Polish Home Army), the underground army still loyal to the Polish government exiled in London.

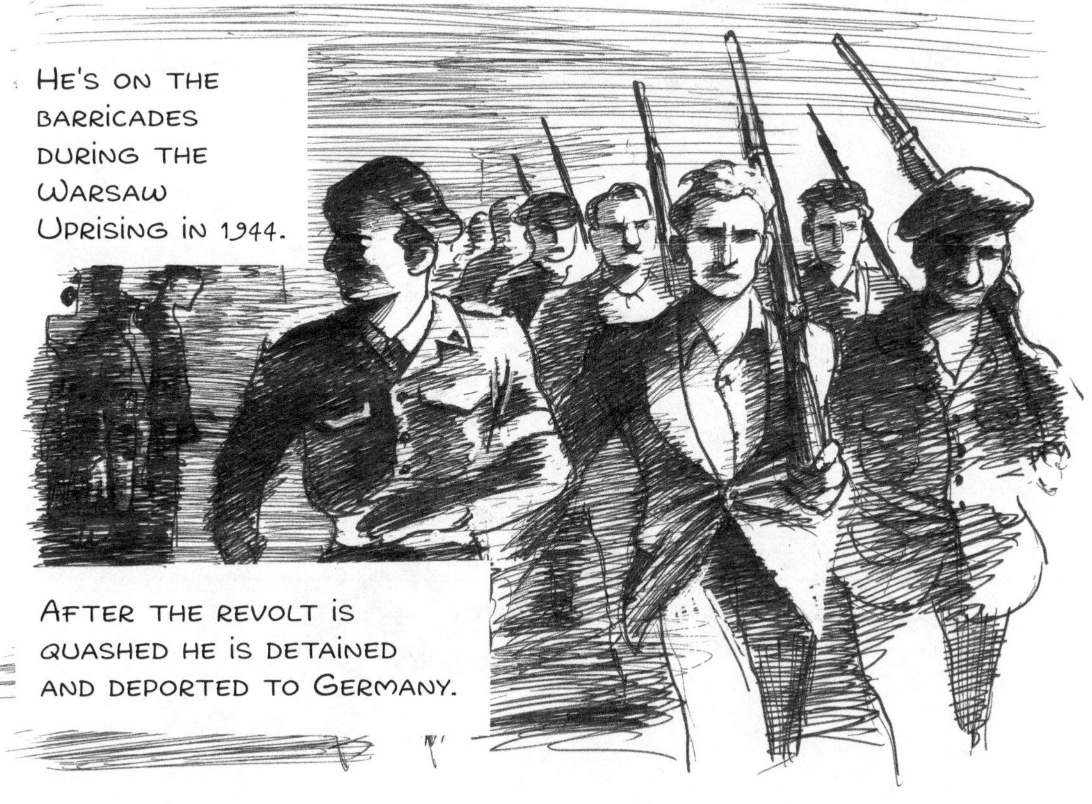
He's on the barricades during the Warsaw Uprising in 1944.
After the revolt is quashed he is detained and deported to Germany.

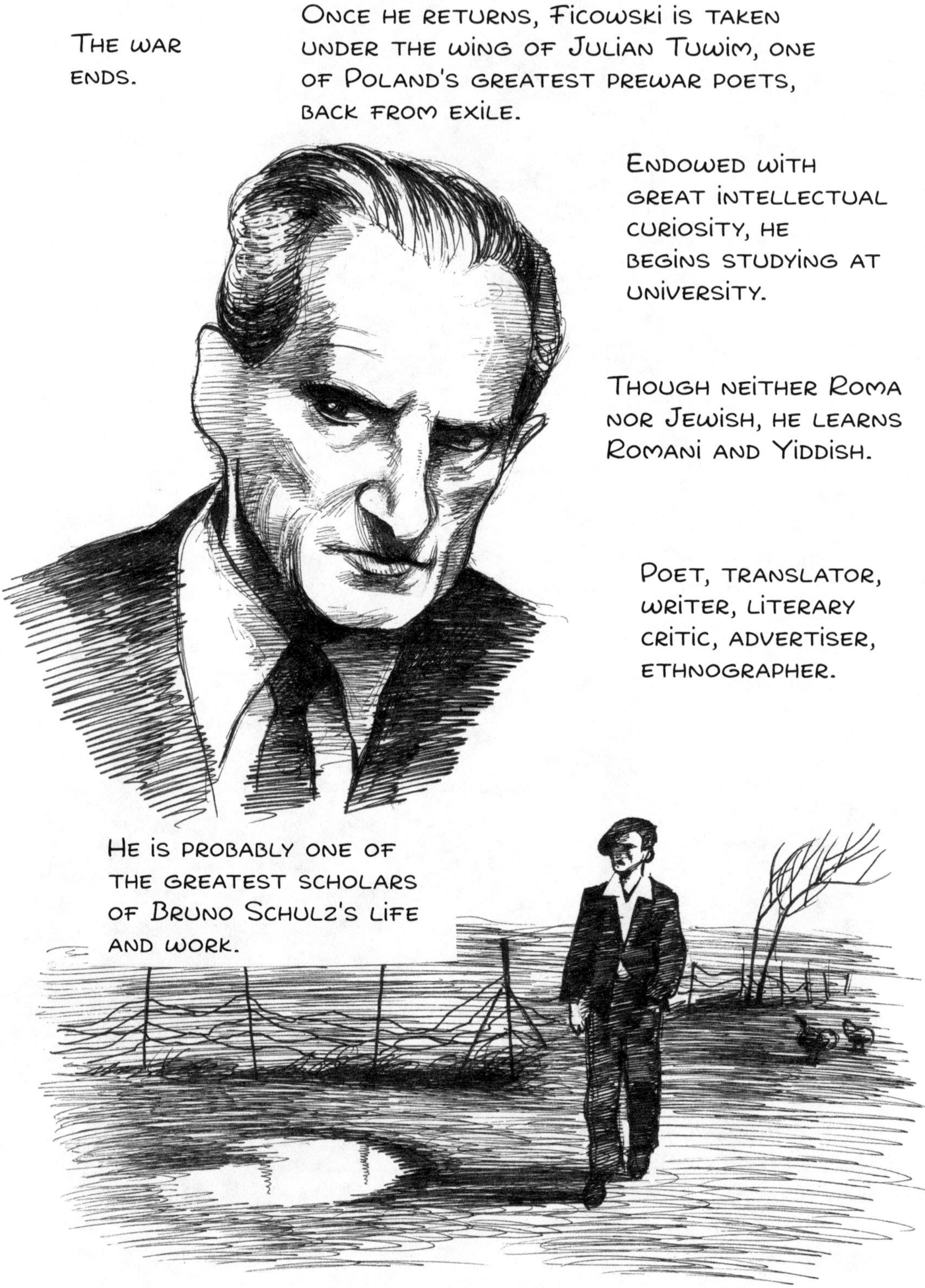
THE WAR ENDS.
ONCE HE RETURNS, FICOWSKI IS TAKEN UNDER THE WING OF JULIAN TUWIM, ONE OF POLAND'S GREATEST PREWAR POETS, BACK FROM EXILE.
ENDOWED WITH GREAT INTELLECTUAL CURIOSITY, HE BEGINS STUDYING AT UNIVERSITY.
THOUGH NEITHER ROMA NOR JEWISH, HE LEARNS ROMANI AND YIDDISH.
POET, TRANSLATOR, WRITER, LITERARY CRITIC, ADVERTISER, ETHNOGRAPHER.
HE IS PROBABLY ONE OF THE GREATEST SCHOLARS OF BRUNO SCHULZ'S LIFE AND WORK.

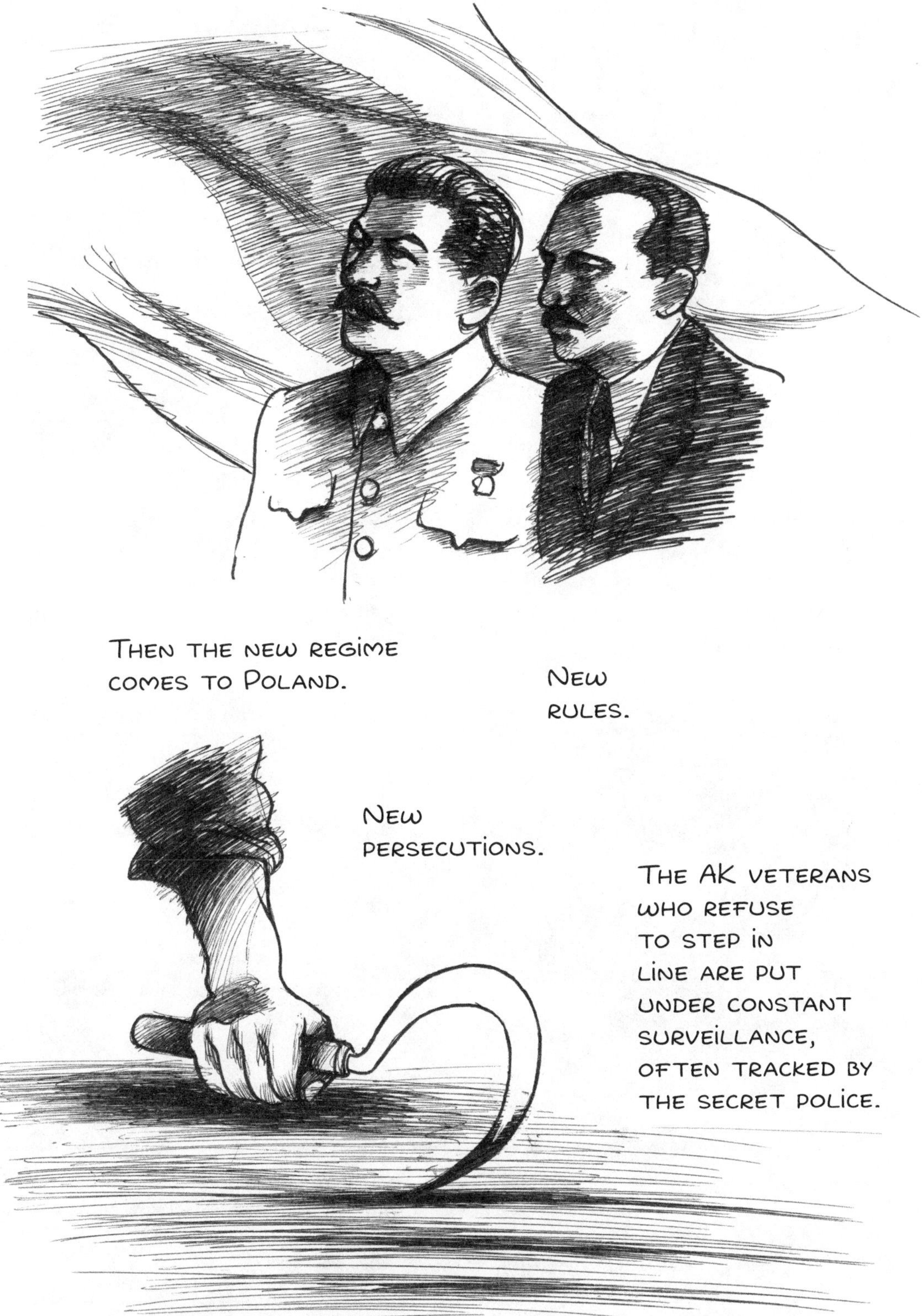
THEN THE NEW REGIME
COMES TO POLAND.
NEW
RULES.
NEW
PERSECUTIONS.
THE AK VETERANS
WHO REFUSE
TO STEP IN
LINE ARE PUT
UNDER CONSTANT
SURVEILLANCE,
OFTEN TRACKED BY
THE SECRET POLICE.

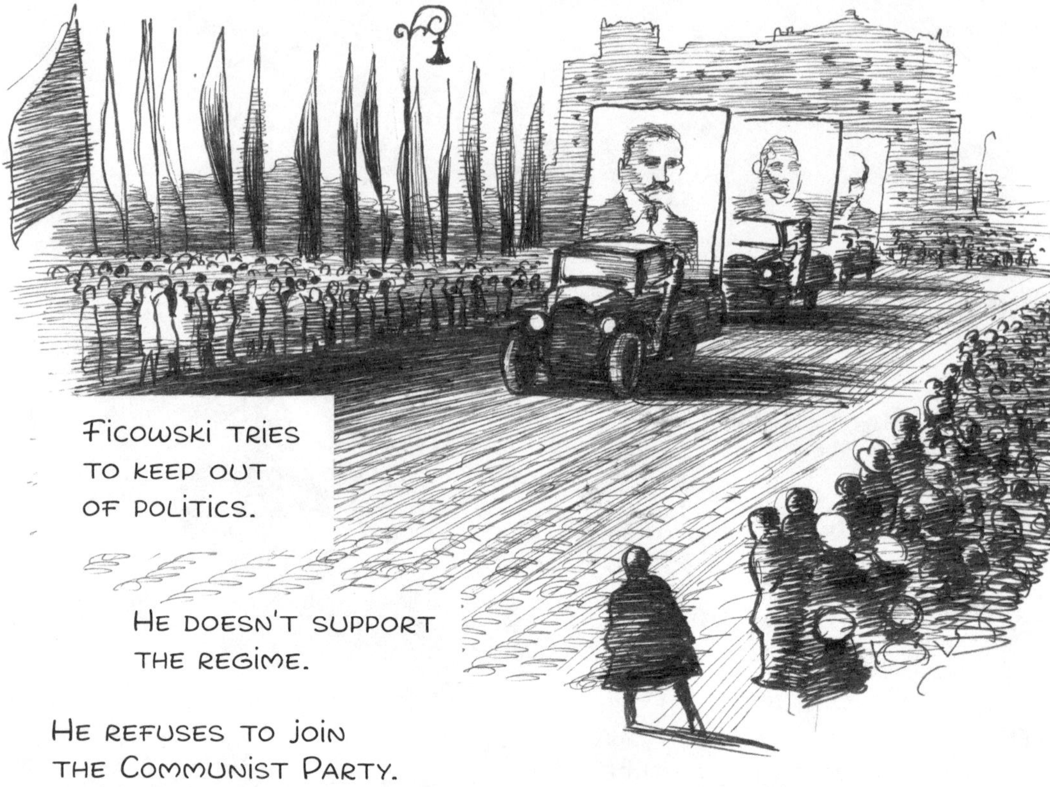

Ficowski tries to keep out of politics.
He doesn't support the regime.
He refuses to join the Communist Party.

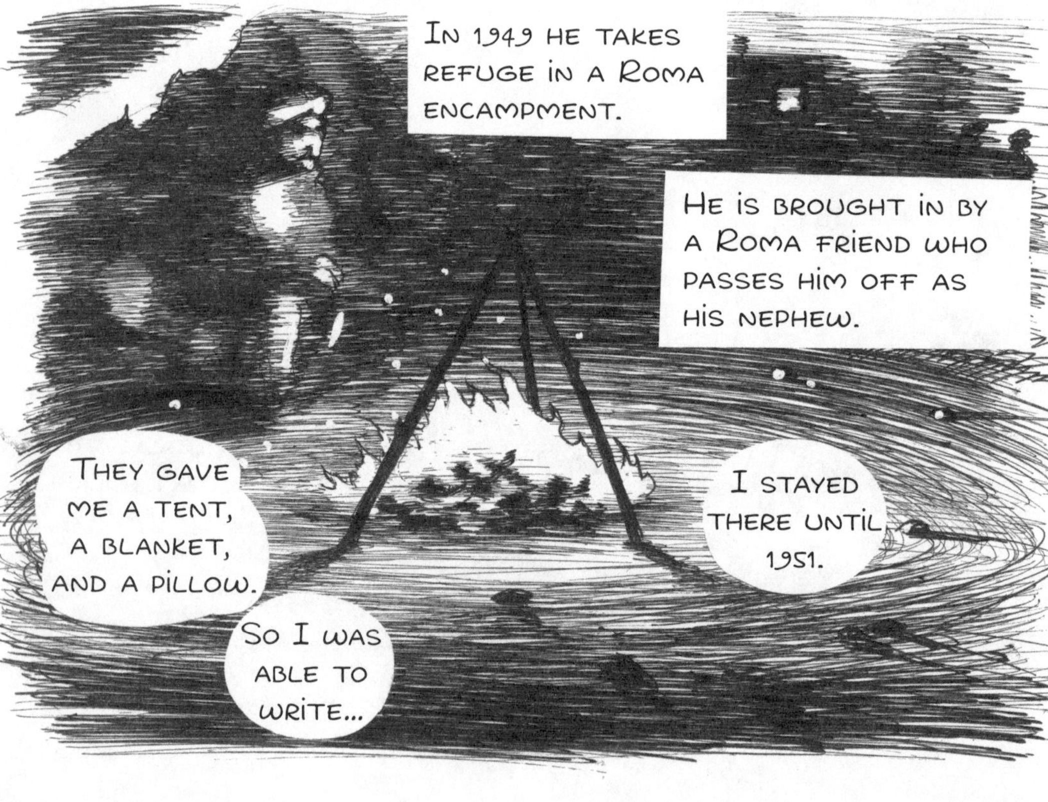

In 1949 he takes refuge in a Roma encampment.
He is brought in by a Roma friend who passes him off as his nephew.
They gave me a tent, a blanket, and a pillow.
So I was able to write...
I stayed there until 1951.

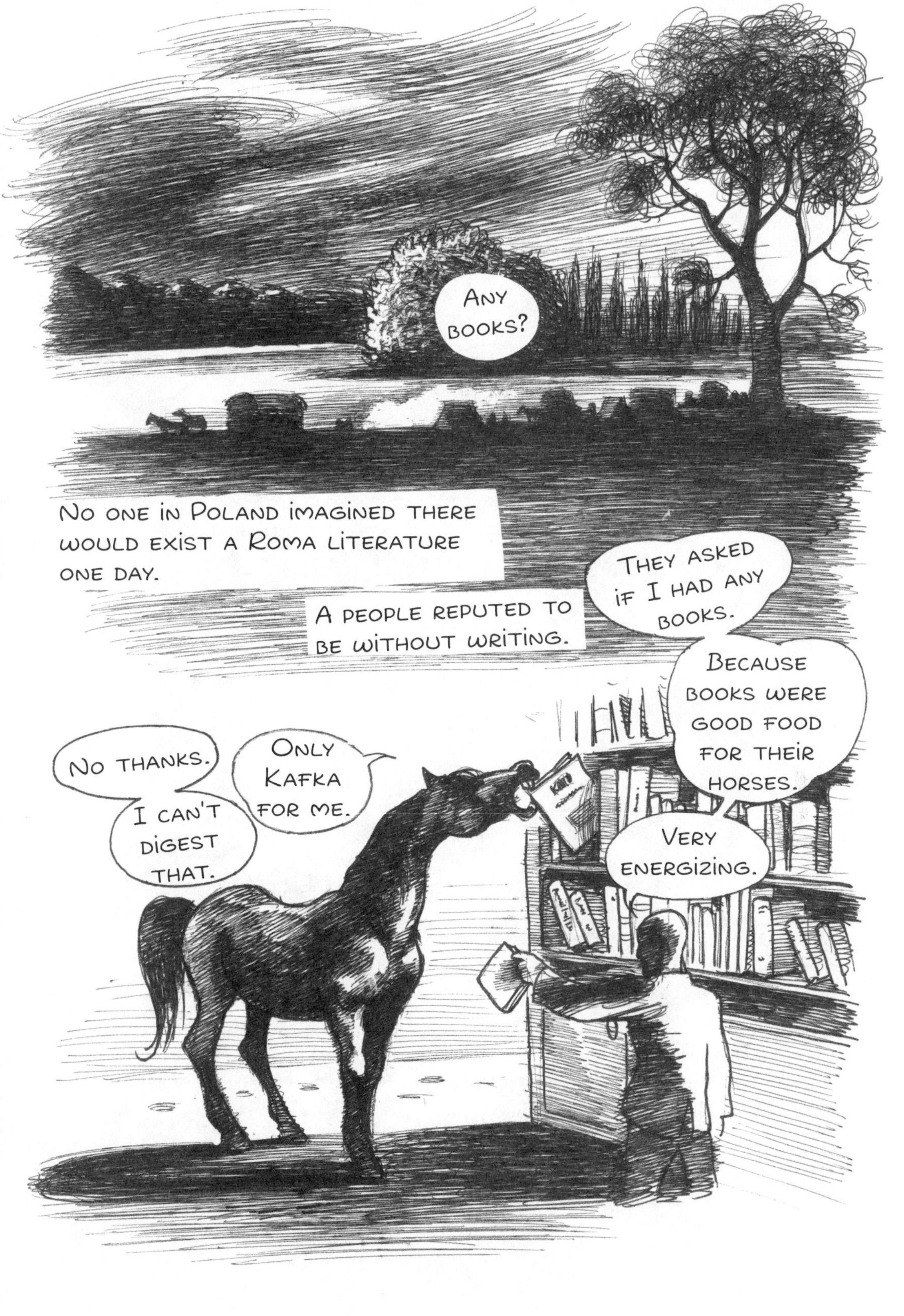
Any books?
No one in Poland imagined there would exist a Roma literature one day.
A people reputed to be without writing.
They asked if I had any books.
Because books were good food for their horses.
No thanks. I can't digest that.
Only Kafka for me.
Very energizing.

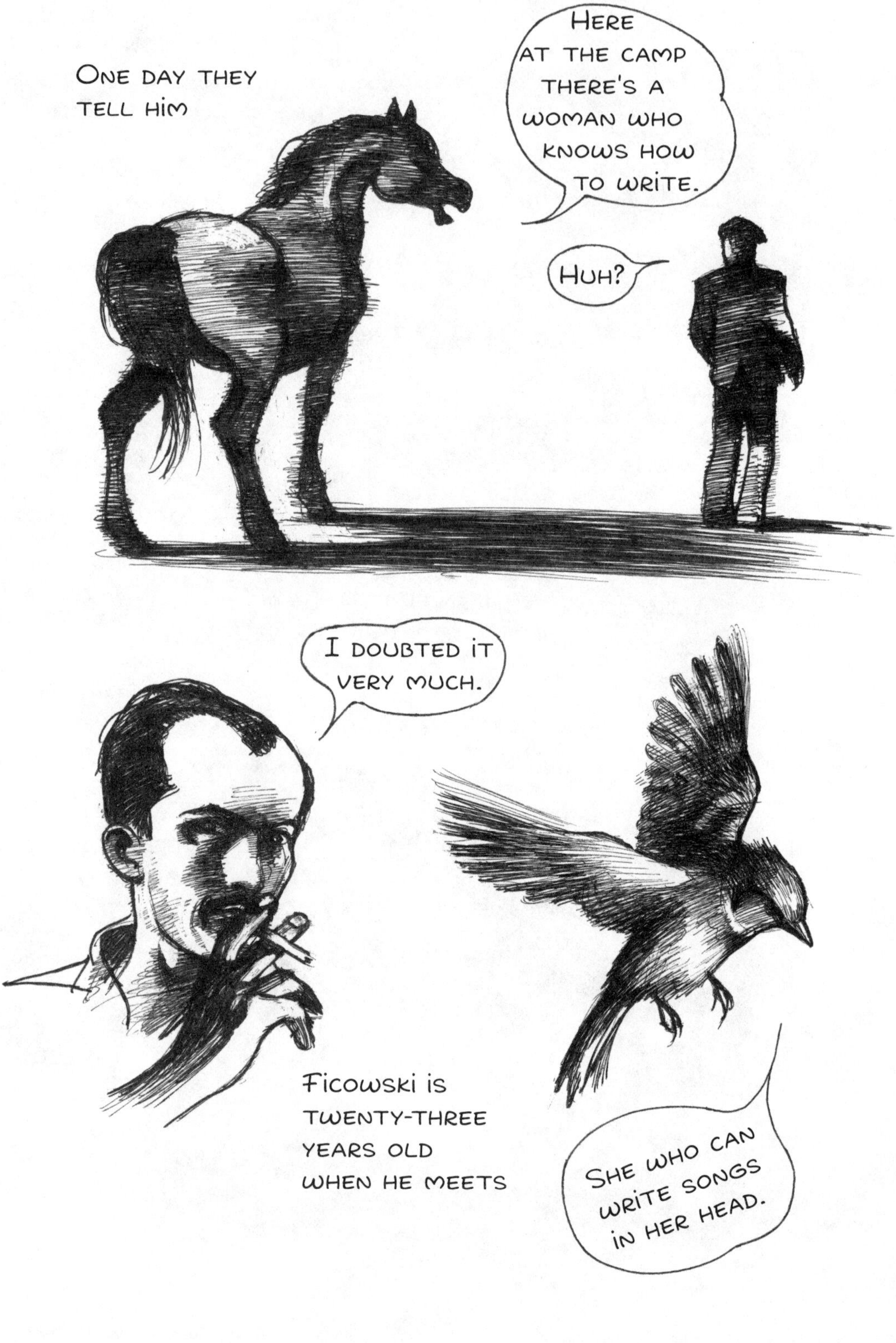
One day they tell him
Here at the camp there's a woman who knows how to write.
Huh?
I doubted it very much.
Ficowski is twenty-three years old when he meets
She who can write songs in her head.

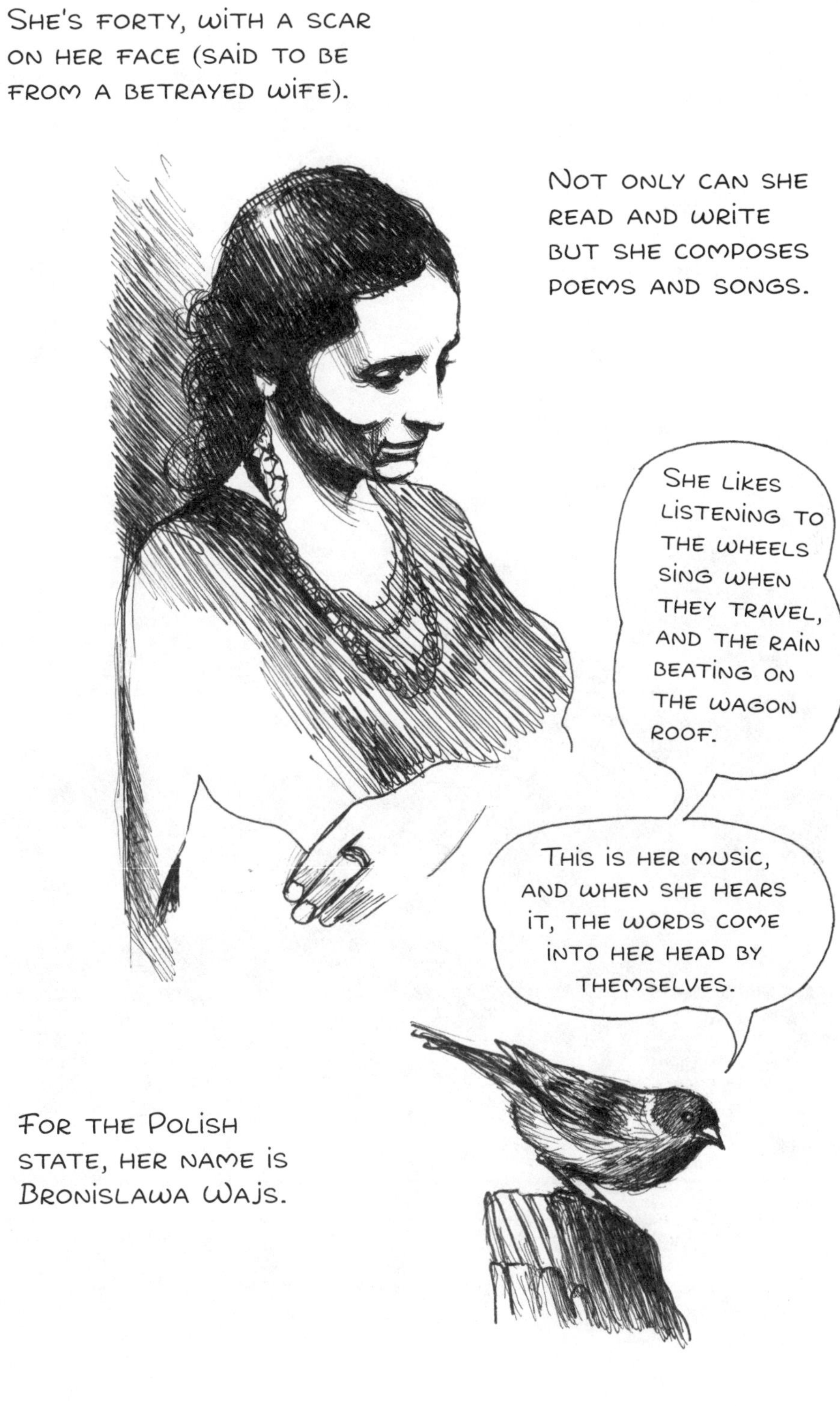
SHE'S FORTY, WITH A SCAR ON HER FACE (SAID TO BE FROM A BETRAYED WIFE).
NOT ONLY CAN SHE READ AND WRITE BUT SHE COMPOSES POEMS AND SONGS.
SHE LIKES LISTENING TO THE WHEELS SING WHEN THEY TRAVEL, AND THE RAIN BEATING ON THE WAGON ROOF.
THIS IS HER MUSIC, AND WHEN SHE HEARS IT, THE WORDS COME INTO HER HEAD BY THEMSELVES.
FOR THE POLISH STATE, HER NAME IS BRONISLAWA WAJS.

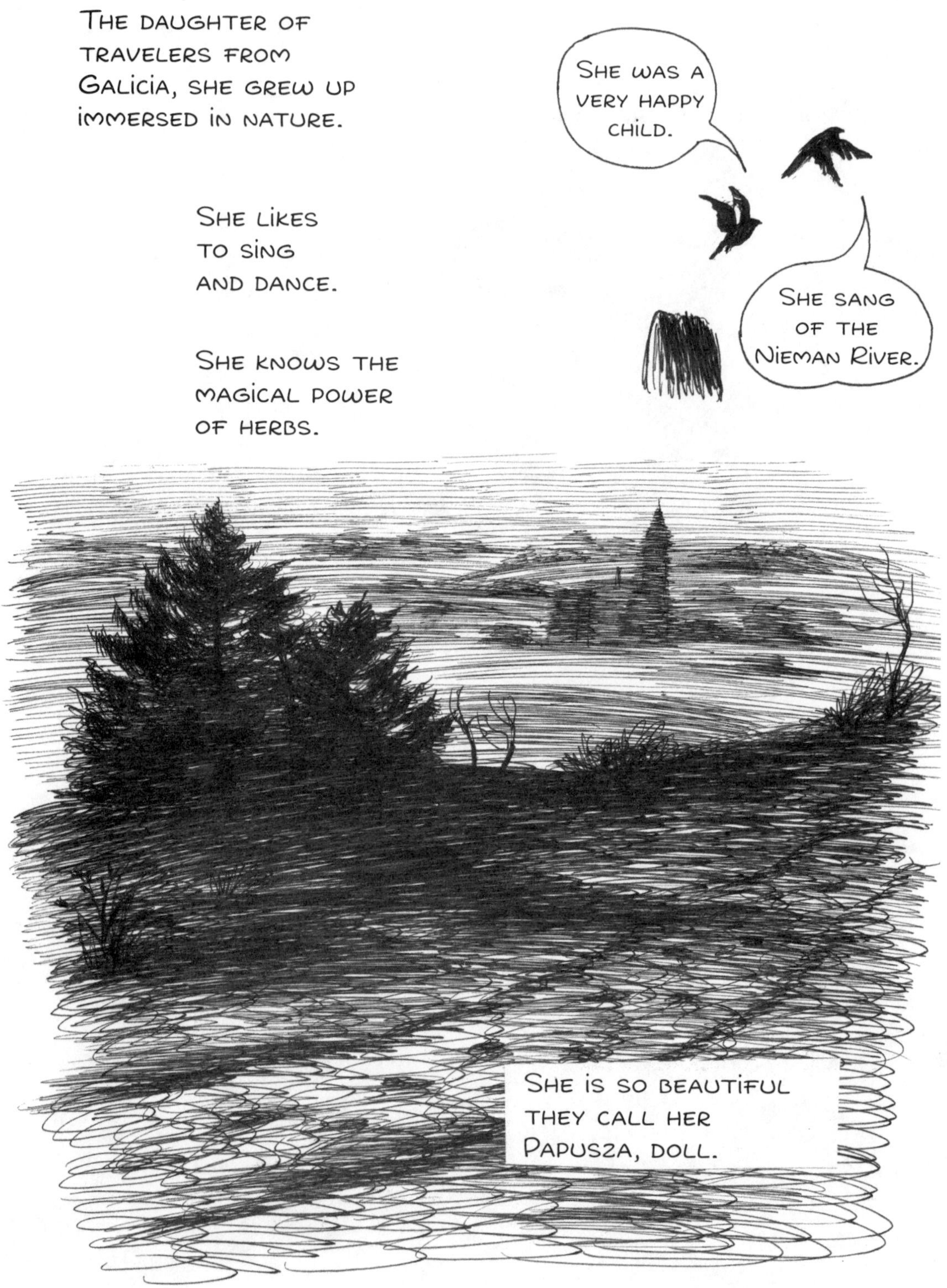
THE DAUGHTER OF TRAVELERS FROM GALICIA, SHE GREW UP IMMERSED IN NATURE.
SHE WAS A VERY HAPPY CHILD.
SHE LIKES TO SING AND DANCE.
SHE SANG OF THE NIEMAN RIVER.
SHE KNOWS THE MAGICAL POWER OF HERBS.
SHE IS SO BEAUTIFUL THEY CALL HER PAPUSZA, DOLL.

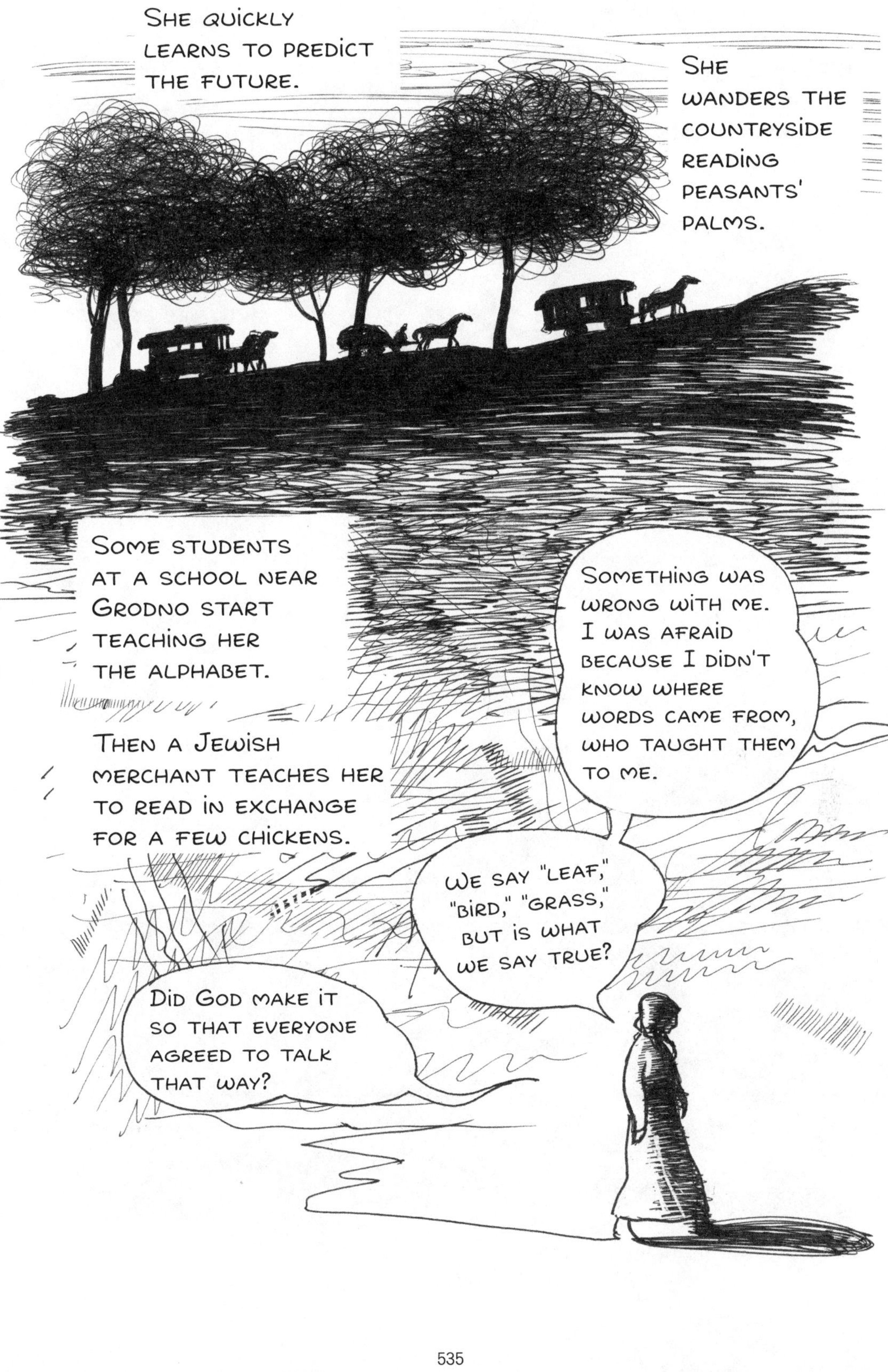

SHE QUICKLY LEARNS TO PREDICT THE FUTURE.
SHE WANDERS THE COUNTRYSIDE READING PEASANTS' PALMS.
SOME STUDENTS AT A SCHOOL NEAR GRODNO START TEACHING HER THE ALPHABET.
THEN A JEWISH MERCHANT TEACHES HER TO READ IN EXCHANGE FOR A FEW CHICKENS.
SOMETHING WAS WRONG WITH ME. I WAS AFRAID BECAUSE I DIDN'T KNOW WHERE WORDS CAME FROM, WHO TAUGHT THEM TO ME.
WE SAY "LEAF," "BIRD," "GRASS," BUT IS WHAT WE SAY TRUE?
DID GOD MAKE IT SO THAT EVERYONE AGREED TO TALK THAT WAY?

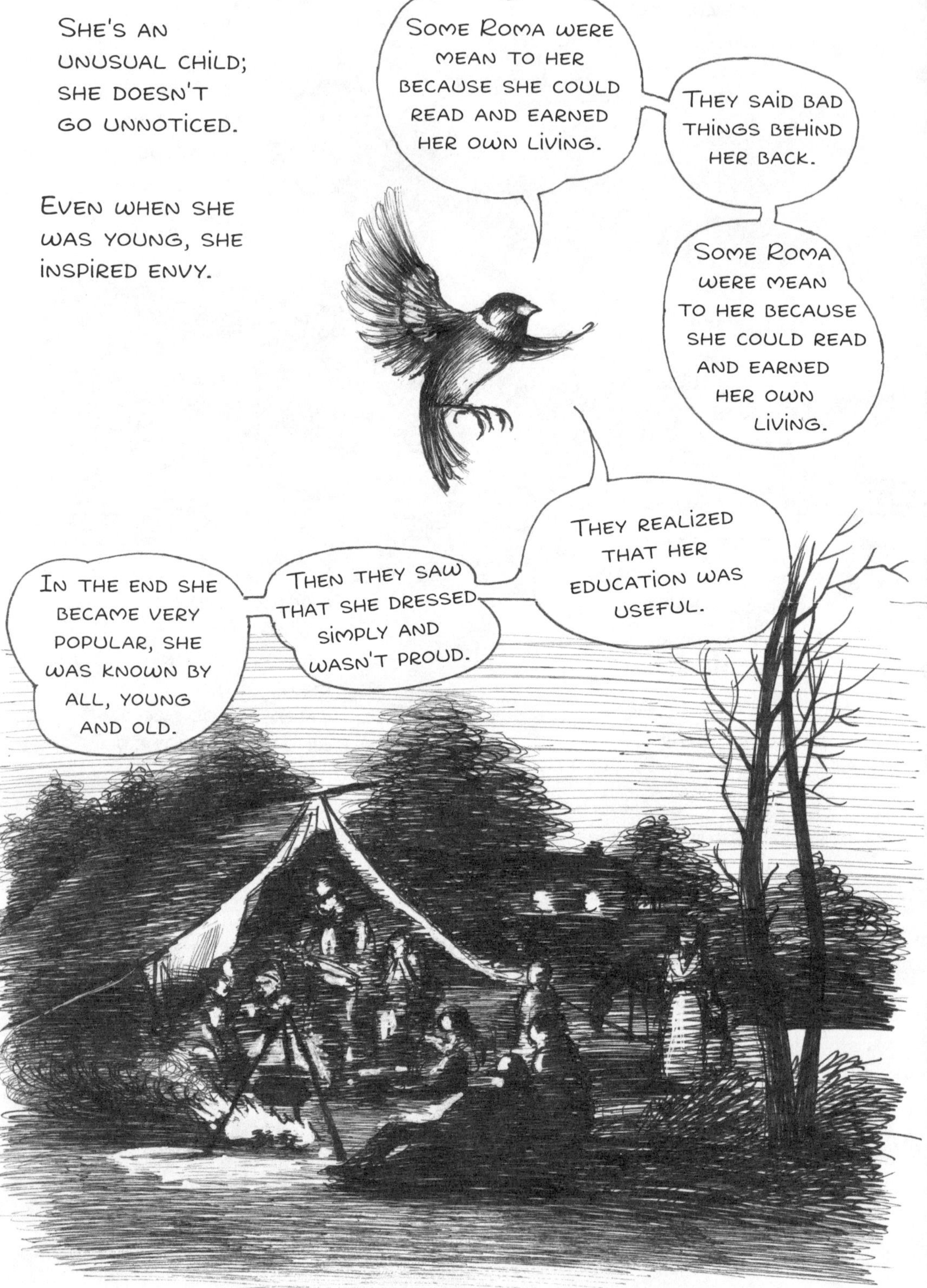
She's an unusual child; she doesn't go unnoticed.
Even when she was young, she inspired envy.
Some Roma were mean to her because she could read and earned her own living.
They said bad things behind her back.
Some Roma were mean to her because she could read and earned her own living.
They realized that her education was useful.
Then they saw that she dressed simply and wasn't proud.
In the end she became very popular, she was known by all, young and old.

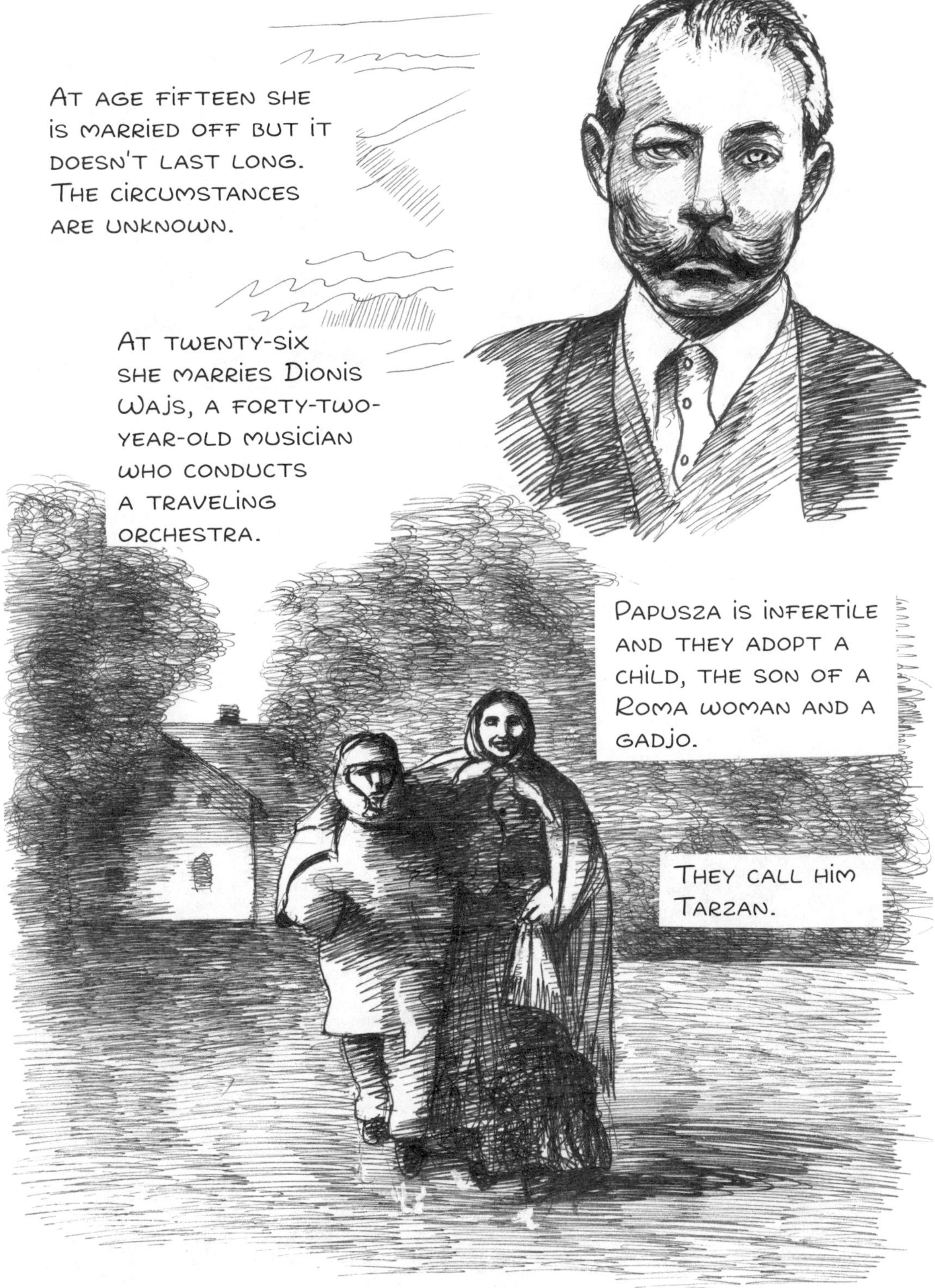
At age fifteen she is married off but it doesn't last long. The circumstances are unknown.
At twenty-six she marries Dionis Wajs, a forty-two-year-old musician who conducts a traveling orchestra.
Papusza is infertile and they adopt a child, the son of a Roma woman and a gadjo.
They call him Tarzan.

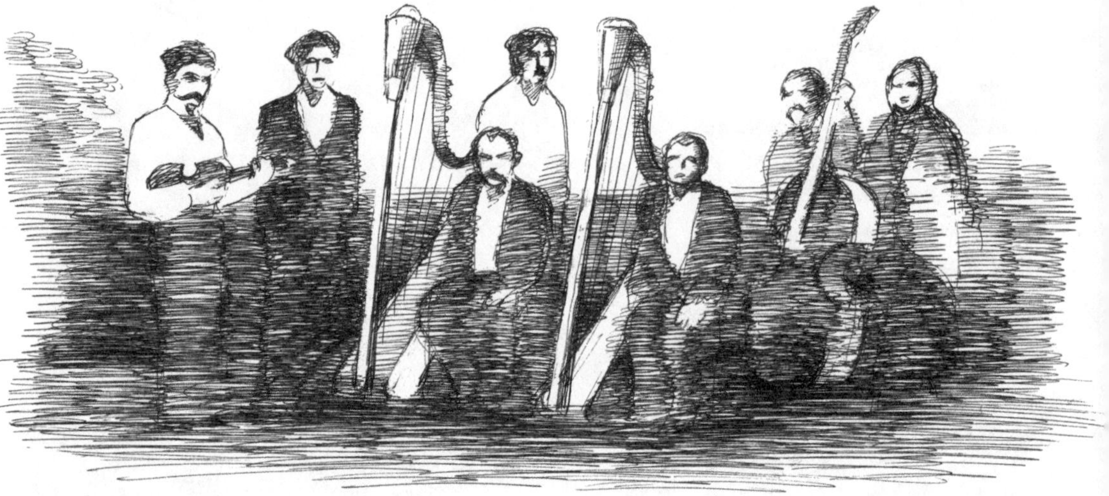

THE WAJS ORCHESTRA PLAYS ON BOATS OR IN TAVERNS.

SHE SINGS AND DANCES AND IMPROVISES LONG POEMS.

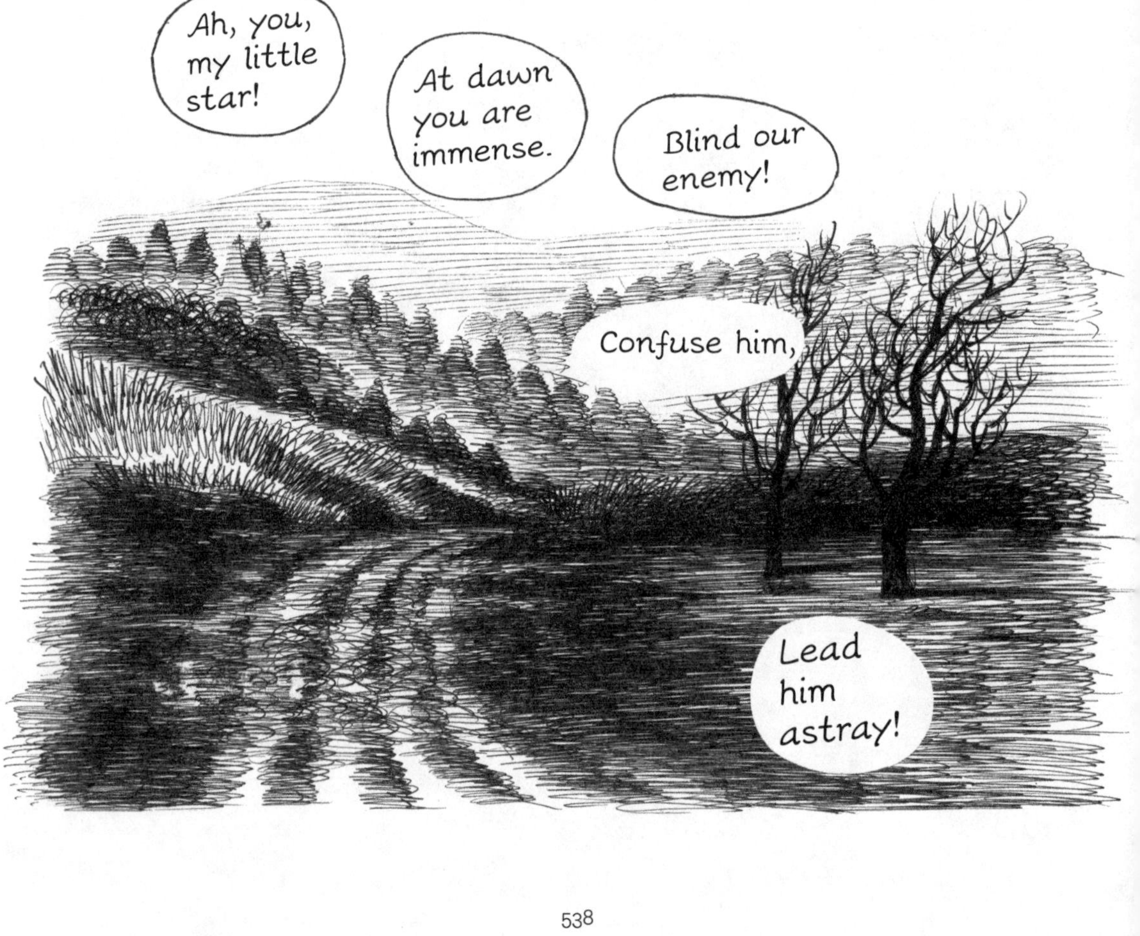
Ah, you, my little star!
At dawn you are immense.
Blind our enemy!
Confuse him,
Lead him astray!

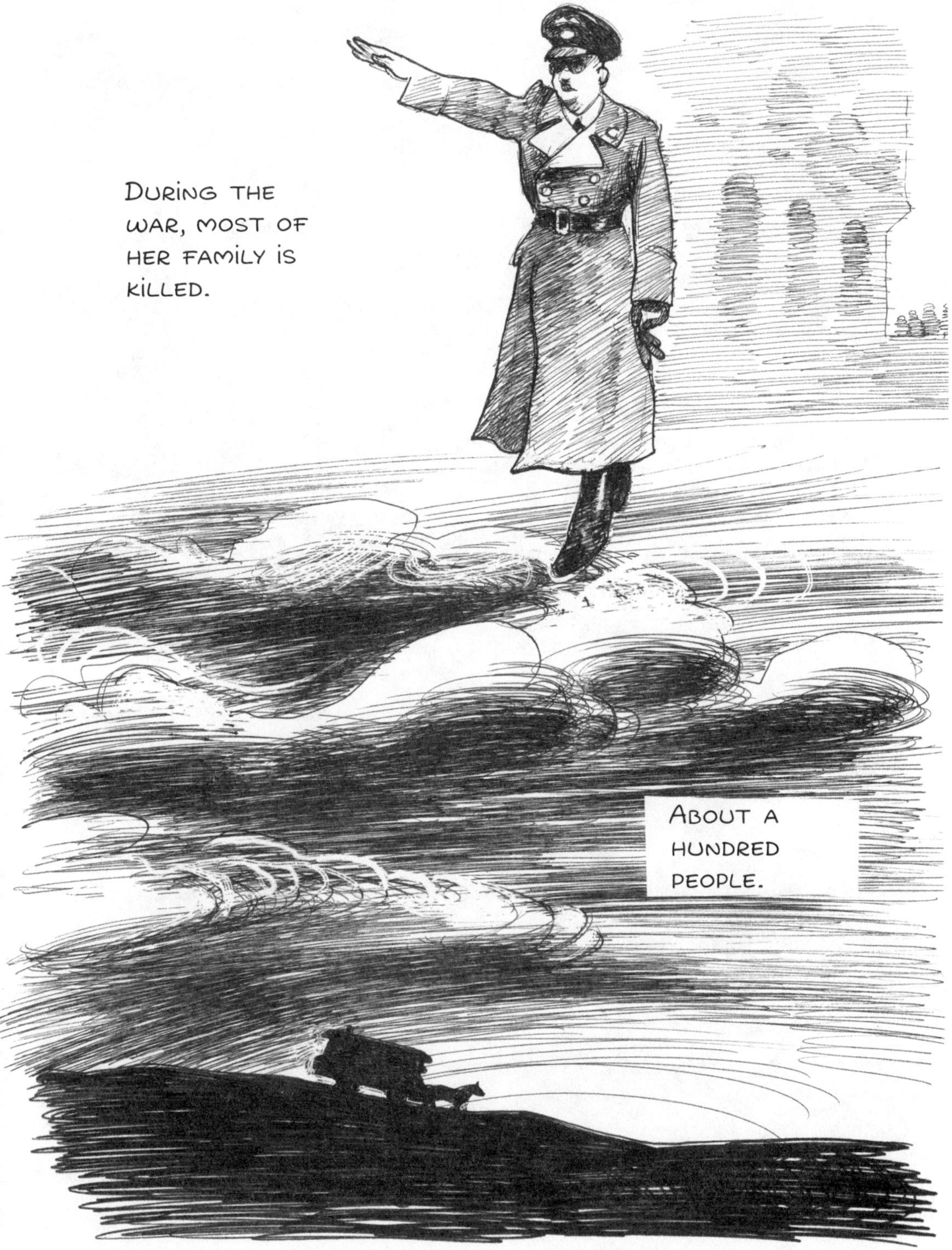
DURING THE WAR, MOST OF HER FAMILY IS KILLED.
ABOUT A HUNDRED PEOPLE.

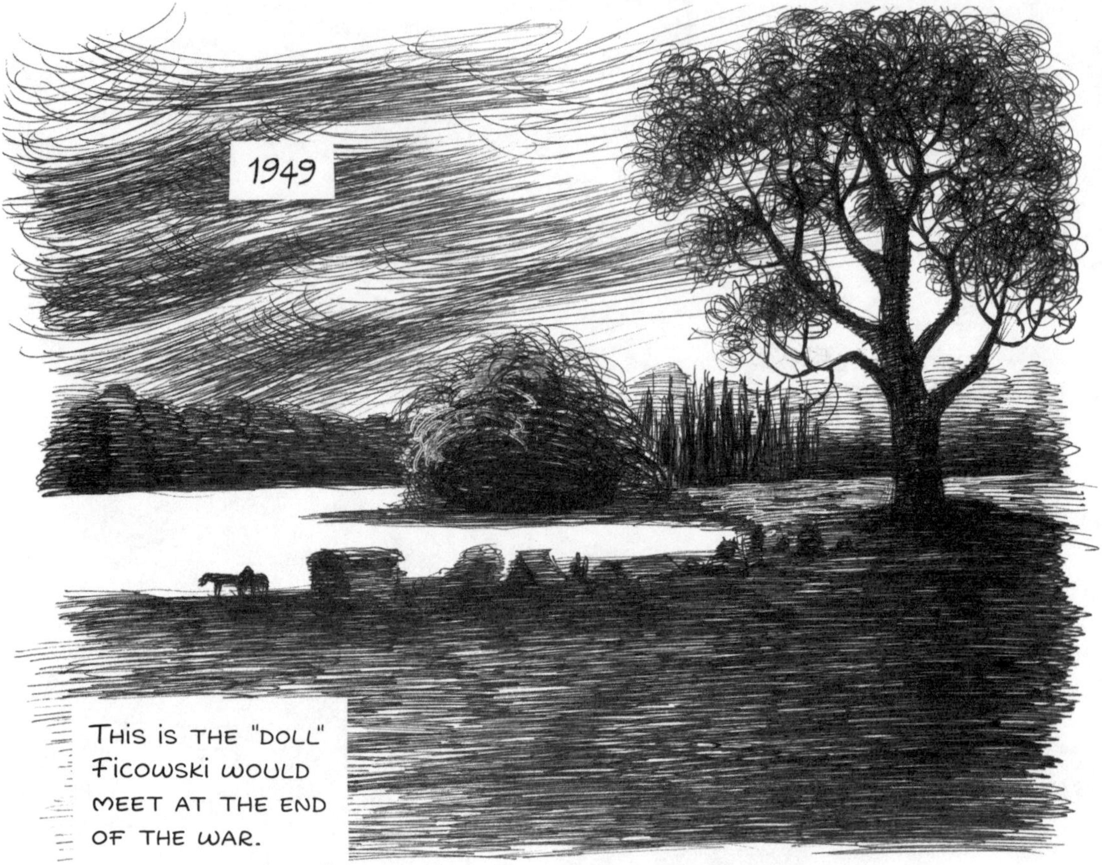
1949
THIS IS THE "DOLL" FICOWSKI WOULD MEET AT THE END OF THE WAR.

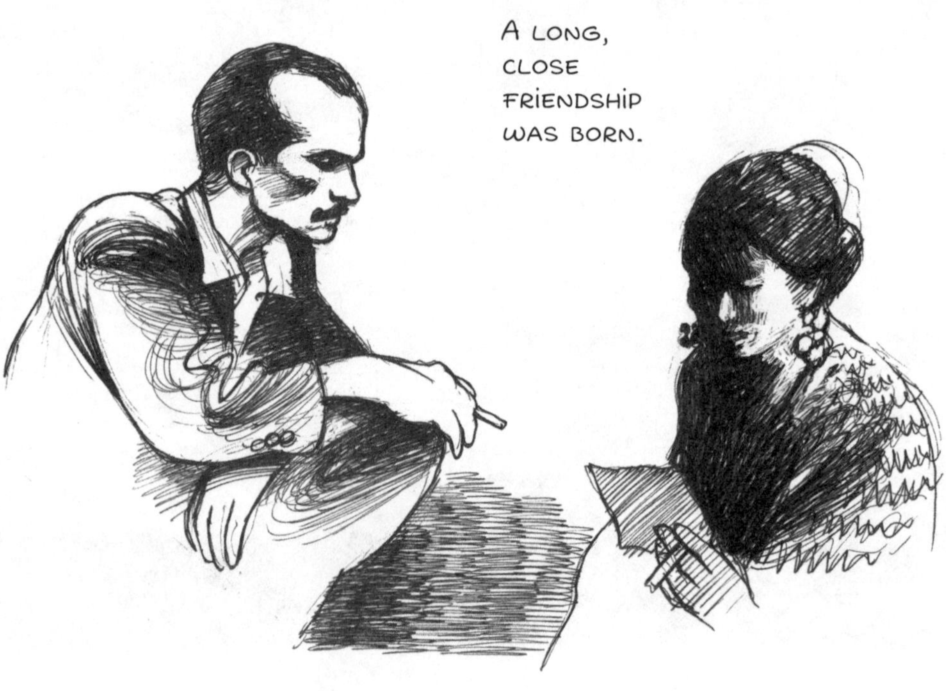
A LONG, CLOSE FRIENDSHIP WAS BORN.

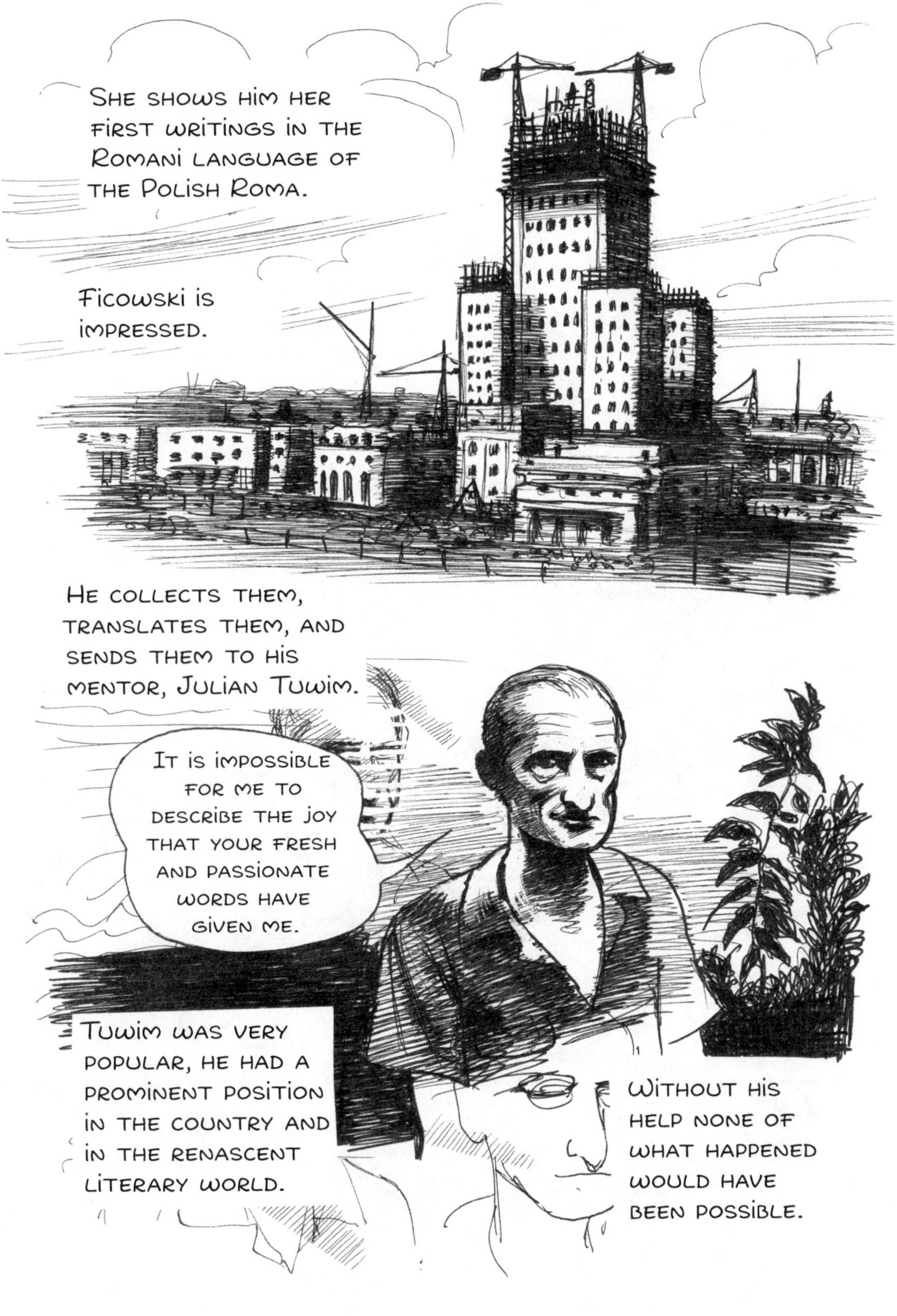

She shows him her first writings in the Romani language of the Polish Roma.
Ficowski is impressed.
He collects them, translates them, and sends them to his mentor, Julian Tuwim.
It is impossible for me to describe the joy that your fresh and passionate words have given me.
Tuwim was very popular, he had a prominent position in the country and in the renascent literary world.
Without his help none of what happened would have been possible.

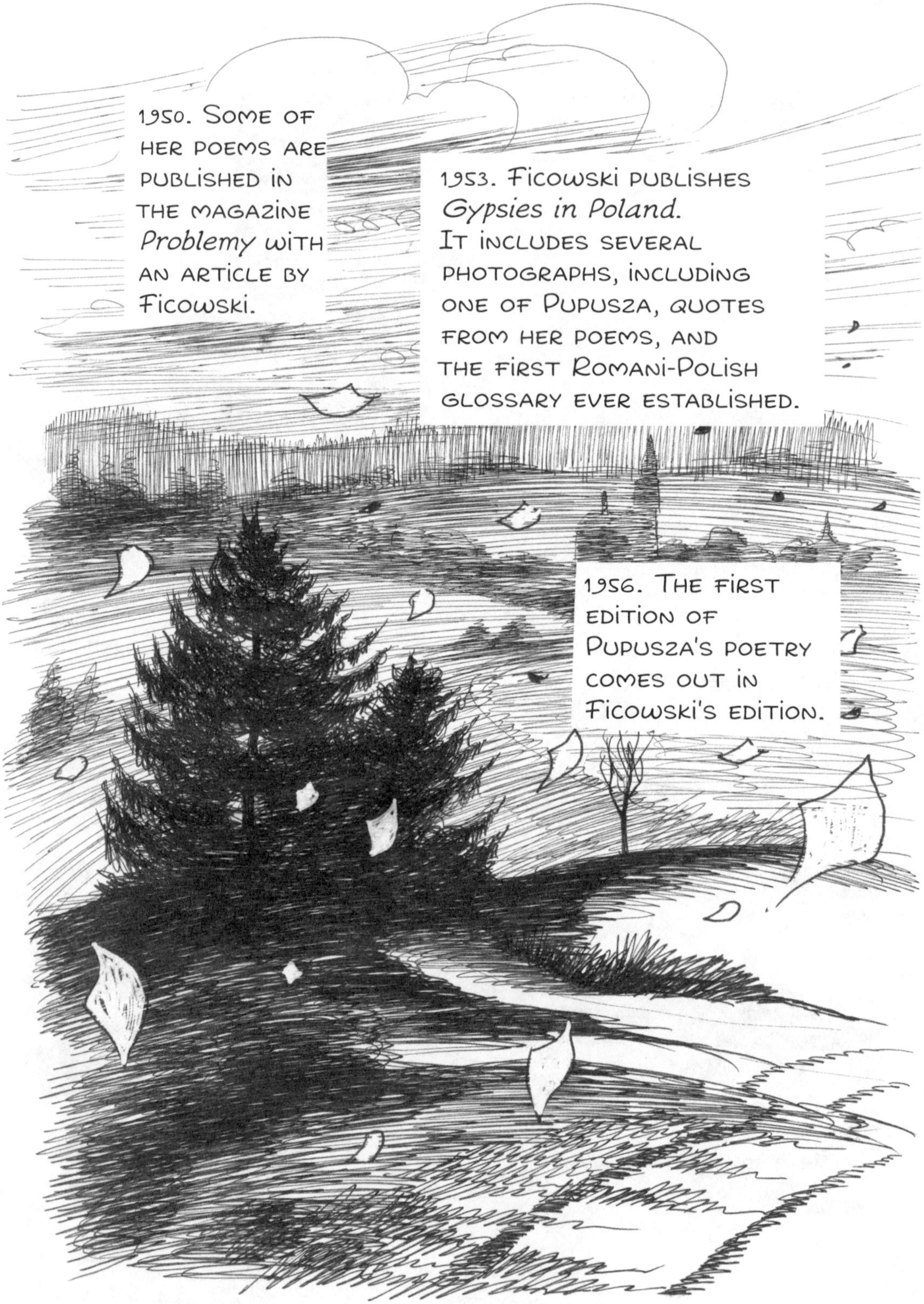
1950. Some of her poems are published in the magazine *Problemy* with an article by Ficowski.
1953. Ficowski publishes *Gypsies in Poland*. It includes several photographs, including one of Pupusza, quotes from her poems, and the first Romani-Polish glossary ever established.
1956. The first edition of Pupusza's poetry comes out in Ficowski's edition.

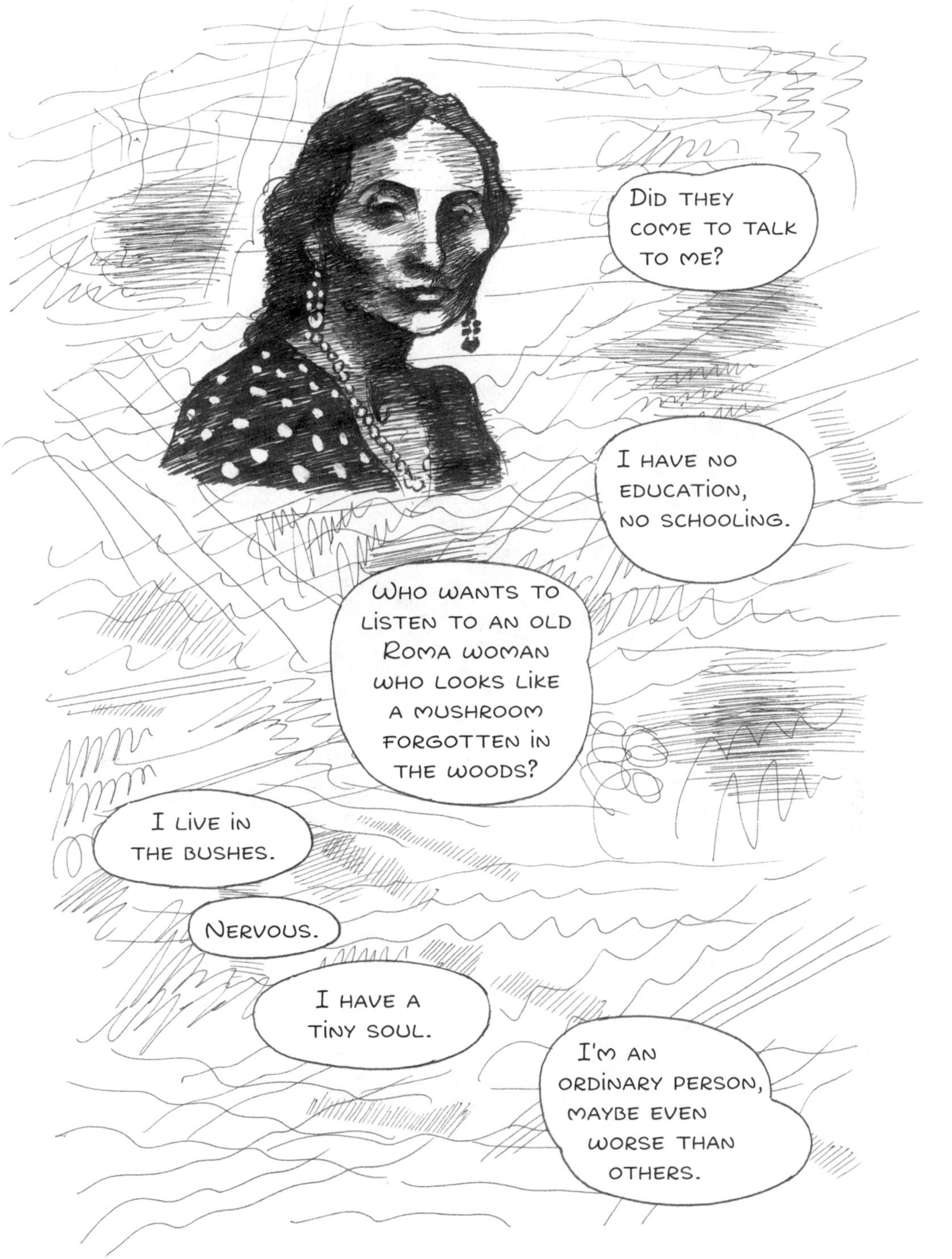
DID THEY COME TO TALK TO ME?
I HAVE NO EDUCATION, NO SCHOOLING.
WHO WANTS TO LISTEN TO AN OLD ROMA WOMAN WHO LOOKS LIKE A MUSHROOM FORGOTTEN IN THE WOODS?
I LIVE IN THE BUSHES.
NERVOUS.
I HAVE A TINY SOUL.
I'M AN ORDINARY PERSON, MAYBE EVEN WORSE THAN OTHERS.

IT'S A
REVELATION.

PAPUSZA WINS
SEVERAL PRIZES

SHE IS REGISTERED
IN THE POLISH
WRITERS' UNION.

SHE RECEIVES A SMALL
STIPEND FROM THE
MINISTRY OF CULTURE.

MANY INTELLECTUALS,
LIKE WISLAWA
SZYMBORSKA, BESTOW
PRAISE ON HER.

TODAY SHE IS
GENERALLY RECOGNIZED
AS A GREAT POET.

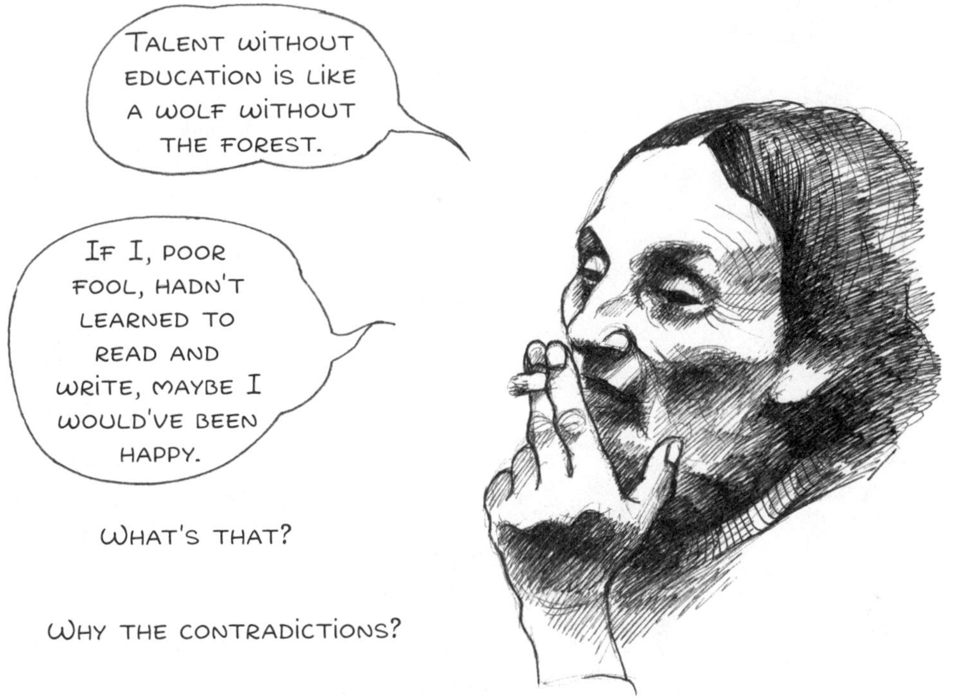
TALENT WITHOUT EDUCATION IS LIKE A WOLF WITHOUT THE FOREST.
IF I, POOR FOOL, HADN'T LEARNED TO READ AND WRITE, MAYBE I WOULD'VE BEEN HAPPY.
WHAT'S THAT?
WHY THE CONTRADICTIONS?

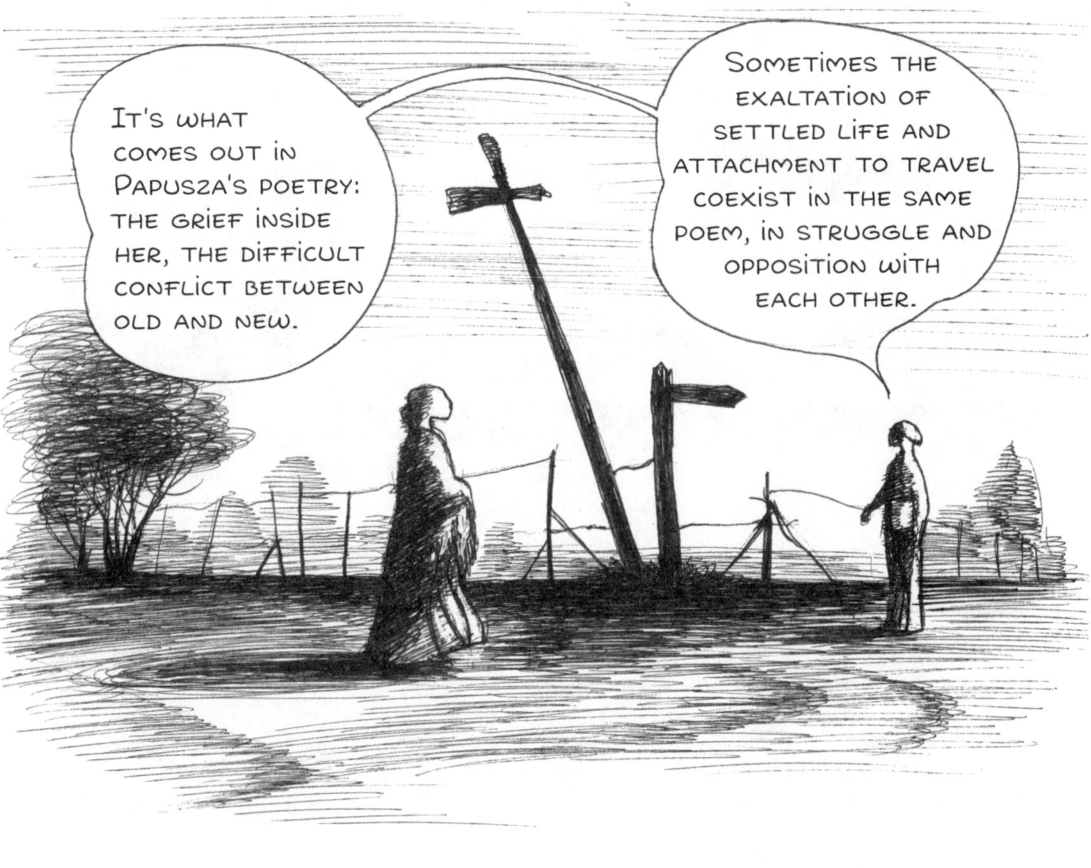
IT'S WHAT COMES OUT IN PAPUSZA'S POETRY: THE GRIEF INSIDE HER, THE DIFFICULT CONFLICT BETWEEN OLD AND NEW.
SOMETIMES THE EXALTATION OF SETTLED LIFE AND ATTACHMENT TO TRAVEL COEXIST IN THE SAME POEM, IN STRUGGLE AND OPPOSITION WITH EACH OTHER.

NOSTALGIA FOR TRAVEL.

ANCESTRAL SYMBIOSIS WITH THE FOREST.

EMOTIONAL AND MENTAL BOND WITH NATURE.

DESIRE FOR STABILITY.

NEED TO BE PRODUCTIVE, CREATIVE.

EDUCATION AS THE ONLY MEANS FOR HER PEOPLE'S EMANCIPATION.

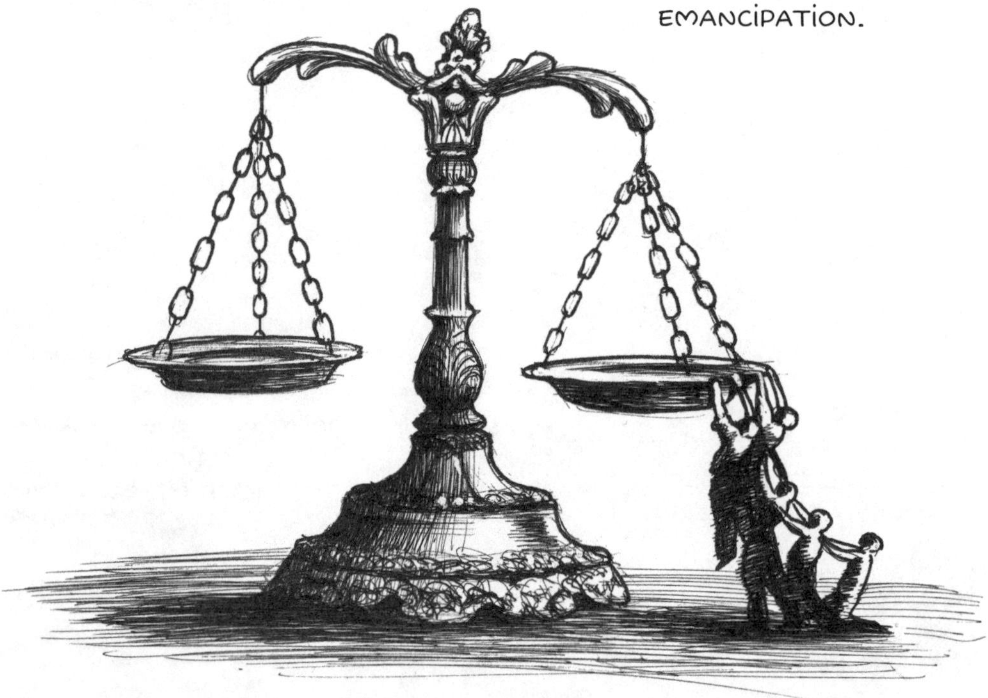

THIS DESIRE FOR STABILITY HAPPENS TO CORRESPOND WITH THE PARTY'S WISHES.

1950. PEAK STALINIST PERIOD. ONE OF THE MOST BRUTAL IN THE COMMUNIST DICTATORSHIP

FOR PUBLICATION, TUWIM ASKS FICOWSKI TO ACCEPT CERTAIN ADDITIONS, LIKE REFERENCES TO THE SOVIET MODEL AND A VERSION OF THE "INTERNATIONALE" IN ROMANI.

JUST TO THROW DUST IN THE EYES OF THE CENSORS.

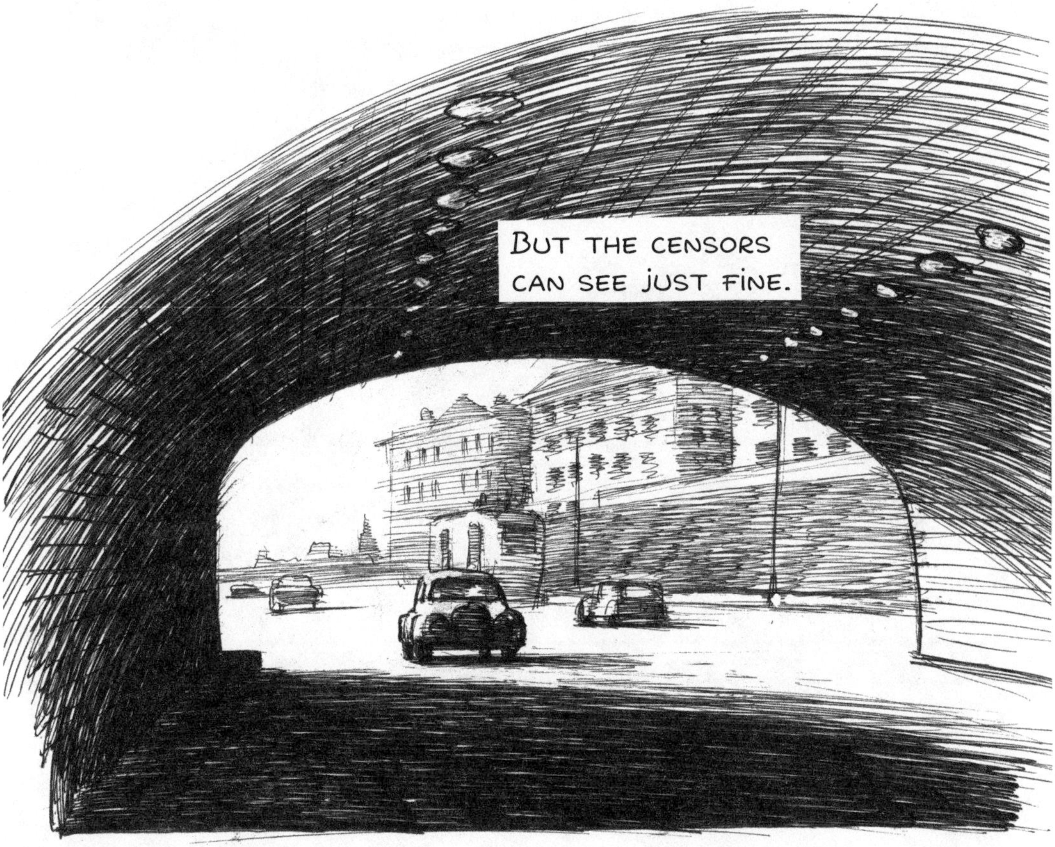
BUT THE CENSORS CAN SEE JUST FINE.

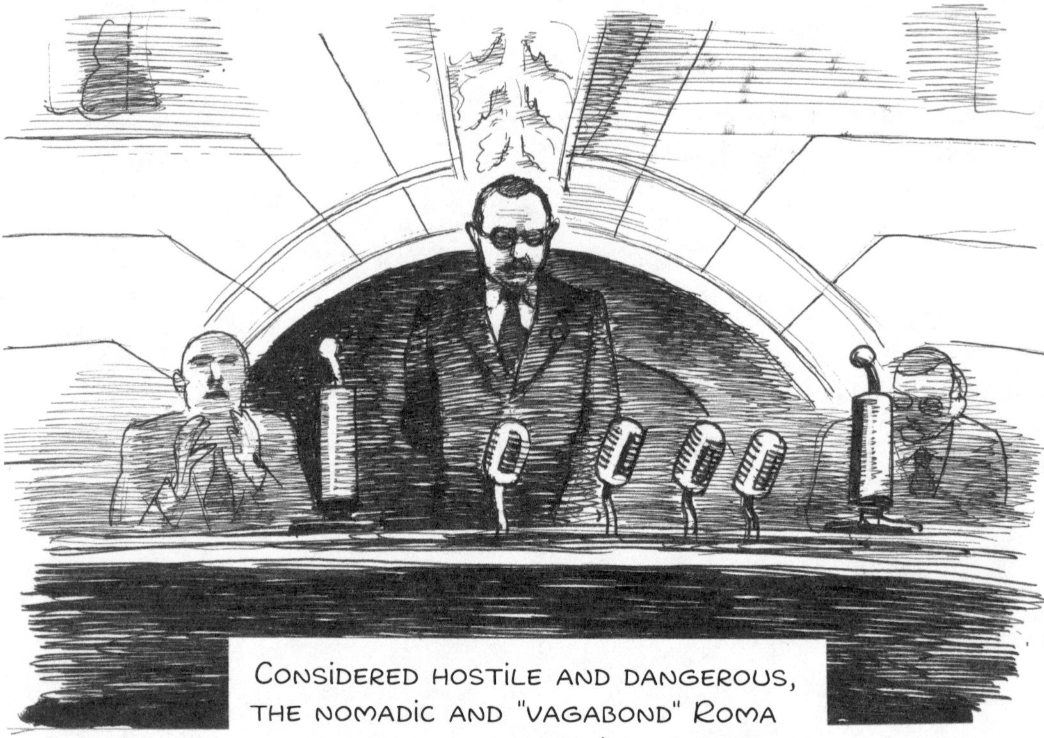
CONSIDERED HOSTILE AND DANGEROUS, THE NOMADIC AND "VAGABOND" ROMA ARE HUNTED BY THE POLICE, FORCED TO LEAVE THEIR CAMPS AND TO SETTLE IN INDIGENT VILLAGES OR PREFABRICATED HOUSING BLOCKS.

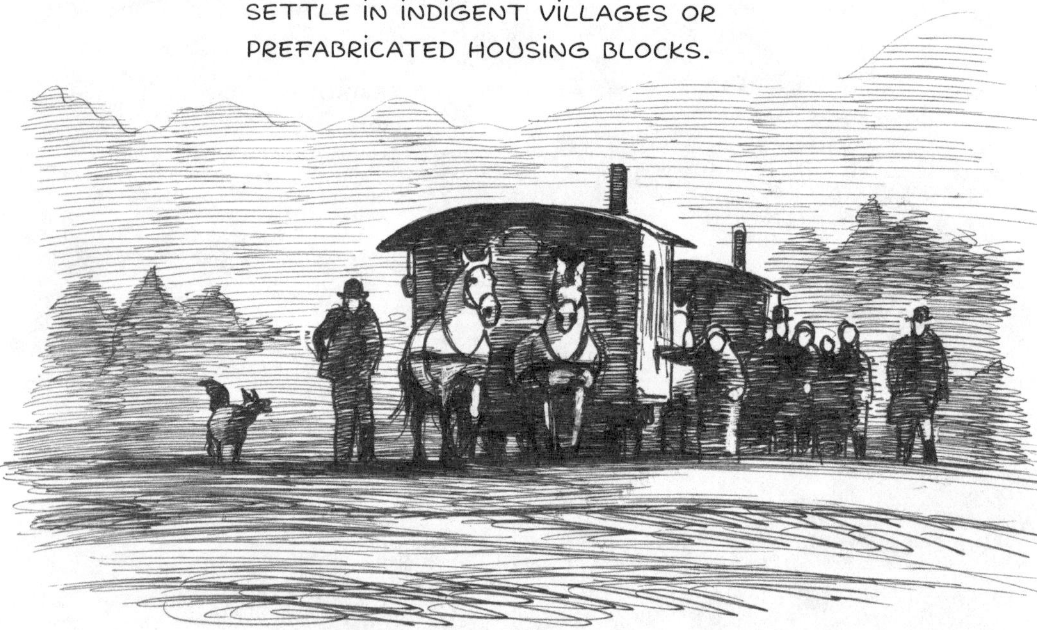

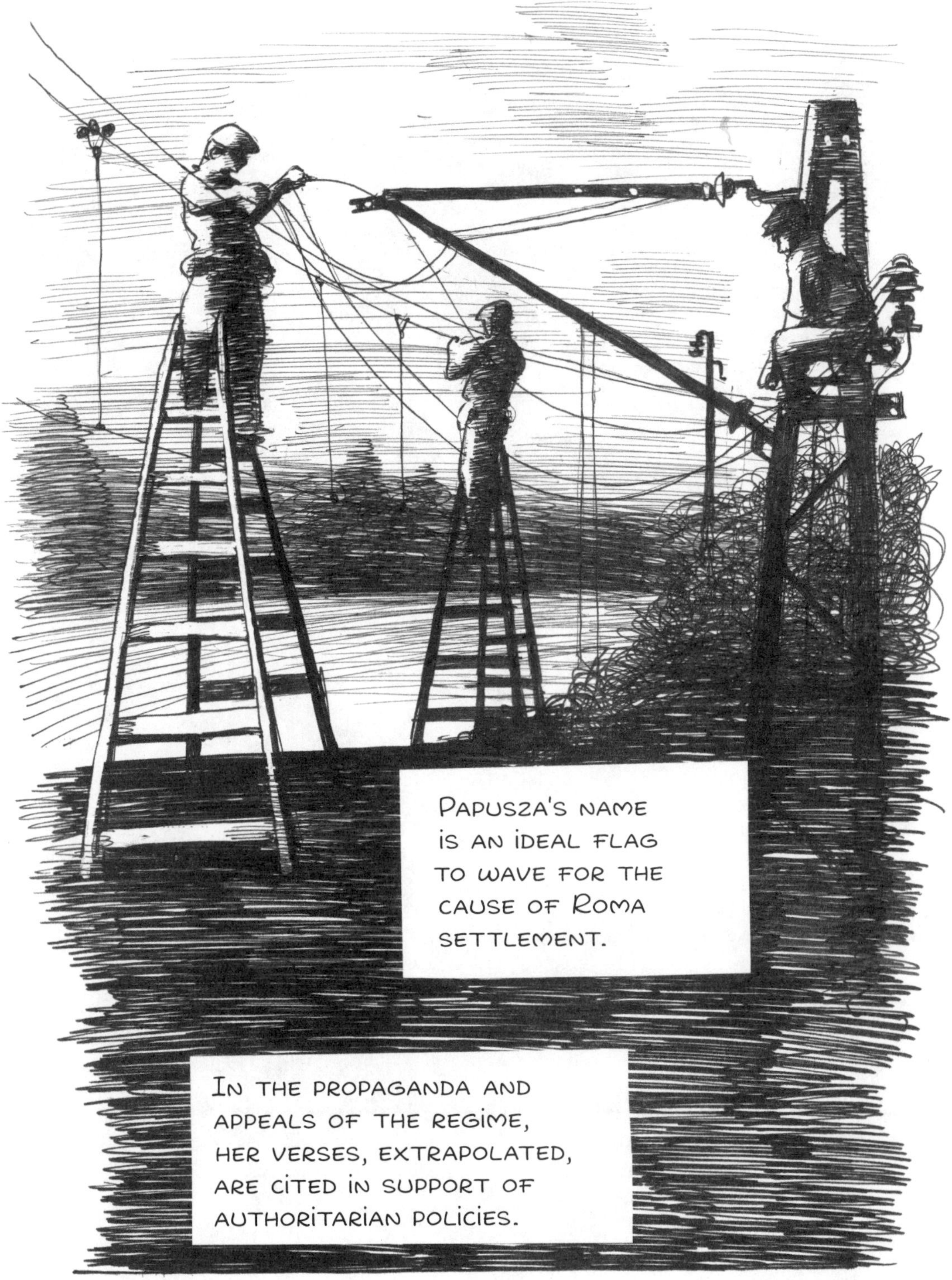
Papusza's name is an ideal flag to wave for the cause of Roma settlement.
In the propaganda and appeals of the regime, her verses, extrapolated, are cited in support of authoritarian policies.

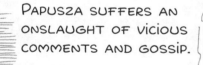

THE ROMA COMMUNITY DOES NOT RESPOND WELL.

PAPUSZA SUFFERS AN ONSLAUGHT OF VICIOUS COMMENTS AND GOSSIP.

SHE IS CONSIDERED A TRAITOR.

THEY DON'T TRUST HER ANYMORE.

THEY TREAT HER LIKE A SPY.

THE ROMA LOOK AT ME IN SUSPICION, AND I CAN'T RECOGNIZE MYSELF ANYMORE.

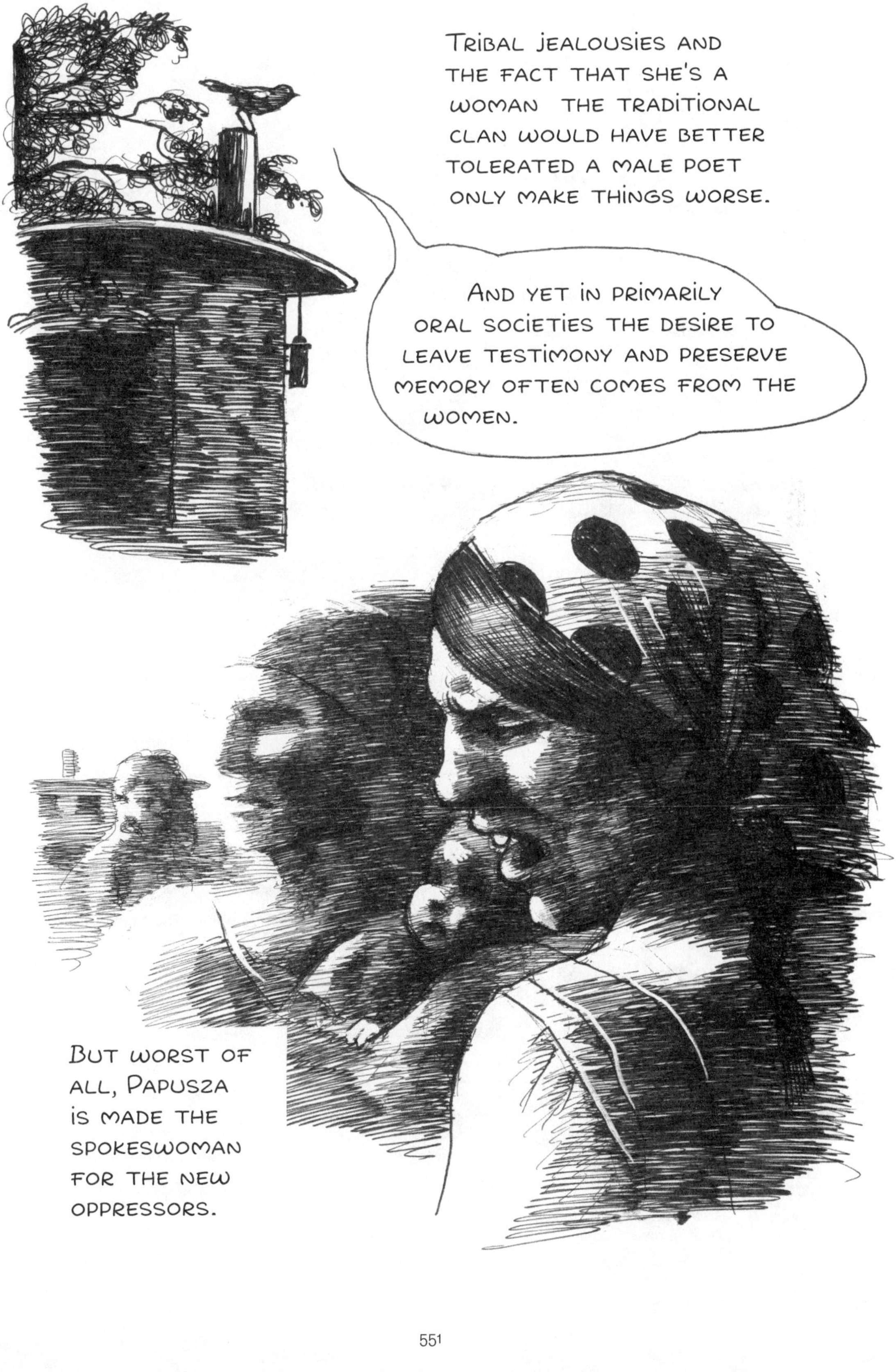
TRIBAL JEALOUSIES AND THE FACT THAT SHE'S A WOMAN THE TRADITIONAL CLAN WOULD HAVE BETTER TOLERATED A MALE POET ONLY MAKE THINGS WORSE.
AND YET IN PRIMARILY ORAL SOCIETIES THE DESIRE TO LEAVE TESTIMONY AND PRESERVE MEMORY OFTEN COMES FROM THE WOMEN.
BUT WORST OF ALL, PAPUSZA IS MADE THE SPOKESWOMAN FOR THE NEW OPPRESSORS.

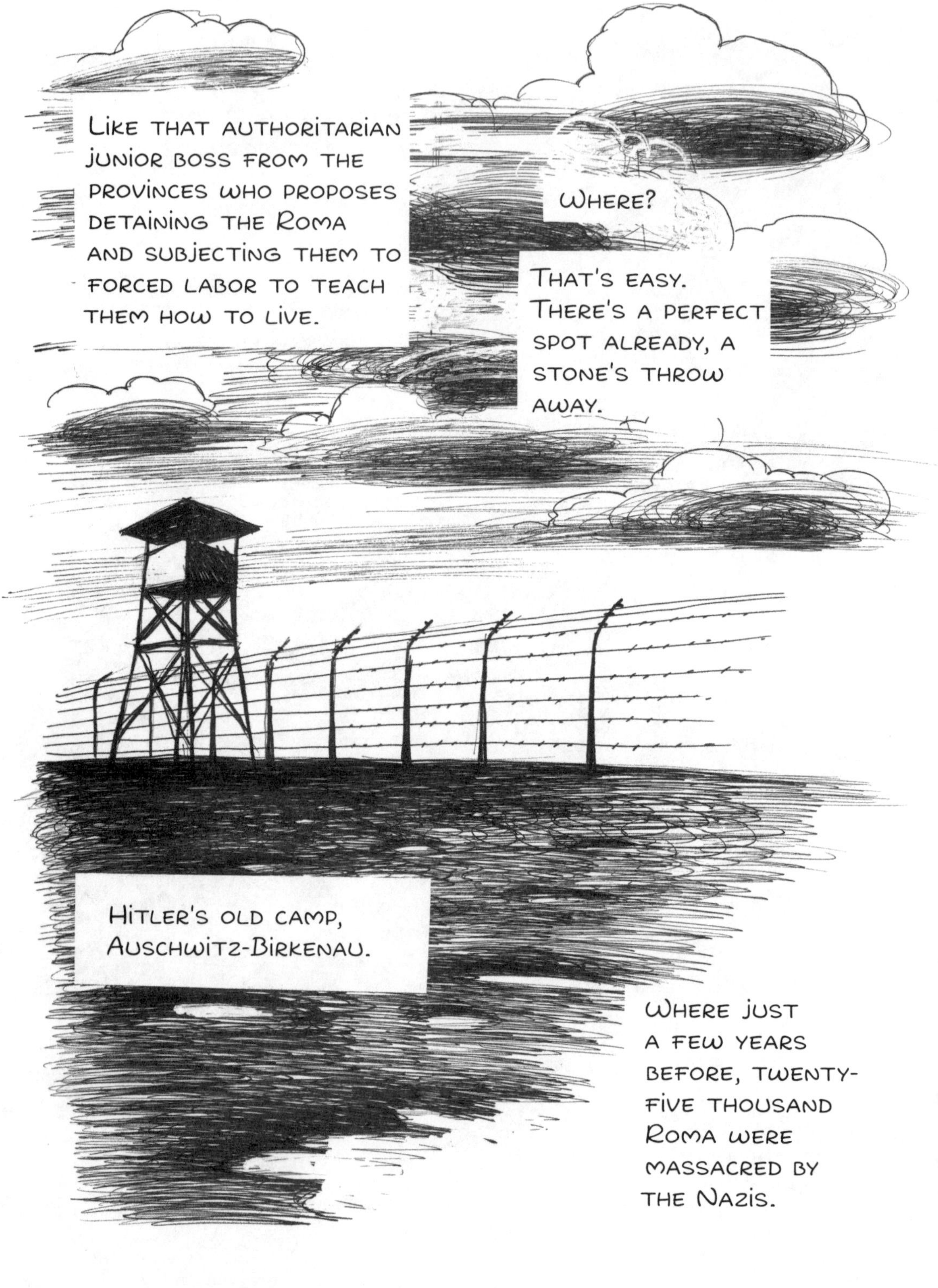
Like that authoritarian junior boss from the provinces who proposes detaining the Roma and subjecting them to forced labor to teach them how to live.
Where?
That's easy. There's a perfect spot already, a stone's throw away.
Hitler's old camp, Auschwitz-Birkenau.
Where just a few years before, twenty-five thousand Roma were massacred by the Nazis.

THE ROMA ARE EXASPERATED.

PAPUSZA IS INSULTED, BEATEN, THREATENED, BANISHED.

SHE LEAVES THE CAMP WITH HER FAMILY, MARCHING THREE HUNDRED KILOMETERS IN THE DECEMBER SNOW. MANY OF THEM FALL ILL.

FINALLY, THEY SET UP THEIR HOME IN ZAGAN.

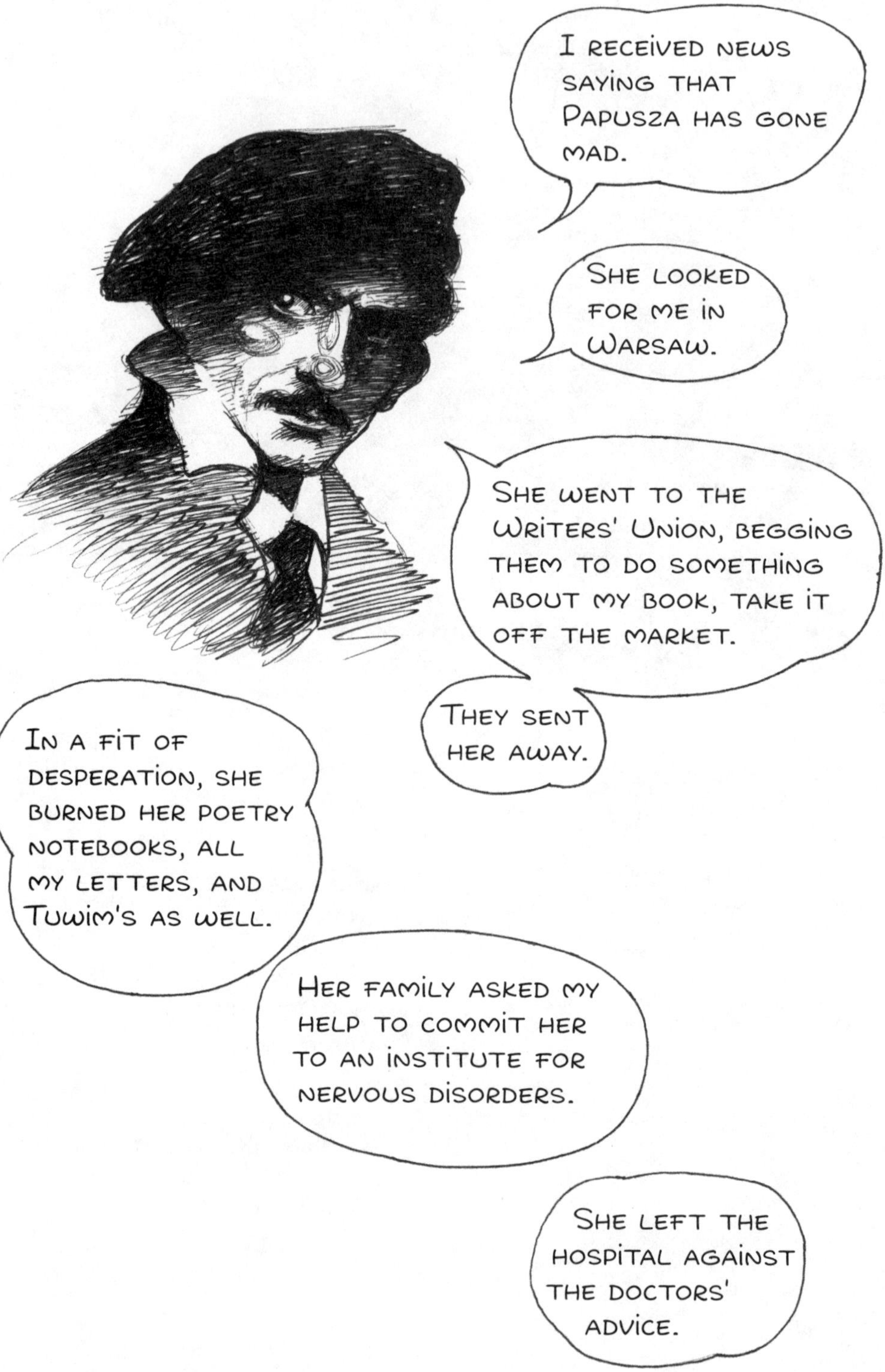
I received news saying that Papusza has gone mad.
She looked for me in Warsaw.
She went to the Writers' Union, begging them to do something about my book, take it off the market.
They sent her away.
In a fit of desperation, she burned her poetry notebooks, all my letters, and Tuwim's as well.
Her family asked my help to commit her to an institute for nervous disorders.
She left the hospital against the doctors' advice.

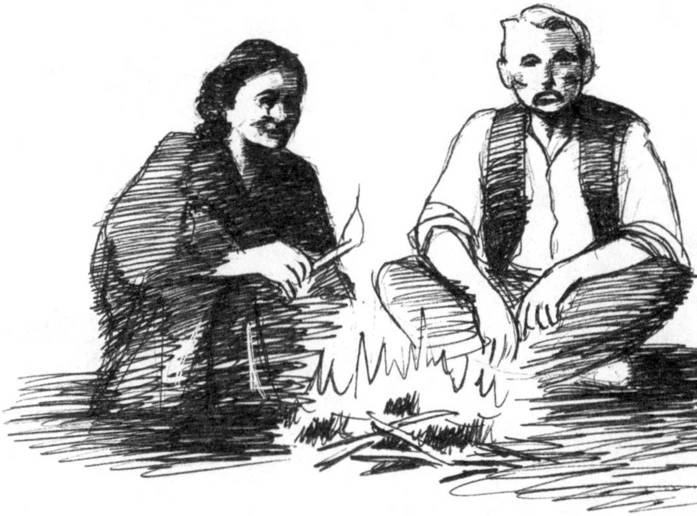

Nervous breakdown.

She falls into a depression and spends months in a psychiatric hospital.

She becomes withdrawn, seeing only her old husband and a few close friends, living away from the Roma and away from the world.

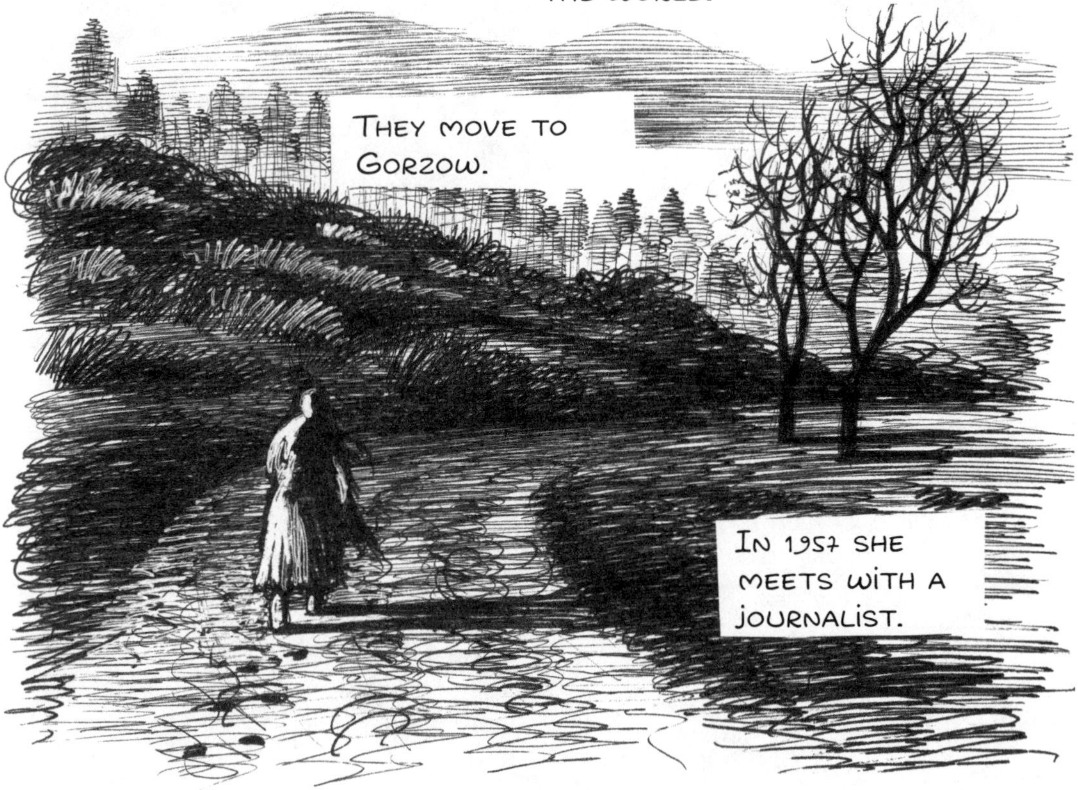
They move to Gorzow.
In 1957 she meets with a journalist.

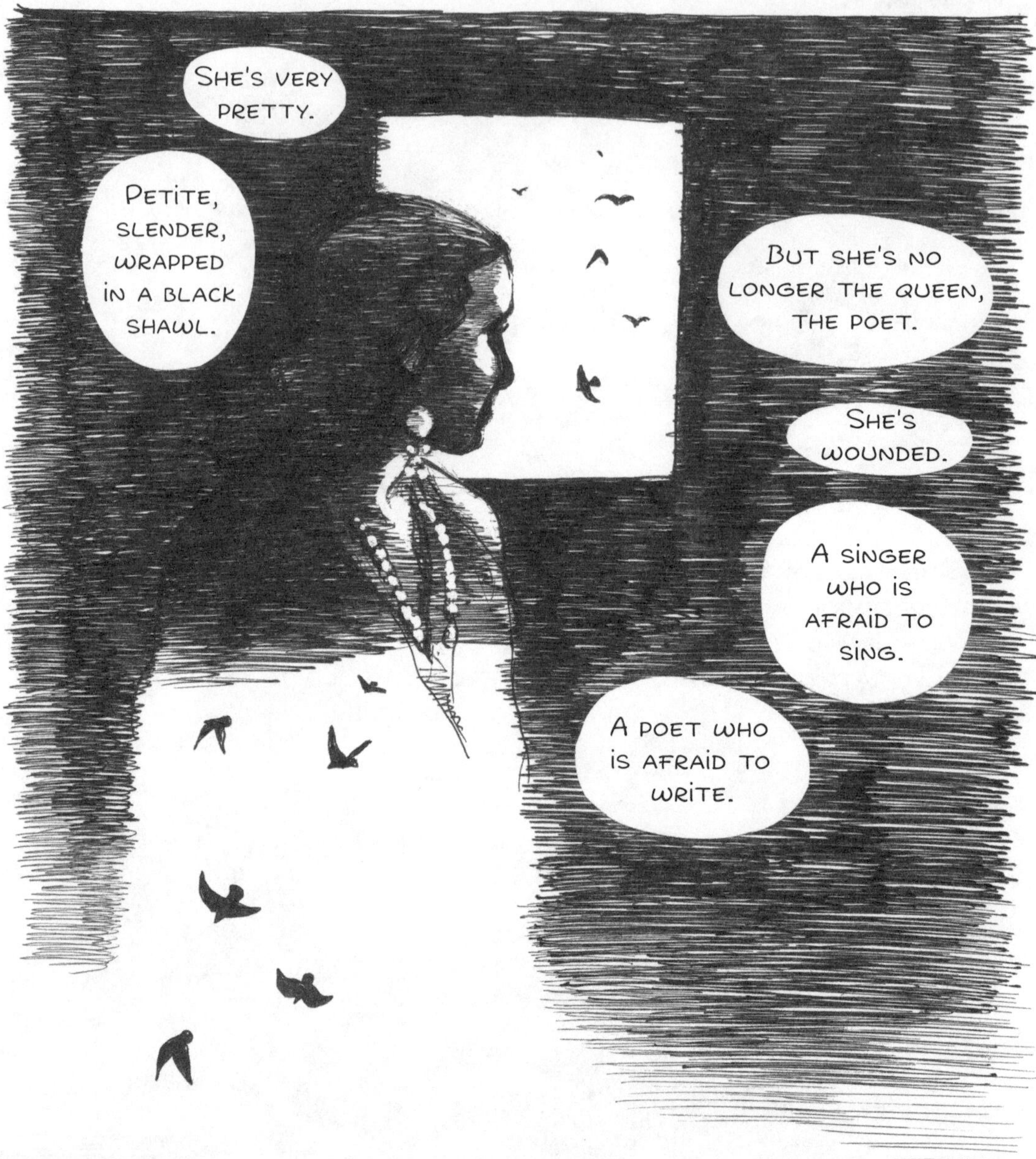
SHE'S VERY PRETTY.
PETITE, SLENDER, WRAPPED IN A BLACK SHAWL.
BUT SHE'S NO LONGER THE QUEEN, THE POET.
SHE'S WOUNDED.
A SINGER WHO IS AFRAID TO SING.
A POET WHO IS AFRAID TO WRITE.

AFTER TUWIM'S DEATH IN 1953 SHE HAS NO ONE TO PROTECT HER.

FICOWSKI HAS HIS OWN TROUBLES WITH THE REGIME DUE TO HIS SUPPORTING THE DEMOCRATIC OPPOSITION.

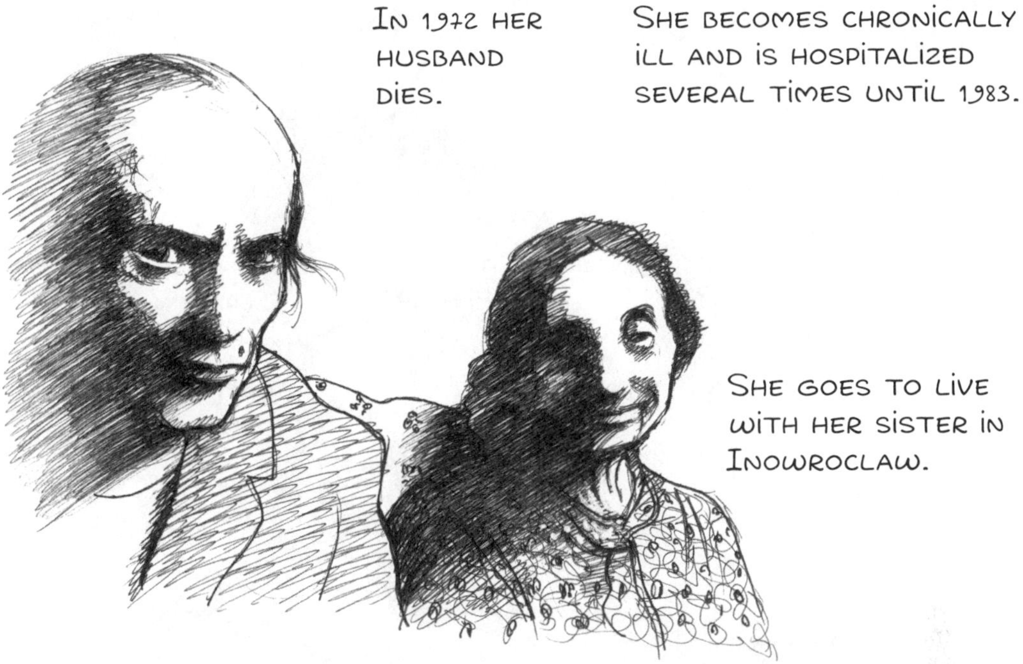
In 1972 her husband dies.
She becomes chronically ill and is hospitalized several times until 1983.
She goes to live with her sister in Inowroclaw.

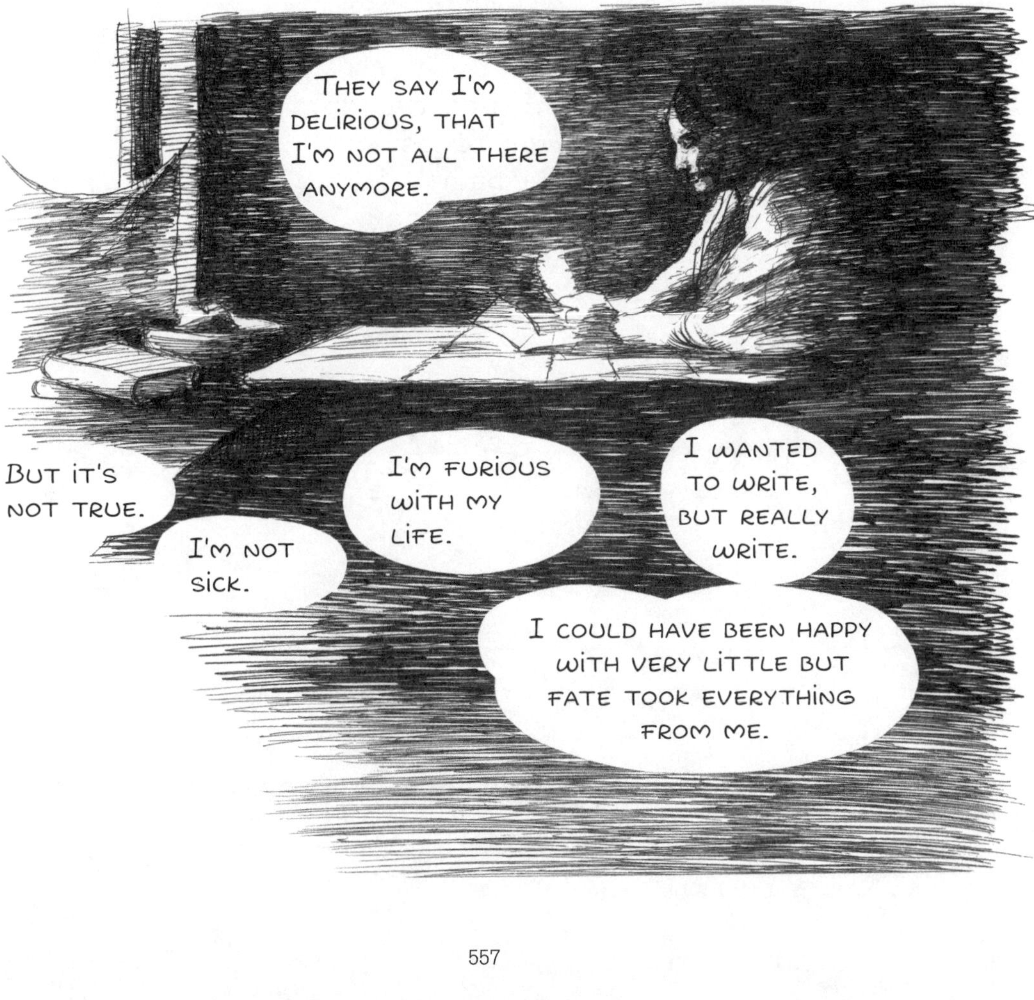
They say I'm delirious, that I'm not all there anymore.
But it's not true.
I'm not sick.
I'm furious with my life.
I wanted to write, but really write.
I could have been happy with very little but fate took everything from me.

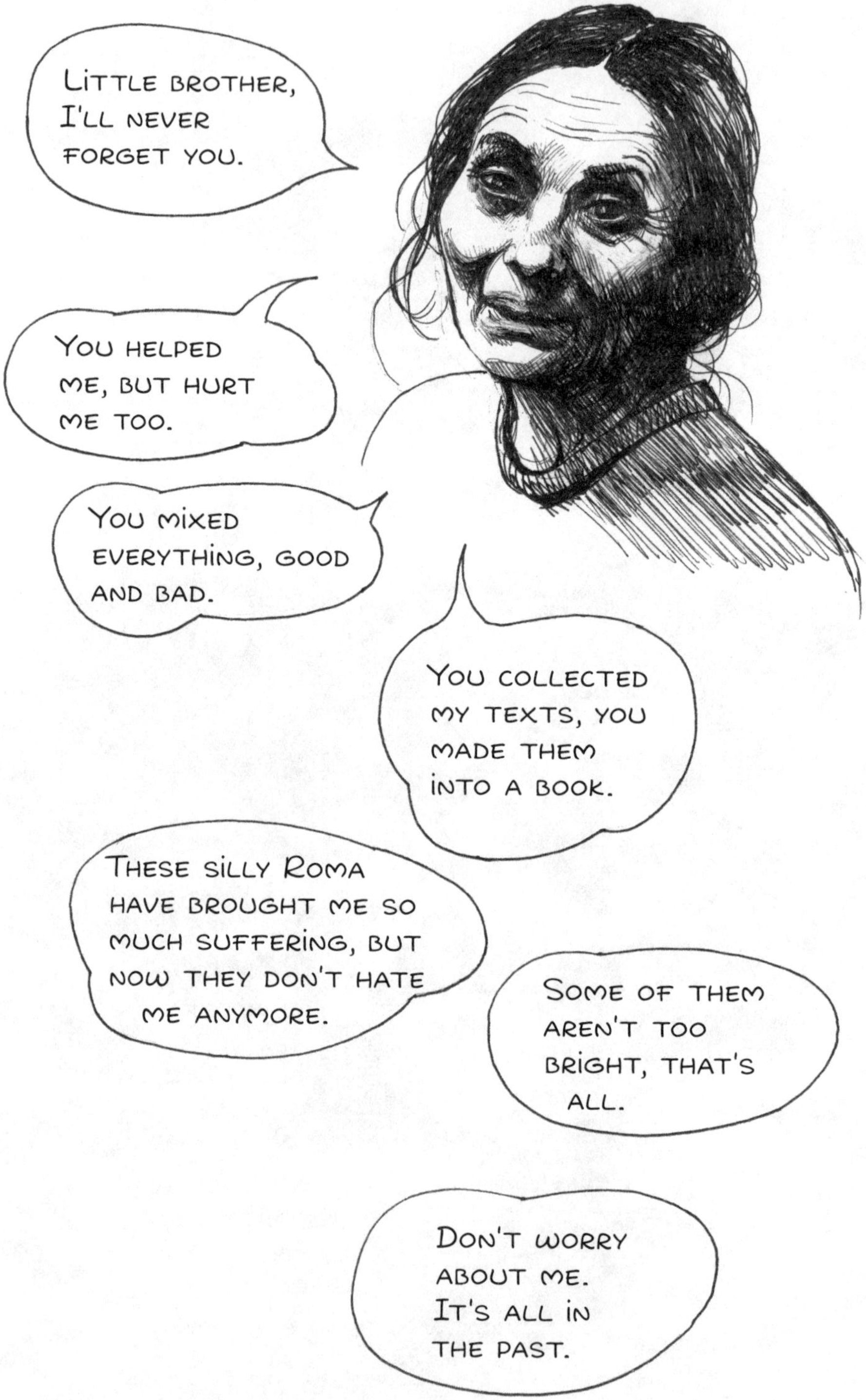
LITTLE BROTHER, I'LL NEVER FORGET YOU.
YOU HELPED ME, BUT HURT ME TOO.
YOU MIXED EVERYTHING, GOOD AND BAD.
YOU COLLECTED MY TEXTS, YOU MADE THEM INTO A BOOK.
THESE SILLY ROMA HAVE BROUGHT ME SO MUCH SUFFERING, BUT NOW THEY DON'T HATE ME ANYMORE.
SOME OF THEM AREN'T TOO BRIGHT, THAT'S ALL.
DON'T WORRY ABOUT ME. IT'S ALL IN THE PAST.

SHE LIVES IN
POVERTY FOR OVER
THIRTY YEARS.

SEPARATED
FROM HER
PEOPLE.

SHE NEVER
WROTE OR
SANG AGAIN.

SHE DIED ON FEBRUARY 8, 1987,
AT THE HOUSE OF AN AUNT,
THE ONLY RELATIVE WHO HAD
AGREED TO TAKE HER IN.

I HAD THE GOOD FORTUNE TO MEET PAPUSZA, THEY SAY I "DISCOVERED" HER.
PAPUSZA HAD THE MISFORTUNE TO MEET ME.
BECAUSE OF ME, SHE WAS THE VICTIM OF A GRAVE INJUSTICE.
DESPITE WHATEVER I COULD SAY IN MY DEFENSE
WHICH WOULD BE A LOT
NOTHING CHANGES THE FACT THAT MY TIME IN THE WAJS CAMP IN 1949 BROUGHT PAPUSZA MORE NEGATIVE CONSEQUENCES THAN ANY OTHER EVENT SHE WENT THROUGH IN HER LIFE.
BUT THE IMPORTANT THING IS THAT WE ARE BOUND BY TRUE FRIENDSHIP.

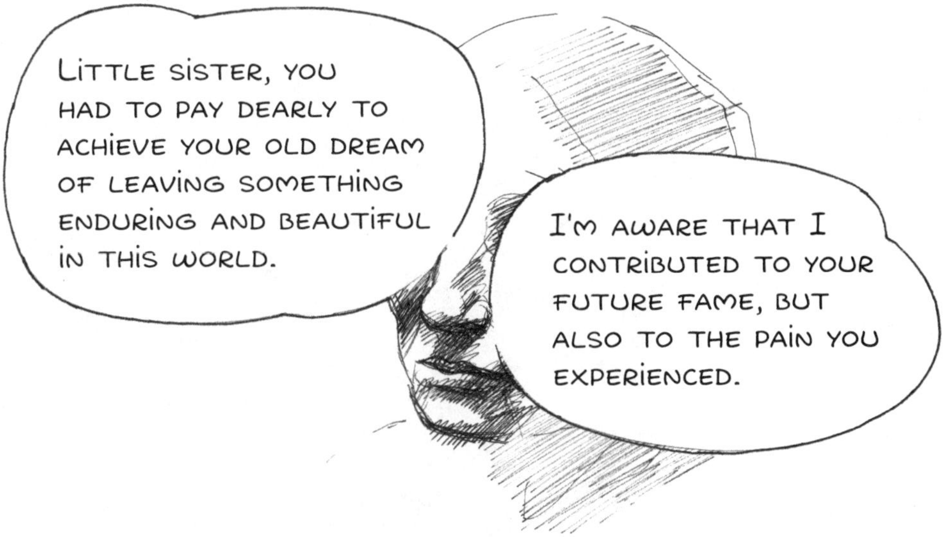
LITTLE SISTER, YOU HAD TO PAY DEARLY TO ACHIEVE YOUR OLD DREAM OF LEAVING SOMETHING ENDURING AND BEAUTIFUL IN THIS WORLD.
I'M AWARE THAT I CONTRIBUTED TO YOUR FUTURE FAME, BUT ALSO TO THE PAIN YOU EXPERIENCED.

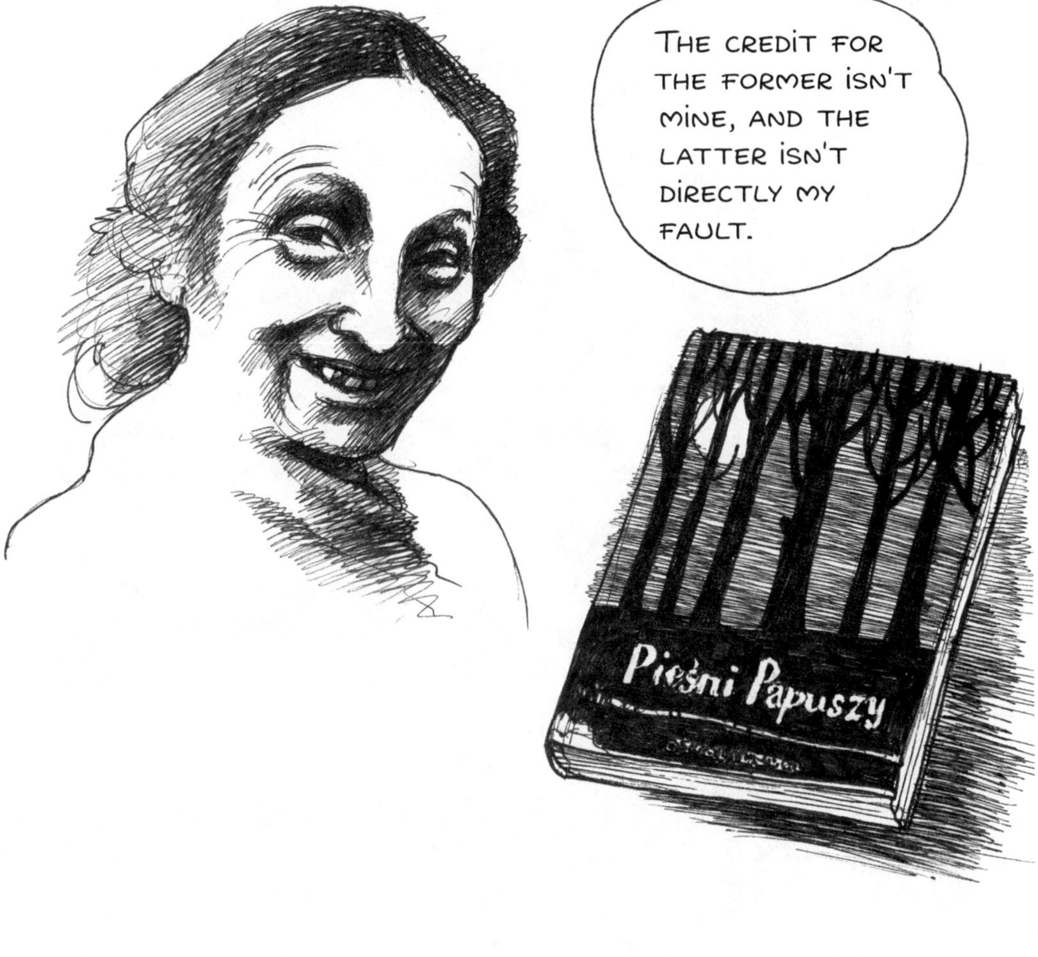
THE CREDIT FOR THE FORMER ISN'T MINE, AND THE LATTER ISN'T DIRECTLY MY FAULT.
Pieśni Papuszy

STILL...
...MY RESPONSIBILITY FOR THE MISFORTUNES HEAPED UPON YOU ALWAYS WEIGHS ON ME.
EVEN IF I REALIZE IT WAS INEVITABLE.
FORGIVE ME, IF YOU CAN.

Acknowledgments

This book and I owe a lot to certain people, to whom I'd like to send my affection and gratitude. It's hard to remember all of them now, so to those who are missing I "humbly ask forgiveness," as the old song goes.

THANKS TO:

Elena Bucci, her keen and always essential eye, but not only that, I should also mention her love. Walter Pretolani and the voice of Pulcino, which came along with me and protected me. Domenico Rosa, who saw seas in puddles and gave me the courage to navigate them. Stefano Ricci, for supporting me and giving of himself with affection and generosity. Alvaro Petricig, for his sensitivity and empathy that were so helpful. Luca Ciarabelli and his enthusiasm, which seemed excessive but has remained in my heart. Valerio Raggi, who said some big things at my house one summer night, even waking up my neighbor. Paolo Gorietti, for his care and sincerity. Doriano Alessandrini, for his always timely and quiet assistance. Umberto Giovannini, who believed even before I did and never wore out. Andrea Bruno, for being there during a difficult time. Giovanni Ferrara and Luca Baldazzi, for their meticulousness and rigor, never taken for granted. Marzena Sowa, Mariagiorgia Ulbar, Silvano De Fanti, Barbara Kowalczyk, Nataliia Danylova, Massimo Giottoli, for their consultation and precious help with the Polish. Falco Bertoni, who gave me a special gift. Leonardo Guardigli, for his technical collaboration at the production stage. Marco Ficarra, for his time and his kindness. Gianni Amadori, Laurence Barthomeuf, Marco Borghesi, Danilo Buscherini, Massimo Caporossi, Gianfranco Casadio, Gigio Dadina, Luca Donelli, Daniele Dradi and Nonno Giovanni, Sira Fanti, Laura Gambi, Iacopo Gardelli, Alice Lucci, Andrea Maestri, Marino Neri, Patrizia Piccino, Beatrice Pucci, Daniele Valentini, and all the friends who contributed in their own way or tolerated my pestering.

Finally, because he was always there, Igor Tuveri, who oversaw and encouraged me for years, and despite the problems that came up, never lost that esteem, for me essential.

I also want to thank Carlotta Saletta Salza and Leonardo Piasere for their useful suggestions, as well as the many authors and texts that helped me get to this point.

Davide Reviati
December 31, 2015

Bibliography

Arlati, Angelo. "Gli zingari e la Resistenza." Calendario del popolo no. 606, 1997

Boursier, Giovanna. "La persecuzione degli zingari da parte del Fascismo." Triangolo Rosso no. 1, January 1998.

—. "Lo sterminio degli zingari durante la seconda guerra mondiale." Studi Storici no. 2, April-June 1995.

Bravi, Luca. Rom e non-zingari. Rome: Cisu editore, 2007.

Capogreco, Carlo Spartaco. I campi del duce. Turin: Einaudi, 2006.

Cossetto, Milena, Elena Farruggia, and Silvia Spada. "L'immagine degli zingari nel tempo." U baro drom no. 3, 2006.

Destro, Adriana, ed. Antropologia dello spazio. Bologna: Pàtron editore, 2002.

Ficowski, Jerzy. Il rametto dell'albero del sole. Trans. Paolo Statuti. Rome: Edizioni e/o, 1985.

Fonseca, Isabel. Seppellitemi in piedi [Bury Me Standing]. Trans. Maura Pizzorno. Milan: Mondadori, 2008.

Galluccio, Fabio. I lager in Italia. Civezzano: Nonluoghi libere edizioni, 2003.

Giannini, Giorgio. Vittime dimenticate - Lo sterminio dei disabili, dei Rom, degli omosessuali e dei testimoni di Geova. Viterbo: Nuovi Equilibri, 2011.

Hancock, Ian. Downplaying the Porrajmos: The Trend to Minimize the Romani Holocaust. A review of Guenther Lewy. The Nazi Persecution of the Gypsies. Oxford: Oxford University Press, 2000.

Innocenzi, Francesca, ed. L'identità sommersa. Rome: Edizioni Progetto Cultura, 2010.

Kosinski, Jerzy. Abitacolo [Cockpit]. Trans. Vincenzo Mantovani. Milan: Longanesi, 1982.

—. Passi [Steps]. Trans. Vincenzo Mantovani. Rome: Elliot, 2013.

—. L'uccello dipinto [The Painted Bird]. Trans. Bruno Oddera. Milan: Longanesi, 1981.

Kowalczyk, Janusz R. "Papusza (Bronislawa Wajs)." Culture.pl, June 2013, https://culture.pl/en/artist/papusza.

Krasnopolska, Zuzanna. "Storia di Papusza, poeta zingara." Societa delle letterate, 2014, http://www.societadelleletterate.it/2014/01/papuska.

Kuzniak, Angelika. Papusza. Wo owiec: Czarne, 2013.

Lewy, Guenther. The Nazi Persecution of the Gypsies. Oxford: Oxford University Press, 2000

Mehr, Mariella. Accusata. Trans. Claudia Costa. Milan: Effigie, 2008.

—. Labambina. Trans. Anna Ruchat. Milan: Effigie, 2006.

—. Il marchio. Trans. Tina D'Agostini. Ferrara: Luciana Tufani Editrice, 2001.

—. Notizie dall'esilio. Trans. Anna Ruchat and Rajko Djuric. Milan: Effigie, 2006.

—. <u>San Colombano e attesa</u>. Trans. Anna Ruchat. Milan: Effigie, 2010.

—. <u>Steinzeit</u>. Trans. Fausta Morganti. Rimini: Guaraldi; San Marino: Aiep, 1995.

Mochi Sismondi, Andrea. <u>Confini diamanti</u>. Verona: Ombre corte, 2012.

Mitrofanov, Il'ja. <u>La fortuna degli zingari</u>. Trans. M.A. Curletto. Milan: Isbn Edizioni, 2009.

Moresco, Antonio. <u>Zingari di merda</u>. Milan: Effigie, 2008.

Mustafa, Demir. <u>Poesie e racconti</u>. Rome: Cisu editore, 2002.

Novitch, Myriam. "Il genocidio degli zingari sotto il regime nazista." <u>Quaderni ANEI</u> no. 1. Rome: Assocazione Nazionale Ex Internati, 1964.

—. "Gypsy Victims of the Nazi Terror." <u>Patrin Web Journal</u>, Excerpted from the UNESCO Courier, October 1984. http://www.geocities.com/Paris/sizi/terror.htm

Pagano, Flavio, and Alessandro Cecchi Paone. <u>La rivolta degli zingari</u>. Milan: Mursia, 2009.

Papusza. <u>Routes d'antan</u> [Xargatune droma]. Trans. Marcel Courthiade. Paris: L'Harmattan, 2010.

Petruzzelli, Pino. <u>Non chiamarmi zingaro</u>. Milan: Chiarelettere, 2008.

Polansky, Paul. <u>La mia vita con gli zingari</u>. Trans. Valentina Confido. Rome: Datanews Editrice, 2011.

Piasere, Leonardo. <u>Buoni da ridere, gli zingari</u>. Rome: Cisu editore, 2006.

—. <u>Popoli delle discariche</u>. Rome: Cisu editore, 2005.

—. <u>I rom d'Europa</u>, Rome: Laterza, 2009.

Pisanty, Valentina. _La difesa della razza_. Pref. Umberto Eco. Milan: Bompiani, 2006.

Potel, Jean-Yves. "Papusza, poète tsigane en Pologne communiste." Presentation at the conference "Tsiganes, nomades, un malentendu européen," Paris, 6-9 October 2011.

Quercioli Mincer, Laura. _101 storie ebraiche che non ti hanno mai raccontato_. Rome: Newton Compton, 2011.

Revelli, Marco. _Fuori luogo: cronaca da un campo rom_. Turin: Bollati Boringhieri, 2008.

Romanès, Alexandre. _Sur l'épaule de l'ange_. Paris: Gallimard, 2010.

—. _Paroles perdues_, Paris: Gallimard, 2004.

—. _Un peuple de promeneurs_. Paris: Gallimard, 2011.

Salza, Carlotta Saletti. _Bambini del campo nomadi_. Rome: Cisu editore, 2003.

Spinelli, Santino. _Rom, genti libere_. Milan: Baldini Castoldi Dalai, 2012.

Toninato, Paola. "Il silenzio e la memoria - Riflessioni sulla memoria culturale fra i Roma." _Achab_ no. 4, 2005.

Tosi Cambini, Sabrina. _La zingara rapitrice_. Rome: Cisu editore, 2008.

Trevisan, Paola, ed. _Storie e vite di Sinti dell'Emilia_. Rome: Cisu editore, 2005.

Williams, Patrick. _Noi, non ne parliamo_ [Nous, on n'en parle pas]. Trans. Leonardo Piasere. Rome: Cisu editore, 2003.

About the Author

DAVIDE REVIATI is an Italian cartoonist, illustrator (for *Il manifesto*, *La Stampa*, and *L'Unità*, among others), and screenwriter. His graphic novel *Morti di sonno* (Coconino Press, 2009) won the 2010 Napoli Comic Con, and the dBD prize for best foreign comic for its French edition (Casterman 2011). *Sputa tre volte* (*Spit Three Times*) was published in Italy in 2016 after seven years of crafting story and illustrations.

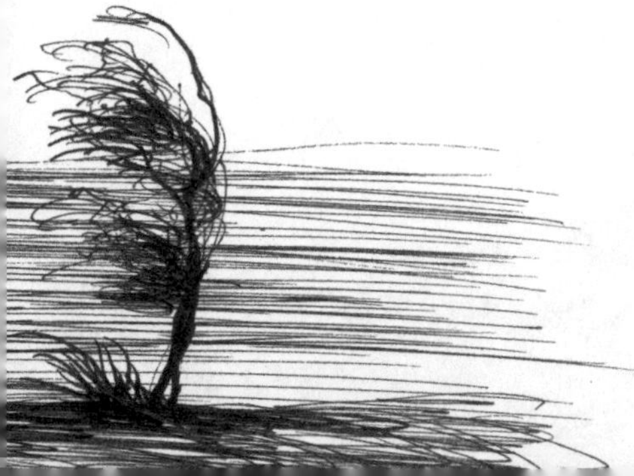

About the Translator

JAMIE RICHARDS is an American literary translator based in Milan. Her translations include Igiaba Scego's novel Adua, Zerocalcare's graphic reportage Kobane Calling, and Serena Vitale's interviews with Viktor Shklovsky, Witness to an Era.

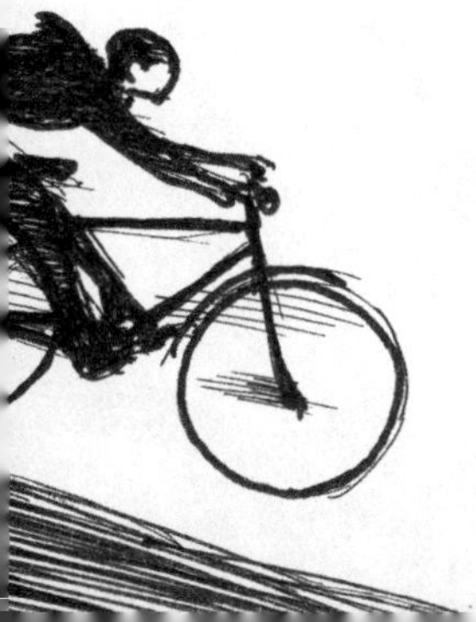